THE NORTON
INTRODUCTION TO
THE SHORT NOVEL

Jerome Beaty
Emory University

THE NORTON
INTRODUCTION TO
THE SHORT NOVEL

W · W · NORTON & COMPANY · NEW YORK · LONDON

W. W. Norton & Company, Inc., 500 Fifth Avenue, New York, N Y 10110
W. W. Norton & Company Ltd., 37 Great Russell Street, London WC1B 3NU

ISBN 0 393 95187 1

1 2 3 4 5 6 7 8 9 0

CONTENTS

FOREWORD

Of the eleven short novels in this collection, five are American (that is, North American), three English, two European (one written in Russian, the other in German), and one South American. They are spread fairly evenly—though with a little bunching at the two ends—over the past century. While there is geographical and historical range, however, the selection is not meant to be representative of the short novel as a whole in space or time, but primarily to offer interesting and challenging reading experiences of various kinds.

Though the novels may be read in any order and may profitably be grouped in a variety of ways, a bound book necessitates some fixed order, so they are arranged here chronologically, by date of publication. This arrangement has the virtue of not imposing an interpretive or editorial order on the novels, while not being entirely arbitrary or meaningless: we can say with some certainty, for example, that Toni Morrison or Philip Roth might have read *Daisy Miller* or *The Death of Iván Ilyich*, but that neither Henry James nor Tolstoy read either *Sula* or *Goodbye, Columbus*.

The "Introduction" defines the short novel in terms of its length, the formal and thematic consequences or corollaries of its length, and the effect of these on the experience of reading such a work. Preceding each novel is a brief headnote with enough biographical and other detail (about the author's other works, his or her theory of fiction—whatever seems fitting and useful) to prepare the reader to experience, appreciate, and understand the novel as fully as possible during a first reading. There are, as is usual in Norton books, informational footnotes designed to help the reader understand the text without either forcing upon the reader the editor's interpretation or unnecessarily burdening the text with what can be found in a standard desk dictionary. Following each novel is an "Afterword" discussing one or more aspects of the work that seem to the editor necessary to experience or understand the novel more fully. These are not meant to be definitive—they are very brief—but to generate thought, discussion, and even, I hope, controversy and excitement.

Just as in choosing the novels I have sought to provide the reader with stimulating and enjoyable material, so in writing the accompanying matter I have aimed at making the full power and pleasure of the novels readily accessible for the college and university student for whom this book is designed. Ready access, however, does not imply effortlessness or passive consumption, but rather an invitation to engage the imagined worlds of the novels actively and deeply, seeking new perspectives on new worlds and new experiences, and consequently new perspectives on our own world, our own experience.

If all my friends, family, colleagues, teachers, students, and acquaintances were to get their due, which of them could escape an acknowledgment of direct or indirect assistance in editing this anthology? I shall here name a few and beg the others to forgive me my debts.

I would like to thank all my colleagues at Emory University, but in particular Michaelyn Burnette, William B. Dillingham, Peter W. Dowell, Ricardo Gutierrez, Leon Mandell, Gayla McGlamery, Sondra O'Neale, Carlos Rojas, John Sitter, and Floyd Watkins. I wish to thank as well T. E. and Margaret Blom (University of British Columbia), Norman Feltes (York University), John Foley (University of Missouri), Kristin Hunter (University of Pennsylvania), George L. Levine (Rutgers University), William Morgan (Illinois State University), Douglas Peterson (Michigan State University), and Melissa Walker (Mercer University).

Andrew Beaty lent many hours of assistance; Mrs. Trudy Kretchman and Margaret Beavers were unfailingly cooperative. For their relief, many thanks.

The Ossabaw Island Project once again offered me hospitality and ideal working conditions; to the project and to Eleanor West and the Ossabaw Island Foundation, as well as the co-directors of the project, Carol Burdick and Albert Bradford, my sincere gratitude.

Robert Kimbrough of the University of Wisconsin was generous and gracious in permitting not only use but adaptation of his splendid annotation of the Norton Critical Edition of *The Nigger of the "Narcissus."* To him, my thanks.

I wish to express my gratitude also to Toni Morrison for granting us permission to reprint her splendid short novel *Sula* and for supplying some information for the notes which would otherwise have eluded me.

At W. W. Norton & Company, I would particularly like to thank my friend and the editor's editor Barry Wade; for advice and encouragement, John Benedict; for assistance and patience, Roberta Flechner, Diane O'Connor, and Nancy Palmquist.

Meaghan and Caelin Beaty gave up many hours of story and play time while their father was reading and editing short novels, and my wife, V. Elaine Beaty, took up the slack cheerfully, and rendered continuous assistance, encouragement, and constructive critical comment. I promise to thank them when I get home.

J.B.

THE NORTON
INTRODUCTION TO
THE SHORT NOVEL

INTRODUCTION

For some readers and some instructional purposes, short stories are too short. And for some, most novels are too long. But short novels are just right. That's one of the reasons I prefer the term *short novel* to *novella* and *novelette:* the adjective echoes *short* story, and the noun tells you it's a *novel,* thus emphasizing its happy position between the two.

The length that normally qualifies a work to be considered a short *novel* rather than short *story* is about 15,000 words (twenty-five or so pages in this volume); when short novels get beyond 50,000 words they sometimes lose the adjective and are novels plain and simple. Length usually allows short novels to have more of everything than a short story. They can accommodate a larger cast of characters and develop them more fully; they can have more incidents or a more complicated plot; they can have more scenes (dramatized incidents in which characters think, talk, or do something over a brief, continuous period of time), or more—and more widely spaced—settings, and they can take place over longer stretches and in more discriminated moments of time. They can thus expand in various ways the scope, breadth, and depth of short stories. The compact form of the short story is particularly suited to stories of initiation, of sudden insight and illumination; the more leisurely novel is better suited to narratives of growth and change, of quest and development. The short novel is happily suited to either, or a blending of both.

The shortest of the short novels in this collection (though the one with the longest title), for example, *The Incredible and Sad Tale of Innocent Eréndira and Her Heartless Grandmother,* has many of the qualities of the full-length novel. It is made up of a goodly number of separate scenes, spread out over a number of years and over a sizable area of Colombia in South America; it has a rather large cast of particularized characters (though it concentrates on two or three) and a rather large number of incidents. It is, however, a story both of development and sudden change. On the other hand, *Daisy Miller* has relatively few dramatized scenes, characters, and incidents, and is primarily a story of discovery or sudden illumination. It is, however, seldom thought of as anything other than a short novel. In its case, primarily length—more than 25,000 words—is no doubt the determining factor. The short novel can be as simple as a short story (but not when it's as short) and as complex as a novel (but not too, too long); it is a happy hybrid.

Sheer length is important not only as one characteristic of the work, but also in our experience of reading the work, something that happens to—but is also created by—the reader. Though one can put down a short story and later pick it up again, it seems designed to be read in a sitting: to absorb the reader for one period of time, come to a point of illumination or reversal and then let the reader go back to a reality that is spatially unchanged from that which was there when the story was begun (you've been sitting in the same spot), temporally changed only slightly (it hasn't taken you long to read it), and psychologically unchanged *except for the effect, vision, insight of the story itself* (not much has happened to you outside the reading).

Though there are novels (novels unmodified by "short") that can be read by nonspeedreading readers in a sitting (a famous critic in the mid-nineteenth century picked up *Jane Eyre* one evening and, as he put it, "married Mr. Rochester at three o'clock the next morning"), the novel as such does not seem to be designed to be read so. Some novels have been published serially, in weekly or monthly installments, so that contemporary readers could not gobble them down; and most are divided into parts or chapters that seem to offer convenient stopping points. This elapsed reading time (and time between sittings) seems to me not insignificant. The reader may or may not resume the same position in chair or bed, may or may not have had illuminating or harrowing or meaningful experiences between readings, but he or she has done something (eaten dinner? answered the phone? gone skiing for a weekend?), and has both left the world of the fiction and, somewhere in the back or front of the mind, thought or felt something about the novel being read. The reader picking up the novel again must make a new entry into the fictional world as a more or less changed and different reader. It is the depth of the experience of reading a novel—more than the depth or breadth of its theme or its analysis of character or its vision—that may be the most significant difference between short story and novel.

Here again, mere length leaves the short novel in between. Short novels such as *Daisy Miller* (though it was serialized and so, on first appearance, could not have been read at once), *Dr. Jekyll and Mr. Hyde*, *The Metamorphosis*, can be read in a single (though fairly long) sitting. However, *Daisy Miller* is divided into two, *Metamorphosis* three, and *Iván Ilyich* twelve numbered chapters, and *Jekyll and Hyde* is divided into ten titled segments. These divisions are invitations to put the book down for a moment or longer, or at least to pause: to prepare for a shift of scene or time or to think back over what has happened so far, and to project some sort of pattern of expectation of what may come next. Even if we do not put a short novel down and let its development—and our expectations—ferment between reading sessions, its relative length requires punctuated pauses to process and store the information, perceptions, emotions, and relationships we are confronting.

Though our capacities differ, and individual works differ markedly, it is often possible to hold not only the details but even the memory of our responses to a *short story* in our minds when we finish it (especially after repeated readings). It is extremely difficult, at least for me, to remember a *short novel* in detail and to recall my point-by-point responses to it fully no matter how many times I have read it; it's like trying to carry an overstuffed bag of groceries or too high a pile of books—something inevitably falls. (And while you're retrieving it, two or three other things fall.) I can remember the witty, worldly tone at the beginning of *Daisy Miller* right now (though I usually don't), but I am not sure I can reconstruct my responses and expectations during the reading of that first page or so of the story.

As you see, when I talk about reading a story or novel, I'm not only talking about understanding it, interpreting it, or abstracting a meaning, but about *experiencing* it. It is difficult to pin down just what one means by the "experience" of reading a work of fiction—everything relevant that is going on in your head and nervous system as you read, perhaps. Reducing this complex activity to its simplest terms, we can talk about your taking in the information or data of the story, going on to gather new data, and making a pattern of what you are taking in, and so anticipating what will happen or be revealed next. When you read on, your expectations are disappointed, altered or fulfilled, new pieces are picked up and new patterns projected. Reading fiction is, then, in part a guessing game.

This reading process is unconscious; we usually do not watch our own minds as we read. But before we begin the eleven short novels in this volume, let's look at the kinds of things that might be happening in our minds as we read them. The beginning is always a good place to begin, but let's begin before the beginning, with the title. There's no fictional "past" here; we have—or so we ought to assume for the sake of the guessing—no prior information as we read *The Strange Case of Dr. Jekyll and Mr. Hyde:* "case" suggests a detective story or crime, "strange" that it will not be like ordinary "cases." Even with only these two counters to go on, a pool of vague possibilities begins to form, waiting for more detail to shape it into a concrete expectation or set of expectations of what is to happen next. Even apparently neutral titles like *Daisy Miller* arouse some anticipation: we know that a person of that name is likely to appear and to be central or significant in the narrative to follow.

Though we can learn something from a title, exploration does not carry us very far in understanding the complex network of activities involved in reading and understanding a long work like a novel, even what we call a short novel. It probably would be not only impractical but misleading to stop to examine our mental activities and pattern-making after reading each word, phrase, or sentence of a prose narrative. To pause to analyze response, recapitulation, and expectation at the end of each paragraph would make some sense—we do, after all, have to shift our eyes back to the beginning of the next line, as we do in reading lines of poetry—but to pause and analyze so often would be cumbersome. Moreover, there is a larger and more appropriate unit of punctuation in a novel, one that is governed—usually consciously so—by the author to control our reading pace, making us pause, and inviting us to recapitulate and to anticipate what is to come. That unit is the chapter. *Eréndira* is divided into units only by spacing—skipped lines—but the other short novels in this volume are all more formally divided into chapters headed by titles, dates, or numbers, and many of them are also divided into smaller units by spacing and other typographical devices. *Daisy Miller* is divided into only two chapters, *The Awakening* into thirty-nine. *Sula* is divided into two parts, eleven chapters headed by dates, and more than three dozen smaller units, mostly by spacing but several times by one or another set of printer's marks.

Let us look briefly at how that form of "punctuation" called the chapter can work in pacing our reading and therefore in generating or controlling our expectations. In Tolstoy's *The Death of Iván Ilyich,* the first chapter ends with Iván Ilyich's best friend, Peter Ivánovich, having just left Iván Ilyich's newly widowed wife, joining his and Iván Ilyich's other friends at cards, finding "them just finishing the first rubber, so that it was quite convenient for him to cut in." The pause forces us to think back over the brief chapter, in which Iván Ilyich's death has been greeted by friends and family with only a show of sorrow but with self-interested questions of how that death will affect their own convenience and material conditions. What developments do we expect? What would surprise us? The punctuation of the chapter-ending has made us, consciously or unconsciously, frame some possibilities if we are reading attentively and following the author's pacing of our reading. Not every one of us will anticipate the same future for the story. Some of us will be drawing a blank not

able to frame an expectation; others will have one plot we are pretty sure will
be followed; still others may have three, five, eight possibilities more or less
vaguely floating through our minds.

Let us settle on just two fairly obvious possibilities. At this point we feel
sorry for Iván Ilyich: neither his friends nor his wife seems truly to mourn him.
Poor Iván: perhaps the rest of the novel will flash back over his life and show
us how the poor man—maybe from the time he was a baby—was mistreated,
misunderstood. We may anticipate, in other words, a sentimental journey into
Iván Ilyich's past. (And perhaps some or all of us are prepared for such a narrative because we have all felt misunderstood, undervalued, ignored, or unrecog-
nized for the splendid person we are, at one time or another.) The second
obvious possibility is that all the selfish nonmourners, friends and widow alike,
will be followed to their unmourned deaths, where each will get his or her just
deserts. We may anticipate, in other words, a tale of moral retaliation. Since
the story has scarcely begun and we can see we have nearly forty pages to go,
either of these expectations—each requiring considerable space and development—would be possible.

But what if we hold both these anticipated plots consciously or unconsciously in mind? One of them is bound to be wrong. Would it not be better
just to have the right one in mind? Or none at all, and just wait and see? Or
suppose both of them are wrong? If we carefully put two and two together
and come up with five, what is the advantage of informed anticipation?

A well-structured novel will play fair with you, offering at appropriate points
all the necessary signals or clues to what will happen next, not just springing
new and essential information on you at the last minute ("Meanwhile, unknown to our hero, the Marines were just on the other side of the hill . . ."). It
is this playing fair that makes an ending satisfying or, when you look back on
it, inevitable. Novels also offer a number of reasonable but false signals, red
herrings, to get you off the scent, so that in a well-structured novel the ending,
though inevitable, is also surprising. When we find that leads are false, that our
expectations or guesses are wrong, we discard them, and with the new evidence we have gathered from the narrative we project a new pattern of events
to come.

Old expectations and patterns seem about as useful as used tubes of tooth-
paste, we may feel: next time through the story we'll know better than to expect Sula to leave Ajax, or to suspect Hyde of forging Jekyll's signature or
blackmailing him. Not so. The "wrong guesses" signalled by the text (not the
free-floating guesses that may from time to time without reason pop into our
heads or be made up) remain part of the text as a reading experience. The false
expectations may be irrelevant to the outcome of the novel, but they are not
irrelevant to the novel: they represent one of the choices made in defining the
world of this particular novel; they represent one of the ways our expectations
of reality is being redefined; they say, "This is a fictional world or view of reality in which two plus two might equal five, but doesn't," and they say, "This is
a fictional world which does not even entertain the possibility that two plus
two might equal three."

Novels differ as much in the questions they raise, in what *might* have happened in them but did not, as they do in what does happen. In a novel there
are a great many more expectations, a great many more things that might have
been than there are in a short story. Even if a short novel and a short story
were to "say" the same thing, embody the same theme or abstraction, the
short novel would usually be the richer. Just as an argument is the more con-

vincing the more objections it raises and rebuts, so a fictional theme or vision may be the more fully realized (made real) the more alternative outcomes, explanations, visions it raises but dismisses. This can be done more readily in a long than in a short work.

So long as you are alert to your own mind's activity as you read, you will notice how breaks, marks, and formal chapter endings will pace your reading, push you to recapitulate and project; the "Afterwords" that follow each of the short novels will occasionally try to describe what happens to the reader at such a pause, as does the "Afterword" to *The Death of Iván Ilyich,* for example. You will notice too that not all the signals come from "inside" the text. We begin a novel usually with the expectation that the world of the fiction resembles our world as we see it, not necessarily in detail—we do not demand the ordinary—but in its "laws" or "physics," as it were. We expect this even of a novel whose title contains such words as "incredible" and "tale," and which begins with a most bizarre setting and set of circumstances, as does *Innocent Eréndira.* We are led by stages in that novel, however, to the extraordinary, the preposterous, and ultimately to the "incredible" or surreal. *The Metamorphosis* rapes rather than seduces our expectations of a more or less normative reality, but then, once we have granted the premise that a young man can wake one morning to find himself an insect, it follows that premise with remorseless "natural" consequences and logic. Reality as we know it outside a work furnishes us with expectations which the work can disappoint, alter, or fulfill like any other expectations.

Our expectations or guesses are also conditioned by literary tradition or our own experience of narratives and narrative patterns. *Goodbye, Columbus* begins when the young male narrator meets a girl named Brenda. Ah, ha! Boy-meets-girl. We know that story, and its various patterns and variations on "loses" and "gets." (We may be a little curious about how the title will figure, however.) *Daisy Miller* is another boy-meets-girl story, but the meeting does not take place quite so quickly: we first meet the "boy," Winterbourne, then Daisy's little brother, then Daisy herself. We are only a few paragraphs into the story, but just as the title of *Goodbye, Columbus* puts in our mind just a little curiosity not clearly related to the love story, so the opening description of Vevey and Lake Geneva in the James novel alerts us to the fashionable, social, cultural scene and its role in the love story and in the novel. So convention alerts us to a love story and detail alerts us to other, related or modifying expectations.

Expectations are not quite so simple, then, as we sometimes think them to be. Our minds can hold at once not only multiple possibilities for the outcome of a story but also have room for other related and unrelated stories or areas of experience. The questions surrounding James Wait and his illness run almost from first to last in *The Nigger of the "Narcissus,"* yet we have room in our heads to follow the course of the horrendous storm and the fierce struggle of the officers, the crew, the ship itself against the elements, and to put Wait in the background. We do not forget him or dismiss him; he's there waiting to emerge again, and in the rescue his story and that of the storm come together.

Just as we began speaking about expectations in terms of the beginning, so, perhaps, we should conclude by talking about endings. In the beginning there is no "past" in our experience of the story: we seek to understand what we are reading in the present and to project the future. It would follow that at the end of the story we take in the last words, remembering all the past of the story, but not projecting a pattern of what will come in the future. The shape of the story is now complete, the final configuration is made (including not only the fulfilled expectations, but also all the things that might have been). At the end of *Daisy Miller* we not only know what she was really like, but we get a view of Winterbourne and of his learning something about her and about himself. The mystery of *Jekyll and Hyde* has been solved long before the ending, but at the conclusion we have the explanation and at least one final version of the meaning of it all.

Not all stories end so definitively, however. Sometimes, especially in a fairly complex novel, while the story has ended, our response to it and understanding of it have not taken final shape; but in other novels, the story itself has not really ended and we are left both with unresolved questions about meaning or vision and unresolved expectations about the future course of the lives with which we have been engaged. It's awkward to talk about endings in an introduction, because I don't want to give too much away and short-circuit any of your first responses or expectations. Let's just say that at the end of *The Fox* one character says to the other that he or she will feel better "over there."

> "Yes, I may. I can't tell. I can't tell what it will be like over there."
> "If only we could go soon!" —— said, with pain in —— voice.

We do not know how it will be "over there," whether the ending will be "happy" or not. We therefore do not know for sure how to interpret or evaluate what has happened to the characters in the story we have just finished reading and we are virtually being invited to complete the story ourselves, to write the ending, or an ending, or a stopping place. We are invited to continue recollecting what we have read, forming it into a present shape, to project a future pattern.

At the very end of *Old Mortality* one of the characters says,

> Let them tell their stories to each other. Let them go on explaining how things happened. I don't care. At least I can know the truth about what happens to me, she assured herself silently, making a promise to herself, in her hopefulness, her ignorance.

We have a double inconclusiveness. The first is a fairly conventional "open" or indefinite ending: we have heard a number of explanations of how things happened and none seems totally satisfactory and none seems totally wrong. We see how people interpret external reality in terms of their own perceptions, prejudices, and needs, so that no subjective explanation is adequate as an objective explanation, if there is such a thing. This is a conclusion, if an inconclusive one: we are invited to review in our minds all the versions of the past to which we have been subjected, perhaps to choose, perhaps to put together like a puzzle, perhaps simply to sigh at the difficulty of it all. But we are not asked to project a pattern of action or incident into the future beyond the moment at which the story ends—until the last five words or so. "Her ignorance"—she will not know the truth even about what will happen to her. We know a little of her life and a good deal about a long-deceased character named Amy and everyone's version of her life, and so we are virtually invited to put these together somehow and project a more or less definite future for the hopeful, ignorant woman who is thinking the final thoughts of the story.

I have some expectations, too. I am looking forward eagerly to your reading these eleven short novels. I do not know (in my ignorance) how intensely you will enjoy them, but I expect (in my hopefulness) that you will enjoy them as much as I have in reading and thinking about them and readying them for you.

HENRY JAMES

Daisy Miller

Henry James (1843-1916) never married, had fairly little formal education, never held down a job, and, though not rich, never had to worry about money. He did little but travel, read and write, go to museums and theaters, dine out, and (with something of a stammer) talk.

The two most interesting things about his life—outside his work—are, perhaps, his famous family and his obscure accident. His father was a philosophic and unorthodox religious writer; his older brother William was one of the first significant American psychologists and a famous philosopher; his sister Alice and two younger brothers rounded out a brilliant, intellectually active family. The accident occurred a few months after the beginning of the Civil War when he was pushed into a fence while trying to put out a small fire in Newport, Rhode Island. The result was what he called a "horrid even if an obscure hurt," and, characteristically, his reticence and ambiguity caused post-Freudian scholars to infer that the accident had something to do with his not marrying. His most authoritative biographer, Leon Edel, believes it was a slipped disc or similar back injury involving recurrent pain.

His travel began early—at six months he was in Paris—and in the late 1850s he spent five of his most formative years in Europe. He returned to Europe a few years after the end of the Civil War and by 1876 had decided to settle in England. Although his writing and reviewing had begun a dozen years before, his first novel, *Roderick Hudson,* did not appear until 1875. The flood was released and he published more than fifty books before his death in 1916.

James had a life-long addiction to the theater and in the early 1890s wrote more than half a dozen plays, two of which were produced and performed—both flopped. His best drama is in his fiction, which is dramatic in that the action takes place in rather lengthy scenes and primarily through dialogue; there is careful, significant, often symbolic use made of setting; and the intermediary or narrator which differentiates fiction from drama is, more and more as James's career progresses, replaced by a center of consciousness, a character spoken of in the third person through whose eye and mind we perceive the action, and, most often, in whose voice we are told of it. We can speak of "the drama of the mind" as characteristic of his novels, for the center *is* in the consciousness, the mind of the beholder; his works are about perception—the perception of the self and others—and if the dramatic nature of his theory and practice in writing fiction assures him a place in the history of literary craft and criticism, so his novels of the mind place him high in the history and development of the psychological novel.

Daisy Miller is an early work of Henry James but one in which several of his themes or preoccupations are already visible: "the international theme" (the American in Europe) and the search by the protagonist for the reality behind the appearance and actions of others. James and his protagonists ask fairly simple questions but the investigation is complex, the answers often tentative, and so the form of the short novel is very congenial to his genius and interests. Though we must name the full-length (even lengthy) novels such as *The Portrait of a Lady* (1881), *The Ambassadors* (1903), and *The Golden Bowl* (1904) among his greatest works, such short novels as *Daisy Miller, The Aspern Papers* (1888), *The Turn of the Screw* (1898), and *The Beast in the Jungle* (1901) are not only excellent examples of the form but are central to James's work.

Daisy Miller
A Study

I

AT THE LITTLE TOWN of Vevey, in Switzerland, there is a particularly comfortable hotel. There are, indeed, many hotels; for the entertainment of tourists is the business of the place, which, as many travellers will remember, is seated upon the edge of a remarkably blue lake[1]—a lake that it behoves every tourist to visit. The shore of the lake presents an unbroken array of establishments of this order, of every category, from the "grand hotel" of the newest fashion, with a chalk-white front, a hundred balconies, and a dozen flags flying from its roof, to the little Swiss *pension* of an elder day, with its name inscribed in German-looking lettering upon a pink or yellow wall, and an awkward summer-house in the angle of the garden. One of the hotels at Vevey, however, is famous, even classical, being distinguished from many of its upstart neighbours by an air both of luxury and of maturity. In this region, in the month of June, American travellers are extremely numerous; it may be said, indeed, that Vevey assumes at this period some of the characteristics of an American watering-place. There are sights and sounds which evoke a vision, an echo, of Newport and Saratoga.[2] There is a flitting hither and thither of "stylish" young girls, a rustling of muslin flounces, a rattle of dance music in the morning hours, a sound of high-pitched voices at all times. You receive an impression of these things at the excellent inn of the "Trois Couronnes,"[3] and are transported in fancy to the Ocean House or to Congress Hall. But at the "Trois Couronnes," it must be added, there are other features that are much at variance with these suggestions: neat German waiters, who look like secretaries of legation; Russian princesses sitting in the garden, little Polish boys walking about, held by the hand, with their governors; a view of the snowy crest of the Dent du Midi and the picturesque towers of the Castle of Chillon.[4]

I hardly know whether it was the analogies or the differences that were uppermost in the mind of a young American, who, two or three years ago, sat in the garden of the "Trois Couronnes," looking about him, rather idly, at some of the graceful objects I have mentioned. It was a beautiful summer morning, and in whatever fashion the young American looked at things, they must have seemed to him charming. He had come from Geneva the day before, by the little steamer, to see his aunt, who was staying at the hotel—Geneva having been for a long time his place of residence. But his aunt had a headache—his aunt had almost always a headache—and now she was shut up in her room, smelling camphor, so

1. Lake Geneva; Vevey is about ten miles east of Lausanne.
2. Newport, R.I., was a fashionable resort for the very rich, studded with palatial mansions; Saratoga Springs, N.Y., about thirty miles from Albany, a summer resort noted for its mineral springs, and from 1850 horse-racing, was considered the social center of America in the middle of the nineteenth century.
3. Three Crowns. Below: Ocean House was a major hotel on Bellevue Avenue in Newport, Congress Hall on Broadway in Saratoga.
4. The ninth- to thirteenth-century castle at the eastern end of Lake Geneva was the residence of the counts of Savoy and the scene of the incarceration of "the prisoner of Chillon" made famous by Byron (see note on Bonivard, below); the Dent or Dents du Midi is a mountain group in Switzerland near the French border.

that he was at liberty to wander about. He was some seven-and-twenty years of age; when his friends spoke of him, they usually said that he was at Geneva, "studying." When his enemies spoke of him they said—but, after all, he had no enemies; he was an extremely amiable fellow, and universally liked. What I should say is, simply, that when certain persons spoke of him they affirmed that the reason of his spending so much time at Geneva was that he was extremely devoted to a lady who lived there— a foreign lady—a person older than himself. Very few Americans—indeed I think none—had ever seen this lady, about whom there were some singular stories. But Winterbourne had an old attachment for the little metropolis of Calvinism;[5] he had been put to school there as a boy, and he had afterwards gone to college there—circumstances which had led to his forming a great many youthful friendships. Many of these he had kept, and they were a source of great satisfaction to him.

After knocking at his aunt's door and learning that she was indisposed, he had taken a walk about the town, and then he had come in to his breakfast. He had now finished his breakfast, but he was drinking a small cup of coffee, which had been served to him on a little table in the garden by one of the waiters, who looked like an *attaché*. At last he finished his coffee and lit a cigarette. Presently a small boy came walking along the path—an urchin of nine or ten. The child, who was diminutive for his years, had an aged expression of countenance, a pale complexion, and sharp little features. He was dressed in knickerbockers, with red stockings, which displayed his poor little spindleshanks; he also wore a brilliant red cravat. He carried in his hand a long alpenstock, the sharp point of which he thrust into everything that he approached—the flower-beds, the garden benches, the trains of the ladies' dresses. In front of Winterbourne he paused, looking at him with a pair of bright penetrating little eyes.

"Will you give me a lump of sugar?" he asked, in a sharp hard little voice—a voice immature, and yet, somehow, not young.

Winterbourne glanced at the small table near him, on which his coffee-service rested, and saw that several morsels of sugar remained. "Yes, you may take one," he answered; "but I don't think sugar is good for little boys."

This little boy stepped forward and carefully selected three of the coveted fragments, two of which he buried in the pocket of his knickerbockers, depositing the other as promptly in another place. He poked his alpenstock, lance-fashion, into Winterbourne's bench, and tried to crack the lump of sugar with his teeth.

"Oh, blazes; it's har-r-d!" he exclaimed, pronouncing the adjective in a peculiar manner.

Winterbourne had immediately perceived that he might have the honour of claiming him as a fellow-countryman. "Take care you don't hurt your teeth," he said, paternally.

"I haven't got any teeth to hurt. They have all come out. I have only got seven teeth. My mother counted them last night, and one came out right afterwards. She said she'd slap me if any more came out. I can't help it. It's this old Europe. It's the climate that makes them come out. In America they didn't come out. It's these hotels."

5. Geneva, after John Calvin (1509–1564), leader of the Protestant Reformation there.

Winterbourne was much amused. "If you eat three lumps of sugar your mother will certainly slap you," he said.

"She's got to give me some candy, then," rejoined his young interlocutor. "I can't get any candy here—any American candy. American candy's the best candy."

"And are American little boys the best little boys?" asked Winterbourne.

"I don't know. I'm an American boy," said the child.

"I see you are one of the best!" laughed Winterbourne.

"Are you an American man?" pursued this vivacious infant. And then, on Winterbourne's affirmative reply—"American men are the best," he declared.

His companion thanked him for the compliment; and the child, who had now got astride of his alpenstock, stood looking about him, while he attacked a second lump of sugar. Winterbourne wondered if he himself had been like this in his infancy, for he had been brought to Europe at about this age.

"Here comes my sister!" cried the child, in a moment. "She's an American girl."

Winterbourne looked along the path and saw a beautiful young lady advancing. "American girls are the best girls," he said, cheerfully, to his young companion.

"My sister ain't the best!" the child declared. "She's always blowing[6] at me."

"I imagine that is your fault, not hers," said Winterbourne. The young lady meanwhile had drawn near. She was dressed in white muslin, with a hundred frills and flounces, and knots of pale-coloured ribbon. She was bare-headed; but she balanced in her hand a large parasol, with a deep border of embroidery; and she was strikingly, admirably pretty. "How pretty they are!" thought Winterbourne, straightening himself in his seat, as if he were prepared to rise.

The young lady paused in front of his bench, near the parapet of the garden, which overlooked the lake. The little boy had now converted his alpenstock into a vaulting-pole, by the aid of which he was springing about in the gravel, and kicking it up not a little.

"Randolph," said the young lady, "What *are* you doing?"

"I'm going up the Alps," replied Randolph. "This is the way!" And he gave another little jump, scattering the pebbles about Winterbourne's ears.

"That's the way they come down," said Winterbourne.

"He's an American man!" cried Randolph, in his little hard voice.

The young lady gave no heed to this announcement, but looked straight at her brother. "Well, I guess you had better be quiet," she simply observed.

It seemed to Winterbourne that he had been in a manner presented. He got up and stepped slowly towards the young girl, throwing away his cigarette. "This little boy and I have made acquaintance," he said, with great civility. In Geneva, as he had been perfectly aware, a young man was not at liberty to speak to a young unmarried lady except under certain rarely-occurring conditions; but here at Vevey, what conditions could

6. Speaking angrily, yelling.

be better than these?—a pretty American girl coming and standing in front of you in a garden. This pretty American girl, however, on hearing Winterbourne's observation, simply glanced at him; she then turned her head and looked over the parapet, at the lake and the opposite mountains. He wondered whether he had gone too far; but he decided that he must advance farther, rather than retreat. While he was thinking of something else to say, the young lady turned to the little boy again.

"I should like to know where you got that pole," she said.

"I bought it!" responded Randolph.

"You don't mean to say you're going to take it to Italy!"

"Yes, I am going to take it to Italy!" the child declared.

The young girl glanced over the front of her dress, and smoothed out a knot or two of ribbon. Then she rested her eyes upon the prospect again. "Well, I guess you had better leave it somewhere," she said, after a moment.

"Are you going to Italy?" Winterbourne inquired, in a tone of great respect.

The young lady glanced at him again. "Yes, sir," she replied. And she said nothing more.

"Are you—a—going over the Simplon?" Winterbourne pursued, a little embarrassed.

"I don't know," she said. "I suppose it's some mountain. Randolph, what mountain are we going over?"

"Going where?" the child demanded.

"To Italy," Winterbourne explained.

"I don't know," said Randolph. "I don't want to go to Italy. I want to go to America."

"Oh, Italy is a beautiful place!" rejoined the young man.

"Can you get candy there?" Randolph loudly inquired.

"I hope not," said his sister. "I guess you have had enough candy, and mother thinks so too."

"I haven't had any for ever so long—for a hundred weeks!" cried the boy, still jumping about.

The young lady inspected her flounces and smoothed her ribbons again; and Winterbourne presently risked an observation upon the beauty of the view. He was ceasing to be embarrassed, for he had begun to perceive that she was not in the least embarrassed herself. There had not been the slightest alteration in her charming complexion; she was evidently neither offended nor fluttered. If she looked another way when he spoke to her, and seemed not particularly to hear him, this was simply her habit, her manner. Yet, as he talked a little more, and pointed out some of the objects of interest in the view, with which she appeared quite unacquainted, she gradually gave him more of the benefit of her glance; and then he saw that this glance was perfectly direct and unshrinking. It was not, however, what would have been called an immodest glance, for the young girl's eyes were singularly honest and fresh. They were wonderfully pretty eyes; and, indeed, Winterbourne had not seen for a long time anything prettier than his fair countrywoman's various features—her complexion, her nose, her ears, her teeth. He had a great relish for feminine beauty; he was addicted to observing and analysing it; and as regards this young lady's face he made several observations. It was not at all insipid, but it was not exactly expressive; and though it was eminently delicate, Winterbourne mentally accused it—very forgivingly—of a want of finish. He thought it very possible that Master Randolph's sister was a coquette; he was sure she had a spirit of her own; but in her bright, sweet, superficial little visage, there was no mockery, no irony. Before long it became obvious that she was much disposed towards conversation. She told him that they were going to Rome for the winter—she and her mother and Randolph. She asked him if he was a "real American"; she wouldn't have taken him for one; he seemed more like a German—this was said after a little hesitation—especially when he spoke. Winterbourne, laughing, answered that he had met Germans who spoke like Americans; but that he had not, so far as he remembered, met an American who spoke like a German. Then he asked her if she would not be more comfortable in sitting upon the bench which he had just quitted. She answered that she liked standing up and walking about; but she presently sat down. She told him she was from New York State—"if you know where that is." Winterbourne learned more about her by catching hold of her small slippery brother and making him stand a few minutes by his side.

"Tell me your name, my boy," he said.

"Randolph C. Miller," said the boy, sharply. "And I'll tell you her name"; and he levelled his alpenstock at his sister.

"You had better wait till you are asked!" said this young lady, calmly.

"I should like very much to know your name," said Winterbourne.

"Her name is Daisy Miller!" cried the child. "But that isn't her real name; that isn't her name on her cards."

"It's a pity you haven't got one of my cards!" said Miss Miller.

"Her real name is Annie P. Miller," the boy went on.

"Ask him *his* name," said his sister, indicating Winterbourne.

But on this point Randolph seemed perfectly indifferent; he continued to supply information with regard to his own family. "My father's name is Ezra B. Miller," he announced. "My father ain't in Europe; my father's in a better place than Europe."

Winterbourne imagined for a moment that this was the manner in which the child had been taught to intimate that Mr. Miller had been removed to the sphere of celestial rewards. But Randolph immediately added, "My father's in Schenectady. He's got a big business. My father's rich, you bet."

"Well!" ejaculated Miss Miller, lowering her parasol and looking at the embroidered border. Winterbourne presently released the child, who departed, dragging his alpenstock along the path. "He doesn't like Europe," said the young girl. "He wants to go back."

"To Schenectady, you mean?"

"Yes; he wants to go right home. He hasn't got any boys here. There is one boy here, but he always goes round with a teacher; they won't let him play."

"And your brother hasn't any teacher?" Winterbourne inquired.

"Mother thought of getting him one, to travel round with us. There was a lady told her of a very good teacher; an American lady—perhaps you know her—Mrs. Sanders. I think she came from Boston. She told her of this teacher, and we thought of getting him to travel round with us. But Randolph said he didn't want a teacher travelling round with us. He

said he wouldn't have lessons when he was in the cars.[7] And we *are* in the
cars about half the time. There was an English lady we met in the cars—I
think her name was Miss Featherstone; perhaps you know her. She
wanted to know why I didn't give Randolph lessons—give him 'instruction,' she called it. I guess he could give me more instruction than I could
give him. He's very smart."

"Yes," said Winterbourne; "he seems very smart."

"Mother's going to get a teacher for him as soon as we get to Italy. Can
you get good teachers in Italy?"

"Very good, I should think," said Winterbourne.

"Or else she's going to find some school. He ought to learn some more.
He's only nine. He's going to college." And in this way Miss Miller continued to converse upon the affairs of her family, and upon other topics.
She sat there with her extremely pretty hands, ornamented with very brilliant rings, folded in her lap, and with her pretty eyes now resting upon
those of Winterbourne, now wandering over the garden, the people who
passed by, and the beautiful view. She talked to Winterbourne as if she
had known him a long time. He found it very pleasant. It was many years
since he had heard a young girl talk so much. It might have been said of
this unknown young lady, who had come and sat down beside him upon a
bench, that she chattered. She was very quiet, she sat in a charming tranquil attitude; but her lips and her eyes were constantly moving. She had a
soft, slender, agreeable voice, and her tone was decidedly sociable. She
gave Winterbourne a history of her movements and intentions, and those
of her mother and brother, in Europe, and enumerated, in particular, the
various hotels at which they had stopped. "That English lady in the cars,"
she said—"Miss Featherstone—asked me if we didn't all live in hotels in
America. I told her I had never been in so many hotels in my life as since
I came to Europe. I have never seen so many—it's nothing but hotels."
But Miss Miller did not make this remark with a querulous accent; she
appeared to be in the best humour with everything. She declared that the
hotels were very good, when once you got used to their ways, and that
Europe was perfectly sweet. She was not disappointed—not a bit. Perhaps
it was because she had heard so much about it before. She had ever so
many intimate friends that had been there ever so many times. And then
she had had ever so many dresses and things from Paris. Whenever she
put on a Paris dress she felt as if she were in Europe.

"It was a kind of a wishing-cap," said Winterbourne.

"Yes," said Miss Miller, without examining this analogy; "it always
made me wish I was here. But I needn't have done that for dresses. I am
sure they send all the pretty ones to America; you see the most frightful
things here. The only thing I don't like," she proceeded, "is the society.
There isn't any society; or, if there is, I don't know where it keeps itself.
Do you? I suppose there is some society somewhere, but I haven't seen
anything of it. I'm very fond of society, and I have always had a great
deal of it. I don't mean only in Schenectady, but in New York. I used to
go to New York every winter. In New York I had lots of society. Last
winter I had seventeen dinners given me; and three of them were by
gentlemen," added Daisy Miller. "I have more friends in New York than
in Schenectady—more gentlemen friends; and more young lady friends

---

7. Railroad cars.

too," she resumed in a moment. She paused again for an instant; she was looking at Winterbourne with all her prettiness in her lively eyes and in her light, slightly monotonous smile. "I have always had," she said, "a great deal of gentlemen's society."

Poor Winterbourne was amused, perplexed, and decidedly charmed. He had never yet heard a young girl express herself in just this fashion; never, at least, save in cases where to say such things seemed a kind of demonstrative evidence of a certain laxity of deportment. And yet was he to accuse Miss Daisy Miller of actual or potential *inconduite*,[8] as they said at Geneva? He felt that he had lived at Geneva so long that he had lost a good deal; he had become dishabituated to the American tone. Never, indeed, since he had grown old enough to appreciate things, had he encountered a young American girl of so pronounced a type as this. Certainly she was very charming; but how deucedly sociable! Was she simply a pretty girl from New York State—were they all like that, the pretty girls who had a good deal of gentlemen's society? Or was she also a designing, an audacious, an unscrupulous young person? Winterbourne had lost his instinct in this matter, and his reason could not help him. Miss Daisy Miller looked extremely innocent. Some people had told him that, after all, American girls were exceedingly innocent; and others had told him that, after all, they were not. He was inclined to think Miss Daisy Miller was a flirt—a pretty American flirt. He had never, as yet, had any relations with young ladies of this category. He had known, here in Europe, two or three women—persons older than Miss Daisy Miller, and provided, for respectability's sake, with husbands—who were great coquettes—dangerous, terrible women, with whom one's relations were liable to take a serious turn. But this young girl was not a coquette in that sense; she was very unsophisticated; she was only a pretty American flirt. Winterbourne was almost grateful for having found the formula that applied to Miss Daisy Miller. He leaned back in his seat; he remarked to himself that she had the most charming nose he had ever seen; he wondered what were the regular conditions and limitations of one's intercourse with a pretty American flirt. It presently became apparent that he was on the way to learn.

"Have you been to that old castle?" asked the young girl, pointing with her parasol to the far-gleaming walls of the Château de Chillon.

"Yes, formerly, more than once," said Winterbourne. "You too, I suppose, have seen it?"

"No; we haven't been there. I want to go there dreadfully. Of course I mean to go there. I wouldn't go away from here without having seen that old castle."

"It's a very pretty excursion," said Winterbourne, "and very easy to make. You can drive, you know, or you can go by the little steamer."

"You can go in the cars," said Miss Miller.

"Yes; you can go in the cars," Winterbourne assented.

"Our courier says they take you right up to the castle," the young girl continued. "We were going last week; but my mother gave out. She suffers dreadfully from dyspepsia. She said she couldn't go. Randolph wouldn't go either; he says he doesn't think much of old castles. But I guess we'll go this week, if we can get Randolph."

8. Improper behavior.

"Your brother is not interested in ancient monuments?" Winterbourne inquired, smiling.

"He says he don't care much about old castles. He's only nine. He wants to stay at the hotel. Mother's afraid to leave him alone, and the courier won't stay with him; so we haven't been to many places. But it will be too bad if we don't go up there." And Miss Miller pointed again at the Château de Chillon.

"I should think it might be arranged," said Winterbourne. "Couldn't you get some one to stay—for the afternoon—with Randolph?"

Miss Miller looked at him a moment; and then, very placidly—"I wish *you* would stay with him!" she said.

Winterbourne hesitated a moment. "I would much rather go to Chillon with you."

"With me?" asked the young girl, with the same placidity.

She didn't rise, blushing, as a young girl at Geneva would have done; and yet Winterbourne, conscious that he had been very bold, thought it possible she was offended. "With your mother," he answered very respectfully.

But it seemed that both his audacity and his respect were lost upon Miss Daisy Miller. "I guess my mother won't go, after all," she said. "She don't like to ride round in the afternoon. But did you really mean what you said just now; that you would like to go up there?"

"Most earnestly," Winterbourne declared.

"Then we may arrange it. If mother will stay with Randolph, I guess Eugenio will."

"Eugenio?" the young man inquired.

"Eugenio's our courier. He doesn't like to stay with Randolph; he's the most fastidious man I ever saw. But he's a splendid courier. I guess he'll stay at home with Randolph if mother does, and then we can go to the castle."

Winterbourne reflected for an instant as lucidly as possible—"we" could only mean Miss Daisy Miller and himself. This programme seemed almost too agreeable for credence; he felt as if he ought to kiss the young lady's hand. Possibly he would have done so—and quite spoiled the project; but at this moment another person—presumably Eugenio—appeared. A tall, handsome man, with superb whiskers, wearing a velvet morning coat and a brilliant watch-chain, approached Miss Miller, looking sharply at her companion. "Oh, Eugenio!" said Miss Miller, with the friendliest accent.

Eugenio had looked at Winterbourne from head to foot; he now bowed gravely to the young lady. "I have the honour to inform Mademoiselle that luncheon is upon the table."

Miss Miller slowly rose. "See here, Eugenio," she said. "I'm going to that old castle, any way."

"To the Château de Chillon, Mademoiselle?" the courier inquired. "Mademoiselle has made arrangements?" he added, in a tone which struck Winterbourne as very impertinent.

Eugenio's tone apparently threw, even to Miss Miller's own apprehension, a slightly ironical light upon the young girl's situation. She turned to Winterbourne, blushing a little—a very little. "You won't back out?" she said.

"I shall not be happy till we go!" he protested.

"And you are staying in this hotel?" she went on. "And you are really an American?"

The courier stood looking at Winterbourne, offensively. The young man, at least, thought his manner of looking an offence to Miss Miller; it conveyed an imputation that she "picked up" acquaintances. "I shall have the honour of presenting to you a person who will tell you all about me," he said, smiling, and referring to his aunt.

"Oh, well, we'll go some day," said Miss Miller. And she gave him a smile and turned away. She put up her parasol and walked back to the inn beside Eugenio. Winterbourne stood looking after her; and as she moved away, drawing her muslin furbelows over the gravel, said to himself that she had the *tournure*[9] of a princess.

He had, however, engaged to do more than proved feasible in promising to present his aunt, Mrs. Costello, to Miss Daisy Miller. As soon as the former lady had got better of her headache he waited upon her in her apartment; and, after the proper inquiries in regard to her health, he asked her if she had observed, in the hotel, an American family—a mamma, a daughter, and a little boy.

"And a courier?" said Mrs. Costello. "Oh yes, I have observed them. Seen them—heard them—and kept out of their way." Mrs. Costello was a widow with a fortune; a person of much distinction, who frequently intimated that, if she were not so dreadfully liable to sick-headaches, she would probably have left a deeper impress upon her time. She had a long pale face, a high nose, and a great deal of very striking white hair, which she wore in large puffs and *rouleaux*[1] over the top of her head. She had two sons married in New York, and another who was now in Europe. This young man was amusing himself at Homburg,[2] and, though he was on his travels, was rarely perceived to visit any particular city at the moment selected by his mother for her own appearance there. Her nephew, who had come up to Vevey expressly to see her, was therefore more attentive than those who, as she said, were nearer to her. He had imbibed at Geneva the idea that one must always be attentive to one's aunt. Mrs. Costello had not seen him for many years, and she was greatly pleased with him, manifesting her approbation by initiating him into many of the secrets of that social sway which, as she gave him to understand, she exerted in the American capital.[3] She admitted that she was very exclusive; but, if he were acquainted with New York, he would see that one had to be. And her picture of the minutely hierarchical constitution of the society of that city, which she presented to him in many different lights, was, to Winterbourne's imagination, almost oppressively striking.

He immediately perceived, from her tone, that Miss Daisy Miller's place in the social scale was low. "I am afraid you don't approve of them," he said.

"They are very common," Mrs. Costello declared. "They are the sort of Americans that one does one's duty by not—not accepting."

"Ah, you don't accept them?" said the young man.

"I can't, my dear Frederick. I would if I could, but I can't."

"The young girl is very pretty," said Winterbourne, in a moment.

"Of course she's pretty. But she is very common."

9. Figure, bearing.
1. Rolls.
2. Bad Homburg, famous spa and resort near
Frankfurt, Germany.
3. American social "capital," New York.

"I see what you mean, of course," said Winterbourne, after another pause.

"She has that charming look they all have," his aunt resumed. "I can't think where they pick it up; and she dresses in perfection—no, you don't know how well she dresses. I can't think where they get their taste."

"But, my dear aunt, she is not, after all, a Comanche savage."

"She is a young lady," said Mrs. Costello, "who has an intimacy with her mamma's courier!"

"An intimacy with the courier?" the young man demanded.

"Oh, the mother is just as bad! They treat the courier like a familiar friend—like a gentleman. I shouldn't wonder if he dines with them. Very likely they have never seen a man with such good manners, such fine clothes, so like a gentleman. He probably corresponds to the young lady's idea of a count. He sits with them in the garden, in the evening. I think he smokes."

Winterbourne listened with interest to these disclosures; they helped him to make up his mind about Miss Daisy. Evidently she was rather wild. "Well," he said, "I am not a courier, and yet she was very charming to me."

"You had better have said at first," said Mrs. Costello with dignity, "that you had made her acquaintance."

"We simply met in the garden, and we talked a bit."

"*Tout bonnement!*[4] And pray what did you say?"

"I said I should take the liberty of introducing her to my admirable aunt."

"I am much obliged to you."

"It was to guarantee my respectability," said Winterbourne.

"And pray who is to guarantee hers?"

"Ah, you are cruel!" said the young man. "She's a very nice girl."

"You don't say that as if you believed it," Mrs. Costello observed.

"She is completely uncultivated," Winterbourne went on. "But she is wonderfully pretty, and, in short, she is very nice. To prove that I believe it, I am going to take her to the Château de Chillon."

"You two are going off there together? I should say it proved just the contrary. How long had you known her, may I ask, when this interesting project was formed? You haven't been twenty-four hours in the house."

"I had known her half an hour!" said Winterbourne, smiling.

"Dear me!" cried Mrs. Costello. "What a dreadful girl!"

Her nephew was silent for some moments. "You really think, then," he began earnestly, and with a desire for trustworthy information—"you really think that—" But he paused again.

"Think what, sir?" said his aunt.

"That she is the sort of young lady who expects a man—sooner or later—to carry her off?"

"I haven't the least idea what such young ladies expect a man to do. But I really think that you had better not meddle with little American girls that are uncultivated, as you call them. You have lived too long out of the country. You will be sure to make some great mistake. You are too innocent."

4. Very simply!

"My dear aunt, I am not so innocent," said Winterbourne, smiling and curling his moustache.

"You are too guilty, then!"

Winterbourne continued to curl his moustache, meditatively. "You won't let the poor girl know you, then?" he asked at last.

"Is it literally true that she is going to the Château de Chillon with you?"

"I think that she fully intends it."

"Then, my dear Frederick," said Mrs. Costello, "I must decline the honour of her acquaintance. I am an old woman, but I am not too old—thank Heaven—to be shocked!"

"But don't they all do these things—the young girls in America?" Winterbourne inquired.

Mrs. Costello stared a moment. "I should like to see my granddaughters do them!" she declared, grimly.

This seemed to throw some light upon the matter, for Winterbourne remembered to have heard that his pretty cousins in New York were "tremendous flirts." If, therefore, Miss Daisy Miller exceeded the liberal license allowed to these young ladies, it was probable that anything might be expected of her. Winterbourne was impatient to see her again, and he was vexed with himself that, by instinct, he should not appreciate her justly.

Though he was impatient to see her, he hardly knew what he should say to her about his aunt's refusal to become acquainted with her; but he discovered, promptly enough, that with Miss Daisy Miller there was no great need of walking on tiptoe. He found her that evening in the garden, wandering about in the warm starlight, like an indolent sylph, and swinging to and fro the largest fan he had ever beheld. It was ten o'clock. He had dined with his aunt, had been sitting with her since dinner, and had just taken leave of her till the morrow. Miss Daisy Miller seemed very glad to see him; she declared it was the longest evening she had ever passed.

"Have you been all alone?" he asked.

"I have been walking round with mother. But mother gets tired walking round," she answered.

"Has she gone to bed?"

"No; she doesn't like to go to bed," said the young girl. "She doesn't sleep—not three hours. She says she doesn't know how she lives. She's dreadfully nervous. I guess she sleeps more than she thinks. She's gone somewhere after Randolph; she wants to try to get him to go to bed. He doesn't like to go to bed."

"Let us hope she will persuade him," observed Winterbourne.

"She will talk to him all she can; but he doesn't like her to talk to him," said Miss Daisy, opening her fan. "She's going to try to get Eugenio to talk to him. But he isn't afraid of Eugenio. Eugenio's a splendid courier, but he can't make much impression on Randolph! I don't believe he'll go to bed before eleven." It appeared that Randolph's vigil was in fact triumphantly prolonged, for Winterbourne strolled about with the young girl for some time without meeting her mother. "I have been looking round for that lady you want to introduce me to," his companion resumed. "She's your aunt." Then, on Winterbourne's admitting the fact,

and expressing some curiosity as to how she had learned it, she said she
had heard all about Mrs. Costello from the chambermaid. She was very
quiet and very *comme il faut;* she wore white puffs; she spoke to no one,
and she never dined at the *table d'hôte*. Every two days she had a headache. "I think that's a lovely description, headache and all!" said Miss
Daisy, chattering along in her thin, gay voice. "I want to know her ever
so much. I know just what *your* aunt would be; I know I should like her.
She would be very exclusive. I like a lady to be exclusive; I'm dying to be
exclusive myself. Well, we *are* exclusive, mother and I. We don't speak to
every one—or they don't speak to us. I suppose it's about the same thing.
Any way, I shall be ever so glad to know your aunt."

Winterbourne was embarrassed. "She would be most happy," he said;
"but I am afraid those headaches will interfere."

The young girl looked at him through the dusk. "But I suppose she
doesn't have a headache every day," she said, sympathetically.

Winterbourne was silent a moment. "She tells me she does," he answered at last—not knowing what to say.

Miss Daisy Miller stopped and stood looking at him. Her prettiness was
still visible in the darkness; she was opening and closing her enormous
fan. "She doesn't want to know me!" she said, suddenly. "Why don't you
say so? You needn't be afraid. I'm not afraid!" And she gave a little laugh.

Winterbourne fancied there was a tremor in her voice; he was touched,
shocked, mortified by it. "My dear young lady," he protested, "she knows
no one. It's her wretched health."

The young girl walked on a few steps, laughing still. "You needn't be
afraid," she repeated. "Why should she want to know me?" Then she
paused again; she was close to the parapet of the garden, and in front of
her was the starlit lake. There was a vague sheen upon its surface, and in
the distance were dimly-seen mountain forms. Daisy Miller looked out
upon the mysterious prospect, and then she gave another little laugh.
"Gracious! she *is* exclusive!" she said. Winterbourne wondered whether
she was seriously wounded, and for a moment almost wished that her
sense of injury might be such as to make it becoming in him to attempt to
reassure and comfort her. He had a pleasant sense that she would be very
approachable for consolatory purposes. He felt then, for the instant, quite
ready to sacrifice his aunt, conversationally; to admit that she was a
proud, rude woman, and to declare that they needn't mind her. But before he had time to commit himself to this perilous mixture of gallantry
and impiety, the young lady, resuming her walk, gave an exclamation in
quite another tone. "Well; here's mother! I guess she hasn't got Randolph
to go to bed." The figure of a lady appeared, at a distance, very indistinct
in the darkness, and advancing with a slow and wavering movement. Suddenly it seemed to pause.

"Are you sure it is your mother? Can you distinguish her in this thick
dusk?" Winterbourne asked.

"Well!" cried Miss Daisy Miller, with a laugh, "I guess I know my own
mother. And when she has got on my shawl, too! She is always wearing
my things."

The lady in question, ceasing to advance, hovered vaguely about the
spot at which she had checked her steps.

"I am afraid your mother doesn't see you," said Winterbourne. "Or
perhaps," he added—thinking, with Miss Miller, the joke permissible—

"perhaps she feels guilty about your shawl."

"Oh, it's a fearful old thing!" the young girl replied, serenely. "I told her she could wear it. She won't come here, because she sees you."

"Ah, then," said Winterbourne, "I had better leave you."

"Oh, no; come on!" urged Miss Daisy Miller.

"I'm afraid your mother doesn't approve of my walking with you."

Miss Miller gave him a serious glance. "It isn't for me; it's for you—that is, it's for *her*. Well; I don't know who it's for! But mother doesn't like any of my gentlemen friends. She's right down timid. She always makes a fuss if I introduce a gentleman. But I *do* introduce them—almost always. If I didn't introduce my gentlemen friends to mother," the young girl added, in her little soft, flat monotone, "I shouldn't think I was natural."

"To introduce me," said Winterbourne, "you must know my name." And he proceeded to pronounce it.

"Oh dear; I can't say all that!" said his companion, with a laugh. But by this time they had come up to Mrs. Miller, who, as they drew near, walked to the parapet of the garden and leaned upon it, looking intently at the lake and turning her back upon them. "Mother!" said the young girl in a tone of decision. Upon this the elder lady turned round. "Mr. Winterbourne," said Miss Daisy Miller, introducing the young man very frankly and prettily. "Common" she was, as Mrs. Costello had pronounced her; yet it was a wonder to Winterbourne that, with her commonness, she had a singularly delicate grace.

Her mother was a small, spare, light person, with a wandering eye, a very exiguous nose, and a large forehead, decorated with a certain amount of thin, much-frizzled hair. Like her daughter, Mrs. Miller was dressed with extreme elegance: she had enormous diamonds in her ears. So far as Winterbourne could observe, she gave him no greeting—she certainly was not looking at him. Daisy was near her, pulling her shawl straight. "What are you doing, poking round here?" this young lady inquired; but by no means with that harshness of accent which her choice of words may imply.

"I don't know," said her mother, turning towards the lake again.

"I shouldn't think you'd want that shawl!" Daisy exclaimed.

"Well—I do!" her mother answered, with a little laugh.

"Did you get Randolph to go to bed?" asked the young girl.

"No; I couldn't induce him," said Mrs. Miller, very gently. "He wants to talk to the waiter. He likes to talk to that waiter."

"I was telling Mr. Winterbourne," the young girl went on; and to the young man's ear her tone might have indicated that she had been uttering his name all her life.

"Oh yes!" said Winterbourne; "I have the pleasure of knowing your son."

Randolph's mamma was silent; she turned her attention to the lake. But at last she spoke. "Well, I don't see how he lives!"

"Anyhow, it isn't so bad as it was at Dover," said Daisy Miller.

"And what occurred at Dover?" Winterbourne asked.

"He wouldn't go to bed at all. I guess he sat up all night—in the public parlour. He wasn't in bed at twelve o'clock: I know that."

"It was half-past twelve," declared Mrs. Miller, with mild emphasis.

"Does he sleep much during the day?" Winterbourne demanded.

"I guess he doesn't sleep much," Daisy rejoined.

"I wish he would!" said her mother. "It seems as if he couldn't."

"I think he's real tiresome," Daisy pursued.

Then, for some moments, there was silence. "Well, Daisy Miller," said the elder lady, presently, "I shouldn't think you'd want to talk against your own brother!"

"Well, he *is* tiresome, mother," said Daisy, quite without the asperity of a retort.

"He's only nine," urged Mrs. Miller.

"Well, he wouldn't go to that castle," said the young girl. "I'm going there with Mr. Winterbourne."

To this announcement, very placidly made, Daisy's mamma offered no response. Winterbourne took for granted that she deeply disapproved of the projected excursion; but he said to himself that she was a simple, easily-managed person, and that a few deferential protestations would take the edge from her displeasure. "Yes," he began; "your daughter has kindly allowed me the honour of being her guide."

Mrs. Miller's wandering eyes atached themselves, with a sort of appealing air, to Daisy, who, however, strolled a few steps farther, gently humming to herself. "I presume you will go in the cars," said her mother.

"Yes; or in the boat," said Winterbourne.

"Well, of course, I don't know," Mrs. Miller rejoined. "I have never been to that castle."

"It is a pity you shouldn't go," said Winterbourne, beginning to feel reassured as to her opposition. And yet he was quite prepared to find that, as a matter of course, she meant to accompany her daughter.

"We've been thinking ever so much about going," she pursued; "but it seems as if we couldn't. Of course Daisy—she wants to go round. But there's a lady here—I don't know her name—she says she shouldn't think we'd want to go to see castles *here;* she should think we'd want to wait till we got to Italy. It seems as if there would be so many there," continued Mrs. Miller, with an air of increasing confidence. "Of course, we only want to see the principal ones. We visited several in England," she presently added.

"Ah yes! in England there are beautiful castles," said Winterbourne. "But Chillon, here, is very well worth seeing."

"Well, if Daisy feels up to it—" said Mrs. Miller, in a tone impregnated with a sense of the magnitude of the enterprise. "It seems as if there was nothing she wouldn't undertake."

"Oh, I think she'll enjoy it!" Winterbourne declared. And he desired more and more to make it a certainty that he was to have the privilege of a *tête-à-tête* with the young lady, who was still strolling along in front of them, softly vocalising. "You are not disposed, madam," he inquired, "to undertake it yourself?"

Daisy's mother looked at him an instant, askance, and then walked forward in silence. Then—"I guess she had better go alone," she said, simply.

Winterbourne observed to himself that this was a very different type of maternity from that of the vigilant matrons who massed themselves in the forefront of social intercourse in the dark old city at the other end of the lake. But his meditations were interrupted by hearing his name very distinctly pronounced by Mrs. Miller's unprotected daughter.

"Mr. Winterbourne!" murmured Daisy.

"Mademoiselle!" said the young man.

"Don't you want to take me out in a boat?"

"At present?" he asked.

"Of course!" said Daisy.

"Well, Annie Miller!" exclaimed her mother.

"I beg you, madam, to let her go," said Winterbourne, ardently; for he had never yet enjoyed the sensation of guiding through the summer starlight a skiff freighted with a fresh and beautiful young girl.

"I shouldn't think she'd want to," said her mother. "I should think she'd rather go indoors."

"I'm sure Mr. Winterbourne wants to take me," Daisy declared. "He's so awfully devoted!"

"I will row you over to Chillon in the starlight."

"I don't believe it!" said Daisy.

"Well!" ejaculated the elder lady again.

"You haven't spoken to me for half an hour," her daughter went on.

"I have been having some very pleasant conversation with your mother," said Winterbourne.

"Well; I want you to take me out in a boat!" Daisy repeated. They had all stopped, and she had turned round and was looking at Winterbourne. Her face wore a charming smile, her pretty eyes were gleaming, she was swinging her great fan about. No; it's impossible to be prettier than that, thought Winterbourne.

"There are half-a-dozen boats moored at that landing-place," he said, pointing to certain steps which descended from the garden to the lake. "If you will do me the honour to accept my arm, we will go and select one of them."

Daisy stood there smiling; she threw back her head and gave a little light laugh. "I like a gentleman to be formal!" she declared.

"I assure you it's a formal offer."

"I was bound I would make you say something," Daisy went on.

"You see it's not very difficult," said Winterbourne. "But I am afraid you are chaffing me."

"I think not, sir," remarked Mrs. Miller, very gently.

"Do, then, let me give you a row," he said to the young girl.

"It's quite lovely, the way you say that!" cried Daisy.

"It will be still more lovely to do it."

"Yes, it would be lovely!" said Daisy. But she made no movement to accompany him; she only stood there laughing.

"I should think you had better find out what time it is," interposed her mother.

"It is eleven o'clock, madam," said a voice, with a foreign accent, out of the neighboring darkness; and Winterbourne, turning, perceived the florid personage who was in attendance upon the two ladies. He had apparently just approached.

"Oh, Eugenio," said Daisy, "I am going out in a boat!"

Eugenio bowed. "At eleven o'clock, Mademoiselle?"

"I am going with Mr. Winterbourne. This very minute."

"Do tell her she can't," said Mrs. Miller to the courier.

"I think you had better not go out in a boat, Mademoiselle," Eugenio declared.

Winterbourne wished to Heaven this pretty girl were not so familiar with her courier; but he said nothing.

"I suppose you don't think it's proper!" Daisy exclaimed. "Eugenio doesn't think anything's proper."

"I am at your service," said Winterbourne.

"Does Mademoiselle propose to go alone?" asked Eugenio of Mrs. Miller.

"Oh no; with this gentleman!" answered Daisy's mamma.

The courier looked for a moment at Winterbourne—the latter thought he was smiling—and then, solemnly, with a bow, "As Mademoiselle pleases!" he said.

"Oh, I hoped you would make a fuss!" said Daisy. "I don't care to go now."

"I myself shall make a fuss if you don't go," said Winterbourne.

"That's all I want—a little fuss!" And the young girl began to laugh again.

"Mr. Randolph has gone to bed!" the courier announced, frigidly.

"Oh, Daisy; now we can go!" said Mrs. Miller.

Daisy turned away from Winterbourne, looking at him, smiling and fanning herself. "Good-night," she said; "I hope you are disappointed, or disgusted, or something!"

He looked at her, taking the hand she offered him. "I am puzzled," he answered.

"Well; I hope it won't keep you awake!" she said, very smartly; and, under the escort of the privileged Eugenio, the two ladies passed towards the house.

Winterbourne stood looking after them; he was indeed puzzled. He lingered beside the lake for a quarter of an hour, turning over the mystery of the young girl's sudden familiarities and caprices. But the only very definite conclusion he came to was that he should enjoy deucedly "going off" with her somewhere.

Two days afterwards he went off with her to the Castle of Chillon. He waited for her in the large hall of the hotel, where the couriers, the servants, the foreign tourists, were lounging about and staring. It was not the place he would have chosen, but she had appointed it. She came tripping downstairs, buttoning her long gloves, squeezing her folded parasol against her pretty figure, dressed in the perfection of a soberly elegant travelling costume. Winterbourne was a man of imagination and, as our ancestors used to say, of sensibility; as he looked at her dress and, on the great staircase, her little rapid, confiding step, he felt as if there were something romantic going forward. He could have believed he was going to elope with her. He passed out with her among all the idle people that were assembled there; they were all looking at her very hard; she had begun to chatter as soon as she joined him. Winterbourne's preference had been that they should be conveyed to Chillon in a carriage; but she expressed a lively wish to go in the little steamer; she declared that she had a passion for steamboats. There was always such a lovely breeze upon the water, and you saw such lots of people. The sail was not long, but Winterbourne's companion found time to say a great many things. To the young man himself their little excursion was so much of an escapade—an adventure—that, even allowing for her habitual sense of freedom, he had some expectation of seeing her regard it in the same way. But it must be confessed that, in this particular, he was disappointed. Daisy Miller was extremely animated, she was in charming spirits; but she was apparently not at all excited; she was not fluttered; she avoided neither his eyes nor those of any one else; she blushed neither when she looked at him nor when she saw that people were looking at her. People continued to look at her a great deal, and Winterbourne took much satisfaction in his pretty companion's distinguished air. He had been a little afraid that she would talk loud, laugh overmuch, and even, perhaps, desire to move about the boat a good deal. But he quite forgot his fears; he sat smiling, with his eyes upon her face, while, without moving from her place, she delivered herself of a great number of original reflections. It was the most charming garrulity he had ever heard. He had assented to the idea that she was "common"; but was she so, after all, or was he simply getting used to her commonness? Her conversation was chiefly of what metaphysicians term the objective cast; but every now and then it took a subjective turn.

"What on *earth* are you so grave about?" she suddenly demanded, fixing her agreeable eyes upon Winterbourne's.

"Am I grave?" he asked. "I had an idea I was grinning from ear to ear."

"You look as if you were taking me to a funeral. If that's a grin, your ears are very near together."

"Should you like me to dance a hornpipe on the deck?"

"Pray do, and I'll carry round your hat. It will pay the expenses of our journey."

"I never was better pleased in my life," murmured Winterbourne.

She looked at him a moment, and then burst into a little laugh. "I like to make you say those things! You're a queer mixture!"

In the castle, after they had landed, the subjective element decidedly prevailed. Daisy tripped about the vaulted chambers, rustled her skirts in the corkscrew staircases, flirted back with a pretty little cry and a shudder from the edge of the *oubliettes*, and turned a singularly well-shaped ear to everything that Winterbourne told her about the place. But he saw that she cared very little for feudal antiquities, and that the dusky traditions of Chillon made but a slight impression upon her. They had the good fortune to have been able to walk about without other companionship than that of the custodian; and Winterbourne arranged with this functionary that they should not be hurried—that they should linger and pause wherever they chose. The custodian interpreted the bargain generously—Winterbourne, on his side, had been generous—and ended by leaving them quite to themselves. Miss Miller's observations were not remarkable for logical consistency; for anything she wanted to say she was sure to find a pretext. She found a great many pretexts in the rugged embrasures of Chillon for asking Winterbourne sudden questions about himself—his family, his previous history, his tastes, his habits, his intentions—and for supplying information upon corresponding points in her own personality. Of her own tastes, habits, and intentions Miss Miller was prepared to give the most definite, and indeed the most favourable, account.

"Well; I hope you know enough!" she said to her companion, after he had told her the history of the unhappy Bonivard.[5] "I never saw a man that knew so much!" The history of Bonivard had evidently, as they say, gone into one ear and out of the other. But Daisy went on to say that she

---

5. François de Bonivard—or Bonnivard—(c. 1493–1570), a priest who supported the revolt of Geneva against Charles III of Savoy, and who late in life became a Protestant, was imprisoned 1530–1536 in the Castle of Chillon; he is the subject of Byron's poem *The Prisoner of Chillon.*

wished Winterbourne would travel with them and "go round" with them;
they might know something, in that case. "Don't you want to come and
teach Randolph?" she asked. Winterbourne said that nothing could possibly please him so much; but that he had unfortunately other occupations.
"Other occupations? I don't believe it!" said Miss Daisy. "What do you
mean? You are not in business." The young man admitted that he was not
in business; but he had engagements which, even within a day or two,
would force him to go back to Geneva. "Oh, bother!" she said, "I don't
believe it!" and she began to talk about something else. But a few moments later, when he was pointing out to her the pretty design of an
antique fireplace, she broke out irrelevantly, "You don't mean to say you
are going back to Geneva?"

"It is a melancholy fact that I shall have to return to Geneva to-
morrow."

"Well, Mr. Winterbourne," said Daisy; "I think you're horrid!"

"Oh, don't say such dreadful things!" said Winterbourne—"just at the
last."

"The last!" cried the young girl; "I call it the first. I have half a mind
to leave you here and go straight back to the hotel alone." And for the
next ten minutes she did nothing but call him horrid. Poor Winterbourne
was fairly bewildered; no young lady had as yet done him the honour to
be so agitated by the announcement of his movements. His companion,
after this, ceased to pay any attention to the curiosities of Chillon or the
beauties of the lake; she opened fire upon the mysterious charmer in Geneva, whom she appeared to have instantly taken it for granted that he
was hurrying back to see. How did Miss Daisy Miller know that there was
a charmer in Geneva? Winterbourne, who denied the existence of such a
person, was quite unable to discover; and he was divided between amazement at the rapidity of her induction and amusement at the frankness of
her *persiflage*. She seemed to him, in all this, an extraordinary mixture of
innocence and crudity. "Does she never allow you more than three days
at a time?" asked Daisy, ironically. "Doesn't she give you a vacation in
summer? There's no one so hard worked, but they can get leave to go off
somewhere at this season. I suppose, if you stay another day, she'll come
after you in the boat. Do wait over till Friday, and I will go down to the
landing to see her arrive!" Winterbourne began to think he had been
wrong to feel disappointed in the temper in which the young lady had
embarked. If he had missed the personal accent, the personal accent was
now making its appearance. It sounded very distinctly, at last, in her telling him she would stop "teasing" him if he would promise her solemnly
to come down to Rome in the winter.

"That's not a difficult promise to make," said Winterbourne. "My aunt
has taken an apartment in Rome for the winter, and has already asked me
to come and see her."

"I don't want you to come for your aunt," said Daisy; "I want you to
come for me." And this was the only allusion that the young man was
ever to hear her make to his invidious kinswoman. He declared that, at
any rate, he would certainly come. After this Daisy stopped teasing. Winterbourne took a carriage, and they drove back to Vevey in the dusk; the
young girl was very quiet.

In the evening Winterbourne mentioned to Mrs. Costello that he had
spent the afternoon at Chillon with Miss Daisy Miller.

"The Americans—of the courier?" asked this lady.

"Ah, happily," said Winterbourne, "the courier stayed at home."

"She went with you all alone?"

"All alone."

Mrs. Costello sniffed a little at her smelling-bottle. "And that," she exclaimed, "is the young person you wanted me to know!"

II

Winterbourne, who had returned to Geneva the day after his excursion to Chillon, went to Rome towards the end of January. His aunt had been established there for several weeks, and he had received a couple of letters from her. "Those people you were so devoted to last summer at Vevey have turned up here, courier and all," she wrote. "They seem to have made several acquaintances, but the courier continues to be the most *intime*. The young lady, however, is also very intimate with some third-rate Italians, with whom she rackets about in a way that makes much talk. Bring me that pretty novel of Cherbuliez's—'Paule Méré'[6]— and don't come later than the 23rd."

In the natural course of events Winterbourne, on arriving in Rome, would presently have ascertained Mrs. Miller's address at the American banker's, and have gone to pay his compliments to Miss Daisy. "After what happened at Vevey I certainly think I may call upon them," he said to Mrs. Costello.

"If, after what happens—at Vevey and everywhere—you desire to keep up the acquaintance, you are very welcome. Of course a man may know every one. Men are welcome to the privilege!"

"Pray, what is it that happens—here, for instance?" Winterbourne demanded.

"The girl goes about alone with her foreigners. As to what happens farther, you must apply elsewhere for information. She has picked up half-a-dozen of the regular Roman fortune-hunters, and she takes them about to people's houses. When she comes to a party she brings with her a gentleman with a good deal of manner and a wonderful moustache."

"And where is the mother?"

"I haven't the least idea. They are very dreadful people."

Winterbourne meditated a moment. "They are very ignorant—very innocent only. Depend upon it they are not bad."

"They are hopelessly vulgar," said Mrs. Costello. "Whether or no being hopelessly vulgar is being 'bad' is a question for the metaphysicians. They are bad enough to dislike, at any rate; and for this short life that is quite enough."

The news that Daisy Miller was surrounded by a half-a-dozen wonderful moustaches checked Winterbourne's impulse to go straightway to see her. He had perhaps not definitely flattered himself that he had made an ineffaceable impression upon her heart, but he was annoyed at hearing of a state of affairs so little in harmony with an image that had lately flitted in and out of his own meditations; the image of a very pretty girl looking out of an old Roman window and asking herself urgently when Mr. Winterbourne would arrive. If, however, he determined to wait a little before

6. The second (1864) in a long series of novels by Victor Cherbuliez (1829–1899), novelist, art critic, and political writer.

reminding Miss Miller of his claims to her consideration, he went very soon to call upon two or three other friends. One of these friends was an American lady who had spent several winters at Geneva, where she had placed her children at school. She was a very accomplished woman, and she lived in the Via Gregoriana. Winterbourne found her in a little crimson drawing-room, on a third floor; the room was filled with southern sunshine. He had not been there ten minutes when the servant came in, announcing "Madame Mila!" This announcement was presently followed by the entrance of little Randolph Miller, who stopped in the middle of the room and stood staring at Winterbourne. An instant later his pretty sister crossed the threshold; and then, after a considerable interval, Mrs. Miller slowly advanced.

"I know you!" said Randolph.

"I'm sure you know a great many things," exclaimed Winterbourne, taking him by the hand. "How is your education coming on?"

Daisy was exchanging greetings very prettily with her hostess; but when she heard Winterbourne's voice she quickly turned her head. "Well, I declare!" she said.

"I told you I should come, you know," Winterbourne rejoined, smiling.

"Well—I didn't believe it," said Miss Daisy.

"I am much obliged to you," laughed the young man.

"You might have come to see me!" said Daisy.

"I arrived only yesterday."

"I don't believe that!" the young girl declared.

Winterbourne turned with a protesting smile to her mother; but this lady evaded his glance, and seating herself, fixed her eyes upon her son. "We've got a bigger place than this," said Randolph. "It's all gold on the walls."

Mrs. Miller turned uneasily in her chair. "I told you if I were to bring you you would say something!" she murmured.

"I told *you!*" Randolph exclaimed. "I tell *you*, sir!" he added jocosely, giving Winterbourne a thump on the knee. "It *is* bigger, too!"

Daisy had entered upon a lively conversation with her hostess; Winterbourne judged it becoming to address a few words to her mother. "I hope you have been well since we parted at Vevey," he said.

Mrs. Miller now certainly looked at him—at his chin. "Not very well, sir," she answered.

"She's got the dyspepsia," said Randolph. "I've got it too. Father's got it. I've got it worst!"

This announcement, instead of embarrassing Mrs. Miller, seemed to relieve her. "I suffer from the liver," she said. "I think it's this climate; it's less bracing than Schenectady, especially in the winter season. I don't know whether you know we reside at Schenectady. I was saying to Daisy that I certainly hadn't found any one like Dr. Davis, and I didn't believe I should. Oh, at Schenectady, he stands first; they think everything of him. He has so much to do, and yet there was nothing he wouldn't do for me. He said he never saw anything like my dyspepsia, but he was bound to cure it. I'm sure there was nothing he wouldn't try. He was just going to try something new when we came off. Mr. Miller wanted Daisy to see Europe for herself. But I wrote to Mr. Miller that it seems as if I couldn't get on without Dr. Davis. At Schenectady he stands at the very top; and there's a great deal of sickness there, too. It affects my sleep."

Winterbourne had a good deal of pathological gossip with Dr. Davis's patient, during which Daisy chattered unremittingly to her own companion. The young man asked Mrs. Miller how she was pleased with Rome. "Well, I must say I am disappointed," she answered. "We had heard so much about it; I suppose we had heard too much. But we couldn't help that. We had been led to expect something different."

"Ah, wait a little, and you will become very fond of it," said Winterbourne.

"I hate it worse and worse every day!" cried Randolph.

"You are like the infant Hannibal,"[7] said Winterbourne.

"No, I ain't!" Randolph declared, at a venture.

"You are not much like an infant," said his mother. "But we have seen places," she resumed, "that I should put a long way before Rome." And in reply to Winterbourne's interrogation, "There's Zurich," she observed; "I think Zurich is lovely; and we hadn't heard half so much about it."

"The best place we've seen is the City of Richmond!" said Randolph.

"He means the ship," his mother explained. "We crossed in that ship. Randolph had a good time on the City of Richmond."

"It's the best place I've seen," the child repeated. "Only it was turned the wrong way."

"Well, we've got to turn the right way some time," said Mrs. Miller, with a little laugh. Winterbourne expressed the hope that her daughter at least found some gratification in Rome, and she declared that Daisy was quite carried away. "It's on account of the society—the society's splendid. She goes round everywhere; she has made a great number of acquaintances. Of course she goes round more than I do. I must say they have been very sociable; they have taken her right in. And then she knows a great many gentlemen. Oh, she thinks there's nothing like Rome. Of course, it's a great deal pleasanter for a young lady if she knows plenty of gentlemen."

By this time Daisy had turned her attention again to Winterbourne. "I've been telling Mrs. Walker how mean you were!" the young girl announced.

"And what is the evidence you have offered?" asked Winterbourne, rather annoyed at Miss Miller's want of appreciation of the zeal of an admirer who on his way down to Rome had stopped neither at Bologna nor at Florence, simply because of a certain sentimental impatience. He remembered that a cynical compatriot had once told him that American women—the pretty ones, and this gave a largeness to the axiom—were at once the most exacting in the world and the least endowed with a sense of indebtedness.

"Why, you were awfully mean at Vevey," said Daisy. "You wouldn't do anything. You wouldn't stay there when I asked you."

"My dearest young lady," cried Winterbourne, with eloquence, "have I come all the way to Rome to encounter your reproaches?"

"Just hear him say that!" said Daisy to her hostess, giving a twist to a bow on this lady's dress. "Did you ever hear anything so quaint?"

"So quaint, my dear?" murmured Mrs. Walker, in the tone of a partisan of Winterbourne.

7. At the age of nine Hannibal was made by his father to swear enmity to Rome, victor over Carthage in the First Punic War (264–241 B.C.); in the Second Punic War (218–201 B.C.), Hannibal successfully led the Carthaginian army over the Alps to attack Rome.

"Well, I don't know," said Daisy, fingering Mrs. Walker's ribbons. "Mrs. Walker, I want to tell you something."

"Motherr," interposed Randolph, with his rough ends to his words, "I tell you you've got to go. Eugenio'll raise something!"

"I'm not afraid of Eugenio," said Daisy, with a toss of her head. "Look here, Mrs. Walker," she went on, "you know I'm coming to your party."

"I am delighted to hear it."

"I've got a lovely dress."

"I am very sure of that."

"But I want to ask a favour—permission to bring a friend."

"I shall be happy to see any of your friends," said Mrs. Walker, turning with a smile to Mrs. Miller.

"Oh, they are not my friends," answered Daisy's mamma, smiling shyly, in her own fashion. "I never spoke to them!"

"It's an intimate friend of mine—Mr. Giovanelli," said Daisy, without a tremor in her clear little voice, or a shadow on her brilliant little face.

Mrs. Walker was silent a moment, she gave a rapid glance at Winterbourne. "I shall be glad to see Mr. Giovanelli," she then said.

"He's an Italian," Daisy pursued, with the prettiest serenity. "He's a great friend of mine—he's the handsomest man in the world—except Mr. Winterbourne! He knows plenty of Italians, but he wants to know some Americans. He thinks ever so much of Americans. He's tremendously clever. He's perfectly lovely!"

It was settled that this brilliant personage should be brought to Mrs. Walker's party, and then Mrs. Miller prepared to take her leave. "I guess we'll go back to the hotel," she said.

"You may go back to the hotel, mother, but I'm going to take a walk," said Daisy.

"She's going to walk with Mr. Giovanelli," Randolph proclaimed.

"I am going to the Pincio,"[8] said Daisy, smiling.

"Alone, my dear—at this hour?" Mrs. Walker asked. The afternoon was drawing to a close—it was the hour for the throng of carriages and of contemplative pedestrians. "I don't think it's safe, my dear," said Mrs. Walker.

"Neither do I," subjoined Mrs. Miller. "You'll get the fever as sure as you live. Remember what Dr. Davis told you!"

"Give her some medicine before she goes," said Randolph.

The company had risen to its feet; Daisy, still showing her pretty teeth, bent over and kissed her hostess. "Mrs. Walker, you are too perfect," she said. "I'm not going alone; I am going to meet a friend."

"Your friend won't keep you from getting the fever," Mrs. Miller observed.

"Is it Mr. Giovanelli?" asked the hostess.

Winterbourne was watching the young girl; at this question his attention quickened. She stood there smiling and smoothing her bonnet-ribbons; she glanced at Winterbourne. Then, while she glanced and smiled, she answered without a shade of hesitation, "Mr. Giovanelli—the beautiful Giovanelli."

"My dear young friend," said Mrs. Walker, taking her hand, pleadingly, "don't walk off to the Pincio at this hour to meet a beautiful Italian."

8. A park in Rome.

"Well, he speaks English," said Mrs. Miller.

"Gracious me!" Daisy exclaimed, "I don't want to do anything improper. There's an easy way to settle it." She continued to glance at Winterbourne. "The Pincio is only a hundred yards distant, and if Mr. Winterbourne were as polite as he pretends he would offer to walk with me!"

Winterbourne's politeness hastened to affirm itself, and the young girl gave him gracious leave to accompany her. They passed downstairs before her mother, and at the door Winterbourne perceived Mrs. Miller's carriage drawn up, with the ornamental courier whose acquaintance he had made at Vevey seated within. "Good-bye, Eugenio!" cried Daisy, "I'm going to take a walk." The distance from the Via Gregoriana to the beautiful garden at the other end of the Pincian Hill is, in fact, rapidly traversed. As the day was splendid, however, and the concourse of vehicles, walkers, and loungers numerous, the young Americans found their progress much delayed. This fact was highly agreeable to Winterbourne, in spite of his consciousness of his singular situation. The slow-moving, idly-gazing Roman crowd, bestowed much attention upon the extremely pretty young foreign lady who was passing through it upon his arm; and he wondered what on earth had been in Daisy's mind when she proposed to expose herself, unattended, to its appreciation. His own mission, to her sense apparently, was to consign her to the hands of Mr. Giovanelli; but Winterbourne, at once annoyed and gratified, resolved that he would do no such thing.

"Why haven't you been to see me?" asked Daisy. "You can't get out of that."

"I have had the honour of telling you that I have only just stepped out of the train."

"You must have stayed in the train a good while after it stopped!" cried the young girl, with her little laugh. "I suppose you were asleep. You have had time to go to see Mrs. Walker."

"I knew Mrs. Walker——" Winterbourne began to explain.

"I knew where you knew her. You knew her at Geneva. She told me so. Well, you knew me at Vevey. That's just as good. So you ought to have come." She asked him no other question than this; she began to prattle about her own affairs. "We've got splendid rooms at the hotel; Eugenio says they're the best rooms in Rome. We are going to stay all winter—if we don't die of the fever; and I guess we'll stay then. It's a great deal nicer than I thought; I thought it would be fearfully quiet; I was sure it would be awfully poky. I was sure we should be going round all the time with one of those dreadful old men that explain about the pictures and things. But we only had about a week of that, and now I'm enjoying myself. I know ever so many people, and they are all so charming. The society's extremely select. There are all kinds—English, and Germans, and Italians. I think I like the English best. I like their style of conversation. But there are some lovely Americans. I never saw anything so hospitable. There's something or other every day. There's not much dancing; but I must say I never thought dancing was everything. I was always fond of conversation. I guess I shall have plenty at Mrs. Walker's—her rooms are so small." When they had passed the gate of the Pincian Gardens, Miss Miller began to wonder where Mr. Giovanelli might be. "We had better go straight to that place in front," she said, "where you look at the view."

"I certainly shall not help you to find him," Winterbourne declared.
"Then I shall find him without you," said Miss Daisy.
"You certainly won't leave me!" cried Winterbourne.
She burst into her little laugh. "Are you afraid you'll get lost—or run over? But there's Giovanelli, leaning against that tree. He's staring at the women in the carriages: did you ever see anything so cool?"
Winterbourne perceived at some distance a little man standing with folded arms, nursing his cane. He had a handsome face, an artfully-poised hat, a glass in one eye and a nosegay in his button-hole. Winterbourne looked at him a moment and then said, "Do you mean to speak to that man?"
"Do I mean to speak to him? Why, you don't suppose I mean to communicate by signs?"
"Pray understand, then," said Winterbourne, "that I intend to remain with you."
Daisy stopped and looked at him, without a sign of troubled consciousness in her face; with nothing but the presence of her charming eyes and her happy dimples. "Well, she's a cool one!" thought the young man.
"I don't like the way you say that," said Daisy, "It's too imperious."
"I beg your pardon if I say it wrong. The main point is to give you an idea of my meaning."
The young girl looked at him more gravely, but with eyes that were prettier than ever. "I have never allowed a gentleman to dictate to me, or to interfere with anything I do."
"I think you have made a mistake," said Winterbourne. "You should sometimes listen to a gentleman—the right one!"
Daisy began to laugh again. "I do nothing but listen to gentlemen!" she exclaimed. "Tell me if Mr. Giovanelli is the right one?"
The gentleman with the nosegay in his bosom had now perceived our two friends, and was approaching the young girl with obsequious rapidity. He bowed to Winterbourne as well as to the latter's companion; he had a brilliant smile, an intelligent eye; Winterbourne thought him not a bad-looking fellow. But he nevertheless said to Daisy—"No, he's not the right one."
Daisy evidently had a natural talent for performing introductions; she mentioned the name of each of her companions to the other. She strolled along with one of them on each side of her; Mr. Giovanelli, who spoke English very cleverly—Winterbourne afterwards learned that he had practiced the idiom upon a great many American heiresses—addressed her a great deal of very polite nonsense; he was extremely urbane, and the young American, who said nothing, reflected upon that profundity of Italian cleverness which enables people to appear more gracious in proportion as they are more acutely disappointed. Giovanelli, of course, had counted upon something more intimate; he had not bargained for a party of three. But he kept his temper in a manner which suggested far-stretching intentions. Winterbourne flattered himself that he had taken his measure. "He is not a gentleman," said the young American; "he is only a clever imitation of one. He is a music-master or a penny-a-liner,[9] or a third-rate artist. Damn his good looks!" Mr. Giovanelli had certainly a very pretty face; but Winterbourne felt a superior indignation at his own lovely fellow-

9. Hack writer.

countrywoman's not knowing the difference between a spurious gentleman and a real one. Giovanelli chattered and jested and made himself wonderfully agreeable. It was true that if he was an imitation the imitation was very skillful. "Nevertheless," Winterbourne said to himself, "a nice girl ought to know!" And then he came back to the question whether this was in fact a nice girl. Would a nice girl—even allowing for her being a little American flirt—make a rendezvous with a presumably low-lived foreigner? The rendezvous in this case, indeed, had been in broad daylight, and in the most crowded corner of Rome; but was it not impossible to regard the choice of these circumstances as a proof of extreme cynicism? Singular though it may seem, Winterbourne was vexed that the young girl, in joining her *amoroso*,[1] should not appear more impatient of his own company, and he was vexed because of his inclination. It was impossible to regard her as a perfectly well-conducted young lady; she was wanting in a certain indispensable delicacy. It would therefore simplify matters greatly to be able to treat her as the object of one of those sentiments which are called by romancers "lawless passions." That she should seem to wish to get rid of him would help him to think more lightly of her, and to be able to think more lightly of her would make her much less perplexing. But Daisy, on this occasion, continued to present herself as an inscrutable combination of audacity and innocence.

She had been walking some quarter of an hour, attended by her two cavaliers, and responding in a tone of very childish gaiety, as it seemed to Winterbourne, to the pretty speeches of Mr. Giovanelli, when a carriage that had detached itself from the revolving train drew up beside the path. At the same moment Winterbourne perceived that his friend Mrs. Walker—the lady whose house he had lately left—was seated in the vehicle and was beckoning to him. Leaving Miss Miller's side, he hastened to obey her summons. Mrs. Walker was flushed; she wore an excited air. "It is really too dreadful," she said. "That girl must not do this sort of thing. She must not walk here with you two men. Fifty people have noticed her."

Winterbourne raised his eyebrows. "I think it's a pity to make too much fuss about it."

"It's a pity to let the girl ruin herself!"

"She is very innocent," said Winterbourne.

"She's very crazy!" cried Mrs. Walker. "Did you ever see anything so imbecile as her mother? After you had all left me, just now, I could not sit still for thinking of it. It seemed too pitiful, not even to attempt to save her. I ordered the carriage and put on my bonnet, and came here as quickly as possible. Thank heaven I have found you!"

"What do you propose to do with us?" asked Winterbourne, smiling.

"To ask her to get in, to drive her about here for half an hour, so that the world may see she is not running absolutely wild, and then to take her safely home."

"I don't think it's a very happy thought," said Winterbourne; "but you can try."

Mrs. Walker tried. The young man went in pursuit of Miss Miller, who had simply nodded and smiled at his interlocutrix in the carriage and had gone her way with her own companion. Daisy, on learning that Mrs.

1. Lover.

Walker wished to speak to her, retraced her steps with a perfect good grace, and with Mr. Giovanelli at her side. She declared that she was delighted to have a chance to present this gentleman to Mrs. Walker. She immediately achieved the introduction, and declared that she had never in her life seen anything so lovely as Mrs. Walker's carriage-rug.

"I am glad you admire it," said this lady, smiling sweetly. "Will you get in and let me put it over you?"

"Oh no, thank you," said Daisy. "I shall admire it much more as I see you driving round with it."

"Do get in and drive with me," said Mrs. Walker.

"That would be charming, but it's so enchanting just as I am!" and Daisy gave a brilliant glance at the gentlemen on either side of her.

"It may be enchanting, dear child, but it is not the custom here," urged Mrs. Walker, leaning forward in her victoria with her hands devoutly clasped.

"Well, it ought to be, then!" said Daisy. "If I didn't walk I should expire."

"You should walk with your mother, dear," cried the lady from Geneva losing patience.

"With my mother dear!" exclaimed the young girl. Winterbourne saw that she scented interference. "My mother never walked ten steps in her life. And then, you know," she added with a laugh, "I am more than five years old."

"You are old enough to be more reasonable. You are old enough, dear Miss Miller, to be talked about."

Daisy looked at Mrs. Walker, smiling intensely. "Talked about? What do you mean?"

"Come into my carriage and I will tell you."

Daisy turned her quickened glance again from one of the gentlemen beside her to the other. Mr. Giovanelli was bowing to and fro, rubbing down his gloves and laughing very agreeably; Winterbourne thought it a most unpleasant scene. "I don't think I want to know what you mean," said Daisy presently. "I don't think I should like it."

Winterbourne wished that Mrs. Walker would tuck in her carriage-rug and drive away; but this lady did not enjoy being defied, as she afterwards told him. "Should you prefer being thought a very reckless girl?" she demanded.

"Gracious me!" exclaimed Daisy. She looked again at Mr. Giovanelli, then she turned to Winterbourne. There was a little pink flush in her cheek; she was tremendously pretty. "Does Mr. Winterbourne think," she asked slowly, smiling, throwing back her head and glancing at him from head to foot, "that—to save my reputation—I ought to get into the carriage?"

Winterbourne coloured; for an instant he hesitated greatly. It seemed so strange to hear her speak that way of her "reputation." But he himself, in fact, must speak in accordance with gallantry. The finest gallantry, here, was simply to tell her the truth; and the truth, for Winterbourne, as the few indications I have been able to give have made him known to the reader, was that Daisy Miller should take Mrs. Walker's advice. He looked at her exquisite prettiness; and then he said very gently, "I think you should get into the carriage."

Daisy gave a violent laugh. "I never heard anything so stiff! If this is improper, Mrs. Walker," she pursued, "then I am all improper, and you must give me up. Good-bye; I hope you'll have a lovely ride!" and, with Mr. Giovanelli, who made a triumphantly obsequious salute, she turned away.

Mrs. Walker sat looking after her, and there were tears in Mrs. Walker's eyes. "Get in here, sir," she said to Winterbourne, indicating the place beside her. The young man answered that he felt bound to accompany Miss Miller; whereupon Mrs. Walker declared that if he refused her this favour she would never speak to him again. She was evidently in earnest. Winterbourne overtook Daisy and her companion, and offering the young girl his hand, told her that Mrs. Walker had made an imperious claim upon his society. He expected that in answer she would say something rather free, something to commit herself still farther to that "recklessness" from which Mrs. Walker had so charitably endeavoured to dissuade her. But she only shook his hand, hardly looking at him, while Mr. Giovanelli bade him farewell with a too emphatic flourish of the hat.

Winterbourne was not in the best possible humour as he took his seat in Mrs. Walker's victoria. "That was not clever of you," he said candidly, while the vehicle mingled again with the throng of carriages.

"In such a case," his companion answered, "I don't wish to be clever, I wish to be *earnest!*"

"Well, your earnestness has only offended her and put her off."

"It has happened very well," said Mrs. Walker. "If she is so perfectly determined to compromise herself, the sooner one knows it the better; one can act accordingly."

"I suspect she meant no harm," Winterbourne rejoined.

"So I thought a month ago. But she has been going too far."

"What has she been doing?"

"Everything that is not done here. Flirting with any man she could pick up; sitting in corners with mysterious Italians; dancing all the evening with the same partners; receiving visits at eleven o'clock at night. Her mother goes away when visitors come."

"But her brother," said Winterbourne, laughing, "sits up till midnight."

"He must be edified by what he sees. I'm told that at their hotel every one is talking about her, and that a smile goes round among the servants when a gentleman comes and asks for Miss Miller."

"The servants be hanged!" said Winterbourne angrily. "The poor girl's only fault," he presently added, "is that she is very uncultivated."

"She is naturally indelicate," Mrs. Walker declared. "Take that example this morning. How long had you known her at Vevey?"

"A couple of days."

"Fancy, then, her making it a personal matter that you should have left the place!"

Winterbourne was silent for some moments; then he said, "I suspect, Mrs. Walker, that you and I have lived too long at Geneva!" And he added a request that she should inform him with what particular design she had made him enter her carriage.

"I wished to beg you to cease your relations with Miss Miller—not to flirt with her—to give her no farther opportunity to expose herself—to let her alone, in short."

"I'm afraid I can't do that," said Winterbourne. "I like her extremely."

"All the more reason that you shouldn't help her to make a scandal."

"There shall be nothing scandalous in my attentions to her."

"There certainly will be in the way she takes them. But I have said what I had on my conscience," Mrs. Walker pursued. "If you wish to rejoin the young lady I will put you down. Here, by the way, you have a chance."

The carriage was traversing that part of the Pincian Garden which overhangs the wall of Rome and overlooks the beautiful Villa Borghese.[2] It is bordered by a large parapet, near which there are several seats. One of the seats, at a distance, was occupied by a gentleman and a lady, towards whom Mrs. Walker gave a toss of her head. At the same moment these persons rose and walked towards the parapet. Winterbourne had asked the coachman to stop; he now descended from the carriage. His companion looked at him a moment in silence; then, while he raised his hat, she drove majestically away. Winterbourne stood there; he had turned his eyes towards Daisy and her cavalier. They evidently saw no one; they were too deeply occupied with each other. When they reached the low garden wall they stood a moment looking off at the great flat-topped pine clusters of the Villa Borghese; then Giovanelli seated himself familiarly upon the broad ledge of the wall. The western sun in the opposite sky sent out a brilliant shaft through a couple of cloud-bars; whereupon Daisy's companion took her parasol out of her hands and opened it. She came a little nearer, and he held the parasol over her; then, still holding it, he let it rest upon her shoulder, so that both of their heads were hidden from Winterbourne. This young man lingered a moment, then he began to walk. But he walked—not towards the couple with the parasol; towards the residence of his aunt, Mrs. Costello.

He flattered himself on the following day that there was no smiling among the servants when he, at least, asked for Mrs. Miller at her hotel. This lady and her daughter, however, were not at home; and on the next day after, repeating his visit, Winterbourne again had the misfortune not to find them. Mrs. Walker's party took place on the evening of the third day, and in spite of the frigidity of his last interview with the hostess Winterbourne was among the guests. Mrs. Walker was one of those American ladies who, while residing abroad, make a point, in their own phrase, of studying European society; and she had on this occasion collected several specimens of her diversely-born fellow-mortals to serve, as it were, as text-books. When Winterbourne arrived Daisy Miller was not there; but in a few moments he saw her mother come in alone, very shyly and ruefully. Mrs. Miller's hair, above her exposed-looking temples, was more frizzled than ever. As she approached Mrs. Walker Winterbourne also drew near.

"You see I've come all alone," said poor Mrs. Miller. "I'm so frightened; I don't know what to do; it's the first time I've ever been to a party alone—especially in this country. I wanted to bring Randolph or Eugenio, or some one, but Daisy just pushed me off by myself. I ain't used to going round alone."

"And does not your daughter intend to favour us with her society?" demanded Mrs. Walker, impressively.

"Well, Daisy's all dressed," said Mrs. Miller, with that accent of the

2. One of the finest of Italian villas, a palace with gardens; though much of its art had been removed to Paris by the time of the story, it still housed many fine paintings.

dispassionate, if not of the philosophic, historian, with which she always recorded the current incidents of her daughter's career. "She got dressed on purpose before dinner. But she's got a friend of hers there; that gentle-man—the Italian—that she wanted to bring. They've got going at the piano; it seems as if they couldn't leave off. Mr. Giovanelli sings splen-didly. But I guess they'll come before very long," concluded Mrs. Miller hopefully.

"I'm sorry she should come—in that way," said Mrs. Walker.

"Well, I told her that there was no use in her getting dressed before dinner if she was going to wait three hours," responded Daisy's mamma. "I didn't see the use of her putting on such a dress as that to sit round with Mr. Giovanelli."

"This is most horrible!" said Mrs. Walker, turning away and addressing herself to Winterbourne. "*Elle s'affiche.*[3] It's her revenge for my having ventured to remonstrate with her. When she comes I shall not speak to her."

Daisy came after eleven o'clock, but she was not, on such an occasion, a young lady to wait to be spoken to. She rustled forward in radiant love-liness, smiling and chattering, carrying a large bouquet, and attended by Mr. Giovanelli. Every one stopped talking, and turned and looked at her. She came straight to Mrs. Walker. "I'm afraid you thought I never was coming, so I sent mother off to tell you. I wanted to make Mr. Giovanelli practise some things before he came; you know he sings beautifully, and I want you to ask him to sing. This is Mr. Giovanelli; you know I intro-duced him to you; he's got the most lovely voice, and he knows the most charming set of songs. I made him go over them this evening, on purpose; we had the greatest time at the hotel." Of all this Daisy delivered herself with the sweetest, brightest audibleness, looking now at her hostess and now round the room, while she gave a series of little pats, round her shoulders, to the edges of her dress. "Is there any one I know?" she asked.

"I think every one knows you!" said Mrs. Walker, pregnantly, and she gave a very cursory greeting to Mr. Giovanelli. This gentleman bore him-self gallantly. He smiled and bowed, and showed his white teeth, he curled his moustaches and rolled his eyes, and performed all the proper functions of a handsome Italian at an evening party. He sang, very pret-tily, half a dozen songs, though Mrs. Walker afterwards declared that she had been quite unable to find out who asked him. It was apparently not Daisy who had given him his orders. Daisy sat at a distance from the piano, and though she had publicly, as it were, professed a high admira-tion for his singing, talked, not inaudibly, while it was going on.

"It's a pity these rooms are so small; we can't dance," she said to Win-terbourne, as if she had seen him five minutes before.

"I am not sorry we can't dance," Winterbourne answered; "I don't dance."

"Of course you don't dance; you're too stiff," said Miss Daisy. "I hope you enjoyed your drive with Mrs. Walker."

"No, I didn't enjoy it; I prefered walking with you."

"We paired off, that was much better," said Daisy. "But did you ever hear anything so cool as Mrs. Walker's wanting me to get into her car-riage and drop poor Mr. Giovanelli; and under the pretext that it was

3. She's trying to get herself talked about.

proper? People have different ideas! It would have been most unkind; he had been talking about that walk for ten days."

"He should not have talked about it at all," said Winterbourne; "he would never have proposed to a young lady of this country to walk about the streets with him."

"About the streets?" cried Daisy, with her pretty stare. "Where, then, would he have proposed to her to walk? The Pincio is not the streets either; and I, thank goodness, am not a young lady of this country. The young ladies of this country have a dreadfully poky time of it, so far as I can learn; I don't see why I should change my habits for *them.*"

"I am afraid your habits are those of a flirt," said Winterbourne, gravely.

"Of course they are," she cried, giving him her little smiling stare again. "I'm a fearful, frightful flirt! Did you ever hear of a nice girl that was not? But I suppose you will tell me now that I am not a nice girl."

"You're a very nice girl, but I wish you would flirt with me, and me only," said Winterbourne.

"Ah! thank you, thank you very much; you are the last man I should think of flirting with. As I have had the pleasure of informing you, you are too stiff."

"You say that too often," said Winterbourne.

Daisy gave a delighted laugh. "If I could have the sweet hope of making you angry, I would say it again."

"Don't do that; when I am angry I'm stiffer than ever. But if you won't flirt with me, do cease at least to flirt with your friend at the piano; they don't understand that sort of thing here."

"I thought they understood nothing else!" exclaimed Daisy.

"Not in young unmarried women."

"It seems to me much more proper in young unmarried women than in old married ones," Daisy declared.

"Well," said Winterbourne, "when you deal with natives you must go by the custom of the place. Flirting is a purely American custom; it doesn't exist here. So when you show yourself in public with Mr. Giovanelli, and without your mother——"

"Gracious! poor mother!" interposed Daisy.

"Though you may be flirting, Mr. Giovanelli is not; he means something else."

"He isn't preaching, at any rate," said Daisy, with vivacity. "And if you want very much to know, we are neither of us flirting; we are too good friends for that; we are very intimate friends."

"Ah!" rejoined Winterbourne, "if you are in love with each other it is another affair."

She had allowed him up to this point to talk so frankly that he had no expectation of shocking her by this ejaculation; but she immediately got up, blushing visibly, and leaving him to exclaim mentally that little American flirts were the queerest creatures in the world. "Mr. Giovanelli, at least," she said, giving her interlocutor a single glance, "never says such very disagreeable things to me."

Winterbourne was bewildered; he stood staring. Mr. Giovanelli had finished singing; he left the piano and came over to Daisy. "Won't you come into the other room and have some tea?" he asked, bending before her, with his decorative smile.

Daisy turned to Winterbourne, beginning to smile again. He was still more preplexed, for this inconsequent smile made nothing clear, though it seemed to prove, indeed, that she had a sweetness and softness that reverted instinctively to the pardon of offences. "It has never occurred to Mr. Winterbourne to offer me any tea," she said, with her little tormenting manner.

"I have offered you advice," Winterbourne rejoined.

"I prefer weak tea!" cried Daisy, and she went off with the brilliant Giovanelli. She sat with him in the adjoining room, in the embrasure of the window, for the rest of the evening. There was an interesting performance at the piano, but neither of these young people gave heed to it. When Daisy came to take leave of Mrs. Walker, this lady conscientiously repaired the weakness of which she had been guilty at the moment of the young girl's arrival. She turned her back straight upon Miss Miller, and left her to depart with what grace she might. Winterbourne was standing near the door; he saw it all. Daisy turned very pale and looked at her mother, but Mrs. Miller was humbly unconscious of any violation of the usual social forms. She appeared, indeed, to have felt an incongruous impulse to draw attention to her own striking observance of them. "Goodnight, Mrs. Walker," she said; "we've had a beautiful evening. You see if I let Daisy come to parties without me, I don't want her to go away without me." Daisy turned away, looking with a pale grave face at the circle near the door; Winterbourne saw that, for the first moment, she was too much shocked and puzzled even for indignation. He on his side was greatly touched.

"That was very cruel," he said to Mrs. Walker.

"She never enters my drawing-room again," replied his hostess.

Since Winterbourne was not to meet her in Mrs. Walker's drawing-room, he went as often as possible to Mrs. Miller's hotel. The ladies were rarely at home, but when he found them the devoted Giovanelli was always present. Very often the polished little Roman was in the drawing-room with Daisy alone, Mrs. Miller being apparently constantly of the opinion that discretion is the better part of surveillance. Winterbourne noted, at first with surprise, that Daisy on these occasions was never embarrassed or annoyed by his own entrance; but he very presently began to feel that she had no more surprises for him; the unexpected in her behaviour was the only thing to expect. She showed no displeasure at her *tête-à-tête* with Giovanelli being interrupted; she could chatter as freshly and freely with two gentlemen as with one; there was always in her conversation the same odd mixture of audacity and puerility. Winterbourne remarked to himself that, if she was seriously interested in Giovanelli, it was very singular that she should not take more trouble to preserve the sanctity of their interviews, and he liked her the more for her innocent-looking indifference and her apparently inexhaustible good-humour. He could hardly have said why, but she seemed to him a girl who would never be jealous. At the risk of exciting a somewhat derisive smile on the reader's part, I may affirm that, with regard to the women who had hitherto interested him, it very often seemed to Winterbourne among the possibilities that, given certain contingencies, he should be afraid—literally afraid—of these ladies. He had a pleasant sense that he should never be afraid of Daisy Miller. It must be added that this sentiment was not altogether flattering to Daisy; it was part of his conviction, or rather of his apprehension, that she would prove a very light young person.

But she was evidently very much interested in Giovanelli. She looked at him whenever he spoke; she was perpetually telling him to do this and to do that; she was constantly "chaffing" and abusing him. She appeared completely to have forgotten that Winterbourne had said anything to displease her at Mrs. Walker's little party. One Sunday afternoon, having gone to St. Peter's with his aunt, Winterbourne perceived Daisy strolling about the great church in company with the inevitable Giovanelli. Presently he pointed out the young girl and her cavalier to Mrs. Costello. This lady looked at them a moment through her eye-glass, and then she said:

"That's what makes you so pensive in these days, eh?"

"I had not the least idea I was pensive," said the young man.

"You are very much preoccupied, you are thinking of something."

"And what is it," he asked, "that you accuse me of thinking of?"

"Of that young lady's—Miss Baker's, Miss Chandler's—what's her name?—Miss Miller's intrigue with that little barber's block."[4]

"Do you call it an intrigue," Winterbourne asked—"an affair that goes on with such peculiar publicity?"

"That's their folly," said Mrs. Costello, "it's not their merit."

"No," rejoined Winterbourne, with something of that pensiveness to which his aunt had alluded. "I don't believe that there is anything to be called an intrigue."

"I have heard a dozen people speak of it; they say she is quite carried away by him."

"They are certainly very intimate," said Winterbourne.

Mrs. Costello inspected the young couple again with her optical instrument. "He is very handsome. One easily sees how it is. She thinks him the most elegant man in the world, the finest gentleman. She has never seen anything like him; he is better even than the courier. It was the courier, probably, who introduced him, and if he succeeds in marrying the young lady, the courier will come in for a magnificent commission."

"I don't believe she thinks of marrying him," said Winterbourne, "and I don't believe he hopes to marry her."

"You may be very sure she thinks of nothing. She goes on from day to day, from hour to hour, as they did in the Golden Age. I can imagine nothing more vulgar. And at the same time," added Mrs. Costello, "depend upon it that she may tell you any moment that she is 'engaged.'"

"I think that is more than Giovanelli expects," said Winterbourne.

"Who is Giovanelli?"

"The little Italian. I have asked questions about him and learned something. He is apparently a perfectly respectable little man. I believe he is in a small way a *cavaliere avvocato*.[5] But he doesn't move in what are called the first circles. I think it is really not absolutely impossible that the courier introduced him. He is evidently immensely charmed with Miss Miller. If she thinks him the finest gentleman in the world, he, on his side, has never found himself in personal contact with such splendour, such opulence, such expensiveness, as this young lady's. And then she must seem to him wonderfully pretty and interesting. I rather doubt whether he dreams of marrying her. That must appear to him too impos-

---

4. Overdressed man.   5. Gentleman-lawyer.

sible a piece of luck. He has nothing but his handsome face to offer, and there is a substantial Mr. Miller in that mysterious land of dollars. Giovanelli knows that he hasn't a title to offer. If he were only a count or a *marchese!* He must wonder at his luck at the way they have taken him up."

"He accounts for it by his handsome face, and thinks Miss Miller a young lady *qui se passe ses fantaisies!*"[6] said Mrs. Costello.

"It is very true," Winterbourne pursued, "that Daisy and her mamma have not yet risen to that stage of—what shall I call it?—of culture, at which the idea of catching a count or a *marchese* begins. I believe that they are intellectually incapable of that conception."

"Ah! but the *cavaliere* can't believe it," said Mrs. Costello.

Of the observation excited by Daisy's "intrigue," Winterbourne gathered that day at St. Peter's sufficient evidence. A dozen of the American colonists in Rome came to talk with Mrs. Costello, who sat on a little portable stool at the base of one of the great pilasters. The vesper-service was going forward in splendid chants and organ-tones in the adjacent choir, and meanwhile, between Mrs. Costello and her friends, there was a great deal said about poor little Miss Miller's going really "too far." Winterbourne was not pleased with what he heard; but when, coming out upon the great steps of the church, he saw Daisy, who had emerged before him, get into an open cab with her accomplice and roll away through the cynical streets of Rome, he could not deny to himself that she was going very far indeed. He felt very sorry for her—not exactly that he believed that she had completely lost her head, but because it was painful to hear so much that was pretty and undefended and natural assigned to a vulgar place among the categories of disorder. He made an attempt after this to give a hint to Mrs. Miller. He met one day in the Corso a friend—a tourist like himself—who had just come out of the Doria Palace,[7] where he had been walking through the beautiful gallery. His friend talked for a moment about the superb portrait of Innocent X. by Velasquez, which hangs in one of the cabinets of the palace, and then said, "And in the same cabinet, by the way, I had the pleasure of contemplating a picture of a different kind—that pretty American girl whom you pointed out to me last week." In answer to Winterbourne's inquiries, his friend narrated that the pretty American girl—prettier than ever—was seated with a companion in the secluded nook in which the great papal portrait is enshrined.

"Who was her companion?" asked Winterbourne.

"A little Italian with a bouquet in his button-hole. The girl is delightfully pretty, but I thought I understood from you the other day that she was a young lady *du meilleur monde.*"[8]

"So she is!" answered Winterbourne; and having assured himself that his informant had seen Daisy and her companion but five minutes before, he jumped into a cab and went to call on Mrs. Miller. She was at home; but she apologised to him for receiving him in Daisy's absence.

"She's gone out somewhere with Mr. Giovanelli," said Mrs. Miller. "She's always going round with Mr. Giovanelli."

---

6. Who is indulging her whims.
7. The gallery contains many art treasures, including the 1649 portrait of Pope Innocent X by the Spanish painter Diego Rodríguez de Silva y Velás-

quez (1599–1669). The Corso is one of the major streets of Rome.
8. Of the better class of society.

"I have noticed that they are very intimate," Winterbourne observed.
"Oh! it seems as if they couldn't live without each other!" said Mrs.
Miller. "Well, he's a real gentleman, anyhow. I keep telling Daisy she's
engaged!"

"And what does Daisy say?"

"Oh, she says she isn't engaged. But she might as well be!" this impar-
tial parent resumed. "She goes on as if she was. But I've made Mr. Giovanelli promise to tell me, if *she* doesn't. I should want to write to Mr.
Miller about it—shouldn't you?"

Winterbourne replied that he certainly should; and the state of mind of
Daisy's mamma struck him as so unprecedented in the annals of parental
vigilance that he gave up as utterly irrelevant the attempt to place her
upon her guard.

After this Daisy was never at home, and Winterbourne ceased to meet
her at the houses of their common acquaintance, because, as he perceived, these shrewd people had quite made up their minds that she was
going too far. They ceased to invite her, and they intimated that they
desired to express to observant Europeans the great truth that, though
Miss Daisy Miller was a young American lady, her behaviour was not
representative—was regarded by her compatriots as abnormal. Winterbourne wondered how she felt about all the cold shoulders that were
turned towards her, and sometimes it annoyed him to suspect that she did
not feel at all. He said to himself that she was too light and childish, too
uncultivated and unreasoning, too provincial, to have reflected upon her
ostracism, or even to have perceived it. Then at other moments he believed that she carried about in her elegant and irresponsible little organism a defiant, passionate, perfectly observant consciousness of the
impression she produced. He asked himself whether Daisy's defiance
came from the consciousness of innocence or from her being, essentially, a
young person of the reckless class. It must be admitted that holding oneself to a belief in Daisy's "innocence" came to seem to Winterbourne
more and more a matter of fine-spun gallantry. As I have already had
occasion to relate, he was angry at finding himself reduced to chopping
logic about this young lady; he was vexed at his want of instinctive certitude as to how far her eccentricities were generic, national, and how far
they were personal. From either view of them he had somehow missed
her, and now it was too late. She was "carried away" by Mr. Giovanelli.

A few days after his brief interview with her mother, he encountered
her in that beautiful abode of flowering desolation known as the Palace of
the Cæsars. The early Roman spring had filled the air with bloom and
perfume, and the rugged surface of the Palatine[9] was muffled with tender
verdure. Daisy was strolling along the top of one of those great mounds of
ruin that are embanked with mossy marble and paved with monumental
inscriptions. It seemed to him that Rome had never been so lovely as just
then. He stood looking off at the enchanting harmony of line and colour
that remotely encircles the city, inhaling the softly humid odours, and
feeling the freshness of the year and the antiquity of the place reaffirm
themselves in mysterious interfusion. It seemed to him also that Daisy
had never looked so pretty; but this had been an observation of his when-

9. One of the seven hills forming the center of ancient Rome.

ever he met her. Giovanelli was at her side, and Giovanelli too wore an aspect of even unwonted brilliancy.

"Well," said Daisy, "I should think you would be lonesome!"

"Lonesome?" asked Winterbourne.

"You are always going round by yourself. Can't you get any one to walk with you?"

"I am not so fortunate," said Winterbourne, "as your companion."

Giovanelli, from the first, had treated Winterbourne with distinguished politeness; he listened with a deferential air to his remarks; he laughed, punctiliously, at his pleasantries; he seemed disposed to testify to his belief that Winterbourne was a superior young man. He carried himself in no degree like a jealous wooer; he had obviously a great deal of tact; he had no objection to your expecting a little humility of him. It even seemed to Winterbourne at times that Giovanelli would find a certain mental relief in being able to have a private understanding with him—to say to him, as an intelligent man, that, bless you, *he* knew how extraordinary was this young lady, and didn't flatter himself with delusive—or at least *too* delusive—hopes of matrimony and dollars. On this occasion he strolled away from his companion to pluck a sprig of almond-blossom, which he carefully arranged in his button-hole.

"I know why you say that," said Daisy, watching Giovanelli. "Because you think I go round too much with *him!*" And she nodded at her attendant.

"Every one thinks so—if you care to know," said Winterbourne.

"Of course I care to know!" Daisy exclaimed seriously. "But I don't believe it. They are only pretending to be shocked. They don't really care a straw what I do. Besides, I don't go round so much."

"I think you will find they do care. They will show it—disagreeably."

Daisy looked at him a moment. "How disagreeably?"

"Haven't you noticed anything?" Winterbourne asked.

"I have noticed you. But I noticed you were as stiff as an umbrella the first time I saw you."

"You will find I am not so stiff as several others," said Winterborne, smiling.

"How shall I find it?"

"By going to see the others."

"What will they do to me?"

"They will give you the cold shoulder. Do you know what that means?"

Daisy was looking at him intently; she began to colour. "Do you mean as Mrs. Walker did the other night?"

"Exactly!" said Winterbourne.

She looked away at Giovanelli, who was decorating himself with his almond-blossom. Then looking back at Winterbourne—"I shouldn't think you would let people be so unkind!" she said.

"How can I help it?" he asked.

"I should think you would say something."

"I do say something;" and he paused a moment. "I say that your mother tells me that she believes you are engaged."

"Well, she does," said Daisy, very simply.

Winterbourne began to laugh. "And does Randolph believe it?" he asked.

"I guess Randolph doesn't believe anything," said Daisy. Randolph's scepticism excited Winterbourne to further hilarity, and he observed that Giovanelli was coming back to them. Daisy, observing it too, addressed herself again to her countryman. "Since you have mentioned it," she said, "I *am* engaged." . . . Winterbourne looked at her; he had stopped laughing. "You don't believe it!" she added.

He was silent a moment; and then, "Yes, I believe it!" he said.

"Oh no, you don't," she answered. "Well, then—I am not!"

The young girl and her cicerone were on their way to the gate of the enclosure, so that Winterbourne, who had but lately entered, presently took leave of them. A week afterwards he went to dine at a beautiful villa on the Cælian Hill, and, on arriving, dismissed his hired vehicle. The evening was charming, and he promised himself the satisfaction of walking home beneath the Arch of Constantine[1] and past the vaguely-lighted monuments of the Forum. There was a waning moon in the sky, and her radiance was not brilliant, but she was veiled in a thin cloud-curtain which seemed to diffuse and equalise it. When, on his return from the villa (it was eleven o'clock), Winterbourne approached the dusky circle of the Colosseum, it occurred to him, as a lover of the picturesque, that the interior, in the pale moonshine, would be well worth a glance. He turned aside and walked to one of the empty arches, near which, as he observed, an open carriage—one of the little Roman street cabs—was stationed. Then he passed in among the cavernous shadows of the great structure, and emerged upon the clear and silent arena. The place had never seemed to him more impressive. One-half of the gigantic circus[2] was in deep shade; the other was sleeping in the luminous dusk. As he stood there he began to murmur Byron's famous lines, out of "Manfred";[3] but before he had finished his quotation he remembered that if nocturnal meditations in the Colosseum are recommended by the poets, they are deprecated by the doctors. The historic atmosphere was there, certainly; but the historic atmosphere, scientifically considered, was no better than a villainous miasma. Winterbourne walked to the middle of the arena, to take a more general glance, intending thereafter to make a hasty retreat. The great cross in the centre was covered with shadow; it was only as he drew near it that he made it out distinctly. Then he saw that two persons were stationed upon the low steps which formed its base. One of these was a woman, seated; her companion was standing in front of her.

Presently the sound of the woman's voice came to him distinctly in the warm night air. "Well, he looks at us as one of the old lions or tigers may have looked at the Christian martyrs!" These were the words he heard, in the familiar accent of Miss Daisy Miller.

"Let us hope he is not very hungry," responded the ingenious Giovanelli. "He will have to take me first; you will serve for dessert!"

Winterbourne stopped, with a sort of horror; and, it must be added, with a sort of relief. It was as if a sudden illumination had been flashed upon the ambiguity of Daisy's behavior and the riddle had become easy to read. She was a young lady whom a gentleman need no longer be at

1. Triumphal arch erected about A.D. 315 honoring Constantine I's victory in 312 over Maxentius in the struggle for control of Rome. The Cælian is one of the seven hills. The Forum, now in ruins, was the marketplace and public area of ancient Rome.

2. Arena.
3. *Manfred* III, iv, 10–41, "I stood within the Coliseum's wall;/ 'Midst the chief relics of almighty Rome;/ The trees which grew along the broken arches/ Waved dark in the blue midnight . . ." etc.

pains to respect. He stood there looking at her—looking at her companion, and not reflecting that though he saw them vaguely, he himself must have been more brightly visible. He felt angry with himself that he had bothered so much about the right way of regarding Miss Daisy Miller. Then, as he was going to advance again, he checked himself; not from the fear that he was doing her injustice, but from a sense of the danger of appearing unbecomingly exhilarated by this sudden revulsion from cautious criticism. He turned away towards the entrance of the place; but as he did so he heard Daisy speak again.

"Why, it was Mr. Winterbourne! He saw me—and he cuts me!"

What a clever little reprobate she was, and how smartly she played an injured innocence! But he wouldn't cut her. Winterbourne came forward again, and went towards the great cross. Daisy had got up; Giovanelli lifted his hat. Winterbourne had now begun to think simply of the craziness, from a sanitary point of view, of a delicate young girl lounging away the evening in this nest of malaria. What if she *were* a clever little reprobate? that was no reason for her dying of the *perniciosa*.[4] "How long have you been here?" he asked, almost brutally.

Daisy, lovely in the flattering moonlight, looked at him a moment. Then—"All the evening," she answered gently. . . . "I never saw anything so pretty."

"I am afraid," said Winterbourne, "that you will not think Roman fever very pretty. This is the way people catch it. I wonder," he added, turning to Giovanelli, "that you, a native Roman, should countenance such a terrible indiscretion."

"Ah," said the handsome native, "for myself, I am not afraid."

"Neither am I—for you! I am speaking for this young lady."

Giovanelli lifted his well-shaped eyebrows and showed his brilliant teeth. But he took Winterbourne's rebuke with docility. "I told the Signorina it was a grave indiscretion; but when was the Signorina ever prudent?"

"I never was sick, and I don't mean to be!" the Signorina declared. "I don't look like much, but I'm healthy! I was bound to see the Colosseum by moonlight; I shouldn't have wanted to go home without that; and we have had the most beautiful time, haven't we, Mr. Giovanelli? If there has been any danger, Eugenio can give me some pills. He has got some splendid pills."

"I should advise you," said Winterbourne, "to drive home as fast as possible and take one!"

"What you say is very wise," Giovanelli rejoined. "I will go and make sure the carriage is at hand." And he went forward rapidly.

Daisy followed with Winterbourne. He kept looking at her; she seemed not in the least embarrassed. Winterbourne said nothing; Daisy chattered about the beauty of the place. "Well, I *have* seen the Colosseum by moonlight!" she exclaimed. "That's one good thing." Then, noticing Winterbourne's silence, she asked him why he didn't speak. He made no answer; he only began to laugh. They passed under one of the dark archways; Giovanelli was in front with the carriage. Here Daisy stopped a moment, looking at the young American. "*Did* you believe I was engaged the other day?" she asked.

4. Pernicious fever, malaria.

"It doesn't matter what I believed the other day," said Winterbourne, still laughing.

"Well, what do you believe now?"

"I believe that it makes very little difference whether you are engaged or not!"

He felt the young girl's pretty eyes fixed upon him through the thick gloom of the archway; she was apparently going to answer. But Giovanelli hurried her forward. "Quick, quick," he said; "if we get in by midnight we are quite safe."

Daisy took her seat in the carriage, and the fortunate Italian placed himself beside her. "Don't forget Eugenio's pills!" said Winterbourne, as he lifted his hat.

"I don't care," said Daisy, in a little strange tone, "whether I have Roman fever or not!" Upon this the cab-driver cracked his whip, and they rolled away over the desultory patches of the antique pavement.

Winterbourne—to do him justice, as it were—mentioned to no one that he had encountered Miss Miller, at midnight, in the Colosseum with a gentleman; but nevertheless, a couple of days later, the fact of her having been there under these circumstances was known to every member of the little American circle, and commented accordingly. Winterbourne reflected that they had of course known it at the hotel, and that, after Daisy's return, there had been an exchange of jokes between the porter and the cab-driver. But the young man was conscious, at the same moment, that it had ceased to be a matter of serious regret to him that the little American flirt should be "talked about" by low-minded menials. These people, a day or two later, had serious information to give: the little American flirt was alarmingly ill. Winterbourne, when the rumour came to him, immediately went to the hotel for more news. He found that two or three charitable friends had preceded him, and that they were being entertained in Mrs. Miller's salon by Randolph.

"It's going round at night," said Randolph—"that's what made her sick. She's always going round at night. I shouldn't think she'd want to—it's so plaguey dark. You can't see anything here at night, except when there's a moon. In America there's always a moon!" Mrs. Miller was invisible: she was now, at least, giving her daughter the advantage of her society. It was evident that Daisy was dangerously ill.

Winterbourne went often to ask for news of her, and once he saw Mrs. Miller, who, though deeply alarmed, was—rather to his surprise—perfectly composed, and, as it appeared, a most efficient and judicious nurse. She talked a good deal about Dr. Davis, but Winterbourne paid her the compliment of saying to himself that she was not, after all, such a monstrous goose. "Daisy spoke of you the other day," she said to him. "Half the time she doesn't know what she's saying, but that time I think she did. She gave me a message; she told me to tell you. She told me to tell you that she never was engaged to that handsome Italian. I am sure I am very glad; Mr. Giovanelli hasn't been near us since she was taken ill. I thought he was so much of a gentleman; but I don't call that very polite! A lady told me that he was afraid I was angry with him for taking Daisy round at night. Well, so I am; but I suppose he knows I'm a lady. I would scorn to scold him. Any way, she says she's not engaged. I don't know why she wanted you to know; but she said to me three times—'Mind you tell Mr. Winterbourne.' And then she told me to ask if you remembered the time you went to that castle, in Switzerland. But I said I wouldn't give any such messages as that. Only, if she is not engaged, I'm sure I'm glad to know it."

But, as Winterbourne had said, it mattered very little. A week after this the poor girl died; it had been a terrible case of the fever. Daisy's grave was in the little Protestant cemetery, in an angle of the wall of imperial Rome, beneath the cypresses and the thick spring flowers. Winterbourne stood there beside it, with a number of other mourners; a number larger than the scandal excited by the young lady's career would have led you to expect. Near him stood Giovanelli, who came nearer still before Winterbourne turned away. Giovanelli was very pale; on this occasion he had no flower in his button-hole; he seemed to wish to say something. At last he said, "She was the most beautiful young lady I ever saw, and the most amiable." And then he added in a moment, "And she was the most innocent."

Winterbourne looked at him, and presently repeated his words, "And the most innocent?"

"The most innocent!"

Winterbourne felt sore and angry. "Why the devil," he asked, "did you take her to that fatal place?"

Mr. Giovanelli's urbanity was apparently imperturbable. He looked on the ground a moment, and then he said, "For myself, I had no fear; and she wanted to go."

"That was no reason!" Winterbourne declared.

The subtle Roman again dropped his eyes. "If she had lived, I should have got nothing. She would never have married me, I am sure."

"She would never have married you?"

"For a moment I hoped so. But no. I am sure."

Winterbourne listened to him; he stood staring at the raw protuberance among the April daisies. When he turned away again Mr. Giovanelli, with his light slow step, had retired.

Winterbourne almost immediately left Rome; but the following summer he again met his aunt, Mrs. Costello, at Vevey. Mrs. Costello was fond of Vevey. In the interval Winterbourne had often thought of Daisy Miller and her mystifying manners. One day he spoke of her to his aunt—said it was on his conscience that he had done her injustice.

"I am sure I don't know," said Mrs. Costello. "How did your injustice affect her?"

"She sent me a message before her death which I didn't understand at the time. But I have understood it since. She would have appreciated one's esteem."

"Is that a modest way," asked Mrs. Costello, "of saying that she would have reciprocated one's affection?"

Winterbourne offered no answer to this question; but he presently said, "You were right in that remark that you made last summer. I was booked to make a mistake. I have lived too long in foreign parts."

Nevertheless, he went back to live at Geneva, whence there continue to come the most contradictory accounts of his motives of sojourn: a report that he is "studying" hard—an intimation that he is much interested in a very clever foreign lady.

1878

AFTERWORD

For a short while *Daisy Miller* promises to be a sophisticated social novel, perhaps a comedy of manners, about Americans in Europe in the mid-1870s. There is a reasonably witty, somewhat cynical first-person narrator on-stage in the second paragraph who seems to know a great deal about the scene and about a certain young American—what his friends say about him, what others say; that he lives in Geneva, has some sort of attachment there and is satisfied, and that at the moment his aunt has (as she often does) a headache. But the narrator does not know quite everything: he is not entirely sure ("I hardly know") of the young man's thoughts. The first-person narrator soon withdraws, leaving us with Winterbourne, the young American, as the center of consciousness in the story, the one through whose eyes and mind we will see and interpret what is to happen. A boy appears, engaging Winterbourne in conversation. Soon his older sister appears, a beautiful American girl. Boy-meets-girl: the "real story" now seems underway.

There are those who say that in novels such as *Daisy Miller* Henry James invented the American Girl, especially the American-Girl-in-Europe. She is (or was) fresher and freer than her European counterpart, or, indeed, than her more "European-like" mother and grandmothers who took their manners and mores from the old country. She thus raises for both Europeans and more conventional Americans certain questions: What are these young girls really like? Independent in words and actions, unchaperoned, are they careless of conventions because of their innocence? Or is their freedom license: are they immoral as well as unconventional? If innocent, are they not in danger of being misunderstood, looked down upon, laughed at, victimized by the more worldly Europeans? These are the questions Winterbourne must ask himself, and since he is the center of consciousness for the rest of the novel, these are also the questions we ask. In this way are our curiosity and suspense aroused and maintained until the very end of the story.

This concern over sexual behavior, especially a woman's sexual behavior, is not necessarily evidence of a kind of prurience on Henry James's part, but rather was part of the contemporary social and moral code, a way of measuring the moral nature of the culture. The "world"—that is, the English-speaking world, which was then the most powerful portion—was then literally and figuratively "Victorian": Victoria had been queen for more than a third of a century. There have been several moral and sexual revolutions in the century that has passed since then, and the kinds of questions Winterbourne and his society upset themselves over may seem rather quaint nowadays, but there are underlying questions that still remain relevant. Where is the line between freedom and license, salutary restraint and tyranny? What can we really learn about others from appearances?

Because this questioning, this curiosity, this lust to know the truth about others is so prevalent in his work, Henry James is sometimes described as an eavesdropper—or even a voyeur—trying, for whatever reason, to live through other people, trying to learn about their lives because he has none of his own. But isn't this interest in others, in knowing what other people are like and how the world looks to them, central to our understanding of ourselves and to the world around us? And isn't it in large measure what literature is almost always about, and one of the chief reasons we read fiction—or look at pictures or films or listen to music or talk at cocktail parties, for that matter? So while "What is Daisy Miller really like?" is the question that drives—or nudges—our interest forward in the "detective" love story, it also pushes us into more profound cultural, moral, and psychological, not to mention literary, questions.

We are never allowed to forget in this "boy-meets-girl" story that the girl is an *American* girl (though we are, interestingly enough, sometimes likely to think that the "boy" is more European than American). The superiority of all things American is a major subject in the first scene, the first bit of dialogue between Winterbourne and Daisy's precocious and patriotic little brother. The Miller family, we soon learn, is typical, almost stereotypical, of one kind of late nineteenth-century American tourist: those with "new," post–Civil War money, for the most part industrially earned, from what might then be considered the American West (that is, any section not on the narrow strand of the Eastern seaboard). Just as Daisy is a "new breed" of American girl, so this family is a new breed of American traveler in Europe—people like these did not tour Europe before the Civil War. Typically enough, too, the father of the family is not touring. He is home in Schenectady making still more of the money that permits his family to travel like their betters, and making it in the rather vulgar way of manufacturing useful objects. The mother is uneducated, obtuse, rather silly, and useless as a chaperone (if it ever dawned on her to act as chaperone). The girl is, as all American girls are, lovely, more gentle and genteel than her mother, more intelligent apparently, but, also apparently, very naïve. She is also spoiled, used to her own way—or is this just to say "free"? Her little brother is spoiled and forward and precocious, a little rude and bratty, but bright and in his way charming.

Winterbourne, our interpreter, is also an American, but a European resident. Daisy at first thinks he might even be a German. She finds him, for better and worse, stiff, formal, most un-American. Having lost touch with American—particularly new American—ways, Winterbourne has as much difficulty "reading" or understanding Daisy as would a true European. Moreover, Winterbourne is from New York—coastal, genteel America. His money, such as it is, no matter how it may have been originally made, we can be sure is "old." Eastern, Anglo-Saxon Americans in those days (and to some extent still?) looked to Europe and England in particular for their social and cultural models. Southern Europe—Latin, Catholic, old, old Europe, honored for its rich history and art, envied for its sensuous weather and flora—was considered as morally decadent as its ancient ruins. Northern Europe—Anglo-Saxon, Protestant, rich, cultured, established, civilized, and honorable—was the genteel American's heaven.

These views are, of course, merely stereotypes, and stereotypes have a bad reputation—deservedly so if all we know or want to know about people ends with pigeonholing them: man/woman, American/European, black/white, old/young, Catholic/Protestant. But, paradoxically, knowing people as individuals often involves first putting them in such a category *and then distinguishing them from other members of the category*. Stereotypes are, after all, only the biggest and coarsest of signs, and if we are going to have to read through appearances—words, gestures, actions, parentage, nationality, milieu—it makes sense to begin with the biggest sign or category, the stereotype, and begin discriminating more and more finely from there. This is what James will do.

Because this story is to a considerable degree about reading signs, we must be alert to those within the story. One such set of signs is that of the settings, the geography of the action. The novel opens in Vevey, described as having become virtually an American social resort, like the fashionable Newport in Rhode Island and Saratoga in New York State. It is into this rather elite society that the Millers "intrude." Visible from Vevey is the Castle of Chillon where centuries before an heroic antiauthoritarian cleric was imprisoned. That hero later became a Protestant, and so for some serves as a symbol of freedom from the tyranny of both church and state. He was commemorated in the early nineteenth century by Lord Byron, noted libertarian, libertine, and Romantic poet. The signs or signals of Vevey here at the very beginning of the novel thus are somewhat mixed, on the borderland between Catholicism and Protestantism, heroism and immorality, rigor and Romanticism.

Offstage is Geneva, where Winterbourne lives: the site of the Calvinist Reformation, it is associated with the most Protestant of Protestantism—the most rigorous intellectually and morally. Northeastern America was largely founded by such Protestants, from within and without the Anglican (or Episcopalian) church. The "Eastern Establishment," genteel America in the late nineteenth century more or less identified with what was seen as the stricter morality and more ethical conduct of that religious orientation when compared to what was seen as the more lax and worldly Catholicism. Winterbourne, whatever his relationship to the older foreign lady, is—in his social standing and demeanor, his stiffness, formality, social and moral values—both a fitting representative of Establishment America and a resident of Calvinist Geneva.

But Geneva remains offstage. The novel's second long chapter (these two chapters are in some editions subdivided) is set in Rome, seat not only of the Roman Catholic church (stereotypically more experienced, worldly, jaded, decadent than the Protestant), but also the site of a great pre-Christian civilization with its long-past days of great power and glory and its long decline and fall into decadence and self-indulgence. The reader of signs, of stereotypes, finds that the settings heighten suspense. Vevey, ambivalently Protestant, moral and Romantic, is only vaguely threatening, just as Eugenio, the Italian guide, does not seem a terribly dangerous threat to Daisy's innocence. Daisy, at worst, is just being blindly indiscreet to let an underling even appear to be on an equal footing; it's enough to cause talk and shaking of heads in the conventional society of Winterbourne's aunt, nothing more. But Winterbourne and we never really take seriously the possibility that Daisy is having an affair with him, do we? In the second half of the story, however, a still (to our eyes) more unworthy and unsuitable suitor, Mr. Giovanelli—so Roman as to be almost sinister— appears. Daisy is equally indiscreet and incomparably more compromised. Even she recognizes that there might be a question of marriage—or something— involved. What is she up to?

Daisy Miller is both an early James novel and a rather short one—just over 25,000 words—and the changes rung on the central question of Daisy's guilt or innocence, vulgarity or freshness (is Annie P. or Daisy the more appropriate name for her?) are not inordinately complex. Later in his career James will leave us more uncertain than he does in *Daisy Miller* (is there any reason to doubt here Mr. Giovanelli's affirmation of Daisy's purity and her love for Winterbourne?). There will be times, too, later in his career, when the national stereotypes will not be so evident or flattering to us. It will be we Americans who, for all our naïveté, are shrewder, less bound by convention than our counterparts in Europe, more able to exploit them. We don't always play by the rules of cricket; poker is our game. Later, too, James will learn to twist and twist again the central interpretive question of character, sometimes to the extent of a very long novel like *The Golden Bowl,* which nonetheless has at its heart not much more of a sophisticated question than does *Daisy Miller* but requires a very much more complex and sophisticated journey in reading, un-reading, rereading, and revising our reading of signs.

So on the one hand, James's questions are as simple as those of short stories: they are, one would think, capable of a yes or no answer, and that rather quickly, and so would not take up very much narrative space; but on the other, getting to that answer means seeing more and more and interpreting what we see at each stage, rigging and unrigging hypotheses—yes, no, maybe—with all the complexity of a full-length novel. Perhaps for that reason—simple ques-tions, complex and tentative answers—James's concerns are very well suited to the intermediate form of the short novel.

Though this collection begins with *Daisy Miller* because the novels are ar-ranged chronologically, it is also a good novel to begin with because of its short-story-like simple center and its novel-like complications, moral, psycho-logical, and social. We can follow it through, watching twist after twist; we can read it both for its narrative interest and its exploration of morality and con-ventions and ask of it such questions as "Why in its narrative and thematic logic does Daisy die?" We can also read it as a study of how the observing mind interprets—suggesting not only the role of stereotypes but of self-inter-est: To what degree does Winterbourne love Daisy? To what extent is his dis-trust of her merely his way of avoiding commitment, of refusing to acknowledge either that she cares for him or that she is capable of or worthy of being taken seriously as a beloved, a subject for a deep and permanent rela-tionship? Is Daisy, finally, the subject or the object of the story?

LEO TOLSTOY

The Death of Iván Ilyich

If there is a "Shakespeare of the Novel," Tolstoy (1828–1910) would be a leading candidate for the title (which would have its own irony, since Tolstoy denied Shakespeare the supreme place in letters most people award him). One might argue whether his vast epic of a novel *War and Peace* (1863–1869) or the more compact (if still lengthy) *Anna Karénina* (1873–1876) is the pinnacle of his career, whether *The Death of Iván Ilyich* (1886) or *The Kreutzer Sonata* (1890) or even *Hadji Murad* (1896–1904) is the greatest of his short novels, but few would want to deny that such works, along with his other novels, short novels, and short stories, constitute a body of fiction of the first magnitude.

No life can "explain" such an accomplishment, but the life of Lyev Nikolayevich Tolstoy does itself read like a novel. Born into a noble family, orphaned before he was ten, studying first Oriental languages and then law at the University of Kazan but taking degrees in neither, Tolstoy settled on the family estate at Yásnaya Polyána, where he tried to improve the lot of his family's serfs—only to be rebuffed, in part by their suspicions. He served in the army in the Caucasian campaign and then around Sevastopol in the early 1850s, returning to Yásnaya Polyána to organize a school and to marry. After writing his two major long novels, the spoiled aristocrat, soldier, famous writer, found, as he tells us in *A Confession* (1884), that his life was "absurd . . . a stupid and spiteful joke," that he saw before him only death. He was "converted," first to the Russian Orthodox church, then along a winding path of theological study toward a "primitive" Christianity like that which he imagined to be the faith of the Russian peasant. He opposed the military, capital punishment, pogroms (massacres, especially of Jews); he gave up alcohol, meat, and as much of his property, including copyrights of his later works, as his family would permit (his wife tried to have him declared incompetent). In 1910 he fled from home intending to enter a monastery but died in the railway station at Astápovo.

Much earlier, in 1859, four years before he himself was married, Tolstoy wrote a story called *Family Happiness* that foreshadows many of the great later scenes of happy marriage in *War and Peace* and *Anna Karénina* which we would otherwise attribute wholly to his own experience of marriage. There are scenes too in *War and Peace* which seem to "predict" what later happened to Tolstoy. Though he wrote about Iván Ilyich's crisis after having gone through his own, Iván's death "predicts" Tolstoy's. As he lay dying at Astápovo, he repeated in his delirium, "I do not understand what it is I have to do."

The Death of Iván Ilyich *

I

D
URING AN INTERVAL in the Melvínski trial in the large building of the Law Courts the members and public prosecutor met in Iván Egórovich Shébek's private room, where the conversation turned on the celebrated Krasóvski case. Fëdor Vasílievich warmly maintained that it was not subject to their jurisdiction, Iván Egórovich maintained the contrary, while Peter Ivánovich, not having entered into the discussion at the start, took no part in it but looked through the *Gazette* which had just been handed in.

"Gentlemen," he said, "Iván Ilyich has died!"

"You don't say!"

"Here, read it yourself," replied Peter Ivánovich, handing Fëdor Vasílievich the paper still damp from the press. Surrounded by a black border were the words: "Praskóvya Fëdorovna Goloviná,[1] with profound sorrow, informs relatives and friends of the demise of her beloved husband Iván Ilyich Golovín, Member of the Court of Justice, which occurred on February the 4th of this year 1882. The funeral will take place on Friday at one o'clock in the afternoon."

Iván Ilyich had been a colleague of the gentlemen present and was liked by them all. He had been ill for some weeks with an illness said to be incurable. His post had been kept open for him, but there had been conjectures that in case of his death Alexéev might receive his appointment, and that either Vínnikov or Shtábel would succeed Alexéev. So on receiving the news of Iván Ilyich's death the first thought of each of the gentlemen in that private room was of the changes and promotions it might occasion among themselves or their acquaintances.

"I shall be sure to get Shtábel's place or Vínnikov's," thought Fëdor Vasílievich. "I was promised that long ago, and the promotion means an extra eight hundred rubles[2] a year for me besides the allowance."

"Now I must apply for my brother-in-law's transfer from Kalúga,"[3] thought Peter Ivánovich. "My wife will be very glad, and then she won't be able to say that I never do anything for her relations."

"I thought he would never leave his bed again," said Peter Ivánovich aloud. "It's very sad."

"But what really was the matter with him?"

"The doctors couldn't say—at least they could, but each of them said something different. When last I saw him I thought he was getting better."

"And I haven't been to see him since the holidays. I always meant to go."

"Had he any property?"

---

* Translated by Louise and Aylmer Maude.
1. Many Russian family names have masculine and feminine endings, so that Iván's name is *Golovín*, his wife's *Goloviná*. Russian "middle" names are patronymics—the father's name plus an ending that means "son of" or "daughter of": *Fëdorovna* = daughter of Fëdor; *Ilyich* = son of Ilya.

2. A ruble was then roughly equivalent to a dollar, though its modern purchasing power is difficult to calculate: perhaps four or five dollars per ruble is close enough.
3. City about one hundred miles southwest of Moscow.

"I think his wife had a little—but something quite trifling."

"We shall have to go to see her, but they live so terribly far away."

"Far away from you, you mean. Everything's far away from your place." "You see, he never can forgive my living on the other side of the river," said Peter Ivánovich, smiling at Shébek. Then, still talking of the distances between different parts of the city, they returned to the Court.

Besides considerations as to the possible transfers and promotions likely to result from Iván Ilyich's death, the mere fact of the death of a near acquaintance aroused, as usual, in all who heard of it the complacent feeling that, "it is he who is dead and not I."

Each one thought or felt, "Well, he's dead but I'm alive!" But the more intimate of Iván Ilyich's acquaintances, his so-called friends, could not help thinking also that they would now have to fulfil the very tiresome demands of propriety by attending the funeral service and paying a visit of condolence to the widow.

Fëdor Vasílievich and Peter Ivánovich had been his nearest acquaintances. Peter Ivánovich had studied law with Iván Ilyich and had considered himself to be under obligations to him.

Having told his wife at dinner-time of Iván Ilyich's death, and of his conjecture that it might be possible to get her brother transferred to their circuit, Peter Ivánovich sacrificed his usual nap, put on his evening clothes, and drove to Iván Ilyich's house.

At the entrance stood a carriage and two cabs. Leaning against the wall in the hall downstairs near the cloak-stand was a coffin-lid covered with cloth of gold, ornamented with gold cord and tassels, that had been polished up with metal powder. Two ladies in black were taking off their fur cloaks. Peter Ivánovich recognized one of them as Iván Ilyich's sister, but the other was a stranger to him. His colleague Schwartz was just coming downstairs, but on seeing Peter Ivánovich enter he stopped and winked at him, as if to say: "Iván Ilyich has made a mess of things—not like you and me."

Schwartz's face with his Piccadilly whiskers,[4] and his slim figure in evening dress, had as usual an air of elegant solemnity which contrasted with the playfulness of his character and had a special piquancy here, or so it seemed to Peter Ivánovich.

Peter Ivánovich allowed the ladies to precede him and slowly followed them upstairs. Schwartz did not come down but remained where he was, and Peter Ivánovich understood that he wanted to arrange where they should play bridge that evening. The ladies went upstairs to the widow's room, and Schwartz with seriously compressed lips but a playful look in his eyes, indicated by a twist of his eyebrows the room to the right where the body lay.

Peter Ivánovich, like everyone else on such occasions, entered feeling uncertain what he would have to do. All he knew was that at such times it is always safe to cross oneself. But he was not quite sure whether one should make obeisances while doing so. He therefore adopted a middle course. On entering the room he began crossing himself and made a slight movement resembling a bow. At the same time, as far as the motion of his

---

4. Sideburns carefully combed out and worn as long as possible, a fashion that died out in the 1880s.

head and arm allowed, he surveyed the room. Two young men—apparently nephews, one of whom was a high-school pupil—were leaving the room, crossing themselves as they did so. An old woman was standing motionless, and a lady with strangely arched eyebrows was saying something to her in a whisper. A vigorous, resolute Church Reader, in a frock-coat, was reading something in a loud voice with an expression that precluded any contradiction. The butler's assistant, Gerásim, stepping lightly in front of Peter Ivánovich, was strewing something on the floor. Noticing this, Peter Ivánovich was immediately aware of a faint odour of a decomposing body.

The last time he had called on Iván Ilyich, Peter Ivánovich had seen Gerásim in the study. Iván Ilyich had been particularly fond of him and he was performing the duty of a sick nurse.

Peter Ivánovich continued to make the sign of the cross slightly inclining his head in an intermediate direction between the coffin, the Reader, and the icons on the table in a corner of the room. Afterwards, when it seemed to him that his movement of his arm in crossing himself had gone on too long, he stopped and began to look at the corpse.

The dead man lay, as dead men always lie, in a specially heavy way, his rigid limbs sunk in the soft cushions of the coffin, with the head forever bowed on the pillow. His yellow waxen brow with bald patches over his sunken temples was thrust up in the way peculiar to the dead, the protruding nose seeming to press on the upper lip. He was much changed and had grown even thinner since Peter Ivánovich had last seen him, but, as is always the case with the dead, his face was handsomer and above all more dignified than when he was alive. The expression on the face said that what was necessary had been accomplished, and accomplished rightly. Besides this there was in that expression a reproach and a warning to the living. This warning seemed to Peter Ivánovich out of place, or at least not applicable to him. He felt a certain discomfort and so he hurriedly crossed himself once more and turned and went out of the door—too hurriedly and too regardless of propriety, as he himself was aware.

Schwartz was waiting for him in the adjoining room with legs spread wide apart and both hands toying with his top-hat behind his back. The mere sight of that playful, well-groomed, and elegant figure refreshed Peter Ivánovich. He felt that Schwartz was above all these happenings and would not surrender to any depressing influences. His very look said that this incident of a church service for Iván Ilyich could not be a sufficient reason for infringing the order of the session—in other words, that it would certainly not prevent his unwrapping a new pack of cards and shuffling them that evening while a footman placed four fresh candles on the table: in fact, that there was no reason for supposing that this incident would hinder their spending the evening agreeably. Indeed he said this in a whisper as Peter Ivánovich passed him, proposing that they should meet for a game at Fëdor Vasílievich's. But apparently Peter Ivánovich was not destined to play bridge that evening. Praskóvya Fëdorovna (a short, fat woman who despite all efforts to the contrary had continued to broaden steadily from her shoulders downwards and who had the same extraordinary arched eyebrows as the lady who had been standing by the coffin), dressed all in black, her head covered with lace, came out of her own room with some other ladies, conducted them to the room where the dead body lay, and said: "The service will begin immediately. Please go in."

Schwartz, making an indefinite bow, stood still, evidently neither accepting nor declining this invitation. Praskóvya Fëdorovna recognizing Peter Ivánovich, sighed, went close up to him, took his hand, and said: "I know you were a true friend to Iván Ilyich . . ." and looked at him awaiting some suitable response. And Peter Ivánovich knew that, just as it had been the right thing to cross himself in that room, so what he had to do here was to press her hand, sigh, and say, "Believe me . . ." So he did all this and as he did it felt that the desired result had been achieved: that both he and she were touched.

"Come with me. I want to speak to you before it begins," said the widow. "Give me your arm."

Peter Ivánovich gave her his arm and they went to the inner rooms, passing Schwartz who winked at Peter Ivánovich compassionately. "That does for our bridge! Don't object if we find another player. Perhaps you can cut in when you do escape," said his playful look.

Peter Ivánovich sighed still more deeply and despondently, and Praskóvya Fëdorovna pressed his arm gratefully. When they reached the drawing-room, upholstered in pink cretonne and lighted by a dim lamp, they sat down at the table—she on a sofa and Peter Ivánovich on a low hassock, the springs of which yielded spasmodically under his weight. Praskóvya Fëdorovna had been on the point of warning him to take another seat, but felt that such a warning was out of keeping with her present condition and so changed her mind. As he sat down on the hassock Peter Ivánovich recalled how Iván Ilyich had arranged this room and had consulted him regarding this pink cretonne with green leaves. The whole room was full of furniture and knick-knacks, and on her way to the sofa the lace of the widow's black shawl caught on the carved edge of the table. Peter Ivánovich rose to detach it, and the springs of the hassock, relieved of his weight, rose also and gave him a push. The widow began detaching her shawl herself, and Peter Ivánovich again sat down, suppressing the rebellious springs of the hassock under him. But the widow had not quite freed herself and Peter Ivánovich got up again, and again the hassock rebelled and even creaked. When this was all over she took out a clean cambric handkerchief and began to weep. The episode with the shawl and the struggle with the hassock had cooled Peter Ivánovich's emotions and he sat there with a sullen look on his face. This awkward situation was interrupted by Sokolóv, Iván Ilyich's butler, who came to report that the plot in the cemetery that Praskóvya Fëdorovna had chosen would cost two hundred rubles. She stopped weeping and, looking at Peter Ivánovich with the air of a victim, remarked in French[5] that it was very hard for her. Peter Ivánovich made a silent gesture signifying his full conviction that it must indeed be so.

"Please smoke," she said in a magnanimous yet crushed voice, and turned to discuss with Sokolóv the price of the plot for the grave.

Peter Ivánovich while lighting his cigarette heard her inquiring very circumstantially into the prices of different plots in the cemetery and finally decide which she would take. When that was done she gave instruc-

---

5. The Russian upper classes commonly spoke French.

tions about engaging the choir. Sokolóv then left the room.

"I look after everything myself," she told Peter Ivánovich, shifting the albums that lay on the table; and noticing that the table was endangered by his cigarette-ash, she immediately passed him an ash-tray, saying as she did so: "I consider it an affectation to say that my grief prevents my attending to practical affairs. On the contrary, if anything can—I won't say console me, but—distract me, it is seeing to everything concerning him." She again took out her handkerchief as if preparing to cry, but suddenly, as if mastering her feeling, she shook herself and began to speak calmly. "But there is something I want to talk to you about."

Peter Ivánovich bowed, keeping control of the springs of the hassock, which immediately began quivering under him.

"He suffered terribly the last few days."

"Did he?" said Peter Ivánovich.

"Oh, terribly! He screamed unceasingly, not for minutes but for hours. For the last three days he screamed incessantly. It was unendurable. I cannot understand how I bore it; you could hear him three rooms off. Oh, what I have suffered!"

"Is it possible that he was conscious all that time?" asked Peter Ivánovich.

"Yes," she whispered. "To the last moment. He took leave of us a quarter of an hour before he died, and asked us to take Vásya[6] away."

The thought of the sufferings of this man he had known so intimately, first as a merry little boy, then as a school-mate, and later as a grown-up colleague, suddenly struck Peter Ivánovich with horror, despite an unpleasant consciousness of his own and this woman's dissimulation. He again saw that brow, and that nose pressing down on the lip, and felt afraid for himself.

"Three days of frightful suffering and then death! Why, that might suddenly, at any time, happen to me," he thought, and for a moment felt terrified. But—he did not himself know how—the customary reflection at once occurred to him that this had happened to Iván Ilyich and not to him, and that it should not and could not happen to him, and that to think that it could would be yielding to depression which he ought not to do, as Schwartz's expression plainly showed. After which reflection Peter Ivánovich felt reassured, and began to ask with interest about the details of Iván Ilyich's death, as though death was an accident natural to Iván Ilyich but certainly not to himself.

After many details of the really dreadful physical sufferings Iván Ilyich had endured (which details he learnt only from the effect those sufferings had produced on Praskóvya Fëdorovna's nerves) the widow apparently found it necessary to get to business.

"Oh, Peter Ivánovich, how hard it is! How terribly, terribly hard!" and she again began to weep.

Peter Ivánovich sighed and waited for her to finish blowing her nose. When she had done so he said, "Believe me . . ." and she again began talking and brought out what was evidently her chief concern with him—namely, to question him as to how she could obtain a grant of money from the government on the occasion of her husband's death. She made it appear that she was asking Peter Ivánovich's advice about her pension,

6. Nickname for Vasílii, Iván Ilyich's son.

but lie soon saw that she already knew about that to the minutest detail, more even than he did himself. She knew how much could be got out of the government in consequence of her husband's death, but wanted to find out whether she could not possibly extract something more. Peter Ivánovich tried to think of some means of doing so, but after reflecting for a while and, out of propriety, condemning the government for its niggardliness, he said he thought that nothing more could be got. Then she sighed and evidently began to devise means of getting rid of her visitor. Noticing this, he put out his cigarette, rose, pressed her hand, and went out into the anteroom.

In the dining-room where the clock stood that Iván Ilyich had liked so much and had bought at an antique shop, Peter Ivánovich met a priest and a few acquaintances who had come to attend the service, and he recognized Iván Ilyich's daughter, a handsome young woman. She was in black and her slim figure appeared slimmer than ever. She had a gloomy, determined, almost angry expression, and bowed to Peter Ivánovich as though he were in some way to blame. Behind her, with the same offended look, stood a wealthy young man, an examining magistrate, whom Peter Ivánovich also knew and who was her fiancé, as he had heard. He bowed mournfully to them and was about to pass into the death-chamber, when from under the stairs appeared the figure of Iván Ilyich's schoolboy son, who was extremely like his father. He seemed a little Iván Ilyich, such as Peter Ivánovich remembered when they studied law together. His tear-stained eyes had in them the look that is seen in the eyes of boys of thirteen or fourteen who are not pure-minded. When he saw Peter Ivánovich he scowled morosely and shamefacedly. Peter Ivánovich nodded to him and entered the death-chamber. The service began: candles, groans, incense, tears, and sobs. Peter Ivánovich stood looking gloomily down at his feet. He did not look once at the dead man, did not yield to any depressing influence, and was one of the first to leave the room. There was no one in the anteroom, but Gerásim darted out of the dead man's room, rummaged with his strong hands among the fur coats to find Peter Ivánovich's and helped him on with it.

"Well, friend Gerásim," said Peter Ivánovich, so as to say something. "It's a sad affair, isn't it?"

"It's God's will. We shall all come to it some day," said Gerásim, displaying his teeth—the even, white teeth of a healthy peasant—and, like a man in the thick of urgent work, he briskly opened the front door, called the coachman, helped Peter Ivánovich into the sledge, and sprang back to the porch as if in readiness for what he had to do next.

Peter Ivánovich found the fresh air particularly pleasant after the smell of incense, the dead body, and carbolic acid.

"Where to, sir?" asked the coachman.

"It's not too late even now.... I'll call on Fëdor Vasílievich."

He accordingly drove there and found them just finishing the first rubber, so that it was quite convenient for him to cut in.

II

Iván Ilyich's life had been most simple and most ordinary and therefore most terrible.

He had been a member of the Court of Justice, and died at the age of forty-five. His father had been an official who after serving in various ministries and departments in Petersburg[7] had made the sort of career which brings men to positions from which by reason of their long service they cannot be dismissed, though they are obviously unfit to hold any responsible position, and for whom therefore posts are specially created, which though fictitious, carry salaries of from six to ten thousand rubles that are not fictitious, and in receipt of which they live on to a great age.

Such was the Privy Councillor and superfluous member of various superfluous institutions, Ilya Epímovich Golovín.

He had three sons, of whom Iván Ilyich was the second. The eldest son was following in his father's footsteps only in another department, and was already approaching that stage in the service at which a similar sinecure would be reached. The third son was a failure. He had ruined his prospects in a number of positions and was now serving in the railway department. His father and brothers, and still more their wives, not merely disliked meeting him, but avoided remembering his existence unless compelled to do so. His sister had married Baron Greff, a Petersburg official of her father's type. Iván Ilyich was *le phénix de la famille*[8] as people said. He was neither as cold and formal as his elder brother nor as wild as the younger, but was a happy mean between them—an intelligent, polished, lively and agreeable man. He had studied with his younger brother at the School of Law, but the latter had failed to complete the course and was expelled when he was in the fifth class. Iván Ilyich finished the course well. Even when he was at the School of Law he was just what he remained for the rest of his life: a capable, cheerful, goodnatured, and sociable man, though strict in the fulfilment of what he considered to be his duty: and he considered his duty to be what was so considered by those in authority. Neither as a boy nor as a man was he a toady, but from early youth was by nature attracted to people of high station as a fly is drawn to the light, assimilating their ways and views of life and establishing friendly relations with them. All the enthusiasms of childhood and youth passed without leaving much trace on him; he succumbed to sensuality, to vanity, and latterly among the highest classes to liberalism, but always within limits which his instinct unfailingly indicated to him as correct.

At school he had done things which had formerly seemed to him very horrid and made him feel disgusted with himself when he did them; but when later on he saw that such actions were done by people of good position and that they did not regard them as wrong, he was able not exactly to regard them as right, but to forget about them entirely or not be at all troubled at remembering them.

Having graduated from the School of Law and qualified for the tenth rank of the civil service, and having received money from his father for his equipment, Iván Ilyich ordered himself clothes at Scharmer's, the fashionable tailor, hung a medallion inscribed *respice finem*[9] on his watchchain, took leave of his professor and the prince who was patron of the school, had a farewell dinner with his comrades at Donon's first-class restaurant, and with his new and fashionable portmanteau, linen, clothes, shaving and other toilet appliances, and a travelling rug, all purchased at the best shops, he set off for one of the provinces where, through his

7. St. Petersburg (now Leningrad), the capital of Russia (1712–1918) and its cultural and social center.

8. Prodigy of the family.

9. Look to (or consider) the end.

father's influence, he had been attached to the governor as an official for special service.

In the province Iván Ilyich soon arranged as easy and agreeable a position for himself as he had had at the School of Law. He performed his official tasks, made his career, and at the same time amused himself pleasantly and decorously. Occasionally he paid official visits to country districts, where he behaved with dignity both to his superiors and inferiors, and performed the duties entrusted to him, which related chiefly to the sectarians,[1] with an exactness and incorruptible honesty of which he could not but feel proud.

In official matters, despite his youth and taste for frivolous gaiety, he was exceedingly reserved, punctilious, and even severe; but in society he was often amusing and witty, and always good-natured, correct in his manner, and *bon enfant*[2] as the governor and his wife—with whom he was like one of the family—used to say of him.

In the province he had an affair with a lady who made advances to the elegant young lawyer, and there was also a milliner; and there were carousals with aides-de-camp who visited the district, and after-supper visits to a certain outlying street of doubtful reputation; and there was too some obsequiousness to his chief and even to his chief's wife, but all this was done with such a tone of good breeding that no hard names could be applied to it. It all came under the heading of the French saying: *Il faut que jeunesse se passe.*"[3] It was all done with clean hands, in clean linen, with French phrases, and above all among people of the best society and consequently with the approval of people of rank.

So Iván Ilyich served for five years and then came a change in his official life. The new and reformed judicial institutions were introduced, and new men were needed. Iván Ilyich became such a new man. He was offered the post of Examining Magistrate, and he accepted it though the post was in another province and obliged him to give up the connexions he had formed and to make new ones. His friends met to give him a send-off; they had a group-photograph taken and presented him with a silver cigarette-case, and he set off to his new post.

As examining magistrate Iván Ilyich was just as *comme il faut* and decorous a man, inspiring general respect and capable of separating his official duties from his private life, as he had been when acting as an official on special service. His duties now as examining magistrate were far more interesting and attractive than before. In his former position it had been pleasant to wear an undress uniform made by Scharmer, and to pass through the crowd of petitioners and officials who were timorously awaiting an audience with the governor, and who envied him as with free and easy gait he went straight into his chief's private room to have a cup of tea and a cigarette with him. But not many people had then been directly dependent on him—only police officials and the sectarians when he went on special missions—and he liked to treat them politely, almost as comrades, as if he were letting them feel that he who had the power to crush them was treating them in this simple, friendly way. There were then but few such people. But now, as an examining magistrate, Iván Ilyich felt that everyone without exception, even the most important and

---

1. A large sect (the "Old Believers") which had broken with the Orthodox church.

2. A good fellow.
3. Youth must have its fling. (Translators' note.)

self-satisfied, was in his power, and that he need only write a few words on a sheet of paper with a certain heading, and this or that important, self-satisfied person would be brought before him in the role of an accused person or a witness, and if he did not choose to allow him to sit down, would have to stand before him and answer his questions. Iván Ilyich never abused his power; he tried on the contrary to soften its expression, but the consciousness of it and of the possibility of softening its effect, supplied the chief interest and attraction of his office. In his work itself, especially in his examinations, he very soon acquired a method of eliminating all considerations irrelevant to the legal aspect of the case, and reducing even the most complicated case to a form in which it would be presented on paper only in its externals, completely excluding his personal opinion of the matter, while above all observing every prescribed formality. The work was new and Iván Ilyich was one of the first men to apply the new Code of 1864.[4]

On taking up the post of examining magistrate in a new town, he made new acquaintances and connexions, placed himself on a new footing, and assumed a somewhat different tone. He took up an attitude of rather dignified aloofness towards the provincial authorities, but picked out the best circle of legal gentlemen and wealthy gentry living in the town and assumed a tone of slight dissatisfaction with the government, of moderate liberalism, and of enlightened citizenship. At the same time, without at all altering the elegance of his toilet, he ceased shaving his chin and allowed his beard to grow as it pleased.

Iván Ilyich settled down very pleasantly in this new town. The society there, which inclined towards opposition to the governor, was friendly, his salary was larger, and he began to play *vint* [a form of bridge], which he found added not a little to the pleasure of life, for he had a capacity for cards, played good-humouredly, and calculated rapidly and astutely, so that he usually won.

After living there for two years he met his future wife, Praskóvya Fëdorovna Míkhel, who was the most attractive, clever, and brilliant girl of the set in which he moved, and among other amusements and relaxations from his labours as examining magistrate, Iván Ilyich established light and playful relations with her.

While he had been an official on special service he had been accustomed to dance, but now as an examining magistrate it was exceptional for him to do so. If he danced now, he did it as if to show that though he served under the reformed order of things, and had reached the fifth official rank, yet when it came to dancing he could do it better than most people. So at the end of an evening he sometimes danced with Praskóvya Fëdorovna, and it was chiefly during these dances that he captivated her. She fell in love with him. Iván Ilyich had at first no definite intention of marrying, but when the girl fell in love with him he said to himself: "Really, why shouldn't I marry?"

Praskóvya Fëdorovna came of a good family, was not bad looking, and had some little property. Iván Ilyich might have aspired to a more brilliant match, but even this was good. He had his salary, and she, he hoped, would have an equal income. She was well connected, and was a sweet,

4. The emancipation of the serfs in 1861 was followed by a thorough all-round reform of judicial proceedings. (Translators' note.)

pretty, and thoroughly correct young woman. To say that Iván Ilyich married because he fell in love with Praskóvya Fëdorovna and found that she sympathized with his views of life would be as incorrect as to say that he married because his social circle approved of the match. He was swayed by both these considerations: the marriage gave him personal satisfaction, and at the same time it was considered the right thing by the most highly placed of his associates.

So Iván Ilyich got married.

The preparations for marriage and the beginning of married life, with its conjugal caresses, the new furniture, new crockery, and new linen, were very pleasant until his wife became pregnant—so that Iván Ilyich had begun to think that marriage would not impair the easy, agreeable, gay, and always decorous character of his life, approved of by society and regarded by himself as natural, but would even improve it. But from the first months of his wife's pregnancy, something new, unpleasant, depressing, and unseemly, and from which there was no way of escape, unexpectedly showed itself.

His wife, without any reason—*de gaieté de coeur*[5] as Iván Ilyich expressed it to himself—began to disturb the pleasure and propriety of their life. She began to be jealous without any cause, expected him to devote his whole attention to her, found fault with everything, and made coarse and ill-mannered scenes.

At first Iván Ilyich hoped to escape from the unpleasantness of this state of affairs by the same easy and decorous relation to life that had served him heretofore: he tried to ignore his wife's disagreeable moods, continued to live in his usual easy and pleasant way, invited friends to his house for a game of cards, and also tried going out to his club or spending his evenings with friends. But one day his wife began upbraiding him so vigorously, using such coarse words, and continued to abuse him every time he did not fulfil her demands, so resolutely and with such evident determination not to give way till he submitted—that is, till he stayed at home and was bored just as she was—that he became alarmed. He now realized that matrimony—at any rate with Praskóvya Fëdorovna—was not always conducive to the pleasures and amenities of life, but on the contrary often infringed both comfort and propriety, and that he must therefore entrench himself against such infringement. And Iván Ilyich began to seek for means of doing so. His official duties were the one thing that imposed upon Praskóvya Fëdorovna, and by means of his official work and the duties attached to it he began struggling with his wife to secure his own independence.

With the birth of their child, the attempts to feed it and the various failures in doing so, and with the real and imaginary illnesses of mother and child, in which Iván Ilyich's sympathy was demanded but about which he understood nothing, the need of securing for himself an existence outside his family life became still more imperative.

As his wife grew more irritable and exacting and Iván Ilyich transferred the centre of gravity of his life more and more to his official work, so did he grow to like his work better and became more ambitious than before.

Very soon, within a year of his wedding, Iván Ilyich had realized that marriage, though it may add some comforts to life, is in fact a very intricate and difficult affair towards which in order to perform one's duty, that is, to lead a decorous life approved of by society, one must adopt a definite attitude just as towards one's official duties.

And Iván Ilyich evolved such an attitude towards married life. He only required of it those conveniences—dinner at home, housewife, and bed—which it could give him, and above all that propriety of external forms required by public opinion. For the rest he looked for light-hearted pleasure and propriety, and was very thankful when he found them, but if he met with antagonism and querulousness he at once retired into his separate fenced-off world of official duties, where he found satisfaction.

Iván Ilyich was esteemed a good official, and after three years was made Assistant Public Prosecutor. His new duties, their importance, the possibility of indicting and imprisoning anyone he chose, the publicity his speeches received, and the success he had in all these things, made his work still more attractive.

More children came. His wife became more and more querulous and ill-tempered, but the attitude Iván Ilyich had adopted towards his home life rendered him almost impervious to her grumbling.

After seven years' service in that town he was transferred to another province as Public Prosecutor. They moved, but were short of money and his wife did not like the place they moved to. Though the salary was higher the cost of living was greater, besides which two of their children died and family life became still more unpleasant for him.

Praskóvya Fëdorovna blamed her husband for every inconvenience they encountered in their new home. Most of the conversations between husband and wife, especially as to the children's education, led to topics which recalled former disputes, and those disputes were apt to flare up again at any moment. There remained only those rare periods of amorousness which still came to them at times but did not last long. These were islets at which they anchored for a while and then again set out upon that ocean of veiled hostility which showed itself in their aloofness from one another. This aloofness might have grieved Iván Ilyich had he considered that it ought not to exist, but he now regarded the position as normal, and even made it the goal at which he aimed in family life. His aim was to free himself more and more from those unpleasantnesses and to give them a semblance of harmlessness and propriety. He attained this by spending less and less time with his family, and when obliged to be at home he tried to safeguard his position by the presence of outsiders. The chief thing however was that he had his official duties. The whole interest of his life now centered in the official world and that interest absorbed him. The consciousness of his power, being able to ruin anybody he wished to ruin, the importance, even the external dignity of his entry into court, or meetings with his subordinates, his success with superiors and inferiors, and above all his masterly handling of cases, of which he was conscious—all this gave him pleasure and filled his life, together with chats with his colleagues, dinners, and bridge. So that on the whole Iván Ilyich's life continued to flow as he considered it should do—pleasantly and properly.

So things continued for another seven years. His eldest daughter was already sixteen, another child had died, and only one son was left, a schoolboy and a subject of dissensions. Iván Ilyich wanted to put him in the School of Law, but to spite him Praskóvya Fëdorovna entered him at the High School. The daughter had been educated at home and had turned out well: the boy did not learn badly either.

III

So Iván Ilyich lived for seventeen years after his marriage. He was already a Public Prosecutor of long standing, and had declined several proposed transfers while awaiting a more desirable post, when an unanticipated and unpleasant occurrence quite upset the peaceful course of his life. He was expecting to be offered the post of presiding judge in a University town, but Hoppe somehow came to the front and obtained the appointment instead. Iván Ilyich became irritable, reproached Hoppe, and quarrelled both with him and with his immediate superiors—who became colder to him and again passed him over when other appointments were made.

This was in 1880, the hardest year of Iván Ilyich's life. It was then that it became evident on the one hand that his salary was insufficient for them to live on, and on the other that he had been forgotten, and not only this, but that what was for him the greatest and most cruel injustice appeared to others a quite ordinary occurrence. Even his father did not consider it his duty to help him. Iván Ilyich felt himself abandoned by everyone, and that they regarded his position with a salary of 3,500 rubles as quite normal and even fortunate. He alone knew that with the consciousness of the injustices done him, with his wife's incessant nagging, and with the debts he had contracted by living beyond his means, his position was far from normal.

In order to save money that summer he obtained leave of absence and went with his wife to live in the country at her brother's place.

In the country, without his work, he experienced *ennui* for the first time in his life, and not only *ennui* but intolerable depression, and he decided that it was impossible to go on living like that, and that it was necessary to take energetic measures.

Having passed a sleepless night pacing up and down the veranda, he decided to go to Petersburg and bestir himself, in order to punish those who had failed to appreciate him and to get transferred to another ministry.

Next day, despite many protests from his wife and her brother, he started for Petersburg with the sole object of obtaining a post with a salary of five thousand rubles a year. He was no longer bent on any particular department, or tendency, or kind of activity. All he now wanted was an appointment to another post with a salary of five thousand rubles, either in the administration, in the banks, with the railways, in one of the Empress Márya's Institutions,[6] or even in the customs—but it had to carry with it a salary of five thousand rubles and be in a ministry other than that in which they had failed to appreciate him.

And this quest of Iván Ilyich's was crowned with remarkable and unexpected success. At Kursk an acquaintance of his, F. I. Ilyín, got into the first-class carriage, sat down beside Iván Ilyich, and told him of a telegram just received by the governor of Kursk announcing that a change was about to take place in the ministry: Peter Ivánovich was to be superseded by Iván Semënovich.

The proposed change, apart from its significance for Russia, had a special significance for Iván Ilyich, because by bringing forward a new man, Peter Petróvich, and consequently his friend Zachár Ivánovich, it was

6. Charitable organization founded nearly a century earlier by the wife of Paul I.

highly favourable for Iván Ilyich, since Zachár Ivánovich was a friend and colleague of his.

In Moscow this news was confirmed, and on reaching Petersburg Iván Ilyich found Zachár Ivánovich and received a definite promise of an appointment in his former department of Justice.

A week later he telegraphed to his wife: "Zachár in Miller's place. I shall receive appointment on presentation of report."

Thanks to this change of personnel, Iván Ilyich had unexpectedly obtained an appointment in his former ministry which placed him two stages above his former colleagues besides giving him five thousand rubles salary and three thousand five hundred rubles for expenses connected with his removal.[7] All his ill humour towards his former enemies and the whole department vanished, and Iván Ilyich was completely happy.

He returned to the country more cheerful and contented than he had been for a long time. Praskóvya Fëdorovna also cheered up and a truce was arranged between them. Iván Ilyich told of how he had been fêted by everybody in Petersburg, how all those who had been his enemies were put to shame and now fawned on him, how envious they were of his appointment, and how much everybody in Petersburg had liked him.

Praskóvya Fëdorovna listened to all this and appeared to believe it. She did not contradict anything, but only made plans for their life in the town to which they were going. Iván Ilyich saw with delight that these plans were his plans, that he and his wife agreed, and that, after a stumble, his life was regaining its due and natural character of pleasant lightheartedness and decorum.

Iván Ilyich had come back for a short time only, for he had to take up his new duties on the 10th of September. Moreover, he needed time to settle into the new place, to move all his belongings from the province, and to buy and order many additional things: in a word, to make such arrangements as he had resolved on, which were almost exactly what Praskóvya Fëdorovna too had decided on.

Now that everything had happened so fortunately, and that he and his wife were at one in their aims and moreover saw so little of one another, they got on together better than they had done since the first years of marriage. Iván Ilyich had thought of taking his family away with him at once, but the insistence of his wife's brother and her sister-in-law, who had suddenly become particularly amiable and friendly to him and his family, induced him to depart alone.

So he departed, and the cheerful state of mind induced by his success and by the harmony between his wife and himself, the one intensifying the other, did not leave him. He found a delightful house, just the thing both he and his wife had dreamt of. Spacious, lofty reception rooms in the old style, a convenient and dignified study, rooms for his wife and daughter, a study for his son—it might have been specially built for them. Iván Ilyich himself superintended the arrangements, chose the wallpapers, supplemented the furniture (preferably with antiques which he considered particularly *comme il faut*), and supervised the upholstering. Everything progressed and progressed and approached the ideal he had set himself: even when things were only half completed they exceeded his expectations. He saw what a refined and elegant character, free from vulgarity, it

7. Moving.

would all have when it was ready. On falling asleep he pictured to himself how the reception-room would look. Looking at the yet unfinished drawing-room he could see the fireplace, the screen, the what-not, the little chairs dotted here and there, the dishes and plates on the walls, and the bronzes, as they would be when everything was in place. He was pleased by the thought of how his wife and daughter, who shared his taste in this matter, would be impressed by it. They were certainly not expecting as much. He had been particularly successful in finding, and buying cheaply, antiques which gave a particularly aristocratic character to the whole place. But in his letters he intentionally understated everything in order to be able to surprise them. All this so absorbed him that his new duties—though he liked his official work—interested him less than he had expected. Sometimes he even had moments of absent-mindedness during the Court Sessions, and would consider whether he should have straight or curved cornices for his curtains. He was so interested in it all that he often did things himself, rearranging the furniture, or rehanging the curtains. Once when mounting a step-ladder to show the upholsterer, who did not understand, how he wanted the hangings draped, he made a false step and slipped, but being a strong and agile man he clung on and only knocked his side against the knob of the window frame. The bruised place was painful but the pain soon passed, and he felt particularly bright and well just then. He wrote: "I feel fifteen years younger." He thought he would have everything ready by September, but it dragged on till mid-October. But the result was charming not only in his eyes but to everyone who saw it.

In reality it was just what is usually seen in the houses of people of moderate means who want to appear rich, and therefore succeed only in resembling others like themselves: there were damasks, dark wood, plants, rugs, and dull and polished bronzes—all the things people of a certain class have in order to resemble other people of that class. His house was so like the others that it would never have been noticed, but to him it all seemed to be quite exceptional. He was very happy when he met his family at the station and brought them to the newly furnished house all lit up, where a footman in a white tie opened the door into the hall decorated with plants, and when they went on into the drawing room and the study uttering exclamations of delight. He conducted them everywhere, drank in their praises eagerly, and beamed with pleasure. At tea that evening, when Praskóvya Fëdorovna among other things asked him about his fall, he laughed, and showed them how he had gone flying and had frightened the upholsterer.

"It's a good thing I'm a bit of an athlete. Another man might have been killed, but I merely knocked myself, just here; it hurts when it's touched, but it's passing off already—it's only a bruise."

So they began living in their new home—in which, as always happens, when they got thoroughly settled in they found they were just one room short—and with the increased income, which as always was just a little (some five hundred rubles) too little, but it was all very nice.

Things went particularly well at first, before everything was finally arranged and while something had still to be done: this thing bought, that thing ordered, another thing moved, and something else adjusted. Though there were some disputes between husband and wife, they were both so well satisfied and had so much to do that it all passed off without any serious quarrels. When nothing was left to arrange it became rather dull and something seemed to be lacking, but they were then making acquaintances, forming habits, and life was growing fuller.

Iván Ilyich spent his mornings at the law court and came home to dinner, and at first he was generally in a good humour, though he occasionally became irritable just on account of his house. (Every spot on the tablecloth or the upholstery, and every broken window-blind string, irritated him. He had devoted so much trouble to arranging it all that every disturbance of it distressed him.) But on the whole his life ran its course as he believed life should do: easily, pleasantly, and decorously.

He got up at nine, drank his coffee, read the paper, and then put on his undress uniform and went to the law courts. There the harness in which he worked had already been stretched to fit him and he donned it without a hitch: petitioners, inquiries at the chancery, the chancery itself, and the sittings public and administrative. In all this the thing was to exclude everything fresh and vital, which always disturbs the regular course of official business, and to admit only official relations with people, and then only on official grounds. A man would come, for instance, wanting some information. Iván Ilyich, as one in whose sphere the matter did not lie, would have nothing to do with him: but if the man had some business with him in his official capacity, something that could be expressed on officially stamped paper, he would do everything, positively everything he could within the limits of such relations, and in doing so would maintain the semblance of friendly human relations, that is, would observe the courtesies of life. As soon as the official relations ended, so did everything else. Iván Ilyich possessed this capacity to separate his real life from the official side of affairs and not mix the two, in the highest degree, and by long practice and natural aptitude had brought it to such a pitch that sometimes, in the manner of a virtuoso, he would even allow himself to let the human and official relations mingle. He let himself do this just because he felt that he could at any time he chose resume the strictly official attitude again and drop the human relation. And he did it all easily, pleasantly, correctly, and even artistically. In the intervals between the sessions he smoked, drank tea, chatted a little about politics, a little about general topics, a little about cards, but most of all about official appointments. Tired, but with the feelings of a virtuoso—one of the first violins who has played his part in an orchestra with precision—he would return home to find that his wife and daughter had been out paying calls, or had a visitor, and that his son had been to school, had done his homework with his tutor, and was duly learning what is taught at High Schools. Everything was as it should be. After dinner, if they had no visitors, Iván Ilyich sometimes read a book that was being much discussed at the time, and in the evening settled down to work, that is, read official papers, compared the depositions of witnesses, and noted paragraphs of the Code applying to them. This was neither dull nor amusing. It was dull when he might have been playing bridge, but if no bridge was available it was at any rate better than doing nothing or sitting with his wife. Iván Ilyich's chief pleasure was giving little dinners to which he invited men and women of good social position, and just as his drawing-room resembled all other drawing-rooms so did his enjoyable little parties resemble all other such parties.

Once they even gave a dance. Iván Ilyich enjoyed it and everything went off well, except that it led to a violent quarrel with his wife about the cakes and sweets. Praskóvya Fëdorovna had made her own plans, but Iván Ilyich insisted on getting everything from an expensive confectioner and ordered too many cakes, and the quarrel occurred because some of those cakes were left over and the confectioner's bill came to forty-five rubles. It was a great and disagreeable quarrel. Praskóvya Fëdorovna called him "a fool and an imbecile," and he clutched at his head and made angry allusions to divorce.

But the dance itself had been enjoyable. The best people were there, and Iván Ilyich had danced with Princess Trúfonova, a sister of the distinguished founder of the Society "Bear my Burden."

The pleasures connected with his work were pleasures of ambition; his social pleasures were those of vanity; but Iván Ilyich's greatest pleasure was playing bridge. He acknowledged that whatever disagreeable incident happened in his life, the pleasure that beamed like a ray of light above everything else was to sit down to bridge with good players, not noisy partners, and of course to four-handed bridge (with five players it was annoying to have to stand out, though one pretended not to mind), to play a clever and serious game (when the cards allowed it) and then to have supper and drink a glass of wine. After a game of bridge, especially if he had won a little (to win a large sum was unpleasant), Iván Ilyich went to bed in specially good humour.

So they lived. They formed a circle of acquaintances among the best people and were visited by people of importance and by young folk. In their views as to their acquaintances, husband, wife, and daughter were entirely agreed, and tacitly and unanimously kept at arm's length and shook off the various shabby friends and relations who, with much show of affection, gushed into the drawing-room with its Japanese plates on the walls. Soon these shabby friends ceased to obtrude themselves and only the best people remained in the Golovíns' set.

Young men made up to Lisa, and Petríshchev, an examining magistrate and Dmítri Ivánovich Petríshchev's son and sole heir, began to be so attentive to her that Iván Ilyich had already spoken to Praskóvya Fëdorovna about it, and considered whether they should not arrange a party for them, or get up some private theatricals.

So they lived, and all went well, without change, and life flowed pleasantly.

IV

They were all in good health. It could not be called ill health if Iván Ilyich sometimes said that he had a queer taste in his mouth and felt some discomfort in his left side.

But this discomfort increased and, though not exactly painful, grew into a sense of pressure in his side accompanied by ill humour. And his irritability became worse and worse and began to mar the agreeable, easy, and correct life that had established itself in the Golovín family. Quarrels between husband and wife became more and more frequent, and soon the ease and amenity disappeared and even the decorum was barely maintained. Scenes again became frequent, and very few of those islets remained on which husband and wife could meet without an explosion. Praskóvya Fëdorovna now had good reason to say that her husband's temper was trying. With characteristic exaggeration she said he had always had a dreadful temper, and that it had needed all her good nature to put up with it for twenty years. It was true that now the quarrels were started by him. His bursts of temper always came just before dinner, often just as he began to eat his soup. Sometimes he noticed that a plate or dish was chipped, or the food was not right, or his son put his elbow on the table, or his daughter's hair was not done as he liked it, and for all this he blamed Praskóvya Fëdorovna. At first she retorted and said disagreeable things to him, but once or twice he fell into such a rage at the beginning of dinner that she realized it was due to some physical derangement brought on by taking food, and so she restrained herself and did not answer, but only hurried to get the dinner over. She regarded this self-restraint as highly praiseworthy. Having come to the conclusion that her husband had a dreadful temper and made her life miserable, she began to feel sorry for herself, and the more she pitied herself the more she hated her husband. She began to wish he would die; yet she did not want him to die because then his salary would cease. And this irritated her against him still more. She considered herself dreadfully unhappy just because not even his death could save her, and though she concealed her exasperation, that hidden exasperation of hers increased his irritation also.

After one scene in which Iván Ilyich had been particularly unfair and after which he had said in explanation that he certainly was irritable but that it was due to his not being well, she said that if he was ill it should be attended to, and insisted on his going to see a celebrated doctor.

He went. Everything took place as he had expected and as it always does. There was the usual waiting and the important air assumed by the doctor, with which he was so familiar (resembling that which he himself assumed in court), and the sounding and listening, and the questions which called for answers that were foregone conclusions and were evidently unnecessary, and the look of importance which implied that "if only you put yourself in our hands we will arrange everything—we know indubitably how it has to be done, always in the same way for everybody alike." It was all just as it was in the law courts. The doctor put on just the same air towards him as he himself put on towards an accused person.

The doctor said that so-and-so indicated that there was so-and-so inside the patient, but if the investigation of so-and-so did not confirm this, then he must assume that and that. If he assumed that and that, then . . . and so on. To Iván Ilyich only one question was important: was his case serious or not? But the doctor ignored that inappropriate question. From his point of view it was not the one under consideration, the real question was to decide between a floating kidney, chronic catarrh, or appendicitis. It was not a question of Iván Ilyich's life or death, but one between a floating kidney and appendicitis. And that question the doctor solved brilliantly, as it seemed to Iván Ilyich, in favour of the appendix, with the reservation that should an examination of the urine give fresh indications the matter would be reconsidered. All this was just what Iván Ilyich had himself brilliantly accomplished a thousand times in dealing with men on trial. The doctor summed up just as brilliantly, looking over his spectacles triumphantly and even gaily at the accused. From the doctor's summing up Iván Ilyich concluded that things were bad, but that for the doctor, and perhaps for everybody else, it was a matter of indifference, though for him it was bad. And this conclusion struck him painfully, arousing in him a great feeling of pity for himself and of bitterness towards the doctor's indifference to a matter of such importance.

He said nothing of this, but rose, placed the doctor's fee on the table, and remarked with a sigh: "We sick people probably often put inappropriate questions. But tell me, in general, is this complaint dangerous, or not? . . ."

The doctor looked at him sternly over his spectacles with one eye, as if to say: "Prisoner, if you will not keep to the questions put to you, I shall be obliged to have you removed from the court."

"I have already told you what I consider necessary and proper. The analysis may show something more." And the doctor bowed.

Iván Ilyich went out slowly, seated himself disconsolately in his sledge, and drove home. All the way home he was going over what the doctor had said, trying to translate those complicated, obscure, scientific phrases into plain language and find in them an answer to the question: "Is my condition bad? Is it very bad? Or is there as yet nothing much wrong?" And it seemed to him that the meaning of what the doctor had said was that it was very bad. Everything in the streets seemed depressing. The cabmen, the houses, the passers-by, and the shops, were dismal. His ache, this dull gnawing ache that never ceased for a moment, seemed to have acquired a new and more serious significance from the doctor's dubious remarks. Iván Ilyich now watched it with a new and oppressive feeling.

He reached home and began to tell his wife about it. She listened, but in the middle of his account his daughter came in with her hat on, ready to go out with her mother. She sat down reluctantly to listen to this tedious story, but could not stand it long, and her mother too did not hear him to the end.

"Well, I am very glad," she said. "Mind now to take your medicine regularly. Give me the prescription and I'll send Gerásim to the chemist's." And she went to get ready to go out.

While she was in the room Iván Ilyich had hardly taken time to breathe, but he sighed deeply when she left it.

"Well," he thought, "perhaps it isn't so bad after all."

He began taking his medicine and following the doctor's directions, which had been altered after the examination of the urine. But then it happened that there was a contradiction between the indications drawn from the examination of the urine and the symptoms that showed themselves. It turned out that what was happening differed from what the doctor had told him, and that he had either forgotten, or blundered, or hidden something from him. He could not, however, be blamed for that, and Iván Ilyich still obeyed his orders implicitly and at first derived some comfort from doing so.

From the time of his visit to the doctor, Iván Ilyich's chief occupation was the exact fulfilment of the doctor's instructions regarding hygiene and the taking of medicine, and the observation of his pain and his excretions. His chief interests came to be people's ailments and people's health. When sickness, deaths, or recoveries were mentioned in his presence, especially when the illness resembled his own, he listened with agitation which he tried to hide, asked questions, and applied what he heard to his own case.

The pain did not grow less, but Iván Ilyich made efforts to force himself to think that he was better. And he could do this so long as nothing agitated him. But as soon as he had any unpleasantness with his wife, any lack of success in his official work, or held bad cards at bridge, he was at once acutely sensible of his disease. He had formerly borne such mischances, hoping soon to adjust what was wrong, to master it and attain success, or make a grand slam. But now every mischance upset him and plunged him into despair. He would say to himself: "There now, just as I was beginning to get better and the medicine had begun to take effect, comes this accursed misfortune, or unpleasantness ..." And he was furious with the mishap, or with the people who were causing the unpleasantness and killing him, for he felt that this fury was killing him but could not restrain it. One would have thought that it should have been clear to him that this exasperation with circumstances and people aggravated his illness, and that he ought therefore to ignore unpleasant occurrences. But he drew the very opposite conclusion: he said that he needed peace, and he watched for everything that might disturb it and became irritable at the slightest infringement of it. His condition was rendered worse by the fact that he read medical books and consulted doctors. The progress of his disease was so gradual that he could deceive himself when comparing one day with another—the difference was so slight. But when he consulted the doctors it seemed to him that he was getting worse, and even very rapidly. Yet despite this he was continually consulting them.

That month he went to see another celebrity, who told him almost the same as the first had done but put his questions rather differently, and the interview with this celebrity only increased Iván Ilyich's doubts and fears. A friend of a friend of his, a very good doctor, diagnosed his illness again quite differently from the others, and though he predicted recovery, his questions and suppositions bewildered Iván Ilyich still more and increased his doubts. A homeopathist diagnosed the disease in yet another way, and prescribed medicine which Iván Ilyich took secretly for a week. But after a week, not feeling any improvement and having lost confidence both in the former doctor's treatment and in this one's, he became still more despondent. One day a lady acquaintance mentioned a cure effected by a wonder-working icon. Iván Ilyich caught himself listening attentively and beginning to believe that it had occurred. This incident alarmed him. "Has my mind really weakened to such an extent?" he asked himself. "Nonsense! It's all rubbish. I mustn't give way to nervous fears but having chosen a doctor must keep strictly to his treatment. That is what I will do. Now it's all settled. I won't think about it, but will follow the treatment seriously till summer, and then we shall see. From now there must be no more of this wavering!" This was easy to say but impossible to carry out. The pain in his side oppressed him and seemed to grow worse and more incessant, while the taste in his mouth grew stranger and stranger. It seemed to him that his breath had a disgusting smell, and he was conscious of a loss of appetite and strength. There was no deceiving himself: something terrible, new, and more important than anything before in his life, was taking place within him of which he alone was aware. Those about him did not understand or would not understand it, but thought everything in the world was going on as usual. That tormented Iván Ilyich more than anything. He saw that his household, especially his wife and daughter who were in a perfect whirl of visiting, did not understand anything of it and were annoyed that he was so depressed and so exacting, as if he were to blame for it. Though they tried to dis-

guise it he saw that he was an obstacle in their path, and that his wife
had adopted a definite line in regard to his illness and kept to it regardless of anything he said or did. Her attitude was this: "You know," she
would say to her friends, "Iván Ilyich can't do as other people do, and
keep to the treatment prescribed for him. One day he'll take his drops
and keep strictly to his diet and go to bed in good time, but the next day
unless I watch him he'll suddenly forget his medicine, eat sturgeon—
which is forbidden—and sit up playing cards till one o'clock in the morning."

"Oh, come, when was that?" Iván Ilyich would ask in vexation. "Only
once at Peter Ivánovich's."

"And yesterday with Shébek."

"Well, even if I hadn't stayed up, this pain would have kept me
awake."

"Be that as it may you'll never get well like that, but will always make
us wretched."

Praskóvya Fëdorovna's attitude to Iván Ilyich's illness, as she expressed
it both to others and to him, was that it was his own fault and was another of the annoyances he caused her. Iván Ilyich felt that this opinion
escaped her involuntarily—but that did not make it easier for him.

At the law courts too, Iván Ilyich noticed, or thought he noticed, a
strange attitude towards himself. It sometimes seemed to him that people
were watching him inquisitively as a man whose place might soon be
vacant. Then again, his friends would suddenly begin to chaff him in a
friendly way about his low spirits, as if the awful, horrible, and unheard-
of thing that was going on within him, incessantly gnawing at him and
irresistibly drawing him away, was a very agreeable subject for jests.
Schwartz in particular irritated him by his jocularity, vivacity, and *savoir-
faire*, which reminded him of what he himself had been ten years ago.

Friends came to make up a set and they sat down to cards. They dealt,
bending the new cards to soften them, and he sorted the diamonds in his
hand and found he had seven. His partner said "No trumps" and supported him with two diamonds. What more could be wished for? It ought
to be jolly and lively. They would make a grand slam. But suddenly Iván
Ilyich was conscious of that gnawing pain, that taste in his mouth, and it
seemed ridiculous that in such circumstances he should be pleased to
make a grand slam.

He looked at his partner Mikháil Mikháylovich, who rapped the table
with his strong hand and instead of snatching up the tricks pushed the
cards courteously and indulgently towards Iván Ilyich that he might have
the pleasure of gathering them up without the trouble of stretching out
his hand for them. "Does he think I am too weak to stretch out my arm?"
thought Iván Ilyich, and forgetting what he was doing he over-trumped
his partner, missing the grand slam by three tricks. And what was most
awful of all was that he saw how upset Mikháil Mikháylovich was about
it but did not himself care. And it was dreadful to realize why he did not
care.

They all saw that he was suffering, and said: "We can stop if you are
tired. Take a rest." Lie down? No, he was not at all tired, and he finished
the rubber. All were gloomy and silent. Iván Ilyich felt that he had dif-
fused this gloom over them and could not dispel it. They had supper and

went away, and Iván Ilyich was left alone with the consciousness that his life was poisoned and was poisoning the lives of others, and that this poison did not weaken but penetrated more and more deeply into his whole being. With this consciousness, and with physical pain besides the terror, he must go to bed, often to lie awake the greater part of the night. Next morning he had to get up again, dress, go to the law courts, speak, and write; or if he did not go out, spend at home those twenty-four hours a day each of which was a torture. And he had to live thus all alone on the brink of an abyss, with no one who understood or pitied him.

V

So one month passed and then another. Just before the New Year his brother-in-law came to town and stayed at their house. Iván Ilyich was at the law courts and Praskóvya Fëdorovna had gone shopping. When Iván Ilyich came home and entered his study he found his brother-in-law there—a healthy, florid man—unpacking his portmanteau himself. He raised his head on hearing Iván Ilyich's footsteps and looked up at him for a moment without a word. That stare told Iván everything. His brother-in-law opened his mouth to utter an exclamation of surprise but checked himself, and that action confirmed it all.

"I have changed, eh?"

"Yes, there is a change."

And after that, try as he would to get his brother-in-law to return to the subject of his looks, the latter would say nothing about it. Praskóvya Fëdorovna came home and her brother went out to her. Iván Ilyich locked the door and began to examine himself in the glass, first full face, then in profile. He took up a portrait of himself taken with his wife, and compared it with what he saw in the glass. The change in him was immense. Then he bared his arms to the elbow, looked at them, drew the sleeves down again, sat down on an ottoman, and grew blacker than night.

"No, no, this won't do!" he said to himself, and jumped up, went to the table, took up some law papers and began to read them, but could not continue. He unlocked the door and went into the reception-room. The door leading to the drawing-room was shut. He approached it on tiptoe and listened.

"No, you are exaggerating!" Praskóvya Fëdorovna was saying.

"Exaggerating! Don't you see it? Why, he's a dead man! Look at his eyes—there's no light in them. But what is it that is wrong with him?"

"No one knows. Nikoláevich [that was another doctor] said something, but I don't know what. And Leshchetítsky [this was the celebrated specialist] said quite the contrary . . ."

Iván Ilyich walked away, went to his own room, lay down and began musing: "The kidney, a floating kidney." He recalled all the doctors had told him of how it detached itself and swayed about. And by an effort of imagination he tried to catch that kidney and arrest it and support it. So little was needed for this, it seemed to him. "No, I'll go to see Peter Ivánovich again." [That was the friend whose friend was a doctor.] He rang, ordered the carriage, and got ready to go.

"Where are you going, Jean?"[8] asked his wife, with a specially sad and exceptionally kind look.
This exceptionally kind look irritated him. He looked morosely at her.
"I must go to see Peter Ivánovich."
He went to see Peter Ivánovich, and together they went to see his friend, the doctor. He was in, and Iván Ilyich had a long talk with him.
Reviewing the anatomical and physiological details of what in the doctor's opinion was going on inside him, he understood it all.
There was something, a small thing, in the vermiform appendix. It might all come right. Only stimulate the energy of one organ and check the activity of another, then absorption would take place and everything would come right. He got home rather late for dinner, ate his dinner, and conversed cheerfully, but could not for a long time bring himself to go back to work in his room. At last, however, he went to his study and did what was necessary, but the consciousness that he had put something aside—an important, intimate matter which he would revert to when his work was done—never left him. When he had finished his work he remembered that this intimate matter was the thought of his vermiform appendix. But he did not give himself up to it, and went to the drawing-room for tea. There were callers there, including the examining magistrate who was a desirable match for his daughter, and they were conversing, playing the piano, and singing. Iván Ilyich, as Praskóvya Fëdorovna remarked, spent that evening more cheerfully than usual, but he never for a moment forgot that he had postponed the important matter of the appendix. At eleven o'clock he said goodnight and went to his bedroom. Since his illness he had slept alone in a small room next to his study. He undressed and took up a novel by Zola,[9] but instead of reading it he fell into thought, and in his imagination that desired improvement in the vermiform appendix occurred. There was the absorption and evacuation and the reestablishment of normal activity. "Yes, that's it!" he said to himself. "One need only assist nature, that's all." He remembered his medicine, rose, took it, and lay down on his back watching for the beneficent action of the medicine and for it to lessen the pain. "I need only take it regularly and avoid all injurious influences. I am already feeling better, much better." He began touching his side: it was not painful to the touch. "There, I really don't feel it. It's much better already." He put out the light and turned on his side . . . "The appendix is getting better, absorption is occurring." Suddenly he felt the old, familiar, dull, gnawing pain, stubborn and serious. There was the same familiar loathsome taste in his mouth. His heart sank and he felt dazed. "My God! My God!" he muttered. "Again, again! And it will never cease." And suddenly the matter presented itself in a quite different aspect. "Vermiform appendix! Kidney!" he said to himself. "It's not a question of appendix or kidney, but of life and . . . death. Yes, life was there and now it is going, going and I cannot stop it. Yes. Why deceive myself? Isn't it obvious to everyone but me that I'm dying, and that it's only a question of weeks, days . . . it may happen this moment. There was light and now there is darkness. I was here and now I'm going there! Where?" A chill came over him, his breathing ceased, and he felt only the throbbing of his heart.

8. French for Iván.
9. The French naturalistic novelist Émile Zola   (1840–1902) saw human life as merely a matter of biological and mechanistic functions.

"When I am not, what will there be? There will be nothing. Then where shall I be when I am no more? Can this be dying? No, I don't want to!" He jumped up and tried to light the candle, felt for it with trembling hands, dropped candle and candlestick on the floor, and fell back on his pillow.

"What's the use? It makes no difference," he said to himself, staring with wide-open eyes into the darkness. "Death. Yes, death. And none of them know or wish to know it, and they have no pity for me. Now they are playing." (He heard through the door the distant sound of a song and its accompaniment.) "It's all the same to them, but they will die too! Fools! I first, and they later, but it will be the same for them. And now they are merry . . . the beasts!"

Anger choked him and he was agonizingly, unbearably miserable. "It is impossible that all men have been doomed to suffer this awful horror!" He raised himself.

"Something must be wrong. I must calm myself—must think it all over from the beginning." And he again began thinking. "Yes, the beginning of my illness: I knocked my side, but I was still quite well that day and the next. It hurt a little, then rather more. I saw the doctors, then followed despondency and anguish, more doctors, and I drew nearer to the abyss. My strength grew less and I kept coming nearer and nearer, and now I have wasted away and there is no light in my eyes. I think of the appendix—but this is death! I think of mending the appendix, and all the while here is death! Can it really be death?" Again terror seized him and he gasped for breath. He leant down and began feeling for the matches, pressing with his elbow on the stand beside the bed. It was in his way and hurt him, he grew furious with it, pressed on it still harder, and upset it. Breathless and in despair he fell on his back, expecting death to come immediately.

Meanwhile the visitors were leaving. Praskóvya Fëdorovna was seeing them off. She heard something fall and came in.

"What has happened?"

"Nothing. I knocked it over accidentally."

She went out and returned with a candle. He lay there panting heavily, like a man who has run a thousand yards, and stared upwards at her with a fixed look.

"What is it, *Jean?*"

"No . . . o . . . thing. I upset it." ("Why speak of it? She won't understand," he thought.)

And in truth she did not understand. She picked up the stand, lit his candle, and hurried away to see another visitor off. When she came back he still lay on his back, looking upwards.

"What is it? Do you feel worse?"

"Yes."

She shook her head and sat down.

"Do you know, *Jean*, I think we must ask Leshchetítsky to come and see you here."

This meant calling in the famous specialist, regardless of expense. He smiled malignantly and said "No." She remained a little longer and then went up to him and kissed his forehead.

While she was kissing him he hated her from the bottom of his soul and with difficulty refrained from pushing her away.

"Good-night. Please God you'll sleep."
"Yes."

VI

Iván Ilyich saw that he was dying, and he was in continual despair.

In the depth of his heart he knew he was dying, but not only was he not accustomed to the thought, he simply did not and could not grasp it. The syllogism he had learned from Kiesewetter's *Logic:*[1] "Caius is a man, men are mortal, therefore Caius is mortal," had always seemed to him correct as applied to Caius, but certainly not as applied to himself. That Caius—man in the abstract—was mortal, was perfectly correct, but he was not Caius, not an abstract man, but a creature quite, quite separate from all others. He had been little Ványa, with a mamma and a papa, with Mítya and Volódya, with the toys, a coachman and a nurse, afterwards with Kátenka and with all the joys, griefs, and delights of childhood, boyhood, and youth. What did Caius know of the smell of that striped leather ball Ványa had been so fond of? Had Caius kissed his mother's hand like that, and did the silk of her dress rustle so for Caius? Had he rioted like that at school when the pastry was bad? Had Caius been in love like that? Could Caius preside at a session as he did? Caius really was mortal, and it was right for him to die; but for me, little Ványa, Iván Ilyich, with all my thoughts and emotions, it's altogether a different matter. It cannot be that I ought to die. That would be too terrible."

Such was his feeling.

"If I had to die like Caius I should have known it was so. An inner voice would have told me so, but there was nothing of the sort in me and I and all my friends felt that our case was quite different from that of Caius. And now here it is!" he said to himself. "It can't be. It's impossible! But here it is. How is this? How is one to understand it?"

He could not understand it, and tried to drive this false, incorrect, morbid thought away and to replace it by other proper and healthy thoughts. But that thought, and not the thought only but the reality itself, seemed to come and confront him.

And to replace that thought he called up a succession of others, hoping to find in them some support. He tried to get back into the former current of thoughts that had once screened the thought of death from him. But strange to say, all that had formerly shut off, hidden, and destroyed, his consciousness of death, no longer had that effect. Iván Ilyich now spent most of his time in attempting to re-establish that old current. He would say to himself: "I will take up my duties again—after all I used to live by them." And banishing all doubts he would go to the law courts, enter into conversation with his colleagues, and sit carelessly as was his wont, scanning the crowd with a thoughtful look and leaning both his emaciated arms on the arms of his oak chair; bending over as usual to a colleague and drawing his papers nearer he would interchange whispers with him, and then suddenly raising his eyes and sitting erect would pronounce certain words and open the proceedings. But suddenly in the midst of those proceedings the pain in his side, regardless of the stage the

---

1. Karl Kiesewetter (1766–1819), *Outline of Logic According to Kantian Principles* (1796), influential in Russia as basis for school textbooks.

proceedings had reached, would begin its own gnawing work. Iván Ilyich would turn his attention to it and try to drive the thought of it away, but without success. *It* would come and stand before him and look at him, and he would be petrified and the light would die out of his eyes, and he would again begin asking himself whether *It* alone was true. And his colleagues and subordinates would see with surprise and distress that he, the brilliant and subtle judge, was becoming confused and making mistakes. He would shake himself, try to pull himself together, manage somehow to bring the sitting to a close, and return home with the sorrowful consciousness that his judicial labours could not as formerly hide from him what he wanted them to hide, and could not deliver him from *It*. And what was worst of all was that *It* drew his attention to itself not in order to make him take some action but only that he should look at *It*, look it straight in the face: look at it without doing anything, suffer inexpressibly.

And to save himself from this condition Iván Ilyich looked for consolations—new screens—and new screens were found and for a while seemed to save him, but then they immediately fell to pieces or rather became transparent, as if *It* penetrated them and nothing could veil *It*.

In these latter days he would go into the drawing-room he had arranged—that drawing-room where he had fallen and for the sake of which (how bitterly ridiculous it seemed) he had sacrificed his life—for he knew that his illness originated with that knock. He would enter and see that something had scratched the polished table. He would look for the cause of this and find that it was the bronze ornamentation of an album, that had got bent. He would take up the expensive album which he had lovingly arranged, and feel vexed with his daughter and her friends for their untidiness—for the album was torn here and there and some of the photographs turned upside down. He would put it carefully in order and bend the ornamentation back into position. Then it would occur to him to place all those things in another corner of the room, near the plants. He would call the footman, but his daughter or wife would come to help him. They would not agree, and his wife would contradict him, and he would dispute and grow angry. But that was all right, for then he did not think about *It*. *It* was invisible.

But then, when he was moving something himself, his wife would say: "Let the servants do it. You will hurt yourself again." And suddenly *It* would flash through the screen and he would see it. It was just a flash, and he hoped it would disappear, but he would involuntarily pay attention to his side. "It sits there as before, gnawing just the same!" And he could no longer forget *It*, but could distinctly see it looking at him from behind the flowers. "What is it all for?"

"It really is so! I lost my life over that curtain as I might have done when storming a fort. Is that possible? How terrible and how stupid. It can't be true! It can't, but it is."

He would go to his study, lie down, and again be alone with *It*: face to face with *It*. And nothing could be done with *It* except to look at it and shudder.

VII

How it happened it is impossible to say because it came about step by step, unnoticed, but in the third month of Iván Ilyich's illness, his wife, his daughter, his son, his acquaintances, the doctors, the servants, and above all he himself, were aware that the whole interest he had for other people was whether he would soon vacate his place, and at last release the living from the discomfort caused by his presence and be himself released from his sufferings.

He slept less and less. He was given opium and hypodermic injections of morphine, but this did not relieve him. The dull depression he experienced in a somnolent condition at first gave him a little relief, but only as something new, afterwards it became as distressing as the pain itself or even more so.

Special foods were prepared for him by the doctors' orders, but all those foods became increasingly distasteful and disgusting to him.

For his excretions also special arrangements had to be made, and this was a torment to him every time—a torment from the uncleanliness, the unseemliness, and the smell, and from knowing that another person had to take part in it.

But just through this most unpleasant matter, Iván Ilyich obtained comfort. Gerásim, the butler's young assistant, always came in to carry the things out. Gerásim was a clean, fresh peasant lad, grown stout on town food and always cheerful and bright. At first the sight of him, in his clean Russian peasant costume, engaged on that disgusting task embarrassed Iván Ilyich.

Once when he got up from the commode too weak to draw up his trousers, he dropped into a soft armchair and looked with horror at his bare, enfeebled thighs with the muscles so sharply marked on them.

Gerásim with a firm light tread, his heavy boots emitting a pleasant smell of tar and fresh winter air, came in wearing a clean Hessian apron,[2] the sleeves of his print shirt tucked up over his strong bare young arms; and refraining from looking at his sick master out of consideration for his feelings, and restraining the joy of life that beamed from his face, he went up to the commode.

"Gerásim!" said Iván Ilyich in a weak voice.

Gerásim started, evidently afraid he might have committed some blunder, and with a rapid movement turned his fresh, kind, simple young face which just showed the first downy signs of a beard.

"Yes, sir?"

"That must be very unpleasant for you. You must forgive me. I am helpless."

"Oh, why, sir," and Gerásim's eyes beamed and he showed his glistening white teeth, "what's a little trouble? It's a case of illness with you, sir."

And his deft strong hands did their accustomed task, and he went out of the room stepping lightly. Five minutes later he as lightly returned.

Iván Ilyich was still sitting in the same position in the armchair.

"Gerásim," he said when the latter had replaced the freshly-washed utensil. "Please come here and help me." Gerásim went up to him. "Lift me up. It is hard for me to get up, and I have sent Dmítri away."

Gerásim went up to him, grasped his master with his strong arms deftly but gently, in the same way that he stepped—lifted him, supported him with one hand, and with the other drew up his trousers and would have

2. Burlap apron.

set him down again, but Iván Ilyich asked to be led to the sofa. Gerásim, without an effort and without apparent pressure, led him, almost lifting him, to the sofa and placed him on it.

"Thank you. How easily and well you do it all!" Gerásim smiled again and turned to leave the room. But Iván Ilyich felt his presence such a comfort that he did not want to let him go.

"One thing more, please move up that chair. No, the other one—under my feet. It is easier for me when my feet are raised."

Gerásim brought the chair, set it down gently in place, and raised Iván Ilyich's legs on to it. It seemed to Iván Ilyich that he felt better while Gerásim was holding up his legs.

"It's better when my legs are higher," he said. "Place that cushion under them."

Gerásim did so. He again lifted the legs and placed them, and again Iván Ilyich felt better while Gerásim held his legs. When he set them down Iván Ilyich fancied he felt worse.

"Gerásim," he said. "Are you busy now?"

"Not at all, sir," said Gerásim, who had learnt from the townsfolk how to speak to gentlefolk.

"What have you still to do?"

"What have I to do? I've done everything except chopping the logs for to-morrow."

"Then hold my legs up a bit higher, can you?"

"Of course I can. Why not?" and Gerásim raised his master's legs higher and Iván Ilyich thought that in that position he did not feel any pain at all.

"And how about the logs?"

"Don't trouble about that, sir. There's plenty of time."

Iván Ilyich told Gerásim to sit down and hold his legs, and began to talk to him. And strange to say it seemed to him that he felt better while Gerásim held his legs up.

After that Iván Ilyich would sometimes call Gerásim and get him to hold his legs on his shoulders, and he liked talking to him. Gerásim did it all easily, willingly, simply, and with a good nature that touched Iván Ilyich. Health, strength, and vitality in other people were offensive to him, but Gerásim's strength and vitality did not mortify but soothed him.

What tormented Iván Ilyich most was the deception, the lie, which for some reason they all accepted, that he was not dying but was simply ill, and that he only need keep quiet and undergo a treatment and then something very good would result. He however knew that do what they would nothing would come of it, only still more agonizing suffering and death. This deception tortured him—their not wishing to admit what they all knew and what he knew, but wanting to lie to him concerning his terrible condition, and wishing and forcing him to participate in that lie. Those lies—lies enacted over him on the eve of his death and destined to degrade this awful, solemn act to the level of their visitings, their curtains, their sturgeon for dinner—were a terrible agony for Iván Ilyich. And strangely enough, many times when they were going through their antics over him he had been within a hairbreadth of calling out to them: "Stop lying! You know and I know that I am dying. Then at least stop lying about it!" But he had never had the spirit to do it. The awful, terrible act of his dying was, he could see, reduced by those about him to the level of

a casual, unpleasant, and almost indecorous incident (as if someone entered a drawing-room diffusing an unpleasant odour) and this was done by
that very decorum which he had served all his life long. He saw that no
one felt for him, because no one even wished to grasp his position. Only
Gerásim recognized and pitied him. And so Iván Ilyich felt at ease only
with him. He felt comforted when Gerásim supported his legs (sometimes
all night long) and refused to go to bed, saying: "Don't you worry, Iván
Ilyich. I'll get sleep enough later on," or when he suddenly became familiar and exclaimed: "If you weren't sick it would be another matter, but as
it is, why should I grudge a little trouble?" Gerásim alone did not lie;
everything showed that he alone understood the facts of the case and did
not consider it necessary to disguise them, but simply felt sorry for his
emaciated and enfeebled master. Once when Iván Ilyich was sending him
away he even said straight out: "We shall all of us die, so why should I
grudge a little trouble?"—expressing the fact that he did not think his
work burdensome, because he was doing it for a dying man and hoped
someone would do the same for him when his time came.

Apart from this lying, or because of it, what most tormented Iván
Ilyich was that no one pitied him as he wished to be pitied. At certain
moments after prolonged suffering he wished most of all (though he
would have been ashamed to confess it) for someone to pity him as a sick
child is pitied. He longed to be petted and comforted. He knew he was
an important functionary, that he had a beard turning grey, and that
therefore what he longed for was impossible, but still he longed for it.
And in Gerásim's attitude towards him there was something akin to what
he wished for, and so that attitude comforted him. Iván Ilyich wanted to
weep, wanted to be petted and cried over, and then his colleague Shébek
would come, and instead of weeping and being petted, Iván Ilyich would
assume a serious, severe, and profound air, and by force of habit would
express his opinion on a decision of the Court of Appeal and would stubbornly insist on that view. This falsity around him and within him did
more than anything else to poison his last days.

VIII

It was morning. He knew it was morning because Gerásim had gone,
and Peter the footman had come and put out the candles, drawn back
one of the curtains, and begun quietly to tidy up. Whether it was morning or evening, Friday or Sunday, made no difference, it was all just the
same: the gnawing, unmitigated, agonizing pain, never ceasing for an instant, the consciousness of life inexorably waning but not yet extinguished, the approach of that ever dreaded and hateful Death which was
the only reality, and always the same falsity. What were days, weeks,
hours, in such a case?

"Will you have some tea, sir?"

"He wants things to be regular, and wishes the gentlefolk to drink tea
in the morning," thought Iván Ilyich, and only said "No."

"Wouldn't you like to move onto the sofa, sir?"

"He wants to tidy up the room, and I'm in the way. I am uncleanliness
and disorder," he thought, and said only:

"No, leave me alone."

The man went on bustling about. Iván Ilyich stretched out his hand. Peter came up, ready to help.

"What is it, sir?"

"My watch."

Peter took the watch which was close at hand and gave it to his master.

"Half-past eight. Are they up?"

"No, sir, except Vasílii Ivánich" (the son) "who has gone to school. Praskóvya Fëdorovna ordered me to wake her if you asked for her. Shall I do so?"

"No, there's no need to." "Perhaps I'd better have some tea," he thought, and added aloud: "Yes, bring me some tea."

Peter went to the door, but Iván Ilyich dreaded being left alone. "How can I keep him here? Oh yes, my medicine." "Peter, give me my medicine." "Why not? Perhaps it may still do me some good." He took a spoonful and swallowed it. "No, it won't help. It's all tomfoolery, all deception," he decided as soon as he became aware of the familiar, sickly, hopeless taste. "No, I can't believe in it any longer. But the pain, why this pain? If it would only cease just for a moment!" And he moaned. Peter turned towards him. "It's all right. Go and fetch me some tea."

Peter went out. Left alone Iván Ilyich groaned not so much with pain, terrible though that was, as from mental anguish. Always and forever the same, always these endless days and nights. If only it would come quicker! If only *what* would come quicker? Death, darkness? . . . No, no! Anything rather than death!

When Peter returned with the tea on a tray, Iván Ilyich stared at him for a time in perplexity, not realizing who and what he was. Peter was disconcerted by that look and his embarrassment brought Iván Ilyich to himself.

"Oh, tea! All right, put it down. Only help me to wash and put on a clean shirt."

And Iván Ilyich began to wash. With pauses for rest, he washed his hands and then his face, cleaned his teeth, brushed his hair, and looked in the glass. He was terrified by what he saw, especially by the limp way in which his hair clung to his pallid forehead.

While his shirt was being changed he knew that he would be still more frightened at the sight of his body, so he avoided looking at it. Finally he was ready. He drew on a dressing-gown, wrapped himself in a plaid, and sat down in the armchair to take his tea. For a moment he felt refreshed, but as soon as he began to drink the tea he was again aware of the same taste, and the pain also returned. He finished it with an effort, and then lay down stretching out his legs, and dismissed Peter.

Always the same. Now a spark of hope flashes up, then a sea of despair rages, and always pain; always pain, always despair, and always the same. When alone he had a dreadful and distressing desire to call someone, but he knew beforehand that with others present it would be still worse. "Another dose of morphine—to lose consciousness. I will tell him, the doctor, that he must think of something else. It's impossible, impossible, to go on like this."

An hour and another pass like that. But now there is a ring at the door bell. Perhaps it's the doctor? It is. He comes in fresh, hearty, plump, and cheerful, with that look on his face that seems to say: "There now, you're in a panic about something, but we'll arrange it all for you directly!" The doctor knows this expression is out of place here, but he has put it on once for all and can't take it off—like a man who has put on a frock-coat in the morning to pay a round of calls.

The doctor rubs his hands vigorously and reassuringly.

"Brr! How cold it is! There's such a sharp frost; just let me warm myself!" he says, as if it were only a matter of waiting till he was warm, and then he would put everything right.

"Well now, how are you?"

Iván Ilyich feels that the doctor would like to say: "Well, how are our affairs?" but that even he feels that this would not do, and says instead: "What sort of a night have you had?"

Iván Ilyich looks at him as much as to say: "Are you really never ashamed of lying?" But the doctor does not wish to understand this question, and Iván Ilyich says: "Just as terrible as ever. The pain never leaves me and never subsides. If only something . . ."

"Yes, you sick people are always like that. . . . There, now I think I'm warm enough. Even Praskóvya Fëdorovna, who is so particular, could find no fault with my temperature. Well, now I can say good-morning," and the doctor presses his patient's hand.

Then, dropping his former playfulness, he begins with a most serious face to examine the patient, feeling his pulse and taking his temperature, and then begins the sounding and auscultation.

Iván Ilyich knows quite well and definitely that all this is nonsense and pure deception, but when the doctor, getting down on his knee, leans over him, putting his ear first higher then lower, and performs various gymnastic movements over him with a significant expression on his face, Iván Ilyich submits to it all as he used to submit to the speeches of the lawyers, though he knew very well that they were all lying and why they were lying.

The doctor, kneeling on the sofa, is still sounding him when Praskóvya Fëdorovna's silk dress rustles at the door and she is heard scolding Peter for not having let her know of the doctor's arrival.

She comes in, kisses her husband, and at once proceeds to prove that she has been up a long time already, and only owing to a misunderstanding failed to be there when the doctor arrived.

Iván Ilyich looks at her, scans her all over, sets against her the whiteness and plumpness and cleanness of her hands and neck, the gloss of her hair, and the sparkle of her vivacious eyes. He hates her with his whole soul. And the thrill of hatred he feels for her makes him suffer from her touch.

Her attitude towards him and his disease is still the same. Just as the doctor had adopted a certain relation to his patient which he could not abandon, so had she formed one towards him—that he was not doing something he ought to do and was himself to blame, and that she reproached him lovingly for this—and she could not now change that attitude.

"You see he doesn't listen to me and doesn't take his medicine at the proper time. And above all he lies in a position that is no doubt bad for him—with his legs up."

She described how he made Gerásim hold his legs up.

The doctor smiled with a contemptuous affability that said: "What's to be done? These sick people do have foolish fancies of that kind, but we must forgive them."

When the examination was over the doctor looked at his watch, and then Praskóvya Fëdorovna announced to Iván Ilyich that it was of course as he pleased, but she had sent to-day for a celebrated specialist who would examine him and have a consultation with Michael Danílovich (their regular doctor).

"Please don't raise any objections. I am doing this for my own sake," she said ironically, letting it be felt that she was doing it all for his sake and only said this to leave him no right to refuse. He remained silent, knitting his brows. He felt that he was so surrounded and involved in a mesh of falsity that it was hard to unravel anything.

Everything she did for him was entirely for her own sake, and she told him she was doing for herself what she actually was doing for herself, as if that was so incredible that he must understand the opposite.

At half-past eleven the celebrated specialist arrived. Again the sounding began and the significant conversations in his presence and in another room, about the kidneys and the appendix, and the questions and answers, with such an air of importance that again, instead of the real question of life and death which now alone confronted him, the question arose of the kidney and the appendix which were not behaving as they ought to and would now be attacked by Michael Danílovich and the specialist and forced to amend their ways.

The celebrated specialist took leave of him with a serious though not hopeless look, and in reply to the timid question Iván Ilyich, with eyes glistening with fear and hope, put to him as to whether there was a chance of recovery, said that he could not vouch for it but there was a possibility. The look of hope with which Iván Ilyich watched the doctor out was so pathetic that Praskóvya Fëdorovna, seeing it, even wept as she left the room to hand the doctor his fee.

The gleam of hope kindled by the doctor's encouragement did not last long. The same room, the same pictures, curtains, wall-paper, medicine bottles, were all there, and the same aching suffering body, and Iván Ilyich began to moan. They gave him a subcutaneous injection and he sank into oblivion.

It was twilight when he came to. They brought him his dinner and he swallowed some beef tea with difficulty, and then everything was the same again and night was coming on.

After dinner, at seven o'clock, Praskóvya Fëdorovna came into the room in evening dress, her full bosom pushed up by her corset, and with traces of powder on her face. She had reminded him in the morning that they were going to the theatre. Sarah Bernhardt was visiting the town and they had a box, which he had insisted on their taking. Now he had forgotten about it and her toilet offended him, but he concealed his vexation when he remembered that he had himself insisted on their securing a box and going because it would be an instructive and aesthetic pleasure for the children.

Praskóvya Fëdorovna came in, self-satisfied but yet with a rather guilty air. She sat down and asked how he was, but, as he saw, only for the sake of asking and not in order to learn about it, knowing that there was nothing to learn—and then went on to what she really wanted to say: that she would not on any account have gone but that the box had been taken and

Helen and their daughter were going, as well as Petríshchev (the examining magistrate, their daughter's fiancé) and that it was out of the question to let them go alone; but that she would have much preferred to sit with him for a while; and he must be sure to follow the doctor's orders while she was away.

"Oh, and Fëdor Petróvich" (the fiancé) "would like to come in. May he? And Lisa?"

"All right."

Their daughter came in in full evening dress, her fresh young flesh exposed (making a show of that very flesh which in his own case caused so much suffering), strong, healthy, evidently in love, and impatient with illness, suffering, and death, because they interfered with her happiness.

Fëdor Petróvich came in too, in evening dress, his hair curled *à la Capoul*,[3] a tight stiff collar round his long sinewy neck, an enormous white shirt-front and narrow black trousers tightly stretched over his strong thighs. He had one white glove tightly drawn on, and was holding his opera hat in his hand.

Following him the schoolboy crept in unnoticed, in a new uniform, poor little fellow, and wearing gloves. Terribly dark shadows showed under his eyes, the meaning of which Iván Ilyich knew well.

His son had always seemed pathetic to him, and now it was dreadful to see the boy's frightened look of pity. It seemed to Iván Ilyich that Vásya was the only one besides Gerásim who understood and pitied him.

They all sat down and again asked how he was. A silence followed. Lisa asked her mother about the opera-glasses, and there was an altercation between mother and daughter as to who had taken them and where they had been put. This occasioned some unpleasantness.

Fëdor Petróvich inquired of Iván Ilyich whether he had ever seen Sarah Bernhardt. Iván Ilyich did not at first catch the question, but then replied: "No, have you seen her before?"

"Yes, in *Adrienne Lecouvreur*."[4]

Praskóvya Fëdorovna mentioned some rôles in which Sarah Bernhardt was particularly good. Her daughter disagreed. Conversation sprang up as to the elegance and realism of her acting—the sort of conversation that is always repeated and is always the same.

In the midst of the conversation Fëdor Petróvich glanced at Iván Ilyich and became silent. The others also looked at him and grew silent. Iván Ilyich was staring with glittering eyes straight before him, evidently indignant with them. This had to be rectified, but it was impossible to do so. The silence had to be broken, but for a time no one dared to break it and they all became afraid that the conventional deception would suddenly become obvious and the truth become plain to all. Lisa was the first to pluck up courage and break that silence, but by trying to hide what everybody was feeling, she betrayed it.

"Well, if we are going it's time to start," she said, looking at her watch, a present from her father, and with a faint and significant smile at Fëdor Petróvich relating to something known only to them. She got up with a rustle of her dress.

---

3. With a part in the middle, hair brushed off the sides of the forehead but with two small curls over the middle of the forehead; after Joseph-Amédée-Victor Capoul (1839–1924), French singer and mati-nee idol.

4. An 1849 play by the prolific and popular French playwright Eugène Scribe (1791–1861), one of Bernhardt's most famous vehicles.

They all rose, said good-night, and went away.

When they had gone it seemed to Iván Ilyich that he felt better; the falsity had gone with them. But the pain remained—that same pain and that same fear that made everything monotonously alike, nothing harder and nothing easier. Everything was worse.

Again minute followed minute and hour followed hour. Everything remained the same and there was no cessation. And the inevitable end of it all became more and more terrible.

"Yes, send Gerásim here," he replied to a question Peter asked.

IX

His wife returned late at night. She came in on tiptoe, but he heard her, opened his eyes, and made haste to close them again. She wished to send Gerásim away and to sit with him herself, but he opened his eyes and said: "No, go away."

"Are you in great pain?"

"Always the same."

"Take some opium."

He agreed and took some. She went away.

Till about three in the morning he was in a state of stupefied misery. It seemed to him that he and his pain were being thrust into a narrow, deep black sack, but though they were pushed further and further in they could not be pushed to the bottom. And this, terrible enough in itself, was accompanied by suffering. He was frightened yet wanted to fall through the sack, he struggled but yet co-operated. And suddenly he broke through, fell, and regained consciousness. Gerásim was sitting at the foot of the bed dozing quietly and patiently, while he himself lay with his emaciated stockinged legs resting on Gerásim's shoulders; the same shaded candle was there and the same unceasing pain.

"Go away, Gerásim," he whispered.

"It's all right, sir. I'll stay a while."

"No. Go away."

He removed his legs from Gerásim's shoulders, turned sideways onto his arm, and felt sorry for himself. He only waited till Gerásim had gone into the next room and then restrained himself no longer but wept like a child. He wept on account of his helplessness, his terrible loneliness, the cruelty of man, the cruelty of God, and the absence of God.

"Why hast Thou done all this? Why hast Thou brought me here? Why dost Thou torment me so terribly?"

He did not expect an answer and yet wept because there was no answer and could be none. The pain again grew more acute, but he did not stir and did not call. He said to himself: "Go on! Strike me! But what is it for? What have I done to Thee? What is it for?"

Then he grew quiet and not only ceased weeping but even held his breath and became all attention. It was as though he were listening not to an audible voice but to a voice of his soul, to the current of thoughts arising within him.

"What is it you want?" was the first clear conception capable of expression in words, that he heard.

"What do you want? What do you want?" he repeated to himself,
"What do I want? To live and not to suffer," he answered.

And again he listened with such concentrated attention that even his
pain did not distract him.

"To live? How?" asked his inner voice.

"Why, to live as I used to—well and pleasantly."

"As you lived before, well and pleasantly?" the voice repeated.

And in imagination he began to recall the best moments of his pleasant
life. But strange to say none of those best moments of his pleasant life
now seemed at all what they had then seemed—none of them except the
first recollections of childhood. There, in childhood, there had been something really pleasant with which it would be possible to live if it could
return. But the child who had experienced that happiness existed no
longer, it was like a reminiscence of somebody else.

As soon as the period began which had produced the present Iván
Ilyich, all that had then seemed joys now melted before his sight and
turned into something trivial and often nasty.

And the further he departed from childhood and the nearer he came to
the present the more worthless and doubtful were the joys. This began
with the School of Law. A little that was really good was still found
there—there was light-heartedness, friendship, and hope. But in the upper
classes there had already been fewer of such good moments. Then during
the first years of his official career, when he was in the service of the
Governor, some pleasant moments again occurred: they were the memories of love for a woman. Then all became confused and there was still
less of what was good; later on again there was still less that was good,
and the further he went the less there was. His marriage, a mere accident, then the disenchantment that followed it, his wife's bad breath and
the sensuality and hypocrisy: then that deadly official life and those
preoccupations about money, a year of it, and two, and ten, and twenty,
and always the same thing. And the longer it lasted the more deadly it
became. "It is as if I had been going downhill while I imagined I was
going up. And that is really what it was. I was going up in public opinion,
but to the same extent life was ebbing away from me. And now it is all
done and there is only death."

"Then what does it mean? Why? It can't be that life is so senseless and
horrible. But if it really has been so horrible and senseless, why must I die
and die in agony? There is something wrong!"

"Maybe I did not live as I ought to have done," it suddenly occurred to
him. "But how could that be, when I did everything properly?" he replied, and immediately dismissed from his mind this, the sole solution of
all the riddles of life and death, as something quite impossible.

"Then what do you want now? To live? Live how? Live as you lived in
the law courts when the usher proclaimed 'The judge is coming!' The
judge is coming, the judge!" he repeated to himself. "Here he is, the
judge. But I am not guilty!" he exclaimed angrily. "What is it for?" And
he ceased crying, but turning his face to the wall continued to ponder on
the same question: Why, and for what purpose, is there all this horror?
But however much he pondered he found no answer. And whenever the
thought occurred to him, as it often did, that it all resulted from his not
having lived as he ought to have done, he at once recalled the correctness
of his whole life, and dismissed so strange an idea.

X

Another fortnight passed. Iván Ilyich now no longer left his sofa. He would not lie in bed but lay on the sofa, facing the wall nearly all the time. He suffered ever the same unceasing agonies and in his loneliness pondered always on the same insoluble question: "What is this? Can it be that it is Death?" And the inner voice answered: "Yes, it is Death."

"Why these sufferings?" And the voice answered, "For no reason—they just are so." Beyond and besides this there was nothing.

From the very beginning of his illness, ever since he had first been to see the doctor, Iván Ilyich's life had been divided between two contrary and alternating moods: now it was despair and the expectation of this uncomprehended and terrible death, and now hope and an intently interested observation of the functioning of his organs. Now before his eyes there was only a kidney or an intestine that temporarily evaded its duty, and now only that incomprehensible and dreadful death from which it was impossible to escape.

These two states of mind had alternated from the very beginning of his illness, but the further it progressed the more doubtful and fantastic became the conception of the kidney, and the more real the sense of impending death.

He had but to call to mind what he had been three months before and what he was now, to call to mind with what regularity he had been going downhill, for every possibility of hope to be shattered.

Latterly during that loneliness in which he found himself as he lay facing the back of the sofa, a loneliness in the midst of a populous town and surrounded by numerous acquaintances and relations but that yet could not have been more complete anywhere—either at the bottom of the sea or under the earth—during that terrible loneliness Iván Ilyich had lived only in memories of the past. Pictures of his past rose before him one after another. They always began with what was nearest in time and then went back to what was most remote—to his childhood—and rested there. If he thought of the stewed prunes that had been offered him that day, his mind went back to the raw shrivelled French plums of his childhood, their peculiar flavour and the flow of saliva when he sucked their stones, and along with the memory of that taste came a whole series of memories of those days: his nurse, his brother, and their toys. "No, I mustn't think of that. . . . It is too painful," Iván Ilyich said to himself, and brought himself back to the present—to the button on the back of the sofa and the creases in its morocco. "Morocco is expensive, but it does not wear well: there had been a quarrel about it. It was a different kind of quarrel and a different kind of morocco that time when we tore father's portfolio and were punished, and mamma brought us some tarts. . . . " And again his thoughts dwelt on his childhood, and again it was painful and he tried to banish them and fix his mind on something else.

Then again together with that chain of memories another series passed through his mind—of how his illness had progressed and grown worse. There also the further back he looked the more life there had been. There had been more of what was good in life and more of life itself. The two merged together. "Just as the pain went on getting worse and worse, so my life grew worse and worse," he thought. "There is one bright spot there at the back, at the beginning of life, and afterwards all becomes blacker and blacker and proceeds more and more rapidly—in inverse ratio to the square of the distance from death," thought Iván Ilyich. And the example of a stone falling downwards with increasing velocity entered his mind. Life, a series of increasing sufferings, flies further and further towards its end—the most terrible suffering. "I am flying. . . . " He shuddered, shifted himself, and tried to resist, but was already aware that resistance was impossible, and again with eyes weary of gazing but unable to cease seeing what was before them, he stared at the back of the sofa and waited—awaiting that dreadful fall and shock and destruction. "Resistance is impossible!" he said to himself. "If I could only understand what it is all for! But that too is impossible. An explanation would be possible if it could be said that I have not lived as I ought to. But it is impossible to say that," and he remembered all the legality, correctitude, and propriety of his life. "That at any rate can certainly not be admitted," he thought, and his lips smiled ironically as if someone could see that smile and be taken in by it. "There is no explanation! Agony, death. . . . What for?"

XI

Another two weeks went by in this way and during that fortnight an event occurred that Iván Ilyich and his wife had desired. Petríshchev formally proposed. It happened in the evening. The next day Praskóvya Fëdorovna came into her husband's room considering how best to inform him of it, but that very night there had been a fresh change for the worse in his condition. She found him still lying on the sofa but in a different position. He lay on his back, groaning and staring fixedly straight in front of him.

She began to remind him of his medicines, but he turned his eyes towards her with such a look that she did not finish what she was saying; so great an animosity, to her in particular, did that look express.

"For Christ's sake let me die in peace!" he said.

She would have gone away, but just then their daughter came in and went up to say good morning. He looked at her as he had done at his wife, and in reply to her inquiry about his health said dryly that he would soon free them all of himself. They were both silent and after sitting with him for a while went away.

"Is it our fault?" Lisa said to her mother. "It's as if we were to blame! I am sorry for papa, but why should we be tortured?"

The doctor came at his usual time. Iván Ilyich answered "Yes" and "No," never taking his angry eyes from him, and at last said: "You know you can do nothing for me, so leave me alone."

"We can ease your sufferings."

"You can't even do that. Let me be."

The doctor went into the drawing-room and told Praskóvya Fëdorovna that the case was very serious and that the only resource left was opium to allay her husband's sufferings, which must be terrible.

It was true, as the doctor said, that Iván Ilyich's physical sufferings were terrible, but worse than the physical sufferings were his mental sufferings which were his chief torture.

His mental sufferings were due to the fact that that night, as he looked at Gerásim's sleepy, good-natured face with its prominent cheek-bones, the question suddenly occurred to him: "What if my whole life has really been wrong?"

It occurred to him that what had appeared perfectly impossible before, namely that he had not spent his life as he should have done, might after all be true. It occurred to him that his scarcely perceptible attempts to struggle against what was considered good by the most highly placed people, those scarcely noticeable impulses which he had immediately suppressed, might have been the real thing, and all the rest false. And his professional duties and the whole arrangement of his life and of his family, and all his social and official interests, might all have been false. He tried to defend all those things to himself and suddenly felt the weakness of what he was defending. There was nothing to defend.

"But if that is so," he said to himself, "and I am leaving this life with the consciousness that I have lost all that was given me and it is impossible to rectify it—what then?"

He lay on his back and began to pass his life in review in quite a new way. In the morning when he saw first his footman, then his wife, then his daughter, and then the doctor, their every word and movement confirmed to him the awful truth that had been revealed to him during the night. In them he saw himself—all that for which he had lived—and saw clearly that it was not real at all, but a terrible and huge deception which had hidden both life and death. This consciousness intensified his physical suffering tenfold. He groaned and tossed about, and pulled at his clothing which choked and stifled him. And he hated them on that account.

He was given a large dose of opium and became unconscious, but at noon his sufferings began again. He drove everybody away and tossed from side to side.

His wife came to him and said:

"Jean, my dear, do this for me. It can't do any harm and often helps. Healthy people often do it."

He opened his eyes wide.

"What? Take communion? Why? It's unnecessary! However . . . "

She began to cry.

"Yes, do, my dear. I'll send for our priest. He is such a nice man."

"All right. Very well," he muttered.

When the priest came and heard his confession, Iván Ilyich was softened and seemed to feel a relief from his doubts and consequently from his sufferings, and for a moment there came a ray of hope. He again began to think of the vermiform appendix and the possibility of correcting it. He received the sacrament with tears in his eyes.

When they laid him down again afterwards he felt a moment's ease, and the hope that he might live awoke in him again. He began to think of the operation that had been suggested to him. "To live! I want to live!" he said to himself.

His wife came in to congratulate him after his communion, and when uttering the usual conventional words she added:

"You feel better, don't you?"

Without looking at her he said "Yes."

Her dress, her figure, the expression of her face, the tone of her voice, all revealed the same thing. "This is wrong, it is not as it should be. All you have lived for and still live for is falsehood and deception, hiding life and death from you." And as soon as he admitted that thought, his hatred and his agonizing physical suffering again sprang up, and with that suffering a consciousness of the unavoidable, approaching end. And to this was added a new sensation of grinding shooting pain and a feeling of suffocation.

The expression of his face when he uttered that "yes" was dreadful. Having uttered it, he looked her straight in the eyes, turned on his face with a rapidity extraordinary in his weak state and shouted:

"Go away! Go away and leave me alone!"

XII

From that moment the screaming began that continued for three days, and was so terrible that one could not hear it through two closed doors without horror. At the moment he answered his wife he realized that he was lost, that there was no return, that the end had come, the very end, and his doubts were still unsolved and remained doubts.

"Oh! Oh! Oh!" he cried in various intonations. He had begun by screaming "I won't!" and continued screaming on the letter "o."

For three whole days, during which time did not exist for him, he struggled in that black sack into which he was being thrust by an invisible, resistless force. He struggled as a man condemned to death struggles in the hands of the executioner, knowing that he cannot save himself. And every moment he felt that despite all his efforts he was drawing nearer and nearer to what terrified him. He felt that his agony was due to his being thrust into that black hole and still more to his not being able to get right into it. He was hindered from getting into it by his conviction that his life had been a good one. That very justification of his life held him fast and prevented his moving forward, and it caused him most torment of all.

Suddenly some force struck him in the chest and side, making it still harder to breathe, and he fell through the hole and there at the bottom was a light. What had happened to him was like the sensation one sometimes experiences in a railway carriage when one thinks one is going backwards while one is really going forwards and suddenly becomes aware of the real direction.

"Yes, it was all not the right thing," he said to himself, "but that's no matter. It can be done. But what *is* the right thing?" he asked himself, and suddenly grew quiet.

This occurred at the end of the third day, two hours before his death. Just then his schoolboy son had crept softly in and gone up to the bedside. The dying man was still screaming desperately and waving his arms. His hand fell on the boy's head, and the boy caught it, pressed it to his lips, and began to cry.

At that very moment Iván Ilyich fell through and caught sight of the light, and it was revealed to him that though his life had not been what it should have been, this could still be rectified. He asked himself, "What *is* the right thing?" and grew still, listening. Then he felt that someone was kissing his hand. He opened his eyes, looked at his son, and felt sorry for him. His wife came up to him and he glanced at her. She was gazing at him open-mouthed, with undried tears on her nose and cheek and a despairing look on her face. He felt sorry for her too.

"Yes, I am making them wretched," he thought. "They are sorry, but it will be better for them when I die." He wished to say this but had not the strength to utter it. "Besides, why speak? I must act," he thought. With a look at his wife he indicated his son and said: "Take him away . . . sorry for him . . . sorry for you too. . . . " He tried to add, "forgive me," but said "forego" and waved his hand, knowing that He whose understanding mattered would understand.

And suddenly it grew clear to him that what had been oppressing him and would not leave him was all dropping away at once from two sides, from ten sides, and from all sides. He was sorry for them, he must act so as not to hurt them: release them and free himself from these sufferings. "How good and how simple!" he thought. "And the pain?" he asked himself. "What has become of it? Where are you, pain?"

He turned his attention to it.

"Yes, here it is. Well, what of it? Let the pain be."

"And death . . . where is it?"

He sought his former accustomed fear of death and did not find it. "Where is it? What death?" There was no fear because there was no death.

In place of death there was light.

"So that's what it is!" he suddenly exclaimed aloud. "What joy!"

To him all this happened in a single instant, and the meaning of that instant did not change. For those present his agony continued for another two hours. Something rattled in his throat, his emaciated body twitched, then the gasping and rattle became less and less frequent.

"It is finished!" said someone near him.

He heard these words and repeated them in his soul.

"Death is finished," he said to himself. "It is no more!"

He drew in a breath, stopped in the midst of a sigh, stretched out, and died.

1886

AFTERWORD

What can one expect from a story called *The Death of ...* ? The title *Daisy Miller* is noncommital; *The Strange Case of ...* promises mystery, arouses curiosity; *The Death of ...* is so specific, so terminal, that it arouses little expectation and only a mild curiosity about how a novel can be made of the subject. Perhaps it will be a story in which, after adventures or trials of some sort, the main character dies at the end, or perhaps "death" will be metaphorical, ironic, somehow not literal.

But just after the very first paragraph of the novel ends, Iván's literal death is announced and our attention shifts to the *effect* of his death. By the end of the third substantial paragraph, we're pretty sure what that will be. We know what kind of society we are dealing with, or at least the tone of the narrator toward that society: all present were Iván's friends, but each first thought "of the changes and promotions it might occasion among themselves or their acquaintances." Such, then, is the governmental, bureaucratic, ruling-class world of the novel. But then, there are responses that do not seem confined to that narrow world: "Each one thought or felt, 'Well, he's dead but I'm alive' "; close friends "could not help thinking also that they would now have to fulfil the very tiresome demands of propriety," attending the funeral, visiting the widow. We join in feeling sympathy for the dead Iván and his grieving widow, distaste for the selfish and superficial others.

We follow Peter Ivánovich on his visit to the widow, which delays his bridge game, and share (or at least recognize as common, if not admirable) his fear of betraying his discomfort and lack of sincere, profound personal feeling. Even the widow, whose grief we assumed was real and deep, and with whom we sympathized, is primarily concerned, it seems, with the price of burial plots—you cannot let these practical things go just because of grief, can you? She does tell Peter about his friend's suffering ("I cannot understand how I bore it," she says!), and for a moment he is terrified—for himself. Still, he just cannot put himself in Iván's place, for he is still alive. Then, no doubt to his relief, he finds that the widow wanted to see him in order to find out if she can get more out of the government than the widow's pension (about which she seems to know in detail). Iván's servant, Gerásim, whose blooming health and efficiency seem to insult poor Iván's memory, appears in his way callous—his master's death was God's will, a conventional way of not thinking about death or feeling for the dead, is it not? The first chapter ends with Peter Ivánovich leaving to join his—and Iván's—friends, finding "them just finishing the first rubber, so that it was quite convenient for him to cut in." Poor Iván is sincerely mourned only by his teenage son who himself is not "pure-minded." The first chapter seems a complete if skimpy short story or vignette in itself—a cynical portrait of the pervasive selfishness of survivors. Poor dead Iván!

This is not a 3500-word short story, however, but a novel about seven or eight times as long (and this chapter is just the first of twelve). Where can it go from here? Tolstoy could conceivably go on to show how the hard-hearted friends, and the widow herself, get their due, but the second chapter sets out to review the life of poor Iván: if his friends or wife do not pity him, we, more feeling human beings, will. About five hundred words into the chapter, however, we begin to wonder whether we should be quite so sorry for him:

At school he had done things which had formerly seemed to him very horrid and made him feel disgusted with himself when he did them; but when later on he saw that such actions were done by people of good position and that they did not regard them as wrong, he was able not exactly to regard them as right, but to forget about them entirely or not be at all troubled at remembering them.

Ironically, as we get to know Iván better, as his becomes the consciousness through which we see the events of his life and milieu, we feel for him less. He's just like the rest of his society; perhaps he deserves the neglect he receives. At the beginning of Chapter 3, when his luck seems to have turned for the worse and he is passed over for a promotion, we are not sure whether we are glad or sorry, and we feel equal ambivalence in his lucky, successful fishing for a job with a higher income and more prestige. That things improve for him after his hardest year we find ironic, since that year was 1880, and we know he will die at the age of forty-five in the year 1882, and our pity may return. We are therefore more apprehensive than Iván himself when he is injured "slightly" while decorating his new home. We see what he does not, what no human being can see, the future; and so we find that final sentence of the chapter ominous, moving, and a little frightening: "So they lived, and all went well, without change, and life flowed pleasantly."

In the fourth chapter Iván recognizes he is seriously ill, but others do not, and the chapter ends, as so many in this novel do, with a sentence which both summarizes and prepares us for a further stage: "And he had to live thus all alone on the brink of an abyss, with no one who understood or pitied him." Here we are almost back to the beginning of the story, the isolated and pitiable dead or dying man surrounded by the callous, on-going, unconcerned world; our sentiments too have shifted all the way back to "poor Iván." He is no longer the prideful magistrate who keeps personal feelings out of all transactions, but only a mortal man. Like ourselves? Are we mortal too? That's what Iván grapples with in the next chapter: can a syllogism be wholly accepted that concludes that an individual is mortal if the individual is Iván Ilyich? or you? . . . or *me*?

We are even yet only into the fifth of the twelve chapters, only in the middle of the novel. It seems we are in for a rather prolonged deathbed scene. Iván Ilyich is still Iván Ilyich, but hasn't our relationship to him changed? It is not that we know him better exactly, but we no longer feel the unqualified pity of Chapter 1 (Conrad's *The Nigger of the "Narcissus"* tells us something about the egoism of such pity); and gone too is the critical distance from which we viewed him as just another bureaucrat as we read Chapters 2 and 3. It is not so much that we identify with Iván, perhaps, as that (like Peter Ivánovich in Chapter 1, when told of Ivan's suffering) we now must be given pause by the syllogism: All men are mortal. Iván is (I am) a man./ Therefore Iván is (I am) mortal. That is, Iván (I) will die. (And women readers, I am sure, will not easily hide behind the word "man" in the traditional syllogism.)

We may no longer be reading simply the story of a nineteenth-century Russian bureaucrat with our entire attention, but we probably are, with some part of our minds, trying to come to terms with our own mortality. From this point on, we will be reading the story rather differently. Iván's character, his faults and virtues, become less important. The way he lived (we live) and the way he dies (we will die) become the center of the story. The sentence with which the story of his life in Chapter 2 begins may at this point come back to us:

"Iván Ilyich's life had been most simple and most ordinary and therefore most terrible." We may want to go back to the very beginning of the story. His surname, Golovín, is mentioned in the *Gazette* announcement of his death early in the story. Why isn't the novel called *The Death of Iván Ilyich Golovín?* Iván is the most common Russian name. Iván Ilyich is not significantly more individualizing than John Smith, or even John Doe. Are we faced with still another irony or twist? That Iván's death is not treated by his friends and loved ones as something that happened to an individual, a human being, a fellow creature, a man, was reprehensible. That Iván in his position in the government did not treat people as individuals but as cases, as abstractions, was reprehensible. But the novel seems to want us to think of him now not just as Iván Ilyich or little Ványa, but as a typical, ordinary human being like the rest of us. Our attention is directed away from Iván the individual and away from our own deaths and toward our common fate, toward the deaths of all humans, of those we love, and those we hate.

But isn't dwelling on the fact that each of us is going to die "morbid"? Doesn't it keep us from living while we're living? What purpose does it serve? What can we learn about *living*—and isn't that the important thing?—by dwelling on the fact of dying?

Are there any examples of "living" in the novel? Only Iván's schoolboy son and the peasant Gerásim come off at all well. The boy is a bit soppy, but he does at least seem capable of love. Gerásim, who we understood at first to treat his master's death almost casually, really meant it when he spoke of God's will. He is willing to face Iván's illness and dying—we will all come to it someday—and do the best for him while he can at considerable cost to himself. He sees Iván Ilyich not primarily as his "master," but as a suffering mortal, like the rest of us, and while he does not deny life and sit mourning or tearing his hair, he performs the services that the living can perform for the dying. Is he merely a sentimentalized version of the unspoiled peasant, the product of the ruling class, a sort of Russian Uncle Tom?

Iván cannot understand the reason for suffering, perhaps cannot die, until he faces the truth that his life was not a proper life (though, we must remember, an ordinary one). Tolstoy does not directly tell us what *is* a proper life, though we may, through negative and positive examples in the story and through what Iván learns, piece together something of a program or rule of conduct. Gerásim clearly believes in God; but his conduct toward Iván some of us may affirm in human as well as (or aside from) religious terms. Iván communes with his soul in his direst hours; to what extent is what he discovers restricted to those who believe in the soul, God, immortality? Tolstoy himself was "converted"—though not to Orthodox or orthodox Christianity—and for several years thereafter studied theology. Why, then, does he not put his conclusions in more forthright, overt Christian terms?

In his essay "What Is Art?" he insists that art is not for art's but for society's sake, is didactic or a form of persuasion or education, but *not* in the form of overt statement or argument:

> the business of art lies just in this,—to make that understood and felt which, in the form of an argument, might be incomprehensible and inaccessible. . . .

Toward the end of that long, profound, disturbing, and exciting work (in which he "throws out" both Shakespeare and his own novels!), he specifies what the *that* is that art must communicate through the feelings:

Art is not a pleasure, a solace, or an amusement; art is a great matter. Art is an organ of human life, transmitting man's reasonable perception into feeling. In our age the common religious perception of men is the consciousness of the brotherhood of man—we know that the well-being of man lies in union with his fellowmen. . . . Art should transform this perception into feeling.

How can a story in which men's selfish concerns are made so manifest be art, if art is the transmission of the feeling of men's fellowship? Is the feeling transmitted in the story contempt or worse for man-in-society? Or is it the brotherhood of man?

ROBERT LOUIS STEVENSON

The Strange Case
of Dr. Jekyll and Mr. Hyde

The congenital weakness of the lungs with which Stevenson was born—in Edinburgh, on November 13, 1850—hampered but did not halt his life's activity. He had to abandon the study of engineering because of ill health, but studied law and was called to the bar in 1875 (though he never practiced). In rapid succession he fell in love with two married women, each of whom was eleven years older than he, each of whom had a tubercular son. Ill health again, and his father's disapproval, caused him to leave the first for a sojourn on the continent, where he met the second, Fanny Osbourne, whom he followed in 1878 to California, where he spent a rather bad year, troubled by ill health and disapproval of friends and family. With reluctant family approval he was able to marry the divorced Mrs. Osbourne and returned to Edinburgh until the death of his father in 1887 provided him with the means of leaving Britain's damp climate. He first went to Saranac, N.Y., where there was a famous tuberculosis sanitarium, then (with money from a generous contract from the American publisher Scribners for a series of articles) sailed from the West Coast for the South Seas, where he traveled widely and where his health improved. In Samoa he bought a plantation and built a home, Vailima, where he died on December 3, 1894, not of lung disease but of a massive cerebral hemorrhage.

Stevenson's first literary accomplishments were in the form of essays written for *Cornhill* magazine in the late 1870s and collected in the volumes *Virginibus Puerisque* (1881) and *Familiar Studies of Men and Books* (1882). Though they did not in his time bring him fame nor are they much remembered now, these essays are, despite some youthful faults, accomplished and promising. The essays he wrote for Scribners a decade later fulfilled that promise. The essays as well as the novels show Stevenson for the stylist he is (Henry James said Stevenson was the only one he knew "who could write a decent English sentence"). It is the novels, however, upon which Stevenson's fame rests. *Treasure Island* appeared in book form in 1883, and both *The Strange Case of Dr. Jekyll and Mr. Hyde* and *Kidnapped* three years later. Even Stevenson's popular *A Child's Garden of Verses* appeared in this same three-year period. The mature but somewhat uneven *The Master of Ballantrae* appeared in 1889, and at his death Stevenson left a number of unfinished works, including the masterful dark fragment of a novel, *Weir of Hermiston*.

The *Doppelgänger*, or double, appears often in nineteenth- and early twentieth-century fiction, from James Hogg's *Confessions of a Justified Sinner* (1824), through Edgar Allan Poe's *William Wilson* (1839), to Joseph Conrad's *The Secret-Sharer* (1912), but *Jekyll and Hyde* is by far the most popular, the most widely known. Has anyone not read (or seen in some adaptation) *The Strange Case of Dr. Jekyll and Mr. Hyde?* Perhaps because it is so well known, we do well to be on our guard so as not to lose sight of the splendid prose and complex structure in which this compelling tale is embodied. Even Stevenson's theme cannot be satisfactorily reduced to Good vs. Evil or any other simple two-part division of the human faculties or psychological or spiritual qualities.

The Strange Case
of Dr. Jekyll and Mr. Hyde

Story of the Door

MR. UTTERSON the lawyer was a man of a rugged countenance that was never lighted by a smile; cold, scanty and embarrassed in discourse; backward in sentiment; lean, long, dusty, dreary and yet somehow lovable. At friendly meetings, and when the wine was to his taste, something eminently human beaconed from his eye; something indeed which never found its way into his talk, but which spoke not only in these silent symbols of the after-dinner face, but more often and loudly in the acts of his life. He was austere with himself; drank gin when he was alone, to mortify a taste for vintages; and though he enjoyed the theatre, had not crossed the doors of one for twenty years. But he had an approved tolerance for others; sometimes wondering, almost with envy, at the high pressure of spirits involved in their misdeeds; and in any extremity inclined to help rather than to reprove. "I incline to Cain's heresy," he used to say quaintly: "I let my brother go to the devil in his own way."[1] In this character, it was frequently his fortune to be the last reputable acquaintance and the last good influence in the lives of downgoing men. And to such as these, so long as they came about his chambers, he never marked a shade of change in his demeanour.

No doubt the feat was easy to Mr. Utterson; for he was undemonstrative at the best, and even his friendship seemed to be founded in a similar catholicity of good-nature. It is the mark of a modest man to accept his friendly circle ready-made from the hands of opportunity; and that was the lawyer's way. His friends were those of his own blood or those whom he had known the longest; his affections, like ivy, were the growth of time, they implied no aptness in the object. Hence, no doubt, the bond that united him to Mr. Richard Enfield, his distant kinsman, the well-known man about town. It was a nut to crack for many, what these two could see in each other, or what subject they could find in common. It was reported by those who encountered them in their Sunday walks, that they said nothing, looked singularly dull, and would hail with obvious relief the appearance of a friend. For all that, the two men put the greatest store by these excursions, counted them the chief jewel of each week, and not only set aside occasions of pleasure, but even resisted the calls of business, that they might enjoy them uninterrupted.

It chanced on one of these rambles that their way led them down a by-street in a busy quarter of London. The street was small and what is called quiet, but it drove a thriving trade on the week-days. The inhabitants were all doing well, it seemed, and all emulously hoping to do better still, and laying out the surplus of their gains in coquetry; so that the shop fronts stood along that thoroughfare with an air of invitation, like rows of smiling saleswomen. Even on Sunday, when it veiled its more

---

1. Genesis 4:9. After Cain killed Abel, "the Lord said, I know not: Am I my brother's keeper?"
said unto Cain, Where is Abel thy brother? And he

florid charms and lay comparatively empty of passage, the street shone
out in contrast to its dingy neighbourhood, like a fire in a forest; and with
its freshly painted shutters, well-polished brasses, and general cleanliness
and gaiety of note, instantly caught and pleased the eye of the passenger.

Two doors from one corner, on the left hand going east, the line was
broken by the entry of a court; and just at that point, a certain sinister
block of building thrust forward its gable on the street. It was two storeys
high; showed no window, nothing but a door on the lower storey and a
blind forehead of discoloured wall on the upper; and bore in every feature, the marks of prolonged and sordid negligence. The door, which was
equipped with neither bell nor knocker, was blistered and distained.
Tramps slouched into the recess and struck matches on the panels; children kept shop upon the steps; the schoolboy had tried his knife on the
mouldings; and for close on a generation, no one had appeared to drive
away these random visitors or to repair their ravages.

Mr. Enfield and the lawyer were on the other side of the by-street; but
when they came abreast of the entry, the former lifted up his cane and
pointed.

"Did you ever remark that door?" he asked; and when his companion
had replied in the affirmative, "It is connected in my mind," added he,
"with a very odd story."

"Indeed?" said Mr. Utterson, with a slight change of voice, "and what
was that?"

"Well, it was this way," returned Mr. Enfield: "I was coming home
from some place at the end of the world, about three o'clock of a black
winter morning, and my way lay through a part of town where there was
literally nothing to be seen but lamps. Street after street, and all the folks
asleep—street after street, all lighted up as if for a procession and all as
empty as a church—till at last I got into that state of mind when a man
listens and listens and begins to long for the sight of a policeman. All at
once, I saw two figures: one a little man who was stumping along eastward at a good walk, and the other a girl of maybe eight or ten who was
running as hard as she was able down a cross street. Well, sir, the two ran
into one another naturally enough at the corner; and then came the horrible part of the thing; for the man trampled calmly over the child's body
and left her screaming on the ground. It sounds nothing to hear, but it
was hellish to see. It wasn't like a man; it was like some damned Juggernaut. I gave a view halloa,[2] took to my heels, collared my gentleman, and
brought him back to where there was already quite a group about the
screaming child. He was perfectly cool and made no resistance, but gave
me one look, so ugly that it brought out the sweat on me like running.
The people who had turned out were the girl's own family; and pretty
soon, the doctor, for whom she had been sent, put in his appearance.
Well, the child was not much the worse, more frightened, according to
the Sawbones; and there you might have supposed would be an end to it.
But there was one curious circumstance. I had taken a loathing to my
gentleman at first sight. So had the child's family, which was only natural.
But the doctor's case was what struck me. He was the usual cut and dry

2. Shout given by a huntsman on seeing the fox break cover.

apothecary, of no particular age and colour, with a strong Edinburgh accent, and about as emotional as a bagpipe. Well, sir, he was like the rest of us; every time he looked at my prisoner, I saw that Sawbones turn sick and white with the desire to kill him. I knew what was in his mind, just as he knew what was in mine; and killing being out of the question, we did the next best. We told the man we could and would make such a scandal out of this, as should make his name stink from one end of London to the other. If he had any friends or any credit, we undertook that he should lose them. And all the time, as we were pitching it in red hot, we were keeping the women off him as best we could, for they were as wild as harpies. I never saw a circle of such hateful faces; and there was the man in the middle, with a kind of black, sneering coolness—frightened too, I could see that—but carrying it off, sir, really like Satan. 'If you choose to make capital out of this accident,' said he, 'I am naturally helpless. No gentleman but wishes to avoid a scene,' says he. 'Name your figure.' Well, we screwed him up to a hundred pounds[3] for the child's family; he would have clearly liked to stick out; but there was something about the lot of us that meant mischief, and at last he struck. The next thing was to get the money; and where do you think he carried us but to that place with the door?—whipped out a key, went in, and presently came back with the matter of ten pounds in gold and a cheque for the balance on Coutts's,[4] drawn payable to bearer and signed with a name that I can't mention, though it's one of the points of my story, but it was a name at least very well known and often printed. The figure was stiff; but the signature was good for more than that, if it was only genuine. I took the liberty of pointing out to my gentleman that the whole business looked apocryphal, and that a man does not, in real life, walk into a cellar door at four in the morning and come out of it with another man's cheque for close upon a hundred pounds. But he was quite easy and sneering. 'Set your mind at rest,' says he, 'I will stay with you till the banks open and cash the cheque myself.' So we all set off, the doctor, and the child's father, and our friend and myself, and passed the rest of the night in my chambers; and next day, when we had breakfasted, went in a body to the bank. I gave in the cheque myself, and said I had every reason to believe it was a forgery. Not a bit of it. The cheque was genuine."

"I see you feel as I do," said Mr. Enfield. "Yes, it's a bad story. For my man was a fellow[5] that nobody could have to do with, a really damnable man; and the person that drew the cheque is the very pink[6] of the proprieties, celebrated too, and (what makes it worse) one of your fellows who do what they call good. Black mail, I suppose; an honest man paying through the nose for some of the capers of his youth. Black Mail House is what I call that place with the door, in consequence. Though even that, you know, is far from explaining all," he added, and with the words fell into a vein of musing.

From this he was recalled by Mr. Utterson asking rather suddenly: "And you don't know if the drawer of the cheque lives there?"

3. About $500 when purchasing power was vastly more, perhaps the equivalent of $3000–$5000 today.
4. A bank.
5. Low sort of person.
6. Highest example.

"A likely place, isn't it?" returned Mr. Enfield. "But I happen to have noticed his address; he lives in some square or other."

"And you never asked about the—place with the door?" said Mr. Utterson.

"No, sir: I had a delicacy," was the reply. "I feel very strongly about putting questions; it partakes too much of the style of the day of judgment. You start a question, and it's like starting a stone. You sit quietly on the top of a hill; and away the stone goes, starting others; and presently some bland old bird (the last you would have thought of) is knocked on the head in his own back garden and the family have to change their name. No, sir, I make it a rule of mine: the more it looks like Queer Street,[7] the less I ask."

"A very good rule, too," said the lawyer.

"But I have studied the place for myself," continued Mr. Enfield. "It seems scarcely a house. There is no other door, and nobody goes in or out of that one but, once in a great while, the gentleman of my adventure. There are three windows looking on the court on the first floor; none below; the windows are always shut but they're clean. And then there is a chimney which is generally smoking; so somebody must live there. And yet it's not so sure; for the buildings are so packed together about that court, that it's hard to say where one ends and another begins."

The pair walked on again for a while in silence; and then "Enfield," said Mr. Utterson, "that's a good rule of yours."

"Yes, I think it is," returned Enfield.

"But for all that," continued the lawyer, "there's one point I want to ask: I want to ask the name of that man who walked over the child."

"Well," said Mr. Enfield, "I can't see what harm it would do. It was a man of the name of Hyde."

"Hm," said Mr. Utterson. "What sort of a man is he to see?"

"He is not easy to describe. There is something wrong with his appearance; something displeasing, something downright detestable. I never saw a man I so disliked, and yet I scarce know why. He must be deformed somewhere; he gives a strong feeling of deformity, although I couldn't specify the point. He's an extraordinary looking man, and yet I really can name nothing out of the way. No, sir; I can make no hand of it; I can't describe him. And it's not want of memory; for I declare I can see him this moment."

Mr. Utterson again walked some way in silence and obviously under a weight of consideration. "You are sure he used a key?" he inquired at last.

"My dear sir . . ." began Enfield, surprised out of himself.

"Yes, I know," said Utterson; "I know it must seem strange. The fact is, if I do not ask you the name of the other party, it is because I know it already. You see, Richard, your tale has gone home. If you have been inexact in any point, you had better correct it."

"I think you might have warned me," returned the other with a touch of sullenness. "But I have been pedantically exact, as you call it. The fellow had a key; and what's more, he has it still. I saw him use it, not a week ago."

Mr. Utterson sighed deeply but said never a word; and the young man presently resumed. "Here is another lesson to say nothing," said he. "I am

7. An imaginary street where people in financial and other trouble live.

ashamed of my long tongue. Let us make a bargain never to refer to this again."

"With all my heart," said the lawyer. "I shake hands on that, Richard."

Search for Mr. Hyde

That evening Mr. Utterson came home to his bachelor house in sombre spirits and sat down to dinner without relish. It was his custom of a Sunday, when this meal was over, to sit close by the fire, a volume of some dry divinity on his reading desk, until the clock of the neighbouring church rang out the hour of twelve, when he would go soberly and gratefully to bed. On this night, however, as soon as the cloth was taken away, he took up a candle and went into his business room. There he opened his safe, took from the most private part of it a document endorsed on the envelope as Dr. Jekyll's Will, and sat down with a clouded brow to study its contents. The will was holograph, for Mr. Utterson, though he took charge of it now that it was made, had refused to lend the least assistance in the making of it; it provided not only that, in case of the decease of Henry Jekyll, M.D., D.C.L., L.L.D., F.R.S., etc., all his possessions were to pass into the hands of his "friend and benefactor Edward Hyde," but that in case of Dr. Jekyll's "disappearance or unexplained absence for any period exceeding three calendar months," the said Edward Hyde should step into the said Henry Jekyll's shoes without further delay and free from any burthen or obligation, beyond the payment of a few small sums to the members of the doctor's household. This document had long been the lawyer's eyesore. It offended him both as a lawyer and as a lover of the sane and customary sides of life, to whom the fanciful was the immodest. And hitherto it was his ignorance of Mr. Hyde that had swelled his indignation; now, by a sudden turn, it was his knowledge. It was already bad enough when the name was but a name of which he could learn no more. It was worse when it began to be clothed upon with detestable attributes; and out of the shifting, insubstantial mists that had so long baffled his eye, there leaped up the sudden, definite presentment of a fiend.

"I thought it was madness," he said, as he replaced the obnoxious paper in the safe, "and now I begin to fear it is disgrace."

With that he blew out his candle, put on a greatcoat, and set forth in the direction of Cavendish Square, that citadel of medicine, where his friend, the great Dr. Lanyon, had his house and received his crowding patients. "If anyone knows, it will be Lanyon," he had thought.

The solemn butler knew and welcomed him; he was subjected to no stage of delay, but ushered direct from the door to the dining-room where Dr. Lanyon sat alone over his wine. This was a hearty, healthy, dapper, red-faced gentleman, with a shock of hair prematurely white, and a boisterous and decided manner. At sight of Mr. Utterson, he sprang up from his chair and welcomed him with both hands. The geniality, as was the way of the man, was somewhat theatrical to the eye; but it reposed on genuine feeling. For those two were old friends, old mates both at school and college, both thorough respecters of themselves and of each other, and, what does not always follow, men who thoroughly enjoyed each other's company.

After a little rambling talk, the lawyer led up to the subject which so disagreeably preoccupied his mind.

"I suppose, Lanyon," said he, "you and I must be the two oldest friends that Henry Jekyll has?"

"I wish the friends were younger," chuckled Dr. Lanyon. "But I suppose we are. And what of that? I see little of him now."

"Indeed?" said Utterson. "I thought you had a bond of common interest."

"We had," was the reply. "But it is more than ten years since Henry Jekyll became too fanciful for me. He began to go wrong, wrong in mind; and though of course I continue to take an interest in him for old sake's sake, as they say, I see and I have seen devilish little of the man. Such unscientific balderdash," added the doctor, flushing suddenly purple, "would have estranged Damon and Pythias."

This little spirit of temper was somewhat of a relief to Mr. Utterson. "They have only differed on some point of science," he thought; and being a man of no scientific passions (except in the matter of conveyancing), he even added: "It is nothing worse than that!" He gave his friend a few seconds to recover his composure, and then approached the question he had come to put. "Did you ever come across a protégé of his—one Hyde?" he asked.

"Hyde?" repeated Lanyon. "No. Never heard of him. Since my time."

That was the amount of information that the lawyer carried back with him to the great, dark bed on which he tossed to and fro, until the small hours of the morning began to grow large. It was a night of little ease to his toiling mind, toiling in mere darkness and besieged by questions.

Six o'clock struck on the bells of the church that was so conveniently near to Mr. Utterson's dwelling, and still he was digging at the problem. Hitherto it had touched him on the intellectual side alone; but now his imagination also was engaged, or rather enslaved; and as he lay and tossed in the gross darkness of the night and the curtained room, Mr. Enfield's tale went by before his mind in a scroll of lighted pictures. He would be aware of the great field of lamps of a nocturnal city; then of the figure of a man walking swiftly; then of a child running from the doctor's; and then these met, and that human Juggernaut trod the child down and passed on regardless of her screams. Or else he would see a room in a rich house, where his friend lay asleep, dreaming and smiling at his dreams; and then the door of that room would be opened, the curtains of the bed plucked apart, the sleeper recalled, and lo! there would stand by his side a figure to whom power was given, and even at that dead hour, he must rise and do its bidding. The figure in these two phases haunted the lawyer all night; and if at any time he dozed over, it was but to see it glide more stealthily through sleeping houses, or move the more swiftly and still the more swiftly, even to dizziness, through wider labyrinths of lamplighted city, and at every street corner crush a child and leave her screaming. And still the figure had no face by which he might know it; even in his dreams, it had no face, or one that baffled him and melted before his eyes; and thus it was that there sprang up and grew apace in the lawyer's mind a singularly strong, almost an inordinate, curiosity to behold the features of the real Mr. Hyde. If he could but once set eyes on him, he thought the mystery would lighten and perhaps roll altogether away, as was the habit of mysterious things when well examined. He might see a reason for his friend's strange preference or bondage (call it which you please) and even for the startling clause of the will. At least it would be a face worth seeing: the face of a man who was without bowels of mercy: a face which had but to show itself to raise up, in the mind of the unimpressionable Enfield, a spirit of enduring hatred.

From that time forward, Mr. Utterson began to haunt the door in the by-street of shops. In the morning before office hours, at noon when business was plenty, and time scarce, at night under the face of the fogged city moon, by all lights and at all hours of solitude or concourse, the lawyer was to be found on his chosen post.

"If he be Mr. Hyde," he had thought, "I shall be Mr. Seek."

And at last his patience was rewarded. It was a fine dry night; frost in the air; the streets as clean as a ballroom floor; the lamps, unshaken by any wind, drawing a regular pattern of light and shadow. By ten o'clock, when the shops were closed, the by-street was very solitary and, in spite of the low growl of London from all round, very silent. Small sounds carried far; domestic sounds out of the houses were clearly audible on either side of the roadway; and the rumour of the approach of any passenger preceded him by a long time. Mr. Utterson had been some minutes at his post, when he was aware of an odd, light footstep drawing near. In the course of his nightly patrols, he had long grown accustomed to the quaint effect with which the footfalls of a single person, while he is still a great way off, suddenly spring out distinct from the vast hum and clatter of the city. Yet his attention had never before been so sharply and decisively arrested; and it was with a strong, superstitious prevision of success that he withdrew into the entry of the court.

The steps drew swiftly nearer, and swelled out suddenly louder as they turned the end of the street. The lawyer, looking forth from the entry, could soon see what manner of man he had to deal with. He was small and very plainly dressed, and the look of him, even at that distance, went somehow strongly against the watcher's inclination. But he made straight for the door, crossing the roadway to save time; and as he came, he drew a key from his pocket like one approaching home.

Mr. Utterson stepped out and touched him on the shoulder as he passed. "Mr. Hyde, I think?"

Mr. Hyde shrank back with a hissing intake of the breath. But his fear was only momentary; and though he did not look the lawyer in the face he answered coolly enough: "That is my name. What do you want?"

"I see you are going in," returned the lawyer. "I am an old friend of Dr. Jekyll's—Mr. Utterson of Gaunt Street—you must have heard of my name; and meeting you so conveniently, I thought you might admit me."

"You will not find Dr. Jekyll; he is from home," replied Mr. Hyde, blowing in the key. And then suddenly, but still without looking up, "How did you know me?" he asked.

"On your side," said Mr. Utterson, "will you do me a favour?"

"With pleasure," replied the other. "What shall it be?"

"Will you let me see your face?" asked the lawyer.

Mr. Hyde appeared to hesitate, and then, as if upon some sudden reflection, fronted about with an air of defiance; and the pair stared at each other pretty fixedly for a few seconds. "Now I shall know you again," said Mr. Utterson. "It may be useful."

"Yes," returned Mr. Hyde, "it is as well we have met; and *à propos*, you should have my address." And he gave a number of a street in Soho.[8]

"Good God!" thought Mr. Utterson, "can he, too, have been thinking of the will?" But he kept his feelings to himself and only grunted in acknowledgment of the address.

"And now," said the other, "how did you know me?"

"By description," was the reply.

"Whose description?"

"We have common friends," said Mr. Utterson.

"Common friends?" echoed Mr. Hyde, a little hoarsely. "Who are they?"

"Jekyll, for instance," said the lawyer.

"He never told you," cried Mr. Hyde, with a flush of anger. "I did not think you would have lied."

"Come," said Mr. Utterson, "that is not fitting language."

The other snarled aloud into a savage laugh; and the next moment, with extraordinary quickness, he had unlocked the door and disappeared into the house.

The lawyer stood awhile when Mr. Hyde had left him, the picture of disquietude. Then he began slowly to mount the street, pausing every step or two and putting his hand to his brow like a man in mental perplexity. The problem he was thus debating as he walked, was one of a class that is rarely solved. Mr. Hyde was pale and dwarfish, he gave an impression of deformity without any nameable malformation, he had a displeasing smile, he had borne himself to the lawyer with a sort of murderous mixture of timidity and boldness, and he spoke with a husky, whispering and somewhat broken voice; all these were points against him, but not all of these together could explain the hitherto unknown disgust, loathing and fear with which Mr. Utterson regarded him. "There must be something else," said the perplexed gentleman. "There *is* something more, if I could find a name for it. God bless me, the man seems hardly human! Something troglodytic, shall we say? or can it be the old story of Dr. Fell?[9] or is it the mere radiance of a foul soul that thus transpires through, and transfigures, its clay continent? The last, I think; for, O my poor old Harry Jekyll, if ever I read Satan's signature upon a face, it is on that of your new friend."

Round the corner from the by-street, there was a square of ancient, handsome houses, now for the most part decayed from their high estate and let in flats and chambers to all sorts and conditions of men; map-engravers, architects, shady lawyers and the agents of obscure enterprises. One house, however, second from the corner, was still occupied entire; and at the door of this, which wore a great air of wealth and comfort, though it was now plunged in darkness except for the fan-light, Mr. Utterson stopped and knocked. A well-dressed, elderly servant opened the door.

"Is Dr. Jekyll at home, Poole?" asked the lawyer.

"I will see, Mr. Utterson," said Poole, admitting the visitor, as he spoke, into a large, low-roofed, comfortable hall, paved with flags,

---

8. Section of London roughly comparable to New York's Greenwich Village: full of good continental restaurants, writers and artists, somewhat shady characters.

9. "I do not love thee, Dr. Fell./ The reason why I cannot tell."; a free translation by Tom Brown (1830–1897) of an epigram by Martial (c. 40–c. 104).

warmed (after the fashion of a country house) by a bright, open fire, and furnished with costly cabinets of oak. "Will you wait here by the fire, sir? or shall I give you a light in the dining-room?"

"Here, thank you," said the lawyer, and he drew near and leaned on the tall fender. This hall, in which he was now left alone, was a pet fancy of his friend the doctor's; and Utterson himself was wont to speak of it as the pleasantest room in London. But tonight there was a shudder in his blood; the face of Hyde sat heavy on his memory; he felt (what was rare with him) a nausea and distaste of life; and in the gloom of his spirits, he seemed to read a menace in the flickering of the firelight on the polished cabinets and the uneasy starting of the shadow on the roof. He was ashamed of his relief, when Poole presently returned to announce that Dr. Jekyll was gone out.

"I saw Mr. Hyde go in by the old dissecting-room door, Poole," he said. "Is that right, when Dr. Jekyll is from home?"

"Quite right, Mr. Utterson, sir," replied the servant. "Mr. Hyde has a key."

"Your master seems to repose a great deal of trust in that young man, Poole," resumed the other musingly.

"Yes, sir, he do indeed," said Poole. "We have all orders to obey him."

"I do not think I ever met Mr. Hyde?" asked Utterson.

"O, dear no, sir. He never *dines* here," replied the butler. "Indeed we see very little of him on this side of the house; he mostly comes and goes by the laboratory."

"Well, good-night, Poole."

"Good-night, Mr. Utterson."

And the lawyer set out homeward with a very heavy heart. "Poor Harry Jekyll," he thought, "my mind misgives me he is in deep waters! He was wild when he was young; a long while ago to be sure; but in the law of God, there is no statute of limitations. Ay, it must be that; the ghost of some old sin, the cancer of some concealed disgrace: punishment coming, *pede claudo,*[1] years after memory has forgotten and self-love condoned the fault." And the lawyer, scared by the thought, brooded awhile on his own past, groping in all the corners of memory, lest by chance some Jack-in-the-Box of an old iniquity should leap to light there. His past was fairly blameless; few men could read the rolls of their life with less apprehension; yet he was humbled to the dust by the many ill things he had done, and raised up again into a sober and fearful gratitude by the many he had come so near to doing, yet avoided. And then by a return on his former subject, he conceived a spark of hope. "This Master Hyde, if he were studied," thought he, "must have secrets of his own, black secrets, by the look of him; secrets compared to which poor Jekyll's worst would be like sunshine. Things cannot continue as they are. It turns me cold to think of this creature stealing like a thief to Harry's bedside; poor Harry, what a wakening! And the danger of it; for if this Hyde suspects the existence of the will, he may grow impatient to inherit. Ay, I must put my shoulder to the wheel—if Jekyll will but let me," he added, "if Jekyll will only let me." For once more he saw before his mind's eye, as clear as transparency, the strange clauses of the will.

1. On limping foot.

Dr. Jekyll Was Quite at Ease

A fortnight later, by excellent good fortune, the doctor gave one of his pleasant dinners to some five or six old cronies, all intelligent, reputable men and all judges of good wine; and Mr. Utterson so contrived that he remained behind after the others had departed. This was no new arrangement, but a thing that had befallen many scores of times. Where Utterson was liked, he was liked well. Hosts loved to detain the dry lawyer, when the light-hearted and loose-tongued had already their foot on the threshold; they liked to sit awhile in his unobtrusive company, practising for solitude, sobering their minds in the man's rich silence after the expense and strain of gaiety. To this rule, Dr. Jekyll was no exception; and as he now sat on the opposite side of the fire—a large, well-made, smooth-faced man of fifty, with something of a slyish cast perhaps, but every mark of capacity and kindness—you could see by his look that he cherished for Mr. Utterson a sincere and warm affection.

"I have been wanting to speak to you, Jekyll," began the latter. "You know that will of yours?"

A close observer might have gathered that the topic was distasteful; but the doctor carried it off gaily. "My poor Utterson," said he, "you are unfortunate in such a client. I never saw a man so distressed as you were by my will; unless it were that hide-bound pedant, Lanyon, at what he called my scientific heresies. O, I know he's a good fellow—you needn't frown—an excellent fellow, and I always mean to see more of him; but a hide-bound pedant for all that; an ignorant, blatant pedant. I was never more disappointed in any man than Lanyon."

"You know I never approved of it," pursued Utterson, ruthlessly disregarding the fresh topic.

"My will? Yes, certainly, I know that," said the doctor, a trifle sharply. "You have told me so."

"Well, I tell you so again," continued the lawyer. "I have been learning something of young Hyde."

The large handsome face of Dr. Jekyll grew pale to the very lips, and there came a blackness about his eyes. "I do not care to hear more," said he. "This is a matter I thought we had agreed to drop."

"What I heard was abominable," said Utterson.

"It can make no change. You do not understand my position," returned the doctor, with a certain incoherency of manner. "I am painfully situated, Utterson; my position is a very strange—a very strange one. It is one of those affairs that cannot be mended by talking."

"Jekyll," said Utterson, "you know me; I am a man to be trusted. Make a clean breast of this in confidence; and I make no doubt I can get you out of it."

"My good Utterson," said the doctor, "this is very good of you, this is downright good of you, and I cannot find words to thank you in. I believe you fully; I would trust you before any man alive, ay, before myself, if I could make the choice; but indeed it isn't what you fancy; it is not as bad as that; and just to put your good heart at rest, I will tell you one thing: the moment I choose, I can be rid of Mr. Hyde. I give you my hand upon that; and I thank you again and again; and I will just add one little word, Utterson, that I'm sure you'll take in good part: this is a private matter, and I beg of you to let it sleep."

Utterson reflected a little, looking in the fire.

"I have no doubt you are perfectly right," he said at last, getting to his feet.

"Well, but since we have touched upon this business, and for the last time I hope," continued the doctor, "there is one point I should like you to understand. I have really a very great interest in poor Hyde. I know you have seen him; he told me so; and I fear he was rude. But I do sincerely take a great, a very great interest in that young man; and if I am taken away, Utterson, I wish you to promise me that you will bear with him and get his rights for him. I think you would, if you knew all; and it would be a weight off my mind if you would promise."

"I can't pretend that I shall ever like him," said the lawyer.

"I don't ask that," pleaded Jekyll, laying his hand upon the other's arm; "I only ask for justice; I only ask you to help him for my sake, when I am no longer here."

Utterson heaved an irrepressible sigh. "Well," said he, "I promise."

The Carew Murder Case

Nearly a year later, in the month of October, 18—, London was startled by a crime of singular ferocity and rendered all the more notable by the high position of the victim. The details were few and startling. A maid servant living alone in a house not far from the river, had gone upstairs to bed about eleven. Although a fog rolled over the city in the small hours, the early part of the night was cloudless, and the lane, which the maid's window overlooked, was brilliantly lit by the full moon. It seems she was romantically given, for she sat down upon her box, which stood immediately under the window, and fell into a dream of musing. Never (she used to say, with streaming tears, when she narrated that experience), never had she felt more at peace with all men or thought more kindly of the world. And as she so sat she became aware of an aged beautiful gentleman with white hair, drawing near along the lane; and advancing to meet him, another and very small gentleman, to whom at first she paid less attention. When they had come within speech (which was just under the maid's eyes) the older man bowed and accosted the other with a very pretty manner of politeness. It did not seem as if the subject of his address were of great importance; indeed, from his pointing, it sometimes appeared as if he were only inquiring his way; but the moon shone on his face as he spoke, and the girl was pleased to watch it, it seemed to breathe such an innocent and old-world kindness of disposition, yet with something high too, as of a well founded self-content. Presently her eye wandered to the other, and she was surprised to recognise in him a certain Mr. Hyde, who had once visited her master and for whom she had conceived a dislike. He had in his hand a heavy cane, with which he was trifling; but he answered never a word, and seemed to listen with an ill-contained impatience. And then all of a sudden he broke out in a great flame of anger, stamping with his foot, brandishing the cane, and carrying on (as the maid described it) like a madman. The old gentleman took a step back, with the air of one very much surprised and a trifle hurt; and at that Mr. Hyde broke out of all bounds and clubbed him to the earth. And next moment, with ape-like fury, he was trampling his victim under foot and hailing down a storm of blows, under which the bones were audibly shattered and the body jumped upon the roadway. At the horror of these sights and sounds, the maid fainted.

It was two o'clock when she came to herself and called for the police. The murderer was gone long ago; but there lay his victim in the middle of the lane, incredibly mangled. The stick with which the deed had been done, although it was of some rare and very tough and heavy wood, had broken in the middle under the stress of this insensate cruelty; and one splintered half had rolled in the neighbouring gutter—the other, without doubt, had been carried away by the murderer. A purse and gold watch were found upon the victim; but no cards or papers, except a sealed and stamped envelope, which he had been probably carrying to the post, and which bore the name and address of Mr. Utterson.

This was brought to the lawyer the next morning, before he was out of bed; and he had no sooner seen it, and been told the circumstances, than he shot out a solemn lip. "I shall say nothing till I have seen the body," said he; "this may be very serious. Have the kindness to wait while I dress." And with the same grave countenance he hurried through his breakfast and drove to the police station, whither the body had been carried. As soon as he came into the cell, he nodded.

"Yes," said he, "I recognise him. I am sorry to say that this is Sir Danver Carew."

"Good God, sir," exclaimed the officer, "is it possible?" And the next moment his eye lighted up with professional ambition. "This will make a deal of noise," he said. "And perhaps you can help us to the man." And he briefly narrated what the maid had seen, and showed the broken stick.

Mr. Utterson had already quailed at the name of Hyde; but when the stick was laid before him, he could doubt no longer; broken and battered as it was, he recognised it for one that he had himself presented many years before to Henry Jekyll.

"Is this Mr. Hyde a person of small stature?" he inquired.

"Particularly small and particularly wicked-looking, is what the maid calls him," said the officer.

Mr. Utterson reflected; and then, raising his head, "If you will come with me in my cab," he said, "I think I can take you to his house."

It was by this time about nine in the morning, and the first fog of the season. A great chocolate-coloured pall lowered over heaven, but the wind was continually charging and routing these embattled vapours; so that as the cab crawled from street to street, Mr. Utterson beheld a marvelous number of degrees and hues of twilight; for here it would be dark like the back-end of evening; and there would be a glow of a rich, lurid brown, like the light of some strange conflagration; and here, for a moment, the fog would be quite broken up, and a haggard shaft of daylight would glance in between the swirling wreaths. The dismal quarter of Soho seen under these changing glimpses, with its muddy ways, and slatternly passengers, and its lamps, which had never been extinguished or had been kindled afresh to combat this mournful reinvasion of darkness, seemed, in the lawyer's eyes, like a district of some city in a nightmare. The thoughts of his mind, besides, were of the gloomiest dye; and when he glanced at the companion of his drive, he was conscious of some touch of that terror of the law and the law's officers, which may at times assail the most honest.

As the cab drew up before the address indicated, the fog lifted a little and showed him a dingy street, a gin palace, a low French eating house, a shop for the retail of penny numbers[2] and twopenny salads, many ragged children huddled in the doorways, and many women of many different nationalities passing out, key in hand, to have a morning glass; and the next moment the fog settled down again upon that part, as brown as umber, and cut him off from his blackguardly surroundings. This was the home of Henry Jekyll's favourite; of a man who was heir to a quarter of a million sterling.

An ivory-faced and silvery-haired old woman opened the door. She had an evil face, smoothed by hypocrisy: but her manners were excellent. Yes, she said, this was Mr. Hyde's, but he was not at home; he had been in that night very late, but he had gone away again in less than an hour; there was nothing strange in that; his habits were very irregular, and he was often absent; for instance, it was nearly two months since she had seen him till yesterday.

"Very well, then, we wish to see his rooms," said the lawyer; and when the woman begin to declare it was impossible, "I had better tell you who this person is," he added. "This is Inspector Newcomen of Scotland Yard."

A flash of odious joy appeared upon the woman's face. "Ah!" said she, "he is in trouble! What has he done?"

Mr. Utterson and the inspector exchanged glances. "He don't seem a very popular character," observed the latter. "And now, my good woman, just let me and this gentleman have a look about us."

In the whole extent of the house, which but for the old woman remained otherwise empty, Mr. Hyde had only used a couple of rooms; but these were furnished with luxury and good taste. A closet was filled with wine; the plate was of silver, the napery elegant; a good picture hung upon the walls, a gift (as Utterson supposed) from Henry Jekyll, who was much of a connoisseur; and the carpets were of many plies and agreeable in colour. At this moment, however, the rooms bore every mark of having been recently and hurriedly ransacked; clothes lay about the floor, with their pockets inside out; lock-fast drawers stood open; and on the hearth there lay a pile of grey ashes, as though many papers had been burned. From these embers the inspector disinterred the butt end of a green cheque book, which had resisted the action of the fire; the other half of the stick was found behind the door; and as this clinched his suspicions, the officer declared himself delighted. A visit to the bank, where several thousand pounds were found to be lying to the murderer's credit, completed his gratification.

"You may depend upon it, sir," he told Mr. Utterson: "I have him in my hand. He must have lost his head, or he never would have left the stick or, above all, burned the cheque book. Why, money's life to the man. We have nothing to do but wait for him at the bank, and get out the handbills."

This last, however, was not so easy of accomplishment; for Mr. Hyde had numbered few familiars—even the master of the servant maid had only seen him twice; his family could nowhere be traced; he had never

2. Sensational popular novels were published in small sections or numbers that sold cheaply. There were 240 pennies to the British pound sterling which was then roughly five American dollars. Though it is difficult to give exact modern equivalents, the differ- ence between two cents for the number, four cents for the salads, and a million and a quarter dollars ("a quarter of a million sterling," below) may give some idea of the proportions.

been photographed, and the few who could describe him differed widely, as common observers will. Only on one point were they agreed; and that was the haunting sense of unexpressed deformity with which the fugitive impressed his beholders.

Incident of the Letter

It was late in the afternoon, when Mr. Utterson found his way to Dr. Jekyll's door, where he was at once admitted by Poole, and carried down by the kitchen offices and across a yard which had once been a garden, to the building which was indifferently known as the laboratory or dissecting rooms. The doctor had bought the house from the heirs of a celebrated surgeon; and his own tastes being rather chemical than anatomical, had changed the destination of the block at the bottom of the garden. It was the first time that the lawyer had been received in that part of his friend's quarters; and he eyed the dingy, windowless structure with curiosity, and gazed round with a distasteful sense of strangeness as he crossed the theatre,[3] once crowded with eager students and now lying gaunt and silent, the tables laden with chemical apparatus, the floor strewn with crates and littered with packing straw, and the light falling dimly through the foggy cupola. At the further end, a flight of stairs mounted to a door covered with red baize; and through this, Mr. Utterson was at last received into the doctor's cabinet. It was a large room fitted round with glass presses,[4] furnished, among other things, with a cheval-glass and a business table, and looking out upon the court by three dusty windows barred with iron. The fire burned in the grate; a lamp was set lighted on the chimney shelf, for even in the houses the fog began to lie thickly; and there, close up to the warmth, sat Dr. Jekyll, looking deadly sick. He did not rise to meet his visitor, but held out a cold hand and bade him welcome in a changed voice.

"And now," said Mr. Utterson, as soon as Poole had left them, "you have heard the news?"

The doctor shuddered. "They were crying it in the square," he said. "I heard them in my dining-room."

"One word," said the lawyer. "Carew was my client, but so are you, and I want to know what I am doing. You have not been mad enough to hide this fellow?"

"Utterson, I swear to God," cried the doctor, "I swear to God I will never set eyes on him again. I bind my honour to you that I am done with him in this world. It is all at an end. And indeed he does not want my help; you do not know him as I do; he is safe, he is quite safe; mark my words, he will never more be heard of."

The lawyer listened gloomily; he did not like his friend's feverish manner. "You seem pretty sure of him," said he; "and for your sake, I hope you may be right. If it came to a trial, your name might appear."

"I am quite sure of him," replied Jekyll; "I have grounds for certainty that I cannot share with anyone. But there is one thing on which you may advise me. I have—I have received a letter; and I am at a loss whether I should show it to the police. I should like to leave it in your hands, Utterson; you would judge wisely, I am sure; I have so great a trust in you."

3. I.e., surgical theater, where lectures were held and autopsies and operations performed before medi-   cal students.
    4. Cases, here used for holding chemicals.

"You fear, I suppose, that it might lead to his detection?" asked the lawyer.

"No," said the other. "I cannot say that I care what becomes of Hyde; I am quite done with him. I was thinking of my own character, which this hateful business has rather exposed."

Utterson ruminated awhile; he was surprised at his friend's selfishness, and yet relieved by it. "Well," said he, at last, "let me see the letter."

The letter was written in an odd, upright hand and signed "Edward Hyde": and it signified, briefly enough, that the writer's benefactor, Dr. Jekyll, whom he had long so unworthily repaid for a thousand generosities, need labour under no alarm for his safety, as he had means of escape on which he placed a sure dependence. The lawyer liked this letter well enough; it put a better colour on the intimacy than he had looked for; and he blamed himself for some of his past suspicions.

"Have you the envelope?" he asked.

"I burned it," replied Jekyll, "before I thought what I was about. But it bore no postmark. The note was handed in."

"Shall I keep this and sleep upon it?" asked Utterson.

"I wish you to judge for me entirely," was the reply. "I have lost confidence in myself."

"Well, I shall consider," returned the lawyer. "And now one word more: it was Hyde who dictated the terms in your will about that disappearance?"

The doctor seemed seized with a qualm of faintness; he shut his mouth tight and nodded.

"I knew it," said Utterson. "He meant to murder you. You had a fine escape."

"I have had what is far more to the purpose," returned the doctor solemnly; "I have had a lesson—O God, Utterson, what a lesson I have had!" And he covered his face for a moment with his hands.

On his way out, the lawyer stopped and had a word or two with Poole. "By the bye," said he, "there was a letter handed in to-day: what was the messenger like?" But Poole was positive nothing had come except by post; "and only circulars by that," he added.

This news sent off the visitor with his fears renewed. Plainly the letter had come by the laboratory door; possibly, indeed, it had been written in the cabinet; and if that were so, it must be differently judged, and handled with the more caution. The newsboys, as he went, were crying themselves hoarse along the footways: "Special edition. Shocking murder of an M.P."[5] That was the funeral oration of one friend and client; and he could not help a certain apprehension lest the good name of another should be sucked down in the eddy of the scandal. It was, at least, a ticklish decision that he had to make; and self-reliant as he was by habit, he began to cherish a longing for advice. It was not to be had directly; but perhaps, he thought, it might be fished for.

Presently after, he sat on one side of his own hearth, with Mr. Guest, his head clerk, upon the other, and midway between, at a nicely calculated distance from the fire, a bottle of a particular old wine that had long dwelt unsunned in the foundations of his house. The fog still slept on the wing above the drowned city, where the lamps glimmered like car-

5. Member of Parliament.

buncles; and through the muffle and smother of these fallen clouds, the procession of the town's life was still rolling in through the great arteries with a sound as of a mighty wind. But the room was gay with firelight. In the bottle the acids were long ago resolved; the imperial dye had softened with time, as the colour grows richer in stained windows; and the glow of hot autumn afternoons on hillside vineyards, was ready to be set free and to disperse the fogs of London. Insensibly the lawyer melted. There was no man from whom he kept fewer secrets than Mr. Guest; and he was not always sure that he kept as many as he meant. Guest had often been on business to the doctor's; he knew Poole; he could scarce have failed to hear of Mr. Hyde's familiarity about the house; he might draw conclusions: was it not as well, then, that he should see a letter which put that mystery to rights? and above all since Guest, being a great student and critic of handwriting, would consider the step natural and obliging? The clerk, besides, was a man of counsel; he could scarce read so strange a document without dropping a remark; and by that remark Mr. Utterson might shape his future course.

"This is a sad business about Sir Danvers," he said.

"Yes, sir, indeed. It has elicited a great deal of public feeling," returned Guest. "The man, of course, was mad."

"I should like to hear your views on that," replied Utterson. "I have a document here in his handwriting; it is between ourselves, for I scarce know what to do about it; it is an ugly business at the best. But there it is; quite in your way: a murderer's autograph."

Guest's eyes brightened, and he sat down at once and studied it with passion. "No sir," he said: "not mad; but it is an odd hand."

"And by all accounts a very odd writer," added the lawyer.

Just then the servant entered with a note.

"Is that from Dr. Jekyll, sir?" inquired the clerk. "I thought I knew the writing. Anything private, Mr. Utterson?"

"Only an invitation to dinner. Why? Do you want to see it?"

"One moment. I thank you, sir;" and the clerk laid the two sheets of paper alongside and sedulously compared their contents. "Thank you, sir," he said at last, returning both; "it's a very interesting autograph."

There was a pause, during which Mr. Utterson struggled with himself. "Why did you compare them, Guest?" he inquired suddenly.

"Well, sir," returned the clerk, "there's a rather singular resemblance; the two hands are in many points identical; only differently sloped."

"Rather quaint," said Utterson.

"It is, as you say, rather quaint," returned Guest.

"I wouldn't speak of this note, you know," said the master.

"No, sir," said the clerk. "I understand."

But no sooner was Mr. Utterson alone that night, than he locked the note into his safe, where it reposed from that time forward. "What!" he thought. "Henry Jekyll forge for a murderer!" And his blood ran cold in his veins.

Remarkable Incident of Dr. Lanyon

Time ran on; thousands of pounds were offered in reward, for the death of Sir Danvers was resented as a public injury; but Mr. Hyde had disappeared out of the ken of the police as though he had never existed. Much of his past was unearthed, indeed, and all disreputable: tales came out of the man's cruelty, at once so callous and violent; of his vile life, of his strange associates, of the hatred that seemed to have surrounded his career; but of his present whereabouts, not a whisper. From the time he had left the house in Soho on the morning of the murder, he was simply blotted out; and gradually, as time drew on, Mr. Utterson began to recover from the hotness of his alarm, and to grow more at quiet with himself. The death of Sir Danvers was, to his way of thinking, more than paid for by the disappearance of Mr. Hyde. Now that that evil influence had been withdrawn, a new life began for Dr. Jekyll. He came out of his seclusion, renewed relations with his friends, became once more their familiar guest and entertainer; and whilst he had always been known for charities, he was now no less distinguished for religion. He was busy, he was much in the open air, he did good; his face seemed to open and brighten, as if with an inward consciousness of service; and for more than two months, the doctor was at peace.

On the 8th of January Utterson had dined at the doctor's with a small party; Lanyon had been there; and the face of the host had looked from one to the other as in the old days when the trio were inseparable friends. On the 12th, and again on the 14th, the door was shut against the lawyer. "The doctor was confined to the house," Poole said, "and saw no one." On the 15th, he tried again, and was again refused; and having now been used for the last two months to see his friend almost daily, he found this return of solitude to weigh upon his spirits. The fifth night he had in Guest to dine with him; and the sixth he betook himself to Dr. Lanyon's.

There at least he was not denied admittance; but when he came in, he was shocked at the change which had taken place in the doctor's appearance. He had his death-warrant written legibly upon his face. The rosy man had grown pale; his flesh had fallen away; he was visibly balder and older; and yet it was not so much these tokens of a swift physical decay that arrested the lawyer's notice, as a look in the eye and quality of manner that seemed to testify to some deep-seated terror of the mind. It was unlikely that the doctor should fear death; and yet that was what Utterson was tempted to suspect. "Yes," he thought; "he is a doctor, he must know his own state and that his days are counted; and the knowledge is more than he can bear." And yet when Utterson remarked on his ill-looks, it was with an air of great firmness that Lanyon declared himself a doomed man.

"I have had a shock," he said, "and I shall never recover. It is a question of weeks. Well, life has been pleasant; I liked it; yes, sir, I used to like it. I sometimes think if we knew all, we should be more glad to get away."

"Jekyll is ill, too," observed Utterson. "Have you seen him?"

But Lanyon's face changed, and he held up a trembling hand. "I wish to see or hear no more of Dr. Jekyll," he said in a loud, unsteady voice. "I am quite done with that person; and I beg that you will spare me any allusion to one whom I regard as dead."

"Tut-tut," said Mr. Utterson; and then after a considerable pause, "Can't I do anything?" he inquired. "We are three very old friends, Lanyon; we shall not live to make others."

"Nothing can be done," returned Lanyon; "ask himself."

"He will not see me," said the lawyer.

"I am not surprised at that," was the reply. "Some day, Utterson, after I am dead, you may perhaps come to learn the right and wrong of this. I cannot tell you. And in the meantime, if you can sit and talk with me of other things, for God's sake, stay and do so; but if you cannot keep clear of this accursed topic, then in God's name, go, for I cannot bear it."

As soon as he got home, Utterson sat down and wrote to Jekyll, complaining of his exclusion from the house, and asking the cause of this unhappy break with Lanyon; and the next day brought him a long answer, often very pathetically worded, and sometimes darkly mysterious in drift. The quarrel with Lanyon was incurable. "I do not blame our old friend," Jekyll wrote, "but I share his view that we must never meet. I mean from henceforth to lead a life of extreme seclusion; you must not be surprised, nor must you doubt my friendship, if my door is often shut even to you. You must suffer me to go my own dark way. I have brought on myself a punishment and a danger that I cannot name. If I am the chief of sinners, I am the chief of sufferers also. I could not think that this earth contained a place for sufferings and terrors so unmanning; and you can do but one thing, Utterson, to lighten this destiny, and that is to respect my silence." Utterson was amazed; the dark influence of Hyde had been withdrawn, the doctor had returned to his old tasks and amities; a week ago, the prospect had smiled with every promise of a cheerful and an honoured age; and now in a moment, friendship, and peace of mind, and the whole tenor of his life were wrecked. So great and unprepared a change pointed to madness; but in view of Lanyon's manner and words, there must lie for it some deeper ground.

A week afterwards Dr. Lanyon took to his bed, and in something less than a fortnight he was dead. The night after the funeral, at which he had been sadly affected, Utterson locked the door of his business room, and sitting there by the light of a melancholy candle, drew out and set before him an envelope addressed by the hand and sealed with the seal of his dead friend. "PRIVATE: for the hands of G. J. Utterson ALONE, and in case of his predecease[6] *to be destroyed unread,*" so it was emphatically superscribed; and the lawyer dreaded to behold the contents. "I have buried one friend to-day," he thought: "what if this should cost me another?" And then he condemned the fear as a disloyalty, and broke the seal. Within there was another enclosure, likewise sealed, and marked upon the cover as "not to be opened till the death or disappearance of Dr. Henry Jekyll." Utterson could not trust his eyes. Yes, it was disappearance; here again, as in the mad will which he had long ago restored to its author, here again were the idea of a disappearance and the name of Henry Jekyll bracketted. But in the will, that idea had sprung from the sinister suggestion of the man Hyde; it was set there with a purpose all too plain and horrible. Written by the hand of Lanyon, what should it mean? A great curiosity came on the trustee, to disregard the prohibition and dive at once to the bottom of these mysteries; but professional honour and faith to his dead friend were stringent obligations; and the packet slept in the inmost corner of his private safe.

It is one thing to mortify curiosity, another to conquer it; and it may be doubted if, from that day forth, Utterson desired the society of his surviving friend with the same eagerness. He thought of him kindly; but his

6. I.e., if Utterson were to die before Lanyon.

thoughts were disquieted and fearful. He went to call indeed; but he was perhaps relieved to be denied admittance; perhaps, in his heart, he preferred to speak with Poole upon the doorstep and surrounded by the air and sounds of the open city, rather than to be admitted into that house of voluntary bondage, and to sit and speak with its inscrutable recluse. Poole had, indeed, no very pleasant news to communicate. The doctor, it appeared, now more than ever confined himself to the cabinet over the laboratory, where he would sometimes even sleep; he was out of spirits, he had grown very silent, he did not read; it seemed as if he had something on his mind. Utterson became so used to the unvarying character of these reports, that he fell off little by little in the frequency of his visits.

Incident at the Window

It chanced on Sunday, when Mr. Utterson was on his usual walk with Mr. Enfield, that their way lay once again through the by-street; and that when they came in front of the door, both stopped to gaze on it.

"Well," said Enfield, "that story's at an end at least. We shall never see more of Mr. Hyde."

"I hope not," said Utterson. "Did I ever tell you that I once saw him, and shared your feeling of repulsion?"

"It was impossible to do the one without the other," returned Enfield. "And by the way, what an ass you must have thought me, not to know that this was a back way to Dr. Jekyll's! It was partly your own fault that I found it out, even when I did."

"So you found it out, did you?" said Utterson. "But if that be so, we may step into the court and take a look at the windows. To tell you the truth, I am uneasy about poor Jekyll; and even outside, I feel as if the presence of a friend might do him good."

The court was very cool and a little damp, and full of premature twilight, although the sky, high up overhead, was still bright with sunset. The middle one of the three windows was half-way open; and sitting close beside it, taking the air with an infinite sadness of mien, like some disconsolate prisoner, Utterson saw Dr. Jekyll.

"What! Jekyll!" he cried. "I trust you are better."

"I am very low, Utterson," replied the doctor drearily, "very low. It will not last long, thank God."

"You stay too much indoors," said the lawyer. "You should be out, whipping up the circulation like Mr. Enfield and me. (This is my cousin— Mr. Enfield—Dr. Jekyll.) Come now; get your hat and take a quick turn with us."

"You are very good," sighed the other. "I should like to very much; but no, no, no, it is quite impossible; I dare not. But indeed, Utterson, I am very glad to see you; this is really a great pleasure; I would ask you and Mr. Enfield up, but the place is really not fit."

"Why then," said the lawyer, good-naturedly, "the best thing we can do is to stay down here and speak with you from where we are."

"That is just what I was about to venture to propose," returned the doctor with a smile. But the words were hardly uttered, before the smile was struck out of his face and succeeded by an expression of such abject terror and despair, as froze the very blood of the two gentlemen below. They saw it but for a glimpse for the window was instantly thrust down;

but that glimpse had been sufficient, and they turned and left the court without a word. In silence, too, they traversed the by-street; and it was not until they had come into a neighbouring thoroughfare, where even upon a Sunday there were still some stirrings of life, that Mr. Utterson at last turned and looked at his companion. They were both pale; and there was an answering horror in their eyes.

"God forgive us, God forgive us," said Mr. Utterson.

But Mr. Enfield only nodded his head very seriously, and walked on once more in silence.

The Last Night

Mr. Utterson was sitting by his fireside one evening after dinner, when he was surprised to receive a visit from Poole.

"Bless me, Poole, what brings you here?" he cried; and then taking a second look at him, "What ails you?" he added; "is the doctor ill?"

"Mr. Utterson," said the man, "there is something wrong."

"Take a seat, and here is a glass of wine for you," said the lawyer. "Now, take your time, and tell me plainly what you want."

"You know the doctor's ways, sir," replied Poole, "and how he shuts himself up. Well, he's shut up again in the cabinet; and I don't like it sir—I wish I may die if I like it. Mr. Utterson, sir, I'm afraid."

"Now, my good man," said the lawyer, "be explicit. What are you afraid of."

"I've been afraid for about a week," returned Poole, doggedly disregarding the question, "and I can bear it no more."

The man's appearance amply bore out his words; his manner was altered for the worse; and except for the moment when he had first announced his terror, he had not once looked the lawyer in the face. Even now, he sat with the glass of wine untasted on his knee, and his eyes directed to a corner of the floor. "I can bear it no more," he repeated.

"Come," said the lawyer, "I see you have some good reason, Poole; I see there is something seriously amiss. Try to tell me what it is."

"I think there's been foul play," said Poole, hoarsely.

"Foul play!" cried the lawyer, a good deal frightened and rather inclined to be irritated in consequence. "What foul play! What does the man mean?"

"I daren't say, sir," was the answer; "but will you come along with me and see for yourself?"

Mr. Utterson's only answer was to rise and get his hat and greatcoat; but he observed with wonder the greatness of the relief that appeared upon the butler's face, and perhaps with no less, that the wine was still untasted when he set it down to follow.

It was a wild, cold, seasonable night of March, with a pale moon, lying on her back as though the wind had tilted her, and a flying wrack[7] of the most diaphanous and lawny texture. The wind made talking difficult, and flecked the blood into the face. It seemed to have swept the streets unusually bare of passengers, besides; for Mr. Utterson thought he had never seen that part of London so deserted. He could have wished it otherwise;

---

7. Mass of broken clouds driven by the wind.

never in his life had he been conscious of so sharp a wish to see and touch his fellow-creatures; for struggle as he might, there was borne in upon his mind a crushing anticipation of calamity. The square, when they got there, was full of wind and dust, and the thin trees in the garden were lashing themselves along the railing. Poole, who had kept all the way a pace or two ahead, now pulled up in the middle of the pavement, and in spite of the biting weather, took off his hat and mopped his brow with a red pocket-handkerchief. But for all the hurry of his coming, these were not the dews of exertion that he wiped away, but the moisture of some strangling anguish; for his face was white and his voice, when he spoke, harsh and broken.

"Well, sir," he said, "here we are, and God grant there be nothing wrong."

"Amen, Poole," said the lawyer.

Thereupon the servant knocked in a very guarded manner; the door was opened on the chain; and a voice asked from within, "Is that you, Poole?"

"It's all right," said Poole. "Open the door."

The hall, when they entered it, was brightly lighted up; the fire was built high; and about the hearth the whole of the servants, men and women, stood huddled together like a flock of sheep. At the sight of Mr. Utterson, the housemaid broke into hysterical whimpering; and the cook, crying out "Bless God! it's Mr. Utterson," ran forward as if to take him in her arms.

"What, what? Are you all here?" said the lawyer peevishly. "Very ir- regular, very unseemly; your master would be far from pleased."

"They're all afraid," said Poole.

Blank silence followed, no one protesting; only the maid lifted up her voice and now wept loudly.

"Hold your tongue!" Poole said to her, with a ferocity of accent that testified to his own jangled nerves; and indeed, when the girl had so sud- denly raised the note of her lamentation, they had all started and turned towards the inner door with faces of dreadful expectation. "And now," continued the butler, addressing the knife-boy,[8] "reach me a candle, and we'll get this through hands at once." And then he begged Mr. Utterson to follow him, and led the way to the back garden.

"Now, sir," said he, "you come as gently as you can. I want you to hear, and I don't want you to be heard. And see here, sir, if by any chance he was to ask you in, don't go."

Mr. Utterson's nerves, at this unlooked-for termination, gave a jerk that nearly threw him from his balance; but he recollected his courage and followed the butler into the laboratory building and through the surgical theatre, with its lumber of crates and bottles, to the foot of the stair. Here Poole motioned him to stand on one side and listen; while he himself, setting down the candle and making a great and obvious call on his reso- lution, mounted the steps and knocked with a somewhat uncertain hand on the red baize of the cabinet door.

"Mr. Utterson, sir, asking to see you," he called; and even as he did so, once more violently signed to the lawyer to give ear.

8. A boy employed to clean table knives.

A voice answered from within: "Tell him I cannot see anyone," it said complainingly.

"Thank you, sir," said Poole, with a note of something like triumph in his voice; and taking up his candle, he led Mr. Utterson back across the yard and into the great kitchen, where the fire was out and the beetles were leaping on the floor.

"Sir," he said, looking Mr. Utterson in the eyes, "was that my master's voice?"

"It seems much changed," replied the lawyer, very pale, but giving look for look.

"Changed? Well, yes, I think so," said the butler. "Have I been twenty years in this man's house, to be deceived about his voice? No, sir; master's made away with; he was made away with eight days ago, when we heard him cry out upon the name of God; and *who's* in there instead of him, and *why* it stays there, is a thing that cries to Heaven, Mr. Utterson!"

"This is a very strange tale, Poole; this is rather a wild tale, my man," said Mr. Utterson, biting his finger. "Suppose it were as you suppose, supposing Dr. Jekyll to have been—well, murdered, what could induce the murderer to stay? That won't hold water; it doesn't commend itself to reason."

"Well, Mr. Utterson, you are a hard man to satisfy, but I'll do it yet," said Poole. "All this last week (you must know) him, or it, whatever it is that lives in that cabinet, has been crying night and day for some sort of medicine and cannot get it to his mind. It was sometimes his way—the master's, that is—to write his orders on a sheet of paper and throw it on the stair. We've had nothing else this week back; nothing but papers, and a closed door, and the very meals left there to be smuggled in when nobody was looking. Well, sir, every day, ay, and twice and thrice in the same day, there have been orders and complaints, and I have been sent flying to all the wholesale chemists in town. Every time I brought the stuff back, there would be another paper telling me to return it, because it was not pure, and another order to a different firm. This drug is wanted bitter bad, sir, whatever for."

"Have you any of these papers?" asked Mr. Utterson.

Poole felt in his pocket and handed out a crumpled note, which the lawyer, bending nearer to the candle, carefully examined. Its contents ran thus: "Dr. Jekyll presents his compliments to Messrs. Maw. He assures them that their last sample is impure and quite useless for his present purpose. In the year 18—, Dr. J. purchased a somewhat large quantity from Messrs. M. He now begs them to search with most sedulous care, and should any of the same quality be left, to forward it to him at once. Expense is no consideration. The importance of this to Dr. J. can hardly be exaggerated." So far the letter had run composedly enough, but here with a sudden splutter of the pen, the writer's emotion had broken loose. "For God's sake," he added, "find me some of the old."

"This is a strange note," said Mr. Utterson; and then sharply, "How do you come to have it open?"

"The man at Maw's was main angry, sir, and he threw it back to me like so much dirt," returned Poole.

"This is unquestionably the doctor's hand, do you know?" resumed the lawyer.

"I thought it looked like it," said the servant rather sulkily; and then, with another voice, "But what matters hand of write?"[9] he said. "I've seen him!"

"Seen him?" repeated Mr. Utterson. "Well?"

"That's it!" said Poole. "It was this way. I came suddenly into the theatre from the garden. It seems he had slipped out to look for this drug or whatever it is; for the cabinet door was open, and there he was at the far end of the room digging among the crates. He looked up when I came in, gave a kind of cry, and whipped upstairs into the cabinet. It was but for one minute that I saw him, but the hair stood upon my head like quills. Sir, if that was my master, why had he a mask upon his face? If it was my master, why did he cry out like a rat, and run from me? I have served him long enough. And then . . ." The man paused and passed his hand over his face.

"These are all very strange circumstances," said Mr. Utterson, "but I think I begin to see daylight. Your master, Poole, is plainly seized with one of those maladies that both torture and deform the sufferer; hence, for aught I know, the alteration of his voice; hence the mask and the avoidance of his friends; hence his eagerness to find this drug, by means of which the poor soul retains some hope of ultimate recovery—God grant that he be not deceived! There is my explanation; it is sad enough, Poole, ay, and appalling to consider; but it is plain and natural, hangs well together, and delivers us from all exorbitant alarms."

"Sir," said the butler, turning to a sort of mottled pallor, "that thing was not my master, and there's the truth. My master"—here he looked round him and began to whisper—"is a tall, fine build of a man, and this was more of a dwarf." Utterson attempted to protest. "O, sir," cried Poole, "do you think I do not know my master after twenty years? Do you think I do not know where his head comes to in the cabinet door, where I saw him every morning of my life? No, sir, that thing in the mask was never Dr. Jekyll—God knows what it was, but it was never Dr. Jekyll; and it is the belief of my heart that there was murder done."

"Poole," replied the lawyer, "if you say that, it will become my duty to make certain. Much as I desire to spare your master's feelings, much as I am puzzled by this note which seems to prove him to be still alive, I shall consider it my duty to break in that door."

"Ah, Mr. Utterson, that's talking!" cried the butler.

"And now comes the second question," resumed Utterson: "Who is going to do it?"

"Why, you and me, sir," was the undaunted reply.

"That's very well said," returned the lawyer; "and whatever comes of it, I shall make it my business to see you are no loser."

"There is an axe in the theatre," continued Poole; "and you might take the kitchen poker for yourself."

The lawyer took that rude but weighty instrument into his hand, and balanced it. "Do you know, Poole," he said, looking up, "that you and I are about to place ourselves in a position of some peril?"

"You may say so, sir, indeed," returned the butler.

"It is well, then, that we should be frank," said the other. "We both think more than we have said; let us make a clean breast. This masked figure that you saw, did you recognise it?"

9. Handwriting.

"Well, sir, it went so quick, and the creature was so doubled up, that I could hardly swear to that," was the answer. "But if you mean, was it Mr. Hyde?—why, yes, I think it was! You see, it was much of the same bigness; and it had the same quick, light way with it; and then who else could have got in by the laboratory door? You have not forgot, sir, that at the time of the murder he had still the key with him? But that's not all. I don't know, Mr. Utterson, if you ever met this Mr. Hyde?"

"Yes," said the lawyer, "I once spoke with him."

"Then you must know as well as the rest of us that there was something queer about that gentleman—something that gave a man a turn—I don't know rightly how to say it, sir, beyond this: that you felt in your marrow kind of cold and thin."

"I own I felt something of what you describe," said Mr. Utterson.

"Quite so, sir," returned Poole. "Well, when that masked thing like a monkey jumped from among the chemicals and whipped into the cabinet, it went down my spine like ice. O, I know it's not evidence, Mr. Utterson; I'm book-learned enough for that; but a man has his feelings, and I give you my bible-word it was Mr. Hyde!"

"Ay, ay," said the lawyer. "My fears incline to the same point. Evil, I fear, founded—evil was sure to come—of that connection. Ay truly, I believe you; I believe poor Harry is killed; and I believe his murderer (for what purpose, God alone can tell) is still lurking in his victim's room. Well, let our name be vengeance. Call Bradshaw."

The footman came at the summons, very white and nervous.

"Pull yourself together, Bradshaw," said the lawyer. "This suspense, I know, is telling upon all of you; but it is now our intention to make an end of it. Poole, here, and I are going to force our way into the cabinet. If all is well, my shoulders are broad enough to bear the blame. Meanwhile, lest anything should really be amiss, or any malefactor seek to escape by the back, you and the boy must go round the corner with a pair of good sticks and take your post at the laboratory door. We give you ten minutes, to get to your stations."

As Bradshaw left, the lawyer looked at his watch. "And now, Poole, let us get to ours," he said; and taking the poker under his arm, led the way into the yard. The scud had banked over the moon, and it was now quite dark. The wind, which only broke in puffs and draughts into that deep well of building, tossed the light of the candle to and fro about their steps, until they came into the shelter of the theatre, where they sat down silently to wait. London hummed solemnly all around; but nearer at hand, the stillness was only broken by the sounds of a footfall moving to and fro along the cabinet floor.

"So it will walk all day, sir," whispered Poole; "ay, and the better part of the night. Only when a new sample comes from the chemist, there's a bit of a break. Ah, it's an ill conscience that's such an enemy to rest! Ah, sir, there's blood foully shed in every step of it! But hark again, a little closer—put your heart in your ears, Mr. Utterson, and tell me, is that the doctor's foot?"

The steps fell lightly and oddly, with a certain swing, for all they went so slowly; it was different indeed from the heavy creaking tread of Henry Jekyll. Utterson sighed. "Is there never anything else?" he asked.

Poole nodded. "Once," he said. "Once I heard it weeping!"

"Weeping? how's that?" said the lawyer, conscious of a sudden chill of horror.

"Weeping like a woman or a lost soul," said the butler. "I came away with that upon my heart, and I could have wept too."

But now the ten minutes drew to an end. Poole disinterred the axe from under a stack of packing straw; the candle was set upon the nearest table to light them to the attack; and they drew near with bated breath to where that patient foot was still going up and down, up and down, in the quiet of the night. "Jekyll," cried Utterson, with a loud voice, "I demand to see you." He paused a moment, but there came no reply. "I give you fair warning, our suspicions are aroused, and I must and shall see you," he resumed; "if not by fair means, then by foul—if not of your consent, then by brute force!"

"Utterson," said the voice, "for God's sake, have mercy!"

"Ah, that's not Jekyll's voice—it's Hyde's!" cried Utterson. "Down with the door, Poole!"

Poole swung the axe over his shoulder; the blow shook the building, and the red baize door leaped against the lock and hinges. A dismal screech, as of mere animal terror, rang from the cabinet. Up went the axe again, and again the panels crashed and the frame bounded; four times the blow fell; but the wood was tough and the fittings were of excellent workmanship; and it was not until the fifth, that the lock burst and the wreck of the door fell inwards on the carpet.

The besiegers, appalled by their own riot and the stillness that had succeeded, stood back a little and peered in. There lay the cabinet before their eyes in the quiet lamplight, a good fire glowing and chattering on the hearth, the kettle singing its thin strain, a drawer or two open, papers neatly set forth on the business table, and nearer the fire, the things laid out for tea; the quietest room, you would have said, and, but for the glazed presses full of chemicals, the most commonplace that night in London.

Right in the midst there lay the body of a man sorely contorted and still twitching. They drew near on tiptoe, turned it on its back and beheld the face of Edward Hyde. He was dressed in clothes far too large for him, clothes of the doctor's bigness; the cords of his face still moved with a semblance of life, but life was quite gone: and by the crushed phial in the hand and the strong smell of kernels[1] that hung upon the air, Utterson knew that he was looking on the body of a self-destroyer.

"We have come too late," he said sternly, "whether to save or punish. Hyde is gone to his account; and it only remains for us to find the body of your master."

The far greater proportion of the building was occupied by the theatre, which filled almost the whole ground storey and was lighted from above, and by the cabinet, which formed an upper storey at one end and looked upon the court. A corridor joined the theatre to the door on the by-street; and with this the cabinet communicated separately by a second flight of stairs. There were besides a few dark closets and a spacious cellar. All these they now thoroughly examined. Each closet needed but a glance, for all were empty, and all, by the dust that fell from their doors, had

---

1. Almonds, the smell of cyanide (prussic acid).

stood long unopened. The cellar, indeed, was filled with crazy lumber, mostly dating from the times of the surgeon who was Jekyll's predecesor; but even as they opened the door they were advertised of the uselessness of further search, by the fall of a perfect mat of cobweb which had for years sealed up the entrance. Nowhere was there any trace of Henry Jekyll, dead or alive.

Poole stamped on the flags of the corridor. "He must be buried here," he said, hearkening to the sound.

"Or he may have fled," said Utterson, and he turned to examine the door in the by-street. It was locked; and lying near by on the flags, they found the key, already stained with rust.

"This does not look like use," observed the lawyer.

"Use!" echoed Poole. "Do you not see, sir, it is broken? much as if a man had stamped on it."

"Ay," continued Utterson, "and the fractures, too, are rusty." The two men looked at each other with a scare. "This is beyond me, Poole," said the lawyer. "Let us go back to the cabinet."

They mounted the stair in silence, and still with an occasional awe-struck glance at the dead body, proceeded more thoroughly to examine the contents of the cabinet. At one table, there were traces of chemical work, various measured heaps of some white salt being laid on glass saucers, as though for an experiment in which the unhappy man had been prevented.

"That is the same drug that I was always bringing him," said Poole, and even as he spoke, the kettle with a startling noise boiled over.

This brought them to the fireside, where the easychair was drawn cosily up, and the tea things stood ready to the sitter's elbow, the very sugar in the cup. There were several books on a shelf; one lay beside the tea things open, and Utterson was amazed to find it a copy of pious work, for which Jekyll had several times expressed a great esteem, annotated, in his own hand, with startling blasphemies.

Next, in the course of their review of the chamber, the searchers came to the cheval-glass, into whose depths they looked with an involuntary horror. But it was so turned as to show them nothing but the rosy glow playing on the roof, the fire sparkling in a hundred repetitions along the glazed front of the presses, and their own pale and fearful countenances stooping to look in.

"This glass has seen some strange things, sir," whispered Poole.

"And surely none stranger than itself," echoed the lawyer in the same tones. "For what did Jekyll"—he caught himself up at the word with a start, and then conquering the weakness—"what could Jekyll want with it?" he said.

"You may say that!" said Poole.

Next they turned to the business table. On the desk, among the neat array of papers, a large envelope was uppermost, and bore, in the doctor's hand, the name of Mr. Utterson. The lawyer unsealed it, and several enclosures fell to the floor. The first was a will, drawn in the same eccentric terms as the one which he had returned six months before, to serve as a testament in case of death and as a deed of gift in case of disappearance; but in place of the name of Edward Hyde, the lawyer, with indescribable amazement, read the name of Gabriel John Utterson. He looked at Poole, and then back at the paper, and last of all at the dead malefactor stretched upon the carpet.

"My head goes round," he said. "He has been all these days in possession; he had no cause to like me; he must have raged to see himself displaced; and he has not destroyed this document."

He caught up the next paper; it was a brief note in the doctor's hand and dated at the top. "O Poole!" the lawyer cried, "he was alive and here this day. He cannot have been disposed of in so short a space; he must be still alive, he must have fled! And then, why fled? and how? and in that case, can we venture to declare this suicide? O, we must be careful. I foresee that we may yet involve your master in some dire catastrophe."

"Why don't you read it, sir?" asked Poole.

"Because I fear," replied the lawyer solemnly. "God grant I have no cause for it!" And with that he brought the paper to his eyes and read as follows:

"MY DEAR UTTERSON,—When this shall fall into your hands, I shall have disappeared, under what circumstances I have not the penetration to foresee, but my instinct and all the circumstances of my nameless situation tell me that the end is sure and must be early. Go then, and first read the narrative which Lanyon warned me he was to place in your hands; and if you care to hear more, turn to the confession of

"Your unworthy and unhappy friend,

"HENRY JEKYLL."

"There was a third enclosure?" asked Utterson.

"Here, sir," said Poole, and gave into his hands a considerable packet sealed in several places.

The lawyer put it in his pocket. "I would say nothing of this paper. If your master has fled or is dead, we may at least save his credit. It is now ten; I must go home and read these documents in quiet; but I shall be back before midnight, when we shall send for the police."

They went out, locking the door of the theatre behind them; and Utterson, once more leaving the servants gathered about the fire in the hall, trudged back to his office to read the two narratives in which this mystery was now to be explained.

Dr. Lanyon's Narrative

On the ninth of January, now four days ago, I received by the evening delivery a registered envelope, addressed in the hand of my colleague and old school companion, Henry Jekyll. I was a good deal surprised by this; for we were by no means in the habit of correspondence; I had seen the man, dined with him, indeed, the night before; and I could imagine nothing in our intercourse that should justify formality of registration. The contents increased my wonder; for this is how the letter ran:

"10th December, 18—.

"DEAR LANYON,—You are one of my oldest friends; and although we may have differed at times on scientific questions, I cannot remember, at least on my side, any break in our affection. There was never a day when, if you had said to me, 'Jekyll, my life, my honour, my reason, depend upon you,' I would not have sacrificed my left hand to help you. Lanyon, my life, my honour, my reason, are all at your mercy; if you fail me to-night, I am lost. You might suppose, after this preface, that I am going to ask you for something dishonourable to grant. Judge for yourself.

"I want you to postpone all other engagements for to-night—ay, even if you were summoned to the bedside of an emperor; to take a cab, unless your carriage should be actually at the door; and with this letter in your hand for consultation, to drive straight to my house. Poole, my butler, has his orders; you will find him waiting your arrival with a locksmith. The door of my cabinet is then to be forced: and you are to go in alone; to open the glazed press (letter E) on the left hand, breaking the lock if it be shut; and to draw out, *with all its contents as they stand,* the fourth drawer from the top or (which is the same thing) the third from the bottom. In my extreme distress of mind, I have a morbid fear of misdirecting you; but even if I am in error, you may know the right drawer by its contents: some powders, a phial and a paper book. This drawer I beg of you to carry back with you to Cavendish Square exactly as it stands.

"That is the first part of the service: now for the second. You should be back, if you set out at once on the receipt of this, long before midnight; but I will leave you that amount of margin, not only in the fear of one of those obstacles that can neither be prevented nor foreseen, but because an hour when your servants are in bed is to be preferred for what will then remain to do. At midnight, then, I have to ask you to be alone in your consulting room, to admit with your own hand into the house a man who will present himself in my name, and to place in his hands the drawer that you will have brought with you from my cabinet. Then you will have played your part and earned my gratitude completely. Five minutes afterwards, if you insist upon an explanation, you will have understood that these arrangements are of capital importance; and that by the neglect of one of them, fantastic as they must appear, you might have charged your conscience with my death or the shipwreck of my reason.

"Confident as I am that you will not trifle with this appeal, my heart sinks and my hand trembles at the bare thought of such a possibility. Think of me at this hour, in a strange place, labouring under a blackness of distress that no fancy can exaggerate, and yet well aware that, if you will but punctually serve me, my troubles will roll away like a story that is told. Serve me, my dear Lanyon, and save

"Your friend,
"H. J.

"P.S.—I had already sealed this up when a fresh terror struck upon my soul. It is possible that the post-office may fail me, and this letter not come into your hands until to-morrow morning. In that case, dear Lanyon, do my errand when it shall be most convenient for you in the course of the day; and once more expect my messenger at midnight. It may then already be too late; and if that night passes without event, you will know that you have seen the last of Henry Jekyll."

Upon the reading of this letter, I made sure my colleague was insane; but till that was proved beyond the possibility of doubt, I felt bound to do as he requested. The less I understood of this farrago, the less I was in a position to judge of its importance; and an appeal so worded could not be set aside without a grave responsibility. I rose accordingly from table, got into a hansom, and drove straight to Jekyll's house. The butler was awaiting my arrival; he had received by the same post as mine a registered letter of instruction, and had sent at once for a locksmith and a carpenter. The tradesmen came while we were yet speaking; and we moved in a body to old Dr. Denman's surgical theatre, from which (as you are doubtless aware) Jekyll's private cabinet is most conveniently entered. The door was very strong, the lock excellent; the carpenter avowed he would have great trouble and have to do much damage, if force were to be used; and the locksmith was near despair. But this last was a handy fellow, and after two hours' work, the door stood open. The press marked E was unlocked; and I took out the drawer, had it filled up with straw and tied in a sheet, and returned with it to Cavendish Square.

Here I proceeded to examine its contents. The powders were neatly enough made up, but not with the nicety of the dispensing chemist; so that it was plain they were of Jekyll's private manufacture: and when I opened one of the wrappers I found what seemed to me a simple crystalline salt of a white colour. The phial, to which I next turned my attention, might have been about half full of a blood-red liquor, which was highly pungent to the sense of smell and seemed to me to contain phosphorus and some volatile ether. At the other ingredients I could make no guess. The book was an ordinary version book[2] and contained little but a series of dates. These covered a period of many years, but I observed that the entries ceased nearly a year ago and quite abruptly. Here and there a brief remark was appended to a date, usually no more than a single word: "double" occurring perhaps six times in a total of several hundred entries; and once very early in the list and followed by several marks of exclamation, "total failure!!!" All this, though it whetted my curiosity, told me little that was definite. Here were a phial of some tincture, a paper of some salt, and the record of a series of experiments that had led (like too many of Jekyll's investigations) to no end of practical usefulness. How could the presence of these articles in my house affect either the honour, the sanity, or the life of my flighty colleague? If his messenger could go to one place, why could he not go to another? And even granting some impediment, why was this gentleman to be received by me in secret? The more I reflected the more convinced I grew that I was dealing with a case of cerebral disease; and though I dismissed my servants to bed, I loaded an old revolver, that I might be found in some posture of self-defence.

Twelve o'clock had scarce rung out over London, ere the knocker sounded very gently on the door. I went myself at the summons, and found a small man crouching against the pillars of the portico.

"Are you come from Dr. Jekyll?" I asked.

He told me "yes" by a constrained gesture; and when I had bidden him enter, he did not obey me without a searching backward glance into the darkness of the square. There was a policeman not far off, advancing with his bull's eye open; and at the sight, I thought my visitor started and made greater haste.

These particulars struck me, I confess, disagreeably; and as I followed him into the bright light of the consulting room, I kept my hand ready on

2. Exercise book.

my weapon. Here, at last, I had a chance of clearly seeing him. I had never set eyes on him before, so much was certain. He was small, as I have said; I was struck besides with the shocking expression of his face, with his remarkable combination of great muscular activity and great apparent debility of constitution, and—last but not least—with the odd, subjective disturbance caused by his neighbourhood. This bore some resemblance to incipient rigour, and was accompanied by a marked sinking of the pulse. At the time, I set it down to some idiosyncratic, personal distaste, and merely wondered at the acuteness of the symptoms; but I have since had reason to believe the cause to lie much deeper in the nature of man, and to turn on some nobler hinge than the principle of hatred.

This person (who had thus, from the first moment of his entrance, struck in me what I can only describe as a disgustful curiosity) was dressed in a fashion that would have made an ordinary person laughable; his clothes, that is to say, although they were of rich and sober fabric, were enormously too large for him in every measurement—the trousers hanging on his legs and rolled up to keep them from the ground, the waist of the coat below his haunches, and the collar sprawling wide upon his shoulders. Strange to relate, this ludicrous accoutrement was far from moving me to laughter. Rather, as there was something abnormal and misbegotten in the very essence of the creature that now faced me—something seizing, surprising and revolting—this fresh disparity seemed but to fit in with and to reinforce it; so that to my interest in the man's nature and character, there was added a curiosity as to his origin, his life, his fortune and status in the world.

These observations, though they have taken so great a space to be set down in, were yet the work of a few seconds. My visitor was, indeed, on fire with sombre excitement.

"Have you got it?" he cried. "Have you got it?" And so lively was his impatience that he even laid his hand upon my arm and sought to shake me.

I put him back, conscious at his touch of a certain icy pang along my blood. "Come, sir," said I. "You forget that I have not yet the pleasure of your acquaintance. Be seated, if you please." And I showed him an example, and sat down myself in my customary seat and with as fair an imitation of my ordinary manner to a patient, as the lateness of the hour, the nature of my preoccupations, and the horror I had of my visitor, would suffer me to muster.

"I beg your pardon, Dr. Lanyon," he replied civilly enough. "What you say is very well founded; and my impatience has shown its heels to my politeness. I come here at the instance of your colleague, Dr. Henry Jekyll, on a piece of business of some moment; and I understood . . ." He paused and put his hand to his throat, and I could see, in spite of his collected manner, that he was wrestling against the approaches of the hysteria—"I understood, a drawer . . ."

But here I took pity on my visitor's suspense, and some perhaps on my own growing curiosity.

"There it is, sir," said I, pointing to the drawer, where it lay on the floor behind a table and still covered with the sheet.

He sprang to it, and then paused, and laid his hand upon his heart; I could hear his teeth grate with the convulsive action of his jaws; and his face was so ghastly to see that I grew alarmed both for his life and reason. "Compose yourself," said I.

He turned a dreadful smile to me, and as if with the decision of despair, plucked away the sheet. At sight of the contents, he uttered one loud sob of such immense relief that I sat petrified. And the next moment, in a voice that was already fairly well under control, "Have you a graduated glass?" he asked.

I rose from my place with something of an effort and gave him what he asked.

He thanked me with a smiling nod, measured out a few minims of the red tincture and added one of the powders. The mixture, which was at first of a reddish hue, began, in proportion as the crystals melted, to brighten in colour, to effervesce audibly, and to throw off small fumes of vapour. Suddenly and at the same moment, the ebullition ceased and the compound changed to a dark purple, which faded again more slowly to a watery green. My visitor, who had watched these metamorphoses with a keen eye, smiled, set down the glass upon the table, and then turned and looked upon me with an air of scrutiny.

"And now," said he, "to settle what remains. Will you be wise? will you be guided? will you suffer me to take this glass in my hand and to go forth from your house without further parley? or has the greed of curiosity too much command of you? Think before you answer, for it shall be done as you decide. As you decide, you shall be left as you were before, and neither richer nor wiser, unless the sense of service rendered to a man in mortal distress may be counted as a kind of riches of the soul. Or, if you shall so prefer to choose, a new province of knowledge and new avenues to fame and power shall be laid open to you, here, in this room, upon the instant; and your sight shall be blasted by a prodigy to stagger the unbelief of Satan."

"Sir," said I, affecting a coolness that I was far from truly possessing, "you speak enigmas, and you will perhaps not wonder that I hear you with no very strong impression of belief. But I have gone too far in the way of inexplicable services to pause before I see the end."

"It is well," replied my visitor. "Lanyon, you remember your vows: what follows is under the seal of our profession. And now, you who have so long been bound to the most narrow and material views, you who have denied the virtue of transcendental medicine, you who have derided your superiors—behold!"

He put the glass to his lips and drank at one gulp. A cry followed; he reeled, staggered, clutched at the table and held on, staring with injected[3] eyes, gasping with open mouth; and as I looked there came, I thought, a change—he seemed to swell—his face became suddenly black and the features seemed to melt and alter—and the next moment, I had sprung to my feet and leaped back against the wall, my arm raised to shield me from that prodigy, my mind submerged in terror.

"O God!" I screamed, and "O God!" again and again; for there before my eyes—pale and shaken, and half fainting, and groping before him with his hands, like a man restored from death—there stood Henry Jekyll!

What he told me in the next hour, I cannot bring my mind to set on paper. I saw what I saw, I heard what I heard, and my soul sickened at it;

3. Bloodshot.

and yet now when that sight has faded from my eyes, I ask myself if I
believe it, and I cannot answer. My life is shaken to its roots; sleep has
left me; the deadliest terror sits by me at all hours of the day and night;
and I feel that my days are numbered, and that I must die; and yet I shall
die incredulous. As for the moral turpitude that man unveiled to me, even
with tears of penitence, I cannot, even in memory, dwell on it without a
start of horror. I will say but one thing, Utterson, and that (if you can
bring your mind to credit it) will be more than enough. The creature who
crept into my house that night was, on Jekyll's own confession, known by
the name of Hyde and hunted for in every corner of the land as the
murderer of Carew.

HASTIE LANYON

Henry Jekyll's Full Statement of the Case

I was born in the year 18— to a large fortune, endowed besides with
excellent parts[4], inclined by nature to industry, fond of the respect of the
wise and good among my fellow-men, and thus, as might have been supposed, with every guarantee of an honourable and distinguished future.
And indeed the worst of my faults was a certain impatient gaiety of disposition, such as has made the happiness of many, but such as I found it
hard to reconcile with my imperious desire to carry my head high, and
wear a more than commonly grave countenance before the public. Hence
it came about that I concealed my pleasures; and that when I reached
years of reflection, and began to look round me and take stock of my
progress and position in the world, I stood already committed to a profound duplicity of life. Many a man would have even blazoned such irreg-
ularities as I was guilty of; but from the high views that I had set before
me, I regarded and hid them with an almost morbid sense of shame. It
was thus rather the exacting nature of my aspirations than any particular
degradation in my faults, that made me what I was, and, with even a
deeper trench than in the majority of men, severed in me those provinces
of good and ill which divide and compound man's dual nature. In this
case, I was driven to reflect deeply and inveterately on that hard law of
life, which lies at the root of religion and is one of the most plentiful
springs of distress. Though so profound a double-dealer, I was in no sense
a hypocrite; both sides of me were in dead earnest; I was no more myself
when I laid aside restraint and plunged in shame, than when I laboured,
in the eye of day, at the furtherance of knowledge or the relief of sorrow
and suffering. And it chanced that the direction of my scientific studies,
which led wholly towards the mystic and the transcendental, reacted and
shed a strong light on this consciousness of the perennial war among my
members. With every day, and from both sides of my intelligence, the
moral and the intellectual, I thus drew steadily nearer to that truth, by
whose partial discovery I have been doomed to such a dreadful shipwreck: that man is not truly one, but truly two. I say two, because the
state of my own knowledge does not pass beyond that point. Others will
follow, others will outstrip me on the same lines; and I hazard the guess
that man will be ultimately known for a mere polity of multifarious, incongruous and independent denizens. I, for my part, from the nature of

4. Personal and mental qualities or endowments.

my life, advanced infallibly in one direction and in one direction only. It was on the moral side, and in my own person, that I learned to recognise the thorough and primitive duality of man; I saw that, of the two natures that contended in the field of my consciousness, even if I could rightly be said to be either, it was only because I was radically both; and from an early date, even before the course of my scientific discoveries had begun to suggest the most naked possibility of such a miracle, I had learned to dwell with pleasure, as a beloved daydream, on the thought of the separation of these elements. If each, I told myself, could be housed in separate identities, life would be relieved of all that was unbearable; the unjust might go his way, delivered from the aspirations and remorse of his more upright twin; and the just could walk steadfastly and securely on his upward path, doing the good things in which he found his pleasure, and no longer exposed to disgrace and penitence by the hands of this extraneous evil. It was the curse of mankind that these incongruous faggots were thus bound together—that in the agonised womb of consciousness, these polar twins should be continuously struggling. How, then, were they dissociated?

I was so far in my reflections when, as I have said, a side light began to shine upon the subject from the laboratory table. I began to perceive more deeply than it has ever yet been stated, the trembling immateriality, the mistlike transience, of this seemingly so solid body in which we walk attired. Certain agents I found to have the power to shake and pluck back that fleshy vestment, even as a wind might toss the curtains of a pavilion. For two good reasons, I will not enter deeply into this scientific branch of my confession. First, because I have been made to learn that the doom and burthen of our life is bound for ever on man's shoulders, and when the attempt is made to cast it off, it but returns upon us with more unfamiliar and more awful pressure. Second, because, as my narrative will make, alas! too evident, my discoveries were incomplete. Enough, then, that I not only recognised my natural body from the mere aura and effulgence of certain of the powers that made up my spirit, but managed to compound a drug by which these powers should be dethroned from their supremacy, and a second form and countenance substituted, none the less natural to me because they were the expression, and bore the stamp of lower elements in my soul.

I hesitated long before I put this theory to the test of practice. I knew well that I risked death; for any drug that so potently controlled and shook the very fortress of identity, might, by the least scruple of an overdose or at the least inopportunity in the moment of exhibition,[5] utterly blot out that immaterial tabernacle which I looked to it to change. But the temptation of a discovery so singular and profound at last overcame the suggestions of alarm. I had long since prepared my tincture; I purchased at once, from a firm of wholesale chemists, a large quantity of a particular salt which I knew, from my experiments, to be the last ingredient required; and late one accursed night, I compounded the elements, watched them boil and smoke together in the glass, and when the ebullition had subsided, with a strong glow of courage, drank off the potion.

The most racking pangs succeeded: a grinding in the bones, deadly nausea, and a horror of the spirit that cannot be exceeded at the hour of

5. In medicine, administration, as of a remedy, etc. *Scruple:* 20 grains or 1/3 dram.

birth or death. Then these agonies began swiftly to subside, and I came to myself as if out of a great sickness. There was something strange in my sensations, something indescribably new and, from its very novelty, incredibly sweet. I felt younger, lighter, happier in body; within I was conscious of a heady recklessness, a current of disordered sensual images running like a millrace in my fancy, a dissolution of the bonds of obligation, an unknown but not an innocent freedom of the soul. I knew myself, at the first breath of this new life, to be more wicked, tenfold more wicked, sold a slave to my original evil; and the thought, in that moment, braced and delighted me like wine. I stretched out my hands, exulting in the freshness of these sensations; and in the act, I was suddenly aware that I had lost in stature.

There was no mirror, at that date, in my room; that which stands beside me as I write, was brought there later on and for the very purpose of these transformations. The night, however, was far gone into the morning—the morning, black as it was, was nearly ripe for the conception of the day—the inmates of my house were locked in the most rigorous hours of slumber; and I determined, flushed as I was with hope and triumph, to venture in my new shape as far as to my bedroom. I crossed the yard, wherein the constellations looked down upon me, I could have thought, with wonder, the first creature of that sort that their unsleeping vigilance had yet disclosed to them; I stole through the corridors, a stranger in my own house; and coming to my room, I saw for the first time the appearance of Edward Hyde.

I must here speak by theory alone, saying not that which I know, but that which I suppose to be most probable. The evil side of my nature, to which I had now transferred the stamping efficacy, was less robust and less developed than the good which I had just deposed. Again, in the course of my life, which had been, after all, nine tenths a life of effort, virtue and control, it had been much less exercised and much less exhausted. And hence, as I think, it came about that Edward Hyde was so much smaller, slighter and younger than Henry Jekyll. Even as good shone upon the countenance of the one, evil was written broadly and plainly on the face of the other. Evil besides (which I must still believe to be the lethal side of man) had left on that body an imprint of deformity and decay. And yet when I looked upon that ugly idol in the glass, I was conscious of no repugnance, rather of a leap of welcome. This, too, was myself. It seemed natural and human. In my eyes it bore a livelier image of the spirit, it seemed more express[6] and single, than the imperfect and divided countenance I had been hitherto accustomed to call mine. And in so far I was doubtless right. I have observed that when I wore the semblance of Edward Hyde, none could come near to me at first without a visible misgiving of the flesh. This, as I take it, was because all human beings, as we meet them, are commingled out of good and evil: and Edward Hyde, alone in the ranks of mankind, was pure evil.

I lingered but a moment at the mirror: the second and conclusive experiment had yet to be attempted; it yet remained to be seen if I had lost my identity beyond redemption and must flee before daylight from a house that was no longer mine; and hurrying back to my cabinet, I once more prepared and drank the cup, once more suffered the pangs of disso-

6. Exact.

lution, and came to myself once more with the character, the stature and the face of Henry Jekyll.

That night I had come to the fatal crossroads. Had I approached my discovery in a more noble spirit, had I risked the experiment while under the empire of generous or pious aspirations, all must have been otherwise, and from these agonies of death and birth, I had come forth an angel instead of a fiend. The drug had no discriminating action; it was neither diabolical nor divine; it but shook the doors of the prisonhouse of my disposition; and like the captives of Philippi,[7] that which stood within ran forth. At that time my virtue slumbered; my evil, kept awake by ambition, was alert and swift to seize the occasion; and the thing that was projected was Edward Hyde. Hence, although I had now two characters as well as two appearances, one was wholly evil, and the other was still the old Henry Jekyll, that incongruous compound of whose reformation and improvement I had already learned to despair. The movement was thus wholly toward the worse.

Even at that time, I had not conquered my aversion to the dryness of a life of study. I would still be merrily disposed at times; and as my pleasures were (to say the least) undignified, and I was not only well known and highly considered, but growing toward the elderly man, this incoherency of my life was daily growing more unwelcome. It was on this side that my new power tempted me until I fell in slavery. I had but to drink the cup, to doff at once the body of the noted professor, and to assume, like a thick cloak, that of Edward Hyde. I smiled at the notion; it seemed to me at the time to be humourous; and I made my preparations with the most studious care. I took and furnished that house in Soho, to which Hyde was tracked by the police; and engaged as a housekeeper a creature whom I knew well to be silent and unscrupulous. On the other side, I announced to my servants that a Mr. Hyde (whom I described) was to have full liberty and power about my house in the square; and to parry mishaps, I even called and made myself a familiar object, in my second character. I next drew up that will to which you so much objected; so that if anything befell me in the person of Dr. Jekyll, I could enter on that of Edward Hyde without pecuniary loss. And thus fortified, as I supposed, on every side, I began to profit by the strange immunities of my position.

Men have before hired bravoes to transact their crimes, while their own person and reputation sat under shelter. I was the first that ever did so for his pleasures. I was the first that could plod in the public eye with a load of genial respectability, and in a moment, like a schoolboy, strip off these lendings and spring headlong into the sea of liberty. But for me, in my impenetrable mantle, the safety was complete. Think of it—I did not even exist! Let me but escape into my laboratory door, give me but a second or two to mix and swallow the draught that I had always standing ready; and whatever he had done, Edward Hyde would pass away like the stain of breath upon a mirror; and there in his stead, quietly at home, trimming the midnight lamp in his study, a man who could afford to laugh at suspicion, would be Harry Jekyll.

The pleasures which I made haste to seek in my disguise were, as I

7. Acts 16:26: "And suddenly there was a great earthquake, so that the foundations of the prison were shaken; and immediately all the doors were opened, and every one's bands were loosed." The biblical captives of Philippi, however, do not flee.

have said, undignified; I would scarce use a harder term. But in the hands of Edward Hyde, they soon began to turn toward the monstrous. When I would come back from these excursions, I was often plunged into a kind of wonder at my vicarious depravity. This familiar that I called out of my own soul, and sent forth alone to do his good pleasure, was a being inherently malign and villainous; his every act and thought centered on self; drinking pleasure with bestial avidity from any degree of torture to another; relentless like a man of stone. Henry Jekyll stood at times aghast before the acts of Edward Hyde; but the situation was apart from ordinary laws, and insidiously relaxed the grasp of conscience. It was Hyde, after all, and Hyde alone, that was guilty. Jekyll was no worse; he woke again to his good qualities seemingly unimpaired; he would even make haste, where it was possible, to undo the evil done by Hyde. And thus his conscience slumbered.

Into the details of the infamy at which I thus connived (for even now I can scarce grant that I committed it) I have no design of entering; I mean but to point out the warnings and the successive steps with which my chastisement approached. I met with one accident which, as it brought on no consequence, I shall no more than mention. An act of cruelty to a child aroused against me the anger of a passerby, whom I recognised the other day in the person of your kinsman; the doctor and the child's family joined him; there were moments when I feared for my life; and at last, in order to pacify their too just resentment, Edward Hyde had to bring them to the door, and pay them in a cheque drawn in the name of Henry Jekyll. But this danger was easily eliminated from the future, by opening an account at another bank in the name of Edward Hyde himself; and when, by sloping my own hand backward, I had supplied my double with a signature, I thought I sat beyond the reach of fate.

Some two months before the murder of Sir Danvers, I had been out for one of my adventures, had returned at a late hour, and woke the next day in bed with somewhat odd sensations. It was in vain I looked about me; in vain I saw the decent furniture and tall proportions of my room in the square; in vain that I recognised the pattern of the bed curtains and the design of the mahogany frame; something still kept insisting that I was not where I was, that I had not wakened where I seemed to be, but in the little room in Soho where I was accustomed to sleep in the body of Edward Hyde. I smiled to myself, and, in my psychological way, began lazily to inquire into the elements of this illusion, occasionally, even as I did so, dropping back into a comfortable morning doze. I was still so engaged when, in one of my more wakeful moments, my eyes fell upon my hand. Now the hand of Henry Jekyll (as you have often remarked) was professional in shape and size: it was large, firm, white and comely. But the hand which I now saw, clearly enough, in the yellow light of a mid-London morning, lying half shut on the bedclothes, was lean, corded, knuckly, of a dusky pallor and thickly shaded with a swart growth of hair. It was the hand of Edward Hyde.

I must have stared upon it for near half a minute, sunk as I was in the mere stupidity of wonder, before terror woke up in my breast as sudden and startling as the crash of cymbals; and bounding from my bed, I rushed to the mirror. At the sight that met my eyes, my blood was changed into something exquisitely thin and icy. Yes, I had gone to bed Henry Jekyll, I had awakened Edward Hyde. How was this to be explained? I asked myself; and then, with another bound of terror—how was it to be remedied? It was well on in the morning; the servants were up; all my drugs were in the cabinet—a long journey down two pairs of stairs, through the back passage, across the open court and through the anatomical theatre, from where I was then standing horror-struck. It might indeed be possible to cover my face; but of what use was that, when I was unable to conceal the alteration in my stature? And then with an overpowering sweetness of relief, it came back upon my mind that the servants were already used to the coming and going of my second self. I had soon dressed, as well as I was able, in clothes of my own size; had soon passed through the house, where Bradshaw stared and drew back at seeing Mr. Hyde at such an hour and in such a strange array; and ten minutes later, Dr. Jekyll had returned to his own shape and was sitting down, with a darkened brow, to make a feint of breakfasting.

Small indeed was my appetite. This inexplicable incident, this reversal of my previous experience, seemed, like the Babylonian finger on the wall,[8] to be spelling out the letters of my judgment; and I began to reflect more seriously than ever before on the issues and possibilities of my double existence. That part of me which I had the power of projecting, had lately been much exercised and nourished; it had seemed to me of late as though the body of Edward Hyde had grown in stature, as though (when I wore that form) I were conscious of a more generous tide of blood; and I began to spy a danger that, if this were much prolonged, the balance of my nature might be permanently overthrown, the power of voluntary change be forfeited, and the character of Edward Hyde become irrevocably mine. The power of the drug had not been always equally displayed. Once, very early in my career, it had totally failed me; since then I had been obliged on more than one occasion to double, and once, with infinite risk of death, to treble the amount; and these rare uncertainties had cast hitherto the sole shadow on my contentment. Now, however, and in the light of that morning's accident, I was led to remark that whereas, in the beginning, the difficulty had been to throw off the body of Jekyll, it had of late gradually but decidedly transferred itself to the other side. All things therefore seemed to point to this: that I was slowly losing hold of my original and better self, and becoming slowly incorporated with my second and worse.

Between these two, I now felt I had to choose. My two natures had memory in common, but all other faculties were most unequally shared between them. Jekyll (who was composite) now with the most sensitive apprehensions, now with a greedy gusto, projected and shared in the pleasures and adventures of Hyde; but Hyde was indifferent to Jekyll, or but remembered him as the mountain bandit remembers the cavern in which he conceals himself from pursuit. Jekyll had more than a father's interest; Hyde had more than a son's indifference. To cast in my lot with Jekyll, was to die to those appetites which I had long secretly indulged and had of late begun to pamper. To cast it in with Hyde, was to die to a thousand interests and aspirations, and to become, at a blow and forever, despised and friendless. The bargain might appear unequal; but there was still another consideration in the scales; for while Jekyll would suffer

8. Daniel 5:25. "The handwriting on the wall" that suddenly appears ("*mene, mene, tekel, upharsin,*" Aramaic for "numbered, numbered, weighed, and di- vided") is interpreted by Daniel as God's judgment on Belshazzar and the Babylonians.

smartingly in the fires of abstinence, Hyde would be not even conscious of all that he had lost. Strange as my circumstances were, the terms of this debate are as old and commonplace as man; much the same inducements and alarms cast the die for any tempted and trembling sinner; and it fell out with me, as it falls with so vast a majority of my fellows, that I chose the better part and was found wanting in the strength to keep to it.

Yes, I preferred the elderly and discontented doctor, surrounded by friends and cherishing honest hopes; and bade a resolute farewell to the liberty, the comparative youth, the light step, leaping impulses and secret pleasures, that I had enjoyed in the disguise of Hyde. I made this choice perhaps with some unconscious reservation, for I neither gave up the house in Soho, nor destroyed the clothes of Edward Hyde, which still lay ready in my cabinet. For two months, however, I was true to my determination; for two months, I led a life of such severity as I had never before attained to, and enjoyed the compensations of an approving conscience. But time began at last to obliterate the freshness of my alarm; the praises of conscience began to grow into a thing of course; I began to be tortured with throes and longings, as of Hyde struggling after freedom; and at last, in an hour of moral weakness, I once again compounded and swallowed the transforming draught.

I do not suppose that, when a drunkard reasons with himself upon his vice, he is once out of five hundred times affected by the dangers that he runs through his brutish, physical insensibility; neither had I, long as I had considered my position, made enough allowance for the complete moral insensibility and insensate readiness to evil, which were the leading characters of Edward Hyde. Yet it was by these that I was punished. My devil had been long caged, he came out roaring. I was conscious, even when I took the draught, of a more unbridled, a more furious propensity to ill. It must have been this, I suppose, that stirred in my soul that tempest of impatience with which I listened to the civilities of my unhappy victim; I declare, at least, before God, no man morally sane could have been guilty of that crime upon so pitiful a provocation; and that I struck in no more reasonable spirit than that in which a sick child may break a plaything. But I had voluntarily stripped myself of all those balancing instincts by which even the worst of us continues to walk with some degree of steadiness among temptations; and in my case, to be tempted, however slightly, was to fall.

Instantly the spirit of hell awoke in me and raged. With a transport of glee, I mauled the unresisting body, tasting delight from every blow; and it was not till weariness had begun to succeed, that I was suddenly, in the top fit of my delirium, struck through the heart by a cold thrill of terror. A mist dispersed; I saw my life to be forfeit; and fled from the scene of these excesses, at once glorying and trembling, my lust of evil gratified and stimulated, my love of life screwed to the topmost peg. I ran to the house in Soho, and (to make assurance doubly sure) destroyed my papers; thence I set out through the lamplit streets, in the same divided ecstasy of mind, gloating on my crime, light-headedly devising others in the future, and yet still hastening and still hearkening in my wake for the steps of the avenger. Hyde had a song upon his lips as he compounded the draught, and as he drank it, pledged the dead man. The pangs of transformation had not done tearing him, before Henry Jekyll, with streaming tears of gratitude and remorse, had fallen upon his knees and lifted his clasped hands to God. The veil of self-indulgence was rent from head to foot. I saw my life as a whole: I followed it up from the days of child-hood, when I had walked with my father's hand, and through the self-denying toils of my professional life, to arrive again and again, with the same sense of unreality, at the damned horrors of the evening. I could have screamed aloud; I sought with tears and prayers to smother down the crowd of hideous images and sounds with which my memory swarmed against me; and still, between the petitions, the ugly face of my iniquity stared into my soul. As the acuteness of this remorse began to die away, it was succeeded by a sense of joy. The problem of my conduct was solved. Hyde was thenceforth impossible; whether I would or not, I was now confined to the better part of my existence; and O, how I rejoiced to think of it! with what willing humility I embraced anew the restrictions of natural life! with what sincere renunciation I locked the door by which I had so often gone and come, and ground the key under my heel!

The next day, came the news that the murder had been overlooked,[9] that the guilt of Hyde was patent to the world, and that the victim was a man high in public estimation. It was not only a crime, it had been a tragic folly. I think I was glad to know it; I think I was glad to have my better impulses thus buttressed and guarded by the terrors of the scaffold. Jekyll was now my city of refuge; let but Hyde peep out an instant, and the hands of all men would be raised to take and slay him.

I resolved in my future conduct to redeem the past; and I can say with honesty that my resolve was fruitful of some good. You know yourself how earnestly, in the last months of the last year, I laboured to relieve suffer-ing; you know that much was done for others, and that the days passed quietly, almost happily for myself. Nor can I truly say that I wearied of this beneficent and innocent life; I think instead that I daily enjoyed it more completely; but I was still cursed with my duality of purpose; and as the first edge of my penitence wore off, the lower side of me, so long indulged, so recently chained down, began to growl for licence. Not that I dreamed of resuscitating Hyde; the bare idea of that would startle me to frenzy: no, it was in my own person that I was once more tempted to trifle with my conscience; and it was as an ordinary secret sinner that I at last fell before the assaults of temptation.

There comes an end to all things; the most capacious measure is filled at last; and this brief condescension to my evil finally destroyed the bal-ance of my soul. And yet I was not alarmed; the fall seemed natural, like a return to the old days before I had made my discovery. It was a fine, clear, January day, wet under foot where the frost had melted, but cloud-less overhead; and the Regent's Park[1] was full of winter chirrupings and sweet with spring odours. I sat in the sun on a bench; the animal within me licking the chops of memory; the spiritual side a little drowsed, prom-ising subsequent penitence, but not yet moved to begin. After all, I re-flected, I was like my neighbours; and then I smiled, comparing myself with other men, comparing my active good-will with the lazy cruelty of their neglect. And at the very moment of that vainglorious thought, a qualm came over me, a horrid nausea and the most deadly shuddering. These passed away, and left me faint; and then, as in its turn faintness subsided, I began to be aware of a change in the temper of my thoughts,

9. Witnessed.   1. Large park in central London.

a greater boldness, a contempt of danger, a solution of the bonds of obligation. I looked down; my clothes hung formlessly on my shrunken limbs; the hand that lay on my knee was corded and hairy. I was once more Edward Hyde. A moment before I had been safe of all men's respect, wealthy, beloved—the cloth laying for me in the dining-room at home; and now I was the common quarry of mankind, hunted, house-less, a known murderer, thrall to the gallows.

My reason wavered, but it did not fail me utterly. I have more than once observed that, in my second character, my faculties seemed sharpened to a point and my spirits more tensely elastic; thus it came about that, where Jekyll perhaps might have succumbed, Hyde rose to the importance of the moment. My drugs were in one of the presses of my cabinet; how was I to reach them? That was the problem that (crushing my temples in my hands) I set myself to solve. The laboratory door I had closed. If I sought to enter by the house, my own servants would consign me to the gallows. I saw I must employ another hand, and thought of Lanyon. How was he to be reached? how persuaded? Supposing that I escaped capture in the streets, how was I to make my way into his presence? and how should I, an unknown and displeasing visitor, prevail on the famous physician to rifle the study of his colleague, Dr. Jekyll? Then I remembered that of my original character, one part remained to me: I could write my own hand; and once I had conceived that kindling spark, the way that I must follow became lighted up from end to end.

Thereupon, I arranged my clothes as best I could, and summoning a passing hansom, drove to an hotel in Portland Street, the name of which I chanced to remember. At my appearance (which was indeed comical enough, however tragic a fate these garments covered) the driver could not conceal his mirth. I gnashed my teeth upon him with a gust of devilish fury; and the smile withered from his face—happily for him—yet more happily for myself, for in another instant I had certainly dragged him from his perch. At the inn, as I entered, I looked about me with so black a countenance as made the attendants tremble; not a look did they exchange in my presence; but obsequiously took my orders, led me to a private room, and brought me wherewithal to write. Hyde in danger of his life was a creature new to me; shaken with inordinate anger, strung to the pitch of murder, lusting to inflict pain. Yet the creature was astute; mastered his fury with a great effort of the will; composed his two important letters, one to Lanyon and one to Poole; and that he might receive actual evidence of their being posted, sent them out with directions that they should be registered. Thenceforward, he sat all day over the fire in the private room, gnawing his nails; there he dined, sitting alone with his fears, the waiter visibly quailing before his eye; and thence, when the night was fully come, he set forth in the corner of a closed cab, and was driven to and fro about the streets of the city. He, I say—I cannot say, I. That child of Hell had nothing human; nothing lived in him but fear and hatred. And when at last, thinking the driver had begun to grow suspicious, he discharged the cab and ventured on foot, attired in his misfitting clothes, an object marked out for observation, into the midst of the nocturnal passengers, these two base passions raged within him like a tempest. He walked fast, hunted by his fears, chattering to himself, skulking through the less frequented thoroughfares, counting the minutes that still divided him from midnight. Once a woman spoke to him, offering, I think, a box of lights. He smote her in the face, and she fled.

When I came to myself at Lanyon's, the horror of my old friend perhaps affected me somewhat: I do not know; it was at least but a drop in the sea to the abhorrence with which I looked back upon these hours. A change had come over me. It was no longer the fear of the gallows, it was the horror of being Hyde that racked me. I received Lanyon's condemnation partly in a dream; it was partly in a dream that I came home to my own house and got into bed. I slept after the prostration of the day, with a stringent and profound slumber which not even the nightmares that wrung me could avail to break. I awoke in the morning shaken, weakened, but refreshed. I still hated and feared the thought of the brute that slept within me, and I had not of course forgotten the appalling dangers of the day before; but I was once more at home, in my own house and close to my drugs; and gratitude for my escape shone so strong in my soul that it almost rivalled the brightness of hope.

I was stepping leisurely across the court after breakfast, drinking the chill of the air with pleasure, when I was seized again with those indescribable sensations that heralded the change; and I had but the time to gain the shelter of my cabinet, before I was once again raging and freezing with the passions of Hyde. It took on this occasion a double dose to recall me to myself; and alas! six hours after, as I sat looking sadly in the fire, the pangs returned, and the drug had to be re-administered. In short, from that day forth it seemed only by a great effort as of gymnastics, and only under the immediate stimulation of the drug, that I was able to wear the countenance of Jekyll. At all hours of the day and night, I would be taken with the premonitory shudder; above all, if I slept, or even dozed for a moment in my chair, it was always as Hyde that I awakened. Under the strain of this continually impending doom and by the sleeplessness to which I now condemned myself, ay, even beyond what I had thought possible to man, I became, in my own person, a creature eaten up and emptied by fever, languidly weak both in body and mind, and solely occupied by one thought: the horror of my other self. But when I slept, or when the virtue of the medicine wore off, I would leap almost without transition (for the pangs of transformation grew daily less marked) into the possession of a fancy brimming with images of terror, a soul boiling with causeless hatreds, and a body that seemed not strong enough to contain the raging energies of life. The powers of Hyde seemed to have grown with the sickliness of Jekyll. And certainly the hate that now divided them was equal on each side. With Jekyll, it was a thing of vital instinct. He had now seen the full deformity of that creature that shared with him some of the phenomena of consciousness, and was co-heir with him to death: and beyond these links of community, which in themselves made the most poignant part of his distress, he thought of Hyde, for all his energy of life, as of something not only hellish but inorganic. This was the shocking thing; that the slime of the pit seemed to utter cries and voices; that the amorphous dust gesticulated and sinned; that what was dead, and had no shape, should usurp the offices of life. And this again, that that insurgent horror was knit to him closer than a wife, closer than an eye; lay caged in his flesh, where he heard it mutter and felt it struggle to be born; and at every hour of weakness, and in the confidence of slumber, prevailed against him, and deposed him out of life. The hatred of Hyde for Jekyll was of a different order. His terror of the gallows drove him continually to commit temporary suicide, and return to his subordinate station of a part instead of a person; but he loathed the necessity, he loathed the despondency into which Jekyll was now fallen, and he resented the dislike with which he was himself regarded. Hence the apelike tricks that he would play me, scrawling in my own hand blasphemies on the pages of my books, burning the letters and destroying the portrait of my father; and indeed, had it not been for his fear of death, he would long ago have ruined himself in order to involve me in the ruin. But his love of life is wonderful; I go further: I, who sicken and freeze at the mere thought of him, when I recall the abjection and passion of this attachment, and when I know how he fears my power to cut him off by suicide, I find it in my heart to pity him.

It is useless, and the time awfully fails me, to prolong this description; no one has ever suffered such torments, let that suffice; and yet even to these, habit brought—no, not alleviation—but a certain callousness of soul, a certain acquiescence of despair; and my punishment might have gone on for years, but for the last calamity which has now fallen, and which has finally severed me from my own face and nature. My provision of the salt, which had never been renewed since the date of the first experiment, began to run low. I sent out for a fresh supply and mixed the draught; the ebullition followed, and the first change of colour, not the second; I drank it and it was without efficacy. You will learn from Poole how I have had London ransacked; it was in vain; and I am now persuaded that my first supply was impure, and that it was that unknown impurity which lent efficacy to the draught.

About a week has passed, and I am now finishing this statement under the influence of the last of the old powders. This, then, is the last time, short of a miracle, that Henry Jekyll can think his own thoughts or see his own face (now how sadly altered!) in the glass. Nor must I delay too long to bring my writing to an end; for if my narrative has hitherto escaped destruction, it has been by a combination of great prudence and great good luck. Should the throes of change take me in the act of writing it, Hyde will tear it in pieces; but if some time shall have elapsed after I have laid it by, his wonderful selfishness and circumscription to the moment will probably save it once again from the action of his ape-like spite. And indeed the doom that is closing on us both has already changed and crushed him. Half an hour from now, when I shall again and forever reindue[2] that hated personality, I know how I shall sit shuddering and weeping in my chair, or continue, with the most strained and fear-struck ecstasy of listening, to pace up and down this room (my last earthly refuge) and give ear to every sound of menace. Will Hyde die upon the scaffold? or will he find courage to release himself at the last moment? God knows; I am careless;[3] this is my true hour of death, and what is to follow concerns another than myself. Here then, as I lay down the pen and proceed to seal up my confession, I bring the life of that unhappy Henry Jekyll to an end.

1886

---

2. Reassume.   3. I do not care.

AFTERWORD

This is no doubt the most widely known story, or tale, in this collection. "Tale" often refers to a narrative whose plot, outline, or situation is paramount, almost to the exclusion of its specific embodiment, structure, or words, and Stevenson's short novel has been told and retold in movies, stage and television plays, and—overtly or covertly—in other stories many, many times. There is a certain amount of irony in the fact that *Jekyll and Hyde* has been treated as a retellable tale, for Robert Louis Stevenson was one of the finest and most self-conscious stylists of his day.

For most of its length, *Jekyll and Hyde* is a mystery story: the reader who does not know the plot (are there any such readers?) is kept guessing as to who Hyde is, what hold he has on Jekyll, and how Jekyll disappears from the closed room. We are as much in the dark as Utterson, the center of consciousness through whose eyes and mind most of the early portions of the story are filtered, and our interests and fears are aroused as his are; or rather, our interest is in part aroused by his fear in the first episode, "Story of the Door," and it is only after we read the will in the second section, "Search for Mr. Hyde," that our fears take form. The possibility that Hyde is blackmailing Dr. Jekyll has been raised earlier by Enfield, but he is a cynical, worldly type whose pronouncements about life we are not disposed to take seriously. We do trust Utterson, however, and share his concern for Jekyll (whom we see surprisingly little of), his fears, and his mystification. His inferences or guesses are reasonable, and for a time convincing. When, in "The Incident of the Letter," for example, he suspects that Hyde has forged Jekyll's hand, or even, much later, when he tries to explain Jekyll's seclusion by the possibility he may have a deforming malady, his explanations seem plausible and guide our expectations—away from the truth, however, as it turns out. Utterson is not the narrator, however, and at one crucial point, in "The Incident at the Window," the narrator withholds what Utterson sees, which may not be playing entirely fair with the reader.

The narrative relies neither on Utterson nor on a narrator telling us the story, in fact. There is a good deal that comes to us through written documents of one kind or another. There is the will, for example, that Utterson dislikes and suspects; there is Hyde's letter promising he will not reappear, and Utterson's clerk, Guest, finds Hyde's and Jekyll's handwriting oddly similar; there is Lanyon's narrative, and of course Jekyll's lengthy statement at the end. Some of these serve to give information not readily available to Utterson, some give other perspectives, some mystify, and some testify or reveal. So different are their perspectives and functions that we might be led to question the validity of the written word in the novel.

The shift of perspective, like the division of the novel into ten narrative segments, each with its own title, punctuates the reading: just as we pause very briefly at a period or other end-punctuation, and a little longer at a paragraph, so we pause still longer at these "chapter" breaks—we may even use the break to take a break and return to our reading later. Even the pause without a break gives us a chance to reassess what we have read and to project more fully or question more fully what is to happen in the rest of the narrative or how the mystery is to be solved. The frequency of shifts and pauses contributes to the sense of duration, and though *Jekyll and Hyde* is only a little over 25,000 words, it has the "feel" of a novel because of the elapsed or punctuated reading time and, possibly, of the nonreading time between "chapters."

Whether we trust Stevenson's words or not, they do from time to time also make us pause, often in admiration. Look at just a single passage, say, that portion of Jekyll's statement beginning "I hesitated long . . ." (p. 127). Look at the precision of the pharmacist's term *scruple* (20 grains or $\frac{1}{3}$ of a dram): "I . . . might, by the least scruple of an overdose . . . utterly blot out that immaterial tabernacle which I looked to it to change." And *tabernacle*, dwelling place of the soul; or in a portion of the sentence I omitted, *exhibition*—the precise medical term for administration of something like a drug but also suggesting here its usual meaning of showing forth, for his identity will soon show forth. And *identity* occurs in another forceful phrase that I have not yet quoted in the same sentence, "the fortress of identity." We might note, too, how *scruple, tabernacle, fortress,* and the areas of experience they suggest play off one another, and how the whole sentence rolls (in a way slightly foreign now to our ears, attuned as they are to the more staccato rhythms of modern American prose):

> I knew very well that I risked death; for any drug that so potently controlled and shook the very fortress of identity, might, by the least scruple of an overdose or at the least inopportunity in the moment of exhibition, utterly blot out that immaterial tabernacle which I looked to it to change.

And let your eye run down the next page or so and note the implication of stiffness in "the most *rigorous* hours of slumber," of *expressive* in the use of *express* to mean *exact*. Or read sentences aloud: "At that time my virtue slumbered; my evil, kept awake by ambition, was alert and swift to seize the occasion; and the thing that was projected was Edward Hyde"; "I was the first that could plod in the public eye with a load of genial respectability, and in a moment, like a schoolboy, strip off these lendings and spring headlong into the sea of liberty."

Perhaps the extraordinary precision of the language, its simultaneously accurate and suggestive diction, and its natural but lyrical rhythms attract our attention; perhaps they affect us unawares; certainly the language stands up to our closest scrutiny, and we have not just a tale but a written narrative, a short novel written in precise words. It is an unfortunate irony that the tale is so universal and effective in itself that we do not often enough go back to the novel in its specificity and appreciate its consummate artistry.

It is the "tale" of *Jekyll*, however, that initially connects most closely with *Daisy*. If *Daisy* raises the question of morality in terms of innocence and sinfulness, *Jekyll* does so in terms of good and evil—comparable but not identical sets of terms. If *Daisy* asks "Is she innocent or guilty?" *Jekyll* asks "Can good and evil be separated?" In *Daisy* sin is incarnate in sex; and though, interestingly enough, in most versions of *Jekyll* Mr. Hyde's career is assumed or shown to be one primarily of sexual debauchery and perversion, and though his name is related to "flesh" and so to some extent justifies that interpretation, in Stevenson's story his only specified evil-doings are those of violence (the first we see of him, he callously knocks over a little girl; later, a witness describes his brutally beating an old man to death). In post-Freudian terms, Hyde is the id, the anarchic, pleasure-seeking, amoral, instinctive portion of the psyche, and Jekyll the superego, and conscience and societal voice of the psyche. Jekyll, in pre-Freudian terms that are not inconsistent with Freud's, calls his two sides *animal* and *spiritual* as well as *good* and *evil*, and he attributes part of his fascination with evil to his repression for social and professional reasons of his natural "gayety" or love of pleasure.

"Translating" the moral into psychological terms may make the novel seem less "dated" or Victorian, and may make some of the questions it raises seem more relevant, even urgent. If the freeing of the instinctual and passional forces in the psyche does or can lead to cruelty, even murder, may this not challenge the widespread modern assumption that all "Victorian" restraints on sexual conduct are somehow wrong and reactionary? Is all freedom good? Is all "government," in the psychological as well as political sense, "bad"? Is there a definable line between liberty and license? What does Stevenson mean by "the restrictions of natural life"? (Isn't "natural" life by definition unrestricted?) These questions may seem strangely familiar to the reader of the not-so-strange "case" of *Daisy Miller* (published just eight years earlier), and may come up again in somewhat different guise as we read a novel published in the decade following *Jekyll and Hyde*, Kate Chopin's *The Awakening*.

In most other versions of the "tale" Hyde is grossly ugly, as if monstrous evil were always readily visible. You will notice that in Stevenson's novel Hyde, though mysteriously "spiritually" repulsive, is younger and handsomer than Jekyll. The "flesh"—Hyde—is of course stronger in youth; the superego is conventionally held to be stronger in later years. So beauty and virtue, ugliness and vice are not so intimately connected in this novel as in many versions of the tale or in our usual stereotypes. You will notice, too, that Hyde is smaller than Jekyll, for Hyde is only part of a human being, as evil or our animal nature is, while Jekyll is not merely the good, as we are sometimes prone to think, but the whole man, good and evil.

There are other significant elements in Stevenson's novel that do not often survive its transformation into the tale. Three-fourths of *The Strange Case of Dr. Jekyll and Mr. Hyde* is, like almost all of *Daisy Miller*, seen through the consciousness of someone other than the title character but is narrated through—but not by—an important observer-character. We asked whether Winterbourne's self-interest or character influenced what he saw or did not see in Daisy. Can we ask the same question of Utterson? What is he like? You might want to look back at the first sentence where he is described as "cold . . . dreary . . . lovable." Why should a story like *Jekyll and Hyde* be largely told by someone like that? He has a weakness for wine; is that the kind of consciousness through which we want to see this moral tale? But he mortifies himself for his fault—with gin! He likes the theater but never goes. That may be a better qualification for a moralist. He's a heretic—not his brother's keeper; but what he seems to mean by that is that he is not censorious. So lots of imperfect men or worse are his friends or acquaintances, including his man-about-town kinsman, Mr. Richard Enfield. Utterson does not become, as Winterbourne may be said to become, the objective as well as the subjective consciousness of the novel; but he is (in addition to being a convenient vehicle for the transmission of the narrative because of his role as everyone's confidant) the model, in a sense, of the mixed human being that Dr. Jekyll refuses to remain. Stevenson thus sets up from the beginning a moral perspective through the center of consciousness that is consonant with the moral values of the novel (but one that is rarely retained in its dramatization or retelling).

This is not to suggest, however, that Utterson is any more morally omniscient than he was intellectually omniscient when the "case" was still a mystery. There may be more reasons than mere narrative convenience for taking the story out of his hands toward the end. A close reading of the last quarter of the novel, "Henry Jekyll's Full Statement," seems to undercut at least some of the implications in the Utterson and other portions of the first three-quarters, and even undercuts some of Jekyll's own inferences. Though the un-happy doctor talks, for example, of the "duplicity of life" and good and evil, he also insists that man is not merely dual in nature but multifarious, that we house not merely what might be called an anarchic id but many potential beings or partial beings of various kinds. This, it seems to me, seriously under-mines most of the fairly simple moral and psychological readings of the story, even if those readings are supported by Utterson's or even Jekyll's own views! Is it accidental, moreover, that in Jekyll's confession he admits that one of his fears is that Hyde can write like him and therefore might "forge" a confession? Can we trust this confession, then? Surely it is not a forgery of a diabolical Edward Hyde?

Though most adaptations of the tale, foregoing the initial mystery and often the intermediary presence of Utterson, concentrate on what is in the novel only the final quarter, the sensational elements of Jekyll's change and Hyde's indulgence in sin—usually adding sexual sins to those specified in the novel—they ignore the undermining of the dualism in Jekyll's confession and the other complications of the straightforward reading that this very portion of the novel suggests. D. H. Lawrence advises us to trust the tale and not the teller; as we have been using the term here, however, we might better warn the reader to trust the telling and not the tale.

JOSEPH CONRAD

The Nigger of the "Narcissus"

Jozef Teodor Konrad Nalecz Korzeniowski (1857–1924) was born in Ber-
dyczew, Polish Ukraine; at five he accompanied his parents into exile to
northern Russia and later the district near Kiev, and was left an orphan at
eleven when his Polish-patriot father (and translator of Shakespeare and
Hugo) died in Cracow, his mother having died four years earlier. Before
he was seventeen he was off to Marseilles, making three trips from that
port to the West Indies as an apprentice seaman. After some veiled troubles in France, involving gambling debts and an apparent suicide attempt,
he sailed on a British ship, landed in England in 1878, and spent the next
sixteen years in the British merchant service, rising to master in 1886, the
same year in which he became a British subject. He began writing in 1889
but did not publish his first novel, *Almayer's Folly*, until 1895, the same
year he married an Englishwoman, Jessie George.

The Nigger of the "Narcissus" (1897) was his third novel and the first of
his major works, which include *Lord Jim* (1900), *Heart of Darkness* (1902),
Nostromo (1904), and *Victory* (1915). Upon completion of *The Nigger of
the "Narcissus,"* Conrad decided finally to leave the life of the sea for that
of the writer, accepting, as he says in "To My Readers in America," the
challenge of the new life and paying tribute to the old: "It is a book by
which, not as a novelist perhaps, but as an artist striving for the utmost
sincerity of expression, I am willing to stand or fall. Its pages are the tribute of my unalterable and profound affection for the ship, the seamen,
the winds and the great sea—the moulders of my youth, the companions
of the best years of my life."

Shortly after he finished the novel and made his decision, he wrote his
manifesto as an artist, "Preface to The Nigger of the 'Narcissus.' " Appropriately, given the choice he was making, it is primarily an attempt to assert his aims as an artist and his sense of or wishes for the place of art in
human life, rather than a philosophic, aesthetic, historical, or technical
essay. Art, he says "is an attempt to find in its forms and colours, in its
light, in its shadows, in the aspects of matter and in the facts of life, what
of each is fundamental, what is enduring and essential . . . the very truth
of their existence." The thinker investigates ideas, the scientist facts, and
both appeal to our intelligence and credulity. "But the artist appeals to
that part of our being which is not dependent on wisdom. . . . He speaks
to our capacity for delight and wonder, to the sense of mystery surrounding our lives; to our sense of pity, and beauty, and pain; to the latent
feeling of fellowship with all creation; and to the subtle but invincible
conviction of solidarity that knits together the loneliness of innumerable
hearts. . . ." Art rescues for a moment from the flux of time that which
endures longer than the transient findings of science and philosophy. The
artist is the see-er and the seer.

The solidarity of mankind at the depths of experience, the permanence
of art, the ability of the artist's imagination to see the reality beneath the
appearance of things, may be expressions of Conrad's hopes as he set out
on his new voyage in a new vessel rather than an accurate chart of the
waters upon which he had set sail. But man-made codes in an indifferent
universe and the solidarity of the human "crew" were the keystones of
Conrad's vision, as well as of his aesthetic.

The Nigger of the "Narcissus"*
A Tale of the Sea

> ... My Lord in his discourse discovered a
> great deal of love to this ship.
> —Diary of Samuel Pepys

Chapter One

MR. BAKER, chief mate of the ship *Narcissus*, stepped
in one stride out of his lighted cabin into the darkness
of the quarter-deck. Above his head on the break of the
poop, the night-watchman rang a double stroke. It was nine o'clock. Mr.
Baker, speaking up to the man above him, asked: "Are all the hands
aboard, Knowles?"

The man limped down the ladder, then said reflectively:

"I think so, sir. All our old chaps are there, and a lot of new men has
come. . . . They must be all there."

"Tell the boatswain to send all hands aft," went on Mr. Baker; "and
tell one of the youngsters to bring a good lamp here. I want to muster our
crowd."

The main deck was dark aft, but half-way from forward, through the
open doors of the forecastle, two streaks of brilliant light cut the shadow
of the quiet night that lay upon the ship. A hum of voices was heard
there, while port and starboard, in the illuminated doorways, silhouettes
of moving men appeared for a moment, very black, without relief, like
figures cut out of sheet tin. The ship was for sea. The carpenter had
driven in the last wedge of the main-hatch battens,[1] and, throwing down
his maul, had wiped his face with great deliberation, just on the stroke of
five. The decks had been swept, the windlass oiled and made ready to
heave up the anchor; the big tow-rope lay in long bights along one side of
the main deck, with one end carried up and hung over the bows, in readiness for the tug that would come paddling and hissing noisily, hot and
smoky, in the limped, cool quietness of the early morning. The captain
was ashore, where he had been engaging some new hands to make up his
full crew; and, the work of the day over, the ship's officers had kept out of
the way, glad of a little breathing-time. Soon after dark the few liberty-
men and the new hands began to arrive in shore-boats rowed by white-
clad Asiatics, who clamoured fiercely for payment before coming
alongside the gangway-ladder. The feverish and shrill babble of Eastern
language struggled against the masterful tones of tipsy seamen, who argued against brazen claims and dishonest hopes by profane shouts. The
resplendent and bestarred peace of the East was torn into squalid tatters
by howls of rage and shrieks of lament raised over sums ranging from five
annas to half a rupee; and every soul afloat in Bombay Harbour became
aware that the new hands were joining the *Narcissus*.

---

* The text is that of the Norton Critical Edition
edited by Robert Kimbrough, and much of the annotation is adapted from the same edition. I am grateful
for Professor Kimbrough's kind permission.

1. Battens are strips of wood that secure the covers
of hatches, square holes in the deck giving access to
storage spaces or living quarters. This novel is full of
sailing terms, most of which are defined in a desk dictionary. Only hard-to-find phrases or passages where
the details are essential for understanding the action
will be annotated; for full explanations of the terms
and seamanship involved, see the Norton Critical Edition.

Gradually the distracting noise had subsided. The boats came no longer
in splashing clusters of three or four together, but dropped alongside singly, in a subdued buzz of expostulation cut short by a "Not a pice more!
You go to the devil!" from some man staggering up the accommodation-
ladder—a dark figure, with a long bag poised on the shoulder. In the forecastle the newcomers, upright and swaying amongst corded boxes and
bundles of bedding, made friends with the old hands, who sat one above
another in the two tiers of bunks, gazing at their future shipmates with
glances critical but friendly. The two forecastle lamps were turned up
high, and shed an intense hard glare; shore-going round hats were pushed
far on the backs of heads, or rolled about on the deck amongst the chain-
cables; white collars, undone, stuck out on each side of red faces; big
arms in white sleeves gesticulated; the growling voices hummed steady
amongst bursts of laughter and hoarse calls. "Here, sonny, take that
bunk!... Don't you do it!... What's your last ship?... I know her....
Three years ago, in Puget Sound.... This here berth leaks, I tell you!...
Come on; give us a chance to swing that chest!... Did you bring a bottle, any of you shore toffs?[2]... Give us a bit of 'baccy.... I know her; her
skipper drank himself to death.... He was a dandy boy!... Liked his
lotion inside, he did!... No!... Hold your row, you chaps.... I tell you,
you came on board a hooker,[3] where they get their money's worth out of
poor Jack,[3] by—!..."
   A little fellow, called Craik and nicknamed Belfast, abused the ship
violently, romancing on principle, just to give the new hands something
to think over. Archie, sitting aslant on his sea-chest, kept his knees out of
the way, and pushed the needle steadily through a white patch in a pair
of blue trousers. Men in black jackets and stand-up collars, mixed with
men bare-footed, bare-armed, with coloured shirts open on hairy chests,
pushed against one another in the middle of the forecastle. The group
swayed, reeled, turning upon itself with the motion of a scrimmage, in a
haze of tobacco smoke. All were speaking together, swearing at every
second word. A Russian Finn, wearing a yellow shirt with pink stripes,
stared upwards, dreamy-eyed, from under a mop of tumbled hair. Two
young giants with smooth, baby faces—two Scandinavians—helped each
other to spread their bedding, silent and smiling placidly at the tempest
of good-humoured and meaningless curses. Old Singleton, the oldest able
seaman in the ship, sat apart on the deck right under the lamps, stripped
to the waist, tattooed like a cannibal chief all over his powerful chest and
enormous biceps. Between the blue and red patterns his white skin
gleamed like satin; his bare back was propped against the heel of the
bow-sprit, and he held a book at arm's length before his big, sunburnt
face. With his spectacles and a venerable white beard, he resembled a
learned and savage patriarch, the incarnation of barbarian wisdom serene
in the blasphemous turmoil of the world. He was intensely absorbed, and,
as he turned the pages, an expression of grave surprise would pass over
his rugged features. He was reading *Pelham*.[4] The popularity of Bulwer
Lytton in the forecastles of Southern-going ships is a wonderful and bizarre phenomenon. What ideas do his polished and so curiously insincere

2. Stylishly dressed person who wants to be
thought a member of the upper class.
3. Slang for a sailor. *Hooker:* clumsy, old-fashioned
vessel.

4. *Pelham; or, Adventures of a Gentleman* (1828),
by Edward Bulwer-Lytton (1803–1873), a fashionable
novel that contributed greatly to the English concept
of the dandy.

sentences awaken in the simple minds of the big children who people
those dark and wandering places of the earth? What meaning can their
rough, inexperienced souls find in the elegant verbiage of his pages? What
excitement?—what forgetfulness?—what appeasement? Mystery! Is it the
fascination of the incomprehensible? is it the charm of the impossible? Or
are those beings who exist beyond the pale of life stirred by his tales as by
an enigmatical disclosure of a resplendent world that exists within the
frontier of infamy and filth, within that border of dirt and hunger, of
misery and dissipation, that comes down on all sides to the water's edge
of the incorruptible ocean, and is the only thing they know of life, the
only thing they see of surrounding land—those lifelong prisoners of the
sea? Mystery!

Singleton, who had sailed to the southward since the age of twelve,
who in the last forty-five years had lived (as we had calculated from his
papers) no more than forty months ashore—old Singleton, who boasted,
with the mild composure of long years well spent, that generally from the
day he was paid off from one ship till the day he shipped in another he
seldom was in a condition to distinguish daylight—old Singleton sat unmoved in the clash of voices and cries, spelling through *Pelham* with slow
labour, and lost in an absorption profound enough to resemble a trance.
He breathed regularly. Every time he turned the book in his enormous
and blackened hands the muscles of his big white arms rolled slightly
under the smooth skin. Hidden by the white moustache, his lips, stained
with tobacco-juice that trickled down the long beard, moved in inward
whisper. His bleared eyes gazed fixedly from behind the glitter of black-
rimmed glasses. Opposite to him, and on a level with his face, the ship's
cat sat on the barrel of the windlass in the pose of a crouching chimera,
blinking its green eyes at its old friend. It seemed to meditate a leap on
to the old man's lap over the bent back of the ordinary seaman who sat at
Singleton's feet. Young Charley was lean and long-necked. The ridge of
his backbone made a chain of small hills under the old shirt. His face of a
street-boy—a face precocious, sagacious, and ironic, with deep downward
folds on each side of the thin, wide mouth—hung low over his bony knees.
He was learning to make a lanyard knot with a bit of an old rope. Small
drops of perspiration stood out on his bulging forehead; he sniffed
strongly from time to time, glancing out of the corners of his restless eyes
at the old seaman, who took no notice of the puzzled youngster muttering
at his work.

The noise increased. Little Belfast seemed, in the heavy heat of the
forecastle, to boil with facetious fury. His eyes danced; in the crimson of
his face, comical as a mask, the mouth yawned black, with strange gri
maces. Facing him, a half-undressed man held his sides, and, throwing his
head back, laughed with wet eyelashes. Others stared with amazed eyes.
Men sitting doubled up in the upper bunks smoked short pipes, swinging
bare brown feet above the heads of those who, sprawling below on sea-
chests, listened, smiling stupidly or scornfully. Over the white rims of
berths stuck out heads with blinking eyes; but the bodies were lost in the
gloom of those places, that resembled narrow niches for coffins in a whitewashed and lighted mortuary. Voices buzzed louder. Archie, with compressed lips, drew himself in, seemed to shrink into a smaller space, and
sewed steadily, industrious and dumb. Belfast shrieked like an inspired
Dervish: ". . . So I seez to him, boys, seez I, 'Beggin' your pardon, sorr,'

seez I to that second mate of that steamer 'beggin' your r r pardon, sorr, the Board of Trade[5] must 'ave been drunk when they granted you your certificate!' 'What do you say, you—!' seez he, comin' at me like a mad bull . . . all in his white clothes; and I up with my tar-pot and capsizes it all over his blamed lovely face and his lovely jacket. . . . 'Take that!' seez I. 'I am a sailor, anyhow, you nosing, skipper-licking, useless, sooperfloos bridge-stanchion, you! That's the kind of man I am!' shouts I. . . . You should have seed him skip boys! Drowned, blind with tar, he was! So . . ."

"Don't 'ee believe him! He never upset no tar; I was there!" shouted somebody. The two Norwegians sat on a chest side by side, alike and placid, resembling a pair of love-birds on a perch, and with round eyes stared innocently; but the Russian Finn, in the racket of explosive shouts and rolling laughter, remained motionless, limp, and dull, like a deaf man without a backbone. Near him Archie smiled at his needle. A broad-chested, slow-eyed newcomer spoke deliberately to Belfast during an exhausted lull in the noise: "I wonder any of the mates here are alive yet with such a chap as you on board! I concloode they ain't that bad now, if you had the taming of them, sonny."

"Not bad! Not bad!" screamed Belfast. "If it wasn't for us sticking together. . . . Not bad! They ain't never bad when they ain't got a chawnce, blast their black 'arts. . . ." He foamed, whirling his arms, then suddenly grinned and, taking a tablet of black tobacco out of his pocket, bit a piece off with a funny show of ferocity. Another new hand—a man with shifty eyes and a yellow hatchet face, who had been listening open-mouthed in the shadow of the midship locker—observed in a squeaky voice: "Well, it's a 'omeward trip, anyhow. Bad or good, I can do it on my 'ed—s'long as I get 'ome. And I can look after my rights! I will show 'em!" All the heads turned towards him. Only the ordinary seaman and the cat took no notice. He stood with arms akimbo, a little fellow with white eyelashes. He looked as if he had known all the degradations and all the furies. He looked as if he had been cuffed, kicked, rolled in the mud; he looked as if he had been scratched, spat upon, pelted with unmentionable filth . . . and he smiled with a sense of security at the faces around. His ears were bending down under the weight of his battered felt hat. The torn tails of his black coat flapped in fringes about the calves of his legs. He unbuttoned the only two buttons that remained and every one saw that he had no shirt under it. It was his deserved misfortune that those rags which nobody could possibly be supposed to own looked on him as if they had been stolen. His neck was long and thin; his eyelids were red; rare hairs hung about his jaws; his shoulders were peaked and drooped like the broken wings of a bird; all his left side was caked with mud, which showed that he had lately slept in a wet ditch. He had saved his inefficient carcass from violent destruction by running away from an American ship[6] where, in a moment of forgetful folly, he had dared to engage himself; and he had knocked about for a fortnight ashore in the native quarter, cadging for drinks, starving, sleeping on rubbish-heaps, wandering in sunshine: a startling visitor from a world of nightmares. He stood repulsive and smiling in the sudden silence. This clean white forecastle was his refuge; the place where he could be lazy; where he could

5. The national ministry in England which supervises and encourages commerce and industry, examines officer candidates, and issues certificates to the successful.
6. Then noted for harsh treatment of crews.

wallow, and lie and eat—and curse the food he ate; where he could display his talents for shirking work, for cheating, for cadging; where he could find surely some one to wheedle and some one to bully—and where he would be paid for doing all this. They all knew him. Is there a spot on earth where such a man is unknown, an ominous survival testifying to the eternal fitness of lies and impudence? A taciturn long-armed shellback,[7] with hooked fingers, who had been lying on his back smoking, turned in his bed to examine him dispassionately, then, over his head, sent a long jet of clear saliva towards the door. They all knew him! He was the man that cannot steer, that cannot splice, that dodges the work on dark nights; that, aloft, holds on frantically with both arms and legs, and swears at the wind, the sleet, the darkness; the man who curses the sea while others work. The man who is the last out and the first in when all hands are called. The man who can't do most things and won't do the rest. The pet of philanthropists and self-seeking landlubbers. The sympathetic and deserving creature that knows all about his rights, but knows nothing of courage, of endurance, and of the unexpressed faith, of the unspoken loyalty that knits together a ship's company. The independent offspring of the ignoble freedom of the slums full of disdain and hate for the austere servitude of the sea.

Some one cried at him: "What's your name?"—"Donkin," he said, looking round with cheerful effrontery.—"What are you?" asked another voice.—"Why, a sailor like you, old man," he replied, in a tone that meant to be hearty but was impudent.—"Blamme if you don't look a blamed sight worse than a broken-down fireman," was the comment in a convinced mutter. Charley lifted his head and piped in a cheeky voice: "He is a man and a sailor"—then, wiping his nose with the back of his hand, bent down industriously over his bit of rope. A few laughed. Others stared doubtfully. The ragged newcomer was indignant—"That's a fine way to welcome a chap into a fo'c'sle," he snarled. "Are you men or a lot of 'artless cannybals?"—"Don't take your shirt off for a word, shipmate," called out Belfast, jumping up in front, fiery, menacing, and friendly at the same time.—"Is that 'ere bloke blind?" asked the indomitable scarecrow, looking right and left with affected surprise. "Can't 'ee see I 'aven't got no shirt?"

He held both his arms out crosswise and shook the rags that hung over his bones with dramatic effect.

" 'Cos why?" he continued very loud. "The bloody Yankees been tryin' to jump my guts out 'cos I stood up for my rights like a good 'un. I am an Englishman, I am. They set upon me an' I 'ad to run. That's why. A'n't yer never seed a man 'ard up? Yah! What kind of blamed ship is this? I'm dead broke. I 'aven't got nothink. No bag, no bed, no blanket, no shirt—not a bloomin' rag but what I stand in. But I 'ad the 'art to stand up agin' them Yankees. 'As any of you 'art enough to spare a pair of old pants for a chum?"

He knew how to conquer the naive instincts of that crowd. In a moment they gave him their compassion, jocularly, contemptuously, or surlily; and at first it took the shape of a blanket thrown at him as he stood there with the white skin of his limbs showing his human kinship through the black fantasy of his rags. Then a pair of old shoes fell at his muddy

7. Old, experienced sailor.

feet. With a cry:—"From under," a rolled up pair of canvas trousers, heavy with tar stains, struck him on the shoulder. The gust of their benevolence sent a wave of sentimental pity through their doubting hearts. They were touched by their own readiness to alleviate a shipmate's misery. Voices cried:—"We will fit you out, old man." Murmurs:—"Never seed seech a hard case. . . . Poor beggar. . . . I've got an old singlet. . . . Will that be of any use to you? . . . Take it, matey. . . ." Those friendly murmurs filled the forecastle. He pawed around with his naked foot, gathering the things in a heap, and looked about for more. Unemotional Archie perfunctorily contributed to the pile an old cloth cap with the peak torn off. Old Singleton, lost in the serene regions of fiction, read on unheeding. Charley, pitiless with the wisdom of youth, squeaked:—"If you want brass buttons for your new unyforms I've got two for you." The filthy object of universal charity shook his fist at the youngster.—"I'll make you keep this 'ere fo'c'sle clean, young feller," he snarled viciously. "Never you fear. I will learn you to be civil to an able seaman, you ignerant ass." He glared harmfully, but saw Singleton shut his book, and his little beady eyes began to roam from berth to berth.—"Take that bunk by the door there—it's pretty fair," suggested Belfast. So advised, he gathered the gifts at his feet, pressed them in a bundle against his breast, then looked cautiously at the Russian Finn, who stood on one side with an unconscious gaze, contemplating, perhaps, one of those weird visions that haunt the men of his race.—"Get out of my road, Dutchy," said the victim of Yankee brutality. The Finn did not move—did not hear. "Get out, blast ye," shouted the other, shoving him aside with his elbow. "Get out, you blanked deaf and dumb fool. Get out." The man staggered, recovered himself, and gazed at the speaker in silence.—"Those damned furriners should be kept under," opined the amiable Donkin to the forecastle. "If you don't teach 'em their place they put on you like anythink." He flung all his worldly possessions into the empty bedplace, gauged with another shrewd look the risks of the proceeding, then leaped up to the Finn, who stood pensive and dull.—"I'll teach you to swell around," he yelled. "I'll plug your eyes for you, you blooming square-head." Most of the men were now in their bunks and the two had the forecastle clear to themselves. The development of the destitute Donkin aroused interest. He danced all in tatters before the amazed Finn, squaring from a distance at the heavy unmoved face. One or two men cried encouragingly: "Go it, Whitechapel!"[8] settling themselves luxuriously in their beds to survey the fight. Others shouted: "Shut yer row! . . . Go an' put yer 'ed in a bag! . . ." The hubbub was recommencing. Suddenly many heavy blows struck with a handspike on the deck above boomed like discharges of small cannon through the forecastle. Then the boatswain's voice rose outside the door with an authoritative note in its drawl:—"D'ye hear, below there? Lay aft! Lay aft to muster all hands!"

There was a moment of surprised stillness. Then the forecastle floor disappeared under men whose bare feet flopped on the planks as they sprang clear out of their berths. Caps were rooted for amongst tumbled blankets. Some, yawning, buttoned waistbands. Half-smoked pipes were knocked hurriedly against woodwork and stuffed under pillows. Voices growled:—"What's up? . . . Is there no rest for us?" Donkin yelped:—"If

8. Boxing term: uppercut, after a district in eastern London, then a desolate, lonely place inhabited chiefly by persons of low character.

that's the way of this ship, we'll 'ave to change all that. ... You leave me alone. ... I will soon. ..." None of the crowd noticed him. They were lurching in twos and threes through the doors, after the manner of merchant Jacks who cannot go out of a door fairly, like mere landsmen. The votary of change followed them. Singleton, struggling into his jacket, came last, tall and fatherly, bearing high his head of a weatherbeaten sage on the body of an old athlete. Only Charley remained alone in the white glare of the empty place, sitting between the two rows of iron links that stretched into the narrow gloom forward. He pulled hard at the strands in a hurried endeavour to finish his knot. Suddenly he started up, flung the rope at the cat, and skipped after the black tom which went off leaping sedately over chain compressors, with its tail carried stiff and upright, like a small flag pole.

Outside the glare of the steaming forecastle the serene purity of the night enveloped the seamen with its soothing breath, with its tepid breath flowing under the stars that hung countless above the mastheads in a thin cloud of luminous dust. On the town side the blackness of the water was streaked with trails of light undulated gently on slight ripples, similar to filaments that float rooted to the shore. Rows of other lights stood away in straight lines as if drawn up on parade between towering buildings; but on the other side of the harbour sombre hills arched high their black spines, on which, here and there, the point of a star resembled a spark fallen from the sky. Far off, Byculla[9] way, the electric lamps at the dock gates shone on the end of lofty standards with a glow blinding and frigid like captive ghosts of some evil moons. Scattered all over the dark polish of the roadstead, the ships at anchor floated in perfect stillness under the feeble gleam of their riding-lights,[1] looming up, opaque and bulky, like strange and monumental structures abandoned by men to an everlasting repose.

Before the cabin door Mr. Baker was mustering the crew. As they stumbled and lurched along past the mainmast, they could see aft his round, broad face with a white paper before it, and beside his shoulder the sleepy head, with dropped eyelids, of the boy, who held, suspended at the end of his raised arm, the luminous globe of a lamp. Even before the shuffle of naked soles had ceased along the decks, the mate began to call over the names. He called distinctly in a serious tone befitting this roll-call to unquiet loneliness, to inglorious and obscure struggle, or to the more trying endurance of small privations and wearisome duties. As the chief mate read out a name, one of the men would answer: "Yes, sir!" or "Here!" and, detaching himself from the shadowy mob of heads visible above the blackness of starboard bulwarks, would stop bare footed into the circle of light, and in two noiseless strides pass into the shadows on the port side of the quarter-deck. They answered in divers tones: in thick mutters, in clear, ringing voices; and some, as if the whole thing had been an outrage on their feelings, used an injured intonation: for discipline is not ceremonious in merchant ships, where the sense of hierarchy is weak, and where all feel themselves equal before the unconcerned immensity of the sea and the exacting appeal of the work.

Mr. Baker read on steadily:—"Hansen—Campbell—Smith—Wamibo. Now, then, Wamibo. Why don't you answer? Always got to call your

9. District in the center of Bombay Island, just west of the docks.

1. White light hoisted in the bow indicating that a vessel is anchored.

name twice." The Finn emitted at last an uncouth grunt, and, stepping out, passed through the patch of light, weird and gaudy, with the face of a man marching through a dream. The mate went on faster:—"Craik—Singleton—Donkin. . . . O Lord!" he involuntarily ejaculated as the incredibly dilapidated figure appeared in the light. It stopped; it uncovered pale gums and long, upper teeth in a malevolent grin.—"Is there anything wrong with me, Mister Mate?" it asked, with a flavour of insolence in the forced simplicity of its tone. On both sides of the deck subdued titters were heard.—"That'll do. Go over," growled Mr. Baker, fixing the new hand with steady blue eyes. And Donkin vanished suddenly out of the light into the dark group of mustered men, to be slapped on the back and to hear flattering whispers:—"He ain't afeard, he'll give sport to 'em, see if he don't. . . . Reg'lar Punch and Judy show. . . . Did ye see the mate start at him? . . . Well! Damme, if I ever! . . ."

The last man had gone over, and there was a moment of silence while the mate peered at his list.—"Sixteen, seventeen," he muttered. "I am one hand short, bo'sun," he said aloud. The big West-countryman[2] at his elbow, swarthy and bearded like a gigantic Spaniard, said in a rumbling bass:—"There's no one left forward, sir. I had a look round. He ain't aboard, but he may turn up before daylight."—"Ay. He may or he may not," commented the mate. "Can't make out that last name. It's all a smudge. . . . That will do, men. Go below."

The distinct and motionless group stirred, broke up, began to move forward.

"Wait!" cried a deep, ringing voice.

All stood still. Mr. Baker, who had turned away yawning, spun round open-mouthed. At last furious, he blurted out:—"What's this? Who said 'Wait'? What . . ."

But he saw a tall figure standing on the rail. It came down and pushed through the crowd, marching with a heavy tread towards the light on the quarter-deck. Then again the sonorous voice said with insistence:— "Wait!" The lamplight lit up the man's body. He was tall. His head was away up in the shadows of lifeboats that stood on skids above the deck. The whites of his eyes and his teeth gleamed distinctly, but the face was indistinguishable. His hands were big and seemed gloved.

Mr. Baker advanced intrepidly. "Who are you? How dare you . . ." he began.

The boy, amazed like the rest, raised the light to the man's face. It was black. A surprised hum—a faint hum that sounded like the suppressed mutter of the word "Nigger"—ran along the deck and escaped out into the night. The nigger seemed not to hear. He balanced himself where he stood in a swagger that marked time. After a moment he said calmly:— "My name is Wait—James Wait."

"Oh!" said Mr. Baker. Then, after a few seconds of smouldering silence, his temper blazed out. "Ah! Your name is Wait. What of that? What do you want? What do you mean, coming shouting here?"

The nigger was calm, cool, towering, superb. The men had approached and stood behind him in a body. He overtopped the tallest by half a head. He said: "I belong to the ship." He enunciated distinctly, with soft precision. The deep, rolling tones of his voice filled the deck without effort. He

2. I.e., from the southwest of England: Somerset, Devon, Cornwall, etc.

was naturally scornful, unaffectedly condescending, as if from his height of six foot three he had surveyed all the vastness of human folly and had made up his mind not to be too hard on it. He went on:—"The captain shipped me this morning. I couldn't get aboard sooner. I saw you all aft as I came up the ladder, and could see directly you were mustering the crew. Naturally I called out my name. I thought you had it on your list, and would understand. You misapprehended." He stopped short. The folly around him was confounded. He was right as ever, and as ever ready to forgive. The disdainful tones had ceased, and, breathing heavily, he stood still, surrounded by all these white men. He held his head up in the glare of the lamp—a head vigorously modelled into deep shadows and shining lights—a head powerful and misshapen, with a tormented and flattened face—a face pathetic and brutal; the tragic, the mysterious, the repulsive mask of a nigger's soul.

Mr. Baker, recovering his composure, looked at the paper close. "Oh yes; that's so. All right, Wait. Take your gear forward," he said.

Suddenly the nigger's eyes rolled wildly, became all whites. He put his hand to his side and coughed twice, a cough metallic, hollow, and tremendously loud; it resounded like two explosions in a vault; the dome of the sky rang to it, and the iron plates of the ship's bulwarks seemed to vibrate in unison; then he marched off forward with the others. The officers lingering by the cabin door could hear him say: "Won't some of you chaps lend a hand with my dunnage? I've got a chest and a bag." The words, spoken sonorously, with an even intonation, were heard all over the ship, and the question was put in a manner that made refusal impossible. The short, quick shuffle of men carrying something heavy went away forward, but the tall figure of the nigger lingered by the main hatch in a knot of smaller shapes. Again he was heard asking: "Is your cook a coloured gentleman?" Then a disappointed and disapproving "Ah! h'm!" was his comment upon the information that the cook happened to be a mere white man. Yet, as they went all together towards the forecastle, he condescended to put his head through the galley door and boom out inside a magnificent "Good evening, doctor!"[3] that made all the saucepans ring. In the dim light the cook dozed on the coal locker in front of the captain's supper. He jumped up as if he had been cut with a whip, and dashed wildly on deck to see the backs of several men going away laughing. Afterwards, when talking about that voyage, he used to say:—"The poor fellow had scared me. I thought I had seen the devil." The cook had been seven years in the ship with the same captain. He was a serious-minded man with a wife and three children, whose society he enjoyed on an average of one month out of twelve. When on shore he took his family to church twice every Sunday. At sea he went to sleep every evening with his lamp turned up full, a pipe in his mouth, and an open Bible in his hand. Some one had always to go during the night to put out the light, take the book from his hand, and the pipe from between his teeth. "For"—Belfast used to say, irritated and complaining—"some night, you stupid cookie, you'll swallow your ould clay, and we will have no cook."— "Ah! sonny, I am ready for my Maker's call . . . wish you all were," the other would answer with a benign serenity that was altogether imbecile and touching. Belfast outside the gallery door danced with vexation. "You

---

3. Nickname (and function) of a cook aboard ship.

holy fool! I don't want you to die," he howled, looking up with furious, quivering face and tender eyes. "What's the hurry? You blessed wooden-headed ould heretic, the divvle will have you soon enough. Think of Us ... of Us ... of Us!" And he would go away, stamping, spitting aside, disgusted and worried; while the other, stepping out, saucepan in hand, hot, begrimed, and placid, watched with a superior cock-sure smile the back of his "queer little man" reeling in a rage. They were great friends..

Mr. Baker, lounging over the after-hatch, sniffed the humid night in the company of the second mate.—"Those West India niggers run fine and large—some of them.... Ough!... Don't they? A fine, big man that, Mr. Creighton. Feel him on a rope. Hey? Ough! I will take him into my watch, I think." The second mate, a fair, gentlemanly young fellow, with a resolute face and a splendid physique, observed quietly that it was just about what he expected. There could be felt in his tone some slight bit-terness which Mr. Baker very kindly set himself to argue away. "Come, come, young man," he said, grunting between the words. "Come! Don't be too greedy. You had that big Finn in your watch all the voyage. I will do what's fair. You may have those two young Scandinavians and I ... Ough!... I get the nigger, and will take that ... Ough! that cheeky cos-termonger chap in a black frockcoat. I'll make him ... Ough!... make him toe the mark, or my ... Ough! ... name isn't Baker. Ough! Ough! Ough!"

He grunted thrice—ferociously. He had that trick of grunting so be-tween his words and at the end of sentences. It was a fine, effective grunt that went well with his menacing utterance, with his heavy, bull-necked frame, his jerky, rolling gait; with his big, seamed face, his steady eyes, and sardonic mouth. But its effect had been long ago discounted by the men. They liked him; Belfast—who was a favourite, and knew it—mim-icked him, not quite behind his back. Charley—but with greater caution—imitated his rolling gait. Some of his sayings became established, daily quotations in the forecastle. Popularity can go no further! Besides, all hands were ready to admit that on a fitting occasion the mate could "jump down a fellow's throat in a reg'lar Western Ocean[4] style."

Now he was giving his last orders. "Ough! ... You, Knowles! Call all hands at four. I want ... Ough! ... to heave short before the tug comes. Look out for the captain. I am going to lie down in my clothes.... Ough! ... Call me when you see the boat coming. Ough! Ough!... The old man is sure to have something to say when he gets aboard," he re-marked to Creighton. "Well, good-night.... Ough! A long day before us to-morrow.... Ough! ... Better turn in now. Ough! Ough!"

Upon the dark deck a band of light flashed, then a door slammed, and Mr. Baker was gone into his neat cabin. Young Creighton stood leaning over the rail, and looked dreamily into the night of the East. And he saw in it a long country lane, a lane of waving leaves and dancing sunshine. He saw stirring boughs of old trees outspread, and framing in their arch the tender, the caressing blueness of an English sky. And through the arch a girl in a light dress, smiling under a sunshade, seemed to be stepping out of the tender sky.

At the other end of the ship the forecastle, with only one lamp burning now, was going to sleep in a dim emptiness traversed by loud breathings,

---

4. North Atlantic.

by sudden, short sighs. The double row of berths yawned black, like graves tenanted by uneasy corpses. Here and there a curtain of gaudy chintz, half drawn, marked the resting-place of a sybarite. A leg hung over the edge very white and lifeless. An arm stuck straight out with a dark palm turned up, and thick fingers half closed. Two light snores, that did not synchronise, quarrelled in funny dialogue. Singleton stripped again—the old man suffered much from prickly heat—stood cooling his back in the doorway, with his arms crossed on his bare and adorned chest. His head touched the beam of the deck above. The nigger, half undressed, was busy casting adrift the lashing of his box, and spreading his bedding in an upper berth. He moved about in his socks, tall and noiseless, with a pair of braces[5] beating about his calves. Amongst the shadows of stanchions and bowsprit, Donkin munched a piece of hard ship's bread, sitting on the deck with upturned feet and restless eyes; he held the biscuit up before his mouth in the whole fist and snapped his jaws at it with a raging face. Crumbs fell between his outspread legs. Then he got up.

"Where's our water-cask?" he asked in a contained voice.

Singleton, without a word, pointed with a big hand that held a short smouldering pipe. Donkin bent over the cask, drank out of the tin, splashing the water, turned round and noticed the nigger looking at him over the shoulder with calm loftiness. He moved up sideways.

"There's a blooming supper for a man," he whispered bitterly. "My dorg at 'ome wouldn't 'ave it. It's fit enouf for you an' me. 'Ere's a big ship's fo'c'sle! . . . Not a blooming scrap of meat in the kids.[6] I've looked in all the lockers. . . ."

The nigger stared like a man addressed unexpectedly in a foreign language. Donkin changed his tone:—"Giv' us a bit of 'baccy, mate," he breathed out confidentially. "I 'aven't 'ad smoke or chew for the last month. I am rampin' mad for it. Come on, old man!"

"Don't be familiar," said the nigger. Donkin started and sat down on a chest near by, out of sheer surprise. "We haven't kept pigs together," continued James Wait in a deep undertone. "Here's your tobacco." Then, after a pause, he inquired:—"What ship?"—"*Golden State*," muttered Donkin indistinctly, biting the tobacco. The nigger whistled low.—"Ran?" he asked curtly. Donkin nodded: one of his cheeks bulged out. "In course I ran," he mumbled. "They booted the life out of one Dago chap on the passage 'ere, then started on me. I cleared out 'ere."—"Left your dunnage behind?"—"Yes, dunnage and money," answered Donkin, raising his voice a little; "I got nothink. No clothes, no bed. A bandy-legged little Irish chap 'ere 'as give me a blanket. . . . Think I'll go an' sleep in the fore topmast staysail to night."

He went on deck trailing behind his back a corner of the blanket. Singleton, without a glance, moved slightly aside to let him pass. The nigger put away his shore togs and sat in clean working clothes on his box, one arm stretched over his knees. After staring at Singleton for some time he asked without emphasis:—"What kind of ship is this? Pretty fair? Eh?"

Singleton didn't stir. A long while after he said, with unmoved face:— "Ship! . . . Ships are all right. It is the men in them!"

He went on smoking in the profound silence. The wisdom of half a century spent in listening to the thunder of the waves had spoken uncon-

---

5. Suspenders.   6. Tublike wooden containers for serving food.

sciously through his old lips. The cat purred on the windlass. Then James
Wait had a fit of roaring, rattling cough, that shook him, tossed him like a
hurricane, and flung him panting with staring eyes headlong on his sea-
chest. Several men woke up. One said sleepily out of his bunk: " 'Struth!
what a blamed row!"—"I have a cold on my chest," gasped Wait.—"Cold!
you call it," grumbled the man; "should think 'twas something
more. . . ."—"Oh! you think so," said the nigger, upright and loftily scornful again. He climbed into his berth and began coughing persistently,
while he put his head out to glare all round the forecastle. There was no
further protest. He fell back on the pillow, and could be heard there
wheezing regularly like a man oppressed in his sleep.

Singleton stood at the door with his face to the light and his back to
the darkness. And alone in the dim emptiness of the sleeping forecastle he
appeared bigger, colossal, very old; old as Father Time himself, who
should have come there into this place as quiet as a sepulchre to contemplate with patient eyes the short victory of sleep, the consoler. Yet he was
only a child of time, a lonely relic of a devoured and forgotten generation. He stood, still strong, as ever unthinking; a ready man with a vast
empty past and with no future, with his childlike impulses and his man's
passions already dead within his tattooed breast. The men who could understand his silence were gone—those men who knew how to exist beyond
the pale of life and within sight of eternity. They had been strong, as
those are strong who know neither doubts nor hopes. They had been impatient and enduring, turbulent and devoted, unruly and faithful. Well-
meaning people had tried to represent those men as whining over every
mouthful of their food; as going about their work in fear of their lives.
But in truth they had been men who knew toil, privation, violence, debauchery—but knew not fear, and had no desire of spite in their hearts.
Men hard to manage, but easy to inspire; voiceless men—but men enough
to scorn in their hearts the sentimental voices that bewailed the hardness
of their fate. It was a fate unique and their own; the capacity to bear it
appeared to them the privilege of the chosen! Their generation lived inar-
ticulate and indispensable, without knowing the sweetness of affections or
the refuge of a home—and died free from the dark menace of a narrow
grave. They were the everlasting children of the mysterious sea. Their
successors are the grown-up children of a discontented earth. They are
less naughty, but less innocent; less profane, but perhaps also less believing; and if they had learned how to speak they have also learned how to
whine. But the others were strong and mute; they were effaced, bowed
and enduring, like stone caryatides that hold up in the night the lighted
halls of a resplendent and glorious edifice. They are gone now—and it
does not matter. The sea and the earth are unfaithful to their children: a
truth, a faith, a generation of men goes—and is forgotten, and it does not
matter! Except, perhaps, to the few of those who believed the truth, confessed the faith—or loved the men.

A breeze was coming. The ship that had been lying tide-rode[7] swung to
a heavier puff; and suddenly the slack of the chain-cable between the
windlass and the hawse-pipe clinked, slipped forward an inch, and rose
gently off the deck with a startling suggestion as of unsuspected life that
had been lurking stealthily in the iron. In the hawse-pipe the grinding

7. Moored with bow pointing in the direction from which tidal current is floating.

links sent through the ship a sound like a low groan of a man sighing under a burden. The strain came on the windlass, the chain tautened like a string, vibrated—and the handle of the screw-brake moved in slight jerks. Singleton stepped forward.

Till then he had been standing meditative and unthinking, reposeful and hopeless, with a face grim and blank—a sixty-year-old child of the mysterious sea. The thoughts of all his lifetime could have been expressed in six words, but the stir of those things that were as much part of his existence as his beating heart called up a gleam of alert understanding upon the sternness of his aged face. The flame of the lamp swayed, and the old man, with knitted and bushy eyebrows, stood over the brake, watchful and motionless in the wild saraband of dancing shadows. Then the ship, obedient to the call of her anchor, forged ahead slightly and eased the strain. The cable, relieved, hung down, and after swaying imperceptibly to and fro dropped with a loud tap on the hard wood planks. Singleton seized the high lever, and, by a violent throw forward of his body, wrung out another half-turn from the brake. He recovered himself, breathed largely, and remained for a while glaring down at the powerful and compact engine that squatted on the deck at his feet like some quiet monster—a creature amazing and tame.

"You . . . hold!" he growled at it masterfully, in the incult tangle of his white beard.

Chapter Two

Next morning, at daylight, the *Narcissus* went to sea.

A slight haze blurred the horizon. Outside the harbour the measureless expanse of smooth water lay sparkling like a floor of jewels, and as empty as the sky. The short black tug gave a pluck to windward, in the usual way, then let go the rope, and hovered for a moment on the quarter[8] with her engines stopped; while the slim, long hull of the ship moved ahead slowly under lower topsails. The loose upper canvas blew out in the breeze with soft round contours, resembling small white clouds snared in the maze of ropes. Then the sheets were hauled home, the yards hoisted, and the ship became a high and lonely pyramid, gliding, all shining and white, through the sunlit mist. The tug turned short round and went away towards the land. Twenty-six pairs of eyes watched her low broad stern crawling languidly over the smooth swell between the two paddle-wheels that turned fast, beating the water with fierce hurry. She resembled an enormous and aquatic black beetle, surprised by the light, overwhelmed by the sunshine, trying to escape with ineffectual effort into the distant gloom of the land. She left a lingering smudge of smoke on the sky, and two vanishing trails of foam on the water. On the place where she had stopped a round patch of soot remained, undulating on the swell—an unclean mark of the creature's rest.

The *Narcissus* left alone, heading south, seemed to stand resplendent and still upon the restless sea, under the moving sun. Flakes of foam swept past her sides; the water struck her with flashing blows; the land glided away, slowly fading; a few birds screamed on motionless wings over the swaying mastheads. But soon the land disappeared, the birds

8. Slightly behind (actually, at an angle 45° behind the ship).

went away; and to the west the pointed sail of an Arab dhow running for
Bombay, rose triangular and upright above the sharp edge of the horizon,
lingered and vanished like an illusion. Then the ship's wake, long and
straight, stretched itself out through a day of immense solitude. The setting sun, burning on the level of the water, flamed crimson below the
blackness of heavy rain clouds. The sunset squall, coming up from behind,
dissolved itself into the short deluge of a hissing shower. It left the ship
glistening from trucks to water-line, and with darkened sails. She ran easily before a fair monsoon, with her decks cleared for the night; and, moving along with her, was heard the sustained and monotonous swishing of
the waves, mingled with the low whispers of men mustered aft for the
setting of watches; the short plaint of some block aloft; or, now and then,
a loud sigh of wind.

Mr. Baker, coming out of his cabin, called out the first name sharply
before closing the door behind him. He was going to take charge of the
deck. On the homeward passage, according to an old custom of the sea,
the chief officer takes the first night-watch—from eight till midnight. So,
Mr. Baker, after he had heard the last "Yes, sir!" said moodily, "Relieve
the wheel and look-out"; and climbed with heavy feet the poop ladder to
windward. Soon after Mr. Creighton came down, whistling softly, and
went into the cabin. On the doorstep the steward lounged, in slippers,
meditative, and with his shirt-sleeves rolled up to the armpits. On the
main deck the cook, locking up the galley doors, had an altercation with
young Charley about a pair of socks. He could be heard saying impressively, in the darkness amidships: "You don't deserve a kindness. I've been
drying them for you, and now you complain about the holes—and you
swear, too! Right in front of me! If I hadn't been a Christian—which you
ain't, you young ruffian—I would give you a clout on the head. . . . Go
away!" Men in couples or threes stood pensive or moved silently along
the bulwarks in the waist. The first busy day of a homeward passage was
sinking into the peace of resumed routine. Aft, on the high poop, Mr.
Baker walked shuffling and grunted to himself in the pauses of his
thoughts. Forward, the look-out man, erect between the flukes of the two
anchors, hummed an endless tune, keeping his eyes fixed dutifully ahead
in a vacant stare. A multitude of stars coming out into the clear night
peopled the emptiness of the sky. They glittered, as if alive above the sea;
they surrounded the running ship on all sides; more intense than the eyes
of a staring crowd, and as inscrutable as the souls of men.

The passage had begun, and the ship, a fragment detached from the
earth, went on lonely and swift like a small planet. Round her the abysses
of sky and sea met in an unattainable frontier. A great circular solitude
moved with her, ever changing and ever the same, always monotonous
and always imposing. Now and then another wandering white speck, burdened with life, appeared far off—disappeared; intent on its own destiny.
The sun looked upon her all day, and every morning rose with a burning,
round stare of undying curiosity. She had her own future; she was alive
with the lives of those beings who trod her decks; like that earth which
had given her up to the sea, she had an intolerable load of regrets and
hopes. On her lived timid truth and audacious lies; and, like the earth,
she was unconscious, fair to see—and condemned by men to an ignoble
fate. The august loneliness of her path lent dignity to the sordid inspiration of her pilgrimage. She drove foaming to the southward, as if guided

by the courage of a high endeavour. The smiling greatness of the sea dwarfed the extent of time. The days raced after one another, brilliant and quick like the flashes of a lighthouse, and the nights, uneventful and short, resembled fleeting dreams.

The men had shaken into their places, and the half-hourly voice of the bells ruled their life of unceasing care. Night and day the head and shoulders of a seaman could be seen aft by the wheel, outlined high against sunshine or starlight, very steady above the stir of revolving spokes. The faces changed, passing in rotation. Youthful faces, bearded faces, dark faces: faces serene, or faces moody, but all akin with the brotherhood of the sea; all with the same attentive expression of eyes, carefully watching the compass or the sails. Captain Allistoun, serious, and with an old red muffler round his throat, all day long pervaded the poop. At night, many times he rose out of the darkness of the companion, such as a phantom above a grave, and stood watchful and mute under the stars, his nightshirt fluttering like a flag—then, without a sound, sank down again. He was born on the shores of the Pentland Firth.[9] In his youth he attained the rank of harpooner in Peterhead whalers. When he spoke of that time his restless grey eyes became still and cold, like the loom of ice. Afterwards he went into the East Indian trade for the sake of change. He had commanded the *Narcissus* since she was built. He loved his ship, and drove her unmercifully; for his secret ambition was to make her accomplish some day a brilliantly quick passage which would be mentioned in nautical papers. He pronounced his owner's name with a sardonic smile, spoke but seldom to his officers, and reproved errors in a gentle voice, with words that cut to the quick. His hair was iron-grey, his face hard and of the colour of pump-leather. He shaved every morning of his life—at six—but once (being caught in a fierce hurricane eighty miles southwest of Mauritius) he had missed three consecutive days. He feared naught but an unforgiving God, and wished to end his days in a little house, with a plot of ground attached—far in the country—out of sight of the sea.

He, the ruler of that minute world, seldom descended from the Olympian heights of his poop. Below him—at his feet, so to speak—common mortals led their busy and insignificant lives. Along the main deck, Mr. Baker grunted in a manner bloodthirsty and innocuous; and kept all our noses to the grindstone, being—as he once remarked—paid for doing that very thing. The men working about the deck were healthy and contented—as most seamen are, when once well out to sea. The true peace of God begins at any spot a thousand miles from the nearest land; and when He sends there the messengers of His might it is not in terrible wrath against crime, presumption, and folly, but paternally, to chasten simple hearts—ignorant hearts that know nothing of life, and beat undisturbed by envy or greed.

In the evening the cleared decks had a reposeful aspect, resembling the autumn of the earth. The sun was sinking to rest, wrapped in a mantle of warm clouds. Forward, on the end of the spare spars, the boatswain and the carpenter sat together with crossed arms; two men friendly, powerful, and deep-chested. Beside them the short, dumpy sailmaker—who had

9. Treacherous channel northeast of Scotland, separating the Orkney Islands from the mainland.

been in the Navy—related, between the whiffs of his pipe, impossible stories about Admirals. Couples tramped backwards and forwards, keeping step and balance without effort, in a confined space. Pigs grunted in the big pigsty. Belfast, leaning thoughtfully on his elbow, above the bars, communed with them through the silence of his meditation. Fellows with shirts open wide on sunburnt breasts sat upon the mooring bits, and all up the steps of the forecastle ladders. By the foremast a few discussed in a circle the characteristics of a gentleman. One said—"It's money as does it." Another maintained:—"No, it's the way they speak." Lame Knowles stumped up with an unwashed face (he had the distinction of being the dirty man of the forecastle), and, showing a few yellow fangs in a shrewd smile, explained craftily that he "had seen some of their pants." The backsides of them—he had observed—were thinner than paper from constant sitting down in offices, yet otherwise they looked first-rate and would last for years. It was all appearance. "It was," he said, "bloomin' easy to be a gentleman when you had a clean job for life." They disputed endlessly, obstinate and childish; they repeated in shouts and with inflamed faces their amazing arguments; while the soft breeze, eddying down the enormous cavity of the foresail, distended above their bare heads, stirred the tumbled hair with a touch passing and light like an indulgent caress.

They were forgetting their toil, they were forgetting themselves. The cook approached to hear, and stood by, beaming with the inward consciousness of his faith, like a conceited saint unable to forget his glorious reward; Donkin, solitary and brooding over his wrongs on the forecastle-head, moved closer to catch the drift of the discussion below him; he turned his sallow face to the sea, and his thin nostrils moved, sniffing the breeze, as he lounged negligently by the rail. In the glow of sunset faces shone with interest, teeth flashed, eyes sparkled. The walking couples stood still suddenly, with broad grins; a man, bending over a wash-tub, sat up, entranced, with the soapsuds flecking his wet arms. Even the three petty officers listened leaning back, comfortably propped, and with superior smiles. Belfast left off scratching the ear of his favourite pig, and, open mouthed, tried with eager eyes to have his say. He lifted his arms, grimacing and baffled. From a distance Charley screamed at the ring:—"I know about gentlemen more'n any of you. I've been intermit with 'em. . . . I've blacked their boots." The cook, craning his neck to hear better, was scandalised. "Keep your mouth shut when your elders speak, you impudent young heathen—you." "All right, old Hallelujah, I'm done," answered Charley soothingly. At some opinion of dirty Knowles, delivered with an air of supernatural cunning, a ripple of laughter ran along, rose like a wave, burst with a startling roar. They stamped with both feet; they turned their shouting faces to the sky; many, spluttering, slapped their thighs; while one or two, bent double, gasped, hugging themselves with both arms like men in pain. The carpenter and the boatswain, without changing their attitude, shook with laughter where they sat; the sail-maker, charged with an anecdote about a Commodore, looked sulky; the cook was wiping his eyes with a greasy rag; and lame Knowles, astonished at his own success, stood in their midst showing a slow smile.

Suddenly the face of Donkin leaning high-shouldered over the after-rail became grave. Something like a weak rattle was heard through the forecastle door. It became a murmur; it ended in a sighing groan. The wash-

erman plunged both his arms into the tub abruptly; the cook became
more crestfallen than an exposed backslider; the boatswain moved his
shoulders uneasily; the carpenter got up with a spring and walked away—
while the sailmaker seemed mentally to give his story up, and began to
puff at his pipe with sombre determination. In the blackness of the doorway a pair of eyes glimmered white, and big, and staring. Then James
Wait's head protruding, became visible, as if suspended between the two
hands that grasped a doorpost on each side of the face. The tassel of his
blue woollen nightcap, cocked forward, danced gaily over his left eyelid.
He stepped out in a tottering stride. He looked powerful as ever, but
showed a strange and affected unsteadiness in his gait; his face was perhaps a trifle thinner, and his eyes appeared rather startlingly prominent.
He seemed to hasten the retreat of departing light by his very presence;
the setting sun dipped sharply, as though fleeing before our nigger; a
black mist emanated from him; a subtle and dismal influence; a something cold and gloomy that floated out and settled on all the faces like a
mourning veil. The circle broke up. The joy of laughter died on stiffened
lips. There was not a smile left among all the ship's company. Not a word
was spoken. Many turned their backs, trying to look unconcerned; others,
with averted heads, sent half-reluctant glances out of the corners of their
eyes. They resembled criminals conscious of misdeeds more than honest
men distracted by doubt; only two or three stared frankly, but stupidly,
with lips slightly open. All expected James Wait to say something, and, at
the same time, had the air of knowing beforehand what he would say. He
leaned his back against the doorpost, and with heavy eyes swept over
them a glance domineering and pained, like a sick tyrant overawing a
crowd of abject but untrustworthy slaves.

No one went away. They waited in fascinated dread. He said ironically,
with gasps between the words:

"Thank you . . . chaps. You . . . are nice . . . and . . . quiet . . . you are!
Yelling so . . . before . . . the door. . . ."

He made a longer pause, during which he worked his ribs in an exaggerated labour of breathing. It was intolerable. Feet were shuffled. Belfast
let out a groan; but Donkin above blinked his red eyelids with invisible
eyelashes, and smiled bitterly over the nigger's head.

The nigger went on again with surprising ease. He gasped no more, and
his voice rang, hollow and loud, as though he had been talking in an
empty cavern. He was contemptuously angry.

"I tried to get a wink of sleep. You know I can't sleep o' nights. And
you come jabbering near the door here like a blooming lot of old
women. . . . You think yourselves good shipmates. Do you? . . . Much you
care for a dying man!"

Belfast spun away from the pigsty. "Jimmy," he cried tremulously, "if
you hadn't been sick I would—"

He stopped. The nigger waited awhile, then said, in a gloomy tone:—
"You would. . . . What? Go an' fight another such one as yourself. Leave
me alone. It won't be for long. I'll soon die. . . . It's coming right enough!"

Men stood around very still and with exasperated eyes. It was just what
they had expected, and hated to hear, that idea of a stalking death, thrust
at them many times a day like a boast and like a menace by this obnoxious nigger. He seemed to take a pride in that death which, so far, had
attended only upon the ease of his life; he was overbearing about it, as if

no one else in the world had ever been intimate with such a companion; he paraded it unceasingly before us with an affectionate persistence that made its presence indubitable, and at the same time incredible. No man could be suspected of such monstrous friendship! Was he a reality—or was he a sham—this ever-expected visitor of Jimmy's? We hesitated between pity and mistrust, while, on the slightest provocation, he shook before our eyes the bones of his bothersome and infamous skeleton. He was for ever trotting him out. He would talk of that coming death as though it had been already there, as if it had been walking the deck outside, as if it would presently come in to sleep in the only empty bunk; as if it had sat by his side at every meal. It interfered daily with our occupations, with our leisure, with our amusements. We had no songs and no music in the evening, because Jimmy (we all lovingly called him Jimmy, to conceal our hate of his accomplice) had managed, with that prospective decease of his, to disturb even Archie's mental balance. Archie was the owner of the concertina; but after a couple of stinging lectures from Jimmy he refused to play any more. He said:—"Yon's an uncanny joker. I dinna ken what's wrang wi' him, but there's something verra wrang, verra wrang. It's nae manner of use asking me. I won't play." Our singers became mute because Jimmy was a dying man. For the same reason no chap—as Knowles remarked—could "drive in a nail to hang his few poor rags upon," without being made aware of the enormity he committed in disturbing Jimmy's interminable last moments. At night, instead of the cheerful yell, "One bell! Turn out! Do you hear there? Hey! hey! hey! Show leg!" the watches were called man by man, in whispers, so as not to interfere with Jimmy's, possibly, last slumber on earth. True, he was always awake, and managed, as we sneaked out on deck, to plant in our backs some cutting remark that, for the moment, made us feel as if we had been brutes, and afterwards made us suspect ourselves of being fools. We spoke in low tones within that fo'c'sle as though it had been a church. We ate our meals in silence and dread, for Jimmy was capricious with his food, and railed bitterly at the salt meat, at the biscuits, at the tea, as at articles unfit for human consumption—"let alone for a dying man!" He would say:—"Can't you find a better slice of meat for a sick man who's trying to get home to be cured—or buried? But there! If I had a chance, you fellows would do away with it. You would poison me. Look at what you have given me!" We served him in his bed with rage and humility, as though we had been the base courtiers of a hated prince; and he rewarded us by his unconciliating criticism. He had found the secret of keeping for ever on the run the fundamental imbecility of mankind; he had the secret of life, that confounded dying man, and he made himself master of every moment of our existence. We grew desperate, and remained submissive. Emotional little Belfast was for ever on the verge of assault or on the verge of tears. One evening he confided to Archie:—"For a ha'-penny I would knock his ugly black head off—the skulking dodger!" And the straightforward Archie pretended to be shocked! Such was the infernal spell which that casual St. Kitt's nigger had cast upon our guileless manhood! But the same night Belfast stole from the galley the officer's Sunday fruit pie, to tempt the fastidious appetite of Jimmy. He endangered not only his long friendship with the cook but also—as it appeared—his eternal welfare. The cook was overwhelmed with grief; he did not know the culprit, but he knew that wickedness flourished; he knew that Satan was abroad amongst those men, whom he looked upon as in some way under his spiritual care. Whenever he saw three or four of us standing together he would leave his stove, to run out and preach. We fled from him; and only Charley (who knew the thief) affronted the cook with a candid gaze which irritated the good man. "It's you, I believe," he groaned, sorrowful and with a patch of soot on his chin. "It's you. You are a brand for the burning! No more of YOUR socks in my galley." Soon, unofficially, the information was spread about that, should there be another case of stealing, our marmalade (an extra allowance: half a pound per man) would be stopped. Mr. Baker ceased to heap jocular abuse upon his favourites, and grunted suspiciously at all. The captain's cold eyes, high up on the poop, glittered mistrustful, as he surveyed us trooping in a small mob from halyards to braces for the usual evening pull at all the ropes. Such stealing in a merchant ship is difficult to check, and may be taken as a declaration by men of their dislike for their officers. It is a bad symptom. It may end in God knows what trouble. The *Narcissus* was still a peaceful ship, but mutual confidence was shaken. Donkin did not conceal his delight. We were dismayed.

Then illogical Belfast reproached our nigger with great fury. James Wait, with his elbow on the pillow, choked, gasped out:—"Did I ask you to bone the dratted thing? Blow[1] your blamed pie. It has made me worse—you little Irish lunatic, you!" Belfast, with scarlet face and trembling lips, made a dash at him. Every man in the forecastle rose with a shout. There was a moment of wild tumult. Some one shrieked piercingly:—"Easy, Belfast! Easy! . . . " We expected Belfast to strangle Wait without more ado. Dust flew. We heard through it the nigger's cough, metallic and explosive like a gong. Next moment we saw Belfast hanging over him. He was saying plaintively:—"Don't! Don't, Jimmy! Don't be like that. An angel couldn't put up with ye—sick as ye are." He looked round at us from Jimmy's bedside, his comical mouth twitching, and through tearful eyes; then he tried to put straight the disarranged blankets. The unceasing whisper of the sea filled the forecastle. Was James Wait frightened, or touched, or repentant? He lay on his back with a hand to his side, and as motionless as if his expected visitor had come at last. Belfast fumbled about his feet, repeating with emotion:—"Yes. We know. Ye are bad, but . . . Just say what ye want done, and . . . We all know ye are bad—very bad. . . . " No! Decidedly James Wait was not touched or repentant. Truth to say, he seemed rather startled. He sat up with incredible suddenness and ease. "Ah! You think I am bad, do you?" he said gloomily, in his clearest baritone voice (to hear him speak sometimes you would never think there was anything wrong with that man). "Do you? . . . Well, act according! Some of you haven't sense enough to put a blanket shipshape over a sick man. There! Leave it alone! I can die anyhow!" Belfast turned away limply with a gesture of discouragement. In the silence of the forecastle, full of interested men, Donkin pronounced distinctly:—"Well, I'm blowed!" and sniggered. Wait looked at him. He looked at him in a quite friendly manner. Nobody could tell what would please our imcomprehensible invalid: but for us the scorn of that snigger was hard to bear.

Donkin's position in the forecastle was distinguished but unsafe. He

1. A curse: "Blast your blamed pie." *Bone*: steal.

stood on the bad eminence of a general dislike. He was left alone, and in his isolation he could do nothing but think of the gales of the Cape of Good Hope and envy us the possession of warm clothing and waterproofs. Our sea-boots, our oilskin coats, our well-filled sea-chests, were to him so many causes for bitter meditation; he had none of those things, and he felt instinctively that no man, when the need arose, would offer to share them with him. He was impudently cringing to us and systematically insolent to the officers. He anticipated the best results, for himself, from such a line of conduct—and was mistaken. Such natures forget that under extreme provocation men will be just—whether they want to be so or not. Donkin's insolence to long-suffering Mr. Baker became at last intolerable to us, and we rejoiced when the mate, one dark night, tamed him for good. It was done neatly, with great decency and decorum, and with little noise. We had been called—just before midnight—to trim the yards, and Donkin—as usual—made insulting remarks. We stood sleepily in a row with the forebrace in our hands waiting for the next order, and heard in the darkness a scuffly trampling of feet, an exclamation of surprise, sounds of cuffs and slaps, suppressed, hissing whispers;—"Ah! Will you!" . . . "Don't! . . . Don't" . . . "Then behave." . . . "Oh! Oh! . . ." Afterwards there were soft thuds mixed with the rattle of iron things as if a man's body had been tumbling helplessly amongst the main-pump rods. Before we could realise the situation, Mr. Baker's voice was heard very near and a little impatient;—"Haul away, men! Lay back on that rope!" And we did lay back on the rope with great alacrity. As if nothing had happened, the chief mate went on trimming the yards with his usual and exasperating fastidiousness. We didn't at the time see anything of Donkin, and did not care. Had the chief officer thrown him overboard, no man would have said as much as "Hallo! he's gone!" But, in truth, no great harm was done—even if Donkin did lose one of his front teeth. We perceived this in the morning, and preserved a ceremonious silence: the etiquette of the forecastle commanded us to be blind and dumb in such a case, and we cherished the decencies of our life more than ordinary landsmen respect theirs. Charley, with unpardonable want of *savoir vivre*,[2] yelled out:— "'Ave you been to your dentyst? . . . Hurt ye, didn't it?" He got a box on the ear from one of his best friends. The boy was surprised, and remained plunged in grief for at least three hours. We were sorry for him, but youth requires even more discipline than age. Donkin grinned venomously. From that day he became pitiless; told Jimmy that he was a "black fraud"; hinted to us that we were an imbecile lot, daily taken in by a vulgar nigger. And Jimmy seemed to like the fellow!

Singleton lived untouched by human emotions. Taciturn and unsmiling, he breathed amongst us—in that alone resembling the rest of the crowd. We were trying to be decent chaps, and found it jolly difficult; we oscillated between the desire of virtue and the fear of ridicule; we wished to save ourselves from the pain of remorse, but did not want to be made the contemptible dupes of our sentiment. Jimmy's hateful accomplice seemed to have blown with his impure breath undreamt-of subtleties into our hearts. We were disturbed and cowardly. That we knew. Singleton seemed to know nothing, understand nothing. We had thought him till then as wise as he looked, but now we dared, at times, suspect him of

2. Good manners.

being stupid—from old age. One day, however, at dinner, as we sat on our boxes round a tin dish that stood on the deck within the circle of our feet, Jimmy expressed his general disgust with men and things in words that were particularly disgusting. Singleton lifted his head. We became mute. The old man, addressing Jimmy, asked:—"Are you dying?" Thus interrogated, James Wait appeared horribly startled and confused. We all were startled. Mouths remained open; hearts thumped; eyes blinked; a dropped tin fork rattled in a dish; a man rose as if to go out, and stood still. In less than a minute Jimmy pulled himself together:—"Why? Can't you see I am?" he answered shakily. Singleton lifted a piece of soaked biscuit ("his teeth"—he declared—"had no edge on them now") to his lips—"Well, get on with your dying," he said, with venerable mildness; "don't raise a blamed fuss with us over that job. We can't help you." Jimmy fell back in his bunk, and for a long time lay very still, wiping the perspiration off his chin. The dinner-tins were put away quickly. On deck we discussed the incident in whispers. Some showed a chuckling exultation. Many looked grave. Wamibo, after long periods of staring dreaminess, attempted abortive smiles; and one of the young Scandinavians, much tormented by doubt, ventured in the second dog-watch to approach Singleton (the old man did not encourage us much to speak to him) and ask sheepishly:—"You think he will die?" Singleton looked up.—"Why, of course he will die," he said deliberately. This seemed decisive. It was promptly imparted to every one by him who had consulted the oracle. Shy and eager, he would step up and with averted gaze recite his formula:—"Old Singleton says he will die." It was a relief! At last we knew that our compassion would not be misplaced, and we could again smile without misgivings—but we reckoned without Donkin. Donkin "didn't want to 'ave no truck with 'em dirty furriners." When Nilsen came to him with the news: "Singleton says he will die," he answered him by a spiteful "And so will you—you fat-headed Dutchman. Wish you Dutchmen were all dead—'stead comin' takin' our money inter your starvin' country." We were appalled. We perceived that after all Singleton's answer meant nothing. We began to hate him for making fun of us. All our certitudes were going; we were on doubtful terms with our officers; the cook had given us up for lost; we had overheard the boatswain's opinion that "we were a crowd of softies." We suspected Jimmy, one another, and even our very selves. We did not know what to do. At every insignificant turn of our humble life we met Jimmy overbearing and blocking the way, arm-in-arm with his awful and veiled familiar. It was a weird servitude.

It began a week after leaving Bombay and came on us stealthily like any other great misfortune. Every one had remarked that Jimmy from the first was very slack at his work; but we thought it simply the outcome of his philosophy of life. Donkin said:—"You put no more weight on a rope than a bloody sparrer." He disdained him. Belfast, ready for a fight, exclaimed provokingly:—"You don't kill yourself, old man!"—"Would you?" he retorted, with extreme scorn—and Belfast retired. One morning, as we were washing decks, Mr. Baker called to him:—"Bring your broom over here, Wait." He strolled languidly. "Move yourself! Ough!" grunted Mr. Baker; "what's the matter with your hind legs?" He stopped dead short. He gazed slowly with eyes that bulged out with an expression audacious and sad.—"It isn't my legs," he said, "it's my lungs." Everybody listened.—"What's . . . Ough! . . . What's wrong with them?" inquired Mr. Baker. All the watch stood around on the wet deck, grinning, and with brooms or buckets in their hands. He said mournfully:—"Going—or gone. Can't you see I'm a dying man? I know it!" Mr. Baker was disgusted.—"Then why the devil did you ship aboard here?"—"I must live till I die—mustn't I?" he replied. The grins became audible. "Go off the deck—get out of my sight," said Mr. Baker. He was nonplussed. It was a unique experience. James Wait, obedient, dropped his broom, and walked slowly forward. A burst of laughter followed him. It was too funny. All hands laughed. . . . They laughed! . . . Alas!

He became the tormentor of all our moments; he was worse than a nightmare. You couldn't see that there was anything wrong with him: a nigger does not show. He was not very fat—certainly—but then he was no leaner than other niggers we had known. He coughed often, but the most prejudiced person could perceive that, mostly, he coughed when it suited his purpose. He wouldn't, or couldn't, do his work—and he wouldn't lie-up. One day he would skip aloft with the best of them, and next time we would be obliged to risk our lives to get his limp body down. He was reported, he was examined; he was remonstrated with, threatened, cajoled, lectured. He was called into the cabin to interview the captain. There were wild rumours. It was said he had cheeked the old man; it was said he had frightened him. Charley maintained that the "skipper, weepin', 'as giv' 'im 'is blessin' an' a pot of jam." Knowles had it from the steward that the unspeakable Jimmy had been reeling against the cabin furniture; that he had groaned; that he had complained of general brutality and disbelief; and had ended by coughing all over the old man's meteorological journals which were then spread on the table. At any rate, Wait returned forward supported by the steward, who, in a pained and shocked voice, entreated us:—"Here! Catch hold of him, one of you. He is to lie-up." Jimmy drank a tin mugful of coffee, and, after bullying first one and then another, went to bed. He remained there most of the time, but when it suited him would come on deck and appear amongst us. He was scornful and brooding; he looked ahead upon the sea, and no one could tell what was the meaning of that black man sitting apart in a meditative attitude and as motionless as a carving.

He refused steadily all medicine; he threw sago and cornflour overboard till the steward got tired of bringing it to him. He asked for paregoric. They sent him a big bottle; enough to poison a wilderness of babies. He kept it between his mattress and the deal lining of the ship's side; and nobody ever saw him take a dose. Donkin abused him to his face, jeered at him while he gasped; and the same day Wait would lend him a warm jersey. Once Donkin reviled him for half an hour; reproached him with the extra work his malingering gave to the watch; and ended by calling him "a black-faced swine." Under the spell of our accursed perversity we were horror-struck. But Jimmy positively seemed to revel in that abuse. It made him look cheerful—and Donkin had a pair of old sea boots thrown at him. "Here, you East-end[3] trash," boomed Wait, "you may have that."

At last Mr. Baker had to tell the captain that James Wait was disturbing the peace of the ship. "Knock discipline on the head—he will, Ough," grunted Mr. Baker. As a matter of fact, the starboard watch came as near

3. Poor section of London inhabited largely by a "marine" population whose life and activity centers   in the docks.

as possible to refusing duty, when ordered one morning by the boatswain to wash out their forecastle. It appears Jimmy objected to a wet floor—and that morning we were in a compassionate mood. We thought the boatswain a brute, and, practically, told him so. Only Mr. Baker's delicate tact prevented an all-fired row; he refused to take us seriously. He came bustling forward, and called us many unpolite names, but in such a hearty and seamanlike manner that we began to feel ashamed of ourselves. In truth, we thought him much too good a sailor to annoy him willingly: and after all Jimmy might have been a fraud—probably was! The forecastle got a clean up that morning; but in the afternoon a sick-bay was fitted up in the deck-house. It was a nice little cabin opening on deck, and with two berths. Jimmy's belongings were transported there, and then—notwithstanding his protests—Jimmy himself. He said he couldn't walk. Four men carried him on a blanket. He complained that he would have to die there alone, like a dog. We grieved for him, and were delighted to have him removed from the forecastle. We attended him as before. The galley was next door, and the cook looked in many times a day. Wait became a little more cheerful. Knowles affirmed having heard him laugh to himself in peals one day. Others had seen him walking about on deck at night. His little place, with the door ajar on a long hook, was always full of tobacco smoke. We spoke through the crack cheerfully, sometimes abusively, as we passed by, intent on our work. He fascinated us. He would never let doubt die. He overshadowed the ship. Invulnerable in his promise of speedy corruption he trampled on our self-respect; he demonstrated to us daily our want of moral courage; he tainted our lives. Had we been a miserable gang of wretched immortals, unhallowed alike by hope and fear, he could not have lorded it over us with a more pitiless assertion of his sublime privilege.

Chapter Three

Meantime the *Narcissus*, with square yards, ran out of the fair monsoon. She drifted slowly, swinging round and round the compass, through a few days of baffling light airs. Under the patter of short warm showers, grumbling men whirled the heavy yards from side to side; they caught hold of the soaked ropes with groans and sighs, while their officers, sulky and dripping with rain water, unceasingly ordered them about in wearied voices. During the short respites they looked with disgust into the smarting palms of their stiff hands, and asked one another bitterly:—"Who would be a sailor if he could be a farmer?" All the tempers were spoilt, and no man cared what he said. One black night, when the watch, panting in the heat and half-drowned with the rain, had been through four mortal hours hunted from brace to brace, Belfast declared that he would "chuck the sea for ever and go in a steamer." This was excessive, no doubt. Captain Allistoun, with great self-control, would mutter sadly to Mr. Baker:—"It is not so bad—not so bad," when he had managed to shove, and dodge, and manoeuvre his smart ship through sixty miles in twenty-four hours. From the doorstep of the little cabin, Jimmy, chin in hand, watched our distasteful labours with insolent and melancholy eyes. We spoke to him gently—and out of his sight exchanged sour smiles.

Then, again, with a fair wind and under a clear sky, the ship went on piling up the South Latitude. She passed outside Madagascar and Mauritius without a glimpse of the land. Extra lashings were put on the spare spars. Hatches were looked to. The steward in his leisure moments and with a worried air tried to fit washboards to the cabin doors. Stout canvas was bent with care. Anxious eyes looked to the westward, towards the cape of storms.[4] The ship began to dip into a south-west swell, and the softly luminous sky of low latitudes took on a harder sheen from day to day above our heads: it arched high above the ship, vibrating and pale, like an immense dome of steel, resonant with the deep voice of freshening gales. The sunshine gleamed cold on the white curls of black waves. Before the strong breath of westerly squalls the ship, with reduced sail, lay slowly over, obstinate and yielding. She drove to and fro in the unceasing endeavour to fight her way through the invisible violence of the winds: she pitched headlong into dark smooth hollows; she struggled upwards over the snowy ridges of great running seas; she rolled restless, from side to side, like a thing in pain. Enduring and valiant, she answered to the call of men; and her slim spars waving for ever in abrupt semicircles, seemed to beckon in vain for help towards the stormy sky.

It was a bad winter off the Cape that year. The relieved helmsmen came off flapping their arms, or ran stamping hard and blowing into swollen, red fingers. The watch on deck dodged the sting of cold sprays or, crouching in sheltered corners, watched dismally the high and merciless seas boarding the ship time after time in unappeasable fury. Water tumbled in cataracts over the forecastle doors. You had to dash through a waterfall to get into your damp bed. The men turned in wet and turned out stiff to face the redeeming ruthless exactions of their glorious and obscure fate. Far aft, and peering watchfully to windward, the officers could be seen through the mist of squalls. They stood by the weather-rail, holding on grimly, straight and glistening in their long coats; and in the disordered plunges of the hard-driven ship, they appeared high up, attentive, tossing violently above the grey line of a clouded horizon in motionless attitudes.

They watched the weather and the ship as men on shore watch the momentous chances of fortune. Captain Allistoun never left the deck, as though he had been part of the ship's fittings. Now and then the steward, shivering, but always in shirt sleeves, would struggle towards him with some hot coffee, half of which the gale blew out of the cup before it reached the master's lips. He drank what was left gravely in one long gulp, while heavy sprays pattered loudly on his oilskin coat, the seas swishing broke about his high boots; and he never took his eyes off the ship. He kept his gaze riveted upon her as a loving man watches the unselfish toil of a delicate woman upon the slender thread of whose existence is hung the whole meaning and joy of the world. We all watched her. She was beautiful and had a weakness. We loved her no less for that. We admired her qualities aloud, we boasted of them to one another, as though they had been our own, and the consciousness of her only fault we kept buried in the silence of our profound affection. She was born in the thundering peal of hammers beating upon iron, in black eddies of smoke, under a grey sky, on the banks of the Clyde.[5] The clamorous and sombre stream gives birth to things of beauty that float away into the sunshine of the world to be loved by men. The *Narcissus* was one of that perfect

4. Cape of Good Hope, at the southern tip of Africa.   5. River in southern Scotland where shipbuilding yards are located.

brood. Less perfect than many perhaps, but she was ours, and, consequently, incomparable. We were proud of her. In Bombay, ignorant landlubbers alluded to her as that "pretty grey ship." Pretty! A scurvy meed of commendation! We knew she was the most magnificent sea-boat ever launched. We tried to forget that, like many good sea-boats, she was at times rather a crank. She was exacting. She wanted care in loading and handling, and no one knew exactly how much care would be enough. Such are the imperfections of mere men! The ship knew, and sometimes would correct the presumptuous human ignorance by the wholesome discipline of fear. We had heard ominous stories about past voyages. The cook (officially a seaman, but in reality no sailor)—the cook, when unstrung by some misfortune, such as the rolling over of a saucepan, would mutter gloomily while he wiped the floor:—"There! Look at what she has done! Some voy'ge she will drown all hands! You'll see if she won't." To which the steward, snatching in the galley a moment to draw breath in the hurry of his worried life, would remark philosophically:—"Those that see won't tell, anyhow. I don't want to see it." We derided those fears. Our hearts went out to the old man when he pressed her hard so as to make her hold her own, hold to every inch gained to windward; when he made her, under reefed sails, leap obliquely at enormous waves. The men, knitted together aft into a ready group by the first sharp order of an officer coming to take charge of the deck in bad weather:—"Keep handy the watch," stood admiring her valiance. Their eyes blinked in the wind; their dark faces were wet with drops of water more salt and bitter than human tears; beards and moustaches, soaked, hung straight and dripping like fine seaweed. They were fantastically misshapen; in high boots, in hats like helmets, and swaying clumsily, stiff and bulky in glistening oilskins, they resembled men strangely equipped for some fabulous adventure. Whenever she rose easily to a towering green sea, elbows dug ribs, faces brightened, lips murmured:—"Didn't she do it cleverly," and all the heads turning like one watched with sardonic grins the foiled wave go roaring to leeward, white with the foam of a monstrous rage. But when she had not been quick enough and, struck heavily, lay over trembling under the blow, we clutched at ropes, and looking up at the narrow bands of drenched and strained sails waving desperately aloft, we thought in our hearts:—"No wonder. Poor thing!"

The thirty-second day out of Bombay began inauspiciously. In the morning a sea smashed one of the galley doors. We dashed in through lots of steam and found the cook very wet and indignant with the ship:— "She's getting worse every day. She's trying to drown me in front of my own stove!" He was very angry. We pacified him, and the carpenter, though washed away twice from there, managed to repair the door. Through that accident our dinner was not ready till late, but it didn't matter in the end because Knowles, who went to fetch it, got knocked down by a sea and the dinner went over the side. Captain Allistoun, looking more hard and thin-lipped than ever, hung on to full topsails and foresail, and would not notice that the ship, asked to do too much, appeared to lose heart altogether for the first time since we knew her. She refused to rise, and bored her way sullenly through the sea. Twice running, as though she had been blind or weary of life, she put her nose deliberately into a big wave and swept the decks from end to end. As the boatswain observed with marked annoyance, while we were splashing about in a body to try and save a worthless wash-tub:—"Every blooming thing in the ship is going overboard this afternoon." Venerable Singleton broke his habitual silence and said, with a glance aloft:—"The old man's in a temper with the weather, but it's no good bein' angry with the winds of heaven." Jimmy had shut his door, of course. We knew he was dry and comfortable within his little cabin, and in our absurd way were pleased one moment, exasperated the next, by that certitude. Donkin skulked shamelessly, uneasy and miserable. He grumbled;—"I'm perishin' with cold outside in bloomin' wet rags, an' that 'ere black sojer sits dry on a blamed chest full of bloomin' clothes; blank his black soul!" We took no notice of him; we hardly gave a thought to Jimmy and his bosom friend. There was no leisure for idle probing of hearts. Sails blew adrift. Things broke loose. Cold and wet, we were washed about the deck while trying to repair damages. The ship tossed about, shaken furiously, like a toy in the hand of a lunatic. Just at sunset there was a rush to shorten sail before the menace of a sombre hail cloud. The hard gust of wind came brutal like the blow of a fist. The ship relieved of her canvas in time received it pluckily: she yielded reluctantly to the violent onset; then, coming up with a stately and irresistible motion, brought her spars to windward in the teeth of the screeching squall. Out of the abysmal darkness of the black cloud overhead white hail streamed on her, rattled on the rigging, leaped in handfuls off the yards, rebounded on the deck—round and gleaming in the murky turmoil like a shower of pearls. It passed away. For a moment a livid sun shot horizontally the last rays of sinister light between the hills of steep rolling waves. Then a wild night rushed in—stamped out in a great howl that dismal remnant of a stormy day.

There was no sleep on board that night. Most seamen remember in their life one or two such nights of a culminating gale. Nothing seems left of the whole universe but darkness, clamour, fury—and the ship. And like the last vestige of a shattered creation she drifts, bearing an anguished remnant of sinful mankind, through the distress, tumult, and pain of an avenging terror. No one slept in the forecastle. The tin oil-lamp suspended on a long string, smoking, described wide circles; wet clothing made dark heaps on the glistening floor; a thin layer of water rushed to and fro. In the bed-places men lay booted, resting on elbows and with open eyes. Hung-up suits of oilskin swung out and in, lively and disquieting like reckless ghosts of decapitated seamen dancing in a tempest. No one spoke and all listened. Outside the night moaned and sobbed to the accompaniment of a continuous loud tremor as of innumerable drums beating far off. Shrieks passed through the air. Tremendous dull blows made the ship tremble while she rolled under the weight of the seas toppling on her deck. At times she soared up swiftly as if to leave this earth for ever, then during interminable moments fell through a void with all the hearts on board of her standing still, till a frightful shock, expected and sudden, started them off again with a big thump. After every dislocating jerk of the ship, Wamibo, stretched full length, his face on the pillow, groaned slightly with the pain of his tormented universe. Now and then, for the fraction of an intolerable second, the ship, in the fiercer burst of a terrible uproar, remained on her side, vibrating and still, with a stillness more appalling than the wildest motion. Then upon all those prone bodies a stir would pass, a shiver of suspense. A man would protrude his anxious head and a pair of eyes glistened in the sway of light, glaring wildly. Some moved their legs a little as if making ready to jump out. But several, motionless on their backs and with one hand gripping hard the edge of the bunk, smoked nervously with quick puffs, staring upwards; immobilised in a great craving for peace.

At midnight, orders were given to furl the fore and mizzen-topsails. With immense efforts men crawled aloft through a merciless buffeting, saved the canvas, and crawled down almost exhausted, to bear in panting silence the cruel battering of the seas. Perhaps for the first time in the history of the merchant service the watch, told to go below, did not leave the deck, as if compelled to remain there by the fascination of a venomous violence. At every heavy gust men, huddled together, whispered to one another:—"It can blow no harder"—and presently the gale would give them the lie with a piercing shriek, and drive their breath back into their throats. A fierce squall seemed to burst asunder the thick mass of sooty vapours; and above the wrack of torn clouds glimpses could be caught of the high moon rushing backwards with frightful speed over the sky, right into the wind's eye. Many hung their heads, muttering that it "turned their inwards out" to look at it. Soon the clouds closed up and the world again became a raging, blind darkness that howled, flinging at the lonely ship salt sprays and sleet.

About half-past seven the pitchy obscurity round us turned a ghastly grey, and we knew that the sun had risen. This unnatural and threatening daylight, in which we could see one another's wild eyes and drawn faces, was only an added tax on our endurance. The horizon seemed to have come on all sides within arm's length of the ship. Into that narrowed circle furious seas leaped in, struck, and leaped out. A rain of salt, heavy drops flew aslant like mist. The main-topsail had to be goose-winged,[6] and with stolid resignation every one prepared to go aloft once more; but the officers yelled, pushed back, and at last we understood that no more men would be allowed to go on the yard than were absolutely necessary for the work. As at any moment the masts were likely to be jumped out or blown overboard, we concluded that the captain didn't want to see all his crowd go over the side at once. That was reasonable. The watch then on duty, led by Mr. Creighton, began to struggle up the rigging. The wind flattened them against the ratlines; then, easing a little, would let them ascend a couple of steps; and again, with a sudden gust, pin all up the shrouds the whole crawling line in attitudes of crucifixion. The other watch plunged down on the main deck to haul up the sail. Men's heads bobbed up as the water flung them irresistibly from side to side. Mr. Baker grunted encouragingly in our midst, spluttering and blowing amongst the tangled ropes like an energetic porpoise. Favoured by an ominous and untrustworthy lull, the work was done without any one being lost either off the deck or from the yard. For the moment the gale seemed to take off, and the ship, as if grateful for our efforts, plucked up heart and made better weather of it.

At eight the men off duty, watching their chance, ran forward over the flooded deck to get some rest. The other half of the crew remained aft for their turn of "seeing her through her trouble," as they expressed it. The two mates urged the master to go below. Mr. Baker grunted in his ear:— "Ough! surely now ... Ough! ... confidence in us ... nothing more to do

6. Half-furled on side of ship from which wind is coming.

... she must lay it out or go. Ough! Ough!" Tall young Mr. Creighton smiled down at him cheerfully:—"... She's as right as a trivet! Take a spell, sir." He looked at them stonily with bloodshot, sleepless eyes. The rims of his eyelids were scarlet, and he moved his jaws unceasingly with a slow effort, as though he had been masticating a lump of indiarubber. He shook his head. He repeated:—"Never mind me. I must see it out—I must see it out," but he consented to sit down for a moment on the skylight, with his hard face turned unflinchingly to windward. The sea spat at it—and stoical, it streamed with water as though he had been weeping. On the weather side of the poop the watch, hanging on to the mizzen-rigging and to one another, tried to exchange encouraging words. Singleton, at the wheel, yelled out:—"Look out for yourselves!" His voice reached them in a warning whisper. They were startled.

A big, foaming sea came out of the mist; it made for the ship, roaring wildly, and in its rush it looked as mischievous and discomposing as a madman with an axe. One or two, shouting, scrambled up the rigging; most, with a convulsive catch of the breath, held on where they stood. Singleton dug his knees under the wheel-box, and carefully eased the helm to the headlong pitch of the ship, but without taking his eyes off the coming wave. It towered close-to and high, like a wall of green grass topped with snow. The ship rose to it as though she had soared on wings, and for a moment rested poised upon the foaming crest as if she had been a great sea-bird. Before we could draw breath a heavy gust struck her, another roller took her unfairly under the weather bow, she gave a toppling lurch, and filled her decks. Captain Allistoun leaped up, and fell; Archie rolled over him, screaming:—"She will rise!" She gave another lurch to leeward; the lower deadeyes[7] dipped heavily; the men's feet flew from under them, and they hung kicking above the slanting poop. They could see the ship putting her side in the water, and shouted all together:—"She's going!" Forward the forecastle doors flew open, and the watch below were seen leaping out one after another, throwing their arms up; and, falling on hands and knees, scrambled aft on all fours along the high side of the deck, sloping more than the roof of a house. From leeward the seas rose, pursuing them; they looked wretched in a hopeless struggle, like vermin fleeing before a flood; they fought up the weather ladder of the poop one after another, half naked and staring wildly; and as soon as they got up they shot to leeward in clusters, with closed eyes, till they brought up heavily with their ribs against the iron stanchions of the rail, when, groaning, they rolled in a confused mass. The immense volume of water thrown forward by the last scend of the ship had burst the lee door of the forecastle. They could see their chests, pillows, blankets, clothing, come out floating upon the sea. While they struggled back to windward they looked in dismay. The straw beds swam high, the blankets, spread out, undulated; while the chests, waterlogged and with a heavy list, pitched heavily like dismasted hulks, before they sank; Archie's big coat passed with outspread arms, resembling a drowned seaman floating with his head under water. Men were slipping down while trying to dig their fingers into the planks; others jammed in corners, rolled enormous eyes. They all yelled unceasingly:—"The masts! Cut! Cut! ... " A black squall howled low over the ship, that lay on her side with the

7. Blocks of wood with holes through them for short ropes holding shrouds to deck railings.

weather yard-arms pointing to the clouds; while the tall masts, inclined nearly to the horizon, seemed to be of an immeasurable length. The carpenter let go his hold, rolled against the skylight, and began to crawl to the cabin entrance, where a big axe was kept ready for just such an emergency. At that moment the topsail sheet parted, the end of the heavy chain racketed aloft, and sparks of red fire streamed down through the flying sprays. The sail flapped once with a jerk that seemed to tear our hearts out through our teeth, and instantly changed into a bunch of fluttering narrow ribbons that tied themselves into knots and became quiet along the yard. Captain Allistoun struggled, managed to stand up with his face near the deck, upon which men swung on the ends of ropes, like nest robbers upon a cliff. One of his feet was on somebody's chest; his face was purple; his lips moved. He yelled also; he yelled, bending down:—"No! No!" Mr. Baker, one leg over the binnacle-stand, roared out:—"Did you say no? Not cut?" He shook his head madly. "No! No!" Between his legs the crawling carpenter heard, collapsed at once, and lay full length in the angle of the skylight. Voices took up the shout—"No! No!" Then all became still. They waited for the ship to turn over altogether, and shake them out into the sea; and upon the terrific noise of wind and sea not a murmur of remonstrance came out from those men, who each would have given ever so many years of life to see "them damned sticks go overboard!" They all believed it their only chance; but a little hard-faced man shook his grey head and shouted "No!" without giving them as much as a glance. They were silent, and gasped. They gripped rails, they had wound ropes'-ends under their arms, they clutched ring-bolts, they crawled in heaps where there was foothold; they held on with both arms, hooked themselves to anything to windward with elbows, with chins, almost with their teeth: and some, unable to crawl away from where they had been flung, felt the sea leap up, striking against their backs as they struggled upwards. Singleton had stuck to the wheel. His hair flew out in the wind; the gale seemed to take its lifelong adversary by the beard and shake his old head. He wouldn't let go, and, with his knees forced between the spokes, flew up and down like a man on a bough. As Death appeared unready, they began to look about. Donkin, caught by one foot in a loop of some rope, hung, head down, below us, and yelled, with his face to the deck:—"Cut! Cut!" Two men lowered themselves cautiously to him; others hauled on the rope. They caught him up, shoved him into a safer place, held him. He shouted curses at the master, shook his fist at him with horrible blasphemies, called upon us in filthy words to "Cut! Don't mind that murdering fool! Cut, some of you!" One of his rescuers struck him a back-handed blow over the mouth; his head banged on the deck, and he became suddenly very quiet, with a white face, breathing hard, and with a few drops of blood trickling from his cut lip. On the lee side another man could be seen stretched out as if stunned; only the washboard prevented him from going over the side. It was the steward. We had to sling him up like a bale, for he was paralysed with fright. He had rushed up out of the pantry when he felt the ship go over, and had rolled down helplessly, clutching a china mug. It was not broken. With difficulty we tore it away from him, and when he saw it in our hands he was amazed. "Where did you get that thing?" he kept on asking us in a trembling voice. His shirt was blown to shreds; the ripped sleeves flapped like wings. Two men made him fast, and, doubled over the rope that held him, he resembled a bundle of wet rags. Mr. Baker crawled along the line of men, asking—"Are you all there?" and looking them over. Some blinked vacantly, others shook convulsively; Wamibo's head hung over his breast; and in painful attitudes, cut by lashings, exhausted with clutching, screwed up in corners, they breathed heavily. Their lips twitched, and at every sickening heave of the overturned ship they opened them wide as if to shout. The cook, embracing a wooden stanchion, unconsciously repeated a prayer. In every short interval of the fiendish noises around he could be heard there, without cap or slippers, imploring in that storm the Master of our lives not to lead him into temptation. Soon he also became silent. In all that crowd of cold and hungry men, waiting wearily for a violent death, not a voice was heard; they were mute, and in sombre thoughtfulness listened to the horrible imprecations of the gale.

Hours passed. They were sheltered by the heavy inclination of the ship from the wind that rushed in one long unbroken moan above their heads, but cold rain showers fell at times into the uneasy calm of their refuge. Under the torment of that new infliction a pair of shoulders would writhe a little. Teeth chattered. The sky was clearing, and bright sunshine gleamed over the ship. After every burst of battering seas, vivid and fleeting rainbows arched over the drifting hull in the flick of sprays. The gale was ending in a clear blow, which gleamed and cut like a knife. Between two bearded shellbacks Charley, fastened with somebody's long muffler to a deck ring-bolt, wept quietly, with rare tears wrung out by bewilderment, cold, hunger, and general misery. One of his neighbours punched him in the ribs, asking roughly:—"What's the matter with your cheek? In fine weather there's no holding you, youngster." Turning about in prudence, he worked himself out of his coat and threw it over the boy. The other man closed up, muttering:—" 'Twill make a bloomin' man of you, sonny." They flung their arms over and pressed against him. Charley drew his feet up and his eyelids dropped. Sighs were heard, as men, perceiving that they were not to be "drowned in a hurry," tried easier positions. Mr. Creighton, who had hurt his leg, lay amongst us with compressed lips. Some fellows belonging to his watch set about securing him better. Without a word or a glance he lifted his arms one after another to facilitate the operation, and not a muscle moved in his stern, young face. They asked him with solicitude:—"Easier now, sir?" He answered with a curt:— "That'll do." He was a hard young officer, but many of his watch used to say they liked him well enough because he had "such a gentlemanly way of damning us up and down the deck." Others, unable to discern such fine shades of refinement, respected him for his smartness. For the first time since the ship had gone on her beam ends Captain Allistoun gave a short glance down at his men. He was almost upright—one foot against the side of the skylight, one knee on the deck; and with the end of the vang[8] round his waist swung back and forth with his gaze fixed ahead, watchful, like a man looking out for a sign. Before his eyes the ship, with half her deck below water, rose and fell on heavy seas that rushed from under her, flashing in the cold sunshine. We began to think she was wonderfully buoyant—considering. Confident voices were heard shouting— "She'll do, boys!" Belfast exclaimed with fervour:—"I would giv' a month's pay for a draw at a pipe!" One or two, passing dry tongues on

8. A rope steadying the gaff or pole which supports the rigging.

their salt lips, muttered something about a "drink of water." The cook, as if inspired, scrambled up with his breast against the poop water-cask and looked in. There was a little at the bottom. He yelled, waving his arms, and two men began to crawl backwards and forwards with the mug. We had a good mouthful all round. The master shook his head impatiently, refusing. When it came to Charley one of his neighbours shouted:—"That bloomin' boy's asleep." He slept as though he had been dosed with narcotics. They let him be. Singleton held to the wheel with one hand while he drank, bending down to shelter his lips from the wind. Wamibo had to be poked and yelled at before he saw the mug held before his eyes. Knowles said sagaciously:—"It's better'n a tot o' rum." Mr. Baker grunted:—"Thank ye." Mr. Creighton drank and nodded. Donkin gulped greedily, glaring over the rim. Belfast made us laugh when with grimacing mouth he shouted:—"Pass it this way. We're all taytottlers here." The master, presented with the mug again by a crouching man, who screamed up at him:—"We all had a drink, captain," groped for it without ceasing to look ahead, and handed it back stiffly as though he could not spare half a glance away from the ship. Faces brightened. We shouted to the cook:— "Well done, doctor!" He sat to leeward, propped by the water-cask and yelled back abundantly, but the seas were breaking in thunder just then, and we only caught snatches that sounded like:—"Providence" and "born again." He was at his old game of preaching. We made friendly but derisive gestures at him, and from below he lifted one arm, holding on with the other, moved his lips; he beamed up to us, straining his voice—earnest, and ducking his head before the sprays.

Suddenly some one cried:—"Where's Jimmy?" and we were appalled once more. On the end of the row the boatswain shouted hoarsely:—"Has any one seed him come out?" Voices exclaimed dismally:—"Drowned—is he? . . . No! In his cabin! . . . Good Lord! . . . Caught like a bloomin' rat in a trap. . . . Couldn't open his door. . . . Ay! She went over too quick and the water jammed it. . . . Poor beggar! . . . No help for 'im. . . . Let's go and see. . . . " "Damn him, who could go?" screamed Donkin.—"Nobody expects you to," growled the man next to him: "you're only a thing."—"Is there half a chance to get at 'im?" inquired two or three men together. Belfast untied himself with blind impetuosity, and all at once shot down to leeward quicker than a flash of lightning. We shouted all together with dismay; but with his legs overboard he held and yelled for a rope. In our extremity nothing could be terrible; so we judged him funny kicking there, and with his scared face. Some one began to laugh, and, as if hysterically infected with screaming merriment, all those haggard men went off laughing, wild eyed, like a lot of maniacs tied up on a wall. Mr. Baker swung off the binnacle-stand and tendered him one leg. He scrambled up rather scared, and consigning us with abominable words to the "divvle." "You are . . . Ough! You're a foul-mouthed beggar, Craik," grunted Mr. Baker. He answered, stuttering with indignation:—"Look at 'em, sorr. The bloomin' dirty images! laughing at a chum going overboard. Call themselves men, too." But from the break of the poop the boatswain called out:—"Come along," and Belfast crawled away in a hurry to join him. The five men, poised and gazing over the edge of the poop, looked for the best way to get forward. They seemed to hesitate. The others, twisting in their lashings, turning painfully, stared with open lips. Captain Allistoun saw nothing; he seemed with his eyes to hold the ship up in a super-human concentration of effort. The wind screamed loud in sunshine; columns of spray rose straight up; and in the glitter of rainbows bursting over the trembling hull the men went over cautiously, disappearing from sight with deliberate movements.

They went swinging from belaying pin to cleat above the seas that beat the half-submerged deck. Their toes scraped the planks. Lumps of green cold water toppled over the bulwark and on their heads. They hung for a moment on strained arms, with the breath knocked out of them, and with closed eyes—then, letting go with one hand, balanced with lolling heads, trying to grab some rope or stanchion futher forward. The long-armed and athletic boatswain swung quickly, gripping things with a fist hard as iron, and remembering suddenly snatches of the last letter from his "old woman." Little Belfast scrambled in a rage, spluttering "Cursed nigger." Wamibo's tongue hung out with excitement; and Archie, intrepid and calm, watched his chance to move with intelligent coolness.

When above the side of the house, they let go one after another, and, falling heavily, sprawled, pressing their palms to the smooth teak wood. Round them the backwash of waves seethed white and hissing. All the doors had become trap-doors, of course. The first was the galley door. The galley extended from side to side, and they could hear the sea splashing with hollow noises in there. The next door was that of the carpenter's shop. They lifted it, and looked down. The room seemed to have been devastated by an earthquake. Everything in it had tumbled on the bulkhead facing the door, and on the other side of that bulkhead there was Jimmy, dead or alive. The bench, a half-finished meat-safe, saws, chisels, wire rods, axes, crowbars, lay in a heap besprinkled with loose nails. A sharp adze stuck up with a shining edge that gleamed dangerously down there like a wicked smile. The men clung to one another, peering. A sickening, sly lurch of the ship nearly sent them overboard in a body. Belfast howled "Here goes!" and leaped down. Archie followed cannily, catching at shelves that gave way with him, and eased himself in a great crash of ripped wood. There was hardly room for three men to move. And in the sunshiny blue square of the door, the boatswain's face, bearded and dark, Wamibo's face, wild and pale, hung over—watching.

Together they shouted: "Jimmy! Jim!" From above the boatswain contributed a deep growl: "You ... Wait!" In a pause, Belfast entreated: "Jimmy, darlin', are ye aloive?" The boatswain said "Again! All together, boys!" All yelled excitedly. Wamibo made noises resembling loud barks. Belfast drummed on the side of the bulkhead with a piece of iron. All ceased suddenly. The sound of screaming and hammering went on, thin and distinct—like a solo after a chorus. He was alive. He was screaming and knocking below us with the hurry of a man prematurely shut up in a coffin. We went to work. We attacked with desperation the abominable heap of things heavy, of things sharp, of things clumsy to handle. The boatswain crawled away to find somewhere a flying end of a rope; and Wamibo, held back by shouts:—"Don't jump! ... Don't come in here, muddle head!"—remained glaring above us—all shining eyes, gleaming fangs, tumbled hair; resembling an amazed and half-witted fiend gloating over the extraordinary agitation of the damned. The boatswain adjured us to "bear a hand,"[9] and a rope descended. We made things fast to it and

9. Get to work, hurry.

they went up spinning, never to be seen by man again. A rage to fling things overboard possessed us. We worked fiercely, cutting our hands and speaking brutally to one another. Jimmy kept up a distracting row; he screamed piercingly, without drawing breath, like a tortured woman; he banged with hands and feet. The agony of his fear wrung our hearts so terribly that we longed to abandon him, to get out of that place deep as a well and swaying like a tree, to get out of his hearing, back on the poop where we could wait passively for death in incomparable repose. We shouted to him to "shut up, for God's sake." He redoubled his cries. He must have fancied we could not hear him. Probably he heard his own clamour but faintly. We could picture him crouching on the edge of the upper berth, letting out with both fists at the wood, in the dark, and with his mouth wide open for that unceasing cry. Those were loathsome moments. A cloud driving across the sun would darken the doorway menacingly. Every movement of the ship was pain. We scrambled about with no room to breathe, and felt frightfully sick. The boatswain yelled down at us:—"Bear a hand! Bear a hand! We two will be washed away from here directly if you ain't quick!" Three times a sea leaped over the high side and flung bucketfuls of water on our heads. Then Jimmy, startled by the shock, would stop his noise for a moment—waiting for the ship to sink, perhaps—and began again, distressingly loud, as if invigorated by the gust of fear. At the bottom the nails lay in a layer several inches thick. It was ghastly. Every nail in the world, not driven in firmly somewhere, seemed to have found its way into that carpenter's shop. There they were, of all kinds, the remnants of stores from seven voyages. Tin-tacks, copper tacks (sharp as needles), pump nails, with big heads, like tiny iron mushrooms; nails without any heads (horrible); French nails polished and slim. They lay in a solid mass more inabordable[1] than a hedgehog. We hesitated, yearning for a shovel, while Jimmy below us yelled as though he had been flayed. Groaning, we dug our fingers in, and very much hurt, shook our hands, scattering nails and drops of blood. We passed up our hats full of assorted nails to the boatswain, who, as if performing a mysterious and appeasing rite, cast them wide upon a raging sea.

We got to the bulkhead at last. Those were stout planks. She was a ship, well finished in every detail—the *Narcissus* was. They were the stoutest planks ever put into a ships's bulkhead—we thought—and then we perceived that, in our hurry, we had sent all the tools overboard. Absurd little Belfast wanted to break it down with his own weight, and with both feet leaped straight up like a springbok, cursing the Clyde shipwrights for not scamping their work. Incidentally he reviled all North Britain, the rest of the earth, the sea—and all his companions. He swore, as he alighted heavily on his heels, that he would never, never any more associate with any fool that "hadn't savee[2] enough to know his knee from his elbow." He managed by this thumping to scare the last remnant of wits out of Jimmy. We could hear the object of our exasperated solicitude darting to and fro under the planks. He had cracked his voice at last, and could only squeak miserably. His back or else his head rubbed the planks, now here, now there, in a puzzling manner. He squeaked as he dodged the invisible blows. It was more heart-rending even than his yells. Suddenly Archie produced a crowbar. He had kept it back; also a small

---

1. Unapproachable.   2. Savvy, good sense.

hatchet. We howled with satisfaction. He struck a mighty blow and small chips flew at our eyes. The boatswain above shouted:—"Look out! Look out there. Don't kill the man. Easy does it!" Wamibo, maddened with excitement, hung head down and insanely urged us:—"Hoo! Strook 'im! Hoo! Hoo!" We were afraid he would fall in and kill one of us, and hurriedly we entreated the boatswain to "shove the blamed Finn overboard." Then, all together, we yelled down at the planks:—"Stand from under! Get forward," and listened. We only heard the deep hum and moan of the wind above us, the mingled roar and hiss of the seas. The ship, as if overcome with despair, wallowed lifelessly, and our heads swam with that unnatural motion. Belfast clamoured:—"For the love of God, Jimmy, where are ye? . . . Knock! Jimmy darlint! . . . Knock! You bloody black beast! Knock!" He was as quiet as a dead man inside a grave; and, like men standing above a grave, we were on the verge of tears—but with vexation, the strain, the fatigue; with the great longing to be done with it, to get away, and lie down to rest somewhere where we could see our danger and breathe. Archie shouted:—"Gi'e me room!" We crouched behind him, guarding our heads, and he struck time after time in the joint of planks. They cracked. Suddenly the crowbar went half-way in through a splintered oblong hole. It must have missed Jimmy's head by less than an inch. Archie withdrew it quickly, and that infamous nigger rushed at the hole, put his lips to it, and whispered "Help" in an almost extinct voice; he pressed his head to it, trying madly to get out through that opening one inch wide and three inches long. In our disturbed state we were absolutely paralysed by his incredible action. It seemed impossible to drive him away. Even Archie at last lost his composure. "If ye don't clear oot I'll drive the crowbar thro' your head," he shouted in a determined voice. He meant what he said, and his earnestness seemed to make an impression on Jimmy. He disappeared suddenly, and we set to prising and tearing at the planks with the eagerness of men trying to get at a mortal enemy, and spurred by the desire to tear him limb from limb. The wood split, cracked, gave way. Belfast plunged in head and shoulders and groped viciously. "I've got 'im! Got 'im," he shouted. "Oh! There! . . . He's gone; I've got 'im! . . . Pull at my legs! . . . Pull!" Wamibo hooted unceasingly. The boatswain shouted directions:—"Catch hold of his hair, Belfast; pull straight up, you two! . . . Pull fair!" We pulled fair. We pulled Belfast out with a jerk, and dropped him with disgust. In a sitting posture purple-faced, he sobbed despairingly:—"How can I hold on to 'is blooming short wool?" Suddenly Jimmy's head and shoulders appeared. He stuck half-way, and with rolling eyes foamed at our feet. We flew at him with brutal impatience, we tore the shirt off his back, we tugged at his ears, we panted over him; and all at once he came away in our hands as though somebody had let go his legs. With the same movement, without a pause, we swung him up. His breath whistled, he kicked our upturned faces, he grasped two pairs of arms above his head, and he squirmed up with such precipitation that he seemed positively to escape from our hands like a bladder full of gas. Streaming with perspiration, we swarmed up the rope, and, coming into the blast of cold wind, gasped like men plunged into icy water. With burning faces we shivered to the very marrow of our bones. Never before had the gale seemed to us more furious, the sea more mad, the sunshine more merciless and mocking, and the position of the ship more hopeless and appalling. Every movement of her was ominous of the end of her agony and of the beginning of ours. We staggered away from the door, and, alarmed by a sudden roll, fell down in a bunch. It appeared to us that the side of the house was more smooth than glass and more slippery than ice. There was nothing to hang on to but a long brass hook used sometimes to keep back an open door. Wamibo held on to it and we held on to Wamibo, clutching our Jimmy. He had completely collapsed now. He did not seem to have the strength to close his hand. We stuck to him blindly in our fear. We were not afraid of Wamibo letting go (we remembered that the brute was stronger than any three men in the ship), but we were afraid of the hook giving way, and we also believed that the ship had made up her mind to turn over at last. But she didn't. A sea swept over us. The boatswain spluttered:—"Up and away. There's a lull. Away aft with you, or we will all go to the devil here." We stood up surrounding Jimmy. We begged him to hold up, to hold on, at least. He glared with his bulging eyes, mute as a fish, and with all the stiffening knocked out of him. He wouldn't stand; he wouldn't even as much as clutch at our necks; he was only a cold black skin loosely stuffed with soft cotton wool; his arms and legs swung jointless and pliable; his head rolled about; the lower lip hung down, enormous and heavy. We pressed round him, bothered and dismayed; sheltering him, we swung here and there in a body; and on the very brink of eternity we tottered all together with concealing and absurd gestures, like a lot of drunken men embarrassed with a stolen corpse.

Something had to be done. We had to get him aft. A rope was tied slack under his armpits, and, reaching up at the risk of our lives, we hung him on the foresheet cleat. He emitted no sound; he looked as ridiculously lamentable as a doll that had lost half its sawdust, and we started on our perilous journey over the main deck, dragging along with care that pitiful, that limp, that hateful burden. He was not very heavy, but had he weighed a ton he could not have been more awkward to handle. We literally passed him from hand to hand. Now and then we had to hang him up on a handy belaying-pin, to draw a breath and reform the line. Had the pin broken he would have irretrievably gone into the Southern Ocean, but he had to take his chance of that; and after a little while, becoming apparently aware of it, he groaned slightly, and with a great effort whispered a few words. We listened eagerly. He was reproaching us with our carelessness in letting him run such risks: "Now, after I got myself out from there," he breathed out weakly. "There" was his cabin. And he got himself out. What had nothing to do with it apparently! . . . No matter. . . . We went on and let him take his chances, simply because we could not help it; for though at that time we hated him more than ever— more than anything under heaven—we did not want to lose him. We had so far saved him; and it had become a personal matter between us and the sea. We meant to stick to him. Had we (by an incredible hypothesis) undergone similar toil and trouble for an empty cask, that cask would have become as precious to us as Jimmy was. More precious, in fact, because we would have had no reason to hate the cask. And we hated James Wait. We could not get rid of the monstrous suspicion that this astounding black man was shamming sick, had been malingering heartlessly in the face of our toil, of our scorn, of our patience—and now was malingering in the face of our devotion—in the face of death. Our vague and imperfect morality rose with disgust at his unmanly lie. But he stuck to it manfully— amazingly. No! It couldn't be. He was at all extremity. His cantankerous temper was only the result of the provoking invincibleness of that death he felt by his side. Any man may be angry with such a masterful chum. But, then, what kind of men were we—with our thoughts! Indignation and doubt grappled within us in a scuffle that trampled upon the finest of our feelings. And we hated him because of the suspicion; we detested him because of the doubt. We could not scorn him safely—neither could we pity him without risk to our dignity. So we hated him, and passed him carefully from hand to hand. We cried, "Got him?"—"Yes. All right. Let go." And he swung from one enemy to another, showing about as much life as an old bolster would do. His eyes made two narrow white slits in the black face. The air escaped through his lips with a noise like the sound of bellows. We reached the poop ladder at last, and it being a comparatively safe place, we lay for a moment in an exhausted heap to rest a little. He began to mutter. We were always incurably anxious to hear what he had to say. This time he mumbled peevishly, "It took you some time to come. I began to think the whole smart lot of you had been washed overboard. What kept you back? Hey? Funk?" We said nothing. With sighs we started again to drag him up. The secret and ardent desire of our hearts was the desire to beat him viciously with our fists about the head; and we handled him as tenderly as though he had been made of glass. . . .

The return on the poop was like the return of wanderers after many years amongst people marked by the desolation of time. Eyes were turned slowly in their sockets, glancing at us. Faint murmurs were heard, "Have you got 'im after all?" The well-known faces looked strange and familiar; they seemed faded and grimy; they had a mingled expression of fatigue and eagerness. They seemed to have become much thinner during our absence, as if all these men had been starving for a long time in their abandoned attitudes. The captain, with a round turn of a rope on his wrist, and kneeling on one knee, swung with a face cold and stiff; but with living eyes he was still holding the ship up, heeding no one, as if lost in the unearthly effort of that endeavour. We fastened up James Wait in a safe place. Mr. Baker scrambled along to lend a hand. Mr. Creighton, on his back, and very pale, muttered, "Well done," and gave us, Jimmy, and the sky a scornful glance, then closed his eyes slowly. Here and there a man stirred a little, but most of them remained apathetic, in cramped positions, muttering between shivers. The sun was setting. A sun enormous, unclouded, and red, declining low as if bending down to look into their faces. The wind whistled across long sunbeams that, resplendent and cold, struck full on the dilated pupils of staring eyes without making them wink. The wisps of hair and the tangled beards were grey with the salt of the sea. The faces were earthy, and the dark patches under the eyes extended to the ears, smudged into the hollows of sunken cheeks. The lips were livid and thin, and when they moved it was with difficulty, as though they had been glued to the teeth. Some grinned sadly in the sunlight, shaking with cold. Others were sad and still. Charley, subdued by the sudden disclosure of the insignificance of his youth, darted fearful glances. The two smoothfaced Norwegians resembled decrepit children, staring stupidly. To leeward, on the edge of the horizon, black seas leaped up towards the glowing sun. It sank slowly, round and blazing, and the crests of waves splashed on the edge of the luminous circle. One of the Norwegians appeared to catch sight of it, and, after giving a violent start, began to speak. His voice, startling the others, made them stir. They moved their heads stiffly, or, turning with difficulty, looked at him with surprise, with fear, or in grave silence. He chattered at the setting sun, nodding his head, while the big seas began to roll across the crimson disc; and over miles of turbulent waters the shadows of high waves swept with a running darkness the faces of men. A crested roller broke with a loud hissing roar, and the sun, as if put out, disappeared. The chattering voice faltered, went out together with the light. There were sighs. In the sudden lull that follows the crash of a broken sea a man said wearily, "Here's that blooming Dutchman gone off his chump." A seaman, lashed by the middle, tapped the deck with his open hand with unceasing quick flaps. In the gathering greyness of twilight a bulky form was seen rising aft, and began marching on all fours with the movements of some big, cautious beast. It was Mr. Baker passing along the line of men. He grunted encouragingly over every one, felt their fastenings. Some, with half-open eyes, puffed like men oppressed by heat; others mechanically and in dreamy voices answered him, "Ay! ay! sir!" He went from one to another grunting, "Ough! . . . See her through it yet"; and unexpectedly, with loud, angry outbursts, blew up Knowles for cutting off a long piece from the fall of the relieving tackle. "Ough! . . . Ashamed of yourself . . . Relieving tackle[3] . . . Don't you know better! . . . Ough! . . . Able seaman! Ough!" The lame man was crushed. He muttered, "Get som'think for a lashing for myself, sir."—"Ough! Lashing . . . yourself. Are you a tinker or a sailor . . . What? Ough! . . . May want that tackle directly . . . Ough! . . . More use to the ship than your lame carcass. Ough! . . . Keep it! . . . Keep it, now you've done it." He crawled away slowly, muttering to himself about some men being "worse than children." It had been a comforting row. Low exclamations were heard: "Hallo . . . Hallo." . . . Those who had been painfully dozing asked with convulsive starts, "What's up? . . . What is it?" The answers came with unexpected cheerfulness: "The mate is going bald-headed[4] for lame Jack about something or other." "No!" . . . "What 'as he done?" Some one even chuckled. It was like a whiff of hope, like a reminder of safe days. Donkin, who had been stupefied with fear, revived suddenly and began to shout:—" 'Ear 'im; that's the way they tawlk to us. Vy donch 'ee 'it 'im—one ov yer? 'It 'im! 'It 'im! Comin' the mate over us. We are as good men as 'ee! We're all goin' to 'ell now. We 'ave been starved in this rotten ship, an' now we're goin' to be drowned for them black-'earted bullies! 'It 'im!" He shrieked in the deepening gloom, he blubbered and sobbed, screaming:—" 'It 'im! 'It 'im!" The rage and fear of his disregarded right to live tried the steadfastness of hearts more than the menacing shadows of the night that advanced through the unceasing clamour of the gale. From aft Mr. Baker was heard:—"Is one of you men going to stop him—must I come along?" "Shut up!" . . . "Keep quiet!" cried various voices, exasperated, trembling with cold.—"You'll get one across the mug from me directly," said an invisible seaman, in a weary tone. "I won't let the mate have the trouble." He ceased and lay still, with the silence of despair. On the black sky the stars, coming out, gleamed over an inky sea that, speckled with foam, flashed back at them the evanescent and pale light of a dazzling whiteness born from the black

3. Arrangement of line and blocks hooked to the tiller to reduce strain on the wheel ropes in heavy weather.
4. Rushing into something impetuously, full-force.

turmoil of the waves. Remote in the eternal calm they glittered hard and cold above the uproar of the earth; they surrounded the vanquished and tormented ship on all sides: more pitiless than the eyes of a triumphant mob, and as unapproachable as the hearts of men.

The icy south wind howled exultingly under the sombre splendour of the sky. The cold shook the men with a resistless violence as though it had tried to shake them to pieces. Short moans were swept, unheard, off the stiff lips. Some complained in mutters of "not feeling themselves below the waist"; while those who had closed their eyes imagined they had a block of ice on their chests. Others, alarmed at not feeling any pain in their fingers, beat the deck feebly with their hands—obstinate and exhausted. Wamibo stared vacant and dreamy. The Scandinavians kept on a meaningless mutter through chattering teeth. The spare Scotchmen, with determined efforts, kept their lower jaws still. The West-country men lay big and stolid in an invulnerable surliness. A man yawned and swore in turns. Another breathed with a rattle in his throat. Two elderly hard-weather shellbacks, fast side by side, whispered dismally to one another about the landlady of a boarding-house in Sunderland,[5] whom they both knew. They extolled her motherliness and her liberality; they tried to talk about the joint of beef and the big fire in the downstairs kitchen. The words, dying faintly on their lips, ended in light sighs. A sudden voice cried into the cold night, "O Lord!" No one changed his position or took any notice of the cry. One or two passed, with a repeated and vague gesture, their hand over their faces, but most of them kept very still. In the benumbed immobility of their bodies they were excessively wearied by their thoughts, which rushed with the rapidity and vividness of dreams. Now and then, by an abrupt and startling exclamation, they answered the weird hail of some illusion; then, again, in silence contemplated the vision of known faces and familiar things. They recalled the aspect of forgotten shipmates and heard the voice of dead-and-gone skippers; they remembered the noise of gaslit streets, the steamy heat of taprooms, or the scorching sunshine of calm days at sea.

Mr. Baker left his insecure place, and crawled, with stoppages, along the poop. In the dark and on all fours he resembled some carnivorous animal prowling amongst corpses. At the break, propped to windward of a stanchion, he looked down on the main deck. It seemed to him that the ship had a tendency to stand up a little more. The wind had eased a little, he thought, but the sea ran as high as ever. The waves foamed viciously, and the lee side of the deck disappeared under a hissing whiteness as of boiling milk, while the rigging sang steadily with a deep vibrating note, and, at every upward swing of the ship, the wind rushed with a long-drawn clamour amongst the spars. Mr. Baker watched very still. A man near him began to make a blabbing noise with his lips, all at once and very loud, as though the cold had broken brutally through him. He went on:—"Ba—ba—ba—brrr—ba—ba."—"Stop that!" cried Mr. Baker, groping in the dark. "Stop it!" He went on shaking the leg he found under his hand.—"What is it, sir?" called out Belfast, in the tone of a man awakened suddenly; "we are looking after that 'ere Jimmy."—"Are you? Ough! Don't make that row then. Who's that near you?"—"It's me—the boatswain, sir," growled the West-country man; "we are trying to keep

5. Shipping center in northern England, on the North Sea.

life in that poor devil."—"Ay, ay!" said Mr. Baker. "Do it quietly, can't you."—"He wants us to hold him up above the rail," went on the boatswain, with irritation, "says he can't breathe here under our jackets."—"If we lift 'im, we drop 'im overboard," said another voice, "we can't feel our hands with cold."—"I don't care. I am choking!" exclaimed James Wait in a clear tone.—"Oh no, my son," said the boatswain desperately, "you don't go till we all go on this fine night."—"You will see yet many a worse," said Mr. Baker cheerfully.—"It's no child's play, sir!" answered the boatswain. "Some of us farther aft, here, are in a pretty bad way."—"If the blamed sticks had been cut out of her she would be running along on her bottom now like any decent ship, an' giv' us all a chance," said some one, with a sigh.—"The old man wouldn't have it . . . much he cares for us," whispered another.—"Care for you!" exclaimed Mr. Baker angrily. "Why should he care for you? Are you a lot of women passengers to be taken care of? We are here to take care of the ship—and some of you ain't up to that. Ough! . . . What have you done so very smart to be taken care of? Ough! . . . Some of you can't stand a bit of a breeze without crying over it."—"Come, sorr. We ain't so bad," protested Belfast, in a voice shaken by shivers; "we ain't . . . brrr . . ."—"Again," shouted the mate, grabbing at the shadowy form; "again! . . . Why, you're in your shirt! What have you done?"—"I've put my oilskin and jacket over that half-dead nayggur—and he says he chokes," said Belfast complainingly.—"You wouldn't call me nigger if I wasn't half dead, you Irish beggar!" boomed James Wait vigorously.—"You . . . brrr . . . You wouldn't be white if you were ever so well . . . I will fight you . . . brrrr . . . in fine weather . . . brrr . . . with one hand tied behind my back . . . brrrrrr . . ."—"I don't want your rags—I want air," gasped out the other faintly, as if suddenly exhausted.

The sprays swept over whistling and pattering. Men disturbed in their peaceful torpor by the pain of quarrelsome shouts, moaned, muttering curses. Mr. Baker crawled off a little way to leeward where a water-cask loomed up big, with something white against it. "Is it you, Podmore?" asked Mr. Baker. He had to repeat the question twice before the cook turned, coughing feebly.—"Yes, sir. I've been praying in my mind for a quick deliverance; for I am prepared for any call. . . . I——"—"Look here, cook," interrupted Mr. Baker, "the men are perishing with cold."—"Cold!" said the cook mournfully; "they will be warm enough before long."—"What?" asked Mr. Baker, looking along the deck into the faint sheen of frothing water.—"They are a wicked lot," continued the cook solemnly, but in an unsteady voice, "about as wicked as any ship's company in this sinful world! Now, I"—he trembled so that he could hardly speak; his was an exposed place, and in a cotton shirt, a thin pair of trousers, and with his knees under his nose, he received, quaking, the flicks of stinging, salt drops; his voice sounded exhausted—"now, I—any time. . . . My eldest youngster, Mr. Baker . . . a clever boy . . . last Sunday on shore before this voyage he wouldn't go to church, sir. Says I, 'You go and clean yourselt, or I'll know the reason why!' What does he do? . . . Pond, Mr. Baker—fell into the pond in his best rig, sir! . . . Accident? . . . 'Nothing will save you, fine scholar though you are!' says I. . . . Accident! . . . I whopped him, sir, till I couldn't lift my arm. . . ." His voice faltered. "I whopped 'im!" he repeated, rattling his teeth; then, after a while, let out a mournful sound that was half a groan, half a snore. Mr. Baker shook him by the shoulders. "Hey! Cook! Hold up, Podmore! Tell me—is there any fresh water in the galley tank? The ship is lying along less, I think; I would try to get forward. A little water would do them good. Hallo! Look out! Look out!" The cook struggled.—"Not you, sir—not you!" He began to scramble to windward. "Galley! . . . my business!" he shouted.—"Cook's going crazy now," said several voices. He yelled:—"Crazy, am I? I am more ready to die than any of you, officers incloosive—there! As long as she swims I will cook! I will get you coffee."—"Cook, ye are a gentleman!" cried Belfast. But the cook was already going over the weather ladder. He stopped for a moment to shout back on the poop:—"As long as she swims I will cook!" and disappeared as though he had gone overboard. The men who had heard sent after him a cheer that sounded like a wail of sick children. An hour or more afterwards some one said distinctly: "He's gone for good."—"Very likely," assented the boatswain; "even in fine weather he was as smart about the deck as a milch-cow[6] on her first voyage. We ought to go and see." Nobody moved. As the hours dragged slowly through the darkness Mr. Baker crawled back and forth along the poop several times. Some men fancied they had heard him exchange murmurs with the master, but at that time the memories were incomparably more vivid than anything actual, and they were not certain whether the murmurs were heard now or many years ago. They did not try to find out. A mutter more or less did not matter. It was too cold for curiosity, and almost for hope. They could not spare a moment on a thought from the great mental occupation of wishing to live. And the desire of life kept them alive, apathetic and enduring under the cruel persistence of wind and cold; while the bestarred black dome of the sky revolved slowly above the ship, that drifted, bearing their patience and their suffering, through the stormy solitude of the sea.

Huddled close to one another, they fancied themselves utterly alone. They heard sustained loud noises, and again bore the pain of existence through long hours of profound silence. In the night they saw sunshine, felt warmth, and suddenly, with a start, thought that the sun would never rise upon a freezing world. Some heard laughter, listened to songs; others, near the end of the poop, could hear loud human shrieks, and opening their eyes, were surprised to hear them still, though very faint, and far away. The boatswain said:—"Why, it's the cook, hailing from forward, I think." He hardly believed his own words or recognised his own voice. It was a long time before the man next to him gave a sign of life. He punched hard his other neighbour and said:—"The cook's shouting!" Many did not understand, others did not care; the majority farther aft did not believe. But the boatswain and another man had the pluck to crawl away forward to see. They seemed to have been gone for hours, and were very soon forgotten. Then suddenly men who had been plunged in a hopeless resignation became as if possessed with a desire to hurt. They belaboured one another with fists. In the darkness they struck persistently anything soft they could feel near, and, with a greater effort than for a shout, whispered excitedly—"They've got some hot coffee. . . . Boss'en got it. . . ." "No! . . . Where?" . . . "It's coming! Cook made it." James Wait moaned. Donkin scrambled viciously, caring not where he kicked, and anxious that the officers should have none of it. It came in a pot, and they

6. Dairy cows were kept aboard ships to supply fresh milk.

drank in turns. It was hot, and while it blistered the greedy palates, it seemed incredible. The men sighed out parting with the mug:—"How 'as he done it?" Some cried weakly:—"Bully for you, doctor!" He had done it somehow. Afterwards Archie declared that the thing was "meeraculous." For many days we wondered, and it was the one ever-interesting subject of conversation to the end of the voyage. We asked the cook, in fine weather, how he felt when he saw his stove "reared up on end." We inquired, in the north-east trade[7] and on serene evenings, whether he had to stand on his head to put things right somewhat. We suggested he had used his breadboard for a raft, and from there comfortably had stoked his grate; and we did our best to conceal our admiration under the wit of fine irony. He affirmed not to know anything about it, rebuked our levity, declared himself, with solemn animation, to have been the object of a special mercy for the saving of our unholy lives. Fundamentally he was right, no doubt; but he need not have been so offensively positive about it—he need not have hinted so often that it would have gone hard with us had he not been there, meritorious and pure, to receive the inspiration and the strength for the work of grace. Had we been saved by his recklessnes or his agility, we could have at length become reconciled to the fact; but to admit our obligation to anybody's virtue and holiness was as difficult for us as for any other handful of mankind. Like many benefactors of humanity, the cook took himself too seriously, and reaped the reward of irreverence. We were not ungrateful, however. He remained heroic. His saying—*the* saying of his life—became proverbial in the mouths of men as are the sayings of conquerors or sages. Later, whenever one of us was puzzled by a task and advised to relinquish it, he would express his determination to persevere and to succeed by the words:—"As long as she swims I will cook!"

The hot drink helped us through the bleak hours that precede the dawn. The sky low by the horizon took on the delicate tints of pink and yellow like the inside of a rare shell. And higher, where it glowed with a pearly sheen, a small black cloud appeared, like a forgotten fragment of the night set in a border of dazzling gold. The beams of light skipped on the crests of waves. The eyes of men turned to the eastward. The sunlight flooded their weary faces. They were giving themselves up to fatigue as though they had done for ever with their work. On Singleton's black oilskin coat the dried salt glistened like hoarfrost. He hung on by the wheel, with open and lifeless eyes. Captain Allistoun, unblinking, faced the rising sun. His lips stirred, opened for the first time in twenty-four hours, and with a fresh firm voice he cried, "Wear ship!"[8]

The commanding sharp tones made all these torpid men start like a sudden flick of a whip. Then again, motionless where they lay, the force of habit made some of them repeat the order in hardly audible murmurs. Captain Allistoun glanced down at his crew, and several, with trembling fingers and hopeless movements, tried to cast themselves adrift. He repeated impatiently, "Wear ship. Now then, Mr. Baker, get the men along. What's the matter with them?"—"Wear ship. Do you hear there?—Wear ship!" thundered out the boatswain suddenly. His voice seemed to break through a deadly spell. Men began to stir and crawl.—"I want the fore-

---

7. Winds from east-northeast, having a steady general direction from the northeast in north latitudes.
8. Bring the vessel on the other tack, swinging her around by means of the wind blowing from behind *into* the sails ("coming before the wind").

top-mast stay sail run up smartly," said the master, very loudly; "if you can't manage it standing up you must do it lying down—that's all. Bear a hand!"—"Come along! Let's give the old girl a chance," urged the boatswain.—"Ay! ay! Wear ship!" exclaimed quavering voices. The forecastle men, with reluctant faces, prepared to go forward. Mr. Baker pushed ahead, grunting, on all fours to show the way, and they followed him over the break. The others lay still with a vile hope in their hearts of not being required to move till they got saved or drowned in peace.

After some time they could be seen forward appearing on the forecastle head, one by one in unsafe attitudes; hanging on to the rails, clambering over the anchors; embracing the cross-head of the windlass or hugging the fore-capstan. They were restless with strange exertions, waved their arms, knelt, lay flat down, staggered up, seemed to strive their hardest to go overboard. Suddenly a small white piece of canvas fluttered amongst them, grew larger, beating. Its narrow head rose in jerks—and at last it stood distended and triangular in the sunshine.—"They have done it!" cried the voices aft. Captain Allistoun let go the rope he had round his wrist and rolled to leeward headlong. He could be seen casting the lee main braces off the pins while the backwash of waves splashed over him.—"Square the main yard!" he shouted up to us—who stared at him in wonder. We hesitated to stir. "The main brace, men. Haul! haul anyhow! Lay on your backs and haul!" he screeched, half drowned down there. We did not believe we could move the main yard, but the strongest and the less discouraged tried to execute the order. Others assisted half-heartedly. Singleton's eyes blazed suddenly as he took a fresh grip of the spokes. Captain Allistoun fought his way up to windward.—"Haul, men! Try to move it! Haul, and help the ship." His hard face worked suffused and furious. "Is she going off, Singleton?" he cried.—"Not a move yet, sir," croaked the old seaman in a horribly hoarse voice.—"Watch the helm, Singleton," spluttered the master. "Haul, men! Have you no more strength than rats? Haul, and earn your salt." Mr. Creighton, on his back, with a swollen leg and a face as white as a piece of paper, blinked his eyes; his bluish lips twitched. In the wild scramble men grabbed at him, crawled over his hurt leg, knelt on his chest. He kept perfectly still, setting his teeth without a moan, without a sigh. The master's ardour, the cries of that silent man inspired us. We hauled and hung in bunches on the rope. We heard him say with violence to Donkin, who sprawled abjectly on his stomach,—"I will brain you with this belaying-pin if you don't catch hold of the brace," and that victim of men's injustice, cowardly and cheeky, whimpered:—"Are you goin' to murder us now?" while with sudden desperation he gripped the rope. Men sighed, shouted, hissed meaningless words, groaned. The yards moved, came slowly square against the wind, that hummed loudly on the yard-arms.—"Going off, sir," shouted Singleton, "she's just started."—"Catch a turn with that brace. Catch a turn!" clamoured the master. Mr. Creighton, nearly suffocated and unable to move, made a mighty effort, and with his left hand managed to nip the rope.—"All fast!" cried some one. He closed his eyes as if going off into a swoon, while huddled together about the brace we watched with scared looks what the ship would do now.

She went off slowly as though she had been weary and disheartened like the men she carried. She paid off very gradually, making us hold our breath till we choked, and as soon as she had brought the wind abaft the beam she started to move, and fluttered our hearts. It was awful to see her, nearly overturned, begin to gather way and drag her submerged side through the water. The dead-eyes of the rigging churned the breaking seas. The lower half of the deck was full of mad whirlpools and eddies; and the long line of the lee rail could be seen showing black now and then in the swirls of a field of foam as dazzling and white as a field of snow. The wind sang shrilly amongst the spars; and at every slight lurch we expected her to slip to the bottom sideways from under our backs. When dead before it she made the first distinct attempt to stand up, and we encouraged her with a feeble and discordant howl. A great sea came running up aft and hung for a moment over us with a curling top; then crashed down under the counter and spread out on both sides into a great sheet of bursting froth. Above its fierce hiss we heard Singleton's croak:— "She is steering!" He had both his feet now planted firmly on the grating, and the wheel spun fast as he eased the helm.—"Bring the wind on the port quarter and steady her!" called out the master, staggering to his feet, the first man up from amongst our prostrate heap. One or two screamed with excitement:—"She rises!" Far away forward, Mr. Baker and three others were seen erect and black on the clear sky, lifting their arms, and with open mouths as though they had been shouting all together. The ship trembled, trying to lift her side, lurched back, seemed to give up with a nerveless dip, and suddenly with an unexpected jerk swung violently to windward, as though she had torn herself out from a deadly grasp. The whole immense volume of water, lifted by her deck, was thrown bodily across to starboard. Loud cracks were heard. Iron ports breaking open thundered with ringing blows. The water topped over the starboard rail with the rush of a river falling over a dam. The sea on deck, and the seas on every side of her, mingled together in a deafening roar. She rolled violently. We got up and were helplessly run or flung about from side to side. Men, rolling over and over, yelled,—"The house will go!"—"She clears herself!" Lifted by a towering sea she ran along with it for a moment, spouting thick streams of water through every opening of her wounded sides. The lee braces having been carried away or washed off the pins, all the ponderous yards on the fore swung from side to side and with appalling rapidity at every roll. The men forward were seen crouching here and there with fearful glances upwards at the enormous spars that whirled about over their heads. The torn canvas and the ends of broken gear streamed in the wind like wisps of hair. Through the clear sunshine, over the flashing turmoil and uproar of the seas, the ship ran blindly, dishevelled and headlong, as if fleeing for her life; and on the poop we spun, we tottered about, distracted and noisy. We all spoke at once in a thin babble; we had the aspects of invalids and the gestures of maniacs. Eyes shone, large and haggard, in smiling, meagre faces that seemed to have been dusted over with powdered chalk. We stamped, clapped our hands, feeling ready to jump and do anything; but in reality hardly able to keep our feet. Captain Allistoun, hard and slim, gesticulated madly from the poop at Mr. Baker: "Steady these fore-yards! Steady them the best you can!" On the main deck, men excited by his cries, splashed, dashing aimlessly here and there with the foam swirling up to their waists. Apart, far aft, and alone by the helm, old Singleton had deliberately tucked his white beard under the top button of his glistening coat. Swaying upon the din and tumult of the seas, with the whole battered length of the ship launched forward in a rolling rush before his steady old eyes, he stood rigidly still, forgotten by all, and with an attentive face. In front of his erect figure only the two arms moved crosswise with a swift and sudden readiness, to check or urge again the rapid stir of circling spokes. He steered with care.

Chapter Four

On men reprieved by its disdainful mercy, the immortal sea confers in its justice the full privilege of desired unrest. Through the perfect wisdom of its grace they are not permitted to meditate at ease upon the complicated and acrid savour of existence. They must without pause justify their life to the eternal pity that commands toil to be hard and unceasing, from sunrise to sunset, from sunset to sunrise; till the weary succession of nights and days tainted by the obstinate clamour of sages, demanding bliss and an empty heaven, is redeemed at last by the vast silence of pain and labour, by the dumb fear and the dumb courage of men obscure, forgetful, and enduring.

The master and Mr. Baker coming face to face stared for a moment, with the intense and amazed looks of men meeting unexpectedly after years of trouble. Their voices were gone, and they whispered desperately at one another.—"Any one missing?" asked Captain Allistoun.—"No. All there,"—"Anybody hurt?"—"Only the second mate."—"I will look after him directly. We're lucky."—"Very," articulated Mr. Baker faintly. He gripped the rail and rolled bloodshot eyes. The little grey man made an effort to raise his voice above a dull mutter, and fixed his chief mate with a cold gaze, piercing like a dart.—"Get sail on the ship," he said, speaking authoritatively and with an inflexible snap of his thin lips. "Get sail on her as soon as you can. This is a fair wind. At once, sir—don't give the men time to feel themselves. They will get done up and stiff, and we will never . . . We must get her along now" . . . He reeled to a long heavy roll; the rail dipped into the glancing hissing water. He caught a shroud, swung helplessly against the mate . . . "Now we have a fair wind at last——Make——sail." His head rolled from shoulder to shoulder. His eyelids began to beat rapidly. "And the pumps——pumps, Mr. Baker." He peered as though the face within a foot of his eyes had been half a mile off. "Keep the men on the move to——to get her along," he mumbled in a drowsy tone, like a man going off into a doze. He pulled himself together suddenly. "Mustn't stand. Won't do," he said, with a painful attempt at a smile. He let go his hold, and, propelled, by the dip of the ship, ran aft unwillingly, with small steps, till he brought up against the binnacle stand. Hanging on there, he looked up in an aimless manner at Singleton, who, unheeding him, watched anxiously the end of the jib-boom.[9]—"Steering gear works all right?" he asked. There was a noise in the old seaman's throat, as though the words had been rattling together before they could come out.—"Steers . . . like a little boat," he said, at last, with hoarse tenderness, without giving the master as much as half a glance—then, watchfully, spun the wheel down, steadied, flung it back again. Captain Allistoun tore himself away from the delight of leaning against the binna-

9. The spar (stout, rounded piece of wood or   of the foresail.
metal) that extends one of the triangular sails forward

cle, and began to walk the poop, swaying and reeling to preserve his balance. . . .

The pump-rods, clanking, stamped in short jumps while the flywheels turned smoothly, with great speed, at the foot of the mainmast, flinging back and forth with a regular impetuosity two limp clusters of men clinging to the handles. They abandoned themselves, swaying from the hip with twitching faces and stony eyes. The carpenter, sounding from time to time, exclaimed mechanically: "Shake her up! Keep her going!" Mr. Baker could not speak, but found his voice to shout; and under the goad of his objurgations, men looked to the lashings, dragged out new sails; and, thinking themselves unable to move, carried heavy blocks aloft— overhauled the gear. They went up the rigging with faltering and desperate efforts. Their heads swam as they shifted their hold, stepped blindly on the yards like men in the dark; or trusted themselves to the first rope at hand with the negligence of exhausted strength. The narrow escapes from falls did not disturb the languid beat of their hearts; the roar of the seas seething far below them sounded continuous and faint like an indistinct noise from another world; the wind filled their eyes with tears, and with heavy gusts tried to push them off from where they swayed in insecure positions. With streaming faces and blowing hair they flew up and down between sky and water, bestriding the ends of yard-arms, crouching on foot-ropes, embracing lifts to have their hands free, or standing up against chain ties. Their thoughts floated vaguely between the desire of rest and the desire of life, while their stiffened fingers cast off head-earrings, fumbled for knives, or held with tenacious grip against the violent shocks of beating canvas. They glared savagely at one another, made frantic signs with one hand while they held their life in the other, looked down on the narrow strip of flooded deck, shouted along to leeward: "Light-to!" . . . "Haul out!" . . . "Make fast!"[1] Their lips moved, their eyes started, furious and eager with the desire to be understood, but the wind tossed their words unheard upon the disturbed sea. In an unendurable and unending strain they worked like men driven by a merciless dream to toil in an atmosphere of ice or flame. They burnt and shivered in turns. Their eyeballs smarted as if in the smoke of a conflagration; their heads were ready to burst with every shout. Hard fingers seemed to grip their throats. At every roll they thought: Now I must let go. It will shake us all off—and thrown about aloft they cried wildly: "Look out, there—catch the end." . . . "Reeve clear." . . . "Turn this block. . . . " They nodded desperately; shook infuriated faces. "No! No! From down up." They seemed to hate one another with a deadly hate. The longing to be done with it all gnawed their breasts, and the wish to do things well was a burning pain. They cursed their fate, contemned their life, and wasted their breath in deadly imprecations upon one another. The sailmaker, with his bald head bared, worked feverishly, forgetting his intimacy with so many admirals. The boatswain, climbing up with marlinspikes and bunches of spunyarn rovings,[2] or kneeling on the yard and ready to take a turn with the midship-stop, had acute and fleeting visions of his old woman and the youngsters in a moorland village. Mr. Baker, feeling very weak, tottered here and there, grunting and inflexible, like a man of iron. He waylaid those who, coming from aloft, stood gasping for breath. He ordered, en-

1. To secure (belay) a rope by turning it around a belaying pin or cleat.   2. Short pieces of rope.

couraged, scolded. "Now then—to the main topsail now! Tally on to that gantline.³ Don't stand about there!"—"Is there no rest for us?" muttered voices. He spun round fiercely, with a sinking heart.—"No! No rest till the work is done. Work till you drop. That's what you're here for." A bowed seaman at his elbow gave a short laugh.—"Do or die," he croaked bitterly, then spat into his broad palms, swung up his long arms, and grasping the rope high above his head sent out a mournful, wailing cry for a pull all together. A sea boarded the quarter-deck and sent the whole lot sprawling to leeward. Caps, handspikes floated. Clenched hands, kicking legs, with here and there a spluttering face, stuck out of the white hiss of foaming water. Mr. Baker, knocked down with the rest, screamed—"Don't let go that rope! Hold on to it! Hold!" And sorely bruised by the brutal fling, they held on to it, as though it had been the fortune of their life. The ship ran, rolling heavily, and the topping crests glanced past port and starboard flashing their white heads. Pumps were freed. Braces were rove. The three topsails and foresail were set. She spurted faster over the water, outpacing the swift rush of waves. The menacing thunder of distanced seas rose behind her—filled the air with the tremendous vibrations of its voice. And devastated, battered and wounded she drove foaming to the northward, as though inspired by the courage of a high endeavour. . . .

The forecastle was a place of damp desolation. They looked at their dwelling with dismay. It was slimy, dripping; it hummed hollow with the wind, and was strewn with shapeless wreckage like a half-tide cavern in a rocky and exposed coast. Many had lost all they had in the world, but most of the starboard watch⁴ had preserved their chests; thin streams of water trickled out of them, however. The beds were soaked; the blankets spread out and saved by some nail squashed under foot. They dragged wet rags from evil-smelling corners, and wringing the water out, recognised their property. Some smiled stiffly. Others looked round blank and mute. There were cries of joy over old waistcoats, and groans of sorrow over shapeless things found among the splinters of smashed bed boards. One lamp was discovered jammed under the bowsprit. Charley whimpered a little. Knowles stumped here and there, sniffing, examining dark places for salvage. He poured dirty water out of a boot, and was concerned to find the owner. Those who, overwhelmed by their losses, sat on the forepeak hatch, remained elbows on knees, and, with a fist against each cheek, disdained to look up. He pushed it under their noses. "Here's a good boot. Yours?" They snarled, "No—get out." One snapped at him, "Take it to hell out of this." He seemed surprised. "Why? It's a good boot," but, remembering suddenly that he had lost every stitch of his clothing, he dropped his find and began to swear. In the dim light cursing voices clashed. A man came in and, dropping his arms, stood still, repeating from the doorstep, "Here's a bloomin' old go!⁵ Here's a bloomin' old go!" A few rooted anxiously in flooded chests for tobacco. They breathed hard, clamoured with heads down. "Look at that, Jack!" . . . "Here! Sam! Here's my shore-going rig spoilt for ever." One blasphemed tearfully, holding up a pair of dripping trousers. No one looked at him. The cat

3. Rope and block attached to the head of a lower mast used to begin the rigging of a ship by making the initial hoists.
4. In the merchant service all hands are divided into two watches, "port" and "starboard," with an officer to command each. First nightwatch, 2000–2400 hours; second nightwatch, 0001–0400 hours, etc.
5. This is a fine state of affairs!

came out from somewhere. He had an ovation. They snatched him from hand to hand, caressed him in a murmur of pet names. They wondered where he had "weathered it out"; disputed about it. A squabbling argument began. Two men brought in a bucket of fresh water, and all crowded round it; but Tom, lean and mewing, came up with every hair astir and had the first drink. A couple of hands went aft for oil and biscuits.

Then in the yellow light and in the intervals of mopping the deck they crunched hard bread, arranging to "worry through somehow." Men chummed as to beds. Turns were settled for wearing boots and having the use of oilskin coats. They called one another "old man" and "sonny" in cheery voices. Friendly slaps resounded. Jokes were shouted. One or two stretched on the wet deck, slept with heads pillowed on their bent arms, and several, sitting on the hatch, smoked. Their weary faces appeared through a thin blue haze, pacified and with sparkling eyes. The boatswain put his head through the door. "Relieve the wheel, one of you"—he shouted inside—"it's six. Blamme if that old Singleton hasn't been there more'n thirty hours. You are a fine lot." He slammed the door again. "Mate's watch on deck," said some one. "Hey, Donkin, it's your relief!" shouted three or four together. He had crawled into an empty bunk and on wet planks lay still. "Donkin, your wheel." He made no sound. "Donkin's dead," guffawed some one. "Sell 'is bloomin' clothes," shouted another. "Donkin, if ye don't go to the bloomin' wheel they will sell your clothes—d'ye hear?" jeered a third. He groaned from his dark hole. He complained about pains in all his bones, he whimpered pitifully. "He won't go," exclaimed a contemptuous voice; "your turn, Davis." The young seaman rose painfully, squaring his shoulders. Donkin stuck his head out, and it appeared in the yellow light fragile and ghastly. "I will giv' yer a pound of tobaccer," he whined in a conciliating voice, "so soon as I draw it from aft. I will—s'elp me. . . . " Davis swung his arm backhanded and the head vanished. "I'll go," he said, "but you will pay for it." He walked unsteady but resolute to the door. "So I will," yelped Donkin, popping out behind him. "So I will—s'elp me . . . a pound . . . three bob⁶ they chawrge." Davis flung the door open. "You will pay my price . . . in fine weather," he shouted over his shoulder. One of the men unbuttoned his wet coat rapidly, threw it at his head. "Here, Taffy—take that, you thief!" "Thank you!" he cried from the darkness above the swish of rolling water. He could be heard splashing; a sea came on board with a thump. "He's got his bath already," remarked a grim shellback. "Ay, ay!" grunted others. Then, after a long silence, Wamibo made strange noises. "Hallo, what' up with you?" said some one grumpily. "He says he would have gone for Davy," explained Archie, who was the Finn's interpreter generally. "I believe him!" cried voices. . . . "Never mind, Dutchy. . . . You'll do, muddle-head. . . . Your turn will come soon enough. . . . You don't know when ye're well off." They ceased and all together turned their faces to the door. Singleton stepped in, advanced two paces, and stood swaying slightly. The sea hissed, flowed roaring past the bows, and the forecastle trembled, full of deep murmurs; the lamp flared, swinging

---

6. Shilling. There were twenty shillings to the British pound, then about five dollars but with purchasing power perhaps ten times that; Donkin is offering a modest but significant sum. Note below that a merchant seaman earned two pounds ten shillings a month above room and board.

like a pendulum. He looked with a dreamy and puzzled stare, as though he could not distinguish the still men from their restless shadows. There were awestruck exclamations:—"Hallo, hallo." . . . "How does it look outside now, Singleton?" Those who sat on the hatch lifted their eyes in silence, and the next oldest seaman in the ship (those two understood one another, though they hardly exchanged three words in a day) gazed up at his friend attentively for a moment, then, taking a short clay pipe out of his mouth, offered it without a word. Singleton put out his arm towards it, missed, staggered, and suddenly fell forward, crashing down, stiff and headlong like an uprooted tree. There was a swift rush. Men pushed, crying:—"He's done!" . . . "Turn him over!" . . . "Stand clear, there!" Under a crowd of startled faces bending over him he lay on his back, staring upwards in a continuous and intolerable manner. In the breathless silence of a general consternation, he said in a grating murmur:—"I am all right," and clutched with his hands. They helped him up. He mumbled despondently:—"I am getting old . . . old."—"Not you," cried Belfast, with ready tact. Supported on all sides, he hung his head.—"Are you better?" they asked. He glared at them from under his eyebrows with large black eyes, spreading over his chest the bushy whiteness of a beard long and thick.— "Old! old!" he repeated sternly. Helped along, he reached his bunk. There was in it a slimy soft heap of something that smelt, as does, at dead low water, a muddy foreshore. It was his soaked straw bed. With a convulsive effort he pitched himself on it, and in the darkness of the narrow place could be heard growling angrily, like an irritated and savage animal uneasy in its den:—"Bit of breeze . . . small thing . . . can't stand up . . . old!" He slept at last, high-booted, sou'wester on head, and his oilskin clothes rustled, when with a deep sighing groan he turned over. Men conversed about him in quiet concerned whispers. "This will break 'im up." . . . "Strong as a horse." . . . "Ay. But he ain't what he used to be." . . . In sad murmurs they gave him up. Yet at midnight he turned out to duty as if nothing had been the matter, and answered to his name with a mournful "Here!" He brooded alone more than ever, in an impenetrable silence and with a saddened face. For many years he had heard himself called "Old Singleton," and had serenely accepted the qualification, taking it as a tribute of respect due to a man who through half a century had measured his strength against the favours and the rages of the sea. He had never given a thought to his mortal self. He lived unscathed, as though he had been indestructible, surrendering to all the temptations, weathering many gales. He had panted in sunshine, shivered in the cold; suffered hunger, thirst, debauch; passed through many trials—known all the furies. Old! It seemed to him he was broken at last. And like a man bound treacherously while he sleeps, he woke up fettered by the long chain of disregarded years. He had to take up at once the burden of all his existence, and found it almost too heavy for his strength. Old! He moved his arms, shook his head, felt his limbs. Getting old . . . and then? He looked upon the immortal sea with the awakened and groping perception of its heartless might; he saw it unchanged, black and foaming under the eternal scrutiny of the stars; he heard its impatient voice calling for him out of a pitiless vastness full of unrest, of turmoil, and of terror. He looked afar upon it, and he saw an immensity tormented and blind, moaning and furious, that claimed all the days of his tenacious life, and, when life was over, would claim the worn-out body of its slave. . . .

This was the last of the breeze. It veered quickly, changed to a black south-easter, and blew itself out, giving the ship a famous shove to the northward into the joyous sunshine of the trade. Rapid and white she ran homewards in a straight path, under a blue sky and upon the plain of a blue sea. She carried Singleton's completed wisdom, Donkin's delicate susceptibilities, and the conceited folly of us all. The hours of ineffective turmoil were forgotten; the fear and anguish of these dark moments were never mentioned in the glowing peace of fine days. Yet from that time our life seemed to start afresh as though we had died and had been resuscitated. All the first part of the voyage, the Indian Ocean on the other side of the Cape, all that was lost in a haze, like an ineradicable suspicion of some previous existence. It had ended—then there were blank hours: a livid blur—and again we lived! Singleton was possessed of sinister truth; Mr. Creighton of a damaged leg; the cook of fame—and shamefully abused the opportunities of his distinction. Donkin had an added grievance. He went about repeating with insistence:—" 'E said 'e would brain me—did yer 'ear? They are goin' to murder us now for the least little thing." We began at last to think it was rather awful. And we were conceited! We boasted of our pluck, of our capacity for work, of our energy. We remembered honourable episodes: our devotion, our indomitable perseverance—and were proud of them as though they had been the outcome of our unaided impulses. We remembered our danger, our toil—and conveniently forgot our horrible scare. We decried our officers—who had done nothing—and listened to the fascinating Donkin. His care for our rights, his disinterested concern for our dignity, were not discouraged by the invariable contumely of our words, by the disdain of our looks. Our contempt for him was unbounded—and we could not but listen with interest to that consummate artist. He told us we were good men—a "bloomin' condemned lot of good men." Who thanked us? Who took any notice of our wrongs? Didn't we lead a "dorg's loife for two poun' ten a month"? Did we think that miserable pay enough to compensate us for the risk to our lives and for the loss of our clothes? "We've lost every rag!" he cried. He made us forget that he, at any rate, had lost nothing of his own. The younger men listened, thinking—this 'ere Donkin's a longheaded chap, though no kind of man, anyhow. The Scandinavians were frightened at his audacities; Wamibo did not understand; and the older seamen thoughtfully nodded their heads, making the thin gold earrings glitter in the fleshy lobes of hairy ears. Severe, sunburnt faces were propped meditatively on tattooed forearms. Veined, brown fists held in their knotted grip the dirty white clay of smouldering pipes. They listened, impenetrable, broad-backed, with bent shoulders, and in grim silence. He talked with ardour, despised and irrefutable. His picturesque and filthy loquacity flowed like a troubled stream from a poisoned source. His beady little eyes danced, glancing right and left, ever on the watch for the approach of an officer. Sometimes Mr. Baker going forward to take a look at the head sheets[7] would roll with his uncouth gait through the sudden stillness of the men; or Mr. Creighton limped along, smooth-faced, youthful, and more stern than ever, piercing our short silence with a keen glance of his clear eyes. Behind his back Donkin would begin again darting stealthy, sidelong looks.—" 'Ere's one of 'em. Some of yer 'as made 'im

7. Lines controlling the headsails (jibs) which are in front of the foremast.

fast that day. Much thanks yer got for it. Ain't 'ee a-driven' yer wusse'n
ever? . . . Let 'im slip overboard. . . .Vy not? It would 'ave been less trouble. Vy not?" He advanced confidentially, backed away with great effect;
he whispered, he screamed, waved his miserable arms no thicker than
pipe-stems—stretched his lean neck—spluttered—squinted. In the pauses
of his impassioned orations the wind sighed quietly aloft, the calm sea
unheeded murmured in a warning whisper along the ship's side. We abo-
minated the creature and could not deny the luminous truth of his con-
tentions. It was all so obvious. We were indubitably good men; our
deserts were great and our pay small. Through our exertions we had saved
the ship and the skipper would get the credit of it. What had he done?
we wanted to know. Donkin asked:—"What 'ee could do without hus?"
and we could not answer. We were oppressed by the injustice of the
world, surprised to perceive how long we had lived under its burden
without realising our unfortunate state, annoyed by the uneasy suspicion
of our undiscerning stupidity. Donkin assured us it was all our "good 'eart-
edness," but we would not be consoled by such shallow sophistry. We
were men enough to courageously admit to ourselves our intellectual
shortcomings; though from that time we refrained from kicking him,
tweaking his nose, or from accidentally knocking him about, which last,
after we had weathered the Cape, had been rather a popular amusement.
Davis ceased to talk at him provokingly about black eyes and flattened
noses. Charley, much subdued since the gale, did not jeer at him. Knowles
deferentially and with a crafty air propounded questions such as:—"Could
we all have the same grub as the mates? Could we all stop ashore till we
got it? What would be the next thing to try for if we got that?" He
answered readily with contemptuous certitude; he strutted with assurance
in clothes that were much too big for him as though he had tried to
disguise himself. These were Jimmy's clothes mostly—though he would
accept anything from anybody; but nobody, except Jimmy, had anything
to spare. His devotion to Jimmy was unbounded. He was for ever dodging
in the little cabin, ministering to Jimmy's wants, humouring his whims,
submitting to his exacting peevishness, often laughing with him. Nothing
could keep him away from the pious work of visiting the sick, especially
when there was some heavy hauling to be done on deck. Mr. Baker had
on two occasions jerked him out from there by the scruff of the neck to
our inexpressible scandal. Was a sick chap to be left without attendance?
Were we to be ill-used for attending a shipmate?—"What?" growled Mr.
Baker, turning menacingly at the mutter, and the whole half-circle like
one man stepped back a pace. "Set the topmast stunsail. Away aloft, Donkin, overhaul the gear," ordered the mate inflexibly. "Fetch the sail
along; bend the down-haul clear. Bear a hand." Then, the sail set, he
would go slowly aft and stand looking at the compass for a long time,
careworn, pensive, and breathing hard as if stifled by the taint of unaccountable ill-will that pervaded the ship. "What's up amongst them?" he
thought. "Can't make out this hanging back and growling. A good crowd,
too, as they go nowadays." On deck the men exchanged bitter words,
suggested by a silly exasperation against something unjust and irremediable that would not be denied, and would whisper into their ears long
after Donkin had ceased speaking. Our little world went on its curved
and unswerving path carrying a discontented and aspiring population.
They found comfort of a gloomy kind in an interminable and conscien-

tious analysis of their unappreciated worth; and inspired by Donkin's hopeful doctrines they dreamed enthusiastically of the time when every lonely ship would travel over a serene sea, manned by a wealthy and well-fed crew of satisfied skippers.

It looked as if it would be a long passage. The south-east trades, light and unsteady, were left behind; and then, on the equator and under a low grey sky, the ship, in close heat, floated upon a smooth sea that resembled a sheet of ground glass. Thunder squalls hung on the horizon, circled round the ship, far off and growling angrily, like a troop of wild beasts afraid to charge home. The invisible sun, sweeping above the upright masts, made on the clouds a blurred stain of rayless light, and a similar patch of faded radiance kept pace with it from east to west over the unglittering level of the waters. At night, through the impenetrable darkness of earth and of heaven, broad sheets of flame waved noiselessly; and for half a second the becalmed craft stood out with its masts and rigging, with every sail and every rope distinct and black in the centre of a fiery outburst, like a charred ship enclosed in a globe of fire. And, again, for long hours, she remained lost in a vast universe of night and silence where gentle sighs wandering here and there like forlorn souls, made the still sails flutter, as in sudden fear, and the ripple of a beshrouded ocean whisper its compassion afar—in a voice mournful, immense, and faint. . . .

When the lamp was put out, and through the door thrown wide open, Jimmy, turning on his pillow, could see vanishing beyond the straight line of top-gallant rail, the quick, repeated visions of a fabulous world made up of leaping fire and sleeping water. The lightning gleamed in his big sad eyes that seemed in a red flicker to burn themselves out in his black face, and then he would lie blinded and invisible in the midst of an intense darkness. He could hear on the quiet deck soft footfalls, the breathing of some man lounging on the doorstep; the low creak of swaying masts; or the calm voice of the watch-officer reverberating aloft, hard and loud, amongst the unstirring sails. He listened with avidity, taking a rest in the attentive perception of the slightest sound from the fatiguing wanderings of his sleeplessness. He was cheered by the rattling of blocks, reassured by the stir and murmur of the watch, soothed by the slow yawn of some sleepy and weary seaman settling himself deliberately for a snooze on the planks. Life seemed an indestructible thing. It went on in darkness, in sunshine, in sleep; tireless, it hovered affectionately round the imposture of his ready death. It was bright, like the twisted flare of lightning, and more full of surprises than the dark night. It made him safe, and the calm of its overpowering darkness was as precious as its restless and dangerous light.

But in the evening, in the dog-watches, and even far into the first night-watch, a knot of men could always be seen congregated before Jimmy's cabin. They leaned on each side of the door peacefully interested, and with crossed legs; they stood astride the doorstep discoursing, or sat in silent couples on his sea-chest; while against the bulwark along the spare topmast, three or four in a row stared meditatively; with their simple faces lit up by the projected glare of Jimmy's lamp. The little place, repainted white, had, in the night, the brilliance of a silver shrine where a black idol, reclining stiffly under a blanket, blinked its weary eyes and received our homage. Donkin officiated. He had the air of a demonstrator showing a phenomenon, a manifestation bizarre, simple, and meritorious that, to the beholders, should be a profound and an everlasting lesson. "Just look at 'im, 'ee knows what's what—never fear!" he exclaimed now and then, flourishing a hand hard and fleshless like the claw of a snipe. Jimmy, on his back, smiled with reserve and without moving a limb. He affected the langour of extreme weakness, so as to make it manifest to us that our delay in hauling him out from his horrible confinement, and then that night spent on the poop among our selfish neglect to his needs, had "done for him." He rather liked to talk about it, and of course we were always interested. He spoke spasmodically, in fast rushes with long pauses between, as a tipsy man walks. . . . "Cook had just given me a pannikin of hot coffee. . . . Slapped it down there, on my chest—banged the door to. . . . I felt a heavy roll coming; tried to save my coffee, burnt my fingers . . . and fell out of my bunk. . . . She went over so quick. . . . Water came in through the ventilator. . . . I couldn't move the door . . . dark as a grave . . . tried to scramble up into the upper berth. . . . Rats . . . a rat bit my finger as I got up. . . . I could hear him swimming below me. . . . I thought you would never come. . . . I thought you were all gone overboard . . . of course. . . . Could hear nothing but the wind. . . . Then you came . . . to look for the corpse, I suppose. A little more and . . ."

"Man! But ye made a rare lot of noise in here," observed Archie thoughtfully.

"You chaps kicked up such a confounded row above. . . . Enough to scare any one. . . . I didn't know what you were up to. . . . Bash in the blamed planks . . . my head. . . . Just what a silly, scary gang of fools would do. . . . Not much good to me, anyhow. . . . Just as well . . . drown. . . . Pah."

He groaned, snapped his big white teeth, and gazed with scorn. Belfast lifted a pair of dolorous eyes, with a broken-hearted smile, clenched his fists stealthily; blue-eyed Archie caressed his red whiskers with a hesitating hand; the boatswain at the door stared a moment, and brusquely went away with a loud guffaw. Wamibo dreamed. . . . Donkin felt all over his sterile chin for the few rare hairs, and said, triumphantly, with a sidelong glance at Jimmy:—"Look at 'im! Wish I was 'arf has 'ealthy as 'ee is—I do." He jerked a short thumb over his shoulder towards the after end of the ship. "That's the blooming way to do 'em!" he yelped, with forced heartiness. Jimmy said:—"Don't be a dam' fool," in a pleasant voice. Knowles, rubbing his shoulder against the doorpost, remarked shrewdly:—"We can't all go an' be took sick—it would be mutiny."—"Mutiny—gawn!" jeered Donkin; "there's no boomin' law against bein' sick."—"There's six weeks' hard for refoosing dooty," argued Knowles. "I mind I once seed in Cardiff the crew of an overloaded ship—leastways she weren't overloaded, only a fatherly old gentleman with a white beard and an umbreller came along the quay and talked to the hands. Said as how it was crool hard to be drownded in winter just for the sake of a few pounds more for the owner—he said. Nearly cried over them—he did; and he had a square mainsail coat, and a gaff-topsail hat[8] too—all proper. So they chaps they said they wouldn't go to be drownded in winter—depending upon that 'ere Plimsoll man[9] to see 'em through the court. They thought

8. Frock coat and silk top hat.
9. Samuel Plimsoll, an English shipping reformer   known as "the sailor's friend."

to have a bloomin' lark and two or three days' spree. And the beak[1] giv' 'em six weeks coss the ship warn't overloaded. Anyways they made it out in court that she wasn't. There wasn't one overloaded ship in Penarth Dock[2] at all. 'Pears that old coon he was only on pay and allowance from some kind people, under orders to look for overloaded ships, and he couldn't see no further than the length of his umbreller. Some of us in the boarding-house, where I live when I'm looking for a ship in Cardiff, stood by to duck that old weeping spunger in the dock. We kept a good look out, too—but he topped his boom[3] directly he was outside the court. . . . Yes. They got six weeks' hard. . . ."

They listened, full of curiosity, nodding in the pauses their rough pensive faces. Donkin opened his mouth once or twice, but restrained himself. Jimmy lay still with open eyes and not at all interested. A seaman emitted the opinion that after a verdict of atrocious partiality, "the bloomin' beaks go an' drink at the skipper's expense." Others assented. It was clear, of course. Donkin said:—"Well, six weeks ain't much trouble. You sleep all night in, reg'lar, in chokey.[4] Do it on my 'ead." "You are used to it ainch'ee, Donkin?" asked somebody. Jimmy condescended to laugh. It cheered up every one wonderfully. Knowles, with surprising mental agility, shifted his ground. "If we all went sick what would become of the ship? eh?" He posed the problem and grinned all round.—"Let 'er go to 'ell," sneered Donkin. "Damn 'er. She ain't yourn."—"What? Just let her drift?" insisted Knowles in a tone of unbelief.—"Ay! Drift, an' be blowed," affirmed Donkin, with fine recklessness. The other did not see it—meditated.—"The stores would run out," he muttered, "and . . . never get anywhere . . . and what about pay-day?" he added, with greater assurance.—"Jack likes a good pay-day," exclaimed a listener on the doorstep. "Ay, because then the girls put one arm round his neck an' t'other in his pocket, and call him ducky. Don't they, Jack?"—"Jack, you're a terror with the gals."—"He takes three of 'em in tow at once, like one of 'em Watkinses[5] two-funnel tugs waddling away with three schooners behind."—"Jack, you're a lame scamp."—"Jack, tell us about that one with a blue eye and a black eye. Do."—"There's plenty of girls with one black eye along the Highway by . . ." "No, that's a speshul one—come, Jack." Donkin looked severe and disgusted; Jimmy very bored; a grey-haired sea-dog shook his head slightly, smiling at the bowl of his pipe, discreetly amused. Knowles turned about bewildered; stammered first at one, then at another.—'No! . . . I never! . . . can't talk sensible sense midst you. . . . Always on the kid." He retired bashfully—muttering and pleased. They laughed, hooting in the crude light, around Jimmy's bed, where on a white pillow his hollowed black face moved to and fro restlessly. A puff of wind came, made the flame of the lamp leap, and outside, high up, the sails fluttered, while near by the block of the foresheet struck a ringing blow on the iron bulwark. A voice far off cried, "Helm up!" another, more faint, answered, "Hard up, sir!" They became silent—waited expectantly. The grey-haired seaman knocked his pipe on the doorstep and stood up. The ship leaned over gently, and the sea seemed to wake up, murmuring drowsily. "Here's a little wind comin'," said some one very

1. Judge, magistrate.
2. Seaport in southeastern Wales.
3. Got boozed up.
4. Jail.

5. William Watkins founded one of the first steam tugboat companies on the Thames in 1833, which soon became (and still is) the largest.

low. Jimmy turned over slowly to face the breeze. The voice in the night cried loud and commanding:—"Haul the spanker out." The group before the door vanished out of the light. They could be heard tramping aft while they repeated with varied intonations:—"Spanker out!"... "Out spanker, sir!" Donkin remained alone with Jimmy. There was silence. Jimmy opened and shut his lips several times as if swallowing draughts of fresher air; Donkin moved the toes of his bare feet and looked at them thoughtfully.

"Ain't you going to give them a hand with the sail?" asked Jimmy.

"No. If six ov 'em ain't 'nough beef to set that blamed, rotten spanker, they ain't fit to live," answered Donkin in a bored, far-away voice, as though he had been talking from the bottom of a hole. Jimmy considered the conical, fowl-like profile with a queer kind of interest; he was leaning out of his bunk with the calculating, uncertain expression of a man who reflects how best to lay hold of some strange creature that looks as though it could sting or bite. But he said only:—"The mate will miss you—and there will be ructions."

Donkin got up to go. "I will do for 'em some dark night; see if I don't," he said over his shoulder.

Jimmy went on quickly:—"You're like a poll-parrot, like a screechin' poll-parrot." Donkin stopped and cocked his head attentively on one side. His big ears stood out, transparent and veined, resembling the thin wings of a bat.

"Yuss!" he said, with his back towards Jimmy.

"Yes! Chatter out all you know—like . . . like a dirty white cockatoo."

Donkin waited. He could hear the other's breathing, long and slow; the breathing of a man with a hundredweight or so on the breastbone. Then he asked calmly:—"What do I know?"

"What? . . . What I tell you . . . not much. What do you want . . . to talk about my health so . . ."

"It's a bloomin' imposyshun. A bloomin', stinkin', first-class imposyshun—but it don't tyke me in. Not it."

Jimmy kept still. Donkin put his hands in his pockets, and in one slouching stride came up to the bunk.

"I talk—what's the odds. They ain't men 'ere—sheep they are. A driven lot of sheep. I 'old you up. . . . Vy not? You're well orf."

"I am . . . I don't say anything about that. . . ."

"Well. Let 'em see it. Let 'em larn what a man can do. I am a man, I know all about yer. . . ." Jimmy threw himself farther away on the pillow; the other stretched out his skinny neck, jerked his birdface down at him as though pecking at the eyes. "I am a man. I've seen the inside of every chokey in the Colonies rather'n give up my rights. . . ."

"You are a jail-prop,"[6] said Jimmy weakly.

"I am . . . an' proud of it too. You! You 'aven't the bloomin' nerve—so you inventyd this 'ere dodge. . . ." He paused; then with marked afterthought accentuated slowly:—"Yer ain't sick—are yer?"

"No," said Jimmy firmly. "Been out of sorts now and again this year," he mumbled, with a sudden drop in his voice.

Donkin closed one eye, amicable and confidential. He whispered:—"Ye 'ave done this afore, 'aven'tchee?" Jimmy smiled—then as if unable to

6. One who supports or holds up the jail.

hold back he let himself go:—"Last ship—yes. I was out of sorts on the passage. See? It was easy. They paid me off in Calcutta, and the skipper made no bones about it either. . . . I got my money all right. Laid up fifty-eight days! The fools! O Lord! The fools! Paid right off." He laughed spasmodically. Donkin chimed in giggling. Then Jimmy coughed violently. "I am as well as ever," he said, as soon as he could draw breath. Donkin made a derisive gesture. "In course," he said profoundly, "any one can see that."—"They don't," said Jimmy, gasping like a fish.—"They would swallow any yarn," affirmed Donkin.—"Don't you let on too much," admonished Jimmy in an exhausted voice.—"Your little gyme? Eh?" commented Donkin jovially. Then with sudden disgust: "Yer all for yerself, s'long as ye're right. . . ."

So charged with egoism James Wait pulled the blanket up to his chin and lay still for a while. His heavy lips protruded in an everlasting black pout. "Why are you so hot on making trouble?" he asked, without much interest.

"'Cos it's a bloomin' shayme. We are put upon . . . bad food, bad pay . . . I want us to kick up a bloomin' row; a blamed 'owling row that would make 'em remember! Knocking people about . . . brain us . . . indeed! Ain't we men?" His altruistic indignation blazed. Then he said calmly:—"I've been airing yer clothes."—"All right," said Jimmy languidly, "bring them in."—"Giv' us the key of your chest, I'll put 'em away for yer," said Donkin, with friendly eagerness.—"Bring 'em in, I will put them away myself," answered James Wait, with severity. Donkin looked down, muttering. . . . "What d'you say? What d'you say?" inquired Wait anxiously.—"Nothink. The night's dry, let 'em 'ang out till the morning," said Donkin, in a strangely trembling voice, as though restraining laughter or rage. Jimmy seemed satisfied.—"Give me a little water for the night in my mug—there," he said. Donkin took a stride over the doorstep.—"Git it yerself," he replied in a surly tone. "You can do it, unless you *are* sick."—"Of course I can do it," said Wait, "only . . ."—"Well, then, do it," said Donkin viciously, "if yer can look after yer clothes, yer can look after yerself." He went on deck without a look back.

Jimmy reached out for the mug. Not a drop. He put it back gently, with a faint sigh—and closed his eyes. He thought:—That lunatic Belfast will bring me some water if I ask. Fool. I am very thirsty. . . . It was very hot in the cabin, and it seemed to turn slowly round, detach itself from the ship, and swing out smoothly into a luminous, arid space where a black sun shone, spinning very fast. A place without any water! No water! A policeman with the face of Donkin drank a glass of beer by the side of an empty well, and flew away flapping vigorously. A ship whose mast-heads protruded through the sky and could not be seen, was discharging grain, and the wind whirled the dry husks in spirals along the quay of a dock with no water in it. He whirled along with the husks—very tired and light. All his inside was gone. He felt lighter than the husks—and more dry. He expanded his hollow chest. The air streamed in, carrying away in its rush a lot of strange things that resembled houses, trees, people, lamp-posts. . . . No more! There was no more air—and he had not finished drawing his long breath. But he was in jail! They were locking him up. A door slammed. They turned the key twice, flung a bucket of water over him— Phoo! What for?

He opened his eyes, thinking the fall had been very heavy for an empty

man empty—empty. He was in his cabin. Ah! All right! His face was
streaming with perspiration, his arms heavier than lead. He saw the cook
standing in the doorway, a brass key in one hand and a bright tin hook-
pot in the other.

"I have locked up the galley for the night," said the cook, beaming
benevolently. "Eight bells just gone. I brought you a pot of cold tea for
your night's drinking, Jimmy. I sweetened it with some white cabin sugar,
too. Well—it won't break the ship."

He came in, hung the pot on the edge of the bunk, asked perfunctorily,
"How goes it?" and sat down on the box.—"H'm," grunted Wait inhospit-
ably. The cook wiped his face with a dirty cotton rag, which, afterwards,
he tied round his neck.—"That's how them firemen do in steamboats," he
said serenely, and much pleased with himself. "My work is as heavy as
theirs—I'm thinking—and longer hours. Did you ever see them down the
stokehold? Like fiends they look—firing—firing—firing—down there."

He pointed his forefinger at the deck. Some gloomy thought darkened
his shining face, fleeting, like the shadow of a travelling cloud over the
light of a peaceful sea. The relieved watch tramped noisily forward, passing in a body across the sheen of the doorway. Some one cried, "Good
night!" Belfast stopped for a moment and looked at Jimmy, quivering and
speechless with repressed emotion. He gave the cook a glance charged
with dismal foreboding, and vanished. The cook cleared his throat. Jimmy
stared upwards and kept as still as a man in hiding.

The night was clear, with a gentle breeze. Above the mastheads the
resplendent curve of the Milky Way spanned the sky like a triumphal
arch of eternal light, thrown over the dark pathway of the earth. On the
forecastle head a man whistled with loud precision a lively jig, while another could be heard faintly, shuffling and stamping in time. There came
from forward a confused murmur of voices, laughter—snatches of song.
The cook shook his head, glanced obliquely at Jimmy, and began to mutter. "Ay. Dance and sing. That's all they think of. I am surprised that
Providence don't get tired. . . . They forget the day that's sure to
come . . . but you. . . ."

Jimmy drank a gulp of tea hurriedly, as though he had stolen it, and
shrank under his blanket, edging away towards the bulkhead. The cook
got up, closed the door, then sat down again and said distinctly:—

"Whenever I poke my galley fire I think of you chaps—swearing, stealing, lying, and worse—as if there was no such thing as another
world. . . . Not bad fellows, either, in a way," he conceded slowly; then,
after a pause of regretful musing, he went on in a resigned tone:—"Well,
well. They will have a hot time of it. Hot! Did I say? The furnaces of one
of them White Star boats[7] ain't nothing to it."

He kept very quiet for a while. There was a great stir in his brain; an
addled vision of bright outlines; an exciting row of rousing songs and
groans of pain. He suffered, enjoyed, admired, approved. He was delighted, frightened, exalted—as on that evening (the only time in his life—
twenty-seven years ago; he loved to recall the number of years) when as a
young man he had—through keeping bad company—become intoxicated
in an East-end music-hall. A tide of sudden feeling swept him clean out of
his body. He soared. He contemplated the secret of the hereafter. It com-

7. The White Star Line, founded in Liverpool in   to New York.
the 1850s, in 1870 initiated "express luxury" service

mended itself to him. It was excellent; he loved it, himself, all hands, and Jimmy. His heart overflowed with tenderness, with comprehension, with the desire to meddle, with anxiety for the soul of that black man, with the pride of possessed eternity, with the feeling of might. Snatch him up in his arms and pitch him right into the middle of salvation ... the black soul—blacker—body—rot—Devil. No! Talk—strength—Samson.... There was a great din as of cymbals in his ears; he flashed through an ecstatic jumble of shining faces, lilies, prayer-books, unearthly joy, white skirts, gold harps, black coats, wings. He saw flowing garments, clean shaved faces, a sea of light—a lake of pitch. There were sweet scents, a smell of sulphur—red tongues of flame licking a white mist. An awesome voice thundered! ... It lasted three seconds.

"Jimmy!" he cried in an inspired tone. Then he hesitated. A spark of human pity glimmered yet through the infernal fog of his supreme conceit.

"What?" said James Wait unwillingly. There was a silence. He turned his head just the least bit, and stole a cautious glance. The cook's lips moved without a sound; his face was rapt, his eyes turned up. He seemed to be mentally imploring deck beams, the brass hook of the lamp, two cockroaches.

"Look here," said Wait. "I want to go to sleep. I think I could."

"This is no time for sleep!" exclaimed the cook, very loud. He had prayerfully divested himself of the last vestige of his humanity. He was a voice—a fleshless and sublime thing, as on that memorable night—the night when he went walking over the sea to make coffee for perishing sinners. "This is no time for sleeping," he repeated, with exaltation. "*I* can't sleep."

"Don't care damn," said Wait, with factitious energy. "I can. Go an' turn in."

"Swear ... in the very jaws! ... In the very jaws! Don't you see the everlasting fire ... don't you feel it? Blind, chockfull of sin! Repent, repent! I can't bear to think of you. I hear the call to save you. Night and day. Jimmy, let me save you!" The words of entreaty and menace broke out of him in a roaring torrent. The cockroaches ran away. Jimmy perspired, wriggling stealthily under his blanket. The cook yelled.... "Your days are numbered! ..."—"Get out of this," boomed Wait courageously.—"Pray with me! ..."—"I won't! ..." The little cabin was as hot as an oven. It contained an immensity of fear and pain; an atmosphere of shrieks and moans; prayers vociferated like blasphemies and whispered curses. Outside, the men called by Charley, who informed them in tones of delight that there was a holy row going on in Jimmy's place, crowded before the closed door, too startled to open it. All hands were there. The watch below had jumped out on deck in their shirts, as after a collision. Men running up, asked:—"What is it?" Others said:—"Listen!" The muffled screaming went on:—"On your knees! On your knees!"—"Shut up!"—"Never! You are delivered into my hands.... Your life has been saved.... Purpose.... Mercy.... Repent."—"You are a crazy fool! ..."—"Account of you ... you ... Never sleep in this world, if I ..."—"Leave off."—"No! ... stokehold ... only think! ..." Then an impassioned screeching babble where words pattered like hail.—"No!" shouted Wait.—"Yes. You are! ... No help.... Everybody says so."—"You lie!"—"I see you dying this minnyt ... before my eyes ... as good as dead already."—

"Help!" shouted Jimmy piercingly.—"Not in this valley . . . look upwards," howled the other.—"Go away! Murder! Help!" clamoured Jimmy. His voice broke. There were moanings, low mutters, a few sobs.

"What's the matter now?" said a seldom-heard voice.—"Fall back, men! Fall back, there!" repeated Mr. Creighton sternly, pushing through.— "Here's the old man," whispered some.—"The cook's in there, sir," exclaimed several, backing away. The door clattered open; a broad stream of light darted out on wondering faces; a warm whiff of vitiated air passed. The two mates towered head and shoulders above the spare, grey-haired man who stood revealed between them, in shabby clothes, stiff and angular, like a small carved figure, and with a thin, composed face. The cook got up from his knees. Jimmy sat high in the bunk, clasping his drawn-up legs. The tassel of the blue night-cap almost imperceptibly trembled over his knees. They gazed astonished at his long, curved back, while the white corner of one eye gleamed blindly at them. He was afraid to turn his head, he shrank within himself; and there was an aspect astounding and animal-like in the perfection of his expectant immobility. A thing of instinct—the unthinking stillness of a scared brute.

"What are you doing here?" asked Mr. Baker sharply.—"My duty," said the cook, with ardour.—"Your . . . what?" began the mate. Captain Allistoun touched his arm lightly.—"I know his caper," he said in a low voice. "Come out of that, Podmore," he ordered, aloud.

The cook wrung his hands, shook his fists above his head, and his arms dropped as if too heavy. For a moment he stood distracted and speechless.—"Never," he stammered, "I . . . he . . . I."—"What—do—you—say?" pronounced Captain Allistoun. "Come out at once—or . . ."—"I am going," said the cook, with a hasty and sombre resignation. He strode over the doorstep firmly—hesitated—made a few steps. They looked at him in silence.—"I make you responsible!" he cried desperately, turning half round. "That man is dying. I make you . . ."—"You there yet?" called the master in a threatening tone.—"No, sir," he exclaimed hurriedly in a startled voice. The boatswain led him away by the arm; some one laughed; Jimmy lifted his head for a stealthy glance, and in one unexpected leap sprang out of his bunk; Mr. Baker made a clever catch and felt him very limp in his arms; the group at the door grunted with surprise.—"He lies," gasped Wait, "he talked about black devils—he is a devil—a white devil—I am all right." He stiffened himself, and Mr. Baker, experimentally, let him go. He staggered a pace or two; Captain Allistoun watched him with a quiet and penetrating gaze; Belfast ran to his support. He did not appear to be aware of any one near him; he stood silent for a moment, battling single-handed with a legion of nameless terrors, amidst the eager looks of excited men who watched him far off, utterly alone in the impenetrable solitude of his fear. The sea gurgled through the scuppers as the ship heeled over to a short puff of wind.

"Keep him away from me," said James Wait at last in his fine baritone voice, and leaning with all his weight on Belfast's neck. "I've been better this last week . . . I am well . . . I was going back to duty . . . to-morrow—now if you like—Captain." Belfast hitched his shoulders to keep him upright.

"No," said the master, looking at him, fixedly.

Under Jimmy's armpit Belfast's red face moved uneasily. A row of eyes, gleaming, stared on the edge of light. They pushed one another with elbows, turned their heads, whispered. Wait let his chin fall on his breast and, with lowered eyelids, looked round in a suspicious manner.

"Why not?" cried a voice from the shadows, "the man's all right, sir." "I am all right," said Wait, with eagerness. "Been sick . . . better . . . turn-to now." He sighed.—"Howly Mother!" exclaimed Belfast, with a heave of the shoulders, "stand up, Jimmy."—"Keep away from me, then," said Wait, giving Belfast a petulant push, and reeling fetched against the door-post. His cheekbones glistened as though they had been varnished. He snatched off his night-cap, wiped his perspiring face with it, flung it on the deck. "I am coming out," he declared, without stirring.

"No. You don't," said the master curtly. Bare feet shuffled, disapproving voices murmured all round; he went on as if he had not heard:—"You have been skulking nearly all the passage and now you want to come out. You think you are near enough to the pay-table now. Smell the shore, hey?"

"I've been sick . . . now—better," mumbled Wait, glaring in the light.— "You have been shamming sick," retorted Captain Allistoun, with severity. "Why . . ." He hesitated for less than half a second. "Why, anybody can see that. There's nothing the matter with you, but you choose to lie-up to please yourself—and now you shall lie-up to please me. Mr. Baker, my orders are that this man is not allowed to be on deck to the end of this passage."

There were exclamations of surprise, triumph, indignation. The dark group of men swung across the light. "What for?" "Told you so . . ."— "Bloomin' shame . . ."—"We've got to say somethink about that," screeched Donkin from the rear.—"Never mind, Jimmy, we will see you righted," cried several together. An elderly seaman stepped to the front. "D'ye mean to say, sir," he asked ominously, "that a sick chap ain't allowed to get well in this 'ere hooker?" Behind him Donkin whispered excitedly amongst a staring crowd where no one spared him a glance, but Captain Allistoun shook a forefinger at the angry bronzed face of the speaker.—"You—you hold your tongue," he said warningly.—"This isn't the way," clamoured two or three younger men.—"Are we bloomin' masheens?" inquired Donkin in a piercing tone, and dived under the elbows of the front rank.—"Soon show 'm we ain't boys . . ."—"The man's a man if he is black."—"We ain't goin' to work this bloomin' ship shorthanded if Snowball's all right . . ."—"He says he is."—"Well then, strike, boys, strike!"—"That's the bloomin' ticket." Captain Allistoun said sharply to the second mate: "Keep quiet, Mr. Creighton," and stood composed in the tumult, listening with profound attention to mixed growls and screeches, to every exclamation and every curse of the sudden outbreak. Somebody slammed the cabin door to with a kick; the darkness full of menacing mutters leaped with a short clatter over the streak of light, and the men became gesticulating shadows that growled, hissed, laughed excitedly. Mr. Baker whispered:—"Get away from them, sir." The big shape of Mr. Creighton hovered silently about the slight figure of the master.— "We have been imposed upon all this voyage," said a gruff voice, "but this 'ere fancy takes the cake."—"That man is a shipmate."—"Are we bloomin' kids?"—"The port watch will refuse duty." Charley carried away by his feelings whistled shrilly, then yelped:—"Giv'us our Jimmy!" This seemed to cause a variation in the disturbance. There was a fresh burst of squabbling uproar. A lot of quarrels were set going at once.—"Yes."—

"No."—"Never been sick."—"Go for them to once."—"Shut yer mouth, youngster—this is men's work."—"Is it?" muttered Captain Allistoun bitterly. Mr. Baker grunted: "Ough! They're gone silly. They've been simmering for the last month."—"I did notice," said the master.—"They have started a row amongst themselves now," said Mr. Creighton, with disdain, "better get aft, sir. We will soothe them."—"Keep your temper, Creighton," said the master. And the three men began to move slowly towards the cabin door.

In the shadows of the fore rigging a dark mass stamped, eddied, advanced, retreated. There were words of reproach, encouragement, unbelief, execration. The elder seamen, bewildered and angry, growled their determination to go through with something or other; but the younger school of advanced thought exposed their and Jimmy's wrongs with confused shouts, arguing amongst themselves. They clustered round that moribund carcass, the fit emblem of their aspirations, and encouraging one another they swayed, they tramped on one spot, shouting that they would not be "put upon." Inside the cabin, Belfast, helping Jimmy into his bunk, twitched all over in his desire not to miss all the row, and with difficulty restrained the tears of his facile emotion. James Wait, flat on his back under the blanket, gasped complaints.—"We will back you up, never fear," assured Belfast, busy about his feet.—"I'll come out to-morrow morning—take my chance—you fellows must——" mumbled Wait, "I come out to-morrow—skipper or no skipper." He lifted one arm with great difficulty, passed the hand over his face; "Don't you let that cook . . ." he breathed out.—"No, no," said Belfast, turning his back on the bunk, "I will put a head on him if he comes near you."—"I will smash his mug!" exclaimed faintly Wait, enraged and weak; "I don't want to kill a man, but . . ." He panted fast like a dog after a run in sunshine. Some one just outside the door shouted, "He's as fit as any ov us!" Belfast put his hand on the door-handle.—"Here!" called James Wait hurriedly and in such a clear voice that the other spun round with a start. James Wait, stretched out black and deathlike in the dazzling light, turned his head on the pillow. His eyes stared at Belfast, appealing and impudent. "I am rather weak from lying-up so long," he said distinctly. Belfast nodded. "Getting quite well now," insisted Wait.—"Yes. I noticed you getting better this . . . last month," said Belfast looking down. "Hallo! What's this?" he shouted and ran out.

He was flattened directly against the side of the house by two men who lurched against him. A lot of disputes seemed to be going on all round. He got clear and saw three indistinct figures standing alone in the fainter darkness under the arched foot of the mainsail, that rose above their heads like a convex wall of a high edifice. Donkin hissed:—"Go for them . . . it's dark!" The crowd took a short run aft in a body—then there was a check. Donkin, agile and thin, flitted past with his right arm going like a windmill—and then stood still suddenly with his arm pointing rigidly above his head. The hurtling flight of some heavy object was heard; it passed between the heads of the two mates, bounded heavily along the deck, struck the after hatch with a ponderous and deadened blow. The bulky shape of Mr. Baker grew distinct. "Come to your senses, men!" he cried, advancing at the arrested crowd. "Come back, Mr. Baker!" called the master's quiet voice. He obeyed unwillingly. There was a minute of silence, then a deafening hubbub arose. Above it Archie was heard ener-

getically:—"If ye do oot ageen I wull tell!" There were shouts. "Don't!"—
"Drop it!"—"We ain't that kind!" The black cluster of human forms
reeled against the bulwark, back again towards the house. Ringbolts rang
under stumbling feet.—"Drop it!"—"Let me!"—"No!"—"Curse
you . . . hah!" Then sounds as of some one's face being slapped; a piece of
iron fell on the deck; a short scuffle, and some one's shadowy body scuttled rapidly across the main hatch before the shadow of a kick. A raging
voice sobbed out a torrent of filthy language. . . . "Throwing things—good
God!" grunted Mr. Baker in dismay.—"That was meant for me," said the
master quietly; "I felt the wind of that thing; what was it—an iron belaying-pin?"—"By Jove!" muttered Mr. Creighton. The confused voices of
men talking amidships mingled with the wash of the sea, ascended between the silent and distended sails—seemed to flow away into the night,
farther than the horizon, higher than the sky. The stars burned steadily
over the inclined mastheads. Trails of light lay on the water, broke before
the advancing hull, and, after she had passed, trembled for a long time as
if in awe of the murmuring sea.

Meantime the helmsman, anxious to know what the row was about, had
let go the wheel, and, bent double, ran with long stealthy footsteps to the
break of the poop. The *Narcissus,* left to herself, came up gently to
the wind without any one being aware of it. She gave a slight roll, and
the sleeping sails woke suddenly, coming all together with a mighty flap
against the masts, then filled again one after another in a quick succession
of loud reports that ran down the lofty spars, till the collapsed mainsail
flew out last with a violent jerk. The ship trembled from trucks to keel;
the sails kept on rattling like a discharge of musketry; the chain sheets
and loose shackles jingled aloft in a thin peal; the gin blocks[8] groaned. It
was as if an invisible hand had given the ship an angry shake to recall the
men that peopled her decks to the sense of reality, vigilance, and duty.—
"Helm up!" cried the master sharply. "Run aft, Mr. Creighton, and see
what that fool there is up to."—"Flatten in the head sheets. Stand by the
weather fore-braces," growled Mr. Baker. Startled men ran swiftly repeating the orders. The watch below, abandoned all at once by the watch on
deck, drifted towards the forecastle in twos and threes, arguing noisily as
they went—"We shall see to-morrow!" cried a loud voice, as if to cover
with a menacing hint an inglorious retreat. And then only orders were
heard, the falling of heavy coils of rope, the rattling of blocks. Singleton's
white head flitted here and there in the night, high above the deck, like
the ghost of a bird.—"Going off, sir!" shouted Mr. Creighton from aft.—
"Full again."—"All right. . . ."—"Ease off the head sheets. That will do the
braces. Coil the ropes up," grunted Mr. Baker, bustling about.

Gradually the tramping noises, the confused sound of voices, died out,
and the officers, coming together on the poop, discussed the events. Mr.
Baker was bewildered and grunted; Mr. Creighton was calmly furious;
but Captain Allistoun was composed and thoughtful. He listened to Mr.
Baker's growling argumentation, to Creighton's interjected and severe remarks, while looking down on the deck he weighed in his hand the iron
belaying-pin—that a moment ago had just missed his head—as if it had
been the only tangible fact of the whole transaction. He was one of those
commanders who speak little, seem to hear nothing, look at no one—and

8. Blocks having large pulleys in open metal frames, used especially to support a cargo tackle.

know everything, hear every whisper, see every floeting shadow of their ship's life. His two big officers towered above his lean, short figure; they talked over his head; they were dismayed, surprised, and angry, while between them the little quiet man seemed to have found his taciturn serenity in the profound depths of a larger experience. Lights were burning in the forecastle; now and then a loud gust of babbling chatter came from forward, swept over the decks, and became faint, as if the unconscious ship, gliding gently through the great peace of the sea, had left behind and for ever the foolish noise of turbulent mankind. But it was renewed again and again. Gesticulating arms, profiles and heads with open mouths appeared for a moment in the illuminated squares of doorways; black fists darted—withdrew.... "Yes. It was most damnable to have such an unprovoked row sprung on one," assented the master.... A tumult of yells rose in the light, abruptly ceased.... He didn't think there would be any further trouble just then.... A bell was struck aft, another, forward, answered in a deeper tone, and the clamour of ringing metal spread round the ship in a circle of wide vibrations that ebbed away into the immeasurable night of an empty sea.... Didn't he know them! Didn't he! In past years. Better men, too. Real men to stand by one in a tight place. Worse than devils too sometimes—downright, horned devils. Pah! This—nothing. A miss as good as a mile.... The wheel was being relieved in the usual way.—"Full and by,"[9] said, very loud, the man going off.— "Full and by," repeated the other, catching hold of the spokes.—"This head wind is my trouble," exclaimed the master, stamping his foot in sudden anger; "head wind! all the rest is nothing." He was calm again in a moment. "Keep them on the move to-night, gentlemen; just to let them feel we've got hold all the time—quietly, you know. Mind you keep your hands off them, Creighton. Tomorrow I will talk to them like a Dutch Uncle. A crazy crowd of tinkers! Yes, tinkers! I could count the real sailors amongst them on the fingers of one hand. Nothing will do but a row— if—you—please." He paused. "Did you think I had gone wrong there, Mr. Baker?" He tapped his forehead, laughed short. "When I saw him standing there, three parts dead and so scared—black amongst the gaping lot— no grit to face what's coming to us all—the notion came to me all at once, before I could think. Sorry for him—as you would be for a sick brute. If ever creature was in a mortal funk to die! ... I thought I would let him go out in his own way. Kind of impulse. It never came into my head, those fools.... H'm! Stand to it now—of course." He stuck the belaying-pin in his pocket, seemed ashamed of himself, then sharply:—"If you see Podmore at his tricks again tell him I will have him put under the pump. Had to do it once before. The fellow breaks out like that now and then. Good cook tho'." He walked away quickly, came back to the companion. The two mates followed him through the starlight with amazed eyes. He went down three steps, and changing his tone, spoke with his head near the deck:—"I shan't turn in to-night, in case of anything; just call out if ... Did you see the eyes of that sick nigger, Mr. Baker? I fancied he begged me for something. What? Past all help. One lone black beggar amongst the lot of us, and he seemed to look through me into the very hell. Fancy, this wretched Podmore! Well, let him die in peace. I am master here after all. Let him be. He might have been half a man

9. Condition of a sailing vessel when she is held as   not shivering.
close to the wind as possible with the sails full and

once. . . . Keep a good look-out." He disappeared down below, leaving his mates facing one another, and more impressed than if they had seen a stone image shed a miraculous tear of compassion over the incertitudes of life and death. . . .

In the blue mist spreading from twisted threads that stood upright in the bowls of pipes, the forecastle appeared as vast as a hall. Between the beams a heavy cloud stagnated; and the lamps surrounded by halos burned each at the core of a purple glow in two lifeless flames without rays. Wreaths drifted in denser wisps. Men sprawled about on the deck, sat in negligent poses, or, bending a knee, drooped with one shoulder against a bulkhead. Lips moved, eyes flashed, waving arms made sudden eddies in the smoke. The murmur of voices seemed to pile itself higher and higher as if unable to run out quick enough through the narrow doors. The watch below in their shirts, and striding on long white legs, resembled raving somnambulists; while now and then one of the watch on deck would rush in, looking strangely overdressed, listen a moment, fling a rapid sentence into the noise and run out again; but a few remained near the door, fascinated, and with one ear turned to the deck. "Stick together, boys," roared Davis. Belfast tried to make himself heard. Knowles grinned in a slow, dazed way. A short fellow with a thick clipped beard kept on yelling periodically:—"Who's afeard? Who's afeard?" Another one jumped up, excited, with blazing eyes, sent out a string of unattached curses and sat down quietly. Two men discussed familiarly, striking one another's breast in turn, to clinch arguments. Three others, with their heads in a bunch, spoke all together with a confidential air, and at the top of their voices. It was a stormy chaos of speech where intelligible fragments tossing, struck the ear. One could hear:—"In the last ship"—"Who cares? Try it on any one of us if——." "Knock under"[1]—"Not a hand's turn"—"He says he is all right"—"I always thought"—"Never mind. . . ." Donkin, crouching all in a heap against the bowsprit, hunched his shoulder blades as high as his ears, and hanging a peaked nose, resembled a sick vulture with ruffled plumes. Belfast, straddling his legs, had a face red with yelling, and with arms thrown up, figured a Maltese cross. The two Scandinavians, in a corner, had the dumbfounded and distracted aspect of men gazing at a cataclysm. And, beyond the light, Singleton stood in the smoke, monumental, indistinct, with his head touching the beam; like a statue of heroic size in the gloom of a crypt.

He stepped forward, impassive and big. The noise subsided like a broken wave: but Belfast cried once more with uplifted arms:—"The man is dying, I tell ye!" then sat down suddenly on the hatch and took his head between his hands. All looked at Singleton, gazing upwards from the deck, staring out of dark corners, or turning their heads with curious glances. They were expectant and appeased as if that old man, who looked at no one, had possessed the secret of their uneasy indignations and desires, a sharper vision, a clearer knowledge. And indeed standing there amongst them, he had the uninterested appearance of one who had seen multitudes of ships, had listened many times to voices such as theirs, had already seen all that could happen on the wide seas. They heard his voice rumble in his broad chest as though the words had been rolling towards them out of a rugged past. "What do you want to do?" he asked.

1. Give up, knuckle under; acknowledge oneself beaten.

No one answered. Only Knowles muttered—"Ay, ay," and somebody said low:—"It's a bloomin' shame." He waited, made a contemptuous gesture.—"I have seen rows aboard ship before some of you were born," he said slowly, "for something or nothing; but never for such a thing."—"The man is dying, I tell ye," repeated Belfast woefully, sitting at Singleton's feet.—"And a black fellow, too," went on the old seaman, "I have seen them die like flies." He stopped, thoughtful, as if trying to recollect gruesome things, details of horrors, hecatombs of niggers. They looked at him fascinated. He was old enough to remember slavers, bloody mutinies, pirates perhaps; who could tell through what violences and terrors he had lived! What would he say? He said:—"You can't help him; die he must." He made another pause. His moustache and beard stirred. He chewed words, mumbled behind tangled white hairs; incomprehensible and exciting, like an oracle behind a veil. . . .—"Stop ashore—sick.—Instead—bringing all this head wind. Afraid. The sea will have her own.—Die in sight of land. Always so. They know it—long passage—more days, more dollars.— You keep quiet.—What do you want? Can't help him." He seemed to wake up from a dream. "You can't help yourselves," he said austerely. "Skipper's no fool. He has something in his mind. Look out—I say! I know 'em!" With eyes fixed in front he turned his head from right to left, from left to right, as if inspecting a long row of astute skippers.—"'Ee said 'ee would brain me!" cried Donkin in a heartrending tone. Singleton peered downwards with puzzled attention, as though he couldn't find him.— "Damn you!" he said vaguely, giving it up. He radiated unspeakable wisdom, hard unconcern, the chilling air of resignation. Round him all the listeners felt themselves somehow completely enlightened by their disappointment, and mute, they lolled about with the careless ease of men who can discern perfectly the irremediable aspect of their existence. He, profound and unconscious, waved his arm once, and strode out on deck without another word.

Belfast was lost in a round-eyed meditation. One or two vaulted heavily into upper berths, and, once there, sighed; others dived head first inside lower bunks—swift, and turning round instantly upon themselves, like animals going into lairs. The grating of a knife scraping burnt clay was heard. Knowles grinned no more. Davis said, in a tone of ardent conviction:—"Then our skipper's looney." Archie muttered:—"My faith! we haven't heard the last of it yet!"

Four bells were struck.—"Half our watch below gone!" cried Knowles in alarm, then reflected. "Well, two hours' sleep is something towards a rest," he observed consolingly. Some already pretended to slumber; and Charley, sound asleep, suddenly said a few slurred words in an arbitrary, blank voice.—"This blamed boy has worrums!" commented Knowles from under a blanket, in a learned manner. Belfast got up and approached Archie's berth.—"We pulled him out," he whispered sadly.—"What?" said the other, with sleepy discontent.—"And now we will have to chuck him overboard," went on Belfast, whose lower lip trembled.—"Chuck what?" asked Archie.—"Poor Jimmy," breathed out Belfast.—"He be blowed!" said Archie with untruthful brutality, and sat up in his bunk; "It's all through him. If it hadn't been for me, there would have been murder on board this ship!"—"'Tain't his fault, is it?" argued Belfast, in a murmur; "I've put him to bed . . . an' he ain't no heavier than an empty beef-cask," he added, with tears in his eyes. Archie looked at him steadily, then turned his nose to the ship's side with determination. Belfast wandered about as though he had lost his way in the dim forecastle, and nearly fell over Donkin. He contemplated him from on high for a while. "Ain't ye going to turn in?" he asked. Donkin looked up hopelessly.—"That black'earted Scotch son of a thief kicked me!" he whispered from the floor, in a tone of utter desolation.—"And a good job, too!" said Belfast, still very depressed. "You were as near hanging as damn-it to-night, sonny. Don't you play any of your murthering games around my Jimmy! You haven't pulled him out. You just mind! 'Cos if I start to kick you"—he brightened up a bit—"if I start to kick you, it will be Yankee fashion—to break something!" He tapped lightly with his knuckles the top of the bowed head. "You moind that, my bhoy!" he concluded cheerily. Donkin let it pass.—"Will they split² on me?" he asked, with pained anxiety.— "Who—split?" hissed Belfast, coming back a step. "I would split your nose this minnyt if I hadn't Jimmy to look after! Who d'ye think we are?" Donkin rose and watched Belfast's back lurch through the doorway. On all sides invisible men slept, breathing calmly. He seemed to draw courage and fury from the peace around him. Venomous and thin-faced, he glared from the ample misfit of borrowed clothes as if looking for something he could smash. His heart leaped wildly in his narrow chest. They slept! He wanted to wring necks, gouge eyes, spit on faces. He shook a dirty pair of meagre fists at the smoking lights. "Ye're no men!" he cried, in a deadened tone. No one moved. "Yer 'aven't the pluck of a mouse!" His voice rose to a husky screech. Wamibo darted out a dishevel- led head, and looked at him wildly. "Ye're sweepings ov ships! I 'ope you will all rot before you die!" Wamibo blinked, uncomprehending but inter- ested. Donkin sat down heavily; he blew with force through quivering nostrils, he ground and snapped his teeth, and, with the chin pressed hard against the breast, he seemed busy gnawing his way through it, as if to get at the heart within. . . .

In the morning the ship, beginning another day of her wandering life, had an aspect of sumptuous freshness, like the spring-time of the earth. The washed decks glistened in the long clear stretch; the oblique sunlight struck the yellow brasses in dazzling splashes, darted over the polished rods in lines of gold, and the single drops of salt water forgotten here and there along the rail were as limpid as drops of dew, and sparkled more than scattered diamonds. The sails slept, hushed by a gentle breeze. The sun, rising lonely and splendid in the blue sky, saw a solitary ship gliding close-hauled³ on the blue sea.

The men pressed three deep abreast of the mainmast and opposite the cabin door. They shuffled, pushed, had an irresolute mien and stolid faces. At every slight movement Knowles lurched heavily on his short leg. Don- kin glided behind backs, restless and anxious, like a man looking for an ambush. Captain Allistoun came out on the quarter-deck suddenly. He walked to and fro before the front. He was grey, slight, alert, shabby in the sunshine, and as hard as adamant. He had his right hand in the side- pocket of his jacket, and also something heavy in there that made folds all down that side. One of the seamen cleared his throat ominously.—"I haven't till now found fault with you men," said the master, stopping

2. Inform, tell.
3. As close to the wind as a vessel will sail, with sails as flat as possible.

short. He faced them with his worn, steely gaze, that by a universal illusion looked straight into every individual pair of the twenty pairs of eyes before his face. At his back Mr. Baker, gloomy and bullnecked, grunted low; Mr. Creighton, fresh as paint, had rosy cheeks and a ready, resolute bearing. "And I don't now," continued the master; "but I am here to drive this ship and keep every man-jack aboard of her up to the mark. If you knew your work as well as I do mine, there would be no trouble. You've been braying in the dark about 'See to-morrow morning!' Well, you see me now. What do you want?" He waited, stepping quickly to and fro, giving them searching glances. What did they want? They shifted from foot to foot, they balanced their bodies; some, pushing back their caps, scratched their heads. What did they want? Jimmy was forgotten; no one thought of him, alone forward in his cabin, fighting great shadows, clinging to brazen lies, chuckling painfully over his transparent deceptions. No, not Jimmy; he was more forgotten than if he had been dead. They wanted great things. And suddenly all the simple words they knew seemed to be lost forever in the immensity of their vague and burning desire. They knew what they wanted, but they could not find anything worth saying. They stirred on one spot, swinging, at the end of muscular arms, big tarry hands with crooked fingers. A murmur died out.—"What is it—food?" asked the master, "you know the stores have been spoiled off the Cape."—"We know that, sir," said a bearded shell-back in the front rank.—"Work too hard—eh? Too much for your strength?" he asked again. There was an offended silence.—"We don't want to go shorthanded, sir," began at last Davis in a wavering voice, "and this 'ere black— . . ."—"Enough!" cried the master. He stood scanning them for a moment, then walking a few steps this way and that began to storm at them coldly, in gusts violent and cutting like the gales of those icy seas that had known his youth.—"Tell you what's the matter? Too big for your boots. Think yourselves damn good men. Know half your work. Do half your duty. Think it too much. If you did ten times as much it wouldn't be enough."—"We did our best by her, sir," cried some one with shaky exasperation.—"Your best!" stormed on the master. "You hear a lot on shore, don't you? They don't tell you there your best isn't much to boast of. I tell you—your best is no better than bad. You can do no more? No, I know, and I say nothing. But you stop your caper or I will stop it for you. I am ready for you! Stop it!" He shook a finger at the crowd. "As to that man," he raised his voice very much; "as to that man, if he puts his nose out on deck without my leave I will clap him in irons. There!" The cook heard him forward, ran out of the galley lifting his arms, horrified, unbelieving, amazed, and ran in again. There was a moment of profound silence during which a bow-legged seaman, stepping aside, expectorated decorously into the scupper. "There is another thing," said the master calmly. He made a quick stride and with a swing took an iron belaying-pin out of his pocket. "This!" His movement was so unexpected and sudden that the crowd stepped back. He gazed fixedly at their faces, and some at once put on a surprised air as though they had never seen a belaying-pin before. He held it up. "This is my affair. I don't ask you any questions, but you all know it; it has got to go where it came from." His eyes became angry. The crowd stirred uneasily. They looked away from the piece of iron, they appeared shy, they were embarrassed and shocked as though it had been something horrid, scandalous, or indelicate, that in common decency should not have been flourished like this in broad daylight. The master watched them attentively. "Donkin," he called out in a short, sharp tone.

Donkin dodged behind one, then behind another, but they looked over their shoulders and moved aside. The ranks kept on opening before him, closing behind, till at last he appeared alone before the master as though he had come up through the deck. Captain Allistoun moved close to him. They were much of a size, and at short range the master exchanged a deadly glance with the beady eyes. They wavered.—"You know this," asked the master.—"No, I don't," answered the other with a cheeky trepidation.—"You are a cur. Take it," ordered the master. Donkin's arms seemed glued to his thighs; he stood, eyes front, as if drawn on parade. "Take it," repeated the master, and stepped closer; they breathed on one another. "Take it," said Captain Allistoun again, making a menacing gesture. Donkin tore away one arm from his side.—"Vy are yer down on me?" he mumbled with effort and as if his mouth had been full of dough.—"If you don't . . ." began the master. Donkin snatched at the pin as though his intention had been to run away with it, and remained stock still holding it like a candle. "Put it back where you took it from," said Captain Allistoun, looking at him fiercely. Donkin stepped back opening wide eyes. "Go, you blackguard, or I will make you," cried the master, driving him slowly backwards by a menacing advance. He dodged, and with the dangerous iron tried to guard his head from a threatening fist. Mr. Baker ceased grunting for a moment.—"Good! By Jove," murmured appreciatively Mr. Creighton in the tone of a connoisseur.—"Don't tech me," snarled Donkin, backing away.—"Then go. Go faster."—"Don't yer 'it me. . . . I will pull yer up afore the magistryt. . . . I'll show yer up." Captain Allistoun made a long stride, and Donkin, turning his back fairly, ran off a little, then stopped and over his shoulder showed yellow teeth.— "Farther on, fore-rigging," urged the master, pointing with his arm.—"Are yer goin' to stand by and see me bullied," screamed Donkin at the silent crowd that watched him. Captain Allistoun walked at him smartly. He started off again with a leap, dashed at the fore-rigging, rammed the pin into its hole violently. "I'll be even with yer yet," he screamed at the ship at large and vanished beyond the foremast. Captain Allistoun spun round and walked back aft with a composed face, as though he had already forgotten the scene. Men moved out of his way. He looked at no one.— "That will do, Mr. Baker. Send the watch below," he said quietly. "And you men try to walk straight for the future," he added in a calm voice. He looked pensively for a while at the backs of the impressed and retreating crowd. "Breakfast, steward," he called in a tone of relief through the cabin door.—"I didn't like to see you—Ough!—give that pin to that chap, sir," observed Mr. Baker; "he could have bust—Ough!—bust your head like an eggshell with it."—"Oh! he!" muttered the master absently. "Queer lot," he went on in a low voice. "I suppose it's all right now. Can never tell tho', nowadays, with such a . . . Years ago—I was a young master then—one China voyage I had a mutiny; real mutiny, Baker. Different men, tho'. I knew what they wanted: they wanted to broach the cargo and get at the liquor. Very simple. . . . We knocked them about for two days, and when they had enough—gentle as lambs. Good crew. And a smart trip I made." He glanced aloft at the yards braced sharp up. "Head wind day after day," he exclaimed bitterly. "Shall we never get a decent slant this passage?"—"Ready, sir," said the steward, appearing before them as if by magic and with a stained napkin in his hand.—"Ah! All right. Come along, Mr. Baker—it's late—with all this nonsense."

Chapter Five

A heavy atmosphere of oppressive quietude pervaded the ship. In the afternoon men went about washing clothes and hanging them out to dry in the unprosperous breeze with the meditative languor of disenchanted philosophers. Very little was said. The problem of life seemed too voluminous for the narrow limits of human speech, and by common consent it was abandoned to the great sea that had from the beginning enfolded it in its immense grip; to the sea that knew all, and would in time infallibly unveil to each the wisdom hidden in all the errors, the certitude that lurks in doubts, the realm of safety and peace beyond the frontiers of sorrow and fear. And in the confused current of impotent thoughts that set unceasingly this way and that through bodies of men, Jimmy bobbed up upon the surface, compelling attention, like a black buoy chained to the bottom of a muddy stream. Falsehood triumphed. It triumphed through doubt, through stupidity, through pity, through sentimentalism. We set ourselves to bolster it up, from compassion, from recklessness, from a sense of fun. Jimmy's steadfastness to his untruthful attitude in the face of the inevitable truth had the proportions of a colossal enigma—of a manifestation grand and incomprehensible that at times inspired a wondering awe; and there was also, to many, something exquisitely droll in fooling him thus to the top of his bent. The latent egoism of tenderness to suffering appeared in the developing anxiety not to see him die. His obstinate non-recognition of the only certitude whose approach we could watch from day to day was as disquieting as the failure of some law of nature. He was so utterly wrong about himself that one could not but suspect him of having access to some source of supernatural knowledge. He was absurd to the point of inspiration. He was unique, and as fascinating as only something inhuman could be; he seemed to shout his denials already from beyond the awful border. He was becoming immaterial like an apparition; his cheekbones rose, the forehead slanted more; the face was all hollows, patches of shade; and the fleshless head resembled a disinterred black skull, fitted with two restless globes of silver in the sockets of eyes. He was demoralising. Through him we were becoming highly humanised, tender, complex, excessively decadent: we understood the subtlety of his fear, sympathised with all his repulsions, shrinkings, evasions, delusions—as though we had been over-civilised, and rotten, and without any knowledge of the meaning of life. We had the air of being initiated in some infamous mysteries; we had the profound grimaces of conspirators, exchanged meaning glances, significant short words. We were inexpressibly vile and very much pleased with ourselves. We lied to him with gravity, with emotion, with unction, as if performing some moral trick with a view to an eternal reward. We made a chorus of affirmation to his wildest assertions, as though he had been a millionaire, a politician, or a reformer—and we a crowd of ambitious lubbers. When we ventured to question his statements we did it after the manner of obsequious sycophants, to the end that his glory should be augmented by the flattery of our dissent. He influenced the moral tone of our world as though he had it in his power to distribute honours, treasures, or pain; and he could give us nothing but his contempt. It was immense; it seemed to grow gradually larger, as his body day by day shrank a little more, while we looked. It was the only thing about him—of him—that gave the impression of durability and vigour. It lived within him with an unquenchable life. It spoke through the eternal pout of his black lips; it looked at us through the impertinent mournfulness of his languid and enormous stare. We watched him intently. He seemed unwilling to move, as if distrustful of his own solidity. The slightest gesture must have disclosed to him (it could not surely be otherwise) his bodily weakness, and caused a pang of mental suffering. He was chary of movements. He lay stretched out, chin on blanket, in a kind of sly, cautious immobility. Only his eyes roamed over faces; his eyes disdainful, penetrating and sad.

It was at that time that Belfast's devotion—and also his pugnacity—secured universal respect. He spent every moment of his spare time in Jimmy's cabin. He tended to him, talked to him; was as gentle as a woman, as tenderly gay as an old philanthropist, as sentimentally careful of his nigger as a model slave-owner. But outside he was irritable, explosive as gunpowder, sombre, suspicious, and never more brutal than when most sorrowful. With him it was a tear and a blow: a tear for Jimmy, a blow for any one who did not seem to take a scrupulously orthodox view of Jimmy's case. We talked about nothing else. The two Scandinavians, even, discussed the situation—but it was impossible to know in what spirit, because they quarrelled in their own language. Belfast suspected one of them of irreverence, and in this incertitude thought that there was no option but to fight them both. They became very much terrified by his truculence, and henceforth lived amongst us, dejected, like a pair of mutes. Wamibo never spoke intelligibly, but he was as smileless as an animal—seemed to know much less about it all than the cat—and consequently was safe. Moreover he had belonged to the chosen band of Jimmy's rescuers, and was above suspicion. Archie was silent generally, but often spent an hour or so talking to Jimmy quietly with an air of proprietorship. At any time of the day and often through the night some man could be seen sitting on Jimmy's box. In the evening, between six and eight, the cabin was crowded, and there was an interested group at the door. Every one stared at the nigger.

He basked in the warmth of our interest. His eyes gleamed ironically, and in a weak voice he reproached us with our cowardice. He would say, "If you fellows had stuck out for me I would be now on deck." We hung our heads. "Yes, but if you think I am going to let them put me in irons just to show you sport..., Well, no... It ruins my health, this lying up, it does. You don't care." We were as abashed as if it had been true. His superb impudence carried all before it. We would not have dared to revolt. We didn't want to, really. We wanted to keep him alive till home—to the end of the voyage.

Singleton as usual held aloof, appearing to scorn the insignificant events of an ended life. Once only he came along, and unexpectedly stopped in the doorway. He peered at Jimmy in profound silence, as if desirous to add that black image to the crowd of Shades that peopled his old memory. We kept very quiet, and for a long time Singleton stood there as though he had come by appointment to call for some one, or to see some important event. James Wait lay perfectly still, and apparently not aware of the gaze scrutinising him with a steadiness full of expectation. There was a sense of a contest in the air. We felt the inward strain of men watching a wrestling bout. At last Jimmy with perceptible apprehension turned his head on the pillow.—"Good evening," he said in a conciliating tone.—"H'm," answered the old seaman, grumpily. For a moment longer he looked at Jimmy with severe fixity, then suddenly went away. It was a long time before any one spoke in the little cabin, though we all breathed more freely as men do after an escape from some dangerous situation. We all knew the old man's ideas about Jimmy, and nobody dared to combat them. They were unsettling, they caused pain; and, what was worse, they might have been true for all we knew. Only once did he condescend to explain them fully, but the impression was lasting. He said that Jimmy was the cause of head winds. Mortally sick men—he maintained—linger till the first sight of land, and then die; and Jimmy knew that the very first land would draw his life from him. It is so in every ship. Didn't we know it? He asked us with austere contempt: what did we know? What would we doubt next? Jimmy's desire encouraged by us and aided by Wamibo's (he was a Finn—wasn't he? Very well!) by Wamibo's spells delayed the ship in the open sea. Only lubberly fools couldn't see it. Whoever heard of such a run of calms and head winds? It wasn't natural. . . . We could not deny that it was strange. We felt uneasy. The common saying, "More days, more dollars," did not give the usual comfort because the stores were running short. Much had been spoiled off the Cape, and we were on half allowance of biscuit. Peas, sugar, and tea had been finished long ago. Salt meat was giving out. We had plenty of coffee but very little water to make it with. We took up another hole in our belts and went on scraping, polishing, painting the ship from morning to night. And soon she looked as though she had come out of a band-box; but hunger lived on board of her. Not dead starvation, but steady, living hunger that stalked about the decks, slept in the forecastle; the tormentor of waking moments, the disturber of dreams. We looked to windward for signs of change. Every few hours of night and day we put her round with the hope that she would come up on that tack at last! She didn't. She seemed to have forgotten the way home; she rushed to and fro, heading north-west, heading east; she ran backwards and forwards, distracted like a timid creature at the foot of a wall. Sometimes, as if tired to death, she would wallow languidly for a day in the smooth swell of an unruffled sea. All up the swinging masts the sails thrashed furiously through the hot stillness of the calm. We were weary, hungry, thirsty; we commenced to believe Singleton, but with unshaken fidelity dissembled to Jimmy. We spoke to him with jocose allusiveness, like cheerful accomplices in a clever plot; but we looked to the westward over the rail with longing eyes for a sign of hope, for a sign of fair wind; even if its first breath should bring death to our reluctant Jimmy. In vain! The universe conspired with James Wait. Light airs from the northward sprang up again; the sky remained clear; and round our weariness the glittering sea, touched by the breeze, basked voluptuously in the great sunshine, as though it had forgotten our life and trouble.

Donkin looked out for a fair wind along with the rest. No one knew the venom of his thoughts now. He was silent, and appeared thinner, as if consumed slowly by an inward rage at the injustice of men and of fate. He was ignored by all and spoke to no one, but his hate for every man

dwelt in his furtive eyes. He talked with the cook only, having somehow
persuaded the good man that he—Donkin—was a much calumniated and
persecuted person. Together they bewailed the immorality of the ship's
company. There could be no greater criminals than we, who by our lies
conspired to send the unprepared soul of a poor ignorant black man to
everlasting perdition. Podmore cooked what there was to cook, remorse-
fully, and felt all the time that by preparing the food of such sinners he
imperilled his own salvation. As to the Captain—he had sailed with him
for seven years, now, he said, and would not have believed it possible that
such a man.... "Well. Well.... There it was.... Can't get out of it.
Judgment capsized all in a minute.... Struck in all his pride.... More
like a sudden visitatioin than anything else." Donkin, perched sullenly on
the coal-locker, swung his legs and concurred. He paid in the coin of
spurious assent for the privilege to sit in the galley; he was disheartened
and scandalised; he agreed with the cook; could find no words severe
enough to criticise our conduct, and when in the heat of reprobation he
swore at us, Podmore, who would have liked to swear also if it hadn't
been for his principles, pretended not to hear. So Donkin, unrebuked,
cursed enough for two, cadged for matches, borrowed tobacco, and loafed
for hours, very much at home, before the stove. From there he could hear
us on the other side of the bulkhead, talking to Jimmy. The cook knocked
the saucepans about, slammed the oven door, muttered prophecies of
damnation for all the ship's company; and Donkin, who did not admit of
any hereafter (except for purposes of blasphemy) listened, concentrated
and angry, gloating fiercely over a called-up image of infinite torment—as
men gloat over the accursed images of cruelty and revenge, of greed, and
of power....

On clear evenings the silent ship, under the cold sheen of the dead
moon, took on a false aspect of passionless repose, resembling the winter
of the earth. Under her a long band of gold barred the black disc of the
sea. Footsteps echoed on her quiet decks. The moonlight clung to her like
a frosted mist, and the white sails stood out in dazzling cones as of stain-
less snow. In the magnificence of the phantom rays the ship appeared
pure like a vision of ideal beauty, illusive like a tender dream of serene
peace. And nothing in her was real, nothing was distinct and solid but the
heavy shadows that filled her decks with their unceasing and noiseless
stir: the shadows darker than the night and more restless than the
thoughts of men.
Donkin prowled spiteful and alone amongst the shadows, thinking that
Jimmy too long delayed to die. That evening land had been reported from
aloft, and the master, while adjusting the tubes of the long glass, had
observed with quiet bitterness to Mr. Baker that, after fighting our way
inch by inch to the Western Islands,[4] there was nothing to expect now
but a spell of calm. The sky was clear and the barometer high. The light
breeze dropped with the sun; and an enormous stillness, forerunner of a
night without wind, descended upon the heated waters of the ocean. As
long as daylight lasted the hands collected on the forecastle-head
watched on the eastern sky the island of Flores, that rose above the level
expanse of the sea with irregular and broken outlines like a sombre ruin

---

4. The Azores, west of Portugal; Flores (below) is one of them.

upon a vast and deserted plain. It was the first land seen for nearly four
months. Charley was excited, and in the midst of general indulgence took
liberties with his betters. Men, strangely elated without knowing why,
talked in groups, and pointed with bared arms. For the first time that
voyage Jimmy's sham existence seemed for a moment forgotten in the
face of a solid reality. We had got so far anyhow. Belfast discoursed, quot-
ing imaginary examples of short homeward runs from the Islands. "Them
smart fruit schooners do it in five days," he affirmed. "What do you
want?—only a good little breeze." Archie maintained that seven days was
the record passage, and they disputed amicably with insulting words.
Knowles declared he could already smell home from there, and with a
heavy list on his short leg laughed fit to split his sides. A group of grizzled
sea-dogs looked out for a time in silence and with grim absorbed faces.
One said suddenly—" 'Tain't far to London now."—"My first night ashore,
blamme if I haven't steak and onions for supper . . . and a pint of bitter,"[5]
said another.—"A barrel ye mean," shouted some one.—"Ham an' eggs
three times a day. That's the way I live!" cried an excited voice. There
was a stir, appreciative murmurs; eyes began to shine; jaws champed;
short nervous laughs were heard. Archie smiled with reserve all to himself. Singleton came up, gave a careless glance, and went down again
without saying a word, indifferent, like a man who had seen Flores an
incalculable number of times. The night travelling from the East blotted
out of the limpid sky the purple stain of the high land. "Dead calm," said
somebody quietly. The murmur of lively talk suddenly wavered, died out;
the clusters broke up; men began to drift away one by one, descending
the ladders slowly and with serious faces as if sobered by that reminder of
their dependence upon the invisible. And when the big yellow moon
ascended gently above the sharp rim of the clear horizon it found the
ship wrapped up in a breathless silence; a fearless ship that seemed to
sleep profoundly, dreamlessly on the bosom of the sleeping and terrible
sea.

Donkin chafed at the peace—at the ship—at the sea that stretching
away on all sides merged into the illimitable silence of all creation. He
felt himself pulled up sharp by unrecognised grievances. He had been
physically cowed, but his injured dignity remained indomitable, and nothing could heal his lacerated feelings. Here was land already—home very
soon—a bad pay-day—no clothes—more hard work. How offensive all this
was. Land! The land that draws away life from sick sailors. That nigger
there had money—clothes—easy times; and would not die. Land draws life
away. . . . He felt tempted to go and see whether it did. Perhaps already. . . . It would be a bit of luck. There was money in the beggar's
chest. He stepped briskly out of the shadows into the moonlight, and instantly, his craving, hungry face from sallow became livid. He opened the
door of the cabin and had a shock. Sure enough, Jimmy was dead! He
moved no more than a recumbent figure with clasped hands, carved on
the lid of a stone coffin. Donkin glared with avidity. Then Jimmy, without
stirring, blinked his eyelids, and Donkin had another shock. Those eyes
were rather startling. He shut the door behind his back with gentle care,
looking intently the while at James Wait as though he had come in there
at a great risk to tell some secret of startling importance. Jimmy did not

5. English beer.

move but glanced languidly out of the corners of his eyes.—"Calm?" he asked. "Yuss," said Donkin, very disappointed, and sat down on the box. Jimmy was used to such visits at all times of night or day. Men succeeded one another. They spoke in clear voices, pronounced cheerful words, repeated old jokes, listened to him; and each, going out, seemed to leave behind a little of his own vitality, surrender some of his own strength, renew the assurance of life—the indestructible thing! He did not like to be alone in his cabin, because, when he was alone, it seemed to him as if he hadn't been there at all. There was nothing. No pain. Not now. Perfectly right—but he couldn't enjoy his healthful repose unless some one was by to see it. This man would do as well as anybody. Donkin watched him stealthily:—"Soon home now," observed Wait.—"Vy d'yer whisper?" asked Donkin with interest, "can't yer speak up?" Jimmy looked annoyed and said nothing for a while; then in a lifeless unringing voice:—"Why should I shout? You ain't deaf that I know."—"Oh! I can 'ear right enough," answered Donkin in a low tone, and looked down. He was thinking sadly of going out when Jimmy spoke again.—"Time we did get home . . . to get something decent to eat . . . I am always hungry." Donkin felt angry all of a sudden.—"What about me?" he hissed, "I am 'ungry too an' got ter work. You, 'ungry!"—"Your work won't kill you," commented Wait feebly; "there's a couple of biscuits in the lower bunk there—you may have one. I can't eat them." Donkin dived in, groped in the corner and when he came up again his mouth was full. He munched with ardour. Jimmy seemed to doze with open eyes. Donkin finished his hard bread and got up.—"You're not going?" asked Jimmy, staring at the ceiling.—"No," said Donkin impulsively, and instead of going out leaned his back against the closed door. He looked at James Wait, and saw him long, lean, dried up, as though all his flesh had shrivelled on his bones in the heat of a white furnace; the meagre fingers of one hand moved lightly upon the edge of the bunk playing an endless tune. To look at him was irritating and fatiguing; he could last like this for days; he was outrageous—belonging wholly neither to death nor life, and perfectly invulnerable in his apparent ignorance of both. Donkin felt tempted to enlighten him.—"What are yer thinkin' of?" he asked surlily. James Wait had a grimacing smile that passed over the deathlike impassiveness of his bony face, incredible and frightful as would, in a dream, have been the sudden smile of a corpse.

"There is a girl," whispered Wait. . . . "Canton Street girl.—She chucked a third engineer of a Rennie boat[6]—for me. Cooks oysters just as I like. . . . She says—she would chuck—any toff—for a coloured gentleman. . . . That's me. I am kind to wimmen," he added, a shade louder.

Donkin could hardly believe his ears. He was scandalised—"Would she? Yer wouldn't be any good to 'er," he said with unrestrained disgust. Wait was not there to hear him. He was swaggering up the East India Dock Road; saying kindly, "Come along for a treat," pushing glass swing-doors, posing with superb assurance in the gaslight above a mahogany counter —"D'yer think yer will ever get ashore?" asked Donkin angrily. Wait came back with a start.—"Ten days," he said promptly, and returned at once to

---

6. Steam, screw-driven ships of the Royal Navy. John Rennie (1761–1821) introduced steam to the British navy; his son George (1791–1866) was an engine designer and shipbuilder for the Royal Navy.

Canton Street is just north of and parallel to East India Dock Road, which services two main basins on the Thames.

the regions of memory that know nothing of time. He felt untired, calm, and safely withdrawn within himself beyond the reach of every grave incertitude. There was something of the immutable quality of eternity in the slow moments of his complete restfulness. He was very quiet and easy amongst his vivid reminiscences which he mistook joyfully for images of an undoubted future. He cared for no one. Donkin felt this vaguely as a blind man feeling in his darkness the fatal antagonism of all the surrounding existences, that to him shall for ever remain unrealisable, unseen, and enviable. He had a desire to assert his importance, to break, to crush; to be even with everybody for everything; to tear the veil, unmask, expose, leave no refuge—a perfidious desire of truthfulness! He laughed in a mocking splutter and said:

"Ten days. Strike me blind if I ever! . . . You will be dead by this time to-morrow p'r'aps. Ten days!" He waited for a while. "D'ye 'ear me? Blamme if yer don't look dead already."

Wait must have been collecting his strength, for he said, almost aloud— "You're a stinking, cadging liar. Every one knows you." And sitting up, against all probability, startled his visitor horribly. But very soon Donkin recovered himself. He blustered.

"What? What? Who's a liar? You are—the crowd are—the skipper—everybody. I ain't! Putting on airs! Who's yer?" He nearly choked himself with indignation. "Who's yer to put on airs," he repeated trembling. " 'Ave one—'ave one, says 'ee—an' cawn't eat 'em 'isself. Now I'll 'ave both. By Gawd—I will! Yer nobody!"

He plunged into the lower bunk, rooted in there and brought to light another dusty biscuit. He held it up before Jimmy—then took a bite defiantly.

"What now?" he asked with feverish impudence. "Yer may take one— says yer. Why not giv' me both? No. I'm a mangy dorg. One fur a mangy dorg. I'll tyke both. Can yer stop me? Try. Come on. Try."

Jimmy was clasping his legs and hiding his face on the knees. His shirt clung to him. Every rib was visible. His emaciated back was shaken in repeated jerks by the panting catches of his breath.

"Yer won't. Yer can't! What did I say?" went on Donkin fiercely. He swallowed another dry mouthful with a hasty effort. The other's silent helplessness, his weakness, his shrinking attitude exasperated him. "Ye're done!" he cried. "Who's yer to be lied to; to be waited on 'and an' foot like a bloomin' ymperor. Yer nobody! Yer no one at all!" he spluttered with such a strength of unerring conviction that it shook him from head to foot in coming out, and left him vibrating like a released string.

James Wait rallied again. He lifted his head and turned bravely at Donkin, who saw a strange face, an unknown face, a fantastic and grimacing mask of despair and fury. Its lips moved rapidly; and hollow, moaning, whistling sounds filled the cabin with a vague mutter full of menace, compaint and desolation, like the far-off murmur of a rising wind. Wait shook his head; rolled his eyes; he denied, cursed, threatened—and not a word had the strength to pass beyond the sorrowful pout of those black lips. It was incomprehensible and disturbing: a gibberish of emotions, a frantic dumb show of speech pleading for impossible things, promising a shadowy vengeance. It sobered Donkin into a scrutinising watchfulness.

"Yer can't oller. See? What did I tell yer?" he said slowly after a moment of attentive examination. The other kept on headlong and unheard, nodding passionately, grinning with grotesque and appalling flashes of big white teeth. Donkin, as if fascinated by the dumb eloquence and anger of that black phantom, approached, stretching his neck out with distrustful curiosity; and it seemed to him suddenly that he was looking only at the shadow of a man crouching high in the bunk on the level with his eyes.— "What? What?" he said. He seemed to catch the shape of some words in the continuous panting hiss. "Yer will tell Belfast! Will yer? Are yer a bloomin' kid?" He trembled with alarm and rage. "Tell yer gran'mother! Yer afeard! Who's yer ter be afeard more'n any one?" His passionate sense of his own importance ran away with a last remnant of caution. "Tell an' be damned! Tell, if yer can!" he cried. "I've been treated worser'n a dorg by your blooming back-lickers. They 'as set me on, only to turn aginst me. I am the only man 'ere. They clouted me, kicked me— an' yer laffed—yer black, rotten incumbrance, you! Yer will pay fur it. They giv' yer their grub, their water—yer will pay fur it to me, by Gawd! Who axed me ter 'ave a drink of water? They put their bloomin' rags on yer that night, an' what did they giv' ter me—a clout on the bloomin' mouth—blast their . . . S'elp me! . . . Yer will pay fur it with yer money. I'm goin' ter 'ave it in a minnyt; as soon as ye're dead, yer bloomin' useless fraud. That's the man I am. An' ye're a thing—a bloody thing! Yah—you corpse!"

He flung at Jimmy's head the biscuit he had been all the time clutching hard, but it only grazed, and striking with a loud crack the bulkhead beyond burst like a hand-grenade into flying pieces. James Wait, as if wounded mortally, fell back on the pillow. His lips ceased to move and the rolling eyes became quiet and stared upwards with an intense and steady persistence. Donkin was surprised; he sat suddenly on the chest, and looked down, exhausted and gloomy. After a moment, he began to mutter to himself, "Die, you beggar—die. Somebody'll come in . . . I wish I was drunk . . . Ten days . . . oysters . . . " He looked up and spoke louder. "No . . . No more for yer . . . no more bloomin' gals to cook oysters. . . . Who's yer? It's my turn now . . . I wish I was drunk; I would soon giv' you a leg up. That's where yer bound to. Feet fust, through a port . . . Splash! Never see yer any more. Overboard! Good 'nuff fur yer."

Jimmy's head moved slightly and he turned his eyes to Donkin's face; a gaze unbelieving, desolated and appealing, of a child frightened by the menace of being shut up alone in the dark. Donkin observed him from the chest with hopeful eyes; then, without rising, tried the lid. Locked. "I wish I was drunk," he muttered and getting up listened anxiously to the distant sound of footsteps on the deck. They approached—ceased. Some one yawned interminably just outside the door, and the footsteps went away shuffling lazily. Donkin's fluttering heart eased its pace, and when he looked towards the bunk again Jimmy was staring as before at the white beam.—" 'Ow d'yer feel now?" he asked.—"Bad," breathed out Jimmy.

Donkin sat down patient and purposeful. Every half-hour the bells spoke to one another ringing along the whole length of the ship. Jimmy's respiration was so rapid that it couldn't be counted, so faint that it couldn't be heard. His eyes were terrified as though he had been looking at unspeakable horrors; and by his face one could see that he was thinking of abominable things. Suddenly with an incredibly strong and heart-breaking voice he sobbed out:

"Overboard! . . . I! . . . My God!"

Donkin writhed a little on the box. He looked unwillingly. James Wait was mute. His two long bony hands smoothed the blanket upwards, as though he had wished to gather it all up under his chin. A tear, a big solitary tear, escaped from the corner of his eye and, without touching the hollow cheek, fell on the pillow. His throat rattled faintly.

And Donkin watching the end of that hateful nigger, felt the anguishing grasp of a great sorrow on his heart at the thought that he himself, some day, would have to go through it all—just like this—perhaps! His eyes became moist. "Poor beggar," he murmured. The night seemed to go by in a flash; it seemed to him he could hear the irremediable rush of precious minutes. How long would this blooming affair last? Too long surely. No luck. He could not restrain himself. He got up and approached the bunk. Wait did not stir. Only his eyes appeared alive and his hands continued their smoothing movement with a horrible and tireless industry. Donkin bent over.

"Jimmy," he called low. There was no answer, but the rattle stopped. "D'yer see me?" he asked trembling. Jimmy's chest heaved. Donkin, looking away, bent his ear to Jimmy's lips, and heard a sound like the rustle of a single dry leaf driven along the smooth sand of a beach. It shaped itself.

"Light . . . the lamp . . . and . . . go," breathed out Wait.

Donkin, instinctively, glanced over his shoulder at the brilliant flame; then, still looking away, felt under the pillow for the key. He got it at once and for the next few minutes remained on his knees shakily but swiftly busy inside the box. When he got up, his face—for the first time in his life—had a pink flush—perhaps of triumph.

He slipped the key under the pillow again, avoiding to glance at Jimmy, who had not moved. He turned his back squarely from the bunk, and started to the door as though he were going to walk a mile. At his second stride he had his nose against it. He clutched the handle cautiously, but at that moment he received the irresistible impression of something happening behind his back. He spun round as though he had been tapped on the shoulder. He was just in time to see Wait's eyes blaze up and go out at once, like two lamps overturned together by a sweeping blow. Something resembling a scarlet thread hung down his chin out of the corner of his lips—and he had ceased to breathe.

Donkin closed the door behind him gently but firmly. Sleeping men, huddled under jackets, made on the lighted deck shapeless dark mounds that had the appearance of neglected graves. Nothing had been done all through the night and he hadn't been missed. He stood motionless and perfectly astounded to find the world outside as he had left it; there was the sea, the ship—sleeping men; and he wondered absurdly at it, as though he had expected to find the men dead, familiar things gone for ever: as though, like a wanderer returning after many years, he had expected to see bewildering changes. He shuddered a little in the penetrating freshness of the air, and hugged himself forlornly. The declining moon dropped sadly in the western board as if withered by the cold touch of a pale dawn. The ship slept. And the immortal sea stretched away, immense and hazy, like the image of life, with a glittering surface and lightless depths. Donkin gave it a defiant glance and slunk off noiselessly as if judged and cast out by the august silence of its might.

Jimmy's death, after all, came as a tremendous surprise. We did not know till then how much faith we had put in his delusions. We had taken his chances of life so much at his own valuation that his death, like the death of an old belief, shook the foundations of our society. A common bond was gone; the strong, effective and respectable bond of a sentimental lie. All that day we mooned at our work, with suspicious looks and a disabused air. In our hearts we thought that in the matter of his departure Jimmy had acted in a perverse and unfriendly manner. He didn't back us up, as a shipmate should. In going he took away with himself the gloomy and solemn shadow in which our folly had posed, with humane satisfaction, as a tender arbiter of fate. And now we saw it was no such thing. It was just common foolishness; a silly and ineffectual meddling with issues of a majestic import—that is, if Podmore was right. Perhaps he was? Doubt survived Jimmy; and, like a community of banded criminals disintegrated by a touch of grace, we were profoundly scandalised with each other. Men spoke unkindly to their best chums. Others refused to speak at all. Singleton only was not surprised. "Dead is he? Of course," he said, pointing at the island right abeam: for the calm still held the ship spell-bound within sight of Flores. Dead—of course. *He* wasn't surprised. Here was the land, and there, on the fore-hatch and waiting for the sail-maker—there was the corpse. Cause and effect. And for the first time that voyage, the old seaman became quite cheery and garrulous, explaining and illustrating from the stores of experience how, in sickness, the sight of an island (even a very small one) is generally more fatal than the view of a continent. But he couldn't explain why.

Jimmy was to be buried at five, and it was a long day till then—a day of mental disquiet and even of physical disturbance. We took no interest in our work and, very properly, were rebuked for it. This, in our constant state of hungry irritation, was exasperating. Donkin worked with his brow bound in a dirty rag, and looked so ghastly that Mr. Baker was touched with compassion at the sight of this plucky suffering.—"Ough! You, Donkin! Put down your work and go lay-up this watch. You look ill."—"I am bad, sir—in my 'ead," he said in a subdued voice, and vanished speedily. This annoyed many, and they thought the mate "bloomin' soft to-day." Captain Allistoun could be seen on the poop watching the sky to the southwest, and it soon got to be known about the decks that the barometer had begun to fall in the night, and that a breeze might be expected before long. This, by a subtle association of ideas, led to violent quarrelling as to the exact moment of Jimmy's death. Was it before or after "that 'ere glass started down"? It was impossible to know, and it caused much contemptuous growling at one another. All of a sudden there was a great tumult forward. Pacific Knowles and good-tempered Davis had come to blows over it. The watch below interfered with spirit, and for ten minutes there was a noisy scrimmage round the hatch, where, in the balancing shade of the sails, Jimmy's body, wrapped up in a white blanket, was watched over by the sorrowful Belfast, who, in his desolation, disdained the fray. When the noise had ceased, and the passions had calmed into surly silence, he stood up at the head of the swathed body, lifting both arms on high, cried with pained indignation:—"You ought to be ashamed of yourselves! . . . " We were.

Belfast took his bereavement very hard. He gave proofs of unextinguishable devotion. It was he, and no other man, who would help the sail-maker to prepare what was left of Jimmy for a solemn surrender to the insatiable sea. He arranged the weights carefully at the feet: two holy-stones, an old anchor-shackle without its pin, some broken links of a worn-out stream cable. He arranged them this way, then that. "Bless my soul! you aren't afraid he will chafe his heel?" said the sailmaker, who hated the job. He pushed the needle, puffing furiously, with his head in a cloud of tobacco smoke; he turned the flaps over, pulled at the stitches, stretched at the canvas.—"Lift his shoulders.... Pull to you a bit.... So—o—o. Steady." Belfast obeyed, pulled, lifted, overcome with sorrow, drop-ping tears on the tarred twine.—"Don't you drag the canvas too taut over his poor face, Sails," he entreated tearfully. "What are you fashing your-self for? He will be comfortable enough," assured the sailmaker, cutting the thread after the last stitch, which came about the middle of Jimmy's forehead. He rolled up the remaining canvas, put away the needles. "What makes you take on so?" he asked. Belfast looked down at the long package of grey sailcloth.—"I pulled him out," he whispered, "and he did not want to go. If I had sat up with him last night he would have kept alive for me . . . but something made me tired." The sailmaker took vigor-ous draws at his pipe and mumbled;—"When I . . . West India Station . . . In the *Blanche* frigate . . . Yellow Jack . . . sewed in twenty men a week . . . Portsmouth—Devonport[7] men—townies—knew their fathers, mothers, sisters—the whole boiling of 'em. Thought nothing of it. And these niggers like this one—you don't know where it comes from. Got nobody. No use to nobody. Who will miss him?"—"I do—I pulled him out," mourned Bel-fast dismally.

On two planks nailed together and apparently resigned and still under the folds of the Union Jack with a white border, James Wait, carried aft by four men, was deposited slowly, with his feet pointing at an open port. A swell had set in from the westward, and following on the roll of the ship, the red ensign, at half-mast, darted out and collapsed again on the grey sky, like a tongue of flickering fire; Charley tolled the bell; and at every swing to starboard the whole vast semicircle of steely waters visible on that side seemed to come up with a rush to the edge of the port, as if impatient to get at our Jimmy. Every one was there but Donkin, who was too ill to come; the Captain and Mr. Creighton stood bareheaded on the break of the poop; Mr. Baker, directed by the master, who had said to him gravely:—"You know more about the prayer book than I do," came out of the cabin door quickly and a little embarrassed. All the caps went off. He began to read in a low tone, and with his usual harmlessly menac-ing utterance, as though he had been for the last time reproving confiden-tially that dead seaman at his feet. The men listened in scattered groups; they leaned on the fife rail, gazing on the deck; they held their chins in their hands thoughtfully, or, with crossed arms and one knee slightly bent, hung their heads in an attitude of upright meditation. Wamibo dreamed. Mr. Baker read on, grunting reverently at the turn of every page. The words, missing the unsteady hearts of men, rolled out to wander without a home upon the heartless sea; and James Wait, silenced for ever, lay uncritical and passive under the hoarse murmur of despair and hopes.

Two men made ready and waited for those words that send so many of

7. Ports in southern and southwestern England respectively. *Yellow Jack:* yellow fever.

our brothers to their last plunge. Mr. Baker began the passage. "Stand by," muttered the boatswain. Mr. Baker read out: "To the deep," and paused. The men lifted the inboard end of the planks, the boatswain snatched off the Union Jack, and James Wait did not move.—"Higher," muttered the boatswain angrily. All the heads were raised; every man stirred uneasily, but James Wait gave no sign of going. In death and swathed up for all eternity, he yet seemed to cling to the ship with the grip of an undying fear. "Higher! Lift!" whispered the boatswain fiercely.—"He won't go," stammered one of the men shakily, and both appeared ready to drop everything. Mr. Baker waited, burying his face in the book, and shuffling his feet nervously. All the men looked profoundly disturbed; from their midst a faint humming noise spread out—growing louder. . . . "Jimmy!" cried Belfast in a wailing tone, and there was a second of shuddering dismay.

"Jimmy, be a man!" he shrieked passionately. Every mouth was wide open, not an eyelid winked. He stared wildly, twitching all over; he bent his body forward like a man peering at an horror. "Go!" he shouted, and sprang out of the crowd with his arm extended. "Go, Jimmy!—Jimmy, go! Go!" His fingers touched the head of the body, and the grey package started reluctantly to whizz off the lifted planks all at once, with the suddenness of a flash of lightning. The crowd stepped forward like one man; a deep Ah—h——h! came out vibrating from the broad chests. The ship rolled as if relieved of an unfair burden; the sails flapped. Belfast, supported by Archie, gasped hysterically; and Charley, who anxious to see Jimmy's last dive, leaped headlong on the rail, was too late to see anything but the faint circle of a vanishing ripple.

Mr. Baker, perspiring abundantly, read out the last prayer in a deep rumour of excited men and fluttering sails. "Amen!" he said in an unsteady growl, and closed the book.

"Square the yards!" thundered a voice above his head. All hands gave a jump; one or two dropped their caps; Mr. Baker looked up surprised. The master, standing on the break of the poop, pointed to the westward. "Breeze coming," he said. "Man the weather braces." Mr. Baker crammed the book hurriedly into his pocket.—"Forward, there—let go the foretack!" he hailed joyfully, bare-headed and brisk; "Square the foreyard, you port watch!"—"Fair wind—fair wind," muttered the men going to the braces.—"What did I tell you?" mumbled old Singleton, flinging down coil after coil with hasty energy; "I knowed it—he's gone, and here it comes."

It came with the sound of a lofty and powerful sigh. The sails filled, the ship gathered way, and the waking sea began to murmur sleepily of home to the ears of men.

That night, while the ship rushed foaming to the northward before a freshening gale, the boatswain unbosomed himself to the petty officers' berth:—"The chap was nothing but trouble," he said, "from the moment he came aboard—d'ye remember—that night in Bombay? Been bullying all that softy crowd—cheeked the old man—we had to go fooling all over a half-drowned ship to save him. Dam' nigh a mutiny all for him—and now the mate abused me like a pickpocket for forgetting to dab a lump of grease on them planks. So I did, but you ought to have known better, too, than to leave a nail sticking up—hey, Chips,"

"And you ought to have known better than to chuck all my tools overboard for 'im, like a skeary greenhorn," retorted the morose carpenter. "Well—he's gone after 'em now," he added in an unforgiving tone.—"On the China Station,[8] I remember once, the Admiral he says to me ... " began the sailmaker.

A week afterwards the *Narcissus* entered the chops of the Channel.

Under white wings she skimmed low over the blue sea like a great tired bird speeding to its nest. The clouds raced with her mastheads; they rose astern enormous and white, soared to the zenith, flew past, and, falling down the wide curve of the sky, seemed to dash headlong into the sea— the clouds swifter than the ship, more free, but without a home. The coast to welcome her stepped out of space into the sunshine. The lofty headlands trod masterfully into the sea; the wide bays smiled in the light; the shadows of homeless clouds ran along the sunny plains, leaped over valleys, without a check darted up the hills, rolled down the slopes; and the sunshine pursued them with patches of running brightness. On the brows of dark cliffs white lighthouses shone in pillars of light. The Channel glittered like a blue mantle shot with gold and starred by the silver of the capping seas. The *Narcissus* rushed past the headlands and the bays. Outward-bound vessels crossed her track, lying over, and with their masts stripped for a slogging fight with the hard sou'wester. And, inshore, a string of smoking steam-boats waddled, hugging the coast, like migrating and amphibious monsters, distrustful of the restless waves.

At night the headlands retreated, the bays advanced into one unbroken line of gloom. The lights of the earth mingled with the lights of heaven; and above the tossing lanterns of a trawling fleet a great lighthouse shone steadily, like an enormous riding light burning above a vessel of fabulous dimensions. Below its steady glow, the coast, stretching away straight and black, resembled the high side of an indestructible craft riding motionless upon the immortal and unresting sea. The dark land lay alone in the midst of waters, like a mighty ship bestarred with vigilant lights—a ship carrying the burden of millions of lives—a ship freighted with dross and with jewels, with gold and with steel. She towered up immense and strong, guarding priceless traditions and untold suffering, sheltering glorious memories and base forgetfulness, ignoble virtues and splendid transgressions. A great ship! For ages had the ocean battered in vain her enduring sides; she was there when the world was vaster and darker, when the sea was great and mysterious, and ready to surrender the prize of fame to audacious men. A ship mother of fleets and nations! The great flagship of the race; stronger than the storms! and anchored in the open sea.

The *Narcissus*, heeling over to off-shore gusts, rounded the South Foreland, passed through the Downs, and, in tow, entered the river.[9] Shorn of the glory of her white wings, she wound obediently after the tug through the maze of invisible channels. As she passed them the red-painted light-vessels, swung at their moorings, seemed for an instant to sail with great speed in the rush of tide, and the next moment were left hopelessly behind. The big buoys on the tails of banks slipped past her sides very low, and, dropping in her wake, tugged at their chains like fierce watchdogs. The reach narrowed; from both sides the land approached the ship. She

8. Service with the Royal Navy in the China Sea.
9. The Thames; the South Foreland is the southern of two headlands in Kent, near Dover; the Downs is an anchorage in the English Channel.

went steadily up the river. On the riverside slopes the houses appeared in groups—seemed to stream down the declivities at a run to see her pass, and, checked by the mud of the foreshore, crowded on the banks. Farther on, the tall factory chimneys appeared in insolent bands and watched her go by, like a straggling crowd of slim giants, swaggering and upright under the black plummets of smoke, cavalierly aslant. She swept round the bends; an impure breeze shrieked a welcome between her stripped spars; and the land, closing in, stepped between the ship and the sea.

A low cloud hung before her—a great opalescent and tremulous cloud, that seemed to rise from the steaming brows of millions of men. Long drifts of smoky vapours soiled it with livid trails; it throbbed to the beat of millions of hearts, and from it came an immense and lamentable murmur—the murmur of millions of lips praying, cursing, sighing, jeering—the undying murmur of folly, regret, and hope exhaled by the crowds of the anxious earth. The Narcissus entered the cloud; the shadows deepened; on all sides there was the clang of iron, the sound of mighty blows, shrieks, yells. Black barges drifted stealthily on the murky stream. A mad jumble of begrimed walls loomed up vaguely in the smoke, bewildering and mournful, like a vision of disaster. The tugs backed and filled in the stream, to hold the ship steady at the dock gates; from her bows two lines went through the air whistling, and struck at the land viciously, like a pair of snakes. A bridge broke in two before her, as if by enchantment; big hydraulic capstans began to turn all by themselves, as though animated by a mysterious and unholy spell. She moved through a narrow lane of water between two low walls of granite, and men with check-ropes in their hands kept pace with her, walking on the broad flagstones. A group waited impatiently on each side of the vanished bridge: rough heavy men in caps; sallow-faced men in high hats; two bareheaded women; ragged children, fascinated, and with wide eyes. A cart coming at a jerky trot pulled up sharply. One of the women screamed at the silent ship—"Hallo, Jack!" without looking at any one in particular, and all hands looked at her from the forecastle head.—"Stand clear! Stand clear of that rope!" cried the dockmen, bending over stone posts. The crowd murmured, stamped where they stood.—"Let go your quarter-checks! Let go!" sang out a ruddy-faced old man on the quay. The ropes splashed heavily falling in the water, and the Narcissus entered the dock.

The stony shores ran away right and left in straight lines, enclosing a sombre and rectangular pool. Brick walls rose high above the water—soulless walls, staring through hundreds of windows as troubled and dull as the eyes of over-fed brutes. At their base monstrous iron cranes crouched, with chains hanging from their long necks, balancing cruel-looking hooks over the decks of lifeless ships. A noise of wheels rolling over stones, the thump of heavy things falling, the racket of feverish winches, the grinding of strained chains, floated on the air. Between high buildings the dust of all the continents soared in short flights; and a penetrating smell of perfumes and dirt, of spices and hides, of things costly and of things filthy, pervaded the space, made for it an atmosphere precious and disgusting. The Narcissus came gently into her berth; the shadows of soulless walls fell upon her, the dust of all the continents leaped upon her deck, and a swarm of strange men, clambering up her sides, took possession of her in the name of the sordid earth. She had ceased to live.

A toff in a black coat and high hat scrambled with agility, came up to the second mate, shook hands, and said:—"Hallo, Herbert." It was his brother. A lady appeared suddenly. A real lady, in a black dress and with a parasol. She looked extremely elegant in the midst of us, and as strange as if she had fallen there from the sky. Mr. Baker touched his cap to her. It was the master's wife. And very soon the Captain, dressed very smartly and in a white shirt, went with her over the side. We didn't recognise him at all till, turning on the quay, he called to Mr. Baker:—"Don't forget to wind up the chronometers to-morrow morning." An underhand lot of seedy-looking chaps with shifty eyes wandered in and out of the forecastle looking for a job—they said.—"More likely for something to steal," commented Knowles cheerfully. Poor beggars! Who cared? Weren't we home! But Mr. Baker went for one of them who had given him some cheek, and we were delighted. Everything was delightful.—"I've finished aft, sir," called out Mr. Creighton.—"No water in the well, sir," reported for the last time the carpenter, sounding-rod in hand. Mr. Baker glanced along the decks at the expectant group of sailors, glanced aloft at the yards.—"Ough! That will do, men," he grunted. The group broke up. The voyage was ended.

Rolled-up beds went flying over the rail; lashed chests went sliding down the gangway—mighty few of both at that. "The rest is having a cruise off the Cape," explained Knowles enigmatically to a dock-loafer with whom he had struck a sudden friendship. Men ran, calling to one another, hailing utter strangers to "lend a hand with the dunnage," then with sudden decorum approached the mate to shake hands before going ashore.—"Good-bye, sir," they repeated in various tones. Mr. Baker grasped hard palms, grunted in a friendly manner at every one, his eyes twinkled.—"Take care of your money, Knowles. Ough! Soon get a nice wife if you do." The lame man was delighted.—"Good-bye, sir," said Belfast, with emotion, wringing the mate's hand, and looked up with swimming eyes. "I thought I would take 'im ashore with me," he went on plaintively. Mr. Baker did not understand, but said kindly:—"Take care of yourself, Craik," and the bereaved Belfast went over the rail mourning and alone.

Mr. Baker, in the sudden peace of the ship, moved about solitary and grunting, trying door handles, peering into dark places, never done—a model chief mate! No one waited for him ashore. Mother dead; father and two brothers, Yarmouth fishermen, drowned together on the Dogger Bank[1], sister married and unfriendly. Quite a lady. Married to the leading tailor of a little town, and its leading politician, who did not think his sailor brother-in-law quite respectable enough for him. Quite a lady, quite a lady, he thought, sitting down for a moment's rest on the quarter-hatch. Time enough to go ashore and get a bite and sup, and a bed somewhere. He didn't like to part with a ship. No one to think about then. The darkness of a misty evening fell, cold and damp, upon the deserted deck; and Mr. Baker sat smoking, thinking of all the successive ships to whom through many long years he had given the best of a seaman's care. And never a command in sight. Not once!—"I haven't somehow the cut of a skipper about me," he meditated placidly, while the shipkeeper (who had taken possession of the galley), a wizened old man with bleared eyes, cursed him in whispers for "hanging about so."—"Now, Creighton," he

---

1. Submerged sand bank about sixty miles east of England. Yarmouth: seaport in eastern England.

pursued the unenvious train of thought, "quite a gentleman ... swell friends ... will get on. Fine young fellow ... a little more experience." He got up and shook himself. "I'll be back first thing to-morrow morning for the hatches. Don't you let them touch anything before I come, ship-keeper," he called out. Then, at last, he also went ashore—a model chief mate!

The men scattered by the dissolving contact of the land came together once more in the shipping office.—"The *Narcissus* pays off," shouted outside a glazed door a brass-bound old fellow, with a crown and the capitals B.T. on his cap. A lot trooped in at once but many were late. The room was large, whitewashed, and bare; a counter surmounted by a brass-wire grating fenced off a third of the dusty space, and behind the grating a pasty-faced clerk, with his hair parted in the middle, had the quick, glittering eyes and the vivacious, jerky movements of a caged bird. Poor Captain Allistoun also in there and sitting before a little table with piles of gold and notes on it, appeared subdued by his captivity. Another Board of Trade bird was perching on a high stool near the door: an old bird that did not mind the chaff of elated sailors. The crew of the *Narcissus*, broken up into knots, pushed in the corners. They had new shore togs, smart jackets that looked as if they had been shaped with an axe, glossy trousers that seemed made of crumpled sheet-iron, collarless flannel shirts, shiny new boots. They tapped on shoulders, button-holed one another, asked:— "Where did you sleep last night?" whispered gaily, slapped their thighs with bursts of subdued laughter. Most had clean radiant faces; only one or two turned up dishevelled and sad; the two young Norwegians looked tidy, meek, and altogether of a promising material for the kind ladies who patronise the Scandinavian Home.[2] Wamibo, still in his working clothes, dreamed, upright and burly in the middle of the room, and, when Archie came in, woke up for a smile. But the wide-awake clerk called out a name, and the paying-off business began.

One by one they came up to the pay-table to get the wages of their glorious and obscure toil. They swept the money with care into broad palms, rammed it trustfully into trousers' pockets, or, turning their backs on the table, reckoned with difficulty in the hollow on their still hands.— "Money right? Sign the release. There—there," repeated the clerk impatiently. "How stupid those sailors are!" he thought. Singleton came up, venerable—and uncertain as to daylight; brown drops of tobacco juice hung in his white beard; his hands, that never hesitated in the great light of the open sea, could hardly find the small pile of gold in the profound darkness of the shore. "Can't write?" said the clerk, shocked. "Make a mark then." Singleton painfully sketched in a heavy cross, blotted the page. "What a disgusting old brute," muttered the clerk. Somebody opened the door for him, and the patriarchal seaman passed through unsteadily, without as much as a glance at any of us.

Archie displayed a pocket-book. he was chaffed. Belfast, who looked wild, as though he had already luffed up[3] through a public-house or two, gave signs of emotion and wanted to speak to the captain privately. The master was surprised. They spoke through the wires, and we could hear the captain saying:—"I've given it up to the Board of Trade." "I should've liked to get something of his," mumbled Belfast. "But you can't, my man. It's given up, locked and sealed, to the Marine Office," expostulated the

2. The Scandinavian Sailor's Temperance Home, by West India Dock.

3. When applied to sails: to shake, from being set too close to the wind.

master; and Belfast stood back, with drooping mouth and troubled eyes. In a pause of the business we heard the master and the clerk talking. We caught: "James Wait—deceased—found no papers of any kind—no relations—no trace—the Office must hold his wages then." Donkin entered. He seemed out of breath, was grave, full of business. He went straight to the desk, talked with animation to the clerk, who thought him an intelligent man. They discussed the account, dropping h's against one another as if for a wager—very friendly. Captain Allistoun paid. "I give you a bad discharge," he said quietly. Donkin raised his voice;—"I don't want your bloomin' discharge—keep it. I'm goin' ter 'ave a job ashore." He turned to us. "No more bloomin' sea fur me," he said aloud. All looked at him. He had better clothes, had an easy air, appeared more at home than any of us; he stared with assurance, enjoying the effect of his declaration. "Yuss. I 'ave friends well off. That's more'n you got. But I am a man. Ye're shipmates for all that. Who's comin' fur a drink?"

No one moved. There was a silence; a silence of blank faces and stony looks. He waited a moment, smiled bitterly, and went to the door. There he faced round once more. "You won't? You bloomin' lot of 'ypocrites. No? What 'ave I done to yer? Did I bully yer? Did I 'urt yer? Did I? . . . You won't drink? . . . No! . . . Then may ye die of thirst, every mother's son of yer! Not one of yer 'as the sperrit of a bug. Ye're the scum of the world. Work and starve!"

He went out, and slammed the door with such violence that the old Board of Trade bird nearly fell off his perch.

"He's mad," declared Archie. "No! No! He's drunk," insisted Belfast, lurching about, and in a maudlin tone. Captain Allistoun sat smiling throughtfully at the cleared pay-table.

Outside, on Tower Hill,[4] they blinked, hesitated clumsily, as if blinded by the strange quality of the hazy light, as if discomposed by the view of so many men; and they who could hear one another in the howl of gales seemed deafened and distracted by the dull roar of the busy earth.—"To the Black Horse! To the Black Horse!" cried some. "Let us have a drink together before we part." They crossed the road, clinging to one another. Only Charley and Belfast wandered off alone. As I came up I saw a red-faced, blowsy woman, in a grey shawl, and with dusty, fluffy hair, fall on Charley's neck. It was his mother. She slobbered over him:—"Oh, my boy! My boy!"—"Leggo of me," said Charley, "Leggo, Mother!" I was passing him at the time, and over the untidy head of the blubbering woman he gave me a humorous smile and a glance ironic, courageous, and profound, that seemed to put all my knowledge of life to shame. I nodded and passed on, but heard him say again, good-naturedly:—"If you leggo of me this minyt—ye shall 'ave a bob for a drink out of my pay." In the next few steps I came upon Belfast. He caught my arm with tremulous enthusiasm.—"I couldn't go wi' 'em," he stammered, indicating by a nod our noisy crowd, that drifted slowly along the other sidewalk. "When I think of Jimmy . . . Poor Jim! When I think of him I have no heart for drink. You were his chum, too . . . but I pulled him out . . . didn't I? Short wool he had. . . . Yes. And I stole the blooming pie. . . . He wouldn't go. . . . He wouldn't go for nobody." He burst into tears. "I never touched him—

4. Above and behind the Tower of London on the Thames. The Black Horse was a pub facing the Board   of Trade on a street next to Tower Hill.

never—never!" he sobbed. "He went for me like . . . like . . . a lamb."
I disengaged myself gently. Belfast's crying fits generally ended in a
fight with some one, and I wasn't anxious to stand the brunt of his inconsolable sorrow. Moreover, two bulky policemen stood near by, looking at
us with a disapproving and incorruptible gaze.—"So long!" I said, and
went on my way.

But at the corner I stopped to take my last look at the crew of the
Narcissus. They were swaying irresolute and noisy on the broad flagstones
before the Mint.[5] They were bound for the Black Horse, where men, in
fur caps, with brutal faces and in shirt sleeves, dispense out of varnished
barrels the illusions of strength, mirth, happiness; the illusion of splendour
and poetry of life, to the paid-off crews of southern-going ships. From afar
I saw them discoursing, with jovial eyes and clumsy gestures, while the
sea of life thundered into their ears ceaseless and unheeded. And swaying
about there on the white stones, surrounded by the hurry and clamour of
men, they appeared to be creatures of another kind—lost, alone, forgetful,
and doomed; they were like castaways, like reckless and joyous castaways,
like mad castaways making merry in the storm and upon an insecure
ledge of a treacherous rock. The roar of the town resembled the roar of
topping breakers, merciless and strong, with a loud voice and cruel purpose; but overhead the clouds broke; a flood of sunshine streamed down
the walls of grimy houses. The dark knot of seamen drifted in sunshine.
To the left of them the trees in Tower Gardens sighed, the stones of the
Tower gleaming, seemed to stir in the play of light, as if remembering
suddenly all the great joys and sorrows of the past, the fighting prototypes
of these men; press-gangs; mutinous cries; the wailing of women by the
riverside, and the shouts of men welcoming victories. The sunshine of
heaven fell like a gift of grace on the mud of the earth, on the remembering and mute stones, on greed, selfishness; on the anxious faces of forgetful men. And to the right of the dark group the stained front of the Mint,
cleansed by the flood of light, stood out for a moment dazzling and white
like a marble palace in a fairy tale. The crew of the *Narcissus* drifted out
of sight.

I never saw them again. The sea took some, the steamers took others,
the graveyards of the earth will account for the rest. Singleton has no
doubt taken with him the long record of his faithful work into the peaceful depths of an hospitable sea. And Donkin, who never did a decent
day's work in his life, no doubt earns his living by discoursing with filthy
eloquence upon the right of labour to live. So be it! Let the earth and the
sea each have its own.

A gone shipmate, like any other man, is gone for ever; and I never met
one of them again. But at times the spring-flood of memory sets with
force up the dark River of the Nine Bends.[6] Then on the waters of the
forlorn stream drifts a ship—a shadowy ship manned by a crew of Shades.
They pass and make a sign, in a shadowy hail. Haven't we, together and
upon the immortal sea, wrung out a meaning from our sinful lives? Goodbye, brothers! You were a good crowd. As good a crowd as ever fisted
with wild cries the beating canvas of a heavy foresail; or tossing aloft,
invisible in the night, gave back yell for yell to a westerly gale.

1897

5. On Tower Hill, northeast of the Tower.
6. Conrad here merges the Thames and the Styx, the river of the dead.

AFTERWORD

Joseph Conrad's prose can be as precise as Stevenson's and as rhythmic. It also frequently seems to have about it an air of mystery or unreality, a sense of having a meaning beyond its statement, even when he is describing routine nautical details: "Above his head on the break of the poop, the night-watchman rang a double stroke"; "The boatswain, climbing with marlinspikes and bunches of spunyard rovings, or kneeling on the yard and ready to take a turn with the midship-stop, had acute and fleeting visions of his old woman and the youngsters in a moorland village." Characteristic of Conrad are sentences in which the sea and its human denizens, the sailors, are explicitly or implicitly contrasted with the more mundane and earthly land and its landlubbers, and are translated into cosmic images or displayed against the mysterious cosmic background. At one point he describes the sea, for example, as " . . . a resplendent world that exists within the frontier of infamy and filth, within that border of dirt and hunger, of misery and dissipation, that comes down on all sides to the water's edge of the incorruptible ocean, and is the only thing they know of life, the only thing they see of surrounding land—those life-long prisoners of the sea."

A small and fragile ship alone in the middle of the vast ocean, its few men surrounded by the sea and sky, seems appropriately to call up images of weak and fallible man in a vast, indifferent or hostile universe. Conrad seems to evoke such images constantly, in statements, in similes and metaphors, in adjectives and adverbs: "And like the last vestige of a shattered creation she drifts, bearing an anguished remnant of sinful mankind, through the distress, tumult, and pain of an avenging terror."

Indeed, man against the implacable universe is the major source of drama in Conrad: directly, in the struggles of ship against calm or storm; indirectly, in the related question of how one conducts oneself in this imperiled community. Do you whine and complain like Donkin? Do you slough off the lonely responsibility of facing life and death by involving others in struggles that are yours to face by yourself, as Wait does? Do you stoically accept the hardness of your lot, the preponderance of pain and paucity of pleasure, the burden of duty and responsibility without the gift of commensurate power, accept all this without complaint or surrender and do your job the best you can, as Singleton does?

It is difficult not to allegorize Conrad, and perhaps one should *not* try not to. The earth itself is no more than a small "ship" in the vastness of the universal "sea," and the "crew," even when made up of a few billions of men and women, is still infinitesimally small in that darkness. Whether by calm or storm, disease or drowning, the end of the voyage is one we all know. Conventionally the sea, or going out to sea, suggests death; in Conrad it is life itself, and the land, especially the city, is, if not death, at least unreality. That the *Narcissus* was the actual name of the ship Conrad sailed which underwent at least part of what he recounts here (he pieced together other characters and events from other voyages) does not prevent our seeing in that name the youth from the Greek myth who saw himself reflected in the water; whether we will fall in love with ourselves as reflected here, is another question.

Some readers see in Conrad an inner as well as outer allegory or symbolic

---

structure, a psychological as well as cosmic dimension. This is often embodied in the form of the journey down or into the interior, as in *Heart of Darkness* or *The Secret-Sharer,* or here in the descent below to rescue "the Nigger," who is our own inner blackness. James Wait has been read as our heart of darkness or original sin or evil (he is once in the novel referred to as Satan); as that which must be brought into the light and exorcised; as death; as the fear of death. He certainly brings out the best in the men—as when they risk their lives to rescue him even though they dislike him and his chance for survival is in any case small—and the worst (especially when assisted by the constantly complaining trouble-maker Donkin)—as when the crew indulges in sentimental pity which Conrad calls "egoism," or threatens mutiny, or neglects necessary tasks. His malingering or pretense at malingering and Donkin's uncooperative shirking are certainly the "wrong way" to face the arduous life of the sea in the novel, just as Singleton's illiterate wisdom, his loyalty and endurance, are the "good" in that nautical world. Wait's refusal to face his own death while yet parading his dying is as bad as cowardice and is opposed to Singleton's stoical acceptance of danger and drudgery. These patterns, like the image of the lonely ship in the cosmic sea, are clearly representative of Conrad's vision of life, morality, value in the world.

Conrad clearly believes some individuals, like Donkin, to be evil; some behavior, like Wait's, wrong; and some people, like Singleton, good. But the generality, the crew, mixed, alternately good and evil, or perhaps readily susceptible to good or evil influences. The sailors pity Wait. Pity is a good, perhaps an essential human quality, but in their pity they are vicariously expressing their own fear or rejection of the reality of death, and so Conrad calls it "egoism." They are capable of heroically endangering their own lives to save another, not necessarily better, or lovable human being; the same crew is capable of mutinous grumbling.

Some see a contradiction in Conrad's narrative of the crew's behavior during the voyage and the final sentence of the novel: "As good a crowd as ever fisted with wild cries the beating canvas of a heavy foresail; or tossing aloft, invisible in the night, gave back yell for yell to a westerly gale" (another of his nautical-cosmic sentences). They did their hard and dangerous work; they fought and even defied the overwhelming power of the hostile elements. They did. They got through the storm and the upsetting and the dangerous and maddening if less dramatic calm. Conrad does not say they are perfectly good or even fundamentally good, but only relatively not bad: "as good a crowd as"—no better, no worse; a typical group of men, of man. "Haven't we, together and upon the immortal sea, wrung out a meaning from our sinful lives?" Their lives are "sinful." If the sea is immortal, they are mere mortals. Still, they have made out of the implacable and dire and meaningless, meaning. That, Conrad seems to say, is what man does.

The narrator who speaks that final sentence that some find dubiously authentic speaks in the first-person singular, "I." For most of the novel the narration is in the first-person plural, "we," and at the very beginning the narrator seems omniscient. Besides certain practical or logical difficulties—how can "we," if we are not omniscient (and not Donkin or Wait), know what these two say to each other when no one else is present?—there is the larger question of the "authority" in the novel. Can we believe that this narrator, who, we assume, is the same throughout—the "I" who just temporarily identifies himself with the rest of the crew during the voyage—and who can see the action in such cosmic terms and describe it in such wonderful language, can we believe that he believes with Singleton the folk or common seaman's superstition that Wait cannot die until the ship is within sight of land? Is this mere coincidence? Has Conrad here opted for allegory over realism?

I believe the problem arises chiefly because *focus,* the camera angle, so to speak, and *voice,* the language in which the story is embodied, are often considered a single fictional element, *point of view.* Here the voice is consistent and is that of the "I" who speaks or writes down the experience of the *Narcissus* in words. The focus is not consistently that of the recording "I," however. The "we" is not "I" plus others of the crew but the composite crew: "we" can know anything any one member of the crew (including Donkin or Wait) knows regardless whether that "I" who writes it all down knew it at the time or not. And the crew as a whole, or at least some of its members severally, including Singleton himself, believed the superstition. The timing of Wait's death may have been a coincidence—such things no doubt happen—but there is no reason for the narrating "I," the voice, to intervene with questions or conjectures, when "we," the crew and the focus of perception during the voyage, are, wholly or partly, permanently or momentarily, convinced that "we" have seen Singleton's folk wisdom confirmed.

Conrad's first novels were not popular successes, and he did not have a great deal of hope for the popularity of *The Nigger of the "Narcissus,"* though he said more than once that he would stand or fall *as an artist* by this novel. The lack of mass appeal is often attributed to the relative absence of plot. There is, it would seem, sufficient *action*—the ship overwhelmed after a monumental struggle by the fiercest of winds, endangered by an agonizingly drawn-out breathless calm; the tense rescue of Jimmy, the threat of mutiny. But action is not the same as plot. Each of these incidents has its own built-in suspense, but the novel as a whole still seems somewhat static because these events are not causally connected—they are sequential but not consequential. If there is not sustained suspense, is there not a pervasive and intensifying curiosity in the mystery of James Wait? Just as we want to know the nature of and truth about Daisy Miller, surely we want to know what Wait is like and whether he is dying or malingering. Why, then, does the novel as a whole not deeply involve or grip us so that, as the saying goes, we cannot put it down? Perhaps we have answered this question by implication already—several times. First of all, though Donkin may be all bad and Singleton all good, and we know Belfast and others of the crew, and the captain and officers by name, and we want them all to survive, we are not invited to share their experiences and feelings, their hopes and fears, their pasts and presents that make up their identity, in any intimate way. The very choice of "we," the crew, as focus gives us essentially a communal but not individual concern. Furthermore, the constant stretching of the prose toward meaning, toward allegory if you will, not only shifts our attention away from the men as individuals but away from incident and outcome toward meaning, or representativeness.

This does not make for a bad novel. It is not only locally exciting—the storm, the rescue—but also morally so. In a suspenseful story we often think of ourselves as the protagonist and suffer or succeed vicariously with his or her pain or victory—we go out to the story in a sense, the way the crew's pity goes out to Wait. But that, says Conrad, is egoism. *The Nigger of the "Narcissus,"* by not allowing us to "identify" and go out to the story, vicariously to see ourselves as Wait or "I," making us stay at home with ourselves, makes us ask about our own conduct, our own values, our own vision of man's reality and role in the universe. The paradoxes of such phrases as "the latent egoism of tenderness to suffering" and "desired unrest" do not merely challenge the assumptions or views of one or more members of the crew, or of the crew of the *Narcissus* as a whole, but of the reader. The reader may not be *on* the *Narcissus,* but he or she *is* Narcissus, reflected and reflecting.

KATE CHOPIN

The Awakening

Born in Saint Louis in 1851, Katherine O'Flaherty was reared primarily by her French Creole mother and great-grandmother, her Irish father having died in an accident when she was only four. At twenty she married another French Creole, Oscar Chopin, who took her to New Orleans where he established a cotton brokerage that was very successful through most of the 1870s until there were consecutive poor cotton crops. They then moved to Natchitoches Parish in northwestern Louisiana where, later, most of her stories would be set. Oscar Chopin died in 1883, and Kate ran the plantation for a while; but at the urging of her mother she returned to St. Louis a year later with her children. In less than a year her mother died, and Kate, in the hope of earning a living, began her literary career. By her death in 1904 she had written two novels, *At Fault* (1890) and *The Awakening* (1899), as well as seven or eight dozen sketches and short stories.

She did not, then, write her Louisiana-drenched fiction while she lived there, but recollected it in the economic untranquility of her widowhood; so her reputation for "local color," her chief reputation during her lifetime, was somewhat ironic. Both insider and outsider, Chopin knew Creole life and society intimately, while having the perspective on the people and places around New Orleans that natives lacked.

The "local color" movement in American literature toward the end of the nineteenth century was at its best a form of regional realism, stressing the particulars of life in a specific locale—dialect, dress, customs. You can see in *The Awakening* Kate Chopin's ability to give a sense of place in her creation of the setting and mood of Grande Isle and New Orleans, and in the relationship of the French Creole society there to its local and cultural traditions. Indeed, Edna Pontellier's awakening is in part the result, one might say, of the collision of her Kentucky Protestantism with the French Catholicism of the people and the semitropical surroundings of New Orleans.

When the locale or environment in "local color" fiction exerts a determining influence on the fictional characters, "local color" virtually becomes a form of "naturalism," a late-nineteenth-century literary movement depicting men and women as the more or less helpless creatures of their heredity and environment. There is a good deal about sleeping and waking, freedom and restriction (or restraint) in *The Awakening*, but Kate Chopin does not resort to didacticism. Her narration is so objective—or, to be more precise, even-handed—that readers must be careful and thorough in deciding just what *The Awakening* "says" or shows.

Chopin's novel was not well received when it first appeared—not so much because it dealt with sex, apparently, as because it did so coolly or objectively, without preaching or promoting, teaching or titillating. It was "rediscovered" about thirty-five years ago and more recently has been incorporated in the feminist reappraisal of the literary tradition. It is challenging reading both in itself and because it is a book that has been read, interpreted, and judged for more than eighty years and yet still does not have a "fixed" position in the canon.

The Awakening

A GREEN AND YELLOW PARROT, which hung in a cage outside the door, kept repeating over and over:

"*Allez vous-en! Allez vous-en! Sapristi!*[1] That's all right!"

He could speak a little Spanish, and also a language which nobody understood, unless it was the mocking-bird that hung on the other side of the door, whistling his fluty notes out upon the breeze with maddening persistence.

Mr. Pontellier, unable to read his newspaper with any degree of comfort, arose with an expression and an exclamation of disgust. He walked down the gallery and across the narrow "bridges" which connected the Lebrun cottages one with the other. He had been seated before the door of the main house. The parrot and the mocking-bird were the property of Madame Lebrun, and they had the right to make all the noise they wished. Mr. Pontellier had the privilege of quitting their society when they ceased to be entertaining.

He stopped before the door of his own cottage, which was the fourth one from the main building and next to the last. Seating himself in a wicker rocker which was there, he once more applied himself to the task of reading the newspaper. The day was Sunday; the paper was a day old. The Sunday papers had not yet reached Grand Isle.[2] He was already acquainted with the market reports, and he glanced restlessly over the editorials and bits of news which he had not had time to read before quitting New Orleans the day before.

Mr. Pontellier wore eye-glasses. He was a man of forty, of medium height and rather slender build; he stooped a little. His hair was brown and straight, parted on one side. His beard was neatly and closely trimmed.

Once in a while he withdrew his glance from the newspaper and looked about him. There was more noise than ever over at the house. The main building was called "the house," to distinguish it from the cottages. The chattering and whistling birds were still at it. Two young girls, the Farival twins, were playing a duet from "Zampa"[3] upon the piano. Madame Lebrun was bustling in and out, giving orders in a high key to a yard boy whenever she got inside the house, and directions in an equally high voice to a dining-room servant whenever she got outside. She was a fresh, pretty woman, clad always in white with elbow sleeves. Her starched skirts crinkled as she came and went. Farther down, before one of the cottages, a lady in black was walking demurely up and down, telling her beads. A good many persons of the *pension* had gone over to the *Chênière Caminada*[4] in Beaudelet's lugger to hear mass. Some young people were out under the water oaks playing croquet. Mr. Pontellier's two children were there—sturdy little fellows of four and five. A quadroon nurse followed them about with a far-away, meditative air.

1. *Go away! Go away! Damn it!*
2. Island resort in the Gulf of Mexico about fifty miles south of New Orleans and devastated by a hurricane in 1893.
3. Opera (1831) by Louis Hérold (1791–1833).
4. Island between Louisiana coast and Grand Isle.

Mr. Pontellier finally lit a cigar and began to smoke, letting the paper drag idly from his hand. He fixed his gaze upon a white sunshade that was advancing at a snail's pace from the beach. He could see it plainly between the gaunt trunks of the water-oaks and across the stretch of yellow camomile. The Gulf looked far away, melting hazily into the blue of the horizon. The sunshade continued to approach slowly. Beneath its pink-lined shelter were his wife, Mrs. Pontellier, and young Robert Lebrun. When they reached the cottage, the two seated themselves with some appearance of fatigue upon the upper step of the porch, facing each other, each leaning against a supporting post.

"What folly! to bathe at such an hour in such heat!" exclaimed Mr. Pontellier. He himself had taken a plunge at daylight. That was why the morning seemed long to him.

"You are burnt beyond recognition," he added, looking at his wife as one looks at a valuable piece of personal property which has suffered some damage. She held up her hands, strong, shapely hands, and surveyed them critically, drawing up her lawn sleeves above the wrists. Looking at them reminded her of her rings, which she had given to her husband before leaving for the beach. She silently reached out to him, and he, understanding, took the rings from his vest pocket and dropped them into her open palm. She slipped them upon her fingers; then clasping her knees, she looked across at Robert and began to laugh. The rings sparkled upon her fingers. He sent back an answering smile.

"What is it?" asked Pontellier, looking lazily and amused from one to the other. It was some utter nonsense; some adventure out there in the water, and they both tried to relate it at once. It did not seem half so amusing when told. They realized this, and so did Mr. Pontellier. He yawned and stretched himself. Then he got up, saying he had half a mind to go over to Klein's hotel and play a game of billiards.

"Come go along, Lebrun," he proposed to Robert. But Robert admitted quite frankly that he preferred to stay where he was and talk to Mrs. Pontellier.

"Well, send him about his business when he bores you, Edna," instructed her husband as he prepared to leave.

"Here, take the umbrella," she exclaimed, holding it out to him. He accepted the sunshade, and lifting it over his head descended the steps and walked away.

"Coming back to dinner?" his wife called after him. He halted a moment and shrugged his shoulders. He felt in his vest pocket; there was a ten-dollar bill there. He did not know; perhaps he would return for the early dinner and perhaps he would not. It all depended upon the company which he found over at Klein's and the size of "the game." He did not say this, but she understood it, and laughed, nodding good-by to him.

Both children wanted to follow their father when they saw him starting out. He kissed them and promised to bring them back bonbons and peanuts.

II

Mrs. Pontellier's eyes were quick and bright; they were a yellowish brown, about the color of her hair. She had a way of turning them swiftly upon an object and holding them there as if lost in some inward maze of contemplation or thought.

Her eyebrows were a shade darker than her hair. They were thick and almost horizontal, emphasizing the depth of her eyes. She was rather handsome than beautiful. Her face was captivating by reason of a certain frankness of expression and a contradictory subtle play of features. Her manner was engaging.

Robert rolled a cigarette. He smoked cigarettes because he could not afford cigars, he said. He had a cigar in his pocket which Mr. Pontellier had presented him with, and he was saving it for his after-dinner smoke. This seemed quite proper and natural on his part. In coloring he was not unlike his companion. A clean-shaved face made the resemblance more pronounced than it would otherwise have been. There rested no shadow of care upon his open countenance. His eyes gathered in and reflected the light and languor of the summer day.

Mrs. Pontellier reached over for a palmleaf fan that lay on the porch and began to fan herself, while Robert sent between his lips light puffs from his cigarette. They chatted incessantly: about the things around them; their amusing adventure out in the water—it had again assumed its entertaining aspect; about the wind, the trees, the people who had gone to the *Chênière;* about the children playing croquet under the oaks, and the Farival twins, who were now performing the overture to "The Poet and the Peasant."[5]

Robert talked a good deal about himself. He was very young, and did not know any better. Mrs. Pontellier talked a little about herself for the same reason. Each was interested in what the other said. Robert spoke of his intention to go to Mexico in the autumn, where fortune awaited him. He was always intending to go to Mexico, but some way never got there. Meanwhile he held on to his modest position in a mercantile house in New Orleans, where an equal familiarity with English, French and Spanish gave him no small value as a clerk and correspondent.

He was spending his summer vacation, as he always did, with his mother at Grand Isle. In former times, before Robert could remember, "the house" had been a summer luxury of the Lebruns. Now, flanked by its dozen or more cottages, which were always filled with exclusive visitors from the *"Quartier Français,"*[6] it enabled Madame Lebrun to maintain the easy and comfortable existence which appeared to be her birthright.

Mrs. Pontellier talked about her father's Mississippi plantation and her girlhood home in the old Kentucky blue-grass country. She was an American woman, with a small infusion of French which seemed to have been lost in dilution. She read a letter from her sister, who was away in the East, and who had engaged herself to be married. Robert was interested, and wanted to know what manner of girls the sisters were, what the father was like, and how long the mother had been dead.

When Mrs. Pontellier folded the letter it was time for her to dress for the early dinner.

"I see Léonce isn't coming back," she said, with a glance in the direc-

---

5. Operetta (1846) by Franz von Suppé (1819–1895).

6. French Quarter, oldest part of New Orleans and home of the Creole population.

tion whence her husband had disappeared. Robert supposed he was not, as there were a good many New Orleans club men over at Klein's.

When Mrs. Pontellier left him to enter her room, the young man descended the steps and strolled over toward the croquet players, where, during the half-hour before dinner, he amused himself with the little Pontellier children, who were very fond of him.

III

It was eleven o'clock that night when Mr. Pontellier returned from Klein's hotel. He was in an excellent humor, in high spirits, and very talkative. His entrance awoke his wife, who was in bed and fast asleep when he came in. He talked to her while he undressed, telling her anecdotes and bits of news and gossip that he had gathered during the day. From his trousers pockets he took a fistful of crumpled bank notes and a good deal of silver coin, which he piled on the bureau indiscriminately with keys, knife, handkerchief, and whatever else happened to be in his pockets. She was overcome with sleep, and answered him with little half utterances.

He thought it very discouraging that his wife, who was the sole object of his existence, evinced so little interest in things which concerned him and valued so little his conversation.

Mr. Pontellier had forgotten the bonbons and peanuts for the boys. Notwithstanding he loved them very much, and went into the adjoining room where they slept to take a look at them and make sure that they were resting comfortably. The result of his investigation was far from satisfactory. He turned and shifted the youngsters about in bed. One of them began to kick and talk about a basket full of crabs.

Mr. Pontellier returned to his wife with the information that Raoul had a high fever and needed looking after. Then he lit a cigar and went and sat near the open door to smoke it.

Mrs. Pontellier was quite sure Raoul had no fever. He had gone to bed perfectly well, she said, and nothing had ailed him all day. Mr. Pontellier was too well acquainted with fever symptoms to be mistaken. He assured her the child was consuming at that moment in the next room.

He reproached his wife with her inattention, her habitual neglect of the children. If it was not a mother's place to look after children, whose on earth was it? He himself had his hands full with his brokerage business. He could not be in two places at once; making a living for his family on the street, and staying at home to see that no harm befell them. He talked in a monotonous, insistent way.

Mrs. Pontellier sprang out of bed and went into the next room. She soon came back and sat on the edge of the bed, leaning her head down on the pillow. She said nothing, and refused to answer her husband when he questioned her. When his cigar was smoked out he went to bed, and in half a minute he was fast asleep.

Mrs. Pontellier was by that time thoroughly awake. She began to cry a little, and wiped her eyes on the sleeve of her *peignoir*. Blowing out the candle, which her husband had left burning, she slipped her bare feet into a pair of satin *mules* at the foot of the bed and went out on the porch, where she sat down in the wicker chair and began to rock gently to and fro.

It was then past midnight. The cottages were all dark. A single faint light gleamed out from the hallway of the house. There was no sound abroad except the hooting of an old owl in the top of a water-oak, and the everlasting voice of the sea, that was not uplifted at that soft hour. It broke like a mournful lullaby upon the night.

The tears came so fast to Mrs. Pontellier's eyes that the damp sleeve of her *peignoir* no longer served to dry them. She was holding the back of her chair with one hand; her loose sleeve had slipped almost to the shoulder of her uplifted arm. Turning, she thrust her face, steaming and wet, into the bend of her arm, and she went on crying there, not caring any longer to dry her face, her eyes, her arms. She could not have told why she was crying. Such experiences as the foregoing were not uncommon in her married life. They seemed never before to have weighed much against the abundance of her husband's kindness and a uniform devotion which had come to be tacit and self-understood.

An indescribable oppression, which seemed to generate in some unfamiliar part of her consciousness, filled her whole being with a vague anguish. It was like a shadow, like a mist passing across her soul's summer day. It was strange and unfamiliar; it was a mood. She did not sit there inwardly upbraiding her husband, lamenting at Fate, which had directed her footsteps to the path which they had taken. She was just having a good cry all to herself. The mosquitoes made merry over her, biting her firm, round arms and nipping at her bare insteps.

The little stinging, buzzing imps succeeded in dispelling a mood which might have held her there in the darkness half a night longer.

The following morning Mr. Pontellier was up in good time to take the rockaway which was to convey him to the steamer at the wharf. He was returning to the city to his business, and they would not see him again at the Island till the coming Saturday. He had regained his composure, which seemed to have been somewhat impaired the night before. He was eager to be gone, as he looked forward to a lively week in Carondelet Street.[7]

Mr. Pontellier gave his wife half the money which he had brought away from Klein's hotel the evening before. She liked money as well as most women, and accepted it with no little satisfaction.

"It will buy a handsome wedding present for Sister Janet!" she exclaimed, smoothing out the bills as she counted them one by one.

"Oh! we'll treat Sister Janet better than that, my dear," he laughed, as he prepared to kiss her good-by.

The boys were tumbling about, clinging to his legs, imploring that numerous things be brought back to them. Mr. Pontellier was a great favorite, and ladies, men, children, even nurses, were always on hand to say good-by to him. His wife stood smiling and waving, the boys shouting, as he disappeared in the old rockaway down the sandy road.

A few days later a box arrived for Mrs. Pontellier from New Orleans. It was from her husband. It was filled with *friandises*,[8] with luscious and toothsome bits—the finest of fruits, *pâtés*, a rare bottle or two, delicious syrups, and bonbons in abundance.

Mrs. Pontellier was always very generous with the contents of such a box; she was quite used to receiving them when away from home. The

---

7. Location of the Cotton Exchange, heart of New Orleans financial district.   8. Delicacies.

pâtés and fruit were brought to the dining-room; the bonbons were passed around. And the ladies, selecting with dainty and discriminating fingers and a little greedily, all declared that Mr. Pontellier was the best husband in the world. Mrs. Pontellier was forced to admit that she knew of none better.

IV

It would have been a difficult matter for Mr. Pontellier to define to his own satisfaction or any one else's wherein his wife failed in her duty toward their children. It was something which he felt rather than perceived, and he never voiced the feeling without subsequent regret and ample atonement.

If one of the little Pontellier boys took a tumble whilst at play, he was not apt to rush crying to his mother's arms for comfort; he would more likely pick himself up, wipe the water out of his eyes and the sand out of his mouth, and go on playing. Tots as they were, they pulled together and stood their ground in childish battles with doubled fists and uplifted voices, which usually prevailed against the other mother-tots. The quadroon nurse was looked upon as a huge encumbrance, only good to button up waists and panties and to brush and part hair; since it seemed to be a law of society that hair must be parted and brushed.

In short, Mrs. Pontellier was not a mother-woman. The mother-women seemed to prevail that summer at Grand Isle. It was easy to know them, fluttering about with extended, protecting wings when any harm, real or imaginary, threatened their precious brood. They were women who idolized their children, worshiped their husbands, and esteemed it a holy privilege to efface themselves as individuals and grow wings as ministering angels.

Many of them were delicious in the rôle; one of them was the embodiment of every womanly grace and charm. If her husband did not adore her, he was a brute, deserving of death by slow torture. Her name was Adèle Ratignolle. There are no words to describe her save the old ones that have served so often to picture the bygone heroine of romance and the fair lady of our dreams. There was nothing subtle or hidden about her charms; her beauty was all there, flaming and apparent: the spun-gold hair that comb nor confining pin could restrain; the blue eyes that were like nothing but sapphires; two lips that pouted, that were so red one could only think of cherries or some other delicious crimson fruit in looking at them. She was growing a little stout, but it did not seem to detract an iota from the grace of every step, pose, gesture. One would not have wanted her white neck a mite less full or her beautiful arms more slender. Never were hands more exquisite than hers, and it was a joy to look at them when she threaded her needle or adjusted her gold thimble to her taper middle finger as she sewed away on the little night-drawers or fashioned a bodice or a bib.

Madame Ratignolle was very fond of Mrs. Pontellier, and often she took her sewing and went over to sit with her in the afternoons. She was sitting there the afternoon of the day the box arrived from New Orleans. She had possession of the rocker, and she was busily engaged in sewing upon a diminutive pair of night-drawers.

She had brought the pattern of the drawers for Mrs. Pontellier to cut out—a marvel of construction, fashioned to enclose a baby's body so effectually that only two small eyes might look out from the garment, like an Eskimo's. They were designed for winter wear, when treacherous drafts came down chimneys and insidious currents of deadly cold found their way through key-holes.

Mrs. Pontellier's mind was quite at rest concerning the present material needs of her children, and she could not see the use of anticipating and making winter night garments the subject of her summer meditations. But she did not want to appear unamiable and uninterested, so she had brought forth newspapers which she spread upon the floor of the gallery, and under Madame Ratignolle's directions she had cut a pattern of the impervious garment.

Robert was there, seated as he had been the Sunday before, and Mrs. Pontellier also occupied her former position on the upper step, leaning listlessly against the post. Beside her was a box of bonbons, which she held out at intervals to Madame Ratignolle.

That lady seemed at a loss to make a selection, but finally settled upon a stick of nougat, wondering if it were not too rich; whether it could possibly hurt her. Madame Ratignolle had been married seven years. About every two years she had a baby. At that time she had three babies, and was beginning to think of a fourth one. She was always talking about her "condition." Her "condition" was in no way apparent, and no one would have known a thing about it but for her persistence in making it the subject of conversation.

Robert started to reassure her, asserting that he had known a lady who had subsisted upon nougat during the entire—but seeing the color mount into Mrs. Pontellier's face he checked himself and changed the subject.

Mrs. Pontellier, though she had married a Creole, was not thoroughly at home in the society of Creoles;[9] never before had she been thrown so intimately among them. There were only Creoles that summer at Lebrun's. They all knew each other, and felt like one large family, among whom existed the most amicable relations. A characteristic which distinguished them and which impressed Mrs. Pontellier most forcibly was their entire absence of prudery. Their freedom of expression was at first incomprehensible to her, though she had no difficulty in reconciling it with a lofty chastity which in the Creole woman seems to be inborn and unmistakable.

Never would Edna Pontellier forget the shock with which she heard Madame Ratignolle relating to old Monsieur Farrival the harrowing story of one of her *accouchements,* withholding no intimate detail. She was growing accustomed to like shocks, but she could not keep the mounting color back from her cheeks. Oftener than once her coming had interrupted the droll story with which Robert was entertaining some amused group of married women.

A book had gone the rounds of the *pension.* When it came her turn to read it, she did so with profound astonishment. She felt moved to read the book in secret and solitude, though none of the others had done so—to hide it from view at the sound of approaching footsteps. It was openly criticised and freely discussed at table. Mrs. Pontellier gave over being astonished, and concluded that wonders would never cease.

9. New Orleans aristocracy, descended from early Spanish and French settlers.

V

They formed a congenial group sitting there that summer afternoon—
Madame Ratignolle sewing away, often stopping to relate a story or incident with much expressive gesture of her perfect hands; Robert and Mrs.
Pontellier sitting idle, exchanging occasional words, glances or smiles
which indicated a certain advanced stage of intimacy and *camaraderie*.
He had lived in her shadow during the past month. No one thought
anything of it. Many had predicted that Robert would devote himself to
Mrs. Pontellier when he arrived. Since the age of fifteen, which was eleven years before, Robert each summer at Grand Isle had constituted himself the devoted attendant of some fair dame or damsel. Sometimes it was
a young girl, again a widow; but as often as not it was some interesting
married woman.

For two consecutive seasons he lived in the sunlight of Mademoiselle
Duvigné's presence. But she died between summers; then Robert posed as
an inconsolable, prostrating himself at the feet of Madame Ratignolle for
whatever crumbs of sympathy and comfort she might be pleased to
vouchsafe.

Mrs. Pontellier liked to sit and gaze at her fair companion as she might
look upon a faultless Madonna.

"Could any one fathom the cruelty beneath that fair exterior?" murmured Robert. "She knew that I adored her once, and she let me adore
her. It was 'Robert, come; go; stand up; sit down; do this; do that; see if
the baby sleeps; my thimble, please, that I left God knows where. Come
and read Daudet to me while I sew.' "

"*Par exemple!*[1] I never had to ask. You were always there under my
feet, like a troublesome cat."

"You mean like an adoring dog. And just as soon as Ratignolle appeared
on the scene, then it was like a dog. '*Passez! Adieu! Allez vous-en!*' "[2]

"Perhaps I feared to make Alphonse jealous," she interjoined, with excessive naïveté. That made them all laugh. The right hand jealous of the
left! The heart jealous of the soul! But for that matter, the Creole husband is never jealous; with him the gangrene passion is one which has
become dwarfed by disuse.

Meanwhile Robert, addressing Mrs. Pontellier, continued to tell of his
one-time hopeless passion for Madame Ratignolle; of sleepless nights, of
consuming flames till the very sea sizzled when he took his daily plunge.
While the lady at the needle kept up a little running, contemptuous comment:

"*Blagueur—farceur—gros bête, va!*"[3]

He never assumed this serio-comic tone when alone with Mrs. Pontellier. She never knew precisely what to make of it; at that moment it was
impossible for her to guess how much of it was jest and what proportion
was earnest. It was understood that he had often spoken words of love to
Madame Ratignolle, without any thought of being taken seriously. Mrs.
Pontellier was glad he had not assumed a similar rôle toward herself. It
would have been unacceptable and annoying.

Mrs. Pontellier had brought her sketching materials, which she sometimes dabbled with in an unprofessional way. She liked the dabbling. She

---

1. *Indeed!* Alphonse Daudet (1840–1897) was a
French novelist and short story writer.

2. *Go on out! Good-by! Go away!*
3. *Fraud—joker—fool, go on with you!*

felt in it satisfaction of a kind which no other employment afforded her. She had long wished to try herself on Madame Ratignolle. Never had that lady seemed a more tempting subject than at that moment, seated there like some sensuous Madonna, with the gleam of the fading day enriching her splendid color.

Robert crossed over and seated himself upon the step below Mrs. Pontellier, that he might watch her work. She handled her brushes with a certain ease and freedom which came, not from long and close acquaintance with them, but from a natural aptitude. Robert followed her work with close attention, giving forth little ejaculatory expressions of appreciation in French, which he addressed to Madame Ratignolle.

"Mais ce n'est pas mal! Elle s'y connait, elle a de la force, oui."[4]

During his oblivious attention he once quietly rested his head against Mrs. Pontellier's arm. As gently she repulsed him. Once again he repeated the offense. She could not but believe it to be thoughtlessness on his part; yet that was no reason she should submit to it. She did not remonstrate, except again to repulse him quietly but firmly. He offered no apology.

The picture completed bore no resemblance to Madame Ratignolle. She was greatly disappointed to find that it did not look like her. But it was a fair enough piece of work, and in many respects satisfying.

Mrs. Pontellier evidently did not think so. After surveying the sketch critically she drew a broad smudge of paint across its surface, and crumpled the paper between her hands.

The youngsters came tumbling up the steps, the quadroon following at the respectful distance which they required her to observe. Mrs. Pontellier made them carry her paints and things into the house. She sought to detain them for a little talk and some pleasantry. But they were greatly in earnest. They had only come to investigate the contents of the bonbon box. They accepted without murmuring what she chose to give them, each holding out two chubby hands scoop-like, in the vain hope that they might be filled; and then away they went.

The sun was low in the west, and the breeze soft and languorous that came up from the south, charged with the seductive odor of the sea. Children, freshly befurbelowed,[5] were gathering for their games under the oaks. Their voices were high and penetrating.

Madame Ratignolle folded her sewing, placing thimble, scissors and thread all neatly together in the roll, which she pinned securely. She complained of faintness. Mrs. Pontellier flew for the cologne water and a fan. She bathed Madame Ratignolle's face with cologne, while Robert plied the fan with unnecessary vigor.

The spell was soon over, and Mrs. Pontellier could not help wondering if there were not a little imagination responsible for its origin, for the rose tint had never faded from her friend's face.

She stood watching the fair woman walk down the long line of galleries with the grace and majesty which queens are sometimes supposed to possess. Her little ones ran to meet her. Two of them clung about her white skirts, the third she took from its nurse and with a thousand endearments bore it along in her own fond, encircling arms. Though, as everybody well knew, the doctor had forbidden her to lift so much as a pin!

---

4. *But that's not bad! She knows what she's doing; yes, she has talent.*

5. Dressed in highly ornamental, showy clothes.

"Are you going bathing?" asked Robert of Mrs. Pontellier. It was not so much a question as a reminder.

"Oh, no," she answered, with a tone of indecision. "I'm tired; I think not." Her glance wandered from his face away toward the Gulf, whose sonorous murmur reached her like a loving but imperative entreaty.

"Oh, come!" he insisted. "You mustn't miss your bath. Come on. The water must be delicious; it will not hurt you. Come."

He reached up for her big, rough straw hat that hung on a peg outside the door, and put it on her head. They descended the steps, and walked away together toward the beach. The sun was low in the west and the breeze was soft and warm.

VI

Edna Pontellier could not have told why, wishing to go to the beach with Robert, she should in the first place have declined, and in the second place have followed in obedience to one of the two contradictory impulses which impelled her.

A certain light was beginning to dawn dimly within her,—the light which, showing the way, forbids it.

At that early period it served but to bewilder her. It moved her to dreams, to thoughtfulness, to the shadowy anguish which had overcome her the midnight when she had abandoned herself to tears.

In short, Mrs. Pontellier was beginning to realize her position in the universe as a human being, and to recognize her relations as an individual to the world within and about her. This may seem like a ponderous weight of wisdom to descend upon the soul of a young woman of twenty-eight—perhaps more wisdom than the Holy Ghost is usually pleased to vouchsafe to any woman.

But the beginning of things, of a world especially, is necessarily vague, tangled, chaotic, and exceedingly disturbing. How few of us ever emerge from such beginning! How many souls perish in its tumult!

The voice of the sea is seductive; never ceasing, whispering, clamoring, murmuring, inviting the soul to wander for a spell in abysses of solitude; to lose itself in mazes of inward contemplation.

The voice of the sea speaks to the soul. The touch of the sea is sensuous, enfolding the body in its soft, close embrace.

VII

Mrs. Pontellier was not a woman given to confidences, a characteristic hitherto contrary to her nature. Even as a child she had lived her own small life all within herself. At a very early period she had apprehended instinctively the dual life—that outward existence which conforms, the inward life which questions.

That summer at Grand Isle she began to loosen a little the mantle of reserve that had always enveloped her. There may have been—there must have been—influences, both subtle and apparent, working in their several ways to induce her to do this; but the most obvious was the influence of Adèle Ratignolle. The excessive physical charm of the Creole had first attracted her, for Edna had a sensuous susceptibility to beauty. Then the candor of the woman's whole existence, which every one might read, and which formed so striking a contrast to her own habitual reserve—this might have furnished a link. Who can tell what metals the gods use in forging the subtle bond which we call sympathy, which we might as well call love.

The two women went away one morning to the beach together, arm in arm, under the huge white sunshade. Edna had prevailed upon Madame Ratignolle to leave the children behind, though she could not induce her to relinquish a diminutive roll of needlework, which Adèle begged to be allowed to slip into the depths of her pocket. In some unaccountable way they had escaped from Robert.

The walk to the beach was no inconsiderable one, consisting as it did of a long, sandy path, upon which a sporadic and tangled growth that bordered it on either side made frequent and unexpected inroads. There were acres of yellow camomile reaching out on either hand. Further away still, vegetable gardens abounded, with frequent small plantations of orange or lemon trees intervening. The dark green clusters glistened from afar in the sun.

The women were both of goodly height, Madame Ratignolle possessing the more feminine and matronly figure. The charm of Edna Pontellier's physique stole insensibly upon you. The lines of her body were long, clean and symmetrical; it was a body which occasionally fell into splendid poses; there was no suggestion of the trim, stereotyped fashion-plate about it. A casual and indiscriminating observer, in passing, might not cast a second glance upon the figure. But with more feeling and discernment he would have recognized the noble beauty of its modeling, and the graceful severity of poise and movement, which made Edna Pontellier different from the crowd.

She wore a cool muslin that morning—white, with a waving vertical line of brown running through it; also a white linen collar and the big straw hat which she had taken from the peg outside the door. The hat rested any way on her yellow-brown hair, that waved a little, was heavy, and clung close to her head.

Madame Ratignolle, more careful of her complexion, had twined a gauze veil about her head. She wore dogskin[6] gloves, with gauntlets that protected her wrists. She was dressed in pure white, with a fluffiness of ruffles that became her. The draperies and fluttering things which she wore suited her rich, luxuriant beauty as a greater severity of line could not have done.

There were a number of bath-houses along the beach, of rough but solid construction, built with small, protecting galleries facing the water. Each house consisted of two compartments, and each family at Lebrun's possessed a compartment for itself, fitted out with all the essential paraphernalia of the bath and whatever other conveniences the owners might desire. The two women had no intention of bathing; they had just strolled down to the beach for a walk and to be alone and near the water. The Pontellier and Ratignolle compartments adjoined one another under the same roof.

Mrs. Pontellier had brought down her key through force of habit. Unlocking the door of her bath-room she went inside, and soon emerged,

---

6. Leather gloves made of dogskin and oiled on the inside to keep the hands moist and cool.

bringing a rug, which she spread upon the floor of the gallery, and two huge hair pillows covered with crash, which she placed against the front of the building.

The two seated themselves there in the shade of the porch, side by side, with their backs against the pillows and their feet extended. Madame Ratignolle removed her veil, wiped her face with a rather delicate handkerchief, and fanned herself with the fan which she always carried suspended somewhere about her person by a long, narrow ribbon. Edna removed her collar and opened her dress at the throat. She took the fan from Madame Ratignolle and began to fan both herself and her companion. It was very warm, and for a while they did nothing but exchange remarks about the heat, the sun, the glare. But there was a breeze blowing, a choppy stiff wind that whipped the water into froth. It fluttered the skirts of the two women and kept them for a while engaged in adjusting, readjusting, tucking in, securing hair-pins and hat-pins. A few persons were sporting some distance away in the water. The beach was very still of human sound at that hour. The lady in black was reading her morning devotions on the porch of a neighboring bath-house. Two young lovers were exchanging their hearts' yearnings beneath the children's tent, which they had found unoccupied.

Edna Pontellier, casting her eyes about, had finally kept them at rest upon the sea. The day was clear and carried the gaze out as far as the blue sky went; there were a few white clouds suspended idly over the horizon. A lateen sail was visible in the direction of Cat Island, and others to the south seemed almost motionless in the far distance.

"Of whom—of what are you thinking?" asked Adèle of her companion, whose countenance she had been watching with a little amused attention, arrested by the absorbed expression which seemed to have seized and fixed every feature into a statuesque repose.

"Nothing," returned Mrs. Pontellier, with a start, adding at once: "How stupid! But it seems to me it is the reply we make instinctively to such a question. Let me see," she went on, throwing back her head and narrowing her fine eyes till they shone like two vivid points of light. "Let me see. I was really not conscious of thinking of anything; but perhaps I can retrace my thoughts."

"Oh! never mind!" laughed Madame Ratignolle. "I am not quite so exacting. I will let you off this time. It is really too hot to think, especially to think about thinking."

"But for the fun of it," persisted Edna. "First of all, the sight of the water stretching so far away, those motionless sails against the blue sky, made a delicious picture that I just wanted to sit and look at. The hot wind beating in my face made me think—without any connection that I can trace—of a summer day in Kentucky, of a meadow that seemed as big as the ocean to the very little girl walking through the grass, which was higher than her waist. She threw out her arms as if swimming when she walked, beating the tall grass as one strikes out in the water. Oh, I see the connection now!"

"Where were you going that day in Kentucky, walking through the grass?"

"I don't remember now. I was just walking diagonally across a big field. My sun-bonnet obstructed the view. I could see only the stretch of green before me, and I felt as if I must walk on forever, without coming to the end of it. I don't remember whether I was frightened or pleased. I must have been entertained.

"Likely as not it was Sunday," she laughed; "and I was running away from prayers, from the Presbyterian service, read in a spirit of gloom by my father that chills me yet to think of."

"And have you been running away from prayers ever since, *ma chère?*"[7] asked Madame Ratignolle, amused.

"No! oh, no!" Edna hastened to say. "I was a little unthinking child in those days, just following a misleading impulse without question. On the contrary, during one period of my life religion took a firm hold upon me; after I was twelve and until—until—why, I suppose until now, though I never thought much about it—just driven along by habit. But do you know," she broke off, turning her quick eyes upon Madame Ratignolle and leaning forward a little so as to bring her face quite close to that of her companion, "sometimes I feel this summer as if I were walking through the green meadow again; idly, aimlessly, unthinking and unguided."

Madame Ratignolle laid her hand over that of Mrs. Pontellier, which was near her. Seeing that the hand was not withdrawn, she clasped it firmly and warmly. She even stroked it a little, fondly, with the other hand, murmuring in an undertone, "*Pauvre chérie.*"

The action was at first a little confusing to Edna, but she soon lent herself readily to the Creole's gentle caress. She was not accustomed to an outward and spoken expression of affection, either in herself or in others. She and her younger sister, Janet, had quarreled a good deal through force of unfortunate habit. Her older sister, Margaret, was matronly and dignified, probably from having assumed matronly and housewifely responsibilities too early in life, their mother having died when they were quite young. Margaret was not effusive; she was practical. Edna had had an occasional girl friend, but whether accidentally or not, they seemed to have been all of one type—the self-contained. She never realized that the reserve of her own character had much, perhaps everything, to do with this. Her most intimate friend at school had been one of rather exceptional intellectual gifts, who wrote fine-sounding essays, which Edna admired and strove to imitate; and with her she talked and glowed over the English classics, and sometimes held religious and political controversies.

Edna often wondered at one propensity which sometimes had inwardly disturbed her without causing any outward show or manifestation on her part. At a very early age—perhaps it was when she traversed the ocean of waving grass—she remembered that she had been passionately enamoured of a dignified and sad-eyed cavalry officer who visited her father in Kentucky. She could not leave his presence when he was there nor remove her eyes from his face, which was something like Napoleon's, with a lock of black hair falling across the forehead. But the cavalry officer melted imperceptibly out of her existence.

At another time her affections were deeply engaged by a young gentleman who visited a lady on a neighboring plantation. It was after they went to Mississippi to live. The young man was engaged to be married to the young lady, and they sometimes called upon Margaret, driving over of

7. *My dear?* Below, *Pauvre chérie:* Poor dear.

afternoons in a buggy. Edna was a little miss, just merging into her teens; and the realization that she herself was nothing, nothing, nothing to the engaged young man was a bitter affliction to her. But he, too, went the way of dreams.

She was a grown young woman when she was overtaken by what she supposed to be the climax of her fate. It was when the face and figure of a great tragedian began to haunt her imagination and stir her senses. The persistence of the infatuation lent it an aspect of genuineness. The hopelessness of it colored it with the lofty tones of a great passion.

The picture of the tragedian stood enframed upon her desk. Any one may possess the portrait of a tragedian without exciting suspicion or comment. (This was a sinister reflection which she cherished.) In the presence of others she expressed admiration for his exalted gifts, as she handed the photograph around and dwelt upon the fidelity of the likeness. When alone she sometimes picked it up and kissed the cold glass passionately.

Her marriage to Léonce Pontellier was purely an accident, in this respect resembling many other marriages which masquerade as the decrees of Fate. It was in the midst of her secret great passion that she met him. He fell in love, as men are in the habit of doing, and pressed his suit with an earnestness and an ardor which left nothing to be desired. He pleased her; his absolute devotion flattered her. She fancied there was a sympathy of thought and taste between them, in which fancy she was mistaken. Add to this the violent opposition of her father and her sister Margaret to her marriage with a Catholic, and we need seek no further for the motives which led her to accept Monsieur Pontellier for her husband.

The acme of bliss, which would have been a marriage with the tragedian, was not for her in this world. As the devoted wife of a man who worshiped her, she felt she would take her place with a certain dignity in the world of reality, closing the portals forever behind her upon the realm of romance and dreams.

But it was not long before the tragedian had gone to join the cavalry officer and the engaged young man and a few others; and Edna found herself face to face with the realities. She grew fond of her husband, realizing with some unaccountable satisfaction that no trace of passion or excessive and fictitious warmth colored her affection, thereby threatening its dissolution.

She was fond of her children in an uneven, impulsive way. She would sometimes gather them passionately to her heart; she would sometimes forget them. The year before they had spent part of the summer with their grandmother Pontellier in Iberville.[8] Feeling secure regarding their happiness and welfare, she did not miss them except with an occasional intense longing. Their absence was a sort of relief, though she did not admit this, even to herself. It seemed to free her of a responsibility which she had blindly assumed and for which Fate had not fitted her.

Edna did not reveal so much as all this to Madame Ratignolle that summer day when they sat with faces turned to the sea. But a good part of it escaped her. She had put her head down on Madame Ratignolle's shoulder. She was flushed and felt intoxicated with the sound of her own voice and the unaccustomed taste of candor. It muddled her like wine, or like a first breath of freedom.

8. Louisiana town fifty miles west of New Orleans.

There was the sound of approaching voices. It was Robert, surrounded by a troop of children, searching for them. The two little Pontelliers were with him, and he carried Madame Ratignolle's little girl in his arms. There were other children beside, and two nursemaids followed, looking disagreeable and resigned.

The women at once rose and began to shake out their draperies and relax their muscles. Mrs. Pontellier threw the cushions and rug into the bath-house. The children all scampered off to the awning, and they stood there in a line, gazing upon the intruding lovers, still exchanging their vows and sighs. The lovers got up, with only a silent protest, and walked slowly away somewhere else.

The children possessed themselves of the tent, and Mrs. Pontellier went over to join them.

Madame Ratignolle begged Robert to accompany her to the house; she complained of cramp in her limbs and stiffness of the joints. She leaned draggingly upon his arm as they walked.

VIII

"Do me a favor, Robert," spoke the pretty woman at his side, almost as soon as she and Robert had started on their slow, homeward way. She looked up in his face, leaning on his arm beneath the encircling shadow of the umbrella which he had lifted.

"Granted; as many as you like," he returned, glancing down into her eyes that were full of thoughtfulness and some speculation.

"I only ask for one; let Mrs. Pontellier alone."

"*Tiens!*" he exclaimed, with a sudden, boyish laugh. "*Voilà que Madame Ratignolle est jalouse!*"[9]

"Nonsense! I'm in earnest; I mean what I say. Let Mrs. Pontellier alone."

"Why?" he asked; himself growing serious at his companion's solicitation.

"She is not one of us; she is not like us. She might make the unfortunate blunder of taking you seriously."

His face flushed with annoyance, and taking off his soft hat he began to beat it impatiently against his leg as he walked. "Why shouldn't she take me seriously?" he demanded sharply. "Am I a comedian, a clown, a jack-in-the-box? Why shouldn't she? You Creoles! I have no patience with you! Am I always to be regarded as a feature of an amusing programme? I hope Mrs. Pontellier does take me seriously. I hope she has discernment enough to find in me something besides the *blagueur*. If I thought there was any doubt—"

"Oh, enough, Robert!" she broke into his heated outburst. "You are not thinking of what you are saying. You speak with about as little reflection as we might expect from one of those children down there playing in the sand. If your attentions to any married women here were ever offered with any intention of being convincing, you would not be the gentleman we all know you to be, and you would be unfit to associate with the wives and daughters of the people who trust you."

9. *Well! So Madame Ratignolle is jealous!*

Madame Ratignolle had spoken what she believed to be the law and
the gospel. The young man shrugged his shoulders impatiently.
"Oh! well! That isn't it," slamming his hat down vehemently upon his
head. "You ought to feel that such things are not flattering to say to a
fellow."
"Should our whole intercourse consist of an exchange of compliments?
Ma foi!"[1]
"It isn't pleasant to have a woman tell you—" he went on, unheedingly,
but breaking off suddenly: "Now if I were like Arobin—you remember
Alcée Arobin and that story of the consul's wife at Biloxi?" And he related the story of Alcée Arobin and the consul's wife; and another about
the tenor of the French Opera,[2] who received letters which should never
have been written; and still other stories, grave and gay, till Mrs. Pontellier and her possible propensity for taking young men seriously was apparently forgotten.
Madame Ratignolle, when they had regained her cottage, went in to
take the hour's rest which she considered helpful. Before leaving her,
Robert begged her pardon for the impatience—he called it rudeness—with
which he had received her well-meant caution.
"You made one mistake, Adèle," he said, with a light smile; "there is
no earthly possibility of Mrs. Pontellier ever taking me seriously. You
should have warned me against taking myself seriously. Your advice might
then have carried some weight and given me subject for some reflection.
Au revoir. But you look tired," he added, solicitously. "Would you like a
cup of bouillon? Shall I stir you a toddy? Let me mix you a toddy with a
drop of Angostura."
She acceded to the suggestion of bouillon, which was grateful and acceptable. He went himself to the kitchen, which was a building apart
from the cottages and lying to the rear of the house. And he himself
brought her the golden-brown bouillon, in a dainty Sèvres cup, with a
flaky cracker or two on the saucer.
She thrust a bare, white arm from the curtain which shielded her open
door, and received the cup from his hands. She told him he was a *bon
garçon,*[3] and she meant it. Robert thanked her and turned away toward
"the house."
The lovers were just entering the grounds of the *pension.* They were
leaning toward each other as the water-oaks bent from the sea. There was
not a particle of earth beneath their feet. Their heads might have been
turned upside-down, so absolutely did they tread upon blue ether. The
lady in black, creeping behind them, looked a trifle paler and more jaded
than usual. There was no sign of Mrs. Pontellier and the children. Robert
scanned the distance for any such apparition. They would doubtless remain away till the dinner hour. The young man ascended to his mother's
room. It was situated at the top of the house, made up of odd angles and
a queer, sloping ceiling. Two broad dormer windows looked out toward
the Gulf, and as far across it as a man's eye might reach. The furnishings
of the room were light, cool, and practical.
Madame Lebrun was busily engaged at the sewing-machine. A little
black girl sat on the floor, and with her hands worked the treadle of the

1. *Really!*
2. A New Orleans opera company.
3. *Nice guy;* also, *good waiter.*

machine. The Creole woman does not take any chances which may be avoided of imperiling her health.

Robert went over and seated himself on the broad sill of one of the dormer windows. He took a book from his pocket and began energetically to read it, judging by the precision and frequency with which he turned the leaves. The sewing-machine made a resounding clatter in the room; it was of a ponderous, by-gone make. In the lulls, Robert and his mother exchanged bits of desultory conversation.

"Where is Mrs. Pontellier?"

"Down at the beach with the children."

"I promised to lend her the Goncourt.[4] Don't forget to take it down when you go; it's there on the bookshelf over the small table." Clatter, clatter, clatter, bang! for the next five or eight minutes.

"Where is Victor going with the rockaway?"

"The rockaway? Victor?"

"Yes; down there in front. He seems to be getting ready to drive away somewhere."

"Call him." Clatter, clatter!

Robert uttered a shrill, piercing whistle which might have been heard back at the wharf.

"He won't look up."

Madame Lebrun flew to the window. She called "Victor!" She waved a handkerchief and called again. The young fellow below got into the vehicle and started the horse off at a gallop.

Madame Lebrun went back to the machine, crimson with annoyance. Victor was the younger son and brother—a *tête montée*,[5] with a temper which invited violence and a will which no ax could break.

"Whenever you say the word I'm ready to thrash any amount of reason into him that he's able to hold."

"If your father had only lived!" Clatter, clatter, clatter, clatter, bang! It was a fixed belief with Madame Lebrun that the conduct of the universe and all things pertaining thereto would have been manifestly of a more intelligent and higher order had not Monsieur Lebrun been removed to other spheres during the early years of their married life.

"What do you hear from Montel?" Montel was a middle-aged gentleman whose vain ambition and desire for the past twenty years had been to fill the void which Monsieur Lebrun's taking off had left in the Lebrun household. Clatter, clatter, bang, clatter!

"I have a letter somewhere," looking in the machine drawer and finding the letter in the bottom of the work-basket. "He says to tell you he will be in Vera Cruz[6] the beginning of next month"—clatter, clatter!— "and if you still have the intention of joining him"—bang! clatter, clatter, bang!

"Why didn't you tell me so before, mother? You know I wanted—" Clatter, clatter, clatter!

"Do you see Mrs. Pontellier starting back with the children? She will be in late to luncheon again. She never starts to get ready for luncheon till the last minute." Clatter, clatter! "Where are you going?"

"Where did you say the Goncourt was?"

---

4. The brothers Goncourt collaborated on a number of novels; Edmond (1822–1896) continued writing after the death of Jules (1830–1870).

5. *Excitable person.*
6. Port in Mexico.

IX

Every light in the hall was ablaze; every lamp turned as high as it could be without smoking the chimney or threatening explosion. The lamps were fixed at intervals against the wall, encircling the whole room. Some one had gathered orange and lemon branches and with these fashioned graceful festoons between. The dark green of the branches stood out and glistened against the white muslin curtains which draped the windows, and which puffed, floated, and flapped at the capricious will of a stiff breeze that swept up from the Gulf.

It was Saturday night a few weeks after the intimate conversation held between Robert and Madame Ratignolle on their way from the beach. An unusual number of husbands, fathers, and friends had come down to stay over Sunday; and they were being suitably entertained by their families, with the material help of Madame Lebrun. The dining tables had all been removed to one end of the hall, and the chairs ranged about in rows and in clusters. Each little family group had had its say and exchanged its domestic gossip earlier in the evening. There was now an apparent disposition to relax; to widen the circle of confidences and give a more general tone to the conversation.

Many of the children had been permitted to sit up beyond their usual bedtime. A small band of them were lying on their stomachs on the floor looking at the colored sheets of the comic papers which Mr. Pontellier had brought down. The little Pontellier boys were permitting them to do so, and making their authority felt.

Music, dancing, and a recitation or two were the entertainments furnished, or rather, offered. But there was nothing systematic about the programme, no appearance of prearrangement nor even premeditation.

At an early hour in the evening the Farival twins were prevailed upon to play the piano. They were girls of fourteen, always clad in the Virgin's colors, blue and white, having been dedicated to the Blessed Virgin at their baptism. They played a duet from "Zampa," and at the earnest solicitation of every one present followed it with the overture to "The Poet and the Peasant."

"Allez vous-en! Sapristi!" shrieked the parrot outside the door. He was the only being present who possessed sufficient candor to admit that he was not listening to these gracious performances for the first time that summer. Old Monsieur Farival, grandfather of the twins, grew indignant over the interruption, and insisted upon having the bird removed and consigned to regions of darkness. Victor Lebrun objected; and his decrees were as immutable as those of Fate. The parrot fortunately offered no further interruption to the entertainment, the whole venom of his nature apparently having been cherished up and hurled against the twins in that one impetuous outburst.

Later a young brother and sister gave recitations, which every one present had heard many times at winter evening entertainments in the city.

A little girl performed a skirt dance in the center of the floor. The mother played her accompaniments and at the same time watched her daughter with greedy admiration and nervous apprehension. She need have had no apprehension. The child was mistress of the situation. She had been properly dressed for the occasion in black tulle and black silk tights. Her little neck and arms were bare, and her hair, artificially crimped, stood out like fluffy black plumes over her head. Her poses were full of grace, and her little black-shod toes twinkled as they shot out and upward with a rapidity and suddenness which were bewildering.

But there was no reason why every one should not dance. Madame Ratignolle could not, so it was she who gaily consented to play for the others. She played very well, keeping excellent waltz time and infusing an expression into the strains which was indeed inspiring. She was keeping up her music on account of the children, she said; because she and her husband both considered it a means of brightening the home and making it attractive.

Almost every one danced but the twins, who could not be induced to separate during the brief period when one or the other should be whirling around the room in the arms of a man. They might have danced together, but they did not think of it.

The children were sent to bed. Some went submissively; others with shrieks and protests as they were dragged away. They had been permitted to sit up till after the ice-cream, which naturally marked the limit of human indulgence.

The ice-cream was passed around with cake—gold and silver cake arranged on platters in alternate slices; it had been made and frozen during the afternoon back of the kitchen by two black women, under the supervision of Victor. It was pronounced a great success—excellent if it had only contained a little less vanilla or a little more sugar, if it had been frozen a degree harder, and if the salt might have been kept out of portions of it. Victor was proud of his achievement, and went about recommending it and urging every one to partake of it to excess.

After Mrs. Pontellier had danced twice with her husband, once with Robert, and once with Monsieur Ratignolle, who was thin and tall and swayed like a reed in the wind when he danced, she went out on the gallery and seated herself on the low window-sill, where she commanded a view of all that went on in the hall and could look out toward the Gulf. There was a soft effulgence in the east. The moon was coming up, and its mystic shimmer was casting a million lights across the distant, restless water.

"Would you like to hear Mademoiselle Reisz play?" asked Robert, coming out on the porch where she was. Of course Edna would like to hear Mademoiselle Reisz play; but she feared it would be useless to entreat her.

"I'll ask her," he said. "I'll tell her that you want to hear her. She likes you. She will come." He turned and hurried away to one of the far cottages, where Mademoiselle Reisz was shuffling away. She was dragging a chair in and out of her room, and at intervals objecting to the crying of a baby, which a nurse in the adjoining cottage was endeavoring to put to sleep. She was a disagreeable little woman, no longer young, who had quarreled with almost every one, owing to a temper which was self-assertive and a disposition to trample upon the rights of others. Robert prevailed upon her without any too great difficulty.

She entered the hall with him during a lull in the dance. She made an awkward, imperious little bow as she went in. She was a homely woman, with a small weazened[7] face and body and eyes that glowed. She had absolutely no taste in dress, and wore a batch of rusty black lace with a bunch of artificial violets pinned to the side of her hair. "Ask Mrs. Pontellier what she would like to hear me play," she requested of Robert. She sat perfectly still before the piano, not touching the keys, while Robert carried her message to Edna at the window. A general air of surprise and genuine satisfaction fell upon every one as they saw the pianist enter. There was a settling down, and a prevailing air of expectancy everywhere. Edna was a trifle embarrassed at being thus signaled out for the imperious little woman's favor. She would not dare to choose, and begged that Mademoiselle Reisz would please herself in her selections.

Edna was what she herself called very fond of music. Musical strains, well rendered, had a way of evoking pictures in her mind. She sometimes liked to sit in the room of mornings when Madame Ratignolle played or practiced. One piece which that lady played Edna had entitled "Solitude." It was a short, plaintive, minor strain. The name of the piece was something else, but she called it "Solitude." When she heard it there came before her imagination the figure of a man standing beside a desolate rock on the seashore. He was naked. His attitude was one of hopeless resignation as he looked toward a distant bird winging its flight away from him.

Another piece called to her mind a dainty young woman clad in an Empire gown, taking mincing dancing steps as she came down a long avenue between tall hedges. Again, another reminded her of children at play, and still another of nothing on earth but a demure lady stroking a cat.

The very first chords which Mademoiselle Reisz struck upon the piano sent a keen tremor down Mrs. Pontellier's spinal column. It was not the first time she had heard an artist at the piano. Perhaps it was the first time she was ready, perhaps the first time her being was tempered to take an impress of the abiding truth.

She waited for the material pictures which she thought would gather and blaze before her imagination. She waited in vain. She saw no pictures of solitude, of hope, of longing, or of despair. But the very passions themselves were aroused within her soul, swaying it, lashing it, as the waves daily beat upon her splendid body. She trembled, she was choking, and the tears blinded her.

Mademoiselle had finished. She arose, and bowing her stiff, lofty bow, she went away, stopping for neither thanks nor applause. As she passed along the gallery she patted Edna upon the shoulder.

"Well, how did you like my music?" she asked. The young woman was unable to answer; she pressed the hand of the pianist convulsively. Mademoiselle Reisz perceived her agitation and even her tears. She patted her again upon the shoulder as she said:

"You are the only one worth playing for. Those others? Bah!" and she went shuffling and sidling on down the gallery toward her room.

But she was mistaken about "those others." Her playing had aroused a fever of enthusiasm. "What passion!" "What an artist!" "I have always

7. Wizened.

said no one could play Chopin like Mademoiselle Reisz!" "That last prelude! Bon Dieu![8] It shakes a man!"

It was growing late, and there was a general disposition to disband. But some one, perhaps it was Robert, thought of a bath[9] at that mystic hour and under that mystic moon.

X

At all events Robert proposed it, and there was not a dissenting voice. There was not one but was ready to follow when he led the way. He did not lead the way, however, he directed the way; and he himself loitered behind with the lovers, who had betrayed a disposition to linger and hold themselves apart. He walked between them, whether with malicious or mischievous intent was not wholly clear, even to himself.

The Pontelliers and Ratignolles walked ahead; the women leaning upon the arms of their husbands. Edna could hear Robert's voice behind them, and could sometimes hear what he said. She wondered why he did not join them. It was unlike him not to. Of late he had sometimes held away from her for an entire day, redoubling his devotion upon the next and the next, as though to make up for hours that had been lost. She missed him the days when some pretext served to take him away from her, just as one misses the sun on a cloudy day without having thought much about the sun when it was shining.

The people walked in little groups toward the beach. They talked and laughed; some of them sang. There was a band playing down at Klein's hotel, and the strains reached them faintly, tempered by the distance. There were strange, rare odors abroad—a tangle of the sea smell and of weeds and damp, new-plowed earth, mingled with the heavy perfume of a field of white blossoms somewhere near. But the night sat lightly upon the sea and the land. There was no weight of darkness; there were no shadows. The white light of the moon had fallen upon the world like the mystery and the softness of sleep.

Most of them walked into the water as though into a native element. The sea was quiet now, and swelled lazily in broad billows that melted into one another and did not break except upon the beach in little foamy crests that coiled back like slow, white serpents.

Edna had attempted all summer to learn to swim. She had received instructions from both the men and women; in some instances from the children. Robert had pursued a system of lessons almost daily; and he was nearly at the point of discouragement in realizing the futility of his efforts. A certain ungovernable dread hung about her when in the water, unless there was a hand near by that might reach out and reassure her.

But that night she was like the little tottering, stumbling, clutching child, who of a sudden realizes its powers, and walks for the first time alone, boldly and with over-confidence. She could have shouted for joy. She did shout for joy, as with a sweeping stroke or two she lifted her body to the surface of the water.

A feeling of exultation overtook her, as if some power of significant import had been given her soul. She grew daring and reckless, overesti-

8. Good Lord!   9. Swim.

mating her strength. She wanted to swim far out, where no woman had swum before.

Her unlooked-for achievement was the subject of wonder, applause, and admiration. Each one congratulated himself that his special teachings had accomplished this desired end.

"How easy it is!" she thought. "It is nothing," she said aloud; "why did I not discover before that it was nothing. Think of the time I have lost splashing about like a baby!" She would not join the groups in their sports and bouts, but intoxicated with her newly conquered power, she swam out alone.

She turned her face seaward to gather in an impression of space and solitude, which the vast expanse of water, meeting and melting with the moonlit sky, conveyed to her excited fancy. As she swam she seemed to be reaching out for the unlimited in which to lose herself.

Once she turned and looked toward the shore, toward the people she had left there. She had not gone any great distance—that is, what would have been a great distance for an experienced swimmer. But to her unaccustomed vision the stretch of water behind her assumed the aspect of a barrier which her unaided strength would never be able to overcome.

A quick vision of death smote her soul, and for a second of time appalled and enfeebled her senses. But by an effort she rallied her staggering faculties and managed to regain the land.

She made no mention of her encounter with death and her flash of terror, except to say to her husband, "I thought I should have perished out there alone."

"You were not so very far, my dear; I was watching you," he told her.

Edna went at once to the bath-house, and she had put on her dry clothes and was ready to return home before the others had left the water. She started to walk away alone. They all called to her and shouted to her. She waved a dissenting hand, and went on, paying no further heed to their renewed cries which sought to detain her.

"Sometimes I am tempted to think that Mrs. Pontellier is capricious," said Madame Lebrun, who was amusing herself immensely and feared that Edna's abrupt departure might put an end to the pleasure.

"I know she is," assented Mr. Pontellier; "sometimes, not often."

Edna had not traversed a quarter of the distance on her way home before she was overtaken by Robert.

"Did you think I was afraid?" she asked him, without a shade of annoyance.

"No; I knew you weren't afraid."

"Then why did you come? Why didn't you stay out there with the others?"

"I never thought of it."

"Thought of what?"

"Of anything. What difference does it make?"

"I'm very tired," she uttered, complainingly.

"I know you are."

"You don't know anything about it. Why should you know? I never was so exhausted in my life. But it isn't unpleasant. A thousand emotions have swept through me to-night. I don't comprehend half of them. Don't mind what I'm saying; I am just thinking aloud. I wonder if I shall ever be stirred again as Mademoiselle Reisz's playing moved me to-night. I won-

der if any night on earth will ever again be like this one. It is like a night
in a dream. The people about me are like some uncanny, half-human
beings. There must be spirits abroad to-night."

"There are," whispered Robert. "Didn't you know this was the twenty-
eighth of August?"

"The twenty-eighth of August?"

"Yes. On the twenty-eighth of August, at the hour of midnight, and if
the moon is shining—the moon must be shining—a spirit that has haunted
these shores for ages rises up from the Gulf. With its own penetrating
vision the spirit seeks some one mortal worthy to hold him company,
worthy of being exalted for a few hours into realms of the semi-celestials.
His search has always hitherto been fruitless, and he has sunk back, disheartened, into the sea. But to-night he found Mrs. Pontellier. Perhaps he
will never wholly release her from the spell. Perhaps she will never again
suffer a poor, unworthy earthling to walk in the shadow of her divine
presence."

"Don't banter me," she said, wounded at what appeared to be his flip-
pancy. He did not mind the entreaty, but the tone with its delicate note
of pathos was like a reproach. He could not explain; he could not tell her
that he had penetrated her mood and understood. He said nothing except
to offer her his arm, for, by her own admission, she was exhausted. She
had been walking alone with her arms hanging limp, letting her white
skirts trail along the dewy path. She took his arm, but she did not lean
upon it. She let her hand lie listlessly, as though her thoughts were elsewhere—somewhere in advance of her body, and she was striving to overtake them.

Robert assisted her into the hammock which swung from the post before her door out to the trunk of a tree.

"Will you stay out here and wait for Mr. Pontellier?" he asked.

"I'll stay out here. Good-night."

"Shall I get you a pillow?"

"There's one here," she said, feeling about, for they were in the
shadow.

"It must be soiled; the children have been tumbling it about."

"No matter." And having discovered the pillow, she adjusted it beneath
her head. She extended herself in the hammock with a deep breath of
relief. She was not a supercilious or an over-dainty woman. She was not
much given to reclining in the hammock, and when she did so it was with
no cat-like suggestion of voluptuous ease, but with a beneficent repose
which seemed to invade her whole body.

"Shall I stay with you till Mr. Pontellier comes?" asked Robert, seating
himself on the outer edge of one of the steps and taking hold of the hammock rope which was fastened to the post.

"If you wish. Don't swing the hammock. Will you get my white shawl
which I left on the window-sill over at the house?"

"Are you chilly?"

"No; but I shall be presently."

"Presently?" he laughed. "Do you know what time it is? How long are
you going to stay out here?"

"I don't know. Will you get the shawl?"

"Of course I will," he said, rising. He went over to the house, walking
along the grass. She watched his figure pass in and out of the strips of

moonlight. It was past midnight. It was very quiet.

When he returned with the shawl she took it and kept it in her hand. She did not put it around her.

"Did you say I should stay till Mr. Pontellier came back?"

"I said you might if you wished to."

He seated himself again and rolled a cigarette, which he smoked in silence. Neither did Mrs. Pontellier speak. No multitude of words could have been more significant than those moments of silence, or more pregnant with the first-felt throbbings of desire.

When the voices of the bathers were heard approaching, Robert said good-night. She did not answer him. He thought she was asleep. Again she watched his figure pass in and out of the strips of moonlight as he walked away.

XI

"What are you doing out here, Edna? I thought I should find you in bed," said her husband, when he discovered her lying there. He had walked up with Madame Lebrun and left her at the house. His wife did not reply.

"Are you asleep?" he asked, bending down close to look at her.

"No." Her eyes gleamed bright and intense, with no sleepy shadows, as they looked into his.

"Do you know it is past one o'clock? Come on," and he mounted the steps and went into their room.

"Edna!" called Mr. Pontellier from within, after a few moments had gone by.

"Don't wait for me," she answered. He thrust his head through the door.

"You will take cold out there," he said, irritably. "What folly is this? Why don't you come in?"

"It isn't cold; I have my shawl."

"The mosquitoes will devour you."

"There are no mosquitoes."

She heard him moving about the room; every sound indicating impatience and irritation. Another time she would have gone in at his request. She would, through habit, have yielded to his desire; not with any sense of submission or obedience to his compelling wishes, but unthinkingly, as we walk, move, sit, stand, go through the daily treadmill of the life which has been portioned out to us.

"Edna, dear, are you not coming in soon?" he asked again, this time fondly, with a note of entreaty.

"No; I am going to stay out here."

"This is more than folly," he blurted out. "I can't permit you to stay out there all night. You must come in the house instantly."

With a writhing motion she settled herself more securely in the hammock. She perceived that her will had blazed up, stubborn and resistant. She could not at that moment have done other than denied and resisted. She wondered if her husband had ever spoken to her like that before, and if she had submitted to his command. Of course she had; she remembered that she had. But she could not realize why or how she should have yielded, feeling as she then did.

"Léonce, go to bed," she said. "I mean to stay out here. I don't wish to go in, and I don't intend to. Don't speak to me like that again; I shall not answer you."

Mr. Pontellier had prepared for bed, but he slipped on an extra garment. He opened a bottle of wine, of which he kept a small and select supply in a buffet of his own. He drank a glass of the wine and went out on the gallery and offered a glass to his wife. She did not wish any. He drew up the rocker, hoisted his slippered feet on the rail, and proceeded to smoke a cigar. He smoked two cigars; then he went inside and drank another glass of wine. Mrs. Pontellier again declined to accept a glass when it was offered to her. Mr. Pontellier once more seated himself with elevated feet, and after a reasonable interval of time smoked some more cigars.

Edna began to feel like one who awakens gradually out of a dream, a delicious, grotesque, impossible dream, to feel again the realities pressing into her soul. The physical need for sleep began to overtake her; the exuberance which had sustained and exalted her spirit left her helpless and yielding to the conditions which crowded her in.

The stillest hour of the night had come, the hour before dawn, when the world seems to hold its breath. The moon hung low, and had turned from silver to copper in the sleeping sky. The old owl no longer hooted, and the water-oaks had ceased to moan as they bent their heads.

Edna arose, cramped from lying so long and still in the hammock. She tottered up the steps, clutching feebly at the post before passing into the house.

"Are you coming in, Léonce?" she asked, turning her face toward her husband.

"Yes, dear," he answered, with a glance following a misty puff of smoke. "Just as soon as I have finished my cigar."

XII

She slept but a few hours. They were troubled and feverish hours, disturbed with dreams that were intangible, that eluded her, leaving only an impression upon her half-awakened senses of something unattainable. She was up and dressed in the cool of the early morning. The air was invigorating and steadied somewhat her faculties. However, she was not seeking refreshment or help from any source, either external or from within. She was blindly following whatever impulse moved her, as if she had placed herself in alien hands for direction, and freed her soul of responsibility.

Most of the people at that early hour were still in bed and asleep. A few, who intended to go over to the *Chênière* for mass, were moving about. The lovers, who had laid their plans the night before, were already strolling toward the wharf. The lady in black, with her Sunday prayer book, velvet and gold-clasped, and her Sunday silver beads, was following them at no great distance. Old Monsieur Farival was up, and was more than half inclined to do anything that suggested itself. He put on his big straw hat, and taking his umbrella from the stand in the hall, followed the lady in black, never overtaking her.

The little negro girl who worked Madame Lebrun's sewing-machine was sweeping the galleries with long, absent-minded strokes of the broom.

Edna sent her up into the house to awaken Robert.

"Tell him I am going to the Chênière. The boat is ready; tell him to hurry."

He had soon joined her. She had never sent for him before. She had never asked for him. She had never seemed to want him before. She did not appear conscious that she had done anything unusual in commanding his presence. He was apparently equally unconscious of anything extraordinary in the situation. But his face was suffused with a quiet glow when he met her.

They went together back to the kitchen to drink coffee. There was no time to wait for any nicety of service. They stood outside the window and the cook passed them their coffee and a roll, which they drank and ate from the window-sill. Edna said it tasted good. She had not thought of coffee nor of anything. He told her he had often noticed that she lacked forethought.

"Wasn't it enough to think of going to the Chênière and waking you up?" she laughed. "Do I have to think of everything?—as Léonce says when he's in a bad humor. I don't blame him; he'd never be in a bad humor if it weren't for me."

They took a short cut across the sands. At a distance they could see the curious procession moving toward the wharf—the lovers, shoulder to shoulder, creeping; the lady in black, gaining steadily upon them; old Monsieur Farival, losing ground inch by inch, and a young barefooted Spanish girl, with a red kerchief on her head and a basket on her arm, bringing up the rear.

Robert knew the girl, and he talked to her a little in the boat. No one present understood what they said. Her name was Mariequita. She had a round, sly, piquant face and pretty black eyes. Her hands were small, and she kept them folded over the handle of her basket. Her feet were broad and coarse. She did not strive to hide them. Edna looked at her feet, and noticed the sand and slime between her brown toes.

Beaudelet grumbled because Mariequita was there, taking up so much room. In reality he was annoyed at having old Monsieur Farival, who considered himself the better sailor of the two. But he would not quarrel with so old a man as Monsieur Farival, so he quarreled with Mariequita. The girl was deprecatory at one moment, appealing to Robert. She was saucy the next, moving her head up and down, making "eyes" at Robert and making "mouths" at Beaudelet.

The lovers were all alone. They saw nothing, they heard nothing. The lady in black was counting her beads for the third time. Old Monsieur Farival talked incessantly of what he knew about handling a boat, and of what Beaudelet did not know on the same subject.

Edna liked it all. She looked Mariequita up and down, from her ugly brown toes to her pretty black eyes, and back again.

"Why does she look at me like that?" inquired the girl of Robert.

"Maybe she thinks you are pretty. Shall I ask her?"

"No. Is she your sweetheart?"

"She's a married lady, and has two children."

"Oh! well! Francisco ran away with Sylvano's wife, who had four children. They took all his money and one of the children and stole his boat."

"Shut up!"

"Does she understand?"

"Oh, hush!"

"Are those two married over there—leaning on each other?"

"Of course not," laughed Robert.

"Of course not," echoed Mariequita, with a serious, confirmatory bob of the head.

The sun was high up and beginning to bite. The swift breeze seemed to Edna to bury the sting of it into the pores of her face and hands. Robert held his umbrella over her.

As they went cutting sidewise through the water, the sails bellied taut, with the wind filling and overflowing them. Old Monsieur Farival laughed sardonically at something as he looked at the sails, and Beaudelet swore at the old man under his breath.

Sailing across the bay to the *Chênière Caminada*, Edna felt as if she were being borne away from some anchorage which had held her fast, whose chains had been loosening—had snapped the night before when the mystic spirit was abroad, leaving her free to drift whithersoever she chose to set her sails. Robert spoke to her incessantly; he no longer noticed Mariequita. The girl had shrimps in her bamboo basket. They were covered with Spanish moss. She beat the moss down impatiently, and muttered to herself sullenly.

"Let us go to Grande Terre to-morrow?" said Robert in a low voice.

"What shall we do there?"

"Climb up the hill to the old fort and look at the little wriggling gold snakes, and watch the lizards sun themselves."

She gazed away toward Grande Terre and thought she would like to be alone there with Robert, in the sun, listening to the ocean's roar and watching the slimy lizards writhe in and out among the ruins of the old fort.

"And the next day or the next we can sail to the Bayou Brulow,"[1] he went on.

"What shall we do there?"

"Anything—cast bait for fish."

"No; we'll go back to Grande Terre. Let the fish alone."

"We'll go wherever you like," he said. "I'll have Tonie come over and help me patch and trim my boat. We shall not need Beaudelet nor any one. Are you afraid of the pirogue?"

"Oh, no."

"Then I'll take you some night in the pirogue when the moon shines. Maybe your Gulf spirit will whisper to you in which of these islands the treasures are hidden—direct you to the very spot, perhaps."

"And in a day we should be rich!" she laughed. "I'd give it all to you, the pirate gold and every bit of treasure we could dig up. I think you would know how to spend it. Pirate gold isn't a thing to be hoarded or utilized. It is something to squander and throw to the four winds, for the fun of seeing the golden specks fly."

"We'd share it, and scatter it together," he said. His face flushed.

They all went together up to the quaint little Gothic church of Our Lady of Lourdes, gleaming all brown and yellow with paint in the sun's glare.

Only Beaudelet remained behind, tinkering at his boat, and Mariequita

---

1. Village built on stilts over marshy area near Grand Isle. Grande Terre is an island near Grand Isle.

walked away with her basket of shrimps, casting a look of childish ill-humor and reproach at Robert from the corner of her eye.

XIII

A feeling of oppression and drowsiness overcame Edna during the service. Her head began to ache, and the lights on the altar swayed before her eyes. Another time she might have made an effort to regain her composure; but her one thought was to quit the stifling atmosphere of the church and reach the open air. She arose, climbing over Robert's feet with a muttered apology. Old Monsieur Farival, flurried, curious, stood up, but upon seeing that Robert had followed Mrs. Pontellier, he sank back into his seat. He whispered an anxious inquiry of the lady in black, who did not notice him or reply, but kept her eyes fastened upon the pages of her velvet prayerbook.

"I felt giddy and almost overcome," Edna said, lifting her hands instinctively to her head and pushing her straw hat up from her forehead. "I couldn't have stayed through the service." They were outside in the shadow of the church. Robert was full of solicitude.

"It was folly to have thought of going in the first place, let alone staying. Come over to Madame Antoine's; you can rest there." He took her arm and led her away, looking anxiously and continuously down into her face.

How still it was, with only the voice of the sea whispering through the reeds that grew in the salt-water pools! The long line of little gray, weather-beaten houses nestled peacefully among the orange trees. It must always have been God's day on that low, drowsy island, Edna thought. They stopped, leaning over a jagged fence made of sea-drift, to ask for water. A youth, a mild-faced Acadian, was drawing water from the cistern, which was nothing more than a rusty buoy, with an opening on one side, sunk in the ground. The water which the youth handed to them in a tin pail was not cold to taste, but it was cool to her heated face, and it greatly revived and refreshed her.

Madame Antoine's cot[2] was at the far end of the village. She welcomed them with all the native hospitality, as she would have opened her door to let the sunlight in. She was fat, and walked heavily and clumsily across the floor. She could speak no English, but when Robert made her understand that the lady who accompanied him was ill and desired to rest, she was all eagerness to make Edna feel at home and to dispose of her comfortably.

The whole place was immaculately clean, and the big, four-posted bed, snow-white, invited one to repose. It stood in a small side room which looked out across a narrow grass plot toward the shed, where there was a disabled boat lying keel upward.

Madame Antoine had not gone to mass. Her son Tonie had, but she supposed he would soon be back, and she invited Robert to be seated and wait for him. But he went and sat outside the door and smoked. Madame Antoine busied herself in the large front room preparing dinner. She was boiling mullets over a few red coals in the huge fireplace.

Edna, left alone in the little side room, loosened her clothes, removing

2. Cottage.

the greater part of them. She bathed her face, her neck and arms in the basin that stood between the windows. She took off her shoes and stockings and stretched herself in the very center of the high, white bed. How luxurious it felt to rest thus in a strange, quaint bed, with its sweet country odor of laurel lingering about the sheets and mattress! She stretched her strong limbs that ached a little. She ran her fingers through her loosened hair for a while. She looked at her round arms as she held them straight up and rubbed them one after the other, observing closely, as if it were something she saw for the first time, the fine, firm quality and texture of her flesh. She clasped her hands easily above her head, and it was thus she fell asleep.

She slept lightly at first, half awake and drowsily attentive to the things about her. She could hear Madame Antoine's heavy, scraping tread as she walked back and forth on the sanded floor. Some chickens were clucking outside the windows, scratching for bits of gravel in the grass. Later she half heard the voices of Robert and Tonie talking under the shed. She did not stir. Even her eyelids rested numb and heavily over her sleepy eyes. The voices went on—Tonie's slow, Acadian drawl, Robert's quick, soft, smooth French. She understood French imperfectly unless directly addressed, and the voices were only part of the other drowsy, muffled sounds lulling her senses.

When Edna awoke it was with the conviction that she had slept long and soundly. The voices were hushed under the shed. Madame Antoine's step was no longer to be heard in the adjoining room. Even the chickens had gone elsewhere to scratch and cluck. The mosquito bar was drawn over her; the old woman had come in while she slept and let down the bar. Edna arose quietly from the bed, and looking between the curtains of the window, she saw by the slanting rays of the sun that the afternoon was far advanced. Robert was out there under the shed, reclining in the shade against the sloping keel of the overturned boat. He was reading from a book. Tonie was no longer with him. She wondered what had become of the rest of the party. She peeped out at him two or three times as she stood washing herself in the little basin between the windows.

Madame Antoine had laid some coarse, clean towels upon a chair, and had placed a box of *poudre de riz*[3] within easy reach. Edna dabbed the powder upon her nose and cheeks as she looked at herself closely in the little distorted mirror which hung on the wall above the basin. Her eyes were bright and wide awake and her face glowed.

When she had completed her toilet she walked into the adjoining room. She was very hungry. No one was there. But there was a cloth spread upon the table that stood against the wall, and a cover was laid for one, with a crusty brown loaf and a bottle of wine beside the plate. Edna bit a piece from the brown loaf, tearing it with her strong, white teeth. She poured some of the wine into the glass and drank it down. Then she went softly out of doors, and plucking an orange from the low-hanging bough of a tree, threw it at Robert who did not know she was awake and up.

An illumination broke over his whole face when he saw her and joined her under the orange tree.

"How many years have I slept?" she enquired. "The whole island seems changed. A new race of beings must have sprung up, leaving only you and

3. Rice powder, a common cosmetic often used as protection against tanning and sunburn.

me as past relics. How many ages ago did Madame Antoine and Tonie die? and when did our people from Grand Isle disappear from the earth?" He familiarly adjusted a ruffle upon her shoulder.

"You have slept precisely one hundred years. I was left here to guard your slumbers; and for one hundred years I have been out under the shed reading a book. The only evil I couldn't prevent was to keep a broiled fowl from drying up."

"If it had turned to stone, still will I eat it," said Edna, moving with him into the house. "But really, what has become of Monsieur Farival and the others?"

"Gone hours ago. When they found that you were sleeping they thought it best not to awake you. Any way, I wouldn't have let them. What was I here for?"

"I wonder if Léonce will be uneasy!" she speculated, as she seated herself at table.

"Of course not; he knows you are with me," Robert replied, as he busied himself among sundry pans and covered dishes which had been left standing on the hearth.

"Where are Madame Antoine and her son?" asked Edna.

"Gone to Vespers, and to visit some friends, I believe. I am to take you back in Tonie's boat whenever you are ready to go."

He stirred the smoldering ashes till the broiled fowl began to sizzle afresh. He served her with no mean repast, dripping the coffee anew and sharing it with her. Madame Antoine had cooked little else than the mullets, but while Edna slept Robert had foraged the island. He was childishly gratified to discover her appetite, and to see the relish with which she ate the food which he had procured for her.

"Shall we go right away?" she asked, after draining her glass and brushing together the crumbs of the crusty loaf.

"The sun isn't as low as it will be in two hours," he answered.

"The sun will be gone in two hours."

"Well, let it go; who cares!"

They waited a good while under the orange trees, till Madame Antoine came back, panting, waddling, with a thousand apologies to explain her absence. Tonie did not dare to return. He was shy, and would not willingly face any woman except his mother.

It was very pleasant to stay there under the orange trees, while the sun dipped lower and lower, turning the western sky to flaming copper and gold. The shadows lengthened and crept out like stealthy, grotesque monsters across the grass.

Edna and Robert both sat upon the ground—that is, he lay upon the ground beside her, occasionally picking at the hem of her muslin gown.

Madame Antoine seated her fat body, broad and squat, upon a bench beside the door. She had been talking all the afternoon and had wound herself up to the story-telling pitch.

And what stories she told them! But twice in her life she had left the *Chênière Caminada*, and then for the briefest span. All her years she had squatted and waddled there upon the island, gathering legends of the Baratarians[4] and the sea. The night came on, with the moon to lighten it.

4. Pirates of Barataria Bay.

Edna could hear the whispering voices of dead men and the click of muffled gold.

When she and Robert stepped into Tonie's boat, with the red lateen sail, misty spirit forms were prowling in the shadows and among the reeds, and upon the water were phantom ships, speeding to cover.

XIV

The youngest boy, Etienne, had been very naughty, Madame Ratignolle said, as she delivered him into the hands of his mother. He had been unwilling to go to bed and had made a scene; whereupon she had taken charge of him and pacified him as well as she could. Raoul had been in bed and asleep for two hours.

The youngster was in his long white nightgown, that kept tripping him up as Madame Ratignolle led him along by the hand. With the other chubby fist he rubbed his eyes, which were heavy with sleep and ill humor. Edna took him in her arms, and seating herself in the rocker, began to coddle and caress him, calling him all manner of tender names, soothing him to sleep.

It was not more than nine o'clock. No one had yet gone to bed but the children.

Léonce had been very uneasy at first, Madame Ratignolle said, and had wanted to start at once for the *Chênière*. But Monsieur Farival had assured him that his wife was only overcome with sleep and fatigue, that Tonie would bring her safely back later in the day; and he had thus been dissuaded from crossing the bay. He had gone over to Klein's, looking up some cotton broker whom he wished to see in regard to securities, exchanges, stocks, bonds, or something of the sort, Madame Ratignolle did not remember what. He said he would not remain away late. She herself was suffering from heat and oppression, she said. She carried a bottle of salts and a large fan. She would not consent to remain with Edna, for Monsieur Ratignolle was alone, and he detested above all things to be left alone.

When Etienne had fallen asleep Edna bore him into the back room, and Robert went and lifted the mosquito bar that she might lay the child comfortably in his bed. The quadroon had vanished. When they emerged from the cottage Robert bade Edna good-night.

"Do you know we have been together the whole livelong day, Robert— since early this morning?" she said at parting.

"All but the hundred years when you were sleeping. Good-night."

He pressed her hand and went away in the direction of the beach. He did not join any of the others, but walked alone toward the Gulf.

Edna stayed outside, awaiting her husband's return. She had no desire to sleep or to retire; nor did she feel like going over to sit with the Ratignolles, or to join Madame Lebrun and a group whose animated voices reached her as they sat in conversation before the house. She let her mind wander back over her stay at Grand Isle; and she tried to discover wherein this summer had been different from any and every other summer of her life. She could only realize that she herself—her present self—was in some way different from the other self. That she was seeing with different eyes and making the acquaintance of new conditions in herself that colored and changed her environment, she did not yet suspect.

She wondered why Robert had gone away and left her. It did not occur to her to think he might have grown tired of being with her the livelong day. She was not tired, and she felt that he was not. She regretted that he had gone. It was so much more natural to have him stay, when he was not absolutely required to leave her.

As Edna waited for her husband she sang low a little song that Robert had sung as they crossed the bay. It began with "Ah! *Si tu savais,*" and every verse ended with "*si tu savais.*"[5]

Robert's voice was not pretentious. It was musical and true. The voice, the notes, the whole refrain haunted her memory.

XV

When Edna entered the dining-room one evening a little late, as was her habit, an unusually animated conversation seemed to be going on. Several persons were talking at once, and Victor's voice was predominating, even over that of his mother. Edna had returned late from her bath, had dressed in some haste, and her face was flushed. Her head, set off by her dainty white gown, suggested a rich, rare blossom. She took her seat at table between old Monsieur Farival and Madame Ratignolle.

As she seated herself and was about to begin to eat her soup, which had been served when she entered the room, several persons informed her simultaneously that Robert was going to Mexico. She laid her spoon down and looked about her bewildered. He had been with her, reading to her all the morning, and had never even mentioned such a place as Mexico. She had not seen him during the afternoon; she had heard some one say he was at the house, upstairs with his mother. This she had thought nothing of, though she was surprised when he did not join her later in the afternoon, when she went down to the beach.

She looked across at him, where he sat beside Madame Lebrun, who presided. Edna's face was a blank picture of bewilderment, which she never thought of disguising. He lifted his eyebrows with the pretext of a smile as he returned her glance. He looked embarrassed and uneasy.

"When is he going?" she asked of everybody in general, as if Robert were not there to answer for himself.

"To-night!" "This very evening!" "Did you ever!" "What possesses him!" were some of the replies she gathered, uttered simultaneously in French and English.

"Impossible!" she exclaimed. "How can a person start off from Grand Isle to Mexico at a moment's notice, as if he were going over to Klein's or to the wharf or down to the beach?"

"I said all along I was going to Mexico; I've been saying so for years!" cried Robert, in an excited and irritable tone, with the air of a man defending himself against a swarm of stinging insects.

Madame Lebrun knocked on the table with her knife handle.

"Please let Robert explain why he is going, and why he is going to-night," she called out. "Really, this table is getting to be more and more like Bedlam every day, with everybody talking at once. Sometimes—I hope God will forgive me—but positively, sometimes I wish Victor would lose the power of speech."

5. "Couldst Thou But Know," song by Michael William Balfe (1808–1870).

Victor laughed sardonically as he thanked his mother for her holy wish, of which he failed to see the benefit to anybody, except that it might afford her a more ample opportunity and license to talk herself.

Monsieur Farival thought that Victor should have been taken out in mid-ocean in his earliest youth and drowned. Victor thought there would be more logic in thus disposing of old people with an established claim for making themselves universally obnoxious. Madame Lebrun grew a trifle hysterical; Robert called his brother some sharp, hard names.

"There's nothing much to explain, mother," he said; though he explained, nevertheless—looking chiefly at Edna—that he could only meet the gentleman whom he intended to join at Vera Cruz by taking such and such a steamer, which left New Orleans on such a day; that Beaudelet was going out with his lugger-load of vegetables that night, which gave him an opportunity of reaching the city and making his vessel on time.

"But when did you make up your mind to all this?" demanded Monsieur Farival.

"This afternoon," returned Robert, with a shade of annoyance.

"At what time this afternoon?" persisted the old gentleman, with nagging determination, as if he were cross-questioning a criminal in a court of justice.

"At four o'clock this afternoon, Monsieur Farival," Robert replied, in a high voice and with a lofty air, which reminded Edna of some gentleman on the stage.

She had forced herself to eat most of her soup, and now she was picking the flaky bits of a *court bouillon*[6] with her fork.

The lovers were profiting by the general conversation on Mexico to speak in whispers of matters which they rightly considered were interesting to no one but themselves. The lady in black had once received a pair of prayer-beads of curious workmanship from Mexico, with very special indulgence attached to them, but she had never been able to ascertain whether the indulgence extended outside the Mexican border. Father Fochel of the Cathedral had attempted to explain it; but he had not done so to her satisfaction. And she begged that Robert would interest himself, and discover, if possible, whether she was entitled to the indulgence accompanying the remarkably curious Mexican prayer-beads.

Madame Ratignolle hoped that Robert would exercise extreme caution in dealing with the Mexicans, who, she considered, were a treacherous people, unscrupulous and revengeful. She trusted she did them no injustice in thus condemning them as a race. She had known personally but one Mexican, who made and sold excellent tamales, and whom she would have trusted implicitly, so soft spoken was he. One day he was arrested for stabbing his wife. She never knew whether he had been hanged or not.

Victor had grown hilarious, and was attempting to tell an anecdote about a Mexican girl who served chocolate one winter in a restaurant in Dauphine Street.[7] No one would listen to him but old Monsieur Farival, who went into convulsions over the droll story.

Edna had wondered if they had all gone mad, to be talking and clamoring at that rate. She herself could think of nothing to say about Mexico or the Mexicans.

6. Fish broth.   7. In the French Quarter, New Orleans.

268   Kate Chopin

"At what time do you leave?" she asked Robert.
"At ten," he told her. "Beaudelet wants to wait for the moon."
"Are you all ready to go?"
"Quite ready. I shall only take a handbag, and shall pack my trunk in the city."
He turned to answer some question put to him by his mother, and Edna, having finished her black coffee, left the table.
She went directly to her room. The little cottage was close and stuffy after leaving the outer air. But she did not mind; there appeared to be a hundred different things demanding her attention indoors. She began to set the toilet-stand to rights, grumbling at the negligence of the quadroon, who was in the adjoining room putting the children to bed. She gathered together stray garments that were hanging on the backs of chairs, and put each where it belonged in closet or bureau drawer. She changed her gown for a more comfortable and commodious wrapper. She rearranged her hair, combing and brushing it with unusual energy. Then she went in and assisted the quadroon in getting the boys to bed.
They were very playful and inclined to talk—to do anything but lie quiet and go to sleep. Edna sent the quadroon away to her supper and told her she need not return. Then she sat and told the children a story. Instead of soothing it excited them, and added to their wakefulness. She left them in heated argument, speculating about the conclusion of the tale which their mother promised to finish the following night.
The little black girl came in to say that Madame Lebrun would like to have Mrs. Pontellier go and sit with them over at the house till Mr. Robert went away. Edna returned answer that she had already undressed, that she did not feel quite well, but perhaps she would go over to the house later. She started to dress again, and got as far advanced as to remove her *peignoir*. But changing her mind once more she resumed the *peignoir*, and went outside and sat down before her door. She was overheated and irritable, and fanned herself energetically for a while. Madame Ratignolle came down to discover what was the matter.
"All that noise and confusion at the table must have upset me," replied Edna, "and moreover, I hate shocks and surprises. The idea of Robert starting off in such a ridiculously sudden and dramatic way! As if it were a matter of life and death! Never saying a word about it all morning when he was with me."
"Yes," agreed Madame Ratignolle. "I think it was showing us all—you especially—very little consideration. It wouldn't have surprised me in any of the others; those Lebruns are all given to heroics. But I must say I should never have expected such a thing from Robert. Are you not coming down? Come on, dear; it doesn't look friendly."
"No," said Edna, a little sullenly. "I can't go to the trouble of dressing again; I don't feel like it."
"You needn't dress; you look all right; fasten a belt around your waist. Just look at me!"
"No," persisted Edna; "but you go on. Madame Lebrun might be offended if we both stayed away."
Madame Ratignolle kissed Edna good-night, and went away, being in truth rather desirous of joining in the general and animated conversation which was still in progress concerning Mexico and the Mexicans.
Somewhat later Robert came up, carrying his hand-bag.

"Aren't you feeling well?" he asked.

"Oh, well enough. Are you going right away?"

He lit a match and looked at his watch. "In twenty minutes," he said. The sudden and brief flare of the match emphasized the darkness for a while. He sat down upon a stool which the children had left out on the porch.

"Get a chair," said Edna.

"This will do," he replied. He put on his soft hat and nervously took it off again, and wiping his face with his handkerchief, complained of the heat.

"Take the fan," said Edna, offering it to him.

"Oh, no! Thank you. It does no good; you have to stop fanning some time, and feel all the more uncomfortable afterward."

"That's one of the ridiculous things which men always say. I have never known one to speak otherwise of fanning. How long will you be gone?"

"Forever, perhaps. I don't know. It depends upon a good many things."

"Well, in case it shouldn't be forever, how long will it be?"

"I don't know."

"This seems to me perfectly preposterous and uncalled for. I don't like it. I don't understand your motive for silence and mystery, never saying a word to me about it this morning." He remained silent, not offering to defend himself. He only said, after a moment:

"Don't part from me in an ill-humor. I never knew you to be out of patience with me before."

"I don't want to part in any ill-humor," she said. "But can't you understand? I've grown used to seeing you, to having you with me all the time, and your action seems unfriendly, even unkind. You don't even offer an excuse for it. Why, I was planning to be together, thinking of how pleasant it would be to see you in the city next winter."

"So was I," he blurted. "Perhaps that's the—" He stood up suddenly and held out his hand. "Good-by, my dear Mrs. Pontellier; good-by. You won't—I hope you won't completely forget me." She clung to his hand, striving to detain him.

"Write to me when you get there, won't you, Robert?" she entreated.

"I will, thank you. Good-by."

How unlike Robert! The merest acquaintance would have said something more emphatic than "I will, thank you; good-by," to such a request.

He had evidently already taken leave of the people over at the house, for he descended the steps and went to join Beaudelet, who was out there with an oar across his shoulder waiting for Robert. They walked away in the darkness. She could only hear Beaudelet's voice; Robert had apparently not even spoken a word of greeting to his companion.

Edna bit her handkerchief convulsively, striving to hold back and to hide, even from herself as she would have hidden from another, the emotion which was troubling—tearing—her. Her eyes were brimming with tears.

For the first time she recognized anew the symptoms of infatuation which she felt incipiently as a child, as a girl in her earliest teens, and later as a young woman. The recognition did not lessen the reality, the poignancy of the revelation by any suggestion or promise of instability. The past was nothing to her; offered no lesson which she was willing to heed. The future was a mystery which she never attempted to penetrate. The present alone was significant; was hers, to torture her as it was doing then with the biting conviction that she had lost that which she had held, that she had been denied that which her impassioned, newly awakened being demanded.

XVI

"Do you miss your friend greatly?" asked Mademoiselle Reisz one morning as she came creeping up behind Edna, who had just left her cottage on her way to the beach. She spent much of her time in the water since she had acquired finally the art of swimming. As their stay at Grand Isle drew near its close, she felt that she could not give too much time to a diversion which afforded her the only real pleasurable moments that she knew. When Mademoiselle Reisz came and touched her upon the shoulder and spoke to her, the woman seemed to echo the thought which was ever in Edna's mind; or, better, the feeling which constantly possessed her.

Robert's going had some way taken the brightness, the color, the meaning out of everything. The conditions of her life were in no way changed, but her whole existence was dulled, like a faded garment which seems to be no longer worth wearing. She sought him everywhere—in others whom she induced to talk about him. She went up in the mornings to Madame Lebrun's room, braving the clatter of the old sewing-machine. She sat there and chatted at intervals as Robert had done. She gazed around the room at the pictures and photographs hanging upon the wall, and discovered in some corner an old family album, which she examined with the keenest interest, appealing to Madame Lebrun for enlightenment concerning the many figures and faces which she discovered between its pages.

There was a picture of Madame Lebrun with Robert as a baby, seated in her lap, a round-faced infant with a fist in his mouth. The eyes alone in the baby suggested the man. And that was he also in kilts, at the age of five, wearing long curls and holding a whip in his hand. It made Edna laugh, and she laughed, too, at the portrait in his first long trousers; while another interested her, taken when he left for college, looking thin, long-faced, with eyes full of fire, ambition and great intentions. But there was no recent picture, none which suggested the Robert who had gone away five days ago, leaving a void and wilderness behind him.

"Oh, Robert stopped having his pictures taken when he had to pay for them himself! He found wiser use for his money, he says," explained Madame Lebrun. She had a letter from him, written before he left New Orleans. Edna wished to see the letter, and Madame Lebrun told her to look for it either on the table or the dresser, or perhaps it was on the mantelpiece.

The letter was on the bookshelf. It possessed the greatest interest and attraction for Edna; the envelope, its size and shape, the postmark, the handwriting. She examined every detail of the outside before opening it. There were only a few lines, setting forth that he would leave the city that afternoon, that he had packed his trunk in good shape, that he was well, and sent her his love and begged to be affectionately remembered to all. There was no special message to Edna except a postscript saying that if Mrs. Pontellier desired to finish the book which he had been reading to her, his mother would find it in his room, among other books there on the table. Edna experienced a pang of jealousy because he had written to his mother rather than to her.

Every one seemed to take for granted that she missed him. Even her husband, when he came down the Saturday following Robert's departure, expressed regret that he had gone.

"How do you get on without him, Edna?" he asked.

"It's very dull without him," she admitted. Mr. Pontellier had seen Robert in the city, and Edna asked him a dozen questions or more. Where had they met? On Carondelet Street, in the morning. They had gone "in" and had a drink and a cigar together. What had they talked about? Chiefly about his prospects in Mexico, which Mr. Pontellier thought were promising. How did he look? How did he seem—grave, or gay, or how? Quite cheerful, and wholly taken up with the idea of his trip, which Mr. Pontellier found altogether natural in a young fellow about to seek fortune and adventure in a strange, queer country.

Edna tapped her foot impatiently, and wondered why the children persisted in playing in the sun when they might be under the trees. She went down and led them out of the sun, scolding the quadroon for not being more attentive.

It did not strike her as in the least grotesque that she should be making of Robert the object of conversation and leading her husband to speak of him. The sentiment which she entertained for Robert in no way resembled that which she felt for her husband, or had ever felt, or ever expected to feel. She had all her life long been accustomed to harbor thoughts and emotions which never voiced themselves. They had never taken the form of struggles. They belonged to her and were her own, and she entertained the conviction that she had a right to them and that they concerned no one but herself. Edna had once told Madame Ratignolle that she would never sacrifice herself for her children, or for any one. Then had followed a rather heated argument; the two women did not appear to understand each other or to be talking the same language. Edna tried to appease her friend, to explain.

"I would give up the unessential; I would give my money, I would give my life for my children; but I wouldn't give myself. I can't make it more clear; it's only something which I am beginning to comprehend, which is revealing itself to me."

"I don't know what you would call the essential, or what you mean by the unessential," said Madame Ratignolle, cheerfully; "but a woman who would give her life for her children could do no more than that—your Bible tells you so. I'm sure I couldn't do more than that."

"Oh, yes you could!" laughed Edna.

She was not surprised at Mademoiselle Reisz's question the morning that lady, following her to the beach, tapped her on the shoulder and asked if she did not greatly miss her young friend.

"Oh, good morning, Mademoiselle; it is you? Why, of course I miss Robert. Are you going down to bathe?"

"Why should I go down to bathe at the very end of the season when I haven't been in the surf all summer?" replied the woman, disagreeably.

"I beg your pardon," offered Edna, in some embarrassment, for she should have remembered that Mademoiselle Reisz's avoidance of the water had furnished a theme for much pleasantry. Some among them thought it was on account of her false hair, or the dread of getting the violets wet, while others attributed it to the natural aversion for water sometimes believed to accompany the artistic temperament. Mademoiselle offered Edna some chocolates in a paper bag, which she took from her pocket, by way of showing that she bore no ill feeling. She habitually ate chocolates for their sustaining quality; they contained much nutriment in small compass, she said. They saved her from starvation, as Madame Lebrun's table was utterly impossible; and no one save so impertinent a woman as Madame Lebrun could think of offering such food to people and requiring them to pay for it.

"She must feel very lonely without her son," said Edna, desiring to change the subject. "Her favorite son, too. It must have been quite hard to let him go."

Mademoiselle laughed maliciously.

"Her favorite son! Oh, dear! Who could have been imposing such a tale upon you? Aline Lebrun lives for Victor, and for Victor alone. She has spoiled him into the worthless creature he is. She worships him and the ground he walks on. Robert is very well in a way, to give up all the money he can earn to the family, and keep the barest pittance for himself. Favorite son, indeed! I miss the poor fellow myself, my dear. I liked to see him and to hear him about the place—the only Lebrun who is worth a pinch of salt. He comes to see me often in the city. I like to play to him. That Victor! hanging would be too good for him. It's a wonder Robert hasn't beaten him to death long ago."

"I thought he had great patience with his brother," offered Edna, glad to be talking about Robert, no matter what was said.

"Oh! he thrashed him well enough a year or two ago," said Mademoiselle. "It was about a Spanish girl, whom Victor considered that he had some sort of claim upon. He met Robert one day talking to the girl, or walking with her, or bathing with her, or carrying her basket—I don't remember what;—and he became so insulting and abusive that Robert gave him a thrashing on the spot that has kept him comparatively in order for a good while. It's about time he was getting another."

"Was her name Mariequita?" asked Edna.

"Mariequita—yes, that was it; Mariequita. I had forgotten. Oh, she's a sly one, and a bad one, that Mariequita!"

Edna looked down at Mademoiselle Reisz and wondered how she could have listened to her venom so long. For some reason she felt depressed, almost unhappy. She had not intended to go into the water; but she donned her bathing suit, and left Mademoiselle alone, seated under the shade of the children's tent. The water was growing cooler as the season advanced. Edna plunged and swam about with an abandon that thrilled and invigorated her. She remained a long time in the water, half hoping that Mademoiselle Reisz would not wait for her.

But Mademoiselle waited. She was very amiable during the walk back, and raved much over Edna's appearance in her bathing suit. She talked about music. She hoped that Edna would go to see her in the city, and wrote her address with the stub of a pencil on a piece of card which she found in her pocket.

"When do you leave?" asked Edna.

"Next Monday; and you?"

"The following week," answered Edna, adding, "It has been a pleasant summer, hasn't it, Mademoiselle?"

"Well," agreed Mademoiselle Reisz, with a shrug, "rather pleasant, if it hadn't been for the mosquitoes and the Farival twins."

XVII

The Pontelliers possessed a very charming home on Esplanade Street[8] in New Orleans. It was a large, double cottage, with a broad front veranda, whose round, fluted columns supported the sloping roof. The house was painted a dazzling white; the outside shutters, or jalousies, were green. In the yard, which was kept scrupulously neat, were flowers and plants of every description which flourishes in South Louisiana. Within doors the appointments were perfect after the conventional type. The softest carpets and rugs covered the floors; rich and tasteful draperies hung at doors and windows. There were paintings, selected with judgment and discrimination, upon the walls. The cut glass, the silver, the heavy damask which daily appeared upon the table were the envy of many women whose husbands were less generous than Mr. Pontellier.

Mr. Pontellier was very fond of walking about his house examining its various appointments and details, to see that nothing was amiss. He greatly valued his possessions, chiefly because they were his, and derived genuine pleasure from contemplating a painting, a statuette, a rare lace curtain—no matter what—after he had bought it and placed it among his household gods.

On Tuesday afternoons—Tuesday being Mrs. Pontellier's reception day[9]—there was a constant stream of callers—women who came in carriages or in the street cars, or walked when the air was soft and distance permitted. A light-colored mulatto boy, in dress coat and bearing a diminutive silver tray for the reception of cards, admitted them. A maid, in white fluted cap, offered the callers liqueur, coffee, or chocolate, as they might desire. Mrs. Pontellier, attired in a handsome reception gown, remained in the drawing-room the entire afternoon receiving her visitors. Men sometimes called in the evening with their wives.

This had been the programme which Mrs. Pontellier had religiously followed since her marriage, six years before. Certain evenings during the week she and her husband attended the opera or sometimes the play.

Mr. Pontellier left his home in the mornings between nine and ten o'clock, and rarely returned before half-past six or seven in the evening dinner being served at half-past seven.

He and his wife seated themselves at table on Tuesday evening, a few weeks after their return from Grand Isle. They were alone together. The boys were being put to bed; the patter of their bare, escaping feet could be heard occasionally, as well as the pursuing voice of the quadroon, lifted in mild protest and entreaty. Mrs. Pontellier did not wear her usual Tuesday reception gown; she was in ordinary house dress. Mr. Pontellier,

8. Socially the best Creole residential street in New Orleans, it forms one border of the French Quarter.

9. A day each week when a lady was "at home" to visitors.

who was observant about such things, noticed it, as he served the soup and handed it to the boy in waiting.

"Tired out, Edna? Whom did you have? Many callers?" he asked. He tasted his soup and began to season it with pepper, salt, vinegar, mustard—everything within reach.

"There were a good many," replied Edna, who was eating her soup with evident satisfaction. "I found their cards when I got home; I was out."

"Out!" exclaimed her husband, with something like genuine consternation in his voice as he laid down the vinegar cruet and looked at her through his glasses. "Why, what could have taken you out on Tuesday? What did you have to do?"

"Nothing. I simply felt like going out, and I went out."

"Well, I hope you left some suitable excuse," said her husband, somewhat appeased, as he added a dash of cayenne pepper to the soup.

"No, I left no excuse. I told Joe to say I was out, that was all."

"Why, my dear, I should think you'd understand by this time that people don't do such things; we've got to observe *les convenances*[1] if we ever expect to get on and keep up with the procession. If you felt that you had to leave home this afternoon, you should have left some suitable explanation for your absence."

"This soup is really impossible; it's strange that woman hasn't learned yet to make a decent soup. Any free-lunch stand in town serves a better one. Was Mrs. Belthrop here?"

"Bring the tray with the cards, Joe. I don't remember who was here."

The boy retired and returned after a moment, bringing the tiny silver tray, which was covered with ladies' visiting cards. He handed it to Mrs. Pontellier.

"Give it to Mr. Pontellier," she said.

Joe offered the tray to Mr. Pontellier, and removed the soup.

Mr. Pontellier scanned the names of his wife's callers, reading some of them aloud, with comments as he read.

" 'The Misses Delasidas.' I worked a big deal in futures for their father this morning; nice girls; it's time they were getting married. 'Mrs. Belthrop.' I tell you what it is, Edna; you can't afford to snub Mrs. Belthrop. Why, Belthrop could buy and sell us ten times over. His business is worth a good, round sum to me. You'd better write her a note. 'Mrs. James Highcamp.' Hugh! the less you have to do with Mrs. Highcamp, the better. 'Madame Laforcé.' Came all the way from Carrolton,[2] too, poor old soul. 'Miss Wiggs,' 'Mrs. Eleanor Boltons.' " He pushed the cards aside.

"Mercy!" exclaimed Edna, who had been fuming. "Why are you taking the thing so seriously and making such a fuss over it?"

"I'm not making any fuss over it. But it's just such seeming trifles that we've got to take seriously; such things count."

The fish was scorched. Mr. Pontellier would not touch it. Edna said she did not mind a little scorched taste. The roast was in some way not to his fancy, and he did not like the manner in which the vegetables were served.

---

1. Social conventions.
2. Area of western New Orleans that was then a separate community.

"It seems to me," he said, "we spend money enough in this house to procure at least one meal a day which a man could eat and retain his self-respect."

"You used to think the cook was a treasure," returned Edna, indifferently.

"Perhaps she was when she first came; but cooks are only human. They need looking after, like any other class of persons that you employ. Suppose I didn't look after the clerks in my office, just let them run things their own way; they'd soon make a nice mess of me and my business."

"Where are you going?" asked Edna, seeing that her husband arose from table without having eaten a morsel except a taste of the highly-seasoned soup.

"I'm going to get my dinner at the club. Good night." He went into the hall, took his hat and stick from the stand, and left the house.

She was somewhat familiar with such scenes. They had often made her very unhappy. On a few previous occasions she had been completely deprived of any desire to finish her dinner. Sometimes she had gone into the kitchen to administer a tardy rebuke to the cook. Once she went to her room and studied the cookbook during an entire evening, finally writing out a menu for the week, which left her harassed with a feeling that, after all, she had accomplished no good that was worth the name.

But that evening Edna finished her dinner alone, with forced deliberation. Her face was flushed and her eyes flamed with some inward fire that lighted them. After finishing her dinner she went to her room, having instructed the boy to tell any other callers that she was indisposed.

It was a large, beautiful room, rich and picturesque in the soft, dim light which the maid had turned low. She went and stood at an open window and looked out upon the deep tangle of the garden below. All the mystery and witchery of the night seemed to have gathered there amid the perfumes and the dusky and tortuous outlines of flowers and foliage. She was seeking herself and finding herself in just such sweet, half-darkness which met her moods. But the voices were not soothing that came to her from the darkness and the sky above and the stars. They jeered and sounded mournful notes without promise, devoid even of hope. She turned back into the room and began to walk to and fro down its whole length, without stopping, without resting. She carried in her hands a thin handkerchief, which she tore into ribbons, rolled into a ball, and flung from her. Once she stopped, and taking off her wedding ring, flung it upon the carpet. When she saw it lying there, she stamped her heel upon it, striving to crush it. But her small boot heel did not make an indenture, not a mark upon the little glittering circlet.

In a sweeping passion she seized a glass vase from the table and flung it upon the tiles of the hearth. She wanted to destroy something. The crash and clatter were what she wanted to hear.

A maid, alarmed at the din of breaking glass, entered the room to discover what was the matter.

"A vase fell upon the hearth," said Edna. "Never mind; leave it till morning."

"Oh! you might get some of the glass in your feet, ma'am," insisted the young woman, picking up bits of the broken vase that were scattered upon the carpet. "And here's your ring, ma'am, under the chair."

Edna held out her hand, and taking the ring, slipped it upon her finger.

XVIII

The following morning Mr. Pontellier, upon leaving for his office, asked Edna if she would not meet him in town in order to look at some new fixtures for the library.

"I hardly think we need new fixtures, Léonce. Don't let us get anything new; you are too extravagant. I don't believe you ever think of saving or putting by."

"The way to become rich is to make money, my dear Edna, not to save it," he said. He regretted that she did not feel inclined to go with him and select new fixtures. He kissed her good-by, and told her she was not looking well and must take care of herself. She was unusually pale and very quiet.

She stood on the front veranda as he quitted the house, and absently picked a few sprays of jessamine that grew upon a trellis near by. She inhaled the odor of the blossoms and thrust them into the bosom of her white morning gown. The boys were dragging along the banquette a small "express wagon," which they had filled with blocks and sticks. The quadroon was following them with little quick steps, having assumed a fictitious animation and alacrity for the occasion. A fruit vender was crying his wares in the street.

Edna looked straight before her with a self-absorbed expression upon her face. She felt no interest in anything about her. The street, the children, the fruit vender, the flowers growing there under her eyes, were all part and parcel of an alien world which had suddenly become antagonistic.

She went back into the house. She had thought of speaking to the cook concerning her blunders of the previous night; but Mr. Pontellier had saved her that disagreeable mission, for which she was so poorly fitted. Mr. Pontellier's arguments were usually convincing with those whom he employed. He left home feeling quite sure that he and Edna would sit down that evening, and possibly a few subsequent evenings, to a dinner deserving of the name.

Edna spent an hour or two in looking over some of her old sketches. She could see their shortcomings and defects, which were glaring in her eyes. She tried to work a little, but found she was not in the humor. Finally she gathered together a few of the sketches—those which she considered the least discreditable; and she carried them with her when, a little later, she dressed and left the house. She looked handsome and distinguished in her street gown. The tan of the seashore had left her face, and her forehead was smooth, white, and polished beneath her heavy, yellow-brown hair. There were a few freckles on her face, and a small, dark mole near the under lip and one on the temple, half-hidden in her hair.

As Edna walked along the street she was thinking of Robert. She was still under the spell of her infatuation. She had tried to forget him, realizing the inutility of remembering. But the thought of him was like an obsession, ever pressing itself upon her. It was not that she dwelt upon details of their acquaintance, or recalled in any special or peculiar way his personality; it was his being, his existence, which dominated her thought, fading sometimes as if it would melt into the midst of the forgotten, reviving again with an intensity which filled her with an incomprehensible longing.

Edna was on her way to Madame Ratignolle's. Their intimacy, begun at Grand Isle, had not declined, and they had seen each other with some frequency since their return to the city. The Ratignolles lived at no great distance from Edna's home, on the corner of a side street, where Monsieur Ratignolle owned and conducted a drug store which enjoyed a steady and prosperous trade. His father had been in the business before him, and Monsieur Ratignolle stood well in the community and bore an enviable reputation for integrity and clear-headedness. His family lived in commodious apartments over the store, having an entrance on the side within the *porte cochère*. There was something which Edna thought very French, very foreign, about their whole manner of living. In the large and pleasant salon which extended across the width of the house, the Ratignolles entertained their friends once a fortnight with a *soirée musicale*,[3] sometimes diversified by card-playing. There was a friend who played upon the 'cello. One brought his flute and another his violin, while there were some who sang and a number who performed upon the piano with various degrees of taste and agility. The Ratignolles' *soirées musicales* were widely known, and it was considered a privilege to be invited to them.

Edna found her friend engaged in assorting the clothes which had returned that morning from the laundry. She at once abandoned her occupation upon seeing Edna, who had been ushered without ceremony into her presence.

" 'Cité can do it as well as I; it is really her business," she explained to Edna, who apologized for interrupting her. And she summoned a young black woman, whom she instructed, in French, to be very careful in checking off the list which she handed her. She told her to notice particularly if a fine linen handkerchief of Monsieur Ratignolle's, which was missing last week, had been returned; and to be sure to set to one side such pieces as required mending and darning.

Then placing an arm around Edna's waist, she led her to the front of the house, to the salon, where it was cool and sweet with the odor of great roses that stood upon the hearth in jars.

Madame Ratignolle looked more beautiful than ever there at home, in a negligé which left her arms almost wholly bare and exposed the rich, melting curves of her white throat.

"Perhaps I shall be able to paint your picture some day," said Edna with a smile when they were seated. She produced the roll of sketches and started to unfold them. "I believe I ought to work again. I feel as if I wanted to be doing something. What do you think of them? Do you think it worth while to take it up again and study some more? I might study for a while with Laidpore."

She knew that Madame Ratignolle's opinion in such a matter would be next to valueless, that she herself had not alone decided, but determined; but she sought the words and praise and encouragement that would help her to put heart into her venture.

"Your talent is immense, dear!"

3. Musical evening.

"Nonsense!" protested Edna, well pleased,

"Immense, I tell you," persisted Madame Ratignolle, surveying the sketches one by one, at close range, then holding them at arm's length, narrowing her eyes, and dropping her head on one side. "Surely, this Bavarian peasant is worthy of framing; and this basket of apples! never have I seen anything more lifelike. One might almost be tempted to reach out a hand and take one."

Edna could not control a feeling which bordered upon complacency at her friend's praise, even realizing, as she did, its true worth. She retained a few of the sketches, and gave all the rest to Madame Ratignolle, who appreciated the gift far beyond its value and proudly exhibited the pictures to her husband when he came up from the store a little later for his midday dinner.

Mr. Ratignolle was one of those men who are called the salt of the earth. His cheerfulness was unbounded, and it was matched by his goodness of heart, his broad charity, and common sense. He and his wife spoke English with an accent which was only discernible through its un-English emphasis and a certain carefulness and deliberation. Edna's husband spoke English with no accent whatever. The Ratignolles understood each other perfectly. If ever the fusion of two human beings into one has been accomplished on this sphere it was surely in their union.

As Edna seated herself at table with them she thought, "Better a dinner of herbs,"[4] though it did not take her long to discover that it was no dinner of herbs, but a delicious repast, simple, choice, and in every way satisfying.

Monsieur Ratignolle was delighted to see her, though he found her looking not so well as at Grand Isle, and he advised a tonic. He talked a good deal on various topics, a little politics, some city news and neighborhood gossip. He spoke with an animation and earnestness that gave an exaggerated importance to every syllable he uttered. His wife was keenly interested in everything he said, laying down her fork the better to listen, chiming in, taking the words out of his mouth.

Edna felt depressed rather than soothed after leaving them. The little glimpse of domestic harmony which had been offered her, gave her no regret, no longing. It was not a condition of life which fitted her, and she could see in it but an appalling and hopeless ennui. She was moved by a kind of commiseration for Madame Ratignolle,—a pity for that colorless existence which never uplifted its possessor beyond the region of blind contentment, in which no moment of anguish ever visited her soul, in which she would never have the taste of life's delirium. Edna vaguely wondered what she meant by "life's delirium." It had crossed her thought like some unsought, extraneous impression.

XIX

Edna could not help but think that it was very foolish, very childish, to have stamped upon her wedding ring and smashed the crystal vase upon the tiles. She was visited by no more outbursts, moving her to such futile expedients. She began to do as she liked and to feel as she liked. She

4. Proverbs 15: 17—"Better is a dinner of herbs   therewith."
where love is, than a stalled ox and hatred

completely abandoned her Tuesdays at home, and did not return the visits of those who had called upon her. She made no ineffectual efforts to conduct her household *en bonne ménagère*,[5] going and coming as it suited her fancy, and, so far as she was able, lending herself to any passing caprice.

Mr. Pontellier had been a rather courteous husband so long as he met a certain tacit submissiveness in his wife. But her new and unexpected line of conduct completely bewildered him. It shocked him. Then her absolute disregard for her duties as a wife angered him. When Mr. Pontellier became rude, Edna grew insolent. She had resolved never to take another step backward.

"It seems to me the utmost folly for a woman at the head of a household, and the mother of children, to spend in an atelier days which would be better employed contriving for the comfort of her family."

"I feel like painting," answered Edna. "Perhaps I shan't always feel like it."

"Then in God's name paint! but don't let the family go to the devil. There's Madame Ratignolle; because she keeps up her music, she doesn't let everything else go to chaos. And she's more of a musician than you are a painter."

"She isn't a musician, and I'm not a painter. It isn't on account of painting that I let things go."

"On account of what, then?"

"Oh! I don't know. Let me alone; you bother me."

It sometimes entered Mr. Pontellier's mind to wonder if his wife were not growing a little unbalanced mentally. He could see plainly that she was not herself. That is, he could not see that she was becoming herself and daily casting aside that fictitious self which we assumed like a garment with which to appear before the world.

Her husband let her alone as she requested, and went away to his office. Edna went up to her atelier—a bright room in the top of the house. She was working with great energy and interest, without accomplishing anything, however, which satisfied her even in the smallest degree. For a time she had the whole household enrolled in the service of art. The boys posed for her. They thought it amusing at first, but the occupation soon lost its attractiveness when they discovered that it was not a game arranged especially for their entertainment. The quadroon sat for hours before Edna's palette, patient as a savage, while the housemaid took charge of the children, and the drawing-room went undusted. But the housemaid, too, served her term as model when Edna perceived that the young woman's back and shoulders were molded on classic lines, and that her hair, loosened from its confining cap, became an inspiration. While Edna worked she sometimes sang low the little air, *"Ah! si tu savais!"*

It moved her with recollections. She could hear again the ripple of the water, the flapping sail. She could see the glint of the moon upon the bay, and could feel the soft, gusty beating of the hot south wind. A subtle current of desire passed through her body, weakening her hold upon the brushes and making her eyes burn.

There were days when she was very happy without knowing why. She was happy to be alive and breathing, when her whole being seemed to be

5. Like a good housewife.

one with the sunlight, the color, the odors, the luxuriant warmth of some perfect Southern day. She liked then to wander alone into strange and unfamiliar places. She discovered many a sunny, sleepy corner, fashioned to dream in. And she found it good to dream and to be alone and unmolested.

There were days when she was unhappy, she did not know why,—when it did not seem worth while to be glad or sorry, to be alive or dead; when life appeared to her like a grotesque pandemonium and humanity like worms struggling blindly toward inevitable annihilation. She could not work on such a day, nor weave fancies to stir her pulses and warm her blood.

XX

It was during such a mood that Edna hunted up Mademoiselle Reisz. She had not forgotten the rather disagreeable impression left upon her by their last interview; but she nevertheless felt a desire to see her—above all, to listen while she played upon the piano. Quite early in the afternoon she started upon her quest for the pianist. Unfortunately she had mislaid or lost Mademoiselle Reisz's card, and looking up her address in the city directory, she found that the woman lived on Bienville Street,[6] some distance away. The directory which fell into her hands was a year or more old, however, and upon reaching the number indicated, Edna discovered that the house was occupied by a respectable family of mulattoes who had *chambres garnies*[7] to let. They had been living there for six months, and knew absolutely nothing of a Mademoiselle Reisz. In fact, they knew nothing of any of their neighbors; their lodgers were all people of the highest distinction, they assured Edna. She did not linger to discuss class distinctions with Madame Pouponne, but hastened to a neighboring grocery store, feeling sure that Mademoiselle would have left her address with the proprietor.

He knew Mademoiselle Reisz a good deal better than he wanted to know her, he informed his questioner. In truth, he did not want to know her at all, anything concerning her—the most disagreeable and unpopular woman who ever lived in Bienville Street. He thanked heaven she had left the neighborhood, and was equally thankful that he did not know where she had gone.

Edna's desire to see Mademoiselle Reisz had increased tenfold since these unlooked-for obstacles had arisen to thwart it. She was wondering who could give her the information she sought, when it suddenly occurred to her that Madame Lebrun would be the one most likely to do so. She knew it was useless to ask Madame Ratignolle, who was on the most distant terms with the musician, and preferred to know nothing concerning her. She had once been almost as emphatic in expressing herself upon the subject as the corner grocer.

Edna knew that Madame Lebrun had returned to the city, for it was the middle of November. And she also knew where the Lebruns lived, on Chartres Street.

Their home from the outside looked like a prison, with iron bars before

6. Across the French Quarter from Edna's home; Chartres Street (below) runs through the middle of the Quarter.

7. Furnished rooms.

the door and lower windows. The iron bars were a relic of the old *régime*,[8] and no one had ever thought of dislodging them. At the side was a high fence enclosing the garden. A gate or door opening upon the street was locked. Edna rang the bell at this side garden gate, and stood upon the banquette, waiting to be admitted.

It was Victor who opened the gate for her. A black woman, wiping her hands upon her apron, was close at his heels. Before she saw them Edna could hear them in altercation, the woman—plainly an anomaly—claiming the right to be allowed to perform her duties, one of which was to answer the bell.

Victor was surprised and delighted to see Mrs. Pontellier, and he made no attempt to conceal either his astonishment or his delight. He was a dark-browed, good-looking youngster of nineteen, greatly resembling his mother, but with ten times her impetuosity. He instructed the black woman to go at once and inform Madame Lebrun that Mrs. Pontellier desired to see her. The woman grumbled a refusal to do part of her duty when she had not been permitted to do it all, and started back to her interrupted task of weeding the garden. Whereupon Victor administered a rebuke in the form of a volley of abuse, which owing to its rapidity and incoherence, was all but incomprehensible to Edna. Whatever it was, the rebuke was convincing, for the woman dropped her hoe and went mumbling into the house.

Edna did not wish to enter. It was very pleasant there on the side porch, where there were chairs, a wicker lounge, and a small table. She seated herself, for she was tired from her long tramp; and she began to rock gently and smooth out the folds of her silk parasol. Victor drew up his chair beside her. He at once explained that the black woman's offensive conduct was all due to imperfect training, as he was not there to take her in hand. He had only come up from the island the morning before, and expected to return next day. He stayed all winter at the island; he lived there, and kept the place in order and got things ready for the summer visitors.

But a man needed occasional relaxation, he informed Mrs. Pontellier, and every now and again he drummed up a pretext to bring him to the city. My! but he had had a time of it the evening before! He wouldn't want his mother to know, and he began to talk in a whisper. He was scintillant with recollections. Of course, he couldn't think of telling Mrs. Pontellier all about it, she being a woman and not comprehending such things. But it all began with a girl peeping and smiling at him through the shutters as he passed by. Oh! but she was a beauty! Certainly he smiled back, and went up and talked to her. Mrs. Pontellier did not know him if she supposed he was one to let an opportunity like that escape him. Despite herself, the youngster amused her. She must have betrayed in her look some degree of interest or entertainment. The boy grew more daring, and Mrs. Pontellier might have found herself, in a little while, listening to a highly colored story but for the timely appearance of Madame Lebrun.

That lady was still clad in white, according to her custom of the summer. Her eyes beamed an effusive welcome. Would not Mrs. Pontellier go

8. The Spanish regime; the French secretly transferred New Orleans to Spain in 1762, getting it back briefly before the United States bought the whole vast territory in 1803 (Louisiana Purchase).

inside? Would she partake of some refreshment? Why had she not been there before? How was that dear Mr. Pontellier and how were those sweet children? Had Mrs. Pontellier ever known such a warm November?

Victor went and reclined on the wicker lounge behind his mother's chair, where he commanded a view of Edna's face. He had taken her parasol from her hands while he spoke to her, and he now lifted it and twirled it above him as he lay on his back. When Madame Lebrun complained that it was *so* dull coming back to the city; that she saw *so* few people now; that even Victor, when he came up from the island for a day or two, had *so* much to occupy him and engage his time; then it was that the youth went into contortions on the lounge and winked mischievously at Edna. She somehow felt like a confederate in crime and tried to look severe and disapproving.

There had been but two letters from Robert, with little in them, they told her. Victor said it was really not worth while to go inside for the letters, when his mother entreated him to go in search of them. He remembered the contents, which in truth he rattled off very glibly when put to the test.

One letter was written from Vera Cruz and the other from the City of Mexico. He had met Montel, who was doing everything toward his advancement. So far, the financial situation was no improvement over the one he had left in New Orleans, but of course the prospects were vastly better. He wrote of the City of Mexico, the buildings, the people and their habits, the conditions of life which he found there. He sent his love to the family. He inclosed a check to his mother, and hoped she would affectionately remember him to all his friends. That was about the substance of the two letters. Edna felt that if there had been a message for her, she would have received it. The despondent frame of mind in which she had left home began again to overtake her, and she remembered that she wished to find Mademoiselle Reisz.

Madame Lebrun knew where Mademoiselle Reisz lived. She gave Edna the address, regretting that she would not consent to stay and spend the remainder of the afternoon, and pay a visit to Mademoiselle Reisz some other day. The afternoon was already well advanced.

Victor escorted her out upon the banquette, lifted her parasol, and held it over her while he walked to the car[9] with her. He entreated her to bear in mind that the disclosures of the afternoon were strictly confidential. She laughed and bantered him a little, remembering too late that she should have been dignified and reserved.

"How handsome Mrs. Pontellier looked!" said Madame Lebrun to her son.

"Ravishing!" he admitted. "The city atmosphere has improved her. Some way she doesn't seem like the same woman."

XXI

Some people contended that the reason Mademoiselle Reisz always chose apartments up under the roof was to discourage the approach of beggars, peddlars and callers. There were plenty of windows in her little front room. They were for the most part dingy, but as they were nearly

9. Street car.

always open it did not make so much difference. They often admitted into the room a good deal of smoke and soot; but at the same time all the light and air that there was came through them. From her windows could be seen the crescent of the river, the masts of ships and the big chimneys of the Mississippi steamers. A magnificent piano crowded the apartment. In the next room she slept, and in the third and last she harbored a gasoline stove on which she cooked her meals when disinclined to descend to the neighboring restaurant. It was there also that she ate, keeping her belongings in a rare old buffet, dingy and battered from a hundred years of use.

When Edna knocked at Mademoiselle Reisz's front room door and entered, she discovered that person standing beside the window, engaged in mending or patching an old prunella gaiter. The little musician laughed all over when she saw Edna. Her laugh consisted of a contortion of the face and all the muscles of the body. She seemed strikingly homely, standing there in the afternoon light. She still wore the shabby lace and the artificial bunch of violets on the side of her head.

"So you remembered me at last," said Mademoiselle. "I had said to myself, 'Ah, bah! she will never come.'"

"Did you want me to come?" asked Edna with a smile.

"I had not thought much about it," answered Mademoiselle. The two had seated themselves on a little bumpy sofa which stood against the wall. "I am glad, however, that you came. I have the water boiling back there, and was just about to make some coffee. You will drink a cup with me. And how is *la belle dame?*[1] Always handsome! always healthy! always contented!" She took Edna's hand between her strong wiry fingers, holding it loosely without warmth, and executing a sort of double theme upon the back and palm.

"Yes," she went on; "I sometimes thought: 'She will never come. She promised as those women in society always do, without meaning it. She will not come.' For I really don't believe you like me, Mrs. Pontellier."

"I don't know whether I like you or not," replied Edna, gazing down at the little woman with a quizzical look.

The candor of Mrs. Pontellier's admission greatly pleased Mademoiselle Reisz. She expressed her gratification by repairing forthwith to the region of the gasoline stove and rewarding her guest with the promised cup of coffee. The coffee and the biscuit accompanying it proved very acceptable to Edna, who had declined refreshment at Madame Lebrun's and was now beginning to feel hungry. Mademoiselle set the tray which she brought in upon a small table near at hand, and seated herself once again on the lumpy sofa.

"I have had a letter from your friend," she remarked, as she poured a little cream into Edna's cup and handed it to her.

"My friend?"

"Yes, your friend Robert. He wrote to me from the City of Mexico."

"Wrote to *you?*" repeated Edna in amazement, stirring her coffee absently.

"Yes, to me. Why not? Don't stir all the warmth out of your coffee; drink it. Though the letter might as well have been sent to you; it was nothing but Mrs. Pontellier from beginning to end."

1. *The beautiful lady.*

"Let me see it," requested the young woman, entreatingly.

"No; a letter concerns no one but the person who writes it and the one to whom it is written."

"Haven't you just said it concerned me from beginning to end?"

"It was written about you, not to you. 'Have you seen Mrs. Pontellier? How is she looking?' he asks. 'As Mrs. Pontellier says,' or 'as Mrs. Pontellier once said.' 'If Mrs. Pontellier should call upon you, play for her that Impromptu of Chopin's, my favorite. I heard it here a day or two ago, but not as you play it. I should like to know how it affects her,' and so on, as if he supposed we were constantly in each other's society."

"Let me see the letter."

"Oh, no."

"Have you answered it?"

"No."

"Let me see the letter."

"No, and again, no."

"Then play the Impromptu for me."

"It is growing late; what time do you have to be home?"

"Time doesn't concern me. Your question seems a little rude. Play the Impromptu."

"But you have told me nothing of yourself. What are you doing?"

"Painting!" laughed Edna. "I am becoming an artist. Think of it!"

"Ah! an artist! You have pretensions, Madame."

"Why pretensions? Do you think I could not become an artist?"

"I do not know you well enough to say. I do not know your talent or your temperament. To be an artist includes much; one must possess many gifts—absolute gifts—which have not been acquired by one's own effort. And, moreover, to succeed, the artist must possess the courageous soul."

"What do you mean by the courageous soul?"

"Courageous, *ma foi!* The brave soul. The soul that dares and defies."

"Show me the letter and play for me the Impromptu. You see that I have persistence. Does that quality count for anything in art?"

"It counts with a foolish old woman whom you have captivated," replied Mademoiselle, with her wriggling laugh.

The letter was right there at hand in the drawer of the little table upon which Edna had just placed her coffee cup. Mademoiselle opened the drawer and drew forth the letter, the topmost one. She placed it in Edna's hands, and without further comment arose and went to the piano.

Mademoiselle played a soft interlude. It was an improvisation. She sat low at the instrument, and the lines of her body settled into ungraceful curves and angles that gave it an appearance of deformity. Gradually and imperceptibly the interlude melted into the soft opening minor chords of the Chopin Impromptu.

Edna did not know when the Impromptu began or ended. She sat in the sofa corner reading Robert's letter by the fading light. Mademoiselle had glided from the Chopin into the quivering love-notes of Isolde's song,[2] and back again to the Impromptu with its soulful and poignant longing.

The shadows deepened in the little room. The music grew strange and fantastic—turbulent, insistent, plaintive and soft with entreaty. The shad-

2. *Liebestod* ("Love-death"), from Richard Wagner's opera *Tristan und Isolde* (1857–1859), sung by Isolde as she dies in her lover's arms.

ows grew deeper. The music filled the room. It floated out upon the night, over the housetops, the crescent of the river, losing itself in the silence of the upper air.

Edna was sobbing, just as she had wept one midnight at Grand Isle when strange, new voices awoke in her. She arose in some agitation to take her departure. "May I come again, Mademoiselle?" she asked at the threshold.

"Come whenever you feel like it. Be careful; the stairs and landings are dark; don't stumble."

Mademoiselle reëntered and lit a candle. Robert's letter was on the floor. She stooped and picked it up. It was crumpled and damp with tears. Mademoiselle smoothed the letter out, restored it to the envelope, and replaced it in the table drawer.

XXII

One morning on his way into town Mr. Pontellier stopped at the house of his old friend and family physician, Doctor Mandelet. The Doctor was a semi-retired physician, resting, as the saying is, upon his laurels. He bore a reputation for wisdom rather than skill—leaving the active practice of medicine to his assistants and younger contemporaries—and was much sought for in matters of consultation. A few families, united to him by bonds of friendship, he still attended when they required the services of a physician. The Pontelliers were among these.

Mr. Pontellier found the Doctor reading at the open window of his study. His house stood rather far back from the street, in the center of a delightful garden, so that it was quiet and peaceful at the old gentleman's study window. He was a great reader. He stared up disapprovingly over his eye-glasses as Mr. Pontellier entered, wondering who had the temerity to disturb him at that hour of the morning.

"Ah, Pontellier! Not sick, I hope. Come and have a seat. What news do you bring this morning?" He was quite portly, with a profusion of gray hair, and small blue eyes which age had robbed of much of their brightness but none of their penetration.

"Oh! I'm never sick, Doctor. You know that I come of tough fiber—of that old Creole race of Pontelliers that dry up and finally blow away. I came to consult—no, not precisely to consult—to talk to you about Edna. I don't know what ails her."

"Madame Pontellier not well?" marveled the Doctor. "Why, I saw her—I think it was a week ago—walking along Canal Street,[3] the picture of health, it seemed to me."

"Yes, yes; she seems quite well," said Mr. Pontellier, leaning forward and whirling his stick between his two hands; "but she doesn't act well. She's odd, she's not like herself. I can't make her out, and I thought perhaps you'd help me."

"How does she act?" inquired the doctor.

"Well, it isn't easy to explain," said Mr. Pontellier, throwing himself back in his chair. "She lets the housekeeping go to the dickens."

"Well, well; women are not all alike, my dear Pontellier. We've got to consider—"

---

3. Major New Orleans thoroughfare, one boundary of the French Quarter.

"I know that; I told you I couldn't explain. Her whole attitude—toward me and everybody and everything—has changed. You know I have a quick temper, but I don't want to quarrel or be rude to a woman, especially my wife; yet I'm driven to it, and feel like ten thousand devils after I've made a fool of myself. She's making it devilishly uncomfortable for me," he went on nervously. "She's got some sort of notion in her head concerning the eternal rights of women; and—you understand—we meet in the morning at the breakfast table."

The old gentleman lifted his shaggy eyebrows, protruded his thick nether lip, and tapped the arms of his chair with his cushioned fingertips.

"What have you been doing to her, Pontellier?"

"Doing! *Parbleu!*"[4]

"Has she," asked the Doctor, with a smile, "has she been associating of late with a circle of pseudo-intellectual women—super-spiritual superior beings? My wife has been telling me about them."

"That's the trouble," broke in Mr. Pontellier, "she hasn't been associating with any one. She has abandoned her Tuesdays at home, has thrown over all her acquaintances, and goes tramping about by herself, moping in the street-cars, getting in after dark. I tell you she's peculiar. I don't like it; I feel a little worried over it."

This was a new aspect for the Doctor. "Nothing hereditary?" he asked, seriously. "Nothing peculiar about her family antecedents, is there?"

"Oh, no, indeed! She comes of sound old Presbyterian Kentucky stock. The old gentleman, her father, I have heard, used to atone for his week-day sins with his Sunday devotions. I know for a fact, that his race horses literally ran away with the prettiest bit of Kentucky farming land I ever laid eyes upon. Margaret—you know Margaret—she has all the Presbyterianism undiluted. And the youngest is something of a vixen. By the way, she gets married in a couple of weeks from now."

"Send your wife up to the wedding," exclaimed the Doctor, foreseeing a happy solution. "Let her stay among her own people for a while; it will do her good."

"That's what I want her to do. She won't go to the marriage. She says a wedding is one of the most lamentable spectacles on earth. Nice thing for a woman to say to her husband!" exclaimed Mr. Pontellier, fuming anew at the recollection.

"Pontellier," said the Doctor, after a moment's reflection, "let your wife alone for a while. Don't bother her, and don't let her bother you. Woman, my dear friend, is a very peculiar and delicate organism—a sensitive and highly organized woman, such as I know Mrs. Pontellier to be, is especially peculiar. It would require an inspired psychologist to deal successfully with them. And when ordinary fellows like you and me attempt to cope with their idiosyncrasies the result is bungling. Most women are moody and whimsical. This is some passing whim of your wife, due to some cause or causes which you and I needn't try to fathom. But it will pass happily over, especially if you let her alone. Send her around to see me."

"Oh! I couldn't do that; there'd be no reason for it," objected Mr. Pontellier.

4. *Good heavens!*

"Then I'll go around and see her," said the Doctor. "I'll drop in to dinner some evening *en bon ami*."[5]

"Do! by all means," urged Mr. Pontellier. "What evening will you come? Say Thursday. Will you come Thursday?" he asked, rising to take his leave.

"Very well; Thursday. My wife may possibly have some engagement for me Thursday. In case she has, I shall let you know. Otherwise, you may expect me."

Mr. Pontellier turned before leaving to say:

"I am going to New York on business very soon. I have a big scheme on hand, and want to be on the field proper to pull the ropes and handle the ribbons. We'll let you in on the inside if you say so, Doctor," he laughed.

"No, I thank you, my dear sir," returned the Doctor. "I leave such ventures to you younger men with the fever of life still in your blood."

"What I wanted to say," continued Mr. Pontellier, with his hand on the knob; "I may have to be absent a good while. Would you advise me to take Edna along?"

"By all means, if she wishes to go. If not, leave her here. Don't contradict her. The mood will pass, I assure you. It may take a month, two, three months—possibly longer, but it will pass; have patience."

"Well, good-by, *à jeudi*,"[6] said Mr. Pontellier, as he let himself out.

The Doctor would have liked during the course of conversation to ask, "Is there any man in the case?" but he knew his Creole too well to make such a blunder as that.

He did not resume his book immediately, but sat for a while meditatively looking out into the garden.

XXIII

Edna's father was in the city, and had been with them several days. She was not very warmly or deeply attached to him, but they had certain tastes in common, and when together they were companionable. His coming was in the nature of a welcome disturbance; it seemed to furnish a new direction for her emotions.

He had come to purchase a wedding gift for his daughter, Janet, and an outfit for himself in which he might make a creditable appearance at her marriage. Mr. Pontellier had selected the bridal gift, as every one immediately connected with him always deferred to his taste in such matters. And his suggestions on the question of dress—which too often assumes the nature of a problem—were of inestimable value to his father-in-law. But for the past few days the old gentleman had been upon Edna's hands, and in his society she was becoming acquainted with a new set of sensations. He had been a colonel in the Confederate army, and still maintained, with the title, the military bearing which had always accompanied it. His hair and mustache were white and silky, emphasizing the rugged bronze of his face. He was tall and thin, and wore his coats padded, which gave a fictitious breadth and depth to his shoulders and chest. Edna and her father looked very distinguished together, and excited a good deal of notice during their perambulations. Upon his arrival she began by introducing him to her atelier and making a sketch of him. He took the whole matter

5. *As a good friend.* 6. *Until Thursday.*

very seriously. If her talent had been ten-fold greater than it was, it would not have surprised him, convinced as he was that he had bequeathed to all of his daughters the germs of a masterful capability, which only depended upon their own efforts to be directed toward successful achievement.

Before her pencil he sat rigid and unflinching, as he had faced the cannon's mouth in days gone by. He resented the intrusion of the children, who gaped with wondering eyes at him, sitting so stiff up there in their mother's bright atelier. When they drew near he motioned them away with an expressive action of the foot, loath to disturb the fixed lines of his countenance, his arms, or his rigid shoulders.

Edna, anxious to entertain him, invited Mademoiselle Reisz to meet him, having promised him a treat in her piano playing; but Mademoiselle declined the invitation. So together they attended a *soirée musicale* at the Ratignolle's. Monsieur and Madame Ratignolle made much of the Colonel, installing him as the guest of honor and engaging him at once to dine with them the following Sunday, or any day which he might select. Madame coquetted with him in the most captivating and naïve manner, with eyes, gestures, and a profusion of compliments, till the Colonel's old head felt thirty years younger on his padded shoulders. Edna marveled, not comprehending. She herself was almost devoid of coquetry.

There were one or two men whom she observed at the *soirée musicale;* but she would never have felt moved to any kittenish display to attract their notice—to any feline or feminine wiles to express herself toward them. Their personality attracted her in an agreeable way. Her fancy selected them, and she was glad when a lull in the music gave them an opportunity to meet her and talk with her. Often on the street the glance of strange eyes had lingered in her memory, and sometimes had disturbed her.

Mr. Pontellier did not attend these *soirées musicales.* He considered them *bourgeois,* and found more diversion at the club. To Madame Ratignolle he said the music dispensed at her *soirées* was too "heavy," too far beyond his untrained comprehension. His excuse flattered her. But she disapproved of Mr. Pontellier's club, and she was frank enough to tell Edna so.

"It's a pity Mr. Pontellier doesn't stay home more in the evenings. I think you would be more—well, if you don't mind my saying it—more united, if he did."

"Oh! dear no!" said Edna, with a blank look in her eyes. "What should I do if he stayed home? We wouldn't have anything to say to each other."

She had not much of anything to say to her father, for that matter; but he did not antagonize her. She discovered that he interested her, though she realized that he might not interest her long; and for the first time in her life she felt as if she were thoroughly acquainted with him. He kept her busy serving him and ministering to his wants. It amused her to do so. She would not permit a servant or one of the children to do anything for him which she might do herself. Her husband noticed, and thought it was the expression of a deep filial attachment which he had never suspected.

The Colonel drank numerous "toddies" during the course of the day, which left him, however, imperturbed. He was an expert at concocting strong drinks. He had even invented some, to which he had given fantastic names, and for whose manufacture he required diverse ingredients that it devolved upon Edna to procure for him.

When Doctor Mandelet dined with the Pontelliers on Thursday he could discern in Mrs. Pontellier no trace of that morbid condition which her husband had reported to him. She was excited and in a manner radiant. She and her father had been to the race course, and their thoughts when they seated themselves at table were still occupied with the events of the afternoon, and their talk was still of the track. The Doctor had not kept pace with turf affairs. He had certain recollections of racing in what he called "the good old times" when the Lecompte stables flourished, and he drew upon this fund of memories so that he might not be left out and seem wholly devoid of the modern spirit. But he failed to impose upon the Colonel, and was even far from impressing him with this trumped-up knowledge of bygone days. Edna had staked her father on his last venture, with the most gratifying results to both of them. Besides, they had met some very charming people, according to the Colonel's impressions. Mrs. Mortimer Merriman and Mrs. James Highcamp, who were there with Alcée Arobin, had joined them and had enlivened the hours in a fashion that warmed him to think of.

Mr. Pontellier himself had no particular leaning toward horse-racing, and was even rather inclined to discourage it as a pastime, especially when he considered the fate of that blue-grass farm in Kentucky. He endeavored, in a general way, to express a particular disapproval, and only succeeded in arousing the ire and opposition of his father-in-law. A pretty dispute followed, in which Edna warmly espoused her father's cause and the Doctor remained neutral.

He observed his hostess attentively from under his shaggy brows, and noted a subtle change which had transformed her from the listless woman he had known into a being who, for the moment, seemed palpitant with the forces of life. Her speech was warm and energetic. There was no repression in her glance or gesture. She reminded him of some beautiful, sleek animal waking up in the sun.

The dinner was excellent. The claret was warm and the champagne was cold, and under their beneficent influence the threatened unpleasantness melted and vanished with the fumes of the wine.

Mr. Pontellier warmed up and grew reminiscent. He told some amusing plantation experiences, recollections of old Iberville and his youth, when he hunted 'possum in company with some friendly darky; thrashed the pecan trees, shot the grosbec,[7] and roamed the woods and fields in mischievous idleness.

The Colonel, with little sense of humor and of the fitness of things, related a somber episode of those dark and bitter days, in which he had acted a conspicuous part and always formed a central figure. Nor was the Doctor happier in his selection, when he told the old, ever new and curious story of the waning of a woman's love, seeking strange, new channels, only to return to its legitimate source after days of fierce unrest. It was one of the many little human documents which had been unfolded to him during his long career as a physician. The story did not seem especially to impress Edna. She had one of her own to tell, of a woman who

7. Grosbeak: birds with large bills.

paddled away with her lover one night in a pirogue and never came back. They were lost amid the Baratarian Islands, and no one ever heard of them or found trace of them from that day to this. It was a pure invention. She said that Madame Antoine had related it to her. That, also, was an invention. Perhaps it was a dream she had had. But every glowing word seemed real to those who listened. They could feel the hot breath of the Southern night; they could hear the long sweep of the pirogue through the glistening moonlit water, the beating of birds' wings, rising startled from among the reeds in the salt-water pools; they could see the faces of the lovers, pale, close together, rapt in oblivious forgetfulness, drifting into the unknown.

The champagne was cold, and its subtle fumes played fantastic tricks with Edna's memory that night.

Outside, away from the glow of the fire and the soft lamplight, the night was chill and murky. The Doctor doubled his old-fashioned cloak across his breast as he strode home through the darkness. He knew his fellow-creatures better than most men; knew that inner life which so seldom unfolds itself to unanointed eyes. He was sorry he had accepted Pontellier's invitation. He was growing old, and beginning to need rest and an imperturbed spirit. He did not want the secrets of other lives thrust upon him.

"I hope it isn't Arobin," he muttered to himself as he walked. "I hope to heaven it isn't Alcée Arobin."

XXIV

Edna and her father had a warm, and almost violent dispute upon the subject of her refusal to attend her sister's wedding. Mr. Pontellier declined to interfere, to interpose either his influence or his authority. He was following Doctor Mandelet's advice, and letting her do as she liked. The Colonel reproached his daughter for her lack of filial kindness and respect, her want of sisterly affection and womanly consideration. His arguments were labored and unconvincing. He doubted if Janet would accept any excuse—forgetting that Edna had offered none. He doubted if Janet would ever speak to her again, and he was sure Margaret would not.

Edna was glad to be rid of her father when he finally took himself off with his wedding garments and his bridal gifts, with his padded shoulders, his Bible reading, his "toddies" and ponderous oaths.

Mr. Pontellier followed him closely. He meant to stop at the wedding on his way to New York and endeavor by every means which money and love could devise to atone somewhat for Edna's incomprehensible action.

"You are too lenient, too lenient by far, Léonce," asserted the Colonel. "Authority, coercion are what is needed. Put your foot down good and hard; the only way to manage a wife. Take my word for it."

The Colonel was perhaps unaware that he had coerced his own wife into her grave. Mr. Pontellier had a vague suspicion of it which he thought it needless to mention at that late day.

Edna was not so consciously gratified at her husband's leaving home as she had been over the departure of her father. As the day approached when he was to leave her for a comparatively long stay, she grew melting and affectionate, remembering his many acts of consideration and his repeated expressions of an ardent attachment. She was solicitous about his health and his welfare. She bustled around, looking after his clothing, thinking about heavy underwear, quite as Madame Ratignolle would have done under similar circumstances. She cried when he went away, calling him her dear, good friend, and she was quite certain she would grow lonely before very long and go to join him in New York.

But after all, a radiant peace settled upon her when she at last found herself alone. Even the children were gone. Old Madame Pontellier had come herself and carried them off to Iberville with their quadroon. The old madame did not venture to say she was afraid they would be neglected during Léonce's absence; she hardly ventured to think so. She was hungry for them—even a little fierce in her attachment. She did not want them to be wholly "children of the pavement," she always said when begging to have them for a space. She wished them to know the country, with its streams, its fields, its woods, its freedom, so delicious to the young. She wished them to taste something of the life their father had lived and known and loved when he, too, was a little child.

When Edna was at last alone, she breathed a big, genuine sigh of relief. A feeling that was unfamiliar but very delicious came over her. She walked all through the house, from one room to another, as if inspecting it for the first time. She tried the various chairs and lounges, as if she had never sat and reclined upon them before. And she perambulated around the outside of the house, investigating, looking to see if windows and shutters were secure and in order. The flowers were like new acquaintances; she approached them in a familiar spirit, and made herself at home among them. The garden walks were damp, and Edna called to the maid to bring out her rubber sandals. And there she stayed, and stooped, digging around the plants, trimming, picking dead, dry leaves. The children's little dog came out, interfering, getting in her way. She scolded him, laughing at him, played with him. The garden smelled so good and looked so pretty in the afternoon sunlight. Edna plucked all the bright flowers she could find, and went into the house with them, she and the little dog.

Even the kitchen assumed a sudden interesting character which she had never before perceived. She went in to give directions to the cook, to say that the butcher would have to bring much less meat, that they would require only half their usual quantity of bread, of milk and groceries. She told the cook that she herself would be greatly occupied during Mr. Pontellier's absence, and she begged her to take all thought and responsibility of the larder upon her own shoulders.

That night Edna dined alone. The candelabra, with a few candles in the center of the table, gave all the light she needed. Outside the circle of light in which she sat, the large dining-room looked solemn and shadowy. The cook, placed upon her mettle, served a delicious repast—a luscious tenderloin broiled à point.[8] The wine tasted good; the marron glacé seemed to be just what she wanted. It was so pleasant, too, to dine in a comfortable *peignoir*.

She thought a little sentimentally about Léonce and the children, and wondered what they were doing. As she gave a dainty scrap or two to the doggie, she talked intimately to him about Etienne and Raoul. He was beside himself with astonishment and delight over these companionable

8. Just right.

advances, and showed his appreciation by his little quick, snappy barks and a lively agitation.

Then Edna sat in the library after dinner and read Emerson until she grew sleepy. She realized that she had neglected her reading, and determined to start anew upon a course of improving studies, now that her time was completely her own to do with as she liked.

After a refreshing bath, Edna went to bed. And as she snuggled comfortably beneath the eiderdown a sense of restfulness invaded her, such as she had not known before.

XXV

When the weather was dark and cloudy Edna could not work. She needed the sun to mellow and temper her mood to the sticking point. She had reached a stage when she seemed to be no longer feeling her way, working, when in the humor, with sureness and ease. And being devoid of ambition, and striving not toward accomplishment, she drew satisfaction from the work in itself.

On rainy or melancholy days Edna went out and sought the society of the friends she had made at Grand Isle. Or else she stayed indoors and nursed a mood with which she was becoming too familiar for her own comfort and peace of mind. It was not despair; but it seemed to her as if life were passing by, leaving its promise broken and unfulfilled. Yet there were other days when she listened, was led on and deceived by fresh promises which her youth held out to her.

She went again to the races, and again. Alcée Arobin and Mrs. Highcamp called for her one bright afternoon in Arobin's drag.[9] Mrs. Highcamp was a worldly but unaffected, intelligent, slim, tall blonde woman in the forties, with an indifferent manner and blue eyes that stared. She had a daughter who served her as a pretext for cultivating the society of young men of fashion. Alcée Arobin was one of them. He was a familiar figure at the race course, the opera, the fashionable clubs. There was a perpetual smile in his eyes, which seldom failed to awaken a corresponding cheerfulness in any one who looked into them and listened to his good-humored voice. His manner was quiet, and at times a little insolent. He possessed a good figure, a pleasing face, not overburdened with depth of thought or feeling; and his dress was that of the conventional man of fashion.

He admired Edna extravagantly, after meeting her at the races with her father. He had met her before on other occasions, but she had seemed to him unapproachable until that day. It was at his instigation that Mrs. Highcamp called to ask her to go with them to the Jockey Club[1] to witness the turf event of the season.

There were possibly a few track men out there who knew the race horse as well as Edna, but there was certainly none who knew it better. She sat between her two companions as one having authority to speak. She laughed at Arobin's pretensions, and deplored Mrs. Highcamp's ignorance. The race horse was a friend and intimate associate of her childhood. The atmosphere of the stables and the breath of the blue-grass paddock revived in her memory and lingered in her nostrils. She did not

9. Large coach with seats inside and on top.
1. The New Louisiana Jockey Club, an exclusive social club.

perceive that she was talking like her father as the sleek geldings ambled in review before them. She played for very high stakes, and fortune favored her. The fever of the game flamed in her cheeks and eyes, and it got into her blood and into her brain like an intoxicant. People turned their heads to look at her, and more than one lent an attentive ear to her utterances, hoping thereby to secure the elusive but ever-desired "tip." Arobin caught the contagion of excitement which drew him to Edna like a magnet. Mrs. Highcamp remained, as usual, unmoved, with her indifferent stare and uplifted eyebrows.

Edna stayed and dined with Mrs. Highcamp upon being urged to do so. Arobin also remained and sent away his drag.

The dinner was quiet and uninteresting, save for the cheerful efforts of Arobin to enliven things. Mrs. Highcamp deplored the absence of her daughter from the races, and tried to convey to her what she had missed by going to the "Dante reading" instead of joining them. The girl held a geranium leaf up to her nose and said nothing, but looked knowing and noncommittal. Mr. Highcamp was a plain, bald-headed man, who only talked under compulsion. He was unresponsive. Mrs. Highcamp was full of delicate courtesy and consideration toward her husband. She addressed most of her conversation to him at table. They sat in the library after dinner and read the evening papers together under the drop-light;[2] while the younger people went into the drawing-room near by and talked. Miss Highcamp played some selections from Grieg upon the piano. She seemed to have apprehended all of the composer's coldness and none of his poetry. While Edna listened she could not help wondering if she had lost her taste for music.

When the time came for her to go home, Mr. Highcamp grunted a lame offer to escort her, looking down at his slippered feet with tactless concern. It was Arobin who took her home. The car ride was long, and it was late when they reached Esplanade Street. Arobin asked permission to enter for a second to light his cigarette—his match safe[3] was empty. He filled his match safe, but did not light his cigarette until he left her, after she had expressed her willingness to go to the races with him again.

Edna was neither tired nor sleepy. She was hungry again, for the Highcamp dinner, though of excellent quality, had lacked abundance. She rummaged in the larder and brought forth a slice of "Gruyère" and some crackers. She opened a bottle of beer which she found in the ice-box. Edna felt extremely restless and excited. She vacantly hummed a fantastic tune as she poked at the wood embers on the hearth and munched a cracker.

She wanted something to happen—something, anything; she did not know what. She regretted that she had not made Arobin stay a half hour to talk over the horses with her. She counted the money she had won. But there was nothing else to do, so she went to bed, and tossed there for hours in a sort of monotonous agitation.

In the middle of the night she remembered that she had forgotten to write her regular letter to her husband; and she decided to do so next day and tell him about her afternoon at the Jockey Club. She lay wide awake composing a letter which was nothing like the one which she wrote next day. When the maid awoke her in the morning Edna was dreaming of Mr.

2. A light (at the time, gas) that can be raised or lowered.   3. Match box.

Highcamp playing the piano at the entrance of a music store on Canal Street, while his wife was saying to Alcée Arobin, as they boarded an Esplanade Street car:

"What a pity that so much talent has been neglected! but I must go." When, a few days later, Alcée Arobin again called for Edna in his drag, Mrs. Highcamp was not with him. He said they would pick her up. But as that lady had not been apprised of his intention of picking her up, she was not at home. The daughter was just leaving the house to attend the meeting of a branch Folk Lore Society, and regretted that she could not accompany them. Arobin appeared nonplused, and asked Edna if there were any one else she cared to ask.

She did not deem it worth while to go in search of any of the fashionable acquaintances from whom she had withdrawn herself. She thought of Madame Ratignolle, but knew that her fair friend did not leave the house, except to take a languid walk around the block with her husband after nightfall. Mademoiselle Reisz would have laughed at such a request from Edna. Madame Lebrun might have enjoyed the outing, but for some reason Edna did not want her. So they went alone, she and Arobin.

The afternoon was intensely interesting to her. The excitement came back upon her like a remittent fever. Her talk grew familiar and confidential. It was no labor to become intimate with Arobin. His manner invited easy confidence. The preliminary stage of becoming acquainted was one which he always endeavored to ignore when a pretty and engaging woman was concerned.

He stayed and dined with Edna. He stayed and sat beside the wood fire. They laughed and talked; and before it was time to go he was telling her how different life might have been if he had known her years before. With ingenuous frankness he spoke of what a wicked, ill-disciplined boy he had been, and impulsively drew up his cuff to exhibit upon his wrist the scar from a saber cut which he had received in a duel outside of Paris when he was nineteen. She touched his hand as she scanned the red cicatrice on the inside of his white wrist. A quick impulse that was somewhat spasmodic impelled her fingers to close in a sort of clutch upon his hand. He felt the pressure of her pointed nails in the flesh of his palm.

She arose hastily and walked toward the mantel.

"The sight of a wound or scar always agitates and sickens me," she said. "I shouldn't have looked at it."

"I beg your pardon," he entreated, following her; "it never occurred to me that it might be repulsive."

He stood close to her, and the effrontery in his eyes repelled the old, vanishing self in her, yet drew all her awakening sensuousness. He saw enough in her face to impel him to take her hand and hold it while he said his lingering good night.

"Will you go to the races again?" he asked.

"No," she said. "I've had enough of the races. I don't want to lose all the money I've won, and I've got to work when the weather is bright, instead of—"

"Yes; work; to be sure. You promised to show me your work. What morning may I come up to your atelier? To-morrow?"

"No!"

"Day after?"

"No, no."

"Oh, please don't refuse me! I know something of such things. I might help you with a stray suggestion or two."

"No. Good night. Why don't you go after you have said good night? I don't like you," she went on in a high, excited pitch, attempting to draw away her hand. She felt that her words lacked dignity and sincerity, and she knew that he felt it.

"I'm sorry you don't like me. I'm sorry I offended you. How have I offended you? What have I done? Can't you forgive me?" And he bent and pressed his lips upon her hand as if he wished never more to withdraw them.

"Mr. Arobin," she complained, "I'm greatly upset by the excitement of the afternoon; I'm not myself. My manner must have misled you in some way. I wish you to go, please." She spoke in a monotonous, dull tone. He took his hat from the table, and stood with eyes turned from her, looking into the dying fire. For a moment or two he kept an impressive silence.

"Your manner has not misled me, Mrs. Pontellier," he said finally. "My own emotions have done that. I couldn't help it. When I'm near you, how could I help it? Don't think anything of it, don't bother, please. You see, I go when you command me. If you wish me to stay away, I shall do so. If you let me come back, I—oh! you will let me come back?"

He cast one appealing glance at her, to which she made no response. Alcée Arobin's manner was so genuine that it often deceived even himself.

Edna did not care or think whether it were genuine or not. When she was alone she looked mechanically at the back of her hand which he had kissed so warmly. Then she leaned her head down on the mantelpiece. She felt somewhat like a woman who in a moment of passion is betrayed into an act of infidelity, and realizes the significance of the act without being wholly awakened from its glamour. The thought was passing vaguely through her mind, "What would he think?"

She did not mean her husband; she was thinking of Robert Lebrun. Her husband seemed to her now like a person whom she had married without love as an excuse.

She lit a candle and went up to her room. Alcée Arobin was absolutely nothing to her. Yet his presence, his manners, the warmth of his glances, and above all the touch of his lips upon her hand had acted like a narcotic upon her.

She slept a languorous sleep, interwoven with vanishing dreams.

XXVI

Alcée Arobin wrote Edna an elaborate note of apology, palpitant with sincerity. It embarrassed her; for in a cooler, quieter moment it appeared to her absurd that she should have taken his action so seriously, so dramatically. She felt sure that the significance of the whole occurrence had lain in her own self-consciousness. If she ignored his note it would give undue importance to a trivial affair. If she replied to it in a serious spirit it would still leave in his mind the impression that she had in a susceptible moment yielded to his influence. After all, it was no great matter to have one's hand kissed. She was provoked at his having written the apology. She answered in as light and bantering a spirit as she fancied it deserved, and said she would be glad to have him look in upon her at work whenever he felt the inclination and his business gave him the opportunity.

He responded at once by presenting himself at her home with all his disarming naïveté. And then there was scarcely a day which followed that she did not see him or was not reminded of him. He was prolific in pretexts. His attitude became one of good-humored subservience and tacit adoration. He was ready at all times to submit to her moods, which were as often kind as they were cold. She grew accustomed to him. They became intimate and friendly by imperceptible degrees, and then by leaps. He sometimes talked in a way that astonished her at first and brought the crimson into her face; in a way that pleased her at last, appealing to the animalism that stirred impatiently within her.

There was nothing which so quieted the turmoil of Edna's senses as a visit to Mademoiselle Reisz. It was then, in the presence of that personality which was offensive to her, that the woman, by her divine art, seemed to reach Edna's spirit and set it free.

It was misty, with heavy, lowering atmosphere, one afternoon, when Edna climbed the stairs to the pianist's apartments under the roof. Her clothes were dripping with moisture. She felt chilled and pinched as she entered the room. Mademoiselle was poking at a rusty stove that smoked a little and warmed the room indifferently. She was endeavoring to heat a pot of chocolate on the stove. The room looked cheerless and dingy to Edna as she entered. A bust of Beethoven, covered with a hood of dust, scowled at her from the mantelpiece.

"Ah! here comes the sunlight!" exclaimed Mademoiselle, rising from her knees before the stove. "Now it will be warm and bright enough; I can let the fire alone."

She closed the stove door with a bang, and approaching, assisted in removing Edna's dripping mackintosh.

"You are cold; you look miserable. The chocolate will soon be hot. But would you rather have a taste of brandy? I have scarcely touched the bottle which you brought me for my cold." A piece of red flannel was wrapped around Mademoiselle's throat; a stiff neck compelled her to hold her head on one side.

"I will take some brandy," said Edna, shivering as she removed her gloves and overshoes. She drank the liquor from the glass as a man would have done. Then flinging herself upon the uncomfortable sofa she said, "Mademoiselle, I am going to move away from my house on Esplanade Street."

"Ah!" ejaculated the musician, neither surprised nor especially interested. Nothing ever seemed to astonish her very much. She was endeavoring to adjust the bunch of violets which had become loose from its fastening in her hair. Edna drew her down upon the sofa, and taking a pin from her own hair, secured the shabby artificial flowers in their accustomed place.

"Aren't you astonished?"

"Passable. Where are you going? To New York? to Iberville? to your father in Mississippi? where?"

"Just two steps away," laughed Edna, "in a little four-room house around the corner. It looks so cozy, so inviting and restful, whenever I pass by; and it's for rent. I'm tired looking after that big house. It never seemed like mine, anyway—like home. It's too much trouble. I have to keep too many servants. I am tired bothering with them."

"That is not your true reason, *ma belle*.[4] There is no use in telling me lies. I don't know your reason, but you have not told me the truth." Edna did not protest or endeavor to justify herself.

"The house, the money that provides for it, are not mine. Isn't that enough reason?"

"They are your husband's," returned Mademoiselle, with a shrug and a malicious elevation of the eyebrows.

"Oh! I see there is no deceiving you. Then let me tell you: It is a caprice. I have a little money of my own from my mother's estate, which my father sends me by driblets. I won a large sum this winter on the races, and I am beginning to sell my sketches. Laidpore is more and more pleased with my work; he says it grows in force and individuality. I cannot judge of that myself, but I feel that I have gained in ease and confidence. However, as I said, I have sold a good many through Laidpore. I can live in the tiny house for little or nothing, with one servant. Old Celestine, who works occasionally for me, says she will come stay with me and do my work. I know I shall like it, like the feeling of freedom and independence."

"What does your husband say?"

"I have not told him yet. I only thought of it this morning. He will think I am demented, no doubt. Perhaps you think so."

Mademoiselle shook her head slowly. "Your reason is not yet clear to me," she said.

Neither was it quite clear to Edna herself; but it unfolded itself as she sat for a while in silence. Instinct had prompted her to put away her husband's bounty in casting off her allegiance. She did not know how it would be when he returned. There would have to be an understanding, an explanation. Conditions would some way adjust themselves, she felt; but whatever came, she had resolved never again to belong to another than herself.

"I shall give a grand dinner before I leave the old house!" Edna exclaimed. "You will have to come to it, Mademoiselle. I will give you everything that you like to eat and to drink. We shall sing and laugh and be merry for once." And she uttered a sigh that came from the very depths of her being.

If Mademoiselle happened to have received a letter from Robert during the interval of Edna's visits, she would give her the letter unsolicited. And she would seat herself at the piano and play as her humor prompted her while the young woman read the letter.

The little stove was roaring; it was red-hot, and the chocolate in the tin sizzled and sputtered. Edna went forward and opened the stove door, and Mademoiselle rising, took a letter from under the bust of Beethoven and handed it to Edna.

"Another! so soon!" she exclaimed, her eyes filled with delight. "Tell me, Mademoiselle, does he know that I see his letters?"

"Never in the world! He would be angry and would never write to me again if he thought so. Does he write to you? Never a line. Does he send

4. *My beauty.*

you a message? Never a word. It is because he loves you, poor fool, and is trying to forget you, since you are not free to listen to him or to belong to him."

"Why do you show me his letters, then?"

"Haven't you begged for them? Can I refuse you anything? Oh! you cannot deceive me," and Mademoiselle approached her beloved instrument and began to play. Edna did not at once read the letter. She sat holding it in her hand, while the music penetrated her whole being like an effulgence, warming and brightening the dark places of her soul. It prepared her for joy and exultation.

"Oh!" she exclaimed, letting the letter fall to the floor. "Why did you not tell me?" She went and grasped Mademoiselle's hands up from the keys. "Oh! unkind! malicious! Why did you not tell me?"

"That he was coming back? No great news, *ma foi*. I wonder he did not come long ago."

"But when, when?" cried Edna, impatiently. "He does not say when."

"He says 'very soon.' You know as much about it as I do; it is all in the letter."

"But why? Why is he coming? Oh, if I thought—" and she snatched the letter from the floor and turned the pages this way and that way, looking for the reason, which was left untold.

"If I were young and in love with a man," said Mademoiselle, turning on the stool and pressing her wiry hands between her knees as she looked down at Edna, who sat on the floor holding the letter, "it seems to me he would have to be some *grand esprit*,[5] a man with lofty aims and ability to reach them; one who stood high enough to attract the notice of his fellow-men. It seems to me if I were young and in love I should never deem a man of ordinary caliber worthy of my devotion."

"Now it is you who are telling lies and seeking to deceive me, Mademoiselle; or else you have never been in love, and know nothing about it. Why," went on Edna, clasping her knees and looking up into Mademoiselle's twisted face, "do you suppose a woman knows why she loves? Does she select? Does she say to herself: 'Go to! Here is a distinguished statesman with presidential possibilities; I shall proceed to fall in love with him.' Or, 'I shall set my heart upon this musician, whose fame is on every tongue?' Or, 'This financier, who controls the world's money markets?'"

"You are purposely misunderstanding me, *ma reine*.[6] Are you in love with Robert?"

"Yes," said Edna. It was the first time she had admitted it, and a glow overspread her face, blotching it with red spots.

"Why?" asked her companion. "Why do you love him when you ought not to?"

Edna, with a motion or two, dragged herself on her knees before Mademoiselle Reisz, who took the glowing face between her two hands.

"Why? Because his hair is brown and grows away from his temples; because he opens and shuts his eyes, and his nose is a little out of drawing; because he has two lips and a square chin, and a little finger which he can't straighten from having played baseball too energetically in his youth. Because—"

5. *Great spirit.*   6. *My lady* (literally, *queen*).

"Because you do, in short," laughed Mademoiselle. "What will you do when he comes back?" she asked.

"Do? Nothing, except feel glad and happy to be alive."

She was already glad and happy to be alive at the mere thought of his return. The murky, lowering sky, which had depressed her a few hours before, seemed bracing and invigorating as she splashed through the streets on her way home.

She stopped at a confectioner's and ordered a huge box of bonbons for the children in Iberville. She slipped a card in the box, on which she scribbled a tender message and sent an abundance of kisses.

Before dinner in the evening Edna wrote a charming letter to her husband, telling him of her intention to move for a while into the little house around the block, and to give a farewell dinner before leaving, regretting that he was not there to share it, to help her out with the menu and assist her in entertaining the guests. Her letter was brilliant and brimming with cheerfulness.

XXVII

"What is the matter with you?" asked Arobin that evening. "I never found you in such a happy mood." Edna was tired by that time, and was reclining on the lounge before the fire.

"Don't you know the weather prophet has told us we shall see the sun pretty soon?"

"Well, that ought to be reason enough," he acquiesced. "You wouldn't give me another if I sat here all night imploring you." He sat close to her on a low tabouret, and as he spoke his fingers lightly touched the hair that fell a little over her forehead. She liked the touch of his fingers through her hair, and closed her eyes sensitively.

"One of these days," she said, "I'm going to pull myself together for a while and think—try to determine what character of a woman I am; for, candidly, I don't know. By all the codes which I am acquainted with, I am a devilishly wicked specimen of the sex. But some way I can't convince myself that I am. I must think about it."

"Don't. What's the use? Why should you bother thinking about it when I can tell you what manner of woman you are." His fingers strayed occasionally down to her warm, smooth cheeks and firm chin, which was growing a little full and double.

"Oh, yes! You will tell me that I am adorable; everything that is captivating. Spare yourself the effort."

"No; I shan't tell you anything of the sort, though I shouldn't be lying if I did."

"Do you know Mademoiselle Reisz?" she asked irrelevantly.

"The pianist? I know her by sight. I've heard her play."

"She says queer things sometimes in a bantering way that you don't notice at the time and you find yourself thinking about afterward."

"For instance?"

"Well, for instance, when I left her today, she put her arms around me and felt my shoulder blades, to see if my wings were strong, she said. 'The bird that would soar above the level plain of tradition and prejudice must have strong wings. It is a sad spectacle to see the weaklings bruised, exhausted, fluttering back to earth.' "

"Whither would you soar?"

"I'm not thinking of any extraordinary flights. I only half comprehend her."

"I've heard she's partially demented," said Arobin.

"She seems to me wonderfully sane," Edna replied.

"I'm told she's extremely disagreeable and unpleasant. Why have you introduced her at a moment when I desired to talk of you?"

"Oh! talk of me if you like," cried Edna, clasping her hands beneath her head; "but let me think of something else while you do."

"I'm jealous of your thoughts to-night. They're making you a little kinder than usual; but some way I feel as if they were wandering, as if they were not here with me." She only looked at him and smiled. His eyes were very near. He leaned upon the lounge with an arm extended across her, while the other hand still rested upon her hair. They continued silently to look into each other's eyes. When he leaned forward and kissed her, she clasped his head, holding his lips to hers.

It was the first kiss of her life to which her nature had really responded. It was a flaming torch that kindled desire.

XXVIII

Edna cried a little that night after Arobin left her. It was only one phase of the multitudinous emotions which had assailed her. There was with her an overwhelming feeling of irresponsibility. There was the shock of the unexpected and the unaccustomed. There was her husband's reproach looking at her from the external things around her which he had provided for her external existence. There was Robert's reproach making itself felt by a quicker, fiercer, more overpowering love, which had awakened within her toward him. Above all, there was understanding. She felt as if a mist had been lifted from her eyes, enabling her to look upon and comprehend the significance of life, that monster made up of beauty and brutality. But among the conflicting sensations which assailed her, there was neither shame nor remorse. There was a dull pang of regret because it was not the kiss of love which had inflamed her, because it was not love which had held this cup of life to her lips.

XXIX

Without even waiting for an answer from her husband regarding his opinion or wishes in the matter, Edna hastened her preparations for quitting her home on Esplanade Street and moving into the little house around the block. A feverish anxiety attended her every action in that direction. There was no moment of deliberation, no interval of repose between the thought and its fulfillment. Early upon the morning following those hours passed in Arobin's society, Edna set about securing her new abode and hurrying her arrangements for occupying it. Within the precincts of her home she felt like one who has entered and lingered within the portals of some forbidden temple in which a thousand muffled voices bade her begone.

Whatever was her own in the house, everything which she had acquired aside from her husband's bounty, she caused to be transported to the other house, supplying simple and meager deficiencies from her own resources.

Arobin found her with rolled sleeves, working in company with the house-maid when he looked in during the afternoon. She was splendid and robust, and had never appeared handsomer than in the old blue gown, with a red silk handkerchief knotted at random around her head to protect her hair from the dust. She was mounted upon a high step-ladder, unhooking a picture from the wall when he entered. He had found the front door open, and had followed his ring by walking in unceremoniously.

"Come down!" he said. "Do you want to kill yourself?" She greeted him with affected carelessness, and appeared absorbed in her occupation.

If he had expected to find her languishing, reproachful, or indulging in sentimental tears, he must have been greatly surprised.

He was no doubt prepared for any emergency, ready for any one of the foregoing attitudes, just as he bent himself easily and naturally to the situation which confronted him.

"Please come down," he insisted, holding the ladder and looking up at her.

"No," she answered; "Ellen is afraid to mount the ladder. Joe is working over at the 'pigeon house'—that's the name Ellen gives it, because it's so small and looks like a pigeon house—and some one has to do this."

Arobin pulled off his coat, and expressed himself ready and willing to tempt fate in her place. Ellen brought him one of her dust-caps, and went into contortions of mirth, which she found it impossible to control, when she saw him put it on before the mirror as grotesquely as he could. Edna herself could not refrain from smiling when she fastened it at his request. So it was he who in turn mounted the ladder, unhooking pictures and curtains, and dislodging ornaments as Edna directed. When he had finished he took off his dust-cap and went out to wash his hands.

Edna was sitting on the tabouret, idly brushing the tips of a feather duster along the carpet when he came in again.

"Is there anything more you will let me do?" he asked.

"That is all," she answered. "Ellen can manage the rest." She kept the young woman occupied in the drawing-room, unwilling to be left alone with Arobin.

"What about the dinner?" he asked; "the grand event, the *coup d'état?*"

"It will be day after to-morrow. Why do you call it the '*coup d'état?*' Oh! it will be very fine; all my best of everything—crystal, silver and gold, Sèvres, flowers, music, and champagne to swim in. I'll let Léonce pay the bills. I wonder what he'll say when he sees the bills."

"And you ask me why I call it a *coup d'état?*" Arobin had put on his coat, and he stood before her and asked if his cravat was plumb. She told him it was, looking no higher than the tip of his collar.

"When do you go to the 'pigeon house?'—with all due acknowledgment to Ellen."

"Day after to-morrow, after the dinner. I shall sleep there."

"Ellen, will you very kindly get me a glass of water?" asked Arobin. "The dust in the curtains, if you will pardon me for hinting such a thing, has parched my throat to a crisp."

"While Ellen gets the water," said Edna, rising, "I will say good-by and let you go. I must get rid of this grime, and I have a million things to do and think of."

"When shall I see you?" asked Arobin, seeking to detain her, the maid having left the room.

"At the dinner, of course. You are invited."

"Not before?—not to-night or to-morrow morning or to-morrow noon or night? or the day after morning or noon? Can't you see yourself, without my telling you, what an eternity it is?"

He had followed her into the hall and to the foot of the stairway, looking up at her as she mounted with her face half turned to him.

"Not an instant sooner," she said. But she laughed and looked at him with eyes that at once gave him courage to wait and made it torture to wait.

XXX

Though Edna had spoken of the dinner as a very grand affair, it was in truth a very small affair and very select, in so much as the guests invited were few and were elected with discrimination. She had counted upon an even dozen seating themselves at her round mahogany board, forgetting for the moment that Madame Ratignolle was to the last degree *souffrante*[7] and unpresentable, and not foreseeing that Madame Lebrun would send a thousand regrets at the last moment. So there were only ten, after all, which made a cozy, comfortable number.

There were Mr. and Mrs. Merriman, a pretty, vivacious little woman in the thirties; her husband, a jovial fellow, something of a shallow-pate, who laughed a good deal at other people's witticisms, and had thereby made himself extremely popular. Mrs. Highcamp had accompanied them. Of course, there was Alcée Arobin; and Mademoiselle Reisz had consented to come. Edna had sent her a fresh bunch of violets with black lace trimmings for her hair. Monsieur Ratignolle brought himself and his wife's excuses. Victor Lebrun, who happened to be in the city, bent upon relaxation, had accepted with alacrity. There was a Miss Mayblunt, no longer in her teens, who looked at the world through lorgnettes and with the keenest interest. It was thought and said that she was intellectual; it was suspected of her that she wrote under a *nom de guerre*. She had come with a gentleman by the name of Gouvernail, connected with one of the daily papers, of whom nothing special could be said, except that he was observant and seemed quiet and inoffensive. Edna herself made the tenth, and at half-past eight they seated themselves at table, Arobin and Monsieur Ratignolle on either side of their hostess.

Mrs. Highcamp sat between Arobin and Victor Lebrun. Then came Mrs. Merriman, Mr. Gouvernail, Miss Mayblunt, Mr. Merriman, and Mademoiselle Reisz next to Monsieur Ratignolle.

There was something extremely gorgeous about the appearance of the table, an effect of splendor conveyed by a cover of pale yellow satin under strips of lace-work. There were wax candles in massive brass candelabra, burning softly under yellow silk shades; full, fragrant roses, yellow and red, abounded. There were silver and gold, as she had said there

7. *Feeling bad.*

would be, and crystal which glittered like the gems which the women wore.

The ordinary stiff dining chairs had been discarded for the occasion and replaced by the most commodious and luxurious which could be collected throughout the house. Mademoiselle Reisz, being exceedingly diminutive, was elevated upon cushions, as small children are sometimes hoisted at table upon bulky volumes.

"Something new, Edna?" exclaimed Miss Mayblunt, with lorgnette directed toward a magnificent cluster of diamonds that sparkled, that almost sputtered, in Edna's hair, just over the center of her forehead.

"Quite new; 'brand' new, in fact; a present from my husband. It arrived this morning from New York. I may as well admit that this is my birthday, and that I am twenty-nine. In good time I expect you to drink my health. Meanwhile, I shall ask you to begin with this cocktail, composed—would you say 'composed?' " with an appeal to Miss Mayblunt—"composed by my father in honor of Sister Janet's wedding."

Before each guest stood a tiny glass that looked and sparkled like a garnet gem.

"Then, all things considered," spoke Arobin, "it might not be amiss to start out by drinking the Colonel's health in the cocktail which he composed, on the birthday of the most charming of women—the daughter whom he invented."

Mr. Merriman's laugh at this sally was such a genuine outburst and so contagious that it started the dinner with an agreeable swing that never slackened.

Miss Mayblunt begged to be allowed to keep her cocktail untouched before her, just to look at. The color was marvelous! She could compare it to nothing she had ever seen, and the garnet lights which it emitted were unspeakably rare. She pronounced the Colonel an artist, and stuck to it.

Monsieur Ratignolle was prepared to take things seriously; the *mets*, the *entre-mets*,[8] the service, the decorations, even the people. He looked up from his pompano and inquired of Arobin if he were related to the gentleman of that name who formed one of the firm of Laitner and Arobin, lawyers. The young man admitted that Laitner was a warm personal friend, who permitted Arobin's name to decorate the firm's letterheads and to appear upon a shingle that graced Perdido Street.

"There are so many inquisitive people and institutions abounding," said Arobin, "that one is really forced as a matter of convenience these days to assume the virtue of an occupation if he has it not."

Monsieur Ratignolle stared a little, and turned to ask Mademoiselle Reisz if she considered the symphony concerts up to the standard which had been set the previous winter. Mademoiselle Reisz answered Monsieur Ratignolle in French, which Edna thought a little rude, under the circumstances but characteristic. Mademoiselle had only disagreeable things to say of the symphony concerts, and insulting remarks to make of all the musicians of New Orleans, singly and collectively. All her interest seemed to be centered upon the delicacies placed before her.

Mr. Merriman said that Mr. Arobin's remark about inquisitive people reminded him of a man from Waco the other day at the St. Charles Hotel—but as Mr. Merriman's stories were always lame and lacking point,

8. *Main courses . . . side-dishes.*

his wife seldom permitted him to complete them. She interrupted him to ask if he remembered the name of the author whose book she had bought the week before to send to a friend in Geneva. She was talking "books" with Mr. Gouvernail and trying to draw from him his opinion upon current literary topics. Her husband told the story of the Waco man privately to Miss Mayblunt, who pretended to be greatly amused and to think it extremely clever.

Mrs. Highcamp hung with languid but unaffected interest upon the warm and impetuous volubility of her left-hand neighbor, Victor Lebrun. Her attention was never for a moment withdrawn from him after seating herself at table; and when he turned to Mrs. Merriman, who was prettier and more vivacious than Mrs. Highcamp, she waited with easy indifference for an opportunity to reclaim his attention. There was the occasional sound of music, of mandolins, sufficiently removed to be an agreeable accompaniment rather than an interruption to the conversation. Outside the soft, monotonous splash of a fountain could be heard; the sound penetrated into the room with the heavy odor of jessamine that came through the open windows.

The golden shimmer of Edna's satin gown spread in rich folds on either side of her. There was a soft fall of lace encircling her shoulders. It was the color of her skin, without the glow, the myriad living tints that one may sometimes discover in vibrant flesh. There was something in her attitude, in her whole appearance when she leaned her head against the high-backed chair and spread her arms, which suggested the regal woman, the one who rules, who looks on, who stands alone.

But as she sat there amid her guests, she felt the old ennui overtaking her; the hopelessness which so often assailed her, which came upon her like an obsession, like something extraneous, independent of volition. It was something which announced itself; a chill breath that seemed to issue from some vast cavern wherein discords wailed. There came over her the acute longing which always summoned into her spiritual vision the presence of the beloved one, overpowering her at once with a sense of the unattainable.

The moments glided on, while a feeling of good fellowship passed around the circle like a mystic cord, holding and binding these people together with jest and laughter. Monsieur Ratignolle was the first to break the pleasant charm. At ten o'clock he excused himself. Madame Ratignolle was waiting for him at home. She was *bien souffrante*, and she was filled with vague dread, which only her husband's presence could allay.

Madameoiselle Reisz arose with Monsieur Ratignolle, who offered to escort her to the car. She had eaten well; she had tasted the good, rich wines, and they must have turned her head, for she bowed pleasantly to all as she withdrew from table. She kissed Edna upon the shoulder, and whispered: *"Bonne nuit, ma reine; soyez sage."*[9] She had been a little bewildered upon rising, or rather, descending from her cushions, and Monsieur Ratignolle gallantly took her arm and led her away.

Mrs. Highcamp was weaving a garland of roses, yellow and red. When she had finished the garland, she laid it lightly upon Victor's black curls. He was reclining far back in the luxurious chair, holding a glass of champagne to the light.

9. *Good night, my dear* (queen), *behave yourself.*

As if a magician's wand had touched him, the garland of roses transformed him into a vision of Oriental beauty. His cheeks were the color of crushed grapes, and his dusky eyes glowed with a languishing fire.

"*Sapristi!*" exclaimed Arobin.

But Mrs. Highcamp had one more touch to add to the picture. She took from the back of her chair a white silken scarf, with which she had covered her shoulders in the early part of the evening. She draped it across the boy in graceful folds, and in a way to conceal his black, conventional evening dress. He did not seem to mind what she did to him, only smiled, showing a faint gleam of white teeth, while he continued to gaze with narrowing eyes at the light through his glass of champagne.

"Oh! to be able to paint in color rather than in words!" exclaimed Miss Mayblunt, losing herself in a rhapsodic dream as she looked at him.

> " 'There was a graven image of Desire
> Painted with red blood on a ground of gold.' "[1]

murmured Gouvernail, under his breath.

The effect of the wine upon Victor was to change his accustomed volubility into silence. He seemed to have abandoned himself to a reverie, and to be seeing pleasing visions in the amber bead.

"Sing," entreated Mrs. Highcamp. "Won't you sing to us?"

"Let him alone," said Arobin.

"He's posing," offered Mr. Merriman; "let him have it out."

"I believe he's paralyzed," laughed Mrs. Merriman. And leaning over the youth's chair, she took the glass from his hand and held it to his lips. He sipped the wine slowly, and when he had drained the glass she laid it upon the table and wiped his lips with her little filmy handkerchief.

"Yes, I'll sing for you," he said, turning in his chair toward Mrs. Highcamp. He clasped his hands behind his head, and looking up at the ceiling began to hum a little, trying his voice like a musician tuning an instrument. Then, looking at Edna, he began to sing:

> "Ah! si tu savais!"

"Stop!" she cried, "don't sing that. I don't want you to sing it," and she laid her glass so impetuously and blindly upon the table as to shatter it against a caraffe. The wine spilled over Arobin's legs and some of it trickled down upon Mrs. Highcamp's black gauze gown. Victor had lost all idea of courtesy, or else he thought his hostess was not in earnest, for he laughed and went on:

> "Ah! si tu savais
> Ce que tes yeux me disent"—[2]

"Oh! you mustn't! you mustn't," exclaimed Edna, and pushing back her chair she got up, and going behind him placed her hand over his mouth. He kissed the soft palm that pressed upon his lips.

"No, no, I won't, Mrs. Pontellier. I didn't know you meant it," looking up at her with caressing eyes. The touch of his lips was like a pleasing sting to her hand. She lifted the garland of roses from his head and flung it across the room.

1. From "A Cameo," sonnet by Algernon Swinburne (1837–1909).   2. *Couldst thou but know/ What thine eyes tell me—*

"Come, Victor; you've posed long enough. Give Mrs. Highcamp her scarf."

Mrs. Highcamp undraped the scarf from about him with her own hands. Miss Mayblunt and Mr. Gouvernail suddenly conceived the notion that it was time to say good night. And Mr. and Mrs. Merriman wondered how it could be so late.

Before parting from Victor, Mrs. Highcamp invited him to call upon her daughter, who she knew would be charmed to meet him and talk French and sing French songs with him. Victor expressed his desire and intention to call upon Miss Highcamp at the first opportunity which presented itself. He asked if Arobin were going his way. Arobin was not.

The mandolin players had long since stolen away. A profound stillness had fallen upon the broad, beautiful street. The voices of Edna's disbanding guests jarred like a discordant note upon the quiet harmony of the night.

XXXI

"Well?" questioned Arobin, who had remained with Edna after the others had departed.

"Well," she reiterated, and stood up, stretching her arms, and feeling the need to relax her muscles after having been so long seated.

"What next?" he asked.

"The servants are all gone. They left when the musicians did. I have dismissed them. The house has to be closed and locked, and I shall trot around to the pigeon house, and shall send Celestine over in the morning to straighten things up."

He looked around, and began to turn out some of the lights.

"What about upstairs?" he inquired.

"I think it is all right; but there may be a window or two unlatched. We had better look; you might take a candle and see. And bring me my wrap and hat on the foot of the bed in the middle room."

He went up with the light, and Edna began closing doors and windows. She hated to shut in the smoke and the fumes of the wine. Arobin found her cape and hat, which he brought down and helped her to put on.

When everything was secured and the lights put out, they left through the front door, Arobin locking it and taking the key, which he carried for Edna. He helped her down the steps.

"Will you have a spray of jessamine?" he asked, breaking off a few blossoms as he passed.

"No; I don't want anything."

She seemed disheartened, and had nothing to say. She took his arm, which he offered her, holding up the weight of her satin train with the other hand. She looked down, noticing the black line of his leg moving in and out so close to her against the yellow shimmer of her gown. There was the whistle of a railway train somewhere in the distance, and the midnight bells were ringing. They met no one in their short walk.

The "pigeon-house" stood behind a locked gate, and a shallow *parterre* that had been somewhat neglected. There was a small front porch, upon which a long window and the front door opened. The door opened directly into the parlor; there was no side entry. Back in the yard was a room for servants, in which old Celestine had been ensconced.

Edna had left a lamp burning low upon the table. She had succeeded in making the room look habitable and homelike. There were some books on the table and a lounge near at hand. On the floor was a fresh matting, covered with a rug or two; and on the walls hung a few tasteful pictures. But the room was filled with flowers. These were a surprise to her. Arobin had sent them, and had had Celestine distribute them during Edna's absence. Her bed-room was adjoining, and across a small passage were the dining-room and kitchen.

Edna seated herself with every appearance of discomfort.

"Are you tired?" he asked.

"Yes, and chilled, and miserable. I feel as if I had been wound up to a certain pitch—too tight—and something inside of me had snapped." She rested her head against the table upon her bare arm.

"You want to rest," he said, "and to be quiet. I'll go; I'll leave you and let you rest."

"Yes," she replied.

He stood up beside her and smoothed her hair with his soft, magnetic hand. His touch conveyed to her a certain physical comfort. She could have fallen quietly asleep there if he had continued to pass his hand over her hair. He brushed the hair upward from the nape of her neck.

"I hope you will feel better and happier in the morning," he said. "You have tried to do too much in the past few days. The dinner was the last straw; you might have dispensed with it."

"Yes," she admitted; "it was stupid."

"No, it was delightful; but it has worn you out." His hand had strayed to her beautiful shoulders, and he could feel the response of her flesh to his touch. He seated himself beside her and kissed her lightly upon the shoulder.

"I thought you were going away," she said, in an uneven voice.

"I am, after I have said good night."

"Good night," she murmured.

He did not answer, except to continue to caress her. He did not say good night until she had become supple to his gentle, seductive entreaties.

XXXII

When Mr. Pontellier learned of his wife's intention to abandon her home and take up her residence elsewhere, he immediately wrote her a letter of unqualified disapproval and remonstrance. She had given reasons which he was unwilling to acknowledge as adequate. He hoped she had not acted upon her rash impulse; and he begged her to consider first, foremost, and above all else, what people would say. He was not dreaming of scandal when he uttered this warning; that was a thing which would never have entered into his mind to consider in connection with his wife's name or his own. He was simply thinking of his financial integrity. It might get noised about that the Pontelliers had met with reverses, and were forced to conduct their *ménage* on a humbler scale than heretofore. It might do incalculable mischief to his business prospects.

But remembering Edna's whimsical turn of mind of late, and foreseeing that she had immediately acted upon her impetuous determination, he grasped the situation with his usual promptness and handled it with his well-known business tact and cleverness.

The same mail which brought to Edna his letter of disapproval carried instructions—the most minute instructions—to a well-known architect concerning the remodeling of his home, changes which he had long contemplated, and which he desired carried forward during his temporary absence.

Expert and reliable packers and movers were engaged to convey the furniture, carpets, pictures—everything movable, in short—to places of security. And in an incredibly short time the Pontellier house was turned over to the artisans. There was to be an addition—a small snuggery; there was to be frescoing, and hardwood flooring was to be put into such rooms as had not yet been subjected to this improvement.

Furthermore, in one of the daily papers appeared a brief notice to the effect that Mr. and Mrs. Pontellier were contemplating a summer sojourn abroad, and that their handsome residence on Esplanade Street was undergoing sumptuous alterations, and would not be ready for occupancy until their return. Mr. Pontellier had saved appearances!

Edna admired the skill of his maneuver, and avoided any occasion to balk his intentions. When the situation as set forth by Mr. Pontellier was accepted and taken for granted, she was apparently satisfied that it should be so.

The pigeon-house pleased her. It at once assumed the intimate character of a home, while she herself invested it with a charm which it reflected like a warm glow. There was with her a feeling of having descended in the social scale, with a corresponding sense of having risen in the spiritual. Every step which she took toward relieving herself from obligations added to her strength and expansion as an individual. She began to look with her own eyes; to see and to apprehend the deeper undercurrents of life. No longer was she content to "feed upon opinion" when her own soul had invited her.

After a little while, a few days, in fact, Edna went up and spent a week with her children in Iberville. They were delicious February days, with all the summer's promise hovering in the air.

How glad she was to see the children! She wept for very pleasure when she felt their little arms clasping her; their hard, ruddy cheeks pressed against her own glowing cheeks. She looked into their faces with hungry eyes that could not be satisfied with looking. And what stories they had to tell their mother! About the pigs, the cows, the mules! About riding to the mill behind Gluglu; fishing back in the lake with their Uncle Jasper; picking pecans with Lidie's little black brood, and hauling chips in their express wagon. It was a thousand times more fun to haul real chips for old lame Susie's real fire than to drag painted blocks along the banquette on Esplanade Street!

She went with them herself to see the pigs and the cows, to look at the darkies laying the cane, to thrash the pecan trees, and catch fish in the back lake. She lived with them a whole week long, giving them all of herself, and gathering and filling herself with their young existence. They listened, breathless, when she told them the house in Esplanade Street was crowded with workmen, hammering, nailing, sawing, and filling the place with clatter. They wanted to know where their bed was; what had been done with their rocking-horse; and where did Joe sleep, and where had Ellen gone, and the cook? But, above all, they were fired with a desire to see the little house around the block. Was there any place to play? Were there any boys next door? Raoul, with pessimistic foreboding, was convinced that there were only girls next door. Where would they sleep, and where would papa sleep? She told them the fairies would fix it all right.

The old Madame was charmed with Edna's visit, and showered all manner of delicate attentions upon her. She was delighted to know that the Esplanade Street house was in a dismantled condition. It gave her the promise and pretext to keep the children indefinitely.

It was with a wrench and a pang that Edna left her children. She carried away with her the sound of their voices and the touch of their cheeks. All along the journey homeward their presence lingered with her like the memory of a delicious song. But by the time she had regained the city the song no longer echoed in her soul. She was again alone.

XXXIII

It happened sometimes when Edna went to see Mademoiselle Reisz that the little musician was absent, giving a lesson or making some small necessary household purchase. The key was always left in a secret hiding-place in the entry, which Edna knew. If Mademoiselle happened to be away, Edna would usually enter and wait for her return.

When she knocked at Mademoiselle Reisz's door one afternoon there was no response; so unlocking the door, as usual, she entered and found the apartment deserted, as she had expected. Her day had been quite filled up, and it was for a rest, for a refuge, and to talk about Robert, that she sought out her friend.

She had worked at her canvas—a young Italian character study—all the morning, completing the work without the model; but there had been many interruptions, some incident to her modest housekeeping, and others of a social nature.

Madame Ratignolle had dragged herself over, avoiding the too public thoroughfares, she said. She complained that Edna had neglected her much of late. Besides, she was consumed with curiosity to see the little house and the manner in which it was conducted. She wanted to hear all about the dinner party; Monsieur Ratignolle had left *so* early. What had happened after he left? The champagne and grapes which Edna sent over were *too* delicious. She had so little appetite; they had refreshed and toned her stomach. Where on earth was she going to put Mr. Pontellier in that little house, and the boys? And then she made Edna promise to go to her when her hour of trial overtook her.

"At any time—any time of the day or night, dear," Edna assured her.

Before leaving Madame Ratignolle said:

"In some way you seem to me like a child, Edna. You seem to act without a certain amount of reflection which is necessary in this life. That is the reason I want to say you mustn't mind if I advise you to be a little careful while you are living here alone. Why don't you have some one come and stay with you? Wouldn't Mademoiselle Reisz come?"

"No; she wouldn't wish to come, and I shouldn't want her always with me."

"Well, the reason—you know how evil-minded the world is—some one was talking of Alcée Arobin visiting you. Of course, it wouldn't matter if Mr. Arobin had not such a dreadful reputation. Monsieur Ratignolle was telling me that his attentions alone are considered enough to ruin a woman's name."

"Does he boast of his successes?" asked Edna, indifferently, squinting at her picture.

"No, I think not. I believe he is a decent fellow as far as that goes. But his character is so well known among the men. I shan't be able to come back and see you; it was very, very imprudent to-day."

"Mind the step!" cried Edna.

"Don't neglect me," entreated Madame Ratignolle; "and don't mind what I said about Arobin, or having some one stay with you."

"Of course not," Edna laughed. "You may say anything you like to me." They kissed each other good-by. Madame Ratignolle had not far to go, and Edna stood on the porch a while watching her walk down the street.

Then in the afternoon Mrs. Merriman and Mrs. Highcamp had made their "party call." Edna felt that they might have dispensed with the formality. They had also come to invite her to play *vingt-et-un* one evening at Mrs. Merriman's. She was asked to go early, to dinner, and Mr. Merriman or Mr. Arobin would take her home. Edna accepted in a half-hearted way. She sometimes felt very tired of Mrs. Highcamp and Mrs. Merriman.

Late in the afternoon she sought refuge with Mademoiselle Reisz, and stayed there alone, waiting for her, feeling a kind of repose invade her with the very atmosphere of the shabby, unpretentious little room.

Edna sat at the window, which looked out over the house-tops and across the river. The window frame was filled with pots of flowers, and she sat and picked the dry leaves from a rose geranium. The day was warm, and the breeze which blew from the river was very pleasant. She removed her hat and laid it on the piano. She went on picking the leaves and digging around the plants with her hat pin. Once she thought she heard Mademoiselle Reisz approaching. But it was a young black girl, who came in, bringing a small bundle of laundry, which she deposited in the adjoining room, and went away.

Edna seated herself at the piano, and softly picked out with one hand the bars of a piece of music which lay open before her. A half-hour went by. There was the occasional sound of people going and coming in the lower hall. She was growing interested in her occupation of picking out the aria, when there was a second rap at the door. She vaguely wondered what these people did when they found Mademoiselle's door locked.

"Come in," she called, turning her face toward the door. And this time it was Robert Lebrun who presented himself. She attempted to rise; she could not have done so without betraying the agitation which mastered her at sight of him, so she fell back upon the stool, only exclaiming, "Why, Robert!"

He came and clasped her hand, seemingly without knowing what he was saying or doing.

"Mrs. Pontellier! How do you happen—oh! how well you look! Is Mademoiselle Reisz not here? I never expected to see you."

"When did you come back?" asked Edna in an unsteady voice, wiping her face with her handkerchief. She seemed ill at ease on the piano stool, and he begged her to take the chair by the window. She did so, mechanically, while he seated himself on the stool.

"I returned day before yesterday," he answered, while he leaned his arm on the keys, bringing forth a crash of discordant sound.

"Day before yesterday!" she repeated, aloud; and went on thinking to herself, "day before yesterday," in a sort of an uncomprehending way. She had pictured him seeking her at the very first hour, and he had lived under the same sky since day before yesterday; while only by accident had he stumbled upon her. Mademoiselle must have lied when she said, "Poor fool, he loves you."

"Day before yesterday," she repeated, breaking off a spray of Mademoiselle's geranium; "then if you had not met me here to-day you wouldn't—when—that is, didn't you mean to come and see me?"

"Of course, I should have gone to see you. There have been so many things—" he turned the leaves of Mademoiselle's music nervously. "I started in at once yesterday with the old firm. After all there is as much chance for me here as there was there—that is, I might find it profitable some day. The Mexicans were not very congenial."

So he had come back because the Mexicans were not congenial; because business was as profitable here as there; because of any reason, and not because he cared to be near her. She remembered the day she sat on the floor, turning the pages of his letter, seeking the reason which was left untold.

She had not noticed how he looked—only feeling his presence; but she turned deliberately and observed him. After all, he had been absent but a few months, and was not changed. His hair—the color of hers—waved back from his temples in the same way as before. His skin was not more burned than it had been at Grand Isle. She found in his eyes, when he looked at her for one silent moment, the same tender caress, with an added warmth and entreaty which had not been there before—the same glance which had penetrated to the sleeping places of her soul and awakened them.

A hundred times Edna had pictured Robert's return, and imagined their first meeting. It was usually at her home, whither he had sought her out at once. She always fancied him expressing or betraying in some way his love for her. And here, the reality was that they sat ten feet apart, she at the window, crushing geranium leaves in her hand and smelling them, he twirling around on the piano stool, saying:

"I was very much surprised to hear of Mr. Pontellier's absence; it's a wonder Mademoiselle Reisz did not tell me; and your moving—mother told me yesterday. I should think you would have gone to New York with him, or to Iberville with the children, rather than be bothered here with housekeeping. And you are going abroad, too, I hear. We shan't have you at Grand Isle next summer; it won't seem—do you see much of Mademoiselle Reisz? She often spoke of you in the few letters she wrote."

"Do you remember that you promised to write to me when you went away?" A flush overspread his whole face.

"I couldn't believe that my letters would be of any interest to you."

"That is an excuse; it isn't the truth." Edna reached for her hat on the piano. She adjusted it, sticking the hat pin through the heavy coil of hair with some deliberation.

"Are you not going to wait for Mademoiselle Reisz?" asked Robert.

"No, I have found when she is absent this long, she is liable not to come back till late." She drew on her gloves, and Robert picked up his hat.

"Won't you wait for her?" asked Edna.

"Not if you think she will not be back till late," adding, as if suddenly aware of some discourtesy in his speech, "and I should miss the pleasure of walking home with you." Edna locked the door and put the key back in its hiding-place.

They went together, picking their way across muddy streets and sidewalks encumbered with the cheap display of small tradesmen. Part of the distance they rode in the car, and after disembarking, passed the Pontellier mansion, which looked broken and half torn asunder. Robert had never known the house, and looked at it with interest.

"I never knew you in your home," he remarked.

"I am glad you did not."

"Why?" She did not answer. They went on around the corner, and it seemed as if her dreams were coming true after all, when he followed her into the little house.

"You must stay and dine with me, Robert. You see I am all alone, and it is so long since I have seen you. There is so much I want to ask you." She took off her hat and gloves. He stood irresolute, making some excuse about his mother who expected him; he even muttered something about an engagement. She struck a match and lit the lamp on the table; it was growing dusk. When he saw her face in the lamp-light, looking pained, with all the soft lines gone out of it, he threw his hat aside and seated himself.

"Oh! you know I want to stay if you will let me!" he exclaimed. All the softness came back. She laughed, and went and put her hand on his shoulder.

"This is the first moment you have seemed like the old Robert. I'll go tell Celestine." She hurried away to tell Celestine to set an extra place. She even sent her off in search of some added delicacy which she had not thought of for herself. And she recommended great care in dripping the coffee and having the omelet done to a proper turn.

When she reëntered, Robert was turning over magazines, sketches, and things that lay upon the table in great disorder. He picked up a photograph, and exclaimed:

"Alcée Arobin! What on earth is his picture doing here?"

"I tried to make a sketch of his head one day," answered Edna, "and he thought the photograph might help me. It was at the other house. I thought it had been left there. I must have packed it up with my drawing materials."

"I should think you would give it back to him if you have finished with it."

"Oh! I have a great many such photographs. I never think of returning them. They don't amount to anything." Robert kept on looking at the picture.

"It seems to me—do you think his head worth drawing? Is he a friend of Mr. Pontellier's? You never said you knew him."

"He isn't a friend of Mr. Pontellier's; he's a friend of mine. I always knew him—that is, it is only of late that I know him pretty well. But I'd rather talk about you, and know what you have been seeing and doing and feeling out there in Mexico." Robert threw aside the picture.

"I've been seeing the waves and the white beach of Grand Isle; the quiet, grassy street of the *Chênière;* the old fort at Grande Terre. I've been working like a machine, and feeling like a lost soul. There was nothing interesting."

She leaned her head upon her hand to shade her eyes from the light.

"And what have you been seeing and doing and feeling all these days?" he asked.

"I've been seeing the waves and the white beach of Grand Isle; the quiet, grassy street of the *Chênière Caminada;* the old sunny fort at Grande Terre. I've been working with little more comprehension than a machine, and still feeling like a lost soul. There was nothing interesting."

"Mrs. Pontellier, you are cruel," he said, with feeling, closing his eyes and resting his head back in his chair. They remained in silence till old Celestine announced dinner.

XXXIV

The dining-room was very small. Edna's round mahogany would have almost filled it. As it was there was but a step or two from the little table to the kitchen, to the mantel, the small buffet, and the side door that opened out on the narrow brick-paved yard.

A certain degree of ceremony settled upon them with the announcement of dinner. There was no return to personalities. Robert related incidents of his sojourn in Mexico, and Edna talked of events likely to interest him, which had occurred during his absence. The dinner was of ordinary quality, except for the few delicacies which she had sent out to purchase. Old Celestine, with a bandana *tignon*[3] twisted about her head, hobbled in and out, taking a personal interest in everything; and she lingered occasionally to talk patois with Robert, whom she had known as a boy.

He went out to a neighboring cigar stand to purchase cigarette papers, and when he came back he found that Celestine had served the black coffee in the parlor.

"Perhaps I shouldn't have come back," he said. "When you are tired of me, tell me to go."

"You never tire me. You must have forgotten the hours and hours at Grand Isle in which we grew accustomed to each other and used to being together."

"I have forgotten nothing at Grand Isle," he said, not looking at her, but rolling a cigarette. His tobacco pouch, which he laid upon the table, was a fantastic embroidered silk affair, evidently the handiwork of a woman.

"You used to carry your tobacco in a rubber pouch," said Edna, picking up the pouch and examining the needlework.

"Yes; it was lost."

"Where did you buy this one? In Mexico?"

"It was given to me by a Vera Cruz girl; they are very generous," he replied, striking a match and lighting his cigarette.

"They are very handsome, I suppose, those Mexican women; very picturesque, with their black eyes and their lace scarfs."

3. *Chignon,* hair coiled at the back of the neck.

"Some are; others are hideous. Just as you find women everywhere."

"What was she like—the one who gave you the pouch? You must have known her very well."

"She was very ordinary. She wasn't of the slightest importance. I knew her well enough."

"Did you visit at her house? Was it interesting? I should like to know and hear about the people you met, and the impressions they made on you."

"There are some people who leave impressions not so lasting as the imprint of an oar upon the water."

"Was she such a one?"

"It would be ungenerous for me to admit that she was of that order and kind." He thrust the pouch back in his pocket, as if to put away the subject with the trifle which had brought it up.

Arobin dropped in with a message from Mrs. Merriman, to say that the card party was postponed on account of the illness of one of her children.

"How do you do, Arobin?" said Robert, rising from the obscurity.

"Oh! Lebrun. To be sure! I heard yesterday you were back. How did they treat you down in Mexique?"

"Fairly well."

"But not well enough to keep you there. Stunning girls, though, in Mexico. I thought I should never get away from Vera Cruz when I was down there a couple of years ago."

"Did they embroider slippers and tobacco pouches and hat-bands and things for you?" asked Edna.

"Oh! my! no! I didn't get so deep in their regard. I fear they made more impression on me than I made on them."

"You were less fortunate than Robert, then."

"I am always less fortunate than Robert. Has he been imparting tender confidences?"

"I've been imposing myself long enough," said Robert, rising, and shaking hands with Edna. "Please convey my regards to Mr. Pontellier when you write."

He shook hands with Arobin and went away.

"Fine fellow, that Lebrun," said Arobin when Robert had gone. "I never heard you speak of him."

"I knew him last summer at Grand Isle," she replied. "Here is that photograph of yours. Don't you want it?"

"What do I want with it? Throw it away." She threw it back on the table.

"I'm not going to Mrs. Merriman's," she said. "If you see her, tell her so. But perhaps I had better write. I think I shall write now, and say that I am sorry her child is sick, and tell her not to count on me."

"It would be a good scheme," acquiesced Arobin. "I don't blame you; stupid lot!"

Edna opened the blotter, and having procured paper and pen, began to write the note. Arobin lit a cigar and read the evening paper, which he had in his pocket.

"What is the date?" she asked. He told her.

"Will you mail this for me when you go out?"

"Certainly." He read to her little bits out of the newspaper, while she straightened things on the table.

"What do you want to do?" he asked, throwing aside the paper. "Do you want to go out for a walk or a drive or anything? It would be a fine night to drive."

"No; I don't want to do anything but just be quiet. You go away and amuse yourself. Don't stay."

"I'll go away if I must; but I shan't amuse myself. You know that I only live when I am near you."

He stood up to bid her good night.

"Is that one of the things you always say to women?"

"I have said it before, but I don't think I ever came so near meaning it," he answered with a smile. There were no warm lights in her eyes; only a dreamy, absent look.

"Good night. I adore you. Sleep well," he said, and he kissed her hand and went away.

She stayed alone in a kind of reverie—a sort of stupor. Step by step she lived over every instant of the time she had been with Robert after he had entered Mademoiselle Reisz's door. She recalled his words, his looks. How few and meager they had been for her hungry heart! A vision—a transcendently seductive vision of a Mexican girl arose before her. She writhed with a jealous pang. She wondered when he would come back. He had not said he would come back. She had been with him, had heard his voice and touched his hand. But some way he had seemed nearer to her off there in Mexico.

XXXV

The morning was full of sunlight and hope. Edna could see before her no denial—only the promise of excessive joy. She lay in bed awake, with bright eyes full of speculation. "He loves you, poor fool." If she could but get that conviction firmly fixed in her mind, what mattered about the rest? She felt she had been childish and unwise the night before in giving herself over to despondency. She recapitulated the motives which no doubt explained Robert's reserve. They were not insurmountable; they would not hold if he really loved her; they could not hold against her own passion, which he must come to realize in time. She pictured him going to his business that morning. She even saw how he was dressed; how he walked down one street, and turned the corner of another; saw him bending over his desk, talking to people who entered the office, going to his lunch, and perhaps watching for her on the street. He would come to her in the afternoon or evening, sit and roll his cigarette, talk a little, and go away as he had done the night before. But how delicious it would be to have him there with her! She would have no regrets, nor seek to penetrate his reserve if he still chose to wear it.

Edna ate her breakfast only half dressed. The maid brought her a delicious printed scrawl from Raoul, expressing his love, asking her to send him some bonbons, and telling her they had found that morning ten tiny white pigs all lying in a row beside Lidie's big white pig.

A letter also came from her husband, saying he hoped to be back early in March, and then they would get ready for that journey abroad which he had promised her so long, which he felt now fully able to afford; he felt able to travel as people should, without any thought of small economies—thanks to his recent speculations in Wall Street.

Much to her surprise she received a note from Arobin, written at midnight from the club. It was to say good morning to her, to hope that she had slept well, to assure her of his devotion, which he trusted she in some faintest manner returned.

All these letters were pleasing to her. She answered the children in a cheerful frame of mind, promising them bonbons, and congratulating them upon their happy find of the little pigs.

She answered her husband with friendly evasiveness,—not with any fixed design to mislead him, only because all sense of reality had gone out of her life; she had abandoned herself to Fate, and awaited the consequences with indifference.

To Arobin's note she made no reply. She put it under Celestine's stovelid.

Edna worked several hours with much spirit. She saw no one but a picture dealer, who asked her if it were true that she was going abroad to study in Paris.

She said possibly she might, and he negotiated with her for some Parisian studies to reach him in time for the holiday trade in December.

Robert did not come that day. She was keenly disappointed. He did not come the following day, nor the next. Each morning she awoke with hope, and each night she was a prey to despondency. She was tempted to seek him out. But far from yielding to the impulse, she avoided any occasion which might throw her in his way. She did not go to Mademoiselle Reisz's nor pass by Madame Lebrun's, as she might have done if he had still been in Mexico.

When Arobin, one night, urged her to drive with him, she went—out to the lake, on the Shell Road.[4] His horses were full of mettle, and even a little unmanageable. She liked the rapid gait at which they spun along, and the quick, sharp sound of the horses' hoofs on the hard road. They did not stop anywhere to eat or to drink. Arobin was not needlessly imprudent. But they ate and they drank when they regained Edna's little dining-room—which was comparatively early in the evening.

It was late when he left her. It was getting to be more than a passing whim with Arobin to see her and be with her. He had detected the latent sensuality, which unfolded under his delicate sense of her nature's requirements like a torpid, torrid, sensitive blossom.

There was no despondency when she fell asleep that night; nor was there hope when she awoke in the morning.

XXXVI

There was a garden out in the suburbs; a small, leafy corner, with a few green tables under the orange trees. An old cat slept all day on the stone step in the sun, and an old *mulatresse*[5] slept her idle hours away in her chair at the open window, till some one happened to knock on one of the green tables. She had milk and cream cheese to sell, and bread and butter. There was no one who could make such excellent coffee or fry a chicken so golden brown as she.

The place was too modest to attract the attention of people of fashion, and so quiet as to have escaped the notice of those in search of pleasure and dissipation. Edna had discovered it accidentally one day when the

4. Road that borders Lake Pontchartrain, a good place to test a horse's speed.   5. Mulatto woman.

high-board gate stood ajar. She caught sight of a little green table, blotched with the checkered sunlight that filtered through the quivering leaves overhead. Within she had found the slumbering *mulatresse*, the drowsy cat, and a glass of milk which reminded her of the milk she had tasted in Iberville.

She often stopped there during her prerambulations; sometimes taking a book with her, and sitting an hour or two under the trees when she found the place deserted. Once or twice she took a quiet dinner there alone, having instructed Celestine beforehand to prepare no dinner at home. It was the last place in the city where she would have expected to meet any one she knew.

Still she was not astonished when, as she was partaking of a modest dinner late in the afternoon, looking into an open book, stroking the cat, which had made friends with her—she was not greatly astonished to see Robert come in at the tall garden gate.

"I am destined to see you only by accident," she said, shoving the cat off the chair beside her. He was surprised, ill at ease, almost embarrassed at meeting her thus so unexpectedly.

"Do you come here often?" he asked.

"I almost live here," she said.

"I used to drop in very often for a cup of Catiche's good coffee. This is the first time since I came back."

"She'll bring you a plate, and you will share my dinner. There's always enough for two—even three." Edna had intended to be indifferent and as reserved as he when she met him; she had reached the determination by a laborious train of reasoning, incident to one of her despondent moods. But her resolve melted when she saw him before her, seated there beside her in the little garden, as if a designing Providence had led him into her path.

"Why have you kept away from me, Robert?" she asked, closing the book that lay open upon the table.

"Why are you so personal, Mrs. Pontellier? Why do you force me to idiotic subterfuges?" he exclaimed with sudden warmth. "I suppose there's no use telling you I've been very busy, or that I've been sick, or that I've been to see you and not found you at home. Please let me off with any one of these excuses."

"You are the embodiment of selfishness," she said. "You save yourself something—I don't know what—but there is some selfish motive, and in sparing yourself you never consider for a moment what I think, or how I feel your neglect and indifference. I suppose this is what you would call unwomanly; but I have got into a habit of expressing myself. It doesn't matter to me, and you may think me unwomanly if you like."

"No; I only think you cruel, as I said the other day. Maybe not intentionally cruel; but you seem to be forcing me into disclosures which can result in nothing; as if you would have me bare a wound for the pleasure of looking at it, without the intention or power of healing it."

"I'm spoiling your dinner, Robert; never mind what I say. You haven't eaten a morsel."

"I only came in for a cup of coffee." His sensitive face was all disfigured with excitement.

"Isn't this a delightful place?" she remarked. "I am so glad it has never actually been discovered. It is so quiet, so sweet, here. Do you notice there is scarcely a sound to be heard? It's so out of the way; and a good walk from the car. However, I don't mind walking. I always feel so sorry for women who don't like to walk; they miss so much—so many rare little glimpses of life; and we women learn so little of life on the whole.

"Catiche's coffee is always hot. I don't know how she manages it, here in the open air. Celestine's coffee gets cold bringing it from the kitchen to the dining-room. Three lumps! how can you drink it so sweet? Take some of the cress with your chop; it's so biting and crisp. Then there's the advantage of being able to smoke with your coffee out here. Now, in the city—aren't you going to smoke?"

"After a while," he said, laying a cigar on the table

"Who gave it to you?" she laughed.

"I bought it. I suppose I'm getting reckless; I bought a whole box." She was determined not to be personal again and make him uncomfortable.

The cat made friends with him, and climbed into his lap when he smoked his cigar. He stroked her silky fur, and talked a little about her. He looked at Edna's book, which he had read; and he told her the end, to save her the trouble of wading through it, he said.

Again he accompanied her back to her home; and it was after dusk when they reached the little "pigeon-house." She did not ask him to remain, which he was grateful for, as it permitted him to stay without the discomfort of blundering through an excuse which he had no intention of considering. He helped her to light the lamp; then she went into her room to take off her hat and to bathe her face and hands.

When she came back Robert was not examining the pictures and magazines as before; he sat off in the shadow, leaning his head back on the chair as if in a reverie. Edna lingered a moment beside the table, arranging the books there. Then she went across the room to where he sat. She bent over the arm of his chair and called his name.

"Robert," she said, "are you asleep?"

"No," he answered, looking up at her.

She leaned over and kissed him—a soft, cool, delicate kiss, whose voluptuous sting penetrated his whole being—then she moved away from him. He followed, and took her in his arms, just holding her close to him. She put her hand up to his face and pressed his cheek against her own. The action was full of love and tenderness. He sought her lips again. Then he drew her down upon the sofa beside him and held her hand in both of his.

"Now you know," he said, "now you know what I have been fighting against since last summer at Grand Isle; what drove me away and drove me back again."

"Why have you been fighting against it?" she asked. Her face glowed with soft lights.

"Why? Because you were not free; you were Léonce Pontellier's wife. I couldn't help loving you if you were ten times his wife; but so long as I went away from you and kept away I could help telling you so." She put her free hand up to his shoulder, and then against his cheek, rubbing it softly. He kissed her again. His face was warm and flushed.

"There in Mexico I was thinking of you all the time, and longing for you."

"But not writing to me," she interrupted.

"Something put into my head that you cared for me; and I lost my senses. I forgot everything but a wild dream of your some way becoming my wife."

"Your wife!"

"Religion, loyalty, everything would give way if only you cared."

"Then you must have forgotten that I was Léonce Pontellier's wife."

"Oh! I was demented, dreaming of wild, impossible things, recalling men who had set their wives free, we have heard of such things."

"Yes, we have heard of such things."

"I came back full of vague, mad intentions. And when I got here—"

"When you got here you never came near me!" She was still caressing his cheek.

"I realized what a cur I was to dream of such a thing, even if you had been willing."

She took his face between her hands and looked into it as if she would never withdraw her eyes more. She kissed him on the forehead, the eyes, the cheeks, and the lips.

"You have been a very, very foolish boy, wasting your time dreaming of impossible things when you speak of Mr. Pontellier setting me free! I am no longer one of Mr. Pontellier's possessions to dispose of or not. I give myself where I choose. If he were to say, 'Here, Robert, take her and be happy; she is yours,' I should laugh at you both."

His face grew a little white. "What do you mean?" he asked.

There was a knock at the door. Old Celestine came in to say that Madame Ratignolle's servant had come around the back way with a message that Madame had been taken sick and begged Mrs. Pontellier to go to her immediately.

"Yes, yes," said Edna, rising; "I promised. Tell her yes—to wait for me. I'll go back with her."

"Let me walk over with you," offered Robert.

"No," she said; "I will go with the servant." She went into her room to put on her hat, and when she came in again she sat once more upon the sofa beside him. He had not stirred. She put her arms about his neck.

"Good-by, my sweet Robert. Tell me good-by." He kissed her with a degree of passion which had not before entered into his caress, and strained her to him.

"I love you," she whispered, "only you; no one but you. It was you who awoke me last summer out of a life-long, stupid dream. Oh! you have made me so unhappy with your indifference. Oh! I have suffered, suffered! Now you are here we shall love each other, my Robert. We shall be everything to each other. Nothing else in the world is of any consequence. I must go to my friend; but you will wait for me? No matter how late; you will wait for me, Robert?"

"Don't go; don't go! Oh! Edna, stay with me," he pleaded. "Why should you go? Stay with me, stay with me."

"I shall come back as soon as I can; I shall find you here." She buried her face in his neck, and said good-by again. Her seductive voice, together with his great love for her, had enthralled his senses, had deprived him of every impulse but the longing to hold her and keep her.

XXXVII

Edna looked in at the drug store. Monsieur Ratignolle was putting up a mixture himself, very carefully, dropping a red liquid into a tiny glass. He was grateful to Edna for having come; her presence would be a comfort to his wife. Madame Ratignolle's sister, who had always been with her at such trying times, had not been able to come up from the plantation, and Adèle had been inconsolable until Mrs. Pontellier so kindly promised to come to her. The nurse had been with them at night for the past week, as she lived a great distance away. And Dr. Mandelet had been coming and going all the afternoon. They were then looking for him any moment.

Edna hastened upstairs by a private stairway that led from the rear of the store to the apartments above. The children were all sleeping in a back room. Madame Ratignolle was in the salon, whither she had strayed in her suffering impatience. She sat on the sofa, clad in an ample white *peignoir*, holding a handkerchief tight in her hand with a nervous clutch. Her face was drawn and pinched, her sweet blue eyes haggard and unnatural. All her beautiful hair had been drawn back and plaited. It lay in a long braid on the sofa pillow, coiled like a golden serpent. The nurse, a comfortable looking *Griffe*[6] woman in white apron and cap, was urging her to return to her bedroom.

"There is no use, there is no use," she said at once to Edna. "We must get rid of Mandelet; he is getting too old and careless. He said he would be here at half-past seven; now it must be eight. See what time it is, Joséphine."

The woman was possessed of a cheerful nature, and refused to take any situation too seriously, especially a situation with which she was so familiar. She urged Madame to have courage and patience. But Madame only set her teeth hard into her under lip, and Edna saw the sweat gather in beads on her white forehead. After a moment or two she uttered a profound sigh and wiped her face with the handkerchief rolled in a ball. She appeared exhausted. The nurse gave her a fresh handkerchief, sprinkled with cologne water.

"This is too much!" she cried. "Mandelet ought to be killed! Where is Alphonse? Is it possible I am to be abandoned like this—neglected by every one?"

"Neglected, indeed!" exclaimed the nurse. Wasn't she there? And here was Mrs. Pontellier leaving, no doubt, a pleasant evening at home to devote to her? And wasn't Monsieur Ratignolle coming that very instant through the hall? And Joséphine was quite sure she had heard Doctor Mandelet's coupé. Yes, there it was, down at the door.

Adèle consented to go back to her room. She sat on the edge of a little low couch next to her bed.

Doctor Mandelet paid no attention to Madame Ratignolle's upbraidings. He was accustomed to them at such times, and was too well convinced of her loyalty to doubt it.

He was glad to see Edna, and wanted her to go with him into the salon and entertain him. But Madame Ratignolle would not consent that Edna should leave her for an instant. Between agonizing moments, she chatted a little, and said it took her mind off her sufferings.

Edna began to feel uneasy. She was seized with a vague dread. Her own like experiences seemed far away, unreal, and only half remembered. She recalled faintly an ecstasy of pain, the heavy odor of chloroform, a stupor which had deadened sensation, and an awakening to find a little

6. Mulatto or person of black and American Indian ancestry.

new life to which she had given being, added to the great unnumbered multitude of souls that come and go.

She began to wish she had not come; her presence was not necessary. She might have invented a pretext for staying away; she might even invent a pretext now for going. But Edna did not go. With an inward agony, with a flaming, outspoken revolt against the ways of Nature, she witnessed the scene of torture.

She was still stunned and speechless with emotion when later she leaned over her friend to kiss her and softly say good-by. Adèle, pressing her cheek, whispered in an exhausted voice: "Think of the children, Edna. Oh think of the children! Remember them!"

XXXVIII

Edna still felt dazed when she got outside in the open air. The Doctor's coupé had returned for him and stood before the *porte cochère*. She did not wish to enter the coupé, and told Doctor Mandelet she would walk; she was not afraid, and would go alone. He directed his carriage to meet him at Mrs. Pontellier's, and he started to walk home with her.

Up—away up, over the narrow street between the tall houses, the stars were blazing. The air was mild and caressing, but cool with the breath of spring and the night. They walked slowly, the Doctor with a heavy, measured tread and his hands behind him; Edna, in an absent-minded way, as she had walked one night at Grand Isle, as if her thoughts had gone ahead of her and she was striving to overtake them.

"You shouldn't have been there, Mrs. Pontellier," he said. "That was no place for you. Adèle is full of whims at such times. There were a dozen women she might have had with her, unimpressionable women. I felt that it was cruel, cruel. You shouldn't have gone."

"Oh, well!" she answered, indifferently. "I don't know that it matters after all. One has to think of the children some time or other; the sooner the better."

"When is Léonce coming back?"

"Quite soon. Some time in March."

"And you are going abroad?"

"Perhaps—no, I am not going. I'm not going to be forced into doing things. I don't want to go abroad. I want to be let alone. Nobody has any right—except children, perhaps—and even then, it seems to me—or it did seem—" She felt that her speech was voicing the incoherency of her thoughts, and stopped abruptly.

"The trouble is," sighed the Doctor, grasping her meaning intuitively, "that youth is given up to illusions. It seems to be a provision of Nature; a decoy to secure mothers for the race. And Nature takes no account of moral consequences, of arbitrary conditions which we create, and which we feel obliged to maintain at any cost."

"Yes," she said. "The years that are gone seem like dreams—if one might go on sleeping and dreaming—but to wake up and find—oh! well! perhaps it is better to wake up after all, even to suffer, rather than to remain a dupe to illusions all one's life."

"It seems to me, my dear child," said the Doctor at parting, holding her hand, "you seem to me to be in trouble. I am not going to ask for your confidence, I will only say that if ever you feel moved to give it to me, perhaps I might help you. I know I would understand, and I tell you there are not many who would—not many, my dear."

"Some way I don't feel moved to speak of things that trouble me. Don't think I am ungrateful or that I don't appreciate your sympathy. There are periods of despondency and suffering which take possession of me. But I don't want anything but my own way. That is wanting a good deal, of course, when you have to trample upon the lives, the hearts, the prejudices of others—but no matter—still, I shouldn't want to trample upon the little lives. Oh! I don't know what I'm saying, Doctor. Good night. Don't blame me for anything."

"Yes, I will blame you if you don't come and see me soon. We will talk of things you never have dreamt of talking about before. It will do us both good. I don't want you to blame yourself, whatever comes. Good night, my child."

She let herself in at the gate, but instead of entering she sat upon the step of the porch. The night was quiet and soothing. All the tearing emotion of the last few hours seemed to fall away from her like a somber, uncomfortable garment, which she had but to loosen to be rid of. She went back to that hour before Adèle had sent for her; and her senses kindled afresh in thinking of Robert's words, the pressure of his arms, and the feeling of his lips upon her own. She could picture at that moment no greater bliss on earth than possession of the beloved one. His expression of love had already given him to her in part. When she thought that he was there at hand, waiting for her, she grew numb with the intoxication of expectancy. It was so late; he would be asleep perhaps. She would awaken him with a kiss. She hoped he would be asleep that she might arouse him with her caresses.

Still, she remembered Adèle's voice whispering, "Think of the children; think of them." She meant to think of them; that determination had driven into her soul like a death wound—but not to-night. To-mmprow would be time to think of everything.

Robert was not waiting for her in the little parlor. He was nowhere at hand. The house was empty. But he had scrawled on a piece of paper that lay in the lamplight:

"I love you. Good-by—because I love you."

Edna grew faint when she read the words. She went and sat on the sofa. Then she stretched herself out there, never uttering a sound. She did not sleep. She did not go to bed. The lamp sputtered and went out. She was still awake in the morning, when Celestine unlocked the kitchen door and came in to light the fire.

XXXIX

Victor, with hammer and nails and scraps of scantling, was patching a corner of one of the galleries. Mariequita sat near by, dangling her legs, watching him work, and handing him nails from the tool-box. The sun was beating down upon them. The girl had covered her head with her apron folded into a square pad. They had been talking for an hour or more. She was never tired of hearing Victor describe the dinner at Mrs. Pontellier's. He exaggerated every detail, making it appear a veritable

Lucullean[7] feast. The flowers were in tubs, he said. The champagne was quaffed from huge golden goblets. Venus rising from the foam[8] could have presented no more entrancing a spectacle than Mrs. Pontellier, blazing with beauty and diamonds at the head of the board, while the other women were all of them youthful houris possessed of incomparable charms.

She got it into her head that Victor was in love with Mrs. Pontellier, and he gave her evasive answers, framed so as to confirm her belief. She grew sullen and cried a little, threatening to go off and leave him to his fine ladies. There were a dozen men crazy about her at the *Chênière;* and since it was the fashion to be in love with married people, why, she could run away any time she liked to New Orleans with Célina's husband.

Célina's husband was a fool, a coward, and a pig, and to prove it to her, Victor intended to hammer his head into a jelly the next time he encountered him. This assurance was very consoling to Mariequita. She dried her eyes, and grew cheerful at the prospect.

They were still talking of the dinner and the allurements of city life when Mrs. Pontellier herself slipped around the corner of the house. The two youngsters stayed dumb with amazement before what they considered to be an apparition. But it was really she in flesh and blood, looking tired and a little travel-stained.

"I walked up from the wharf," she said, "and heard the hammering. I supposed it was you, mending the porch. It's a good thing. I was always tripping over those loose planks last summer. How dreary and deserted everything looks!"

It took Victor some little time to comprehend that she had come in Beaudelet's lugger, that she had come alone, and for no purpose but to rest.

"There's nothing fixed up yet, you see. I'll give you my room; it's the only place."

"Any corner will do," she assured him.

"And if you can stand Philomel's cooking," he went on, "though I might try to get her mother while you are here. Do you think she would come?" turning to Mariequita.

Mariequita thought that perhaps Philomel's mother might come for a few days, and money enough.

Beholding Mrs. Pontellier make her appearance, the girl had at once suspected a lovers' rendezvous. But Victor's astonishment was so genuine, and Mrs. Pontellier's indifference so apparent, that the disturbing notion did not lodge long in her brain. She contemplated with the greatest interest this woman who gave the most sumptuous dinners in America, and who had all the men in New Orleans at her feet.

"What time will you have dinner?" asked Edna. "I'm very hungry; but don't get anything extra."

"I'll have it ready in little or no time," he said, bustling and packing away his tools. "You may go to my room to brush up and rest yourself. Mariequita will show you."

"Thank you," said Edna. "But, do you know, I have a notion to go

7. Sumptuous feast, after Lucius Licinius Lucullus Ponticus (c. 110–56 B.C.), Roman general and epicure, noted in retirement for his lavish entertainments.

8. The Roman goddess of love and beauty was born rising from the sea in foam.

down to the beach and take a good wash and even a little swim, before dinner?"

"The water is too cold!" they both exclaimed. "Don't think of it."

"Well I might go down and try—dip my toes in. Why, it seems to me the sun is hot enough to have warmed the very depths of the ocean. Could you get me a couple of towels? I'd better go right away, so as to be back in time. It would be a little too chilly if I waited till this afternoon."

Mariequita ran over to Victor's room, and returned with some towels, which she gave to Edna.

"I hope you have fish for dinner," said Edna, as she started to walk away; "but don't do anything extra if you haven't."

"Run and find Philomel's mother," Victor instructed the girl. "I'll go to the kitchen and see what I can do. By Gimminy! Women have no consideration! She might have sent me word."

Edna walked on down to the beach rather mechanically, not noticing anything special except that the sun was hot. She was not dwelling upon any particular train of thought. She had done all the thinking which was necessary after Robert went away, when she lay awake upon the sofa till morning.

She had said over and over to herself: "To-day it is Arobin; to-morrow it will be some one else. It makes no difference to me, it doesn't matter about Léonce Pontellier—but Raoul and Etienne!" She understood now clearly what she had meant long ago when she said to Adèle Ratignolle that she would give up the unessential, but she would never sacrifice herself for her children.

Despondency had come upon her there in the wakeful night, and had never lifted. There was no one thing in the world that she desired. There was no human being whom she wanted near her except Robert; and she even realized that the day would come when he, too, and the thought of him would melt out of her existence, leaving her alone. The children appeared before her like antagonists who had overcome her; who had overpowered and sought to drag her into the soul's slavery for the rest of her days. But she knew a way to elude them. She was not thinking of these things when she walked down to the beach.

The water of the Gulf stretched out before her, gleaming with the million lights of the sun. The voice of the sea is seductive, never ceasing, whispering, clamoring, murmuring, inviting the soul to wander in abysses of solitude. All along the white beach, up and down, there was no living thing in sight. A bird with a broken wing was beating the air above, reeling, fluttering, circling disabled down, down to the water.

Edna had found her old bathing suit still hanging, faded, upon its accustomed peg.

She put it on, leaving her clothing in the bath-house. But when she was there beside the sea, absolutely alone, she cast the unpleasant, pricking garments from her, and for the first time in her life she stood naked in the open air, at the mercy of the sun, the breeze that beat upon her, and the waves that invited her.

How strange and awful it seemed to stand naked under the sky! how delicious! She felt like some new-born creature, opening its eyes in a familiar world that it had never known.

The foamy wavelets curled up to her white feet, and coiled like serpents about her ankles. She walked out. The water was chill, but she walked on. The water was deep, but she lifted her white body and reached out with a long, sweeping stroke. The touch of the sea is sensuous, enfolding the body in its soft, close embrace.

She went on and on. She remembered the night she swam far out, and recalled the terror that seized her at the fear of being unable to regain the shore. She did not look back now, but went on and on, thinking of the blue-grass meadow that she had traversed when a little child, believing that it had no beginning and no end.

Her arms and legs were growing tired.

She thought of Léonce and the children. They were a part of her life. But they need not have thought that they could possess her, body and soul. How Mademoiselle Reisz would have laughed, perhaps sneered, if she knew! "And you call yourself an artist! What pretensions, Madame! The artist must possess the courageous soul that dares and defies."

Exhaustion was pressing upon and over-powering her.

"Good-by—because, I love you." He did not know; he did not understand. He would never understand. Perhaps Doctor Mandelet would have understood if she had seen him—but it was too late; the shore was far behind her, and her strength was gone.

She looked into the distance, and the old terror flamed up for an instant, then sank again. Edna heard her father's voice and her sister Margaret's. She heard the barking of an old dog that was chained to the sycamore tree. The spurs of the cavalry officer clanged as he walked across the porch. There was the hum of bees, and the musky odor of pinks filled the air.

1899

AFTERWORD

The question we asked at the end of *Daisy Miller* was whether Winterbourne, the character through whose eyes and mind we focused on Daisy and her actions, on the other characters, and on events, was the subject or the object, the seer, or the seen. The question for Winterbourne, and for us through a good part of the story, is what kind of person Daisy is, that is, what the reality is behind her appearance and behavior. That question is answered at the end of the novel and we are left with another question: What kind of person is Winterbourne? (Was his behavior—his reticence, "gentlemanliness"—proper, puritanical, prurient, or priggishly protective?) James's novel illustrates the extremes of independence and conformity but does not define the golden mean, the precisely proper degree of moderation.

It should be easier to figure out the moral norm of *The Awakening*, for Edna Pontellier is both the object, like Daisy, and often, like Winterbourne, the subject, the mind and eye through which the characters (including herself) and the actions (including her own) are seen. Moreover, though the focus is often on and through Edna, the narration is omniscient, not nearly so restricted to the central consciousness as is that of *Daisy Miller*. The narrator's freedom to enter the minds of other characters, you would think, would clarify what the more restricted focus of the James novel leaves doubtful. Finally, though Winterbourne is spoken of in the third person, and though there is presumed to be a narrator other than he, the *voice* or *tone of voice*—the language of the novel itself—is rarely separated from that of Winterbourne (we can imagine his actually writing the novel); in *The Awakening* there is rather consistently a voice other than Edna's that makes statements and offers or implies judgments that are not specifically Edna's, and that we can therefore assume belong to the narrator and are consequently authoritative. If the narrative focus and voice can see all, know all, tell all, how can there be any doubt about the novel's attitude toward or judgment of Edna Pontellier that a careful reading cannot dispell?

Like *Madame Bovary*, a work that *The Awakening* in many ways resembles and to which it has often been compared, Chopin's novel is at first focused not on the heroine but on her husband (and Edna, until the seventh chapter, is consistently called "Mrs. Pontellier"). Unlike Charles Bovary, however, Léonce Pontellier is not presented as a dolt, even a pitiable dolt. Defining just what sort of person he is, indeed, presents the reader with an immediate problem of evaluation, one that will be of some significance in understanding and evaluating Edna and her actions. We first see Mr. Pontellier reading the paper. His wife and young Robert Lebrun approach from the beach where they have, foolishly in his view, been swimming in the heat of the day. She has got too much sun, is "'burnt beyond recognition,'" he says, "looking at his wife as one looks at a valuable piece of personal property." There would seem to be no problem of understanding or allegiance here. The possessive, materialist, bourgeois husband—that is Léonce Pontellier. He wanders off to amuse himself at billiards, not sure whether he will be home for dinner, not consciously asserting his will to dominate, but, what may be worse, unconsciously assuming the absolute privilege of a nineteenth-century middle-class husband. He comes home late at night. and, again unconsciously, tries to tell his sleepy wife anecdotes and gossip that he self-centeredly believes will amuse her. She barely responds. It is difficult to sympathize with his displeasure: "He thought it very discouraging that his wife . . . evinced so little interest in things which concerned him and valued so little his conversation." Poor Edna.

And yet, even in these early chapters there are qualifications, or indicators that point in a somewhat different direction. In a phrase omitted from the most recently quoted passage, for example, Pontellier's wife is described as "the sole object of his existence." He is not, then, the stereotype of the businessman who is so wrapped up in work and making money that he neglects his wife and family. He is well liked by others, including his own children. Both sons want to follow their father when he goes off to play billiards (Chapter 1), and when he has to return to New Orleans and the workaday world from the vacation area of Grand Isle, everyone comes to see him off: "Mr. Pontellier was a great favorite, and ladies, men, children, even nurses, were always on hand to say good-by to him." Well, good guys don't always make good husbands.

Edna is quite aware of her husband's devotion, and indeed she married him not because of her love for him but because of his for her. If at issue is the question of blame for the unsatisfactory marriage, the novel, even Edna herself, seems quite clear in seeing that the fault was hers.

> He fell in love, as men are in the habit of doing, and pressed his suit with an earnestness and an ardor which left nothing to be desired. He pleased her; his absolute devotion flattered her. She fancied there was a sympathy of thought and taste between them, in which fancy she was mistaken. Add to this the violent opposition of her father and her sister Margaret to her marriage with a Catholic, and we need seek no further for the motives which led her to accept Monsieur Pontellier for her husband.

Her assertion of her selfhood, of her independence from the opinion of her father and sister, helps lead her into the mistaken marriage. So does her imagination or fancy. This may serve to warn us, perhaps, that in *The Awakening,* as in *Daisy Miller,* not all unconventional behavior, not all assertions of independence and will are unquestionably good, a warning that it may be important to remember later in the novel. We are not shown Léonce during the courtship or the grounds for Edna's fancy that misinterprets his thought and taste. We are also not shown, remember, Mr. Pontellier telling the anecdotes and gossip he brings home from his evening at billiards, so we have no way of knowing for sure whether they are boring or amusing, trivial or significant. Nor are we presented with what amuses Edna and Robert so when they are returning from the beach, though here we have some indication:

> they both tried to relate it at once. It did not seem half so amusing when told. They realized this, and so did Mr. Pontellier. He yawned and stretched himself.

It's hard to tell the boring from the bored.

Whether Edna's taste is provincial, ordinary, bourgeois, like Emma Bovary's, or extraordinary and out of place in her mediocre environment, we must judge for ourselves, and because some significant scenes are not dramatized, we do not have an abundance of concrete, objective evidence to go on. We know little of her response to literature, for example, except that she is shocked at how freely the Creoles in mixed society discuss what she considers the "scandalous" novels of the French realists. We know a bit more about her response

to music, but, characteristically, there are what seem to be contradictory indicators in the narration and we are again left on our own—with too much rather
than too little to go on.

She "was what she herself called very fond of music." Why does the narrator
pass off responsibility for this statement to Edna? Can we assume the narrator
wants to show that Edna is herself aware that her feelings toward music are
foolish or excessive—as the precise meaning of "fond" would indicate? Probably not, since Edna is also described as having grown very "fond" of her husband, and whatever she feels for him it is not excessive. Is the narrator, by
allowing her to use the ambiguous word unconsciously, judging Edna to be a
bit foolish, and unaware that her emotionalism is foolish? The precise tone is
most difficult to identify here.

Edna's characteristic form of enjoying music is shown to be rather superficial
and romantic: while she listens, she makes pictures in her mind which have
little to do with the music. She also makes up romantic titles for musical
pieces. Still, when she hears Mademoiselle Reisz play she makes no mental
pictures and responds deeply and directly to the passion of the music. Mademoiselle Reisz believes Edna different from and superior to those around her;
she tells her, "'You are the only one worth playing for. Those others. Bah!' and
she went shuffling and sliding on down the gallery toward her room." As soon
as we feel we have at last grasped something solid—a good musician finds
Edna's appreciation of music exceptional, so our heroine's sensibility is affirmed at last—it melts in our grasp. The next sentence tells us that Mademoiselle Reisz "was mistaken about 'those others.' Her playing had aroused a fever
of enthusiasm." Well, Edna is sensitive, anyway, even if not extraordinarily so
in the society of Grand Isle. When Iván Ilyich prides himself on his individual
taste in furnishing and decorating his new house, Tolstoy ironically tells us that
it looks exactly like the homes of others who want to look better off than they
are. Is something like this what Chopin is ironically suggesting about Edna Pontellier's response to the passion of the music?

How about Edna's painting? Once more the narration seems to follow a zig-
zag course. Painting, we are told, gives her a "satisfaction of a kind which no
other employment afforded her." She handles her brushes with ease "from a
natural aptitude," yet she paints "in an unprofessional way," indeed she "dab-
bles." Robert says she has talent, but while he has been watching her paint he
has been touching her (a move which she repulses). Edna's portrait of Madame
Ratignolle does not look like her, but the subject thinks it "a fair enough piece
of work, and in many respects satisfying." Edna does not think so and she destroys the portrait. She has aptitude and is capable of self-criticism. She's an
unprofessional dabbler. The judgment that she has talent comes from a prejudiced and self-serving source; later in the novel, however, she does have an
agent who is selling some of her work. Though there is certainly no evidence
that the novel wants us to feel she is potentially a Rosa Bonheur or Mary Cas-
satt born to blush unseen in the humid air of Grand Isle, she does have some
technical aptitude or dexterity, and she does enjoy painting as she seems to
enjoy little else about her life except talking to Robert Lebrun. She is an amateur in the best as well as in the ordinary sense of the term.

One role that she clearly does not enjoy as those around her expect her to is
motherhood. In her attitude and behavior toward her children in the summer
society of Grand Isle, Louisiana, she is exceptional. We learn this very early.
When Mr. Pontellier returns home from billiards late that first night (Chapter
3), in saying good night to the children he discovers their son Raoul seems to
have a fever.

He reproached his wife with her inattention, her habitual neglect of the children. If it was not a mother's place to look after children, whose on earth was it? He himself had his hands full with his brokerage business. He could not be in two places at once; making a living for his family on the street, and staying home to see that no harm befell them. He talked in a monotonous, insistent way.

Who says this last, the narrator or Edna? Can one be insistent in a monotone? This would seem to be a conclusion of the listener rather than the objective description of speech. If he is monotonous and insistent, is he then necessarily wrong? Whose place *is* it to look after the children? That evening he has not been at his brokerage business but playing billiards. Could he not have stayed home? But if the neglect is more or less habitual, can we deny the implications of his charge? the justice of it?

We are never told whether Raoul does have a fever, so once more we are not given the external evidence to judge even this instance. Edna goes out on the porch to cry, knowing the cause is primarily her own mood and not injustice on her husband's part: "She was just having a good cry all to herself." To what extent does her mood suggest the subjective quality of this whole scene?

"Mrs. Pontellier was not a mother-woman" like the Creole mothers, we are told:

> They were women who idolized their children, worshiped their husbands, and esteemed it a holy privilege to efface themselves as individuals and grow wings as ministering angels.

Whose extravagant language is this, Edna's or the narrator's? Is being a parent necessarily to "idolize" children, being a wife to "worship," being either necessarily to "efface" the self? It is probably Edna's language, for later (Chapter 16) she gets into an argument with her good friend Adèle Ratignolle, having told her she would not sacrifice herself for her children:

> the two women did not appear to understand each other, or to be talking the same language. Edna tried to appease her friend, to explain:
> "I would give up the unessential; I would give my money, I would give my life for my children; but I wouldn't give myself. I can't make it more clear; it's only something which I am beginning to comprehend, which is revealing itself to me."

Earlier (Chapter 7) she is described as

> fond of her children in an uneven, impulsive way. She would sometimes gather them passionately to her heart; she would sometimes forget them. . . . Their absence was a sort of relief, though she did not admit this, even to herself. It seemed to free her of a responsibility which she had blindly assumed and for which Fate had not fitted her.

Is it the narrator, Edna, or both who believe "Fate" somehow fits us or fails to fit us for motherhood or other responsibilities? As in the Raoul and mother-woman passages, Chopin seems to be letting Edna serve as both focus and voice. What is this "self" that Edna Pontellier will not sacrifice? What is this "freedom" she seeks? The self seems to have little connection with others, the external world, society—it is random impulse, an in-dwelling essence, a soul. And freedom seems to be freedom *from* rather than freedom *to*—a freedom from responsibility:

> She was blindly following whatever impulse moved her, as if she had

placed herself in alien hands for direction, and freed her soul of responsibility.

Is freedom then blindness, slavery to alien hands? The narrative voice seems separate from Edna (who would not describe herself as blind, surely). The narrator identifies Edna's confusion as such—a common state, the narrator says, when one is "awakening," is at the beginning of something:

> But the beginning of things, of a world especially, is necessarily vague, tangled, chaotic, and exceedingly disturbing. How few of us ever emerge from such a beginning! How many souls perish in its tumult!

Edna, alas, will be one of those who perish.

Suppose she had not. What would have happened? Would she have "found" herself? And what does that mean? Is there an essential self separate from others, from commitments and consequences? What would the self be like that Edna Pontellier found? We usually assume that our "self" is something pristine and perfect. Is that necessarily true? Is the self merely its chaotic bundle of impulses? Is it an essence? Is it naturally good? naturally corrupt? Is there a self in isolation from time, place, society? Is it created by its environment, by its genes, by its will? Can you be whatever you choose to be? *The Awakening* implicitly raises such questions; does it explicitly or implicitly answer them? Should it attempt to?

Whatever the narrator thinks about Edna Pontellier's thoughts, feelings, character, actions, it is clear that Edna is seen sympathetically, if not always uncritically. At times, however, the narrator seems to tell us things about the protagonist for which there is little concrete or dramatized evidence in the narrative (just as we are not shown what amuses Edna and Robert or interests Léonce). Perhaps it is the narrator's knowledge that Edna will be one of those souls which perish in the tumult that prompts the narrator early in the novel to step forth from the narrative surface of the fiction (as in the most recently quoted passage) to generalize and exclaim, and (in the following passage) to state what the novel itself does not support:

> Mrs. Pontellier was beginning to realize her position in the universe as a human being, and to recognize her relations as an individual to the world within and about her. This may seem like a ponderous weight of wisdom to descend upon the soul of a young woman of twenty-eight—perhaps more wisdom than the Holy Ghost is usually pleased to vouchsafe to any woman.

Edna is distanced (here in Chapter 6 she is still "Mrs. Pontellier"), and we can accept the observation that she is at the beginning of something and that it may have to do with recognizing something inside herself. But is there any evidence that she is beginning to recognize her position *in the universe* or her relations to *the world about her*? Isn't the uncharacteristic pomposity of the rhetoric here a symptom of irony (which does not seem too likely) or of special pleading or mere assertion? Is there any evidence that what Edna Pontellier is acquiring is more than awareness of her sexuality, her boredom, her unhappiness and unsuitability for her lot? Does it seem a ponderous weight of wisdom? And how do we read the irony at the end of the passage? Does it undercut the statement? Does it mean that of course all women do have this ponderous weight of wisdom? The narrator, often content to let Edna's voice determine the language of the novel while at the same time giving us clues for judging the reliability of that language, seems here not to have stepped back to see Edna more clearly, but to have stepped forward to tell us what the novel does not show or support. Our problems with tone are thus further complicated.

All the incidents and passages cited so far are from only the first fifth of the novel. It is here that the reader's expectations are schooled, that he or she is oriented to the characters, values, world of the novel—or is disoriented, uncertain just what kind of world it is. The shifting, sometimes contradictory perspectives and judgments keep us alert—and puzzled; it is perhaps more to learn how Edna Pontellier is finally to be judged than to discover what happens next that is the major interest and suspense in *The Awakening*. Is she a sensitive young woman trapped in a narrow bourgeois world? a foolish, romantic woman trapped in that world? Is she a middle-class wife bored because she does not have anything much to do, without sufficient training or resources of her own, and who therefore finds in sexual excitement something to give her the illusion of life and purpose? Is she a Victorian wife who was offered no vocation but marriage? a Victorian woman offered no education in or socially acceptable channel for passion and sexual fulfilment? Is Robert Lebrun worth loving? Would marriage to him be any different from marriage to Léonce? Could she earn a livelihood and a respected place in the world of art by her painting? Should lust and love, which are sometimes separable, be separated? How is Edna seen and understood by her husband? her children? Robert? Madame Lebrun? Adèle? Arobin? Why does Edna commit suicide? Do women who dare, like Daisy Miller, Emma Bovary, Anna Karénina, always die young? From the discussion of the early portions of the novel it should be evident that the reader's problem is not that these questions cannot be answered and passages from the text marshalled to support such an answer, but that in many instances an equal and equally sound number of passages can document a quite different, even contradictory answer.

No two readers read any book in precisely the same way; we each "perform" a text somewhat differently, based on our own real and reading experiences, our interests, and our prejudices. This may not be a "distortion": the text may no more exist as a narrative until it is read than a symphony exists as music until it is performed. This is not to say, however, that, like Humpty-Dumpty's words in Lewis Carroll, a novel can mean whatever one chooses for it to mean. We are obliged to play the notes that are there—all of them, not just the ones we like to play or are good at playing or have played before. Nonetheless, no two performances may be exactly alike, and when a text or score has as many gaps or grace notes as *The Awakening*, our humility and open-mindedness are severely put to the test.

Often when the tone or meaning of a work of literature is in question we can discover a likely answer beyond the text in the context. The context of *The Awakening*, however, is almost as complicated as the text. A feminist reading of Chopin's novel, for example, supported by substantial evidence from the text, can be reinforced by history. The first international meeting of the women's movement had been held half a century before the writing of this novel, and the "Woman Question" was current throughout the rest of the century. In the third quarter of the nineteenth century two great novels, Flaubert's *Madame Bovary* and Tolstoy's *Anna Karénina*, treated the subject of adultery by wives of middle-class or provincial husbands, both novels ending with the heroine's suicide. There were a great many such novels, written by men and women, which ranged widely in describing, defining, evaluating women's feelings, including sexual feelings, women's social and sexual behavior, women's roles, restrictions, and rights. We must be as careful in adducing historical evidence as we are in using the text.

Kate Chopin has until recently been considered a "local color" writer, one of those American novelists in the realist-naturalist school or schools who concentrate on the social and geographical milieu as the conditioning agent if not the determinant of human behavior. Chopin's local color is undeniably superb; here the ambience of Grand Isle, the New Orleans vacationland, and of New Orleans itself, is captured accurately and lyrically. In attempting, with some justice, to take her out of that confining and somewhat denigrating pigeon-hole, however, we may have taken her out of the context of her own time and her own canon. What if we were to read the treatment of Edna Pontellier's awakening sexuality, for example, in terms of the naturalistic novel? The naturalists would have it that man's animal or biological nature determines his conduct much more than does his reason or civilization. Edna's awakening, then, is an awakening to Nature as well as to her own sexual nature. *The Awakening*, read so, is not only an awakening to sexuality but also to those instinctive, impulsive, pleasure-seeking forces which are as potentially destructive as they are potentially creative—forces that about this very time Freud was naming the id. These forces are often likened to the life-giving and life-destroying properties of the sea, that same sea that attracts, buoys, and destroys Edna Pontellier. To awaken to unconscious forces is somewhat paradoxical, and it has also seemed odd to some that the heroine of this novel about wakening should so often be sleepy or asleep, not just when she is enmeshed in her old, unwakened life, but even at times when she is waking to the new.

If this is a novel of universal, biological, and metaphysical issues, why the local color? Is it merely a mode left over from Chopin's earlier work? Edna Pontellier is, remember, a Kentucky Presbyterian. New Orleans Creole—largely French—Catholic culture is foreign to her. We have already mentioned how shocked she is by public discussion of "risqué" books. Adèle Ratignolle warns Robert not to indulge in the kind of courtly love homage he has been paying to her and other women since he was fifteen, because Edna might take him seriously. Creole husbands, we are told, are not jealous—they know, apparently, the rules of the game. Edna does not. It is this cultural clash which arouses, wakes her. She *is* Winterbourne; Robert, at least, is as innocent as Daisy. Unlike Winterbourne, Edna answers the signals she mistakenly receives; as Daisy does, she flaunts the conventional and the prudent, but Arobin is no Giovanelli. As in *Daisy Miller*, neither culture is socially or morally "correct," the other "wrong" or vicious. Here, each has apparently come to terms with the primitive forces which threaten to subvert it in a different, though practically successful way. Even as Edna wakes the dawn reveals both the possibility of a new life and the necessity of restraint: "A certain light was beginning to dawn dimly within her,—the light which, showing the way, forbids it."

To see in the text and context of *The Awakening* the multiplicity of signals may serve to restrain our imposing our own more or less simplistic reading upon it, and may make it less what we want to hear, less "modern" and doctrinaire. This does not, however, necessarily reduce its stature as a literary work (whatever it does to its status as a "document"). On the contrary, its resonance may move us and more of us the more deeply, its complexity may awaken us to its—and our—wider world.

FRANZ KAFKA

The Metamorphosis

His father a butcher, Hermann Kafka worked his way up from peddlar to owner of a wholesale women's wear company. The story of the life and work of his only son, Franz (born on July 3, 1883, in Prague, then part of the Austro-Hungarian Empire), begins and in a sense virtually ends with the Father. This overbearing, powerful, aggressive, worldly man terrified his rather sickly intellectual son, so that even at thirty-six years of age the "boy" was writing a long, long letter (never delivered) to his father explaining why he was afraid of him, and the son's strange fiction is dominated by a powerful father-figure—father of the family, of the political state, or Father of the Universe. This fear, and guilt at the fear and lack of love, this smouldering rebellion and sense of both helplessness and unworthiness, whatever its cause, and however we read it—psychologically, politically, religiously—seems to speak to our experience of the modern world, to reflect how we sometimes see ourselves. Many other writers have reflected this aspect of the modern world, but Kafka, perhaps because his works both contain, yet are not reducible to, any of the interpretive modes or systems, seems to stand as *the* symbol—the irreducible embodiment—of that vision.

Franz Kafka, whatever his inner fears, was not an insect or an ineffectual angel, however. He earned a doctorate in law from Karl-Ferdinand University in Prague, entered the Austrian civil service, rising in the government's Workers' Accident Insurance Company in fourteen years as far as his training would permit, to the post of senior secretary. No doubt in opposition to his father's secularism and identification with the dominant German culture, Franz studied Judaism, Hebrew, and Czech. Though he never married, he was often enough engaged—three times between 1912 and 1917 to Felice Bauer of Belin, for example; he had an equally inconclusive relationship with another Jewish girl, Julie Wohryzek, from 1918 to 1920, a stormy love affair with a married Czech woman, Melenia Jesenska, who was translating part of his unfinished novel *Amerika*, and toward the very end of his life, he lived with a very young Hasidic girl, Dora Dymant, whom he had met in a tuberculosis sanitorium and who nursed him through his last illness.

Though his full-length novels, *The Trial, The Castle*, and *Amerika* (published in 1925, 1926, and 1927, respectively), which he had been working on during the last decade of his life, were all left incomplete and had to be pieced together posthumously by his best friend and literary executor Max Brod (who had been ordered by Kafka to burn his work but didn't), Kafka had published *The Metamorphosis* in 1915, a volume of short stories called *The Country Doctor* the following year, a longish story (about 12,500 words), "In the Penal Colony," published as a separate work in 1919, and had fully prepared for publication before his death a second volume of short stories, *A Hunger Artist* (1924).

The fragmentary novels and the fragmentary love affairs were no doubt indicative of a deep psychological disturbance evident in his work, but Franz Kafka died on his forty-first birthday, had a law degree, a full-time job from the age of twenty-five, poor health throughout his life and was known to have tuberculosis as early as 1917, so his published work, though far from voluminous, was not negligible in quantity, and is certainly monumental in quality.

The Metamorphosis[*]

A S GREGOR SAMSA awoke one morning from uneasy dreams he found himself transformed in his bed into a gigantic insect. He was lying on his hard, as it were armor-plated, back and when he lifted his head a little he could see his dome-like brown belly divided into stiff arched segments on top of which the bed quilt could hardly keep in position and was about to slide off completely. His numerous legs, which were pitifully thin compared to the rest of his bulk, waved helplessly before his eyes.

What has happened to me? he thought. It was no dream. His room, a regular human bedroom, only rather too small, lay quiet between the four familiar walls. Above the table on which a collection of cloth samples was unpacked and spread out—Samsa was a commercial traveler—hung the picture which he had recently cut out of an illustrated magazine and put into a pretty gilt frame. It showed a lady, with a fur cap on and a fur stole, sitting upright and holding out to the spectator a huge fur muff into which the whole of her forearm had vanished!

Gregor's eyes turned next to the window, and the overcast sky—one could hear rain drops beating on the window gutter—made him quite melancholy. What about sleeping a little longer and forgetting all this nonsense, he thought, but it could not be done, for he was accustomed to sleep on his right side and in his present condition he could not turn himself over. However violently he forced himself towards his right side he always rolled on to his back again. He tried it at least a hundred times, shutting his eyes to keep from seeing his struggling legs, and only desisted when he began to feel in his side a faint dull ache he had never experienced before.

Oh God, he thought, what an exhausting job I've picked on! Traveling about day in, day out. It's much more irritating work than doing the actual business in the office, and on top of that there's the trouble of constant traveling, of worrying about train connections, the bed and irregular meals, casual acquaintances that are always new and never become intimate friends. The devil take it all! He felt a slight itching up on his belly; slowly pushed himself on his back neared to the top of the bed so that he could lift his his head more easily; identified the itching place which was surrounded by many small white spots the nature of which he could not understand and made to touch it with a leg, but drew the leg back immediately, for the contact made a cold shiver run through him.

He slid down again into his former position. This getting up early, he thought, makes one quite stupid. A man needs his sleep. Other commercials live like harem women. For instance, when I come back to the hotel of a morning to write up the orders I've got, these others are only sitting down to breakfast. Let me just try that with my chief; I'd be sacked on the spot. Anyhow, that might be quite a good thing for me, who can tell? If I didn't have to hold my hand because of my parents I'd have given notice long ago, I'd have gone to the chief and told him exactly what I

[*] Translated by Willa and Edwin Muir.

think of him. That would knock him endways from his desk! It's a queer way of doing, too, this sitting on high at a desk and talking down to employees, especially when they have to come quite near because the chief is hard of hearing. Well, there's still hope; once I've saved enough money to pay back my parents' debts to him—that should take another five or six years—I'll do it without fail. I'll cut myself completely loose then. For the moment, though, I'd better get up, since my train goes at five.

He looked at the alarm clock ticking on the chest. Heavenly Father! he thought. It was half-past six o'clock and the hands were quickly moving on, it was even past the half-hour, it was getting on toward a quarter to seven. Had the alarm clock not gone off? From the bed one could see that it had been properly set for four o'clock; of course it must have gone off. Yes, but was it possible to sleep quietly through that ear-splitting noise? Well, he had not slept quietly, yet apparently all the more soundly for that. But what was he to do now? The next train went at seven o'clock; to catch that he would need to hurry like mad and his samples weren't even packed up, and he himself wasn't feeling particularly fresh and active. And even if he did catch the train he wouldn't avoid a row with the chief, since the firm's porter would have been waiting for the five o'clock train and would have long since reported his failure to turn up. The porter was a creature of the chief's, spineless and stupid. Well, supposing he were to say he was sick? But that would be most unpleasant and would look suspicious, since during his five years' employment he had not been ill once. The chief himself would be sure to come with the sick-insurance doctor, and reproach his parents with their son's laziness and would cut all excuses short by referring to the insurance doctor, who of course regarded all mankind as perfectly healthy malingerers. And would he be so far wrong on this occasion? Gregor really felt quite well, apart from a drowsiness that was utterly superfluous after such a long sleep, and he was even unusually hungry.

As all this was running through his mind at top speed without his being able to decide to leave his bed—the alarm clock had just struck a quarter to seven—there came a cautious tap at the door behind the head of his bed. "Gregor," said a voice—it was his mother's—"it's a quarter to seven. Hadn't you a train to catch?" That gentle voice! Gregor had a shock as he heard his own voice answering hers, unmistakably his own voice, it was true, but with a persistent horrible twittering squeak behind it like an undertone, that left the words in their clear shape only for the first moment and then rose up reverberating around them to destroy their sense, so that one could not be sure one had heard them rightly. Gregor wanted to answer at length and explain everything, but in the circumstances he confined himself to saying: "Yes, yes, thank you, Mother, I'm getting up now." The wooden door between them must have kept the change in his voice from being noticeable outside, for his mother contented herself with this statement and shuffled away. Yet this brief exchange of words had made the other members of the family aware that Gregor was still in the house, as they had not expected, and at one of the side doors his father was already knocking, gently, yet with his fist. "Gregor, Gregor," he called, "what's the matter with you?" And after a little while he called again in a deeper voice: "Gregor! Gregor!" At the other side door his sister was saying in a low, plaintive tone: "Gregor? Aren't you well? Are you needing anything?" He answered them both at once: "I'm just ready," and did his best to make his voice sound as normal as possible by enunciating the words very clearly and leaving long pauses between them. So his father went back to his breakfast, but his sister whispered: "Gregor, open the door, do." However, he was not thinking of opening the door, and felt thankful for the prudent habit he had acquired in traveling of locking all doors during the night, even at home.

His immediate intention was to get up quietly without being disturbed, to put on his clothes and above all eat his breakfast, and only then to consider what else was to be done, since in bed, he was well aware, his meditations would come to no sensible conclusion. He remembered that often enough in bed he had felt small aches and pains, probably caused by awkward postures, which had proved purely imaginary once he got up, and he looked forward eagerly to seeing this morning's delusions gradually fall away. That the change in his voice was nothing but the precursor of a severe chill, a standing ailment of commercial travelers, he had not the least possible doubt.

To get rid of the quilt was quite easy; he had only to inflate himself a little and it fell off by itself. But the next move was difficult, especially because he was so uncommonly broad. He would have needed arms and hands to hoist himself up; instead he had only the numerous little legs which never stopped waving in all directions and which he could not control in the least. When he tried to bend one of them it was the first to stretch itself straight; and did he succeed at last in making it do what he wanted, all the other legs meanwhile waved the more wildly in a high degree of unpleasant agitation. "But what's the use of lying idle in bed," said Gregor to himself.

He thought that he might get out of bed with the lower part of his body first, but this lower part, which he had not yet seen and of which he could form no clear conception, proved too difficult to move; it shifted so slowly; and when finally, almost wild with annoyance, he gathered his forces together and thrust out recklessly, he had miscalculated the direction and bumped heavily against the lower end of the bed, and the stinging pain he felt informed him that precisely this lower part of his body was at the moment probably the most sensitive.

So he tried to get the top part of himself out first, and cautiously moved his head towards the edge of the bed. That proved easy enough, and despite its breadth and mass the bulk of his body at last slowly followed the movement of his head. Still, when he finally got his head free over the edge of the bed he felt too scared to go on advancing, for after all if he let himself fall in this way it would take a miracle to keep his head from being injured. And at all costs he must not lose consciousness now, precisely now; he would rather stay in bed.

But when after a repetition of the same efforts he lay in his former position again, sighing, and watched his little legs struggling against each other more wildly than ever, if that were possible, and saw no way of bringing any order into this arbitrary confusion, he told himself again that it was impossible to stay in bed and that the most sensible course was to risk everything for the smallest hope of getting away from it. At the same time he did not forget meanwhile to remind himself that cool reflection, the coolest possible, was much better than desperate resolves. In such moments he focused his eyes as sharply as possible on the window, but, unfortunately, the prospect of the morning fog, which muffled even the other side of the narrow street, brought him little encouragement and comfort. "Seven o'clock already," he said to himself when the alarm clock chimed again, "seven o'clock already and still such a thick fog." And for a little while he lay quiet, breathing lightly, as if perhaps expecting such complete repose to restore all things to their real and normal condition. But then he said to himself: "Before it strikes a quarter past seven I must be quite out of this bed, without fail. Anyhow, by that time someone will have come from the office to ask for me, since it opens before seven." And he set himself to rocking his whole body at once in a regular rhythm, with the idea of swinging it out of the bed. If he tipped himself out in that way he could keep his head from injury by lifting it at an acute angle when he fell. His back seemed to be hard and was not likely to suffer from a fall on the carpet. His biggest worry was the loud crash he would not be able to help making, which would probably cause anxiety, if not terror, behind all the doors. Still, he must take the risk.

When he was already half out of the bed—the new method was more a game than an effort, for he needed only to hitch himself across by rocking to and fro—it struck him how simple it would be if he could get help. Two strong people—he thought of his father and the servant girl—would be amply sufficient; they would only have to thrust their arms under his convex back, lever him out of the bed, bend down with their burden and then be patient enough to let him turn himself right over on the floor, where it was to be hoped his legs would then find their proper function. Well, ignoring the fact that the doors were all locked, ought he really to call for help? In spite of his misery he could not suppress a smile at the very idea of it.

He had got so far that he could barely keep his equilibrium when he rocked himself strongly, and he would have to nerve himself very soon for the final decision since in five minutes' time it would be a quarter past seven—when the front door bell rang. "That's someone from the office," he said to himself, and grew almost rigid, while his little legs only jigged about all the faster. For a moment everything stayed quiet. "They're not going to open the door," said Gregor to himself, catching at some kind of irrational hope. But then of course the servant girl went as usual to the door with her heavy tread and opened it. Gregor needed only to hear the first good morning of the visitor to know immediately who it was—the chief clerk himself. What a fate, to be condemned to work for a firm where the smallest omission at once gave rise to the gravest suspicion! Were all employees in a body nothing but scoundrels, was there not among them one single loyal devoted man who, had he wasted only an hour or so of the firm's time in a morning, was so tormented by conscience as to be driven out of his mind and actually incapable of leaving his bed? Wouldn't it really have been sufficient to send an apprentice to inquire—if any inquiry were necessary at all—did the chief clerk himself have to come and thus indicate to the entire family, an innocent family, that this suspicious circumstance could be investigated by no one less versed in affairs than himself? And more through the agitation caused by these reflections than through any act of will Gregor swung himself out of bed with all his strength. There was a loud thump, but it was not really a crash. His fall was broken to some extent by the carpet, his back, too, was less stiff than he thought, and so there was merely a dull thud, not so very startling. Only he had not lifted his head carefully enough and had hit it; he turned it and rubbed it on the carpet in pain and irritation.

"That was something falling down in there," said the chief clerk in the next room to the left. Gregor tried to suppose to himself that something like what had happened to him today might some day happen to the chief clerk; one really could not deny that it was possible. But as if in brusque reply to this supposition the chief clerk took a couple of firm steps in the next-door room and his patent leather boots creaked. From the right-hand room his sister was whispering to inform him of the situation: "Gregor, the chief clerk's here." "I know," muttered Gregor to himself; but he didn't dare to make his voice loud enough for his sister to hear it.

"Gregor," said his father now from the left-hand room, "the chief clerk has come and wants to know why you didn't catch the early train. We don't know what to say to him. Besides, he wants to talk to you in person. So open the door, please. He will be good enough to excuse the untidiness of your room." "Good morning. Mr. Samsa," the chief clerk was calling amiably meanwhile. "He's not well," said his mother to the visitor, while his father was still speaking through the door, "he's not well, sir, believe me. What else would make him miss a train! The boy thinks about nothing but his work. It makes me almost cross the way he never goes out in the evenings; he's been here the last eight days and has stayed at home every single evening. He just sits there quietly at the table reading a newspaper or looking through railway timetables. The only amusement he gets is doing fretwork. For instance, he spent two or three evenings cutting out a little picture frame; you would be surprised to see how pretty it is; it's hanging in his room; you'll see it in a minute when Gregor opens the door. I must say I'm glad you've come, sir; we should never have got him to unlock the door by ourselves; he's so obstinate; and I'm sure he's unwell, though he wouldn't have it to be so this morning." "I'm just coming," said Gregor slowly and carefully, not moving an inch for fear of losing one word of the conversation. "I can't think of any other explanation, madam," said the chief clerk, "I hope it's nothing serious. Although on the other hand I must say that we men of business—fortunately or unfortunately—very often simply have to ignore any slight indisposition, since business must be attended to." "Well, can the chief clerk come in now?" asked Gregor's father impatiently, again knocking on the door. "No," said Gregor. In the left-hand room a painful silence followed this refusal, in the right-hand room his sister began to sob.

Why didn't his sister join the others? She was probably newly out of bed and hadn't even begun to put on her clothes yet. Well, why was she crying? Because he wouldn't get up and let the chief clerk in, because he was in danger of losing his job, and because the chief would begin dunning his parents again for the old debts? Surely these were things one didn't need to worry about for the present. Gregor was still at home and not in the least thinking of deserting the family. At the moment, true, he was lying on the carpet and no one who knew the condition he was in could seriously expect him to admit the chief clerk. But for such a small discourtesy, which could plausibly be explained away somehow later on, Gregor could hardly be dismissed on the spot. And it seemed to Gregor that it would be much more sensible to leave him in peace for the present than to trouble him with tears and entreaties. Still, of course, their uncertainty bewildered them all and excused their behavior.

"Mr. Samsa," the chief clerk called now in a louder voice, "what's the matter with you? Here you are, barricading yourself in your room, giving only 'yes' and 'no' for answers, causing your parents a lot of unnecessary trouble and neglecting—I mention this only in passing—neglecting your business duties in an incredible fashion. I am speaking here in the name of your parents and of your chief, and I beg you quite seriously to give me an immediate and precise explanation. You amaze me, you amaze me. I thought you were a quiet, dependable person, and now all at once you seem bent on making a disgraceful exhibition of yourself. The chief did hint to me early this morning a possible explanation for your disappearance—with reference to the cash payments that were entrusted to you recently—but I almost pledged my solemn word of honor that this could not be so. But now that I see how incredibly obstinate you are, I no longer have the slightest desire to take your part at all. And your position in the firm is not so unassailable. I came with the intention of telling you all this in private, but since you are wasting my time so needlessly I don't see why your parents shouldn't hear it too. For some time past your work has been most unsatisfactory; this is not the season of the year for a business boom, of course, we admit that, but a season of the year for doing no business at all, that does not exist, Mr. Samsa, must not exist."

"But, sir," cried Gregor, beside himself and in his agitation forgetting everything else, "I'm just going to open the door this very minute. A slight illness, an attack of giddiness, has kept me from getting up. I'm still lying in bed. But I feel all right again. I'm getting out of bed now. Just give me a moment or two longer! I'm not quite so well as I thought. But I'm all right, really. How a thing like that can suddenly strike one down! Only last night I was quite well, my parents can tell you, or rather I did have a slight presentiment. I must have showed some sign of it. Why didn't I report it at the office! But one always thinks that an indisposition can be got over without staying in the house. Oh sir, do spare my parents! All that you're reproaching me with now has no foundation; no one has ever said a word to me about it. Perhaps you haven't looked at the last orders I sent in. Anyhow, I can still catch the eight o'clock train, I'm much the better for my few hours' rest. Don't let me detain you here, sir; I'll be attending to business very soon, and do be good enough to tell the chief so and to make my excuses to him!"

And while all this was tumbling out pell-mell and Gregor hardly knew what he was saying, he had reached the chest quite easily, perhaps because of the practice he had had in bed, and was now trying to lever himself upright by means of it. He meant actually to open the door, actually to show himself and speak to the chief clerk; he was eager to find out what the others, after all their insistence, would say at the sight of him. If they were horrified then the responsibility was no longer his and he could stay quiet. But if they took it calmly, then he had no reason either to be upset, and could really get to the station for the eight o'clock train if he hurried. At first he slipped down a few times from the polished surface of the chest, but at length with a last heave he stood upright; he paid no more attention to the pains in the lower part of his body, however they smarted. Then he let himself fall against the back of a near-by chair, and clung with his little legs to the edges of it. That brought him into control of himself again and he stopped speaking, for now he could listen to what the chief clerk was saying.

"Did you understand a word of it?" the chief clerk was asking; "surely

he can't be trying to make fools of us?" "Oh dear," cried his mother, in
tears, "perhaps he's terribly ill and we're tormenting him. Grete! Grete!"
she called out then. "Yes Mother?" called his sister from the other side.
They were calling to each other across Gregor's room. "You must go this
minute for the doctor, quick. Did you hear how he was speaking?" "That
was no human voice," said the chief clerk in a voice noticeably low beside the shrillness of the mother's. "Anna! Anna!" his father was calling
through the hall to the kitchen, clapping his hands, "get a locksmith at
once!" And the two girls were already running through the hall with a
swish of skirts—how could his sister have got dressed so quickly?—and
were tearing the front door open. There was no sound of its closing again;
they had evidently left it open, as one does in houses where some great
misfortune has happened.

But Gregor was now much calmer. The words he uttered were no
longer understandable, apparently, although they seemed clear enough to
him, even clearer than before, perhaps because his ear had grown accustomed to the sound of them. Yet at any rate people now believed that
something was wrong with him, and were ready to help him. The positive
certainty with which these first measures had been taken comforted him.
He felt himself drawn once more into the human circle and hoped for
great and remarkable results from both the doctor and the locksmith,
without really distinguishing precisely between them. To make his voice
as clear as possible for the decisive conversation that was now imminent
he coughed a little, as quietly as he could, of course, since this noise too
might not sound like a human cough for all he was able to judge. In the
next room meanwhile there was complete silence. Perhaps his parents
were sitting at the table with the chief clerk, whispering, perhaps they
were all leaning against the door and listening.

Slowly Gregor pushed the chair towards the door, then let go of it,
caught hold of the door for support—the soles at the end of his little legs
were somewhat sticky—and rested against it for a moment after his efforts. Then he set himself to turning the key in the lock with his mouth.
It seemed, unhappily, that he hadn't really any teeth—what could he grip
the key with?—but on the other hand his jaws were certainly very strong;
with their help he did manage to set the key in motion, heedless of the
fact that he was undoubtedly damaging them somewhere, since a brown
fluid issued from his mouth, flowed over the key and dripped on the floor.
"Just listen to that," said the chief clerk next door; "he's turning the key."
That was a great encouragement to Gregor; but they should all have
shouted encouragement to him, his father and mother too: "Go on, Gregor," they should have called out, "keep going, hold on to that key!" And
in the belief that they were all following his efforts intently, he clenched
his jaws recklessly on the key with all the force at his command. As the
turning of the key progressed he circled round the lock, holding on now
only with his mouth, pushing on the key, as required, or pulling it down
again with all the weight of his body. The louder click of the finally
yielding lock literally quickened Gregor. With a deep breath of relief he
said to himself: "So I didn't need the locksmith," and laid his head on the
handle to open the door wide.

Since he had to pull the door towards him, he was still invisible when
it was really wide open. He had to edge himself slowly round the near
half of the double door, and to do it very carefully if he was not to fall

plump upon his back just on the threshold. He was still carrying out this difficult manoeuvre, with no time to observe anything else, when he heard the chief clerk utter a loud "Oh!"—it sounded like a gust of wind— and now he could see the man, standing as he was nearest to the door, clapping one hand before his open mouth and slowly backing away as if driven by some invisible steady pressure. His mother—in spite of the chief clerk's being there her hair was still undone and sticking up in all direc- tions—first clasped her hands and looked at his father, then took two steps towards Gregor and fell on the floor among her outspread skirts, her face quite hidden on her breast. His father knotted his fist with a fierce expres- sion on his face as if he meant to knock Gregor back into his room, then looked uncertainly round the living room, covered his eyes with his hands and wept till his great chest heaved.

Gregor did not go now into the living room, but leaned against the inside of the firmly shut wing of the door, so that only half his body was visible and his head above it bending sideways to look at the others. The light had meanwhile strengthened; on the other side of the street one could see clearly a section of the endlessly long, dark gray building oppo- site—it was a hospital—abruptly punctuated by its row of regular win- dows; the rain was still falling, but only in large singly discernible and literally singly splashing drops. The breakfast dishes were set out on the table lavishly, for breakfast was the most important meal of the day to Gregor's father, who lingered it out for hours over various newspapers. Right opposite Gregor on the wall hung a photograph of himself on mili- tary service, as a lieutenant, hand on sword, a carefree smile on his face, inviting one to respect his uniform and military bearing. The door leading to the hall was open, and one could see that the front door stood open too, showing the landing beyond and the beginning of the stairs going down.

"Well," said Gregor, knowing perfectly that he was the only one who had retained any composure, "I'll put my clothes on at once, pack up my samples and start off. Will you only let me go? You see, sir, I'm not obsti- nate, and I'm willing to work; traveling is a hard life, but I couldn't live without it. Where are you going, sir? To the office? Yes? Will you give a true account of all this? One can be temporarily incapacitated, but that's just the moment for remembering former services and bearing in mind that later on, when the incapacity has been got over, one will certainly work with all the more industry and concentration. I'm loyally bound to serve the chief, you know that very well. Besides, I have to provide for my parents and my sister. I'm in great difficulties, but I'll get out of them again. Don't make things any worse for me than they are. Stand up for me in the firm. Travelers are not popular there, I know. People think they earn sacks of money and just have a good time. A prejudice there's no particular reason for revising. But you, sir, have a more comprehensive view of affairs than the rest of the staff, yes, let me tell you in confidence, a more comprehensive view than the chief himself, who, being the owner, lets his judgment easily be swayed against one of his employees. And you know very well that the traveler, who is never seen in the office almost the whole year round, can so easily fall a victim to gossip and ill luck and unfounded complaints, which he mostly knows nothing about, except when he comes back exhausted from his rounds, and only then suffers in person from their evil consequences, which he can no longer trace back to the original causes. Sir, sir, don't go away without a word to me to show that you think me in the right at least to some extent!"

But at Gregor's very first words the chief clerk had already backed away and only stared at him with parted lips over one twitching shoulder. And while Gregor was speaking he did not stand still one moment but stole away towards the door, without taking his eyes off Gregor, yet only an inch at a time, as if obeying some secret injunction to leave the room. He was already at the hall, and the suddenness with which he took his last step out of the living room would have made one believe he had burned the sole of his foot. Once in the hall he stretched his right arm before him towards the staircase, as if some supernatural power were waiting there to deliver him.

Gregor perceived that the chief clerk must on no account be allowed to go away in this frame of mind if his position in the firm were not to be endangered to the utmost. His parents did not understand this so well; they had convinced themselves in the course of years that Gregor was settled for life in this firm, and besides they were so preoccupied with their immediate troubles that all foresight had forsaken them. Yet Gregor had this foresight. The chief clerk must be detained, soothed, persuaded and finally won over; the whole future of Gregor and his family depended on it! If only his sister had been there! She was intelligent; she had begun to cry while Gregor was still lying quietly on his back. And no doubt the chief clerk, so partial to ladies, would have been guided by her; she would have shut the door of the flat and in the hall talked him out of his horror. But she was not there, and Gregor would have to handle the situation himself. And without remembering that he was still unaware what powers of movement he possessed, without even remembering that his words in all possibility, indeed in all likelihood, would again be unintelligible, he let go the wing of the door, pushed himself through the opening, started to walk towards the chief clerk, who was already ridiculously clinging with both hands to the railing on the landing; but immediately, as he was feeling for a support, he fell down with a little cry upon all his numerous legs. Hardly was he down when he experienced for the first time this morning a sense of physical comfort; his legs had firm ground under them; they were completely obedient, as he noted with joy; they even strove to carry him forward in whatever direction he chose; and he was inclined to believe that a final relief from all his sufferings was at hand. But in the same moment as he found himself on the floor, rocking with suppressed eagerness to move, not far from his mother, indeed just in front of her, she, who had seemed so completely crushed, sprang all at once to her feet, her arms and fingers outspread, cried: "Help, for God's sake, help!" bent her head down as if to see Gregor better, yet on the contrary kept backing senselessly away; had quite forgotten that the laden table stood behind her; sat upon it hastily, as if in absence of mind, when she bumped into it; and seemed altogether unaware that the big coffee pot beside her was upset and pouring coffee in a flood over the carpet.

"Mother, Mother," said Gregor in a low voice, and looked up at her. The chief clerk, for the moment, had quite slipped from his mind; instead, he could not resist snapping his jaws together at the sight of the streaming coffee. That made his mother scream again, she fled from the table and fell into the arms of his father, who hastened to catch her. But

Gregor had now no time to spare for his parents; the chief clerk was already on the stairs; with his chin on the banisters he was taking one last backward look. Gregor made a spring, to be as sure as possible of overtaking him; the chief clerk must have divined his intention, for he leaped down several steps and vanished; he was still yelling "Ugh!" and it echoed through the whole staircase.

Unfortunately, the flight of the chief clerk seemed completely to upset Gregor's father, who had remained relatively calm until now, for instead of running after the man himself, or at least not hindering Gregor in his pursuit, he seized in his right hand the walking stick which the chief clerk had left behind on a chair, together with a hat and greatcoat, snatched in his left hand a large newspaper from the table and began stamping his feet and flourishing the stick and the newspaper to drive Gregor back into his room. No entreaty of Gregor's availed, indeed no entreaty was even understood, however humbly he bent his head his father only stamped on the floor the more loudly. Behind his father his mother had torn open a window, despite the cold weather, and was leaning far out of it with her face in her hands. A strong draught set in from the street to the staircase, the window curtains blew in, the newspapers on the table fluttered, stray pages whisked over the floor. Pitilessly Gregor's father drove him back, hissing and crying "Shoo!" like a savage. But Gregor was quite unpracticed in walking backwards, it really was a slow business. If he only had a chance to turn round he could get back to his room at once, but he was afraid of exasperating his father by the slowness of such a rotation and at any moment the stick in his father's hand might hit him a fatal blow on the back or on the head. In the end, however, nothing else was left for him to do since to his horror he observed that in moving backwards he could not even control the direction he took; and so, keeping an anxious eye on his father all the time over his shoulder, he began to turn round as quickly as he could, which was in reality very slowly. Perhaps his father noted his good intentions, for he did not interfere except every now and then to help him in the manoeuvre from a distance with the point of the stick. If only he would have stopped making that unbearable hissing noise! It made Gregor quite lose his head. He had turned almost completely round when the hissing noise so distracted him that he even turned a little the wrong way again. But when at last his head was fortunately right in front of the doorway, it appeared that his body was too broad simply to get through the opening. His father, of course in his present mood was far from thinking of such a thing as opening the other half of the door, to let Gregor have enough space. He had merely the fixed idea of driving Gregor back into his room as quickly as possible. He would never have suffered Gregor to make the circumstantial preparations for standing up on end and perhaps slipping his way through the door. Maybe he was now making more noise than ever to urge Gregor forward, as if no obstacle impeded him; to Gregor, anyhow, the noise in his rear sounded no longer like the voice of one single father; this was really no joke, and Gregor thrust himself—come what might—into the doorway. One side of his body rose up, he was tilted at an angle in the doorway, his flank was quite bruised, horrid blotches stained the white door, soon he was stuck fast and, left to himself, could not have moved at all, his legs on one side fluttered trembling in the air, those on the other were crushed painfully to the floor—when from behind his father gave him a strong push which was literally a deliverance and he flew far into the room, bleeding freely. The door was slammed behind him with the stick, and then at last there was silence.

II

Not until it was twilight did Gregor awake out of a deep sleep, more like a swoon than a sleep. He would certainly have waked up of his own accord not much later, for he felt himself sufficiently rested and well-slept, but it seemed to him as if a fleeting step and a cautious shutting of the door leading into the hall had aroused him. The electric lights in the street cast a pale sheen here and there on the ceiling and the upper surfaces of the furniture, but down below, where he lay, it was dark. Slowly, awkwardly trying out his feelers, which he now first learned to appreciate, he pushed his way to the door to see what had been happening there. His left side felt like one single long, unpleasantly tense scar, and he had actually to limp on his two rows of legs. One little leg, moreover, had been severely damaged in the course of that morning's events—it was almost a miracle that only one had been damaged—and trailed uselessly behind him.

He had reached the door before he discovered what had really drawn him to it: the smell of food. For there stood a basin filled with fresh milk in which floated little sops of white bread. He could almost have laughed with joy, since he was now still hungrier than in the morning, and he dipped his head almost over the eyes straight into the milk. But soon in disappointment he withdrew it again; not only did he find it difficult to feed because of his tender left side—and he could only feed with the palpitating collaboration of his whole body—he did not like the milk either, although milk had been his favorite drink and that was certainly why his sister had set it there for him, indeed it was almost with repulsion that he turned away from the basin and crawled back to the middle of the room.

He could see through the crack of the door that the gas was turned on in the living room, but while usually at this time his father made a habit of reading the afternoon newspaper in a loud voice to his mother and occasionally to his sister as well, not a sound was now to be heard. Well, perhaps his father had recently given up this habit of reading aloud, which his sister had mentioned so often in conversation and in her letters. But there was the same silence all around, although the flat was certainly not empty of occupants. "What a quiet life our family has been leading," said Gregor to himself, and as he sat there motionless staring into the darkness he felt great pride in the fact that he had been able to provide such a life for his parents and sister in such a fine flat. But what if all the quiet, the comfort, the contentment were now to end in horror? To keep himself from being lost in such thoughts Gregor took refuge in movement and crawled up and down the room.

Once during the long evening one of the side doors was opened a little and quickly shut again, later the other side door too; someone had apparently wanted to come in and then thought better of it. Gregor now stationed himself immediately before the living room door, determined to persuade any hesitating visitor to come in or at least to discover who it might be; but the door was not opened again and he waited in vain. In the early morning, when the doors were locked, they had all wanted to

come in, now that he had opened one door and the other had apparently
been opened during the day, no one came in and even the keys were on
the other side of the doors.

It was late at night before the gas went out in the living room, and
Gregor could easily tell that his parents and his sister had all stayed
awake until then, for he could clearly hear the three of them stealing
away on tiptoe. No one was likely to visit him, not until the morning, that
was certain; so he had plenty of time to meditate at his leisure on how he
was to arrange his life afresh. But the lofty, empty room in which he had
to lie flat on the floor filled him with an apprehension he could not account for, since it had been his very own room for the past five years—and
with a half-unconscious action, not without a slight feeling of shame, he
scuttled under the sofa, where he felt comfortable at once, although his
back was a little cramped and he could not lift his head up, and his only
regret was that his body was too broad to get the whole of it under the
sofa.

He stayed there all night, spending the time partly in a light slumber,
from which his hunger kept waking him up with a start, and partly in
worrying and sketching vague hopes, which all led to the same conclusion, that he must lie low for the present and, by exercising patience and
the utmost consideration, help the family to bear the inconvenience he
was bound to cause them in his present condition.

Very early in the morning, it was still almost night, Gregor had the
chance to test the strength of his new resolutions, for his sister, nearly
fully dressed, opened the door from the hall and peered in. She did not
see him at once, yet when she caught sight of him under the sofa—well,
he had to be somewhere, he couldn't have flown away, could he?—she
was so startled that without being able to help it she slammed the door
shut again. But as if regretting her behavior she opened the door again
immediately and came in on tiptoe, as if she were visiting an invalid or
even a stranger. Gregor had pushed his head forward to the very edge of
the sofa and watched her. Would she notice that he had left the milk
standing, and not for lack of hunger, and would she bring in some other
kind of food more to his taste? If she did not do it of her own accord, he
would rather starve than draw her attention to the fact, although he felt a
wild impulse to dart out from under the sofa, throw himself at her feet
and beg her for something to eat. But his sister at once noticed, with
surprise, that the basin was still full, except for a little milk that had been
spilt all around it, she lifted it immediately, not with her bare hands,
true, but with a cloth and carried it away. Gregor was wildly curious to
know what she would bring instead, and made various speculations about
it. Yet what she actually did next, in the goodness of her heart, he could
never have guessed at. To find out what he liked she brought him a whole
selection of food, all set on an old newspaper. There were old, half-
decayed vegetables, bones from last night's supper covered with a white
sauce that had thickened; some raisins and almonds; a piece of cheese
that Gregor would have called uneatable two days ago; a dry roll of
bread, a buttered roll, and a roll both buttered and salted. Besides all
that, she set down again the same basin, into which she had poured some
water, and which was apparently to be reserved for his exclusive use. And
with fine tact, knowing that Gregor would not eat in her presence, she
withdrew quickly and even turned the key, to let him understand that he

could take his ease as much as he liked. Gregor's legs all whizzed towards the food. His wounds must have healed completely, moreover, for he felt no disability, which amazed him and made him reflect how more than a month ago he had cut one finger a little with a knife and had still suffered pain from the wound only the day before yesterday. Am I less sensitive now? he thought, and sucked greedily at the cheese, which above all the other edibles attracted him at once and strongly. One after another and with tears of satisfaction in his eyes he quickly devoured the cheese, the vegetables and the sauce; the fresh food, on the other hand, had no charms for him, he could not even stand the smell of it and actually dragged away to some little distance the things he could eat. He had long finished his meal and was only lying lazily on the same spot when his sister turned the key slowly as a sign for him to retreat. That roused him at once, although he was nearly asleep, and he hurried under the sofa again. But it took considerable self-control for him to stay under the sofa, even for the short time his sister was in the room, since the large meal had swollen his body somewhat and he was so cramped he could hardly breathe. Slight attacks of breathlessness afflicted him and his eyes were starting a little out of his head as he watched his unsuspecting sister sweeping together with a broom not only the remains of what he had eaten but even the things he had not touched, as if these were now of no use to anyone, and hastily shoveling it all into a bucket, which she covered with a wooden lid and carried away. Hardly had she turned her back when Gregor came from under the sofa and stretched and puffed himself out.

In this manner Gregor was fed, once in the early morning while his parents and the servant girl were still asleep, and a second time after they had all had their midday dinner, for then his parents took a short nap and the servant girl could be sent out on some errand or other by his sister. Not that they would have wanted him to starve, of course, but perhaps they could not have borne to know more about his feeding than from hearsay, perhaps too his sister wanted to spare them such little anxieties wherever possible, since they had quite enough to bear as it was.

Under what pretext the doctor and the locksmith had been got rid of on that first morning Gregor could not discover, for since what he said was not understood by the others it never struck any of them, not even his sister, that he could understand what they said, and so whenever his sister came into his room he had to content himself with hearing her utter only a sigh now and then and an occasional appeal to the saints. Later on, when she had got a little used to the situation—of course she could never get completely used to it—she sometimes threw out a remark which was kindly meant or could be so interpreted. "Well, he liked his dinner today," she would say when Gregor had made a good clearance of his food; and when he had not eaten, which gradually happened more and more often, she would say almost sadly: "Everything's been left standing again."

But although Gregor could get no news directly, he overheard a lot from the neighboring rooms, and as soon as voices were audible, he would run to the door of the room concerned and press his whole body against it. In the first few days especially there was no conversation that did not refer to him somehow, even if only indirectly. For two whole days there were family consultations at every mealtime about what should be done;

but also between meals the same subject was discussed, for there were always at least two members of the family at home, since no one wanted to be alone in the flat and to leave it quite empty was unthinkable. And on the very first of these days the household cook—it was not quite clear what and how much she knew of the situation—went down on her knees to his mother and begged leave to go, and when she departed, a quarter of an hour later, gave thanks for her dismissal with tears in her eyes as if for the greatest benefit that could have been conferred on her, and without any prompting swore a solemn oath that she would never say a single word to anyone about what had happened.

Now Gregor's sister had to cook too, helping her mother; true, the cooking did not amount to much, for they ate scarcely anything. Gregor was always hearing one of the family vainly urging another to eat and getting no answer but: "Thanks, I've had all I want," or something similar. Perhaps they drank nothing either. Time and again his sister kept asking his father if he wouldn't like some beer and offered kindly to go and fetch it herself, and when he made no answer suggested that she could ask the concierge to fetch it, so that he need feel no sense of obligation, but then a round "No" came from his father and no more was said about it.

In the course of that very first day Gregor's father explained the family's financial position and prospects to both his mother and his sister. Now and then he rose from the table to get some voucher or memorandum out of the small safe he had rescued from the collapse of his business five years earlier. One could hear him opening the complicated lock and rustling papers out and shutting it again. This statement made by his father was the first cheerful information Gregor had heard since his imprisonment. He had been of the opinion that nothing at all was left from his father's business, at least his father had never said anything to the contrary, and of course he had not asked him directly. At that time Gregor's sole desire was to do his utmost to help the family to forget as soon as possible the catastrophe which had overwhelmed the business and thrown them all into a state of complete despair. And so he had set to work with unusual ardor and almost overnight had become a commercial traveler instead of a little clerk, with of course much greater chances of earning money, and his success was immediately translated into good round coin which he could lay on the table for his amazed and happy family. These had been fine times, and they had never recurred, at least not with the same sense of glory, although later on Gregor had earned so much money that he was able to meet the expenses of the whole household and did so. They had simply got used to it, both the family and Gregor; the money was gratefully accepted and gladly given, but there was no special uprush of warm feeling. With his sister alone had he remained intimate, and it was a secret plan of his that she, who loved music, unlike himself, and could play movingly on the violin, should be sent next year to study at the Conservatorium, despite the great expense that would entail, which must be made up in some other way. During his brief visits home the Conservatorium was often mentioned in the talks he had with his sister, but always merely as a beautiful dream which could never come true, and his parents discouraged even these innocent references to it; yet Gregor had made up his mind firmly about it and meant to announce the fact with due solemnity on Christmas Day.

Such were the thoughts, completely futile in his present condition, that went through his head as he stood clinging upright to the door and listening. Sometimes out of sheer weariness he had to give up listening and let his head fall negligently against the door, but he always had to pull himself together again at once, for even the slight sound his head made was audible next door and brought all conversation to a stop. "What can he be doing now?" his father would say after a while, obviously turning towards the door, and only then would the interrupted conversation gradually be set going agian.

Gregor was now informed as amply as he could wish—for his father tended to repeat himself in his explanations, partly because it was a long time since he had handled such matters and partly because his mother could not always grasp things at once—that a certain amount of investments, a very small amount it was true, had survived the wreck of their fortunes and had even increased a little because the dividends had not been touched meanwhile. And besides that, the money Gregor brought home every month—he had kept only a few dollars for himself—had never been quite used up and now amounted to a small capital sum. Behind the door Gregor nodded his head eagerly, rejoiced at this evidence of unexpected thrift and foresight. True, he could really have paid off some more of his father's debts to the chief with this extra money, and so brought much nearer the day on which he could quit his job, but doubtless it was better the way his father had arranged it.

Yet this capital was by no means sufficient to let the family live on the interest of it; for one year, perhaps, or at the most two, they could live on the principal, that was all. It was simply a sum that ought not to be touched and should be kept for a rainy day; money for living expenses would have to be earned. Now his father was still hale enough but an old man, and he had done no work for the past five years and could not be expected to do much; during these five years, the first years of leisure in his laborious though unsuccessful life, he had grown rather fat and become sluggish. And Gregor's old mother, how was she to earn a living with her asthma, which troubled her even when she walked through the flat and kept her lying on a sofa every other day panting for breath beside an open window? And was his sister to earn her bread, she who was still a child of seventeen and whose life hitherto had been so pleasant, consisting as it did in dressing herself nicely, sleeping long, helping in the housekeeping, going out to a few modest entertainments and above all playing the violin? At first whenever the need for earning money was mentioned Gregor let go his hold on the door and threw himself down on the cool leather sofa beside it, he felt so hot with shame and grief.

Often he just lay there the long nights through without sleeping at all, scrabbling for hours on the leather. Or he nerved himself to the great effort of pushing an armchair to the window, then crawled up over the window sill and, braced against the chair, leaned against the window panes, obviously in some recollection of the sense of freedom that looking out of a window always used to give him. For in reality day by day things that were even a little way off were growing dimmer to his sight; the hospital across the street, which he used to execrate for being all too often before his eyes, was now quite beyond his range of vision, and if he had not known that he lived in Charlotte Street, a quiet street but still a city street, he might have believed that his window gave on a desert waste where gray sky and gray land blended indistinguishably into each other. His quick-witted sister only needed to observe twice that the arm-chair stood by the window; after that whenever she had tidied the room she always pushed the chair back to the same place at the window and even left the inner casements open.

If he could have spoken to her and thanked her for all she had to do for him, he could have borne her ministrations better; as it was, they oppressed him. She certainly tried to make as light as possible of whatever was disagreeable in her task, and as time went on she succeeded, of course, more and more, but time brought more enlightenment to Gregor too. The very way she came in distressed him. Hardly was she in the room when she rushed to the window, without even taking time to shut the door, careful as she was usually to shield the sight of Gregor's room from the others, and as if she were almost suffocating tore the casements open with hasty fingers, standing then in the open draught for a while even in the bitterest cold and drawing deep breaths. This noisy scurry of hers upset Gregor twice a day; he would crouch trembling under the sofa all the time, knowing quite well that she would certainly have spared him such a disturbance had she found it at all possible to stay in his presence without opening the window.

On one occasion, about a month after Gregor's metamorphosis, when there was surely no reason for her to be still startled at his appearance, she came a little earlier than usual and found him gazing out of the window, quite motionless, and thus well placed to look like a bogey. Gregor would not have been surprised had she not come in at all, for she could not immediately open the window while he was there, but not only did she retreat, she jumped back as if in alarm and banged the door shut; a stranger might have thought that he had been lying in wait for her there meaning to bite her. Of course he hid himself under the sofa at once, but he had to wait until midday before she came again, and she seemed more ill at ease than usual. This made him realize how repulsive the sight of him still was to her, and that it was bound to go on being repulsive, and what an effort it must cost her not to run away even from the sight of the small portion of his body that stuck out from under the sofa. In order to spare her that, therefore, one day he carried a sheet on his back to the sofa—it cost him four hours' labor—and arranged it there in such a way as to hide him completely, so that even if she were to bend down she could not see him. Had she considered the sheet unnecessary, she would certainly have stripped it off the sofa again, for it was clear enough that this curtaining and confining of himself was not likely to conduce to Gregor's comfort, but she left it where it was, and Gregor even fancied that he caught a thankful glance from her eye when he lifted the sheet carefully a very little with his head to see how she was taking the new arrangement.

For the first fortnight his parents could not bring themselves to the point of entering his room, and he often heard them expressing their appreciation of his sister's activities, whereas formerly they had frequently scolded her for being as they thought a somewhat useless daughter. But now, both of them waited outside the door, his father and his mother, while his sister tidied his room, and as soon as she came out she had to tell them exactly how things were in the room, what Gregor had eaten, how he had conducted himself this time and whether there was not perhaps some slight improvement in his condition. His mother, moreover, began relatively soon to want to visit him, but his father and sister dissuaded her at first with arguments which Gregor listened to very attentively and altogether approved. Later, however, she had to be held back by main force, and when she cried out: "Do let me in to Gregor, he is my unfortunate son! Can't you understand that I must go to him?" Gregor thought that it might be well to have her come in, not every day, of course, but perhaps once a week; she understood things, after all, much better than his sister, who was only a child despite the efforts she was making and had perhaps taken on so difficult a task merely out of childish thoughtlessness.

Gregor's desire to see his mother was soon fulfilled. During the daytime he did not want to show himself at the window, out of consideration for his parents, but he could not crawl very far around the few square yards of floor space he had, nor could he bear lying quietly at rest all during the night, while he was fast losing any interest he had ever taken in food, so that for mere recreation he had formed the habit of crawling crisscross over the walls and ceiling. He especially enjoyed hanging suspended from the ceiling; it was much better than lying on the floor; one could breathe more freely; one's body swung and rocked lightly; and in the almost blissful absorption induced by this suspension it could happen to his own surprise that he let go and fell plump on the floor. Yet he now had his body much better under control than formerly, and even such a big fall did him no harm. His sister had once remarked the new distraction Gregor had found for himself—he left traces behind him of the sticky stuff on his soles wherever he crawled—and she got the idea in her head of giving him as wide a field as possible to crawl in and of removing the pieces of furniture that hindered him, above all the chest of drawers and the writing desk. But that was more than she could manage all by herself; she did not dare ask her father to help her; and as for the servant girl, a young creature of sixteen who had had the courage to stay on after the cook's departure, she could not be asked to help, for she had begged as an especial favor that she might keep the kitchen door locked and open it only on a definite summons; so there was nothing left but to apply to her mother at an hour when her father was out. And the old lady did come, with exclamations of joyful eagerness, which, however, died away at the door of Gregor's room. Gregor's sister, of course, went in first, to see that everything was in order before letting his mother enter. In great haste Gregor pulled the sheet lower and rucked it more in folds so that it really looked as if it had been thrown accidentally over the sofa. And this time he did not peer out from under it; he renounced the pleasure of seeing his mother on this occasion and was only glad she had come at all. "Come in, he's out of sight," said his sister, obviously leading her mother in by the hand. Gregor could now hear the two women struggling to shift the heavy old chest from its place, and his sister claiming the greater part of the labor for herself, without listening to the admonitions of her mother who feared she might overstrain herself. It took a long time. After at least a quarter of an hour's tugging his mother objected that the chest had better be left where it was, for in the first place it was too heavy and could never be got out before his father came home, and standing in the middle of the room like that it would only hamper Gregor's movements, while in the second place it was not at all certain that removing the furniture would be doing a service to Gregor. She was inclined to think to the contrary; the sight of the naked walls made her own heart heavy and why shouldn't Gregor have the same feeling, considering that he had been used to his furniture for so long and might feel forlorn without it. "And doesn't it look," she concluded in a low voice—in fact she had been almost whispering all the time as if to avoid letting Gregor, whose exact whereabouts she did not know, hear even the tones of her voice, for she was convinced that he could not understand her words—"doesn't it look as if we were showing him, by taking away his furniture, that we have given up hope of his ever getting better and are just leaving him coldly to himself? I think it would be best to keep his room exactly as it has always been, so that when he comes back to us he will find everything unchanged and be able all the more easily to forget what has happened in between."

On hearing these words from his mother Gregor realized that the lack of all direct human speech for the past two months together with the monotony of family life must have confused his mind, otherwise he could not account for the fact that he had quite earnestly looked forward to having his room emptied of furnishing. Did he really want his warm room, so comfortably fitted with old family furniture, to be turned into a naked den in which he would certainly be able to crawl unhampered in all directions but at the price of shedding simultaneously all recollection of his human background? He had indeed been so near the brink of forgetfulness that only the voice of his mother, which he had not heard for so long, had drawn him back from it. Nothing should be taken out of his room; everything must stay as it was; he could not dispense with the good influence of the furniture on his state of mind; and even if the furniture did hamper him in his senseless crawling round and round, that was no drawback but a great advantage.

Unfortunately his sister was of the contrary opinion; she had grown accustomed, and not without reason, to consider herself an expert in Gregor's affairs as against her parents, and so her mother's advice was now enough to make her determined on the removal not only of the chest and the writing desk, which had been her first intention, but of all the furniture except the indispensable sofa. This determination was not, of course, merely the outcome of childish recalcitrance and of the self-confidence she had recently developed so unexpectedly and at such cost; she had in fact perceived that Gregor needed a lot of space to crawl about in, while on the other hand he never used the furniture at all, so far as could be seen. Another factor might have been also the enthusiastic temperament of an adolescent girl, which seeks to indulge herself on every opportunity and which now tempted Grete to exaggerate the horror of her brother's circumstances in order that she might do all the more for him. In a room where Gregor lorded it all alone over empty walls no one save herself was likely ever to set foot.

And so she was not to be moved from her resolve by her mother, who seemed moreover to be ill at ease in Gregor's room and therefore unsure of herself, was soon reduced to silence and helped her daughter as best she could to push the chest outside. Now, Gregor could do without the chest, if need be, but the writing desk he must retain. As soon as the two women had got the chest out of his room, groaning as they pushed it, Gregor stuck his head out from under the sofa to see how he might intervene as kindly and cautiously as possible. But as bad luck would have it, his mother was the first to return, leaving Grete clasping the chest in the room next door where she was trying to shift it all by herself, without of course moving it from the spot. His mother however was not accustomed to the sight of him, it might sicken her and so in alarm Gregor backed quickly to the other end of the sofa, yet could not prevent the sheet from swaying a little in front. That was enough to put her on the alert. She paused, stood still for a moment and then went back to Grete.

Although Gregor kept reassuring himself that nothing out of the way was happening, but only a few bits of furniture were being changed around, he soon had to admit that all this trotting to and fro of the two women, their little ejaculations and the scraping of furniture along the floor affected him like a vast disturbance coming from all sides at once, and however much he tucked in his head and legs and cowered to the very floor he was bound to confess that he would not be able to stand it for long. They were clearing his room out; taking away everything he loved; the chest in which he kept his fret saw and other tools was already dragged off; they were now loosening the writing desk which had almost sunk into the floor, the desk at which he had done all his homework when he was at the commercial academy, at the grammar school before that, and, yes, even at the primary school—he had no more time to waste in weighing the good intentions of the two women, whose existence he had by now almost forgotten, for they were so exhausted that they were laboring in silence and nothing could be heard but the heavy scuffling of their feet.

And so he rushed out—the women were just leaning against the writing desk in the next room to give themselves a breather—and four times changed his direction, since he really did not know what to rescue first, then on the wall opposite, which was already otherwise cleared, he was struck by the picture of the lady muffled in so much fur and quickly crawled up to it and pressed himself to the glass, which was a good surface to hold on to and comforted his hot belly. This picture at least, which was entirely hidden beneath him, was going to be removed by nobody. He turned his head towards the door of the living room so as to observe the women when they came back.

They had not allowed themselves much of a rest and were already coming; Grete had twined her arm round her mother and was almost supporting her. "Well, what shall we take now?" said Grete, looking round. Her eyes met Gregor's from the wall. She kept her composure, presumably because of her mother, bent her head down to her mother, to keep her from looking up, and said, although in a fluttering, unpremeditated voice: "Come, hadn't we better go back to the living room for a moment?" Her intentions were clear enough to Gregor, she wanted to bestow her mother in safety and then chase him down from the wall. Well, just let her try it! He clung to his picture and would not give it up. He would rather fly in Grete's face.

But Grete's words had succeeded in disquieting her mother, who took a step to one side, caught sight of the huge brown mass on the flowered wallpaper, and before she was really conscious that what she saw was Gregor screamed in a loud, hoarse voice: "Oh God, oh God!" fell with outspread arms over the sofa as if giving up and did not move. "Gregor!"

cried his sister, shaking her fist and glaring at him This was the first time she had directly addressed him since his metamorphosis. She ran into the next room for some aromatic essence with which to rouse her mother from her fainting fit. Gregor wanted to help too—there was still time to rescue the picture—but he was stuck fast to the glass and had to tear himself loose; he then ran after his sister into the next room as if he could advise her, as he used to do; but then had to stand helplessly behind her; she meanwhile searched among various small bottles and when she turned round started in alarm at the sight of him; one bottle fell on the floor and broke; a splinter of glass cut Gregor's face and some kind of corrosive medicine splashed him; without pausing a moment longer Grete gathered up all the bottles she could carry and ran to her mother with them; she banged the door shut with her foot. Gregor was now cut off from his mother, who was perhaps nearly dying because of him; he dared not open the door for fear of frightening away his sister, who had to stay with her mother; there was nothing he could do but wait; and harassed by self-reproach and worry he began now to crawl to and fro, over everything, walls, furniture and ceiling, and finally in his despair, when the whole room seemed to be reeling round him, fell down on the middle of the big table.

A little while elapsed, Gregor was still lying there feebly and all around was quiet, perhaps that was a good omen. Then the doorbell rang. The servant girl was of course locked in her kitchen, and Grete would have to open the door. It was his father. "What's been happening?" were his first words; Grete's face must have told him everything. Grete answered in a muffled voice, apparently hiding her head on his breast: "Mother has been fainting, but she's better now. Gregor's broken loose." "Just what I expected," said his father, "just what I've been telling you, but you women would never listen." It was clear to Gregor that his father had taken the worst interpretation of Grete's all too brief statement and was assuming that Gregor had been guilty of some violent act. Therefore Gregor must now try to propitiate his father, since he had neither time nor means for an explanation. And so he fled to the door of his own room and crouched against it, to let his father see as soon as he came in from the hall that his son had the good intention of getting back into his room immediately and that it was not necessary to drive him there, but that if only the door were opened he would disappear at once.

Yet his father was not in the mood to perceive such fine distinctions. "Ah!" he cried as soon as he appeared, in a tone which sounded at once angry and exultant. Gregor drew his head back from the door and lifted it to look at his father. Truly, this was not the father he had imagined to himself; admittedly he had been too absorbed of late in his new recreation of crawling over the ceiling to take the same interest as before in what was happening elsewhere in the flat, and he ought really to be prepared for some changes. And yet, and yet, could that be his father? The man who used to lie wearily sunk in bed whenever Gregor set out on a business journey; who welcomed him back of an evening lying in a long chair in a dressing gown; who could not really rise to his feet but only lifted his arms in greeting, and on the rare occasions when he did go out with his family, on one or two Sundays a year and on high holidays, walked between Gregor and his mother, who were slow walkers anyhow, even more slowly than they did, muffled in his old greatcoat, shuffling laboriously forward with the help of his crook-handled stick which he set down most cautiously at every step and, whenever he wanted to say anything, nearly always came to a full stop and gathered his escort around him? Now he was standing there in fine shape; dressed in a smart blue uniform with gold buttons, such as bank messengers wear; his strong double chin bulged over the stiff high collar of his jacket; from under his bushy eyebrows his black eyes darted fresh and penetrating glances; his onetime tangled white hair had been combed flat on either side of a shining and carefully exact parting. He pitched his cap, which bore a gold monogram, probably the badge of some bank, in a wide sweep across the whole room on to a sofa and with the tail-ends of his jacket thrown back, his hands in his trouser pockets, advanced with a grim visage towards Gregor. Likely enough he did not himself know what he meant to do, at any rate he lifted his feet uncommonly high, and Gregor was dumbfounded at the enormous size of his shoe soles. But Gregor could not risk standing up to him, aware as he had been from the very first day of his new life that his father believed only the severest measures suitable for dealing with him. And so he ran before his father, stopping when he stopped and scuttling forward again when his father made any kind of move. In this way they circled the room several times without anything decisive happening, indeed the whole operation did not even look like a pursuit because it was carried out so slowly. And so Gregor did not leave the floor, for he feared that his father might take as a piece of peculiar wickedness any excursion of his over the walls or the ceiling. All the same, he could not stay this course much longer, for while his father took one step he had to carry out a whole series of movements. He was already beginning to feel breathless, just as in his former life his lungs had not been very dependable. As he was staggering along, trying to concentrate his energy on running, hardly keeping his eyes open; in his dazed state never even thinking of any other escape than simply going forward; and having almost forgotten that the walls were free to him, which in this room were well provided with finely carved pieces of furniture full of knobs and crevices—suddenly something lightly flung landed close behind him and rolled before him. It was an apple; a second apple followed immediately; Gregor came to a stop in alarm; there was no point in running on, for his father was determined to bombard him. He had filled his pockets with fruit from the dish on the sideboard and was now shying apple after apple, without taking particularly good aim for the moment. The small red apples rolled about the floor as if magnetized and cannoned into each other. An apple thrown without much force grazed Gregor's back and glanced off harmlessly. But another following immediately landed right on his back and sank in; Gregor wanted to drag himself forward, as if this startling, incredible pain could be left behind him; but he felt as if nailed to the spot and flattened himself out in a complete derangement of all his senses. With his last conscious look he saw the door of his room being torn open and his mother rushing out ahead of his screaming sister, in her underbodice, for her daughter had loosened her clothing to let her breathe more freely and recover from her swoon, he saw his mother rushing towards his father, leaving one after another behind her on the floor her loosened petticoats, stumbling over her petticoats straight to his father and embracing him, in complete union with him—but here Gregor's sight began to fail—with her hands clasped round his father's neck as she begged for her son's life.

III

The serious injury done to Gregor, which disabled him for more than a month—the apple went on sticking in his body as a visible reminder, since no one ventured to remove it—seemed to have made even his father recollect that Gregor was a member of the family, despite his present unfortunate and repulsive shape, and ought not to be treated as an enemy, that, on the contrary, family duty required the suppression of disgust and the exercise of patience, nothing but patience.

And although his injury had impaired, probably for ever, his powers of movement, and for the time being it took him long, long minutes to creep across his room like an old invalid—there was no question now of crawling up the wall—yet in his opinion he was sufficiently compensated for this worsening of his condition by the fact that towards evening the living-room door, which he used to watch intently for an hour or two beforehand, was always thrown open, so that lying in the darkness of his room, invisible to the family, he could see them all at the lamp-lit table and listen to their talk, by general consent as it were, very different from his earlier eavesdropping.

True, their intercourse lacked the lively character of former times, which he had always called to mind with a certain wistfulness in the small hotel bedrooms where he had been wont to throw himself down, tired out, on damp bedding. They were now mostly very silent. Soon after supper his father would fall asleep in his armchair; his mother and sister would admonish each other to be silent; his mother, bending low over the lamp, stitched at fine sewing for an underwear firm; his sister, who had taken a job as a salesgirl, was learning shorthand and French in the evenings on the chance of bettering herself. Sometimes his father woke up, and as if quite unaware that he had been sleeping said to his mother: "What a lot of sewing you're doing today!" and at once fell asleep again, while the two women exchanged a tired smile.

With a kind of mulishness his father persisted in keeping his uniform on even in the house; his dressing gown hung uselessly on its peg and he slept fully dressed where he sat, as if he were ready for service at any moment and even here only at the beck and call of his superior. As a result, his uniform, which was not brand-new to start with, began to look dirty, despite all the loving care of the mother and sister to keep it clean, and Gregor often spent whole evenings gazing at the many greasy spots on the garment, gleaming with gold buttons always in a high state of polish, in which the old man sat sleeping in extreme discomfort and yet quite peacefully.

As soon as the clock struck ten his mother tried to rouse his father with gentle words and to persuade him after that to get into bed, for sitting there he could not have a proper sleep and that was what he needed most, since he had to go on duty at six. But with the mulishness that had obsessed him since he became a bank messenger he always insisted on staying longer at the table, although he regularly fell asleep again and in the end only with the greatest trouble could be got out of his armchair and into his bed. However insistently Gregor's mother and sister kept urging him with gentle reminders, he would go on slowly shaking his head for a quarter of an hour, keeping his eyes shut, and refuse to get to his feet. The mother plucked at his sleeve, whispering endearments in his ear, the sister left her lessons to come to her mother's help, but Gregor's father was not to be caught. He would only sink down deeper in his chair. Not until the two women hoisted him up by the armpits did he open his eyes and look at them both, one after the other, usually with the remark: "This is a life. This is the peace and quiet of my old age." And leaning on the two of them he would heave himself up, with difficulty, as if he were a great burden to himself, suffer them to lead him as far as the door and then wave them off and go on alone, while the mother abandoned her needlework and the sister her pen in order to run after him and help him farther.

Who could find time, in this overworked and tired-out family, to bother about Gregor more than was absolutely needful? The household was reduced more and more; the servant girl was turned off; a gigantic bony charwoman with white hair flying round her head came in morning and evening to do the rough work; everything else was done by Gregor's mother, as well as great piles of sewing. Even various family ornaments, which his mother and sister used to wear with pride at parties and celebrations, had to be sold, as Gregor discovered of an evening from hearing them all discuss the prices obtained. But what they lamented most was the fact that they could not leave the flat which was much too big for their present circumstances, because they could not think of any way to shift Gregor. Yet Gregor saw well enough that consideration for him was not the main difficulty preventing the removal, for they could have easily shifted him in some suitable box with a few air holes in it; what really kept them from moving into another flat was rather their own complete hopelessness and the belief that they had been singled out for a misfortune such as had never happened to any of their relations or acquaintances. They fulfilled to the uttermost all that the world demands of poor people, the father fetched breakfast for the small clerks in the bank, the mother devoted her energy to making underwear for strangers, the sister trotted to and fro behind the counter at the behest of customers, but more than this they had not the strength to do. And the wound in Gregor's back began to nag at him afresh when his mother and sister, after getting his father into bed, came back again, left their work lying, drew close to each other and sat cheek to cheek; when his mother, pointing towards his room, said: "Shut that door now, Grete," and he was left again in darkness, while next door the women mingled their tears or perhaps sat dry-eyed staring at the table.

Gregor hardly slept at all by night or by day. He was often haunted by the idea that next time the door opened he would take the family's affairs in hand again just as he used to do; once more, after this long interval, there appeared in his thoughts the figures of the chief and the chief clerk, the commercial travelers and the apprentices, the porter who was so dull-witted, two or three friends in other firms, a chambermaid in one of the rural hotels, a sweet and fleeting memory, a cashier in a milliner's shop, whom he had wooed earnestly but too slowly—they all appeared, together with strangers or people he had quite forgotten, but instead of helping him and his family they were one and all unapproachable and he was glad when they vanished. At other times he would not be in the mood to bother about his family, he was only filled with rage at the way they were neglecting him, and although he had no clear idea of what he might care to eat he would make plans for getting into the larder to take the food that was after all his due, even if he were not hungry. His sister no longer took thought to bring him what might especially please him, but in the morning and at noon before she went to business hurriedly pushed into his room with her foot any food that was available, and in the evening cleared it out again with one sweep of the broom, heedless of whether it had been merely tasted, or—as most frequently happened—left untouched. The cleaning of his room, which she now did always in the evenings, could not have been more hastily done. Streaks of dirt stretched along the walls, here and there lay balls of dust and filth. At first Gregor used to station himself in some particularly filthy corner when his sister arrived, in order to reproach her with it, so to speak. But he could have sat there for weeks without getting her to make any improvement; she could see the dirt as well as he did, but she had simply made up her mind to leave it alone. And yet, with a touchiness that was new to her, which seemed anyhow to have infected the whole family, she jealously guarded her claim to be the sole caretaker of Gregor's room. His mother once subjected his room to a thorough cleaning, which was achieved only by means of several buckets of water—all this dampness of course upset Gregor too and he lay widespread, sulky and motionless on the sofa—but she was well punished for it. Hardly had his sister noticed the changed aspect of his room that evening than she rushed in high dudgeon into the living room and, despite the imploringly raised hands of her mother, burst into a storm of weeping, while her parents—her father had of course been startled out of his chair—looked on at first in helpless amazement; then they too began to go into action; the father reproached the mother on his right for not having left the cleaning of Gregor's room to his sister; shrieked at the sister on his left that never again was she to be allowed to clean Gregor's room; while the mother tried to pull the father into his bedroom, since he was beyond himself with agitation; the sister, shaken with sobs, then beat upon the table with her small fists; and Gregor hissed loudly with rage because not one of them thought of shutting the door to spare him such a spectacle and so much noise.

Still, even if the sister, exhausted by her daily work, had grown tired of looking after Gregor as she did formerly, there was no need for his mother's intervention or for Gregor's being neglected at all. The charwoman was there. This old widow, whose strong bony frame had enabled her to survive the worst a long life could offer, by no means recoiled from Gregor. Without being in the least curious she had once by chance opened the door of his room and at the sight of Gregor, who, taken by surprise, began to rush to and fro although no one was chasing him, merely stood there with her arms folded. From that time she never failed to open his door a little for a moment, morning and evening, to have a look at him. At first she even used to call him to her, with words which apparently she took to be friendly, such as: "Come along, then, you old dung beetle!" or "Look at the old dung beetle, then!" To such allocutions Gregor made no answer, but stayed motionless where he was, as if the door had never been opened. Instead of being allowed to disturb him so senselessly whenever the whim took her, she should rather have been ordered to clean out his room daily, that charwoman! Once, early in the morning—heavy rain was lashing on the windowpanes, perhaps a sign that spring was on the way—Gregor was so exasperated when she began addressing him again that he ran at her, as if to attack her, although slowly and feebly enough. But the charwoman instead of showing fright merely lifted high a chair that happened to be beside the door, and as she stood there with her mouth wide open it was clear that she meant to shut it only when she brought the chair down on Gregor's back. "So you're not coming any nearer?" she asked, as Gregor turned away again, and quietly put the chair back into the corner.

Gregor was now eating hardly anything. Only when he happened to pass the food laid out for him did he take a bit of something in his mouth as a pastime, kept it there for an hour at a time and usually spat it out again. At first he thought it was chagrin over the state of his room that prevented him from eating, yet he soon got used to the various changes in his room. It had become a habit in the family to push into his room things there was no room for elsewhere, and there were plenty of these now, since one of the rooms had been let to three lodgers. These serious gentlemen—all three of them with full beards, as Gregor once observed through a crack in the door—had a passion for order, not only in their own room but, since they were now members of the household, in all its arrangements, especially in the kitchen. Superfluous, not to say dirty, objects they could not bear. Besides, they had brought with them most of the furnishings they needed. For this reason many things could be dispensed with that it was no use trying to sell but that should not be thrown away either. All of them found their way into Gregor's room. The ash can likewise and the kitchen garbage can. Anything that was not needed for the moment was simply flung into Gregor's room by the charwoman, who did everything in a hurry; fortunately Gregor usually saw only the object, whatever it was, and the hand that held it. Perhaps she intended to take the things away again as time and opportunity offered, or to collect them until she could throw them all out in a heap, but in fact they just lay wherever she happened to throw them, except when Gregor pushed his way through the junk heap and shifted it somewhat, at first out of necessity, because he had not room enough to crawl, but later with increasing enjoyment, although after such excursions, being sad and weary to death, he would lie motionless for hours. And since the lodgers often ate their supper at home in the common living room, the living-room door stayed shut many an evening, yet Gregor reconciled himself quite easily to the shutting of the door, for often enough on evenings when it was opened he had disregarded it entirely and lain in the darkest corner of his room, quite unnoticed by the family. But on one occasion the charwoman left the door open a little and it stayed ajar even when the lodgers came in for supper and the lamp was lit. They set themselves at the top end of the table where formerly Gregor and his father and mother had eaten their meals, unfolded their napkins and took knife and fork in hand. At once his mother appeared in the other doorway with a dish of meat and close behind her his sister with a dish of potatoes piled high. The food steamed with a thick vapor. The lodgers bent over the food set before them as if to scrutinize it before eating, in fact the man in the middle, who seemed to pass for an authority with the other two, cut a piece of meat as it lay on the dish, obviously to discover if it were tender or should be sent back to the kitchen. He showed satisfaction, and Gregor's mother and sister, who had been watching anxiously, breathed freely and began to smile. The family itself took its meals in the kitchen. None the less, Gregor's father came into the living room before going into the kitchen and with one prolonged bow, cap in hand, made a round of the table. The lodgers all stood up and murmured something in their beards. When they were alone again they ate their food in almost complete silence. It seemed remarkable to Gregor that among the various noises coming from the table he could always distinguish the sound of their masticating teeth, as if this were a sign to Gregor that one needed teeth in order to eat, and that with toothless jaws even of the finest make one could do nothing. "I'm hungry enough," said Gregor sadly to himself, "but not for that kind of food. How these lodgers are stuffing themselves, and here am I dying of starvation!"

On that very evening—during the whole of his time there Gregor could not remember ever having heard the violin—the sound of violin-playing came from the kitchen. The lodgers had already finished their supper, the one in the middle had brought out a newspaper and given the other two a page apiece, and now they were leaning back at ease reading and smoking. When the violin began to play they pricked up their ears, got to their feet, and went on tiptoe to the hall door where they stood huddled together. Their movements must have been heard in the kitchen, for Gregor's father called out: "Is the violin-playing disturbing you, gentlemen? It can be stopped at once." "On the contrary," said the middle lodger, "could not Fräulein Samsa come and play in this room, beside us, where it is much more convenient and comfortable?" "Oh certainly," cried Gregor's father, as if he were the violin-player. The lodgers came back into the living room and waited. Presently Gregor's father arrived with the music stand, his mother carrying the music and his sister with the violin. His sister quietly made everything ready to start playing; his parents, who had never let rooms before and so had an exaggerated idea of the courtesy due to lodgers, did not venture to sit down on their own chairs; his father leaned against the door, the right hand thrust between two buttons of his livery coat, which was formally buttoned up; but his mother was offered a chair by one of the lodgers and, since she left the chair just where he had happened to put it, sat down in a corner to one side.

Gregor's sister began to play; the father and mother, from either side, intently watched the movements of her hands. Gregor, attracted by the playing, ventured to move forward a little until his head was actually inside the living room. He felt hardly any surprise at his growing lack of consideration for the others; there had been a time when he prided himself on being considerate. And yet just on this occasion he had more reason than ever to hide himself, since owing to the amount of dust which lay thick in his room and rose into the air at the slightest movement, he too was covered with dust; fluff and hair and remnants of food trailed with him, caught on his back and along his sides; his indifference to everything was much too great for him to turn on his back and scrape himself clean on the carpet, as once he had done several times a day. And in spite of his condition, no shame deterred him from advancing a little over the spotless floor in the living room.

To be sure, no one was aware of him. The family was entirely absorbed in the violin-playing; the lodgers, however, who first of all had stationed themselves, hands in pockets, much too close behind the music stand so that they could all have read the music, which must have bothered his sister, had soon retreated to the window, half-whispering with downbent heads, and stayed there while his father turned an anxious eye on them. Indeed, they were making it more than obvious that they had been disappointed in their expectation of hearing good or enjoyable violin-playing, that they had had more than enough of the performance and only out of courtesy suffered a continued disturbance of their peace. From the way they all kept blowing the smoke of their cigars high in the air through nose and mouth one could divine their irritation. And yet Gregor's sister was playing so beautifully. Her face leaned sideways, intently and sadly her eyes followed the notes of music. Gregor crawled a little farther forward and lowered his head to the ground so that it might be possible for his eyes to meet hers. Was he an animal, that music had such an effect upon him? He felt as if the way were opening before him to the unknown nourishment he craved. He was determined to push forward till he reached his sister, to pull at her skirt and so let her know that she was to come into his room with her violin, for no one here appreciated her playing as he could appreciate it. He would never let her out of his room, at least, not so long as he lived; his frightful appearance would become, for the first time, useful to him; he would watch all the doors of his room at once and spit at intruders; but his sister should need no constraint, she should stay with him of her own free will; she should sit beside him on the sofa; bend down her ear to him and hear him confide that he had had the firm intention of sending her to the Conservatorium, and that, but for his mishap, last Christmas—surely Christmas was long past?—he would have announced it to everybody without allowing a single objection. After this confession his sister would be so touched that she would burst into tears, and Gregor would then raise himself to her shoulder and kiss her on the neck, which, now that she went to business, she kept free of any ribbon or collar.

"Mr. Samsa!" cried the middle lodger, to Gregor's father, and pointed, without wasting any more words, at Gregor, now working himself slowly forwards. The violin fell silent, the middle lodger first smiled at his friends with a shake of the head and then looked at Gregor again. Instead of driving Gregor out, his father seemed to think it more needful to begin by soothing down the lodgers, although they were not at all agitated and apparently found Gregor more entertaining than the violin-playing. He hurried towards them and spreading out his arms, tried to urge them back into their own room and at the same time to block their view of Gregor. They now began to be really a little angry, one could not tell whether because of the old man's behavior or because it had just dawned on them that all unwittingly they had such a neighbor as Gregor next door. They demanded explanations of his father, they waved their arms like him, tugged uneasily at their beards, and only with reluctance backed towards their room. Meanwhile Gregor's sister, who stood there as if lost when her playing was so abruptly broken off, came to life again, pulled herself together all at once after standing for a while holding violin and bow in nervelessly hanging hands and staring at her music, pushed her violin into the lap of her mother, who was still sitting in her chair fighting asthmatically for breath, and ran into the lodgers' rooms to which they were now being shepherded by her father rather more quickly than before. One could see the pillows and blankets on the beds flying under her accustomed fingers and being laid in order. Before the lodgers had actually reached their rooms she had finished making the beds and slipped out.

The old man seemed once more to be so possessed by his mulish self-assertiveness that he was forgetting all the respect he should show to his lodgers. He kept driving them on and driving them on until in the very door of the bedroom the middle lodger stamped his foot loudly on the floor and so brought him to a halt. "I beg to announce," said the lodger, lifting one hand and looking also at Gregor's mother and sister, "that because of the disgusting conditions prevailing in this household and family"—here he spat on the floor with emphatic brevity—"I give you notice on the spot. Naturally I won't pay you a penny for the days I have lived here, on the contrary I shall consider bringing an action for damages against you, based on claims—believe me—that will be easily susceptible of proof." He ceased and stared straight in front of him, as if he expected something. In fact his two friends at once rushed into the breach with these words: "And we too give notice on the spot." On that he seized the door-handle and shut the door with a slam.

Gregor's father, groping with his hands, staggered forward and fell into his chair; it looked as if he were stretching himself there for his ordinary evening nap, but the marked jerkings of his head, which was as if uncontrollable, showed that he was far from asleep. Gregor had simply stayed quietly all the time on the spot where the lodgers had espied him. Disappointment at the failure of his plan, perhaps also the weakness arising from extreme hunger, made it impossible for him to move. He feared, with a fair degree of certainty, that at any moment the general tension would discharge itself in a combined attack upon him, and he lay waiting. He did not react even to the noise made by the violin as it fell off his mother's lap from under her trembling fingers and gave out a resonant note.

"My dear parents," said his sister, slapping her hand on the table by way of introduction, "things can't go on like this. Perhaps you don't realize that, but I do. I won't utter my brother's name in the presence of this creature, and so all I say is: we must try to get rid of it. We've tried to look after it and to put up with it as far as is humanly possible, and I don't think anyone could reproach us in the slightest."

"She is more than right," said Gregor's father to himself. His mother, who was still choking for lack of breath, began to cough hollowly into her hand with a wild look in her eyes.

His sister rushed over to her and held her forehead. His father's thoughts seemed to have lost their vagueness at Grete's words, he sat more upright, fingering his service cap that lay among the plates still lying on the table from the lodgers' supper, and from time to time looked at the still form of Gregor.

"We must try to get rid of it," his sister now said explicitly to her father, since her mother was coughing too much to hear a word, "it will be the death of both of you, I can see that coming. When one has to work as hard as we do, all of us, one can't stand this continual torment at home on top of it. At least I can't stand it any longer." And she burst into such a passion of sobbing that her tears dropped on her mother's face, where she wiped them off mechanically.

"My dear," said the old man sympathetically, and with evident understanding, "but what can we do?"

Gregor's sister merely shrugged her shoulders to indicate the feeling of helplessness that had now overmastered her during her weeping fit, in contrast to her former confidence.

"If he could understand us," said her father, half questioningly; Grete, still sobbing, vehemently waved a hand to show how unthinkable that was.

"If he could understand us," repeated the old man, shutting his eyes to consider his daughter's conviction that understanding was impossible, "then perhaps we might come to some agreement with him. But as it is—"

"He must go," cried Gregor's sister, "that's the only solution, Father. You must just try to get rid of the idea that this is Gregor. The fact that we've believed it for so long is the root of all our trouble. But how can it be Gregor? If this were Gregor, he would have realized long ago that human beings can't live with such a creature, and he'd have gone away on his own accord. Then we wouldn't have any brother, but we'd be able to go on living and keep his memory in honor. As it is, this creature persecutes us, drives away our lodgers, obviously wants the whole apartment to himself and would have us all sleep in the gutter. Just look, Father," she shrieked all at once, "he's at it again!" And in an access of panic that was quite incomprehensible to Gregor she even quitted her mother, literally thrusting the chair from her as if she would rather sacrifice her mother than stay so near to Gregor, and rushed behind her father, who also rose up, being simply upset by her agitation, and half-spread his arms out as if to protect her.

Yet Gregor had not the slightest intention of frightening anyone, far less his sister. He had only begun to turn round in order to crawl back to his room, but it was certainly a startling operation to watch, since because of his disabled condition he could not execute the difficult turning movements except by lifting his head and then bracing it against the floor over and over again. He paused and looked round. His good intentions seemed to have been recognized; the alarm had only been momentary. Now they were all watching him in melancholy silence. His mother lay in her chair, her legs stiffly outstretched and pressed together, her eyes almost closing for sheer weariness; his father and his sister were sitting beside each other, his sister's arm around the old man's neck.

Perhaps I can go on turning round now, thought Gregor, and began his labors again. He could not stop himself from panting with the effort, and had to pause now and then to take breath. Nor did anyone harass him, he was left entirely to himself. When he had completed the turn-round he began at once to crawl straight back. He was amazed at the distance separating him from his room and could not understand how in his weak state he had managed to accomplish the same journey so recently, almost without remarking it. Intent on crawling as fast as possible, he barely noticed that not a single word, not an ejaculation from his family, interfered with his progress. Only when he was already in the doorway did he turn his head round, not completely, for his neck muscles were getting stiff, but enough to see that nothing had changed behind him except that his sister had risen to her feet. His last glance fell on his mother, who was not quite overcome by sleep.

Hardly was he well inside his room when the door was hastily pushed shut, bolted and locked. The sudden noise in his rear startled him so much that his little legs gave beneath him. It was his sister who had shown such haste. She had been standing ready waiting and had made a light spring forward, Gregor had not even heard her coming, and she cried "At last!" to her parents as she turned the key in the lock.

"And what now?" said Gregor to himself, looking round in the darkness. Soon he made the discovery that he was now unable to stir a limb. This did not surprise him, rather it seemed unnatural that he should ever actually have been able to move on these feeble little legs. Otherwise he felt relatively comfortable. True, his whole body was aching, but it seemed that the pain was gradually growing less and would finally pass away. The rotting apple in his back and the inflamed area around it, all covered with soft dust, already hardly troubled him. He thought of his family with tenderness and love. The decision that he must disappear was one that he held to even more strongly than his sister, if that were possible. In this state of vacant and peaceful meditation he remained until the tower clock struck three in the morning. The first broadening of light in the world outside the window entered his consciousness once more. Then his head sank to the floor of its own accord and from his nostrils came the last faint flicker of his breath.

When the charwoman arrived early in the morning—what between her strength and her impatience she slammed all the doors so loudly, never mind how often she had been begged not to do so, that no one in the whole apartment could enjoy any quiet sleep after her arrival—she noticed nothing unusual as she took her customary peep into Gregor's room. She thought he was lying motionless on purpose, pretending to be in the sulks; she credited him with every kind of intelligence. Since she happened to have the long-handled broom in her hand she tried to tickle him up with it from the doorway. When that too produced no reaction she felt provoked and poked at him a little harder, and only when she had pushed him along the floor without meeting any resistance was her attention aroused. It did not take her long to establish the truth of the matter, and her eyes widened, she let out a whistle, yet did not waste much time over it but tore open the door of the Samsas' bedroom and yelled into the darkness at the top of her voice: "Just look at this, it's dead; it's lying here dead and done for!"

Mr. and Mrs. Samsa started up in their double bed and before they realized the nature of the charwoman's announcement had some difficulty in overcoming the shock of it. But then they got out of bed quickly, one on either side, Mr. Samsa throwing a blanket over his shoulders, Mrs. Samsa in nothing but her nightgown; in this array they entered Gregor's room. Meanwhile the door of the living room opened, too, where Grete had been sleeping since the advent of the lodgers; she was completely dressed as if she had not been to bed, which seemed to be confirmed also by the paleness of her face. "Dead?" said Mrs. Samsa, looking questioningly at the charwoman, although she could have investigated for herself, and the fact was obvious enough without investigation. "I should say so," said the charwoman, proving her words by pushing Gregor's corpse a long way to one side with her broomstick. Mrs. Samsa made a movement as if to stop her, but checked it. "Well," said Mr. Samsa, "now thanks be to God." He crossed himself, and the three women followed his example. Grete, whose eyes never left the corpse, said: "Just see how thin he was. It's such a long time since he's eaten anything. The food came out again just as it went in." Indeed, Gregor's body was completely flat and dry, as could only now be seen when it was no longer supported by the legs and nothing prevented one from looking closely at it.

"Come in beside us, Grete, for a little while," said Mrs. Samsa with a tremulous smile, and Grete, not without looking back at the corpse, followed her parents into their bedroom. The charwoman shut the door and opened the window wide. Although it was so early in the morning a certain softness was perceptible in the fresh air. After all, it was already the end of March.

The three lodgers emerged from their room and were surprised to see no breakfast; they had been forgotten. "Where's our breakfast?" said the middle lodger peevishly to the charwoman. But she put her finger to her lips and hastily, without a word, indicated by gestures that they should go into Gregor's room. They did so and stood, their hands in the pockets of their somewhat shabby coats, around Gregor's corpse in the room where it was now fully light.

At that the door of the Samsas' bedroom opened and Mr. Samsa appeared in his uniform, his wife on one arm, his daughter on the other. They all looked a little as if they had been crying; from time to time Grete hid her face on her father's arm.

"Leave my house at once!" said Mr. Samsa, and pointed to the door without disengaging himself from the women. "What do you mean by that?" said the middle lodger, taken somewhat aback, with a feeble smile. The two others put their hands behind them and kept rubbing them together, as if in gleeful expectation of a fine set-to in which they were bound to come off the winners. "I mean just what I say," answered Mr. Samsa, and advanced in a straight line with his two companions towards the lodger. He stood his ground at first quietly, looking at the floor as if his thoughts were taking a new pattern in his head. "Then let us go, by all means," he said, and looked up at Mr. Samsa as if in a sudden access of humility he were expecting some renewed sanction for this decision. Mr. Samsa merely nodded briefly once or twice with meaning eyes. Upon that the lodger really did go with long strides into the hall, his two friends had been listening and had quite stopped rubbing their hands for some moments and now went scuttling after him as if afraid that Mr. Samsa might get into the hall before them and cut them off from their leader. In the hall they all three took their hats from the rack, their sticks from the umbrella stand, bowed in silence and quitted the apartment. With a suspiciousness which proved quite unfounded Mr. Samsa and the two women followed them out to the landing; leaning over the banister they watched the three figures slowly but surely going down the long stairs, vanishing from sight at a certain turn of the staircase on every floor and coming into view again after a moment or so; the more they dwindled, the more the Samsa family's interest in them dwindled, and when a butcher's boy met them and passed them on the stairs coming up proudly with a tray on his head, Mr. Samsa and the two women soon left the landing and as if a burden had been lifted from them went back into their apartment.

They decided to spend this day in resting and going for a stroll; they had not only deserved such a respite from work, but absolutely needed it. And so they sat down at the table and wrote three notes of excuse, Mr. Samsa to his board of management, Mrs. Samsa to her employer and Grete to the head of her firm. While they were writing, the charwoman came in to say that she was going now, since her morning's work was finished. At first they only nodded without looking up, but as she kept hovering there they eyed her irritably. "Well?" said Mr. Samsa. The charwoman stood grinning in the doorway as if she had good news to impart to the family but meant not to say a word unless properly questioned. The small ostrich feather standing upright on her hat, which had annoyed Mr. Samsa ever since she was engaged, was waving gaily in all directions. "Well, what is it then?" asked Mrs. Samsa, who obtained more respect from the charwoman than the others. "Oh," said the charwoman, giggling so amiably that she could not at once continue, "just this, you don't need to bother about how to get rid of the thing next door. It's been seen to already." Mrs. Samsa and Grete bent over their letters again, as if preoccupied; Mr. Samsa, who perceived that she was eager to begin describing it all in detail, stopped her with a decisive hand. But since she was not allowed to tell her story, she remembered the great hurry she was in, being obviously deeply huffed: "Bye, everybody," she said, whirling off violently, and departed with a frightful slamming of doors.

"She'll be given notice tonight," said Mr. Samsa, but neither from his wife nor his daughter did he get any answer, for the charwoman seemed to have shattered again the composure they had barely achieved. They rose, went to the window and stayed there, clasping each other tight. Mr. Samsa turned in his chair to look at them and quietly observed them for a little. Then he called out: "Come along, now, do. Let bygones be bygones. And you might have some consideration for me." The two of them complied at once, hastened to him, caressed him and quickly finished their letters.

Then they all three left the apartment together, which was more than they had done for months, and went by tram into the open country outside the town. The tram, in which they were the only passengers, was filled with warm sunshine. Leaning comfortably back in their seats they canvassed their prospects for the future, and it appeared on closer inspection that these were not at all bad, for the jobs they had got, which so far they had never really discussed with each other, were all three admirable and likely to lead to better things later on. The greatest immediate improvement in their condition would of course arise from moving to another house; they wanted to take a smaller and cheaper but also better situated and more easily run apartment than the one they had, which Gregor had selected. While they were thus conversing, it struck both Mr. and Mrs. Samsa, almost at the same moment, as they became aware of their daughter's increasing vivacity, that in spite of all the sorrow of recent times, which had made her cheeks pale, she had bloomed into a pretty girl with a good figure. They grew quieter and half unconsciously exchanged glances of complete agreement, having come to the conclusion that it would soon be time to find a good husband for her. And it was like a confirmation of their new dreams and excellent intentions that at the end of their journey their daughter sprang to her feet first and stretched her young body.

1915

AFTERWORD

"As Gregor Samsa awoke one morning from uneasy dreams he found himself transformed in his bed into a gigantic insect." Not how you would expect one of the great short novels of the twentieth century to begin, right? But of course, the canny reader notices, "awoke . . . from uneasy dreams"; he didn't really wake, right? and this is just another dream, right? Suppose not: in the second paragraph Samsa says it is no dream. Suppose he stays a giant insect, a beetle or bedbug, say, throughout the story? How do we come to terms with it? How can we take it seriously? Indeed, if the protagonist—usually the person we like to identify with—is going to remain a bug the whole time, how can we even be interested enough to read the story? The adventures, survival, sex life of bugs just don't seem all that fascinating.

Gregor Samsa was, when he went to bed, a human being, and still thinks he's human; but he has awakened to find himself transformed. He both believes and does not believe he is an insect. His mind is still functioning as a human mind and his feelings are human, so we can relate to him there. From time to time he even seems to forget about his predicament—if it is a real one—and complains to himself about his job and his boss, worries about catching his train. Interwoven with these half-awake thoughts are Gregor's attempts to roll over, to get out of bed, to control his voice, which is becoming a kind of "twittering squeak" and less and less comprehensible to others. So mixed are the human and realistic with the inhuman and fantastic, most readers find themselves fully engaged with Gregor Samsa's consciousness, his worries, likes, and dislikes, despite his new, distasteful form. For the sake of his human self we accept his insect self.

Meanwhile, there's another question about the reader's relation to the story, especially in the early passages. Is the story supposed to be funny? The manner in which the human and insect concerns are mixed or juxtaposed, it sometimes seems that way. While Gregor is struggling to turn over, for example, his legs kicking uncontrollably in the air, he thinks, "Oh God . . . what an exhausting job I've picked on!" He doesn't mean turning over, but his job as a traveling salesman, "Traveling about day in, day out. It's much more irritating work than doing the actual business in the office. . . . " And in the midst of going on about his job his belly begins to itch. Isn't there something ludicrous about the infiltrating of the real and the fantastic, the fantastic and the real? He even sees something comic in the situation himself. When he cannot get out of bed he thinks, "Well, ignoring the fact that the doors were all locked, ought he really to call for help? In spite of his misery he could not suppress a smile at the very idea of it." Later, he tries to stand up and open the door; there's a kind of Hitchcock suspense and absurdity in the posture and possibility: the door seems to separate the worlds of fantasy and reality, and the imminence of their mingling seems frightening and funny.

At times, too, the confusion of those outside the room seems comic—their failure to understand his increasingly insectlike speech, for example. This is, of course, another means by which the reader is engaged with Gregor: we begin to feel impatient with the chief clerk and the members of the family because they do not understand that behind that door is not an obstinate, rebellious Gregor Samsa but a giant bug struggling to move, to speak, to come to terms with his metamorphosis. The "outsiders," those outside the room, here seem as lacking in understanding and sympathy as Iván Ilyich's circle of friends when they hear of his death. And just as Iván's widow seeks out his friend not for consolation but to discover if she can get more from the government than a widow's pension, so Gregor's sister is concerned for Gregor because she fears he will lose his job and the family will be dunned for debts; and so, too, Gregor's boss suspects that Gregor's absence has something to do with his having some of the customers' cash in his hands.

When Gregor manages to open the door there is another slapstick scene as the horrified witnesses fall all over each other. The comedy is reinforced by Gregor's trying to speak to the terrified chief clerk, to get him to speak up for Gregor in the firm, not for his having been transformed into a repulsive insect, but because "Travelers are not popular there, I know." When the chief clerk eludes Gregor, Gregor's father is "upset." The tone begins to change. His father tries to drive him back into his room, and when Gregor gets stuck in the doorway, pushes him violently from behind, a "push which was literally a deliverance and he flew far into the room, bleeding freely." It is still ludicrous but doesn't seem quite so funny any more; it's a little frightening.

So ends the first chapter. We are more than likely not so concerned any longer about whether this story is fantasy or reality as we are about whether it is comic or tragic, whether Gregor will successfully reassume his human shape, or . . . ? Escape into the insect world seems as unlikely as returning to the human world while in this form; all other possibilities seem rather dreadful.

Our sympathies for Gregor are further reinforced by the evidence in the second chapter of his sweetness of temper—or is it his naïveté or passivity?—when it is disclosed that his father has been holding out from him some money he has salvaged from the ruin of his business, money that could have shortened Gregor's virtual indentured servitude had it been paid to the chief. Though we learn of this with Gregor and through his consciousness, we see more in it than he does, understand the callousness of his father and indeed of the family, and how they all have taken advantage of him. His father has not worked for five years and has grown fat; his mother complains of asthma; his sister is only seventeen: the whole burden for supporting the family has been on Gregor's shoulders, and to make matters even worse—though Gregor does not think so—his father has actually been saving money from the sums Gregor had given him for support.

While our pity has been deepened, Gregor is sinking more deeply into his insect state: he uses his feelers, does not like milk or fresh food or the spaciousness of his room; he has learned how to crawl over the walls and ceiling; his eyesight is dimming. Less and less is said about his occupation. Still, he does not want to part with the encumbering furniture, for it preserves his memories of his human state, and that he wants to cling to. He even turns a little hostile to his sister Grete as she comes to take the picture out of the room.

Despite the decline in his condition, then, we are led to expect that he might indeed regain his former identity. But toward the end of the chapter, after his resistance to Grete, things take a serious turn for the worse and a less happy eventuality seems the more likely. Another metamorphosis has taken place: his father, now a bank guard, has flourished and become more authoritative. He tries to force Gregor back into his room and throws apples at him. One sticks in Gregor's insect back. If his mother had not intervened Gregor might well have been killed right then and there.

There is still one more up and a final down in Gregor's fortunes and our hopes before what we must have known all along was the inevitable end. Rather surprisingly, Grete, the one who from the beginning seemed to understand him best, is the one who turns against him—or as she says, "it." What are we to feel about her "betrayal"? There is even a final indignity: after Gregor's death, the new charwoman is eager but unable to tell the family and us how "it" was disposed of. It is astonishing how, through the repellent and the comic, our sympathies have been engaged on the side of Gregor, and how moving and pathetic the end of his story is.

But that is not the end of *The Metamorphosis.* Gregor's consciousness and plight removed, we see the family better off than they were—not just better off than when the insect loomed in the inner room, but better off than when Gregor, working as a traveling salesman, supported them. They are all in reasonably good jobs and hopeful of improvement in the future. Grete has grown up to be a pretty young lady during the ordeal; her parents plan to find a husband for her. The story ends, "And it was like a confirmation of their new dreams and excellent intentions that at the end of their journey their daughter sprang to her feet first and stretched her young body." Have they forgotten already? have we? Is this an affirmation of life? a condemnation of Gregor? a tribute to his "sacrifice"? a cynical view of human selfishness and separateness? The ambivalence or mixture of mode and tone continues right to the end. We are not even absolutely certain which "metamorphosis" the title is referring to.

When we close the book and think about what we have read and how we have responded to what we have read, how do we answer the unanswered question we asked at the beginning? We know that it is no dream, no comedy, so how do we come to terms with a story that tells us that a traveling salesman woke one morning to find he was an insect? It's a delicate operation at best. On the one hand, you probably need to bring it into "ordinary" terms: Gregor is not *really* turned into a bug—cockroach, bedbug, dung beetle, whatever—but falls ill or falls in love or he just wakes up one morning and says to hell with it all and decides not to go to work (even though he's frightened no to), or in some other way separates himself from his family and his job, his role as provider, and he becomes repulsive, or unnecessary. He is rejected, and the family, which seemed dependent on him, survives and even flourishes. Or can it be Gregor's revulsion at himself and at the role forced upon him by the family, the feeling that they are exploiting him and will exploit him until he dies, but that they can, if they want, get along very well without him and without exploiting him? Some such reductive "realistic" or psychological reading is possible and in a sense perhaps necessary so that we can connect the story to our own lives or world.

But we cannot exterminate the bug without destroying the story. The preservation of the narrative surface is not just homage to some icon sacred to art or literature but necessary to preserve the emotional and imaginative impact of the story, the feelings—repulsion, frustration, horror, contempt, pity, impatience, humor—all mixed and separate, simultaneous and alternating which *define the experience* more accurately than the reductive realistic or psychological interpretation can. As Tolstoy might have it, art is a more effective form of transmission of perception through feeling than is any argument or statement into which we can translate (or metamorphose) it. Gregor Samsa is a traveling salesman who supports his family, *and* an insect, a mutant of the imagination essential for understanding the world of human experience.

D. H. LAWRENCE

The Fox

His father a coal miner, his mother middle class, young "Bertie" Lawrence won a scholarship to Nottingham High School in 1898 when he was thirteen, but had to leave school a few years later when his elder brother died. He worked for a surgical-appliance manufacturer, became a pupil-teacher, and attended Nottingham College, where in 1906 he earned his certificate; he left Nottinghamshire for Croydon, near London, where he taught school. When, in 1911, his first novel, *The White Peacock,* was published, he left teaching to devote his time to writing. The next year he eloped to the continent with Frieda, wife of Prof. Ernest Weekley and daughter of Baron von Richthofen; in 1914, after her divorce, they were married. During World War I both his novels and the fact that his wife was German gave him trouble: *The Rainbow* was published in September 1915 and suppressed in November; in 1917 he and his wife were ordered away from the Cornish coast, suspected of spying for the Germans. Understandably, in November 1919 the Lawrences left England. Their years of wandering began: first Italy, then Ceylon and Australia, Mexico and New Mexico, then back to England and Italy. His troubles with publishers were not ended by his exile, however: *Women in Love* was published in a subscription edition in New York in 1920, and *Lady Chatterley's Lover* in a similar edition eight years later, but even that was not enough to stem the outrage that lasted for more than a quarter-century after his death; even a volume of his poems was seized in the mails. Through it all he suffered from tuberculosis, the disease from which he finally died, in France in 1930. His other major novels include *Sons and Lovers, Aaron's Rod, The Plumed Serpent;* he is as well an acknowledged twentieth-century master of the short novel and of the short story; his poetry, long neglected, is gaining greater and greater recognition; even his plays have been revived in London, and he is a brilliant, profound, eccentric, and disturbing critic. He seems to speak for and to recent generations even more directly than does his rival as the greatest British fiction writer of the twentieth century, James Joyce.

He believed the novel the highest form of knowing, dealing with the whole living human being. "And being a novelist, I consider myself superior to the saint, the scientist, the philosopher, and the poet, who are all great masters of different bits of man alive, but never get the whole thing." Because he felt novels dealt with particulars, lived life at a specific time and place, he did not believe in the "well-made novel," or rules for writing narrative: "all rules of construction hold good only for novels which are copies of other novels," he wrote. His great subject was, of course, heterosexual love, not because it made great novels, but because it was *the* important human relationship and art is, he thought, "the relation between man and his circumambient universe, at the living moment. . . . The great relationship for humanity will always be the relation between man and woman. The relation between man and man, woman and woman, parent and child, will always be subsidiary."

The Fox was written not long after World War I, which Lawrence, along with most others of his generation, found a cataclysmic upheaval, changing life forever. It is, characteristically, a love story—a Lawrencian love story, which means like no other.

The Fox

THE TWO GIRLS were usually known by their sur-
names, Banford and March. They had taken the farm
together, intending to work it all by themselves: that
is, they were going to rear chickens, make a living by poultry, and add to
this by keeping a cow, and raising one or two young beasts. Unfortunately
things did not turn out well.

Banford was a small, thin, delicate thing with spectacles. She, however,
was the principal investor, for March had little or no money. Banford's
father, who was a tradesman in Islington,[1] gave his daughter the start, for
her health's sake, and because he loved her, and because it did not look as
if she would marry. March was more robust. She had learned carpentry
and joinery at the evening classes in Islington. She would be the man
about the place. They had, moreover, Banford's old grandfather living
with them at the start. He had been a farmer. But unfortunately the old
man died after he had been at Bailey Farm for a year. Then the two girls
were left alone.

They were neither of them young: that is, they were near thirty. But
they certainly were not old. They set out quite gallantly with their enterprise. They had numbers of chickens, black Leghorns and white Leghorns,
Plymouths and Wyandots; also some ducks; also two heifers in the fields.
One heifer, unfortunately, refused absolutely to stay in the Bailey Farm
closes. No matter how March made up the fences, the heifer was out,
wild in the woods, or trespassing on the neighbouring pasture, and March
and Banford were away, flying after her, with more haste than success. So
this heifer they sold in despair. And just before the other beast was expecting her first calf, the old man died, and the girls, afraid of the coming
event, sold her in a panic, and limited their attentions to fowls and ducks.

In spite of a little chagrin, it was a relief to have no more cattle on
hand. Life was not made merely to be slaved away. Both girls agreed in
this. The fowls were quite enough trouble. March had set up her carpenter's bench at the end of the open shed. Here she worked, making coops
and doors and other appurtenances. The fowls were housed in the bigger
building, which had served as barn and cowshed in old days. They had a
beautiful home, and should have been perfectly content. Indeed, they
looked well enough. But the girls were disgusted at their tendency to
strange illnesses, at their exacting way of life, and at their refusal, obstinate refusal, to lay eggs.

March did most of the outdoor work. When she was out and about, in
her puttees and breeches, her belted coat and her loose cap, she looked
almost like some graceful, loose-balanced young man, for her shoulders
were straight, and her movements easy and confident, even tinged with a
little indifference, or irony. But her face was not a man's face, ever. The
wisps of her crisp dark hair blew about her as she stooped, her eyes were
big and wide and dark, when she looked up again, strange, startled, shy
and sardonic at once. Her mouth, too, was almost pinched as if in pain

1. Heavily populated, residential borough of London with some commerce and light industry.

373

and irony. There was something odd and unexplained about her. She would stand balanced on one hip, looking at the fowls pottering about in the obnoxious fine mud of the sloping yard, and calling to her favourite white hen, which came in answer to her name. But there was an almost satirical flicker in March's big, dark eyes as she looked at her three-toed flock pottering about under her gaze, and the same slight dangerous satire in her voice as she spoke to the favoured Patty, who pecked at March's boot by way of friendly demonstration.

Fowls did not flourish at Bailey Farm, in spite of all that March did for them. When she provided hot food for them, in the morning, according to rule, she noticed that it made them heavy and dozy for hours. She expected to see them lean against the pillars of the shed in their languid processes of digestion. And she knew quite well that they ought to be busily scratching and foraging about, if they were to come to any good. So she decided to give them their hot food at night, and let them sleep on it. Which she did. But it made no difference.

War conditions, again, were very unfavourable to poultry keeping. Food was scarce and bad. And when the Daylight Saving Bill was passed, the fowls obstinately refused to go to bed as usual, about nine o'clock in the summer time. That was late enough, indeed, for there was no peace till they were shut up and asleep. Now they cheerfully walked around, without so much as glancing at the barn, until ten o'clock or later. Both Banford and March disbelieved in living for work alone. They wanted to read or take a cycle-ride in the evening, or perhaps March wished to paint curvilinear swans on porcelain, with green background, or else make a marvellous fire-screen by processes of elaborate cabinet work. For she was a creature of odd whims and unsatisfied tendencies. But from all these things she was prevented by the stupid fowls.

One evil there was greater than any other. Bailey Farm was a little homestead, with ancient wooden barn and low gabled farm-house, lying just one field removed from the edge of the wood. Since the War[2] the fox was a demon. He carried off the hens under the very noses of March and Banford. Banford would start and stare through her big spectacles with all her eyes, as another squawk and flutter took place at her heels. Too late! Another white Leghorn gone. It was disheartening.

They did what they could to remedy it. When it became permitted to shoot foxes, they stood sentinel with their guns, the two of them, at the favoured hours. But it was no good. The fox was too quick for them. So another year passed, and another, and they were living on their losses, as Banford said. They let their farm-house one summer, and retired to live in a railway-carriage that was deposited as a sort of out-house in a corner of the field. This amused them, and helped their finances. None the less, things looked dark.

Although they were usually the best of friends, because Banford, though nervous and delicate, was a warm, generous soul, and March, though so odd and absent in herself, had a strange magnanimity, yet, in the long solitude, they were apt to become a little irritable with one another, tired of one another. March had four-fifths of the work to do, and though she did not mind, there seemed no relief, and it made her eyes flash curiously sometimes. Then Banford, feeling more nerve-worn than

---

2. World War I, 1914–1918.

ever, would become despondent, and March would speak sharply to her. They seemed to be losing ground, somehow, losing hope as the months went by. There alone in the fields by the wood, with the wide country stretching hollow and dim to the round hills of the White Horse,[3] in the far distance, they seemed to have to live too much off themselves. There was nothing to keep them up—and no hope.

The fox really exasperated them both. As soon as they had let the fowls out, in the early summer mornings, they had to take their guns and keep guard: and then again, as soon as evening began to mellow, they must go once more. And he was so sly. He slid along in the deep grass, he was difficult as a serpent to see. And he seemed to circumvent the girls deliberately. Once or twice March had caught sight of the white tip of his brush, or the ruddy shadow of him in the deep grass, and she had let fire at him. But he made no account of this.

One evening March was standing with her back to the sunset, her gun under her arm, her hair pushed under her cap. She was half watching, half musing. It was her constant state. Her eyes were keen and observant, but her inner mind took no notice of what she saw. She was always lapsing into this odd, rapt state, her mouth rather screwed up. It was a question, whether she was there, actually consciously present, or not.

The trees on the wood-edge were a darkish, brownish green in the full light—for it was the end of August. Beyond, the naked, copper-like shafts and limbs of the pine-trees shone in the air. Nearer, the rough grass, with its long brownish stalks all agleam, was full of light. The fowls were round about—the ducks were still swimming on the pond under the pine-trees. March looked at it all, saw it all, and did not see it. She heard Banford speaking to the fowls, in the distance—and she did not hear. What was she thinking about? Heaven knows. Her consciousness was, as it were, held back.

She lowered her eyes, and suddenly saw the fox. He was looking up at her. His chin was pressed down, and his eyes were looking up. They met her eyes. And he knew her. She was spell-bound—she knew he knew her. So he looked into her eyes, and her soul failed her. He knew her, he was not daunted.

She struggled, confusedly she came to herself, and saw him making off, with slow leaps over some fallen boughs, slow, impudent jumps. Then he glanced over his shoulder, and ran smoothly away. She saw his brush held smooth like a feather, she saw his white buttocks twinkle. And he was gone, softly, soft as the wind.

She put her gun to her shoulder, but even then pursed her mouth, knowing it was nonsense to pretend to fire. So she began to walk slowly after him, in the direction he had gone, slowly, pertinaciously. She expected to find him. In her heart she was determined to find him. What she would do when she saw him again she did not consider. But she was determined to find him. So she walked abstractedly about on the edge of the wood, with wide, vivid dark eyes, and a faint flush in her cheeks. She did not think. In strange mindlessness she walked hither and thither.

At last she became aware that Banford was calling her. She made an effort of attention, turned, and gave some sort of screaming call in an-

3. Hills fifty to seventy-five miles west of London; the White Horse is a large figure (over 350 feet long) made by cutting away the turf on an escarpment of the Chalk Downs in Berkshire.

swer. Then again she was striding off towards the homestead. The red sun was setting, the fowls were retiring towards their roost. She watched them, white creatures, black creatures, gathering to the barn. She watched them spell-bound, without seeing them. But her automatic intelligence told her when it was time to shut the door.

She went indoors to supper, which Banford had set on the table. Banford chatted easily. March seemed to listen, in her distant, manly way. She answered a brief word now and then. But all the time she was as if spell-bound. And as soon as supper was over, she rose again to go out, without saying why.

She took her gun again and went to look for the fox. For he had lifted his eyes upon her, and his knowing look seemed to have entered her brain. She did not so much think of him: she was possessed by him. She saw his dark, shrewd, unabashed eye looking into her, knowing her. She felt him invisibly master her spirit. She knew the way he lowered his chin as he looked up, she knew his muzzle, the golden brown, and the greyish white. And again, she saw him glance over his shoulder at her, half-inviting, half-contemptuous and cunning. So she went, with her great startled eyes glowing, her gun under her arm, along the wood-edge. Meanwhile the night fell, and a great moon rose above the pine-trees. And again Banford was calling.

So she went indoors. She was silent and busy. She examined her gun, and cleaned it, musing abstractedly by the lamp-light. Then she went out again, under the great moon, to see if everything was right. When she saw the dark crests of the pine-trees against the blood-red sky, again her heart beat to the fox, the fox. She wanted to follow him, with her gun.

It was some days before she mentioned the affair to Banford. Then suddenly, one evening, she said:

"The fox was right at my feet on Saturday night."

"Where?" said Banford, her eyes opening behind her spectacles.

"When I stood just above the pond."

"Did you fire?" cried Banford.

"No, I didn't."

"Why not?"

"Why, I was too much surprised, I suppose."

It was the same old, slow, laconic way of speech March always had. Banford stared at her friend for a few moments.

"You saw him?" she cried.

"Oh, yes! He was looking up at me, cool as anything."

"I tell you," cried Banford—"the cheek!—They're not afraid of us, Nellie."

"Oh, no," said March.

"Pity you didn't get a shot at him," said Banford.

"Isn't it a pity! I've been looking for him ever since. But I don't suppose he'll come so near again."

"I don't suppose he will," said Banford.

And she proceeded to forget about it, except that she was more indignant than ever at the impudence of the beggar. March also was not conscious that she thought of the fox. But whenever she fell into her half-musing, when she was half-rapt, and half-intelligently aware of what passed under her vision, then it was the fox which somehow dominated her unconsciousness, possessed the blank half of her musing. And so it was

for weeks, and months. No matter whether she had been climbing the
trees for the apples, or beating down the last of the damsons, or whether
she had been digging out the ditch from the duck-pond, or clearing out
the barn, when she had finished, or when she straightened herself, and
pushed the wisps of hair away again from her forehead, and pursed up
her mouth again in an odd, screwed fashion, much too old for her years,
there was sure to come over her mind the old spell of the fox, as it came
when he was looking at her. It was as if she could smell him at these
times. And it always recurred, at unexpected moments, just as she was
going to sleep at night, or just as she was pouring the water into the
tea-pot, to make tea—it was the fox, it came over her like a spell.

So the months passed. She still looked for him unconsciously when
she went towards the wood. He had become a settled effect in her spirit,
a state permanently established, not continuous, but always recurring. She
did not know what she felt or thought: only the state came over her, as
when he looked at her.

The months passed, the dark evenings came, heavy, dark November,
when March went about in high boots, ankle deep in mud, when the
night began to fall at four o'clock, and the day never properly dawned.
Both girls dreaded these times. They dreaded the almost continuous darkness that enveloped them on their desolate little farm near the wood.
Banford was physically afraid. She was afraid of tramps, afraid lest someone should come prowling round. March was not so much afraid, as uncomfortable, and disturbed. She felt discomfort and gloom in all her
physique.

Usually the two girls had tea in the sitting room. March lighted a fire
at dusk, and put on the wood she had chopped and sawed during the day.
Then the long evening was in front, dark, sodden, black outside, lonely
and rather oppressive inside, a little dismal. March was content not to
talk, but Banford could not keep still. Merely listening to the wind in the
pines outside, or the drip of water, was too much for her.

One evening the girls had washed up the tea things in the kitchen, and
March had put on her house-shoes, and taken up a roll of crochet-work,
which she worked at slowly from time to time. So she lapsed into silence.
Banford stared at the red fire, which, being of wood, needed constant
attention. She was afraid to begin to read too early, because her eyes
would not bear any strain. So she sat staring at the fire, listening to the
distant sounds, sound of cattle lowing, of a dull, heavy moist wind, of the
rattle of the evening train on the little railway not far off. She was almost
fascinated by the red glow of the fire.

Suddenly both girls started, and lifted their heads. They heard a footstep—distinctly a footstep. Banford recoiled in fear. March stood listening.
Then rapidly she approached the door that led into the kitchen. At the
same time they heard the footsteps approach the back door. They waited
a second. The back door opened softly. Banford gave a loud cry. A man's
voice said softly:

"Hello!"

March recoiled, and took a gun from a corner.

"What do you want?" she cried, in a sharp voice.

Again the soft, softly-vibrating man's voice said:

"Hello! What's wrong?"

"I shall shoot!" cried March. "What do you want?"

"Why, what's wrong? What's wrong?" came the soft, wondering, rather scared voice: and a young soldier, with his heavy kit on his back, advanced into the dim light. "Why," he said, "who lives here then?"

"We live here," said March. "What do you want?"

"Oh!" came the long, melodious, wonder-note from the young soldier. "Doesn't William Grenfel live here then?"

"No—you know he doesn't."

"Do I?—Do I? I don't, you see.—He *did* live here, because he was my grandfather, and I lived here myself five years ago. What's become of him then?"

The young man—or youth, for he would not be more than twenty, now advanced and stood in the inner doorway. March, already under the influence of his strange, soft, modulated voice, stared at him spell-bound. He had a ruddy, roundish face, with fairish hair, rather long, flattened to his forehead with sweat. His eyes were blue, and very bright and sharp. On his cheeks, on the fresh ruddy skin were fine, fair hairs, like a down, but sharper. It gave him a slightly glistening look. Having his heavy sack on his shoulders, he stooped, thrusting his head forward. His hat was loose in one hand. He stared brightly, very keenly from girl to girl, particularly at March, who stood pale, with great dilated eyes, in her belted coat and puttees, her hair knotted in a big crisp knot behind. She still had the gun in her hand. Behind her, Banford, clinging to the sofa-arm, was shrinking away, with half-averted head.

"I thought my grandfather still lived here?—I wonder if he's dead."

"We've been here for three years," said Banford, who was beginning to recover her wits, seeing something boyish in the round head with its rather long sweaty hair.

"Three years! you don't say so!—And you don't know who was here before you?"

"I know it was an old man, who lived by himself."

"Ay! Yes, that's him!—And what became of him then?"

"He died.—I know he died—"

"Ay! He's dead then!"

The youth stared at them without changing colour or expression. If he had any expression, besides a slight baffled look of wonder, it was one of sharp curiosity concerning the two girls; sharp impersonal curiosity, the curiosity of that round young head.

But to March he was the fox. Whether it was the thrusting forward of his head, or the glisten of fine whitish hairs on the ruddy cheek-bones, or the bright, keen eyes, that can never be said: but the boy was to her the fox, and she could not see him otherwise.

"How is it you didn't know if your grandfather was alive or dead?" asked Banford, recovering her natural sharpness.

"Ay, that's it," replied the softly-breathing youth. "You see I joined up in Canada, and I hadn't heard for three or four years.—I ran away to Canada."

"And now have you just come from France?"

"Well—from Salonika really."

There was a pause, nobody knowing quite what to say.

"So you've nowhere to go now?" said Banford rather lamely.

"Oh, I know some people in the village. Anyhow, I can go to the Swan."

"You came on the train, I suppose.—Would you like to sit down a bit?"

"Well—I don't mind."

He gave an odd little groan as he swung off his kit. Banford looked at March.

"Put the gun down," she said. "We'll make a cup of tea."

"Ay," said the youth. "We've seen enough of rifles."

He sat down rather tired on the sofa, leaning forward.

March recovered her presence of mind, and went into the kitchen. There she heard the soft young voice musing:

"Well, to think I should come back and find it like this!" He did not seem sad, not at all—only rather interestedly surprised.

"And what a difference in the place, eh?" he continued, looking round the room.

"You see a difference, do you?" said Banford.

"Yes,—don't I!"

His eyes were unnaturally clear and bright, though it was the brightness of abundant health.

March was busy in the kitchen preparing another meal. It was about seven o'clock. All the time, while she was active, she was attending to the youth in the sitting-room, not so much listening to what he said, as feeling the soft run of his voice. She primmed up her mouth tighter and tighter, puckering it as if it was sewed, in her effort to keep her will uppermost. Yet her large eyes dilated and glowed in spite of her; she lost herself. Rapidly and carelessly she prepared the meal, cutting large chunks of bread and margarine—for there was no butter. She racked her brain to think of something else to put on the tray—she had only bread, margarine, and jam, and the larder was bare. Unable to conjure anything up, she went into the sitting-room with her tray.

She did not want to be noticed. Above all, she did not want him to look at her. But when she came in, and was busy setting the table just behind him, he pulled himself up from his sprawling, and turned and looked over his shoulder. She became pale and wan.

The youth watched her as she bent over the table, looked at her slim, well-shapen legs, at the belted coat dropping around her thighs, at the knot of dark hair, and his curiosity, vivid and widely alert, was again arrested by her.

The lamp was shaded with a dark-green shade, so that the light was thrown downwards, the upper half of the room was dim. His face moved bright under the light, but March loomed shadowy in the distance.

She turned round, but kept her eyes sideways, dropping and lifting her dark lashes. Her mouth unpuckered, as she said to Banford:

"Will you pour out?"

Then she went into the kitchen again.

"Have your tea where you are, will you?" said Banford to the youth—"unless you'd rather come to the table."

"Well," said he, "I'm nice and comfortable here, aren't I? I will have it here, if you don't mind."

"There's nothing but bread and jam," she said. And she put his plate on a stool by him. She was very happy now, waiting on him. For she loved company. And now she was no more afraid of him than if he were her own younger brother. He was such a boy.

"Nellie," she cried. "I've poured you a cup out."

March appeared in the doorway, took her cup, and sat down in a corner, as far from the light as possible. She was very sensitive in her knees. Having no skirts to cover them, and being forced to sit with them boldly exposed, she suffered. She shrank and shrank, trying not to be seen. And the youth, sprawling low on the couch, glanced up at her, with long, steady, penetrating looks, till she was almost ready to disappear. Yet she held her cup balanced, she drank her tea, screwed up her mouth and held her head averted. Her desire to be invisible was so strong that it quite baffled the youth. He felt he could not see her distinctly. She seemed like a shadow within the shadow. And ever his eyes came back to her, searching, unremitting, with unconscious fixed attention.

Meanwhile he was talking softly and smoothly to Banford, who loved nothing so much as gossip, and who was full of perky interest, like a bird. Also he ate largely and quickly and voraciously, so that March had to cut more chunks of bread and margarine, for the roughness of which Banford apologized.

"Oh, well," said March, suddenly speaking, "if there's no butter to put on it, it's no good trying to make dainty pieces."

Again the youth watched her, and he laughed, with a sudden, quick laugh, showing his teeth and wrinkling his nose.

"It isn't, is it?" he answered, in his soft, near voice.

It appeared he was Cornish by birth and upbringing. When he was twelve years old he had come to Bailey Farm with his grandfather, with whom he had never agreed very well. So he had run away to Canada, and worked far away in the West. Now he was here—and that was the end of it.

He was very curious about the girls, to find out exactly what they were doing. His questions were those of a farm youth; acute, practical, a little mocking. He was very much amused by their attitude to their losses: for they were amusing on the score of heifers and fowls.

"Oh, well," broke in March, "we don't believe in living for nothing but work."

"Don't you?" he answered. And again the quick young laugh came over his face. He kept his eyes steadily on the obscure woman in the corner.

"But what will you do when you've used up all your capital?" he said.

"Oh, I don't know," answered March laconically. "Hire ourselves out for landworkers, I suppose."

"Yes, but there won't be any demand for women landworkers, now the war's over," said the youth.

"Oh, we'll see. We shall hold on a bit longer yet," said March, with a plangent, half-sad, half-ironical indifference.

"There wants a man about the place," said the youth softly. Banford burst out laughing.

"Take care what you say," she interrupted. "We consider ourselves quite efficient."

"Oh," came March's slow, plangent voice, "It isn't a case of efficiency, I'm afraid. If you're going to do farming you must be at it from morning till night, and you might as well be a beast yourself."

"Yes, that's it," said the youth. "You aren't willing to put yourselves into it."

"We aren't," said March, "and we know it."

"We want some of our time for ourselves," said Banford.

The youth threw himself back on the sofa, his face tight with laughter, and laughed silently but thoroughly. The calm scorn of the girls tickled him tremendously.

"Yes," he said, "but why did you begin then?"

"Oh," said March, "we had a better opinion of the nature of fowls then, than we have now."

"Of Nature altogether, I'm afraid," said Banford. "Don't talk to me about Nature."

Again the face of the youth tightened with delighted laughter.

"You haven't a very high opinion of fowls and cattle, have you?" he said.

"Oh, no—quite a low one," said March.

He laughed out.

"Neither fowls nor heifers," said Banford, "nor goats nor the weather."

The youth broke into a sharp yap of laughter, delighted. The girls began to laugh too, March turning aside her face and wrinkling her mouth in amusement.

"Oh, well," said Banford, "we don't mind, do we, Nellie?"

"No," said March, "we don't mind."

The youth was very pleased. He had eaten and drunk his fill. Banford began to question him. His name was Henry Grenfel—no, he was not called Harry, always Henry. He continued to answer with courteous simplicity, grave and charming. March, who was not included, cast long, slow glances at him from her recess, as he sat there on the sofa, his hands clasping his knees, his face under the lamp bright and alert, turned to Banford. She became almost peaceful, at last. He was identified with the fox—and he was here in full presence. She need not go after him any more. There in the shadow of her corner she gave herself up to a warm, relaxed peace, almost like sleep, accepting the spell that was on her. But she wished to remain hidden. She was only fully at peace whilst he forgot her, talking with Banford. Hidden in the shadow of the corner, she need not any more be divided in herself, trying to keep up two planes of consciousness. She could at last lapse into the odour of the fox.

For the youth, sitting before the fire in his uniform, sent a faint but distinct odour into the room, indefinable, but something like a wild creature. March no longer tried to reserve herself from it. She was still and soft in her corner like a passive creature in its cave.

At last the talk dwindled. The youth relaxed his clasp of his knees, pulled himself together a little, and looked round. Again he became aware of the silent, half-invisible woman in the corner.

"Well," he said, unwillingly, "I suppose I'd better be going, or they'll be in bed at the Swan."

"I'm afraid they're in bed anyhow," said Banford. "They've all got this influenza."

"Have they!" he exclaimed. And he pondered. "Well," he continued, "I shall find a place somewhere."

"I'd say you could stay here, only—" Banford began.

He turned and watched her, holding his head forward.

"What—?" he asked.

"Oh, well," she said, "propriety, I suppose—" She was rather confused.

"It wouldn't be improper, would it?" he said, gently surprised.

"Not as far as we're concerned," said Banford.

"And not as far as *I'm* concerned," he said, with grave naïveté. "After all, it's my own home, in a way."

Banford smiled at this.

"It's what the village will have to say," she said.

There was a moment's blank pause.

"What do you say, Nellie?" asked Banford

"I don't mind," said March, in her distinct tone. "The village doesn't matter to me, anyhow."

"No," said the youth, quick and soft. "Why should it?—I mean, what should they say?"

"Oh, well," came March's plangent, laconic voice, "they'll easily find something to say. But it makes no difference, what they say. We can look after ourselves."

"Of course you can," said the youth.

"Well then, stop if you like," said Banford. "The spare room is quite ready."

His face shone with pleasure.

"If you're quite sure it isn't troubling you too much," he said, with that soft courtesy which distinguished him.

"Oh, it's no trouble," they both said.

He looked, smiling with delight, from one to another.

"It's awfully nice not to have to turn out again, isn't it?" he said gratefully.

"I suppose it is," said Banford.

March disappeared to attend to the room. Banford was as pleased and thoughtful as if she had her own young brother home from France. It gave her just the same kind of gratification to attend on him, to get out the bath for him, and everything. Her natural warmth and kindliness had now an outlet. And the youth luxuriated in her sisterly attention. But it puzzled him slightly to know that March was silently working for him too. She was so curiously silent and obliterated. It seemed to him he had not really seen her. He felt he should not know her if he met her in the road.

That night March dreamed vividly. She dreamed she heard a singing outside, which she could not understand, a singing that roamed round the house, in the fields and in the darkness. It moved her so, that she felt she must weep. She went out, and suddenly she knew it was the fox singing. He was very yellow and bright, like corn. She went nearer to him, but he ran away and ceased singing. He seemed near, and she wanted to touch him. She stretched out her hand, but suddenly he bit her wrist, and at the same instant, as she drew back, the fox, turning round to bound away, whisked his brush across her face, and it seemed his brush was on fire, for it seared and burned her mouth with a great pain. She awoke with the pain of it, and lay trembling as if she were really seared.

In the morning, however, she only remembered it as a distant memory. She arose and was busy preparing the house and attending to the fowls. Banford flew into the village on her bicycle, to try and buy food. She was a hospitable soul. But alas in the year 1918 there was not much food to buy. The youth came downstairs in his shirt-sleeves. He was young and fresh, but he walked with his head thrust forward, so that his shoulders seemed raised and rounded, as if he had a slight curvature of the spine. It must have been only a manner of bearing himself, for he was young and vigorous. He washed himself and went outside, whilst the women were preparing breakfast.

He saw everything, and examined everything. His curiosity was quick and insatiable. He compared the state of things with that which he remembered before, and cast over in his mind the effect of the changes. He watched the fowls and the ducks, to see their condition, he noticed the flight of wood-pigeons overhead: they were very numerous; he saw the few apples high up, which March had not been able to reach; he remarked that they had borrowed a draw-pump, presumably to empty the big soft-water cistern which was on the north side of the house.

"It's a funny, dilapidated old place," he said to the girls, as he sat at breakfast.

His eyes were wise and childish, with thinking about things. He did not say much, but ate largely. March kept her face averted. She, too, in the early morning, could not be aware of him, though something about the glint of his khaki reminded her of the brilliance of her dream-fox.

During the day the girls went about their business. In the morning, he attended to the guns, shot a rabbit and a wild duck that was flying high, towards the wood. That was a great addition to the empty larder. The girls felt that already he had earned his keep. He said nothing about leaving, however. In the afternoon he went to the village. He came back at tea-time. He had the same alert, forward-reaching look on his roundish face. He hung his hat on a peg with a little swinging gesture. He was thinking about something.

"Well," he said to the girls, as he sat at table. "What am I going to do?"

"How do you mean—what are you going to do?" said Banford.

"Where am I going to find a place in the village to stay?" he said.

"I don't know," said Banford. "Where do you think of staying?"

"Well—" he hesitated—"at the Swan they've got this flu, and at the Plough and Harrow they've got the soldiers who are collecting the hay for the army: besides in the private houses, there's ten men and a corporal altogether billeted in the village, they tell me. I'm not sure where I could get a bed."

He left the matter to them. He was rather calm about it. March sat with her elbows on the table, her two hands supporting her chin, looking at him unconsciously. Suddenly he lifted his clouded blue eyes, and unthinking looked straight into March's eyes. He was startled as well as she. He, too, recoiled a little. March felt the same sly, taunting, knowing spark leap out of his eyes as he turned his head aside, and fall into her soul, as it had fallen from the dark eyes of the fox. She pursed her mouth as if in pain, as if asleep too.

"Well, I don't know—" Banford was saying. She seemed reluctant, as if she were afraid of being imposed upon. She looked at March. But, with her weak, troubled sight, she only saw the usual semi-abstraction on her friend's face. "Why don't you speak, Nellie?" she said.

But March was wide-eyed and silent, and the youth, as if fascinated, was watching her without moving his eyes.

"Go on—answer something," said Banford. And March turned her head slightly aside, as if coming to consciousness, or trying to come to consciousness.

"What do you expect me to say?" she asked automatically.

"Say what you think," said Banford.

"It's all the same to me," said March.

And again there was silence. A pointed light seemed to be on the boy's eyes, penetrating like a needle.

"So it is to me," said Banford. "You can stop on here if you like."

A smile like a cunning little flame came over his face, suddenly and involuntarily. He dropped his head quickly to hide it, and remained with his head dropped, his face hidden.

"You can stop on here if you like. You can please yourself, Henry," Banford concluded.

Still he did not reply, but remained with his head dropped. Then he lifted his face. It was bright with a curious light, as if exultant, and his eyes were strangely clear as he watched March. She turned her face aside, her mouth suffering as if wounded, and her consciousness dim.

Banford became a little puzzled. She watched the steady, pellucid gaze of the youth's eyes, as he looked at March, with the invisible smile gleaming on his face. She did not know how he was smiling, for no feature moved. It seemed only in the gleam, almost the glitter of the fine hairs on his cheeks. Then he looked with quite a changed look, at Banford.

"I'm sure," he said in his soft, courteous voice, "you're awfully good. You're too good. You don't want to be bothered with me, I'm sure."

"Cut a bit of bread, Nellie," said Banford uneasily; adding: "It's no bother, if you like to stay. It's like having my own brother here for a few days. He's a boy like you are."

"That's awfully kind of you," the lad repeated. "I should like to stay, ever so much, if you're sure I'm not a trouble to you."

"No, of course you're no trouble. I tell you, it's a pleasure to have somebody in the house besides ourselves," said warm-hearted Banford.

"But Miss March?" he said in his soft voice, looking at her.

"Oh, it's quite all right as far as I'm concerned," said March vaguely.

His face beamed, and he almost rubbed his hands with pleasure.

"Well, then," he said, "I should love it, if you'd let me pay my board and help with the work."

"You've no need to talk about board," said Banford.

One or two days went by, and the youth stayed on at the farm. Banford was quite charmed by him. He was so soft and courteous in speech, not wanting to say much himself, preferring to hear what she had to say, and to laugh in his quick, half-mocking way. He helped readily with the work—but not too much. He loved to be out alone with the gun in his hands, to watch, to see. For his sharp-eyed, impersonal curiosity was insatiable, and he was most free when he was quite alone, half-hidden, watching.

Particularly he watched March. She was a strange character to him. Her figure, like a graceful young man's, piqued him. Her dark eyes made something rise in his soul, with a curious elate excitement, when he looked into them, an excitement he was afraid to let be seen, it was so keen and secret. And then her odd, shrewd speech made him laugh outright. He felt he must go further, he was inevitably impelled. But he put away the thought of her, and went off towards the wood's edge with the gun.

The dusk was falling as he came home, and with the dusk, a fine, late November rain. He saw the fire-light leaping in the window of the sitting-room, a leaping light in the little cluster of the dark buildings. And he thought to himself, it would be a good thing to have this place for his own. And then the thought entered him shrewdly: why not marry March? He stood still in the middle of the field for some moments, the dead rabbit hanging still in his hand, arrested by this thought. His mind waited in amazement—it seemed to calculate . . . then he smiled curiously to himself in acquiescence. Why not? Why not, indeed? It was a good idea. What if it was rather ridiculous? What did it matter? What if she was older than he? It didn't matter. When he thought of her dark, startled, vulnerable eyes he smiled subtly to himself. He was older than she, really. He was master of her.

He scarcely admitted his intention even to himself. He kept it as a secret even from himself. It was all too uncertain as yet. He would have to see how things went. Yes, he would have to see how things went. If he wasn't careful, she would just simply mock at the idea. He knew, sly and subtle as he was, that if he went to her plainly and said: "Miss March, I love you and want you to marry me," her inevitable answer would be: "Get out. I don't want any of that tomfoolery." This was her attitude to men and their "tomfoolery." If he was not careful, she would turn round on him with her savage, sardonic ridicule, and dismiss him from the farm and from her own mind, for ever. He would have to go gently. He would have to catch her as you catch a deer or a wood-cock when you go out shooting. It's no good walking out into the forest and saying to the deer: "Please fall to my gun." No, it is a slow, subtle battle. When you really go out to get a deer, you gather yourself together, you coil yourself inside yourself, and you advance secretly, before dawn, into the mountains. It is not so much what you do, when you go out hunting, as how you feel. You have to be subtle and cunning and absolutely fatally ready. It becomes like a fate. Your own fate overtakes and determines the fate of the deer you are hunting. First of all, even before you come in sight of your quarry, there is a strange battle, like mesmerism. Your own soul, as a hunter, has gone out to fasten on the soul of the deer, even before you see any deer. And the soul of the deer fights to escape. Even before the deer has any wind of you, it is so. It is a subtle, profound battle of wills, which takes place in the invisible. And it is a battle never finished till your bullet goes home. When you are *really* worked up to the true pitch, and you come at last into range, you don't then aim as you do when you are firing at a bottle. It is your own *will* which carries the bullet into the heart of your quarry. The bullet's flight home is a sheer projection of your own fate into the fate of the deer. It happens like a supreme wish, a supreme act of volition, not as a dodge of cleverness.

He was a huntsman in spirit, not a farmer, and not a soldier stuck in a regiment. And it was as a young hunter, that he wanted to bring down March as his quarry, to make her his wife. So he gathered himself subtly together, seemed to withdraw into a kind of invisibility. He was not quite sure how he would go on. And March was suspicious as a hare. So he remained in appearance just the nice, odd stranger-youth, staying for a fortnight on the place.

He had been sawing logs for the fire, in the afternoon. Darkness came very early. It was still a cold, raw mist. It was getting almost too dark to see. A pile of short sawed logs lay beside the trestle. March came to carry them indoors, or into the shed, as he was busy sawing the last log. He was working in his shirt-sleeves, and did not notice her approach. She came unwillingly, as if shy. He saw her stooping to the bright-ended logs, and he stopped sawing. A fire like lightning flew down his legs in the nerves.

"March?" he said, in his quiet young voice.

She looked up from the logs she was piling.

"Yes!" she said.

He looked down on her in the dusk. He could see her not too distinctly.

"I wanted to ask you something," he said.

"Did you? What was it?" she said. Already the fright was in her voice. But she was too much mistress of herself.

"Why—" his voice seemed to draw out soft and subtle, it penetrated her nerves—"why, what do you think it is?"

She stood up, placed her hands on her hips, and stood looking at him transfixed, without answering. Again he burned with a sudden power.

"Well," he said, and his voice was so soft it seemed rather like a subtle touch, like the merest touch of a cat's paw, a feeling rather than a sound. "Well—I wanted to ask you to marry me."

March felt rather than heard him. She was trying in vain to turn aside her face. A great relaxation seemed to have come over her. She stood silent, her head slightly on one side. He seemed to be bending towards her, invisibly smiling. It seemed to her fine sparks came out of him.

Then very suddenly, she said:

"Don't try any of your tomfoolery on me."

A quiver went over his nerves. He had missed. He waited a moment to collect himself again. Then he said, putting all the strange softness into his voice, as if he were imperceptibly stroking her:

"Why, it's not tomfoolery. It's not tomfoolery. I mean it. I mean it. What makes you disbelieve me?"

He sounded hurt. And his voice had such a curious power over her; making her feel loose and relaxed. She struggled somewhere for her own power. She felt for a moment that she was lost—lost—lost. The word seemed to rock in her as if she were dying. Suddenly again she spoke.

"You don't know what you are talking about," she said, in a brief and transient stroke of scorn. "What nonsense! I'm old enough to be your mother."

"Yes, I do know what I'm talking about. Yes, I do," he persisted softly, as if he were producing his voice in her blood. "I know quite well what I'm talking about. You're not old enough to be my mother. That isn't true. And what does it matter even if it was? You can marry me whatever age we are. What is age to me? And what is age to you! Age is nothing."

A swoon went over her as he concluded. He spoke rapidly—in the rapid Cornish fashion—and his voice seemed to sound in her somewhere where she was helpless against it. "Age is nothing!" The soft, heavy insistence of it made her sway dimly out there in the darkness. She could not answer.

A great exultance leaped like fire over his limbs. He felt he had won.

"I want to marry you, you see. Why shouldn't I?" he proceeded, soft and rapid. He waited for her to answer. In the dusk he saw her almost phosphorescent. Her eyelids were dropped, her face half-averted and unconscious. She seemed to be in his power. But he waited, watchful. He dared not yet touch her.

"Say then," he said. "Say then you'll marry me. Say—say!" He was softly insistent.

"What?" she asked, faint, from a distance, like one in pain. His voice was now unthinkably near and soft. He drew very near to her.

"Say yes."

"Oh, I can't," she wailed helplessly, half articulate, as if semi-conscious, and as if in pain, like one who dies. "How can I?"

"You can," he said softly, laying his hand gently on her shoulder as she stood with her head averted and dropped, dazed. "You can. Yes, you can. What makes you say you can't? You can. You can." And with awful softness he bent forward and just touched her neck with his mouth and his chin.

"Don't!" she cried, with a faint mad cry like hysteria, starting away and facing round on him. "What do you mean?" But she had no breath to speak with. It was as if she were killed.

"I mean what I say," he persisted softly and cruelly. "I want you to marry me. I want you to marry me. You know that, now, don't you? You know that, now? Don't you? Don't you?"

"What?" she said.

"Know," he replied.

"Yes," she said. "I know you say so."

"And you know I mean it, don't you?"

"I know you say so."

"You believe me?" he said.

She was silent for some time. Then she pursed her lips.

"I don't know what I believe," she said.

"Are you out there?" came Banford's voice, calling from the house.

"Yes, we're bringing in the logs," he answered.

"I thought you'd gone lost," said Banford disconsolately. "Hurry up, do, and come and let's have tea. The kettle's boiling."

He stooped at once, to take an armful of little logs and carry them into the kitchen, where they were piled in a corner. March also helped, filling her arms and carrying the logs on her breast as if they were some heavy child. The night had fallen cold.

When the logs were all in, the two cleaned their boots noisily on the scraper outside, then rubbed them on the mat. March shut the door and took off her old felt hat—her farm-girl hat. Her thick, crisp black hair was loose, her face was pale and strained. She pushed back her hair vaguely, and washed her hands. Banford came hurrying into the dimly-lighted kitchen, to take from the oven the scones she was keeping hot.

"Whatever have you been doing all this time?" she asked fretfully. "I thought you were never coming in. And it's ages since you stopped sawing. What were you doing out there?"

"Well," said Henry, "we had to stop that hole in the barn, to keep the rats out."

"Why, I could see you standing there in the shed. I could see your shirt-sleeves," challenged Banford.

"Yes, I was just putting the saw away."

They went in to tea. March was quite mute. Her face was pale and strained and vague. The youth, who always had the same ruddy, self-contained look on his face, as though he were keeping himself to himself, had come to tea in his shirt-sleeves as if he were at home. He bent over his plate as he ate his food.

"Aren't you cold?" said Banford spitefully. "In your shirt-sleeves."

He looked up at her, with his chin near his plate, and his eyes very clear, pellucid, and unwavering as he watched her.

"No, I'm not cold," he said with his usual soft courtesy. "It's much warmer in here than it is outside, you see."

"I hope it is," said Banford, feeling nettled by him. He had a strange suave assurance, and a wide-eyed bright look that got on her nerves this evening.

"But perhaps," he said softly and courteously, "you don't like me coming to tea without my coat. I forgot that."

"Oh, I don't mind," said Banford: although she *did*.

"I'll go and get it, shall I?" he said.

March's dark eyes turned slowly down to him.

"No, don't you bother," she said in her queer, twanging tone. "If you feel all right as you are, stop as you are." She spoke with a crude authority.

"Yes," said he, "I *feel* all right, if I'm not rude."

"It's usually considered rude," said Banford. "But we don't mind."

"Go along, 'considered rude,'" ejaculated March. "Who considers it rude?"

"Why you do, Nellie, in anybody else," said Banford, bridling a little behind her spectacles, and feeling her food stick in her throat.

But March had again gone vague and unheeding, chewing her food as if she did not know she was eating at all. And the youth looked from one to another, with bright, watchful eyes.

Banford was offended. For all his suave courtesy and soft voice, the youth seemed to her impudent. She did not like to look at him. She did not like to meet his clear, watchful eyes, she did not like to see the strange glow in his face, his cheeks with their delicate fine hair, and his ruddy skin that was quite dull and yet which seemed to burn with a curious heat of life. It made her feel a little ill to look at him: the quality of his physical presence was too penetrating, too hot.

After tea the evening was very quiet. The youth rarely went into the village. As a rule he read: he was a great reader, in his own hours. That is, when he did begin, he read absorbedly. But he was not very eager to begin. Often he walked about the fields and along the hedges alone in the dark at night, prowling with a queer instinct for the night, and listening to the wild sounds.

To-night, however, he took a Captain Mayne Reid[4] book from Banford's shelf and sat down with knees wide apart and immersed himself in his story. His brownish fair hair was long, and lay on his head like a thick cap, combed sideways. He was still in his shirt-sleeves, and bending forward under the lamp-light, with his knees stuck wide apart and the book in his hand and his whole figure absorbed in the rather strenuous business of reading, he gave Banford's sitting-room the look of a lumber-camp. She resented this. For on her sitting-room floor she had a red Turkey rug and dark stain round, the fire-place had fashionable green tiles, the piano stood open with the latest dance-music—she played quite well—and on the walls were March's hand-painted swans and water-lilies. Moreover, with the logs nicely, tremulously burning in the grate, the thick curtains drawn,

---

4. A British novelist (1818–1883) who served as captain in the U.S. Army in the Mexican war, and wrote such tales of adventure as *The Rifle Rangers* (1850), *The Scalp-Hunters* (1851), and *The Boy Hunters* (1852).

the doors all shut, and the pine-trees hissing and shuddering in the wind outside, it was cosy, it was refined and nice. She resented the big, raw, long-legged youth sticking his khaki knees out and sitting there with his soldier's shirt-cuffs buttoned on his thick red wrists. From time to time he turned a page, and from time to time he gave a sharp look at the fire, settling the logs. Then he immersed himself again in the intense and isolated business of reading.

March, on the far side of the table, was spasmodically crochetting. Her mouth was pursed in an odd way, as when she had dreamed the fox's brush burned it, her beautiful, crisp black hair strayed in wisps. But her whole figure was absorbed in its bearing, as if she herself were miles away. In a sort of semi-dream she seemed to be hearing the fox singing round the house in the wind, singing wildly and sweetly and like a madness. With red but well-shaped hands she slowly crochetted the white cotton, very slowly, awkwardly.

Banford was also trying to read, sitting in her low chair. But between those two she felt fidgety. She kept moving and looking round and listening to the wind and glancing secretly from one to the other of her companions. March, seated on a straight chair, with her knees in their close breeches crossed, and slowly, laboriously crochetting, was also a trial.

"Oh, dear!" said Banford. "My eyes are bad tonight." And she pressed her fingers on her eyes.

The youth looked up at her with his clear bright look, but did not speak.

"Are they, Jill?" said March absently.

Then the youth began to read again, and Banford perforce returned to her book. But she could not keep still. After a while she looked up at March, and a queer, almost malignant little smile was on her thin face.

"A penny for them, Nell," she said suddenly.

March looked round with big, startled black eyes, and went pale as if with terror. She had been listening to the fox singing so tenderly, so tenderly, as he wandered round the house.

"What?" she said vaguely.

"A penny for them," said Banford sarcastically. "Or twopence, if they're as deep as all that."

The youth was watching with bright clear eyes from beneath the lamp.

"Why," came March's vague voice, "what do you want to waste your money for?"

"I thought it would be well spent," said Branford.

"I wasn't thinking of anything except the way the wind was blowing," said March.

"Oh, dear," replied Banford. "I could have had as original thoughts as that myself. I'm afraid I *have* wasted my money this time."

"Well, you needn't pay," said March.

The youth suddenly laughed. Both women looked at him: March rather surprised-looking, as if she had hardly known he was there.

"Why, do you ever pay up on these occasions?" he asked.

"Oh, yes," said Banford. "We always do. I've sometimes had to pass a shilling[5] a week to Nellie, in the winter time. It costs much less in summer."

5. Twelve pence.

"What, paying for each other's thoughts?" he laughed.

"Yes, when we've absolutely come to the end of everything else."

He laughed quickly, wrinkling his nose sharply like a puppy and laughing with quick pleasure, his eyes shining.

"It's the first time I ever heard of that," he said.

"I guess you'd hear of it often enough if you stayed a winter on Bailey Farm," said Banford lamentably.

"Do you get so tired, then?" he asked.

"So bored," said Banford.

"Oh!" he said gravely. "But why should you be bored?"

"Who wouldn't be bored?" said Banford.

"I'm sorry to hear that," he said gravely.

"You must be, if you were hoping to have a lively time here," said Banford.

He looked at her long and gravely.

"Well," he said, with his odd young seriousness, "it's quite lively enough for me."

"I'm glad to hear it," said Banford.

And she returned to her book. In her thin, frail hair were already many threads of grey, though she was not yet thirty. The boy did not look down, but turned his eyes to March, who was sitting with pursed mouth laboriously crochetting, her eyes wide and absent. She had a warm, pale, fine skin, and a delicate nose. Her pursed mouth looked shrewish. But the shrewish look was contradicted by the curious lifted arch of her dark brows, and the wideness of her eyes; a look of startled wonder and vagueness. She was listening again for the fox, who seemed to have wandered farther off into the night.

From under the edge of the lamp-light the boy sat with his face looking up, watching her silently, his eyes round and very clear and intent. Banford, biting her fingers irritably, was glancing at him under her hair. He sat there perfectly still, his ruddy face tilted up from the low level under the light, on the edge of the dimness, and watching with perfect abstract intentness. March suddenly lifted her great dark eyes from her crochetting, and saw him. She started, giving a little exclamation.

"There he is!" she cried, involuntarily, as if terribly startled.

Banford looked around in amazement, sitting up straight.

"Whatever has got you, Nellie?" she cried.

But March, her face flushed a delicate rose colour, was looking away to the door.

"Nothing! Nothing!" she said crossly. "Can't one speak?"

"Yes, if you speak sensibly," said Banford. "Whatever did you mean?"

"I don't know what I meant," cried March testily.

"Oh, Nellie, I hope you aren't going jumpy and nervy. I feel I can't stand another *thing!*—Whoever did you mean? Did you mean Henry?" cried poor frightened Banford.

"Yes. I suppose so," said March laconically. She would never confess to the fox.

"Oh, dear, my nerves are all gone for to-night," wailed Banford.

At nine o'clock March brought in a tray with bread and cheese and tea—Henry had confessed that he liked a cup of tea. Banford drank a glass of milk, and ate a little bread. And soon she said:

"I'm going to bed, Nellie. I'm all nerves to-night. Are you coming?"

"Yes, I'm coming the minute I've taken the tray away," said March.

"Don't be long then," said Banford fretfully. "Good-night, Henry. You'll see the fire is safe, if you come up last, won't you?"

"Yes, Miss Banford, I'll see it's safe," he replied in his reassuring way.

March was lighting the candle to go to the kitchen. Banford took her candle and went upstairs. When March came back to the fire she said to him:

"I suppose we can trust you to put out the fire and everything?" She stood there with her hand on her hip, and one knee loose, her head averted shyly, as if she could not look at him. He had his face lifted, watching her.

"Come and sit down a minute," he said softly.

"No, I'll be going. Jill will be waiting, and she'll get upset if I don't come."

"What made you jump like that this evening?" he asked.

"When did I jump?" she retorted, looking at him.

"Why, just now you did," he said. "When you cried out."

"Oh!" she said. "Then!—Why, I thought you were the fox!" And her face screwed into a queer smile, half ironic.

"The fox! Why the fox?" he asked softly.

"Why, one evening last summer when I was out with the gun I saw the fox in the grass nearly at my feet, looking straight up at me. I don't know—I suppose he made an impression on me." She turned aside her head again, and let one foot stray loose, self-consciously.

"And did you shoot him?" asked the boy.

"No, he gave me such a start, staring straight at me as he did, and then stopping to look back at me over his shoulder with a laugh on his face."

"A laugh on his face!" repeated Henry, also laughing. "He frightened you, did he?"

"No, he didn't frighten me. He made an impression on me, that's all."

"And you thought I was the fox, did you?" he laughed, with the same queer quick little laugh, like a puppy wrinkling its nose.

"Yes, I did, for the moment," she said. "Perhaps he'd been in my mind without my knowing."

"Perhaps you think I've come to steal your chickens or something," he said, with the same young laugh.

But she only looked at him with a wide, dark, vacant eye.

"It's the first time," he said, "that I've ever been taken for a fox. Won't you sit down for a minute?" His voice was very soft and cajoling.

"No," she said. "Jill will be waiting." But still she did not go, but stood with one foot loose and her face turned aside, just outside the circle of light.

"But won't you answer my question?" he said, lowering his voice still more.

"I don't know what question you mean."

"Yes, you do. Of course you do. I mean the question of you marrying me."

"No, I shan't answer that question," she said flatly.

"Won't you?" The queer young laugh came on his nose again. "Is it because I'm like the fox? Is that why?" And still he laughed.

She turned and looked at him with a long, slow look.

"I wouldn't let that put you against me," he said. "Let me turn the lamp low, and come and sit down a minute."

He put his red hand under the glow of the lamp, and suddenly made the light very dim. March stood there in the dimness quite shadowy, but unmoving. He rose silently to his feet, on his long legs. And now his voice was extraordinarily soft and suggestive, hardly audible.

"You'll stay a moment," he said. "Just a moment." And he put his hand on her shoulder.—She turned her face from him. "I'm sure you don't really think I'm like the fox," he said, with the same softness and with a suggestion of laughter in his tone, a subtle mockery. "Do you now?"—And he drew her gently towards him and kissed her neck, softly. She winced and trembled and hung away. But his strong young arm held her, and he kissed her softly again, still on the neck, for her face was averted.

"Won't you answer my question? Won't you now?" came his soft, lingering voice. He was trying to draw her near to kiss her face. And he kissed her cheek softly, near the ear.

At that moment Banford's voice was heard calling fretfully, crossly, from upstairs.

"There's Jill!" cried March, starting and drawing erect.

And as she did so, quick as lightning he kissed her on the mouth, with a quick brushing kiss. It seemed to burn through her every fibre. She gave a queer little cry.

"You will, won't you? You will?" he insisted softly.

"Nellie! *Nellie!* Whatever are you so long for?" came Banford's faint cry from the outer darkness.

But he held her fast, and was murmuring with that intolerable softness and insistency:

"You will, won't you? Say yes! Say yes!"

March, who felt as if the fire had gone through her and scathed her, and as if she could do no more, murmured:

"Yes! Yes! Anything you like! Anything you like! Only let me go! Only let me go! Jill's calling."

"You know you've promised," he said insidiously.

"Yes! Yes! I do!—" Her voice suddenly rose into a shrill cry. "All right, Jill, I'm coming."

Startled, he let her go, and she went straight upstairs.

In the morning at breakfast, after he had looked round the place and attended to the stock and thought to himself that one could live easily enough here, he said to Banford:

"Do you know what, Miss Banford?"

"Well, what?" said the good-natured, nervy Banford.

He looked at March, who was spreading jam on her bread.

"Shall I tell?" he said to her.

She looked up at him, and a deep pink colour flushed over her face.

"Yes, if you mean Jill," she said. "I hope you won't go talking all over the village, that's all." And she swallowed her dry bread with difficulty.

"Whatever's coming?" said Banford, looking up with wide, tired, slightly reddened eyes. She was a thin, frail little thing, and her hair, which was delicate and thin, was bobbed, so it hung softly by her worn face in its faded brown and grey.

"Why, what do you think?" he said, smiling like one who has a secret.

"How do I know!" said Banford.

"Can't you guess?" he said, making bright eyes, and smiling, pleased with himself.

"I'm sure I can't. What's more, I'm not going to try."

"Nellie and I are going to be married."

Banford put down her knife, out of her thin, delicate fingers, as if she would never take it up to eat any more. She stared with blank, reddened eyes.

"You what?" she exclaimed.

"We're going to get married. Aren't we, Nellie?" and he turned March.

"You say so, anyway," said March laconically. But again she flushed with an agonized flush. She, too, could swallow no more.

Banford looked at her like a bird that has been shot: a poor little sick bird. She gazed at her with all her wounded soul in her face, at the deep-flushed March.

"Never!" she exclaimed, helpless.

"It's quite right," said the bright and gloating youth.

Banford turned aside her face, as if the sight of the food on the table made her sick. She sat like this for some moments, as if she were sick. Then, with one hand on the edge of the table, she rose to her feet.

"I'll *never* believe it, Nellie," she cried. "It's absolutely impossible!"

Her plaintive, fretful voice had a thread of hot anger and despair.

"Why? Why shouldn't you believe it?" asked the youth, with all his soft, velvety impertinence in his voice.

Banford looked at him from her wide vague eyes, as if he were some creature in a museum.

"Oh," she said languidly, "because she can never be such a fool. She can't lose her self-respect to such an extent." Her voice was cold and plaintive, drifting.

"In what way will she lose her self-respect?" asked the boy.

Banford looked at him with vague fixity from behind her spectacles.

"If she hasn't lost it already," she said.

He became very red, vermilion, under the slow vague stare from behind the spectacles.

"I don't see it at all," he said.

"Probably you don't. I shouldn't expect you would," said Banford, with that straying mild tone of remoteness which made her words even more insulting.

He sat stiff in his chair, staring with hot blue eyes from his scarlet face. An ugly look had come on his brow.

"My word, she doesn't know what she's letting herself in for," said Banford, in her plaintive, drifting, insulting voice.

"What has it got to do with you, anyway?" said the youth in a temper.

"More than it has to do with you, probably," she replied, plaintive and venomous.

"Oh, has it! I don't see that at all," he jerked out.

"No, you wouldn't," she answered, drifting.

"Anyhow," said March, pushing back her chair and rising uncouthly, "it's no good arguing about it." And she seized the bread and the tea-pot, and strode away to the kitchen.

Banford let her fingers stray across her brow and along her hair, like one bemused. Then she turned and went away upstairs.

Henry sat stiff and sulky in his chair, with his face and his eyes on fire. March came and went, clearing the table. But Henry sat on, stiff with temper. He took no notice of her. She had regained her composure and her soft, even, creamy complexion. But her mouth was pursed up. She glanced at him each time as she came to take things from the table, glanced from her large, curious eyes, more in curiosity than anything. Such a long, red-faced sulky boy! That was all he was. He seemed as remote from her as if his red face were a red chimney-pot on a cottage across the fields, and she looked at him just as objectively, as remotely.

At length he got up and stalked out into the fields with the gun. He came in only at dinner-time, with the devil still in his face, but his manners quite polite. Nobody said anything particular: they sat each one at the sharp corner of a triangle, in obstinate remoteness. In the afternoon he went out again at once with the gun. He came in at nightfall with a rabbit and a pigeon. He stayed in all evening, but hardly opened his mouth. He was in the devil of a temper, feeling he had been insulted.

Banford's eyes were red, she had evidently been crying. But her manner was more remote and supercilious than ever; the way she turned her head if he spoke at all, as if he were some tramp or inferior intruder of that sort, made his blue eyes go almost black with rage. His face looked sulkier. But he never forgot his polite intonation, if he opened his mouth to speak.

March seemed to flourish in this atmosphere. She seemed to sit between the two antagonists with a little wicked smile on her face, enjoying herself. There was even a sort of complacency in the way she laboriously crochetted this evening.

When he was in bed, the youth could hear the two women talking and arguing in their room. He sat up in bed and strained his ears to hear what they said. But he could hear nothing, it was too far off. Yet he could hear the soft, plaintive drip of Banford's voice, and March's deeper note.

The night was quiet, frosty. Big stars were snapping outside, beyond the ridge-tops of the pine-trees. He listened and listened. In the distance he heard a fox yelping: and the dogs from the farms barking in answer. But it was not that he wanted to hear. It was what the two women were saying.

He got stealthily out of bed, and stood by his door. He could hear no more than before. Very, very carefully he began to lift the door-latch. After quite a time he had his door open. Then he stepped stealthily out into the passage. The old oak planks were cold under his feet, and they creaked preposterously. He crept very, very gently up the one step, and along by the wall, till he stood outside their door. And there he held his breath and listened. Banford's voice:

"No, I simply couldn't stand it. I should be dead in a month. Which is just what he would be aiming at, of course. That would just be his game, to see me in the churchyard. No, Nellie, if you were to do such a thing as to marry him, you could never stop here. I couldn't, I couldn't live in the same house with him. Oh-h! I feel quite sick with the smell of his clothes. And his red face simply turns me over. I can't eat my food when he's at the table. What a fool I was ever to let him stop. One ought *never* to try to do a kind action. It always flies back in your face like a boomerang."

"Well, he's only got two more days," said March.

"Yes, thank heaven. And when he's gone he'll never come in this house

again. I feel so bad while he's here. And I know, I know he's only counting what he can get out of you. I know that's all it is. He's just a good-for-
nothing, who doesn't want to work, and who thinks he'll live on us. But
he won't live on me. If you're such a fool, then it's your own lookout.
Mrs. Burgess knew him all the time he was here. And the old man could
never get him to do any steady work. He was off with the gun on every
occasion, just as he is now. Nothing but the gun! Oh, I do hate it. You
don't know what you're doing, Nellie, you don't. If you marry him he'll
just make a fool of you. He'll go off and leave you stranded. I know he
will. If he can't get Bailey Farm out of us—and he's not going to, while I
live. While I live he's never going to set foot here. I know what it would
be. He'd soon think he was master of both of us, as he thinks he's master
of you already."

"But he isn't," said Nellie.

"He thinks he is, anyway. And that's what he wants: to come and be
master here. Yes, imagine it! That's what we've got the place together
for, is it, to be bossed and bullied by a hateful red-faced boy, a beastly
labourer? Oh, we *did* make a mistake when we let him stop. We ought
never to have lowered ourselves. And I've had such a fight with all the
people here, not to be pulled down to their level. No, he's not coming
here.—And then you see—if he can't have the place, he'll run off to Canada or somewhere again, as if he'd never known you. And here you'll be,
absolutely ruined and made a fool of. I know I shall never have any peace
of mind again."

"We'll tell him he can't come here. We'll tell him that," said March.

"Oh, don't you bother; I'm going to tell him that, and other things as
well, before he goes. He's not going to have all his own way, while I've
got the strength left to speak. Oh, Nellie, he'll despise you, he'll despise
you like the awful little beast he is, if you give way to him. I'd no more
trust him than I'd trust a cat not to steal. He's deep, he's deep, and he's
bossy, and he's selfish through and through, as cold as ice. All he wants is
to make use of you. And when you're no more use to him, then I pity
you."

"I don't think he's as bad as all that," said March.

"No, because he's been playing up to you. But you'll find out, if you see
much more of him. Oh, Nellie, I can't bear to think of it."

"Well, it won't hurt you, Jill darling."

"Won't it! Won't it! I shall never know a moment's peace again while I
live, nor a moment's happiness. No, Nellie—" and Banford began to weep
bitterly.

The boy outside could hear the stifled sound of the woman's sobbing,
and could hear March's soft, deep, tender voice comforting, with wonderful gentleness and tenderness, the weeping woman.

His eyes were so round and wide that he seemed to see the whole
night, and his ears were almost jumping off his head. He was frozen stiff.
He crept back to bed, but felt as if the top of his head were coming off.
He could not sleep. He could not keep still. He rose, quietly dressed him-
self, and crept out on to the landing once more. The women were silent.
He went softly downstairs and out to the kitchen.

Then he put on his boots and his overcoat, and took the gun. He did
not think to go away from the farm. No, he only took the gun. As softly as
possible he unfastened the door and went out into the frosty December

night, The air was still, the stars bright, the pine-trees seemed to bristle audibly in the sky. He went stealthily away down a fence-side, looking for something to shoot. At the same time he remembered that he ought not to shoot and frighten the women.

So he prowled round the edge of the gorse cover, and through the grove of tall old hollies, to the woodside. There he skirted the fence, peering through the darkness with dilated eyes that seemed to be able to grow black and full of sight in the dark, like a cat's. An owl was slowly and mournfully whooing round a great oak tree. He stepped stealthily with his gun, listening, listening, watching.

As he stood under the oaks of the wood-edge he heard the dogs from the neighbouring cottage, up the hill, yelling suddenly and startlingly, and the wakened dogs from the farms around barking answer. And suddenly, it seemed to him England was little and tight, he felt the landscape was constricted even in the dark, and that there were too many dogs in the night, making a noise like a fence of sound, like the network of English hedges netting the view. He felt the fox didn't have a chance. For it must be the fox that had started all this hullabaloo.

Why not watch for him, anyhow! He would no doubt be coming sniffing round. The lad walked downhill to where the farmstead with its few pine-trees crouched blackly. In the angle of the long shed, in the black dark, he crouched down. He knew the fox would be coming. It seemed to him it would be the last of the foxes in this loudly-barking, thick-voiced England, tight with innumerable little houses.

He sat a long time with his eyes fixed unchanging upon the open gateway, where a little light seemed to fall from the stars or from the horizon, who knows? He was sitting on a log in a dark corner with the gun across his knees. The pine-trees snapped. Once a chicken fell off its perch in the barn, with a loud crawk and cackle and commotion that startled him, and he stood up, watching with all his eyes, thinking it might be a rat. But he *felt* it was nothing. So he sat down again with the gun on his knees and his hands tucked in to keep them warm, and his eyes fixed unblinking on the pale reach of the open gateway. He felt he could smell the hot, sickly, rich smell of live chickens on the cold air.

And then—a shadow. A sliding shadow in the gateway. He gathered all his vision into a concentrated spark, and saw the shadow of the fox, the fox creeping on his belly through the gate. There he went, on his belly like a snake. The boy smiled to himself and brought the gun to his shoulder. He knew quite well what would happen. He knew the fox would go to where the fowl-door was boarded up, and sniff there. He knew he would lie there for a minute, sniffing the fowls within. And then he would start again prowling under the edge of the old barn, waiting to get in.

The fowl-door was at the top of a slight incline. Soft, soft as a shadow the fox slid up this incline, and crouched with his nose to the boards. And at the same moment there was the awful crash of a gun reverberating between the old buildings, as if all the night had gone smash. But the boy watched keenly. He saw even the white belly of the fox as the beast beat his paws in death. So he went forward.

There was a commotion everywhere. The fowls were scuffling and crawking, the ducks were quark-quarking, the pony had stamped wildly to his feet. But the fox was on his side, struggling in his last tremors. The boy bent over him and smelt his foxy smell.

There was a sound of a window opening upstairs, then March's voice calling:

"Who is it?"

"It's me," said Henry; "I've shot the fox."

"Oh, goodness! You nearly frightened us to death."

"Did I? I'm awfully sorry."

"Whatever made you get up?"

"I heard him about."

"And have you shot him?"

"Yes, he's here," and the boy stood in the yard holding up the warm, dead brute. "You can't see, can you? Wait a minute." And he took his flash-light from his pocket, and flashed it on to the dead animal. He was holding it by the brush. March saw, in the middle of the darkness, just the reddish fleece and the white belly and the white underneath of the pointed chin, and the queer, dangling paws. She did not know what to say.

"He's a beauty," he said. "He will make you a lovely fur."

"You don't catch me wearing a fox fur," she replied.

"Oh!" he said. And he switched off the light.

"Well, I should think you'd come in and go to bed again now," she said.

"Probably I shall. What time is it?"

"What time is it, Jill?" called March's voice. It was a quarter to one.

That night March had another dream. She dreamed that Banford was dead, and that she, March, was sobbing her heart out. Then she had to put Banford into her coffin. And the coffin was the rough wood-box in which the bits of chopped wood were kept in the kitchen, by the fire. This was the coffin, and there was no other, and March was in agony and dazed bewilderment, looking for something to line the box with, something to make it soft with, something to cover up the poor dead darling. Because she couldn't lay her in there just in her white thin nightdress, in the horrible wood box. So she hunted and hunted, and picked up thing after thing, and threw it aside in the agony of dream-frustration. And in her dream-despair all she could find that would do was a fox-skin. She knew that it wasn't right, that this was not what she should have. But it was all she could find. And so she folded the brush of the fox, and laid her darling Jill's head on this, and she brought round the skin of the fox and laid it on the top of the body, so that it seemed to make a whole ruddy, fiery coverlet, and she cried and cried and woke to find the tears streaming down her face.

The first thing that both she and Banford did in the morning was to go out to see the fox. He had hung it up by the heels in the shed, with its poor brush falling backwards. It was a lovely dog-fox in its prime, with a handsome thick winter coat: a lovely golden-red colour, with grey as it passed to the belly, and belly all white, and a great full brush with a delicate black and grey and pure white tip.

"Poor brute!" said Banford. "If it wasn't such a thieving wretch, you'd feel sorry for it."

March said nothing, but stood with her foot trailing aside, one hip out; her face was pale and her eyes big and black, watching the dead animal that was suspended upside down. White and soft as snow his belly: white and soft as snow. She passed her hand softly down it. And his wonderful black-glinted brush was full and frictional, wonderful. She passed her hand down this also, and quivered. Time after time she took the full fur of that thick tail between her hand, and passed her hand slowly downwards. Wonderful sharp thick splendour of a tail! And he was dead! She pursed her lips, and her eyes went black and vacant. Then she took the head in her hand.

Henry was sauntering up, so Banford walked rather pointedly away. March stood there bemused, with the head of the fox in her hand. She was wondering, wondering, wondering over his long fine muzzle. For some reason it reminded her of a spoon or a spatula. She felt she could not understand it. The beast was a strange beast to her, incomprehensible, out of her range. Wonderful silver whiskers he had, like ice-threads. And pricked ears with hair inside.—But that long, long slender spoon of a nose!—and the marvellous white teeth beneath! It was to thrust forward and bite with,—deep, deep into the living prey, to bite and bite the blood.

"He's a beauty, isn't he?" said Henry, standing by.

"Oh, yes, he's a fine big fox. I wonder how many chickens he's responsible for," she replied.

"A good many. Do you think he's the same one you saw in the summer?"

"I should think very likely he is," she replied.

He watched her, but he could make nothing of her. Partly she was so shy and virgin, and partly she was so grim, matter-of-fact, shrewish. What she said seemed to him so different from the look of her big, queer dark eyes.

"Are you going to skin him?" she asked.

"Yes, when I've had breakfast, and got a board to peg him on."

"My word, what a strong smell he's got! Pooo!—It'll take some washing off one's hands. I don't know why I was so silly as to handle him."—And she looked at her right hand, that had passed down his belly and along his tail, and had even got a tiny streak of blood from one dark place in his fur.

"Have you seen the chickens when they smell him, how frightened they are?" he said.

"Yes, aren't they!"

"You must mind you don't get some of his fleas."

"Oh, fleas!" she replied, nonchalant.

Later in the day she saw the fox's skin nailed flat on a board, as if crucified. It gave her an uneasy feeling.

The boy was angry. He went about with his mouth shut, as if he had swallowed part of his chin. But in behaviour he was polite and affable. He did not say anything about his intentions. And he left March alone.

That evening they sat in the dining-room. Banford wouldn't have him in her sitting-room any more. There was a very big log on the fire. And everybody was busy. Banford had letters to write, March was sewing a dress, and he was mending some little contrivance.

Banford stopped her letter-writing from time to time to look round and rest her eyes. The boy had his head down, his face hidden over his job.

"Let's see," said Banford. "What train do you go by, Henry?"

He looked up straight at her.

"The morning train. In the morning," he said.

"What, the eight-ten or the eleven-twenty?"

"The eleven-twenty, I suppose," he said.

"That is the day after to-morrow?" said Banford.

"Yes, the day after to-morrow."

"Mmm!" murmured Banford, and she returned to her writing. But as she was licking her envelope, she asked:

"And what plans have you made for the future, if I may ask?"

"Plans?" he said, his face very bright and angry.

"I mean about you and Nellie, if you are going on with this business. When do you expect the wedding to come off?" She spoke in a jeering tone.

"Oh, the wedding!" he replied. "I don't know."

"Don't you know anything?" said Banford. "Are you going to clear out on Friday and leave things no more settled than they are?"

"Well, why shouldn't I? We can always write letters."

"Yes, of course you can. But I wanted to know because of this place. If Nellie is going to get married all of a sudden, I shall have to be looking round for a new partner."

"Couldn't she stay on here if she was married?" he said. He knew quite well what was coming.

"Oh," said Banford, "this is no place for a married couple. There's not enough work to keep a man going, for one thing. And there's no money to be made. It's quite useless your thinking of staying on here if you marry. Absolutely!"

"Yes, but I wasn't thinking of staying on here," he said.

"Well, that's what I want to know. And what about Nellie, then? How long is *she* going to be here with me, in that case?"

The two antagonists looked at one another.

"That I can't say," he answered.

"Oh, go along," she cried petulantly. "You must have some idea what you are going to do, if you ask a woman to marry you. Unless it's all a hoax."

"Why should it be a hoax?—I am going back to Canada."

"And taking her with you?"

"Yes, certainly."

"You hear that, Nellie?" said Banford.

March, who had had her head bent over her sewing, now looked up with a sharp pink blush on her face and a queer, sardonic laugh in her eyes and on her twisted mouth.

"That's the first time I've heard that I was going to Canada," she said.

"Well, you have to hear it for the first time, haven't you?" said the boy.

"Yes, I suppose I have," she said nonchalantly. And she went back to her sewing.

"You're quite ready, are you, to go to Canada? Are you, Nellie?" asked Banford.

March looked up again. She let her shoulders go slack, and let her hand that held the needle lie loose in her lap.

"It depends on *how* I'm going," she said. "I don't think I want to go jammed up in the steerage, as a soldier's wife. I'm afraid I'm not used to that way."

The boy watched her with bright eyes.

"Would you rather stay over here while I go first?" he asked.

"I would, if that's the only alternative," she replied.

"That's much the wisest. Don't make it any fixed engagement," said Banford. "Leave yourself free to go or not after he's got back and found you a place, Nellie. Anything else is madness, madness."

"Don't you think," said the youth, "we ought to get married before I go—and then go together, or separate, according to how it happens?"

"I think it's a terrible idea," cried Banford.

But the boy was watching March.

"What do you think?" he asked her.

She let her eyes stray vaguely into space.

"Well, I don't know," she said. "I shall have to think about it."

"Why?" he asked, pertinently.

"Why?"—She repeated his question in a mocking way, and looked at him laughing, though her face was pink again. "I should think there's plenty of reasons why."

He watched her in silence. She seemed to have escaped him. She had got into league with Banford against him. There was again the queer sardonic look about her; she would mock stoically at everything he said or which life offered.

"Of course," he said, "I don't want to press you to do anything you don't wish to do."

"I should think not, indeed," cried Banford indignantly.

At bedtime Banford said plaintively to March:

"You take my hot bottle up for me, Nellie, will you?"

"Yes, I'll do it," said March, with the kind of willing unwillingness she so often showed towards her beloved but uncertain Jill.

The two women went upstairs. After a time March called from the top of the stairs: "Good-night, Henry. I shan't be coming down. You'll see to the lamp and the fire, won't you?"

The next day Henry went about with the cloud on his brow and his young cub's face shut up tight. He was cogitating all the time. He had wanted March to marry him and go back to Canada with him. And he had been sure she would do it. Why he wanted her he didn't know. But he did want her. He had set his mind on her. And he was convulsed with a youth's fury at being thwarted. To be thwarted, to be thwarted! It made him so furious inside, that he did not know what to do with himself. But he kept himself in hand. Because even now things might turn out differently. She might come over to him. Of course she might. It was her business to do so.

Things drew to a tension again towards evening. He and Banford had avoided each other all day. In fact Banford went in to the little town by the 11.20 train. It was market day. She arrived back on the 4.25. Just as the night was falling Henry saw her little figure in a dark-blue coat and a dark-blue tam-o'-shanter hat crossing the first meadow from the station. He stood under one of the wild pear-trees, with the old dead leaves round his feet. And he watched the little blue figure advancing persistently over the rough winter-ragged meadow. She had her arms full of parcels, and advanced slowly, frail thing she was, but with that devilish little certainty which he so detested in her. He stood invisible under the pear-tree, watching her every step. And if looks could have affected her, she would have felt a log of iron on each of her ankles as she made her way forward. "You're a nasty little thing, you are," he was saying softly, across the distance. "You're a nasty little thing. I hope you'll be paid back for all the harm you've done me for nothing. I hope you will—you nasty little thing. I hope you'll have to pay for it. You will, if wishes are anything. You nasty little creature that you are."

She was toiling slowly up the slope. But if she had been slipping back at every step towards the Bottomless Pit, he would not have gone to help her with her parcels. Aha! there went March, striding with her long, land stride in her breeches and her short tunic! Striding down hill at a great pace, and even running a few steps now and then, in her great solicitude and desire to come to the rescue of the little Banford. The boy watched her with rage in his heart. See her leap a ditch, and run, run as if a house was on fire, just to get to that creeping dark little object down there! So, the Banford just stood still and waited. And March strode up and took *all* the parcels except a bunch of yellow chrysanthemums. These the Banford still carried—yellow chrysanthemums!

"Yes, you look well, don't you," he said softly into the dusk air. "You look well, pottering up there with a bunch of flowers, you do. I'd make you eat them for your tea, if you hug them so tight. And I'd give them you for breakfast again, I would. I'd give you flowers. Nothing but flowers."

He watched the progress of the two women. He could hear their voices: March always outspoken and rather scolding in her tenderness, Banford murmuring rather vaguely. They were evidently good friends. He could not hear what they said till they came to the fence of the home meadow, which they must climb. Then he saw March manfully climbing over the bars with all her packages in her arms, and on the still air he heard Banford's fretful:

"Why don't you let me help you with the parcels?" She had a queer plaintive hitch in her voice.—Then came March's robust and reckless:

"Oh, I can manage. Don't you bother about me. You've all you can do to get yourself over."

"Yes, that's all very well," said Banford fretfully. "You say '*Don't you bother about me*' and then all the while you feel injured because nobody thinks of you."

"When do I feel injured?" said March.

"Always. You always feel injured. Now you're feeling injured because I won't have that boy to come and live on the farm."

"I'm not feeling injured at all," said March.

"I know you are. When he's gone you'll sulk over it. I know you will."

"Shall I?" said March. "We'll see."

"Yes, we *shall* see, unfortunately.—I can't think how you can make yourself so cheap. I can't *imagine* how you can lower yourself like it."

"I haven't lowered myself," said March.

"I don't know what you call it, then. Letting a boy like that come so cheeky and impudent and make a mug of you. I don't know what you think of yourself. How much respect do you think he's going to have for you afterwards?—My word, I wouldn't be in your shoes, if you married him."

"Of course you wouldn't. My boots are a good bit too big for you, and not half dainty enough," said March, with rather a miss-fire sarcasm.

D. H. Lawrence

"I thought you had too much pride, really I did. A woman's got to hold herself high, especially with a youth like that. Why, he's impudent. Even the way he forced himself on us at the start."

"We asked him to stay," said March.

"Not till he'd almost forced us to.—And then he's so cocky and self-assured. My word, he puts my back up. I simply can't imagine how you can let him treat you so cheaply."

"I don't let him treat me cheaply," said March. "Don't you worry yourself, nobody's going to treat me cheaply. And even you aren't, either." She had a tender defiance, and a certain fire in her voice.

"Yes, it's sure to come back to me," said Banford bitterly. "That's always the end of it. I believe you only do it to spite me."

They went now in silence up the steep grassy slope and over the brow through the gorse bushes. On the other side of the hedge the boy followed in the dusk, at some little distance. Now and then, through the huge ancient hedge of hawthorn, risen into trees, he saw the two dark figures creeping up the hill. As he came to the top of the slope he saw the homestead dark in the twilight, with a huge old pear-tree leaning from the near gable, and a little yellow light twinkling in the small side windows of the kitchen. He heard the clink of the latch and saw the kitchen door open into light as the two women went indoors. So, they were at home.

And so!—this was what they thought of him. It was rather in his nature to be a listener, so he was not at all suprised whatever he heard. The things people said about him always missed him personally. He was only rather surprised at the women's way with one another. And he disliked the Banford with an acid dislike. And he felt drawn to the March again. He felt again irresistibly drawn to her. He felt there was a secret bond, a secret thread between him and her, something very exclusive, which shut out everybody else and made him and her possess each other in secret.

He hoped again that she would have him. He hoped with his blood suddenly firing up that she would agree to marry him quite quickly: at Christmas, very likely. Christmas was not far off. He wanted, whatever else happened, to snatch her into a hasty marriage and a consummation with him. Then for the future, they could arrange later. But he hoped it would happen as he wanted it. He hoped that to-night she would stay a little while with him, after Banford had gone upstairs. He hoped he could touch her soft, creamy cheek, her strange, frightened face. He hoped he could look into her dilated, frightened dark eyes, quite near. He hoped he might even put his hand on her bosom and feel her soft breasts under her tunic. His heart beat deep and powerful as he thought of that. He wanted very much to do so. He wanted to make sure of her soft woman's breasts under her tunic. She always kept the brown linen coat buttoned so close up to her throat. It seemed to him like some perilous secret, that her soft woman's breasts must be buttoned up in that uniform. It seemed to him moreover that they were so much softer, tenderer, more lovely and lovable, shut up in that tunic, than were the Banford's breasts, under her soft blouses and chiffon dresses. The Banford would have little iron breasts, he said to himself. For all her frailty and fretfulness and delicacy, she would have tiny iron breasts. But March under her crude, fast, workman's tunic, would have soft white breasts, white and unseen. So he told himself, and his blood burned.

When he went in to tea, he had a surprise. He appeared at the inner door, his face very ruddy and vivid and his blue eyes shining, dropping his head forward as he came in, in his usual way, and hesitating in the doorway to watch the inside of the room, keenly and cautiously, before he entered. He was wearing a long-sleeved waistcoat. His face seemed extraordinarily like a piece of the out-of-doors come indoors: as holly-berries do. In his second of pause in the doorway he took in the two women sitting at table, at opposite ends, saw them sharply. And to his amazement March was dressed in a dress of dull, green silk crêpe. His mouth came open in surprise. If she had suddenly grown a moustache he could not have been more surprised.

"Why," he said, "do you wear a dress, then?"

She looked up, flushing a deep rose colour, and twisting her mouth with a smile, said:

"Of course I do. What else do you expect me to wear, but a dress?"

"A land girl's uniform, of course," said he.

"Oh," she cried nonchalant, "that's only for this dirty mucky work about here."

"Isn't it your proper dress, then?" he said.

"No, not indoors it isn't," she said. But she was blushing all the time as she poured out his tea. He sat down in his chair at table, unable to take his eyes off her. Her dress was a perfectly simple slip of bluey-green crêpe, with a line of gold stitching round the top and round the sleeves, which came to the elbow. It was cut just plain and round at the top, and showed her white soft throat. Her arms he knew, strong and firm muscled, for he had often seen her with her sleeves rolled up. But he looked her up and down, up and down.

Banford, at the other end of the table, said not a word, but piggled[6] with the sardine on her plate. He had forgotten her existence. He just simply stared at March, while he ate his bread and margarine in huge mouthfuls, forgetting even his tea.

"Well, I never knew anything make such a difference!" he murmured, across his mouthfuls.

"Oh, goodness!" cried March, blushing still more. "I might be a pink monkey!"

And she rose quickly to her feet and took the tea-pot to the fire, to the kettle. And as she crouched on the hearth with her green slip about her, the boy stared more wide-eyed than ever. Through the crêpe her woman's form seemed soft and womanly. And when she stood up and walked he saw her legs move soft within her modernly short skirt. She had on black silk stockings and small, patent-leather shoes with little gold buckles.

No, she was another being. She was something quite different. Seeing her always in the hard-cloth breeches, wide on the hips, buttoned on the knee, strong as armour, and in the brown puttees and thick boots, it had never occurred to him that she had a woman's legs and feet. Now it came upon him. She had a woman's soft, skirted legs, and she was accessible. He blushed to the roots of his hair, shoved his nose in his teacup and drank his tea with a little noise that made Banford simply squirm: and strangely, suddenly he felt a man, no longer a youth. He felt a man, with

---

6. Picked at; touched continually.

all a man's grave weight of responsibility. A curious quietness and gravity came over his soul. He felt a man, quiet, with a little of the heaviness of male destiny upon him.

She was soft and accessible in her dress. The thought went home in him like an everlasting responsibility.

"Oh, for goodness sake, say something, somebody," cried Banford fretfully. "It might be a funeral." The boy looked at her, and she could not bear his face.

"A funeral!" said March, with a twisted smile. "Why, that breaks my dream."

Suddenly she had thought of Banford in the wood-box for a coffin.

"What, have you been dreaming of a wedding?" said Banford sarcastically.

"Must have been," said March.

"Whose wedding?" asked the boy.

"I can't remember," said March.

She was shy and rather awkward that evening, in spite of the fact that, wearing a dress, her bearing was much more subdued than in her uniform. She felt unpeeled and rather exposed. She felt almost improper.

They talked desultorily about Henry's departure next morning, and made the trivial arrangement. But of the matter on their minds, none of them spoke. They were rather quiet and friendly this evening; Banford had practically nothing to say. But inside herself she seemed still, perhaps kindly.

At nine o'clock March brought in the tray with the everlasting tea and a little cold meat which Banford had managed to procure. It was the last supper, so Banford did not want to be disagreeable. She felt a bit sorry for the boy, and felt she must be as nice as she could.

He wanted her to go to bed. She was usually the first. But she sat on in her chair under the lamp, glancing at her book now and then, and staring into the fire. A deep silence had come into the room. It was broken by March asking, in a rather small tone:

"What time is it, Jill?"

"Five past ten," said Banford, looking at her wrist.

And then not a sound. The boy had looked up from the book he was holding between his knees. His rather wide, cat-shaped face had its obstinate look, his eyes were watchful.

"What about bed?" said March at last.

"I'm ready when you are," said Banford.

"Oh, very well," said March. "I'll fill your bottle."

She was as good as her word. When the hot-water bottle was ready, she lit a candle and went upstairs with it. Banford remained in her chair, listening acutely. March came downstairs again.

"There you are then," she said. "Are you going up?"

"Yes, in a minute," said Banford. But the minute passed, and she sat on in her chair under the lamp.

Henry, whose eyes were shining like a cat's as he watched from under his brows, and whose face seemed wider, more chubbed[7] and cat-like with unalterable obstinacy, now rose to his feet to try his throw.

_____
7. Rounded.

"I think I'll go and look if I can see the she-fox," he said. "She may be creeping round. Won't you come as well for a minute, Nellie, and see if we see anything?"

"Me!" cried March, looking up with her startled, wondering face.

"Yes. Come on," he said. It was wonderful how soft and warm and coaxing his voice could be, how near. The very sound of it made Banford's blood boil.

"Come on for a minute," he said, looking down into her uplifted, unsure face.

And she rose to her feet as if drawn up by his young, ruddy face that was looking down on her.

"I should think you're never going out at this time of night, Nellie!" cried Banford.

"Yes, just for a minute," said the boy, looking round on her, and speaking with an odd sharp yelp in his voice.

March looked from one to the other, as if confused, vague. Banford rose to her feet for a battle.

"Why, it's ridiculous. It's bitter cold. You'll catch your death in that thin frock. And in those slippers. You're not going to do any such thing."

There was a moment's pause. Banford turtled up like a little fighting cock, facing March and the boy.

"Oh, I don't think you need worry yourself," he replied. "A moment under the stars won't do anybody any damage. I'll get the rug off the sofa in the dining-room. You're coming, Nellie."

His voice had so much anger and contempt and fury in it as he spoke to Banford: and so much tenderness and proud authority as he spoke to March, that the latter answered:

"Yes, I'm coming."

And she turned with him to the door.

Banford, standing there in the middle of the room, suddenly burst into a long wail and a spasm of sobs. She covered her face with her poor thin hands, and her thin shoulders shook in an agony of weeping. March looked back from the door.

"Jill!" she cried in a frantic tone, like someone just coming awake. And she seemed to start towards her darling.

But the boy had March's arm in his grip, and she could not move. She did not know why she could not move. It was as in a dream when the heart strains and the body cannot stir.

"Never mind," said the boy, softly. "Let her cry. Let her cry. She will have to cry sooner or later. And the tears will relieve her feelings. They will do her good."

So he drew March slowly through the door-way. But her last look was back to the poor little figure which stood in the middle of the room with covered face and thin shoulders shaken with bitter weeping.

In the dining-room he picked up the rug and said:

"Wrap yourself up in this."

She obeyed—and they reached the kitchen door, he holding her soft and firm by the arm, though she did not know it. When she saw the night outside she started back.

"I must go back to Jill," she said. "I *must!* Oh, yes, I must!"

Her tone sounded final. The boy let go of her and she turned indoors.

106   D. H. Lawrence

But he seized her again and arrested her.

"Wait a minute," he said. "Wait a minute. Even if you go you're not going yet."

"Leave go! Leave go!" she cried. "My place is at Jill's side. Poor little thing, she's sobbing her heart out."

"Yes," said the boy bitterly. "And your heart, too, and mine as well."

"Your heart?" said March. He still gripped her and detained her.

"Isn't it as good as her heart?" he said. "Or do you think it's not?"

"Your heart?" she said again, incredulous.

"Yes, mine! Mine! Do you think I haven't *got* a heart?"—And with his hot grasp he took her hand and pressed it under his left breast. "There's my heart," he said, "if you don't believe in it."

It was wonder which made her attend. And then she felt the deep, heavy, powerful stroke of his heart, terrible, like something from beyond. It was like something from beyond, something awful from outside, signalling to her. And the signal paralysed her. It beat upon her very soul, and made her helpless. She forgot Jill. She could not think of Jill any more. She could not think of her. That terrible signalling from outside!

The boy put his arm round her waist.

"Come with me," he said gently. "Come and let us say what we've got to say."

And he drew her outside, closed the door. And she went with him darkly down the garden path. That he should have a beating heart! And that he should have his arm round her, outside the blanket! She was too confused to think who he was or what he was.

He took her to a dark corner of the shed, where there was a tool-box with a lid, long and low.

"We'll sit here a minute," he said.

And obediently she sat down by his side.

"Give me your hand," he said.

She gave him both her hands, and he held them between his own. He was young, and it made him tremble.

"You'll marry me. You'll marry me before I go back, won't you?" he pleaded.

"Why, aren't we both a pair of fools!" she said.

He had put her in the corner, so that she should not look out and see the lighted window of the house, across the dark yard and garden. He tried to keep her all there inside the shed with him.

"In what way a pair of fools?" he said. "If you go back to Canada with me, I've got a job and a good wage waiting for me, and it's a nice place, near the mountains. Why shouldn't you marry me? Why shouldn't we marry? I should like to have you there with me. I should like to feel I'd got somebody there, at the back of me, all my life."

"You'd easily find somebody else, who'd suit you better," she said.

"Yes, I might easily find another girl. I know I could. But not one I really wanted. I've never met one I really wanted, for good. You see, I'm thinking of all my life. If I marry, I want to feel it's for all my life. Other girls: well, they're just girls, nice enough to go a walk with now and then. Nice enough for a bit of play. But when I think of my life, then I should be very sorry to have to marry one of them, I should indeed."

"You mean they wouldn't make you a good wife."

"Yes, I mean that. But I don't mean they wouldn't do their duty by me.

I mean—I don't know what I mean. Only when I think of my life, and of you, then the two things go together."

"And what if they didn't?" she said, with her odd sardonic touch.

"Well, I think they would."

They sat for some time silent. He held her hands in his, but he did not make love to her. Since he had realized that she was a woman, and vulnerable, accessible, a certain heaviness had possessed his soul. He did not want to make love to her. He shrank from any such performance, almost with fear. She was a woman, and vulnerable, accessible to him finally, and he held back from that which was ahead, almost with dread. It was a kind of darkness he knew he would enter finally, but of which he did not want as yet even to think. She was the woman, and he was responsible for the strange vulnerability he had suddenly realized in her.

"No," she said at last, "I'm a fool. I know I'm a fool."

"What for?" he asked.

"To go on with this business."

"Do you mean me?" he asked.

"No, I mean myself. I'm making a fool of myself, and a big one."

"Why, because you don't want to marry me, really?"

"Oh, I don't know whether I'm against it, as a matter of fact. That's just it. I don't know."

He looked at her in the darkness, puzzled. He did not in the least know what she meant.

"And don't you know whether you like to sit here with me this minute, or not?" he asked.

"No, I don't, really. I don't know whether I wish I was somewhere else, or whether I like being here. I don't know, really."

"Do you wish you were with Miss Banford? Do you wish you'd gone to bed with her?" he asked, as a challenge.

She waited a long time before she answered:

"No," she said at last. "I don't wish that."

"And do you think you would spend all your life with her—when your hair goes white, and you are old?" he said.

"No," she said, without much hesitation. "I don't see Jill and me two old women together."

"And don't you think, when I'm an old man, and you're an old woman, we might be together still, as we are now?" he said.

"Well, not as we are now," she replied. "But I could imagine—no, I can't. I can't imagine you an old man. Besides, it's dreadful!"

"What, to be an old man?"

"Yes, of course."

"Not when the time comes," he said. "But it hasn't come. Only it will. And when it does, I should like to think you'd be there as well."

"Sort of old age pensions," she said drily.

Her kind of witless humour always startled him. He never knew what she meant. Probably she didn't quite know herself.

"No," he said, hurt.

"I don't know why you harp on old age," she said. "I'm not ninety."

"Did anybody ever say you were?" he asked, offended.

They were silent for some time, pulling different ways in the silence.

"I don't want you to make fun of me," he said.

"Don't you?" she replied, enigmatic.

"No, because just this minute I'm serious. And when I'm serious, I believe in not making fun of it."

"You mean nobody else must make fun of you," she replied.

"Yes, I mean that. And I mean I don't believe in making fun of it
myself. When it comes over me so that I'm serious, then—there it is, I
don't want it to be laughed at."

She was silent for some time. Then she said, in a vague, almost pained
voice:

"No, I'm not laughing at you."

A hot wave rose in his heart.

"You believe me, do you?" he asked.

"Yes, I believe you," she replied, with a twang of her old tired noncha-
lance, as if she gave in because she was tired.—But he didn't care. His
heart was hot and clamorous.

"So you agree to marry me before I go?—perhaps at Christmas?"

"Yes, I agree."

"There!" he exclaimed. "That's settled it."

And he sat silent, unconscious, with all the blood burning in all his
veins, like fire in all the branches and twigs of him. He only pressed her
two hands to his chest, without knowing. When the curious passion began
to die down, he seemed to come awake to the world.

"We'll go in, shall we?" he said: as if he realized it was cold.

She rose without answering.

"Kiss me before we go, now you've said it," he said.

And he kissed her gently on the mouth, with a young, frightened kiss. It
made her feel so young, too, and frightened, and wondering: and tired,
tired, as if she were going to sleep.

They went indoors. And in the sitting-room, there, crouched by the fire
like a queer little witch, was Banford. She looked round with reddened
eyes as they entered, but did not rise. He thought she looked frightening,
unnatural, crouching there and looking round at them. Evil he thought
her look was, and he crossed his fingers.

Banford saw the ruddy, elate face of the youth: he seemed strangely
tall and bright and looming. And March had a delicate look on her face;
she wanted to hide her face, to screen it, to let it not be seen.

"You've come at last," said Banford uglily.

"Yes, we've come," said he.

"You've been long enough for anything," she said.

"Yes, we have. We've settled it. We shall marry as soon as possible," he
replied.

"Oh, you've settled it, have you! Well, I hope you won't live to repent
it," said Banford.

"I hope so too," he replied.

"Are you going to bed *now*, Nellie?" said Banford.

"Yes, I'm going now."

"Then for goodness sake come along."

March looked at the boy. He was glancing with his very bright eyes at
her and at Banford. March looked at him wistfully. She wished she could
stay with him. She wished she had married him already, and it was all
over. For oh, she felt suddenly so safe with him. She felt so strangely safe
and peaceful in his presence. If only she could sleep in his shelter, and
not with Jill. She felt afraid of Jill. In her dim, tender state, it was agony

to have to go with Jill and sleep with her. She wanted the boy to save her. She looked again at him.

And he, watching with bright eyes, divined something of what she felt. It puzzled and distressed him that she must go with Jill.

"I shan't forget what you've promised," he said, looking clear into her eyes, right into her eyes, so that he seemed to occupy all her self with his queer, bright look.

She smiled to him, faintly, gently. She felt safe again—safe with him.

But in spite of all the boy's precautions, he had a set-back. The morning he was leaving the farm he got March to accompany him to the market-town, about six miles away, where they went to the registrar and had their names stuck up as two people who were going to marry. He was to come at Christmas, and the wedding was to take place then. He hoped in the spring to be able to take March back to Canada with him, now the war was really over. Though he was so young, he had saved some money.

"You never have to be without *some* money at the back of you, if you can help it," he said.

So she saw him off in the train that was going West: his camp was on Salisbury plains. And with big dark eyes she watched him go, and it seemed as if everything real in life was retreating as the train retreated with his queer, chubby, ruddy face, that seemed so broad across the cheeks, and which never seemed to change its expression, save when a cloud of sulky anger hung on the brow, or the bright eyes fixed themselves in their stare. This was what happened now. He leaned there out of the carriage window as the train drew off, saying good-bye and staring back at her, but his face quite unchanged. There was no emotion on his face. Only his eyes tightened and became fixed and intent in their watching, as a cat when suddenly she sees something and stares. So the boy's eyes stared fixedly as the train drew away, and she was left feeling intensely forlorn. Failing his physical presence, she seemed to have nothing of him. And she had nothing of anything. Only his face was fixed in her mind: the full, ruddy, unchanging cheeks, and the straight snout of a nose, and the two eyes staring above. All she could remember was how he suddenly wrinkled his nose when he laughed, as a puppy does when he is playfully growling. But him, himself, and what he was—she knew nothing, she had nothing of him when he left her.

On the ninth day after he had left her he received this letter:

"DEAR HENRY,

"I have been over it all again in my mind, this business of me and you, and it seems to me impossible. When you aren't there I see what a fool I am. When you are there you seem to blind me to things as they actually are. You make me see things all unreal and I don't know what. Then when I am alone again with Jill I seem to come to my own senses and realize what a fool I am making of myself and how I am treating you unfairly. Because it must be unfair to you for me to go on with this affair when I can't feel in my heart that I really love you. I know people talk a lot of stuff and nonsense about love, and I don't want to do that. I want to keep to plain facts and act in a sensible way. And that seems to me what I'm not doing. I don't see on what grounds I am going to marry you. I know I am not head over heels in love with you, as I have fancied myself to be with fellows when I was a young fool of a girl. You are an absolute stranger to me, and it seems to me you will always be one. So on what grounds am I going to marry you? When I think of Jill, she is ten times more real to me. I know her and I'm awfully fond of her and I hate myself for a beast if I ever hurt her little finger. We have a life together. And even if it can't last for ever, it is a life while it does last. And it might last as long as either of us lives. Who knows how long we've got to live? She is a delicate little thing, perhaps nobody but me knows how delicate. And as for me, I feel I might fall down the well any day. What I don't seem to see at all is you. When I think of what I've been and what I've done with you, I'm afraid I am a few screws loose. I should be sorry to think that softening of the brain is setting in so soon, but that is what it seems like. You are such an absolute stranger and so different from what I'm used to and we don't seem to have a thing in common. As for love, the very word seems impossible. I know what love means even in Jill's case, and I know that in this affair with you it's an absolute impossibility. And then going to Canada. I'm sure I must have been clean off my chump when I promised such a thing. It makes me feel fairly frightened of myself. I feel I might do something really silly, that I wasn't responsible for. And end my days in a lunatic asylum. You may think that's all I'm fit for after the way I've gone on, but it isn't a very nice thought for me. Thank goodness Jill is here and her being here makes me feel sane again, else I don't know what I might do; I might have an accident with the gun one evening. I love Jill and she makes me feel safe and sane, with her loving anger against me for being such a fool. Well, what I want to say is, won't you let us cry the whole thing off? I can't marry you, and really, I won't do such a thing if it seems to me wrong. It is all a great mistake. I've made a complete fool of myself, and all I can do is to apologize to you and ask you please to forget it and please to take no further notice of me. Your fox skin is nearly ready and seems all right. I will post it to you if you will let me know if this address is still right, and if you will accept my apology for the awful and lunatic way I have behaved with you, and then let the matter rest.

"Jill sends her kindest regards. Her mother and father are staying with us over Christmas.

"Yours very sincerely,
"ELLEN MARCH."

The boy read this letter in camp as he was cleaning his kit. He set his teeth and for a moment went almost pale, yellow round the eyes with fury. He said nothing and saw nothing and felt nothing but a livid rage that was quite unreasoning. Balked! Balked again! Balked! He wanted the woman, he had fixed like doom upon having her. He felt that was his doom, his destiny, and his reward, to have this woman. She was his heaven and hell on earth, and he would have none elsewhere. Sightless with rage and thwarted madness he got through the morning. Save that in his mind he was lurking and scheming towards an issue, he would have committed some insane act. Deep in himself he felt like roaring and howling and gnashing his teeth and breaking things. But he was too intelligent. He knew society was on top of him, and he must scheme. So with his teeth bitten together and his nose curiously slightly lifted, like some creature that is vicious, and his eyes fixed and staring, he went through the morning's affairs drunk with anger and suppression. In his mind was one thing—Banford. He took no heed of all March's outpouring: none. One thorn rankled, stuck in his mind. Banford. In his mind, in his soul, in his whole being, one thorn rankling to insanity. And he would have to get it out. He would have to get the thorn of Banford out of his life, if he died for it.

With this one fixed idea in his mind, he went to ask for twenty-four hours' leave of absence. He knew it was not due to him. His consciousness was supernaturally keen. He knew where he must go—he must go to the captain. But how could he get at the captain? In that great camp of wooden huts and tents, he had no idea where his captain was.

But he went to the officers' canteen. There was his captain standing talking with three other officers. Henry stood in the door-way at attention.

"May I speak to Captain Berryman?"—The captain was Cornish like himself.

"What do you want?" called the captain.

"May I speak to you, Captain?"

"What do you want?" replied the captain, not stirring from among his group of fellow officers.

Henry watched his superior for a minute without speaking.

"You won't refuse me, sir, will you?" he asked gravely.

"It depends what it is."

"Can I have twenty-four hours' leave?"

"No, you've no business to ask."

"I know I haven't. But I must ask you."

"You've had your answer."

"Don't send me away, Captain."

There was something strange about the boy as he stood there so everlasting in the door-way. The Cornish captain felt the strangeness at once, and eyed him shrewdly.

"Why, what's afoot?" he said, curious.

"I'm in trouble about something. I must go to Blewbury," said the boy.

"Blewbury, eh? After the girls?"

"Yes, it is a woman, Captain." And the boy, as he stood there with his head reaching forward a little, went suddenly terribly pale, or yellow, and his lips seemed to give off pain. The captain saw and paled a little also. He turned aside.

"Go on then," he said. "But for God's sake don't cause any trouble of any sort."

"I won't, Captain, thank you."

He was gone. The captain, upset, took a gin and bitters. Henry managed to hire a bicycle. It was twelve o'clock when he left the camp. He had sixty miles of wet and muddy cross-roads to ride. But he was in the saddle and down the road without a thought of food.

At the farm, March was busy with a work she had had some time in hand. A bunch of Scotch fir-trees stood at the end of the open shed, on a little bank where ran the fence between two of the gorse-shaggy meadows. The furthest of these trees was dead—it had died in the summer and stood with all its needles brown and sere in the air. It was not a very big tree. And it was absolutely dead. So March determined to have it, although they were not allowed to cut any of the timber. But it would make such splendid firing, in these days of scarce fuel.

She had been giving a few stealthy chops at the trunk for a week or more, every now and then hacking away for five minutes, low down, near the ground, so no one should notice. She had not tried the saw, it was such hard work, alone. Now the tree stood with a great yawning gap in his base, perched as it were on one sinew, and ready to fall. But he did not fall.

It was late in the damp December afternoon, with cold mists creeping out of the woods and up the hollows, and darkness waiting to sink in from above. There was a bit of yellowness where the sun was fading away beyond the low woods of the distance. March took her axe and went to the tree. The small thud-thud of her blows resounded rather ineffectual about the wintry homestead. Banford came out wearing her thick coat, but with no hat on her head, so that her thin, bobbed hair blew on the uneasy wind that sounded in the pines and in the wood.

"What I'm afraid of," said Banford, "is that it will fall on the shed and we'll have another job repairing that."

"Oh, I don't think so," said March, straightening herself and wiping her arm over her hot brow. She was flushed red, her eyes were very wide-open and queer, her upper lip away from her two white front teeth with a curious, almost rabbit-look.

A little stout man in a black overcoat and a bowler hat came pottering across the yard. He had a pink face and a white beard and smallish, pale-blue eyes. He was not very old, but nervy, and he walked with little short steps.

"What do you think, father?" said Banford. "Don't you think it might hit the shed in falling?"

"Shed, no!" said the old man. "Can't hit the shed. Might as well say the fence."

"The fence doesn't matter," said March, in her high voice.

"Wrong as usual, am I?" said Banford, wiping her straying hair from her eyes.

The tree stood as it were on one spelch[8] of itself, leaning, and creaking in the wind. It grew on the bank of a little dry ditch between the two meadows. On the top of the bank straggled one fence, running to the bushes uphill. Several trees clustered there in the corner of the field near the shed and near the gate which led into the yard. Towards this gate, horizontal across the weary meadows, came the grassy, rutted approach from the highroad. There trailed another rickety fence, long split poles joining the short, thick, wide-apart uprights. The three people stood at the back of the tree, in the corner of the shed meadow, just above the yard gate. The house with its two gables and its porch stood tidy in a little grassed garden across the yard. A little stout rosy-faced woman in a little red woollen shoulder shawl had come and taken her stand in the porch.

"Isn't it down yet?" she cried, in a high little voice.

"Just thinking about it," called her husband. His tone towards the two girls was always rather mocking and satirical. March did not want to go

8. Spelk, splinter.

on with her hitting while he was there. As for him, he wouldn't lift a stick from the ground if he could help it, complaining, like his daughter, of rheumatics in his shoulder. So the three stood there a moment silent in the cold afternoon, in the bottom corner near the yard.

They heard the far-off taps of a gate, and craned to look. Away across, on the green horizontal approach, a figure was just swinging on to a bicycle again, and lurching up and down over the grass, approaching.

"Why it's one of our boys—it's Jack," said the old man.

"Can't be," said Banford.

March craned her head to look. She alone recognized the khaki figure. She flushed, but said nothing.

"No, it isn't Jack, I don't think," said the old man, staring with little round blue eyes under his white lashes.

In another moment the bicycle lurched into sight, and the rider dropped off at the gate. It was Henry, his face wet and red and spotted with mud. He was altogether a muddy sight.

"Oh!" cried Banford, as if afraid. "Why, it's Henry!"

"What!" muttered the old man. He had a thick, rapid, muttering way of speaking, and was slightly deaf. "What? What? Who is it? Who is it, do you say? That young fellow? That young fellow of Nellie's? Oh! Oh!" And the satiric smile came on his pink face and white eyelashes.

Henry, pushing the wet hair off his steaming brow, had caught sight of them and heard what the old man said. His hot young face seemed to flame in the cold light.

"Oh, are you all there!" he said, giving his sudden, puppy's little laugh. He was so hot and dazed with cycling he hardly knew where he was. He leaned the bicycle against the fence and climbed over into the corner on to the bank, without going in to the yard.

"Well, I must say, we weren't expecting *you*," said Banford laconically.

"No, I suppose not," said he, looking at March.

She stood aside, slack, with one knee drooped and the axe resting its head loosely on the ground. Her eyes were wide and vacant, and her upper lip lifted from her teeth in that helpless, fascinated rabbit-look. The moment she saw his glowing red face it was all over with her. She was as helpless as if she had been bound. The moment she saw the way his head seemed to reach forward.

"Well, who is it? Who is it, anyway?" asked the smiling, satiric old man in his muttering voice.

"Why, Mr. Grenfel, whom you've heard us tell about, father," said Banford coldly.

"Heard you tell about, I should think so. Heard of nothing else practically," muttered the elderly man with his queer little jeering smile on his face. "How do you do," he added, suddenly reaching out his hand to Henry.

The boy shook hands just as startled. Then the two men fell apart.

"Cycled over from Salisbury Plain have you?" asked the old man.

"Yes."

"Ha! Longish ride. How long d'it take you, eh? Some time, eh? Several hours, I suppose."

"About four."

"Eh? Four! Yes, I should have thought so. When are you going back then?"

"I've got till to-morrow evening."

"Till to-morrow evening, eh? Yes. Ha! Girls weren't expecting you, were they?"

And the old man turned his pale-blue, round little eyes under their white lashes mockingly towards the girls. Henry also looked round. He had become a little awkward. He looked at March, who was still staring away into the distance as if to see where the cattle were. Her hand was on the pommel of the axe, whose head rested loosely on the ground.

"What were you doing there?" he asked in his soft, courteous voice. "Cutting a tree down?"

March seemed not to hear, as if in a trance.

"Yes," said Banford. "We've been at it for over a week."

"Oh! And have you done it all by yourselves, then?"

"Nellie's done it all, I've done nothing," said Banford.

"Really!—You must have worked quite hard," he said, addressing himself in a curious gentle tone direct to March. She did not answer, but remained half averted, staring away towards the woods above as if in a trance.

"*Nellie!*" cried Banford sharply. "Can't you answer?"

"What—me?" cried March, starting round, and looking from one to the other. "Did anyone speak to me?"

"Dreaming!" muttered the old man, turning aside to smile. "Must be in love, eh, dreaming in the day-time!"

"Did you say anything to me?" said March, looking at the boy as from a strange distance, her eyes wide and doubtful, her face delicately flushed.

"I said you must have worked hard at the tree," he replied courteously.

"Oh, that! Bit by bit. I thought it would have come down by now."

"I'm thankful it hasn't come down in the night, to frighten us to death," said Banford.

"Let me just finish it for you, shall I?" said the boy.

March slanted the axe-shaft in his direction.

"Would you like to?" she said.

"Yes, if you wish it," he said.

"Oh, I'm thankful when the thing's down, that's all," she replied, nonchalant.

"Which way is it going to fall?" said Banford. "Will it hit the shed?"

"No, it won't hit the shed," he said. "I should think it will fall there—quite clear. Though it might give a twist and catch the fence."

"Catch the fence!" cried the old man. "What, catch the fence! When it's leaning at that angle?—Why it's further off than the shed. It won't catch the fence."

"No," said Henry, "I don't suppose it will. It has plenty of room to fall quite clear, and I suppose it will fall clear."

"Won't tumble backwards on top of *us*, will it?" asked the old man sarcastic.

"No, it won't do that," said Henry, taking off his short overcoat and his tunic. "Ducks! Ducks! Go back!"

A line of four brown-speckled ducks led by a brown-and-green drake were stemming away downhill from the upper meadow, coming like boats running on a ruffled sea, cackling their way top speed downwards towards the fence and towards the little group of people, and cackling as excitedly as if they brought news of the Spanish Armada.

"Silly things! Silly things!" cried Banford going forward to turn them off. But they came eagerly towards her, opening their yellow-green beaks and quacking as if they were so excited to say something.

"There's no food. There's nothing here. You must wait a bit," said Banford to them. "Go away. Go away. Go round to the yard."

They didn't go, so she climbed the fence to swerve them round under the gate and into the yard. So off they waggled in an excited string once more, wagging their rumps like the sterns of little gondolas ducking under the bar of the gate. Banford stood on the top of the bank, just over the fence, looking down on the other three.

Henry looked up at her, and met her queer, round-pupilled, weak eyes staring behind her spectacles. He was perfectly still. He looked away, up at the weak, leaning tree. And as he looked into the sky, like a huntsman who is watching a flying bird, he thought to himself: "If the tree falls in just such a way, and spins just so much as it falls, then the branch there will strike her exactly as she stands on top of that bank."

He looked at her again. She was wiping the hair from her brow again, with that perpetual gesture. In his heart he had decided her death. A terrible still force seemed in him, and a power that was just his. If he turned even a hair's breadth in the wrong direction, he would lose the power.

"Mind yourself, Miss Banford," he said. And his heart held perfectly still, in the terrible pure will that she should not move.

"Who me, mind myself?" she cried, her father's jeering tone in her voice. "Why, do you think you might hit me with the axe?"

"No, it's just possible the tree might, though," he answered soberly. But the tone of his voice seemed to her to imply that he was only being falsely solicitous and trying to make her move because it was his will to move her.

"Absolutely impossible," she said.

He heard her. But he held himself icy still, lest he should lose his power.

"No, it's just possible. You'd better come down this way."

"Oh, all right. Let us see some crack Canadian tree felling," she retorted.

"Ready then," he said, taking the axe, looking round to see he was clear.

There was a moment of pure, motionless suspense, when the world seemed to stand still. Then suddenly his form seemed to flash up enormously tall and fearful, he gave two swift, flashing blows, in immediate succession, the tree was severed, turning slowly, spinning strangely in the air and coming down like a sudden darkness on the earth. No one saw what was happening except himself. No one heard the strange little cry which the Banford gave as the dark end of the bough swooped down, down on her. No one saw her crouch a little and receive the blow on the back of the neck. No one saw her flung outwards and laid, a little twitching heap, at the foot of the fence. No one except the boy. And he watched with intense bright eyes, as he would watch a wild goose he had shot. Was it winged, or dead? Dead!

Immediately he gave a loud cry. Immediately March gave a wild shriek that went far, far down the afternoon. And the father started a strange bellowing sound.

The boy leapt the fence and ran to the figure. The back of the neck and head was a mass of blood, of horror. He turned it over. The body was quivering with little convulsions. But she was dead really. He knew it, that it was so. He knew it in his soul and his blood. The inner necessity of his life was fulfilling itself, it was he who was to live. The thorn was drawn out of his bowels. So, he put her down gently. She was dead.

He stood up. March was standing there petrified and absolutely motionless. Her face was dead white, her eyes big black pools. The old man was scrambling horribly over the fence.

"I'm afraid it's killed her," said the boy.

The old man was making curious, blubbering noises as he huddled over the fence.

"What!" cried March, starting electric.

"Yes, I'm afraid," repeated the boy.

March was coming forward. The boy was over the fence before she reached it.

"What do you say, killed her?" she asked in a sharp voice.

"I'm afraid so," he answered softly.

She went still whiter, fearful. The two stood facing each other. Her black eyes gazed on him with the last look of resistance. And then in a last agonized failure she began to grizzle, to cry in a shivery little fashion of a child that doesn't want to cry, but which is beaten from within, and gives that little first shudder of sobbing which is not yet weeping, dry and fearful.

He had won. She stood there absolutely helpless, shuddering her dry sobs and her mouth trembling rapidly. And then, as in a child, with a little crash came the tears and the blind agony of sightless weeping. She sank down on the grass and sat there with her hands on her breast and her face lifted in sightless, convulsed weeping. He stood above her, looking down on her, mute, pale, and everlasting seeming. He never moved, but looked down on her. And among all the torture of the scene, the torture of his own heart and bowels, he was glad, he had won.

After a long time he stooped to her and took her hands.

"Don't cry," he said softly. "Don't cry."

She looked up at him with tears running from her eyes, a senseless look of helplessness and submission. So she gazed on him as if sightless, yet looking up to him. She would never leave him again. He had won her. And he knew it and was glad, because he wanted her for his life. His life must have her. And now he had won her. It was what his life must have.

But if he had won her, he had not yet got her. They were married at Christmas as he had planned, and he got again ten days' leave. They went to Cornwall, to his own village, on the sea. He realized that it was awful for her to be at the farm any more.

But though she belonged to him, though she lived in his shadow, as if she could not be away from him, she was not happy. She did not want to leave him: and yet she did not feel free with him. Everything around her seemed to watch her, seemed to press on her. He had won her, he had her with him, she was his wife. And she—she belonged to him, she knew it. But she was not glad. And he was still foiled. He realized that though he was married to her and possessed her in every possible way, apparently, and though she *wanted* him to possess her, she wanted it, she wanted nothing else, now, still he did not quite succeed.

Something was missing. Instead of her soul swaying with new life, it seemed to droop, to bleed, as if it were wounded. She would sit for a long time with her hand in his, looking away at the sea. And in her dark, vacant eyes was a sort of wound, and her face looked a little peaked. If he spoke to her, she would turn to him with a faint new smile, the strange, quivering little smile of a woman who has died in the old way of love, and can't quite rise to the new way. She still felt she ought to *do* something, to strain herself in some direction. And there was nothing to do, and no direction in which to strain herself. And she could not quite accept the submergence which his new love put upon her. If she was in love, she ought to *exert* herself, in some way, loving. She felt the weary need of our day to *exert* herself in love. But she knew that in fact she must no more exert herself in love. He would not have the love which exerted itself towards him. It made his brow go black. No, he wouldn't let her exert her love towards him. No, she had to be passive, to acquiesce, and to be submerged under the surface of love. She had to be like the seaweed she saw as she peered down from the boat, swaying for ever delicately under water, with all their delicate fibrils put tenderly out upon the flood, sensitive, utterly sensitive and receptive within the shadowy sea, and never, never rising and looking forth above water while they lived. Never. Never looking forth from the water until they died, only then washing corpses, upon the surface. But while they lived, always submerged, always beneath the wave. Beneath the wave they might have powerful roots, stronger than iron, they might be tenacious and dangerous in their soft waving within the flood. Beneath the water they might be stronger, more indestructible than resistant oak trees are on land. But it was always under-water, always under-water. And she, being a woman, must be like that.

And she had been so used to the very opposite. She had had to take all the thought for love and for life, and all the responsibility. Day after day she had been responsible for the coming day, for the coming year: for her dear Jill's health and happiness and well-being. Verily, in her own small way, she had felt herself responsible for the well-being of the world. And this had been her great stimulant, this grand feeling that, in her own small sphere, she was responsible for the well-being of the world.

And she had failed. She knew that, even in her small way, she had failed. She had failed to satisfy her own feeling of responsibility. It was so difficult. It seemed so grand and easy at first. And the more you tried, the more difficult it became. It had seemed so easy to make one beloved creature happy. And the more you tried, the worse the failure. It was terrible. She had been all her life reaching, reaching, and what she reached for seemed so near, until she had stretched to her utmost limit. And then it was always beyond her.

Always beyond her, vaguely, unrealizably beyond her, and she was left with nothingness at last. The life she reached for, the happiness she reached for, the well-being she reached for, all slipped back, became unreal, the further she stretched her hand. She wanted some goal, some finality—and there was none. Always this ghastly reaching, reaching, striving for something that might be just beyond. Even to make Jill happy.

She was glad Jill was dead. For she had realized that she could never make her happy. Jill would always be fretting herself thinner and thinner, weaker and weaker. Her pains grew worse instead of less. It would be so for ever. She was glad she was dead.

And if she had married a man it would have been just the same. The woman striving, striving to make the man happy, striving within her own limits for the well-being of her world. And always achieving failure. Little, foolish successes in money or in ambition. But at the very point where she most wanted success, in the anguished effort to make some one beloved human being happy and perfect, there the failure was almost catastrophic. You wanted to make your beloved happy, and his happiness seemed always achievable. If only you did just this, that and the other. And you did this, that, and the other, in all good faith, and every time the failure became a little more ghastly. You could love yourself to ribbons, and strive and strain yourself to the bone, and things would go from bad to worse, bad to worse, as far as happiness went. The awful mistake of happiness.

Poor March, in her goodwill and her responsibility, she had strained herself till it seemed to her that the whole of life and everything was only a horrible abyss of nothingness. The more you reached after the fatal flower of happiness, which trembles so blue and lovely in a crevice just beyond your grasp, the more fearfully you become aware of the ghastly and awful gulf of the precipice below you, into which you will inevitably plunge, as into the bottomless pit, if you reach any further. You pluck flower after flower—it is never *the* flower. The flower itself—its calyx is a horrible gulf, it is the bottomless pit.

That is the whole history of the search for happiness, whether it be your own or somebody else's that you want to win. It ends, and it always ends, in the ghastly sense of the bottomless nothingness into which you will inevitably fall if you strain any further.

And women?—what goal can any woman conceive, except happiness? Just happiness, for herself and the whole world. That, and nothing else. And so, she assumes the responsibility, and sets off towards her goal. She can see it there, at the foot of the rainbow. Or she can see it a little way beyond, in the blue distance. Not far, not far.

But the end of the rainbow is a bottomless gulf down which you can fall for ever without arriving, and the blue distance is a void pit which can swallow you and all your efforts into its emptiness, and still be no emptier. You and all your efforts. So, the illusion of attainable happiness!

Poor March, she had set off so wonderfully, towards the blue goal. And the further and further she had gone, the more fearful had become the realization of emptiness. An agony, an insanity at last.

She was glad it was over. She was glad to sit on the shore and look westwards over the sea, and know the great strain had ended. She would never strain for love and happiness any more. And Jill was safely dead. Poor Jill, poor Jill. It must be sweet to be dead.

For her own part, death was not her destiny. She would have to leave her destiny to the boy. But then, the boy. He wanted more than that. He wanted her to give herself without defences, to sink and become submerged in him. And she—she wanted to sit still, like a woman on the last milestone, and watch. She wanted to see, to know, to understand. She wanted to be alone: with him at her side.

And he! He did not want her to watch any more, to see any more, to understand any more. He wanted to veil her woman's spirit, as Orientals veil the woman's face. He wanted her to commit herself to him, and to put her independent spirit to sleep. He wanted to take away from her all her effort, all that seemed her very *raison d'être*. He wanted to make her submit, yield, blindly pass away out of all her strenuous consciousness. He wanted to take away her consciousness, and make her just his woman. Just his woman.

And she was so tired, so tired, like a child that wants to go to sleep, but which fights against sleep as if sleep were death. She seemed to stretch her eyes wider in the obstinate effort and tension of keeping awake. She *would* keep awake. She *would* know. She *would* consider and judge and decide. She *would* have the reins of her own life between her own hands. She *would* be an independent woman, to the last. But she was so tired, so tired of everything. And sleep seemed near. And there was such rest in the boy.

Yet there, sitting in a niche of the high wild cliffs of West Cornwall, looking over the westward sea, she stretched her eyes wider and wider. Away to the West, Canada, America. She *would* know and she *would* see what was ahead. And the boy, sitting beside her staring down at the gulls, had a cloud between his brows and the strain of discontent in his eyes. He wanted her asleep, at peace in him. He wanted her at peace, asleep in him. And *there* she was, dying with the strain of her own wakefulness. Yet she would not sleep: no, never. Sometimes he thought bitterly that he ought to have left her. He ought never to have killed Banford. He should have left Banford and March to kill one another.

But that was only impatience: and he knew it. He was waiting, waiting to go west. He was aching almost in torment to leave England, to go west, to take March away. To leave this shore! He believed that as they crossed the seas, as they left this England which he so hated, because in some way it seemed to have stung him with poison, she would go to sleep. She would close her eyes at last, and give in to him.

And then he would have her and he would have his own life at last. He chafed, feeling he hadn't got his own life. He would never have it till she yielded and slept in him. Then he would have all his own life as a young man and a male, and she would have all her own life as a woman and a female. There would be no more of this awful straining. She would not be a man any more, an independent woman with a man's responsibility. Nay, even the responsibility for her own soul she would have to commit to him. He knew it was so, and obstinately held out against her, waiting for the surrender.

"You'll feel better when once we get over the seas, to Canada, over there," he said to her as they sat among the rocks on the cliff.

She looked away to the sea's horizon, as if it were not real. Then she looked round at him, with the strained, strange look of a child that is struggling against sleep.

"Shall I?" she said.

"Yes," he answered quietly.

And her eyelids dropped with the slow motion, sleep weighing them unconscious. But she pulled them open again to say:

"Yes, I may. I can't tell. I can't tell what it will be like over there."

"If only we could go soon!" he said, with pain in his voice.

1923

AFTERWORD

> She heard Banford speaking to the fowls, in the distance—and she did not
> hear. What was she thinking about? Heaven knows. Her consciousness
> was, as it were, held back.
>   She lowered her eyes, and suddenly saw the fox. He was looking up at
> her. His chin was pressed down, and his eyes were looking up. They met
> her eyes. And he knew her. She was spell-bound—she knew he knew her.
> So he looked into her eyes, and her soul failed her. He knew her, he was
> not daunted.

This is Lawrence country: easy to parody, easy to misunderstand, but difficult
to deny.

It is August 1918, World War I is drawing to an end at long last. Nellie March
and Jill Banford have been living on the farm for the last three years of the
war, at first with Banford's grandfather who died after the first year. At first
they had cattle too, but one heifer turned wild, another got pregnant and troublesome, so they since have had only chickens and ducks. March, loose-
limbed, graceful, like a young man, "did most of the outside work."
Banford—like March, nearly thirty—tends the house, pours the tea, likes company and gossip; it is her money that runs the farm. But the farm is not
flourishing. The hens won't lay. The two women, generally compatible, are
starting to get irritated with one another. A fox preys on the chickens.

"There was something odd and unexplained about [March]," with her boy's
figure, her woman's face, her mouth "almost pinched as if in pain and irony,"
her eyes big, wide, deep, "strange, startled, shy and sardonic at once." What is
this odd and unexplained element? What does the fox know about her? What
is the "she" the fox knows? Why does her soul fail in looking at the fox? Is it
because he knows her and she knows he knows her? And what does that
mean? How can a fox know a person, whatever "know" means? And what
does Lawrence mean by March's soul? And how does a soul "fail"?

The incident is clearly important to March, and whenever she goes into one
of her rapt or trancelike states thereafter she thinks of the fox. About three
months (but only a few pages) later, a twenty-year-old soldier shows up. He
used to live on the farm with his grandfather. He ran away to Canada, joined
the army, and has been serving in Greece, but the war is over now. He has a
"ruddy, roundish face, with fairish hair" and bright blue eyes.

> But to March he was the fox. Whether it was the thrusting forward of his
> head, or the glisten of fine whitish hairs on the ruddy cheek-bones, or the
> bright, keen eyes, that can never be said: but the boy was to her the fox,
> and she could not see him otherwise.

The narrative focus is rather odd if you think about it. We seem to know
what is going on inside March (and the other characters) to some degree,
more, certainly, than we or the narrator could learn merely by observing. Yet
"Heaven knows" what she was thinking about when the fox first appeared;
there's something about her "unexplained," and just what makes her think the
boy is the fox "can never be said." The depth yet limitation of the narrator's
knowledge is rather puzzling. Is it a mere awkwardness or arbitrariness in the

narration, or does it have some significance in the world of the fiction, in Lawrence's vision of reality?

Other things are beginning to clear up, however, or so it seems. This is to be a love story, of sorts, or at least a story about sex. The fox is male (a dog-fox, as we learn) and what he "knows" about her—having caught her unawares, with her defenses of intelligence and consciousness down—is that she needs a male, a man. She needs a man to help run the farm; she needs a man to protect her—and the "other" chickens—from the marauders, the hunters, the male foxes—she has a rifle with her but cannot shoot, she's so startled and absorbed. She needs a man sexually; she's nearly thirty, very womanly despite her boyish grace, and has been living with another woman for three years. There's something unnatural about her life, her role; Nature, in the form of the fox, can sense it. When Henry Grenfel the soldier shows up, it all falls into place. He is the fox, the male, what March wants (both in the sense of "desires" and "needs"). She identifies him with the fox. She dreams the fox is bright yellow and singing; he bites her on the wrist and flicks his brush across her face, burning her mouth. Henry's khaki uniform, glinting in sun, reminds her of the fox's yellowness. When, later, Henry kisses her on the mouth, the kiss burns like the fox's brush.

It's all very simple, not to say crude. March and Banford have a lesbian or lesbianlike arrangement. That's "unnatural." March is cast in the role of the male and that perverts her natural self. She needs to be dominated by a male, sexually and otherwise. Henry Grenfel fills the bill perfectly: he's young and vigorous—only twenty; he's a soldier and natural-born "hunter" or predator (that is, macho male); he knows how to put food on the table and run the farm. The fox is a literary symbol, crude, perhaps as crude as the theme, but an obvious symbol, and the coincidence of the fox scene and the advent of Henry is almost ludicrous. (The heavy-handedness of the symbol may lead us to believe that the problematical focus is, too, mere awkwardness.) *Voilà!* The Lawrence we all know: all about sex; sexist; formally negligent or nearly inept; simple, obvious, and repetitive (we're less than halfway into the story) in theme, narration, and language (why is the fox described as looking up in two consecutive sentences: "He was looking up at her. His chin was pressed down, and his eyes were looking up"?).

This is a great writer? This a great short novel?

Still, even thus far there are items difficult to explain away as merely Lawrence's ineptitude. The schema we (or, let me take the blame, I) have rigged casts Banford in something of the villain's role. She's not going to marry, her family has decided, so that's where she got the money that set up the farm and put March in the role of "husband." She's the "unnatural" one, one would think. Shouldn't she then resent Henry from the beginning? consciously or unconsciously try to get rid of him even before he makes a move toward March? She *is* a bit concerned about the propriety of his staying with them at first, but seems as reluctantly agreeable as March. She enjoys waiting on him, enjoys the company and the gossip, treats him as if he were her brother and is "naturally warm and kind." She will fight March's intention to marry the boy, but she is not instinctively, unnaturally, bitchily hostile—yet. But perhaps that's just Lawrence's chauvinist way of making her more womanly—warm, kind, accommodating, that sort of sexist palaver.

What about Henry, the soldier, the hunter, the macho male, the fox? Are we not supposed to admire him, the natural one fulfilling his natural role and offering March the opportunity to live a natural, fulfilled life? How or why does

he fall in love with March? Or is "love" too soft and feminine an emotion?
Given the schema he should probably just want her, want to possess her, dominate her sexually. That's not exactly how Lawrence presents his "courtship."
Henry has noticed March all right, but we do not know too much about what
he thinks of her. Then one evening he's returning from hunting and sees the
cozy home:

> And he thought to himself, it would be a good thing to have this place for
> his own. And then the thought entered him shrewdly: why not marry
> March? . . . His mind . . . seemed to calculate. . . .
> He scarcely admitted his intention even to himself. He kept it as a secret
> even from himself [repetition again]. It was all too uncertain as yet. He
> would have to see how things went. Yes, he would have to see how things
> went [and again].

Is this our macho hero? Well, he is the fox. Foxes are cunning, aren't they? But
calculation seems somehow a bit less admirable than "cunning," especially
putting profit or at least economic security or domesticity before sex. He
doesn't even say, "Yeah, this farm and cozy house, and, wow! March too," and
go off into scenes of love and such. Too cool, Henry is, for the perfect hero in
our Lawrencian scheme, isn't he? What's Lawrence up to?

Henry does not identify himself with the fox. "'Perhaps you think I've come
to steal your chickens or something,' he said. . . .'" This is the first time anyone
has ever identified him with a fox (and he is often described here in terms of a
cat or puppy). He, with his Canadian sense of space, sympathizes with the fox
in constricted England; the fox doesn't have a chance. But it is Henry who
shoots the fox, kills him. It is only the middle of the story, the fox is dead, and
after March fondles the pelt for a bit, the creature gets scarcely a mention. The
fox is shot and Henry is leaving the farm; the predators—or is there only one?—
are going. But March dreams that it is Banford who is dead, not Henry; it's
Banford who is put in the wood-box as in a coffin, with the fox's brush beneath her head and the skin on top the body.

The battle between Banford and Henry over March is now intense. It is his
last day. He watches the two women return from shopping, March carrying all
the packages, acting "the male." His hatred for Banford wells.

Then, in the middle of the scene there is a break on the page, like this one,
the first in the novel; the scene does not change, nor the time, nor the focus,
but there is a break. Nothing is said or implied that explains the break. The
new section simply begins, "He watched the progress of the two women. He
could hear their voices. . . ." He eavesdrops. Banford is trying to talk March out
of marrying him.

> And he disliked the Banford with an acid dislike. And he felt drawn to the
> March again. He felt again irresistibly drawn to her. He felt there was a
> secret bond, a secret thread between him and her, something very exclu-
> sive, which shut out everybody else and made him and her possess each
> other in secret.

There is another change, a costume change—March that evening wears a
dress. And still another—Henry changes from boy to man, feeling "a little of
the heaviness of male destiny upon him." His battle with Banford over March
is now overt. When March goes out into the night with Henry, Banford sobs.
Her heart is breaking, March says, but Henry says theirs—March's and his—are

breaking too. She never thought of Henry's having a heart—and we have had little reason to think so either—but he puts her hand on his chest and she feels his heart "like a thing far beyond ... signalling to her." He tells her he had never before met a woman "'I really wanted, for good. You see, I'm thinking of all my life.'" In his new maturity he does not take advantage of her vulnerability; he feels responsible for her. He is born into a new world. She is "his heaven and hell on earth, and he would have none elsewhere."

There is another break on the page; Henry leaves the farm for camp; March, out from under the influence of his presence, reneges on her promise to marry him; and the final dramatic act in the struggle of Henry against Banford for March ensues. We see the struggle largely through Henry and his consciousness or subconsciousness—he feels winning March is the "inner necessity of his life fulfilling itself," or "His life must have her. And now he had won her. It was what his life must have." March must "submit"; she must not, as she has been doing, "exert herself." We see little that is going on inside her. The story ends but the struggle does not. (This indecisiveness is typical of a Lawrence conclusion.)

Surely this is a male chauvinist story, the kind of thing popularly believed to be characteristic of Lawrence. Nellie—not March, androgynous name—must be saved from being (an ineffectual) male, running things (the farm), exerting (or asserting) herself; she must submit to the superior and protective and responsible male predator or hunter. Even though the story is left unresolved, surely its vision (or "message") is clear. We may think we see in this single work a global world or vision or position that we take to be Lawrence's own, but we ought to remember that if he, like the later Tolstoy, believes in art as essentially truth-telling, the irresolution of the ending is as honest and uncontrived as the internal argument. That is, Lawrence does not know precisely how to extrapolate the "contest" between March and Henry, does not know precisely how to conclude. His fiction is a progress or pilgrimage, seeking and testing, trying and adjusting his vision and its articulation.

It seems clear from such short stories as "Tickets, Please" and novels as *Aaron's Rod*, written in the war and postwar years, as was *The Fox*, that Lawrence saw a disruption or perversion of the relationship between the sexes generated or intensified by the Great War. Aaron's wife Lottie, he thinks, believes "that she, as woman, was the centre of creation, the man was but an adjunct. She, as woman, and particularly as mother, was the first great source of life and being, and also of culture. . . . It is the substantial and professed belief of the whole white world: . . . the life-centrality of woman. Woman, the life-bearer, the life-source." If Henry Grenfel had been able to think or even feel in general terms, this could have been his what he might have said he was fighting against in March. But Aaron also says that love is not a goal but a process, and that "The completion of the process of love is the arrival at a state of simple, pure self-possession, *for man and woman.*" Would Henry have said this? Did Lawrence see this in the years 1918-1921 when he was writing *The Fox?* Could Henry and March have come to see this after their novel-time was over, in Canada perhaps? When we read *The Fox* are we getting a global view of Lawrence's whole vision, or even his vision of man-woman relationships? or even his vision of man-woman relationships during or just after World War I? Or are we seeing how the conditions of the war and of relationships, of their individual lives and their states of growth, make things appear to Henry, perhaps to March, or to one within the confines of their time and place? What was March thinking before she saw the fox? Heaven knows? *Is* Henry the fox or only in March's eyes? Or is Banford the fox? Should woman submit, "be submerged under the surface of love ... like the seaweed she saw as she peered down from the boat, swaying for ever delicately under water, with all their delicate fibrils put tenderly out upon the flood, sensitive, utterly sensitive and receptive within the shadowy sea, and never, never rising and looking forth above water while they lived"? Or should she be an eagle, bearing herself on her own wings, consummating love in mid-air, as Aaron puts it:

> Two eagles in mid-air, grappling, whirling, coming to their intensification of love-oneness there in mid-air. In mid-air the love consummation. But all the time each lifted on its own wings: each bearing itself on its own wings at every moment of the mid-air love consummation. That is the splendid love-way.

KATHERINE ANNE PORTER

Old Mortality

It took Katherine Anne Porter about twenty-five years to write her only lengthy novel, *The Ship of Fools,* parts of which (when it was to have been called *No Safe Harbor*) appeared from time to time in literary magazines. Even her short novels, such as *Pale Horse, Pale Rider* and *Old Mortality,* are at the shorter rather than longer end of the short novel spectrum. Yet this is not because the range of experience or vision in her works is narrow or thin, but because her diction and style are precise, concise, pure, and resonant; deftly, with few but sufficient details, and no wasted words, she can capture a character with its contradictions, strata of a culture, life and its chaos. So beautifully wrought and perfect are her stories and short novels that she has assured herself a high and permanent place among the writers of her generation, and in America alone her generation includes Faulkner, Fitzgerald, and Hemingway. Indeed, in 1967 the National Institute of Arts and Letters gave her fiction its Gold Medal, an award it offers only every five years and had given five years earlier to Faulkner.

"Human life is mostly pure chaos," she once said, and her own life she once described as "jumbled." Part of the jumble, no doubt, was her three marriages (the first when she was sixteen), each of which lasted only three or four years. Part was the variety of occupations she engaged in to keep herself afloat: journalism, hack writing, acting, lecturing. Part was travel: she reached Mexico in 1920 in the middle of a revolution, stayed for two years, during which time she managed to get a Los Angeles dealer to exhibit huge quantities of Mexican art on behalf of the Mexican government, and wrote several of her early stories. She returned to Mexico almost ten years later (on a Guggenheim Fellowship) and sailed from there to Europe for five or six years. She lectured in Mexico, Trinidad, Belgium, and in Asia, taught and lectured in universities all over the United States, and received a number of honorary degrees (though she never attended college). Besides the Guggenheim Fellowship and Fulbright and Department of State grants, and the Gold Medal, she won many other awards, including both the Pulitzer and National Book Awards in 1966 for *The Collected Stories of Katherine Anne Porter.* She translated from the French and the Spanish, wrote nonfiction as well as essays and autobiography; but she wrote rather little fiction, given her long life and great fame and accomplishment.

Her early stories were published in the *Century Magazine* in the early 1920s, her first volume, *Flowering Judas,* in 1930 (to critical acclaim). Her last volume of stories (except for the *Collected Stories* which included some unpublished early works and others) was *The Leaning Tower* in 1944, in bulk what a Dickens or a Henry James might turn out in a year or eighteen months. These stories are the order she distilled from the jumble and chaos of her experience.

"My one aim is to tell a straight story and give true testimony," she said, but "true" did not mean "actual" or "autobiographical." Though Miranda in *Old Mortality,* who also appears in *Pale Horse, Pale Rider,* admittedly resembles her author rather closely, Katherine Anne Porter, with her usual nicety of distinction, warned that "the reviewers are much mistaken when they insist on identifying me with any and every woman that appears in my stories.... I am a considerably more complicated person than they. They were not writers."

Old Mortality

Part I: 1885-1902

S HE WAS a spirited-looking young woman, with dark curly hair cropped and parted on the side, a short oval face with straight eyebrows, and a large curved mouth. A round white collar rose from the neck of her tightly buttoned black basque, and round white cuffs set off lazy hands with dimples in them, lying at ease in the folds of her flounced skirt which gathered around to a bustle. She sat thus, forever in the pose of being photographed, a motionless image in her dark walnut frame with silver oak leaves in the corners, her smiling gray eyes following one about the room. It was a reckless indifferent smile, rather disturbing to her nieces Maria and Miranda. Quite often they wondered why every older person who looked at the picture said, "How lovely"; and why everyone who had known her thought her so beautiful and charming.

There was a kind of faded merriment in the background, with its vase of flowers and draped velvet curtains, the kind of vase and the kind of curtains no one would have any more. The clothes were not even romantic looking, but merely most terribly out of fashion, and the whole affair was associated, in the minds of the little girls, with dead things: the smell of Grandmother's medicated cigarettes and her furniture that smelled of beeswax, and her old-fashioned perfume, Orange Flower. The woman in the picture had been Aunt Amy, but she was only a ghost in a frame, and a sad, pretty story from old times. She had been beautiful, much loved, unhappy, and she had died young.

Maria and Miranda, aged twelve and eight years, knew they were young, though they felt they had lived a long time. They had lived not only their own years; but their memories, it seemed to them, began years before they were born, in the lives of the grown-ups around them, old people above forty, most of them, who had a way of insisting that they too had been young once. It was hard to believe.

Their father was Aunt Amy's brother Harry. She had been his favorite sister. He sometimes glanced at the photograph and said, "It's not very good. Her hair and her smile were her chief beauties, and they aren't shown at all. She was much slimmer than that, too. There were never any fat women in the family, thank God."

When they heard their father say things like that, Maria and Miranda simply wondered, without criticism, what he meant. Their grandmother was thin as a match; the pictures of their mother, long since dead, proved her to have been a candle-wick, almost. Dashing young ladies, who turned out to be, to Miranda's astonishment, merely more of Grandmother's grandchildren, like herself, came visiting from school for the holidays, boasting of their eighteen-inch waists. But how did their father account for great-aunt Eliza, who quite squeezed herself through doors, and who, when seated, was one solid pyramidal monument from floor to neck? What about great-aunt Keziah, in Kentucky? Her husband, great-uncle John Jacob, had refused to allow her to ride his good horses after she had achieved two hundred and twenty pounds. "No," said great-uncle

John Jacob, "my sentiments of chivalry are not dead in my bosom; but
neither is my common sense, to say nothing of charity to our faithful
dumb friends. And the greatest of these is charity."[1] It was suggested to
great-uncle John Jacob that charity should forbid him to wound great-aunt
Keziah's female vanity by such a comment on her figure. "Female vanity
will recover," said great-uncle John Jacob, callously, "but what about my
horses' backs? And if she had the proper female vanity in the first place,
she would never have got into such shape." Well, great-aunt Keziah was
famous for her heft, and wasn't she in the family? But something seemed
to happen to their father's memory when he thought of the girls he had
known in the family of his youth, and he declared steadfastly they had all
been, in every generation without exception, as slim as reeds and graceful
as sylphs.

This loyalty of their father's in the face of evidence contrary to his
ideal had its springs in family feeling, and a love of legend that he shared
with the others. They loved to tell stories, romantic and poetic, or comic
with a romantic humor; they did not gild the outward circumstance, it
was the feeling that mattered. Their hearts and imaginations were captivated by their past, a past in which worldly considerations had played a
very minor role. Their stories were almost always love stories against a
bright blank heavenly blue sky.

Photographs, portraits by inept painters who meant earnestly to flatter,
and the festival garments folded away in dried herbs and camphor were
disappointing when the little girls tried to fit them to the living beings
created in their minds by the breathing words of their elders. Grandmother, twice a year compelled in her blood by the change of seasons,
would sit nearly all of one day beside old trunks and boxes in the lumber
room, unfolding layers of garments and small keepsakes; she spread them
out on sheets on the floor around her, crying over certain things, nearly
always the same things, looking again at pictures in velvet cases, unwrapping locks of hair and dried flowers, crying gently and easily as if tears
were the only pleasure she had left.

If Maria and Miranda were very quiet, and touched nothing until it
was offered, they might sit by her at these times, or come and go. There
was a tacit understanding that her grief was strictly her own, and must
not be noticed or mentioned. The little girls examined the objects, one by
one, and did not find them, in themselves, impressive. Such dowdy little
wreaths and necklaces, some of them made of pearly shells; such moth-
eaten bunches of pink ostrich feathers for the hair; such clumsy big breast
pins and bracelets of gold and colored enamel; such silly-looking combs,
standing up on tall teeth capped with seed pearls and French paste.[2]
Miranda, without knowing why, felt melancholy. It seemed such a pity
that these faded things, these yellowed long gloves and misshapen satin
slippers, these broad ribbons cracking where they were folded, should
have been all those vanished girls had to decorate themselves with. And
where were they now, those girls, and the boys in the odd-looking collars?
The young men seemed even more unreal than the girls, with their high-
buttoned coats, their puffy neckties, their waxed mustaches, their waving

---

1. 1 Corinthians 13:12—"And now abideth faith,
hope, charity, these three; but the greatest of these is
charity."
2. Lead-glass compound used for imitation jewelry,
perfected in France in the eighteenth century; seed
pearls are very small, often irregularly shaped, and
used decoratively.

thick hair combed carefully over their foreheads. Who could have taken them seriously, looking like that?

No, Maria and Miranda found it impossible to sympathize with those young persons, sitting rather stiffly before the camera, hopelessly out of fashion; but they were drawn and held by the mysterious love of the living, who remembered and cherished these dead. The visible remains were nothing; they were dust, perishable as the flesh; the features stamped on paper and metal were nothing, but their living memory enchanted the little girls. They listened, all ears and eager minds, picking here and there among the floating ends of narrative, patching together as well as they could fragments of tales that were like bits of poetry or music, indeed were associated with the poetry they had heard or read, with music, with the theater.

"Tell me again how Aunt Amy went away when she was married." "She ran into the gray cold and stepped into the carriage and turned and smiled with her face as pale as death, and called out 'Good-by, good-by,' and refused her cloak, and said, 'Give me a glass of wine.' And none of us saw her alive again." "Why wouldn't she wear her cloak, Cousin Cora?" "Because she was not in love, my dear." Ruin hath taught me thus to ruminate, that time will come and take my love away.[3] "Was she really beautiful, Uncle Bill?" "As an angel, my child." There were golden-haired angels with long blue pleated skirts dancing around the throne of the Blessed Virgin. None of them resembled Aunt Amy in the least, nor the type of beauty they had been brought up to admire. There were points of beauty by which one was judged severely. First, a beauty must be tall; whatever color the eyes, the hair must be dark, the darker the better; the skin must be pale and smooth. Lightness and swiftness of movement were important points. A beauty must be a good dancer, superb on horseback, with a serene manner, an amiable gaiety tempered with dignity at all hours. Beautiful teeth and hands, of course, and over and above all this, some mysterious crown of enchantment that attracted and held the heart. It was all very exciting and discouraging.

Miranda persisted through her childhood in believing, in spite of her smallness, thinness, her little snubby nose saddled with freckles, her speckled gray eyes and habitual tantrums, that by some miracle she would grow into a tall, cream-colored brunette, like cousin Isabel; she decided always to wear a trailing white satin gown. Maria, born sensible, had no such illusions. "We are going to take after Mamma's family," she said. "It's no use, we are. We'll never be beautiful, we'll always have freckles. And *you*," she told Miranda, "haven't even a good disposition."

Miranda admitted both truth and justice in this unkindness, but still secretly believed that she would one day suddenly receive beauty, as by inheritance, riches laid suddenly in her hands through no deserts of her own. She believed for quite a while that she would one day be like Aunt Amy, not as she appeared in the photograph, but as she was remembered by those who had seen her.

When Cousin Isabel came out in her tight black riding habit, surrounded by young men, and mounted gracefully, drawing her horse up and around so that he pranced learnedly on one spot while the other riders sprang to their saddles in the same sedate flurry, Miranda's heart

3. Shakespeare, Sonnet 64.

would close with such a keen dart of admiration, envy, vicarious pride it was almost painful; but there would always be an elder present to lay a cooling hand upon her emotions. "She rides almost as well as Amy, doesn't she? But Amy had the pure Spanish style, she could bring out paces in a horse no one else knew he had." Young namesake Amy, on her way to a dance, would swish through the hall in ruffled white taffeta, glimmering like a moth in the lamplight, carrying her elbows pointed backward stiffly as wings, sliding along as if she were on rollers, in the fashionable walk of her day. She was considered the best dancer at any party, and Maria, sniffing the wave of perfume that followed Amy, would clasp her hands and say, "Oh, I can't *wait* to be grown up." But the elders would agree that the first Amy had been lighter, more smooth and delicate in her waltzing; young Amy would never equal her. Cousin Molly Parrington, far past her youth, indeed she belonged to the generation before Aunt Amy, was a noted charmer. Men who had known her all her life still gathered about her; now that she was happily widowed for the second time there was no doubt that she would yet marry again. But Amy, said the elders, had the same high spirits and wit without boldness, and you really could not say that Molly had ever been discreet. She dyed her hair, and made jokes about it. She had a way of collecting the men around her in a corner, where she told them stories. She was an unnatural mother to her ugly daughter Eva, an old maid past forty while her mother was still the belle of the ball. "Born when I was fifteen, you remember," Molly would say shamelessly, looking an old beau straight in the eye, both of them remembering that he had been best man at her first wedding when she was past twenty-one. "Everyone said I was like a little girl with her doll."

Eva, shy and chinless, straining her upper lip over two enormous teeth, would sit in corners watching her mother. She looked hungry, her eyes were strained and tired. She wore her mother's old clothes, made over, and taught Latin in a Female Seminary. She believed in votes for women, and had traveled about, making speeches. When her mother was not present, Eva bloomed out a little, danced prettily, smiled, showing all her teeth, and was like a dry little plant set out in a gentle rain. Molly was merry about her ugly duckling. "It's lucky for me my daughter is an old maid. She's not so apt," said Molly naughtily, "to make a grandmother of me." Eva would blush as if she had been slapped.

Eva was a blot, no doubt about it, but the little girls felt she belonged to their everyday world of dull lessons to be learned, stiff shoes to be limbered up, scratchy flannels to be endured in cold weather, measles and disappointed expectations. Their Aunt Amy belonged to the world of poetry. The romance of Uncle Gabriel's long, unrewarded love for her, her early death, was such a story as one found in old books: unworldly books, but true, such as the Vita Nuova, the Sonnets of Shakespeare and the Wedding Song of Spenser; and poems by Edgar Allan Poe. "Her tantalized spirit now blandly reposes, Forgetting or never regretting its roses. . . . "⁴ Their father read that to them, and said, "He was our greatest poet," and they knew that "our" meant he was Southern. Aunt Amy was real as the pictures in the old Holbein and Dürer books were real. The little girls lay flat on their stomachs and peered into a world of wonder,

4. Slightly altered from Poe's "For Annie" (1849);   *Epithalamion* by Edmund Spenser (1552-1599).
Vita Nuova, by Dante Alighiere (1265-1321); *The*

turning the shabby leaves that fell apart easily, not surprised at the sight of the Mother of God sitting on a hollow log nursing her Child; not doubting either Death or the Devil riding at the stirrups of the grim knight;[5] not questioning the propriety of the stiffly dressed ladies of Sir Thomas More's household, seated in dignity on the floor, or seeming to be. They missed all the dog and pony shows, and lantern-slide entertainments, but their father took them to see "Hamlet," and "The Taming of the Shrew," and "Richard the Third," and a long sad play with Mary, Queen of Scots, in it. Miranda thought the magnificent lady in black velvet was truly the Queen of Scots, and was pained to learn that the real Queen had died long ago, and not at all on the night she, Miranda, had been present.

The little girls loved the theater, that world of personages taller than human beings, who swept upon the scene and invested it with their presences, their more than human voices, their gestures of gods and goddesses ruling a universe. But there was always a voice recalling other and greater occasions. Grandmother in her youth had heard Jenny Lind, and thought that Nellie Melba was much overrated.[6] Father had seen Bernhardt, and Madame Modjeska was no sort of rival. When Paderewski played for the first time in their city, cousins came from all over the state and went from the grandmother's house to hear him. The little girls were left out of this great occasion. They shared the excitement of the going away, and shared the beautiful moment of return, when cousins stood about in groups, with coffee cups and glasses in their hands, talking in low voices, awed and happy. The little girls, struck with the sense of a great event, hung about in their nightgowns and listened, until someone noticed and hustled them away from the sweet nimbus of all that glory. One old gentleman, however, had heard Rubinstein frequently. He could not but feel that Rubinstein had reached the final height of musical interpretation, and, for him, Paderewski had been something of an anticlimax. The little girls heard him muttering on, holding up one hand, patting the air as if he were calling for silence. The others looked at him, and listened, without any disturbance of their grave tender mood. They had never heard Rubinstein; they had, one hour since, heard Paderewski, and why should anyone need to recall the past? Miranda, dragged away, half understanding the old gentleman, hated him. She felt that she too had heard Paderewski.

There was then a life beyond a life in this world, as well as in the next; such episodes confirmed for the little girls the nobility of human feeling, the divinity of man's vision of the unseen, the importance of life and death, the depths of the human heart, the romantic value of tragedy. Cousin Eva, on a certain visit, trying to interest them in the study of Latin, told them the story of John Wilkes Booth, who, handsomely garbed in a long black cloak, had leaped to the stage after assassinating President Lincoln. "Sic semper tyrannis,"[7] he had shouted superbly, in spite of his broken leg. The little girls never doubted that it had happened in just that way, and the moral seemed to be that one should always have Latin, or at least a good classical poetry quotation, to depend upon in great or

---

5. *Death and the Devil*, print by Albrecht Dürer (1471–1528); following is a description of a painting by Hans Holbein (1465–1524).
6. Two nineteenth-century sopranos. Father com-

pares two actresses, and the old gentleman (below) two pianists.
7. "Thus always to tyrants."

desperate moments, Cousin Eva reminded them that no one, not even a good Southerner, could possibly approve of John Wilkes Booth's deed. It was murder, after all. They were to remember that. But Miranda, used to tragedy in books and in family legends—two great-uncles had committed suicide and a remote ancestress had gone mad for love—decided that, without the murder, there would have been no point to dressing up and leaping to the stage shouting in Latin. So how could she disapprove of the deed? It was a fine story. She knew a distantly related old gentleman who had been devoted to the art of Booth, had seen him in a great many plays, but not, alas, at his greatest moment. Miranda regretted this; it would have been so pleasant to have the assassination of Lincoln in the family.

Uncle Gabriel, who had loved Aunt Amy so desperately, still lived somewhere, though Miranda and Maria had never seen him. He had gone away, far away, after her death. He still owned racehorses, and ran them at famous tracks all over the country, and Miranda believed there could not possibly be a more brilliant career. He had married again, quite soon, and had written to Grandmother, asking her to accept his new wife as a daughter in place of Amy. Grandmother had written coldly, accepting, inviting them for a visit, but Uncle Gabriel had somehow never brought his bride home. Harry had visited them in New Orleans, and reported that the second wife was a very good-looking well-bred blonde girl who would undoubtedly be a good wife for Gabriel. Still, Uncle Gabriel's heart was broken. Faithfully once a year he wrote a letter to someone of the family, sending money for a wreath for Amy's grave. He had written a poem for her gravestone, and had come home, leaving his second wife in Atlanta, to see that it was carved properly. He could never account for having written this poem; he had certainly never tried to write a single rhyme since leaving school. Yet one day when he had been thinking about Amy, the verse occurred to him, out of the air. Maria and Miranda had seen it, printed in gold on a mourning card. Uncle Gabriel had sent a great number of them to be handed around among the family.

> "She lives again who suffered life,
>   Then suffered death, and now set free
>   A singing angel, she forgets
>   The griefs of old mortality."

"Did she really sing?" Maria asked her father.

"Now what has that to do with it?" he asked. "It's a poem."

"I think it's very pretty," said Miranda, impressed. Uncle Gabriel was second cousin to her father and Aunt Amy. It brought poetry very near.

"Not so bad for tombstone poetry," said their father, "but it should be better."

Uncle Gabriel had waited five years to marry Aunt Amy. She had been ill, her chest was weak; she was engaged twice to other young men and broke her engagements for no reason; and she laughed at the advice of older and kinder-hearted persons who thought it very capricious of her not to return the devotion of such a handsome and romantic young man as Gabriel, her second cousin, too; it was not as if she would be marrying a stranger. Her coldness was said to have driven Gabriel to a wild life and even to drinking. His grandfather was wealthy and Gabriel was his favorite; they had quarreled over the racehorses, and Gabriel had shouted, "By God, I must have *something.*" As if he had not everything already: youth, health, good looks, the prospect of riches, and a devoted family circle. His grandfather pointed out to him that he was little better than an ingrate, and showed signs of being a wastrel as well. Gabriel said, "You had race-horses, and made a good thing of them." "I never depended upon them for a livelihood, sir," said his grandfather.

Gabriel wrote letters about this and many other things to Amy from Saratoga[8] and from Kentucky and from New Orleans, sending her presents, and flowers packed in ice, and telegrams. The presents were amusing, such as a huge cage full of small green lovebirds; or, as an ornament for her hair, a full-petaled enameled rose with paste dewdrops, with an enameled butterfly in brilliant colors suspended quivering on a gold wire about it; but the telegrams always frightened her mother, and the flowers, after a journey by train and then by stage into the country, were much the worse for wear. He would send roses when the rose garden at home was in full bloom. Amy could not help smiling over it, though her mother insisted it was touching and sweet of Gabriel. It must prove to Amy that she was always in his thoughts.

"That's no place for me," said Amy, but she had a way of speaking, a tone of voice, which made it impossible to discover what she meant by what she said. It was possible always that she might be serious. And she would not answer questions.

"Amy's wedding dress," said the grandmother, unfurling an immense cloak of dove-colored cut velvet, spreading beside it a silvery-gray watered-silk frock, and a small gray velvet toque with a dark red breast of feathers. Cousin Isabel, the beauty, sat with her. They talked to each other, and Miranda could listen if she chose.

"She would not wear white, nor a veil," said Grandmother. "I couldn't oppose her, for I had said my daughters should each have exactly the wedding dress they wanted. But Amy surprised me. 'Now what would I look like in white satin?' she asked. It's true she was pale, but she would have been angelic in it, and all of us told her so, 'I shall wear mourning if I like,' she said, 'it is *my* funeral, you know.' I reminded her that Lou and your mother had worn white with veils and it would please me to have my daughters all alike in that. Amy said, 'Lou and Isabel are not like me,' but I could not persuade her to explain what she meant. One day when she was ill she said, 'Mammy, I'm not long for this world,' but not as if she meant it. I told her, 'You might live as long as anyone, if only you will be sensible.' 'That's the whole trouble,' said Amy. 'I feel sorry for Gabriel,' she told me. 'He doesn't know what he's asking for.'

"I tried to tell her once more," said the grandmother, "that marriage and children would cure her of everything. 'All women of our family are delicate when they are young,' I said. 'Why, when I was your age no one expected me to live a year. It was called greensickness, and everybody knew there was only one cure.' 'If I live for a hundred years and turn green as grass,' said Amy, 'I still shan't want to marry Gabriel,' So I told her very seriously that if she truly felt that way she must never do it, and Gabriel must be told once for all, and sent away. He would get over it. 'I

8. Saratoga Springs, N.Y., site of a race track and a socially prestigious resort.

have told him, and I have sent him away,' said Amy. 'He just doesn't listen.' We both laughed at that, and I told her young girls found a hundred ways to deny they wished to be married, and a thousand more to test their power over men, but that she had more than enough of that, and now it was time for her to be entirely sincere and make her decision. As for me," said the grandmother, "I wished with all my heart to marry your grandfather, and if he had not asked me, I should have asked him most certainly. Amy insisted that she could not imagine wanting to marry anybody. She would be, she said, a nice old maid like Eva Parrington. For even then it was pretty plain that Eva was an old maid, born. Harry said, 'Oh, Eva—Eva has no chin, that's her trouble. If you had no chin, Amy, you'd be in the same fix as Eva, no doubt.' Your Uncle Bill would say, 'When women haven't anything else, they'll take a vote for consolation. A pretty thin bed-fellow,' said your Uncle Bill. 'What I really need is a good dancing partner to guide me through life,' said Amy, 'that's the match I'm looking for,' It was no good trying to talk to her."

Her brothers remembered her tenderly as a sensible girl. After listening to their comments on her character and ways, Maria decided that they considered her sensible because she asked their advice about her apprearance when she was going out to dance. If they found fault in any way, she would change her dress or her hair until they were pleased, and say, "You are an angel not to let your poor sister go out looking like a freak." But she would not listen to her father, nor to Gabriel. If Gabriel praised the frock she was wearing, she was apt to disappear and come back in another. He loved her long black hair, and once, lifting it up from her pillow when she was ill, said, "I love your hair, Amy, the most beautiful hair in the world." When he returned on his next visit, he found her with her hair cropped and curled close to her head. He was horrified, as if she had willfully mutilated herself. She would not let it grow again, not even to please her brothers. The photograph hanging on the wall was one she had made at that time to send to Gabriel, who sent it back without a word. This pleased her, and she framed the photograph. There was a thin inky scrawl low in one corner, "To dear brother Harry, who likes my hair cut."

This was a mischievous reference to a very grave scandal. The little girls used to look at their father, and wonder what would have happened if he had really hit the young man he shot at. The young man was believed to have kissed Aunt Amy, when she was not in the least engaged to him. Uncle Gabriel was supposed to have had a duel with the young man, but Father had got there first. He was a pleasant, everyday sort of father, who held his daughters on his knee if they were prettily dressed and well behaved, and pushed them away if they had not freshly combed hair and nicely scrubbed fingernails. "Go away, you're disgusting," he would say, in a matter-of-fact voice. He noticed if their stocking seams were crooked. He caused them to brush their teeth with a revolting mixture of prepared chalk, powdered charcoal and salt. When they behaved stupidly he could not endure the sight of them. They understood dimly that all this was for their own future good; and when they were snively with colds, he prescribed delicious hot toddy for them, and saw that it was given them. He was always hoping they might not grow up to be so silly as they seemed to him at any given moment, and he had a disconcerting way of inquiring, "How do you *know?*" when they forgot and made dogmatic statements in his presence. It always came out embarrassingly that they did not know at all, but were repeating something they had heard. This made conversation with him difficult, for he laid traps and they fell into them, but it became important to them that their father should not believe them to be fools. Well, this very father had gone to Mexico once and stayed there for nearly a year, because he had shot at a man with whom Aunt Amy had flirted at a dance. It had been very wrong of him, because he should have challenged the man to a duel, as Uncle Gabriel had done. Instead, he just took a shot at him, and this was the lowest sort of manners. It had caused great disturbance in the whole community and had almost broken up the affair between Aunt Amy and Uncle Gabriel for good. Uncle Gabriel insisted that the young man had kissed Aunt Amy, and Aunt Amy insisted that the young man had merely paid her a compliment on her hair.

During the Mardi Gras holidays there was to be a big gay fancy-dress ball. Harry was going as a bull-fighter because his sweetheart, Mariana, had a new black lace mantilla and high comb from Mexico. Maria and Miranda had seen a photograph of their mother in this dress, her lovely face without a trace of coquetry looking gravely out from under a tremendous fall of lace from the peak of the comb, a rose tucked firmly over her ear. Amy copied her costume from a small Dresden-china shepherdess which stood on the mantelpiece in the parlor; a careful copy with ribboned hat, gilded crook, very low-laced bodice, short basket skirts, green slippers and all. She wore it with a black half-mask, but it was no disguise. "You would have known it was Amy at any distance," said Father. Gabriel, six feet three in height as he was, had got himself up to match, and a spectacle he provided in pale blue satin knee breeches and a blond curled wig with a hair ribbon. "He felt a fool, and he looked like one," said Uncle Bill, "and he behaved like one before the evening was over."

Everything went beautifully until the party gathered downstairs to leave for the ball. Amy's father—he must have been born a grandfather, thought Miranda—gave one glance at his daughter, her white ankles shining, bosom deeply exposed, two round spots of paint on her cheeks, and fell into a frenzy of outraged propriety. "It's disgraceful," he pronounced, loudly. "No daughter of mine is going to show herself in such a rig-out. It's bawdy," he thundered. "Bawdy!"

Amy had taken off her mask to smile at him. "Why, Papa," she said very sweetly, "what's wrong with it? Look on the mantelpiece. She's been there all along, and you were never shocked before."

"There's all the difference in the world," said her father, "all the difference, young lady, and you know it. You go upstairs this minute and pin up that waist in front and let down those skirts to a decent length before you leave this house. *And wash your face!*"

"I see nothing wrong with it," said Amy's mother, firmly, "and you shouldn't use such language before innocent young girls." She and Amy sat down with several females of the household to help, and they made short work of the business. In ten minutes Amy returned, face clean, bodice filled in with lace, shepherdess skirt modestly sweeping the carpet behind her.

When Amy appeared from the dressing room for her first dance with Gabriel, the lace was gone from her bodice, her skirts were tucked up more daringly than before, and the spots on her cheeks were like pomegranates. "Now Gabriel, tell me truly, wouldn't it have been a pity to spoil my costume?" Gabriel, delighted that she had asked his opinion, declared it was perfect. They agreed with kindly tolerance that old people were often tiresome, but one need not upset them by open disobedience: their youth was gone, what had they to live for?

Harry, dancing with Mariana who swung a heavy train around her expertly at every turn of the waltz, began to be uneasy about his sister Amy. She was entirely too popular. He saw young men make beelines across the floor, eyes fixed on those white silk ankles. Some of the young men he did not know at all, others he knew too well and could not approve of for his sister Amy. Gabriel, unhappy in his lyric satin and wig, stood about holding his ribboned crook as though it had sprouted thorns. He hardly danced at all with Amy, he did not enjoy dancing with anyone else, and he was having a thoroughly wretched time of it.

There appeared late, alone, got up as Jean Lafitte,[9] a young Creole gentleman who had, two years before, been for a time engaged to Amy. He came straight to her, with the manner of a happy lover, and said, clearly enough for everyone near by to hear him, "I only came because I knew you were to be here. I only want to dance with you and I shall go again." Amy, with a face of delight, cried out, "Raymond!" as if to a lover. She had danced with him four times, and had then disappeared from the floor on his arm.

Harry and Mariana, in conventional disguise of romance, irreproachably betrothed, safe in their happiness, were waltzing slowly to their favorite song, the melancholy farewell of the Moorish King on leaving Granada. They sang in whispers to each other, in their uncertain Spanish, a song of love and parting and that sword's point of grief that makes the heart tender towards all other lost and disinherited creatures: Oh, mansion of love, my earthly paradise ... that I shall see no more ... whither flies the poor swallow, weary and homeless, seeking for shelter where no shelter is? I too am far from home without the power to fly.... Come to my heart, sweet bird, beloved pilgrim, build your nest near my bed, let me listen to your song, and weep for my lost land of joy....

Into this bliss broke Gabriel. He had thrown away his shepherd's crook and he was carrying his wig. He wanted to speak to Harry at once, and before Mariana knew what was happening she was sitting beside her mother and the two excited young men were gone. Waiting, disturbed and displeased, she smiled at Amy who waltzed past with a young man in Devil costume, including ill-fitting scarlet cloven hoofs. Almost at once, Harry and Gabriel came back, with serious faces, and Harry darted on the dance floor, returning with Amy. The girls and the chaperones were asked to come at once, they must be taken home. It was all mysterious and sudden, and Harry said to Mariana, "I will tell you what is happening, but not now—"

The grandmother remembered of this disgraceful affair only that Gabriel brought Amy home alone and that Harry came in somewhat later. The other members of the party straggled in at various hours, and the story came out piecemeal. Amy was silent and, her mother discovered later, burning with fever. "I saw at once that something was very wrong.

9. Pirate (1780–1825) who refused a handsome offer by the British in order to join the American side in the Battle of New Orleans (1814). A Creole is a descendant of French or Spanish early settlers of the New Orleans area.

'What has happened, Amy?' 'Oh, Harry goes about shooting at people at a party,' she said, sitting down as if she were exhausted. 'It was on your account, Amy,' said Gabriel. 'Oh, no, it was not,' said Amy. 'Don't believe him, Mammy.' So I said, 'Now enough of this. Tell me what happened, Amy.' And Amy said, 'Mammy, this is it. Raymond came in, and you know I like Raymond, and he is a good dancer. So we danced together, too much, maybe. We went on the gallery for a breath of air, and stood there. He said, "How well your hair looks. I like this new shingled style."' She glanced at Gabriel. 'And then another young man came out and said, "I've been looking everywhere. This is our dance, isn't it?" And I went in to dance. And now it seems that Gabriel went out at once and challenged Raymond to a duel about something or other, but Harry doesn't wait for that. Raymond had already gone out to have his horse brought, I suppose one doesn't duel in fancy dress,' she said, looking at Gabriel, who fairly shriveled in his blue satin shepherd's costume, 'and Harry simply went out and shot at him. I don't think that was fair,' said Amy."

Her mother agreed that indeed it was not fair; it was not even decent, and she could not imagine what her son Harry thought he was doing. "It isn't much of a way to defend your sister's honor," she said to him afterward. "I didn't want Gabriel to go fighting duels," said Harry. "That wouldn't have helped much, either."

Gabriel had stood before Amy, leaning over, asking once more the question he had apparently been asking her all the way home. "Did he kiss you, Amy?"

Amy took off her shepherdess hat and pushed her hair back. "Maybe he did," she answered, "and maybe I wished him to."

"Amy, you must not say such things," said her mother. "Answer Gabriel's question."

"He hasn't the right to ask it," said Amy, but without anger.

"Do you love him, Amy?" asked Gabriel, the sweat standing out on his forehead.

"It doesn't matter," answered Amy, leaning back in her chair.

"Oh, it does matter; it matters terribly," said Gabriel. "You must answer me now." He took both of her hands and tried to hold them. She drew her hands away firmly and steadily so that he had to let go.

"Let her alone, Gabriel," said Amy's mother. "You'd better go now. We are all tired. Let's talk about it tomorrow."

She helped Amy to undress, noticing the changed bodice and the shortened skirt. "You shouldn't have done that, Amy. That was not wise of you. It was better the other way.'"

Amy said, "Mammy, I'm sick of this world. I don't like anything in it. It's so *dull*," she said, and for a moment she looked as if she might weep. She had never been tearful, even as a child, and her mother was alarmed. It was then she discovered that Amy had fever.

"Gabriel is dull, Mother—he sulks," she said. "I could see him sulking every time I passed. It spoils things," she said. "Oh, I want to go to sleep."

Her mother sat looking at her and wondering how it had happened she had brought such a beautiful child into the world. "Her face," said her mother, "was angelic in sleep."

Some time during that fevered night, the projected duel between Gabriel and Raymond was halted by the offices of friends on both sides.

There remained the open question of Harry's impulsive shot, which was not so easily settled. Raymond seemed vindictive about that, it was possible he might choose to make trouble. Harry, taking the advice of Gabriel, his brothers and friends, decided that the best way to avoid further scandal was for him to disappear for a while. This being decided upon, the young men returned about daybreak, saddled Harry's best horse and helped him pack a few things; accompanied by Gabriel and Bill, Harry set out for the border, feeling rather gay and adventurous.

Amy, being wakened by the stirring in the house, found out the plan. Five minutes after they were gone, she came down in her riding dress, had her own horse saddled, and struck out after them. She rode almost every morning; before her parents had time to be uneasy over her prolonged absence, they found her note.

What had threatened to be a tragedy became a rowdy lark. Amy rode to the border, kissed her brother Harry good-bye, and rode back again with Bill and Gabriel. It was a three days' journey, and when they arrived Amy had to be lifted from the saddle. She was really ill by now, but in the gayest of humors. Her mother and father had been prepared to be severe with her, but, at sight of her, their feelings changed. They turned on Bill and Gabriel. "Why did you let her do this?" they asked.

"You know we could not stop her," said Gabriel helplessly, "and she did enjoy herself so much!"

Amy laughed. "Mammy, it was splendid, the most delightful trip I ever had. And if I am to be the heroine of this novel, why shouldn't I make the most of it?"

The scandal, Maria and Miranda gathered, had been pretty terrible. Amy simply took to bed and stayed there, and Harry had skipped out blithely to wait until the little affair blew over. The rest of the family had to receive visitors, write letters, go to church, return calls, and bear the whole brunt, as they expressed it. They sat in the twilight of scandal in their little world, holding themselves very rigidly, in a shared tension as if all their nerves began at a common center. This center had received a blow, and family nerves shuddered, even into the farthest reaches of Kentucky. From whence in due time great-great-aunt Sally Rhea addressed a letter to *Mifs*[1] *Amy Rhea*. In deep brown ink like dried blood, in a spidery hand adept at archaic symbols and abbreviations, great-great-aunt Sally informed Amy that she was fairly convinced that this calamity was only the forerunner of a series shortly to be visited by the Almighty God upon a race already condemned through its own wickedness, a warning that man's time was short, and that they must all prepare for the end of the world. For herself, she had long expected it, she was entirely resigned to the prospect of meeting her Maker; and Amy, no less than her wicked brother Harry, must likewise place herself in God's hands and prepare for the worst. "*Oh, my dear unfortunate young relative,*" twittered great-great-aunt Sally, "*we must in our Extremty join hands and appr before ye Dread Throne of Jdgmnt a United Fmly, if One is Mssg from ye Flock, what will Jesus say?*"

Great-great-aunt Sally's religious career had become comic legend. She

1. Old-fashioned double *s*; the *y* in *ye*, below, is old-fashioned *th*.

had forsaken her Catholic rearing for a young man whose family were Cumberland Presbyterians. Unable to accept their opinions, however, she was converted to the Hard-Shell Baptists,[2] a sect as loathsome to her husband's family as the Catholic could possibly be. She had spent a life of vicious self-indulgent martyrdom to her faith; as Harry commented: "Religion put claws on Aunt Sally and gave her a post to whet them on." She had out-argued, out-fought, and out-lived her entire generation, but she did not miss them. She bedeviled the second generation without ceasing, and was beginning hungrily on the third.

Amy, reading this letter, broke into her gay full laugh that always caused everyone around her to laugh too, even before they knew why, and her small green lovebirds in their cage turned and eyed her solemnly. "Imagine drawing a pew in heaven beside Aunt Sally," she said. "What a prospect."

"Don't laugh too soon," said her father. "Heaven was made to order for Aunt Sally. She'll be on her own territory there."

"For my sins," said Amy, "I must go to heaven with Aunt Sally."

During the uncomfortable time of Harry's absence, Amy went on refusing to marry Gabriel. Her mother could hear their voices going on in their endless colloquy, during many long days. One afternoon Gabriel came out, looking very sober and discouraged. He stood looking down at Amy's mother as she sat sewing, and said, "I think it is all over, I believe now that Amy will never have me." The grandmother always said afterward, "Never have I pitied anyone as I did poor Gabriel at that moment. But I told him, very firmly, 'Let her alone, then, she is ill.' " So Gabriel left, and Amy had no word from him for more than a month.

The day after Gabriel was gone, Amy rose looking extremely well, went hunting with her brothers Bill and Stephen, bought a velvet wrap, had her hair shingled and curled again, and wrote long letters to Harry, who was having a most enjoyable exile in Mexico City.

After dancing all night three times in one week, she woke one morning in a hemorrhage. She seemed frightened and asked for the doctor, promising to do whatever he advised. She was quiet for a few days, reading. She asked for Gabriel. No one knew where he was. "You should write him a letter; his mother will send it on." "Oh, no," she said. "I miss him coming in with his sour face. Letters are no good."

Gabriel did come in, only a few days later, with a very sour face and unpleasant news. His grandfather had died, after a day's illness. On his death bed, in the name of God, being of a sound and disposing mind, he had cut off his favorite grandchild Gabriel with one dollar. "In the name of God, Amy," said Gabriel, "the old devil has ruined me in one sentence."

It was the conduct of his immediate family in the matter that had embittered him, he said. They could hardly conceal their satisfaction. They had known and envied Gabriel's quite just, well-founded expectations. Not one of them offered to make any private settlement. No one even thought of repairing this last-minute act of senile vengeance. Privately they blessed their luck. "I have been cut off with a dollar," said Gabriel,

2. Or Primitive Baptists, extreme Calvinists who split from the church in the middle of the nineteenth century. The Cumberland Presbyterians originated in revival preaching in Cumberland County, Kentucky, in 1810.

"and they are all glad of it. I think they feel somehow that this justifies every criticism they ever made against me. They were right about me all along. I am a worthless poor relation," said Gabriel. "My God, I wish you could see them."

Amy said, "I wonder how you will ever support a wife, now."

Gabriel said, "Oh, it isn't so bad as that. If you would, Amy—"

Amy said, "Gabriel, if we get married now there'll be just time to be in New Orleans for Mardi Gras. If we wait until after Lent, it may be too late."

"Why, Amy," said Gabriel, "how could it ever be too late?"

"You might change your mind," said Amy. "You know how fickle you are."

There were two letters in the grandmother's many packets of letters that Maria and Miranda read after they were grown. One of them was from Amy. It was dated ten days after her marriage.

"Dear Mammy, New Orleans hasn't changed as much as I have since we saw each other last. I am now a staid old married woman, and Gabriel is very devoted and kind. Footlights won a race for us yesterday, she was the favorite, and it was wonderful. I go to the races every day, and our horses are doing splendidly; I had my choice of Erin Go Bragh[3] or Miss Lucy, and I chose Miss Lucy. She is mine now, she runs like a streak. Gabriel says I made a mistake, Erin Go Bragh will stay better. I think Miss Lucy will stay my time.

"We are having a lovely visit. I'm going to put on a domino and take to the streets with Gabriel sometime during Mardi Gras. I'm tired of watching the show from a balcony. Gabriel says it isn't safe. He says he'll take me if I insist, but I doubt it. Mammy, he's very nice. Don't worry about me. I have a beautiful black-and-rose-colored velvet gown for the Proteus Ball.[4] Madame, my new mother-in-law, wanted to know if it wasn't a little dashing. I told her I hoped so or I had been cheated. It is fitted perfectly smooth in the bodice, very low in the shoulders—Papa would not approve—and the shirt is looped with wide silver ribbons between the waist and knees in front, and then it surges around and is looped enormously in the back, with a train just one yard long. I now have an eighteen-inch waist, thanks to Madame Duré. I expect to be so dashing that my mother-in-law will have an attack. She has them quite often. Gabriel sends love. Please take good care of Graylie and Fiddler. I want to ride them again when I come home. We're going to Saratoga, I don't know just when. Give everybody my dear dear love. It rains all the time here, of course. . . .

"P.S. Mammy, as soon as I get a minute to myself, I'm going to be terribly homesick. Good-by, my darling Mammy."

The other was from Amy's nurse, dated six weeks after Amy's marriage.

"I cut off the lock of hair because I was sure you would like to have it. And I do not want you to think I was careless, leaving her medicine where she could get it, the doctor has written and explained. It would not have done her any harm except that her heart was weak. She did not know how much she was taking, often she said to me, one more of those

3. Irish motto meaning "Ireland Forever."   4. Final party of the New Orleans Mardi Gras.

little capsules wouldn't do any harm, and so I told her to be careful and not take anything except what I gave her. She begged me for them sometimes but I would not give her more than the doctor said. I slept during the night because she did not seem to be so sick as all that and the doctor did not order me to sit up with her. Please accept my regrets for your great loss and please do not think that anybody was careless with your dear daughter. She suffered a great deal and now she is at rest. She could not get well but she might have lived longer. Yours respectfully. . . . "

The letters and all the strange keepsakes were packed away and forgotten for a great many years. They seemed to have no place in the world.

Part II: 1904

During vacation on their grandmother's farm, Maria and Miranda, who read as naturally and constantly as ponies crop grass, and with much the same kind of pleasure, had by some happy chance laid hold of some forbidden reading matter, brought in and left there with missionary intent, no doubt, by some Protestant cousin. It fell into the right hands if enjoyment had been its end. The reading matter was printed in poor type on spongy paper, and was ornamented with smudgy illustrations all the more exciting to the little girls because they could not make head or tail of them. The stories were about beautiful but unlucky maidens, who for mysterious reasons had been trapped by nuns and priests in dire collusion; they were then "immured" in convents, where they were forced to take the veil—an appalling rite during which the victims shrieked dreadfully— and condemned forever after to most uncomfortable and disorderly existences. They seemed to divide their time between lying chained in dark cells and assisting other nuns to bury throttled infants under stones in moldering rat-infested dungeons.

Immured! It was the word Maria and Miranda had been needing all along to describe their condition at the Convent of the Child Jesus, in New Orleans, where they spent the long winters trying to avoid an education. There were no dungeons at the Child Jesus, and this was only one of numerous marked differences between convent life as Maria and Miranda knew it and the thrilling paper-backed version. It was no good at all trying to fit the stories to life, and they did not even try. They had long since learned to draw the lines between life, which was real and earnest, and the grave was not its goal;[5] poetry, which was true but not real; and stories, or forbidden reading matter, in which things happened as nowhere else, with the most sublime irrelevance and unlikelihood, and one need not turn a hair, because there was not a word of truth in them.

It was true the little girls were hedged and confined, but in a large garden with trees and a grotto; they were locked at night into a long cold dormitory, with all the windows open, and a sister sleeping at either end. Their beds were curtained with muslin, and small night-lamps were so arranged that the sisters could see through the curtains, but the children could not see the sisters. Miranda wondered if they ever slept, or did they sit there all night quietly watching the sleepers through the muslin? She tried to work up a little sinister thrill about this, but she found it impossi-

5. "Life is real! Life is earnest!/ And the grave is not its goal"; from *A Psalm of Life* by Henry Wadsworth Longfellow (1807–1882).

ble to care much what either of the sisters did. They were very dull good natured women who managed to make the whole dormitory seem dull. All days and all things in the Convent of the Child Jesus were dull, in fact, and Maria and Miranda lived for Saturdays.

No one had even hinted that they should become nuns. On the contrary Miranda felt that the discouraging attitude of Sister Claude and Sister Austin and Sister Ursula towards her expressed ambition to be a nun barely veiled a deeply critical knowledge of her spiritual deficiencies. Still Maria and Miranda had got a fine new word out of their summer reading, and they referred to themselves as "immured." It gave a romantic glint to what was otherwise a very dull life for them, except for blessed Saturday afternoons during the racing season.

If the nuns were able to assure the family that the deportment and scholastic achievements of Maria and Miranda were at least passable, some cousin or other always showed up smiling, in holiday mood, to take them to the races, where they were given a dollar each to bet on any horse they chose. There were black Saturdays now and then, when Maria and Miranda sat ready, hats in hand, curly hair plastered down and slicked behind their ears, their stiffly pleated navy-blue skirts spread out around them, waiting with their hearts going down slowly into their high-topped laced-up black shoes. They never put on their hats until the last minute, for somehow it would have been too horrible to have their hats on, when, after all, Cousin Henry and Cousin Isabel, or Uncle George and Aunt Polly, were not coming to take them to the races. When no one appeared, and Saturday came and went a sickening waste, they were then given to understand that it was a punishment for bad marks during the week. They never knew until it was too late to avoid the disappointment. It was very wearing.

One Saturday they were sent down to wait in the visitor's parlor, and there was their father. He had come all the way from Texas to see them. They leaped at sight of him, and then stopped short, suspiciously. Was he going to take them to the races? If so, they were happy to see him.

"Hello," said father, kissing their cheeks. "Have you been good girls? Your Uncle Gabriel is running a mare at the Crescent City[6] today, so we'll all go and bet on her. Would you like that?"

Maria put on her hat without a word, but Miranda stood and addressed her father sternly. She had suffered many doubts about this day. "*Why* didn't you send word yesterday? I could have been looking forward all this time."

"We didn't know," said father, in his easiest paternal manner, "that you were going to deserve it. Remember Saturday before last?"

Miranda hung her head and put on her hat, with the round elastic under the chin. She remembered too well. She had, in midweek, given way to despair over her arithmetic and had fallen flat on her face on the classroom floor, refusing to rise until she was carried out. The rest of the week had been a series of novel deprivations, and Saturday a day of mourning; secret mourning, for if one mourned too noisily, it simply meant another bad mark against deportment.

"Never mind," said father, as if it were the smallest possible matter, "today you're going. Come along now. We've barely time."

6. Nickname from New Orleans, here the name of a horse race.

These expeditions were all joy, every time, from the moment they stepped into a closed one-horse cab, a treat in itself with its dark, thick upholstery, soaked with strange perfumes and tobacco smoke, until the thrilling moment when they walked into a restaurant under big lights and were given dinner with things to eat they never had at home, much less at the convent. They felt worldly and grown up, each with her glass of water colored pink with claret.

The great crowd was always exciting as if they had never seen it before, with the beautiful, incredibly dressed ladies, all plumes and flowers and paint, and the elegant gentlemen with yellow gloves. The bands played in turn with thundering drums and brasses, and now and then a wild beautiful horse would career around the track with a tiny, monkey-shaped boy on his back, limbering up for his race.

Miranda had a secret personal interest in all this which she knew better than to confide to anyone, even Maria. Least of all to Maria. In ten minutes the whole family would have known. She had lately decided to be a jockey when she grew up. Her father had said one day that she was going to be a little thing all her life, she would never be tall; and this meant, of course, that she would never be a beauty like Aunt Amy, or Cousin Isabel. Her hope of being a beauty died hard, until the notion of being a jockey came suddenly and filled all her thoughts. Quietly, blissfully, at night before she slept, and too often in the daytime when she should have been studying, she planned her career as jockey. It was dim in detail, but brilliant at the right distance. It seemed too silly to be worried about arithmetic at all, when what she needed for her future was to ride better—much better. "You ought to be ashamed of yourself," said father, after watching her gallop full tilt down the lane at the farm, on Trixie, the mustang mare. "I can see the sun, moon and stars between you and the saddle every jump." Spanish style meant that one sat close to the saddle, and did all kinds of things with the knees and reins. Jockeys bounced lightly, their knees almost level with the horse's back, rising and falling like a rubber ball. Miranda felt she could do that easily. Yes, she would be a jockey, like Tod Sloan,[7] winning every other race at least. Meantime, while she was training, she would keep it a secret, and one day she would ride out, bouncing lightly, with the other jockeys, and win a great race, and surprise everybody, her family most of all.

On that particular Saturday, her idol, the great Tod Sloan, was riding, and he won two races. Miranda longed to bet her dollar on Tod Sloan, but father said, "Not now, honey. Today you must bet on Uncle Gabriel's horse. Save your dollar for the fourth race, and put it on Miss Lucy. You've got a hundred to one shot. Think if she wins."

Miranda knew well enough that a hundred to one shot was no bet at all. She sulked, the crumpled dollar in her hand grew damp and warm. She could have won three dollars already on Tod Sloan. Maria said virtuously, "It wouldn't be nice not to bet on Uncle Gabriel. That way, we keep the money in the family." Miranda put out her under lip at her sister. Maria was too prissy for words. She wrinkled her nose back at Miranda.

They had just turned their dollar over to the bookmaker for the fourth race when a vast bulging man with a red face and immense tan ragged

7. James Foreman Sloan (1874–1933), known for his "monkey crouch" riding form.

mustaches fading into gray hailed them from a lower level of the grand-stand, over the heads of the crowd, "Hey, there, Harry?" Father said, "Bless my soul, there's Gabriel." He motioned to the man, who came pushing his way heavily up the shallow steps. Maria and Miranda stared, first at him, then at each other. "Can that be our Uncle Gabriel?" their eyes asked. "Is that Aunt Amy's handsome romantic beau? Is that the man who wrote the poem about our Aunt Amy?" Oh, what did grown-up people *mean* when they talked, anyway?

He was a shabby fat man with bloodshot blue eyes, sad beaten eyes, and a big melancholy laugh, like a groan. He towered over them shouting to their father, "Well, for God's sake, Harry, it's been a coon's age. You ought to come out and look 'em over. You look just like yourself, Harry, how are you?"

The band struck up "Over the River" and Uncle Gabriel shouted louder. "Come on, let's get out of this. What are you doing up here with the pikers?"

"Can't," shouted Father. "Brought my little girls. Here they are."

Uncle Gabriel's bleared eyes beamed blindly upon them. "Fine looking set, Harry," he bellowed, "pretty as pictures, how old are they?"

"Ten and fourteen now," said Father; "awkward ages. Nest of vipers," he boasted, "perfect batch of serpent's teeth.[8] Can't do a thing with 'em." He fluffed up Miranda's hair, pretending to tousle it.

"Pretty as pictures," bawled Uncle Gabriel, "but rolled into one they don't come up to Amy, do they?"

"No, they don't," admitted their father at the top of his voice, "but they're only half-baked." *Over the river, over the river,* moaned the band, *my sweetheart's waiting for me.*

"I've got to get back now," yelled Uncle Gabriel. The little girls felt quite deaf and confused. "Got the God-damnedest jockey in the world, Harry, just my luck. Ought to tie him on. Fell off Fiddler yesterday, just plain fell off on his tail—Remember Amy's mare, Miss Lucy? Well, this is her namesake, Miss Lucy IV. None of 'em ever came up to the first one, though. Stay right where you are, I'll be back."

Maria spoke up boldly. "Uncle Gabriel, tell Miss Lucy we're betting on her." Uncle Gabriel bent down and it looked as if there were tears in his swollen eyes. "God bless your sweet heart," he bellowed, "I'll tell her." He plunged down through the crowd again, his fat back bowed slightly in his loose clothes, his thick neck rolling over his collar.

Miranda and Maria, disheartened by the odds, by their first sight of their romantic Uncle Gabriel, whose language was so coarse, sat listlessly without watching, their chances missed, their dollars gone, their hearts sore. They didn't even move until their father leaned over and hauled them up. "Watch your horse," he said, in a quick warning voice, "watch Miss Lucy come home."

They stood up, scrambled to their feet on the bench, every vein in them suddenly beating so violently they could hardly focus their eyes, and saw a thin little mahogany-colored streak flash by the judges' stand, only a neck ahead, but their Miss Lucy, oh, their darling, their lovely—oh, Miss Lucy, their Uncle Gabriel's Miss Lucy, had won, had won. They

8. Shakespeare, *King Lear* I, iv, 371–72—"How sharper than a serpent's tooth it is/ To have a thank- less child."

leaped up and down screaming and clapping their hands, their hats falling back on their shoulders, their hair flying wild. *Whoa, you heifer,* squalled the band with snorting brasses, and the crowd broke into a long roar like the falling of the walls of Jericho.[9]

The little girls sat down, feeling quite dizzy, while their father tried to pull their hats straight, and taking out his handkerchief held it to Miranda's face, saying very gently, "Here, blow your nose," and he dried her eyes while he was about it. He stood up then and shook them out of their daze. He was smiling with deep laughing wrinkles around his eyes, and spoke to them as if they were grown young ladies he was squiring around.

"Let's go out and pay our respects to Miss Lucy," he said. "She's the star of the day."

The horses were coming in, looking as if their hides had been drenched and rubbed with soap, their ribs heaving, their nostrils flaring and closing. The jockeys sat bowed and relaxed, their faces calm, moving a little at the waist with the movement of their horses. Miranda noted this for future use; that was the way you came in from a race, easy and quiet, whether you had won or lost. Miss Lucy came last, and a little handful of winners applauded her and cheered the jockey. He smiled and lifted his whip, his eyes and shriveled brown face perfectly serene. Miss Lucy was bleeding at the nose, two thick red rivulets were stiffening her tender mouth and chin, the round velvet chin that Miranda thought the nicest kind of chin in the world. Her eyes were wild and her knees were trembling, and she snorted when she drew her breath.

Miranda stood staring. That was winning, too. Her heart clinched tight; that was winning, for Miss Lucy. So instantly and completely did her heart reject that victory, she did not know when it happened, but she hated it, and was ashamed that she had screamed and shed tears for joy when Miss Lucy, with her bloodied nose and bursting heart had gone past the judges' stand a neck ahead. She felt empty and sick and held to her father's hand so hard that he shook her off a little impatiently and said, "What is the matter with you? Don't be so fidgety."

Uncle Gabriel was standing there waiting, and he was completely drunk. He watched the mare go in, then leaned against the fence with its white-washed posts and sobbed openly. "She's got the nosebleed, Harry," he said. "Had it since yesterday. We thought we had her all fixed up. But she did it, all right. She's got a heart like a lion. I'm going to breed her, Harry. Her heart's worth a million dollars, by itself, God bless her." Tears ran over his brick-colored face and into his straggling mustaches. "If anything happens to her now I'll blow my brains out. She's my last hope. She saved my life. I've had a run," he said, groaning into a large handkerchief and mopping his face all over, "I've had a run of luck that would break a brass billy goat. God, Harry, let's go somewhere and have a drink."

"I must get the children back to school first, Gabriel," said their father, taking each by a hand.

"No, no, don't go yet," said Uncle Gabriel desperately. "Wait here a minute, I want to see the vet and take a look at Miss Lucy, and I'll be

---

9. Joshua 6:20—"So the people shouted when the priests blew the trumpets: and it came to pass, when the people heard the sound of the trumpet, and the people shouted with a great shout, that the wall fell down flat, so that the people went up into the city, every man straight before him, and they took the city."

right back. Don't go, Harry, for God's sake, I want to talk to you a few minutes."

Maria and Miranda, watching Uncle Gabriel's lumbering, unsteady back, were thinking that this was the first time they had ever seen a man that they knew to be drunk. They had seen pictures and read descriptions, and had heard descriptions, so they recognized the symptoms at once. Miranda felt it was an important moment in a great many ways. "Uncle Gabriel's a drunkard, isn't he?" she asked her father, rather proudly.

"Hush, don't say such things," said father with a heavy frown, "or I'll never bring you here again." He looked worried and unhappy, and, above all, undecided. The little girls stood stiff with resentment against such obvious injustice. They loosed their hands from his and moved away coldly, standing together in silence. Their father did not notice, watching the place where Uncle Gabriel had disappeared. In a few minutes he came back, still wiping his face, as if there were cobwebs on it, carrying his big black hat. He waved at them from a short distance, calling out in a cheerful way, "She's going to be all right, Harry. It's stopped now. Lord, this will be good news for Miss Honey. Come on, Harry, let's all go home and tell Miss Honey. She deserves some good news."

Father said, "I'd better take the children back to school first, then we'll go."

"No, no," said Uncle Gabriel, fondly. "I want her to see the girls. She'll be tickled pink to see them, Harry. Brimg 'em along."

"Is it another race horse we're going to see?" whispered Miranda in her sister's ear.

"Don't be silly," said Maria. "It's Uncle Gabriel's second wife."

"Let's find a cab, Harry," said Uncle Gabriel, "and take your little girls out to cheer up Miss Honey. Both of 'em rolled into one look a lot like Amy, I swear they do. I want Miss Honey to see them. She's always liked our family, Harry, though of course she's not what you'd call an expansive kind of woman."

Maria and Miranda sat facing the driver, and Uncle Gabriel squeezed himself in facing them beside their father. The air became at once bitter and sour with his breathing. He looked sad and poor. His necktie was on crooked and his shirt was rumpled. Father said, "You're going to see Uncle Gabriel's second wife, children," exactly if they had not heard everything; and to Gabriel, "How *is* your wife nowadays? It must be twenty years since I saw her last."

"She's pretty gloomy, and that's a fact," said Uncle Gabriel. "She's been pretty gloomy for years now, and nothing seems to shake her out of it. She never did care for horses, Harry, if you remember; she hasn't been near the track three times since we were married. When I think how Amy wouldn't have missed a race for anything ... She's very different from Amy, Harry, a very different kind of woman. As fine a woman as ever lived in her own way, but she hates change and moving around, and she just lives in the boy."

"Where is Gabe now?" asked father.

"Finishing college," said Uncle Gabriel; "a smart boy, but awfully like his mother. Awfully like," he said, in a melancholy way. "She hates being away from him. Just wants to sit down in the same town and wait for him to get through with his education. Well, I'm sorry it can't be done if that's what she wants, but God Almighty—And this last run of luck has about got her down. I hope you'll be able to cheer her up a little, Harry, she needs it."

The little girls sat watching the streets grow duller and dingier and narrower, and at last the shabbier and shabbier white people gave way to dressed-up Negroes, and then to shabby Negroes, and after a long way the cab stopped before a desolate-looking little hotel in Elysian Fields.[1] Their father helped Maria and Miranda out, told the cabman to wait, and they followed Uncle Gabriel through a dirty damp-smelling patio, down a long gas-lighted hall full of a terrible smell, Miranda couldn't decide what it was made of but it had a bitter taste even, and up a long staircase with a ragged carpet. Uncle Gabriel pushed open a door without warning, saying, "Come in, here we are."

A tall pale-faced woman with faded straw-colored hair and pink-rimmed eyelids rose suddenly from a squeaking rocking chair. She wore a stiff blue-and-white striped shirtwaist and a still black skirt of some hard shiny material. Her large knuckled hands rose to her round, neat pompadour at sight of her visitors.

"Honey," said Uncle Gabriel, with large false heartiness, "you'll never guess who's come to see you." He gave her a clumsy hug. Her face did not change and her eyes rested steadily on the three strangers. "Amy's brother Harry, Honey, you remember, don't you?"

"Of course," said Miss Honey, putting out her hand straight as a paddle, "of course I remember you, Harry." She did not smile.

"And Amy's two little nieces," went on Uncle Gabriel, bringing them forward. They put out their hands limply, and Miss Honey gave each one a slight flip and dropped it. "And we've got good news for you," went on Uncle Gabriel, trying to bolster up the painful situation. "Miss Lucy stepped out and showed 'em today, Honey. We're rich again, old girl, cheer up."

Miss Honey turned her long, despairing face towards her visitors. "Sit down," she said with a heavy sigh, seating herself and motioning towards various rickety chairs. There was a big lumpy bed, with a grayish-white counterpane on it, a marble-topped washstand, grayish coarse lace curtains on strings at the two small windows, a small closed fireplace with a hole in it for a stovepipe, and two trunks, standing at odds as if somebody were just moving in, or just moving out. Everything was dingy and soiled and neat and bare; not a pin out of place.

"We'll move to the St. Charles[2] tomorrow," said Uncle Gabriel, as much to Harry as to his wife. "Get your best dresses together, Honey, the long dry spell is over."

Miss Honey's nostrils pinched together and she rocked slightly, with her arms folded. "I've lived in the St. Charles before, and I've lived here before," she said, in a tight deliberate voice, "and this time I'll just stay where I am, thank you. I prefer it to moving back here in three months. I'm settled now, I feel at home here," she told him, glancing at Harry, her pale eyes kindling with blue fire, a stiff white line around her mouth.

The little girls sat trying not to stare, miserably ill at ease. Their grandmother had pronounced Harry's children to be the most unteachable she had ever seen in her long experience with the young; but they had

1. Run-down section of New Orleans.   2. Expensive New Orleans hotel.

learned by indirection one thing well—nice people did not carry on quarrels before outsiders. Family quarrels were sacred, to be waged privately in fierce hissing whispers, low choked mutters and growls. If they did yell and stamp, it must be behind closed doors and windows. Uncle Gabriel's second wife was hopping mad and she looked ready to fly out at Uncle Gabriel any second, with him sitting there like a hound when someone shakes a whip at him.

"She loathes and despises everybody in this room," thought Miranda, coolly, "and she's afraid we won't know it. She needn't worry, we knew it when we came in." With all her heart she wanted to go, but her father, though his face was a study, made no move. He seemed to be trying to think of something pleasant to say. Maria, feeling guilty, though she couldn't think why, was calculating rapidly, "Why, she's only Uncle Gabriel's second wife, and Uncle Gabriel was only married before to Aunt Amy, why, she's no kin at all, and I'm glad of it." Sitting back easily, she let her hands fall open in her lap; they would be going in a few minutes, undoubtedly, and they need never come back.

Then father said, "We mustn't be keeping you, we just dropped in for a few minutes. We wanted to see how you are."

Miss Honey said nothing, but she made a little gesture with her hands, from the wrist, as if to say, "Well, you see how I am, and now what next?"

"I must take these young ones back to school," said father, and Uncle Gabriel said stupidly, "Look, Honey, don't you think they resemble Amy a little? Especially around the eyes, especially Maria, don't you think, Harry?"

Their father glanced at them in turn. "I really couldn't say," he decided, and the little girls saw he was more monstrously embarrassed than ever. He turned to Miss Honey, "I hadn't seen Gabriel for so many years," he said, "we thought of getting out for a talk about old times together. You know how it is."

"Yes, I know," said Miss Honey, rocking a little, and all that she knew gleamed forth in a pallid, unquenchable hatred and bitterness that seemed enough to bring her long body straight up out of the chair in a fury, "I know," and she sat staring at the floor. Her mouth shook and straightened. There was a terrible silence, which was broken when the little girls saw their father rise. They got up, too, and it was all they could do to keep from making a dash for the door.

"I must get the young ones back," said their father. "They've had enough excitement for one day. They each won a hundred dollars on Miss Lucy. It was a good race," he said, in complete wretchedness, as if he simply could not extricate himself from the situation. "Wasn't it, Gabriel?"

"It was a grand race," said Gabriel, brokenly, "a grand race."

Miss Honey stood up and moved a step towards the door. "Do you take them to the races, actually?" she asked, and her lids flickered towards them as if they were loathsome insects, Maria felt.

"If I feel they deserve a little treat, yes," said their father, in an easy tone but with wrinkled brow.

"I had rather, much rather," said Miss Honey clearly, "see my son dead at my feet than hanging around a race track."

The next few moments were rather a blank, but at last they were out of it, going down the stairs, across the patio, with Uncle Gabriel seeing them back into the cab. His face was sagging, the features had fallen as if the flesh had slipped from the bones, and his eyelids were puffed and blue. "Good-by, Harry," he said soberly. "How long you expect to be here?"

"Starting back tomorrow," said Harry. "Just dropped in on a little business and to see how the girls were getting along."

"Well," said Uncle Gabriel, "I may be dropping into your part of the country one of these days. Good-by, children," he said, taking their hands one after the other in his big warm paws. "They're nice children, Harry. I'm glad you won on Miss Lucy," he said to the little girls, tenderly. "Don't spend your money foolishly, now. Well, so long, Harry." As the cab jolted away he stood there fat and sagging, holding up his arm and wagging his hand at them.

"Goodness," said Maria, in her most grown-up manner, taking her hat off and hanging it over her knee, "I'm glad that's over."

"What I want to know is," said Miranda, "*is* Uncle Gabriel a real drunkard?"

"Oh, hush," said their father, sharply, "I've got the heartburn."

There was a respectful pause, as before a public monument. When their father had the heartburn it was time to lay low. The cab rumbled on, back to clean gay streets, with the lights coming on in the early February darkness, past shimmering shop windows, smooth pavements, on and on, past beautiful old houses set in deep gardens, on, on back to the dark walls with the heavy-topped trees hanging over them. Miranda sat thinking so hard she forgot and spoke out in her thoughtless way: "I've decided I'm not going to be a jockey, after all." She could as usual have bitten her tongue, but as usual it was too late.

Father cheered up and twinkled at her knowingly, as if that didn't surprise him in the least. "Well, well," said he, "so you aren't going to be a jockey! That's very sensible of you. I think she ought to be a lion-tamer, don't you, Maria? That's a nice, womanly profession."

Miranda, seeing Maria from the height of her fourteen years suddenly joining with their father to laugh at her, made an instant decision and laughed with them at herself. That was better. Everybody laughed and it was such a relief.

"Where's my hundred dollars?" asked Maria, anxiously.

"It's going in the bank," said their father, "and yours too," he told Miranda. "That is your nest-egg."

"Just so they don't buy my stockings with it," said Miranda, who had long resented the use of her Christmas money by their grandmother. "I've got enough stockings to last me a year."

"I'd like to buy a racehorse," said Maria, "but I know it's not enough." The limitations of wealth oppressed her. "*What* could you buy with a hundred dollars?" she asked fretfully.

"Nothing, nothing at all," said their father, "a hundred dollars is just something you put in the bank."

Maria and Miranda lost interest. They had won a hundred dollars on a horse race once. It was already in the far past. They began to chatter about something else.

The lay sister opened the door on a long cord, from behind the grille; Maria and Miranda walked in silently to their familiar world of shining bare floors and insipid wholesome food and cold-water washing and regu-

lar prayers; their world of poverty, chastity and obedience, of early to bed
and early to rise, of sharp little rules and tittle-tattle. Resignation was in
their childish faces as they held them up to be kissed.

"Be good girls," said their father, in the strange serious, rather helpless
way he always had when he told them good-by. "Write to your daddy,
now, nice long letters," he said, holding their arms firmly for a moment
before letting go for good. Then he disappeared, and the sister swung the
door closed after him.

Maria and Miranda went upstairs to the dormitory to wash their faces
and hands and slick down their hair again before supper.

Miranda was hungry. "We didn't have a thing to eat, after all," she
grumbled. "Not even a chocolate nut bar. I think that's mean. We didn't
even get a quarter to spend," she said.

"Not a living bite," said Maria. "Not a nickel." She poured out cold
water into the bowl and rolled up her sleeves.

Another girl about her own age came in and went to a washbowl near
another bed. "Where have you been?" she asked. "Did you have a good
time?"

"We went to the races, with our father," said Maria, soaping her hands.

"Our uncle's horse won," said Miranda.

"My goodness," said the other girl, vaguely, "that must have been
grand."

Maria looked at Miranda, who was rolling up her own sleeves. She
tried to feel martyred, but it wouldn't go. "Immured for another week,"
she said, her eyes sparkling over the edge of her towel.

Part III: 1912

Miranda followed the porter down the stuffy aisle of the sleeping-car,
where the berths were nearly all made down and the dusty green curtains
buttoned, to a seat at the further end. "Now yo' berth's ready any time,
Miss," said the porter.

"But I want to sit up a while," said Miranda. A very thin old lady
raised choleric black eyes and fixed upon her a regard of unmixed disapproval. She had two immense front teeth and a receding chin, but she did
not lack character. She had piled her luggage around her like a barricade,
and she glared at the porter when he picked some of it up to make room
for his new passenger. Miranda sat, saying mechanically, "May I?"

"You may, indeed," said the old lady, for she seemed old in spite of a
certain brisk, rustling energy. Her taffeta petticoats creaked like hinges
every time she stirred. With ferocious sarcasm, after a half second's
pause, she added, "You may be so good as to get off my hat!"

Miranda rose instantly in horror, and handed to the old lady a wilted
contrivance of black horsehair braid and shattered white poppies. "I'm
dreadfully sorry," she stammered, for she had been brought up to treat
ferocious old ladies respectfully, and this one seemed capable of spanking
her, then and there. "I didn't dream it was your hat."

"And whose hat did you dream it might be?" inquired the old lady,
baring her teeth and twirling the hat on a forefinger to restore it.

"I didn't think it was a hat at all," said Miranda with a touch of
hysteria.

"Oh, you didn't think it was a hat? Where on earth are your eyes, child?" and she proved the nature and function of the object by placing it on her head at a somewhat tipsy angle, though still it did not much resemble a hat. "Now can you see what it is?"

"Yes, oh, yes," said Miranda, with a meekness she hoped was disarming. She ventured to sit again after a careful inspection of the narrow space she was to occupy.

"Well, well," said the old lady, "let's have the porter remove some of these encumbrances," and she stabbed the bell with a lean sharp forefinger. There followed a flurry of rearrangements, during which they both stood in the aisle, the old lady giving a series of impossible directions to the Negro which he bore philosophically while he disposed of the luggage exactly as he had meant to do. Seated again, the old lady asked in a kindly, authoritative tone, "And what might your name be, child?"

At Miranda's answer, she blinked somewhat, unfolded her spectacles, straddled them across her high nose competently, and took a good long look at the face beside her.

"If I'd had my spectacles on," she said, in an astonishingly changed voice, "I might have known. I'm Cousin Eva Parrington," she said, "Cousin Molly Parrington's daughter, remember? I knew you when you were a little girl. You were a lively little girl," she added as if to console her, "and very opinionated. The last thing I heard about you, you were planning to be a tight-rope walker. You were going to play the violin and walk the tight rope at the same time."

"I must have seen it at the vaudeville show," said Miranda. "I couldn't have invented it. Now I'd like to be an air pilot!"

"I used to go to dances with your father," said Cousin Eva, busy with her own thoughts, "and to big holiday parties at your grandmother's house, long before you were born. Oh, indeed, yes, a long time before."

Miranda remembered several things at once. Aunt Amy had threatened to be an old maid like Eva. Oh, Eva, the trouble with her is she has no chin. Eva has given up, and is teaching Latin in a Female Seminary. Eva's gone out for votes for women, God help her. The nice thing about an ugly daughter is, she's not apt to make me a grandmother.... "They didn't do you much good, those parties, dear Cousin Eva," thought Miranda.

"They didn't do me much good, those parties," said Cousin Eva aloud as if she were a mind-reader, and Miranda's head swam for a moment with fear that she had herself spoken aloud. "Or at least, they didn't serve their purpose, for I never got married; but I enjoyed them, just the same. I had a good time at those parties, even if I wasn't a belle. And so you are Harry's child, and here I was quarreling with you. You do remember me, don't you?"

"Yes," said Miranda, and thinking that even if Cousin Eva had been really an old maid ten years before, still she couldn't be much past fifty now, and she looked so withered and tired, so famished and sunken in the cheeks, so *old*, somehow. Across the abyss separating Cousin Eva from her own youth, Miranda looked with painful premonition. "Oh, must I ever be like that?" She said aloud, "Yes, you used to read Latin to me, and tell me not to bother about the sense, to get the sound in my mind, and it would come easier later."

"Ah, so I did," said Cousin Eva, delighted. "So I did. You don't happen to remember that I once had a beautiful sapphire velvet dress with a train on it?"

"No, I don't remember that dress," said Miranda.

"It was an old dress of my mother's made over and cut down to fit," said Eva, "and it wasn't in the least becoming to me, but it was the only really good dress I ever had, and I remember it as if it were yesterday. Blue was never my color." She sighed with a humorous bitterness. The humor seemed momentary, but the bitterness was a constant state of mind.

Miranda, trying to offer the sympathy of fellow suffering, said, "I know. I've had Maria's dresses made over for me, and they were never right. It was dreadful."

"Well," said Cousin Eva, in the tone of one who did not wish to share her unique disappointments. "How is your father? I always liked him. He was one of the finest-looking young men I ever saw. Vain, too, like all his family. He wouldn't ride any but the best horses he could buy, and I used to say he made them prance and then watched his own shadow. I used to tell this on him at dinner parties, and he hated me for it. I feel pretty certain he hated me." An overtone of complacency in Cousin Eva's voice explained better than words that she had her own method of commanding attention and arousing emotion. "How *is* your father, I asked you, my dear?"

"I haven't seen him for nearly a year," answered Miranda, quickly, before Cousin Eva could get ahead again. "I'm going home now to Uncle Gabriel's funeral; you know, Uncle Gabriel died in Lexington[3] and they have brought him back to be buried beside Aunt Amy."

"So that's how we meet," said Cousin Eva. "Yes, Gabriel drank himself to death at last. I'm going to the funeral, too. I haven't been home since I went to Mother's funeral, it must be, let's see, yes, it will be nine years next July. I'm going to Gabriel's funeral, though. I wouldn't miss that. Poor fellow, what a life he had. Pretty soon, they'll all be gone."

Miranda said, "We're left, Cousin Eva," meaning those of her own generation, the young, and Cousin Eva said, "Pshaw, you'll live forever, and you won't bother to come to our funerals." She didn't seem to think this was a misfortune, but flung the remark from her like a woman accustomed to saying what she thought.

Miranda sat thinking, "Still, I suppose it would be pleasant if I could say something to make her believe that she and all of them would be lamented, but—but—" With a smile which she hoped would be her denial of Cousin Eva's cynicism about the younger generation, she said, "You were right about the Latin, Cousin Eva, your reading did help when I began with it. I still study," she said. "Latin, too."

"And why shouldn't you?" asked Cousin Eva, sharply, adding at once mildly, "I'm glad you are going to use your mind a little, child. Don't let yourself rust away. Your mind outwears all sorts of things you may set your heart upon; you can enjoy it when all other things are taken away." Miranda was chilled by her melancholy. Cousin Eva went on: "In our part of the country, in my time, we were so provincial—a woman didn't dare to think or act for herself. The whole world was a little that way,"

---

3. The center of Kentucky horse country.

she said, "but we were the worst, I believe. I suppose you must know how I fought for votes for women when it almost made a pariah of me—I was turned out of my chair at the Seminary, but I'm glad I did it and I would do it again. You young things don't realize. You'll live in a better world because we worked for it."

Miranda knew something of Cousin Eva's career. She said sincerely, "I think it was brave of you, and I'm glad you did it, too. I loved your courage."

"It wasn't just showing off, mind you," said Cousin Eva, rejecting praise, fretfully. "Any fool can be brave. We were working for something we knew was right, and it turned out that we needed a lot of courage for it. That was all. I didn't expect to go to jail, but I went three times, and I'd go three times three more if it were necessary. We aren't voting yet," she said, "but we will be."

Miranda did not venture any answer, but she felt convinced that indeed women would be voting soon if nothing fatal happened to Cousin Eva. There was something in her manner which said such things could be left safely to her. Miranda was dimly fired for the cause herself; it seemed heroic and worth suffering for, but discouraging, too, to those who came after: Cousin Eva so plainly had swept the field clear of opportunity.

They were silent for a few minutes, while Cousin Eva rummaged in her handbag, bringing up odds and ends: peppermint drops, eye drops, a packet of needles, three handkerchiefs, a little bottle of violet perfume, a book of addresses, two buttons, one black, one white, and, finally, a packet of headache powders.

"Bring me a glass of water, will you, my dear?" she asked Miranda. She poured the headache powder on her tongue, swallowed the water, and put two peppermints in her mouth.

"So now they're going to bury Gabriel near Amy," she said after a while, as if her eased headache had started her on a new train of thought. "Miss Honey would like that, poor dear, if she could know. After listening to stories about Amy for twenty-five years, she must lie alone in her grave in Lexington while Gabriel sneaks off to Texas to make his bed with Amy again. It was a kind of life-long infidelity, Miranda, and now an eternal infidelity on top of that. He ought to be ashamed of himself."

"It was Aunt Amy he loved," said Miranda, wondering what Miss Honey could have been like before her long troubles with Uncle Gabriel. "First, anyway."

"Oh, that Amy," said Cousin Eva, her eyes glittering. "Your Aunt Amy was a devil and a mischief-maker, but I loved her dearly. I used to stand up for Amy when her reputation wasn't worth that." Her fingers snapped like castanets. "She used to say to me, in that gay soft way she had, 'Now, Eva, don't go talking votes for women when the lads ask you to dance. Don't recite Latin poems to 'em,' she would say, 'they got sick of that in school. Dance and say nothing, Eva,' she would say, her eyes perfectly devilish, 'and hold your chin up, Eva.' My chin was my weak point, you see. 'You'll never catch a husband if you don't look out,' she would say. Then she would laugh and fly away, and where did she fly to?" demanded Cousin Eva, her sharp eyes pinning Miranda down to the bitter facts of the case, "To scandal and to death, nowhere else."

"She was joking, Cousin Eva," said Miranda, innocently, "and everybody loved her."

"Not everybody, by a long shot," said Cousin Eva in triumph. "She had enemies. If she knew, she pretended she didn't. If she cared, she never said. You couldn't make her quarrel. She was sweet as a honeycomb to everybody. *Everybody,*" she added, "that was the trouble. She went through life like a spoiled darling, doing as she pleased and letting other people suffer for it, and pick up the pieces after her. I never believed for one moment," said Cousin Eva, putting her mouth close to Miranda's ear and breathing peppermint hotly into it, "that Amy was an impure woman. Never! But let me tell you, there were plenty who did believe it. There were plenty to pity poor Gabriel for being so completely blinded by her. A great many persons were not suprised when they heard that Gabriel was perfectly miserable all the time, on their honeymoon, in New Orleans. Jealousy. And why not? But I used to say to such persons that, no matter what the appearances were, I had faith in Amy's virtue. Wild, I said, indiscreet, I said, heartless, I said, but *virtuous,* I feel certain. But you could hardly blame anyone for being mystified. The way she rose up suddenly from death's door to marry Gabriel Breaux, after refusing him and treating him like a dog for years, looked odd, to say the least. To say the very least," she added, after a moment, "odd is a mild word for it. And there was something very mysterious about her death, only six weeks after marriage."

Miranda roused herself. She felt she knew this part of the story and could set Cousin Eva right about one thing. "She died of a hemorrhage from the lungs," said Miranda. "She had been ill for five years, don't you remember?"

Cousin Eva was ready for that. "Ha, that was the story, indeed. The official account, you might say. Oh, yes, I heard that often enough. But did you ever hear about that fellow Raymond somebody-or-other from Calcasieu Parish,[4] almost a stranger, who persuaded Amy to elope with him from a dance one night, and she just ran out into the darkness without even stopping for her cloak, and your poor dear nice father Harry— you weren't even thought of then—had to run him down to earth and shoot him?"

Miranda leaned back from the advancing flood of speech. "Cousin Eva, my father shot *at* him, don't you remember? He didn't hit him. . . . "

"Well, that's a pity."

" . . . and they had only gone out for a breath of air between dances. It was Uncle Gabriel's jealousy. And my father shot at the man because he thought that was better than letting Uncle Gabriel fight a duel about Aunt Amy. There was *nothing* in the whole affair except Uncle Gabriel's jealousy."

"You poor baby," said Cousin Eva, and pity gave a light like daggers to her eyes, "you dear innocent, you—do you believe that? How old are you, anyway?"

"Just past eighteen," said Miranda.

"If you don't understand what I tell you," said Cousin Eva portentously, "you will later. Knowledge can't hurt you. You mustn't live in a romantic haze about life. You'll understand when you're married, at any rate."

"I'm marrried now, Cousin Eva," said Miranda, feeling for almost the

4. Parish (county) about 200 miles due west of New Orleans, on the Texas border.

first time that it might be an advantage, "nearly a year. I eloped from school." It seemed very unreal even as she said it, and seemed to have nothing at all to do with the future; still, it was important, it must be declared, it was a situation in life which people seemed to be most exacting about, and the only feeling she could rouse in herself about it was an immense weariness as if it were an illness that she might one day hope to recover from.

"Shameful, shameful," cried Cousin Eva, genuinely repelled. "If you had been my child I should have brought you home and spanked you."

Miranda laughed out. Cousin Eva seemed to believe things could be arranged like that. She was so solemn and fierce, so comic and baffled.

"And you must know I should have just gone straight out again, through the nearest window," she taunted her. "If I went the first time, why not the second?"

"Yes, I suppose so," said Cousin Eva. "I hope you married rich."

"Not so very," said Miranda. "Enough." As if anyone could have stopped to think of such a thing!

Cousin Eva adjusted her spectacles and sized up Miranda's dress, her luggage, examined her engagement ring and wedding ring, with her nostrils fairly quivering as if she might smell out wealth on her.

"Well, that's better than nothing," said Cousin Eva. "I thank God every day of my life that I have a small income. It's a Rock of Ages.[5] What would have become of me if I hadn't a cent of my own? Well, you'll be able now to do something for your family."

Miranda remembered what she had always heard about the Parringtons. They were money-hungry, they loved money and nothing else, and when they had got some they kept it. Blood was thinner than water between the Parringtons where money was concerned.

"We're pretty poor," said Miranda, stubbornly allying herself with her father's family instead of her husband's, "but a rich marriage is no way out," she said, with the snobbishness of poverty. She was thinking, "You don't know my branch of the family, dear Cousin Eva, if you think it is."

"Your branch of the family," said Cousin Eva, with that terrifying habit she had of lifting phrases out of one's mind, "has no more practical sense than so many children. Everything for love," she said, with a face of positive nausea, "that was it. Gabriel would have been rich if his grandfather had not disinherited him, but would Amy be sensible and marry him and make him settle down so the old man would have been pleased with him? No. And what could Gabriel do without money? I wish you could have seen the life he led Miss Honey, one day buying her Paris gowns and the next day pawning her earrings. It just depended on how the horses ran, and they ran worse and worse, and Gabriel drank more and more."

Miranda did not say, "I saw a little of it." She was trying to imagine Miss Honey in a Paris gown. She said, "But Uncle Gabriel was so mad about Aunt Amy, there was no question of her not marrying him at last, money or no money."

Cousin Eva strained her lips tightly over her teeth, let them fly again and leaned over, gripping Miranda's arm. "What I ask myself, what I ask myself over and over again," she whispered, "is, what connection did this

<hr />

5. Solid support; the 1775 hymn of that title by Augustus Montague Toplady (1740–1778) begins, "Rock of Ages, cleft for me,/ Let me hide myself in thee."

man Raymond from Calcasieu have with Amy's sudden marriage to Gabriel, and *what* did Amy do to make away with herself so soon afterward? For mark my words, child, Amy wasn't so ill as all that. She'd been flying around for years after the doctors said her lungs were weak. Amy did away with herself to escape some disgrace, some exposure that she faced."

The beady black eyes glinted; Cousin Eva's face was quite frightening, so near and so intent. Miranda wanted to say, "Stop. Let her rest. What harm did she ever do you?" but she was timid and unnerved, and deep in her was a horrid fascination with the terrors and the darkness Cousin Eva had conjured up. What was the end of this story?

"She was a bad, wild girl, but I was fond of her to the last," said Cousin Eva. "She got into trouble somehow, and she couldn't get out again, and I have every reason to believe she killed herself with the drug they gave her to keep her quiet after a hemorrhage. If she didn't, what happened, what happened?"

"I don't know," said Miranda. "How should I know? She was very beautiful," she said, as if this explained everything. "Everybody said she was very beautiful."

"Not everybody," said Cousin Eva, firmly, shaking her head. "I for one never thought so. They made entirely too much fuss over her. She was good-looking enough, but why did they think she was beautiful? I cannot understand it. She was too thin when she was young, and later I always thought she was too fat, and again in her last year she was altogether too thin. She always got herself up to be looked at, and so people looked, of course. She rode too hard, and she danced too freely, and she talked too much, and you'd have to be blind, deaf and dumb not to notice her. I don't mean she was loud or vulgar, she wasn't, but she was *too free*," said Cousin Eva. She stopped for breath and put a peppermint in her mouth. Miranda could see Cousin Eva on the platform, making her speeches, stopping to take a peppermint. But why did she hate Aunt Amy so, when Aunt Amy was dead and she alive? Wasn't being alive enough?

"And her illness wasn't romantic either," said Cousin Eva, "though to hear them tell it she faded like a lily. Well, she coughed blood, if that's romantic. If they had made her take proper care of herself, if she had been nursed sensibly, she might have been alive today. But no, nothing of the kind. She lay wrapped in beautiful shawls on a sofa with flowers around her, eating as she liked or not eating, getting up after a hemorrhage and going out to ride or dance, sleeping with the windows closed; with crowds coming in and out laughing and talking at all hours, and Amy sitting up so her hair wouldn't get out of curl. And why wouldn't that sort of thing kill a well person in time? I have almost died twice in my life," said Cousin Eva, "and both times I was sent to a hospital where I belonged and left there until I came out. And I came out," she said, her voice deepening to a bugle note, "and I went to work again."

"Beauty goes, character stays," said the small voice of axiomatic morality in Miranda's ear. It was a dreary prospect; why was a strong character so deforming? Miranda felt she truly wanted to be strong, but how could she face it, seeing what it did to one?

"She had a lovely complexion," said Cousin Eva, "perfectly transparent with a flush on each cheekbone. But it was tuberculosis, and is disease beautiful? And she brought it on herself by drinking lemon and salt to stop her periods when she wanted to go to dances. There was a superstition among young girls about that. They fancied that young men could tell what ailed them by touching their hands, or even by looking at them. As if it mattered? But they were terribly self-conscious and they had immense respect for man's worldly wisdom in those days. My own notion is that a man couldn't—but anyway, the whole thing was stupid."

"I should have thought they'd have stayed at home if they couldn't manage better than that," said Miranda, feeling very knowledgeable and modern.

"They didn't dare. Those parties and dances were their market, a girl couldn't afford to miss out, there were always rivals waiting to cut the ground from under her. The rivalry—" said Cousin Eva, and her head lifted, she arched like a cavalry horse getting a whiff of the battlefield— "you can't imagine what the rivalry was like. The way those girls treated each other—nothing was too mean, nothing too false—"

Cousin Eva wrung her hands. "It was just sex," she said in despair; "their minds dwelt on nothing else. They didn't call it that, it was all smothered under pretty names, but that's all it was, sex." She looked out of the window into the darkness, her sunken cheek near Miranda flushed deeply. She turned back. "I took to the soap box and the platform when I was called upon," she said proudly, "and I went to jail when it was necessary, and my condition didn't make any difference. I was booed and jeered and shoved around just as if I had been in perfect health. But it was part of our philosophy not to let our physical handicaps make any difference to our work. You know what I mean," she said, as if until now it was all mystery. "Well, Amy carried herself with more spirit than the others, and she didn't seem to be making any sort of fight, but she was simply sex-ridden, like the rest. She behaved as if she hadn't a rival on earth, and she pretended not to know what marriage was about, but I know better. None of them had, and they didn't want to have, anything else to think about, and they didn't really know anything about that, so they simply festered inside—they festered—"

Miranda found herself deliberately watching a long procession of living corpses, festering women stepping gaily towards the charnel house, their corruption concealed under laces and flowers, their dead faces lifted smiling, and thought quite coldly, "Of course it was not like that. This is no more true than what I was told before, it's every bit as romantic," and she realized that she was tired of her intense Cousin Eva, she wanted to go to sleep, she wanted to be at home, she wished it were tomorrow and she could see her father and her sister, who were so alive and solid; who would mention her freckles and ask her if she wanted something to eat.

"My mother was not like that," she said, childishly. "My mother was a perfectly natural woman who liked to cook. I have seen some of her sewing," she said. "I have read her diary."

"Your mother was a saint," said Cousin Eva, automatically.

Miranda sat silent, outraged. "My mother was nothing of the sort," she wanted to fling in Cousin Eva's big front teeth. But Cousin Eva had been gathering bitterness until more speech came of it.

" 'Hold your chin up, Eva,' Amy used to tell me," she began, doubling up both her fists and shaking them a little. "All my life the whole family bedeviled me about my chin. My entire girlhood was spoiled by it. Can you imagine," she asked, with a ferocity that seemed much too deep for this one cause, "people who call themselves civilized spoiling life for a young girl because she had one unlucky feature? Of course, you understand perfectly it was all in the very best humor, everybody was very amusing about it, no harm meant—oh, no, no harm at all. That is the hellish thing about it. It is that I can't forgive," she cried out, and she twisted her hands together as if they were rags. "Ah, the family," she said, releasing her breath and sitting back quietly, "the whole hideous institution should be wiped from the face of the earth. It is the root of all human wrongs," she ended, and relaxed, and her face became calm. She was trembling. Miranda reached out and took Cousin Eva's hand and held it. The hand fluttered and lay still, and Cousin Eva said, "You've not the faintest idea what some of us went through, but I wanted you to hear the other side of the story. And I'm keeping you up when you need your beauty sleep," she said grimly, stirring herself with an immense rustle of petticoats.

Miranda pulled herself together, feeling limp, and stood up. Cousin Eva put out her hand again, and drew Miranda down to her. "Good night, you dear child," she said, "to think you're grown up." Miranda hesitated, then quite suddenly kissed her Cousin Eva on the cheek. The black eyes shown brightly through water for an instant, and Cousin Eva said with a warm note in her sharp clear orator's voice, "Tomorrow we'll be at home again. I'm looking forward to it, aren't you? Good night."

Miranda fell asleep while she was getting off her clothes. Instantly it was morning again. She was still trying to close her suitcase when the train pulled into the small station, and there on the platform she saw her father, looking tired and anxious, his hat pulled over his eyes. She rapped on the window to catch his attention, then ran out and threw herself upon him. He said, "Well, here's my big girl," as if she were still seven, but his hands on her arms held her off, the tone was forced. There was no welcome for her, and there had not been since she had run away. She could not persuade herself to remember how it would be; between one home-coming and the next her mind refused to accept its own knowledge. Her father looked over her head and said, without surprise, "Why, hello, Eva, I'm glad somebody sent you a telegram." Miranda, rebuffed again, let her arms fall away again, with the same painful dull jerk of the heart.

"No one in my family," said Eva, her face framed in the thin black veil she reserved, evidently, for family funerals, "ever sent me a telegram in my life. I had the news from young Keziah who had it from young Gabriel. I suppose Gabe is here?"

"Everybody seems to be here," said Father. "The house is getting full."

"I'll go to the hotel if you like," said Cousin Eva.

"Damnation, no," said Father. "I didn't mean that. You'll come with us where you belong."

Skid, the handy man, grabbed the suitcases and started down the rocky village street. "We've got the car," said Father. He took Miranda by the hand, then dropped it again, and reached for Cousin Eva's elbow.

"I'm perfectly able, thank you," said Cousin Eva, shying away.

"If you're so independent now, said Father, "God help us when you get that vote."

Cousin Eva pushed back her veil. She was smiling merrily. She liked Harry, she always had liked him, he could tease as much as he liked. She slipped her arm through his. "So it's all over with poor Gabriel, isn't it?"

"Oh, yes," said Father, "it's all over, all right. They're pegging out pretty regularly now. It will be our turn next, Eva?"

"I don't know, and I don't care," said Eva, recklessly. "It's good to be back now and then, Harry, even if it is only for funerals. I feel sinfully cheerful."

"Oh, Gabriel wouldn't mind, he'd like seeing you cheerful. Gabriel was the cheerfulest cuss I ever saw, when we were young. Life for Gabriel," said Father, "was just one perpetual picnic."

"Poor fellow," said Cousin Eva.

"Poor old Gabriel," said Father, heavily.

Miranda walked along beside her father, feeling homeless, but not sorry for it. He had not forgiven her, she knew that. When would he? She could not guess, but she felt it would come of itself, without words and without acknowledgment on either side, for by the time it arrived neither of them would need to remember what had caused their division, nor why it had seemed so important. Surely old people cannot hold their grudges forever because the young want to live, too, she thought, in her arrogance, her pride. I will make my own mistakes, not yours; I cannot depend upon you beyond a certain point, why depend at all? There was something more beyond, but this was a first step to take, and she took it, walking in silence beside her elders who were no longer Cousin Eva and Father, since they had forgotten her presence, but had become Eva and Harry, who knew each other well, who were comfortable with each other, being contemporaries on equal terms, who occupied by right their place in this world, at the time of life to which they had arrived by paths familiar to them both. They need not play their roles of daughter, of son, to aged persons who did not understand them; nor of father and elderly female cousin to young persons whom they did not understand. They were precisely themselves; their eyes cleared, their voices relaxed into perfect naturalness, they need not weigh their words or calculate the effect of their manner. "It is I who have no place," thought Miranda. "Where are my own people and my own time?" She resented, slowly and deeply and in profound silence, the presence of these aliens who lectured and admonished her, who loved her with bitterness and denied her the right to look at the world with her own eyes, who demanded that she accept their version of life and yet could not tell her the truth, not in the smallest thing. "I hate them both," her most inner and secret mind said plainly, *"I will be free of them, I shall not even remember them."*

She sat in the front seat with Skid, the Negro boy. "Come back with us, Miranda," said Cousin Eva, with the sharp little note of elderly command, "there is plenty of room."

"No, thank you," said Miranda, in a firm cold voice. "I'm quite comfortable. Don't disturb yourself."

Neither of them noticed her voice or her manner. They sat back and went on talking steadily in their friendly family voices, talking about their dead, their living, their affairs, their prospects, their common memories, interrupting each other, catching each other up on small points of dispute, laughing with a gaiety and freshness Miranda had not known they were capable of, going over old stories and finding new points of interest in them.

Miranda could not hear the stories above the noisy motor, but she felt she knew them well, or stories like them. She knew too many stories like them, she wanted something new of her own. The language was familiar to them, but not to her, not any more. The house, her father had said, was full. It would be full of cousins, many of them strangers. Would there be any young cousins there, to whom she could talk about things they both knew? She felt a vague distaste for seeing cousins. There were too many of them and her blood rebelled against the ties of blood. She was sick to death of cousins. She did not want any more ties with this house, she was going to leave it, and she was not going back to her husband's family either. She would have no more bonds that smothered her in love and hatred. She knew now why she had run away to marriage, and she knew that she was going to run away from marriage, and she was not going to stay in any place, with anyone, that threatened to forbid her making her own discoveries, that said "No" to her. She hoped no one had taken her old room, she would like to sleep there once more, she would say good-by there where she had loved sleeping once, sleeping and waking and waiting to be grown, to begin to live. Oh, what is life, she asked herself in desperate seriousness, in those childish unanswerable words, and what shall I do with it? It is something of my own, she thought in a fury of jealous possessiveness, what shall I make of it? She did not know that she asked herself this because all her earliest training had argued that life was a substance, a material to be used, it took shape and direction and meaning only as the possessor guided and worked it; living was a progress of continuous and varied acts of the will directed towards a definite end. She had been assured that there were good and evil ends, one must make a choice. But what was good, and what was evil? I hate love, she thought, as if this were the answer, I hate loving and being loved, I hate it. And her disturbed and seething mind received a shock of comfort from this sudden collapse of an old painful structure of distorted images and misconceptions. "You don't know anything about it," said Miranda to herself, with extraordinary clearness as if she were an elder admonishing some younger misguided creature. "You have to find out about it." But nothing in her prompted her to decide, "I will now do this, I will be that, I will go yonder, I will take a certain road to a certain end." There are questions to be asked first, she thought, but who will answer them? No one, or there will be too many answers, none of them right. What is the truth, she asked herself as intently as if the question had never been asked, the truth, even about the smallest, the least important of all the things I must find out? and where shall I begin to look for it? Her mind closed stubbornly against remembering, not the past but the legend of the past, other people's memory of the past, at which she had spent her life peering in wonder like a child at a magic-lantern show. Ah, but there is my own life to come yet, she thought, my own life now and beyond. I don't want any promises, I won't have false hopes, I won't be romantic about myself. I can't live in their world any longer, she told herself, listening to the voices back of her. Let them tell their stories to each other. Let them go on explaining how things happened. I don't care. At least I can know the truth about what happens to me, she assured herself silently, making a promise to herself, in her hopefulness, her ignorance.

1937

AFTERWORD

Reading this anthology in isolation, you would have to believe that Katherine Anne Porter wrote *Old Mortality* with *Daisy Miller* in mind. Both novels concern themselves with the reality behind the unconventional behavior of a beautiful American girl. In both, that "reality" has to do more or less directly with the girl's sexual conduct, her "purity"; in both, the "threat" comes from a "Latin lover," someone outside her own (and therefore "proper") society. Both girls die soon after, both possibly as a result of their "misconduct." Both narratives are presented through centers of consciousness which learn or believe they learn something about themselves and their own lives from the stories of the girls.

Katherine Anne Porter may indeed have had the James novel in mind, and since her conclusions are so different, may have been "answering" it. Even if she were not consciously responding to James, by comparing the two stories we may bring out depths and nuances in each that might otherwise be missed. We must remember, however, that in the sixty years between the two there were not only drastic changes in American society and mores, but that there were a significant number of narratives by writers such as Edith Wharton and F. Scott Fitzgerald, centering on just such American girls as Daisy and Amy.

The change in social customs and mores from roughly the Civil War to the eve of World War I (seen by an author writing on the eve of World War II) underlies the structure of the story. The three chapters have, instead of verbal titles, dates: "1885–1902," "1904," "1912." And not long after the scandal represented by the first date, Amy receives a letter from Great-great-aunt Sally, a representative of the moral values and mores (including handwriting and abbreviations) of two generations earlier, the generation that fought the Civil War. So, whereas James uses space or geography to indicate moral attitudes—Winterbourne lives in Geneva, center of Calvinism; he meets Daisy in Vevey, where a romantic hero had been imprisoned; Daisy's "scandal" and death take place in "corrupt" Rome—Porter does so historically or chronologically. The audience for which the novels were written may be presumed to be close to the centers of consciousness in the novels—American Protestant for James, twentieth rather than nineteenth century for Porter. If this is so, then both novels may be intentionally instructive, teaching their readers something, for both centers of consciousness learn not only about "reality" but about themselves.

The focus in Porter's novel, however, is closer to that of *The Nigger of the "Narcissus"* than it is to that of *Daisy Miller*. Conrad, you will remember, begins with what seems to be an omniscient narrator, slides to "we" (the crew), and ends with a single crew member speaking in the first-person singular. There is no first-person narration, singular or plural (except for interior monologue), in *Old Mortality*, but in the first two chapters Maria and Miranda seem, like the crew of the *Narcissus*, to share the focus of the narration, in the third the consciousness is for the most part Miranda's alone, until very near the end of the novel when the focus seems to pull back from her, toward an omniscience similar to Conrad's at the beginning of his novel. At the end of *Old Mortality*, we see that her way of looking at things, her "truth," is limited by her youth and inexperience: "I won't be romantic about myself. I can't live in their world any longer. . . . At least I can know the truth about what happens to me, she assured herself silently, making a promise to herself in her hopefulness, her ignorance."

What does Miranda learn, then? What is the truth? What is the story?

The story seems to be about telling stories. At the very beginning, though Maria and Miranda cannot see in the old-fashioned picture of their Aunt Amy why all the "old" people think she was so beautiful and so charming, they do share their father's and their family's love of legend, love of romantic stories, that were like poetry, music, theater. "Their Aunt Amy belonged to the world of poetry. The romance of Uncle Gabriel's long, unrewarded love for her, her early death, was such a story as one found in old books. . . ." The first chapter tells the story of this romantic tragedy more or less according to how the twelve-year-old Maria and eight-year-old Miranda, nieces of Amy's, reconstruct it from family tradition. The second chapter narrates the encounter of the fourteen-year-old Maria and ten-year-old Miranda with their Uncle Gabriel, Amy's husband. The girls are in a convent school in New Orleans, and

> had long since learned to draw the lines between life, which was real and earnest, and the grave was not its goal; poetry, which was true but not real; and stories, or forbidden reading matter, in which things happened as nowhere else, with the most sublime irrelevance and unlikelihood, and one need not turn a hair, because there was not a word of truth in them.

That life's reality is described in terms of Longfellow's rather pietistic poem suggests that the girls have yet a way to go toward seeing things as they really are, and the central incident in this chapter does reveal that the romantic hero of Amy's story, Gabriel, is now a fat, sentimental, hard-drinking, seedy horse-owner and gambler. Their experience at the track and after cures Miranda of her childish fantasy of becoming a jockey, and reveals, through the horse Miss Lucy (named after Amy's horse), that even the reality of winning may mean not glamour and joy but pain and bleeding. Gabriel's romanticizing of Amy and the past has ruined him and embittered his second wife.

Though the romance of remembering is undercut by the damage it does to the living, the memory itself, Amy's story, is not reviewed or revised in this chapter; but it is in the final chapter, however. Miranda, eighteen and having herself been through an unhappy marriage, is alone on a train, on her way home to Uncle Gabriel's funeral, when she meets her chinless, feminist, Latin-teaching, spinster Aunt Eva. From her she hears that Amy was no innocent romantic heroine; that she and all her friends thought of nothing but sex; that Amy, everyone's darling, was spoiled, but not an "impure" woman; that the scandal was not that the outsider had complemented Amy on her looks or even that he had kissed her (as in the family's versions) but that he had persuaded her to elope with him; that her death was mysterious, that it was not the result of her weak lungs, may have had something to do with pills, and that Eva believes   " 'Amy did away with herself to escape some disgrace, some exposure that she faced.' "

What's this, now? Pregnancy and suicide? Abortion, perhaps? We are now in the modern world, the harsh world of twentieth-century reality. We have had a familiar enlightenment: in the good old days before the First World War, especially in such already anachronistic societies as that of the Old South, people lived by romantic myths, covering up unpalatable or embarrassing truths— from slavery to sex, from drunkenness to death—with poetry, fiction, lies. The title of the novel comes from the one poem the prosaic Gabriel wrote in which he sentimentally transforms the saucy, head-strong reality of Amy to a saccharine angel:

> She lives again who suffered life,
> Then suffered death, and now set free
> A singing angel, she forgets
> The griefs of old mortality.

"Did she really sing?" Maria asked her father.
"Now what has that to do with it?" he asked. "It's a poem."

We might also note that *Old Mortality* is the title of one of Sir Walter Scott's finest historical novels, itself a mixture of the barbarous putting down of the Scottish Covenanters by the forces of Charles II and a sentimental romantic plot in which the hero returns from supposed death just in the nick of time, etc. Mark Twain, in one of those truth-bearing comic extravagances of his, blamed the Civil War on Scott's novels: the romantic sense of the chivalry of combat and the inevitable triumph of the well-born good over whatever odds led the South, where every gentleman's library had a set of Scott's Waverley novels, to undertake an unrealistic war for a sentimentalized cause.

Most short stories and some novels would have been content with this "epiphany" or moment of illumination, fulfilling one of the most common functions of fiction—to say, "You have been told reality is like this, but I say it is otherwise." Even our imagined response to James is complete: you call "her" Daisy, the innocent; I call her Amy, the loved. Miranda, however, finds Eva's version "no more true than what I was told before, it's every bit as romantic." Is it Eva, then, who is obsessed with sex? Or is she merely driven by a bitterness toward the beautiful Amy, loved by all, who used to tell her with unwitting cruelty how to minimize her chinlessness? She transforms Miranda's mother into a saint—which Miranda rejects as a lie, loving her human mother too much—just as Gabriel transformed Amy into an angel. And though she wishes, she says, to do away with the family as an institution, she has not only come to Gabriel's funeral, but she sinks back into her old relationship with Miranda's father.

Miranda's father greets Miranda herself somewhat coolly because she ran away from the family to marry, and as he talks comfortably to his contemporary, Eva, both of them "precisely themselves," not needing to play the roles of son or daughter, of father or elderly cousin, Miranda rejects them both. They are the ones who have "denied her the right to look at the world with her own eyes, who demanded that she accept their version of life and yet could not tell her the truth, not in the smallest thing. 'I hate them both,' her innermost and secret mind said plainly, '*I will be free of them, I shall not even remember them.*'"

That's it, then. There is the romance of chivalry, and the romance of the sex-starved "festering woman stepping gaily toward the charnel house, their corruption concealed under laces and flowers, their dead faces lifted smiling. . . ." Miranda will be free of their memory, will live her own life, find her own truths if not about the past, at least about her own life. Youth, freedom, seeing things for oneself, that's what Miranda comes up with in rejection of the past her family has created in its stories.

But what about Miranda's own story? She has given up as childish her ambition to be a jockey—she wants to be an airline pilot instead (or is she kidding?). She says she will not even remember her family, but isn't this story a testimonial to the fact that she has not forgotten them? Eva tells her that her branch of the family " 'has no more practical sense than so many children. Everything for love. . . .' " Has Miranda escaped her family? Has she no practical sense, eloping, everything for love? Has she reenacted Amy's mistake, *mutatis mutandis*? The date *in* the story is 1912, the date *of* the story is 1937. How far removed from the eighteen-year-old Miranda is the focus of the story?

> Surely old people cannot hold their grudges forever because the young want to live, too, she thought, in her arrogance, her pride. I will make my own mistakes, not yours; I cannot depend upon you beyond a certain point, why depend at all?

What is arrogant and proud about Miranda's wanting to live her own life? declaring her independence? awakening?

> At least I can know the truth about what happens to me, she assured herself silently, making a promise to herself, in her hopefulness, her ignorance.

That's the last word in the story, "ignorance." In the eyes of the narrator of 1937, Miranda is telling herself stories too. Is she as romantic as Gabriel? her father? Eva? And while the truth recedes still farther, who *is* that narrator of 1937, whose voice is telling us the story? Is it Miranda looking back at her youthfully arrogant and innocent self? a member of a still newer generation, Miranda's son or daughter or niece, perhaps? And what myth, what "chinlessness" distorts that narrator's vision, writing out of the depths of a world-shaking depression, the earth, even in America, echoing to the sound of marching boots and rumbling tanks in central Europe?

PHILIP ROTH

Goodbye, Columbus

It is difficult to write a biographical note about a living, indeed relatively young author without its sounding like an obituary, so let's begin with Philip Roth (born 1933) at twenty-three, about the same age as his protagonist, Neil Klugman, in *Goodbye, Columbus*. Roth, like Klugman, is Jewish, was also born in Newark, attended Rutgers, and was in the army in 1955–1956. Unlike Neil, he had graduated from Bucknell University (not Rutgers, Newark), and before he entered the army he had earned a master's degree from the University of Chicago. After getting out of the army he did more graduate work at Chicago and taught there. But the big difference between Philip and Neil was that in 1956 Roth published his first short story, "Defender of the Faith," in the *New Yorker*. And he went on very soon thereafter to write *Goodbye, Columbus*, which won the National Book Award in 1959. Ten years and two books later, *Portnoy's Complaint* brought him fame, fortune, and plenty to complain about. His early work had been criticized for being anti-Semitic in its portrayal of the humor and the agonies of being a second- or third-generation American Jew: after a half-century of striving for subsistence, success, and acceptance, American Jews just after the defeat of Hitler and the "liberation" of the living and dead bones from the concentration camps almost literally did not know which way to turn. Alienated from what they felt was a clannish, claustrophobic tradition, ashamed of their survival and Americanization, they added to the sardonic self-deprecating humor of the ghetto a new bitterness and shame, a sense of being betrayed by history and betraying their own past. Roth's humor and thrashing around between defiance and self-hatred was too close to the bone. With *Portnoy* the complaint was different: it was that Roth had not lived up to his early promise. His response seems to have been to move to Connecticut and seclusion, and to publish eight books in the next ten years, including *The Great American Novel, My Life as a Man, The Professor of Desire,* and *The Ghost Writer.*

Roth told an interviewer that in recent years he has been struck by "the uses to which literature is put in this country. The writer in his isolation publishes a book, the book goes out into the world, and the strangest things begin to happen. . . . What I write has a particular purpose and use for me, but I've learned that what it means to me isn't what it means to others. When you publish a book, it's the world's book. The world edits it."

Perhaps Roth's purpose in writing *Goodbye, Columbus* was no more than to exorcise his own painful experience of being a young Jew caught in the identity crisis of the 1950s, but sympathetic readers will see in it both that experience and more; they will "edit" it into a novel about a more universal American experience—coming to terms with American myth and American reality—a novel in its way not unlike *The Great Gatsby.*

Goodbye, Columbus

T HE FIRST TIME I saw Brenda she asked me to hold her glasses. Then she stepped out to the edge of the diving board and looked foggily into the pool; it could have been drained, myopic Brenda would never have known it. She dove beautifully, and a moment later she was swimming back to the side of the pool, her head of short clipped auburn hair held up, straight ahead of her, as though it were a rose on a long stem. She glided to the edge and then was beside me. "Thank you," she said, her eyes watery though not from the water. She extended a hand for her glasses but did not put them on until she turned and headed away. I watched her move off. Her hands suddenly appeared behind her. She caught the bottom of her suit between thumb and index finger and flicked what flesh had been showing back where it belonged. My blood jumped.

That night, before dinner, I called her.

"Who are you calling?" my Aunt Gladys asked.

"Some girl I met today."

"Doris introduced you?"

"Doris wouldn't introduce me to the guy who drains the pool, Aunt Gladys."

"Don't criticize all the time. A cousin's a cousin. How did you meet her?"

"I didn't really meet her. I saw her."

"Who is she?"

"Her last name is Patimkin."

"Patimkin I don't know," Aunt Gladys said, as if she knew anybody who belonged to the Green Lane Country Club. "You're going to call her you don't know her?"

"Yes," I explained. "I'll introduce myself."

"Casanova," she said, and went back to preparing my uncle's dinner. None of us ate together: my Aunt Gladys ate at five o'clock, my cousin Susan at five-thirty, me at six, and my uncle at six-thirty. There is nothing to explain this beyond the fact that my aunt is crazy.

"Where's the suburban phone book?" I asked after pulling out all the books tucked under the telephone table.

"What?"

"The suburban phone book. I want to call Short Hills."[1]

"That skinny book? What, I gotta clutter my house with that, I never use it?"

"Where is it?"

"Under the dresser where the leg came off."

"For God's sake," I said.

"Call information better. You'll go yanking around there, you'll mess up my drawers. Don't bother me, you see your uncle'll be home soon. I haven't even fed *you* yet."

---

1. Posh New Jersey suburb of New York City.

468 Philip Roth

"Aunt Gladys, suppose tonight we all eat together. It's hot, it'll be easier for you."

"Sure, I should serve four different meals at once. You eat pot roast, Susan with the cottage cheese, Max has steak. Friday night is his steak night, I wouldn't deny him. And I'm having a little cold chicken. I should jump up and down twenty different times? What am I, a workhorse?"

"Why don't we all have steak, or cold chicken—"

"Twenty years I'm running a house. Go call your girl friend."

But when I called, Brenda Patimkin wasn't home. She's having dinner at the club, a woman's voice told me. Will she be home after (my voice was two octaves higher than a choirboy's)? I don't know, the voice said, she may go driving golf balls. Who is this? I mumbled some words—nobody she wouldn't know I'll call back no message thank you sorry to bother . . . I hung up somewhere along in there. Then my aunt called me and I steeled myself for dinner.

She pushed the black whirring fan up to *High* and that way it managed to stir the cord that hung from the kitchen light.

"What kind of soda you want? I got ginger ale, plain seltzer, black raspberry, and a bottle cream soda I could open up."

"None, thank you."

"You want water?"

"I don't drink with my meals. Aunt Gladys, I've told you that every day for a year already—"

"Max could drink a whole case with his chopped liver only. He works hard all day. If you worked hard you'd drink more."

At the stove she heaped up a plate with pot roast, gravy, boiled potatoes, and peas and carrots. She put it in front of me and I could feel the heat of the food in my face. Then she cut two pieces of rye bread and put that next to me, on the table.

I forked a potato in half and ate it, while Aunt Gladys, who had seated herself across from me, watched. "You don't want bread," she said, "I wouldn't cut it it should go stale."

"I *want* bread," I said.

"You don't like with seeds, do you?"

I tore a piece of bread in half and ate it.

"How's the meat?" she said.

"Okay. Good."

"You'll fill yourself with potatoes and bread, the meat you'll leave over I'll have to throw it out."

Suddenly she leaped up from the chair. "Salt!" When she returned to the table she plunked a salt shaker down in front of me—pepper wasn't served in her home: she'd heard on Galen Drake[2] that it was not absorbed by the body, and it was disturbing to Aunt Gladys to think that anything she served might pass through a gullet, stomach, and bowel just for the pleasure of the trip.

"You're going to pick the peas out is all? You tell me that, I wouldn't buy with the carrots."

"I love carrots," I said, "I love them." And to prove it, I dumped half of them down my throat and the other half onto my trousers.

"Pig," she said.

2. Host of daytime radio talk show of interest primarily to housewives.

Though I am very fond of desserts, especially fruit, I chose not to have any. I wanted, this hot night, to avoid the conversation that revolved around my choosing fresh fruit over canned fruit, or canned fruit over fresh fruit; whichever I preferred, Aunt Gladys always had an abundance of the other jamming her refrigerator like stolen diamonds. "He wants canned peaches, I have a refrigerator full of grapes I have to get rid of . . ." Life was a throwing off for poor Aunt Gladys, her greatest joys were taking out the garbage, emptying her pantry, and making threadbare bundles for what she still referred to as the Poor Jews in Palestine. I only hope she dies with an empty refrigerator, otherwise she'll ruin eternity for everyone else, what with her Velveeta turning green, and her navel oranges growing fuzzy jackets down below.

My Uncle Max came home and while I dialed Brenda's number once again, I could hear soda bottles being popped open in the kitchen. The voice that answered this time was high, curt, and tired. "Hullo."

I launched into my speech. "Hello-Brenda-Brenda-you-don't-know-me-that-is-you-don't-know-my-name-but-I-held-your-glasses-for-you-this-afternoon-at-the-club . . . You-asked-me-to-I'm-not-a-member-my-cousin-Doris-is-Doris-Klugman-I-asked-who-you-were . . ." I breathed, gave her a chance to speak, and then went ahead and answered the silence on the other end. "Doris? She's the one who's always reading *War and Peace*. That's how I know it's the summer, when Doris is reading *War and Peace*." Brenda didn't laugh; right from the start she was a practical girl.

"What's your name?" she said.

"Neil Klugman. I held your glasses at the board, remember?"

She answered me with a question of her own, one, I'm sure, that is an embarrassment to both the homely and the fair. "What do you look like?"

"I'm . . . dark."

"Are you a Negro?"

"No," I said.

"What *do* you look like?"

"May I come see you tonight and show you?"

"That's nice," she laughed. "I'm playing tennis tonight."

"I thought you were driving golf balls."

"I drove them already."

"How about after tennis?"

"I'll be sweaty after," Brenda said.

It was not to warn me to clothespin my nose and run in the opposite direction, it was a fact; it apparently didn't bother Brenda, but she wanted it recorded.

"I don't mind," I said, and hoped by my tone to earn a niche somewhere between the squeamish and the grubby. "Can I pick you up?"

She did not answer a minute; I heard her muttering, "Doris Klugman, Doris Klugman . . ." Then she said, "Yes, Briarpath Hills, eight-fifteen."

"I'll be driving a—" I hung back with the year, "a tan Plymouth. So you'll know me. How will I know you?" I said with a sly, awful laugh.

"I'll be sweating," she said and hung up.

Once I'd driven out of Newark, past Irvington and the packed-in tangle of railroad crossings, switchmen shacks, lumberyards, Dairy Queens, and used-car lots, the night grew cooler. It was, in fact, as though the hundred and eighty feet that the suburbs rose in altitude above Newark brought one closer to heaven, for the sun itself became bigger, lower, and rounder, and soon I was driving past long lawns which seemed to be twirling water on themselves, and past houses where no one sat on stoops, where lights were on but no windows open, for those inside, refusing to share the very texture of life with those of us outside, regulated with a dial the amounts of moisture that were allowed access to their skin. It was only eight o'clock, and I did not want to be early, so I drove up and down the streets whose names were those of eastern colleges, as though the township, years ago, when things were named, had planned the destinies of the sons of its citizens. I thought of my Aunt Gladys and Uncle Max sharing a Mounds bar in the cindery darkness of their alley, on beach chairs, each cool breeze sweet to them as the promise of afterlife, and after a while I rolled onto the gravel roads of the small park where Brenda was playing tennis. Inside my glove compartment it was as though the map of *The City Streets of Newark* had metamorphosed into crickets, for those mile-long tarry streets did not exist for me any longer, and the night noises sounded loud as the blood whacking at my temples.

I parked the car under the black-green canopy of three oaks, and walked towards the sound of the tennis balls. I heard an exasperated voice say, "Deuce *again*." It was Brenda and she sounded as though she was sweating considerably. I crackled slowly up the gravel and heard Brenda once more. "My ad," and then just as I rounded the path, catching a cuff full of burrs, I heard, "Game!" Her racket went spinning up in the air and she caught it neatly as I came into sight.

"Hello," I called.

"Hello, Neil. One more game," she called. Brenda's words seemed to infuriate her opponent, a pretty brown-haired girl, not quite so tall as Brenda, who stopped searching for the ball that had been driven past her, and gave both Brenda and myself a dirty look. In a moment I learned the reason why: Brenda was ahead five games to four, and her cocksureness about there being just one game remaining aroused enough anger in her opponent for the two of us to share.

As it happened, Brenda finally won, though it took more games than she'd expected. The other girl, whose name sounded like Simp, seemed happy to end it at six all, but Brenda, shifting, running, up on her toes, would not stop, and finally all I could see moving in the darkness were her glasses, a glint of them, the clasp of her belt, her socks, her sneakers, and, on occasion, the ball. The darker it got the more savagely did Brenda rush the net, which seemed curious, for I had noticed that earlier, in the light, she had stayed back, and even when she had had to rush, after smashing back a lob, she didn't look entirely happy about being so close to her opponent's racket. Her passion for winning a point seemed out-matched by an even stronger passion for maintaining her beauty as it was. I suspected that the red print of a tennis ball on her cheek would pain her more than losing all the points in the world. Darkness pushed her in, however, and she stroked harder, and at last Simp seemed to be running on her ankles. When it was all over, Simp refused my offer of a ride home and indicated with a quality of speech borrowed from some old Katharine Hepburn movie that she could manage for herself; apparently her manor lay no further than the nearest briar patch. She did not like me and I her, though I worried about it, I'm sure, more than she did.

"Who is *she?*"

"Laura Simpson Stolowitch."

"Why don't you call her Stolo?" I asked.

"Simp is her Bennington[3] name. The ass."

"Is that where you go to school?" I asked.

She was pushing her shirt up against her skin to dry the perspiration. "No. I go to school in Boston."

I disliked her for the answer. Whenever anyone asks me where I went to school I come right out with it: Newark Colleges of Rutgers University. I may say it a bit too ringingly, too fast, too up-in-the-air, but I say it. For an instant Brenda reminded me of the pug-nosed little bastards from Montclair who come down to the library during vacations, and while I stamp out their books, they stand around tugging their elephantine scarves until they hang to their ankles, hinting all the while at "Boston" and "New Haven."

"Boston University?" I asked, looking off at the trees.

"Radcliffe."[4]

We were still standing on the court, bounded on all sides by white lines. Around the bushes back of the court, fireflies were cutting figure eights in the thorny-smelling air and then, as the night suddenly came all the way in, the leaves on the trees shone for an instant, as though they'd just been rained upon. Brenda walked off the court, with me a step behind her. Now I had grown accustomed to the dark, and as she ceased being merely a voice and turned into a sight again, some of my anger at her "Boston" remark floated off and I let myself appreciate her. Her hands did not twitch at her bottom, but the form revealed itself, covered or not, under the closeness of her khaki Bermudas. There were two wet triangles on the back of her tiny-collared white polo shirt, right where her wings would have been if she'd had a pair. She wore, to complete the picture, a tartan belt, white socks, and white tennis sneakers.

As she walked she zipped the cover on her racket.

"Are you anxious to get home?" I said.

"No."

"Let's sit here. It's pleasant."

"Okay."

We sat down on a bank of grass slanted enough for us to lean back without really leaning; from the angle it seemed as though we were preparing to watch some celestial event, the christening of a new star, the inflation to full size of a half-ballooned moon. Brenda zipped and unzipped the cover while she spoke; for the first time she seemed edgy. Her edginess coaxed mine back, and so we were ready now for what, magically, it seemed we might be able to get by without: a meeting.

"What does your cousin Doris look like?" she asked.

"She's dark—"

"Is she—"

"No," I said. "She has freckles and dark hair and she's very tall."

"Where does she go to school?"

"Northampton."[5]

3. Prestigious Vermont college, at the time exclusively for women.
4. The woman's college of Harvard University. Rutgers is the state university of New Jersey. Montclair, like Short Hills and (below) Livingston, is a suburb for the well-to-do.
5. Massachusetts site of Smith College, a prestigious college for women.

She did not answer and I don't know how much of what I meant she had understood.

"I guess I don't know her," she said after a moment. "Is she a new member?"

"I think so. They moved to Livingston only a couple of years ago."

"Oh."

No new star appeared, at least for the next five minutes.

"Did you remember me from holding your glasses?" I said.

"Now I do," she said. "Do you live in Livingston too?"

"No. Newark."

"We lived in Newark when I was a baby," she offered.

"Would you like to go home?" I was suddenly angry.

"No. Let's walk though."

Brenda kicked a stone and walked a step ahead of me.

"Why is it you rush the net only after dark?" I said.

She turned to me and smiled. "You noticed? Old Simp the Simpleton doesn't."

"Why do you?"

"I don't like to be up too close, unless I'm sure she won't return it."

"Why?"

"My nose."

"What?"

"I'm afraid of my nose. I had it bobbed."

"What?"

"I had my nose fixed."

"What was the matter with it?"

"It was bumpy."

"A lot?"

"No," she said, "I was pretty. Now I'm prettier. My brother's having his fixed in the fall."

"Does he want to be prettier?"

She didn't answer and walked ahead of me again.

"I don't mean to sound facetious. I mean why's he doing it?"

"He *wants* to . . . unless he becomes a gym teacher . . . but he won't," she said. "We all look like my father."

"Is he having his fixed?"

"Why are you so nasty?"

"I'm not. I'm sorry." My next question was prompted by a desire to sound interested and thereby regain civility; it didn't quite come out as I'd expected—I said it too loud. "How much does it cost?"

Brenda waited a moment but then she answered. "A thousand dollars. Unless you go to a butcher."

"Let me see if you got your money's worth."

She turned again; she stood next to a bench and put the racket down on it. "If I let you kiss me would you stop being nasty?"

We had to take about two too many steps to keep the approach from being awkward, but we pursued the impulse and kissed. I felt her hand on the back of my neck and so I tugged her towards me, too violently perhaps, and slid my own hands across the side of her body and around to her back. I felt the wet spots on her shoulder blades, and beneath them, I'm sure of it, a faint fluttering, as though something stirred so deep in her breasts, so far back it could make itself felt through her shirt. It was like the fluttering of wings, tiny wings no bigger than her breasts. The smallness of the wings did not bother me—it would not take an eagle to carry me up those lousy hundred and eighty feet to make summer nights so much cooler in Short Hills than they are in Newark.

2

The next day I held Brenda's glasses for her once again, this time not as momentary servant but as afternoon guest; or perhaps as both, which still was an improvement. She wore a black tank suit and went barefooted, and among the other women, with their Cuban heels and boned-up breasts, their knuckle-sized rings, their straw hats, which resembled immense wicker pizza plates and had been purchased, as I heard one deeply tanned woman rasp, "from the cutest little *shvartze*[6] when we docked at Barbados," Brenda among them was elegantly simple, like a sailor's dream of a Polynesian maiden, albeit one with prescription sun glasses and the last name of Patimkin. She brought a little slurp of water with her when she crawled back towards the pool's edge, and at the edge she grabbed up with her hands and held my ankles, tightly and wet.

"Come in," she said up to me, squinting. "We'll play."

"Your glasses," I said.

"Oh break the goddam things. I hate them."

"Why don't you have your eyes fixed?"

"There you go again."

"I'm sorry," I said. "I'll give them to Doris."

Doris, in the surprise of the summer, had gotten past Prince Andrey's departure from his wife, and now sat brooding, not, it turned out, over the lonely fate of poor Princess Liza,[7] but at the skin which she had lately discovered to be peeling off her shoulders.

"Would you watch Brenda's glasses?" I said.

"Yes." She fluffed little scales of translucent flesh into the air. "Damn it."

I handed her the glasses.

"Well, for God's sake," she said, "I'm not going to hold them. Put them down. *I'm* not her slave."

"You're a pain in the ass, you know that, Doris?" Sitting there, she looked a little like Laura Simpson Stolowitch, who was, in fact, walking somewhere off at the far end of the pool, avoiding Brenda and me because (I liked to think) of the defeat Brenda had handed her the night before; or maybe (I didn't like to think) because of the strangeness of my presence. Regardless, Doris had to bear the weight of my indictment of both Simp and herself.

"Thank you," she said. "After I invite you up for the day."

"That was yesterday."

"What about last year?"

"That's right, your mother told you last year too—invite Esther's boy so when he writes his parents they won't complain we don't look after him. Every summer I get my day."

"You should have gone with them. That's not our fault. You're not our charge," and when she said it, I could just tell it was something she'd

6. A black.
7. Events at the end of the first of the fifteen sections, or "books," of *War and Peace*.

heard at home, or received in a letter one Monday mail, after she'd returned to Northampton from Stowe, or Dartmouth, or perhaps from that weekend when she'd taken a shower with her boyfriend in Lowell House.[8]

"Tell your father not to worry. Uncle Aaron, the sport. I'll take care of myself," and I ran on back to the pool, ran into a dive, in fact, and came up like a dolphin beside Brenda, whose legs I slid upon with my own.

"How's Doris?" she said.

"Peeling," I said. "She's going to have her skin fixed."

"*Stop* it," she said, and dove down beneath us till I felt her clamping her hands on the soles of my feet. I pulled back and then down too, and then, at the bottom, no more than six inches above the wiggling black lines that divided the pool into lanes for races, we bubbled a kiss into each other's lips. She was smiling there, at *me*, down at the bottom of the swimming pool of the Green Lane Country Club. Way above us, legs shimmied in the water and a pair of fins skimmed greenly by: my cousin Doris could peel away to nothing for all I cared, my Aunt Gladys have twenty feedings every night, my father and mother could roast away their asthma down in the furnace of Arizona, those penniless deserters—I didn't care for anything but Brenda. I went to pull her towards me just as she started fluttering up; my hand hooked on to the front of her suit and the cloth pulled away from her. Her breasts swam towards me like two pink-nosed fish and she let me hold them. Then, in a moment, it was the sun who kissed us both, and we were out of the water, too pleased with each other to smile. Brenda shook the wetness of her hair onto my face and with the drops that touched me I felt she had made a promise to me about the summer, and, I hoped, beyond.

"Do you want your sun glasses?"

"You're close enough to see," she said. We were under a big blue umbrella, side-by-side on two chaise longues, whose plastic covers sizzled against out suits and flesh; I turned my head to look at Brenda and smelled that pleasant little burning odor in the skin of my shoulders. I turned back up to the sun, as did she, and as we talked, and it grew hotter and brighter, the colors splintered under my closed eyelids.

"This is all very fast," she said.

"Nothing's happened," I said softly.

"No. I guess not. I sort of feel something has."

"In eighteen hours?"

"Yes. I feel . . . pursued," she said after a moment.

"*You* invited *me*, Brenda."

"Why do you always sound a little nasty to me?"

"Did I sound nasty? I don't mean to. Truly."

"You do! *You* invited *me*, Brenda. So what?" she said. "That isn't what I mean anyway."

"I'm sorry."

"Stop apologizing. You're so automatic about it, you don't even mean it."

"Now you're being nasty to me," I said.

"No. Just stating the facts. Let's not argue. I like you." She turned her head and looked as though she too paused a second to smell the summer

8. A Harvard College residence for upperclassmen.   college in New Hampshire.
Stowe: Vermont ski resort. Dartmouth: Ivy League

on her own flesh. "I like the way you look." She saved it from embarrassing me with that factual tone of hers.

"Why?" I said.

"Where did you get those fine shoulders? Do you play something?"

"No," I said. "I just grew up and they came with me."

"I like your body. It's fine."

"I'm glad," I said.

"You like mine, don't you?"

"No," I said.

"Then it's denied you," she said.

I brushed her hair flat against her ear with the back of my hand and then we were silent a while.

"Brenda," I said, "you haven't asked me anything about me."

"How you feel? Do you want me to ask you how you feel?"

"Yes," I said, accepting the back door she gave me, though probably not for the same reasons she had offered it.

"How *do* you feel?"

"I want to swim."

"Okay," she said.

We spent the rest of the afternoon in the water. There were eight of those long lines painted down the length of the pool and by the end of the day I think we had parked for a while in every lane, close enough to the dark stripes to reach out and touch them. We came back to the chairs now and then and sang hesitant, clever, nervous, gentle dithyrambs about how we were beginning to feel towards one another. Actually we did not have the feelings we said we had until we spoke them—at least I didn't; to phrase them was to invent them and own them. We whipped our strangeness and newness into a froth that resembled love, and we dared not play too long with it, talk too much of it, or it would flatten and fizzle away. So we moved back and forth from chairs to water, from talk to silence, and considering my unshakable edginess with Brenda, and the high walls of ego that rose, buttresses and all, between her and her knowledge of herself, we managed pretty well.

At about four o'clock, at the bottom of the pool, Brenda suddenly wrenched away from me and shot up to the surface. I shot up after her.

"What's the matter?" I said.

First she whipped the hair off her forehead. Then she pointed a hand down towards the base of the pool. "My brother," she said, coughing some water free inside her.

And suddenly, like a crew-cut Proteus rising from the sea, Ron Patimkin emerged from the lower depths we'd just inhabited and his immensity was before us.

"Hey, Bren," he said, and pushed a palm flat into the water so that a small hurricane beat up against Brenda and me.

"What are you so happy about?" she said.

"The Yankees took two."

"Are we going to have Mickey Mantle for dinner?" she said. "When the Yankees win," she said to me, treading so easily she seemed to have turned the chlorine to marble beneath her, "we set an extra place for Mickey Mantle."

"You want to race?" Ron asked.

"No, Ronald. Go race alone."

Nobody had as yet said a word about me. I treaded unobtrusively as I could, as a third party, unintroduced, will step back and say nothing, awaiting the amenities. I was tired, however, from the afternoon's sport, and wished to hell brother and sister would not tease and chat much longer. Fortunately Brenda introduced me. "Ronald, this is Neil Klugman. This is my brother, Ronald Patimkin."

Of all things there in the fifteen feet water, Ron reached out his hand to shake. I returned the shake, not quite as monumentally as he apparently expected; my chin slipped an inch into the water and all at once I was exhausted.

"Want to race?" Ron asked me good-naturedly.

"Go ahead, Neil, race with him. I want to call home and tell them you're coming to dinner."

"Am I? I'll have to call my aunt. You didn't say anything. My clothes—"

"We dine *au naturel*."

"What?" Ronald said.

"Swim, baby," Brenda said to him and it ached me some when she kissed him on the face.

I begged out of the race, saying I had to make a phone call myself, and once upon the tiled blue border of the pool, looked back to see Ron taking the length in sleek, immense strokes. He gave one the feeling that after swimming the length of the pool a half dozen times he would have earned the right to drink its contents; I imagined he had, like my Uncle Max, a colossal thirst and a gigantic bladder.

Aunt Gladys did not seem relieved when I told her she'd have only three feedings to prepare that night. "Fancy-shmancy" was all she said to me on the phone.

We did not eat in the kitchen; rather, the six of us—Brenda, myself, Ron, Mr. and Mrs. Patimkin, and Brenda's little sister, Julie—sat around the dining room table, while the maid, Carlota, a Navaho-faced Negro who had little holes in her ears but no earrings, served us the meal. I was seated next to Brenda, who was dressed in what was *au naturel* for her: Bermudas, the close ones, white polo shirt, tennis sneakers and white socks. Across from me was Julie, ten, round-faced, bright, who before dinner, while the other little girls on the street had been playing with jacks and boys and each other, had been on the back lawn putting golf balls with her father. Mr. Patimkin reminded me of my father, except that when he spoke he did not surround each syllable with a wheeze. He was tall, strong, ungrammatical, and a ferocious eater. When he attacked his salad—after drenching it in bottled French dressing—the veins swelled under the heavy skin of his forearm. He ate three helpings of salad, Ron had four, Brenda and Julie had two, and only Mrs. Patimkin and I had one each. I did not like Mrs. Patimkin, though she was certainly the handsomest of all of us at the table. She was disastrously polite to me, and with her purple eyes, her dark hair, and large, persuasive frame, she gave me the feeling of some captive beauty, some wild princess, who has been tamed and made the servant to the king's daughter—who was Brenda.

Outside, through the wide picture window, I could see the back lawn with its twin oak trees. I say oaks, though fancifully, one might call them sporting-goods trees. Beneath their branches, like fruit dropped from their limbs, were two irons, a golf ball, a tennis can, a baseball bat, a basketball, a first-baseman's glove, and what was apparently a riding crop. Further back, near the scrubs that bounded the Patimkin property and in front of the small basketball court, a square red blanket, with a white O stitched in the center, looked to be on fire against the green grass. A breeze must have blown outside, for the net on the basket moved; inside we ate in the steady coolness of air by Westinghouse. It was a pleasure, except that eating among those Brobdingnags,[9] I felt for quite a while as though four inches had been clipped from my shoulders, three inches from my height, and for good measure, someone had removed my ribs and my chest had settled meekly in towards my back.

There was not much dinner conversation; eating was heavy and methodical and serious, and it would be just as well to record all that was said in one swoop, rather than indicate the sentences lost in the passing of food, the words gurgled into mouthfuls, the syntax chopped and forgotten in heapings, spillings, and gorgings.

TO RON: When's Harriet calling?

RON: Five o'clock.

JULIE: It *was* five o'clock.

RON: Their time.

JULIE: Why is it that it's earlier in Milwaukee? Suppose you took a plane back and forth all day. You'd never get older.

BRENDA: That's right, sweetheart.

MRS. P.: What do you give the child misinformation for? Is that why she goes to school?

BRENDA: I don't know why she goes to school.

MR. P. *(lovingly)*: College girl.

RON: Where's Carlota? Carlota!

MRS. P.: Carlota, give Ronald more.

CARLOTA *(calling)*: More what?

RON: Everything.

MR. P.: Me too.

MRS. P.: They'll have to *roll* you on the links.

MR. P. *(pulling his shirt up and slapping his black, curved belly)*: What are you talking about? Look at that.

RON *(yanking his T-shirt up)*: Look at *this.*

BRENDA *(to me)*: Would you care to bare your middle?

ME *(the choir boy again)*: No.

MRS. P.: That's right, Neil.

ME: Yes. Thank you.

CARLOTA *(over my shoulder, like an unsummoned spirit)*: Would *you* like more?

ME: No.

MR. P.: He eats like a bird.

JULIE: Certain birds eat a lot.

BRENDA: Which ones?

MRS. P.: Let's not talk about animals at the dinner table. Brenda, why do you encourage her?

RON: Where's Carlota, I gotta play tonight.

MR. P.: Tape your wrist, don't forget.

MRS. P.: Where do you live, Bill?

BRENDA: Neil.

9. The giants in Jonathan Swift's *Gulliver's Travels* (1726).

MRS. P.: Didn't I say Neil?
JULIE: You said "Where do you live, *Bill?*"
MRS. P.: I must have been thinking of something else.
RON: I hate tape. How the hell can I play in tape?
JULIE: Don't curse.
MRS. P.: That's right.
MR. P.: What is Mantle batting now?
JULIE: Three twenty-eight.
RON: Three twenty-five.
JULIE: Eight!
RON: Five, jerk! He got three for four in the second game.
JULIE: *Four* for four.
RON: That was an error, Minoso[1] should have had it.
JULIE: *I* didn't think so.
BRENDA *(to me)*: See?
MRS. P.: See what?
BRENDA: I was talking to Bill.
JULIE: Neil.
MR. P.: Shut up and eat.
MRS. P.: A little less talking, young lady.
JULIE: *I* didn't say anything.
BRENDA: She was talking to me, sweetie.
MR. P.: What's this *she* business. Is that how you call your mother?
What's dessert?

The phone rings, and though we are awaiting dessert, the meal seems at a formal end, for Ron breaks for his room, Julie shouts "Harriet!" and Mr. Patimkin is not wholly successful in stifling a belch, though the failure even more than the effort ingratiates him to me. Mrs. Patimkin is directing Carlota not to mix the milk silverware and the meat silverware[2] again, and Carlota is eating a peach while she listens; under the table I feel Brenda's fingers tease my calf. I am full.

We sat under the biggest of the oak trees while out on the basketball court Mr. Patimkin played five and two[3] with Julie. In the driveway Ron was racing the motor of the Volkswagen. "Will somebody *please* move the Chrysler out from behind me?" he called angrily. "I'm late as it is."

"Excuse me," Brenda said, getting up.

"I think I'm behind the Chrysler," I said.

"Let's go," she said.

We backed the cars out so that Ron could hasten on to his game. Then we reparked them and went back to watching Mr. Patimkin and Julie.

"I like your sister," I said.

"So do I," she said. "I wonder what she'll turn out to be."

"Like you," I said.

"I don't know," she said. "Better probably." And then she added, "Or maybe worse. How can you tell? My father's nice to her, but I'll give her another three years with my mother . . . Bill," she said, musingly.

"I didn't mind that," I said. "She's very beautiful, your mother."

---

1. Minnie Minoso, then left fielder for the Chicago White Sox.
2. According to Jewish dietary laws, meat and dairy products may not be eaten together, and their respective dishes and utensils are kept separate.
3. Basketball game played by shooting longer (set) shots from the foul line for five points each and shorter (lay-up) shots for two points each.

"I can't even think of her as my mother. She hates me. Other girls, when they pack in September, at least their mothers help them. Not mine. She'll be busy sharpening pencils for Julie's pencil box while I'm carrying my trunk around upstairs. And it's so obvious why. It's practically a case study."

"Why?"

"She's jealous. It's so corny I'm ashamed to say it. Do you know my mother had the best back-hand in New Jersey? Really, she was the best tennis player in the state, man or woman. You ought to see the pictures of her when she was a girl. She was so healthy-looking. But not chubby or anything. She was soulful, truly. I love her in those pictures. Sometimes I say to her how beautiful the pictures are. I even asked to have one blown up so I could have it at school. 'We have other things to do with our money, young lady, than spend it on old photographs.' Money! My father's up to here with it, but whenever I buy a coat you should hear her. 'You don't have to go to Bonwit's, young lady, Ohrbach's[4] has the strongest fabrics of any of them.' Who *wants* a strong fabric! Finally I get what I want, but not till she's had a chance to aggravate me. Money is a waste for her. She doesn't even know how to enjoy it. She still thinks we live in Newark."

"But you get what you want," I said.

"Yes. Him," and she pointed out to Mr. Patimkin who had just swished his third straight set shot through the basket to the disgruntlement, apparently, of Julie, who stamped so hard at the ground that she raised a little dust storm around her perfect young legs.

"He's not too smart but he's sweet at least. He doesn't treat my brother the way she treats me. Thank God, for that. Oh, I'm tired of talking about them. Since my freshman year I think every conversation I've ever had has always wound up about my parents and how awful it is. It's universal. The only trouble is they don't know it."

From the way Julie and Mr. Patimkin were laughing now, out on the court, no problem could ever have seemed less universal; but, of course, it was universal for Brenda, more than that, cosmic—it made every cashmere sweater a battle with her mother, and her life, which, I was certain, consisted to a large part of cornering the market on fabrics that felt soft to the skin, took on the quality of a Hundred Years' War . . .

I did not intend to allow myself such unfaithful thoughts, to line up with Mrs. Patimkin while I sat beside Brenda, but I could not shake from my elephant's brain that she-still-thinks-we-live-in-Newark remark. I did not speak, however, fearful that my tone would shatter our post-dinner ease and intimacy. It had been so simple to be intimate with water pounding and securing all our pores, and later, with the sun heating them and drugging our senses, but now, in the shade and the open, cool and clothed on her own grounds, I did not want to voice a word that would lift the cover and reveal that hideous emotion I always felt for her, and is the underside of love. It will not always *stay* the underside—but I am skipping ahead.

Suddenly, little Julie was upon us. "Want to play?" she said to me. "Daddy's tired."

<hr />

4. Clothing store on 34th Street, out of the fashionable district; Bonwit Teller was a more prestigious and expensive Fifth Avenue women's specialty shop.

"C'mon," Mr Patimkin called. "Finish for me."

I hesitated—I hadn't held a basketball since high school—but Julie was dragging at my hand, and Brenda said, "Go ahead."

Mr. Patimkin tossed the ball towards me while I wasn't looking and it bounced off my chest, leaving a round dust spot, like the shadow of a moon, on my shirt. I laughed, insanely.

"Can't you catch?" Julie said.

Like her sister, she seemed to have a knack for asking practical, infuriating questions.

"Yes."

"Your turn," she said. "Daddy's behind forty-seven to thirty-nine. Two hundred wins."

For an instant, as I placed my toes in the little groove that over the years had been nicked into a foul line, I had one of those instantaneous waking dreams that plague me from time to time, and send, my friends tell me, deadly cataracts over my eyes: the sun had sunk, crickets had come and gone, the leaves had blackened, and still Julie and I stood alone on the lawn, tossing the ball at the basket; "Five hundred wins," she called, and then when she beat me to five hundred she called, "Now *you* have to reach it," and I did, and the night lengthened, and she called, "*Eight* hundred wins," and we played on and then it was eleven hundred that won and we played on and it never was morning.

"Shoot," Mr. Patimkin said. "You're me."

That puzzled me, but I took my set shot and, of course, missed. With the Lord's blessing and a soft breeze, I made the lay-up.

"You have forty-one. I go," Julie said.

Mr. Patimkin sat on the grass at the far end of the court. He took his shirt off, and in his undershirt, and his whole day's growth of beard, looked like a trucker. Brenda's old nose fitted him well. There was a bump in it, all right; up at the bridge it seemed as though a small eight-sided diamond had been squeezed in under the skin. I knew Mr. Patimkin would never bother to have that stone cut from his face, and yet, with joy and pride, no doubt, had paid to have Brenda's diamond removed and dropped down some toilet in Fifth Avenue Hospital.

Julie missed her set shot, and I admit to a slight, gay, flutter of heart.

"Put a little spin on it," Mr. Patimkin told her.

"Can I take it again?" Julie asked me.

"Yes." What with paternal directions from the sidelines and my own grudging graciousness on the court, there did not seem much of a chance for me to catch up. And I wanted to, suddenly, I wanted to win, to run little Julie into the ground. Brenda was back on one elbow, under the tree, chewing on a leaf, watching. And up in the house, at the kitchen window, I could see that the curtain had swished back—the sun too low now to glare off electrical appliances—and Mrs. Patimkin was looking steadily out at the game. And then Carlota appeared on the back steps, eating a peach and holding a pail of garbage in her free hand. She stopped to watch too.

It was my turn again. I missed the set shot and laughingly turned to Julie and said, "Can I take it again?"

"No!"

So I learned how the game was played. Over the years Mr. Patimkin had taught his daughters that free throws were theirs for the asking; he could afford to. However, with the strange eyes of Short Hills upon me, matrons, servants, and providers, I somehow felt I couldn't. But I had to and I did.

"Thanks a lot, Neil," Julie said when the game was ended—at 100—and the crickets had come.

"You're welcome."

Under the trees, Brenda smiled. "Did you let her win?"

"I think so," I said. "I'm not sure."

There was something in my voice that prompted Brenda to say, comfortingly, "Even Ron lets her win."

"It's all nice for Julie," I said.

3

The next morning I found a parking space on Washington Street directly across from the library. Since I was twenty minutes early I decided to stroll in the park rather than cross over to work; I didn't particularly care to join my colleagues, who I knew would be sipping early morning coffee in the binding room, smelling still of all the orange crush they'd drunk that weekend at Asbury Park.[5] I sat on a bench and looked out towards Broad Street and the morning traffic. The Lackawanna commuter trains were rumbling in a few blocks to the north and I could hear them, I thought—the sunny green cars, old and clean, with windows that opened all the way. Some mornings, with time to kill before work, I would walk down to the tracks and watch the open windows roll in, on their sills the elbows of tropical suits and the edges of briefcases, the properties of businessmen arriving in town from Maplewood, the Oranges, and the suburbs beyond.

The park, bordered by Washington Street on the west and Broad on the east, was empty and shady and smelled of trees, night, and dog leavings; and there was a faint damp smell too, indicating that the huge rhino of a water cleaner had passed by already, soaking and whisking the downtown streets. Down Washington Street, behind me, was the Newark Museum—I could see it without even looking: two oriental vases in front like spittoons for a rajah, and next to it the little annex to which we had traveled on special buses as schoolchildren. The annex was a brick building, old and vine-covered, and always reminded me of New Jersey's link with the beginning of the country, with George Washington, who had trained his scrappy army—a little bronze tablet informed us children—in the very park where I now sat. At the far end of the park, beyond the Museum, was the bank building where I had gone to college. It had been converted some years before into an extension of Rutgers University; in fact, in what once had been the bank president's waiting room I had taken a course called Contemporary Moral Issues. Though it was summer now, and I was out of college three years, it was not hard for me to remember the other students, my friends, who had worked evenings in Bamberger's and Kresge's and had used the commissions they'd earned pushing ladies' out-of-season shoes to pay their laboratory fees. And then I looked out to Broad Street again. Jammed between a grimy-windowed bookstore and a cheesy luncheonette was the marquee of a tiny art the-

5. New Jersey seaside resort.

ator how many years had passed since I'd stood beneath that marquee, lying about the year of my birth so as to see Hedy Lamarr swim naked in *Ecstasy;* and then, having slipped the ticket taker an extra quarter, what disappointment I had felt at the frugality of her Slavic charm . . .[6] Sitting there in the park, I felt a deep knowledge of Newark, an attachment so rooted that it could not help but branch out into affection.

Suddenly it was nine o'clock and everything was scurrying. Wobbly-heeled girls revolved through the doors of the telephone building across the way, traffic honked desperately, policemen barked, whistled, and waved motorists to and fro. Over at St. Vincent's Church the huge dark portals swung back and those bleary-eyes that had risen early for Mass now blinked at the light. Then the worshipers had stepped off the church steps and were racing down the streets towards desks, filing cabinets, secretaries, bosses, and—if the Lord had seen fit to remove a mite of harshness from their lives—to the comfort of air-conditioners pumping at their windows. I got up and crossed over to the library, wondering if Brenda was awake yet.

The pale cement lions stood unconvincing guard on the library steps, suffering their usual combination of elephantiasis and arteriosclerosis, and I was prepared to pay them as little attention as I had for the past eight months were it not for a small colored boy who stood in front of one of them. The lion had lost all of its toes the summer before to a safari of juvenile delinquents, and now a new tormentor stood before him, sagging a little in his knees, and growling. He would growl, low and long, drop back, wait, then growl again. Then he would straighten up, and, shaking his head, he would say to the lion, "Man, you's a coward . . . " Then, once again, he'd growl.

The day began the same as any other. From behind the desk on the main floor, I watched the hot high-breasted teen-age girls walk twitchingly up the wide flight of marble stairs that led to the main reading room. The stairs were an imitation of a staircase somewhere in Versailles, though in their toreador pants and sweaters these young daughters of Italian leatherworkers, Polish brewery hands, and Jewish furriers were hardly duchesses. They were not Brenda either, and any lust that sparked inside me through the dreary day was academic and time-passing. I looked at my watch occasionally, thought of Brenda, and waited for lunch and then for after lunch, when I would take over the Information Desk upstairs and John McKee, who was only twenty-one but wore elastic bands around his sleeves, would march starchily down the stairs to work assiduously at stamping books in and out. John McRubberbands was in his last year at Newark State Teachers College where he was studying at the Dewey Decimal System[7] in preparation for his lifework. The library was not going to be my lifework, I knew it. Yet, there had been some talk—from Mr. Scapello, an old eunuch who had learned somehow to disguise his voice as a man's—that when I returned from my summer vacation I would be put in charge of the Reference Room, a position that had been empty ever since that morning when Martha Winney had fallen off a high stool in the Encyclopedia Room and shattered all those frail bones that come together to form what in a woman half her age we would call the hips.

6. In this 1933 Czech film the slim beauty Hedy Lamarr (b. 1913) appears, though rather indistinctly, nude.

7. Method for cataloguing and shelving library books.

I had strange fellows at the library and, in truth, there were many hours when I never quite knew how I'd gotten there or why I stayed. But I did stay and after a while waited patiently for that day when I would go into the men's room on the main floor for a cigarette and, studying myself as I expelled smoke into the mirror, would see that at some moment during the morning I had gone pale, and that under my skin, as under McKee's and Scapello's and Miss Winney's, there was a thin cushion of air separating the blood from the flesh. Someone had pumped it there while I was stamping out a book, and so life from now on would be not a throwing off, as it was for Aunt Gladys, and not a gathering in, as it was for Brenda, but a bouncing off, a numbness. I began to fear this, and yet, in my muscleless devotion to my work, seemed edging towards it, silently, as Miss Winney used to edge up to the *Britannica*. Her stool was empty now and awaited me.

Just before lunch the lion tamer came wide-eyed into the library. He stood still for a moment, only his fingers moving, as though he were counting the number of marble stairs before him. Then he walked creepily about on the marble floor, snickering at the clink of his taps and the way his little noise swelled up to the vaulted ceiling. Otto, the guard at the door, told him to make less noise with his shoes, but that did not seem to bother the little boy. He clacked on his tiptoes, high, secretively, delighted at the opportunity Otto had given him to practice this posture. He tiptoed up to me.

"Hey," he said, "where's the heart section?"

"The what?" I said.

"The heart section. Ain't you got no heart section?"

He had the thickest sort of southern Negro dialect and the only word that came clear to me was the one that sounded like heart.

"How do you spell it?" I said.

"*Heart.* Man, pictures. Drawing books. Where you got them?"

"You mean art books? Reproductions?"

He took my polysyllabic word for it. "Yea, they's them."

"In a couple of places," I told him. "Which artist are you interested in?"

The boy's eyes narrowed so that his whole face seemed black. He started backing away, as he had from the lion. "All of them . . ." he mumbled.

"That's okay," I said. "You go look at whichever ones you want. The next flight up. Follow the arrow to where it says Stack Three. You remember that? Stack Three. Ask somebody upstairs."

He did not move; he seemed to be taking my curiosity about his taste as a kind of poll-tax investigation.[8] "Go ahead," I said, slashing my face with a smile, "right up there . . ."

And like a shot he was scuffling and tapping up towards the heart section.

After lunch I came back to the in-and-out desk and there was John McKee, waiting, in his pale blue slacks, his black shoes, his barber-cloth shirt with the elastic bands, and a great knit tie, green, wrapped into a Windsor knot, that was huge and jumped when he talked. His breath smelled of hair oil and his hair of breath and when he spoke, spittle cob-

---

8. A voting eligibility tax used for years in some states to keep blacks from voting; outlawed for fed- eral elections by the Twenty-fourth Amendment (1964).

webbed the corners of his mouth. I did not like him and at times had the urge to yank back on his armbands and slingshoot him out past Otto and the lions into the street.

"Has a little Negro boy passed the desk? With a thick accent? He's been hiding in the art books all morning. You know what those boys *do* in there."

"I saw him come in, John."

"So did I. Has he gone *out* though?"

"I haven't noticed. I guess so."

"Those are *very* expensive books."

"Don't be so nervous, John. People are supposed to touch them."

"There is touching," John said sententiously, "and there is touching. Someone should check on him. I was afraid to leave the desk here. You know the way they treat the housing projects we give them."

"*You* give them?"

"The city. Have you seen what they do at Seth Boyden? They threw *beer* bottles, those big ones, on the *lawn*. They're taking over the city."

"Just the Negro sections."

"It's easy to laugh, you don't live near them. I'm going to call Mr. Scapello's office to check the Art Section. Where did he ever find out about art?"

"You'll give Mr. Scapello an ulcer, so soon after his egg-and-pepper sandwich. I'll check, I have to go upstairs anyway."

"You know what they do in there," John warned me.

"Don't worry, Johnny, *they're* the ones who'll get warts on their dirty little hands."

"Ha ha. Those books happen to cost—"

So that Mr. Scapello would not descend upon the boy with his chalky fingers, I walked up the three flights to Stack Three, past the receiving room where rheumy-eyed Jimmy Boylen, our fifty-one-year-old boy, unloaded books from a cart; past the reading room, where bums off Mulberry Street slept over *Popular Mechanics;* past the smoking corridor where damp-browed summer students from the law school relaxed, some smoking, others trying to rub the colored dye from their tort texts off their fingertips; and finally, past the periodical room, where a few ancient ladies who'd been motored down from Upper Montclair now huddled in their chairs, pince-nezing over yellowed, fraying society pages in old old copies of the Newark *News.* Up on Stack Three I found the boy. He was seated on the glass-brick floor holding an open book in his lap, a book, in fact, that was bigger than his lap and had to be propped up by his knees. By the light of the window behind him I could see the hundreds of spaces between the hundreds of tiny black corkscrews that were his hair. He was very black and shiny, and the flesh of his lips did not so much appear to be a different color as it looked to be unfinished and awaiting another coat. The lips were parted, the eyes wide, and even the ears seemed to have a heightened receptivity. He looked ecstatic—until he saw me, that is. For all he knew I was John McKee.

"That's okay," I said before he could even move, "I'm just passing through. You read."

"Ain't nothing *to* read. They's pictures."

"Fine." I fished around the lowest shelves a moment, playing at work. "Hey, mister," the boy said after a minute, "where is this?"

"Where is what?"

"Where is these pictures? These people, man, they sure does look cool. They ain't no yelling or shouting here, you could just see it."

He lifted the book so I could see. It was an expensive large-sized edition of Gauguin reproductions. The page he had been looking at showed an 8½ x 11 print, in color, of three native women standing knee-high in a rose-colored stream. It *was* a silent picture, he was right.

"That's Tahiti. That's an island in the Pacific Ocean."

"That ain't no place you could go, is it? Like a ree-*sort?*"

"You could go there, I suppose. It's very far. People live there . . ."

"Hey, *look*, look here at this one." He flipped back to a page where a young brown-skinned maid was leaning forward on her knees, as though to dry her hair. "Man," the boy said, "that's the fuckin life." The euphoria of his diction would have earned him eternal banishment from the Newark Public Library and its branches had John or Mr. Scapello—or, God forbid, the hospitalized Miss Winney—come to investigate.

"Who took these pictures?" he asked me.

"Gauguin. He didn't take them, he painted them. Paul Gauguin. He was a Frenchman."

"Is he a white man or a colored man?"

"He's white."

"Man," the boy smiled, chuckled almost, "I knew that. He don't *take* pictures like no colored men would. He's a good picture taker . . . *Look, look*, look here at this one. Ain't that the fuckin *life?*"

I agreed it was and left.

Later I sent Jimmy Boylen hopping down the stairs to tell McKee that everything was all right. The rest of the day was uneventful. I sat at the Information Desk thinking about Brenda and reminding myself that that evening I would have to get gas before I started up to Short Hills, which I could see now, in my mind's eye, at dusk, rose-colored, like a Gauguin stream.

When I pulled up to the Patimkin house that night, everybody but Julie was waiting for me on the front porch: Mr. and Mrs., Ron, and Brenda, wearing a dress. I had not seen her in a dress before and for an instant she did not look like the same girl. But that was only half the surprise. So many of those Lincolnesque college girls turn out to be limbed for shorts alone. Not Brenda. She looked, in a dress, as though she'd gone through life so attired, as though she'd never worn shorts, or bathing suits, or pajamas, or anything but that pale linen dress. I walked rather bouncingly up the lawn, past the huge weeping willow, towards the waiting Patimkins, wishing all the while that I'd had my car washed. Before I'd even reached them, Ron stepped forward and shook my hand, vigorously, as though he hadn't seen me since the Diaspora. Mrs. Patimkin smiled and Mr. Patimkin grunted something and continued twitching his wrists before him, then raising an imaginary golf club and driving a ghost of a golf ball up and away towards the Orange Mountains, that are called Orange, I'm convinced, because in that various suburban light that's the *only* color they do not come dressed in.

"We'll be right back," Brenda said to me. "You have to sit with Julie. Carlota's off."

"Okay," I said.

"We're taking Ron to the airport."

"Okay."

"Julie doesn't want to go. She says Ron pushed her in the pool this afternoon. We've been waiting for you, so we don't miss Ron's plane. Okay?"

"*Okay.*"

Mr. and Mrs. Patimkin and Ron moved off, and I flashed Brenda just the hint of a glare. She reached out and took my hand a moment.

"How do you like me?" she said.

"You're great to baby-sit for. Am I allowed all the milk and cake I want?"

"Don't be angry, baby. We'll be right back." Then she waited a moment, and when I failed to deflate the pout from my mouth, she gave *me* a glare, no hints about it. "I *meant* how do you like me in a dress!" Then she ran off towards the Chrysler, trotting in her high heels like a colt.

When I walked into the house, I slammed the screen door behind me.

"Close the other door too," a little voice shouted. "The air-conditioning."

I closed the other door, obediently.

"Neil?" Julie called.

"Yes."

"Hi. Want to play five and two?"

"No."

"Why not?"

I did not answer.

"I'm in the television room," she called.

"Good."

"Are you supposed to stay with me?"

"Yes."

She appeared unexpectedly through the dining room. "Want to read a book report I wrote?"

"Not now."

"What do you want to do?" she said.

"Nothing, honey. Why don't you watch TV?"

"All right," she said disgustedly, and kicked her way back to the television room.

For a while I remained in the hall, bitten with the urge to slide quietly out of the house, into my car, and back to Newark, where I might even sit in the alley and break candy with my own. I felt like Carlota; no, not even as comfortable as that. At last I left the hall and began to stroll in and out of rooms on the first floor. Next to the living room was the study, a small knotty-pine room jammed with cater-cornered leather chairs and a complete set of *Information Please Almanacs*. On the wall hung three colored photo-paintings; they were the kind which, regardless of the subjects, be they vital or infirm, old or youthful, are characterized by bud-cheeks, wet lips, pearly teeth, and shiny, metallized hair. The subjects in this case were Ron, Brenda, and Julie at about ages fourteen, thirteen, and two. Brenda had long auburn hair, her diamond-studded nose, and no glasses; all combined to make her look a regal thirteen-year-old who'd just gotten smoke in her eyes. Ron was rounder and his hairline was lower, but that love of spherical objects and lined courts twinkled in his boyish eyes. Poor little Julie was lost in the photo-painter's Platonic idea of childhood; her tiny humanity was smothered somewhere back of gobs of pink and white.

There were other pictures about, smaller ones, taken with a Brownie Reflex before photo-paintings had become fashionable. There was a tiny picture of Brenda on a horse; another of Ron in bar mitzvah suit, *yamalkah,* and *tallas;*[9] and two pictures framed together—one of a beautiful, faded woman, who must have been, from the eyes, Mrs. Patimkin's mother, and the other of Mrs. Patimkin herself, her hair in a halo, her eyes joyous and not those of a slowly aging mother with a quick and lovely daughter.

I walked through the archway into the dining room and stood a moment looking out at the sporting goods tree. From the television room that winged off the dining room, I could hear Julie listening to *This Is Your Life.*[1] The kitchen, which winged off the other side, was empty, and apparently, with Carlota off, the Patimkins had had dinner at the club. Mr. and Mrs. Patimkin's bedroom was in the middle of the house, down the hall, next to Julie's, and for a moment I wanted to see what size bed those giants slept in—I imagined it wide and deep as a swimming pool— but I postponed my investigation while Julie was in the house, and instead opened the door in the kitchen that led down to the basement.

The basement had a different kind of coolness from the house, and it had a smell, which was something the upstairs was totally without. It felt cavernous down there, but in a comforting way, like the simulated caves children make for themselves on rainy days, in hall closets, under blankets, or in between the legs of dining room tables. I flipped on the light at the foot of the stairs and was not surprised at the pine paneling, the bamboo furniture, the ping-pong table, and the mirrored bar that was stocked with every kind and size of glass, ice bucket, decanter, mixer, swizzle stick, shot glass, pretzel bowl—all the bacchanalian paraphernalia, plentiful, orderly, and untouched, as it can be only in the bar of a wealthy man who never entertains drinking people, who himself does not drink, who, in fact, gets a fishy look from his wife when every several months he takes a shot of schnapps before dinner. I went behind the bar where there was an aluminum sink that had not seen a dirty glass, I'm sure, since Ron's bar mitzvah party, and would not see another, probably, until one of the Patimkin children was married or engaged. I would have poured myself a drink—just as a wicked wage for being forced into servantry—but I was uneasy about breaking the label on a bottle of whiskey. You had to break a label to get a drink. On the shelf back of the bar were two dozen bottles—twenty-three to be exact—of Jack Daniels, each with a little booklet tied to its collared neck informing patrons how patrician of them it was to drink the stuff. And over the Jack Daniels were more photos: there was a blown-up newspaper photo of Ron palming a basketball in one hand like a raisin; under the picture it said, "Center, Ronald Patimkin, Milburn High School, 6'4", 217 pounds." And there was another picture of Brenda on a horse, and next to that, a velvet mounting board with ribbons and medals clipped to it: Essex County Hose Show 1949, Union County Horse Show 1950, Garden State Fair 1952, Morris-

9. Prayer shawl. *Yamalkah:* skullcap worn by Jews in synagogue and at prayers (and by the very orthodox in and out of doors).
1. Popular television program in which the guest was surprised by a review of the highlights of his or her life and the presence of old friends, colleagues, relatives.

town Horse Show 1950, and so on all for Brenda, for jumping and run-, ning or galloping or whatever else young girls receive ribbons for. In the entire house I hadn't seen one picture of Mr. Patimkin.

The rest of the basement, back of the wide pine-paneled room, was gray cement walls and linoleum floor and contained innumerable electrical appliances, including a freezer big enough to house a family of Eskimos. Beside the freezer, incongruously, was a tall old refrigerator; its ancient presence was a reminder to me of the Patimkin roots in Newark. This same refrigerator had once stood in the kitchen of an apartment in some four-family house, probably in the same neighborhood where I had lived all my life, first with my parents and then, when the two of them went wheezing off to Arizona, with my aunt and uncle. After Pearl Harbor the refrigerator had made the move up to Short Hills; Patimkin Kitchen and Bathroom Sinks had gone to war: no new barracks was complete until it had a squad of Patimkin sinks lined up in its latrine.

I opened the door of the old refrigerator; it was not empty. No longer did it hold butter, eggs, herring in cream sauce, ginger ale, tuna fish salad, an occasional corsage—rather it was heaped with fruit, shelves swelled with it, every color, every texture, and hidden within, every kind of pit. There were greengage plums, black plums, red plums, apricots, nectarines, peaches, long horns of grapes, black, yellow, red, and cherries, cherries flowing out of boxes and staining everything scarlet. And there were melons—cantaloupes and honeydews—and on the top shelf, half of a huge watermelon, a thin sheet of wax paper clinging to its bare red face like a wet lip. Oh Patimkin! Fruit grew in their refrigerator and sporting goods dropped from their trees!

I grabbed a handful of cherries and then a nectarine, and I bit right down to its pit.

"You better wash that or you'll get diarrhea."

Julie was standing behind me in the pine-paneled room. She was wearing *her* Bermudas and *her* white polo shirt which was unlike Brenda's only in that it had a little dietary history of its own.

"What?" I said.

"They're not washed yet," Julie said, and in such a way that it seemed to place the refrigerator itself out-of-bounds, if only for me.

"That's all right," I said, and devoured the nectarine and put the pit in my pocket and stepped out of the refrigerator room, all in one second. I still didn't know what to do with the cherries. "I was just looking around," I said.

Julie didn't answer.

"Where's Ron going?" I asked, dropping the cherries into my pocket, among my keys and change.

"Milwaukee."

"For long?"

"To see Harriet. They're in love."

We looked at each other for longer than I could bear. "Harriet?" I asked.

"Yes."

Julie was looking at me as though she were trying to look behind me, and then I realized that I was standing with my hands out of sight. I brought them around to the front, and, I swear it, she did peek to see if they were empty.

We confronted one another again; she seemed to have a threat in her face.

Then she spoke. "Want to play ping-pong?"

"God, yes," I said, and made for the table with two long, bounding steps. "You can serve."

Julie smiled and we began to play.

I have no excuses to offer for what happened next. I began to win and I liked it.

"Can I take that one over?" Julie said. "I hurt my finger yesterday and it just hurt when I served."

"No."

I continued to win.

"That wasn't fair, Neil. My shoelace came untied. Can I take it—"

"No."

We played, I ferociously.

"Neil, you leaned over the table. That's illegal—"

"I didn't lean and it's not illegal."

I felt the cherries hopping among my nickels and pennies.

"Neil, you gypped me out of a point. You have nineteen and I have eleven—"

"Twenty and *ten*," I said. "Serve!"

She did and I smashed my return past her—it zoomed off the table and skittered into the refrigerator room.

"You're a cheater!" she screamed at me. "You cheat!" Her jaw was trembling as though she carried a weight on top of her pretty head. "*I hate* you!" And she threw the racket across the room and it clanged off the bar, just as, outside, I heard the Chrysler crushing gravel in the driveway.

"The game isn't over," I said to her.

"You cheat! And you were stealing fruit!" she said, and ran away before I had my chance to win.

Later that night, Brenda and I made love, our first time. We were sitting on the sofa in the television room and for some ten minutes had not spoken a word to each other. Julie had long since gone to a weepy bed, and though no one had said anything to me about her crying, I did not know if the child had mentioned my fistful of cherries, which, some time before, I had flushed down the toilet. The television set was on and though the sound was off and the house quiet, the gray pictures still wiggled at the far end of the room. Brenda was quiet and her dress circled her legs, which were tucked back beneath her. We sat there for some while and did not speak. Then she went into the kitchen and when she came back she said that it sounded as though everyone was asleep. We sat a while longer, watching the soundless bodies on the screen eating a silent dinner in someone's silent restaurant. When I began to unbutton her dress she resisted me, and I like to think it was because she knew how lovely she looked in it. But she looked lovely, my Brenda, anyway, and we folded it carefully and held each other close and soon there we were, Brenda falling, slowly but with a smile, and me rising.

How can I describe loving Brenda? It was so sweet, as though I'd finally scored that twenty-first point.

When I got home I dialed Brenda's number, but not before my aunt heard and rose from her bed.

"Who are you calling at this hour? The doctor?"

"No."

"What kind phone calls, one o'clock at night?"

"Shhh!" I said.

"He tells *me* shhh. Phone calls one o'clock at night, we haven't got a big enough bill," and then she dragged herself back into bed, where with a martyr's heart and bleary eyes she had resisted the downward tug of sleep until she'd heard my key in the door.

Brenda answered the phone.

"Neil?" she said.

"Yes," I whispered. "You didn't get out of bed, did you?"

"No," she said, "the phone is next to the bed."

"Good. How is it in bed?"

"Good. Are you in bed?"

"Yes," I lied, and tried to right myself by dragging the phone by its cord as close as I could to my bedroom.

"I'm in bed with you," she said.

"That's right," I said, "and I'm with you."

"I have the shades down, so it's dark and I don't see you."

"I don't see you either."

"That was so nice, Neil."

"Yes. Go to sleep, sweet, I'm here," and we hung up without goodbyes. In the morning, as planned, I called again, but I could hardly hear Brenda or myself for that matter, for Aunt Gladys and Uncle Max were going on a Workmen's Circle[2] picnic in the afternoon, and there was some trouble about grape juice that had dripped all night from a jug in the refrigerator and by morning had leaked out onto the floor. Brenda was still in bed and so could play our game with some success, but I had to pull down all the shades of my senses to imagine myself beside her. I could only pray our nights and mornings would come, and soon enough they did.

4

Over the next week and a half there seemed to be only two people in my life: Brenda and the little colored kid who liked Gauguin. Every morning before the library opened, the boy was waiting; sometimes he seated himself on the lion's back, sometimes under his belly, sometimes he just stood around throwing pebbles at his mane. Then he would come inside, tap around the main floor until Otto stared him up on tiptoes, and finally headed up the long marble stairs that led to Tahiti. He did not always stay to lunch time, but one very hot day he was there when I arrived in the morning and went through the door behind me when I left at night. The next morning, it was, that he did not show up, and as though in his place, a very old man appeared, white, smelling of Life Savers, his nose and jowls showing erupted veins beneath them. "Could you tell me where I'd find the art section?"

"Stack Three," I said.

In a few minutes, he returned with a big brown-covered book in his

2. A predominantly but not exclusively Jewish fraternal benefit life insurance society with many social   and educational activities.

hand. He placed it on my desk, withdrew his card from a long moneyless billfold and waited for me to stamp out the book.

"Do you want to take this book *out?*" I said.

He smiled.

I took his card and jammed the metal edge into the machine; but I did not stamp down. "Just a minute," I said. I took a clipboard from under the desk and flipped through a few pages, upon which were games of battleship and tick-tack-toe that I'd been playing through the week with myself. "I'm afraid there's a hold on this book."

"A what?"

"A hold. Someone's called up and asked that we hold it for them. Can I take your name and address and drop a card when it's free . . ."

And so I was able, not without flushing once or twice, to get the book back in the stacks. When the colored kid showed up later in the day, it was just where he'd left it the afternoon before.

As for Brenda, I saw her every evening and when there was not a night game that kept Mr. Patimkin awake and in the TV room, or a Hadassah[3] card party that sent Mrs. Patimkin out of the house and brought her in at unpredictable hours, we made love before the silent screen. One muggy, low-skied night Brenda took me swimming at the club. We were the only ones in the pool, and all the chairs, the cabañas, the lights, the diving boards, the very water seemed to exist only for our pleasure. She wore a blue suit that looked purple in the lights and down beneath the water it flashed sometimes green, sometimes black. Late in the evening a breeze came up off the golf course and we wrapped ourselves in one huge towel, pulled two chaise lounges together, and despite the bartender, who was doing considerable pacing back and forth by the bar window, which over-looked the pool, we rested side by side on the chairs. Finally the bar light itself flipped off, and then, in a snap, the lights around the pool went down and out. My heart must have beat faster, or something, for Brenda seemed to guess my sudden doubt—*we should go*, I thought.

She said: "That's okay."

It was very dark, the sky was low and starless, and it took a while for me to see, once again, the diving board a shade lighter than the night, and to distinguish the water from the chairs that surrounded the far side of the pool.

I pushed the straps of her bathing suit down but she said no and rolled an inch away from me, and for the first time in two weeks I'd known her she asked me a question about me.

"Where are your parents?" she said.

"Tucson," I said. "Why?"

"My mother asked me."

I could see the life guard's chair now, white almost.

"Why are you still here? Why aren't you with them?" she asked.

"I'm not a child any more, Brenda," I said, more sharply than I'd intended. "I just can't go wherever my parents are."

"But then why do you stay with your aunt and uncle?"

"They're not my parents."

"They're better?"

"No. Worse. I don't *know* why I stay with them."

3. Women's Zionist organization, which in the United States engages in educational and charitable   work.

"Why?" she said.

"Why don't I know?"

"Why do you stay? You do know, don't you?"

"My job, I suppose. It's convenient from there, and it's cheap, and it pleases my parents. My aunt's all right really . . . Do I really have to explain to your mother why I live where I do?"

"It's not for my mother. I want to know. I wondered why you weren't with your parents, that's all."

"Are you cold?" I asked.

"No."

"Do you want to go home?"

"No, not unless you do. Don't you feel well, Neil?"

"I feel all right," and to let her know that I was still me, I held her to me, though that moment I was without desire.

"Neil?"

"What?"

"What about the library?"

"Who wants to know that?"

"My father," she laughed.

"And you?"

She did not answer a moment. "And me," she said finally.

"Well, what about it? Do I like it? It's okay. I sold shoes once and like the library better. After the Army they tried me for a couple of months at Uncle Aaron's real estate company—Doris' father—and I like the library better than that . . ."

"How did you get a job *there?*"

"I worked there for a little while when I was in college, then when I quit Uncle Aaron's, oh, I don't know . . ."

"What did you take in college?"

"At Newark Colleges of Rutgers University I majored in philosophy. I am twenty-three years old. I—"

"Why do you sound nasty again?"

"Do I?"

"Yes."

I didn't say I was sorry.

"Are you planning on making a career of the library?"

"Bren, I'm not planning anything. I haven't planned a thing in three years. At least for the year I've been out of the Army. In the Army I used to plan to go away weekends. I'm—I'm not a planner." After all the truth I'd suddenly given her, I shouldn't have ruined it for myself with that final lie. I added, "I'm a liver."

"I'm a pancreas," she said.

"I'm a—"

And she kissed the absurd game away; she wanted to be serious.

"Do you love me, Neil?"

I did not answer.

"I'll sleep with you whether you do or not, so tell me the truth."

"That was pretty crude."

"Don't be prissy," she said.

"No, I mean a crude thing to say about me."

"I don't understand," she said, and she didn't, and that she didn't pained me; I allowed myself the minor subterfuge, however, of forgiving

Brenda her obtuseness. "Do you?" she said.

"No."

"I want you to."

"What about the library?"

"What about it?" she said.

Was it obtuseness again? I thought not—and it wasn't, for Brenda said, "When you love me, there'll be nothing to worry about."

"Then of course I'll love you." I smiled.

"I know you will," she said. "Why don't you go in the water, and I'll wait for you and close my eyes, and when you come back you'll surprise me with the wet. Go ahead."

"You like games, don't you?"

"Go ahead. I'll close my eyes."

I walked down to the edge of the pool and dove in. The water felt colder than it had earlier, and when I broke through and was headed blindly down I felt a touch of panic. At the top again, I started to swim the length of the pool and then turned at the end and started back, but suddenly I was sure that when I left the water Brenda would be gone. I'd be alone in this damn place. I started for the side and pulled myself up and ran to the chairs and Brenda was there and I kissed her.

"God," she shivered, "you didn't stay long."

"I know."

"My turn," she said, and then she was up and a second later I heard a little crack of water and then nothing. Nothing for quite a while.

"Bren," I called softly, "are you all right?" but no one answered.

I found her glasses on the chair beside me and held them in my hands. "Brenda?"

Nothing.

"Brenda?"

"No fair calling," she said and gave me her drenched self. "Your turn," she said.

This time I stayed below the water for a long while and when I surfaced again my lungs were ready to pop. I threw my head back for air and above me saw the sky, low like a hand pushing down, and I began to swim as though to move out from under its pressure. I wanted to get back to Brenda, for I worried once again—and there was no evidence, was there?—that if I stayed away too long she would not be there when I returned. I wished that I had carried her glasses away with me, so she would have to wait for me to lead her back home. I was having crazy thoughts, I knew, and yet they did not seem uncalled for in the darkness and strangeness of that place. Oh how I wanted to call out to her from the pool, but I knew she would not answer and I forced myself to swim the length a third time, and then a fourth, but midway through the fifth I felt a weird fright again, had momentary thoughts of my own extinction, and that time when I came back I held her tighter than either of us expected.

"Let go, let go," she laughed, "my turn—"

"But Brenda—"

But Brenda was gone and this time it seemed as though she'd never come back. I settled back and waited for the sun to dawn over the ninth hole, prayed it would if only for the comfort of its light, and when Brenda finally returned to me I would not let her go, and her cold wetness crept into me somehow and made me shiver "That's it, Brenda. Please, no more games," I said, and then when I spoke again I held her so tightly I almost dug my body into hers, "I love you," I said, "I do."

So the summer went on. I saw Brenda every evening: we went swimming, we went for walks, we went for rides, up through the mountains so far and so long that by the time we started back the fog had begun to emerge from the trees and push out into the road, and I would tighten my hands on the wheel and Brenda would put on her glasses and watch the white line for me. And we would eat—a few nights after my discovery of the fruit refrigerator Brenda led me to it herself. We would fill huge soup bowls with cherries, and in serving dishes for roast beef we would heap slices of watermelon. Then we would go up and out the back doorway of the basement and onto the back lawn and sit under the sporting-goods tree, the light from the TV room the only brightness we had out there. All we would hear for a while were just the two of us spitting pits. "I wish they would take root overnight and in the morning there'd just be watermelons and cherries."

"If they took root in this yard, sweetie, they'd grow refrigerators and Westinghouse Preferred. I'm not being nasty," I'd add quickly, and Brenda would laugh, and say she felt like a greengage plum, and I would disappear down into the basement and the cherry bowl would now be a greengage plum bowl, and then a nectarine bowl, and then a peach bowl, until, I have to admit it, I cracked my frail bowel, and would have to spend the following night, sadly, on the wagon. And then too we went out for corned beef sandwiches, pizza, beer and shrimp, ice cream sodas, and hamburgers. We went to the Lions Club Fair one night and Brenda won a Lions Club ashtray by shooting three baskets in a row. And when Ron came home from Milwaukee we went from time to time to see him play basketball in the semi-pro summer league, and it was those evenings that I felt a stranger with Brenda, for she knew all the players' names, and though for the most part they were gawky-limbed and dull, there was one named Luther Ferrari who was neither, and whom Brenda had dated for a whole year in high school. He was Ron's closest friend and I remembered his name from the Newark *News:* he was one of the great Ferrari brothers, All State all of them in at least two sports. It was Ferrari who called Brenda Buck, a nickname which apparently went back to her ribbon-winning days. Like Ron, Ferrari was exceedingly polite, as though it were some affliction of those over six feet three; he was gentlemanly towards me and gentle towards Brenda, and after a while I balked when the suggestion was made that we go to see Ron play. And then one night we discovered that at eleven o'clock the cashier of the Hilltop Theatre went home and the manager disappeared into his office, and so that summer we saw the last quarter of at least fifteen movies, and then when we were driving home—driving Brenda home, that is—we would try to reconstruct the beginnings of the films. Our favorite last quarter of a movie was *Ma and Pa Kettle in the City,*[4] our favorite fruit, greengage plums, and our favorite, our only, people, each other. Of course we ran into others from time to time, some of Brenda's friends, and occasionally, one or two of mine. One night in August we even went to a bar out on Route 6 with

4. One of the nine comic Ma and Pa Kettle films made between 1949 and 1957 starring salty Marjorie Main (1890–1975) and peppery Percy Kilbride (1888–1964) as earthy rural characters.

Laura Simpson Stolowitch and her fiancé, but it was a dreary evening.
Brenda and I seemed untrained in talking to others, and so we danced a
great deal, which we realized was one thing we'd never done before.
Laura's boyfriend drank stingers pompously and Simp—Brenda wanted me
to call her Stolo but I didn't—Simp drank a tepid combination of something like ginger ale and soda. Whenever we returned to the table, Simp
would be talking about "the dance" and her fiancé about "the film," until
finally Brenda asked him "Which film?" and then we danced till closing
time. And when we went back to Brenda's we filled a bowl with cherries
which we carried into the TV room and ate sloppily for a while; and
later, on the sofa, we loved each other and when I moved from the darkened room to the bathroom I could always feel cherry pits against my
bare soles. At home, undressing for the second time that night, I would
find red marks on the undersides of my feet.

And how did her parents take all of this? Mrs. Patimkin continued to
smile at me and Mr. Patimkin continued to think I ate like a bird. When
invited to dinner I would, for his benefit, eat twice what I wanted, but
the truth seemed to be that after he'd characterized my appetite that first
time, he never really bothered to look again. I might have eaten ten times
my normal amount, have finally killed myself with food, he would still
have considered me not a man but a sparrow. No one seemed distressed
by my presence, though Julie had cooled considerably; consequently,
when Brenda suggested to her father that at the end of August I spend a
week of my vacation at the Patimkin house, he pondered a moment, decided on the five iron, made his approach shot, and said yes. And when
she passed on to her mother the decision of Patimkin Sink, there wasn't
much Mrs. Patimkin could do. So, through Brenda's craftiness, I was
invited.

On that Friday morning that was to be my last day of work, my Aunt
Gladys saw me packing my bag and she asked where I was going. I told
her. She did not answer and I thought I saw awe in those red-rimmed
hysterical eyes—I had come a long way since that day she'd said to me on
the phone, "Fancy-shmancy."

"How long you going, I should know how to shop I wouldn't buy too
much. You'll leave me with a refrigerator full of milk it'll go bad it'll
stink up the refrigerator—"

"A week," I said.

"A *week?*" she said. "They got room for a week?"

"Aunt Gladys, they don't live over the store."

"I lived over a store I wasn't ashamed. Thank God we always had a
roof. We never went begging in the streets," she told me as I packed the
Bermudas I'd just bought, "and your cousin Susan we'll put through college, Uncle Max should live and be well. We didn't send her away to
camp for August, she doesn't have shoes when she wants them, sweaters
she doesn't have a drawerful—"

"I didn't say anything, Aunt Gladys."

"You don't get enough to eat here? You leave over sometimes I show
your Uncle Max your plate it's a shame. A child in Europe could make a
four-course meal from what you leave over."

"Aunt Gladys." I went over to her. "I get everything I want here. I'm
just taking a vacation. Don't I deserve a vacation?"

She held herself to me and I could feel her trembling. "I told your mother I would take care of her Neil she shouldn't worry. And now you go running—"

I put my arms around her and kissed her on the top of her head. "C'mon," I said, "you're being silly. I'm not running away. I'm just going away for a week, on a vacation."

"You'll leave their telephone number God forbid you should get sick."

"Okay."

"Milburn they live?"

"Short Hills. I'll leave the number."

"Since when do Jewish people live in Short Hills? They couldn't be real Jews believe me."

"They're real Jews," I said.

"I'll see it I'll believe it." She wiped her eyes with the corner of her apron, just as I was zipping up the sides of the suitcase. "Don't close the bag yet. I'll make a little package with some fruit in it, you'll take with you."

"Okay, Aunt Gladys," and on the way to work that morning I ate the orange and the two peaches that she'd put in a bag for me.

A few hours later Mr. Scapello informed me that when I returned from my vacation after Labor Day, I would be hoisted up onto Martha Winney's stool. He himself, he said, had made the same move some twelve years ago, and so it appeared that if I could manage to maintain my balance I might someday be Mr. Scapello. I would also get an eight-dollar increase in salary which was five dollars more than the increase Mr. Scapello had received years before. He shook my hand and then started back up the long flight of marble stairs, his behind barging against his suit jacket like a hoop. No sooner had he left my side then I smelled spearmint and looked up to see the old man with veiny nose and jowls.

"Hello, young man," he said pleasantly. "Is the book back?"

"What book?"

"The Gauguin. I was shopping and I thought I'd stop by to ask. I haven't gotten the card yet. It's two weeks already."

"No," I said, and as I spoke I saw that Mr. Scapello had stopped midway up the stairs and turned as though he'd forgotten to tell me something. "Look," I said to the old man, "it should be back any day." I said it with a finality that bordered on rudeness, and I alarmed myself, for suddenly I saw what would happen: the old man making a fuss, Mr. Scapello gliding down the stairs, Mr. Scapello scampering up to the stacks, Scapello scandalized, Scapello profuse, Scapello presiding at the ascension of John McKee to Miss Winney's stool. I turned to the old man, "Why don't you leave your phone number and I'll try to get a hold of it this afternoon—" but my attempt at concern and courtesy came too late, and the man growled some words about public servants, a letter to the Mayor, snotty kids, and left the library, thank God, only a second before Mr. Scapello returned to my desk to remind me that everyone was chipping in for a present for Miss Winney and that if I liked I should leave a half dollar on his desk during the day.

After lunch the colored kid came in. When he headed past the desk for the stairs, I called over to him. "Come here," I said. "Where are you going?"

"The heart section."

"What book are you reading?"

"That Mr. Go-again's book. Look, man, I ain't doing nothing wrong. I didn't do *no* writing in *any*thing. You could search me—"

"I know you didn't. Listen, if you like that book so much why don't you please take it home? Do you have a library card?"

"No, sir, I didn't take *nothing*."

"No, a library card is what we give to you so you can take books home. Then you won't have to come down here every day. Do you go to school?"

"Yes, sir. Miller Street School. But this here's summertime. It's okay I'm not in school. I ain't *supposed* to be in school."

"I know. As long as you go to school you can *have* a library card. You could take the book home."

"What you keep telling me take that book home for? At home somebody dee-*stroy* it."

"You could hide it someplace, in a desk—"

"Man," he said, squinting at me, "why don't you want me to come round here?"

"I didn't say you shouldn't."

"I *likes* to come here. I likes them stairs."

"I like them too," I said. "But the trouble is that someday somebody's going to take that book out."

He smiled. "Don't you worry," he said to me. "Ain't nobody done that yet," and he tapped off to the stairs and Stack Three.

Did I perspire that day! It was the coolest of the summer, but when I left work in the evening my shirt was sticking to my back. In the car I opened my bag, and while the rush-hour traffic flowed down Washington Street, I huddled in the back and changed into a clean shirt so that when I reached Short Hills I'd look as though I was deserving of an interlude in the suburbs. But driving up Central Avenue I could not keep my mind on my vacation, or for that matter on my driving: to the distress of pedestrians and motorists, I ground gears, overshot crosswalks, hesitated at green and red lights alike. I kept thinking that while I was on vacation that jowly bastard would return to the library, that the colored kid's book would disappear, that my new job would be taken away from me, that, in fact my old job—but then why should I worry about all that: the library wasn't going to be my life.

5

"Ron's getting married!" Julie screamed at me when I came through the door. "Ron's getting married!"

"Now?" I said.

"Labor Day! He's marrying Harriet, he's marrying Harriet." She began to sing it like a jump-rope song, nasal and rhythmic. "I'm going to be a sister-in-law!"

"Hi," Brenda said, "I'm going to be a sister-in-law."

"So I hear. When did it happen?"

"This afternoon he told us. They spoke long distance for forty minutes last night. She's flying here next week, and there's going to be a *huge* wedding. My parents are flittering all over the place. They've got to arrange everything in about a day or two. And my father's taking Ron in the business—but he's going to have to start at two hundred a week and then work himself up. That'll take till October."

"I thought he was going to be a gym teacher."

"He was. But now he has responsibilities . . ."

And at dinner Ron expanded on the subject of responsibilities and the future.

"We're going to have a boy," he said, to his mother's delight, "and when he's about six months old I'm going to sit him down with a basketball in front of him, and a football, and a baseball, and then whichever one he reaches for, that's the one we're going to concentrate on."

"Suppose he doesn't reach for any of them," Brenda said.

"Don't be funny, young lady," Mrs. Patimkin said.

"I'm going to be an aunt," Julie sang, and she stuck her tongue out at Brenda.

"When is Harriet coming?" Mr. Patimkin breathed through a mouthful of potatoes.

"A week from yesterday."

"Can she sleep in my room?" Julie cried. *"Can* she?"

"No, the guest room—" Mrs. Patimkin began, but then she remembered me—with a crushing side glance from those purple eyes, and said, "Of course."

Well, I did eat like a bird. After dinner my bag was carried—by me—up to the guest room which was across from Ron's room and right down the hall from Brenda. Brenda came along to show me the way.

"Let me see your bed, Bren."

"Later," she said.

"Can we? Up here?"

"I think so," she said. "Ron sleeps like a log."

"Can I stay the night?"

"I don't know."

"I could get up early and come back in here. We'll set the alarm."

"It'll wake everybody up."

"I'll remember to get up. I can do it."

"I better not stay up here with you too long," she said. "My mother'll have a fit. I think she's nervous about your being here."

"So am I. I hardly know them. Do you think I should really stay a whole week?"

"A whole week? Once Harriet gets here it'll be so chaotic you can probably stay two months."

"You think so?"

"Yes."

"Do you want me to?"

"Yes," she said, and went down the stairs so as to ease her mother's conscience.

I unpacked my bag and dropped my clothes into a drawer that was empty except for a packet of dress shields and a high school yearbook. In the middle of my unpacking, Ron came clunking up the stairs.

"Hi," he called into my room.

"Congratulations," I called back. I should have realized that any word of ceremony would provoke a handshake from Ron; he interrupted whatever it was he was about to do in his room, and came into mine.

"Thanks." He pumped me. "Thanks."

Then he sat down on my bed and watched me as I finished unpacking. I have one shirt with a Brooks Brothers label and I let it linger on the bed a while; the Arrows[5] I heaped in the drawer. Ron sat there rubbing his forearm and grinning. After a while I was thoroughly unsettled by the silence.

"Well," I said, "that's something."

He agreed, to *what* I don't know.

"How does it feel?" I asked, after another longer silence.

"Better. Ferrari smacked it under the boards."

"Oh. Good," I said. "How does getting married feel?"

"Ah, okay, I guess."

I leaned against the bureau and counted stitches in the carpet.

Ron finally risked a journey into language. "Do you know anything about music?" he asked.

"Something, yes."

"You can listen to my phonograph if you want."

"Thanks, Ron. I didn't know you were interested in music."

"Sure. I got all the Andre Kostelanetz records ever made. You like Mantovani?[6] I got all of him too. I like semi-classical a lot. You can hear my Columbus record if you want . . ." he dwindled off. Finally he shook my hand and left.

Downstairs I could hear Julie singing. "I'm going to be an a-a-aunt," and Mrs. Patimkin saying to her, "No, honey, you're going to be a sister-in-law. Sing that, sweetheart," but Julie continued to sing, "I'm going to be an a-a-aunt," and then I heard Brenda's voice joining hers, singing, "We're going to be an a-a-aunt," and then Julie joined that, and finally Mrs. Patimkin called to Mr. Patimkin, "Will you make her stop encouraging her . . ." and soon the duet ended.

And then I heard Mrs. Patimkin again. I couldn't make out the words but Brenda answered her. Their voices grew louder; finally I could hear perfectly. "I need a houseful of company at a time like this?" It was Mrs. Patimkin. "I asked you, Mother." "You asked your father. I'm the one you should have asked first. He doesn't know how much extra work this is for me . . ." "My God, Mother, you'd think we didn't have Carlota and Jenny." "Carlota and Jenny can't do everything. This is not the Salvation Army!" "What the hell does that mean?" "Watch your tongue, young lady. That may be very well for your college friends." "Oh, *stop* it, Mother!" "Don't raise your voice to me. When's the last time you lifted a finger to help around here?" "I'm not a slave . . . I'm a daughter." "You ought to learn what a day's work means." "Why?" Brenda said. "*Why?*" "Because you're lazy," Mrs. Patimkin answered, "and you think the world owes you a living." "Whoever said *that?*" "You ought to earn some money and buy your own clothes." "Why? Good God, Mother, Daddy could live off the stocks alone, for God's sake. What are you complaining about?" "When's the last time you washed the dishes!" "Jesus Christ!" Brenda flared, "Carlota washes the dishes!" "Don't Jesus Christ me!" "Oh, Mother!" and Brenda was crying. "Why the hell are you like this!" "That's it," Mrs. Patimkin said, "cry in front of your company . . ." "My

5. An ordinary label; Brooks Brothers is an exclusive one.

6. Both the Russian-born American conductor, pianist, composer Andre Kostelanetz (1901–1980) and the Italian-born English bandleader Annunzio Paulo Mantovani (b. 1908) are best known for their radio broadcasts and recordings; both Kostelanetz's arrangements of semiclassical music and Mantovani's large orchestra, dominated by strings, have been described as "lush."

company . . ." Brenda wept, "why don't you go yell at him too . . . why is everyone so nasty to me . . ."

From across the hall I heard Andre Kostelanetz let several thousand singing violins loose on "Night and Day." Ron's door was open and I saw he was stretched out, colossal, on his bed; he was singing along with the record. The words belonged to "Night and Day," but I didn't recognize Ron's tune. In a minute he picked up the phone and asked the operator for a Milwaukee number. While she connected him, he rolled over and turned up the volume on the record player, so that it would carry the nine hundred miles west.

I heard Julie downstairs. "Ha, ha, Brenda's crying, ha, ha, Brenda's crying."

And then Brenda was running up the stairs. "Your day'll come, you little bastard!" she called.

"Brenda!" Mrs. Patimkin called.

"Mommy!" Julie cried. "Brenda cursed at me!"

"What's going *on* here!" Mr. Patimkin shouted.

"You call *me*, Mrs. P?" Carlota shouted.

And Ron, in the other room, said, "Hello, Har, I told them . . ."

I sat down on my Brooks Brothers shirt and pronounced my own name out loud.

"Goddam her!" Brenda said to me as she paced up and down my room.

"Bren, do you think I should go—"

"Shhh . . ." She went to the door of my room and listened. "They're going visiting, thank God."

"Brenda—"

"Shhh . . . They've gone."

"Julie too?"

"Yes," she said. "Is Ron in his room? His door is closed."

"He went out."

"You can't hear anybody move around here. They all creep around in *sneakers*. Oh Neil."

"Bren, I asked you, maybe I should just stay through tomorrow and then go."

"Oh, it isn't you she's angry about."

"I'm not helping any."

"It's Ron, really. That he's getting married just has her flipped. And me. Now with that goody-good Harriet around she'll just forget I ever exist."

"Isn't that okay with you?"

She walked off to the window and looked outside. It was dark and cool; the trees rustled and flapped as though they were sheets that had been hung out to dry. Everything outside hinted at September, and for the first time I realized how close we were to Brenda's departure for school.

"Is it, Bren?" but she was not listening to me.

She walked across the room to a door at the far end of the room. She opened it.

"I thought it was a closet," I said.

"Come here."

She held the door back and we leaned into the darkness and could hear the strange wind hissing in the eaves of the house.

"What's in here?" I said.

"Money."

Brenda went into the room. When the puny sixty-watt bulb was twisted on, I saw that the place was full of old furniture—two wing chairs with hair-oil lines at the back, a sofa with a paunch in its middle, a bridge table, two bridge chairs with their stuffing showing, a mirror whose backing had peeled off, shadeless lamps, lampless shades, a coffee table with a cracked glass top, and a pile of rolled up shades.

"What is this?" I said.

"A storeroom. Our old furniture."

"How old?"

"From Newark," she said. "Come here." She was on her hands and knees in front of the sofa and was holding up its paunch to peek beneath.

"Brenda, what the hell are we doing here? You're getting filthy."

"It's not here."

"*What?*"

"The money. I told you."

I sat down on a wing chair, raising some dust. It had begun to rain outside, and we could smell the fall dampness coming through the vent that was outlined at the far end of the storeroom. Brenda got up from the floor and sat down on the sofa. Her knees and Bermudas were dirty and when she pushed her hair back she dirtied her forehead. There among the disarrangement and dirt I had the strange experience of seeing us, *both* of us, placed among disarrangement and dirt: we looked like a young couple who had just moved into a new apartment; we had suddenly taken stock of our furniture, finances, and future, and all we could feel any pleasure about was the clean smell of outside, which reminded us we were alive, but which, in a pinch, would not feed us.

"What money?" I said again.

"The hundred-dollar bills. From when I was a little girl . . ." and she breathed deeply. "When I was little and we'd just moved from Newark, my father took me up here one day. He took me into this room and told me that if anything should ever happen to him, he wanted me to know where there was some money that I should have. He said it wasn't for anybody else but me, and that I should never tell anyone about it, not even Ron. Or my mother."

"How much was it?"

"Three hundred-dollar bills. I'd never seen them before. I was nine, around Julie's age. I don't think we'd been living here a month. I remember I used to come up here about once a week, when no one was home but Carlota, and crawl under the sofa and make sure it was still here. And it always was. He never mentioned it once again. Never."

"Where is it? Maybe someone stole it."

"I don't know, Neil. I suppose he took it back."

"When it was gone," I said, "my God, didn't you tell him? Maybe Carlota—"

"I never knew it was gone, until just now. I guess I stopped looking at one time or another . . . And then I forgot about it. Or just didn't think about it. I mean I always had enough, I didn't need this. I guess one day *he* figured I wouldn't need it."

Brenda paced up to the narrow, dust-covered window and drew her initials on it.

"Why did you want it now?" I said.

"I don't know . . ." she said and went over and twisted the bulb off.

I didn't move from the chair and Brenda, in her tight shorts and shirt, seemed naked standing there a few feet away. Then I saw her shoulders shaking. "I wanted to find it and tear it up in little pieces and put the goddam pieces in her purse! If it was there, I swear it, I would have done it."

"I wouldn't have let you, Bren."

"Wouldn't you have?"

"No."

"Make love to me, Neil. Right now."

"Where?"

"Do it! *Here*. On this cruddy cruddy cruddy sofa."

And I obeyed her.

The next morning Brenda made breakfast for the two of us. Ron had gone off to his first day of work—I'd heard him singing in the shower only an hour after I'd returned to my own room; in fact, I had still been awake when the Chrysler had pulled out of the garage, carrying boss and son down to the Patimkin works in Newark. Mrs. Patimkin wasn't home either; she had taken her car and had gone off to the Temple to talk to Rabbi Kranitz about the wedding. Julie was on the back lawn playing at helping Carlota hang the clothes.

"You know what I want to do this morning?" Brenda said. We were eating a grapefruit, sharing it rather sloppily, for Brenda couldn't find a paring knife, and so we'd decided to peel it down like an orange and eat the segments separately.

"What?" I said.

"Run," she said. "Do you ever run?"

"You mean on a track? God, yes. In high school we had to run a mile every month. So we wouldn't be Momma's boys. I think the bigger your lungs get the more you're supposed to hate your mother."

"I want to run," she said, "and I want you to run. Okay?"

"Oh, Brenda . . ."

But an hour later, after a breakfast that consisted of another grapefruit, which apparently is all a runner is supposed to eat in the morning, we had driven the Volkswagen over to the high school, behind which was a quarter-mile track. Some kids were playing with a dog out in the grassy center of the track, and at the far end, near the woods, a figure in white shorts with slits in the side, and no shirt, was twirling, twirling, and then flinging a shot put as far as he could. After it left his hand he did a little eagle-eyed tap dance while he watched it arch and bend and land in the distance.

"You know," Brenda said, "you look like me. Except bigger."

We were dressed similarly, sneakers, sweat socks, khaki Bermudas, and sweat shirts, but I had the feeling that Brenda was not talking about the accidents of our dress—if they were accidents. She meant, I was sure, that I was somehow beginning to look the way she wanted me to. Like herself.

"Let's see who's faster," she said, and then we started along the track. Within the first eighth of a mile the three little boys and their dog were following us. As we passed the corner where the shot putter was, he waved at us; Brenda called "Hi!" and I smiled, which, as you may or may not know, makes one engaged in serious running feel inordinately silly. At the quarter mile the kids dropped off and retired to the grass, the dog turned and started the other way, and I had a tiny knife in my side. Still I was abreast of Brenda, who as we started on the second lap, called "Hi!" once again to the lucky shot putter, who was reclining in the grass now, watching us, and rubbing his shot like a crystal ball. Ah, I thought, there's the sport.

"How about us throwing the shot put?" I panted.

"After," she said, and I saw beads of sweat clinging to the last strands of hair that shagged off her ear. When we approached the half mile Brenda suddenly swerved off the track onto the grass and tumbled down; her departure surprised me and I was still running.

"Hey, Bob Mathias,"[7] she called, "let's lie in the sun . . ."

But I acted as though I didn't hear her and though my heart pounded in my throat and my mouth was dry as a drought, I made my legs move, and swore I would not stop until I'd finished one more lap. As I passed the shot putter for the third time, I called "Hi!"

She was excited when I finally pulled up alongside of her. "You're good," she said. My hands were on my hips and I was looking at the ground and sucking air—rather, air was sucking me, I didn't have much to say about it.

"Uh-huh," I breathed.

"Let's do this every morning," she said. "We'll get up and have two grapefruit, and then you'll come out here and run. I'll time you. In two weeks you'll break four minutes, won't you sweetie? I'll get Ron's stop watch." She was so excited—she'd slid over on the grass and was pushing my socks up against my wet ankles and calves. She bit my kneecap.

"Okay," I said.

"Then we'll go back and have a real breakfast."

"Okay."

"You drive back," she said, and suddenly she was up and running ahead of me, and then we were headed back in the car.

And the next morning, my mouth still edgy from the grapefruit segments, we were at the track. We had Ron's stop watch and a towel for me, for when I was finished.

"My legs are a little sore," I said.

"Do some exercises," Brenda said. "I'll do them with you." She heaped the towel on the grass and together we did deep knee bends, and sit-ups, and push-ups, and some high-knee raising in place. I felt overwhelmingly happy.

"I'm just going to run a half today, Bren. We'll see what I do . . ." and I heard Brenda click the watch, and then when I was on the far side of the track, the clouds trailing above me like my own white, fleecy tail, I saw that Brenda was on the ground, hugging her knees, and alternately checking the watch and looking out at me. We were the only ones there, and it all reminded me of one of those scenes in race-horse movies, where an old trainer like Walter Brennan[8] and a young handsome man clock the beautiful girl's horse in the early Kentucky morning, to see if it really is the fastest two-year-old alive. There were differences all right—one being sim-

7. American athlete (b. 1930), Olympic decathlon champion in 1948 and 1952.
8. A famous Hollywood character actor, Brennan (1894–1974) played a horse-trainer in the film *Kentucky* (1938).

ply that at the quarter mile Brenda shouted out to me, "A minute and fourteen seconds," but it was pleasant and exciting and clean and when I was finished Brenda was standing up and waiting for me. Instead of a tape to break I had Brenda's sweet flesh to meet, and I did, and it was the first time she said that she loved me.

We ran—I ran—every morning, and by the end of the week I was running a 7:02 mile, and always at the end there was the little click of the watch and Brenda's arms.

At night, I would read in my pajamas, while Brenda, in her room, read, and we would wait for Ron to go to sleep. Some nights we had to wait longer than others, and I would hear the leaves swishing outside, for it had grown cooler at the end of August, and the air-conditioning was turned off at night and we were all allowed to open our windows. Finally Ron would be ready for bed. He would stomp around his room and then he would come to the door in his shorts and T-shirt and go into the bathroom where he would urinate loudly and brush his teeth. After he brushed his teeth I would go in to brush mine. We would pass in the hall and I would give him a hearty and sincere "Goodnight." Once in the bathroom, I would spend a moment admiring my tan in the mirror; behind me I could see Ron's jock straps hanging out to dry on the Hot and Cold knobs of the shower. Nobody ever questioned their tastefulness as adornment, and after a few nights I didn't even notice them.

While Ron brushed his teeth and I waited in my bed for my turn, I could hear the record player going in his room. Generally, after coming in from basketball, he would call Harriet—who was now only a few days away from us—and then would lock himself up with *Sports Illustrated* and Mantovani; however, when he emerged from his room for his evening toilet, it was not a Mantovani record I would hear playing, but something else, apparently what he'd once referred to as his Columbus record. I *imagined* that was what I heard, for I could not tell much from the last moments of sound. All I heard were bells moaning evenly and soft patriotic music behind them, and riding over it all, a deep kind of Edward R. Murrow[9] gloomy voice: *"And so goodbye, Columbus,"* the voice intoned, *". . . goodbye, Columbus . . . goodbye . . ."* Then there would be silence and Ron would be back in his room; the light would switch off and in only a few minutes I would hear him rumbling down into that exhilarating, restorative, vitamin-packed sleep that I imagined athletes to enjoy.

One morning near sneaking-away time I had a dream and when I awakened from it, there was just enough dawn coming into the room for me to see the color of Brenda's hair. I touched her in her sleep, for the dream had unsettled me: it had taken place on a ship, an old sailing ship like those you see in pirate movies. With me on the ship was the little colored kid from the library—I was the captain and he my mate, and we were the only crew members. For a while it was a pleasant dream; we were anchored in the harbor of an island in the Pacific and it was very sunny. Upon the beach there were beautiful bare-skinned Negresses, and none of them moved; but suddenly *we* were moving, our ship, out of the harbor, and the Negresses moved slowly down to the shore and began to throw leis at us and say "Goodbye, Columbus . . . goodbye, Columbus . . . good-

---

9. Murrow (1908–1965) formed and headed the CBS radio news-reporting team that in the World War II years revolutionized news broadcasting; after the war he had his own news and documentary programs on both radio and television.

bye . . ." and though we did not want to go, the little boy and I, the boat
was moving and there was nothing we could do about it, and he shouted
at me that it was my fault and I shouted it was his for not having a
library card, but we were wasting our breath, for we were further and
further from the island, and soon the natives were nothing at all. Space
was all out of proportion in the dream, and things were sized and squared
in no way I'd ever seen before, and I think it was that more than anything else that steered me into consciousness. I did not want to leave
Brenda's side that morning, and for a while I played with the little point
at the nape of her neck, where she'd had her hair cut. I stayed longer
than I should have, and when finally I returned to my room I almost ran
into Ron who was preparing for his day at Patimkin Kitchen and Bathroom Sinks.

6

That morning was supposed to have been my last at the Patimkin
house; however, when I began to throw my things into my bag late in the
day, Brenda told me I could unpack—somehow she'd managed to inveigle
another week out of her parents, and I would be able to stay right
through till Labor Day, when Ron would be married; then, the following
morning Brenda would be off to school and I would go back to work. So
we would be with each other until the summer's last moment.

This should have made me overjoyed, but as Brenda trotted back down
the stairs to accompany her family to the airport—where they were to
pick up Harriet—I was not joyful but disturbed, as I had been more and
more with the thought that when Brenda went back to Radcliffe, that
would be the end for me. I was convinced that even Miss Winney's stool
was not high enough for me to see clear up to Boston. Nevertheless, I
tossed my clothing back into the drawer and was able, finally, to tell
myself that there'd been no hints of ending our affair from Brenda, and
any suspicions I had, any uneasiness, was spawned in my own uncertain
heart. Then I went into Ron's room to call my aunt.

"Hello?" she said.

"Aunt Gladys," I said, "how are you?"

"You're sick."

"No, I'm having a fine time. I wanted to call you, I'm going to stay
another week."

"Why?"

"I told you. I'm having a good time. Mrs. Patimkin asked me to stay
until Labor Day."

"You've got clean underwear?"

"I'm washing it at night. I'm okay, Aunt Gladys."

"By hand you can't get it clean."

"It's clean enough. Look, Aunt Gladys, I'm having a wonderful time."

"*Shmutz*[1] he lives in and I shouldn't worry."

"How's Uncle Max?" I asked.

"What should he be? Uncle Max is Uncle Max. You, I don't like the
way your voice sounds."

"Why? Do I sound like I've got on dirty underwear?"

---

1. Dirt.

"Smart guy. Someday you'll learn."

"What?"

"What do you mean *what?* You'll find out. You'll stay there too long you'll be too good for us."

"Never, sweetheart," I said.

"I'll see it I'll believe it."

"Is it cool in Newark, Aunt Gladys?"

"It's snowing," she said.

"Hasn't it been cool all week?"

"You sit around all day it's cool. For me it's not February, believe me."

"Okay, Aunt Gladys. Say hello to everybody."

"You got a letter from your mother."

"Good. I'll read it when I get home."

"You couldn't take a ride down you'll read it?"

"It'll wait. I'll drop them a note. Be a good girl," I said.

"What about your socks?

"I go barefoot. Goodbye, honey." And I hung up.

Down in the kitchen Carlota was getting dinner ready. I was always amazed at how Carlota's work never seemed to get in the way of her life. She made household chores seem like illustrative gestures of whatever it was she was singing, even, if as now, it was "I Get a Kick out of You."[2] She moved from the oven to the automatic dishwasher—she pushed buttons, turned dials, peeked in the glass-doored oven, and from time to time picked a big black grape out of a bunch that lay on the sink. She chewed and chewed, humming all the time, and then, with a deliberated casualness, shot the skin and the pit directly into the garbage disposal unit. I said hello to her as I went out the back door, and though she did not return the greeting, I felt a kinship with one who, like me, had been partially wooed and won on Patimkin fruit.

Out on the lawn I shot baskets for a while; then I picked up an iron and drove a cotton golf ball limply up into the sunlight; then I kicked a soccer ball towards the oak tree; then I tried shooting foul shots again. Nothing diverted me—I felt open-stomached, as though I hadn't eaten for months, and though I went back inside and came out with my own handful of grapes, the feeling continued, and I knew it had nothing to do with my caloric intake; it was only a rumor of the hollowness that would come when Brenda was away. The fact of her departure had, of course, been on my mind for a while, but overnight it had taken on a darker hue. Curiously, the darkness seemed to have something to do with Harriet, Ron's intended, and I thought for a time that it was simply the reality of Harriet's arrival that had dramatized the passing of time: we had been talking about it and now suddenly it was here—just as Brenda's departure would be here before we knew it.

But it was more than that: the union of Harriet and Ron reminded me that separation need not be a permanent state. People could marry each other, even if they were young! And yet Brenda and I had never mentioned marriage, except perhaps for that night at the pool when she'd said, "When you love me, everything will be all right." Well, I loved her, and she me, and things didn't seem all right at all. Or was I inventing troubles again? I supposed I should really have thought my lot improved

---

2. Song (1934) by Cole Porter (1893–1964) from the musical *Anything Goes;* the second movie version   of the play was released in 1956.

considerably; yet, there on the lawn, the August sky seemed too beautiful and temporary to bear, and I wanted Brenda to marry me. Marriage, though, was not what I proposed to her when she drove the car up the driveway, alone, some fifteen minutes later. That proposal would have taken a kind of courage that I did not think I had. I did not feel myself prepared for any answer but "Hallelujah!" Any other kind of yes wouldn't have satisfied me, and any kind of no, even one masked behind the words, "Let's wait, sweetheart," would have been my end. So I imagine that's why I proposed the surrogate, which turned out finally to be far more daring than I knew it to be at the time.

"Harriet's plane is late, so I drove home," Brenda called.

"Where's everyone else?"

"They're going to wait for her and have dinner at the airport. I have to tell Carlota," and she went inside.

In a few minutes she appeared on the porch. She wore a yellow dress that cut a wide-bottomed U across her shoulders and neck, and showed where the tanned flesh began above her breasts. On the lawn she stepped out of her heels and walked barefoot over to where I was sitting under the oak tree.

"Women who wear high heels all the time get tipped ovaries," she said.

"Who told you that?"

"I don't remember. I like to think everything's shipshape in there."

"Brenda, I want to ask you something . . . "

She yanked the blanket with the big O on it over to us and sat down. "What?" she said.

"I know this is out of the blue, though really it's not . . . I want you to buy a diaphragm. To go to a doctor and get one."

She smiled. "Don't worry, sweetie, we're careful. Everything is okay."

"But that's the safest."

"We're safe. It'd be a waste."

"Why take chances?"

"But we *aren't?* How many things do you need."

"Honey, it isn't bulk I'm interested in. It's not even safety," I added.

"You just want me to own one, is that it? Like a walking stick, or a pith helmet—"

"Brenda, I want you to own one for . . . for the sake of pleasure."

"Pleasure? Whose? The doctor's?"

"Mine," I said.

She did not answer me, but rubbed her fingers along the ridge of her collarbone to wipe away the tiny globes of perspiration that had suddenly formed there.

"No, Neil, it's silly."

"Why?"

"Why? It just is."

"You know why it's silly, Brenda—because *I* asked you to do it?"

"That's sillier."

"If you asked *me* to buy a diaphragm we'd have to go straight to the Yellow Pages and find a gynecologist open on Saturday afternoon."

"I would never ask you to do that, baby."

"It's the truth," I said, though I was smiling. "It's the truth."

"It's not," she said, and got up and walked over to the basketball court, where she walked on the white lines that Mr. Patimkin had laid the day before.

"Come back here," I said.

"Neil, it's silly and I don't want to talk about it."

"Why are you being so selfish?"

"Selfish? You're the one who's being selfish. It's your pleasure . . . "

"That's right. My pleasure. Why not!"

"Don't raise your voice. Carlota."

"Then get the hell over here," I said.

She walked over to me, leaving white footprints on the grass. "I didn't think you were such a creature of the flesh," she said.

"Didn't you?" I said. "I'll tell you something that you ought to know. It's not even the pleasures of the flesh I'm talking about."

"Then frankly, I don't know *what* you're talking about. Why you're even bothering. Isn't what we use sufficient?"

"I'm bothering just because I want you to go to a doctor and get a diaphragm. That's all. No explanation. Just do it. Do it because I asked you to."

"You're not being reasonable—"

"Goddamit, Brenda!"

"Goddamit yourself!" she said and went up into the house.

I closed my eyes and leaned back and in fifteen minutes, or maybe less, I heard somebody stroking at the cotton golf ball. She had changed into shorts and a blouse and was still barefoot.

We didn't speak with each other, but I watched her bring the club back of her ear, and then swing through, her chin tilted up with the line of flight a regular golf ball would have taken.

"That's five hundred yards," I said.

She didn't answer but walked after the cotton ball and then readied for another swing.

"Brenda. Please come here."

She walked over, dragging the club over the grass.

"What?"

"I don't want to argue with you."

"Nor I with you," she said. "It was the first time."

"Was it such an awful thing for me to ask?"

She nodded.

"Bren, I know it was probably a surprise. It was for me. But we're not children."

"Neil, I just don't want to. It's not because you asked me to, either. I don't know where you get that from. That's not it."

"Then why is it?"

"Oh everything. I just don't feel *old* enough for all that equipment."

"What does age have to do with it?"

"I don't mean age. I just mean—well, *me*. I mean it's so conscious a thing to do."

"Of course it's conscious. That's exactly it. Don't you see? It would change us."

"It would change me."

"Us. Together."

"Neil, how do you think I'd feel lying to some doctor."

"You can go to Margaret Sanger,[3] in New York. They don't ask any questions."

"You've done this before?"

"No, I said. "I just know. I read Mary McCarthy."[4]

"That's exactly right. That's just what I'd feel like, somebody out of *her*."

"Don't be dramatic," I said.

"You're the one who's being dramatic. You think there would be something affairish about it, then. Last summer I went with this whore who I sent out to buy—"

"Oh, Brenda, you're a selfish egotistical bitch! You're the one who's thinking about 'last summer,' about an end for us. In fact, that's the whole thing, isn't it—"

"That's right, I'm a bitch. I want this to end. That's why I ask you to stay another week, that's why I let you sleep with me in my own house. What's the *matter* with you! Why don't you and my mother take turns—one day she can plague me, the next you—"

"Stop it!"

"Go to hell, all of you!" Brenda said, and now she was crying and I knew when she ran off I would not see her, as I didn't, for the rest of the afternoon.

Harriet Ehrlich impressed me as a young lady singularly unconscious of a motive in others or herself. All was surfaces, and she seemed a perfect match for Ron, and too for the Patimkins. Mrs. Patimkin, in fact, did just as Brenda prophesied: Harriet appeared, and Brenda's mother lifted one wing and pulled the girl in towards the warm underpart of her body, where Brenda herself would have liked to nestle. Harriet was built like Brenda, although a little chestier, and she nodded her head insistently whenever anyone spoke. Sometimes she would even say the last few words of your sentence with you, though that was infrequent; for the most part she nodded and kept her hands folded. All evening, as the Patimkins planned where the newlyweds should live, what furniture they should buy, how soon they should have a baby—all through this I kept thinking that Harriet was wearing white gloves, but she wasn't.

Brenda and I did not exchange a word or a glance; we sat, listening, Brenda somewhat more impatient than me. Near the end Harriet began calling Mrs. Patimkin "Mother," and once, "Mother Patimkin," and that was when Brenda went to sleep. I stayed behind, mesmerized almost by the dissection, analysis, reconsideration, and finally, the embracing of the trivial. At last Mr. and Mrs. Patimkin tumbled off to bed, and Julie, who had fallen asleep on her chair, was carried into her room by Ron. That left us two non-Patimkins together.

"Ron tells me you have a very interesting job."

"I work in the library."

"I've always liked reading."

"That'll be nice, married to Ron."

3. Clinic named for Sanger (1883–1966), longtime advocate of birth control education.

4. Though her most notorious work, *The Group*, was not published until 1963, McCarthy (b. 1912) was already well known in the 1950s for her explicit autobiographical fiction, such as *Cast a Cold Eye* (1950), and nonfiction, such as *Memories of a Catholic Girlhood* (1959), which, though it appeared in book form the same year as *Goodbye, Columbus*, had been appearing in the *New Yorker*.

"Ron likes music."

"Yes," I said. What had I *said?*

"You must get first crack at the best-sellers," she said.

"Sometimes," I said.

"Well," she said, flapping her hands on her knees, "I'm sure we'll all have a good time together. Ron and I hope you and Brenda will double with us soon."

"Not tonight." I smiled. "Soon. Will you excuse me?"

"Good night. I like Brenda very much."

"Thank you," I said as I started up the stairs.

I knocked gently on Brenda's door.

"I'm sleeping."

"Can I come in?" I asked.

Her door opened an inch and she said, "Ron will be up soon."

"We'll leave the door open. I only want to talk."

She let me in and I sat in the chair that faced the bed.

"How do you like your sister-in-law?"

"I've met her before."

"Brenda, you don't have to sound so damn terse."

She didn't answer and I just sat there yanking the string on the shade up and down.

"Are you still angry?" I asked at last.

"Yes."

"Don't be," I said. "You can forget about my suggestion. It's not worth it if this is what's going to happen."

"What did you expect to happen?"

"Nothing. I didn't think it would be so horrendous."

"That's because you can't understand my side."

"Perhaps."

"No perhaps about it."

"*Okay,*" I said. "I just wish you'd realize what it is you're getting angry about. It's not my suggestion, Brenda."

"No? What is it?"

"It's me."

"Oh don't start that again, will you? I can't win, no matter what I say."

"Yes, you can," I said. "You have."

I walked out of her room, closing the door behind me for the night.

When I got downstairs the following morning there was a great deal of activity. In the living room I heard Mrs. Patimkin reading a list to Harriet while Julie ran in and out of rooms in search of a skate key. Carlota was vacuuming the carpet; every appliance in the kitchen was bubbling, twisting, and shaking. Brenda greeted me with a perfectly pleasant smile and in the dining room, where I walked to look out at the back lawn and the weather, she kissed me on the shoulder.

"Hello," she said.

"Hello."

"I have to go with Harriet this morning," Brenda told me. "So we can't run. Unless you want to go alone."

"No. I'll read or something. Where are you going?"

"We're going to New York. Shopping. She's going to buy a wedding dress. For after the wedding. To go away in."

"What are *you* going to buy?"

"A dress to be maid of honor in. If I go with Harriet then I can go to Bergdorf's[5] without all that Ohrbach's business with my mother."

"Get me something, will you?" I said.

"Oh, Neil, are you going to bring that up again!"

"I was only *fooling*. I wasn't even thinking about that."

"Then why did you say it?"

"Oh Jesus!" I said, and went outside and drove my car down into Millburn Center where I had some eggs and coffee.

When I came back, Brenda was gone, and there were only Carlota, Mrs. Patimkin, and myself in the house. I tried to stay out of whichever rooms they were in, but finally Mrs. Patimkin and I wound up sitting opposite each other in the TV room. She was checking off names on a long sheet of paper she held; next to her, on the table, were two thin phone books which she consulted from time to time.

"No rest for the weary," she said to me.

I smiled hugely, embracing the proverb as though Mrs. Patimkin had just then coined it. "Yes. Of course," I said. "Would you like some help? Maybe I could help you check something."

"Oh, no," she said with a little head-shaking dismissal, "it's for Hadassah."

"Oh," I said.

I sat and watched her until she asked, "Is your mother in Hadassah?"

"I don't know if she is now. She was in Newark."

"Was she an active member?"

"I guess so, she was always planting trees in Israel for someone."[6]

"Really?" Mrs. Patimkin said. "What's her name?"

"Esther Klugman. She's in Arizona now. Do they have Hadassah there?"

"Wherever there are Jewish women."

"Then I guess she is. She's with my father. They went there for their asthma. I'm staying with my aunt in Newark. She's not in Hadassah. My Aunt Sylvia is, though. Do you know her, Aaron Klugman and Sylvia? They belong to your club. They have a daughter, my cousin Doris—" I couldn't stop myself "—They live in Livingston. Maybe it isn't Hadassah my Aunt Sylvia belongs to. I think it's some TB organization. Or cancer. Muscular dystrophy, maybe. I know she's interested in *some* disease."

"That's very nice," Mrs. Patimkin said.

"Oh yes."

"They do very good work."

"I know."

Mrs. Patimkin, I thought, had begun to warm to me; she let the purple eyes stop peering and just look out at the world for a while without judging. "Are you interested in B'nai B'rith?"[7] she asked me. "Ron is joining, you know, as soon as he gets married."

"I think I'll wait till then," I said.

Petulantly, Mrs. Patimkin went back to her lists, and I realized it had been foolish of me to risk lightheartedness with her about Jewish affairs. "You're active in the Temple, aren't you?" I asked with all the interest I could muster.

5. Bergdorf Goodman, exclusive Fifth Avenue clothing store.
6. The Hadassah (mentioned earlier) does indeed collect money for planting memorial trees in Israel in the name of a loved one.
7. A Jewish fraternity founded in New York in 1843, now international.

"Yes," she said.

"What Temple do *you* belong to?" she asked in a moment.

"We used to belong to Hudson Street Synagogue. Since my parents left, I haven't had much contact."

I didn't know whether Mrs. Patimkin caught a false tone in my voice. Personally I thought I had managed my rueful confession pretty well, especially when I recalled the decade of paganism prior to my parents' departure. Regardless, Mrs. Patimkin asked immediately—and strategically it seemed—"We're all going to Temple Friday night. Why don't you come with us? I mean, are you orthodox or conservative?"

I considered. "Well, I haven't gone in a long time . . . I sort of switch . . . " I smiled. "I'm just Jewish," I said well-meaningly, but that too sent Mrs. Patimkin back to her Hadassah work. Desperately I tried to think of something that would convince her I wasn't an infidel. Finally I asked: "Do you know Martin Buber's[8] work?"

"Buber . . . Buber," she said, looking at her Hadassah list. "Is he orthodox or conservative?" she asked.

" . . . He's a philosopher."

"Is he *reformed?*" she asked, piqued either at my evasiveness or at the possibility that Buber attended Friday night services without a hat, and Mrs. Buber had only one set of dishes in her kitchen.

"Orthodox," I said faintly.

"That's very nice," she said.

"Yes."

"Isn't Hudson Street Synagogue orthodox?" she asked.

"I don't know."

"I thought you belonged."

"I was bar-mitzvahed there."

"And you don't know that it's orthodox?"

"Yes. I do. It is."

"Then *you* must be."

"Oh, yes, I am," I said. "What are you?" I popped, flushing.

"Orthodox. My husband is conservative," which meant, I took it, that he didn't care. "Brenda is nothing, as you probably know."

"Oh?" I said. "No, I didn't know that."

"She was the best Hebrew student I've ever seen," Mrs. Patimkin said, "but then, of course, she got too big for her britches."

Mrs. Patimkin looked at me, and I wondered whether courtesy demanded that I agree. "Oh, I don't know," I said at last, "I'd say Brenda is conservative. Maybe a little reformed . . . "

The phone rang, rescuing me, and I spoke a silent orthodox prayer to the Lord.

"Hello," Mrs. Patimkin said. " . . . no . . . I can *not*, I have all the Hadassah calls to make . . . "

I acted as though I were listening to the birds outside, though the closed windows let no natural noises in.

"Have Ronald drive them up . . . But we can't wait, not if we want it on time . . . "

Mrs. Patimkin glanced up at me; then she put one hand over the mouthpiece. "Would you ride down to Newark for me?"

---

8. Eminent Jewish philosopher and biblical commentator (1878–1965), best known for his book *I and Thou* (1923; 2nd ed. 1958), in which he describes the relation between God and man as a direct and personal dialogue, not a matter of "It," or institutions.

I stood. "Yes. Surely."

"Dear?" she said back into the phone, "Neil will come for it ... No, *Neil*, Brenda's friend ... Yes ... Goodbye.

"Mr. Patimkin has some silver patterns I have to see. Would you drive down to his place and pick them up?"

"Of course."

"Do you know where the shop is?"

"Yes."

"Here," she said, handing a key ring to me, "take the Volkswagen."

"My car is right outside."

"Take these," she said.

Patimkin Kitchen and Bathroom Sinks was in the heart of the Negro section of Newark. Years ago, at the time of the great immigration, it had been the Jewish section, and still one could see the little fish stores, the kosher delicatessens, the Turkish baths, where my grandparents had shopped and bathed at the beginning of the century. Even the smells had lingered: whitefish, corned beef, sour tomatoes—but now, on top of these, was the grander greasier smell of auto wrecking shops, the sour stink of a brewery, the burning odor from a leather factory; and on the streets, instead of Yiddish, one heard the shouts of Negro children playing at Willie Mays with a broom handle and half a rubber ball.[9] The neighborhood had changed: the old Jews like my grandparents had struggled and died, and their offspring had struggled and prospered, and moved further and further west, towards the edge of Newark, then out of it, and up the slope of the Orange Mountains, until they had reached the crest and started down the other side, pouring into Gentile territory as the Scotch-Irish had poured through the Cumberland Gap. Now, in fact, the Negroes were making the same migration, following the steps of the Jews, and those who remained in the Third Ward lived the most squalid of lives and dreamed in their fetid mattresses of the piny smell of Georgia nights.

I wondered, for an instant only, if I would see the colored kid from the library on the streets here. I didn't, of course, though I was sure he lived in one of the scabby, peeling buildings out of which dogs, children, and aproned women moved continually. On the top floors, windows were open, and the very old, who could no longer creak down the long stairs to the street, sat where they had been put, in the screenless windows, their elbows resting on fluffless pillows, and their heads tipping forward on their necks, watching the push of the young and the pregnant and the unemployed. Who would come after the Negroes? Who was left? No one, I thought, and someday these streets, where my grandmother drank hot tea from an old *jahrzeit* glass,[1] would be empty and we would all of us have moved to the crest of the Orange Mountains, and wouldn't the dead stop kicking at the slats in their coffins then?

I pulled the Volkswagen up in front of a huge garage door that said across the front of it:

PATIMKIN KITCHEN AND BATHROOM SINKS
"Any Size—Any Shape"

Inside I could see a glass-enclosed office; it was in the center of an im-

9. The great centerfielder (b. 1931) for the New York and San Francisco Giants developed his skills as a child playing stickball in the New York streets.

1. Glass for holding a candle that memorializes the anniversary of a loved one's death.

mense warehouse. Two trucks were being loaded in the rear, and Mr. Patimkin, when I saw him, had a cigar in his mouth and was shouting at someone. It was Ron, who was wearing a white T-shirt that said Ohio State Athletic Association across the front. Though he was taller than Mr. Patimkin, and almost as stout, his hands hung weakly at his sides like a small boy's; Mr. Patimkin's cigar locomoted in his mouth. Six Negroes were loading one of the trucks feverishly, tossing—my stomach dropped—sink bowls at one another.

Ron left Mr. Patimkin's side and went back to directing the men. He thrashed his arms about a good deal, and though on the whole he seemed rather confused, he didn't appear to be at all concerned about anybody dropping a sink. Suddenly I could see myself directing the Negroes—I would have an ulcer in an hour. I could almost hear the enamel surfaces shattering on the floor. And I could hear myself: "Watch it, you guys. Be careful, will you? *Whoops!* Oh, please be—*watch* it! Watch! Oh!" Suppose Mr. Patimkin should come up to me and say, "Okay, boy, you want to marry my daughter, let's see what you can do." Well, he would see: in a moment that floor would be a shattered mosaic, a crunchy path of enamel. "Klugman, what kind of worker are you? You work like you eat!" "That's right, that's right, I'm a sparrow, let me go." "Don't you even know how to load and unload?" "Mr. Patimkin, even breathing gives me trouble, sleep tires me out, let me go, let me go . . ."

Mr. Patimkin was headed back to the fish bowl to answer a ringing phone, and I wrenched myself free of my reverie and headed towards the office too. When I entered, Mr. Patimkin looked up from the phone with his eyes; the sticky cigar was in his free hand—he moved it at me, a greeting. From outside I heard Ron call in a high voice, "You can't all go to lunch at the same time. We haven't got all day!"

"Sit down," Mr. Patimkin shot at me, though when he went back to his conversation I saw there was only one chair in the office, his. People did not sit at Patimkin Sink—here you earned your money the hard way, standing up. I busied myself looking at the several calendars that hung from filing cabinets; they showed illustrations of women so dreamy, so fantastically thighed and uddered, that one could not think of them as pornographic. The artist who had drawn the calendar girls for "Lewis Construction Company," and "Earl's Truck and Auto Repair," and "Grossman and Son, Paper Box" had been painting some third sex I had never seen.

"Sure, sure, sure," Mr. Patimkin said into the phone. "Tomorrow, don't tell me tomorrow. Tomorrow the world could blow up."

At the other end someone spoke. Who was it? Lewis from the construction company? Earl from truck repair?

"I'm running a business, Grossman, not a charity."

So it was Grossman being browbeaten at the other end.

"Shit on that," Mr. Patimkin said. "You're not the only one in town, my good friend," and he winked at me.

Ah-ha, a conspiracy against Grossman. Me and Mr. Patimkin. I smiled as collusively as I knew how.

"All right then, we're here till five . . . No later."

He wrote something on a piece of paper. It was only a big X.

"My kid'll be here," he said. "Yea, he's in the business."

Whatever Grossman said on the other end, it made Mr. Patimkin laugh.

Mr. Patimkin hung up without a goodbye.

He looked out the back to see how Ron was doing. "Four years in college he can't unload a truck."

I didn't know what to say but finally chose the truth. "I guess I couldn't either."

"You could learn. What am I, a genius? I learned. Hard work never killed anybody."

To that I agreed.

Mr. Patimkin looked at his cigar. "A man works hard he's got something. You don't get anywhere sitting on your behind, you know ... The biggest men in the country worked hard, believe me. Even Rockefeller. Success don't come easy ..." He did not say this so much as he mused it out while he surveyed his dominion. He was not a man enamored of words, and I had the feeling that what had tempted him into this barrage of universals was probably the combination of Ron's performance and my presence—me, the outsider who might one day be an insider. But did Mr. Patimkin even consider that possibility? I did not know; I only knew that these few words he did speak could hardly transmit all the satisfaction and surprise he felt about the life he had managed to build for himself and his family.

He looked out at Ron again. "Look at him, if he played basketball like that they'd throw him the hell off the court." But he was smiling when he said it.

He walked over to the door. "Ronald, let them go to lunch."

Ron shouted back, "I thought I'd let some go now, and some later."

"Why?"

"Then somebody'll always be—"

"No fancy deals here," Mr. Patimkin shouted. "We all go to lunch at once."

Ron turned back. "All right, boys, lunch!"

His father smiled at me. "Smart boy? Huh?" He tapped his head. "That took brains, huh? He ain't got the stomach for business. He's an idealist," and then I think Mr. Patimkin suddenly realized who I was, and eagerly corrected himself so as not to offend. "That's all right, you know, if you're a schoolteacher, or like you, you know, a student or something like that. Here you need a little of the *gonif* in you. You know what that means? *Gonif?*"

"Thief," I said.

"You know more than my own kids. They're *goyim,*[2] my kids, that's how much they understand." He watched the Negro loading gang walk past the office and shouted out to them, "You guys know how long an hour is? All right, you'll be back in an hour!"

Ron came into the office and of course shook my hand.

"Do you have that stuff for Mrs. Patimkin?" I asked.

"Ronald, get him the silver patterns." Ron turned away and Mr. Patimkin said, "When I got married we had forks and knives from the five and ten. This kid needs gold to eat off," but there was no anger; far from it.

I drove to the mountains in my own car that afternoon, and stood for a while at the wire fence watching the deer lightly prance, coyly feed,

2. Gentiles.

under the protection of signs that read, Do Not Feed the Deer, *By Order of South Mountain Reservation.* Alongside me at the fence were dozens of kids; they giggled and screamed when the deer licked the popcorn from their hands, and then were sad when their own excitement sent the young loping away towards the far end of the field where their tawny-skinned mothers stood regally watching the traffic curl up the mountain road. Young white-skinned mothers, hardly older than I, and in many instances younger, chatted in their convertibles behind me, and looked down from time to time to see what their children were about. I had seen them before, when Brenda and I had gone out for a bite in the afternoon, or had driven up here for lunch: in clotches of three and four they sat in the rustic hamburger joints that dotted the Reservation area while their children gobbled hamburgers and malteds and were given dimes to feed the jukebox. Though none of the little ones were old enough to read the song titles, almost all of them could holler out the words, and they did, while the mothers, a few of whom I recognized as high school mates of mine, compared suntans, supermarkets, and vacations. They looked immortal sitting there. Their hair would always stay the color they desired, their clothes the right texture and shade; in their homes they would have simple Swedish modern when that was fashionable, and if huge, ugly baroque ever came back, out would go the long, midget-legged marble coffee table and in would come Louis Quatorze. These were the goddesses, and if I were Paris I could not have been able to choose among them,[3] so microscopic were the differences. Their fates had collapsed them into one. Only Brenda shone. Money and comfort would not erase her singleness—they hadn't yet, or had they? What was I loving, I wondered, and since I am not one to stick scalpels into myself, I wiggled my hands in the fence and allowed a tiny-nosed buck to lick my thoughts away.

When I returned to the Patimkin house, Brenda was in the living room looking more beautiful than I had ever seen her. She was modeling her new dress for Harriet and her mother. Even Mrs. Patimkin seemed softened by the sight of her; it looked as though some sedative had been injected into her, and so relaxed the Brenda-hating muscles around her eyes and mouth.

Brenda, without glasses, modeled in place; when she looked at me it was a kind of groggy, half-waking look I got, and though others might have interpreted it as sleepiness it sounded in my veins as lust. Mrs. Patimkin told her finally that she'd bought a very nice dress and I told her she looked lovely and Harriet told her she was very beautiful and that *she* ought to be the bride, and then there was an uncomfortable silence while all of us wondered who ought to be the groom.

Then when Mrs. Patimkin had led Harriet out to the kitchen, Brenda came up to me and said, "I *ought* to be the bride."

"You ought, sweetheart." I kissed her, and suddenly she was crying.

"What is it, honey?" I said.

"Let's go outside."

On the lawn, Brenda was no longer crying but her voice sounded very tired.

"Neil, I called Margaret Sanger Clinic," she said. "When I was in New York."

---

3. In Greek myth Paris had to choose the fairest of the goddesses from among Hera, Athena, and Aphro-   dite.

I didn't answer.

"Neil, they *did* ask if I was married. God, the woman sounded like my mother . . ."

"What did you say?"

"I said *no.*"

"What did she say?"

"I don't know. I hung up." She walked away and around the oak tree. When she appeared again she'd stepped out of her shoes and held one hand on the tree, as though it were a Maypole she were circling.

"You can call them back," I said.

She shook her head. "No, I can't. I don't even know why I called in the first place. We were shopping and I just walked away, looked up the number, and called."

"Then you can go to a doctor."

She shook again.

"Look, Bren," I said, rushing to her, "we'll go together, to a doctor. In New York—"

"I don't want to go to some dirty little office—"

"We won't. We'll go to the most posh gynecologist in New York. One who gets *Harper's Bazaar* for the reception room. How does that sound?"

She bit her lower lip.

"You'll come with me?" she asked.

"I'll come with you."

"To the office?"

"Sweetie, your husband wouldn't come to the office."

"No?"

"He'd be working."

"But you're not," she said.

"I'm on vacation," I said, but I had answered the wrong question. "Bren, I'll wait and when you're all done we'll buy a drink. We'll go out to dinner."

"Neil, I shouldn't have called Margaret Sanger—it's not right."

"It is, Brenda. It's the most right thing we can do." She walked away and I was exhausted from pleading. Somehow I felt I could have convinced her had I been a bit more crafty; and yet I did not want it to be craftiness that changed her mind. I was silent when she came back, and perhaps it was just that, my *not* saying anything, that prompted her finally to say, "I'll ask Mother Patimkin if she wants us to take Harriet too . . ."

7

I shall never forget the heat and mugginess of that afternoon we drove into New York. It was four days after the day she'd called Margaret Sanger—she put it off and put it off, but finally on Friday, three days before Ron's wedding and four before her departure, we were heading through the Lincoln Tunnel, which seemed longer and fumier than ever, like Hell with tiled walls. Finally we were in New York and smothered again by the thick day. I pulled around the policeman who directed traffic in his shirt sleeves and up onto the Port Authority[4] roof to park the car.

4. Bus terminal at the Manhattan end of the Lincoln Tunnel.

"Do you have cab fare?" I said.

"Aren't you going to come with me?"

"I thought I'd wait in the bar. Here, downstairs."

"You can wait in Central Park. His office is right across the street."

"Bren, what's the diff—" But when I saw the look that invaded her eyes I gave up the air-conditioned bar to accompany her across the city. There was a sudden shower while our cab went crosstown, and when the rain stopped the streets were sticky and shiny, and below the pavement was the rumble of the subways, and in all it was like entering the ear of a lion.

The doctor's office was in the Squibb Building, which is across from Bergdorf Goodman's and so was a perfect place for Brenda to add to her wardrobe. For some reason we had never once considered her going to a doctor in Newark, perhaps because it was too close to home and might allow for possiblities of discovery. When Brenda got to the revolving door she looked back at me; her eyes were very watery, even with her glasses, and I did not say a word, afraid what a word, any word, might do. I kissed her hair and motioned that I would be across the street by the Plaza fountain, and then I watched her revolve through the doors. Out on the street the traffic moved slowly as though the humidity were a wall holding everything back. Even the fountain seemed to be bubbling boiling water on the people who sat at its edge, and in an instant I decided against crossing the street, and turned south on Fifth and began to walk the steaming pavement towards St. Patrick's. On the north steps a crowd was gathered; everyone was watching a model being photographed. She was wearing a lemon-colored dress and had her feet pointed like ballerina, and as I passed into the church I heard some lady say, "If I ate cottage cheese *ten* times a day, I couldn't be that skinny."

It wasn't much cooler inside the church, though the stillness and the flicker of the candles made me think it was. I took a seat at the rear and while I couldn't bring myself to kneel, I did lean forward onto the back of the bench before me, and held my hands together and closed my eyes. I wondered if I looked like a Catholic, and in my wonderment I began to make a little speech to myself. Can I call the self-conscious words I spoke prayer? At any rate, I called my audience God. God, I said, I am twenty-three years old. I want to make the best of things. Now the doctor is about to wed Brenda to me, and I am not entirely certain this is all for the best. What is it I love, Lord? Why have I chosen? Who is Brenda? The race is to the swift.[5] Should I have stopped to think?

I was getting no answers, but I went on. If we meet You at all, God, it's that we're carnal, and acquisitive, and thereby partake of You. I am carnal, and I know You approve, I just know it. But how carnal can I get? I am acquisitive. Where do I turn now in my acquisitiveness? Where do we meet? Which prize is You?

It was an ingenious meditation, and suddenly I felt ashamed. I got up and walked outside, and the noise of Fifth Avenue met me with an answer:

Which prize do you think, *schmuck?*[6] Gold dinnerware, sporting-goods trees, nectarines, garbage disposals, bumpless noses, Patimkin Sink, Bonwit Teller—

5. Cp. Ecclesiastes 9:11—"The race is not to the swift, nor the battle to the strong."

6. *Jerk* or *dope*, but somewhat obscene.

But damn it, God, that *is* You!

And God only laughed, that clown.

On the steps around the fountain I sat in a small arc of a rainbow that the sun had shot through the spray of the water. And then I saw Brenda coming out of the Squibb Building. She carried nothing with her, like a woman who's only been window shopping, and for a moment I was glad that in the end she had disobeyed my desire.

As she crossed the street, though, that little levity passed, and then I was myself again.

She walked up before me and looked down at where I sat; when she inhaled she filled her entire body, and then let her breath out with a "Whew!"

"Where is it?" I said.

My answer, at first, was merely that victorious look of hers, the one she'd given Simp the night she'd beaten her, the one I'd gotten the morning I finished the third lap alone. At last she said, "I'm wearing it."

"Oh, Bren."

"He said shall I wrap it or will you take it with you?"

"Oh Brenda, I love you."

We slept together that night, and so nervous were we about our new toy that we performed like kindergartners, or (in the language of that country) like a lousy double-play combination. And then the next day we hardly saw one another at all, for with the last-minute wedding preparations came scurrying, telegramming, shouting, crying, rushing—in short, lunacy. Even the meals lost their Patimkin fullness, and were tortured out of Kraft cheese, stale onion rolls, dry salami, a little chopped liver, and fruit cocktail. It was hectic all weekend, and I tried as best I could to keep clear of the storm, at whose eye, Ron, clumsy and smiling, and Harriet, flittering and courteous, were being pulled closer and closer together. By Sunday night fatigue had arrested hysteria and all of the Patimkins, Brenda included, had gone off to an early sleep. When Ron went into the bathroom to brush his teeth I decided to go in and brush mine. While I stood over the sink he checked his supports for dampness; then he hung them on the shower knobs and asked me if I would like to listen to his records for a while. It was not out of boredom and loneliness that I accepted; rather a brief spark of locker-room comradery had been struck there among the soap and the water and the tile, and I thought that perhaps Ron's invitation was prompted by a desire to spend his last moments as a Single Man with another Single Man. If I was right, then it was the first real attestation he'd given to my masculinity. How could I refuse?

I sat on the unused twin bed.

"You want to hear Mantovani?"

"Sure," I said.

"Who do you like better, him or Kostolanetz?"

"It's a toss-up."

Ron went to his cabinet. "Hey, how about the Columbus record? Brenda ever play it for you?"

"No. I don't think so."

He extracted a record from its case, and like a giant with a sea shell, placed it gingerly on the phonograph. Then he smiled at me and leaned

520 *Philip Roth*

back onto his bed. His arms were behind his head and his eyes fixed on the ceiling. "They give this to all the seniors. With the yearbook—" but he hushed as soon as the sound began. I watched Ron and listened to the record.

At first there was just a roll of drums, then silence, then another drum roll—and then softly, a marching song, the melody of which was very familiar. When the song ended, I heard the bells, soft, loud, then soft again. And finally there came a Voice, bowel-deep and historic, the kind one associates with documentaries about the rise of Fascism.

"The year, 1956. The season, fall. The place, Ohio State University . . ."

Blitzkrieg! Judgment Day! The Lord had lowered his baton and the Ohio State Glee Club were lining out the Alma Mater as if their souls depended on it. After one desperate chorus, they fell, still screaming, into bottomless oblivion, and the Voice resumed:

"The leaves had begun to turn and redden on the trees. Smoky fires line Fraternity Row, as pledges rake the leaves and turn them to a misty haze. Old faces greet new ones, new faces meet old, and another year has begun . . ."

Music. Glee Club in great comeback. Then the Voice: "The place, the banks of the Olentangy. The event, Homecoming Game, 1956. The opponent, the ever dangerous Illini . . ."

Roar of crowd. New voice—Bill Stern:[7] "Illini over the ball. The snap. Linday fading to pass, he finds a receiver, he passes long *long* down field— and IT'S INTERCEPTED BY NUMBER 43, HERB CLARK OF OHIO STATE! Clark evades one tackler, he evades another as he comes up to midfield. Now he's picking up blockers, he's down to the 45, the 40, the 35—"

And as Bill Stern egged on Clark, and Clark, Bill Stern, Ron, on his bed, with just a little body-english, eased Herb Clark over the goal.

"And it's the Buckeyes ahead now, 21 to 19. *What a game!*"

The Voice of History baritoned in again: "But the season was up and down, and by the time the first snow had covered the turf, it was the sound of dribbling and the cry *Up and In!* that echoed through the field-house . . ."

Ron closed his eyes.

"The Minnesota game," a new, high voice announced, "and for some of our seniors, their last game for the red and white . . . The players are ready to come out on the floor and into the spotlight. There'll be a big hand of appreciation from this capacity crowd for some of the boys who won't be back next year. Here comes Larry Gardner, big Number 7, out onto the floor, Big Larry from Akron, Ohio . . ."

"Larry—" announced the P.A. system; "Larry," the crowd roared back.

"And here comes Ron Patimkin dribbling out. Ron, Number 11, from Short Hills, New Jersey. Big Ron's last game, and it'll be some time before Buckeye fans forget him . . ."

Big Ron tightened on his bed as the loudspeaker called his name; his ovation must have set the nets to trembling. Then the rest of the players were announced, and then basketball season was over, and it was Religious Emphasis Week, the Senior Prom (Billy May[8] blaring at the gymna-

7. Famous radio sportcaster, Stern (1907–1971) was noted for his "embroidering" both sports history and play-by-play accounts.
8. Trumpeter, and arranger for Glenn Miller, Les Brown, and Frank Sinatra, Williams E. ("Billy") May (b. 1916) had a studio and touring band in the early fifties, before going to Hollywood as a freelance arranger for films and television.

sium roof), Fraternity Skit Night, E. E. Cummings reading to students (verse, silence, applause); and then, finally, commencement:

"The campus is hushed this day of days. For several thousand young men and women it is a joyous yet a solemn occasion. And for their parents a day of laughter and a day of tears. It is a bright green day, it is June the seventh of the year one thousand nine hundred and fifty-seven and for these young Americans the most stirring day of their lives. For many this will be their last glimpse of the campus, of Columbus, for many many years. Life calls us, and anxiously if not nervously we walk out into the world and away from the pleasures of these ivied walls. But not from its memories. They will be the concomitant, if not the fundament, of our lives. We shall choose husbands and wives, we shall choose jobs and homes, we shall sire children and grandchildren, but we will not forget you, Ohio State. In the years ahead we will carry with us always memories of thee, Ohio State . . . "

Slowly, softly, the OSU band begins the Alma Mater, and then the bells chime that last hour. Soft, very soft, for it is spring.

There was goose flesh on Ron's veiny arms as the Voice continued. "We offer ourselves to you then, world, and come at you in search of Life. And to you, Ohio State, to you Columbus, we say thank you, thank you and goodbye. We will miss you, in the fall, in the winter, in the spring, but some day we shall return. Till then, goodbye, Ohio State, goodbye, red and white, goodbye, Columbus . . . goodbye, Columbus . . . goodbye . . . "

Ron's eyes were closed. The band was upending its last truckload of nostalgia, and I tiptoed from the room, in step with the 2163 members of the Class of '57.

I closed my door, but then opened it and looked back at Ron: he was still humming on his bed. Thee! I thought, my brother-in-law!

The wedding.
Let me begin with the relatives.

There was Mrs. Patimkin's side of the family: her sister Molly, a tiny buxom hen whose ankles swelled and ringed her shoes, and who would remember Ron's wedding if for no other reason than she'd martyred her feet in three-inch heels, and Molly's husband, the butter and egg man, Harry Grossbart, who had earned his fortune with barley and corn in the days of Prohibition. Now he was active in the Temple and whenever he saw Brenda he swatted her on the can; it was a kind of physical bootlegging that passed, I guess, for familial affection. Then there was Mrs. Patimkin's brother, Marty Kreiger, the Kosher Hot-Dog King, an immense man, as many stomachs as he had chins, and already, at fifty-five, with as many heart attacks as chins and stomachs combined. He had just come back from a health cure in the Catskills,[9] where he said he'd eaten nothing but All-Bran and had won $1500 at gin rummy. When the photographer came by to take pictures, Marty put his hand on his wife's pancake breasts and said, "Hey, how about a picture of this!" His wife, Sylvia, was a frail, spindly woman with bones like a bird's. She had cried throughout the ceremony and sobbed openly, in fact, when the rabbi had pronounced Ron and Harriet "man and wife in the eyes of God and the State of New Jersey." Later, at dinner, she had hardened enough to slap her husband's

9. Mountains in southern New York State, site of numerous, primarily Jewish resorts well known for their generous quantities of food and their entertainment (the "Borscht Belt").

hand as it reached out for a cigar. However, when he reached across to hold her breast she just looked aghast and said nothing.

Also there were Mrs. Patimkin's twin sisters, Rose and Pearl, who both had white hair, the color of Lincoln convertibles, and nasal voices, and husbands who followed after them but talked only to each other, as though, in fact, sister had married sister, and husband had married husband. The husbands, named Earl Klein and Manny Kartzman, sat next to each other during the ceremony, then at dinner, and once, in fact, while the band was playing between courses, they rose, Klein and Kartzman, as though to dance, but instead walked to the far end of the hall where together they paced off the width of the floor. Earl, I learned later, was in the carpet business, and apparently he was trying to figure how much money he would make if the Hotel Pierre[1] favored him with a sale.

On Mr. Patimkin's side there was only Leo, his half-brother. Leo was married to a woman named Bea whom nobody seemed to talk to. Bea kept hopping up and down during the meal and running over to the kiddie table to see if her little girl, Sharon, was being taken care of. "I told her not to take the kid. Get a baby-sitter, I said." Leo told me this while Brenda danced with Ron's best man, Ferrari. "She says what are we, millionaires? No, for Christ sake, but my brother's kids gets married, I can have a little celebration. No, we gotta *shelp*[2] the kid with us. Aah, it gives her something to do! . . . " He looked around the hall. Upon the stage Harry Winters (né Weinberg) was leading his band in a medley from *My Fair Lady*; on the floor, all ages, all sizes, all shapes were dancing. Mr. Patimkin was dancing with Julie, whose dress had slipped down from her shoulders to reveal her soft small back, and long neck, like Brenda's. He danced in little squares and was making considerable effort not to step on Julie's toes. Harriet, who was, as everyone said, a beautiful bride, was dancing with her father. Ron danced with Harriet's mother, Brenda with Ferrari, and I had sat down for a while in the empty chair beside Leo so as not to get maneuvered into dancing with Mrs. Patimkin, which seemed to be the direction towards which things were moving.

"You're Brenda's boy friend? Huh?" Leo said.

I nodded—earlier in the evening I'd stopped giving blushing explanations. "You gotta deal there, boy," Leo said, "you don't louse it up."

"She's very beautiful," I said.

Leo poured himself a glass of champagne, and then waited as though he expected a head to form on it; when one didn't, he filled the glass to the brim.

"Beautiful, not beautiful, what's the difference. I'm a practical man. I'm on the bottom, so I gotta be. You're Aly Khan[3] you worry about marrying movie stars. I wasn't born yesterday . . . You know how old I was when I got married? Thirty-five years old. I don't know what the hell kind of hurry I was in." He drained his glass and refilled it. "I'll tell you something, one good thing happened to me in my whole life. Two maybe. Before I came back from overseas I got a letter from my wife—she wasn't my wife then. My mother-in-law found an apartment for us in Queens. Sixty-two fifty a month it cost. That's the last good thing that happened."

---

1. Very posh New York hotel.
2. Drag.
3. Playboy son of Moslem spiritual leader who in 1949, after a courtship conducted rather publicly while he was still married, wed Rita Hayworth (b. 1918), torrid Hollywood dancer, movie star, and sex symbol.

"What was the first?"

"What first?"

"You said *two* things," I said.

"I don't remember. I say two because my wife tells me I'm sarcastic and a cynic. That way maybe she won't think I'm such a wise guy."

I saw Brenda and Ferrari separate, and so excused myself and started for Brenda, but just then Mr. Patimkin separated from Julie and it looked as though the two men were going to switch partners. Instead the four of them stood on the dance floor and when I reached them they were laughing and Julie was saying, "What's so funny!" Ferrari said "Hi" to me and whisked Julie away, which sent her into peals of laughter.

Mr. Patimkin had one hand on Brenda's back and suddenly the other one was on mine. "You kids having a good time?" he said.

We were sort of swaying, the three of us, to "Get Me to the Church on Time."

Brenda kissed her father. "Yes," she said. "I'm so drunk my head doesn't even need my neck."

"It's a fine wedding, Mr. Patimkin."

"You want anything just ask me . . . " he said, a little drunken himself. "You're two good kids . . . How do you like that brother of yours getting married? . . . Huh? . . . Is that a girl or is that a girl?"

Brenda smiled, and though she apparently thought her father had spoken of her, I was sure he'd been referring to Harriet.

"You like weddings, Daddy?" Brenda said.

"I like my kids' weddings . . . " He slapped me on the back. "You two kids, you want anything? Go have a good time. Remember," he said to Brenda, "you're my honey . . . " Then he looked at me. "Whatever my Buck wants is good enough for me. There's no business too big it can't use another head."

I smiled, though not directly at him, and beyond I could see Leo sopping up champagne and watching the three of us; when he caught my eye he made a sign with his hand, a circle with his thumb and forefinger, indicating, "That a boy, that a boy!"

After Mr. Patimkin departed, Brenda and I danced closely, and we only sat down when the waiters began to circulate with the main course. The head table was noisy, particularly at our end where the men were almost all teammates of Ron's, in one sport or another; they ate a fantastic number of rolls. Tank Feldman, Ron's roommate, who had flown in from Toledo, kept sending the waiter back for rolls, for celery, for olives, and always to the squealing delight of Gloria Feldman, his wife, a nervous, undernourished girl who continually looked down the front of her gown as though there was some sort of construction project going on under her clothes. Gloria and Tank, in fact, seemed to be self-appointed precinct captains at our end. They proposed toasts, burst into wild song, and continually referred to Brenda and me as "love birds." Brenda smiled at this with her eyeteeth and I brought up a cheery look from some fraudulent auricle of my heart.

And the night continued: we ate, we drank, we danced—Rose and Pearl did the Charleston with one another (while their husbands examined woodwork and chandeliers), and then I did the Charleston with none other than Gloria Feldman, who made coy, hideous faces at me all the time we danced. Near the end of the evening, Brenda, who'd been drinking champagne like her Uncle Leo, did a Rita Hayworth tango with herself, and Julie fell asleep on some ferns she'd whisked off the head table and made into a mattress at the far end of the hall. I felt a numbness creep into my hard palate, and by three o'clock people were dancing in their coats, shoeless ladies were wrapping hunks of wedding cake in napkins for their children's lunch, and finally Gloria Feldman made her way over to our end of the table and said, freshly, "Well, our little Radcliffe smarty, what have *you* been doing all summer?"

"Growing a penis."

Gloria smiled and left as quickly as she'd come, and Brenda without another word headed shakily away for the ladies' room and the rewards of overindulgence. No sooner had she left than Leo was beside me, a glass in one hand, a new bottle of champagne in the other.

"No sign of the bride and groom?" he said, leering. He'd lost most of his consonants by this time and was doing the best he could with long, wet vowels. "Well, you're next, kid, I see it in the cards ... You're nobody's sucker ... " And he stabbed me in the side with the top of the bottle, spilling champagne onto the side of my rented tux. He straightened up, poured more onto his hand and glass, but then suddenly he stopped. He was looking into the lights which were hidden beneath a long bank of flowers that adorned the front of the table. He shook the bottle in his hand as though to make it fizz. "The son of a bitch who invented the fluorescent bulb should drop dead!" He set the bottle down and drank.

Up on the stage Harry Winters brought his musicians to a halt. The drummer stood up, stretched, and they all began to open up cases and put their instruments away. On the floor, relatives, friends, associates, were holding each other around the waists and the shoulders, and small children huddled around their parents' legs. A couple of kids ran in and out of the crowd, screaming at tag, until one was grabbed by an adult and slapped soundly on the behind. He began to cry, and couple by couple the floor emptied. Our table was a tangle of squashed everything: napkins, fruits, flowers; there were empty whiskey bottles, droopy ferns, and dishes puddled with unfinished cherry jubilee, gone sticky with the hours. At the end of the table Mr. Patimkin was sitting next to his wife, holding her hand. Opposite them, on two bridge chairs that had been pulled up, sat Mr. and Mrs. Ehrlich. They spoke quietly and evenly, as though they had known each other for years and years. Everything had slowed down now, and from time to time people would come up to the Patimkins and Ehrlichs, wish them *mazel tov*,[4] and then drag themselves and their families out into the September night, which was cool and windy, someone said, and reminded me that soon would come winter and snow.

"They never wear out, those things, you know that." Leo was pointing to the fluorescent lights that shone through the flowers. "They last for years. They could make a car like that if they wanted, that could never wear out. It would run on water in the summer and snow in the winter. But they wouldn't do it, the big boys ... Look at me," Leo said, splashing his suit front with champagne, "I sell a good bulb. You can't get the kind of bulb I sell in the drugstores. It's a quality bulb. But I'm the little guy. I don't even own a car. His brother, and I don't even own an automobile. I

4. Congratulations.

take a train wherever I go. I'm the only guy I know who wears out three pairs of rubbers every winter. Most guys get new ones when they lose the old ones. I wear them out, like shoes. Look," he said, leaning into me, "I could sell a crappy bulb, it wouldn't break my heart. But it's not good business."

The Ehrlichs and Patimkins scraped back their chairs and headed away, all except Mr. Patimkin who came down the table towards Leo and me.

He slapped Leo on the back. "Well, how you doing, *shtarke*?"[5]

"All right, Ben. All right . . ."

"You have a good time?"

"You had a nice affair, Ben, it must've cost a pretty penny, believe me . . ."

Mr. Patimkin laughed. "When I make out my income tax I go to see Leo. He knows just how much money I spent . . . You need a ride home?" he asked me.

"No, thanks. I'm waiting for Brenda. We have my car."

"Good night," Mr. Patimkin said.

I watched him step down off the platform that held the head table, and then start towards the exit. Now the only people in the hall—the shambles of a hall—were myself, Leo, and his wife and child who slept, both of them, with their heads pillowed on a crumpled tablecloth at a table down on the floor before us. Brenda still wasn't around.

"When you got it," Leo said, rubbing his fingers together, "you can afford to talk like a big shot. Who needs a guy like me any more? Salesmen, you spit on them. You can go to the supermarket and buy anything. Where my wife shops you can buy sheets and pillowcases. Imagine, a grocery store! Me, I sell to gas stations, factories, small businesses, all up and down the east coast. Sure, you can sell a guy in a gas station a crappy bulb that'll burn out in a week. For inside the pumps I'm talking, it takes a certain kind of bulb. A utility bulb. All right, so you sell him a crappy bulb, and then a week later he puts in a new one, and while he's screwing it in he still remembers your name. Not me. I sell a quality bulb. It lasts a month, five weeks, before it even flickers, then it gives you another couple days, dim maybe, but so you shouldn't go blind. It hangs on, it's a quality bulb. Before it even burns out you notice it's getting darker, so you put a new one in. What people don't like is when one minute it's sunlight and the next dark. Let it glimmer a few days and they don't feel so bad. Nobody ever throws out my bulb—they figure they'll save them, can always use them in a pinch. Sometimes I say to a guy, you ever throw out a bulb you bought from Leo Patimkin? You gotta use psychology. That's why I'm sending my kid to college. You don't know a little psychology these days, you're licked . . ."

He lifted an arm and pointed out to his wife; then he slumped down in his seat. "Aaach!" he said, and drank off half a glass of champagne. "I'll tell you, I go as far as New London, Connecticut.[6] That's as far as I'll go, and when I come home at night I stop first for a couple drinks. Martinis. Two I have, sometimes three. That seems fair, don't it? But to her a little sip or a bathtubful, it smells the same. She says it's bad for the kid if I come home smelling. The kid's a baby, for God's sake, she thinks that's

---

5. "Stud" (literally, strong man).   6. About one hundred miles from New York City.

the way I'm *supposed* to smell. A forty-eight-year-old man with a three-year-old kid! She'll give me a thrombosis that kid. My wife, she wants me to come home early and play with the kid before she goes to bed. Come home, she says, and *I'll* make you a drink. Hah! I spend all day sniffing gas, leaning under hoods with grimy *poilishehs*[7] in New London, trying to force a lousy bulb into a socket—I'll screw it in myself, I tell them—and she thinks I want to come home and drink a martini from a jelly glass! How long are you going to stay in bars, she says. Till a Jewish girl is Miss Rheingold![8]

"Look," he went on after another drink, "I love my kid like Ben loves his Brenda. It's not that I don't want to play with her. But if I play with the kid and then at night get into bed with my wife, then she can't expect fancy things from me. It's one or the other. I'm no movie star."

Leo looked at his empty glass and put it on the table; he tilted the bottle up and drank the champagne like soda water. "How much do you think I make a week?" he said.

"I don't know."

"Take a guess."

"A hundred dollars."

"Sure, and tomorrow they're gonna let the lions out of the cage in Central Park. What do you think I make?"

"I can't tell."

"A cabdriver makes more than me. That's a fact. My wife's brother is a cabdriver, *he* lives in Kew Gardens.[9] And he don't take no crap, no sir, not those cabbies. Last week it was raining one night and I said the hell with it, I'm taking a cab. I'd been all day in Newton, Mass.[1] I don't usually go so far, but on the train in the morning I said to myself, stay on, go further, it'll be a change. And I know all the time I'm kidding myself. I wouldn't even make up the extra fare it cost me. But I stay on. And at night I still had a couple boxes with me, so when the guy pulls up at Grand Central there's like a genie inside me says get in. I even threw the bulbs in, not caring if they broke. And this cabbie says, Whatya want to do, buddy, rip the leather? Those are brand new seats I got. No, I said. Jesus Christ, he says, some goddam people. I get in and give him a Queens address which ought to shut him up, but no, all the way up the Drive he was Jesus Christing me. It's hot in the cab, so I open a window and *then* he turns around and says, Whatya want to do, give me a cold in the neck? I just got over a goddam cold . . ." Leo looked at me, bleary-eyed. "This city is crazy! If I had a little money I'd get out of here in a minute. I'd go to California. They don't need bulbs out there it's so light. I went to New Guinea during the war from San Francisco. *There*," he burst, "there is the other good thing that happened to me, that night in San Francisco with this Hannah Schreiber. That's the both of them, you asked me I'm telling you—the apartment my mother-in-law got us, and this Hannah Schreiber. One night was all. I went to a B'nai B'rith dance for servicemen in the basement of some big temple, and I met her. I wasn't married then, so don't make faces."

"I'm not."

"She had a nice little room by herself. She was going to school to be a

7. Poles.

8. Rheingold Beer commercials, subway posters, etc., featured a series of beautiful girls, each called in turn "Miss Rheingold."

9. A middle-class section of Queens.

1. Near Boston, some 220 miles from New York.

teacher. Already I knew something was up because she let me feel inside her slip in the cab. Listen to me, I sound like I'm always in cabs. Maybe two other times in my life. To tell the truth I don't even enjoy it. All the time I'm riding I'm watching the meter. Even the pleasures I can't enjoy!"

"What about Hannah Schreiber?"

He smiled, flashing some gold in his mouth. "How do you like that name? She was only a girl, but she had an old lady's name. In the room she says to me she believes in oral love. I can still hear her: Leo Patimkin, I believe in oral love. I don't know what the hell she means. I figure she was one of those Christian Scientists or some cult or something. So I said, But what about for soldiers, guys going overseas who may get killed, God forbid." He shrugged his shoulders. "The smartest guy in the world I wasn't. But that's twenty years almost, I was still wet behind the ears. I'll tell you, every once in a while my wife—you know, she does for me what Hannah Schreiber did. I don't like to force her, she works hard. That to her is like a cab to me. I wouldn't force her. I can remember every time, I'll bet. Once after a Seder, my mother was still living, she should rest in peace. My wife was up to here with Mogen David.[2] In fact, *twice* after Seders. Aachhh! Everything good in my life I can count on my fingers! God forbid some one should leave me a million dollars, I wouldn't even have to take off my shoes. I got a whole other hand yet."

He pointed to the fluorescent bulbs with the nearly empty champagne bottle. "You call that a light? That's a light to *read* by? It's purple, for God's sake! Half the blind men in the world ruined themselves by those damn things. You know who's behind them? The optometrists! I'll tell you, if I could get a couple hundred for all my stock and the territory, I'd sell tomorrow. That's right, Leo A. Patimkin, one semester accounting, City College nights, will sell equipment, territory, good name. I'll buy two inches in the *Times*. The territory is from here to everywhere. I go where I want, my own boss, no one tells me what to do. You know the Bible? 'Let there be light—and there's Leo Patimkin!'[3] That's my trademark, I'll sell that too. I tell them that slogan, the *poilishehs*, they think I'm making it up. What good is it to be smart unless you're in on the ground floor! I got more brains in my pinky than Ben got in his whole *head*. Why is it he's on top and I'm on the bottom! *Why!* Believe me, if you're born lucky, you're lucky!" And then he exploded into silence.

I had the feeling that he was going to cry, so I leaned over and whispered to him, "You better go home." He agreed, but I had to raise him out of his seat and steer him by one arm down to his wife and child. The little girl could not be awakened, and Leo and Bea asked me to watch her while they went out into the lobby to get their coats. When they returned, Leo seemed to have dragged himself back to the level of human communication. He shook my hand with real feeling. I was very touched.

"You'll go far," he said to me. "You're a smart boy, you'll play it safe. Don't louse things up."

"I won't."

"Next time we see you it'll be *your* wedding," and he winked at me. Bea stood alongside, muttering goodbye all the while he spoke. He shook

2. A wine (literally, Star of David). Seder: Passover ritual meal.

3. Genesis 1:3—"And God said, Let there be light: and there was light."

my hand again and then picked the child out of her seat, and they turned
towards the door. From the back, round-shouldered, burdened, child-
carrying, they looked like people fleeing a captured city.

Brenda, I discovered, was asleep on a couch in the lobby. It was almost
four o'clock and the two of us and the desk clerk were the only ones in
the hotel lobby. At first I did not waken Brenda, for she was pale and
wilted and I knew she had been sick. I sat beside her, smoothing her hair
back off her ears. How would I ever come to know her, I wondered, for as
she slept I felt I knew no more of her than what I could see in a photograph. I stirred her gently and in a half-sleep she walked beside me out to
the car.

It was almost dawn when we came out of the Jersey side of the Lincoln
Tunnel. I switched down to my parking lights, and drove on to the Turn-
pike, and there out before me I could see the swampy meadows that
spread for miles and miles, watery, blotchy, smelly, like an oversight of
God. I thought of that other oversight, Leo Patimkin, half-brother to Ben.
In a few hours he would be on a train heading north, and as he passed
Scarsdale and White Plains, he would belch and taste champagne and let
the flavor linger in his mouth. Alongside him on the seat, like another
passenger, would be cartons of bulbs. He would get off at New London,
or maybe, inspired by the sight of his half-brother, he would stay on
again, hoping for some new luck further north. For the world was Leo's
territory, every city, every swamp, every road and highway. He could go
on to Newfoundland if he wanted, Hudson Bay, and on up to Thule, and
then slide down the other side of the globe and rap on frosted windows
on the Russian steppes, if he wanted. But he wouldn't. Leo was forty-
eight years old and he had learned. He pursued discomfort and sorrow, all
right, but if you had a heartful by the time you reached New London,
what new awfulness could you look forward to in Vladivostok?

The next day the wind was blowing the fall in and the branches of the
weeping willow were fingering at the Patimkin front lawn. I drove
Brenda to the train at noon, and she left me.

8

Autumn came quickly. It was cold and in Jersey the leaves turned and
fell overnight. The following Saturday I took a ride up to see the deer,
and did not even get out of the car, for it was too brisk to be standing at
the wire fence, and so I watched the animals walk and run in the dimness
of the late afternoon, and after a while everything, even the objects of
nature, the trees, the clouds, the grass, the weeds, reminded me of
Brenda, and I drove back down to Newark. Already we had sent our first
letters and I had called her late one night, but in the mail and on the
phone we had some difficulty discovering one another; we had not the
style yet. That night I tried her again, and someone on her floor said she
was out and would not be in till late.

Upon my return to the library I was questioned by Mr. Scapello about
the Gauguin book. The jowly gentleman *had* sent a nasty letter about my
discourtesy, and I was only able to extricate myself by offering a confused
story in an indignant tone. In fact, I even managed to turn it around so
that Mr. Scapello was apologizing to me as he led me up to my new post,
there among the encyclopedias, the bibliographies, the indexes and

guides. My bullying surprised me, and I wondered if some of it had not been learned from Mr. Patimkin that morning I'd heard him giving Grossman an earful on the phone. Perhaps I was more of a businessman than I thought. Maybe I could learn to become a Patimkin with ease ...

Days passed slowly; I never did see the colored kid again, and when, one noon, I looked in the stacks, Gauguin was gone, apparently charged out finally by the jowly man. I wondered what it had been like that day the colored kid had discovered the book was gone. Had he cried? For some reason I imagined that he had blamed it on me, but then I realized that I was confusing the dream I'd had with reality. Chances were he had discovered someone else, Van Gogh, Vermeer ... But no, they were not his kind of artists. What had probably happened was that he'd given up on the library and gone back to playing Willie Mays in the streets. He was better off, I thought. No sense carrying dreams of Tahiti in your head, if you can't afford the fare.

Let's see, what else did I do? I ate, I slept, I went to the movies, I sent broken-spined books to the bindery—I did everything I'd ever done before, but now each activity was surrounded by a fence, existed alone, and my life consisted of jumping from one fence to the next. There was no flow, for that had been Brenda.

And then Brenda wrote saying that she would be coming in for the Jewish holidays which were only a week away. I was so overjoyed I wanted to call Mr. and Mrs. Patimkin, just to tell them of my pleasure. However, when I got to the phone and had actually dialed the first two letters, I knew that at the other end there would be silence; if there was anything said, it would only be Mrs. Patimkin asking, "What is it you want?" Mr. Patimkin had probably forgotten my name.

That night, after dinner, I gave Aunt Gladys a kiss and told her she shouldn't work so hard.

"In less than a week it's Rosh Hashana and he thinks I should take a vacation. Ten people I'm having. What do you think, a chicken cleans itself? Thank God, the holidays come once a year, I'd be an old woman before my time."

But then it was only nine people Aunt Gladys was having, for only two days after her letter Brenda called.

"Oy, Gut!"[4] Aunt Gladys called. "Long *distance!*"

"Hello?" I said.

"Hello, sweetie?"

"Yes," I said.

"What *is* it?" Aunt Gladys tugged at my shirt. "What is it?"

"It's for me."

"Who?" Aunt Gladys said, pointing into the receiver.

"Brenda," I said.

"Yes?" Brenda said.

"Brenda?" Aunt Gladys said. "What does she call long distance, I almost had a heart attack."

"Because she's in Boston," I said. "Please, Aunt Gladys ... "

And Aunt Gladys walked off, mumbling, "These kids ... "

"Hello," I said again into the phone.

"Neil, how are you?"

4. *O, God!*

"I love you."

"Neil, I have bad news. I can't come in this week."

"But, honey, it's the Jewish holidays."

"Sweet*heart*," she laughed.

"Can't you say that, for an excuse?"

"I have a test Saturday, and a paper, and you know if I went home I wouldn't get anything done . . ."

"You would."

"Neil, I just *can't*. My mother'd make me go to Temple, and I wouldn't even have enough time to see *you*."

"Oh God, Brenda."

"Sweetie?"

"Yes?"

"Can't you come up here?" she asked.

"I'm working."

"The Jewish holidays," she said.

"Honey, I can't. Last year I didn't take them off, I can't all—"

"You can say you had a conversion."

"Besides, my aunt's having all the family for dinner, and you know what with my parents—"

"Come up, Neil."

"I can't just take two days off, Bren. I just got promoted and a raise—"

"The hell with the raise."

"Baby, it's my job."

"Forever?" she said.

"No."

"Then come. I've got a hotel room."

"For me?"

"For us."

"Can you do that?"

"No and yes. People do it."

"Brenda, you tempt me."

"Be tempted."

"I could take a train Wednesday right from work."

"You could stay till Sunday night."

"Bren, I can't. I still have to be back to work on Saturday."

"Don't you ever get a day *off?*" she said.

"Tuesdays," I said glumly.

"God."

"And Sunday," I added.

Brenda said something but I did not hear her, for Aunt Gladys called, "You talk all day long distance?"

"Quiet!" I shouted back to her.

"Neil, will you?"

"Damn it, yes," I said.

"Are you angry?"

"I don't think so. I'm going to come up."

"Till Sunday."

"We'll see."

"Don't feel upset, Neil. You sound upset. It is the Jewish holidays. I mean you *should* be off."

"That's right," I said. "I'm an orthodox Jew, for God's sake, I ought to take advantage of it."

"That's right," she said.

"Is there a train around six?"

"Every hour, I think."

"Then I'll be on the one that leaves at six."

"I'll be at the station," she said. "How will I know you?"

"I'll be disguised as an orthodox Jew."

"Me too," she said.

"Good night, love," I said.

Aunt Gladys cried when I told her I was going away for Rosh Hashana.

"And I was preparing a big meal," she said.

"You can still prepare it."

"What will I tell your mother?"

"I'll tell her, Aunt Gladys. Please. You have no right to get upset ... "

"Someday you'll have a family you'll know what it's like."

"I have a family now."

"What's a matter," she said, blowing her nose. "That girl couldn't come home to see her family it's the holidays?"

"She's in school, she just can't—"

"If she loved her family she'd find time. We don't live six hundred years."

"She does love her family."

"Then one day a year you could break your heart and pay a visit."

"Aunt Gladys, you don't understand."

"Sure," she said, "when I'm twenty-three years old I'll understand everything."

I went to kiss her and she said, "Go away from me, go run to Boston ... "

The next morning I discovered that Mr. Scapello didn't want me to leave on Rosh Hashana either, but I unnerved him, I think, by hinting that his coldness about my taking the two days off might just be so much veiled anti-Semitism, so on the whole he was easier to manage. At lunch time I took a walk down to Penn Station and picked up a train schedule to Boston. That was my bedtime reading for the next three nights.

She did not look like Brenda, at least for the first minute. And probably to her I did not look like me. But we kissed and held each other, and it was strange to feel the thickness of our coats between us.

"I'm letting my hair grow," she said in the cab, and that in fact was all she said. Not until I helped her out of the cab did I notice the thin gold band shining on her left hand.

She hung back, strolling casually about the lobby while I signed the register "Mr. and Mrs. Neil Klugman," and then in the room we kissed again.

"Your heart's pounding," I said to her.

"I know," she said.

"Are you nervous?"

"No."

"Have you done this before?" I said.

"I read Mary McCarthy."

She took off her coat and instead of putting it in the closet, she tossed it across the chair. I sat down on the bed; she didn't.

"What's the matter?"

Brenda took a deep breath and walked over to the window, and I thought that perhaps it would be best for me to ask nothing—for us to get used to each other's presence in quiet. I hung her coat and mine in the empty closet, and left the suitcases—mine and hers—standing by the bed.

Brenda was kneeling backwards in the chair, looking out the window as though out the window was where she'd rather be. I came up behind her and put my hands around her body and held her breasts, and when I felt the cool draft that swept under the sill, I realized how long it had been since that first warm night when I had put my arms around her and felt the tiny wings beating in her back. And then I realized why I'd really come to Boston—it had been long enough. It was time to stop kidding about marriage.

"Is something the matter?" I said.

"Yes."

It wasn't the answer I'd expected; I wanted no answer really, only to soothe her nervousness with my concern.

But I asked, "What is it? Why didn't you mention it on the phone?"

"It only happened today."

"School?"

"Home. They found out about us."

I turned her face up to mine. "That's okay. I told my aunt I was coming here too. What's the difference?"

"About the summer. About our sleeping together."

"Oh?"

"Yes."

" . . . Ron?"

"No."

"That night, you mean, did Julie—"

"No," she said, "it wasn't *anybody*."

"I don't get it."

Brenda got up and walked over to the bed where she sat down on the edge. I sat in the chair.

"My mother found the thing."

"The diaphragm?"

She nodded.

"When?" I asked.

"The other day, I guess." She walked to the bureau and opened her purse. "Here, you can read them in the order I got them." She tossed an envelope at me; it was dirty-edged and crumpled, as though it had been in and out of her pockets a good many times. "I got this one this morning," she said. "Special delivery."

I took out the letter and read:

PATIMKIN KITCHEN AND BATHROOM SINKS
"Any Size—Any Shape"

Dear Brenda—

Don't pay any Attention to your Mother's Letter when you get it. I love you honey if you want a coat I'll buy You a coat. You could always have anything you wanted. We have every faith in you so you won't be too upset by what your mother says in her Letter. Of course she is a little hysterical because of the shock and she has been Working so hard for Hadassah. She is a Woman and it is hard for her to understand some of the Shocks in life. Of course I can't say We weren't all surprised because from the beginning I was nice to him and Thought he would appreciate the nice vacation we supplied for him. Some People never turn out the way you hope and pray but I am willing to forgive and call Buy Gones, Buy Gones, You have always up till now been a good Buck and got good scholastic Grades and Ron has always been what we wanted a Good Boy, most important, and a Nice boy. This late in my life believe me I am not going to start hating my own flesh and blood. As for your mistake it takes Two to make a mistake and now that you will be away at school and from him and what you got involved in you will probably do all right I have every faith you will. You have to have faith in your children like in a Business or any serious undertaking and there is nothing that is so bad that we can't forgive especially when Our own flesh and blood is involved. We have a nice close nitt family and why not???? Have a nice Holiday and in Temple I will say a Prayer for you as I do every year. On Monday I want you to go into Boston and buy a coat. Whatever you need because I know how Cold it gets up where you are ... Give my regards to Linda and remember to bring her home with you on Thanksgiving like last year. You two had such a nice time. I have always never said bad things about any of your friends or Rons and that this should happen is only the exception that proves the rule. Have a Happy Holiday.

YOUR FATHER

And then it was signed BEN PATIMKIN, but that was crossed out and written beneath "Your Father" were again, like an echo, the words, "Your Father."

"Who's Linda?" I asked.

"My roommate, last year." She tossed another envelope to me. "Here. I got this one in the afternoon. Air Mail."

The letter was from Brenda's mother. I started to read it and then put it down a moment. "You got this *after?*"

"Yes," she said. "When I got his I didn't know what was happening. Read hers."

I began again.

Dear Brenda:

I don't even know how to begin. I have been crying all morning and have had to skip my board meeting this afternoon because my eyes are so red. I never thought this would happen to a daughter of mine. I wonder if you know what I mean, if it is at least on your conscience, so I won't have to degrade either of us with a description. All I can say is that this morning when I was cleaning out the drawers and putting away your summer clothing I came upon something in your bottom drawer, *under* some sweaters which you probably remember leaving there. I cried the minute I saw it and I haven't stopped crying yet. Your father called a while ago and now he is driving home because he heard how upset I was on the phone.

I don't know what we ever did that you should reward us this way. We gave you a nice home and all the love and respect a child needs. I always was proud when you were a little girl that you could take care of yourself so well. You took care of Julie so beautifully it was a treat to see, when you were only fourteen years old. But you drifted away from your family, even though we sent you to the best schools and gave you the best money could buy. Why you should reward us this way is a question I'll carry with me to the grave.

About your friend I have no words. He is his parents' responsibility and I cannot imagine what kind of home life he had that he could act that way. Certainly that was a fine way to repay us for the hospitality we were nice enough to show to him, a perfect stranger. That the two of you should be carrying on like that in our very house I will never in my life be able to understand. Times certainly have changed since I was a girl that this kind of thing could go on. I keep asking myself if at least you didn't think of us while you were doing that. If not for me, how could you do this to your father? God forbid Julie should ever learn of this.

God only knows what you have been doing all these years we put our trust in you.

You have broken your parents' hearts and you should know that. This is some thank you for all we gave you.

MOTHER

She only signed "Mother" once, and that was in an extraordinarily miniscule hand, like a whisper.

"Brenda," I said.

"What?"

"Are you starting to cry?"

"No. I cried already."

"Don't start again."

"I'm trying not to, for God's sake."

"Okay ... Brenda, can I ask you one question?"

"What?"

"Why did you leave it home?"

"Because I didn't plan on using it here, that's why."

"Suppose I'd come up. I mean I have come up, what about that?"

"I thought I'd come down first."

"So then couldn't you have carried it down then? Like a toothbrush?"

"Are you trying to be funny?"

"No. I'm just asking you why you left it home."

"I told you," Brenda said. "I thought I'd come home."

"But, Brenda, that doesn't make any sense. Suppose you did come home, and then you came back again. Wouldn't you have taken it with you then?"

"I don't *know*."

"Don't get angry," I said.

"You're the one who's angry."

"I'm upset, I'm not angry."

"I'm upset then too."

I did not answer but walked to the window and looked out. The stars and moon were out, silver and hard, and from the window I could see over to the Harvard campus where lights burned and then seemed to flicker when the trees blew across them.

"Brenda ... "

"What?"

"Knowing how your mother feels about you, wasn't it silly to leave it home? Risky?"

"What does how she feels about me have to do with it?"

"You can't trust her."

"Why can't I?"

"Don't you see. You *can't*."

"Neil, she was only cleaning out the drawers."

"Didn't you know she would?"

"She never did before. Or maybe she did. Neil, I couldn't think of everything. We slept together night after night and nobody heard or noticed—"

"Brenda, why the hell are you willfully confusing things?"

"I'm not!"

"Okay," I said softly. "All right."

"It's you who's confusing things," Brenda said. "You act as though I wanted her to find it."

I didn't answer.

"Do you believe *that?*" she said, after neither of us had spoken for a full minute.

"I don't know."

"Oh, Neil, you're *crazy*."

"What was crazier than leaving that damn thing around?"

"It was an oversight."

"Now it's an oversight, before it was deliberate."

"It was an oversight about the drawer. It wasn't an oversight about leaving it," she said.

"Brenda, sweetheart, wouldn't the safest, smartest, easiest, simplest thing been to have taken it with you? Wouldn't it?"

"It didn't make any difference either way."

"Brenda, this is the most frustrating argument of my life!"

"You keep making it seem as though I *wanted* her to find it. Do you think I need this? Do you? I can't even go home any more."

"Is that so?"

"Yes!"

"No," I said. "You can go home—your father will be waiting with two coats and a half-dozen dresses."

"What about my mother?"

"It'll be the same with her."

"Don't be absurd. How can I face them!"

"Why can't you face them? Did you do anything wrong?"

"Neil, look at the reality of the thing, will you?"

"*Did* you do anything wrong?"

"Neil, *they* think it's wrong. They're my parents."

"But do you think it's wrong—"

"That doesn't *matter*."

"It does to me, Brenda . . ."

"Neil, why are *you* confusing things? You keep accusing me of things."

"Damn it, Brenda, you're guilty of some things."

"*What?*"

"Of leaving that damn diaphragm there. How can you call it an oversight!"

"Oh, Neil, don't start any of that psychoanalytic crap!"

"Then why else did you do it? You wanted her to find it!"

"Why?"

"I don't know, Brenda, *why?*"

"Oh!" she said, and she picked up the pillow and threw it back on to the bed.

"What happens now, Bren?" I said.

"What does that mean?"

"Just that. What happens now?"

She rolled over on to the bed and buried her head in it.

"Don't start crying," I said.

"I'm *not.*"

I was still holding the letters and took Mr. Patimkin's from its envelope.

"Why does your father capitalize all these letters?"

She didn't answer.

" 'As for your mistake,' " I read aloud to Brenda, " 'it takes Two to make a mistake and now that you will be away at school and from him and what you got involved in you will probably do all right I have every faith you will. Your father. Your father.' "

She turned and looked at me; but silently.

" 'I have always never said bad things about any of your friends or Rons and that this should happen is only the exception that proves the rule. Have a Happy Holiday.' " I stopped; in Brenda's face there was positively no threat of tears; she looked, suddenly, solid and decisive. "Well, what are you going to do?" I asked.

"Nothing."

"Who are you going to bring home Thanksgiving—Linda?" I said, "or me?"

"Who *can* I bring home, Neil?"

"I don't know, who can you?"

"Can I bring you home?"

"I don't know," I said, "can you?"

"Stop repeating the question!"

"I sure as hell can't give you the answer."

"Neil, be realistic. After this, can I bring you home? Can you see us all sitting around the table?"

"I can't if you can't, and I can if you can."

"Are you going to speak Zen,[5] for God's sake!"

"Brenda, the choices aren't mine. You can bring Linda or me. You can go home or not go home. That's another choice. Then you don't even have to worry about choosing between me and Linda."

"Neil, you don't understand. They're still my parents. They did send me to the best schools, didn't they? They have given me everything I've wanted, haven't they?"

"Yes."

"Then how can I not go home? I *have* to go home."

"Why?"

"You don't understand. Your parents don't bother you any more. You're lucky."

5. Meditative, antirationalist Buddhist sect especially strong in Japan which stresses oral instruction through paradox, impossible riddles, nonsensical proposition (the *koan*) to subvert logic and expand the mind. Rinsai Zen was popular in the United States in the 1950s.

"Oh, sure. I live with my crazy aunt, that's a real bargain."

"Families are different. You don't understand."

"Goddamit, I understand more than you think. I understand why the hell you left that thing lying around. Don't you? Can't you put two and two together?"

"Neil, what are you talking about! You're the one who doesn't understand. You're the one who from the very beginning was accusing me of things? Remember? Isn't it so? Why don't you have your eyes fixed? Why don't you have this fixed, that fixed? As if it were my fault that I *could* have them fixed. You kept acting as if I was going to run away from you every minute. And now you're doing it again, telling me I planted that thing on purpose."

"I loved you, Brenda, so I cared."

"I loved *you*. That's why I got that damn thing in the first place."

And then we heard the tense in which we'd spoken and we settled back into ourselves and silence.

A few minutes later I picked up my bag and put on my coat. I think Brenda was crying too when I went out the door.

Instead of grabbing a cab immediately, I walked down the street and out towards the Harvard Yard which I had never seen before. I entered one of the gates and then headed out along a path, under the tired autumn foliage and the dark sky. I wanted to be alone, in the dark; not because I wanted to think about anything, but rather because, for just a while, I wanted to think about nothing. I walked clear across the Yard and up a little hill and then I was standing in front of the Lamont Library, which, Brenda had once told me, had Patimkin Sinks in its rest rooms. From the light of the lamp on the path behind me I could see my reflection in the glass front of the building. Inside, it was dark and there were no students to be seen, no librarians. Suddenly, I wanted to set down my suitcase and pick up a rock and heave it right through the glass, but of course I didn't. I simply looked at myself in the mirror the light made of the window. I was only that substance, I thought, those limbs, that face that I saw in front of me. I looked, but the outside of me gave up little information about the inside of me. I wished I could scoot around to the other side of the window, faster than light or sound or Herb Clark on Homecoming Day, to get behind that image and catch whatever it was that looked through those eyes. What was it inside me that had turned pursuit and clutching into love, and then turned it inside out again? What was it that had turned winning into losing, and losing—who knows—into winning? I was sure I had loved Brenda, though standing there, I knew I couldn't any longer. And I knew it would be a long while before I made love to anyone the way I had made love to her. With anyone else, could I summon up such a passion? Whatever spawned my love for her, had that spawned such lust too? If she had only been slightly *not* Brenda ... but then would I have loved her? I looked hard at the image of me, at that darkening of the glass, and then my gaze pushed through it, over the cool floor, to a broken wall of books, imperfectly shelved.

I did not look very much longer, but took a train that got me into Newark just as the sun was rising on the first day of the Jewish New Year. I was back in plenty of time for work.

1959

AFTERWORD

This is a love story, or, I guess you could say, the story of what turns out to have been just a summer romance. It spans the summer and a bit of the fall, so there's enough time to warrant a narrative the length of a novel, at least a short novel. There are eight chapters and the chapters are often divided by white space into discrete scenes, giving a reading pace and sense of time and space sufficient to make the reading feel like the reading of a novel. There are a number of settings: Aunt Gladys's apartment in Newark, the city library, the Short Hills Country Club, the Patimkin house, Central Park in New York City, the hotel in Boston, Harvard Yard. So there's certainly enough development and detail, scene and setting, to meaningfully fill out a novel about a young couple's brief love affair.

But there's more, and perhaps we ought to look at what else is here before focusing on the central story. Though the novel begins, as we would expect a love story to, when boy (Neil) meets girl (Brenda), after the first fairly brief paragraph the scene shifts to a Newark apartment and the boy's conversation with his aunt. Though the topic is chiefly the girl, the reader's attention is likely to be diverted from the romance by the brilliantly mimetic and characterizing dialogue. There is, first of all, Aunt Gladys's Yiddish-American accent (or rather, syntax and rhythm): not "Did Doris introduce you?" but "Doris introduced you?"; not "I don't know the Patimkins," but "Patimkin I don't know" (without even a comma); not "Are you going to call her even though you don't know her?" but "You're going to call her you don't know her?"

There's more to this than mere delight in mimicry, for, it becomes clear, the love story is also about social class and climbing, about second- and third-generation Jewish immigrant families climbing not only from the lower to the middle class but from the urban ghetto to the suburban one and, tentatively, into the American "mainstream." Aunt Gladys's language identifies her as a first-generation lower- or lower-middle-class Jewish housewife. Compare her language to Mrs. Patimkin's standard American (with pretensions to culture). Though we are not specifically told, her tennis-playing youth does suggest that she's at least second generation and middle class (the "masses" did not play tennis forty or fifty years ago, when she was a girl). Though she is as least as religious as Aunt Gladys, she's not as "Jewish"—in the ethnic sense, that is—just as her husband, a "self-made man" (that is, one who made lots of money during the Second World War), is economically but not socially middle class.

Class differences and their social and psychological nuances are an important element in the love story itself. Though Neil is first attracted to Brenda sexually (by her snapping her bathing-suit back into place), her relative gentility and sensibility, the absence of vulgarity in any obvious sense, are also a major part of her attraction for him. It is his half-conscious sense that this is true that generates his jokes, or what Brenda somewhat justifiably calls his "nastiness," about such things as her ostentatiously wealthy bourgeois surroundings, her and her friends' swanky schools, her "nose-job." He is also inordinately sensitive to real or imagined references to his lower social and economic status. We applaud his puncturing pretentiousness, but he is sometimes guilty of what has been called "working-class snobbery," and his own awareness and sense of guilt that his is a love-hate relationship to higher social status gives his humor an aftertaste of bitterness that more or less justifies Brenda's criticism.

Lovers separated by or in conflict with social stratification are not rare in love stories. In *Goodbye, Columbus,* however, the social theme is so pervasive we may question whether this is a love story in which social distinctions play an important part, or whether it is a story of ethnic social movement into the American "mainstream," embodied in a love story. The "Americanization" of the sons and daughters, grandsons and granddaughters of Jewish immigrants is not treated here through intermarriage or "mixing." All the major characters are Jewish, both lovers are Jewish, and even Ronald's Harriet from Milwaukee is Jewish. This could, then, just be the anatomy or portrait of eastern Jewish society soon after World War II. But that is a society on the move, and the move is into Establishment schools like Radcliffe and Smith, and into "gentile" living areas—Aunt Gladys wants to know if Jews live in Short Hills: they didn't used to.

Roth, like James, uses geography to suggest different ways of life as well as mere setting. Newark and Short Hills function here much as Geneva and Vevey in *Daisy Miller,* and Columbus, Ohio, we might say, is the "Rome" in this novel. This is not to suggest that they "stand for" the same things: Roth's counters are more economic and social than moral. Newark is lower or lower middle class, just a step above the old Jewish ghetto where Neil's grandparents lived; Short Hills is upper middle class Jewish suburban; Columbus is America. (If there are those who think there's nothing much west of the Hudson until you get to California, there are others who believe that America only begins west of the Appalachians.) Though the novel never leaves the East Coast and Ron is not one of the major characters, the title comes from a record of Ron's bidding farewell to Ohio State University (where he played varsity basketball) in Columbus, Ohio. Why should that extraneous detail serve as the title of this novel?

The last scene of the novel *is* a farewell, but not in Columbus: it takes place in the Harvard Yard in Cambridge, Massachusetts, and the farewell is not to Columbus or Cambridge, but to Brenda and Neil's love for her. The novel begins and ends with the love story, and so clearly *is* the love story, isn't it? Why, then, *Goodbye, Columbus*? Is it a Rothian joke? Is the love affair being judged as mawkishly sentimental like Ron's record? Perhaps, but Neil, though he no longer loves Brenda, affirms in the last scene that what he felt that summer *was* love. It was love, and lust, and both had been generated in him by something in Brenda, but also something in her that spoke to something he cannot identify in himself. And it seems to be a flaw of some sort that doomed as well as generated the love and lust:

> Whatever spawned my love for her, had that spawned such lust too? If she had only been slightly *not* Brenda . . . but then would I have loved her?

What does Neil—what do we?—want to be different in Brenda? Her faults all seem associated with her bourgeois surrounding, her being spoiled by her father, her irresponsibility and lack of commitment. But, then, would he have loved her if she had not been so surrounded, so spoiled, so irresponsible, and therefore not Brenda?

The story is not quite at an end. Neil looks through the Lamont Library window, "to a broken wall of books, imperfectly shelved." Though he is only three years out of college where he majored in philosophy, and a year out of the army, he is—only for a time, he has been insisting—a librarian. He is on his way back to the library in Newark, and the last word of the novel is "work."

Is the farewell only to Brenda, then, and is the ending only the ending of the love story? Hasn't Neil been almost as irresponsible as Brenda? If he is not a librarian, what is he? To what has he made a commitment? Wasn't his love at least in part the love of the bourgeois life? Perhaps the social theme is broader than eastern American Jewish society in the 1950s. Perhaps even the town named after the wealth-seeking discoverer of our country, and that country and its postwar materialist culture are also being bid farewell. Work is certainly not un-American; even working in a library may not be wholly un-American, but Neil does seem at the end to be saying goodbye to the scramble for wealth and status. He's even going back to Newark!

Novels that are both love stories and stories about America or the American Way of Life are not uncommon, as readers of *Daisy Miller, The Great Gatsby, An American Tragedy,* well know. Reading *Goodbye, Columbus* as such a novel helps explain not only the somewhat puzzling title but also the apparently extraneous story of the black boy and the art books that threads through the novel. The boy is not only divorced from the love story but also from the whole Short Hills section of the novel, except at one point of intersection: when Neil visits Mr. Patimkin's sink business in the black ghetto, he wonders whether he will see the boy. That strand is, however, more tightly connected to the larger social theme: that section of Newark was, in Neil's grandfather's time, the Jewish ghetto, and the movement from there to Aunt Gladys's apartment in Newark, to Short Hills, and beyond, is the same journey Neil foresees American blacks will now be undertaking, and that, presumably, Americans have undertaken before the Jewish journey: at the very beginning, George Washington had trained his scraggly army on the site of the park in front of where the Newark library now stands. (There is also some suggestion that the climb is not necessarily aided by those who have recently made the same effort: remember the rather derogatory reference of one of the women at the country club to having bought her straw hat in Barbados from "the cutest little *shvartze*"?)

The other librarians' racism, their suspicion that the boy will do something nasty or destructive in the art section, and Neil's passive resistance to their racism, his protection of the black boy's right to look at Gauguin prints, and even his "affirmative action" on the boy's behalf by not letting the book be withdrawn from the library, establish Neil as a "good guy" and his conduct as something of a norm or yardstick for measuring social, or rather human, relations. To show a first-person narrator to be good, more moral and sensitive than the other characters, poses difficulties for an author. We accept Dickens's Pip in *Great Expectations* not only because he's small and put-upon, but because as he grows up he becomes an ungrateful snob and has to learn his lesson; we accept David Copperfield more readily when we recognize that his innocence is a fault once he grows up. If we read *Goodbye, Columbus* believing that Neil is telling us that he is the intelligent, sensitive, human, faultless hero, doesn't he seem a bit of a prig (like Winterbourne), or a bit too self-righteous? Do we feel his smugness about not being a racist (or bourgeois, or a fat or unvirile librarian, or old, or ugly) off-putting, or do we so identify with him that it makes us feel good all over to think how good we are, just like Neil-baby? Is it okay to be nasty if you're funny? Do we ever believe Neil truly loves Brenda? When does he fall in love with her? when she flicks her bathing suit? when he's lying by the pool at night and fears she will not come back to him?

Henry, in *The Fox,* seems to set out to marry March to get the farm, and we never know exactly why or how he falls in love with her, but somehow, as he watches her bringing packages home with Banford, he, and we, realize he does, or at least that his life and hers are tied to each other, that he's committed. Is Neil "committed"? The diaphragm is to him a symbol that Brenda will commit herself; how does he? Do you think we could find him if we were to go to the Newark library?

We get no indication just who Neil is or what he will become. Now he can take only the first step, go back to work, be for a time at least the librarian; when he looks for himself in the mirroring window of Lamont Library, he sees not into the outer image of himself, but through himself to his "duty":

> I looked hard at the image of me, at that darkening of the glass, and then my gaze pushed through it, over the cool floor, to a broken wall of books, imperfectly shelved.

GABRIEL GARCÍA MÁRQUEZ

The Incredible and Sad Tale
of Innocent Eréndira and
Her Heartless Grandmother

Gabriel García Márquez was born on March 6, 1928, in Aracataca near the Caribbean coast of Colombia, and he was reared there by his maternal grandparents until he went to school near Bogotá at the age of eight. (His parents were alive and living in Riohacha, but they were too poor and had too many children apparently—eleven more after Gabriel—to be able to care for him themselves.) Aracataca is the basis for his Macondo where so much of his fiction is set, and the stories of his grandfather, a retired colonel, about war, and of his grandmother about ancestors and ghosts, as well as the realities of Colombian dictatorships, civil wars, and banana companies pervade that mythic world. "Surrealism comes from the reality of Latin America," García Márquez has said.

Though he studied law and journalism and worked for some time as a journalist, and during his "dry" period in the early 1960s as copywriter, editor, and screenwriter, he says he has been trying to tell stories ever since he can remember. He was, indeed, only nineteen when his first story was published. La hojarasca, a short novel (translated in 1972 as Leaf Storm), was written in 1948, or shortly thereafter, but was not published until 1955. Whether because he was published so early or because he had such difficulty with Leaf Storm, García Márquez is rather careless about publishing; El Colonel no tiene quien le escriba (translated as No One Writes to the Colonel, 1968), a short novel, appeared in a magazine in Colombia in 1958, as a book in Bogotá in 1961, in a mutilated version in Madrid in 1962, and finally in an authorized version in Mexico City in 1966. His most famous work, a novel that has had such extravagant, world-wide praise that to call it a masterpiece might seem understatement, is Cien años de soledad (1967; translated as One Hundred Years of Solitude in 1970), a surreal century-long saga of the Buendías family of Macondo, which has been read as everything from a history of Latin America to a history of the human race, readings not fully undercut by the author's insistence that he is merely a storyteller: "The writer is not here to make declarations but to tell about things," he has said. Another novel, El otoño del patriarca, appeared in 1975 and was almost immediately translated into English as The Autumn of the Patriarch (1976), and a novel of 1962, La mala hora was finally translated in 1979 (In Evil Hour).

La increible y triste historia de la candida Eréndira y de su abuela desalmada (1972, translated as The Incredible and Sad Tale of Innocent Eréndira and Her Heartless Grandmother in 1973, and first published in book form in English in 1978) was the first work García Márquez published after Solitude. It is in his mature style, not so flamboyant as Leaf Storm nor so terse as the style of the stories of the 1950s but rich and ranging, with a wealth of natural detail in strange juxtapositions and interpenetrated by the supernatural or surreal.

The Incredible and Sad Tale of Innocent Eréndira and Her Heartless Grandmother*

ERÉNDIRA[1] WAS BATHING her grandmother when the wind of her misfortune began to blow. The enormous mansion of moonlike concrete lost in the solitude of the desert trembled down to its foundations with the first attack. But Eréndira and her grandmother were used to the risks of the wild nature there, and in the bathroom decorated with a series of peacocks and childish mosaics of Roman baths they scarcely paid any attention to the caliber of the wind.

The grandmother, naked and huge in the marble tub, looked like a handsome white whale. The granddaughter had just turned fourteen and was languid, soft-boned, and too meek for her age. With a parsimony that had something like sacred rigor about it, she was bathing her grandmother with water in which purifying herbs and aromatic leaves had been boiled, the latter clinging to the succulent back, the flowing metal-colored hair, and the powerful shoulders which were so mercilessly tattooed as to put sailors to shame.

"Last night I dreamt I was expecting a letter," the grandmother said.

Eréndira, who never spoke except when it was unavoidable, asked:

"What day was it in the dream?"

"Thursday."

"Then it was a letter with bad news," Eréndira said, "but it will never arrive."

When she had finished bathing her grandmother, she took her to her bedroom. The grandmother was so fat that she could only walk by leaning on her granddaughter's shoulder or on a staff that looked like a bishop's crosier, but even during her most difficult efforts the power of an antiquated grandeur was evident. In the bedroom, which had been furnished with an excessive and somewhat demented taste, like the whole house, Eréndira needed two more hours to get her grandmother ready. She untangled her hair strand by strand, perfumed and combed it, put an equatorially flowered dress on her, put talcum powder on her face, bright red lipstick on her mouth, rouge on her cheeks, musk on her eyelids, and mother-of-pearl polish on her nails, and when she had her decked out like a larger than life-size doll, she led her to an artificial garden with suffocating flowers that were like the ones on the dress, seated her in a large chair that had the foundation and the pedigree of a throne, and left her listening to elusive records on a phonograph that had a speaker like a megaphone.

While the grandmother floated through the swamps of the past, Eréndira busied herself sweeping the house, which was dark and motley, with bizarre furniture and statues of invented Caesars, chandeliers of teardrops and alabaster angels, a gilded piano, and numerous clocks of unthinkable

* Translated by Gregory Rabassa.
1. The name suggests the Spanish verb *rendir*, meaning "to surrender."

sizes and shapes. There was a cistern in the courtyard for the storage of water carried over many years from distant springs on the backs of Indians, and hitched to a ring on the cistern wall was a broken-down ostrich, the only feathered creature who could survive the torment of that accursed climate. The house was far away from everything, in the heart of the desert, next to a settlement with miserable and burning streets where the goats committed suicide from desolation when the wind of misfortune blew.

That incomprehensible refuge had been built by the grandmother's husband, a legendary smuggler whose name was Amadís,[2] by whom she had a son whose name was also Amadís and who was Eréndira's father. No one knew either the origins or the motivations of that family. The best known version in the language of the Indians was that Amadís the father had rescued his beautiful wife from a house of prostitution in the Antilles, where he had killed a man in a knife fight, and that he had transplanted her forever in the impunity of the desert. When the Amadíses died, one of melancholy fevers and the other riddled with bullets in a fight over a woman, the grandmother buried their bodies in the courtyard, sent away the fourteen barefoot servant girls, and continued ruminating on her dreams of grandeur in the shadows of the furtive house, thanks to the sacrifices of the bastard granddaughter whom she had reared since birth.

Eréndira needed six hours just to set and wind the clocks. The day when her misfortune began she didn't have to do that because the clocks had enough winding left to last until the next morning, but on the other hand, she had to bathe and overdress her grandmother, scrub the floors, cook lunch, and polish the crystalware. Around eleven o'clock, when she was changing the water in the ostrich's bowl and watering the desert weeds around the twin graves of the Amadíses, she had to fight off the anger of the wind, which had become unbearable, but she didn't have the slightest feeling that it was the wind of her misfortune. At twelve o'clock she was wiping the last champagne glasses when she caught the smell of broth and had to perform the miracle of running to the kitchen without leaving a disaster of Venetian glass in her wake.

She just managed to take the pot off the stove as it was beginning to boil over. Then she put on a stew she had already prepared and took advantage of a chance to sit down and rest on a stool in the kitchen. She closed her eyes, opened them again with an unfatigued expression, and began pouring the soup into the tureen. She was working as she slept.

The grandmother had sat down alone at the head of a banquet table with silver candlesticks set for twelve people. She shook her little bell and Eréndira arrived almost immediately with the steaming tureen. As Eréndira was serving the soup, her grandmother noticed the somnambulist look and passed her hand in front of her eyes as if wiping an invisible pane of glass. The girl didn't see the hand. The grandmother followed her with her look and when Eréndira turned to go back to the kitchen, she shouted at her:

"Eréndira!"

Having been awakened all of a sudden, the girl dropped the tureen onto the rug.

---

2. Echoing *Amadís de Gaula*, a thirteenth- or fourteenth-century Spanish or Portuguese chivalric prose romance and model for its code of honor and knightly perfection.

"That's all right, child," the grandmother said to her with assuring tenderness. "You fell asleep while you were walking about again."

"My body has that habit," Eréndira said by way of an excuse.

Still hazy with sleep, she picked up the tureen, and tried to clean the stain on the rug.

"Leave it," he grandmother dissuaded her. "You can wash it this afternoon."

So in addition to her regular afternoon chores, Eréndira had to wash the dining room rug, and she took advantage of her presence at the washtub to do Monday's laundry as well, while the wind went around the house looking for a way in. She had so much to do that night came upon her without her realizing it, and when she put the dining room rug back in its place it was time to go to bed.

The grandmother had been fooling around on the piano all afternoon, singing the songs of her times to herself in a falsetto, and she had stains of musk and tears on her eyelids. But when she lay down on her bed in her muslin nightgown, the bitterness of fond memories returned.

"Take advantage of tomorrow to wash the living room rug too," she told Eréndira. "It hasn't seen the sun since the days of all the noise."

"Yes, Grandmother," the girl answered.

She picked up a feather fan and began to fan the implacable matron, who recited the list of nighttime orders to her as she sank into sleep.

"Iron all the clothes before you go to bed so you can sleep with a clear conscience."

"Yes, Grandmother."

"Check the clothes closets carefully, because moths get hungrier on windy nights."

"Yes, Grandmother."

"With the time you have left, take the flowers out into the courtyard so they can get a breath of air."

"Yes, Grandmother."

"And feed the ostrich."

She had fallen asleep but she was still giving orders, for it was from her that the granddaughter had inherited the ability to be alive while sleeping. Eréndira left the room without making any noise and did the final chores of the night, still replying to the sleeping grandmother's orders.

"Give the graves some water."

"Yes, Grandmother."

"And if the Amadíses arrive, tell them not to come in," the grandmother said, "because Porfirio Galán's gang is waiting to kill them."

Eréndira didn't answer her any more because she knew that the grandmother was getting lost in her delirium, but she didn't miss a single order. When she finished checking the window bolts and put out the last lights, she took a candlestick from the dining room and lighted her way to her bedroom as the pauses in the wind were filled with the peaceful and enormous breathing of her sleeping grandmother.

Her room was also luxurious, but not so much as her grandmother's, and it was piled high with the rag dolls and wind-up animals of her recent childhood. Overcome by the barbarous chores of the day, Eréndira didn't have the strength to get undressed and she put the candlestick on the night table and fell onto the bed. A short while later the wind of her misfortune came into the bedroom like a pack of hounds and knocked the candle over against the curtain.

At dawn, when the wind finally stopped, a few thick and scattered drops of rain began to fall, putting out the last embers and hardening the smoking ashes of the mansion. The people in the village, Indians for the most part, tried to rescue the remains of the disaster: the charred corpse of the ostrich, the frame of the gilded piano, the torso of a statue. The grandmother was contemplating the residue of her fortune with an impenetrable depression. Eréndira, sitting between the two graves of the Amadíses, had stopped weeping. When the grandmother was convinced that very few things remained intact among the ruins, she looked at her granddaughter with sincere pity.

"My poor child," she sighed. "Life won't be long enough for you to pay me back for this mishap."

She began to pay it back that very day, beneath the noise of the rain, when she was taken to the village storekeeper, a skinny and premature widower who was quite well known in the desert for the good price he paid for virginity. As the grandmother waited undauntedly, the widower examined Eréndira with scientific austerity: he considered the strength of her thighs, the size of her breasts, the diameter of her hips. He didn't say a word until he had some calculation of what she was worth.

"She's still quite immature," he said then. "She has the teats of a bitch."

Then he had her get on a scale to prove his decision with figures. Eréndira weighed ninety pounds.

"She isn't worth more than a hundred pesos," the widower said.

The grandmother was scandalized.

"A hundred pesos for a girl who's completely new!" she almost shouted. "No, sir, that shows a great lack of respect for virtue on your part."

"I'll make it a hundred and fifty," the widower said.

"This girls caused me damages amounting to more than a million pesos," the grandmother said. "At this rate she'll need two hundred years to pay me back."

"You're lucky that the only good feature she has is her age," the widower said.

The storm threatened to knock the house down, and there were so many leaks in the roof that it was raining almost as much inside as out. The grandmother felt all alone in a world of disaster.

"Just raise it to three hundred," she said.

"Two hundred and fifty."

Finally they agreed on two hundred and twenty pesos in cash and some provisions. The grandmother then signaled Eréndira to go with the widower and he led her by the hand to the back room as if he were taking her to school.

"I'll wait for you here," the grandmother said.

"Yes, Grandmother," said Eréndira.

The back room was a kind of shed with four brick columns, a roof of rotted palm leaves, and an adobe wall three feet high, through which outdoor disturbances got into the building. Placed on top of the adobe wall were pots with cacti and other plants of aridity. Hanging between two columns and flapping like the free sail of a drifting sloop was a faded hammock. Over the whistle of the storm and the lash of the water one could hear distant shouts, the howling of far-off animals, the cries of a shipwreck.

When Eréndira and the widower went into the shed they had to hold on so as not to be knocked down by a gust of rain which left them soaked. Their voices could not be heard but their movements became clear in the roar of the squall. At the widower's first attempt, Eréndira shouted something inaudible and tried to get away. The widower answered her without any voice, twisted her arm by the wrist, and dragged her to the hammock. She fought him off with a scratch on the face and shouted in silence again, but he replied with a solemn slap which lifted her off the ground and suspended her in the air for an instant with her long Medusa hair[3] floating in space. He grabbed her about the waist before she touched ground again, flung her into the hammock with a brutal heave, and held her down with his knees. Eréndira then succumbed to terror, lost consciousness, and remained as if fascinated by the moonbeams from a fish that was floating through the storm air, while the widower undressed her, tearing off her clothes with a methodical clawing, as if he were pulling up grass, scattering them with great tugs of color that waved like streamers and went off with the wind.

When there was no other man left in the village who could pay anything for Eréndira's love, her grandmother put her on a truck to go where the smugglers were. They made the trip on the back of the truck in the open, among sacks of rice and buckets of lard and what had been left by the fire: the headboard of the viceregal bed, a warrior angel, the scorched throne, and other pieces of useless junk. In a trunk with two crosses painted in broad strokes they carried the bones of the Amadíses.

The grandmother protected herself from the sun with a tattered umbrella and it was hard for her to breathe because of the torment of sweat and dust, but even in that unhappy state she kept control of her dignity. Behind the pile of cans and sacks of rice Eréndira paid for the trip and the cartage by making love for twenty pesos a turn with the truck's loader. At first her system of defense was the same as she had used against the widower's attack, but the loader's approach was different, slow and wise, and he ended up taming her with tenderness. So when they reached the first town after a deadly journey, Eréndira and the loader were relaxing from good love behind the parapet of cargo. The driver shouted to the grandmother:

"Here's where the world begins."

The grandmother observed with disbelief the miserable and solitary streets of a town somewhat larger but just as sad as the one they had abandoned.

"It doesn't look like it to me," she said.

"It's mission country," the driver said.

"I'm not interested in charity, I'm interested in smugglers," said the grandmother.

Listening to the dialogue from behind the load, Eréndira dug into a sack of rice with her finger. Suddenly she found a string, pulled on it, and drew out a necklace of genuine pearls. She looked at it amazed, holding it

---

3. In Greek mythology, Medusa had snakes for hair.

between her fingers like a dead snake, while the driver answered her grandmother:

"Don't be daydreaming, ma'am. There's no such thing as smugglers."

"Of course not," the grandmother said. "I've got your word for it."

"Try to find one and you'll see," the driver bantered. "Everybody talks about them, but no one's ever seen one."

The loader realized that Eréndira had pulled out the necklace and hastened to take it away from her and stick it back into the sack of rice. The grandmother, who had decided to stay in spite of the poverty of the town, then called to her granddaughter to help her out of the truck. Eréndira said good-bye to the loader with a kiss that was hurried but spontaneous and true.

The grandmother waited, sitting on her throne in the middle of the street, until they finished unloading the goods. The last item was the trunk with the remains of the Amadíses.

"This thing weighs almost as much as a dead man," said the driver, laughing.

"There are two of them," the grandmother said, "so treat them with the proper respect."

"I bet they're marble statues." The driver laughed again.

He put the trunk with bones down carelessly among the singed furniture and held out his open hand to the grandmother.

"Fifty pesos," he said.

"Your slave has already paid on the right-hand side."

The driver looked at his helper with surprise and the latter made an affirmative sign. The driver then went back to the cab, where a woman in mourning was riding, in her arms a baby who was crying from the heat. The loader, quite sure of himself, told the grandmother:

"Eréndira is coming with me, if it's all right by you. My intentions are honorable."

The girl intervened, surprised:

"I didn't say anything!"

"The idea was all mine," the loader said.

The grandmother looked him up and down, not to make him feel small but trying to measure the true size of his guts.

"It's all right by me," she told him, "provided you pay me what I lost because of her carelessness. It's eight hundred seventy-two thousand three hundred fifteen pesos, less the four hundred and twenty she's already paid me, making it eight hundred seventy-one thousand eight hundred ninety-five."

The truck started up.

"Believe me, I'd give you that pile of money if I had it," the loader said seriously. "The girl is worth it."

The grandmother was pleased with the boy's decision.

"Well, then, come back when you have it, son," she answered in a sympathetic tone. "But you'd better go now, because if we figure out accounts again you'll end up owing me ten pesos."

The loader jumped onto the back of the truck and it went off. From there he waved good-bye to Eréndira, but she was still so surprised that she didn't answer him.

In the same vacant lot where the truck had left them, Eréndira and her grandmother improvised a shelter to live in from sheets of zinc and the remains of Oriental rugs. They laid two mats on the ground and slept as well as they had in the mansion until the sun opened holes in the ceiling and burned their faces.

Just the opposite of what normally happened, it was the grandmother who busied herself that morning fixing up Eréndira. She made up her face in the style of sepulchral beauty that had been the vogue in her youth and touched her up with artificial fingernails and an organdy bow that looked like a butterfly on her head.

"You look awful," she admitted, "but it's better that way: men are quite stupid when it comes to female matters."

Long before they saw them they both recognized the sound of two mules walking on the flint of the desert. At a command from her grandmother, Eréndira lay down on the mat the way an amateur actress might have done at the moment when the curtain was about to go up. Leaning on her bishop's crosier, the grandmother went out of the shelter and sat down on the throne to wait for the mules to pass.

The mailman was coming. He was only twenty years old, but his work had aged him, and he was wearing a khaki uniform, leggings, a pith helmet, and had a military pistol on his cartridge belt. He was riding a good mule and leading by the halter another, more timeworn one, on whom the canvas mailbags were piled.

As he passed by the grandmother he saluted her and kept on going, but she signaled him to look inside the shelter. The man stopped and saw Eréndira lying on the mat in her posthumous make-up and wearing a purple-trimmed dress.

"Do you like it?" the grandmother asked.

The mailman hadn't understood until then what the proposition was. "It doesn't look bad to someone who's been on a diet," he said, smiling.

"Fifty pesos," the grandmother said.

"Boy, you're asking a mint!" he said. "I can eat for a whole month on that."

"Don't be a tightwad," the grandmother said. "The airmail pays even better than being a priest."

"I'm the domestic mail," the man said. "The airmail man travels in a pickup truck."

"In any case, love is just as important as eating," the grandmother said.

"But it doesn't feed you."

The grandmother realized that a man who lived from what other people were waiting for had more than enough time for bargaining.

"How much have you got?" she asked him.

The mailman dismounted, took some chewed-up bills from his pocket, and showed them to the grandmother. She snatched them up all together with a rapid hand just as if they had been a ball.

"I'll lower the price for you," she said, "but on one condition: that you spread the word all around."

"All the way to the other side of the world," the mailman said. "That's what I'm for."

Eréndira, who had been unable to blink, then took off her artificial eyelashes and moved to one side of the mat to make room for the chance boyfriend. As soon as he was in the shelter, the grandmother closed the entrance with an energetic tug on the sliding curtain.

It was an effective deal. Taken by the words of the mailman, men came

from very far away to become acquainted with the newness of Eréndira.
Behind the men came gambling tables and food stands, and behind them
all came a photographer on a bicycle, who, across from the encampment,
set up a camera with a mourning sleeve on a tripod and a backdrop of a
lake with listless swans.

The grandmother, fanning herself on her throne, seemed alien to her
own bazaar. The only thing that interested her was keeping order in the
line of customers who were waiting their turn and checking the exact
amount of money they paid in advance to go in to Eréndira. At first she
had been so strict that she refused a good customer because he was five
pesos short. But with the passage of months she was assimilating the lessons of reality and she ended up letting people in who completed their
payment with religious medals, family relics, wedding rings, and anything
her bite could prove was bona-fide gold even if it didn't shine.

After a long stay in that first town, the grandmother had sufficient
money to buy a donkey, and she went off into the desert in search of
places more propitious for the payment of the debt. She traveled on a
litter that had been improvised on top of the donkey and she was protected from the motionless sun by the half-spoked umbrella that Eréndira
held over her head. Behind them walked four Indian bearers with the
remnants of the encampment: the sleeping mats, the restored throne, the
alabaster angel, and the trunks with the remains of the Amadíses. The
photographer followed the caravan on his bicycle, but never catching up,
as if he were going to a different festival.

Six months had passed since the fire when the grandmother was able to
get a complete picture of the business.

"If things go on like this," she told Eréndira, "you will have paid me
the debt inside of eight years, seven months, and eleven days."

She went back over her calculations with her eyes closed, fumbling
with the seeds she was taking out of a cord pouch where she also kept the
money, and she corrected herself:

"All that, of course, not counting the pay and board of the Indians and
other minor expenses."

Eréndira, who was keeping in step with the donkey, bowed down by
the heat and dust, did not reproach her grandmother for her figures, but
she had to hold back her tears.

"I've got ground glass in my bones," she said.

"Try to sleep."

"Yes, Grandmother."

She closed her eyes, took in a deep breath of scorching air, and went on
walking in her sleep.

A small truck loaded with cages appeared, frightening goats in the dust
of the horizon, and the clamor of the birds was like a splash of cool water
for the Sunday torpor of San Miguel del Desierto. At the wheel was a
corpulent Dutch farmer, his skin splintered by the outdoors, and with a
squirrel-colored mustache he had inherited from some great-grandfather.
His son Ulises,[4] who was riding in the other seat, was a gilded adolescent
with lonely maritime eyes and with the appearance of a furtive angel.
The Dutchman noticed a tent in front of which all the soldiers of the

---

4. Ulysses. *San Miguel del Desierto:* Saint Michael of the Desert.

local garrison were awaiting their turn. They were sitting on the ground, drinking out of the same bottle, which passed from mouth to mouth, and they had almond branches on their heads as if camouflaged for combat. The Dutchman asked in his language:

"What the devil can they be selling there?"

"A woman," his son answered quite naturally. "Her name is Eréndira."

"How do you know?"

"Everybody in the desert knows," Ulises answered..

The Dutchman stopped at the small hotel in town and got out. Ulises stayed in the truck. With agile fingers he opened a briefcase that his father had left on the seat, took out a roll of bills, put several in his pocket, and left everything just the way it had been. That night, while his father was asleep, he climbed out the hotel window and went to stand in line in front of Eréndira's tent.

The festivities were at their height. The drunken recruits were dancing by themselves so as not to waste the free music, and the photographer was taking nighttime pictures with magnesium papers. As she watched over her business, the grandmother counted the bank notes in her lap, dividing them into equal piles and arranging them in a basket. There were only twelve soldiers at that time, but the evening line had grown with civilian customers. Ulises was the last one.

It was the turn of a soldier with a woeful appearance. The grandmother not only blocked his way but avoided contact with his money.

"No, son," she told him. "You couldn't go in for all the gold in the world. You bring bad luck."

The soldier, who wasn't from those parts, was puzzled.

"What do you mean?"

"You bring down the evil shadows," the grandmother said. "A person only has to look at your face."

She waved him off with her hand, but without touching him, and made way for the next soldier.

"Go right in, handsome," she told him good naturedly, "but don't take too long, your country needs you."

The soldier went in but he came right out again because Eréndira wanted to talk to her grandmother. She hung the basket of money on her arm and went into the tent, which wasn't very roomy, but which was neat and clean. In the back, on an army cot, Eréndira was unable to repress the trembling in her body, and she was in sorry shape, all dirty with soldier sweat.

"Grandmother," she sobbed, "I'm dying."

The grandmother felt her forehead and when she saw she had no fever, she tried to console her.

"There are only ten soldiers left," she said.

Eréndira began to weep with the shrieks of a frightened animal. The grandmother realized then that she had gone beyond the limits of horror and, stroking her head, she helped her calm down.

"The trouble is that you're weak," she told her. "Come on, don't cry any more, take a bath in sage water to get your blood back into shape."

She left the tent when Eréndira was calmer and she gave the soldier waiting his money back. "That's all for today," she told him. "Come back tomorrow and I'll give you the first place in line." Then she shouted to those lined up:

"That's all, boys. Tomorrow morning at nine."

Soldiers and civilians broke ranks with shouts of protest. The grandmother confronted them, in a good mood but brandishing the devastating crosier in earnest.

"You're an inconsiderate bunch of slobs!" she shouted. "What do you think the girl is made of, iron? I'd like to see you in her place. You perverts! You shitty bums!"

The men answered her with even cruder insults, but she ended up controlling the revolt and stood guard with her staff until they took away the snack tables and dismantled the gambling stands. She was about to go back into the tent when she saw Ulises, as large as life, all by himself in the dark and empty space where the line of men had been before. He had an unreal aura about him and he seemed to be visible in the shadows because of the very glow of his beauty.

"You," the grandmother asked him. "What happened to your wings?"

"The one who had wings was my grandfather,"[5] Ulises answered in his natural way, "but nobody believed it."

The grandmother examined him again with fascination. "Well, I do," she said. "Put them on and come back tomorrow." She went into the tent and left Ulises burning where he stood.

Eréndira felt better after her bath. She had put on a short, lace-trimmed slip and she was drying her hair before going to bed, but she was still making an effort to hold back her tears. Her grandmother was asleep.

Behind Eréndira's bed, very slowly, Ulises' head appeared. She saw the anxious and diaphanous eyes, but before saying anything she rubbed her head with the towel in order to prove that it wasn't an illusion. When Ulises blinked for the first time, Eréndira asked him in a very low voice:

"Who are you?"

Ulises showed himself down to his shoulders. "My name is Ulises," he said. He showed her the bills he had stolen and added:

"I've got money."

Eréndira put her hands on the bed, brought her face close to that of Ulises, and went on talking to him as if in a kindergarten game.

"You were supposed to get in line," she told him.

"I waited all night long," Ulises said.

"Well, now you have to wait until tomorrow," Eréndira said. "I feel as if someone had been beating me on the kidneys."

At that instant the grandmother began to talk in her sleep.

"It's going on twenty years since it rained last," she said. "It was such a terrible storm that the rain was all mixed in with sea water, and the next morning the house was full of fish and snails and your grandfather Amadís, may he rest in peace, saw a glowing manta ray floating through the air."

Ulises hid behind the bed again. Eréndira showed an amused smile.

"Take it easy," she told him. "She always acts kind of crazy when she's asleep, but not even an earthquake can wake her up."

Ulises reappeared. Eréndira looked at him with a smile that was naughty and even a little affectionate and took the soiled sheet off the mattress.

"Come," she said. "Help me change the sheet."

---

5. See García Márquez's story "A Very Old Man with Enormous Wings" for a possible reference. Márquez often refers to other works from his fictional world of Macondo.

Then Ulises came from behind the bed and took one end of the sheet. Since the sheet was much larger than the mattress, they had to fold it several times. With every fold Ulises drew closer to Eréndira.

"I was going crazy wanting to see you," he suddenly said. "Everybody says you're very pretty and they're right."

"But I'm going to die," Eréndira said.

"My mother says that people who die in the desert don't go to heaven but to the sea," Ulises said.

Eréndira put the dirty sheet aside and covered the mattress with another, which was clean and ironed.

"I never saw the sea," she said.

"It's like the desert but with water," said Ulises.

"Then you can't walk on it."

"My father knew a man who could," Ulises said, "but that was a long time ago."

Eréndira was fascinated but she wanted to sleep.

"If you come very early tomorrow you can be first in line," she said.

"I'm leaving with my father at dawn," said Ulises.

"Won't you be coming back this way?"

"Who can tell?" Ulises said. "We just happened along now because we got lost on the road to the border."

Eréndira looked thoughtfully at her sleeping grandmother.

"All right," she decided. "Give me the money."

Ulises gave it to her. Eréndira lay down on the bed but he remained trembling where he was: at the decisive moment his determination had weakened. Eréndira took him by the hand to hurry him up and only then did she notice his tribulation. She was familiar with that fear.

"Is it the first time?" she asked him.

Ulises didn't answer but he smiled in desolation. Eréndira became a different person.

"Breathe slowly," she told him. "That's the way it always is the first time. Afterwards you won't even notice."

She laid him down beside her and while she was taking his clothes off she was calming him maternally.

"What's your name?"

"Ulises."

"That's a gringo name," Eréndira said.

"No, a sailor name."

Eréndira uncovered his chest, gave a few little orphan kisses, sniffed him.

"It's like you were made of gold all over," she said, "but you smell of flowers."

"It must be the oranges," Ulises said.

Calmer now, he gave a smile of complicity.

"We carry a lot of birds along to throw people off the track," he added, "but what we're doing is smuggling a load of oranges across the border."

"Oranges aren't contraband," Eréndira said.

"These are," said Ulises. "Each one is worth fifty thousand pesos."

Eréndira laughed for the first time in a long while.

"What I like about you," she said, "is the serious way you make up nonsense."

She had become spontaneous and talkative again, as if Ulises' innorence had changed not only her mood but her character. The grandmother, such a short distance away from misfortune, was still talking in her sleep.

"Around those times, at the beginning of March, they brought you home," she said. "You looked like a lizard wrapped in cotton. Amadís, your father, who was young and handsome, was so happy that afternoon that he sent for twenty carts loaded with flowers and arrived strewing them along the street until the whole village was gold with flowers like the sea."

She ranted on with great shouts and with a stubborn passion for several hours. But Ulises couldn't hear her because Eréndira had loved him so much and so truthfully that she loved him again for half price while her grandmother was raving and kept on loving him for nothing until dawn.

A group of missionaries holding up their crucifixes stood shoulder to shoulder in the middle of the desert. A wind as fierce as the wind of misfortune shook their burlap habits and their rough beards and they were barely able to stand on their feet. Behind them was the mission, a colonial pile of stone with a tiny belfry on top of the harsh whitewashed walls.

The youngest missionary, who was in charge of the group, pointed to a natural crack in the glazed clay ground.

"You shall not pass beyond this line!" he shouted.

The four Indian bearers carrying the grandmother in a litter made of boards stopped when they heard the shout. Even though she was uncomfortable sitting on the planks of the litter and her spirit was dulled by the dust and sweat of the desert, the grandmother maintained her haughtiness intact. Eréndira was on foot. Behind the litter came a file of eight Indians carrying the baggage and at the very end the photographer on his bicycle.

"The desert doesn't belong to anyone," the grandmother said.

"It belongs to God," the missionary said, "and you are violating his sacred laws with your filthy business."

The grandmother then recognized the missionary's peninsular[6] usage and diction and avoided a head-on confrontation so as not to break her head against his intransigence. She went back to being herself.

"I don't understand your mysteries, son."

The missionary pointed at Eréndira.

"That child is underage."

"But she's my granddaughter."

"So much the worse," the missionary replied. "Put her under our care willingly or we'll have to seek recourse in other ways."

The grandmother had not expected them to go so far.

"All right, if that's how it is." She surrendered in fear. "But sooner or later I'll pass, you'll see."

Three days after the encounter with the missionaries, the grandmother and Eréndira were sleeping in a village near the mission when a group of stealthy, mute bodies, creeping along like an infantry patrol, slipped into the tent. They were six Indian novices, strong and young, their rough cloth habits seeming to glow in the moonlight. Without making a sound

6. Colombia's Península de la Guajira.

they cloaked Eréndira in a mosquito netting, picked her up without waking her, and carried her off wrapped like a large, fragile fish caught in a lunar net.

There were no means left untried by the grandmother in an attempt to rescue her granddaughter from the protection of the missionaries. Only when they had all failed, from the most direct to the most devious, did she turn to the civil authority, which was vested in a military man. She found him in the courtyard of his home, his chest bare, shooting with an army rifle at a dark and solitary cloud in the burning sky. He was trying to perforate it to bring on rain, and his shots were furious and useless, but he did take the necessary time out to listen to the grandmother.

"I can't do anything," he explained to her when he had heard her out. "The priesties, according to the concordat, have the right to keep the girl until she comes of age. Or until she gets married."

"Then why do they have you here as mayor?" the grandmother asked.

"To make it rain," was the mayor's answer.

Then, seeing that the cloud had moved out of range, he interrupted his official duties and gave his full attention to the grandmother.

"What you need is someone with a lot of weight who will vouch for you," he told her. "Someone who can swear to your moral standing and your good behavior in a signed letter. Do you know Senator Onésimo Sánchez?"

Sitting under the naked sun on a stool that was too narrow for her astral buttocks, the grandmother answered with a solemn rage:

"I'm just a poor woman all alone in the vastness of the desert."

The mayor, his right eye twisted from the heat, looked at her with pity.

"Then don't waste your time, ma'am," he said. "You'll rot in hell."

She didn't rot, of course. She set up her tent across from the mission and sat down to think, like a solitary warrior besieging a fortified city. The wandering photographer, who knew her quite well, loaded his gear onto the carrier of his bicycle and was ready to leave all alone when he saw her in the full sun with her eyes fixed on the mission.

"Let's see who gets tired first," the grandmother said, "they or I."

"They've been here for three hundred years and they can still take it," the photographer said. "I'm leaving."

Only then did the grandmother notice the loaded bicycle.

"Where are you going?"

"Wherever the wind takes me," the photographer said, and he left. "It's a big world."

The grandmother sighed.

"Not as big as you think, you ingrate."

But she didn't move her head in spite of her anger so as not to lose sight of the mission. She didn't move it for many, many days of mineral heat, for many, many nights of wild winds, for all the time she was meditating and no one came out of the mission. The Indians built a lean-to of palm leaves beside the tent and hung their hammocks there, but the grandmother stood watch until very late, nodding on her throne and chewing the uncooked grain in her pouch with the invincible laziness of a resting ox.

One night a convoy of slow covered trucks passed very close to her and the only lights they carried were wreaths of colored bulbs which gave them the ghostly size of sleepwalking altars. The grandmother recognized them at once because they were just like the trucks of the Amadíses. The last truck in the convoy slowed, stopped, and a man got out of the cab to adjust something in back. He looked like a replica of the Amadíses, wearing a hat with a turned-up brim, high boots, two crossed cartridge belts across his chest, an army rifle, and two pistols. Overcome by an irresistible temptation, the grandmother called to the man.

"Don't you know who I am?" she asked him.

The man lighted her pitilessly with a flashlight. For an instant he studied the face worn out by vigil, the eyes dim from fatigue, the withered hair of the woman who, even at her age, in her sorry state, and with that crude light on her face, could have said that she had been the most beautiful woman in the world. When he examined her enough to be sure that he had never seen her before, he turned out the light.

"The only thing I know for sure is that you're not the Virgin of Perpetual Help."

"Quite the contrary," the grandmother said with a very sweet voice. "I'm the Lady."

The man put his hand to his pistol out of pure instinct.

"What lady?"

"Big Amadís's."

"Then you're not of this world," he said, tense. "What is it you want?"

"For you to help me rescue my granddaughter, Big Amadís's granddaughter, the daughter of our son Amadís, held captive in that mission."

The man overcame his fear.

"You knocked on the wrong door," he said. "If you think we're about to get mixed up in God's affairs, you're not the one you say you are, you never knew the Amadíses, and you haven't got the whoriest notion of what smuggling's all about."

Early that morning the grandmother slept less than before. She lay awake pondering things, wrapped in a wool blanket while the early hour got her memory all mixed up and the repressed raving struggled to get out even though she was awake, and she had to tighten her heart with her hand so as not to be suffocated by the memory of a house by the sea with great red flowers where she had been happy. She remained that way until the mission bell rang and the first lights went on in the windows and the desert became saturated with the smell of the hot bread of matins. Only then did she abandon her fatigue, tricked by the illusion that Eréndira had got up and was looking for a way to escape and come back to her.

Eréndira, however, had not lost a single night's sleep since they had taken her to the mission. They had cut her hair with pruning shears until her head was like a brush, they put a hermit's rough cassock on her and gave her a bucket of whitewash and a broom so that she could whitewash the stairs every time someone went up or down. It was mule work because there was an incessant coming and going of muddied missionaries and novice carriers, but Eréndira felt as if every day were Sunday after the fearsome galley that had been her bed. Besides, she wasn't the only one worn out at night, because the mission was dedicated to fighting not against the devil but against the desert. Eréndira had seen the Indian novices bulldogging cows in the barn in order to milk them, jumping up and down on planks for days on end in order to press cheese, helping a

goat through a difficult birth. She had seen them sweat like tanned steve-
dores hauling water from the cistern, watering by hand a bold garden that
other novices cultivated with hoes in order to plant vegetables in the
flintstone of the desert. She had seen the earthly inferno of the ovens for
baking bread and the rooms for ironing clothes. She had seen a nun chase
a pig through the courtyard, slide along holding the runaway animal by
the ears, and roll in a mud puddle without letting go until two novices in
leather aprons helped her get it under control and one of them cut its
throat with a butcher knife as they all became covered with blood and
mire. In the isolation ward of the infirmary she had seen tubercular nuns
in their nightgown shrouds, waiting for God's last command as they embroidered bridal sheets on the terraces while the men preached in the
desert. Eréndira was living in her shadows and discovering other forms of
beauty and horror that she had never imagined in the narrow world of
her bed, but neither the coarsest nor the most persuasive of the novices
had managed to get her to say a word since they had taken her to the
mission. One morning, while she was preparing the whitewash in her
bucket, she heard string music that was like a light even more diaphanous
than the light of the desert. Captivated by the miracle, she peeped into
an immense and empty salon with bare walls and large windows through
which the dazzling June light poured in and remained still, and in the
center of the room she saw a very beautiful nun whom she had never seen
before playing an Easter oratorio on the clavichord. Eréndira listened to
the music without blinking, her heart hanging by a thread, until the
lunch bell rang. After eating, while she whitewashed the stairs with her
reed brush, she waited until all the novices had finished going up and
coming down, and she was alone, with no one to hear her, and then she
spoke for the first time since she had entered the mission.

"I'm happy," she said.

So that put an end to the hopes the grandmother had that Eréndira
would run away to rejoin her, but she maintained her granite siege without having made any decision until Pentecost. During that time the missionaries were combing the desert in search of pregnant concubines in
order to get them married. They traveled all the way to the most remote
settlements in a broken-down truck with four well-armed soldiers and a
chest of cheap cloth. The most difficult part of that Indian hunt was to
convince the women, who defended themselves against divine grace with
the truthful argument that men, sleeping in their hammocks with legs
spread, felt they had the right to demand much heavier work from legitimate wives than from concubines. It was necessary to seduce them with
trickery, dissolving the will of God in the syrup of their own language so
that it would seem less harsh to them, but even the most crafty of them
ended up being convinced by a pair of flashy earrings. The men, on the
other hand, once the women's acceptance had been obtained, were
routed out of their hammocks with rifle butts, bound, and hauled away in
the back of the truck to be married by force.

For several days the grandmother saw the little truck loaded with pregnant Indian women heading for the mission, but she failed to recognize
her opportunity. She recognized it on Pentecost Sunday itself, when she
heard the rockets and the ringing of the bells and saw the miserable and
merry crowd that was going to the festival, and she saw that among the

crowds there were pregnant women with the veil and crown of a bride holding the arms of their casual mates, whom they would legitimize in the collective wedding.

Among the last in the procession a boy passed, innocent of heart, with gourd-cut Indian hair and dressed in rags, carrying an Easter candle with a silk bow in his hand. The grandmother called him over.

"Tell me something, son," she asked with her smoothest voice. "What part do you have in this affair?"

The boy felt intimidated by the candle and it was hard for him to close his mouth because of his donkey teeth.

"The priests are going to give me my first communion," he said.

"How much did they pay you?"

"Five pesos."

The grandmother took a roll of bills from her pouch and the boy looked at them with surprise.

"I'm going to give you twenty," the grandmother said. "Not for you to make your first communion, but for you to get married."

"Who to?"

"My granddaughter."

So Eréndira was married in the courtyard of the mission in her hermit's cassock and a silk shawl that the novices gave her, and without even knowing the name of the groom her grandmother had bought for her. With uncertain hope she withstood the torment of kneeling on the saltpeter ground, the goat-hair stink of the two hundred pregnant brides, the punishment of the Epistle of Saint Paul hammered out in Latin under the motionless and burning sun, because the missionaries had found no way to oppose the wile of that unforeseen marriage, but had given her a promise as a last attempt to keep her in the mission. Nevertheless, after the ceremony in the presence of the apostolic prefect, the military mayor who shot at the clouds, her recent husband, and her impassive grandmother, Eréndira found herself once more under the spell that had dominated her since birth. When they asked her what her free, true, and definitive will was, she didn't even give a sigh of hesitation.

"I want to leave," she said. And she clarified things by pointing at her husband. "But not with him, with my grandmother."

Ulises had wasted a whole afternoon trying to steal an orange from his father's grove, because the older man wouldn't take his eyes off him while they were pruning the sick trees, and his mother kept watch from the house. So he gave up his plan, for that day at least, and grudgingly helped his father until they had pruned the last orange trees.

The extensive grove was quiet and hidden, and the wooden house with a tin roof had copper grating over the windows and a large porch set on pilings, with primitive plants bearing intense flowers. Ulises' mother was on the porch sitting back in a Viennese rocking chair[7] with smoked leaves on her temples to relieve her headache, and her full-blooded-Indian look followed her son like a beam of invisible light to the most remote corners of the orange grove. She was quite beautiful, much younger than her husband, and not only did she still wear the garb of her tribe, but she knew the most ancient secrets of her blood.

---

7. One with back and seat made of tied straw.

When Ulises returned to the house with the pruning tools, his mother asked him for her four o'clock medicine, which was on a nearby table. As soon as he touched them, the glass and the bottle changed color. Then, out of pure play, he touched a glass pitcher that was on the table beside some tumblers and the pitcher also turned blue. His mother observed him while she was taking her medicine and when she was sure that it was not a delirium of her pain, she asked him in the Guajiro Indian language:

"How long has that been happening to you?"

"Ever since we came back from the desert," Ulises said, also in Guajiro. "It only happens with glass things."

In order to demonstrate, one after the other he touched the glasses that were on the table and they all turned different colors.

"Those things happen only because of love," his mother said. "Who is it?"

Ulises didn't answer. His father, who couldn't understand the Guajiro language, was passing by the porch at that moment with a cluster of oranges.

"What are you two talking about?" he asked Ulises in Dutch.

"Nothing special," Ulises answered.

Ulises' mother didn't know any Dutch. When her husband went into the house, she asked her son in Guajiro:

"What did he say?"

"Nothing special," Ulises answered.

He lost sight of his father when he went into the house, but he saw him again through a window of the office. The mother waited until she was alone with Ulises and then repeated:

"Tell me who it is."

"It's nobody," Ulises said.

He answered without paying attention because he was hanging on his father's movements in the office. He had seen him put the oranges on top of the safe when he worked out the combination. But while he was keeping an eye on his father, his mother was keeping an eye on him.

"You haven't eaten any bread for a long time," she observed.

"I don't like it."

The mother's face suddenly took on an unaccustomed liveliness. "That's a lie," she said. "It's because you're lovesick and people who are lovesick can't eat bread." Her voice, like her eyes, had passed from entreaty to threat.

"It would be better if you told me who it was," she said, "or I'll make you take some purifying baths."

In the office the Dutchman opened the safe, put the oranges inside, and closed the armoured door. Ulises moved away from the window then and answered his mother impatiently.

"I already told you there wasn't anyone," he said. "If you don't believe me, ask Papa."

The Dutchman appeared in the office doorway lighting his sailor's pipe and carrying his threadbare Bible under his arm. His wife asked him in Spanish:

"Who did you meet in the desert?"

"Nobody," her husband answered, a little in the clouds. "If you don't believe me, ask Ulises."

He sat down at the end of the hall and sucked on his pipe until the tobacco was used up. Then he opened the Bible at random and recited spot passages for almost two hours in flowing and ringing Dutch.

At midnight Ulises was still thinking with such intensity that he couldn't sleep. He rolled about in his hammock for another hour, trying to overcome the pain of memories until the very pain gave him the strength he needed to make a decision. Then he put on his cowboy pants, his plaid shirt, and his riding boots, jumped through the window, and fled from the house in the truck loaded with birds. As he went through the groves he picked the three ripe oranges he had been unable to steal that afternoon.

He traveled across the desert for the rest of the night and at dawn he asked in towns and villages about the whereabouts of Eréndira, but no one could tell him. Finally they informed him that she was traveling in the electoral campaign retinue of Senator Onésimo Sánchez and that on that day he was probably in Nueva Castilla.[8] He didn't find him there but in the next town and Eréndira was no longer with him, for the grandmother had managed to get the senator to vouch for her morality in a letter written in his own hand, and with it she was going about opening the most tightly barred doors in the desert. On the third day he came across the domestic mailman and the latter told him what direction to follow.

"They're heading toward the sea," he said, "and you'd better hurry because the goddamned old woman plans to cross over to the island of Aruba."[9]

Following that direction, after half a day's journey Ulises spotted the broad, stained tent that the grandmother had bought from a bankrupt circus. The wandering photographer had come back to her, convinced that the world was really not as large as he had thought, and he had set up his idyllic backdrops near the tent. A band of brass-blowers was captivating Eréndira's clientele with a taciturn waltz.

Ulises waited for his turn to go in, and the first thing that caught his attention was the order and cleanliness of the inside of the tent. The grandmother's bed had recovered its viceregal splendor, the statue of the angel was in its place beside the funerary trunk of the Amadíses, and in addition, there was a pewter bathtub with lion's feet. Lying on her new canopied bed, Eréndira was naked and placid, irradiating a childlike glow under the light that filtered through the tent. She was sleeping with her eyes open. Ulises stopped beside her, the oranges in his hand, and he noticed that she was looking at him without seeing him. Then he passed his hand over her eyes and called her by the name he had invented when he wanted to think about her:

"Arídnere."[1]

Eréndira woke up. She felt naked in front of Ulises, let out a squeak, and covered herself with the sheet up to her neck.

"Don't look at me," she said. "I'm horrible."

"You're the color of an orange all over," Ulises said. He raised the fruits to her eyes so that she could compare. "Look."

8. New Castile (after the province in Spain).
9. Off the coast of Venezuela, and about eighty miles from the Península de la Guajira.

1. *Eréndira* backwards; the root of the name means "dryness, aridity."

Eréndira uncovered her eyes and saw that indeed the oranges did have her color.

"I don't want you to stay now," she said.

"I only came to show you this," Ulises said. "Look here."

He broke open an orange with his nails, split it in two with his hands, and showed Eréndira what was inside: stuck in the heart of the fruit was a genuine diamond.

"These are the oranges we take across the border," he said.

"But they're living oranges!" Eréndira exclaimed.

"Of course." Ulises smiled. "My father grows them."

Eréndira couldn't believe it. She uncovered her face, took the diamond in her fingers and contemplated it with surprise.

"With three like these we can take a trip around the world," Ulises said.

Eréndira gave him back the diamond with a look of disappointment. Ulises went on:

"Besides, I've got a pickup truck," he said. "And besides that . . . Look!"

From underneath his shirt he took an ancient pistol.

"I can't leave for ten years," Eréndira said.

"You'll leave," Ulises said. "Tonight, when the white whale falls asleep, I'll be outside there calling like an owl."

He made such a true imitation of the call of an owl that Eréndira's eyes smiled for the first time.

"It's my grandmother," she said.

"The owl?"

"The whale."

They both laughed at the mistake, but Eréndira picked up the thread again.

"No one can leave for anywhere without her grandmother's permission."

"There's no reason to say anything."

"She'll find out in any case," Eréndira said. "She can dream things."

"When she starts to dream that you're leaving we'll already be across the border. We'll cross over like smugglers," Ulises said.

Grasping the pistol with the confidence of a movie gunfighter, he imitated the sounds of the shots to excite Eréndira with his audacity. She didn't say yes or no, but her eyes gave a sigh and she sent Ulises away with a kiss. Ulises, touched, whispered:

"Tomorrow we'll be watching the ships go by."

That night, a little after seven o'clock, Eréndira was combing her grandmother's hair when the wind of her misfortune blew again. In the shelter of the tent were the Indian bearers and the leader of the brass band, waiting to be paid. The grandmother finished counting out the bills on a chest she had within reach, and after consulting a ledger she paid the oldest of the Indians.

"Here you are," she told him. "Twenty pesos for the week, less eight for meals, less three for water, less fifty cents on account for the new shirts, that's eight fifty. Count it."

The oldest Indian counted the money and they all withdrew with a bow.

"Thank you, white lady."

Next came the leader of the band. The grandmother consulted her ledger and turned to the photographer, who was trying to repair the bellows of his camera with wads of gutta-percha.

"What's it going to be?" she asked him. "Will you or won't you pay a quarter of the cost of the music?"

The photographer didn't even raise his head to answer.

"Music doesn't come out in pictures."

"But it makes people want to have their pictures taken," the grandmother answered.

"On the contrary," said the photographer. "It reminds them of the dead and then they come out in the picture with their eyes closed."

The bandleader intervened.

"What makes them close their eyes isn't the music," he said. "It's the lightning you make taking pictures at night."

"It's the music," the photographer insisted.

The grandmother put an end to the dispute. "Don't be a cheapskate," she said to the photographer. "Look how well things have been going for Senator Onésimo Sánchez and it's thanks to the musicians he has along." Then, in a harsh tone, she concluded:

"So pay what you ought to or go follow your fortune by yourself. It's not right for that poor child to carry the whole burden of expenses."

"I'll follow my fortune by myself," the photographer said. "After all, an artist is what I am."

The grandmother shrugged her shoulders and took care of the musician. She handed him a bundle of bills that matched the figure written in her ledger.

"Two hundred and fifty-four numbers," she told him. "At fifty cents apiece, plus thirty-two on Sundays and holidays at sixty cents apiece, that's one hundred fifty-six twenty."

The musician wouldn't accept the money.

"It's one hundred eighty-two forty," he said. "Waltzes cost more."

"Why is that?"

"Because they're sadder," the musician said.

The grandmother made him take the money.

"Well, this week you'll play us two happy numbers for each waltz I owe you for and we'll be even."

The musician didn't understand the grandmother's logic, but he accepted the figures while he unraveled the tangle. At that moment the fearsome wind threatened to uproot the tent, and in the silence that it left in its wake, outside, clear and gloomy, the call of an owl was heard.

Eréndira didn't know what to do to disguise her upset. She closed the chest with the money and hid it under the bed, but the grandmother recognized the fear in her hand when she gave her the key. "Don't be frightened," she told her. "There are always owls on windy nights." Still she didn't seem so convinced when she saw the photographer go out with the camera on his back.

"Wait till tomorrow if you'd like," she told him. "Death is on the loose tonight."

The photographer had also noticed the call of the owl, but he didn't change his intentions.

"Stay, son," the grandmother insisted. "Even if it's just because of the liking I have for you."

"But I won't pay for the music," the photographer said.

"Oh, no," the grandmother said. "Not that."

"You see?" the photographer said. "You've got no love for anybody."

The grandmother grew pale with rage.

"Then beat it!" she said. "You lowlife!"

She felt so outraged that she was still venting her rage on him while Eréndira helped her go to bed. "Son of an evil mother," she muttered. "What does that bastard know about anyone else's heart?" Eréndira paid no attention to her, because the owl was calling her with tenacious insistence during the pauses in the wind and she was tormented by uncertainty. The grandmother finally went to bed with the same ritual that had been *de rigueur* in the ancient mansion, and while her granddaughter fanned her she overcame her anger and once more breathed her sterile breath.

"You have to get up early," she said then, "so you can boil the infusion for my bath before the people get here."

"Yes, Grandmother."

"With the time you have left, wash the Indians' dirty laundry and that way we'll have something else to take off their pay next week."

"Yes, Grandmother," Eréndira said.

"And sleep slowly so that you won't get tired, because tomorrow is Thursday, the longest day of the week."

"Yes, Grandmother."

"And feed the ostrich."

"Yes, Grandmother," Eréndira said.

She left the fan at the head of the bed and lighted two altar candles in front of the chest with their dead. The grandmother, asleep now, was lagging behind with her orders.

"Don't forget to light the candles for the Amadíses."

"Yes, Grandmother."

Eréndira knew then that she wouldn't wake up, because she had begun to rave. She heard the wind barking about the tent, but she didn't recognize it as the wind of her misfortune that time either. She looked out into the night until the owl called again and her instinct for freedom in the end prevailed over her grandmother's spell.

She hadn't taken five steps outside the tent when she came across the photographer, who was lashing his equipment to the carrier of his bicycle. His accomplice's smile calmed her down.

"I don't know anything," the photographer said, "I haven't seen anything, and I won't pay for the music."

He took his leave with a blessing for all. Then Eréndira ran toward the desert, having decided once and for all, and she was swallowed up in the shadows of the wind where the owl was calling.

That time the grandmother went to the civil authorities at once. The commandment of the local detachment leaped out of his hammock at six in the morning when she put the senator's letter before his eyes. Ulises' father was waiting at the door.

"How in hell do you expect me to know what it says!" the commandant shouted. "I can't read."

"It's a letter of recommendation from Senator Onésimo Sánchez," the grandmother said.

Without further questions, the commandant took down a rifle he had near his hammock and began to shout orders to his men. Five minutes later they were all in a military truck flying toward the border against a contrary wind that had erased all trace of the fugitives. The commandant rode in the front seat beside the driver. In back were the Dutchman and the grandmother, with an armed policeman on each running board.

Close to town they stopped a convoy of trucks covered with waterproof canvases. Several men who were riding concealed in the rear raised the canvas and aimed at the small vehicle with machine guns and army rifles. The commandant asked the driver of the first truck how far back they had passed a farm truck loaded with birds.

The driver started up before he answered.

"We're not stool pigeons," he said indignantly, "we're smugglers."

The commandant saw the sooty barrels of the machine guns pass close to his eyes and he raised his arms and smiled.

"At least," he shouted at them, "you could have the decency not to go around in broad daylight."

The last truck had a sign on its rear bumper: I THINK OF YOU, ERÉNDIRA.

The wind became drier as they headed north and the sun was fiercer than the wind. It was hard to breathe because of the heat and dust inside the closed-in truck.

The grandmother was the first to spot the photographer: he was pedaling along in the same direction in which they were flying, with no protection against the sun except for a handkerchief tied around his head.

"There he is." She pointed. "He was their accomplice, the lowlife."

The commandant ordered one of the policemen on the running board to take charge of the photographer.

"Grab him and wait for us here," he said. "We'll be right back."

The policeman jumped off the running board and shouted twice for the photographer to halt. The photographer didn't hear him because of the wind blowing in the opposite direction. When the truck went on, the grandmother made an enigmatic gesture to him, but he confused it with a greeting, smiled, and waved. He didn't hear the shot. He flipped into the air and fell dead on top of his bicycle, his head blown apart by a rifle bullet, and he never knew where it came from.

Before noon they began to see feathers. They were passing by in the wind and they were feathers from young birds. The Dutchman recognized them because they were from his birds, plucked out by the wind. The driver changed direction, pushed the gas pedal to the floor, and in half an hour they could make out the pickup truck on the horizon.

When Ulises saw the military vehicle appear in the rear-view mirror, he made an effort to increase the distance between them, but the motor couldn't do any better. They had traveled with no sleep and were done in from fatigue and thirst. Eréndira, who was dozing on Ulises' shoulder, woke up in fright. She saw the truck that was about to overtake them and with innocent determination she took the pistol from the glove compartment.

"It's no good," Ulises said. "It used to belong to Sir Francis Drake."

She pounded it several times and threw it out the window. The military patrol passed the broken-down truck loaded with birds plucked by the wind, turned sharply, and cut it off.

It was around that time that I came to know them, their moment of greatest splendor, but I wouldn't look into the details of their lives until many years later when Rafael Escalona, in a song, revealed the terrible ending of the drama and I thought it would be good to tell the tale. I was traveling about selling encyclopedias and medical books in the province of Riohacha.[2] Álvaro Cepeda Samudio, who was also traveling in the region, selling beer-cooling equipment, took me through the desert towns in his truck with the intention of talking to me about something and we talked so much about nothing and drank so much beer that without knowing when or where we crossed the entire desert and reached the border. There was the tent of wandering love under hanging canvas signs: ERÉNDIRA IS BEST; LEAVE AND COME BACK—ERÉNDIRA WAITS FOR YOU; THERE'S NO LIFE WITHOUT ERÉNDIRA. The endless wavy line composed of men of diverse races and ranks looked like a snake with human vertebrae dozing through vacant lots and squares, through gaudy bazaars and noisy marketplaces, coming out of the streets of that city, which was noisy with passing merchants. Every street was a public gambling den, every house a saloon, every doorway a refuge for fugitives. The many undecipherable songs and the shouted offerings of wares formed a single roar of panic in the hallucinating heat.

Among the throng of men without a country and sharpers was Blacamán the Good, up on a table and asking for a real serpent in order to test an antidote of his invention on his own flesh. There was the woman who had been changed into a spider[3] for having disobeyed her parents, who would let herself be touched for fifty cents so that people would see there was no trick, and she would answer questions of those who might care to ask about her misfortune. There was an envoy from the eternal life who announced the imminent coming of the fearsome astral bat, whose burning brimstone breath would overturn the order of nature and bring the mysteries of the sea to the surface.

The one restful backwater was the red-light district, reached only by the embers of the urban din. Women from the four quadrants of the nautical rose[4] yawned with boredom in the abandoned cabarets. They had slept their siestas sitting up, unawakened by people who wanted them, and they were still waiting for the astral bat under the fans that spun on the ceilings. Suddenly one of them got up and went to a balcony with pots of pansies that overlooked the street. Down there the rows of Eréndira's suitors was passing.

"Come on," the woman shouted at them. "What's that one got that we don't have?"

"A letter from a senator," someone shouted.

Attracted by the shouts and the laughter, other women came out onto the balcony.

"The line's been like that for days," one of them said. "Just imagine, fifty pesos apiece."

---

2. Capital of the province of La Guajira, in northeastern Colombia. Rafael Escalona: Not identified, possibly fictitious.
3. The spider woman, Blacamán, and other elements appear elsewhere in García Márquez's fictional works, in the world of Macondo.
4. Compass card.

The one who had come out first made a decision:

"Well, I'm going to go find out what jewel that seven-month baby has got."

"Me, too," another said. "It'll be better than sitting here warming our chairs for free."

On the way others joined them and when they got to Eréndira's tent they made up a rowdy procession. They went in without any announcement, used pillows to chase away the man they found spending himself as best he could for his money, and they picked up Eréndira's bed and carried it out into the street like a litter.

"This is an outrage!" the grandmother shouted. "You pack of traitors, you bandits!" And then, turning to the men in line: "And you, you sissies, where do you keep your balls, letting this attack against a poor defenseless child go on? Damned fags!"

She kept on shouting as far as her voice would carry, distributing whacks with her crosier against all who came within reach, but her rage was inaudible amongst the shouts and mocking whistles of the crowd.

Eréndira couldn't escape the ridicule because she was prevented by the dog chain that the grandmother used to hitch her to a slat of the bed ever since she had tried to run away. But they didn't harm her. They exhibited her on the canopied altar along the noisiest streets like the allegorical passage of the enchained penitent and finally they set her down like a catafalque in the center of the main square. Eréndira was all coiled up, her face hidden, but not weeping, and she stayed that way under the terrible sun in the square, biting with shame and rage at the dog chain of her evil destiny until someone was charitable enough to cover her with a shirt.

That was the only time I saw them, but I found out that they had stayed in that border town under the protection of the public forces until the grandmother's chests were bursting and then they left the desert and headed toward the sea. Never had such opulence been seen gathered together in that realm of poor people. It was a procession of ox-drawn carts on which cheap replicas of the paraphernalia lost in the disaster of the mansion were piled, not just the imperial busts and rare clocks, but also a secondhand piano and a Victrola with a crank and the records of nostalgia. A team of Indians took care of the cargo and a band of musicians announced their triumphal arrival in the villages.

The grandmother traveled on a litter with paper wreaths, chomping on the grains in her pouch, in the shadow of a church canopy. Her monumental size had increased, because under her blouse she was wearing a vest of sailcloth in which she kept the gold bars the way one keeps cartridges in a bandoleer. Eréndira was beside her, dressed in gaudy fabrics and with trinkets hanging, but with the dog chain still on her ankle.

"You've got no reason to complain," her grandmother had said to her when they left the border town. "You've got the clothes of a queen, a luxurious bed, a musical band of your own, and fourteen Indians at your service. Don't you think that's splendid?"

"Yes, Grandmother."

"When you no longer have me," the grandmother went on, "you won't be left to the mercy of men because you'll have your own home in an important city. You'll be free and happy."

It was a new and unforeseen vision of the future. On the other hand, she no longer spoke about the original debt, whose details had become twisted and whose installments had grown as the costs of the business became more complicated. Still Eréndira didn't let slip any sigh that would have given a person a glimpse of her thoughts. She submitted in silence to the torture of the bed in the saltpeter pits, in the torpor of the lakeside towns, in the lunar craters of the talcum mines, while her grandmother sang the vision of the future to her as if she were reading cards. One afternoon, as they came out of an oppressive canyon, they noticed a wind of ancient laurels and they caught snatches of Jamaica conversations and felt an urge to live and a knot in their hearts. They had reached the sea.

"There it is," the grandmother said, breathing in the glassy light of the Caribbean after half a lifetime of exile. "Don't you like it?"

"Yes, Grandmother."

They pitched the tent there. The grandmother spent the night talking without dreaming and sometimes she mixed up her nostalgia with clairvoyance of the future. She slept later than usual and awoke relaxed by the sound of the sea. Nevertheless, when Eréndira was bathing her she again made predictions of the future and it was such a feverish clairvoyance that it seemed like the delirium of a vigil.

"You'll be a noble lady," she told her. "A lady of quality, venerated by those under your protection and favored and honored by the highest authorities. Ships' captains will send you postcards from every port in the world."

Eréndira wasn't listening to her. The warm water perfumed with oregano was pouring into the bathtub through a tube fed from outside. Eréndira picked it up in a gourd, impenetrable, not even breathing, and poured it over her grandmother with one hand while she soaped her with the other.

"The prestige of your house will fly from mouth to mouth from the string of the Antilles to the realm of Holland," the grandmother was saying. "And it will be more important than the presidential palace, because the affairs of government will be discussed there and the fate of the nation will be decided."

Suddenly the water in the tube stopped. Eréndira left the tent to find out what was going on and saw the Indian in charge of pouring water into the tube chopping wood by the kitchen.

"It ran out," the Indian said. "We have to cool more water."

Eréndira went to the stove, where there was another large pot with aromatic herbs boiling. She wrapped her hands in a cloth and saw that she could lift the pot without the help of the Indian.

"You can go," she told him. "I'll pour the water."

She waited until the Indian had left the kitchen. Then she took the boiling pot off the stove, lifted it with great effort to the height of the tube, and was about to pour the deadly water into the conduit to the bathtub when the grandmother shouted from inside the tent:

"Eréndira!"

It was as if she had seen. The granddaughter, frightened by the shout, repented at the last minute.

"Coming, Grandmother," she said. "I'm cooling off the water."

That night she lay thinking until quite late while her grandmother sang in her sleep, wearing the golden vest. Eréndira looked at her from her bed with intense eyes that in the shadows resembled those of a cat. Then she went to bed like a person who had drowned, her arms on her breast and her eyes open, and she called with all the strength of her inner voice: "Ulises!"

Ulises woke up suddenly in the house on the orange plantation. He had heard Eréndira's voice so clearly that he was looking for her in the shadows of the room. After an instant of reflection, he made a bundle of his clothing and shoes and left the bedroom. He had crossed the porch when his father's voice surprised him:

"Where are you going?"

Ulises saw him blue in the moonlight.

"Into the world," he answered.

"This time I won't stop you," the Dutchman said. "But I warn you of one thing: wherever you go your father's curse will follow you."

"So be it," said Ulises.

Surprised and even a little proud of his son's resolution, the Dutchman followed him through the orange grove with a look that slowly began to smile. His wife was behind him with her beautiful Indian woman's way of standing. The Dutchman spoke when Ulises closed the gate.

"He'll be back," he said, "beaten down by life, sooner than you think."

"You're so stupid," she sighed. "He'll never come back."

On that occasion Ulises didn't have to ask anyone where Eréndira was. He crossed the desert hiding in passing trucks, stealing to eat and sleep and stealing many times for the pure pleasure of the risk until he found the tent in another seaside town which the glass buildings gave the look of an illuminated city and where resounded the nocturnal farewells of ships weighing anchor for the island of Aruba. Eréndira was asleep chained to the slat and in the same position of a drowned person on the beach from which she had called him. Ulises stood looking at her for a long time without waking her up, but he looked at her with such intensity that Eréndira awoke. Then they kissed in the darkness, caressed each other slowly, got undressed wearily, with a silent tenderness and a hidden happiness that was more than ever like love.

At the other end of the tent the sleeping grandmother gave a monumental turn and began to rant.

"That was during the time the Greek ship arrived," she said. "It was a crew of madmen who made the women happy and didn't pay them with money but with sponges, living sponges that later on walked about the houses moaning like patients in a hospital and making the children cry so that they could drink the tears."

She made a subterranean movement and sat up in bed.

"That was when he arrived, my God," she shouted, "stronger, taller, and much more of a man than Amadís."

Ulises, who until then had not paid any attention to the raving, tried to hide when he saw the grandmother sitting up in bed. Eréndira calmed him.

"Take it easy," she told him. "Every time she gets to that part she sits up in bed, but she doesn't wake up."

Ulises leaned on her shoulder.

"I was singing with the sailors that night and I thought it was an earthquake," the grandmother went on. "They all must have thought the same thing because they ran away shouting, dying with laughter, and only he

remained under the starsong canopy. I remember as if it had been yesterday that I was singing the song that everyone was singing those days.
Even the parrots in the courtyard sang it."

Flat as a mat, as one can sing only in dreams, she sang the lines of her
bitterness:

> *Lord, oh, Lord, give me back the innocence I had*
> *So I can feel his love all over again from the start.*

Only then did Ulises become interested in the grandmother's nostalgia.

"There he was," she was saying, "with a macaw on his shoulder and a
cannibal-killing blunderbuss, the way Guatarral arrived in the Guianas,[5]
and I felt his breath of death when he stood opposite me and said: 'I've
been around the world a thousand times and seen women of every nation,
so I can tell you on good authority that you are the haughtiest and the
most obliging, the most beautiful woman on earth.' "

She lay down again and sobbed on her pillow. Ulises and Eréndira remained silent for a long time, rocked in the shadows by the sleeping old
woman's great breathing. Suddenly Eréndira, without the slightest quiver
in her voice, asked:

"Would you dare to kill her?"

Taken by surprise, Ulises didn't know what to answer.

"Who knows," he said. "Would you dare?"

"I can't," Eréndira said. "She's my grandmother."

Then Ulises looked once more at the enormous sleeping body as if
measuring its quantity of life and decided:

"For you I'd be capable of anything."

Ulises bought a pound of rat poison, mixed it with whipped cream and
raspberry jam, and poured that fatal cream into a piece of pastry from
which he had removed the original filling. Then he put some thicker
cream on top, smoothing it with a spoon until there was no trace of his
sinister maneuver, and he completed the trick with seventy-two little
pink candles.

The grandmother sat up on her throne waving her threatening crosier
when she saw him come into the tent with the birthday cake.

"You brazen devil!" she shouted. "How dare you set foot in this
place?"

Ulises hid behind his angel face.

"I've come to ask your forgiveness," he said, "on this day, your birthday."

Disarmed by his lie, which had hit its mark, the grandmother had the
table set as it for a wedding feast. She sat Ulises down on her right while
Eréndira served them, and after blowing out the candles with one devastating gust, she cut the cake into two equal parts. She served Ulises.

"A man who knows how to get himself forgiven has earned half of
heaven," she said. "I give you the first piece, which is the piece of happiness."

"I don't like sweet things," he said. "You take it."

The grandmother offered Eréndira a piece of cake. She took it into the
kitchen and threw it in the garbage.

The grandmother ate the rest all by herself. She put whole pieces into

5. Not identified, possibly fictitious.

her mouth and swallowed them without chewing, moaning with delight and looking at Ulises from the limbo of her pleasure. When there was no more on her plate she also ate what Ulises had turned down. While she was chewing the last bit, with her fingers she picked up the crumbs from the tablecloth and put them into her mouth.

She had eaten enough arsenic to exterminate a whole generation of rats. And yet she played the piano and sang until midnight, went to bed happy, and was able to have a normal sleep. The only thing new was a rocklike scratch in her breathing.

Eréndira and Ulises kept watch over her from the other bed, and they were only waiting for her death rattle. But the voice was as alive as ever when she began to rave.

"I went crazy, my God, I went crazy!" she shouted. "I put two bars on the bedroom door so he couldn't get in; I put the dresser and table against the door and the chairs on the table, and all he had to do was give a little knock with his ring for the defenses to fall apart, the chairs to fall off the table by themselves, the table and dresser to separate by themselves, the bars to move out of their slots by themselves."

Eréndira and Ulises looked at her with growing surprise as the delirium became more profound and dramatic and the voice more intimate.

"I felt I was going to die, soaked in the sweat of fear, begging inside for the door to open without opening, for him to enter without entering, for him never to go away but never to come back either so I wouldn't have to kill him!"

She went on repeating her drama for several hours, even the most intimate details, as if she had lived it again in her dream. A little before dawn she rolled over in bed with a movement of seismic accommodation and the voice broke with the imminence of sobs.

"I warned him and he laughed," she shouted. "I warned him again and he laughed again, until he opened his eyes in terror, saying, 'Agh, queen! Agh, queen!' and his voice wasn't coming out of his mouth but through the cut the knife had made in his throat."

Ulises, terrified at the grandmother's fearful evocation, grabbed Eréndira's hand.

"Murdering old woman!" he exclaimed.

Eréndira didn't pay any attention to him because at that instant dawn began to break. The clocks struck five.

"Go!" Eréndira said. "She's going to wake up now."

"She's got more life in her than an elephant," Ulises exclaimed. "It can't be!"

Eréndira cut him with a knifing look.

"The whole trouble," she said, "is that you're no good at all for killing anybody."

Ulises was so affected by the crudeness of the reproach that he left the tent. Eréndira kept on looking at the sleeping grandmother with her secret hate, with the rage of her frustration, as the sun rose and the bird air awakened. Then the grandmother opened her eyes and looked at her with a placid smile.

"God be with you, child."

The only noticeable change was a beginning of disorder in the daily routine. It was Wednesday, but the grandmother wanted to put on a Sunday dress, decided that Eréndira would receive no customers before eleven o'clock, and asked her to paint her nails garnet and give her a pontifical coiffure.

"I never had so much of an urge to have my picture taken," she exclaimed.

Eréndira began to comb her grandmother's hair, but as she drew the comb through the tangles a clump of hair remained between the teeth. She showed it to her grandmother in alarm. The grandmother examined it, pulled on another clump with her fingers, and another bush of hair was left in her hand. She threw it on the ground, tried again and pulled out a larger lock. Then she began to pull her hair with both hands, dying with laughter, throwing the handfuls into the air with an incomprehensible jubliation until her head looked like a peeled coconut.

Eréndira had no more news of Ulises until two weeks later when she caught the call of the owl outside the tent. The grandmother had begun to play the piano and was so absorbed in her nostalgia that she was unaware of reality. She had a wig of radiant feathers on her head.

Eréndira answered the call and only then did she notice the wick that came out of the piano and went on through the underbrush and was lost in the darkness. She ran to where Ulises was, hid next to him among the bushes, and with tight hearts they both watched the little blue flame that crept along the wick, crossed the dark space, and went into the tent.

"Cover your ears," Ulises said.

They both did, without any need, for there was no explosion. The tent lighted up inside with a radiant glow, burst in silence, and disappeared in a whirlwind of wet powder. When Eréndira dared enter, thinking that her grandmother was dead, she found her with her wig singed and her nightshirt in tatters, but more alive than ever, trying to put out the fire with a blanket.

Ulises slipped away under the protection of the shouts of the Indians, who didn't know what to do, confused by the grandmother's contradictory orders. When they finally managed to conquer the flames and get rid of the smoke, they were looking at a shipwreck.

"It's like the work of the evil one," the grandmother said. "Pianos don't explode just like that."

She made all kinds of conjectures to establish the causes of the new disaster, but Eréndira's evasions and her impassive attitude ended up confusing her. She couldn't find the slightest crack in her granddaughter's behavior, nor did she consider the existence of Ulises. She was awake until dawn, threading suppositions together and calculating the loss. She slept little and poorly. On the following morning, when Eréndira took the vest with the gold bars off her grandmother, she found fire blisters on her shoulders and raw flesh on her breast. "I had good reason to be turning over in my sleep," she said as Eréndira put egg whites on the burns. "And besides, I had a strange dream." She made an effort at concentration to evoke the image until it was as clear in her memory as in the dream.

"It was a peacock in a white hammock," she said.

Eréndira was surprised but she immediately assumed her everyday expression once more.

"It's a good sign," she lied. "Peacocks in dreams are animals with long lives."

"May God hear you," the grandmother said, "because we're back where we started. We have to begin all over again."

Eréndira didn't change her expression. She went out of the tent with the plate of compresses and left her grandmother with her torso soaked in egg white and her skull daubed with mustard. She was putting more egg whites in the plate under the palm shelter that served as a kitchen when she saw Ulises' eyes appear behind the stove as she had seen them the first time behind the bed. She wasn't startled, but told him in a weary voice:

"The only thing you've managed to do is increase my debt."

Ulises' eyes clouded over with anxiety. He was motionless, looking at Eréndira in silence, watching her crack the eggs with a fixed expression of absolute disdain, as if he didn't exist. After a moment the eyes moved, looked over the things in the kitchen, the hanging pots, the strings of annatto, the carving knife. Ulises stood up, still not saying anything, went in under the shelter, and took down the knife.

Eréndira didn't look at him again, but when Ulises left the shelter she told him in a very low voice:

"Be careful, because she's already had a warning of death. She dreamed about a peacock in a white hammock."

The grandmother saw Ulises come in with the knife, and making a supreme effort, she stood up without the aid of her staff and raised her arms.

"Boy!" she shouted. "Have you gone mad?"

Ulises jumped on her and plunged the knife into her naked breast. The grandmother moaned, fell on him, and tried to strangle him with her powerful bear arms.

"Son of a bitch," she growled. "I discovered too late that you have the face of a traitor angel."

She was unable to say anything more because Ulises managed to free the knife and stab her a second time in the side. The grandmother let out a hidden moan and hugged her attacker with more strength. Ulises gave her a third stab, without pity, and a spurt of blood, released by high pressure, sprinkled his face: it was oily blood, shiny and green, just like mint honey.

Eréndira appeared at the entrance with the plate in her hand and watched the struggle with criminal impassivity.

Huge, monolithic, roaring with pain and rage, the grandmother grasped Ulises' body. Her arms, her legs, even her hairless skull were green with blood. Her enormous bellows-breathing, upset by the first rattles of death, filled the whole area. Ulises managed to free his arm with the weapon once more, opened a cut in her belly, and an explosion of blood soaked him in green from head to toe. The grandmother tried to reach the open air which she needed in order to live now and fell face down. Ulises got away from the lifeless arms and without pausing a moment gave the vast fallen body a final thrust.

Eréndira then put the plate on a table and leaned over her grandmother, scrutinizing her without touching her. When she was convinced that she was dead her face suddenly acquired all the maturing of an older person which her twenty years of misfortune had not given her. With quick and precise movements she grabbed the gold vest and left the tent.

Ulises remained sitting by the corpse, exhausted by the fight, and the more he tried to clean his face the more it was daubed with the green and living matter that seemed to be flowing from his fingers. Only when he saw Eréndira go out with the gold vest did he become aware of his state.

He shouted to her but got no answer. He dragged himself to the entrance to the tent and he saw Eréndira starting to run along the shore away from the city. Then he made a last effort to chase her, calling her with painful shouts that were no longer those of a lover but of a son, yet he was overcome by the terrible drain of having killed a woman without anybody's help. The grandmother's Indians caught up to him lying face down on the beach, weeping from solitude and fear.

Eréndira had not heard him. She was running into the wind, swifter than a deer, and no voice of this world could stop her. Without turning her head she ran past the saltpeter pits, the talcum craters, the torpor of the shacks, until the natural science of the sea ended and the desert began, but she still kept on running with the gold vest beyond the arid winds and the never-ending sunsets and she was never heard of again nor was the slightest trace of her misfortune ever found.

1972

AFTERWORD

The title warns us that García Márquez's story will be incredible, and *that* it certainly.is. Unlike Kafka's novel, which began with the fantastic proposition that the protagonist woke one morning to find he was an insect, there is nothing fantastic or clearly surreal in the first sentence, paragraph, or "chapter"—that is, to the break on page 548 after the knocking over of the candle (I shall call the sections marked by breaks "Chapters"). This is not to say that all is ordinary. The concrete mansion in the desert, complete with ostrich, marble tub, statues of fictional Caesars, and so many clocks of all shapes and sizes that it takes six hours just to wind them; the grandmother huge as a whale, grossly tattooed, decked out like a doll, dining alone at a banquet table for twelve with silver candlesticks, giving orders even in her sleep and dreaming deliriously; even Eréndira's working in her sleep, are not your run-of-the-mill everyday setting, situation, and cast of characters, exactly. Still, there is nothing here so improbable as to be "incredible." (The reference to the goats' committing suicide may be taken as hyperbolic or figurative.)

The second chapter (to the appearance of Ulises) is also bizarre, a bit more surreal, but not yet fantastic. Still, how do you read this sentence: "Over the whistle of the storm and the lash of the water one could hear distant shouts, the howling of far-off animals, the cries of a shipwreck"? Or this passage: "Eréndira then succumbed to terror, lost consciousness, and remained as if fascinated by the moonbeams from a fish that was floating through the storm air . . ."? Does she merely remain as if fascinated at a fish really flying through the air, or fascinated as if by a fish flying. . .? By the end of the third chapter we are at or over the border of fantasy: Ulises looks like a furtive angel and the grandmother asks him where his wings are; it isn't he, he says, but his grandfather who is the winged one; he cannot walk on water, but his father knew a man who could. Still, like the oranges that Ulises says are worth 50,000 pesos, these are all reports or superstitions; nothing incredible has yet happened on the literal surface in the action of the story.

Perhaps we've all heard of mayors who have done rather less reasonable things than shoot at clouds to bring rain (Chapter 4), but in Chapter 5 Ulises the angel is changing the color of everything glass that he touches. Perhaps we find that fantastic, but his Indian mother accepts it as a familiar symptom of being in love. This first bit of "on-stage," verified fantasy on the surface of the narrative occurs in the middle of the novel; in the next chapter (the sixth of seven) the fantastic comes to the fore: the woman who has been turned into a spider (or is this just a carnival stunt?); Eréndira calling Ulises in the night across miles and miles, summoning him to her (but remember *Jane Eyre*); the sponges that walk around the house moaning, making the children cry and drinking their tears (but that's just the crazy grandmother remembering—or fantasizing—in her dreams again); the grandmother's surviving the huge dose of arsenic and the dynamite blast (almost like the coyote or cat in cartoons), and then the final horrible scene with its torrents of green blood. That, surely, is incredible.

Kafka proceeds logically, even realistically after his opening sentence: if we accept Gregor Samsa's metamorphosis, all else in the story follows. Here we begin with the extraordinary, with what seems like exaggeration or distortion of reality but not with the wholly impossible or incredible, and we are led deeper and deeper into the fantastic world of García Márquez's Macondo.

How do we take such a story? As a fairy tale with an innocent heroine, wicked grand- (not step-) mother, and occasional "magic"? As a folk tale or legend? If we want to reduce Kafka to the mundane and rational we treat his world as allegorically or psychologically symbolic. I don't think many readers do this sort of thing with García Márquez. We either reject it, or we accept it as an imaginative creation without any paraphrasable or interpretable meaning, as something outside the rules or "physics" of phenomenal reality. It is enough, perhaps, that it is the creation of a human mind and therefore part of human reality in the largest sense. The characters, moreover, have human traits, emotions, and, usually, responses, and the story creates in most readers feelings of considerable intensity.

What are those feelings, precisely? The title says the tale is "sad," and there's certainly enough unhappiness in the story to justify that part of the title. The heartless grandmother's exploitation of Eréndira even before the "misfortune" is pitiable. The list of Eréndira's duties, so overwhelming that she works even in her sleep, surely moves us despite—or perhaps more so because of—the girl's stoic acceptance of her lot. The grandmother's plan for making Eréndira pay her back for the losses incurred in the fire is disgusting; the image of Eréndira being led by the storekeeper who has bought her virginity "to the back room as if he were taking her to school" is wrenchingly pathetic. Eréndira endures her rape in a daze, benumbed, so we are spared the detailed account of her feelings; just as her first "misfortune," the burning-down of the mansion, occurs in the white space between the first two chapters, so the details of her sale to and use by all the men in the village passes in the silent space between paragraphs. Are our horror and pity made more or less intense by these stoic silences?

We do not get the full sense of Eréndira's pain until, in Chapter 3, she tells her grandmother she is dying, and when her heartless grandmother "consoles" her with the information that there are only ten more soldiers in line, "Eréndira began to weep with the shrieks of a frightened animal." When, later, the "mule work" endlessly whitewashing the busy stairs of the mission feels to her "as if every day were Sunday after the fearsome galley that had been her bed," we get a rare glimpse into her consciousness of her earlier oppression. During this "interlude," when she hears a nun playing an Easter oratorio on the clavichord, she speaks for the first time since leaving her grandmother: she says aloud that she's happy! Is this just inexpressibly sad? Does it make us furious at what has been done to her by emphasizing her "innocence"? Is it, possibly, exhilarating, a tribute to human endurance and the resiliency of the human spirit? Pathos, anger, horror, even exultation seem as commingled as the realistic, the extraordinary, and the fantastic in this novel.

As in *The Metamorphosis*, alternating and even mixed with the horror there also runs a bizarre streak of humor. The terrible and comic are mixed in the grandmother's shrewd wit in bargaining with the village shopkeeper over Eréndira's virginity: his low offer, she says, shows a lack of respect for virtue. More purely humorous is the musician's attempt to outwit the grandmother by claiming that waltzes cost more because they're sadder, only to be vanquished by her dizzying calculations. The grotesqueness of the moaning sponges and even of the grandmother's surviving the explosion is ludicrous, but the mixture of fantasy and humor has a tinge of feelings more sinister. The nun wrestling the pig begins as slapstick but ends with the pig's throat being cut. The horror of the photographer's head being blown apart is presented like a scene from a slapstick comedy in a silent film.

All of this, perhaps, prepares us for the climactic events of the story and its conclusion. Eréndira can stand her life no longer and calls Ulises to kill her grandmother but the heartless one seems invulnerable—arsenic results only in her loss of hair (compensated for by a wig of feathers!), the piano blast is ineffective. Finally, however, she and the story come to an end in a fantastic sea of green blood. Does that make the scene more horrible or less? funnier or nauseating? And how about Eréndira's taking off with the gold at the very end, skipping out on the angelic murderer Ulises? What are we to think of that? of her? of the novel? Is she no longer "innocent"? Is she now (has she always been?) like her grandmother (who was also a prostitute in her youth)? Where do you imagine she is? Is she off somewhere living a life of luxury? growing old and fat and being bathed in exotic and decadent surroundings by an overworked girl? Is she wandering in the desert laden with the vest of gold, mad and screaming? Has she died, or will she die there? We'll never know.

Why do we care? Is Eréndira a "real" person to us, despite the fantasy, the bewildering mix of emotional stimuli, the challenge to (if not an attack on) our sense of psychological and phenomenal reality, the orderliness of the universe? There is even an affront to conventional narrative decorum: Who is the book salesman who wanders into the story in the next-to-last chapter as a momentary first-person narrator and takes authority for reconstructing the story? It is from this narrator that we get some of the details from other García Márquez stories of Macondo—the spider-woman, for example. Does this remind us of the actual author and so undermine the authenticity of the story, or does it verify or substantiate that fictional world? If it is the first-person narrator's function to make the incredible a bit more credible, to "authenticate" it, why does he wander off again? Does this brief appearance not raise questions about the narration and thus call our attention to the novel as a fiction? Do we somehow find it wonderful (in the literal sense) and moving? Do we, because of its unreality, its fictionality, reduce it to the status of a fairy tale—"just a story"—or to a clever manipulation of narrative devices, a spoof on storytelling? García Márquez's fiction seems to raise some of the same questions that have been raised from time to time about the paintings of Picasso (or Salvador Dali, or perhaps Andy Warhol). Are modern audiences too sophisticated to believe fictions to be real or to be fooled by what Henry James called "the illusion of reality," or has modern reality become so bizarre, the actions of supposedly sane and civilized men and nations so irrational, that only fantasy seems real?

TONI MORRISON

Sula

When you are enthusiastic about a writer who is still in mid-career, who is known but whose name is not yet a household word, whose third novel, *Song of Solomon,* won the National Book Critics' Award as the best work of fiction in 1977, but who is not yet an inevitable part of the college curriculum, subject for doctoral dissertations, or fixture in anthologies, it is difficult not to sound as if you are writing a blurb for a dust-jacket.

Toni Morrison was born on February 18, 1931, in Lorain, Ohio, as Chloe Anthony Wofford. She has a B.A. from Howard University and an M.A. from Cornell, has taught at Texas Southern University, Howard, Yale, and Bard College. She is a senior editor at Random House, having worked as a textbook editor for one of their subsidiaries soon after she left Howard and her marriage in 1964. Her first novel, *The Bluest Eye* (1970), was well received by the critics and *Sula* (1974) was widely acclaimed. Though she was taken seriously by the critics—being compared to such established writers as Vladimir Nabokov and Doris Lessing—her first truly popular success was *Song of Solomon* (1977). The eagerly awaited *Tar Baby* was published in 1981.

Sula was named an alternate Book-of-the-Month Club selection, was condensed in *Redbook,* and was nominated for the 1975 National Book Award in fiction. Like all her novels to date, *Sula* is about the experience of black Americans—their history and mythology, their contemporary reality, mores, and methods of coping as a visible and exploited minority. *Sula* is also about Sula, an individual—black, female, growing up in the Midwest between the World Wars: all of these, but also herself. It is also about her friend Nel—black, female, growing up in the Midwest between the wars, but as different from Sula in the life she chooses and the values she holds as two people can be. Or is she?

Just as *Daisy Miller* is the object of that short novel and, as it turns out, Winterbourne the subject, so Sula moves from subject to object and toward the end it is Nel whose examined life we are closer to. Are Nel and Sula doubles? mirror images? Jekyll and Hyde? Like *Old Mortality,* the chapters are dated rather than titled and the action spreads over years; both novels are one woman's quest to understand another woman, and herself, and are images of complex, traditional societies seen changing and enduring over time. Sula even has an awakening in New Orleans, coincidentally a site the three women novelists here represented all use. Like *Goodbye, Columbus,* this is a novel of cultural transition. Is the price of survival, much less success, worth the cost? Toni Morrison explores not only the cost of rebellion or difference for Sula—as James does for Daisy, Chopin for Edna, and Porter for Amy—but the hidden cost few explore: that of living according to traditional values. In this last, most recent short novel in the collection, many of the themes, issues, and structures represented in the earlier selections emerge from rich new experiences and are embodied in a supple lyric prose with compelling narrative interest to create a new vision. When an interviewer recently asked her to describe what is distinctive about her fiction, Toni Morrison replied: "The language, only the language. The language must be careful and must appear effortless. It must not sweat."

Sula

> "Nobody knew my rose of the world
> but me. . . . I had too much glory.
> They don't want glory like that
> in nobody's heart."
> —The Rose Tattoo[1]

Part One

IN THAT PLACE, where they tore the nightshade and blackberry patches from their roots to make room for the Medallion City Golf Course, there was once a neighborhood. It stood in the hills above the valley town of Medallion and spread all the way to the river. It is called the suburbs now, but when black people lived there it was called the Bottom. One road, shaded by beeches, oaks, maples and chestnuts, connected it to the valley. The beeches are gone now, and so are the pear trees where children sat and yelled down through the blossoms to passersby. Generous funds have been allotted to level the stripped and faded buildings that clutter the road from Medallion up to the golf course. They are going to raze the Time and a Half Pool Hall, where feet in long tan shoes once pointed down from chair rungs. A steel ball will knock to dust Irene's Palace of Cosmetology, where women used to lean their heads back on sink trays and doze while Irene lathered Nu Nile into their hair. Men in khaki work clothes will pry loose the slats of Reba's Grill, where the owner cooked in her hat because she couldn't remember the ingredients without it.

There will be nothing left of the Bottom (the footbridge that crossed the river is already gone), but perhaps it is just as well, since it wasn't a town anyway: just a neighborhood where on quiet days people in valley houses could hear singing sometimes, banjos sometimes, and, if a valley man happened to have business up in those hills—collecting rent or insurance payments—he might see a dark woman in a flowered dress doing a bit of cakewalk, a bit of black bottom,[2] a bit of "messing around" to the lively notes of a mouth organ. Her bare feet would raise the saffron dust that floated down on the coveralls and bunion-split shoes of the man breathing music in and out of his harmonica. The black people watching her would laugh and rub their knees, and it would be easy for the valley man to hear the laughter and not notice the adult pain that rested somewhere under the eyelids, somewhere under their head rags and soft felt hats, somewhere in the palm of the hand, somewhere behind the frayed lapels, somewhere in the sinew's curve. He'd have to stand in the back of Greater Saint Matthew's and let the tenor's voice dress him in silk, or touch the hands of the spoon carvers (who had not worked in eight years) and let the fingers that danced on wood kiss his skin. Otherwise the pain would escape him even though the laughter was part of the pain.

A shucking, knee-slapping, wet-eyed laughter that could even describe

---

1. 1951 play by Tennessee Williams (b. 1911).
2. The cakewalk was a syncopated dance that originated among southern blacks in the 1890s and was popular through the 1920s, the black bottom from the 1920s through the 1930s.

and explain how they came to be where they were.

A joke. A nigger joke. That was the way it got started. Not the town, of course, but that part of town where the Negroes lived, the part they called the Bottom in spite of the fact that it was up in the hills. Just a nigger joke. The kind white folks tell when the mill closes down and they're looking for a little comfort somewhere. The kind colored folks tell on themselves when the rain doesn't come, or comes for weeks, and they're looking for a little comfort somehow.

A good white farmer promised freedom and a piece of bottom land to his slave if he would perform some very difficult chores. When the slave completed the work, he asked the farmer to keep his end of the bargain. Freedom was easy—the farmer had no objection to that. But he didn't want to give up any land. So he told the slave that he was very sorry that he had to give him valley land. He had hoped to give him a piece of the Bottom. The slave blinked and said he thought valley land was bottom land. The master said, "Oh, no! See those hills? That's bottom land, rich and fertile."

"But it's high up in the hills," said the slave.

"High up from us," said the master, "but when God looks down, it's the bottom. That's why we call it so. It's the bottom of heaven—best land there is."

So the slave pressed his master to try to get him some. He preferred it to the valley. And it was done. The nigger got the hilly land, where planting was backbreaking, where the soil slid down and washed away the seeds, and where the wind lingered all through the winter.

Which accounted for the fact that white people lived on the rich valley floor in that little river town in Ohio, and the blacks populated the hills above it, taking small consolation in the fact that every day they could literally look down on the white folks.

Still, it was lovely up in the Bottom. After the town grew and the farm land turned into a village and the village into a town and the streets of Medallion were hot and dusty with progress, those heavy trees that sheltered the shacks up in the Bottom were wonderful to see. And the hunters who went there sometimes wondered in private if maybe the white farmer was right after all. Maybe it was the bottom of heaven.

The black people would have disagreed, but they had no time to think about it. They were mightily preoccupied with earthly things—and each other, wondering even as early as 1920 what Shadrack was all about, what that little girl Sula who grew into a woman in their town was all about, and what they themselves were all about, tucked up there in the Bottom.

1919

Except for World War II, nothing ever interfered with the celebration of National Suicide Day. It had taken place every January third since 1920, although Shadrack, its founder, was for many years the only celebrant. Blasted and permanently astonished by the events of 1917, he had returned to Medallion handsome but ravaged, and even the most fastidious people in the town sometimes caught themselves dreaming of what he must have been like a few years back before he went off to war. A young man of hardly twenty, his head full of nothing and his mouth recalling the taste of lipstick, Shadrack had found himself in December,

1917, running with his comrades across a field in France. It was his first encounter with the enemy and he didn't know whether his company was running toward them or away. For several days they had been marching, keeping close to a stream that was frozen at its edges. At one point they crossed it, and no sooner had he stepped foot on the other side than the day was adangle with shouts and explosions. Shellfire was all around him, and though he knew that this was something called *it,* he could not muster up the proper feeling—the feeling that would accommodate *it.* He expected to be terrified or exhilarated—to feel *something* very strong. In fact, he felt only the bite of a nail in his boot, which pierced the ball of his foot whenever he came down on it. The day was cold enough to make his breath visible, and he wondered for a moment at the purity and whiteness of his own breath among the dirty, gray explosions surrounding him. He ran, bayonet fixed, deep in the great sweep of men flying across this field. Wincing at the pain in his foot, he turned his head a little to the right and saw the face of a soldier near him fly off. Before he could register shock, the rest of the soldier's head disappeared under the inverted soup bowl of his helmet. But stubbornly, taking no direction from the brain, the body of the headless soldier ran on, with energy and grace, ignoring altogether the drip and slide of brain tissue down its back.

When Shadrack opened his eyes he was propped up in a small bed. Before him on a tray was a large tin plate divided into three triangles. In one triangle was rice, in another meat, and in the third stewed tomatoes. A small round depression held a cup of whitish liquid. Shadrack stared at the soft colors that filled these triangles: the lumpy whiteness of rice, the quivering blood tomatoes, the grayish-brown meat. All their repugnance was contained in the neat balance of the triangles—a balance that soothed him, transferred some of its equilibrium to him. Thus reassured that the white, the red and the brown would stay where they were—would not explode or burst forth from their restricted zones—he suddenly felt hungry and looked around for his hands. His glance was cautious at first, for he had to be very careful—anything could be anywhere. Then he noticed two lumps beneath the beige blanket on either side of his hips. With extreme care he lifted one arm and was relieved to find his hand attached to his wrist. He tried the other and found it also. Slowly he directed one hand toward the cup and, just as he was about to spread his fingers, they began to grow in higgledy-piggledy fashion like Jack's beanstalk all over the tray and the bed. With a shriek he closed his eyes and thrust his huge growing hands under the covers. Once out of sight they seemed to shrink back to their normal size. But the yell had brought a male nurse.

"Private? We're not going to have any trouble today, are we? Are we, Private?"

Shadrack looked up at a balding man dressed in a green-cotton jacket and trousers. His hair was parted low on the right side so that some twenty or thirty yellow hairs could discreetly cover the nakedness of his head.

"Come on. Pick up that spoon. Pick it up, Private. Nobody is going to feed you forever."

Sweat slid from Shadrack's armpits down his sides. He could not bear to see his hands grow again and he was frightened of the voice in the apple-green suit.

"Pick it up, I said. There's no point to this . . ." The nurse reached under the cover for Shadrack's wrist to pull out the monstrous hand. Shadrack jerked it back and overturned the tray. In panic he raised himself to his knees and tried to fling off and away his terrible fingers, but succeeded only in knocking the nurse into the next bed.

When they bound Shadrack into a straitjacket, he was both relieved and grateful, for his hands were at last hidden and confined to whatever size they had attained.

Laced and silent in his small bed, he tried to tie the loose cords in his mind. He wanted desperately to see his own face and connect it with the word "private"—the word the nurse (and the others who helped bind him) had called him. "Private" he thought was something secret, and he wondered why they looked at him and called him a secret. Still, if his hands behaved as they had done, what might he expect from his face? The fear and longing were too much for him, so he began to think of other things. That is, he let his mind slip into whatever cave mouths of memory it chose.

He saw a window that looked out on a river which he knew was full of fish. Someone was speaking softly just outside the door . . .

Shadrack's earlier violence had coincided with a memorandum from the hospital executive staff in reference to the distribution of patients in high-risk areas. There was clearly a demand for space. The priority or the violence earned Shadrack his release, $217 in cash, a full suit of clothes and copies of very official-looking papers.

When he stepped out of the hospital door the grounds overwhelmed him: the cropped shrubbery, the edged lawns, the undeviating walks. Shadrack looked at the cement stretches: each one leading clearheadedly to some presumably desirable destination. There were no fences, no warnings, no obstacles at all between concrete and green grass, so one could easily ignore the tidy sweep of stone and cut out in another direction—a direction of one's own.

Shadrack stood at the foot of the hospital steps watching the heads of trees tossing ruefully but harmlessly, since their trunks were rooted too deeply in the earth to threaten him. Only the walks made him uneasy. He shifted his weight, wondering how he could get to the gate without stepping on the concrete. While plotting his course—where he would have to leap, where to skirt a clump of bushes—a loud guffaw startled him. Two men were going up the steps. Then he noticed that there were many people about, and that he was just now seeing them, or else they had just materialized. They were thin slips, like paper dolls floating down the walks. Some were seated in chairs with wheels, propelled by other paper figures from behind. All seemed to be smoking, and their arms and legs curved in the breeze. A good high wind would pull them up and away and they would land perhaps among the tops of the trees.

Shadrack took the plunge. Four steps and he was on the grass heading for the gate. He kept his head down to avoid seeing the paper people swerving and bending here and there, and he lost his way. When he looked up, he was standing by a low red building separated from the main building by a covered walkway. From somewhere came a sweetish smell which reminded him of something painful. He looked around for the gate and saw that he had gone directly away from it in his complicated journey over the grass. Just to the left of the low building was a graveled driveway that appeared to lead outside the grounds. He trotted quickly to it and left, at last, a haven of more than a year, only eight days of which he fully recollected.

Once on the road, he headed west. The long stay in the hospital had left him weak—too weak to walk steadily on the gravel shoulders of the road. He shuffled, grew dizzy, stopped for breath, started again, stumbling and sweating but refusing to wipe his temples, still afraid to look at his hands. Passengers in dark, square cars shuttered their eyes at what they took to be a drunken man.

The sun was already directly over his head when he came to a town. A few blocks of shaded streets and he was already at its heart—a pretty, quietly regulated downtown.

Exhausted, his feet clotted with pain, he sat down at the curbside to take off his shoes. He closed his eyes to avoid seeing his hands and fumbled with the laces of the heavy high-topped shoes. The nurse had tied them into a double knot, the way one does for children, and Shadrack, long unaccustomed to the manipulation of intricate things, could not get them loose. Uncoordinated, his fingernails tore away at the knots. He fought a rising hysteria that was not merely anxiety to free his aching feet; his very life depended on the release of the knots. Suddenly without raising his eyelids, he began to cry. Twenty-two years old, weak, hot, frightened, not daring to acknowledge the fact that he didn't even know who or what he was ... with no past, no language, no tribe, no source, no address book, no comb, no pencil, no clock, no pocket handkerchief, no rug, no bed, no can opener, no faded postcard, no soap, no key, no tobacco pouch, no soiled underwear and nothing nothing nothing to do ... he was sure of one thing only: the unchecked monstrosity of his hands. He cried soundlessly at the curbside of a small Midwestern town wondering where the window was, and the river, and the soft voices just outside the door ...

Through his tears he saw the fingers joining the laces, tentatively at first, then rapidly. The four fingers of each hand fused into the fabric, knotted themselves and zig-zagged in and out of the tiny eyeholes.

By the time the police drove up, Shadrack was suffering from a blinding headache, which was not abated by the comfort he felt when the policemen pulled his hands away from what he thought was a permanent entanglement with his shoelaces. They took him to jail, booked him for vagrancy and intoxication, and locked him in a cell. Lying on a cot, Shadrack could only stare helplessly at the wall, so paralyzing was the pain in his head. He lay in this agony for a long while and then realized he was staring at the painted-over letters of a command to fuck himself. He studied the phrase as the pain in his head subsided.

Like moonlight stealing under a window shade an idea insinuated itself: his earlier desire to see his own face. He looked for a mirror; there was none. Finally, keeping his hands carefully behind his back he made his way to the toilet bowl and peeped in. The water was unevenly lit by the sun so he could make nothing out. Returning to his cot he took the blanket and covered his head, rendering the water dark enough to see his reflection. There in the toilet water he saw a grave black face. A black so definite, so unequivocal, it astonished him. He had been harboring a skittish apprehension that he was not real—that he didn't exist at all. But

when the blackness greeted him with its indisputable presence, he
wanted nothing more. In his joy he took the risk of letting one edge of the
blanket drop and glanced at his hands. They were still. Courteously still.

Shadrack rose and returned to the cot, where he fell into the first sleep
of his new life. A sleep deeper than the hospital drugs; deeper than the
pits of plums, steadier than the condor's wing; more tranquil than the
curve of eggs.

The sheriff looked through the bars at the young man with the matted
hair. He had read through his prisoner's papers and hailed a farmer.
When Shadrack awoke, the sheriff handed him back his papers and
escorted him to the back of a wagon. Shadrack got in and in less than
three hours he was back in Medallion, for he had been only twenty-two
miles from his window, his river, and his soft voices just outside the door.

In the back of the wagon, supported by sacks of squash and hills of
pumpkins, Shadrack began a struggle that was to last for twelve days, a
struggle to order and focus experience. It had to do with making a place
for fear as a way of controlling it. He knew the smell of death and was
terrified of it, for he could not anticipate it. It was not death or dying
that frightened him, but the unexpectedness of both. In sorting it all out,
he hit on the notion that if one day a year were devoted to it, everybody
could get it out of the way and the rest of the year would be safe and
free. In this manner he instituted National Suicide Day.

On the third day of the new year, he walked through the Bottom down
Carpenter's Road with a cowbell and a hangman's rope calling the people
together. Telling them that this was their only chance to kill themselves
or each other.

At first the people in the town were frightened; they knew Shadrack
was crazy but that did not mean that he didn't have any sense or, even
more important, that he had no power. His eyes were so wild, his hair so
long and matted, his voice was so full of authority and thunder that he
caused panic on the first, or Charter, National Suicide Day in 1920. The
next one, in 1921, was less frightening but still worrisome. The people
had seen him a year now in between. He lived in a shack on the riverbank that had once belonged to his grandfather long time dead. On Tuesday and Friday he sold the fish he had caught that morning, the rest of
the week he was drunk, loud, obscene, funny and outrageous. But he
never touched anybody, never fought, never caressed. Once the people
understood the boundaries and nature of his madness, they could fit him,
so to speak, into the scheme of things.

Then, on subsequent National Suicide Days, the grown people looked
out from behind curtains as he rang his bell; a few stragglers increased
their speed, and little children screamed and ran. The tetter heads[3] tried
goading him (although he was only four or five years older than they) but
not for long, for his curses were stingingly personal.

As time went along, the people took less notice of these January thirds,
or rather they thought they did, thought they had no attitudes or feelings
one way or another about Shadrack's annual solitary parade. In fact they
had simply stopped remarking on the holiday because they had absorbed
it into their thoughts, into their language, into their lives.

3. Heads with itchy sores.

Someone said to a friend, "You sure was a long time delivering that baby. How long was you in labor?"

And the friend answered, " 'Bout three days. The pains started on Suicide Day and kept up till the following Sunday. Was borned on Sunday. All my boys is Sunday boys."

Some lover said to his bride-to-be, "Let's do it after New Years, 'stead of before. I get paid New Year's Eve."

And his sweetheart answered, "OK, but make sure it ain't on Suicide Day. I ain't 'bout to be listening to no cowbells whilst the weddin's going on."

Somebody's grandmother said her hens always started a laying of double yolks right after Suicide Day.

Then Reverend Deal took it up, saying the same folks who had sense enough to avoid Shadrack's call were the ones who insisted on drinking themselves to death or womanizing themselves to death. "May's well go on with Shad and save the Lamb the trouble of redemption."

Easily, quietly, Suicide Day became a part of the fabric of life up in the Bottom of Medallion, Ohio.

1920

It had to be as far away from the Sundown House as possible. And her grandmother's middle-aged nephew who lived in a Northern town called Medallion was the one chance she had to make sure it would be. The red shutters had haunted both Helene Sabat and her grandmother for sixteen years. Helene was born behind those shutters, daughter of a Creole whore who worked there. The grandmother took Helene away from the soft lights and flowered carpets of the Sundown House and raised her under the dolesome eyes of a multicolored Virgin Mary, counseling her to be constantly on guard for any sign of her mother's wild blood.

So when Wiley Wright came to visit his Great Aunt Cecile in New Orleans, his enchantment with the pretty Helene became a marriage proposal—under the pressure of both women. He was a seaman (or rather a lakeman, for he was a ship's cook on one of the Great Lakes lines), in port only three days out of every sixteen.

He took his bride to his home in Medallion and put her in a lovely house with a brick porch and real lace curtains at the window. His long absences were quite bearable for Helene Wright, especially when, after some nine years of marriage, her daughter was born.

Her daughter was more comfort and purpose than she had ever hoped to find in this life. She rose grandly to the occasion of motherhood—grateful, deep down in her heart, that the child had not inherited the great beauty that was hers: that her skin had dusk in it, that her lashes were substantial but not undignified in their length, that she had taken the broad flat nose of Wiley (although Helene expected to improve it somewhat) and his generous lips.

Under Helene's hand the girl became obedient and polite. Any enthusiasms that little Nel showed were calmed by the mother until she drove her daughter's imagination underground.

Helene Wright was an impressive woman, at least in Medallion she was. Heavy hair in a bun, dark eyes arched in a perpetual query about other people's manners. A woman who won all social battles with presence and a conviction of the legitimacy of her authority. Since there was no Catholic church in Medallion then, she joined the most conservative black church. And held sway. It was Helene who never turned her head in church when latecomers arrived; Helene who established the practice of seasonal altar flowers; Helene who introduced the giving of banquets of welcome to returning Negro veterans. She lost only one battle—the pronunciation of her name. The people in the Bottom refused to say Helene. They called her Helen Wright and left it at that.

All in all her life was a satisfactory one. She loved her house and enjoyed manipulating her daughter and her husband. She would sigh sometimes just before falling asleep, thinking that she had indeed come far enough away from the Sundown House.

So it was with extremely mixed emotions that she read a letter from Mr. Henri Martin describing the illness of her grandmother, and suggesting she come down right away. She didn't want to go, but could not bring herself to ignore the silent plea of the woman who had rescued her.

It was November. November, 1920.[4] Even in Medallion there was a victorious swagger in the legs of white men and a dull-eyed excitement in the eyes of colored veterans.

Helene thought about the trip South with heavy misgiving but decided that she had the best protection: her manner and her bearing, to which she would add a beautiful dress. She bought some deep-brown wool and three-fourths of a yard of matching velvet. Out of this she made herself a heavy but elegant dress with velvet collar and pockets.

Nel watched her mother cutting the pattern from newspapers and moving her eyes rapidly from a magazine model to her own hands. She watched her turn up the kerosene lamp at sunset to sew far into the night.

The day they were ready, Helene cooked a smoked ham, left a note for her lake-bound husband, in case he docked early, and walked head high and arms stiff with luggage ahead of her daughter to the train depot.

It was a longer walk than she remembered, and they saw the train steaming up just as they turned the corner. They ran along the track looking for the coach pointed out to them by the colored porter. Even at that they made a mistake. Helene and her daughter entered a coach peopled by some twenty white men and women. Rather than go back and down the three wooden steps again, Helene decided to spare herself some embarrassment and walk on through to the colored car. She carried two pieces of luggage and a string purse; her daughter carried a covered basket of food.

As they opened the door marked COLORED ONLY, they saw a white conductor coming toward them. It was a chilly day but a light skim of sweat glistened on the woman's face as she and the little girl struggled to hold the door open, hang on to their luggage and enter all at once. The conductor let his eyes travel over the pale yellow woman and then stuck his little finger into his ear, jiggling it free of wax. "What you think you doin', gal?"

Helene looked up at him.

So soon. So soon. She hadn't even begun the trip back. Back to her grandmother's house in the city where the red shutters glowed, and already she had been called "gal." All the old vulnerabilities, all the old

4. Second anniversary of the armistice ending World War I.

fears of being somehow flawed gathered in her stomach and made her hands tremble. She had heard only that one word; it dangled above her wide-brimmed hat, which had slipped, in her exertion, from its carefully leveled placement and was now tilted in a bit of a jaunt over her eye.

Thinking he wanted her tickets, she quickly dropped both the cowhide suitcase and the straw one in order to search for them in her purse. An eagerness to please and an apology for living met in her voice. "I have them. Right here somewhere, sir . . ."

The conductor looked at the bit of wax his fingernail had retrieved. "What was you doin' back in there? What was you doin' in that coach yonder?"

Helene licked her lips. "Oh . . . I . . . " Her glance moved beyond the white man's face to the passengers seated behind him. Four or five black faces were watching, two belonging to soldiers still in their shit-colored uniforms and peaked caps. She saw their closed faces, their locked eyes, and turned for compassion to the gray eyes of the conductor.

"We made a mistake, sir. You see, there wasn't no sign. We just got in the wrong car, that's all. Sir."

"We don't 'low no mistakes on this train. Now git your butt on in there."

He stood there staring at her until she realized that he wanted her to move aside. Pulling Nel by the arm, she pressed herself and her daughter into the foot space in front of a wooden seat. Then, for no earthly reason, at least no reason that anybody could understand, certainly no reason that Nel understood then or later, she smiled. Like a street pup that wags its tail at the very doorjamb of the butcher shop he has been kicked away from only moments before, Helene smiled. Smiled dazzlingly and coquettishly at the salmon-colored face of the conductor.

Nel looked away from the flash of pretty teeth to the other passengers. The two black soldiers, who had been watching the scene with what appeared to be indifference, now looked stricken. Behind Nel was the bright and blazing light of her mother's smile; before her the midnight eyes of the soldiers. She saw the muscles of their faces tighten, a movement under the skin from blood to marble. No change in the expression of the eyes, but a hard wetness that veiled them as they looked at the stretch of her mother's foolish smile.

As the door slammed on the conductor's exit, Helene walked down the aisle to a seat. She looked about for a second to see whether any of the men would help her put the suitcases in the overhead rack. Not a man moved. Helene sat down, fussily, her back toward the men. Nel sat opposite, facing both her mother and the soldiers, neither of whom she could look at. She felt both pleased and ashamed to sense that these men, unlike her father, who worshiped his graceful, beautiful wife, were bubbling with a hatred for her mother that had not been there in the beginning but had been born with the dazzling smile. In the silence that preceded the train's heave, she looked deeply at the folds of her mother's dress. There in the fall of the heavy brown wool she held her eyes. She could not risk letting them travel upward for fear of seeing that the hooks and eyes in the placket of the dress had come undone and exposed the custard-colored skin underneath. She stared at the hem, wanting to believe in its weight but knowing that custard was all that it hid. If this tall, proud woman, this woman who was very particular about her friends, who slipped into church with unequaled elegance, who could quell a roustabout with a look, if *she* were really custard, then there was a chance that Nel was too.

It was on that train, shuffling toward Cincinnati, that she resolved to be on guard—always. She wanted to make certain that no man ever looked at her that way. That no midnight eyes or marbled flesh would ever accost her and turn her into jelly.

For two days they rode; two days of watching sleet turn to rain, turn to purple sunsets, and one night knotted on the wooden seats (their heads on folded coats), trying not to hear the snoring soldiers. When they changed trains in Birmingham for the last leg of the trip, they discovered what luxury they had been in through Kentucky and Tennessee, where the rest stops had all had colored toilets. After Birmingham there were none. Helene's face was drawn with the need to relieve herself, and so intense was her distress she finally brought herself to speak about her problem to a black woman with four children who had got on in Tuscaloosa.

"Is there somewhere we can go to use the restroom?"

The woman looked up at her and seemed not to understand. "Ma'am?" Her eyes fastened on the thick velvet collar, the fair skin, the high-tone voice.

"The restroom," Helene repeated. Then, in a whisper, "The toilet."

The woman pointed out the window and said, "Yes, ma'am. Yonder."

Helene looked out of the window halfway expecting to see a comfort station in the distance; instead she saw gray-green trees leaning over tangled grass. "Where?"

"Yonder," the woman said. "Meridian. We be pullin' in direc'lin." Then she smiled sympathetically and asked, "Kin you make it?"

Helene nodded and went back to her seat trying to think of other things—for the surest way to have an accident would be to remember her full bladder.

At Meridian the women got out with their children. While Helene looked about the tiny stationhouse for a door that said COLORED WOMEN, the other woman stalked off to a field of high grass on the far side of the track. Some white men were leaning on the railing in front of the stationhouse. It was not only their tongues curling around toothpicks that kept Helene from asking information of them. She looked around for the other woman and, seeing just the top of her head rag in the grass, slowly realized where "yonder" was. All of them, the fat woman and her four children, three boys and a girl, Helene and her daughter, squatted there in the four o'clock Meridian sun. They did it again in Ellisville, again in Hattiesburg, and by the time they reached Slidell, not too far from Lake Pontchartrain, Helene could not only fold leaves as well as the fat woman, she never felt a stir as she passed the muddy eyes of the men who stood like wrecked Dorics[5] under the station roofs of those towns.

The lift in spirit that such an accomplishment produced in her quickly disappeared when the train finally pulled into New Orleans.

Cecile Sabat's house leaned between two others just like it on Elysian Fields. A Frenchified shotgun house,[6] it sported a magnificent garden in the back and a tiny wrought-iron fence in the front. On the door hung a

---

5. Heavy Greek columns.
6. House in which all the rooms are in line front to   back. Elysian Fields is a major street running through the poor section of New Orleans.

black crepe wreath with purple ribbon. They were too late. Helene
reached up to touch the ribbon, hesitated, and knocked. A man in a collarless shirt opened the door. Helene identified herself and he said he was
Henri Martin and that he was there for the settin'-up.[7] They stepped into
the house. The Virgin Mary clasped her hands in front of her neck three
times in the front room and once in the bedroom where Cecile's body lay.
The old woman had died without seeing or blessing her granddaughter.

No one other than Mr. Martin seemed to be in the house, but a sweet
odor as of gardenias told them that someone else had been. Blotting her
lashes with a white handkerchief, Helene walked through the kitchen to
the back bedroom where she had slept for sixteen years. Nel trotted along
behind, enchanted with the smell, the candles and the strangeness. When
Helene bent to loosen the ribbons of Nel's hat, a woman in a yellow dress
came out of the garden and onto the back porch that opened into the
bedroom. The two women looked at each other. There was no recognition
in the eyes of either. Then Helene said, "This is your . . . grandmother,
Nel." Nel looked at her mother and then quickly back at the door they
had just come out of.

"No. That was your great-grandmother. This is your grandmother. My
. . . mother."

Before the child could think, her words were hanging in the gardenia
air. "But she looks so young."

The woman in the canary-yellow dress laughed and said she was forty-
eight, "an old forty-eight."

Then it was she who carried the gardenia smell. This tiny woman with
the softness and glare of a canary. In that somber house that held four
Virgin Marys, where death sighed in every corner and candles sputtered,
the gardenia smell and canary-yellow dress emphasized the funeral atmosphere surrounding them.

The woman smiled, glanced in the mirror and said, throwing her voice
toward Helene, "That your only one?"

"Yes," said Helene.

"Pretty. A lot like you."

"Yes. Well. She's ten now."

"Ten? Vrai?[8] Small for her age, no?"

Helene shrugged and looked at her daughter's questioning eyes. The
woman in the yellow dress leaned forward. "Come. Come, chère."

Helene interrupted. "We have to get cleaned up. We been three days
on the train with no chance to wash or . . . "

"Comment t'appelle?"

"She doesn't talk Creole."

"Then you ask her."

"She wants to know your name, honey."

With her head pressed into her mother's heavy brown dress, Nel told
her and then asked, "What's yours?"

"Mine's Rochelle. Well. I must be going on." She moved closer to the
mirror and stood there sweeping hair up from her neck back into its halo-
like roll, and wetting with spit the ringlets that fell over her ears. "I been
here, you know, most of the day. She pass on yesterday. The funeral to-

---

7. Wake; a watch held over the body prior to the funeral.

8. *Is that the truth?* Below: *Chère—dear; Comment t'appelle?—What's your name?*

morrow. Henri takin' care." She struck a match, blew it out and darkened her eyebrows with the burnt head. All the while Helene and Nel watched her. The one in a rage at the folded leaves she had endured, the wooden benches she had slept on, all to miss seeing her grandmother and seeing instead that painted canary who never said a word of greeting or affection or . . .

Rochelle continued. "I don't know what happen to de house. Long time paid for. You be thinkin' on it? Oui?"[9] Her newly darkened eyebrows queried Helene.

"Oui." Helene's voice was chilly. "I be thinkin' on it."

"Oh, well. Not for me to say . . ."

Suddenly she swept around and hugged Nel—a quick embrace tighter and harder than one would have imagined her thin soft arms capable of.

" 'Voir! 'Voir!" and she was gone.

In the kitchen, being soaped head to toe by her mother, Nel ventured an observation. "She smelled so nice. And her skin was so soft."

Helene rinsed the cloth. "Much handled things are always soft."

"What does 'vwah' mean?"

"I don't know," her mother said. "I don't talk Creole." She gazed at her daughter's wet buttocks. "And neither do you."

When they got back to Medallion and into the quiet house they saw the note exactly where they had left it and the ham dried out in the icebox.

"Lord, I've never been so glad to see this place. But look at the dust. Get the rags, Nel. Oh, never mind. Let's breathe awhile first. Lord, I never thought I'd get back here safe and sound. Whoo. Well it's over. Good and over. Praise His name. Look at that. I told that old fool not to deliver any milk and there's the can curdled to beat all. What gets into people? I told him not to. Well, I got other things to worry 'bout. Got to get a fire started. I left it ready so I wouldn't have to do nothin' but light it. Lord, it's cold. Don't just sit there, honey. You could be pulling your nose . . ."

Nel sat on the red-velvet sofa listening to her mother but remembering the smell and the tight, tight hug of the woman in yellow who rubbed burned matches over her eyes.

Late that night after the fire was made, the cold supper eaten, the surface dust removed, Nel lay in bed thinking of her trip. She remembered clearly the urine running down and into her stockings until she learned how to squat properly; the disgust on the face of the dead woman and the sound of the funeral drums. It had been an exhilarating trip but a fearful one. She had been frightened of the soldiers' eyes on the train, the black wreath on the door, the custard pudding she believed lurked under her mother's heavy dress, the feel of unknown streets and unknown people. But she had gone on a real trip, and now she was different. She got out of bed and lit the lamp to look in the mirror. There was her face, plain brown eyes, three braids and the nose her mother hated. She looked for a long time and suddenly a shiver ran through her.

"I'm me," she whispered. "Me."

Nel didn't know quite what she meant, but on the other hand she knew exactly what she meant.

9. *Will you?* (literally, *Yes?*) Below: *'Voir* (and *"vwah"*), short for *Au revoir—see you again.*

"I'm me. I'm not their daughter. I'm not Nel. I'm me. Me."

Each time she said the word *me* there was a gathering in her like power, like joy, like fear. Back in bed with her discovery, she stared out the window at the dark leaves of the horse chestnut.

"Me," she murmured. And then, sinking deeper into the quilts, "I want . . . I want to be . . . wonderful. Oh, Jesus, make me wonderful."

The many experiences of her trip crowded in on her. She slept. It was the last as well as the first time she was ever to leave Medallion.

For days afterward she imagined other trips she would take, alone though, to faraway places. Contemplating them was delicious. Leaving Medallion would be her goal. But that was before she met Sula, the girl she had seen for five years at Garfield Primary but never played with, never knew, because her mother said that Sula's mother was sooty. The trip, perhaps, or her new found me-ness, gave her the strength to cultivate a friend in spite of her mother.

When Sula first visited the Wright house, Helene's curdled scorn turned to butter. Her daughter's friend seemed to have none of the mother's slackness. Nel, who regarded the oppressive neatness of her home with dread, felt comfortable in it with Sula, who loved it and would sit on the red-velvet sofa for ten to twenty minutes at a time—still as dawn. As for Nel, she preferred Sula's woolly house, where a pot of something was always cooking on the stove; where the mother, Hannah, never scolded or gave directions; where all sorts of people dropped in; where newspapers were stacked in the hallway, and dirty dishes left for hours at a time in the sink, and where a one-legged grandmother named Eva handed you goobers from deep inside her pockets or read you a dream.

1921

Sula Peace lived in a house of many rooms that had been built over a period of five years to the specifications of its owner, who kept on adding things: more stairways—there were three sets to the second floor—more rooms, doors and stoops. There were rooms that had three doors, others that opened out on the porch only and were inaccessible from any other part of the house; others that you could get to only by going through somebody's bedroom. The creator and sovereign of this enormous house with the four sickle-pear trees in the front yard and the single elm in the back yard was Eva Peace, who sat in a wagon on the third floor directing the lives of her children, friends, strays, and a constant stream of boarders. Fewer than nine people in the town remembered when Eva had two legs, and her oldest child, Hannah, was not one of them. Unless Eva herself introduced the subject, no one ever spoke of her disability; they pretended to ignore it, unless, in some mood of fancy, she began some fearful story about it—generally to entertain children. How the leg got up by itself one day and walked on off. How she hobbled after it but it ran too fast. Or how she had a corn on her toe and it just grew and grew and grew until her whole foot was a corn and then it traveled on up her leg and wouldn't stop growing until she put a red rag at the top by that time it was already at her knee.

Somebody said Eva stuck it under a train and made them pay off. Another said she sold it to a hospital for $10,000—at which Mr. Reed opened his eyes and asked, "Nigger gal legs goin' for $10,000 a *piece?*" as though he could understand $10,000 a *pair*—but for *one?*

Whatever the fate of her lost leg, the remaining one was magnificent. It was stockinged and shod at all times and in all weather. Once in a while she got a felt slipper for Christmas or her birthday, but they soon disappeared, for Eva always wore a black lace-up shoe that came well above her ankle. Nor did she wear overlong dresses to disguise the empty place on her left side. Her dresses were mid-calf so that her one glamorous leg was always in view as well as the long fall of space below her left thigh. One of her men friends had fashioned a kind of wheelchair for her: a rocking-chair top fitted into a large child's wagon. In this contraption she wheeled around the room, from bedside to dresser to the balcony that opened out the north side of her room or to the window that looked out on the back yard. The wagon was so low that children who spoke to her standing up were eye level with her, and adults, standing or sitting, had to look down at her. But they didn't know it. They all had the impression that they were looking up at her, up into the open distances of her eyes, up into the soft black of her nostrils and up at the crest of her chin.

Eva had married a man named BoyBoy and had three children: Hannah, the eldest, and Eva, whom she named after herself but called Pearl, and a son named Ralph, whom she called Plum.

After five years of a sad and disgruntled marriage BoyBoy took off. During the time they were together he was very much preoccupied with other women and not home much. He did whatever he could that he liked, and he liked womanizing best, drinking second, and abusing Eva third. When he left in November, Eva had $1.65, five eggs, three beets and no idea of what or how to feel. The children needed her; she needed money, and needed to get on with her life. But the demands of feeding her three children were so acute she had to postpone her anger for two years until she had both the time and the energy for it. She was confused and desperately hungry. There were very few black families in those low hills then. The Suggs, who lived two hundred yards down the road, brought her a warm bowl of peas, as soon as they found out, and a plate of cold bread. She thanked them and asked if they had a little milk for the older ones. They said no, but Mrs. Jackson, they knew, had a cow still giving. Eva took a bucket over and Mrs. Jackson told her to come back and fill it up in the morning, because the evening milking had already been done. In this way, things went on until near December. People were very willing to help, but Eva felt she would soon run her welcome out; winters were hard and her neighbors were not that much better off. She would lie in bed with the baby boy, the two girls wrapped in quilts on the floor, thinking. The oldest child, Hannah, was five and too young to take care of the baby alone, and any housework Eva could find would keep her away from them from five thirty or earlier in the morning until dark—way past eight. The white people in the valley weren't rich enough then to want maids; they were small farmers and tradesmen and wanted hard-labor help if anything. She thought also of returning to some of her people in Virginia, but to come home dragging three young ones would have to be a step one rung before death for Eva. She would have to scrounge around and beg through the winter, until her baby was at least nine months old, then she could plant and maybe hire herself out to valley farms to weed or sow or feed stock until something steadier came along at harvest time. She thought she had probably been a fool to let

BoyBoy haul her away from her people, but it had seemed so right at the time. He worked for a white carpenter and toolsmith who insisted on BoyBoy's accompanying him when he went West and set up in a squinchy little town called Medallion. BoyBoy brought his new wife and built them a one-room cabin sixty feet back from the road that wound up out of the valley, on up into the hills and was named for the man he worked for. They lived there a year before they had an outhouse.

Sometime before the middle of December, the baby, Plum, stopped having bowel movements. Eva massaged his stomach and gave him warm water. Something must be wrong with my milk, she thought. Mrs. Suggs gave her castor oil, but even that didn't work. He cried and fought so they couldn't get much down his throat anyway. He seemed in great pain and his shrieks were pitched high in outrage and suffering. At one point, maddened by his own crying, he gagged, choked and looked as though he was strangling to death. Eva rushed to him and kicked over the earthen slop jar, washing a small area of the floor with the child's urine. She managed to soothe him, but when he took up the cry again late that night, she resolved to end his misery once and for all. She wrapped him in blankets, ran her finger around the crevices and sides of the lard can and stumbled to the outhouse with him. Deep in its darkness and freezing stench she squatted down, turned the baby over on her knees, exposed his buttocks and shoved the last bit of food she had in the world (besides three beets) up his ass. Softening the insertion with the dab of lard, she probed with her middle finger to loosen his bowels. Her fingernail snagged what felt like a pebble; she pulled it out and others followed. Plum stopped crying as the black hard stools ricocheted onto the frozen ground. And now that it was over, Eva squatted there wondering why she had come all the way out there to free his stools, and what was she doing down on her haunches with her beloved baby boy warmed by her body in the almost total darkness, her shins and teeth freezing, her nostrils assailed. She shook her head as though to juggle her brains around, then said aloud, "Uh uh. Nooo." Thereupon she returned to the house and her bed. As the grateful Plum slept, the silence allowed her to think.

Two days later she left all of her children with Mrs. Suggs, saying she would be back the next day.

Eighteen months later she swept down from a wagon with two crutches, a new black pocketbook, and one leg. First she reclaimed her children, next she gave the surprised Mrs. Suggs a ten-dollar bill, later she started building a house on Carpenter's Road, sixty feet from BoyBoy's one-room cabin, which she rented out.

When Plum was three years old, BoyBoy came back to town and paid her a visit. When Eva got the word that he was on his way, she made some lemonade. She had no idea what she would do or feel during that encounter. Would she cry, cut his throat, beg him to make love to her? She couldn't imagine. So she just waited to see. She stirred lemonade in a green pitcher and waited.

BoyBoy danced up the steps and knocked on the door.

"Come on in," she hollered.

He opened the door and stood smiling, a picture of prosperity and good will. His shoes were a shiny orange, and he had on a citified straw hat, a light-blue suit, and a cat's-head stickpin in his tie. Eva smiled and told him to sit himself down. He smiled too.

"How you been, girl?"

"Pretty fair. What you know good?" When she heard those words come out of her own mouth she knew that their conversation would start off polite. Although it remained to be seen whether she would still run the ice pick through the cat's-head pin.

"Have some lemonade."

"Don't mind if I do." He swept his hat off with a satisfied gesture. His nails were long and shiny. "Sho is hot, and I been runnin' around all day."

Eva looked out of the screen door and saw a woman in a pea-green dress leaning on the smallest pear tree. Glancing back at him, she was reminded of Plum's face when he managed to get the meat out of a walnut all by himself. Eva smiled again, and poured the lemonade.

Their conversation was easy: she catching him up on all the gossip, he asking about this one and that one, and like everybody else avoiding any reference to her leg. It was like talking to somebody's cousin who just stopped by to say howdy before getting on back to wherever he came from. BoyBoy didn't ask to see the children, and Eva didn't bring them into the conversation.

After a while he rose to go. Talking about his appointments and exuding an odor of new money and idleness, he danced down the steps and strutted toward the pea-green dress. Eva watched. She looked at the back of his neck and the set of his shoulders. Underneath all of that shine she saw defeat in the stalk of his neck and the curious tight way he held his shoulders. But still she was not sure what she felt. Then he leaned forward and whispered into the ear of the woman in the green dress. She was still for a moment and then threw back her head and laughed. A high-pitched big-city laugh that reminded Eva of Chicago. It hit her like a sledge hammer, and it was then that she knew what to feel. A liquid trail of hate flooded her chest.

Knowing that she would hate him long and well filled her with pleasant anticipation, like when you know you are going to fall in love with someone and you wait for the happy signs. Hating BoyBoy, she could get on with it, and have the safety, the thrill, the consistency of that hatred as long as she wanted or needed it to define and strengthen her or protect her from routine vulnerabilities. (Once when Hannah accused her of hating colored people, Eva said she only hated one, Hannah's father BoyBoy, and it was hating him that kept her alive and happy.)

Happy or not, after BoyBoy's visit she began her retreat to her bedroom, leaving the bottom of the house more and more to those who lived there: cousins who were passing through, stray folks, and the many, many newly married couples she let rooms to with housekeeping privileges, and after 1910 she didn't willingly set foot on the stairs but once and that was to light a fire, the smoke of which was in her hair for years.

Among the tenants in that big old house were the children Eva took in. Operating on a private scheme of preference and prejudice, she sent off for children she had seen from the balcony of her bedroom or whose circumstances she had heard about from the gossipy old men who came to play checkers or read the *Courier*, or write her number.[1] In 1921, when her granddaughter Sula was eleven, Eva had three such children. They

1. (Illegal) lottery number.

came with woolen caps and names given to them by their mothers, or grandmothers, or somebody's best friend. Eva snatched the caps off their heads and ignored their names. She looked at the first child closely, his wrists, the shape of his head and the temperament that showed in his eyes and said, "Well. Look at Dewey. My my mymymy." When later that same year she sent for a child who kept falling down off the porch across the street, she said the same thing. Somebody said, "But, Miss Eva, you calls the other one Dewey."

"So? This here's another one."

When the third one was brought and Eva said "Dewey" again, everybody thought she had simply run out of names or that her faculties had finally softened.

"How is anybody going to tell them apart?" Hannah asked her.

"What you need to tell them apart for? They's all deweys."

When Hannah asked the question it didn't sound very bright, because each dewey was markedly different from the other two. Dewey one was a deeply black boy with a beautiful head and the golden eyes of chronic jaundice. Dewey two was light-skinned with freckles everywhere and a head of tight red hair. Dewey three was half Mexican with chocolate skin and black bangs. Besides, they were one and two years apart in age. It was Eva saying things like, "Send one of them deweys out to get me some Garret, if they don't have Garret, get Buttercup,"[2] or, "Tell them deweys to cut out that noise," or, "Come here, you dewey you," and, "Send me a dewey," that gave Hannah's question its weight.

Slowly each boy came out of whatever cocoon he was in at the time his mother or somebody gave him away, and accepted Eva's view, becoming in fact as well as in name a dewey—joining with the other two to become a trinity with a plural name ... inseparable, loving nothing and no one but themselves. When the handle from the icebox fell off, all the deweys got whipped, and in dry-eyed silence watched their own feet as they turned their behinds high up into the air for the stroke. When the golden-eyed dewey was ready for school he would not go without the others. He was seven, freckled dewey was five, and Mexican dewey was only four. Eva solved the problem by having them all sent off together. Mr. Buckland Reed said, "But one of them's only four."

"How you know? They all come here the same year," Eva said.

"But that one there was one year old when he came, and that was three years ago."

"You don't know how old he was when he come here and neither do the teacher. Send 'em."

The teacher was startled but not unbelieving, for she had long ago given up trying to fathom the ways of the colored people in town. So when Mrs. Reed said that their names were Dewey King, that they were cousins, and all were six years old, the teacher gave only a tiny sigh and wrote them in the record book for the first grade. She too thought she would have no problem distinguishing among them, because they looked nothing alike, but like everyone else before her, she gradually found that she could not tell one from the other. The deweys would not allow it. They got all mixed up in her head, and finally she could not literally believe her eyes. They spoke with one voice, thought with one mind, and maintained an annoying privacy. Stoutheated, surly, and wholly unpre-

2. Brands of snuff.

dictable, the deweys remained a mystery not only during all of their lives in Medallion but after as well.

The deweys came in 1921, but the year before Eva had given a small room off the kitchen to Tar Baby, a beautiful, slight, quiet man who never spoke above a whisper. Most people said he was half white, but Eva said he was all white. That she knew blood when she saw it, and he didn't have none. When he first came to Medallion, the people called him Pretty Johnnie, but Eva looked at his milky skin and cornsilk hair and out of a mixture of fun and meanness called him Tar Baby. He was a mountain boy who stayed to himself, bothering no one, intent solely on drinking himself to death. At first he worked in a poultry market, and after wringing the necks of chickens all day, he came home and drank until he slept. Later he began to miss days at work and frequently did not have his rent money. When he lost his job altogether, he would go out in the morning, scrounge around for money doing odd jobs, bumming or whatever, and come home to drink. Because he was no bother, ate little, required nothing, and was a lover of cheap wine, no one found him a nuisance. Besides, he frequently went to Wednesday-night prayer meetings and sang with the sweetest hill voice imaginable "In the Sweet By-and-By."[3] He sent the deweys out for his liquor and spent most of his time in a heap on the floor or sitting in a chair staring at the wall.

Hannah worried about him a little, but only a very little. For it soon became clear that he simply wanted a place to die privately but not quite alone. No one thought of suggesting to him that he pull himself together or see a doctor or anything. Even the women at prayer meeting who cried when he sang "In the Sweet By-and-By" never tried to get him to participate in the church activities. They just listened to him sing, wept and thought very graphically of their own imminent deaths. The people either accepted his own evaluation of his life, or were indifferent to it. There was, however, a measure of contempt in their indifference, for they had little patience with people who took themselves that seriously. Seriously enough to try to die. And it was natural that he, after all, became the first one to join Shadrack—Tar Baby and the deweys—on National Suicide Day.

Under Eva's distant eye, and prey to her idiosyncrasies, her own children grew up stealthily: Pearl married at fourteen and moved to Flint, Michigan, from where she posted frail letters to her mother with two dollars folded into the writing paper. Sad little nonsense letters about minor troubles, her husband's job and who the children favored. Hannah married a laughing man named Rekus who died when their daughter Sula was about three years old, at which time Hannah moved back into her mother's big house prepared to take care of it and her mother forever.

With the exception of BoyBoy, those Peace women loved all men. It was manlove that Eva bequeathed to her daughters. Probably, people said, because there were no men in the house, no men to run it. But actually that was not true. The Peace women simply loved maleness, for its own sake. Eva, old as she was, and with one leg, had a regular flock of gentleman callers, and although she did not participate in the act of love, there

---

3. Hymn by Sanford Fillmore Bennett (1836–1896) regarding death as release: "In the sweet by-and-by/   There's a land that is fairer than day."

was a good deal of teasing and pecking and laughter. The men wanted to see her lovely calf, that neat shoe, and watch the focusing that sometimes swept down out of the distances in her eyes. They wanted to see the joy in her face as they settled down to play checkers, knowing that even when she beat them, as she almost always did, somehow, in her presence, it was they who had won something. They would read the newspaper aloud to her and make observations on its content, and Eva would listen feeling no obligation to agree and, in fact, would take them to task about their interpretation of events. But she argued with them with such an absence of bile, such a concentration of manlove, that they felt their convictions solidified by her disagreement.

With other people's affairs Eva was equally prejudiced about men. She fussed interminably with the brides of the newly wed couples for not getting their men's supper ready on time; about how to launder shirts, press them, etc. "Yo' man be here direc'lin. Ain't it 'bout time you got busy?"

"Aw, Miss Eva. It'll be ready. We just having spaghetti."

"Again?" Eva's eyebrows fluted up and the newlywed pressed her lips together in shame.

Hannah simply refused to live without the attentions of a man, and after Rekus' death had a steady sequence of lovers, mostly the husbands of her friends and neighbors. Her flirting was sweet, low and guileless. Without ever a pat of the hair, a rush to change clothes or a quick application of paint, with no gesture whatsoever, she rippled with sex. In her same old print wraparound, barefoot in the summer, in the winter her feet in a man's leather slippers with the backs flattened under her heels, she made men aware of her behind, her slim ankles, the dew-smooth skin and the incredible length of neck. Then the smile-eyes, the turn of the head—all so welcoming, light and playful. Her voice trailed, dipped and bowed; she gave a chord to the simplest words. Nobody, but nobody, could say "hey sugar" like Hannah. When he heard it, the man tipped his hat down a little over his eyes, hoisted his trousers and thought about the hollow place at the base of her neck. And all this without the slightest confusion about work and responsibilities. While Eva tested and argued with her men, leaving them feeling as though they had been in combat with a worthy, if amiable, foe, Hannah rubbed no edges, made no demands, made the man feel as though he were complete and wonderful just as he was—he didn't need fixing—and so he relaxed and swooned in the Hannah-light that shone on him simply because he was. If the man entered and Hannah was carrying a coal scuttle up from the basement, she handled it in such a way that it became a gesture of love. He made no move to help her with it simply because he wanted to see how her thighs looked when she bent to put it down, knowing that she wanted him to see them too.

But since in that crowded house there were no places for private and spontaneous lovemaking, Hannah would take the man down into the cellar in the summer where it was cool back behind the coal bin and the newspapers, or in the winter they would step into the pantry and stand up against the shelves she had filled with canned goods, or lie on the flour sack just under the rows of tiny green peppers. When those places were not available, she would slip into the seldom-used parlor, or even up to her bedroom. She liked the last place least, not because Sula slept in the room with her but because her love mate's tendency was always to fall asleep afterward and Hannah was fastidious about whom she slept with. She would fuck practically anything, but sleeping with someone implied for her a measure of trust and a definite commitment. So she ended up a daylight lover, and it was only once actually that Sula came home from school and found her mother in the bed, curled spoon in the arms of a man.

Seeing her step so easily into the pantry and emerge looking precisely as she did when she entered, only happier, taught Sula that sex was pleasant and frequent, but otherwise unremarkable. Outside the house, where children giggled about underwear, the message was different. So she watched her mother's face and the face of the men when they opened the pantry door and made up her own mind.

Hannah exasperated the women in the town—the "good" women, who said, "One thing I can't stand is a nasty woman"; the whores, who were hard put to find trade among black men anyway and who resented Hannah's generosity; the middling women, who had both husbands and affairs, because Hannah seemed too unlike them, having no passion attached to her relationships and being wholly incapable of jealousy. Hannah's friendships with women were, of course, seldom and short-lived, and the newly married couples whom her mother took in soon learned what a hazard she was. She could break up a marriage before it had even become one—she would make love to the new groom and wash his wife's dishes all in an afternoon. What she wanted, after Rekus died, and what she succeeded in having more often than not, was some touching every day.

The men, surprisingly, never gossiped about her. She was unquestionably a kind and generous woman and that, coupled with her extraordinary beauty and funky elegance of manner, made them defend her and protect her from any vitriol that newcomers or their wives might spill.

Eva's last child, Plum, to whom she hoped to bequeath everything, floated in a constant swaddle of love and affection, until 1917 when he went to war. He returned to the States in 1919 but did not get back to Medallion until 1920. He wrote letters from New York, Washington, D.C., and Chicago full of promises of homecomings, but there was obviously something wrong. Finally some two or three days after Christmas, he arrived with just the shadow of his old dip-down walk. His hair had been neither cut nor combed in months, his clothes were pointless and he had no socks. But he did have a black bag, a paper sack, and a sweet, sweet smile. Everybody welcomed him and gave him a warm room next to Tar Baby's and waited for him to tell them whatever it was he wanted them to know. They waited in vain for his telling but not long for the knowing. His habits were much like Tar Baby's but there were no bottles, and Plum was sometimes cheerful and animated. Hannah watched and Eva waited. Then he began to steal from them, take trips to Cincinnati and sleep for days in his room with the record player going. He got even thinner, since he ate only snatches of things at beginnings or endings of meals. It was Hannah who found the bent spoon black from steady cooking.

So late one night in 1921, Eva got up from her bed and put on her clothes. Hoisting herself up on her crutches, she was amazed to find that she could still manage them, although the pain in her armpits was severe. She practiced a few steps around the room, and then opened the door. Slowly, she manipulated herself down the long flights of stairs, two crutches under her left arm, the right hand grasping the banister. The sound of her foot booming in comparison to the delicate pat of the crutch tip. On each landing she stopped for breath. Annoyed at her physical condition, she closed her eyes and removed the crutches from under her arms to relieve the unaccustomed pressure. At the foot of the stairs she redistributed her weight between the crutches and swooped on through the front room, to the dining room, to the kitchen, swinging and swooping like a giant heron, so graceful sailing about in its own habitat but awkward and comical when it folded its wings and tried to walk. With a swing and a swoop she arrived at Plum's door and pushed it open with the tip of one crutch. He was lying in bed barely visible in the light coming from a single bulb. Eva swung over to the bed and propped her crutches at its foot. She sat down and gathered Plum into her arms. He woke, but only slightly.

"Hey, man. Hey. You holdin' me Mamma?" His voice was drowsy and amused. He chuckled as though he had heard some private joke. Eva held him closer and began to rock. Back and forth she rocked him, her eyes wandering around his room. There in the corner was a half-eaten store-bought cherry pie. Balled-up candy wrappers and empty pop bottles peeped from under the dresser. On the floor by her foot was a glass of strawberry crush and a *Liberty* magazine. Rocking, rocking, listening to Plum's occasional chuckles, Eva let her memory spin, loop and fall. Plum in the tub that time as she leaned over him. He reached up and dripped water into her bosom and laughed. She was angry, but not too, and laughed with him.

"Mamma, you so purty. You so purty, Mamma."

Eva lifted her tongue to the edge of her lip to stop the tears from running into her mouth. Rocking, rocking. Later she laid him down and looked at him a long time. Suddenly she was thirsty and reached for the glass of strawberry crush. She put it to her lips and discovered it was blood-tainted water and threw it to the floor. Plum woke up and said, "Hey, Mamma, whyn't you go on back to bed? I'm all right. Didn't I tell you? I'm all right. Go on, now."

"I'm going, Plum," she said. She shifted her weight and pulled her crutches toward her. Swinging and swooping, she left his room. She dragged herself to the kitchen and made grating noises.

Plum on the rim of a warm light sleep was still chuckling. Mamma. She sure was somethin'. He felt twilight. Now there seemed to be some kind of wet light traveling over his legs and stomach with a deeply attractive smell. It wound itself—this wet light—all about him, splashing and running into his skin. He opened his eyes and saw what he imagined was the great wing of an eagle pouring a wet lightness over him. Some kind of baptism, some kind of blessing, he thought. Everything is going to be all right, it said. Knowing that it was so he closed his eyes and sank back into the bright hole of sleep.

Eva stepped back from the bed and let the crutches rest under her arms. She rolled a bit of newspaper into a tight stick about six inches long, lit it and threw it onto the bed where the kerosene-soaked Plum lay in snug delight. Quickly, as the *whoosh* of flames engulfed him, she shut the door and made her slow and painful journey back to the top of the house.

Just as she got to the third landing she could hear Hannah and some child's voice. She swung along, not even listening to the voices of alarm and the cries of the deweys. By the time she got to her bed someone was bounding up the stairs after her. Hannah opened the door. "Plum! Plum! He's burning, Mamma! We can't even open the door! Mamma!"

Eva looked into Hannah's eyes. "Is? My baby? Burning?" The two women did not speak, for the eyes of each were enough for the other. Then Hannah closed hers and ran toward the voices of neighbors calling for water.

1922

It was too cool for ice cream. A hill wind was blowing dust and empty Camels wrappers about their ankles. It pushed their dresses into the creases of their behinds, then lifted the hems to peek at their cotton underwear. They were on their way to Edna Finch's Mellow House, an ice-cream parlor catering to nice folks—where even children would feel comfortable, you know, even though it was right next to Reba's Grill and just one block down from the Time and a Half Pool Hall. It sat in the curve of Carpenter's Road, which, in four blocks, made up all the sporting life available in the Bottom. Old men and young ones draped themselves in front of the Elmira Theater, Irene's Palace of Cosmetology, the pool hall, the grill and the other sagging business enterprises that lined the street. On sills, on stoops, on crates and broken chairs they sat tasting their teeth and waiting for something to distract them. Every passerby, every motorcar, every alteration in stance caught their attention and was commented on. Particularly they watched women. When a woman approached, the older men tipped their hats; the younger ones opened and closed their thighs. But all of them, whatever their age, watched her retreating view with interest.

Nel and Sula walked through this valley of eyes chilled by the wind and heated by the embarrassment of appraising stares. The old men looked at their stalklike legs, dwelled on the cords in the backs of their knees and remembered old dance steps they had not done in twenty years. In their lust, which age had turned to kindness, they moved their lips as though to stir up the taste of young sweat on tight skin.

Pig meat. The words were in all their minds. And one of them, one of the young ones, said it aloud. Softly but definitively and there was no mistaking the compliment. His name was Ajax, a twenty-one-year-old pool haunt of sinister beauty. Graceful and economical in every movement, he held a place of envy with men of all ages for his magnificently foul mouth. In fact he seldom cursed, and the epithets he chose were dull, even harmless. His reputation was derived from the way he handled the words. When he said "hell" he hit the *h* with his lungs and the impact was greater than the achievement of the most imaginative foul mouth in the town. He could say "shit" with a nastiness impossible to imitate. So, when he said "pig meat" as Nel and Sula passed, they guarded their eyes lest someone see their delight.

It was not really Edna Finch's ice cream that made them brave the stretch of those panther eyes. Years later their own eyes would glaze as they cupped their chins in remembrance of the inchworm smiles, the squatting haunches, the track-rail legs straddling broken chairs. The cream-colored trousers marking with a mere seam the place where the mystery curled. Those smooth vanilla crotches invited them; those lemon-yellow gabardines beckoned to them.

They moved toward the ice-cream parlor like tightrope walkers, as thrilled by the possibility of a slip as by the maintenance of tension and balance. The least sideways glance, the merest toe stub, could pitch them into those creamy haunches spread wide with welcome. Somewhere beneath all of that daintiness, chambered in all that neatness, lay the thing that clotted their dreams.

Which was only fitting, for it was in dreams that the two girls had first met. Long before Edna Finch's Mellow House opened, even before they marched through the chocolate halls of Garfield Primary School out onto the playground and stood facing each other through the ropes of the one vacant swing ("Go on." "No. You go."), they had already made each other's acquaintance in the delirium of their noon dreams. They were solitary little girls whose loneliness was so profound it intoxicated them and sent them stumbling into Technicolored visions that always included a presence, a someone, who, quite like the dreamer, shared the delight of the dream. When Nel, an only child, sat on the steps of her back porch surrounded by the high silence of her mother's incredibly orderly house, feeling the neatness pointing at her back, she studied the poplars and fell easily into a picture of herself lying on a flowered bed, tangled in her own hair, waiting for some fiery prince. He approached but never quite arrived. But always, watching the dream along with her, were some smiling sympathetic eyes. Someone as interested as she herself in the flow of her imagined hair, the thickness of the mattress of flowers, the voile sleeves that closed below her elbows in gold-threaded cuffs.

Similarly, Sula, also an only child, but wedged into a household of throbbing disorder constantly awry with things, people, voices and the slamming of doors, spent hours in the attic behind a roll of linoleum galloping through her own mind on a gray-and-white horse tasting sugar and smelling roses in full view of a someone who shared both the taste and the speed.

So when they met, first in those chocolate halls and next through the ropes of the swing, they felt the ease and comfort of old friends. Because each had discovered years before that they were neither white nor male, and that all freedom and triumph was forbidden to them, they had set about creating something else to be. Their meeting was fortunate, for it let them use each other to grow on. Daughters of distant mothers and incomprehensible fathers (Sula's because he was dead; Nel's because he wasn't), they found in each other's eyes the intimacy they were looking for.

Nel Wright and Sula Peace were both twelve in 1922, wishbone thin and easy-assed. Nel was the color of wet sandpaper—just dark enough to escape the blows of the pitch-black truebloods and the contempt of old women who worried about such things as bad blood mixtures and knew that the origins of a mule and a mulatto were one and the same. Had she been any lighter-skinned she would have needed either her mother's protection on the way to school or a streak of mean to defend herself. Sula was a heavy brown with large quiet eyes, one of which featured a birthmark that spread from the middle of the lid toward the eyebrow, shaped something like a stemmed rose. It gave her otherwise plain face a broken excitement and blue-blade threat like the keloid scar of the razored man who sometimes played checkers with her grandmother. The birthmark was to grow darker as the years passed, but now it was the same shade as her gold-flecked eyes, which, to the end, were as steady and clean as rain.

Their friendship was as intense as it was sudden. They found relief in each other's personality. Although both were unshaped, formless things, Nel seemed stronger and more consistent than Sula, who could hardly be counted on to sustain any emotion for more than three minutes. Yet there was one time when that was not true, when she held on to a mood for weeks, but even that was in defense of Nel.

Four white boys in their early teens, sons of some newly arrived Irish people, occasionally entertained themselves in the afternoon by harassing black schoolchildren. With shoes that pinched and woolen knickers that made red rings on their calves, they had come to this valley with their parents believing as they did that it was a promised land—green and shimmering with welcome. What they found was a strange accent, a pervasive fear of their religion and firm resistance to their attempts to find work. With one exception the older residents of Medallion scorned them. The one exception was the black community. Although some of the Negroes had been in Medallion before the Civil War (the town didn't even have a name then), if they had any hatred for these newcomers it didn't matter because it didn't show. As a matter fact, baiting them was the one activity that the white Protestant residents concurred in. In part their place in this world was secured only when they echoed the old residents' attitude toward blacks.

These particular boys caught Nel once, and pushed her from hand to hand until they grew tired of the frightened helpless face. Because of that incident, Nel's route home from school became elaborate. She, and then Sula, managed to duck them for weeks until a chilly day in November when Sula said, "Let's us go on home the shortest way."

Nel blinked, but acquiesced. They walked up the street until they got to the bend of Carpenter's Road where the boys lounged on a disused well. Spotting their prey, the boys sauntered forward as though there were nothing in the world on their minds but the gray sky. Hardly able to control their grins, they stood like a gate blocking the path. When the girls were three feet in front of the boys, Sula reached into her coat pocket and pulled out Eva's paring knife. The boys stopped short, exchanged looks and dropped all pretense of innocence. This was going to be better than they thought. They were going to try and fight back, and with a knife. Maybe they could get an arm around one of their waists, or tear . . .

Sula squatted down in the dirt road and put everything down on the ground: her lunchpail, her reader, her mittens, her slate. Holding the knife in her right hand, she pulled the slate toward her and pressed her left forefinger down hard on its edge. Her aim was determined but inaccurate. She slashed off only the tip of her finger. The four boys stared open-mouthed at the wound and the scrap of flesh, like a button mushroom, curling in the cherry blood that ran into the corners of the slate.

Sula raised her eyes to them. Her voice was quiet. "If I can do that to myself, what you suppose I'll do to you?"

The shifting dirt was the only way Nel knew that they were moving away; she was looking at Sula's face, which seemed miles and miles away.

But toughness was not their quality—adventuresomeness was—and a mean determination to explore everything that interested them, from one-eyed chickens high-stepping in their penned yards to Mr. Buckland Reed's gold teeth, from the sound of sheets flapping in the wind to the labels on Tar Baby's wine bottles. And they had no priorities. They could be distracted from watching a fight with mean razors by the glorious smell of hot tar being poured by roadmen two hundred yards away.

In the safe harbor of each other's company they could afford to abandon the ways of other people and concentrate on their own perceptions of things. When Mrs. Wright reminded Nel to pull her nose, she would do it enthusiastically but without the least hope in the world.

"While you sittin' there, honey, go 'head and pull your nose."

"It hurts, Mamma."

"Don't you want a nice nose when you grow up?"

After she met Sula, Nel slid the clothespin under the blanket as soon as she got in the bed. And although there was still the hateful hot comb to suffer through each Saturday evening, its consequences—smooth hair—no longer interested her.

Joined in mutual admiration they watched each day as though it were a movie arranged for their amusement. The new theme they were now discovering was men. So they met regularly, without even planning it, to walk down the road to Edna Finch's Mellow House, even though it was too cool for ice cream.

Then summer came. A summer limp with the weight of blossomed things. Heavy sunflowers weeping over fences; iris curling and browning at the edges far away from their purple hearts; ears of corn letting their auburn hair wind down to their stalks. And the boys. The beautiful, beautiful boys who dotted the landscape like jewels, split the air with their shouts in the field, and thickened the river with their shining wet backs. Even their footsteps left a smell of smoke behind.

It was in that summer, the summer of their twelfth year, the summer of the beautiful black boys, that they became skittish, frightened and bold—all at the same time.

In that mercury mood in July, Sula and Nel wandered about the Bottom barefoot looking for mischief. They decided to go down by the river where the boys sometimes swam. Nel waited on the porch of 7 Carpenter's Road while Sula ran into the house to go to the toilet. On the way up the stairs, she passed the kitchen where Hannah sat with two friends, Patsy and Valentine. The two women were fanning themselves and watching Hannah put down some dough, all talking casually about one thing and another, and had gotten around, when Sula passed by, to the problems of child rearing.

"They a pain."

"Yeh. Wish I'd listened to mamma. She told me not to have 'em too soon."

"Any time at all is too soon for me."

"Oh, I don't know. My Rudy minds his daddy. He just wild with me. Be glad when he growed and gone."

Hannah smiled and said, "Shut your mouth. You love the ground he pee on."

"Sure I do. But he still a pain. Can't help loving your own child. No matter what they do."

"Well, Hester grown now and I can't say love is exactly what I feel."

"Sure you do. You love her, like I love Sula. I just don't like her. That's the difference."

"Guess so. Likin' them is another thing."

"Sure. They different people, you know . . . "

She only heard Hannah's words, and the pronouncement sent her flying up the stairs. In bewilderment, she stood at the window fingering the curtain edge, aware of a sting in her eye. Nel's call floated up and into the window, pulling her away from dark thoughts back into the bright, hot daylight.

They ran most of the way.

Heading toward the wide part of the river where trees grouped themselves in families darkening the earth below. They passed some boys swimming and clowning in the water, shrouding their words in laughter. They ran in the sunlight, creating their own breeze, which pressed their dresses into their damp skin. Reaching a kind of square of four leaf-locked trees which promised cooling, they flung themselves into the four-cornered shade to taste their lip sweat and contemplate the wildness that had come upon them so suddenly. They lay in the grass, their foreheads almost touching, their bodies stretched away from each other at a 180-degree angle. Sula's head rested on her arm, an undone braid coiled around her wrist. Nel leaned on her elbows and worried long blades of grass with her fingers. Underneath their dresses flesh tightened and shivered in the high coolness, their small breasts just now beginning to create some pleasant discomfort when they were lying on their stomachs.

Sula lifted her head and joined Nel in the grass play. In concert, without ever meeting each other's eyes, they stroked the blades up and down, up and down. Nel found a thick twig and, with her thumbnail, pulled away its bark until it was stripped to a smooth, creamy innocence. Sula looked about and found one too. When both twigs were undressed Nel moved easily to the next stage and began tearing up rooted grass to make a bare spot of earth. When a generous clearing was made, Sula traced intricate patterns in it with her twig. At first Nel was content to do the same. But soon she grew impatient and poked her twig rhythmically and intensely into the earth, making a small neat hole that grew deeper and wider with the least manipulation of her twig. Sula copied her, and soon each had a hole the size of a cup. Nel began a more strenuous digging and, rising to her knee, was careful to scoop out the dirt as she made her hole deeper. Together they worked until the two holes were one and the same. When the depression was the size of a small dishpan, Nel's twig broke. With a gesture of disgust she threw the pieces into the hole they had made. Sula threw hers in too. Nel saw a bottle cap and tossed it in as well. Each then looked around for more debris to throw into the hole: paper, bits of glass, butts of cigarettes, until all of the small defiling things they could find were collected there. Carefully they replaced the soil and covered the entire grave with uprooted grass.

Neither one had spoken a word.

They stood up, stretched, then gazed out over the swift dull water as an unspeakable restlessness and agitation held them. At the same instant each girl heard footsteps in the grass. A little boy in too big knickers was coming up from the lower bank of the river. He stopped when he saw them and picked his nose.

"Your mamma tole you to stop eatin' snot, Chicken," Nel hollered at him through cupped hands.

"Shut up," he said, still picking.

"Come up here and say that."

"Leave him 'lone, Nel. Come here, Chicken. Lemme show you something."

"Naw."

"You scared we gone take your bugger away?"

"Leave him 'lone, I said. Come on, Chicken. Look. I'll help you climb a tree."

Chicken looked at the tree Sula was pointing to—a big double beech with low branches and lots of bends for sitting.

He moved slowly toward her.

"Come on, Chicken, I'll help you up."

Still picking his nose, his eyes wide, he came to where they were standing. Sula took him by the hand and coaxed him along. When they reached the base of the beech, she lifted him to the first branch, saying, "Go on. Go on. I got you." She followed the boy, steadying him, when he needed it, with her hand and her reassuring voice. When they were as high as they could go, Sula pointed to the far side of the river.

"See? Bet you never saw that far before, did you?"

"Uh uh."

"Now look down there." They both leaned a little and peered through the leaves at Nel standing below, squinting up at them. From their height she looked small and fore-shortened.

Chicken Little laughed.

"Y'all better come on down before you break your neck," Nel hollered.

"I ain't never coming down," the boy hollered back.

"Yeah. We better. Come on, Chicken."

"Naw. Lemme go."

"Yeah, Chicken. Come on, now."

Sula pulled his leg gently.

"Lemme go."

"OK, I'm leavin' you." She started on.

"Wait!" he screamed.

Sula stopped and together they slowly worked their way down.

Chicken was still elated. "I was way up there, wasn't I? Wasn't I? I'm a tell my brovver."

Sula and Nel began to mimic him: "I'm a tell my brovver; I'm a tell my brovver."

Sula picked him up by his hands and swung him outward then around and around. His knickers ballooned and his shrieks of frightened joy startled the birds and the fat grasshoppers. When he slipped from her hands and sailed away out over the water they could still hear his bubbly laughter.

The water darkened and closed quickly over the place where Chicken Little sank. The pressure of his hard and tight little fingers was still in Sula's palms as she stood looking at the closed place in the water. They expected him to come back up, laughing. Both girls stared at the water.

Nel spoke first. "Somebody saw." A figure appeared briefly on the opposite shore.

The only house over there was Shadrack's. Sula glanced at Nel. Terror widened her nostrils. Had he seen?

The water was so peaceful now. There was nothing but the baking sun and something newly missing. Sula cupped her face for an instant, then turned and ran up to the little plank bridge that crossed the river to Shadrack's house. There was no path. It was as though neither Shadrack nor anyone else ever came this way.

Her running was swift and determined, but when she was close to the three little steps that led to his porch, fear crawled into her stomach and only the something newly missing back there in the river made it possible for her to walk up the three steps and knock at the door.

No one answered. She started back, but thought again of the peace of the river. Shadrack would be inside, just behind the door ready to pounce on her. Still she could not go back. Ever so gently she pushed the door with the tips of her fingers and heard only the hinges weep. More. And then she was inside. Alone. The neatness, the order startled her, but more surprising was the restfulness. Everything was so tiny, so common, so unthreatening. Perhaps this was not the house of the Shad. The terrible Shad who walked about with his penis out, who peed in front of ladies and girl-children, the only black who could curse white people and get away with it, who drank in the road from the mouth of the bottle, who shouted and shook in the streets. This cottage? This sweet old cottage? With its made-up bed? With its rag rug and wooden table? Sula stood in the middle of the little room and in her wonder forgot what she had come for until a sound at the door made her jump. He was there in the doorway looking at her. She had not heard his coming and now he was looking at her.

More in embarrassment than terror she averted her glance. When she called up enough courage to look back at him, she saw his hand resting upon the door frame. His fingers, barely touching the wood, were arranged in a graceful arc. Relieved and encouraged (no one with hands like that, no one with fingers that curved around wood so tenderly could kill her), she walked past him out of the door, feeling his gaze turning, turning with her.

At the edge of the porch, gathering the wisps of courage that were fast leaving her, she turned once more to look at him, to ask him . . . had he . . . ?

He was smiling, a great smile, heavy with lust and time to come. He nodded his head as though answering a question, and said, in a pleasant conversational tone, a tone of cooled butter, "Always."

Sula fled down the steps, and shot through the greenness and the baking sun back to Nel and the dark closed place in the water. There she collapsed in tears.

Nel quieted her. "Sh, sh. Don't, don't. You didn't mean it. It ain't your fault. Sh. Sh. Come on, le's go, Sula. Come on, now. Was he there? Did he see? Where's the belt to your dress?"

Sula shook her head while she searched her waist for the belt.

Finally she stood up and allowed Nel to lead her away. "He said, 'Always. Always.'"

"What?"

Sula covered her mouth as they walked down the hill. Always. He had answered a question she had not asked, and its promise licked at her feet.

A bargeman, poling away from the shore, found Chicken late that afternoon stuck in some rocks and weeds, his knickers ballooning about his legs. He would have left him there but noticed that it was a child, not an old black man, as it first appeared, and he prodded the body loose, netted it and hauled it aboard. He shook his head in disgust at the kind of parents who would drown their own children. When, he wondered, will those people ever be anything but animals, fit for nothing but substitutes for mules, only mules didn't kill each other the way niggers did. He dumped Chicken Little into a burlap sack and tossed him next to some egg crates and boxes of wool cloth. Later, sitting down to smoke on an empty lard tin, still bemused by God's curse and the terrible burden his own kind had of elevating Ham's sons,[4] he suddenly became alarmed by the thought that the corpse in this heat would have a terrible odor, which might get into the fabric of his woolen cloth. He dragged the sack away and hooked it over the side, so that the Chicken's body was half in and half out of the water.

Wiping the sweat from his neck, he reported his find to the sheriff at Porter's Landing, who said they didn't have no niggers in their country, but that some lived in those hills 'cross the river, up above Medallion. The bargeman said he couldn't go all the way back there, it was every bit of two miles. The sheriff said whyn't he throw it on back into the water. The bargeman said he never shoulda taken it out in the first place. Finally they got the man who ran the ferry twice a day to agree to take it over in the morning.

That was why Chicken Little was missing for three days and didn't get to the embalmer's until the fourth day, by which time he was unrecognizable to almost everybody who once knew him, and even his mother wasn't deep down sure, except that it just had to be him since nobody could find him. When she saw his clothes lying on the table in the basement of the mortuary, her mouth snapped shut, and when she saw his body her mouth flew wide open again and it was seven hours before she was able to close it and make the first sound.

So the coffin was closed.

The Junior Choir, dressed in white, sang "Nearer My God to Thee" and "Precious Memories,"[5] their eyes fastened on the songbooks they did not need, for this was the first time their voices had presided at a real-life event.

Nel and Sula did not touch hands or look at each other during the funeral. There was a space, a separateness, between them. Nel's legs had turned to granite and she expected the sheriff or Reverend Deal's pointing finger at any moment. Although she knew she had "done nothing,"

4. Because Ham, the ancestor of the African tribes, saw his father Noah naked, the patriarch curses Ham's son Canaan: "a servant of servants shall he be unto his brethren" (Genesis 9:22–25).

5. Hymn by J. B. F. Wright, which speaks of memories as "unseen angels"; the 1841 hymn by Sarah Flower Adams (1805–1848) consoles the sufferer (". . . So by my woes to be/ Nearer, my God, to thee").

she felt convicted and hanged right there in the pew—two rows down
from her parents in the children's section.

Sula simply cried. Soundlessly and with no heaving and gasping for
breath, she let the tears roll into her mouth and slide down her chin to
dot the front of her dress.

As Reverend Deal moved into his sermon, the hands of the women unfolded like pairs of raven's wings and flew high above their hats in the air.
They did not hear all of what he said; they heard the one word, or
phrase, or inflection that was for them the connection between the event
and themselves. For some it was the term "Sweet Jesus." And they saw
the Lamb's eye and the truly innocent victim: themselves. They acknowledged the innocent child hiding in the corner of their hearts, holding a
sugar-and-butter sandwich. That one. The one who lodged deep in their
fat, thin, old, young skin, and was the one the world had hurt. Or they
thought of their son newly killed and remembered his legs in short pants
and wondered where the bullet went in. Or they remembered how dirty
the room looked when their father left home and wondered if that is the
way the slim, young Jew felt, he who for them was both son and lover
and in whose downy face they could see the sugar-and-butter sandwiches
and feel the oldest and most devastating pain there is: not the pain of
childhood, but the remembrance of it.

Then they left their pews. For with some emotions one has to stand.
They spoke, for they were full and needed to say. They swayed, for the
rivulets of grief or of ecstasy must be rocked. And when they thought of
all that life and death locked into that little closed coffin they danced and
screamed, not to protest God's will but to acknowledge it and confirm
once more their conviction that the only way to avoid the Hand of God is
to get in it.

In the colored part of the cemetery, they sank Chicken Little in between his grandfather and an aunt. Butterflies flew in and out of the
bunches of field flowers now loosened from the top of the bier and lying
in a small heap at the edge of the grave. The heat had gone, but there
was still no breeze to lift the hair of the willows.

Nel and Sula stood some distance away from the grave, the space that
had sat between them in the pews had dissolved. They held hands and
knew that only the coffin would lie in the earth; the bubbly laughter and
the press of fingers in the palm would stay aboveground forever. At first,
as they stood there, their hands were clenched together. They relaxed
slowly until during the walk back home their fingers were laced in as
gentle a clasp as that of any two young girlfriends trotting up the road on
a summer day wondering what happened to butterflies in the winter.

1923

The second strange thing was Hannah's coming into her mother's room
with an empty bowl and a peck of Kentucky Wonders[6] and saying,
"Mamma, did you ever love us?" She sang the words like a small child
saying a piece at Easter, then knelt to spread a newspaper on the floor
and set the basket on it; the bowl she tucked in the space between her
legs. Eva, who was just sitting there fanning herself with the cardboard

6. A kind of green bean.

fan from Mr. Hodges' funeral parlor, listened to the silence that followed Hannah's words, then said, "Scat!" to the deweys who were playing chain gang near the window. With the shoelaces of each of them tied to the laces of the others, they stumbled and tumbled out of Eva's room.

"Now," Eva looked up across from her wagon at her daughter. "Give me that again. Flat out to fit my head."

"I mean, did you? You know. When we was little."

Eva's hand moved snail-like down her thigh toward her stump, but stopped short of it to realign a pleat. "No. I don't reckon I did. Not the way you thinkin'."

"Oh, well. I was just wonderin'." Hannah appeared to be through with the subject.

"An evil wonderin' if I ever heard one." Eva was not through.

"I didn't mean nothing by it, Mamma."

"What you mean you didn't *mean* nothing by it? How you gone not mean something by it?"

Hannah pinched the tips off the Kentucky Wonders and snapped their long pods. What with the sound of the cracking and snapping and her swift-fingered movements, she seemed to be playing a complicated instrument. Eva watched her a moment and then said, "You gone can them?"

"No. They for tonight."

"Thought you was gone can some."

"Uncle Paul ain't brought me none yet. A peck ain't enough to can. He say he got two bushels for me."

"Triflin'."

"Oh, he all right."

"Sho he all right. Everybody all right. 'Cept Mamma. Mamma the only one ain't all right. Cause she didn't *love* us."

"Awww, Mamma."

"Awww, Mamma? Awww, Mamma? You settin' here with your healthy-ass self and ax me did I love you? Them big old eyes in your head would a been two holes full of maggots if I hadn't."

"I didn't mean that, Mamma. I know you fed us and all. I was talkin' 'bout something else. Like. Like. Playin' with us. Did you ever, you know, play with us?"

"Play? Wasn't nobody playin' in 1895. Just 'cause you got it good now you think it was always this good? 1895 was a killer, girl. Things was bad. Niggers was dying like flies. Stepping tall, ain't you? Uncle Paul gone bring me *two* bushels. Yeh. And they's a melon downstairs, ain't they? And I bake every Saturday, and Shad brings fish on Friday, and they's a pork barrel full of meal, and we float eggs in a crock of vinegar . . ."

"Mamma, what you talkin' 'bout?"

"I'm talkin' 'bout 18 and 95 when I set in that house five days with you and Pearl and Plum and three beets, you snake-eyed ungrateful hussy. What would I look like leapin' 'round that little old room playin' with youngins with three beets to my name?"

"I know 'bout them beets, Mamma. You told us that a million times."

"Yeah? Well? Don't that count? Ain't that love? You want me to tinkle you under the jaw and forget 'bout them sores in your mouth? Pearl was shittin' worms and I was supposed to play rang-around-the-rosie?"

"But Mamma, they had to be some time when you wasn't thinkin' 'bout . . ."

"No time. They wasn't no time. Not none. Soon as I got one day done here come a night. With you all coughin' and me watchin' so TB wouldn't take you off and if you was sleepin' quiet I thought, O Lord, they dead and put my hand over your mouth to feel if the breath was comin' what you talkin' 'bout did I love you girl I stayed alive for you can't you get that through your thick head or what is that between your ears, heifer?"

Hannah had enough beans now. With some tomatoes and hot bread, she thought, that would be enough for everybody, especially since the deweys didn't eat vegetables no how and Eva never made them and Tar Baby was living off air and music these days. She picked up the basket and stood with it and the bowl of beans over her mother. Eva's face was still asking her last question. Hannah looked into her mother's eyes.

"But what about Plum? What'd you kill Plum for, Mamma?"

It was a Wednesday in August and the ice wagon was coming and coming. You could hear bits of the driver's song. Now Mrs. Jackson would be tipping down her porch steps. "Jes a piece. You got a lil ole piece layin' 'round in there you could spare?" And as he had since the time of the pigeons, the iceman would hand her a lump of ice saying, "Watch it now, Mrs. Jackson. That straw'll tickle your pretty neck to death."

Eva listened to the wagon coming and thought about what it must be like in the icehouse. She leaned back a little and closed her eyes trying to see the insides of the icehouse. It was a dark, lovely picture in this heat, until it reminded her of that winter night in the outhouse holding her baby in the dark, her fingers searching for his asshole and the last bit of lard scooped from the sides of the can, held deliberately on the tip of her middle finger, the last bit of lard to keep from hurting him when she slid her finger in and all because she had broken the slop jar and the rags had frozen. The last food staple in the house she had rammed up her baby's behind to keep from hurting him too much when she opened up his bowels to pull the stools out. He had been screaming fit to kill, but when she found his hole at last and stuck her finger up in it, the shock was so great he was suddenly quiet. Even now on the hottest day anyone in Medallion could remember—a day so hot flies slept and cats were splaying their fur like quills, a day so hot pregnant wives leaned up against trees and cried, and women remembering some three-month-old hurt put ground glass in their lovers' food and the men looked at the food and wondered if there was glass in it and ate it anyway because it was too hot to resist eating it—even on this hottest of days in the hot spell, Eva shivered from the biting cold and stench of that outhouse.

Hannah was waiting. Watching her mother's eyelids. When Eva spoke at last it was with two voices. Like two people were talking at the same time, saying the same thing, one a fraction of a second behind the other.

"He give me such a time. Such a time. Look like he didn't even want to be born. But he come on out. Boys is hard to bear. You wouldn't know that but they is. It was such a carryin' on to get him born and to keep him alive. Just to keep his little heart beating and his little old lungs cleared and look like when he came back from that war he wanted to git back in. After all that carryin' on, just gettin' him out and keepin' him alive, he wanted to crawl back in my womb and well . . . I ain't got the room no more even if he could do it. There wasn't space for him in my womb. And he was crawlin' back. Being helpless and thinking baby

thoughts and dreaming baby dreams and messing up his pants again and
smiling all the time. I had room enough in my heart, but not in my
womb, not no more. I birthed him once. I couldn't do it again. He was
growed, a big old thing. Godhavemercy, I couldn't birth him twice. I'd be
laying here at night and he be downstairs in that room, but when I closed
my eyes I'd see him ... six feet tall smilin' and crawlin' up the stairs
quietlike so I wouldn't hear and opening the door soft so I wouldn't hear
and he'd be creepin' to the bed trying to spread my legs trying to get
back up in my womb. He was a man, girl, a big old growed-up man. I
didn't have that much room. I kept on dreaming it. Dreaming it and
I knowed it was true. One night it wouldn't be no dream. It'd be true and I
would have done it, would have let him if I'd've had the room but a big
man can't be a baby all wrapped up inside his mamma no more; he suffo-
cate. I done everything I could to make him leave me and go on and live
and be a man but he wouldn't and I had to keep him out so I just thought
of a way he could die like a man not all scrunched up inside my womb,
but like a man."

Eva couldn't see Hannah clearly for the tears, but she looked up at her
anyway and said, by way of apology or explanation or perhaps just by
way of neatness, "But I held him close first. Real close. Sweet Plum. My
baby boy."

Long after Hannah turned and walked out of the room, Eva continued
to call his name while her fingers lined up the pleats in her dress.

Hannah went off to the kitchen, her old man's slippers plopping down
the stairs and over the hardwood floors. She turned the spigot on, letting
water break up the tight knots of Kentucky Wonders and float them to
the top of the bowl. She swirled them about with her fingers, poured the
water off and repeated the process. Each time the green tubes rose to the
surface she felt elated and collected whole handfuls at a time to drop in
twos and threes back into the water.

Through the window over the sink she could see the deweys still playing chain gang; their ankles bound one to the other, they tumbled, struggled back to their feet and tried to walk single file. Hens strutted by with
one suspicious eye on the deweys, another on the brick fireplace where
sheets and mason jars were boiled. Only the deweys could play in this
heat. Hannah put the Kentucky Wonders over the fire and, struck by a
sudden sleepiness, she went off to lie down in the front room. It was even
hotter there, for the windows were shut to keep out the sunlight. Hannah
straightened the shawl that draped the couch and lay down. She dreamed
of a wedding in a red bridal gown until Sula came in and woke her.

But before the second strange thing, there had been the wind, which
was the first. The very night before the day Hannah had asked Eva if she
had ever loved them, the wind tore over the hills rattling roofs and loosening doors. Everything shook, and although the people were frightened
they thought it meant rain and welcomed it. Windows fell out and trees
lost arms. People waited up half the night for the first crack of lightning.
Some had even uncovered barrels to catch the rain water, which they
loved to drink and cook in. They waited in vain, for no lightning no
thunder no rain came. The wind just swept through, took what dampness
there was out of the air, messed up the yards, and went on. The hills of
the Bottom, as always, protected the valley part of town where the white
people lived, and the next morning all the people were grateful because

there was a dryer heat. So they set about their work early, for it was canning time, and who knew but what the wind would come back this time with a cooling rain. The men who worked in the valley got up at four thirty in the morning and looked at the sky where the sun was already rising like a hot white bitch. They beat the brims of their hats against their legs before putting them on and trudged down the road like old promises nobody wanted kept.

On Thursday, when Hannah brought Eva her fried tomatoes and soft scrambled eggs with the white left out for good luck, she mentioned her dream of the wedding in the red dress. Neither one bothered to look it up for they both knew the number was 522.[7] Eva said she'd play it when Mr. Buckland Reed came by. Later she would remember it as the third strange thing. She had thought it odd even then, but the red in the dream confused her. But she wasn't certain that it was third or not because Sula was acting up, fretting the deweys and meddling the newly married couple. Because she was thirteen, everybody supposed her nature was coming down, but it was hard to put up with her sulking and irritation. The birthmark over her eye was getting darker and looked more and more like a stem and rose. She was dropping things and eating food that belonged to the newly married couple and started in to worrying everybody that the deweys needed a bath and she was going to give it to them. The deweys, who went wild at the thought of water, were crying and thundering all over the house like colts.

"We ain't got to, do we? Do we got to do what she says? It ain't Saturday." They even woke up Tar Baby, who came out of his room to look at them and then left the house in search of music.

Hannah ignored them and kept on bringing mason jars out of the cellar and washing them. Eva banged on the floor with her stick but nobody came. By noon it was quiet. The deweys had escaped, Sula was either in her room or gone off somewhere. The newly married couple, energized by their morning lovemaking, had gone to look for a day's work happily certain that they would find none.

The air all over the Bottom got heavy with peeled fruit and boiling vegetables. Fresh corn, tomatoes, string beans, melon rinds. The women, the children and the old men who had no jobs were putting up for a winter they understood so well. Peaches were stuffed into jars and black cherries (later, when it got cooler, they would put up jellies and preserves). The greedy canned as many as forty-two a day even though some of them, like Mrs. Jackson, who ate ice, had jars from 1920.

Before she trundled her wagon over to the dresser to get her comb, Eva looked out the window and saw Hannah bending to light the yard fire. And that was the fifth (or fourth, if you didn't count Sula's craziness) strange thing. She couldn't find her comb. Nobody moved stuff in Eva's room except to clean and then they put everything right back. But Eva couldn't find it anywhere. One hand pulling her braids loose, the other searching the dresser drawers, she had just begun to get irritated when she felt it in her blouse drawer. Then she trundled back to the window to catch a breeze, if one took a mind to come by, while she combed her hair. She rolled up to the window and it was then she saw Hannah burning. The flames from the yard fire were licking the blue cotton dress,

7. The reference is apparently to a dream book in which Hannah's dream is #522 and well known; Eva plans to buy #522 in the daily "numbers" lottery.

making her dance. Eva knew there was time for nothing in this world
other than the time it took to get there and cover her daughter's body
with her own. She lifted her heavy frame up on her good leg, and with
fists and arms smashed the windowpane. Using her stump as a support on
the window sill, her good leg as a lever, she threw herself out of the
window. Cut and bleeding she clawed the air trying to aim her body
toward the flaming, dancing figure. She missed and came crashing down
some twelve feet from Hannah's smoke. Stunned but still conscious, Eva
dragged herself toward her firstborn, but Hannah, her senses lost, went
flying out of the yard gesturing and bobbing like a spring jack-in-the-box.

Mr. and Mrs. Suggs, who had set up their canning apparatus in their
front yard, saw her running, dancing toward them. They whispered,
"Jesus, Jesus," and together hoisted up their tub of water in which tight
red tomatoes floated and threw it on the smoke-and-flame-bound woman.
The water did put out the flames, but it also made steam, which seared to
sealing all that was left of the beautiful Hannah Peace. She lay there on
the wooden sidewalk planks, twitching lightly among the smashed tomatoes, her face a mask of agony so intense that for years the people who
gathered 'round would shake their heads at the recollection of it.

Somebody covered her legs with a shirt. A woman unwrapped her head
rag and placed it on Hannah's shoulder. Somebody else ran to Dick's
Fresh Food and Sundries to call the ambulance. The rest stood there as
helpless as sunflowers leaning on a fence. The deweys came and stepped
in the tomatoes, their eyes raked with wonder. Two cats sidled through
the legs of the crowd, sniffing the burned flesh. The vomiting of a young
girl finally broke the profound silence and caused the women to talk to
each other and to God. In the midst of calling Jesus they heard the hollow clang of the ambulance bell struggling up the hill, but not the "Help
me, ya'll" that the dying woman whispered. Then somebody remembered
to go and see about Eva. They found her on her stomach by the forsythia
bushes calling Hannah's name and dragging her body through the sweet
peas and clover that grew under the forsythia by the side of the house.
Mother and daughter were placed on stretchers and carried to the ambulance. Eva was wide awake. The blood from her face cuts filled her eyes
so she could not see, could only smell the familiar odor of cooked flesh.

Hannah died on the way to the hospital. Or so they said. In any case,
she had already begun to bubble and blister so badly that the coffin had
to be kept closed at the funeral and the women who washed the body and
dressed it for death wept for her burned hair and wrinkled breasts as
though they themselves had been her lovers.

When Eva got to the hospital they put her stretcher on the floor, so
preoccupied with the hot and bubbling flesh of the other (some of them
had never seen so extreme a burn case before) they forgot Eva, who
would have bled to death except Old Willy Fields, the orderly, saw blood
staining his just-mopped floors and went to find out where it was coming
from. Recognizing Eva at once he shouted to a nurse, who came to see if
the bloody one-legged black woman was alive or dead. From then on
Willy boasted that he had saved Eva's life—an indisputable fact which
she herself admitted and for which she cursed him every day for thirty-
seven years thereafter and would have cursed him for the rest of her life
except by then she was already ninety years old and forgot things.

Lying in the colored ward of the hospital, which was a screened corner of a larger ward, Eva mused over the perfection of the judgment against her. She remembered the wedding dream and recalled that weddings always meant death. And the red gown, well that was the fire, as she should have known. She remembered something else too, and try as she might to deny it, she knew that as she lay on the ground trying to drag herself through the sweet peas and clover to get to Hannah, she had seen Sula standing on the back porch just looking. When Eva, who was never one to hide the faults of her children, mentioned what she thought she'd seen to a few friends, they said it was natural. Sula was probably struck dumb, as anybody would be who saw her own mamma burn up. Eva said yes, but inside she disagreed and remained convinced that Sula had watched Hannah burn not because she was paralyzed, but because she was interested.

1927

Old people were dancing with little children. Young boys with their sisters, and the church women who frowned on any bodily expression of joy (except when the hand of God commanded it) tapped their feet. Somebody (the groom's father, everybody said) had poured a whole pint jar of cane liquor into the punch, so even the men who did not sneak out the back door to have a shot, as well as the women who let nothing stronger than Black Draught enter their blood, were tipsy. A small boy stood at the Victrola turning its handle and smiling at the sound of Bert Williams' "Save a Little Dram for Me."[8]

Even Helene Wright had mellowed with the cane, waving away apologies for drinks spilled on her rug and paying no attention whatever to the chocolate cake lying on the arm of her red-velvet sofa. The tea roses above her left breast had slipped from the brooch that fastened them and were hanging heads down. When her husband called her attention to the children wrapping themselves into her curtains, she merely smiled and said, "Oh, let them be." She was not only a little drunk, she was weary and had been for weeks. Her only child's wedding—the culmination of all she had been, thought or done in this world—had dragged from her energy and stamina even she did not know she possessed. Her house had to be thoroughly cleaned, chickens had to be plucked, cakes and pies made, and for weeks she, her friends and her daughter had been sewing. Now it was all happening and it took only a little cane juice to snap the chords of fatigue and damn the white curtains that she had pinned on the stretcher only the morning before. Once this day was over she would have a lifetime to rattle around in that house and repair the damage.

A real wedding, in a church, with a real reception afterward, was rare among the people of the Bottom. Expensive for one thing, and most newlyweds just went to the courthouse if they were not particular, or had the preacher come in and say a few words if they were. The rest just "took up" with one another. No invitations were sent. There was no need for formality. Folks just came, bringing a gift if they had one, none if they didn't. Except for those who worked in valley houses, most of them had never been to a big wedding; they simply assumed it was rather like a

8. Egbert Austin Williams (1874–1922), a great vaudeville and Broadway comedian, wrote as well as performed novelty songs. Black Draught: a vegetable laxative.

funeral except afterward you didn't have to walk all the way out to Beechnut Cemetery.

This wedding offered a special attraction, for the bridegroom was a handsome, well-liked man—the tenor of Mount Zion's Men's Quartet, who had an enviable reputation among the girls and a comfortable one among men. His name was Jude Greene, and with the pick of some eight or ten girls who came regularly to services to hear him sing, he had chosen Nel Wright.

He wasn't really aiming to get married. He was twenty then, and although his job as a waiter at the Hotel Medallion was a blessing to his parents and their seven other children, it wasn't nearly enough to support a wife. He had brought the subject up first on the day the word got out that the town was building a new road, tarmac, that would wind through Medallion on down to the river, where a great new bridge was to be built to connect Medallion to Porter's Landing, the town on the other side. The war over, a fake prosperity was still around. In a state of euphoria, with a hunger for more and more, the council of founders cast its eye toward a future that would certainly include trade from cross-river towns. Towns that needed more than a house raft to get to the merchants of Medallion. Work had already begun on the New River Road (the city had always meant to name it something else, something wonderful, but ten years later when the bridge idea was dropped for a tunnel it was still called the New River Road).

Along with a few other young black men, Jude had gone down to the shack where they were hiring. Three old colored men had already been hired, but not for the road work, just to do the picking up, food bringing and other small errands. These old men were close to feeble, not good for much else, and everybody was pleased they were taken on; still it was a shame to see those white men laughing with their grandfathers but shying away from the young black men who could tear that road up. The men like Jude who could do real work. Jude himself longed more than anybody else to be taken. Not just for the good money, more for the work itself. He wanted to swing the pick or kneel down with the string or shovel the gravel. His arms ached for something heavier than trays, for something dirtier than peelings; his feet wanted the heavy work shoes, not the thin-soled black shoes that the hotel required. More than anything he wanted the camaraderie of the road men: the lunch buckets, the hollering, the body movement that in the end produced something real, something he could point to. "I built that road," he could say. How much better sun-down would be than the end of a day in the restaurant, where a good day's work was marked by the number of dirty plates and the weight of the garbage bin. "I built that road." People would walk over his sweat for years. Perhaps a sledge hammer would come crashing down on his foot, and when people asked him how come he limped, he could say, "Got that building the New Road."

It was while he was full of such dreams, his body already feeling the rough work clothes, his hands already curved to the pick handle, that he spoke to Nel about getting married. She seemed receptive but hardly anxious. It was after he stood in lines for six days running and saw the gang boss pick out thin-armed white boys from the Virginia hills and the bull-necked Greeks and Italians and heard over and over, "Nothing else today. Come back tomorrow," that he got the message. So it was rage, rage and a determination to take on a man's role anyhow that made him press Nel about settling down. He needed some of his appetites filled, some posture of adulthood recognized, but mostly he wanted someone to care about his hurt, to care very deeply. Deep enough to hold him, deep enough to rock him, deep enough to ask, "How you feel? You all right? Want some coffee?" And if he were to be a man, that someone could no longer be his mother. He chose the girl who had always been kind, who had never seemed hell-bent to marry, who made the whole venture seem like his idea, his conquest.

The more he thought about marriage, the more attractive it became. Whatever his fortune, whatever the cut of his garment, there would always be the hem—the tuck and fold that hid his raveling edges; a someone sweet, industrious and loyal to shore him up. And in return he would shelter her, love her, grow old with her. Without that someone he was a waiter hanging around a kitchen like a woman. With her he was head of a household pinned to an unsatisfactory job out of necessity. The two of them together would make one Jude.

His fears lest his burst dream of road building discourage her were never realized. Nel's indifference to his hints about marriage disappeared altogether when she discovered his pain. Jude could see himself taking shape in her eyes. She actually wanted to help, to soothe, and was it true what Ajax said in the Time and a Half Pool Hall? That "all they want, man, is they own misery. Ax em to die for you and they yours for life."

Whether he was accurate in general, Ajax was right about Nel. Except for an occasional leadership role with Sula, she had no aggression. Her parents had succeeded in rubbing down to a dull glow any sparkle or splutter she had. Only with Sula did that quality have free reign, but their friendship was so close, they themselves had difficulty distinguishing one's thoughts from the other's. During all of her girlhood the only respite Nel had had from her stern and undemonstrative parents was Sula. When Jude began to hover around, she was flattered—all the girls liked him—and Sula made the enjoyment of his attentions keener simply because she seemed always to want Nel to shine. They never quarreled, those two, the way some girlfriends did over boys, or competed against each other for them. In those days a compliment to one was a compliment to the other, and cruelty to one was a challenge to the other.

Nel's response to Jude's shame and anger selected her away from Sula. And greater than her friendship was this new feeling of being needed by someone who saw her singly. She didn't even know she had a neck until Jude remarked on it, or that her smile was anything but the spreading of her lips until he saw it as a small miracle.

Sula was no less excited about the wedding. She thought it was the perfect thing to do following their graduation from general school. She wanted to be the bridesmaid. No others. And she encouraged Mrs. Wright to go all out, even to borrowing Eva's punch bowl. In fact, she handled most of the details very efficiently, capitalizing on the fact that most people were anxious to please her since she had lost her mamma only a few years back and they still remembered the agony in Hannah's face and the blood on Eva's.

So they danced up in the Bottom on the second Saturday in June, danced at the wedding where everybody realized for the first time that except for their magnificent teeth, the deweys would never grow. They had been forty-eight inches tall for years now, and while their size was unusual it was not unheard of. The realization was based on the fact that they remained boys in mind. Mischievous, cunning, private and completely unhousebroken, their games and interests had not changed since Hannah had them all put into the first grade together.

Nel and Jude, who had been the stars all during the wedding, were forgotten finally as the reception melted into a dance, a feed, a gossip session, a playground and a love nest. For the first time that day they relaxed and looked at each other, and liked what they saw. They began to dance, pressed in among the others, and each one turned his thoughts to the night that was coming on fast. They had taken a housekeeping room with one of Jude's aunts (over the protest of Mrs. Wright, who had rooms to spare, but Nel didn't want to make love to her husband in her mother's house) and were getting restless to go there.

As if reading her thoughts, Jude leaned down and whispered, "Me too." Nel smiled and rested her cheek on his shoulder. The veil she wore was too heavy to allow her to feel the core of the kiss he pressed on her head. When she raised her eyes to him for one more look of reassurance, she saw through the open door a slim figure in blue, gliding, with just a hint of a strut, down the path toward the road. One hand was pressed to the head to hold down the large hat against the warm June breeze. Even from the rear Nel could tell that it was Sula and that she was smiling; that something deep down in that litheness was amused. It would be ten years before they saw each other again, and their meeting would be thick with birds.

Part Two

1937

Accompanied by a plague of robins, Sula came back to Medallion. The little yam-breasted shuddering birds were everywhere, exciting very small children away from their usual welcome into a vicious stoning. Nobody knew why or from where they had come. What they did know was that you couldn't go anywhere without stepping in their pearly shit, and it was hard to hang up clothes, pull weeds or just sit on the front porch when robins were flying and dying all around you.

Although most of the people remembered the time when the sky was black for two hours with clouds and clouds of pigeons, and although they were accustomed to excesses in nature—too much heat, too much cold, too little rain, rain to flooding—they still dreaded the way a relatively trivial phenomenon could become sovereign in their lives and bend their minds to its will.

In spite of their fear, they reacted to an oppressive oddity, or what they called evil days, with an acceptance that bordered on welcome. Such evil must be avoided, they felt, and precautions must naturally be taken to protect themselves from it. But they let it run its course, fulfill itself, and never invented ways either to alter it, to annihilate it or to prevent its happening again. So also were they with people.

What was taken by outsiders to be slackness, slovenliness or even generosity was in fact a full recognition of the legitimacy of forces other than
good ones. They did not believe doctors could heal—for them, none ever
had done so. They did not believe death was accidental—life might be,
but death was deliberate. They did not believe Nature was ever askew—
only inconvenient. Plague and drought were as "natural" as springtime. If
milk could curdle, God knows robins could fall. The purpose of evil was
to survive it and they determined (without ever knowing they had made
up their minds to do it) to survive floods, white people, tuberculosis, fam-
ine and ignorance. They knew anger well but not despair, and they didn't
stone sinners for the same reason they didn't commit suicide—it was beneath them.

Sula stepped off the Cincinnati Flyer into the robin shit and began the
long climb up into the Bottom. She was dressed in a manner that was as
close to a movie star as anyone would ever see. A black crepe dress
splashed with pink and yellow zinnias, foxtails, a black felt hat with the
veil of net lowered over one eye. In her right hand was a black purse
with a beaded clasp and in her left a red leather traveling case, so small,
so charming—no one had seen anything like it ever before, including the
mayor's wife and the music teacher, both of whom had been to Rome.

Walking up the hill toward Carpenter's Road, the heels and sides of
her pumps edged with drying bird shit, she attracted the glances of old
men sitting on stone benches in front of the courthouse, housewives
throwing buckets of water on their sidewalks, and high school students on
their way home for lunch. By the time she reached the Bottom, the news
of her return had brought the black people out on their porches or to
their windows. There were scattered hellos and nods but mostly stares. A
little boy ran up to her saying, "Carry yo' bag, ma'am?" Before Sula could
answer his mother had called him, "You, John. Get back in here."

At Eva's house there were four dead robins on the walk. Sula stopped
and with her toe pushed them into the bordering grass.

Eva looked at Sula pretty much the same way she had looked at Boy-
Boy that time when he returned after he'd left her without a dime or a
prospect of one. She was sitting in her wagon, her back to the window
she had jumped out of (now all boarded up) setting fire to the hair she
had combed out of her head. When Sula opened the door she raised her
eyes and said, "I might have knowed them birds meant something.
Where's your coat?"

Sula threw herself on Eva's bed. "The rest of my stuff will be on later."

"I should hope so. Them little old furry tails ain't going to do you no
more good than they did the fox that was wearing them."

"Don't you say hello to nobody when you ain't seen them for ten
years?"

"If folks let somebody know where they is and when they coming, then
other folks can get ready for them. If they don't—if they just pop in all
sudden like—then they got to take whatever mood they find."

"How you been doing, Big Mamma?"

"Gettin' by. Sweet of you to ask. You was quick enough when you
wanted something. When you needed a little change or . . ."

"Don't talk to me about how much you gave me, Big Mamma, and how
much I owe you or none of that."

"Oh? I ain't supposed to mention it?"

"OK. Mention it." Sula shrugged and turned over on her stomach, her buttocks toward Eva.

"You ain't been in this house ten seconds and already you starting something."

"Takes two, Big Mamma."

"Well, don't let your mouth start nothing that your ass can't stand. When you gone to get married? You need to have some babies. It'll settle you."

"I don't want to make somebody else. I want to make myself."

"Selfish. Ain't no woman got no business floatin' around without no man."

"You did."

"Not by choice."

"Mamma did."

"Not by choice, I said. It ain't right for you to want to stay off by yourself. You need . . . I'm a tell you what you need."

Sula sat up. "I need you to shut your mouth."

"Don't nobody talk to me like that. Don't nobody . . ."

"This body does. Just 'cause you was bad enough to cut off your own leg you think you got a right to kick everybody with the stump."

"Who said I cut off my leg?"

"Well, you stuck it under a train to collect insurance."

"Hold on, you lyin' heifer!"

"I aim to."

"Bible say honor thy father and thy mother that thy days may be long upon the land thy God giveth thee."[9]

"Mamma must have skipped that part. Her days wasn't too long."

"Pus mouth! God's going to strike you!"

"Which God? The one watched you burn Plum?"

"Don't talk to me about no burning. You watched your own mamma. You crazy roach! You the one should have been burnt!"

"But I ain't. Got that? I ain't. Any more fires in this house, I'm lighting them!"

"Hellfire don't need lighting and it's already burning in you . . ."

"Whatever's burning in me is mine!"

"Amen!"

"And I'll split this town in two and everything in it before I'll let you put it out!"

"Pride goeth before a fall."

"What the hell do I care about falling?"

"Amazing Grace."[1]

"You sold your life for twenty-three dollars a month."

"You throwed yours away."

"It's mine to throw."

"One day you gone need it."

"But not you. I ain't never going to need you. And you know what?

9. Exodus 20:12.
1. Hymn (1779) by John Newton (1725–1807)—"Amazing grace! how sweet the sound/ That saved a wretch like me!/ I once was lost, but now am found,/ Was blind, but now I see." Above: a paraphrase of Proverbs 16:18—"Pride goeth before destruction, and an haughty spirit before a fall."

Maybe one night when you dozing in that wagon flicking flies and swallowing spit, maybe I'll just tip on up here with some kerosene and—who knows—you may make the brightest flame of them all."

So Eva locked her door from then on. But it did no good. In April two men came with a stretcher and she didn't even have time to comb her hair before they strapped her to a piece of canvas.

When Mr. Buckland Reed came by to pick up the number, his mouth sagged at the sight of Eva being carried out and Sula holding some papers against the wall, at the bottom of which, just above the word "guardian," she very carefully wrote Miss Sula Mae Peace.

◉ ◉ ◉

Nel alone noticed the peculiar quality of the May that followed the leaving of the birds. It had a sheen, a glimmering as of green, rain-soaked Saturday nights (lit by the excitement of newly installed street lights); of lemon-yellow afternoons bright with iced drinks and splashes of daffodils. It showed in the damp faces of her children and the river-smoothness of their voices. Even her own body was not immune to the magic. She would sit on the floor to sew as she had done as a girl, fold her legs up under her or do a little dance that fitted some tune in her head. There were easy sun-washed days and purple dusks in which Tar Baby sang "Abide With Me" at prayer meetings, his lashes darkened by tears, his silhouette limp with regret against the whitewashed walls of Greater Saint Matthew's. Nel listened and was moved to smile. To smile at the sheer loveliness that pressed in from the windows and touched his grief, making it a pleasure to behold.

Although it was she alone who saw this magic, she did not wonder at it. She knew it was all due to Sula's return to the Bottom. It was like getting the use of an eye back, having a cataract removed. Her old friend had come home. Sula. Who made her laugh, who made her see old things with new eyes, in whose presence she felt clever, gentle and a little raunchy. Sula, whose past she had lived through and with whom the present was a constant sharing of perceptions. Talking to Sula had always been a conversation with herself. Was there anyone else before whom she could never be foolish? In whose view inadequacy was mere idiosyncrasy, a character trait rather than a deficiency? Anyone who left behind that aura of fun and complicity? Sula never competed; she simply helped others define themselves. Other people seemed to turn their volume on and up when Sula was in the room. More than any other thing, humor returned. She could listen to the crunch of sugar underfoot that the children had spilled without reaching for the switch; and she forgot the tear in the living-room window shade. Even Nel's love for Jude, which over the years had spun a steady gray web around her heart, became a bright and easy affection, a playfulness that was reflected in their lovemaking.

Sula would come by of an afternoon, walking along with her fluid stride, wearing a plain yellow dress the same way her mother, Hannah, had worn those too-big house dresses—with a distance, an absence of a relationship to clothes which emphasized everything the fabric covered. When she scratched the screen door, as in the old days, and stepped inside, the dishes piled in the sink looked as though they belonged there; the dust on the lamps sparkled; the hair brush lying on the "good" sofa in the living room did not have to be apologetically retrieved, and Nel's grimy intractable children looked like three wild things happily insouciant in the May shine.

"Hey, girl." The rose mark over Sula's eye gave her glance a suggestion of startled pleasure. It was darker than Nel remembered.

"Hey yourself. Come on in here."

"How you doin'?" Sula moved a pile of ironed diapers from a chair and sat down.

"Oh, I ain't strangled nobody yet so I guess I'm all right."

"Well, if you change your mind call me."

"Somebody need killin'?"

"Half this town need it."

"And the other half?"

"A drawn-out disease."

"Oh, come on. Is Medallion that bad?"

"Didn't nobody tell you?"

"You been gone too long, Sula."

"Not too long, but maybe too far."

"What's that supposed to mean?" Nel dipped her fingers into the bowl of water and sprinkled a diaper.

"Oh, I don't know."

"Want some cool tea?"

"Mmmm. Lots of ice, I'm burnin' up."

"Iceman don't come yet, but it's good and cold."

"That's fine."

"Hope I didn't speak too soon. Kids run in and out of here so much." Nel bent to open the icebox.

"You puttin' it on, Nel. Jude must be wore out."

"*Jude* must be wore out? You don't care nothin' 'bout my back, do you?"

"Is that where it's at, in your back?"

"Hah! Jude thinks it's everywhere."

"He's right, it is everywhere. Just be glad he found it, wherever it is. Remember John L.?"

"When Shirley said he got her down by the well and tried to stick it in her hip?" Nel giggled at the remembrance of that teen-time tale. "She should have been grateful. Have you seen her since you been back?"

"Mmm. Like a ox."

"That was one dumb nigger, John L."

"Maybe. Maybe he was just sanitary."

"Sanitary?"

"Well. Think about it. Suppose Shirley was all splayed out in front of you? Wouldn't you go for the hipbone instead?"

Nel lowered her head onto crossed arms while tears of laughter dripped into the warm diapers. Laughter that weakened her knees and pressed her bladder into action. Her rapid soprano and Sula's dark sleepy chuckle made a duet that frightened the cat and made the children run in from the back yard, puzzled at first by the wild free sounds, then delighted to see their mother stumbling merrily toward the bathroom, holding on to her stomach, fairly singing through the laughter: "Aw. Aw. Lord. Sula. Stop." And the other one, the one with the scary black thing over her eye, laughing softly and egging their mother on: "Neatness counts. You know what cleanliness is next to . . ."

"Hush." Nel's plea was clipped off by the slam of the bathroom door.

"What y'all laughing at?"

"Old time-y stuff. Long gone, old time-y stuff."

"Tell us."

"Tell *you?*" The black mark leaped.

"Uh huh. Tell us."

"What tickles us wouldn't tickle you."

"Uh huh, it would."

"Well, we was talking about some people we used to know when we was little."

"Was my mamma little?"

"Of course."

"What happened?"

"Well, some old boy we knew name John L. and a girl name . . ."

Damp-faced, Nel stepped back into the kitchen. She felt new, soft and new. It had been the longest time since she had had a rib-scraping laugh. She had forgotten how deep and down it could be. So different from the miscellaneous giggles and smiles she had learned to be content with these past few years.

"Oh Lord, Sula. You haven't changed none." She wiped her eyes. "What was all that about, anyway? All that scramblin' we did trying to do it and not do it at the same time?"

"Beats me. Such a simple thing."

"But we sure made a lot out of it, and the boys were dumber than we were."

"Couldn't nobody be dumber than I was."

"Stop lying. All of 'em liked you best."

"Yeah? Where are they?"

"They still here. You the one went off."

"Didn't I, though?"

"Tell me about it. The big city."

"Big is all it is. A big Medallion."

"No. I mean the life. The nightclubs, and parties . . ."

"I was in college, Nellie. No nightclubs on campus."

"Campus? That what they call it? Well. You wasn't in no college for—what—ten years now? And you didn't write to nobody. How come you never wrote?"

"You never did either."

"Where was I going to write to? All I knew was that you was in Nashville. I asked Miss Peace about you once or twice."

"What did *she* say?"

"I couldn't make much sense out of her. You know she been gettin' stranger and stranger after she come out the hospital. How is she anyway?"

"Same, I guess. Not so hot."

"No? Laura, I know, was doing her cooking and things. Is she still?"

"No. I put her out."

"Put her out? What for?"

"She made me nervous."

"But she was doing it for nothing, Sula."

"That's what you think. She was stealing right and left."

"Since when did you get froggy[2] about folks' stealing?"

Sula smiled. "OK. I lied. You wanted a reason."

"Well, give me the real one."

"I don't know the real one. She just didn't belong in that house. Digging around in the cupboards, picking up pots and ice picks . . ."

"You sure have changed. That house was always full of people digging in cupboards and carrying on."

"That's the reason, then."

"Sula. Come on, now."

"You've changed, too. I didn't used to have to explain everything to you."

Nel blushed. "Who's feeding the deweys and Tar Baby? You?"

"Sure me. Anyway Tar Baby don't eat and the deweys still crazy."

"I heard one of 'em's mamma came to take him back but didn't know which was hern."

"Don't nobody know."

"And Eva? You doing the work for her too?"

"Well, since you haven't heard it, let me tell you. Eva's real sick. I had her put where she could be watched and taken care of."

"Where would that be?"

"Out by Beechnut."

"You mean that home the white church run? Sula! That ain't no place for Eva. All them women is dirt poor with no people at all. Mrs. Wilkens and them. They got dropsy and can't hold their water—crazy as loons. Eva's odd, but she got sense. I don't think that's right, Sula."

"I'm scared of her, Nellie. That's why . . ."

"Scared? Of Eva?"

"You don't know her. Did you know she burnt Plum?"

"Oh, I heard that years ago. But nobody put no stock in it."

"They should have. It's true. I saw it. And when I got back here she was planning to do it to me too."

"Eva? I can't hardly believe that. She almost died trying to get to your mother."

Sula leaned forward, her elbows on the table. "You ever known me to lie to you?"

"No. But you could be mistaken. Why would Eva . . ."

"All I know is I'm scared. And there's no place else for me to go. We all that's left, Eva and me. I guess I should have stayed gone. I didn't know what else to do. Maybe I should have talked to you about it first. You always had better sense than me. Whenever I was scared before, you knew just what to do."

The closed place in the water spread before them. Nel put the iron on the stove. The situation was clear to her now. Sula, like always, was incapable of making any but the most trivial decisions. When it came to matters of grave importance, she behaved emotionally and irresponsibly and left it to others to straighten out. And when fear struck her, she did unbelievable things. Like that time with her finger. Whatever those hunkies[3] did, it wouldn't have been as bad as what she did to herself. But Sula was so scared she had mutilated herself, to protect herself.

"What should I do, Nellie? Take her back and sleep with my door locked again?"

"No. I guess it's too late anyway. But let's work out a plan for taking care of her. So she won't be messed over."

"Anything you say."

"What about money? She got any?"

Sula shrugged. "The checks come still. It's not much, like it used to be. Should I have them made over to me?"

"Can you? Do it, then. We can arrange for her to have special comforts. That place is a mess, you know. A doctor don't never set foot in there. I ain't figured out yet how they stay alive in there as long as they do."

"Why don't I have the checks made over to you, Nellie? You better at this than I am."

"Oh no. People will say I'm scheming. You the one to do it. Was there insurance from Hannah?"

"Yes. Plum too. He had all that army insurance."

"Any of it left?"

"Well I went to college on some. Eva banked the rest. I'll look into it, though."

". . . and explain it all to the bank people."

"Will you go down with me?"

"Sure. It's going to be all right."

"I'm glad I talked to you 'bout this. It's been bothering me."

"Well, tongues will wag, but so long as we know the truth, it don't matter."

Just at that moment the children ran in announcing the entrance of their father. Jude opened the back door and walked into the kitchen. He was still a very good-looking man, and the only difference Sula could see was the thin pencil mustache under his nose, and a part in his hair.

"Hey, Jude. What you know good?"

"White man running it—nothing good."

Sula laughed while Nel, high-tuned to his moods, ignored her husband's smile saying, "Bad day, honey?"

"Same old stuff," he replied and told them a brief tale of some personal insult done him by a customer and his boss—a whiney tale that peaked somewhere between anger and a lapping desire for comfort. He ended it with the observation that a Negro man had a hard row to hoe in this world. He expected his story to dovetail into milkwarm commiseration, but before Nel could excrete it, Sula said she didn't know about that—it looked like a pretty good life to her.

"Say what?" Jude's temper flared just a bit as he looked at this friend of his wife's, this slight woman, not exactly plain, but not fine either, with a copperhead over her eye. As far as he could tell, she looked like a woman roaming the country trying to find some man to burden down with a lot of lip and a lot of mouths.

Sula was smiling. "I mean, I don't know what the fuss is about. I mean, everything in the world loves you. White men love you. They spend so much time worrying about your penis they forget their own. The only thing they want to do is cut off a nigger's privates. And if that ain't love

and respect I don't know what is. And white women? They chase you all
to every corner of the earth, feel for you under every bed. I knew a white
woman wouldn't leave the house after 6 o'clock for fear one of you would
snatch her. Now ain't that love? They think rape soon's they see you, and
if they don't get the rape they looking for, they scream it anyway just so
the search won't be in vain. Colored women worry themselves into bad
health just trying to hang on to your cuffs. Even little children—white and
black, boys and girls—spend all their childhood eating their hearts out
'cause they think you don't love them. And if that ain't enough, you love
yourselves. Nothing in this world loves a black man more than another
black man. You hear of solitary white men, but niggers? Can't stay away
from one another a whole day. So. It looks to me like you the envy of the
world."

Jude and Nel were laughing, he saying, "Well, if that's the only way
they got to show it—cut off my balls and throw me in jail—I'd just as soon
they left me alone." But thinking that Sula had an odd way of looking at
things and that her wide smile took some of the sting from that rattle-
snake over her eye. A funny woman, he thought, not that bad-looking.
But he could see why she wasn't married; she stirred a man's mind
maybe, but not his body.

◉ ◉ ◉

He left his tie. The one with the scriggly yellow lines running lopsided
across the dark-blue field. It hung over the top of the closet door pointing
steadily downward while it waited with every confidence for Jude to return.

Could he be gone if his tie is still here? He will remember it and come
back and then she would . . . uh. Then she could . . . tell him. Sit down
quietly and tell him. "But Jude," she would say, "you *knew* me. All those
days and years, Jude, you *knew* me. My ways and my hands and how my
stomach folded and how we tried to get Mickey to nurse and how about
that time when the landlord said . . . but you said . . . and I cried, Jude.
You knew me and had listened to the things I said in the night, and heard
me in the bathroom and laughed at my raggedy girdle and I laughed too
because I knew you too, Jude. So how could you leave me when you
knew me?"

But they had been down on all fours naked, not touching except their
lips right down there on the floor where the tie is pointing to, on all fours
like (uh huh, go on, say it) like dogs. Nibbling at each other, not even
touching, not even looking at each other, just their lips, and when I
opened the door they didn't even look for a minute and I thought the
reason they are not looking up is because they are not doing that. So it's
all right. I am just standing here. They are not doing that. I am just standing here and seeing it, but they are not really doing it. But then they did
look up. Or you did. You did, Jude. And if only you had not looked at me
the way the soldiers did on the train, the way you look at the children
when they come in while you are listening to Gabriel Heatter[4] and break

---

4. Longtime popular radio news commentator who always had "good news tonight."

your train of thought—not focusing exactly but giving them an instant, a piece of time, to remember what they are doing, what they are interrupting, and to go on back to wherever they were and let you listen to Gabriel Heatter. And I did not know how to move my feet or fix my eyes or what. I just stood there seeing it and smiling, because maybe there was some explanation, something important that I did not know about that would have made it all right. I waited for Sula to look up at me any minute and say one of those lovely college words like *aesthetic* or *rapport*, which I never understood but which I loved because they sounded so comfortable and firm. And finally you just got up and started putting on your clothes and your privates were hanging down, so soft, and you buckled your pants belt but forgot to button the fly and she was sitting on the bed not even bothering to put on her clothes because actually she didn't need to because somehow she didn't look naked to me, only you did. Her chin was in her hand and she sat like a visitor from out of town waiting for the hosts to get some quarreling done and over with so the card game could continue and me wanting her to leave so I could tell you privately that you had forgotten to button your fly because I didn't want to say it in front of her, Jude. And even when you began to talk, I couldn't hear because I was worried about you not knowing that your fly was open and scared too because your eyes looked like the soldiers' that time on the train when my mother turned to custard.

Remember how big that bedroom was? Jude? How when we moved here we said, Well, at least we got us a real big bedroom, but it was small then, Jude, and so shambly, and maybe it was that way all along but it would have been better if I had gotten the dust out from under the bed because I was ashamed of it in that small room. And then you walked past me saying, "I'll be back for my things." And you did but you left your tie.

The clock was ticking. Nel looked at it and realized that it was two thirty, only forty-five minutes before the children would be home and she hadn't even felt anything right or sensible and now there was no time or wouldn't be until nighttime when they were asleep and she could get into bed and maybe she could do it then. Think. But who could think in that bed where *they* had been and where they *also* had been and where only she was now?

She looked around for a place to be. A small place. The closet? No. Too dark. The bathroom. It was both small and bright, and she wanted to be in a very small, very bright place. Small enough to contain her grief. Bright enough to throw into relief the dark things that cluttered her. Once inside, she sank to the tile floor next to the toilet. On her knees, her hand on the cold rim of the bathtub, she waited for something to happen . . . inside. There was stirring, a movement of mud and dead leaves. She thought of the women at Chicken Little's funeral. The women who shrieked over the bier and at the lip of the open grave. What she had regarded since as unbecoming behavior seemed fitting to her now; they were screaming at the neck of God, his giant nape, the vast back-of-the-head that he had turned on them in death. But it seemed to her now that it was not a fist-shaking grief they were keening but rather a simple obligation to say something, do something, feel something about the dead. They could not let that heart-smashing event pass unrecorded, unidentified. It was poisonous, unnatural to let the dead go with a mere whimpering, a slight murmur, a rose bouquet of good taste. Good taste was out of place in the company of death, death itself was the essence of bad taste. And there must be much rage and saliva in its presence. The body must move and throw itself about, the eyes must roll, the hands should have no peace, and the throat should release all the yearning, despair and outrage that accompany the stupidity of loss.

"The real hell of Hell is that it is forever." Sula said that. She said doing anything forever and ever was hell. Nel didn't understand it then, but now in the bathroom, trying to feel, she thought, "If I could be sure that I could stay here in this small white room with the dirty tile and water gurgling in the pipes and my head on the cool rim of this bathtub and never have to go out the door, I would be happy. If I could be certain that I never had to get up and flush the toilet, go in the kitchen, watch my children grow up and die, see my food chewed on my plate . . . Sula was wrong. Hell ain't things lasting forever. Hell is change." Not only did men leave and children grow up and die, but even the misery didn't last. One day she wouldn't even have that. This very grief that had twisted her into a curve on the floor and flayed her would be gone. She would lose that too.

"Why, even in hate here I am thinking of what Sula said."

Hunched down in the small bright room Nel waited. Waited for the oldest cry. A scream not for others, not in sympathy for a burnt child, or a dead father, but a deeply personal cry for one's own pain. A loud, strident: "Why me?" She waited. The mud shifted, the leaves stirred, the smell of overripe green things enveloped her and announced the beginnings of her very own howl.

But it did not come.

The odor evaporated; the leaves were still, the mud settled. And finally there was nothing, just a flake of something dry and nasty in her throat. She stood up frightened. There was something just to the right of her, in the air, just out of view. She could not see it, but she knew exactly what it looked like. A gray ball hovering just there. Just there. To the right. Quiet, gray, dirty. A ball of muddy strings, but without weight, fluffy but terrible in its malevolence. She knew she could not look, so she closed her eyes and crept past it out of the bathroom, shutting the door behind her. Sweating with fear, she stepped to the kitchen door and onto the back porch. The lilac bushes preened at the railing, but there were no lilacs yet. Wasn't it time? Surely it was time. She looked over the fence to Mrs. Rayford's yard. Hers were not in bloom either. Was it too late? She fastened on this question with enthusiasm, all the time aware of something she was not thinking. It was the only way she could get her mind off the flake in her throat.

She spent a whole summer with the gray ball, the little ball of fur and string and hair always floating in the light near her but which she did not see because she never looked. But that was the terrible part, the effort it took not to look. But it was there anyhow, just to the right of her head and maybe further down by her shoulder, so when the childern went to a monster movie at the Elmira Theater and came home and said, "Mamma, can you sleep with us tonight?" she said all right and got into bed with the two boys, who loved it, but the girl did not. For a long time she could not stop getting in the bed with her children and told herself each time that they might dream a dream about dragons and would need her to

comfort them. It was so nice to think about their scary dreams and not
about a ball of fur. She even hoped their dreams would rub off on her and
give her the wonderful relief of a nightmare so she could stop going
around scared to turn her head this way or that lest she see it. That was
the scary part—seeing it. It was not coming at her; it never did that, or
tried to pounce on her. It just floated there for the seeing, if she wanted
to, and O my God for the touching if she wanted to. But she didn't want
to see it, ever, for if she saw it, who could tell but what she might actually touch it, or want to, and then what would happen if she actually
reached out her hand and touched it? Die probably, but no, worse than
that. Dying was OK because it was sleep and there wasn't no gray ball in
death, was there? Was there? She would have to ask somebody about
that, somebody she could confide in and who knew a lot of things, like
Sula, for Sula would know or if she didn't she would say something funny
that would make it all right. Ooo no, not Sula. Here she was in the midst
of it, hating it, scared of it, and again she thought of Sula as though they
were still friends and talked things over. That was too much. To lose Jude
and not have Sula to talk to about it because it was Sula that he had left
her for.

Now her thighs were really empty. And it was then that what those
women said about never looking at another man made some sense to her,
for the real point, the heart of what they said, was the word *looked*. Not
to promise never to make love to another man, not to refuse to marry
another man, but to promise and know that she could never afford to look
again, to see and accept the way in which their heads cut the air or see
moons and tree limbs framed by their necks and shoulders . . . never to
look, for now she could not risk looking—and anyway, so what? For now
her thighs were truly empty and dead too, and it was Sula who had taken
the life from them and Jude who smashed her heart and the both of them
who left her with no thighs and no heart just her brain raveling away.

And what am I supposed to do with these old thighs now, just walk up
and down these rooms? What good are they, Jesus? They will never give
me the peace I need to get from sunup to sundown, what good are they,
are you trying to tell me that I am going to have to go all the way
through these days all the way, O my god, to that box with four handles
with never nobody settling down between my legs even if I sew up those
old pillow cases and rinse down the porch and feed my children and beat
the rugs and haul the coal up out of the bin even then nobody, O Jesus, I
could be a mule or plow the furrows with my hands if need be or hold
these rickety walls up with my back if need be if I knew that somewhere
in this world in the pocket of some night I could open my legs to some
cowboy lean hips but you are trying to tell me no and O my sweet Jesus
what kind of cross is that?

1939

When the word got out about Eva being put in Sunnydale, the people
in the Bottom shook their heads and said Sula was a roach. Later, when
they saw how she took Jude, then ditched him for others, and heard how
he bought a bus ticket to Detroit (where he bought but never mailed
birthday cards to his sons), they forgot all about Hannah's easy ways (or
their own) and said she was a bitch. Everybody remembered the plague

of robins that announced her return, and the tale about her watching Hannah burn was stirred up again.

But it was the men who gave her the final label, who fingerprinted her for all time. They were the ones who said she was guilty of the unforgivable thing—the thing for which there was no understanding, no excuse, no compassion. The route from which there was no way back, the dirt that could not ever be washed away. They said that Sula slept with white men. It may not have been true, but it certainly could have been. She was obviously capable of it. In any case, all minds were closed to her when that word was passed around. It made the old women draw their lips together; made small children look away from her in shame; made young men fantasize elaborate torture for her—just to get the saliva back in their mouths when they saw her.

Every one of them imagined the scene, each according to his own predilections—Sula underneath some white man—and it filled them with choking disgust. There was nothing lower she could do, nothing filthier. The fact that their own skin color was proof that it had happened in their own families was no deterrent to their bile. Nor was the willingness of black men to lie in the beds of white women a consideration that might lead them toward tolerance. They insisted that all unions between white men and black women be rape; for a black woman to be willing was literally unthinkable. In that way, they regarded integration with precisely the same venom that white people did.

So they laid broomsticks across their doors at night and sprinkled salt on porch steps.[5] But aside from one or two unsuccessful efforts to collect the dust from her footsteps, they did nothing to harm her. As always the black people looked at evil stony-eyed and let it run.

Sula acknowledged none of their attempts at counter-conjure or their gossip and seemed to need the services of nobody. So they watched her far more closely than they watched any other roach or bitch in the town, and their alertness was gratified. Things began to happen.

First off, Teapot knocked on her door to see if she had any bottles. He was the five-year-old son of an indifferent mother, all of whose interests sat around the door of the Time and a Half Pool Hall. Her name was Betty but she was called Teapot's Mamma because being his mamma was precisely her major failure. When Sula said no, the boy turned around and fell down the steps. He couldn't get up right away and Sula went to help him. His mother, just then tripping home, saw Sula bending over her son's pained face. She flew into a fit of concerned, if drunken, motherhood, and dragged Teapot home. She told everybody that Sula had pushed him, and talked so strongly about it she was forced to abide by the advice of her friends and take him to the county hospital. The two dollars she hated to release turned out to be well spent, for Teapot did have a fracture, although the doctor said poor diet had contributed substantially to the daintiness of his bones. Teapot's Mamma got a lot of attention anyway and immersed herself in a role she had shown no inclination for: motherhood. The very idea of a grown woman hurting her boy kept her teeth on edge. She became the most devoted mother: sober, clean and industrious. No more nickels for Teapot to go to Dick's for a breakfast of Mr. Goodbars[6] and soda pop: no more long hours of him alone or wandering the roads while she was otherwise engaged. Her

5. To keep evil away.　　　　　6. Candy bars.

change was a distinct improvement, although little Teapot did miss those quiet times at Dick's.

Other things happened. Mr. Finley sat on his porch sucking chicken bones, as he had done for thirteen years, looked up, saw Sula, choked on a bone and died on the spot. That incident, and Teapot's Mamma, cleared up for everybody the meaning of the birthmark over her eye; it was not a stemmed rose, or a snake, it was Hannah's ashes marking her from the very beginning.

She came to their church suppers without underwear, bought their steaming platters of food and merely picked at it—relishing nothing, exclaiming over no one's ribs or cobbler. They believed that she was laughing at their God.

And the fury she created in the women of the town was incredible—for she would lay their husbands once and then no more. Hannah had been a nuisance, but she was complimenting the women, in a way, by wanting their husbands. Sula was trying them out and discarding them without any excuse the men could swallow. So the women, to justify their own judgment, cherished their men more, soothed the pride and vanity Sula had bruised.

Among the weighty evidence piling up was the fact that Sula did not look her age. She was near thirty and, unlike them, had lost no teeth, suffered no bruises, developed no ring of fat at the waist or pocket at the back of her neck. It was rumored that she had had no childhood diseases, was never known to have chicken pox, croup or even a runny nose. She had played rough as a child—where were the scars? Except for a funny-shaped finger and that evil birthmark, she was free of any normal signs of vulnerability. Some of the men, who as boys had dated her, remembered that on picnics neither gnats nor mosquitoes would settle on her. Patsy, Hannah's one-time friend, agreed and said not only that, but she had witnessed the fact that when Sula drank beer she never belched.

The most damning evidence, however, came from Dessie, who was a big Daughter Elk[7] and knew things. At one of the social meetings she revealed something to her friends.

"Yeh, well I noticed something long time ago. Ain't said nothing 'bout it 'cause I wasn't sure what it meant. Well ... I did mention it to Ivy but not nobody else. I disremember how long ago. 'Bout a month or two I guess 'cause I hadn't put down my new linoleum yet. Did you see it, Cora? It's that kind we saw in the catalogue."

"Naw."

"Get on with it, Dessie."

"Well, Cora was with me when we looked in the catalogue ..."

"We all know 'bout your linoleum. What we don't know is ..."

"OK. Let me tell it, will you? Just before the linoleum come I was out front and seed Shadrack carryin' on as usual ... up by the well ... walkin' 'round it salutin' and carryin' on. You know how he does ... hollerin' commands and ..."

"Will you get on with it?"

"Who's tellin' this? Me or you?"

"You."

"Well, let me tell it then. Like I say, he was just cuttin' up as usual

7. Member of a black social organization.

when Miss Sula Mae walks by on the other side of the road. And quick as that"—she snapped her fingers—"he stopped and cut on over 'cross the road, steppin' over to her like a tall turkey in short corn. And guess what? He tips his hat."

"Shadrack don't wear no hat."

"I know that but he tipped it anyway. You know what I mean. He acted like he had a hat and reached up for it and tipped it at her. Now you know Shadrack ain't civil to nobody!"

"Sure ain't."

"Even when you buyin' his fish he's cussin'. If you ain't got the right change he cussin' you. If you act like a fish ain't too fresh he snatch it out of your hand like he doin' you the favor."

"Well, everybody know he a reprobate."

"Yeh, so how come he tip his hat to Sula? How come he don't cuss her?"

"Two devils."

"Exactly!"

"What'd she do when he tipped it? Smile and give him a curtsey?"

"No, and that was the other thing. It was the first time I see her look anything but hateful. Like she smellin' you with her eyes and don't like your soap. When he tipped his hat she put her hand on her throat for a minute and *cut* out. Went runnin' on up the road to home. And him still standin' there tippin' away. And—this the point I was comin' to—when I went back in the house a big sty come on my eye. And I ain't never had no sty before. Never!"

"That's 'cause you saw it."

"Exactly."

"Devil all right."

"No two ways about it," Dessie said, and she popped the rubber band off the deck of cards to settle them down for a nice long game of bid whist.

Their conviction of Sula's evil changed them in accountable yet mysterious ways. Once the source of their personal misfortune was identified, they had leave to protect and love one another. They began to cherish their husbands and wives, protect their children, repair their homes and in general band together against the devil in their midst. In their world, aberrations were as much a part of nature as grace. It was not for them to expel or annihilate it. They would no more run Sula out of town than they would kill the robins that brought her back, for in their secret awareness of Him, He was not the God of three faces they sang about. They knew quite well that He had four, and that the fourth explained Sula. They had lived with various forms of evil all their days, and it wasn't that they believed God would take care of them. It was rather that they knew God had a brother and that brother hadn't spared God's son, so why should he spare them?

There was no creature so ungodly as to make them destroy it. They could easily if provoked to anger, but not by design, which explained why they could not "mob kill" anyone. To do so was not only unnatural, it was undignified. The presence of evil was something to be first recognized, then dealt with, survived, outwitted, triumphed over.

Their evidence against Sula was contrived, but their conclusions about

her were not. Sula was distinctly different. Eva's arrogance and Hannah's
self-indulgence merged in her and, with a twist that was all her own
imagination, she lived out her days exploring her own thoughts and emotions, giving them full reign, feeling no obligation to please anybody unless their pleasure pleased her. As willing to feel pain as to give pain, to
feel pleasure as to give pleasure, hers was an experimental life—ever since
her mother's remarks sent her flying up those stairs, ever since her one
major feeling of responsibility had been exorcised on the bank of a river
with a closed place in the middle. The first experience taught her there
was no other that you could count on; the second that there was no self
to count on either. She had no center, no speck around which to grow. In
the midst of a pleasant conversation with someone she might say, "Why
do you chew with your mouth open?" not because the answer interested
her but because she wanted to see the person's face change rapidly. She
was completely free of ambition, with no affection for money, property or
things, no greed, no desire to command attention or compliments—no ego.
For that reason she felt no compulsion to verify herself—be consistent
with herself.

She had clung to Nel as the closest thing to both an other and a self,
only to discover that she and Nel were not one and the same thing. She
had no thought at all of causing Nel pain when she bedded down with
Jude. They had always shared the affection of other people: compared
how a boy kissed, what line he used with one and then the other. Marriage, apparently, had changed all that, but having had no intimate
knowledge of marriage, having lived in a house with women who thought
all men available, and selected from among them with a care only for
their tastes, she was ill prepared for the possessiveness of the one person
she felt close to. She knew well enough what other women said and felt,
or said they felt. But she and Nel had always seen through them. They
both knew that those women were not jealous of other women; that they
were only afraid of losing their jobs. Afraid their husbands would discover
that no uniqueness lay between their legs.

Nel was the one person who had wanted nothing from her, who had
accepted all aspects of her. Now she wanted everything, and all because of
that. Nel was the first person who had been real to her, whose name she
knew, who had seen as she had the slant of life that made it possible to
stretch it to its limits. Now Nel was one of *them.* One of the spiders
whose only thought was the next rung of the web, who dangled in dark
dry places suspended by their own spittle, more terrified of the free fall
than the snake's breath below. Their eyes so intent on the wayward
stranger who trips into their net, they were blind to the cobalt on their
own backs, the moonshine fighting to pierce their corners. If they were
touched by the snake's breath, however fatal, they were merely victims
and knew how to behave in that role (just as Nel knew how to behave as
the wronged wife). But the free fall, oh no, that required—demanded—invention: a thing to do with the wings, a way of holding the legs and most
of all a full surrender to the downward flight if they wished to taste their
tongues or stay alive. But alive was what they, and now Nel, did not want
to be. Too dangerous. Now Nel belonged to the town and all of its ways.
She had given herself over to them, and the flick of their tongues would
drive her back into her little dry corner where she would cling to her
spittle high above the breath of the snake and the fall.

It had surprised her a little and saddened her a good deal when Nel behaved the way the others would have. Nel was one of the reasons she had drifted back to Medallion, that and the boredom she found in Nashville, Detroit, New Orleans, New York, Philadelphia, Macon and San Diego. All those cities held the same people, working the same mouths, sweating the same sweat. The men who took her to one or another of those places had merged into one large personality: the same language of love, the same entertainments of love, the same cooling of love. Whenever she introduced her private thoughts into their rubbings or goings, they hooded their eyes. They taught her nothing but love tricks, shared nothing but worry, gave nothing but money. She had been looking all along for a friend, and it took her a while to discover that a lover was not a comrade and could never be—for a woman. And that no one would ever be that version of herself which she sought to reach out to and touch with an ungloved hand. There was only her own mood and whim, and if that was all there was, she decided to turn the naked hand toward it, discover it and let others become as intimate with their own selves as she was.

In a way, her strangeness, her naïveté, her craving for the other half of her equation was the consequence of an idle imagination. Had she paints, or clay, or knew the discipline of the dance, or strings; had she anything to engage her tremendous curiosity and her gift for metaphor, she might have exchanged the restlessness and preoccupation with whim for an activity that provided her with all she yearned for. And like any artist with no art form, she became dangerous.

She had lied only once in her life—to Nel about the reason for putting Eva out, and she could lie to her only because she cared about her. When she had come back home, social conversation was impossible for her because she could not lie. She could not say to those old acquaintances, "Hey, girl, you looking good," when she saw how the years had dusted their bronze with ash, the eyes that had once opened wide to the moon bent into grimy sickles of concern. The narrower their lives, the wider their hips. Those with husbands had folded themselves into starched coffins, their sides bursting with other people's skinned dreams and bony regrets. Those without men were like sour-tipped needles featuring one constant empty eye. Those with men had had the sweetness sucked from their breath by ovens and steam kettles. Their children were like distant but exposed wounds whose aches were no less intimate because separate from their flesh. They had looked at the world and back at their children, back at the world and back again at their children, and Sula knew that one clear young eye was all that kept the knife away from the throat's curve.

She was pariah, then, and knew it. Knew that they despised her and believed that they framed their hatred as disgust for the easy way she lay with men. Which was true. She went to bed with men as frequently as she could. It was the only place where she could find what she was looking for: misery and the ability to feel deep sorrow. She had not always been aware that it was sadness that she yearned for. Lovemaking seemed to her, at first, the creation of a special kind of joy. She thought she liked the sootiness of sex and its comedy; she laughed a great deal during the raucous beginnings, and rejected those lovers who regarded sex as healthy or beautiful. Sexual aesthetics bored her. Although she did not regard sex as ugly (ugliness was boring also), she liked to think of it as wicked. But as her experiences multiplied she realized that not only was it not wicked, it was not necessary for her to conjure up the idea of wickedness in order to participate fully. During the lovemaking she found and needed to find the cutting edge. When she left off cooperating with her body and began to assert herself in the act, particles of strength gathered in her like steel shavings drawn to a spacious magnetic center, forming a tight cluster that nothing, it seemed, could break. And there was utmost irony and outrage in lying under someone, in a position of surrender, feeling her own abiding strength and limitless power. But the cluster did break, fall apart, and in her panic to hold it together she leaped from the edge into soundlessness and went down howling, howling in a stinging awareness of the endings of things: an eye of sorrow in the midst of all that hurricane rage of joy. There, in the center of that silence was not eternity but the death of time and a loneliness so profound the word itself had no meaning. For loneliness assumed the absence of other people, and the solitude she found in that desperate terrain had never admitted the possibility of other people. She wept then. Tears for the deaths of the littlest things: the castaway shoes of children; broken stems of marsh grass battered and drowned by the sea; prom photographs of dead women she never knew; wedding rings in pawnshop windows; the tidy bodies of Cornish hens in a nest of rice.

When her partner disengaged himself, she looked up at him in wonder trying to recall his name; and he looked down at her, smiling with tender understanding of the state of tearful gratitude to which he believed he had brought her. She waiting impatiently for him to turn away and settle into a wet skim of satisfaction and light disgust, leaving her to the postcoital privateness in which she met herself, welcomed herself, and joined herself in matchless harmony.

At twenty-nine she knew it would be no other way for her, but she had not counted on the footsteps on the porch, and the beautiful black face that stared at her through the blue-glass window. Ajax.

Looking for all the world as he had seventeen years ago when he had called her pig meat. He was twenty-one then, she twelve. A universe of time between them. Now she was twenty-nine, he thirty-eight, and the lemon-yellow haunches seemed not so far away after all.

She opened the heavy door and saw him standing on the other side of the screen door with two quarts of milk tucked into his arms like marble statues. He smiled and said, "I been lookin' all over for you."

"Why?" she asked.

"To give you these," and he nodded toward one of the quarts of milk.

"I don't like milk," she said.

"But you like bottles don't you?" He held one up. "Ain't that pretty?"

And indeed it was. Hanging from his fingers, framed by a slick blue sky, it looked precious and clean and permanent. She had the distinct impression that he had done something dangerous to get them.

Sula ran her fingernails over the screen thoughtfully for a second and then, laughing, she opened the screen door.

Ajax came in and headed straight for the kitchen. Sula followed slowly. By the time she got to the door he had undone the complicated wire cap and was letting the cold milk run into his mouth.

Sula watched him—or rather the rhythm in his throat—with growing interest. When he had had enough, he poured the rest into the sink, rinsed the bottle out and presented it to her. She took the bottle with one hand and his wrist with the other and pulled him into the pantry. There was no need to go there, for not a soul was in the house, but the gesture came to Hannah's daughter naturally. There in the pantry, empty now of flour sacks, void of row upon row of canned goods, free forever of strings of tiny green peppers, holding the wet milk bottle tight in her arm she stood wide-legged against the wall and pulled from his track-lean hips all the pleasure her thighs could hold.

He came regularly then, bearing gifts: clusters of black berries still on their branches, four meal-fried porgies wrapped in a salmon-colored sheet of the Pittsburgh *Courier,* a handful of jacks, two boxes of lime Jell-Well, a hunk of ice-wagon ice, a can of Old Dutch Cleanser with the bonneted woman chasing dirt with her stick; a page of Tillie the Toiler comics, and more gleaming white bottles of milk.

Contrary to what anybody would have suspected from just seeing him lounging around the pool hall, or shooting at Mr. Finley for beating his own dog, or calling filthy compliments to passing women, Ajax was very nice to women. His women, of course, knew it, and it provoked them into murderous battles over him in the streets, brawling thick-thighed women with knives disturbed many a Friday night with their bloodletting and attracted whooping crowds. On such occasions Ajax stood, along with the crowd, and viewed the fighters with the same golden-eyed indifference with which he watched old men playing checkers. Other than his mother, who sat in her shack with six younger sons working roots,[8] he had never met an interesting woman in his life.

His kindness to them in general was not due to a ritual of seduction (he had no need for it) but rather to the habit he acquired in dealing with his mother, who inspired thoughtfulness and generosity in all her sons.

She was an evil conjure woman, blessed with seven adoring children whose joy it was to bring her the plants, hair, underclothing, fingernail parings, white hens, blood, camphor, pictures, kerosene and footstep dust that she needed, as well as to order Van Van, High John the Conqueror, Little John to Chew, Devil's Shoe String, Chinese Wash, Mustard Seed and the Nine Herbs[9] from Cincinnati. She knew about the weather, omens, the living, the dead, dreams and all illnesses and made a modest living with her skills. Had she any teeth or ever straightened her back, she would have been the most gorgeous thing alive, worthy of her sons' worship for her beauty alone, if not for the absolute freedom she allowed them (known in some quarters as neglect) and the weight of her hoary knowledge.

This woman Ajax loved, and after her airplanes. There was nothing in between. And when he was not sitting enchanted listening to his mother's words, he thought of airplanes, and pilots, and the deep sky that held them both. People thought that those long trips he took to large cities in the state were for some sophisticated good times they could not imagine but only envy; actually he was leaning against the barbed wire of airports, or nosing around hangars just to hear the talk of the men who were fortunate enough to be in the trade. The rest of the time, the time he was not watching his mother's magic or thinking of airplanes, he spent in the

8. Making folk medicine.   strength, health.
9. Powders, charms, and so forth sold for luck,

idle pursuits of bachelors without work in small towns. He had heard all the stories about Sula, and they aroused his curiosity. Her elusiveness and indifference to established habits of behavior reminded him of his mother, who was as stubborn in her pursuits of the occult as the women of Greater Saint Matthew's were in the search for redeeming grace. So when his curiosity was high enough he picked two bottles of milk off the porch of some white family and went to see her, suspecting that this was perhaps the only other woman he knew whose life was her own, who could deal with life efficiently, and who was not interested in nailing him.

Sula, too, was curious. She knew nothing about him except the word he had called out to her years ago and the feeling he had excited in her then. She had grown quite accustomed to the clichés of other people's lives as well as her own increasing dissatisfaction with Medallion. If she could have thought of a place to go, she probably would have left, but that was before Ajax looked at her through the blue glass and held the milk aloft like a trophy.

But it was not the presents that made her wrap him up in her thighs. They were charming, of course (especially the jar of butterflies he let loose in the bedroom), but her real pleasure was the fact that he talked to her. They had genuine conversations. He did not speak down to her or at her, nor content himself with puerile questions about her life or monologues of his own activities. Thinking she was possibly brilliant, like his mother, he seemed to expect brilliance from her, and she delivered. And in all of it, he listened more than he spoke. His clear comfort at being in her presence, his lazy willingness to tell her all about fixes and the powers of plants, his refusal to baby or protect her, his assumption that she was both tough and wise—all of that coupled with a wide generosity of spirit only occasionally erupting into vengeance sustained Sula's interest and enthusiasm.

His idea of bliss (on earth as opposed to bliss in the sky) was a long bath in piping-hot water—his head on the cool white rim, his eyes closed in reverie.

"Soaking in hot water give you a bad back." Sula stood in the doorway looking at his knees glistening just at the surface of the soap-gray water.

"Soaking in Sula give me a bad back."

"Worth it?"

"Don't know yet. Go 'way."

"Airplanes?"

"Airplanes."

"Lindbergh know about you?"

"Go 'way."

She went and waited for him in Eva's high bed, her head turned to the boarded-up window. She was smiling, thinking how like Jude's was his craving to do the white man's work, when two deweys came in with their beautiful teeth and said, "We sick."

Sula turned her head slowly and murmured, "Get well."

"We need some medicine."

"Look in the bathroom."

"Ajax in there."

"Then wait."

"We sick now."

Sula leaned over the bed, picked up a shoe and threw it at them.

"Cocksucker!" they screamed, and she leaped out of the bed naked as a yard dog. She caught the redheaded dewey by his shirt and held him by the heels over the banister until he wet his pants. The other dewey was joined by the third, and they delved into their pockets for stones, which they threw at her. Sula, ducking and tottering with laughter, carried the wet dewey to the bedroom and when the other two followed her, deprived of all weapons except their teeth, Sula had dropped the first dewey on the bed and was fishing in her purse. She gave each of them a dollar bill which they snatched and then scooted off down the stairs to Dick's to buy the catarrh remedy they loved to drink.

Ajax came sopping wet into the room and lay down on the bed to let the air dry him. They were both still for a long time until he reached out and touched her arm.

He liked for her to mount him so he could see her towering above him and call soft obscenities up into her face. As she rocked there, swayed there, like a Georgia pine on its knees, high above the slipping, falling smile, high above the golden eyes and the velvet helmet of hair, rocking, swaying, she focused her thoughts to bar the creeping disorder that was flooding her hips. She looked down, down from what seemed an awful height at the head of the man whose lemon-yellow gabardines had been the first sexual excitement she'd known. Letting her thoughts dwell on his face in order to confine, for just a while longer, the drift of her flesh toward the high silence of orgasm.

If I take a chamois and rub real hard on the bone, right on the ledge of your cheek bone, some of the black will disappear. It will flake away into the chamois and underneath there will be gold leaf. I can see it shining through the black. I know it is there . . .

How high she was over his wand-lean body, how slippery was his sliding sliding smile.

And if I take a nail file or even Eva's old paring knife—that will do—and scrape away at the gold, it will fall away and there will be alabaster. The alabaster is what gives your face its planes, its curves. That is why your mouth smiling does not reach your eyes. Alabaster is giving it a gravity that resists a total smile.

The height and the swaying dizzied her, so she bent down and let her breasts graze his chest.

Then I can take a chisel and small tap hammer and tap away at the alabaster. It will crack then like ice under the pick, and through the breaks I will see the loam, fertile, free of pebbles and twigs. For it is the loam that is giving you that smell.

She slipped her hands under his armpits, for it seemed as though she would not be able to dam the spread of weakness she felt under her skin without holding on to something.

I will put my hand deep into your soil, lift it, sift it with my fingers, feel its warm surface and dewy chill below.

She put her head under his chin with no hope in the world of keeping anything at all at bay.

I will water your soil, keep it rich and moist. But how much? How much water to keep the loam moist? And how much loam will I need to keep my water still? And when do the two make mud?

He swallowed her mouth just as her thighs had swallowed his genitals, and the house was very, very quiet.

◉ ◉ ◉

Sula began to discover what possession was. Not love, perhaps, but possession or at least the desire for it. She was astounded by so new and alien a feeling. First there was the morning of the night before when she actually wondered if Ajax would come by that day. Then there was an afternoon when she stood before the mirror finger-tracing the laugh lines around her mouth and trying to decide whether she was good-looking or not. She ended this deep perusal by tying a green ribbon in her hair. The green silk made a rippling whisper as she slid it into her hair—a whisper that could easily have been Hannah's chuckle, a soft slow nasal hiss she used to emit when something amused her. Like women sitting for two hours under the marcelling irons only to wonder two days later how soon they would need another appointment. The ribbon-tying was followed by other activity, and when Ajax came that evening, bringing her a reed whistle he had carved that morning, not only was the green ribbon still in her hair, but the bathroom was gleaming, the bed was made, and the table was set for two.

He gave her the reed whistle, unlaced his shoes and sat in the rocking chair in the kitchen.

Sula walked toward him and kissed his mouth. He ran his fingers along the nape of her neck.

"I bet you ain't even missed Tar Baby, have you?" he asked.

"Missed? No. Where is he?"

Ajax smiled at her delicious indifference. "Jail."

"Since when?"

"Last Saturday."

"Picked up for drunk?"

"Little bit more than that," he answered and went ahead to tell her about his own involvement in another of Tar Baby's misfortunes.

On Saturday afternoon Tar Baby had stumbled drunk into traffic on the New River Road. A woman driver swerved to avoid him and hit another car. When the police came, they recognized the woman as the mayor's niece and arrested Tar Baby. Later, after the word got out, Ajax and two other men went to the station to see about him. At first they wouldn't let them in. But they relented after Ajax and the other two just stood around for one hour and a half and repeated their request at regular intervals. When they finally got permission to go in and looked in at him in the cell, he was twisted up in a corner badly beaten and dressed in nothing but extremely soiled underwear. Ajax and the other men asked the officer why Tar Baby couldn't have back his clothes. "It ain't right," they said, "to let a grown man lay around in his own shit."

The policeman, obviously in agreement with Eva, who had always maintained that Tar Baby was white, said that if the prisoner didn't like to live in shit, he should come down out of those hills, and live like a decent white man.

More words were exchanged, hot words and dark, and the whole thing ended with the arraignment of the three black men, and an appointment to appear in civil court Thursday next.

Ajax didn't seem too bothered by any of it. More annoyed and inconvenienced than anything else. He had had several messes with the police, mostly in gambling raids, and regarded them as the natural hazards of Negro life.

But Sula, the green ribbon shining in her hair, was flooded with an awareness of the impact of the outside world on Ajax. She stood up and arranged herself on the arm of the rocking chair. Putting her fingers deep into the velvet of his hair, she murmured, "Come on. Lean on me."

Ajax blinked. Then he looked swiftly into her face. In her words, in her voice, was a sound he knew well. For the first time he saw the green ribbon. He looked around and saw the gleaming kitchen and the table set for two and detected the scent of the nest. Every hackle on his body rose, and he knew that very soon she would, like all of her sisters before her, put to him the death-knell question "Where you been?" His eyes dimmed with a mild and momentary regret.

He stood and mounted the stairs with her and entered the spotless bathroom where the dust had been swept from underneath the claw-foot tub. He was trying to remember the date of the air show in Dayton. As he came into the bedroom, he saw Sula lying on fresh white sheets, wrapped in the deadly odor of freshly applied cologne.

He dragged her under him and made love to her with the steadiness and the intensity of a man about to leave for Dayton.

Every now and then she looked around for tangible evidence of his having ever been there. Where were the butterflies? the blueberries? the whistling reed? She could find nothing, for he had left nothing but his stunning absence. An absence so decorative, so ornate, it was difficult for her to understand how she had ever endured, without falling dead or being consumed, his magnificent presence.

The mirror by the door was not a mirror by the door, it was an altar where he stood for only a moment to put on his cap before going out. The red rocking chair was a rocking of his own hips as he sat in the kitchen. Still, there was nothing of his—his own—that she could find. It was as if she were afraid she had hallucinated him and needed proof to the contrary. His absence was everywhere, stinging everything, giving the furnishings primary colors, sharp outlines to the corners of rooms and gold light to the dust collecting on table tops. When he was there he pulled everything toward himself. Not only her eyes and all her senses but also inanimate things seemed to exist because of him, backdrops to his presence. Now that he had gone, these things, so long subdued by his presence, were glamorized in his wake.

Then one day, burrowing in a dresser drawer, she found what she had been looking for: proof that he had been there, his driver's license. It contained just what she needed for verification—his vital statistics: Born 1901, height 5'11", weight 152 lbs., eyes brown, hair black, color black. Oh yes, skin black. Very black. So black that only a steady careful rubbing with steel wool would remove it, and as it was removed there was the glint of gold leaf and under the gold leaf the cold alabaster and deep, deep down under the cold alabaster more black only this time the black of warm loam.

But what was this? Albert Jacks? His name was Albert Jacks? A. Jacks. She had thought it was Ajax. All those years. Even from the time she walked by the pool hall and looked away from him sitting astride a wooden chair, looked away to keep from seeing the wide space of intolerable orderliness between his legs; the openness that held no sign, no sign at all, of the animal that lurked in his trousers; looked away from the insolent nostrils and the smile that kept slipping and falling, falling, falling so she wanted to reach out with her hand to catch it before it fell to the pavement and was sullied by the cigarette butts and bottle caps and spittle at his feet and the feet of other men who sat or stood around outside the pool hall, calling, singing out to her and Nel and grown women too with lyrics like *pig meat* and *brown sugar* and *jailbait* and *O Lord, what have I done to deserve the wrath,* and *Take me, Jesus, I have seen the promised land,* and *Do, Lord, remember me* in voices mellowed by hopeless passion into gentleness. Even then, when she and Nel were trying hard not to dream of him and not to think of him when they touched the softness in their underwear or undid their braids as soon as they left home to let the hair bump and wave around their ears, or wrapped the cotton binding around their chests so the nipples would not break through their blouses and give him cause to smile his slipping, falling smile, which brought the blood rushing to their skin. And even later, when for the first time in her life she had lain in bed with a man and said his name involuntarily or said it truly meaning *him,* the name she was screaming and saying was not his at all.

Sula stood with a worn slip of paper in her fingers and said aloud to no one, "I didn't even know his name. And if I didn't know his name, then there is nothing I did know and I have known nothing ever at all since the one thing I wanted was to know his name so how could he help but leave me since he was making love to a woman who didn't even know his name.

"When I was a little girl the heads of my paper dolls came off, and it was a long time before I discovered that my own head would not fall off if I bent my neck. I used to walk around holding it very stiff because I thought a strong wind or a heavy push would snap my neck. Nel was the one who told me the truth. But she was wrong. I did not hold my head stiff enough when I met him and so I lost it just like the dolls.

"It's just as well he left. Soon I would have torn the flesh from his face just to see if I was right about the gold and nobody would have understood that kind of curiosity. They would have believed that I wanted to hurt him just like the little boy who fell down the steps and broke his leg and the people think I pushed him just because I looked at it."

Holding the driver's license she crawled into bed and fell into a sleep full of dreams of cobalt blue.

When she awoke, there was a melody in her head she could not identify or recall ever hearing before. "Perhaps I made it up," she thought. Then it came to her—the name of the song and all its lyrics just as she had heard it many times before. She sat on the edge of the bed thinking, "There aren't any more new songs and I have sung all the ones there are. I have sung them all. I have sung all the songs there are." She lay down again on the bed and sang a little wandering tune made up of the words *I have sung all the songs all the songs I have sung all the songs there are* until, touched by her own lullaby, she grew drowsy, and in the hollow of near-sleep she tasted the acridness of gold, left the chill of alabaster and smelled the dark, sweet stench of loam.

1940

"I heard you was sick. Anything I can do for you?"

She had practiced not just the words but the tone, the pitch of her voice. It should be calm, matter-of-fact, but strong in sympathy—for the illness though, not for the patient.

The sound of her voice as she heard it in her head betrayed no curiosity, no pride, just the inflection of any good woman come to see about a sick person who, incidentally, had such visits from nobody else.

For the first time in three years she would be looking at the stemmed rose that hung over the eye of her enemy. Moreover, she would be doing it with the taste of Jude's exit in her mouth, with the resentment and shame that even yet pressed for release in her stomach. She would be facing the black rose that Jude had kissed and looking at the nostrils of the woman who had twisted her love for her own children into something so thick and monstrous she was afraid to show it lest it break loose and smother them with its heavy paw. A cumbersome bear-love that, given any rein, would suck their breath away in its crying need for honey.

Because Jude's leaving was so complete, the full responsibility of the household was Nel's. There were no more fifty dollars in brown envelopes to count on, so she took to cleaning rather than fret away the tiny seaman's pension her parents lived on. And just this past year she got a better job working as a chambermaid in the same hotel Jude had worked in. The tips were only fair, but the hours were good—she was home when the children got out of school.

At thirty her hot brown eyes had turned to agate, and her skin had taken on the sheen of maple struck down, split and sanded at the height of its green. Virtue, bleak and drawn, was her only mooring. It brought her to Number 7 Carpenter's Road and the door with the blue glass; it helped her to resist scratching the screen as in days gone by; it hid from her the true motives for her charity, and, finally, it gave her voice the timbre she wanted it to have: free of delight or a lip-smacking "I told you so" with which the news of Sula's illness had been received up in the Bottom—free of the least hint of retribution.

Now she stood in Eva's old bedroom, looking down at that dark rose, aware of the knife-thin arms sliding back and forth over the quilt and the boarded-up window Eva had jumped out of.

Sula looked up and without a second's pause followed Nel's example of leaving out the greeting when she spoke.

"As a matter of fact, there is. I got a prescription. Nathan usually goes for me but he . . . school don't let out till three. Could you run it over to the drugstore?"

"Where is it?" Nel was glad to have a concrete errand. Conversation would be difficult. (Trust Sula to pick up a relationship exactly where it lay.)

"Look in my bag. No. Over there."

Nel walked to the dresser and opened the purse with the beaded clasp. She saw only a watch and the folded prescription down inside. No wallet, no change purse. She turned to Sula: "Where's your . . ."

But Sula was looking at the boarded-up window. Something in her eye right there in the corner stopped Nel from completing her question. That and the slight flare of the nostrils—a shadow of a snarl. Nel took the piece of paper and picked up her own purse, saying, "OK. I'll be right back."

As soon as the door was shut, Sula breathed through her mouth. While Nel was in the room the pain had increased. Now that this new pain killer, the one she had been holding in reserve, was on the way her misery was manageable. She let a piece of her mind lay on Nel. It was funny, sending Nel off to that drugstore right away like that, after she had not seen her to speak to for years. The drugstore was where Edna Finch's Mellow House used to be years back when they were girls. Where they used to go, the two of them, hand in hand, for the 18-cent ice-cream sundaes, past the Time and a Half Pool Hall, where the sprawling men said "pig meat," and they sat in that cool room with the marble-top tables and ate the first ice-cream sundaes of their lives. Now Nel was going back there alone and Sula was waiting for the medicine the doctor said not to take until the pain got really bad. And she supposed "really bad" was now. Although you could never tell. She wondered for an instant what Nellie wanted; why she had come. Did she want to gloat? Make up? Following this line of thought required more concentration than she could muster. Pain was greedy; it demanded all of her attention. But it was good that this new medicine, the reserve, would be brought to her by her old friend. Nel, she remembered, always thrived on a crisis. The closed place in the water; Hannah's funeral. Nel was the best. When Sula imitated her, or tried to, those long years ago, it always ended up in some action noteworthy not for its coolness but mostly for its being bizarre. The one time she tried to protect Nel, she had cut off her own finger tip and earned not Nel's gratitude but her disgust. From then on she had let her emotions dictate her behavior.

She could hear Nel's footsteps long before she opened the door and put the medicine on the table near the bed.

As Sula poured the liquid into a sticky spoon, Nel began the sickroom conversation.

"You look fine, Sula."

"You lying, Nellie. I look bad." She gulped the medicine.

"No. I haven't seen you for a long time, but you look . . . "

"You don't have to do that, Nellie. It's going to be all right."

"What ails you? Have they said?"

Sula licked the corners of her lips. "You want to talk about that?"

Nel smiled, slightly, at the bluntness she had forgotten. "No. No, I don't, but you sure you should be staying up here alone?"

"Nathan comes by. The deweys sometimes, and Tar Baby . . . "

"That ain't help, Sula. You need to be with somebody grown. Somebody who can . . . "

"I'd rather be here, Nellie."

"You know you don't have to be proud with me."

"Proud?" Sula's laughter broke through the phlegm. "What you talking about? I like my own dirt, Nellie. I'm not proud. You sure have forgotten me."

"Maybe. Maybe not. But you a woman and you alone."

"And you? Ain't you alone?"

"I'm not sick. I work."

"Yes. Of course you do. Work's good for you, Nellie. It don't do nothing for me."

"You never *had* to."

"I never would."

"There's something to say for it, Sula. 'Specially if you don't want people to have to do for you."

"Neither one, Nellie. Neither one."

"You can't have it all, Sula." Nel was getting exasperated with her arrogance, with her lying at death's door still smart-talking.

"Why? I can do it all, why can't I have it all?"

"You *can't* do it all. You a woman and a colored woman at that. You can't act like a man. You can't be walking around all independent-like, doing whatever you like, taking what you want, leaving what you don't."

"You repeating yourself."

"How repeating myself?"

"You say I'm a woman and colored. Ain't that the same as being a man?"

"I don't think so and you wouldn't either if you had children."

"Then I really would act like what you call a man. Every man I ever knew left his children."

"Some were taken."

"Wrong, Nellie. The word is 'left.' "

"You still going to know everything, ain't you?"

"I don't know everything, I just do everything."

"Well, you don't do what I do."

"You think I don't know what your life is like just because I ain't living it? I know what every colored woman in this country is doing."

"What's that?"

"Dying. Just like me. But the difference is they dying like a stump. Me, I'm going down like one of those redwoods. I sure did live in this world."

"Really? What have you got to show for it?"

"Show? To who? Girl, I got my mind. And what goes on in it. Which is to say, I got me."

"Lonely, ain't it?"

"Yes. But my lonely is *mine*. Now your lonely is somebody else's. Made by somebody else and handed to you. Ain't that something? A secondhand lonely."

Nel sat back on the little wooden chair. Anger skipped but she realized that Sula was probably just showing off. No telling what shape she was really in, but there was no point in saying anything other than what was the truth. "I always understood how you could take a man. Now I understand why you can't keep none."

"Is that what I'm supposed to do? Spend my life keeping a man?"

"They worth keeping, Sula."

"They ain't worth more than me. And besides, I never loved no man because he was worth it. Worth didn't have nothing to do with it."

"What did?"

"My mind did. That's all."

"Well I guess that's it. You own the world and the rest of us is renting. You ride the pony and we shovel the shit. I didn't come up here for this kind of talk, Sula . . . "

"No?"

"No. I come to see about you. But now that you opened it up, I may as well close it." Nel's fingers closed around the brass rail of the bed. Now she would ask her. "How come you did it, Sula?"

There was a silence but Nel felt no obligation to fill it.

Sula stirred a little under the covers. She looked bored as she sucked her teeth. "Well, there was this space in front of me, behind me, in my head. Some space. And Jude filled it up. That's all. He just filled up the space."

"You mean you didn't even love him?" The feel of the brass was in Nel's mouth. "It wasn't even loving him?"

Sula looked toward the boarded-up window again. Her eyes fluttered as if she were about to fall off into sleep.

"But . . . " Nel held her stomach in. "But what about me? What about me? Why didn't you think about me? Didn't I count? I never hurt you. What did you take him for if you didn't love him and why didn't you think about me?" And then, "I was good to you, Sula, why don't that matter?"

Sula turned her head away from the boarded window. Her voice was quiet and the stemmed rose over her eye was very dark. "It matters, Nel, but only to you. Not to anybody else. Being good to somebody is just like being mean to somebody. Risky. You don't get nothing for it."

Nel took her hands from the brass railing. She was annoyed with herself. Finally when she had gotten the nerve to ask the question, the right question, it made no difference. Sula couldn't give her a sensible answer because she didn't know. Would be, in fact, the last to know. Talking to her about right and wrong was like talking to the deweys. She picked at the fringe on Sula's bedspread and said softly, "We were friends."

"Oh, yes. Good friends," Sula said.

"And you didn't love me enough to leave him alone. To let him love me. You had to take him away."

"What you mean take him away? I didn't kill him, I just fucked him. If we were such good friends, how come you couldn't get over it?"

"You laying there in that bed without a dime or a friend to your name having done all the dirt you did in this town and you still expect folks to love you?"

Sula raised herself up on her elbows. Her face glistened with the dew of fever. She opened her mouth as though to say something, then fell back on the pillows and sighed. "Oh, they'll love me all right. It will take time, but they'll love me." The sound of her voice was as soft and distant as the look in her eyes. "After all the old women have lain with the teen-agers; when all the young girls have slept with their old drunken uncles; after all the black men fuck all the white ones; when all the white women kiss all the black ones; when the guards have raped all the jailbirds and after all the whores make love to their grannies; after all the faggots get their mothers' trim;[1] when Lindbergh sleeps with Bessie Smith and Norma Shearer makes it with Stepin Fetchit;[2] after all the dogs have fucked all the cats and every weathervane on every barn flies off the roof to mount the hogs . . . then there'll be a little love left over for me. And I know just what it will feel like."

She closed her eyes then and thought of the wind pressing her dress

---

1. Ornaments and clothing; *faggots*—derogatory term for male homosexuals.

2. Charles Lindbergh (1902–1974) became an All-American hero when, in 1927, he was the first man to fly solo and nonstop across the Atlantic; Bessie Smith (1895–1937), a black, was perhaps the greatest of all blues singers; Norma Shearer (b. 1900), an elegant film star of the thirties, was called by her studio (MGM) "The First Lady of the Films," while Lincoln Theodore Monroe Andrew Perry (b. 1902), known as Stepin Fetchit, played stereotyped lazy, readily frightened black roles in films from the late 1920s to the early 1950s.

between her legs as she ran up the bank of the river to four leaf-locked trees and the digging of holes in the earth.

Embarrassed, irritable and a little bit ashamed, Nel rose to go. "Good-bye, Sula. I don't reckon I'll be back."

She opened the door and heard Sula's low whisper. "Hey, girl." Nel paused and turned her head but not enough to see her.

"How you know?" Sula asked.

"Know what?" Nel still wouldn't look at her.

"About who was good. How you know it was you?"

"What you mean?"

"I mean maybe it wasn't you. Maybe it was me."

Nel took two steps out the door and closed it behind her. She walked down the hall and down the four flights of steps. The house billowed around her light then dark, full of presences without sounds. The deweys, Tar Baby, the newly married couples, Mr. Buckland Reed, Patsy, Valentine, and the beautiful Hannah Peace. Where were they? Eva out at the old folks' home, the deweys living anywhere, Tar Baby steeped in wine, and Sula upstairs in Eva's bed with a boarded-up window and an empty pocketbook on the dresser.

● ● ●

When Nel closed the door, Sula reached for more medicine. Then she turned the pillow over to its cool side and thought about her old friend. "So she will walk on down that road, her back so straight in that old green coat, the strap of her handbag pushed back all the way to the elbow, thinking how much I have cost her and never remember the days when we were two throats and one eye and we had no price."

Pictures drifted through her head as lightly as dandelion spores: the blue eagle that swallowed the E of the Sherman's Mellowe wine[3] that Tar Baby drank; the pink underlid of Hannah's eye as she probed for a fleck of coal dust or a lash. She thought of looking out of the windows of all those trains and buses, looking at the feet and backs of all those people. Nothing was ever different. They were all the same. All of the words and all of the smiles, every tear and every gag just something to do.

"That's the same sun I looked at when I was twelve, the same pear trees. If I live a hundred years my urine will flow the same way, my armpits and breath will smell the same. My hair will grow from the same holes. I didn't mean anything. I never meant anything. I stood there watching her burn and was thrilled. I wanted her to keep on jerking like that, to keep on dancing."

Then she had the dream again. The Clabber Girl Baking Powder lady was smiling and beckoning to her, one hand under her apron. When Sula came near she disintegrated into white dust, which Sula was hurriedly trying to stuff into the pockets of her blue-flannel housecoat. The disintegration was awful to see, but worse was the feel of the powder—its starchy slipperiness as she tried to collect it by handfuls. The more she scooped, the more it billowed. At last it covered her, filled her eyes, her nose, her throat, and she woke gagging and overwhelmed with the smell of smoke.

3. Cheap brand of wine.

Pain took hold. First a fluttering as of doves in her stomach, then a kind of burning, followed by a spread of thin wires to other parts of her body. Once the wires of liquid pain were in place, they jelled and began to throb. She tried concentrating on the throbs, identifying them as waves, hammer strokes, razor edges or small explosions. Soon even the variety of the pain bored her and there was nothing to do, for it was joined by fatigue so great she could not make a fist or fight the taste of oil at the back of her tongue.

Several times she tried to cry out, but the fatigue barely let her open her lips, let alone take the deep breath necessary to scream. So she lay there wondering how soon she would gather enough strength to lift her arm and push the rough quilt away from her chin and whether she should turn her cheek to the cooler side of the pillow now or wait till her face was thoroughly soaked and the move would be more refreshing. But she was reluctant to move her face for another reason. If she turned her head, she would not be able to see the boarded-up window Eva jumped out of. And looking at those four wooden planks with the steel rod slanting across them was the only peace she had. The sealed window soothed her with its sturdy termination, its unassailable finality. It was as though for the first time she was completely alone—where she had always wanted to be—free of the possibility of distraction. It would be here, only here, held by this blind window high above the elm tree, that she might draw her legs up to her chest, close her eyes, put her thumb in her mouth and float over and down the tunnels, just missing the dark walls, down, down until she met a rain scent and would know the water was near, and she would curl into its heavy softness and it would envelop her, carry her, and wash her tired flesh always. Always. Who said that? She tried hard to think. Who was it that had promised her a sleep of water always? The effort to recall was too great; it loosened a knot in her chest that turned her thoughts again to the pain.

While in this state of weary anticipation, she noticed that she was not breathing, that her heart had stopped completely. A crease of fear touched her breast, for any second there was sure to be a violent explosion in her brain, a gasping for breath. Then she realized, or rather she sensed, that there was not going to be any pain. She was not breathing because she didn't have to. Her body did not need oxygen. She was dead.

Sula felt her face smiling. "Well, I'll be damned," she thought, "it didn't even hurt. Wait'll I tell Nel."

1941

The death of Sula Peace was the best news folks up in the Bottom had had since the promise of work at the tunnel. Of the few who were not afraid to witness the burial of a witch and who had gone to the cemetery, some had come just to verify her being put away but stayed to sing "Shall We Gather at the River"[4] for politeness' sake, quite unaware of the bleak promise of their song. Others came to see that nothing went awry, that the shallow-minded and small-hearted kept their meanness at bay, and that the entire event be characterized by that abiding gentleness of spirit to which they themselves had arrived by the simple determination not to

---

4. Popular hymn (1864) written by Robert Lowry (1826–1899) amid an epidemic; the river ("where angel feet have trod") is the river of death.

let anything—anything at all: not failed crops, not rednecks, lost jobs, sick children, rotten potatoes, broken pipes, bug-ridden flour, third-class coal, educated social workers, thieving insurance men, garlic-ridden hunkies, corrupt Catholics, racist Protestants, cowardly Jews, slaveholding Moslems, jack-leg[5] nigger preachers, squeamish Chinamen, cholera, dropsy or the Black Plague, let alone a strange woman—keep them from their God.

In any case, both the raw-spirited and the gentle who came—not to the white funeral parlor but to the colored part of the Beechnut Cemetery— felt that either *because* Sula was dead or just *after* she was dead a brighter day was dawning. There were signs. The rumor that the tunnel spanning the river would use Negro workers became an announcement. Planned, abandoned and replanned for years, this project had finally begun in 1937. For three years there were rumors that blacks would work it, and hope was high in spite of the fact that the River Road leading to the tunnel had encouraged similar hopes in 1927 but had ended up being built entirely by white labor—hillbillies and immigrants taking even the lowest jobs. But the tunnel itself was another matter. The craft work—no, they would not get that. But it was a major job, and the government seemed to favor opening up employment to black workers. It meant black men would not have to sweep Medallion to eat, or leave the town altogether for the steel mills in Akron and along Lake Erie.

The second sign was the construction begun on an old people's home. True, it was more renovation than construction, but the blacks were free, or so it was said, to occupy it. Some said that the very transfer of Eva from the ramshackle house that passed for a colored women's nursing home to the bright new one was a clear sign of the mystery of God's ways, His mighty thumb having been seen at Sula's throat.

So it was with a strong sense of hope that the people in the Bottom watched October close.

Then Medallion turned silver. It seemed sudden, but actually there had been days and days of no snow—just frost—when, late one afternoon, a rain fell and froze. Way down Carpenter's Road, where the concrete sidewalks started, children hurried to the sliding places before shopkeepers and old women sprinkled stove ashes, like ancient onyx, onto the new-minted silver. They hugged trees simply to hold for a moment all that life and largeness stilled in glass, and gazed at the sun pressed against the gray sky like a worn doubloon, wondering all the while if the world were coming to an end. Grass stood blade by blade, shocked into separateness by an ice that held for days.

Late-harvesting things were ruined, of course, and fowl died of both chill and rage. Cider turned to ice and split the jugs, forcing the men to drink their cane liquor too soon. It was better down in the valley, since, as always, the hills protected it, but up in the Bottom black folks suffered heavily in their thin houses and thinner clothes. The ice-cold wind bled what little heat they had through windowpanes and ill-fitting doors. For days on end they were virtually housebound, venturing out only to coal-bins or right next door for the trading of vital foodstuffs. Never to the stores. No deliveries were being made anyway, and when they were, the items were saved for better-paying white customers. Women could not

5. Unordained.

make it down the icy slopes and therefore missed days of wages they sorely needed.

The consequence of all that ice was a wretched Thanksgiving of tiny tough birds, heavy pork cakes, and pithy sweet potatoes. By the time the ice began to melt and the first barge was seen shuddering through the ice skim on the river, everybody under fifteen had croup, or scarlet fever, and those over had chilblains, rheumatism, pleurisy, earaches and a world of other ailments.

Still it was not those illnesses or even the ice that marked the beginning of the trouble, that self-fulfilled prophecy that Shadrack carried on his tongue. As soon as the silvering began, long before the cider cracked the jugs, there was something wrong. A falling away, a dislocation was taking place. Hard on the heels of the general relief that Sula's death brought a restless irritability took hold. Teapot, for example, went into the kitchen and asked his mother for some sugar-butter-bread. She got up to fix it and found that she had no butter, only oleomargarine. Too tired to mix the saffron-colored powder into the hard cake of oleo,[6] she simply smeared the white stuff on the bread and sprinkled the sugar over it. Teapot tasted the difference and refused to eat it. This keenest of insults that a mother can feel, the rejection by a child of her food, bent her into fury and she beat him as she had not done since Sula knocked him down the steps. She was not alone. Other mothers who had defended their children from Sula's malevolence (or who had defended their positions as mothers from Sula's scorn for the role) now had nothing to rub up against. The tension was gone and so was the reason for the effort they had made. Without her mockery, affection for others sank into flaccid disrepair. Daughters who had complained bitterly about the responsibilities of taking care of their aged mothers-in-law had altered when Sula locked Eva away, and they began cleaning those old women's spittoons without a murmur. Now that Sula was dead and done with, they returned to a steeping resentment of the burdens of old people. Wives uncoddled their husbands; there seemed no further need to reinforce their vanity. And even those Negroes who had moved down from Canada to Medallion, who remarked every chance they got that they had never been slaves, felt a loosening of the reactionary compassion for Southern-born blacks Sula had inspired in them. They returned to their original claims of superiority.

The normal meanness that the winter brought was compounded by the small-spiritedness that hunger and scarlet fever produced. Even a definite and witnessed interview of four colored men (and the promise of more in the spring) at the tunnel site could not break the cold vise of that lean and bitter year's end.

Christmas came one morning and haggled everybody's nerves like a dull ax—too shabby to cut clean but too heavy to ignore. The children lay wall-eyed on creaking beds or pallets near the stove, sucking peppermint and oranges in between coughs while their mothers stomped the floors in rage at the cakes that did not rise because the stove fire had been so stingy; at the curled bodies of men who chose to sleep the day away rather than face the silence made by the absence of Lionel trains, drums, crybaby dolls and rocking horses. Teen-agers sneaked into the Elmira

6. In many states until quite recently oleomargarine could be sold only uncolored, a dead-white; small capsules or bits of powder were often included in the package to be squeezed or mixed in for coloring.

Theater in the afternoon and let Tex Ritter[7] free them from the recollection of their father's shoes, yawning in impotence under the bed. Some of
them had a bottle of wine, which they drank at the feet of the glittering
Mr. Ritter, making such a ruckus the manager had to put them out. The
white people who came with Christmas bags of rock candy and old
clothes were hard put to get a *Yes'm, thank you,* out of those sullen
mouths.

Just as the ice lingered in October, so did the phlegm of December—
which explained the enormous relief brought on by the first three days of
1941. It was as though the season had exhausted itself, for on January first
the temperature shot up to sixty-one degrees and slushed the whiteness
overnight. On January second drab patches of grass could be seen in the
fields. On January third the sun came out—and so did Shadrack with his
rope, his bell and his childish dirge.

He had spent the night before watching a tiny moon. The people, the
voices that kept him company, were with him less and less. Now there
were long periods when he heard nothing except the wind in the trees
and the plop of buckeyes on the earth. In the winter, when the fish were
too hard to get to, he did picking-up jobs for small businessmen (nobody
would have him in or even near their homes), and thereby continued to
have enough money for liquor. Yet the drunk times were becoming
deeper but more seldom. It was as though he no longer needed to drink
to forget whatever it was he could not remember. Now he could not remember that he had ever forgotten anything. Perhaps that was why for
the first time after that cold day in France he was beginning to miss the
presence of other people. Shadrack had improved enough to feel lonely. If
he was lonely before, he didn't know it because the noise he kept up, the
roaring, the busyness, protected him from knowing it. Now the compulsion to activity, to filling up the time when he was not happily fishing on
the riverbank, had dwindled. He sometimes fell asleep before he got
drunk; sometimes spent whole days looking at the river and the sky; and
more and more he relinquished the military habits of cleanliness in his
shack. Once a bird flew into his door—one of the robins during the time
there was a plague of them. It stayed, looking for an exit, for the better
part of an hour. When the bird found the window and flew away, Shadrack was grieved and actually waited and watched for its return. During
those days of waiting, he did not make his bed, or sweep, or shake out the
little rag-braid rug, and almost forgot to slash with his fish knife the passing day on his calendar. When he did return to housekeeping, it was not
with the precision he had always insisted upon. The messier his house
got, the lonelier he felt, and it was harder and harder to conjure up ser-
geants, and orderlies, and invading armies; harder and harder to hear the
gunfire and keep the platoon marching in time. More frequently now he
looked at and fondled the one piece of evidence that he once had a visitor in his house: a child's purple-and-white belt. The one the little girl
left behind when she came to see him. Shadrack remembered the scene
clearly. He had stepped into the door and there was a tear-stained face
turning, turning toward him; eyes hurt and wondering; mouth parted in
an effort to ask a question. She had wanted something—from him. Not

7. "America's Most Beloved Cowboy" (1905–1974),   Country Music Halls of Fame.
film star of the 1940s elected both to the Cowboy and

fish, not work, but something only he could give. She had a tadpole over her eye (that was how he knew she was a friend—she had the mark of the fish he loved), and one of her braids had come undone. But when he looked at her face he had seen also the skull beneath, and thinking she saw it too—knew it was there and was afraid—he tried to think of something to say to comfort her, something to stop the hurt from spilling out of her eyes. So he had said "always," so she would not have to be afraid of the change—the falling away of skin, the drip and slide of blood, and the exposure of bone underneath. He had said "always" to convince her, assure her, of permanency.

It worked, for when he said it her face lit up and the hurt did leave. She ran then, carrying his knowledge, but her belt fell off and he kept it as a memento. It hung on a nail near his bed—unfrayed, unsullied after all those years, with only the permanent bend in the fabric made by its long life on a nail. It was pleasant living with that sign of a visitor, his only one. And after a while he was able to connect the belt with the face, the tadpole-over-the-eye-face that he sometimes saw up in the Bottom. His visitor, his company, his guest, his social life, his woman, his daughter, his friend—they all hung there on a nail near his bed.

Now he stared at the tiny moon floating high over the ice-choked river. His loneliness had dropped down somewhere around his ankles. Some other feeling possessed him. A feeling that touched his eyes and made him blink. He had seen her again months? weeks? ago. Raking leaves for Mr. Hodges, he had gone into the cellar for two bushel baskets to put them in. In the hallway he passed an open door leading to a small room. She lay on a table there. It was surely the same one. The same little-girl face, same tadpole over the eye. So he had been wrong. Terribly wrong. No "always" at all. Another dying away of someone whose face he knew.

It was then he began to suspect that all those years of rope hauling and bell ringing were never going to do any good. He might as well sit forever on his riverbank and stare out of the window at the moon.

By his day-slashed calendar he knew that tomorrow was the day. And for the first time he did not want to go. He wanted to stay with the purple-and-white belt. Not go. Not go.

Still, when the day broke in an incredible splash of sun, he gathered his things. In the early part of the afternoon, drenched in sunlight and certain that this would be the last time he would invite them to end their lives neatly and sweetly, he walked over the rickety bridge and on into the Bottom. But it was not heartfelt this time, not loving this time, for he no longer cared whether he helped them or not. His rope was improperly tied; his bell had a tinny unimpassioned sound. His visitor was dead and would come no more.

Years later people would quarrel about who had been the first to go. Most folks said it was the deweys, but one or two knew better, knew that Dessie and Ivy had been first. Said that Dessie had opened her door first and stood there shielding her eyes from the sun while watching Shadrack coming down the road. She laughed.

Maybe the sun; maybe the clots of green showing in the hills promising so much; maybe the contrast between Shadrack's doomy, gloomy bell glinting in all that sweet sunshine. Maybe just a brief moment, for once, of not feeling fear, of looking at death in the sunshine and being unafraid. She laughed.

Upstairs, Ivy heard her and looked to see what caused the thick music that rocked her neighbor's breasts. Then Ivy laughed too. Like the scarlet fever that had touched everybody and worn them down to gristle, their laughter infected Carpenter's Road. Soon children were jumping about giggling and men came to the porches to chuckle. By the time Shadrack reached the first house, he was facing a line of delighted faces.

Never before had they laughed. Always they had shut their doors, pulled down the shades and called their children out of the road. It frightened him, this glee, but he stuck to his habit—singing his song, ringing his bell and holding fast to his rope. The deweys with their magnificent teeth ran out from Number 7 and danced a little jig around the befuddled Shadrack, then cut into a wild aping of his walk, his song and his bell-ringing. By now women were holding their stomachs, and the men were slapping their knees. It was Mrs. Jackson, who ate ice, who tripped down off her porch and marched—actually marched—along behind him. The scene was so comic the people walked into the road to make sure they saw it all. In that way the parade started.

Everybody, Dessie, Tar Baby, Patsy, Mr. Buckland Reed, Teapot's Mamma, Valentine, the deweys, Mrs. Jackson, Irene, the proprietor of the Palace of Cosmetology, Reba, the Herrod brothers and flocks of teen-agers got into the mood and, laughing, dancing, calling to one another, formed a pied piper's band behind Shadrack. As the initial group of about twenty people passed more houses, they called to the people standing in doors and leaning out of windows to join them; to help them open further this slit in the veil, this respite from anxiety, from dignity, from gravity, from the weight of that very adult pain that had undergirded them all those years before. Called to them to come out and play in the sunshine—as though the sunshine would last, as though there really was hope. The same hope that kept them picking beans for other farmers; kept them from finally leaving as they talked of doing; kept them knee-deep in other people's dirt; kept them excited about other people's wars; kept them solicitous of white people's children; kept them convinced that some magic "government" was going to lift them up, out and away from that dirt, those beans, those wars.

Some, of course, like Helene Wright, would not go. She watched the ruckus with characteristic scorn. Others, who understood the Spirit's touch which made them dance, who understood whole families bending their backs in a field while singing as from one throat, who understood the ecstasy of river baptisms under suns just like this one, did not understand this curious disorder, this headless display and so refused also to go.

Nevertheless, the sun splashed on a larger and larger crowd that strutted, skipped, marched, and shuffled down the road. When they got down to where the sidewalk started, some of them stopped and decided to turn back, too embarrassed to enter the white part of town whooping like banshees. But except for three or four, the fainthearted were put to shame by the more aggressive and abandoned, and the parade danced down Main Street past Woolworth's and the old poultry house, turned right and moved on down the New River Road.

At the mouth of the tunnel excavation, in a fever pitch of excitement

and joy, they saw the timber, the bricks, the steel ribs and the tacky wire
gate that glittered under ice struck to diamond in the sun. It dazzled
them, at first, and they were suddenly quiet. Their hooded eyes swept
over the place where their hope had lain since 1927. There was the promise: leaf-dead. The teeth unrepaired, the coal credit cut off, the chest
pains unattended, the school shoes unbought, the rush-stuffed mattresses,
the broken toilets, the leaning porches, the slurred remarks and the staggering childish malevolence of their employers. All there in blazing sunlit
ice rapidly becoming water.

Like antelopes they leaped over the little gate—a wire barricade that
was never intended to bar anything but dogs, rabbits and stray children—
and led by the tough, the enraged and the young they picked up the
lengths of timber and thin steel ribs and smashed the bricks they would
never fire in yawning kilns, split the sacks of limestone they had not
mixed or even been allowed to haul; tore the wire mesh, tipped over
wheelbarrows and rolled forepoles[8] down the bank, where they sailed far
out on the icebound river.

Old and young, women and children, lame and hearty, they killed, as
best they could, the tunnel they were forbidden to build.

They didn't mean to go in, to actually go down into the lip of the
tunnel, but in their need to kill it all, all of it, to wipe from the face of
the earth the work of the thin-armed Virginia boys, the bull-necked
Greeks and the knife-faced men who waved the leaf-dead promise, they
went too deep, too far . . .

A lot of them died there. The earth, now warm, shifted; the first fore-
pole slipped; loose rock fell from the face of the tunnel and caused a
shield to give way. They found themselves in a chamber of water, deprived of the sun that had brought them there. With the first crack and
whoosh of water, the clamber to get out was so fierce that others who
were trying to help were pulled to their deaths. Pressed up against steel
ribs and timber blocks young boys strangled when the oxygen left them to
join the water. Outside, others watched in terror as ice split and earth
shook beneath their feet. Mrs. Jackson, weighing less than 100 pounds,
slid down the bank and met with an open mouth the ice she had craved
all her life. Tar Baby, Dessie, Ivy, Valentine, the Herrod boys, some of
Ajax's younger brothers and the deweys (at least it was supposed; their
bodies were never found)—all died there. Mr. Buckland Reed escaped, so
did Patsy and her two boys, as well as some fifteen or twenty who had not
gotten close enough to fall, or whose timidity would not let them enter an
unfinished tunnel.

And all the while Shadrack stood there. Having forgotten his song and
his rope, he just stood there high up on the bank ringing, ringing his bell.

1965

Things were so much better in 1965. Or so it seemed. You could go
downtown and see colored people working in the dime store behind the
counters, even handling money with cash-register keys around their
necks. And a colored man taught mathematics at the junior high school.

8. Where there is danger of a cave-in during excavation, a pole or plank is sometimes thrust into the
ground ahead of the digging and used as support.

The young people had a look about them that everybody said was new but which reminded Nel of the deweys, whom nobody had ever found. Maybe, she thought, they had gone off and seeded the land and growed up in these young people in the dime store with the cash-register keys around their necks.

They were so different, these young people. So different from the way she remembered them forty years ago.

Jesus, there were some beautiful boys in 1921! Look like the whole world was bursting at the seams with them. Thirteen, fourteen, fifteen years old. Jesus, they were fine. L. P., Paul Freeman and his brother Jake, Mrs. Scott's twins—and Ajax had a whole flock of younger brothers. They hung out of attic windows, rode on car fenders, delivered the coal, moved into Medallion and moved out, visited cousins, plowed, hoisted, lounged on the church steps, careened on the school playground. The sun heated them and the moon slid down their backs. God, the world was *full* of beautiful boys in 1921.

Nothing like these kids. Everything had changed. Even the whores were better then: tough, fat, laughing women with burns on their cheeks and wit married to their meanness: or widows couched in small houses in the woods with eight children to feed and no man. These modern-day whores were pale and dull before those women. These little clothes-crazy things were always embarrassed. Nasty but shamed. They didn't know what shameless was. They should have known those silvery widows in the woods who would get up from the dinner table and walk into the trees with a customer with as much embarrassment as a calving mare.

Lord, how time flies. She hardly recognized anybody in the town any more. Now there was another old people's home. Look like this town just kept on building homes for old people. Every time they built a road they built a old folks' home. You'd think folks was living longer, but the fact of it was, they was just being put out faster.

Nel hadn't seen the insides of this most recent one yet, but it was her turn in Circle Number 5 to visit some of the old women there. The pastor visited them regularly, but the circle thought private visits were nice too. There were just nine colored women out there, the same nine that had been in the other one. But a lot of white ones. White people didn't fret about putting their old ones away. It took a lot for black people to let them go, and even if somebody was old and alone, others did the dropping by, the floor washing, the cooking. Only when they got crazy and unmanageable were they let go. Unless it was somebody like Sula, who put Eva away out of meanness. It was true that Eva was foolish in the head, but not so bad as to need locking up.

Nel was more than a little curious to see her. She had been really active in church only a year or less, and that was because the children were grown now and took up less time and less space in her mind. For over twenty-five years since Jude walked out she had pinned herself into a tiny life. She spent a little time trying to marry again, but nobody wanted to take her on with three children, and she simply couldn't manage the business of keeping boyfriends. During the war she had had a rather long relationship with a sergeant stationed at the camp twenty miles down river from Medallion, but then he got called away and everything was reduced to a few letters—then nothing. Then there was a bartender at the hotel. But now she was fifty-five and hard put to remember what all that had been about.

It didn't take long, after Jude left, for her to see what the future would be. She had looked at her children and knew in her heart that that would be all. That they were all she would ever know of love. But it was a love that, like a pan of syrup kept too long on the stove, had cooked out, leaving only its odor and a hard, sweet sludge, impossible to scrape off. For the mouths of her children quickly forgot the taste of her nipples, and years ago they had begun to look past her face into the nearest stretch of sky.

In the meantime the Bottom had collapsed. Everybody who had made money during the war moved as close as they could to the valley, and the white people were buying down river, cross river, stretching Medallion like two strings on the banks. Nobody colored lived much up in the Bottom any more. White people were building towers for television stations up there and there was a rumor about a golf course or something. Anyway, hill land was more valuable now, and those black people who had moved down right after the war and in the fifties couldn't afford to come back even if they wanted to. Except for the few blacks still huddled by the river bend, and some undemolished houses on Carpenter's Road, only rich white folks were building homes in the hills. Just like that, they had changed their minds and instead of keeping the valley floor to themselves, now they wanted a hilltop house with a river view and a ring of elms. The black people, for all their new look, seemed awfully anxious to get to the valley, or leave town, and abandon the hills to whoever was interested. It was sad, because the Bottom had been a real place. These young ones kept talking about the community, but they left the hills to the poor, the old, the stubborn—and the rich white folks. Maybe it hadn't been a community, but it had been a place. Now there weren't any places left, just separate houses with separate televisions and separate telephones and less and less dropping by.

These were the same thoughts she always had when she walked down into the town. One of the last true pedestrians, Nel walked the shoulder road while cars slipped by. Laughed at by her children, she still walked wherever she wanted to go, allowing herself to accept rides only when the weather required it.

Now she went straight through the town and turned left at its farthest end, along a tree-lined walk that turned into a country road farther on and passed the cemetery, Beechnut Park.

When she got to Sunnydale, the home for the aged, it was already four o'clock and turning chill. She would be glad to sit down with those old birds and rest her feet.

A red-haired lady at the desk gave her a pass card and pointed to a door that opened onto a corridor of smaller doors. It looked like what she imagined a college dormitory to be. The lobby was luxurious—modern—but the rooms she peeped into were sterile green cages. There was too much light everywhere; it needed some shadows. The third door, down the hall, had a little name tag over it that read EVA PEACE. Nel twisted the knob and rapped a little on the door at the same time, then listened a moment before she opened it.

At first she couldn't believe it. She seemed so small, sitting at that table in a black-vinyl chair. All the heaviness had gone and the height. Her once beautiful leg had no stocking and the foot was in a slipper. Nel wanted to cry—not for Eva's milk-dull eyes or her floppy lips, but for the once proud foot accustomed for over a half century to a fine well-laced shoe, now stuffed gracelessly into a pink terrycloth slipper.

"Good evening, Miss Peace. I'm Nel Greene come to pay a call on you. You remember me, don't you?"

Eva was ironing and dreaming of stairwells. She had neither iron nor clothes but did not stop her fastidious lining up of pleats or pressing out of wrinkles even when she acknowledged Nel's greeting.

"Howdy. Sit down."

"Thank you." Nel sat on the edge of the little bed.

"You've got a pretty room, a real pretty room, Miss Peace."

"You eat something funny today?"

"Ma'am?"

"Some chop suey? Think back."

"No, ma'am."

"No? Well, you gone be sick later on."

"But I didn't have no chop suey."

"You think I come all the way over here for you to tell me that? I can't make visits too often. You should have some respect for old people."

"But Miss Peace, I'm visiting *you*. This is *your* room." Nel smiled.

"What you say your name was?"

"Nel Greene."

"Wiley Wright's girl?"

"Uh huh. You do remember. That makes me feel good, Miss Peace. You remember me and my father."

"Tell me how you killed that little boy."

"What? What little boy?"

"The one you threw in the water. I got oranges. How did you get him to go in the water?"

"I didn't throw no little boy in the river. That was Sula."

"You. Sula. What's the difference? You was there. You watched, didn't you? Me, I never would've watched."

"You're confused, Miss Peace. I'm Nel. Sula's dead."

"It's awful cold in the water. Fire is warm. How did you get him in?" Eva wet her forefinger and tested the iron's heat.

"Who told you all these lies? Miss Peace? Who told you? Why are you telling lies on me?"

"I got oranges. I don't drink they old orange juice. They puts something in it."

"Why are you trying to make out like I did it?"

Eva stopped ironing and looked at Nel. For the first time her eyes looked sane.

"You think I'm guilty?" Nel was whispering.

Eva whispered back, "Who would know that better than you?"

"I want to know who you been talking to." Nel forced herself to speak normally.

"Plum. Sweet Plum. He tells me things." Eva laughed a light, tinkly giggle—girlish.

"I'll be going now, Miss Peace." Nel stood.

"You ain't answered me yet."

"I don't know what you're talking about."

"Just alike. Both of you. Never was no difference between you. Want some oranges? It's better for you than chop suey. Sula? I got oranges."

Nel walked hurriedly down the hall, Eva calling after her, "Sula?" Nel couldn't see the other women today. That woman had upset her. She handed her pass back to the lady, avoiding her look of surprise.

Outside she fastened her coat against the rising wind. The top button was missing so she covered her throat with her hand. A bright space opened in her head and memory seeped into it.

Standing on the riverbank in a purple-and-white dress, Sula swinging Chicken Little around and around. His laughter before the hand-slip and the water closing quickly over the place. What had she felt then, watching Sula going around and around and then the little boy swinging out over the water? Sula had cried and cried when she came back from Shadrack's house. But Nel had remained calm.

"*Shouldn't we tell?*"

"*Did he see?*"

"*I don't know. No.*"

"*Let's go. We can't bring him back.*"

What did old Eva mean by *you watched?* How could she help seeing it? She was right there. But Eva didn't say *see*, she said *watched.* "I did not watch it. I just saw it." But it was there anyway, as it had always been, the old feeling and the old question. The good feeling she had had when Chicken's hand slipped. She hadn't wondered about that in years. "Why didn't I feel bad when it happened? How come it felt so good to see him fall?"

All these years she had been secretly proud of her calm, controlled behavior when Sula was uncontrollable, her compassion for Sula's frightened and shamed eyes. Now it seemed that what she had thought was maturity, serenity and compassion was only the tranquillity that follows a joyful stimulation. Just as the water closed peacefully over the turbulence of Chicken Little's body, so had contentment washed over her enjoyment.

She was walking too fast. Not watching where she placed her feet, she got into the weeds by the side of the road. Running almost, she approached Beechnut Park. Just over there was the colored part of the cemetery. She went in. Sula was buried there along with Plum, Hannah and now Pearl. With the same disregard for name changes by marriage that the black people of Medallion always showed, each flat slab had one word carved on it. Together they read like a chant: PEACE 1895–1921, PEACE 1890–1923, PEACE 1910–1940, PEACE 1892–1959.

They were not dead people. They were words. Not even words. Wishes, longings.

All these years she had been harboring good feelings about Eva; sharing, she believed, her loneliness and unloved state as no one else could or did. She, after all, was the only one who really understood why Eva refused to attend Sula's funeral. The others thought they knew; thought the grandmother's reasons were the same as their own—that to pay respect to someone who had caused them so much pain was beneath them. Nel, who did go, believed Eva's refusal was not due to pride or vengeance but to a plain unwillingness to see the swallowing of her own flesh into the dirt, a determination not to let the eyes see what the heart could not hold.

Now, however, after the way Eva had just treated her, accused her, she wondered if the townspeople hadn't been right the first time. Eva *was* mean. Sula had even said so. There was no good reason for her to speak so. Feeble-minded or not. Old. Whatever. Eva knew what she was doing. Always had. She had stayed away from Sula's funeral and accused Nel of drowning Chicken Little for spite. The same spite that galloped all over the Bottom. That made every gesture an offense, every off-center smile a threat, so that even the bubbles of relief that broke in the chest of practically everybody when Sula died did not soften their spite and allow them to go to Mr. Hodges' funeral parlor or send flowers from the church or bake a yellow cake.

She thought about Nathan opening the bedroom door the day she had visited her, and finding the body. He said he knew she was dead right away not because her eyes were open but because her mouth was. It looked to him like a giant yawn that she never got to finish. He had run across the street to Teapot's Mamma, who, when she heard the news, said "Ho!" like the conductor on the train when it was about to take off except louder, and then did a little dance. None of the women left their quilt patches in disarray to run to the house. Nobody left the clothes halfway through the wringer to run to the house. Even the men just said "uhn," when they heard. The day passed and no one came. The night slipped into another day and the body was still lying in Eva's bed gazing at the ceiling trying to complete a yawn. It was very strange, this stubbornness about Sula. For even when China, the most rambunctious whore in the town, died (whose black son and white son said, when they heard she was dying, "She ain't dead yet?"), even then everybody stopped what they were doing and turned out in numbers to put the fallen sister away.

It was Nel who finally called the hospital, then the mortuary, then the police, who were the ones to come. So the white people took over. They came in a police van and carried the body down the steps past the four pear trees and into the van for all the world as with Hannah. When the police asked questions nobody gave them any information. It took them hours to find out the dead woman's first name. The call was for a Miss Peace at 7 Carpenter's Road. So they left with that: a body, a name and an address. The white people had to wash her, dress her, prepare her and finally lower her. It was all done elegantly, for it was discovered that she had a substantial death policy. Nel went to the funeral parlor, but was so shocked by the closed coffin she stayed only a few minutes.

The following day Nel walked to the burying and found herself the only black person there, steeling her mind to the roses and pulleys. It was only when she turned to leave that she saw the cluster of black folk at the lip of the cemetery. Not coming in, not dressed for mourning, but there waiting. Not until the white folks left—the gravediggers, Mr. and Mrs. Hodges, and their young son who assisted them—did those black people from up in the Bottom enter with hooded hearts and filled eyes to sing "Shall We Gather at the River" over the curved earth that cut them off from the most magnificent hatred they had ever known. Their question clotted the October air, Shall We Gather at the River? The beautiful, the beautiful river? Perhaps Sula answered them even then, for it began to rain, and the women ran in tiny leaps through the grass for fear their straightened hair would beat them home.

Sadly, heavily, Nel left the colored part of the cemetery. Further along the road Shadrack passed her by. A little shaggier, a little older, still energetically mad, he looked at the woman hurrying along the road with the sunset in her face.

He stopped. Trying to remember where he had seen her before. The effort of recollection was too much for him and he moved on. He had to haul some trash out at Sunnydale and it would be good and dark before he got home. He hadn't sold fish in a long time now. The river had killed them all. No more silver-gray flashes, no more flat, wide, unhurried look. No more slowing down of gills. No more tremor on the line.

Shadrack and Nel moved in opposite directions, each thinking separate thoughts about the past. The distance between them increased as they both remembered gone things.

Suddenly Nel stopped. Her eye twitched and burned a little.

"Sula?" she whispered, gazing at the tops of trees. "Sula?"

Leaves stirred; mud shifted; there was the smell of overripe green things. A soft ball of fur broke and scattered like dandelion spores in the breeze.

"All that time, all that time, I thought I was missing Jude." And the loss pressed down on her chest and came up into her throat. "We was girls together," she cried as though explaining something. "O Lord, Sula," she cried, "girl, girl, girlgirlgirl."

It was a fine cry—loud and long—but it had no bottom and it had not top, just circles and circles of sorrow.

1973

AFTERWORD

Sula is, first of all, a novel about being black and female in America in the early and middle years of the twentieth century. When Sula Peace and Nel Wright are twelve years old they meet each other in school, and immediately "they felt the ease and comfort of old friends. Because each had discovered years before that they were neither white nor male, and that all freedom and triumph was forbidden to them, they set about creating something else to be." Eighteen years later, when Nel visits the ill Sula, she tells her she cannot both be independent and not work; she can't have it all.

> "Why? I can do it all, why can't I have it all?"
> "You *can't* do it all. You a woman and a colored woman at that. You can't act like a man. You can't be walking around all independent-like, doing whatever you like, taking what you want, leaving what you don't."

Both women want to be themselves. As a girl, even before meeting Sula, Nel says to herself. "'I'm me. I'm not their daughter, I'm not Nel. I'm me. Me.'" When, at twenty-seven, Sula returns to her hometown after an absence of ten years, her grandmother tells her she needs to settle down and have babies, but Sula responds, "'I don't want to make somebody else. I want to make myself.'"

Nel chooses the conventional path: she marries and has children, lives in her hometown, is a member of the church. Sula goes off to college and wanders over the country before she returns, dressed like a movie star but without a husband or "visible means of support." She lives as she can, never letting anyone tell her what to do, never making demands—"Sula never competed; she simply helped others define themselves." She accepted people as they were, made Nel, at least, feel good about herself, and made her laugh, a deep "rib-scraping laugh." For her, however, anything forever is hell (just as for Nel change is hell); she scorns others for having safety nets, fearing the "free fall," which to her means fearing life: "she lived out her days exploring her own thoughts and emotions, giving them full reign, feeling no obligation to please anybody unless their pleasure pleased her." She takes men as she wants them, doubly offending the community wives by sleeping with their husbands just once, and then rejecting them as if she had found them wanting. Without loving him, she even seduces the husband of her only friend, Nel, whose whole life is built around her domesticity. Sula does not really seem to understand that Nel will be bothered by her husband's adultery, that it will virtually ruin her life; after all, Sula says, "I didn't kill him." When Nel asks her how she could do such a thing when Nel had been so good to her, Sula replies, "'Being good to somebody is just like being mean to somebody. Risky. You don't get nothing for it.'"

Yet despite their differences the two women are bonded. None of Sula's men will talk to her (until Ajax comes into her life), and she craves that other half of self. With Nel she talks and laughs, or, as on one summer day when they are twelve, walks and plays an unpremeditated game, digging a hole, together, communicating, acting in concert, without speaking. Nel has been the only real "other" person to her. When death comes to Sula but comes without pain, despite their estrangement, she thinks, "'Wait'll I tell Nel.'" And twenty-five years after Sula's death, the "soft ball of fur" that has been on the periphery of Nel's vision since her husband left her breaks.

"All that time, all that time, I thought I was missing Jude." And the loss pressed down on her chest and came up into her throat. "We were girls together," she said as though explaining something. "O Lord, Sula," she cried, "girl, girl, girlgirlgirl."

It was a fine cry—loud and long—but it had no bottom and it had no top, just circles and circles of sorrow.

And that is how this moving, tough, tender, and powerful novel ends.

It's certainly a novel about growing up female, and growing up black, and about bonding. But let's look a moment at that bonding. Domesticity, security, virtue are the cornerstones of Nel's rational life. In moments of crisis, she is cool, while Sula, governed by emotions, is ineffectual. Sula, who cuts the tip of her finger off to demonstrate her courage to a group of boys who are hassling them; who watches her mother burn to death "with interest," and who callously puts her grandmother into a home; who sleeps around and seduces Nel's husband; who seems a sociopath, with no sense of right or wrong—Sula says, in her last conversation with Nel:

"About who was good. How you know it was you?"
"What you mean?"
"I mean maybe it wasn't you. Maybe it was me."

Those are the last words of Sula *Peace* to Nel *Wright*.

Twenty-five years later Nel visits Sula's ancient grandmother in the home. The old lady accuses Nel of having thrown a little boy, Chicken Little, into the river more than forty years earlier.

"I didn't throw no little boy in the river. That was Sula."
"You. Sula. What's the difference? . . ."

She repeats herself, and in her senility confuses Nel with Sula. Nel questions herself and finds that she had not just *seen* but *watched* Chicken Little arc into the water and disappear, as Sula had watched her mother burn.

All these years she had been secretly proud of her calm, controlled behavior when Sula was uncontrollable, her compassion for Sula's frightened and shamed eyes. Now it seemed that what she had thought was maturity, serenity and compassion was only the tranquillity that follows a joyful stimulation.

Who is the virtuous one? Is the head or the heart the seat of virtue?

Do we see Sula the sociopath (the Devil, as the black community believed her to be) as good? Is she admirable? Is she right in the way she chose to live? Why, then, does she get her come-uppance? Why, when she finally finds a man for whom she wants to build a nest, does he—her male equivalent—leave her, just as Jude Greene left Nel? If we make her representative of a way of life—uncommitted, free, amoral—is the outcome of her life representative too? Why does she, like the unconventional Daisy and Amy and the "awakened" Edna Pontellier, die young, and apparently as a result of her independent mode of life? She tells Nel she knows she's dying, but she's "going down like one of those redwoods" while all the other black women, who are also dying, are going down like stumps. And if her independent life is a lonely one, she says, Nel is lonely too, but Nel is lonely by another's choosing and Sula by her own. We know Sula has not really chosen to have Ajax go away; Nel believes Sula's bravado is just showing off. Is it?

If the wages of sin are death, the wages of virtue as Nel practices it are loveless survival; all she has of love is her children—a love described in one of those brilliant homey images that sparkle through the novel like bright thread— "a love that, like a pan of syrup kept too long on the stove, had cooked out, leaving only its odor and a hard, sweet sludge, impossible to scrape off." Which (if either) is virtuous? Which (if either) chooses the proper path? Eventually, these seem almost meaningless questions. Falling free and going down like a redwood may be mere romantic bravado covering a somewhat lonely and sordid life and death; going down like a stump is all too painfully real. Growing up black and female, there is no freedom and triumph, no "right" way. Sula and Nel, Peace and Wright, are alternative paths to similar goals. The two women are in effect doubles, in which we are not sure which is Jekyll and which Hyde, in each of which good and evil can neither be separated nor even defined.

We may be able to outline the way the novel educates us in Sula's character and evaluates her career by controlling our expectations and pattern-making. Four times in *Sula* our reading is punctuated by three dots stopping us (on three of the four occasions each dot being enclosed in a small circle). The first three punctuation marks, those with the circles, mark time breaks. Just before the first Sula callously has her grandmother put, against her will, into a home. Though Eva, Sula's grandmother, is tough, Sula is tougher. Eva's toughness has usually been exercised to help her children live (or die). Sula's toughness here is to help herself. The mark is followed by her friend Nel's feeling a special magic in that May time and attributing it to the good effect, the magic of Sula's recent return home. Before the marks we pause and put together what seems to be the completed life story of Eva (it is not the last we hear of her, but it looks that way); we think about Sula: Is she as cruel as she seems, or as wonderful as Nel thinks her?

On the second occasion, Jude, Nel's husband, is sizing up Sula too: "A funny woman, he thought, not that bad-looking. But he could see why she wasn't married; she stirred a man's mind maybe, but not his body." What goes on in your mind as you pause there? You think back about what you know of Jude's marriage, Nel's friendship with Sula, Sula's way with men, her mother's way with men, and you think, "Oh, no, Sula wouldn't do that, not to her best friend. . . . Would she?" You remember what she did to her own grandmother, and you think, "Okay, man, your body isn't stirred, but I know Sula better than you do, and you're in for it." And more, much more. Whether these are exactly the thoughts and feelings you have, the author's stop sign is designed to and is likely to make you stop, think back, perhaps to the three dots and Eva, evaluate the situation and its implications, and frame some sort of expectation of what is to come next.

The timing of the next appearance of the encircled dots could not be more different: Sula and her man, her free and independent male counterpart Ajax, have just made love, "and the house was very, very quiet." Then we see the three dots. By now we know they signal a change and we remember that they have been associated with an act of self-indulgence or amorality on Sula's part. We think back, we make a pattern, we anticipate. What? Some of us will probably expect Sula to tire of Ajax, cast him off as she has others, or—since in her love she has thought of getting beneath his skin, beneath the black to the gold, and with "a nail file or even Eva's old paring knife," getting beneath the gold to the alabaster, and with hammer and chisel, beneath the alabaster to the loam—we may expect her to commit some act of violence on her lover, to cut, burn, murder him. After all, she is the woman who, as a girl, cut off the tip of her own finger, and who watched with interest as her mother burned to death.

We're wrong. Beyond the dots the paragraph begins, "Sula began to discover what possession was." She starts to make a nest, and a few hundred words later, just before the next break (though without dots), Ajax makes "love to her with the steadiness and intensity of a man about to leave for Dayton." This time it is Sula who is abandoned. These divisions may help us, then, answer some of the questions we have asked about the evaluation of Sula's behavior or way of life.

Though Nel and Sula may be representative, they are also highly individualized, and though each seeks to be herself, the novel embeds each in a history and community. The novel is one-sixth over before they meet and almost a third over before they assume center stage. Nel may deny being her parents' daughter, she may delight in the female household of the Peace family and its warm slovenliness, but she is Helene Wright's daughter in her respectability, rejecting as her mother did the gaudy hell of her grandmother's life in a New Orleans whorehouse or its equivalent. Her respectability is her independence; she lives so that she will never have to smile that obsequious, flirtatious smile her mother gives the brutal white trainman to appease him, will never bring the look to the eyes of black men her mother's behavior did to the eyes of the black soldiers on the train. But she does bring that look to the eyes of her husband when she interrupts his sex-play with Sula.

A great deal more time in the novel is spent on the Peace family than on the Wrights, and Sula's grandmother Eva and mother Hannah are two of the triumphs of the novel. Eva is tough, some would say mean. She endures, but not like Faulkner's stolid Dilsey. She manages to have her own leg cut off by a train for the pension money to support her father-abandoned children. One of those children, her "boy," whose life she had saved as an infant by using the last of her food as a suppository to relieve his life-threatening constipation, she "executes" when he returns home after World War I a helpless drug addict. When Sula cuts off the tip of her finger to protect herself, we are reminded of Eva. Hannah Peace is an easy-going sexy woman who takes lovers casually and warmly, making men feel good about themselves. Sula is not so gentle and not at all submissive like her mother, but some of her casual attitudes toward sex, her seductiveness, and her carelessness she has learned from her mother. Though Sula is different, is herself, "Eva's arrogance and Hannah's self-indulgence merged in her. . . ."

The portrait of Sula without Eva and Hannah would not only deprive us of two memorable and fully realized characterizations, but even if its abstraction would make it seem more representative, it would lack the vibrancy, resonance, and reality that it now has and that makes the novel significant, in the full sense of that word. "The novel," D. H. Lawrence says, "is the highest example of subtle interrelatedness that man has discovered. Everything is true in its own time, place, and circumstance, and untrue outside of its own place, time, circumstance." *Sula* shows that interrelatedness and particularity.

Like *Old Mortality* it uses dates for chapter titles. It begins, after a brief prelude, in 1919, not with Sula, Nel, or anyone from either family, but with a "shell-shock" victim of World War I, Shadrack, and a thumbnail sketch of the incident in 1917 that deranged him, a scene in hospital, his release, and his founding of National Suicide Day, a day he thought would get the fear of unexpected death out of the way for the rest of the year. A fair amount of time early in the novel is spent on Shadrack and we may expect him to play a greater role in the novel than he in fact does. He does, indeed, thread his way through the rest of the novel without being entirely necessary for any of the major action. Sula goes to his hermit's cabin on the river when Chicken Little is drowned to see if he has seen anything; they speak at cross-purposes but with an eerie sense of significance; Sula accidentally leaves her belt, and she, his one visitor, he singles out in the town for unique attention.

The townspeople, years later, think his respect a sign that Sula, like the mad Shadrack, is a devil. Indeed, these two do seem to have a special relationship as outsiders inside the community. When Sula dies, Shadrack loses his enthusiasm for Suicide Day, and he is now greeted with laughter rather than fear. At the very end of the novel, it is Nel's passing Shadrack, "each thinking separate thoughts about the past," that triggers Nel's whispering "Sula?" and her final recognition that it is her friend and not her husband she has been missing all these years. So Shadrack, while not being a double or a symbol, is an important pigment in the portrait of Sula, and to get just the right tone, we must see him too in significant particularity.

Sula, her family, her friend Nel and her family, her lover Ajax, the people in the community, the times are in subtle interrelatedness, so it makes no sense to ask whether the novel is about Sula, the community, being black in the Midwest from 1919 to 1965, being black and female, because the answer to all these questions is yes. There is, however, little historical background in the usual sense. There is the World War I scene, but no specific mention of the Depression, though more than half the novel occurs between 1937 and 1941— the black community of Medallion was always, in its fashion, depressed. World War II, so far as I can remember, is represented only by the casual mention that Nel had a boyfriend who was a sergeant stationed nearby and by its later effect on the town's growth. The only "political" event is the unpremeditated attack on the tunnel construction site where no blacks have been hired for honorable labor, ending with a cave-in and the deaths of a good many blacks. The undated prefatory chapter describes the disappearance of the black neighborhood in the hills above Medallion known as the Bottom and gives a bit of its history.

The final chapter, "1965," begins,

> Things were so much better in 1965. Or so it seemed. You could go downtown and see colored people working in the dime store behind the counters, even handling money with cash-register keys around their necks. And a colored man taught mathematics at the junior high school.

To Nel's fifty-five-year-old eyes, however, things were not better than they were forty years earlier. The beautiful boys of 1921 were no more, "Nothing like these kids." Even the whores in the old days were better, truly shameless, getting "up from the dinner table and walk[ing] into the trees with a customer with as much embarrassment as a calving mare." The "good old days" of Medallion in 1921 were no more truly good or better than any nostalgic memory of the good old days, but Nel's nostalgia is true to her, and even the reader, who has seen the calendar turning and the times changing throughout the novel, shares it to a degree.

There is a deep sense of time and of time passing conveyed in this short novel. Perhaps one of the ways in which it is achieved is in the rhythmic repetition or recollection of early events throughout the later portions of the novel.

Nor is this merely a device for rendering time—repeatedly the recollection not only mimics the reader's recapitulation of the past as he moves through the novel, but also shows the conditioning power of the past on the lives of the characters. Nel's final "'We was girls together'" is only a summary of the effect of experience, lived life, the past on the present. Sula's swinging the boy Chicken Little by the hands, letting go, only to see him disappear under the waters of the river, is recalled time and again through the novel.

Earlier that day, Sula, passing the room in which her mother was talking to neighbors, all of them complaining about their children, hears her mother say she loves Sula but does not like her. Seventeen years later, the events of that day in 1922 serve to explain what the community feels is Sula's "evil."

> Their evidence against Sula was contrived, but their conclusions about her were not. Sula was distinctly different. . . . hers was an experimental life— ever since her mother's remarks sent her flying up those stairs, ever since her one major feeling of responsibility had been exorcised on the bank of a river with a closed place in the middle. The first experience taught her there was no other that you could count on; the second that there was no self to count on either. She had no center, no speck around which to grow.

National Suicide Day and Shadrack, the look of the soldiers on the train headed for New Orleans, the burning of Hannah Peace, Sula cutting off her fingertip, the death of Chicken Little stitch the novel together with a rhythm as subtle and supple as the prose, creating a sense of depth in the characters and in their lived experience, a sense of causal and emotional connection in the events in their lives, forcing the reader to remember what he or she has read and so linking his or her own past to that of the characters, lending to *Sula* that depth, scope, and emotional as well as intellectual complexity that realizes the potentiality of the novel as a form and marks the short novel off from the short story.